THE SOUL-CATCHER'S CALLING

THE SOUL-CATCHER'S CALLING

Sponsored by Supreme Command

As reported (LDO:803926) by
Leading Agent (Third Class) in the Field

Nigel J. Jamieson, LLD (Otago)

The Marsyas Press Dunedin
2020
Encouraging Prophetic Readership beyond 20/20 Vision

Library of Congress Control Number: 2019920245
ISBN: Hardcover   978-1-5434-9592-8
               Softcover   978-1-5434-9591-1
               eBook   978-1-5434-9590-4

Print information available on the last page.

Rev. date: 01/03/2020

To order additional copies of this book, contact:
Xlibris
0-800-443-678
www.Xlibris.co.nz
Orders@Xlibris.co.nz
803926

This very slight and short report
made whilst under heavy fire
is dedicated
to the grace and favour of
Heaven's Supreme Command.

* * *

FOREWORD
From Origins to Outcomes

First premise: origins without objectives don't always lead to outcomes. Second premise: without actively operating objectives origins can be purloined or diverted to counterfeit outcomes. Third premise: counterfeit outcomes can be so much at odds with their origins as to deceive their incumbents as to their objectives. Conclusion: this is just a foreword. So then, beware—we haven't even started yet.

For aspiring to angelic heights (and not just a means of securing intellectual property), this book (however slight) presents a stellar series (or constellation) of twelve interplanetary handbooks. It does so in the still creative context of this world's continuously growing diversity of people and places. And it does so also for the sometimes comic, yet other times tragic, but always divine purpose of explaining the origins and outcomes of today's constantly changing cosmic constellation—which it does by means of these twelve interplanetary handbooks.

After all, there are no longer just eight planets (as once thought) but instead (not counting moons, satellites, and other space debris) now twelve scientifically recognisable planets in this Earth's solar system. Nevertheless, don't mistake the physicality of this Earth's fast-declining solar system, either figuratively for the divine hand of creation or else literally for the cosmological outcome of any self-referential big bang. That would be to mistake your own creative origins for someone else's entropic outcomes.

Vouched for by our own angelic acclamation, together with the stellar song still being sung to celebrate all creation, there's been no big bang to account for what most of you humans now dismiss as the fairy tale of divine creation. This little boy's idea of creating some big bang is largely a guilt-edged notion devised to assuage the human conscience for the death and destruction brought about by nuclear warfare. Why, there's more creative power in the smallest mustard seed than in any humanly conjectured big bang!

Dearest humans, you flatter yourselves to be forever at home here—in what you assume to own for yourselves as planet Earth. We know this for sure since some of us angels can likewise mistake the demonic for being the heavenly, the virtual for being the real, and so go on to make similarly false claims to property (which fallen angels measure in terms of captive human souls).

For the most part, the whole fallen concept of what constitutes 'our very own' property (whether so-called real, personal, collective, or intellectual property) either verges on or transgresses deeply into the realm of the demonic. Well now, was it not Cain (both by name and nature) who stood for 'possession being nine-tenths of the law'?

For most humans, the whole false concept of property is no more than a self-reverential and idolatrous anthropomorphism. Now, if you would know more about how some of the biggest bangs are brought about to break up families, capture the souls of the disinherited, and blow up unsuspecting lives to kingdom come, then in each case caused by the hugely explosive qualities built up by your own anthropocentric self-reverence, read again the age-old story of Cain and Abel, the midlife parable of the prodigal son, or for modernists, then John Galsworthy's novel entitled *The Man of Property*.

As an anthropomorphism, we can revere property as if that false concept (for being made by ourselves in our very own image) were to be substituted subjectively for being only what we less like to see of ourselves as self-made men and women. Whether for being then completely fallen humans or completely fallen angels, we can then quite truly be described as being 'possessed'. [Fyodor Dostoyevsky's masterwork (for so long erroneously referred to in its English translation as *The Devils*) is more tellingly told in its original Russian for being entitled *The Possessed*.]

As humans, most of us claim the planet Earth to be our home (just as most of us angels claim heaven to be our home), but what (it may be asked) really constitutes any such 'proper claim' to either being 'our home'? In short, a claim is no more than a self-assertion (until proven valid, as every lawyer knows)!

Without there being any more objective predication, however, this sort of unjustified property claim (the bane of every lawyer) might risk what most scholars would dismiss for being a self-centred solipsism. This is the sort of invalidity which sooner or later arises in any argument from presuming, say, mankind to be its own earthly measure or, say, the angelic host to be its own heavenly measure. In each case, the self-centred solipsism is void for lack of any predicated objectivity.

Many scientists and scholars look to *scientia* (or the state of their own advancing knowledge) to substitute for this external objectivity; but arguments in favour of such self-substitution, once again of their 'own claim' to settle the scientific or scholarly score from within themselves, pose as many problems of infinite regression, self-centred circularity, or indeterminate advancement than they afford any least likelihood of more objective certainty.

No man can be the ultimate measure of his own worthiness (whether in terms of human science, scholarship, artistry, expertise, wisdom, or anything else). And with no more validity can the same self-validation be done more collectively of mankind by mankind.

Looking to everyone's own, as well as to mankind's collective *philosophia* (or life experience), in pursuit of not just *scientia* (human knowledge) but also of *sophia* (always a wisdom more externally divine than internally human) then allows for no other way than to search for some other means by which to predicate some more authentic objectivity of ourselves than we could give by self-reference.

Indeed, it is in our continued pursuit of this otherworldly or cosmic wisdom (in some external shape or deistic form) down and throughout all earlier ages of both human and angelic endeavour that we come to learn more of who we each are in terms of origins, objectives, and outcomes.

In all this, the fundamental question of all time (aside from this passing moment) is not just 'What is man?' by which when asked only by man of man (as if the unseeing eye could see the all-seeing eye) is in itself meaningless. On the contrary, the fundamental question is rather, as the Psalmist asks, 'What is man that man should still be meaningful and this even to some supremely sovereign being?'

Here in this question we have a metaphysical conundrum of considerable magnitude. First comes the search for individuation by which to distinguish, not only the human self, but also one's human limitations. Then, disatisfied with what we find out of our limitations, next comes the search for humanity unlimited.

Ultimately, however, through wisdom passed on by our predecessors or by our own personal life experience, we come to learn that it is only through the presence of a fully sovereign person in our lives—that is to say, someone who, for being sufficiently known to mankind as someone superlatively superior to mankind, and yet who by deigning himself to serve as man's fullest and only possible measure of perfection will have, as they say, the power to cut the mustard in resolving the already mentioned metaphysical conundrum—which we may now begin to appreciate for being one of the first magnitude to us humans.

At the very least then, at which point you could read *Man's Search for Himself* by Rollo May (about what then becomes man's sovereign struggle to find out and to know exactly who he is and what it means to be human), the same man starts to learn who it is that he's looking for through whom he too must find the same way of his sharing in this same sovereign and absolute measure.

In other words, when the meaning of meaning (suborned to itself by the Delphic Oracle) is left to be decided by whoever it may be who asks the question, then whether determined by a Procrustean sidekick given to physicality or by a Pythagorean conjuring trick of intellectuality, the meaning of meaning then becomes meaningless.

On the other hand, our God (when finally found) is one to whom we, for having been created in his image, are inherently meaningful, and from whom, therefore, we, in turn, acquire our greatest meaning.

Nevertheless, even just for the sake of the record, who are these people, such as Procrustes, Pythagoras, and those prophetic celebrants, who served the Delphic Oracle?

In terms of both popular as well as scholastic opinion, Procrustes was a Greek robber baron who either cut down or stretched all his victims to all one size as measured by his own bed. Thus, Procrustes operates the mechanism of death (just as did Adolf Hitler with the Jews and Slavs) to serve as this world's great leveller.

Whereas Procrustes relied on brute physicality, Pythagoras (covenanted or dedicated by name to the conjoint god Python-Apollo) relied on intellectuality. As a brilliant mathematician, he performed amazing tricks with numbers, although in the end, as later collated by the geometrician, Euclid, his plane geometry would prove reductive and thence constrictive rather than expansive.

As for the Delphic Oracle, whose celebrants also followed Python-Apollo in their search (for 'the meaning of meaning' as they described it), they specialised in the production of prophecy, which they proclaimed under the same drug-induced state of ecstasy as employed more trivially by addicts today. This road to Delphi to experience and participate in this otherworldly prophetic measure (whether authentic or spurious) would present itself as a very crowded pathway (dating back to one and a half thousand years before the birth of Jesus Christ).

Along this path of pilgrimage to Delphi would pass many ancient pilgrims seeking to find the measure of meaning by which to resolve their issues and answer their questions. As often as not (or so it was said), it would happen that through meetings with each other along this pathway leading to Delphi, the disputes and differences of opinion between supplicants, which had brought about their mutual travel, would be negotiated or compromised or resolved by themselves along the way.

However primitive, and still overmuch occult, there's a breakthrough here in the human spirit to find a measure more spiritual than either just brutally physical or smartly intellectual by which to operate as an objective and external measure for all suffering mankind. Since ever the fall of mankind, the search has always been on to discover the one and only means of man's redemption.

Since, with hope (both angelic and human) in the substance of things as yet unseen, we have hailed this attempt of mankind to consult some prophetic power as the distinctive measure of mankind to be some sort of a breakthrough from that of mankind presuming to be its own self-measure, then we shall say just a little more as to the origins and objectives of this radically different way of handling, if not yet all human affairs, nevertheless those at the highest level of requiring dispute resolution.

Now every oracular utterance, whether authentic or spurious, is decided not by those who utter it but by those who interpret it—as in the same way that the significance of any book is decided by those who read the book rather than by those who write it. And that, like it or not by those students who hear it, is first-class teaching practice (as preached in the parables by our Lord and Saviour, Jesus Christ).

This glamorous conclusion of all creation (through all time) that we should learn to search for our master and maker and not to expect him to flaunt himself before us both all day and every night is one of the greatest measures of freedom and trust he could invest in us by which to demonstrate both his significance to us and our significance to him. Likewise, that he should have chosen to measure himself by his making of us, and that we should be measured in turn by the great delight he takes in our being measured by him, is for us (both angels and humans) one of the greatest glories of all creation.

What better than this light of love with which he made us and this great delight in consequence with which he follows our doings as closely as we follow his could we have by which to measure ourselves (both angels and humans).

There's no measure that makes sense without an earth for the sake of heaven together with that heaven for the sake of earth, which far-seeing mutuality, in turn, explains the need for both a new heaven and a new earth and, in turn, for any hell to see itself as a sole survivor making only for nonsense without measure.

For both angels and humans, this is what we mean for this celestial hierarchy being vested in the Supreme Command. We do so essentially: first, by recognising our own personal calling from the Supreme Command (emboldening us to share in its own righteous measure of supreme creation) and, secondly, by its providing an immutable touchstone with which to identify ourselves in Christ and so then avoid those subversive wiles of the Counterfeit Command which would otherwise stultify our righteous calling.

Supreme Command? Well, what's in a name, as may be so frequently asked by those who—to the cost of their own personality, character, individuality, and every other means of identifying who they are and to what exactly is their foretold calling or ultimate destiny—remain at a loss (either partial or total) for being unable to relate to what ought to be their own explicitly understood and fully covenanted name.

Covenanted name? Yes, by what we're dedicated, named, and known by, we each have a covenanted name. We won't fully know or understand this name whilst yet on earth, but in terms of our calling and destiny and whether we like it or get to like it, dispute it, ignore it, or repudiate it, it's still our covenanted name. It's often something of a threshold (as to a family household) which we must first cross to engage and prosper in our calling.

Likewise, the same goes for this book or report, since by what name and by what dedication it ought to be known will best ensure every reader's understanding as to its purpose. This will be done by virtue of drawing your own human spirit as close as you freely can to its own explicitly covenanted name or dedication.

So then, what shall we call this present work in progress (for being yet barely a foreword to introduce a total of twelve books) each emanating out of at least one almost infinitely longer, more deeply detailed, and far more widely commissioned report? Well, unless you've illegitimately bought a coverless or rebound remaindered copy, you'll already have its present working title of *The Soul-Catcher's Calling* to ponder on.

Of course, in terms of sheer practicality, there's no *Soul-Catcher's Calling* that could be carried through otherwise than by action (although some who are called may not hear their calling or, even if heard, be still disposed to non-action).

By granting free will to both angels and humans, the all-knowing, all-seeing, and yet mercifully redemptive Supreme Command indicates its own extremely experimental and open-ended outlook towards its own strongly scientific, scholarly, and conscientiously designed creation. You'd hardly believe that open-ended outlook on earth for being God's own truth, but it's a fitting biblical commentary on earth's own ridiculously lowered standard of truth that not even the much-celebrated Ripley records it for being a matter of 'believe it or not'.

You baulk, don't you, dearest readers, at any suggestion of an all-powerful, all-seeing, and all-present God (as you see it) being an even just minimally, far less an even extremely experimental person? You think perhaps or else prefer to see or experience your God as being extremely determinative and your own lives as being either decisively ordained or determinedly predestined. By means of his instruction manual, you look for a safe passage, but perhaps not much more than your own most comfortable passage, in his Word, through his Word, and by his Word. Bon voyage!

However, this might just indicate that you don't exercise as much of your own free will to identify yourself with a far more adventuresome and awesome God, as he grants you that freedom to exercise in your deciding how and by what personal and most intimate means you should identify yourself with him. It's even possible you've never listened to his everyday voice, far less heard his clarion calling, or have felt the need to search and identify yourself with him for the purpose of fulfilling your own lifelong vocation or calling. As one of his first-class leading agents, Bill Johnston (no, not the dramatist Ben Johnson) has so often encouraged us to venture, the privilege is ours when we are called on to *strengthen ourselves in the Lord!*

We won't enquire here into your own personal philosophy (love of wisdom), personal philology (love of learning), or personal psychology (whether behaviourally influenced, theoretically taught, or experientially processed), although all these soul-markers are extremely relevant to your own highly personal identification with God. Instead, we'll take yet another passing look at the Ten Commandments (as can never be done too often) lest we still run in fear of falling victim to any god who sees us (both angels and humans) as providing no more than the raw material for yet another of his all-powerful, all-seeing, and all-present experiments.

Why, however great the Ten Commandments are in the march of many different civilisations and in the development of many different cultures (which is not disputed here), these by now tedious ten have long ago served their purpose. Let it be seen now, as Jesus showed in so many very different yet fundamentally jurisprudential ways that the full complement of these ten commandments could never be more than experimental. This hard enough fact (to understand) is actually made to be so, since their outcomes depend not just on the right human responses to those commandments but also on developing that right loving relationship between their maker and mankind to allow the implementation of his heavenly justice through the very best of well-made laws.

Break any one of these commandments, and you've broken the whole lot. Try keeping the whole caboodle of Ten Commandments in all their ever-proliferating detail, and likewise you've broken the whole lot for just your smallest breach of one (besides deductively of every least likely detail)—since (as every lawyer knows) the devil is in the details. Likewise, try to hedge around, bolster up, or ring around the whole caboodle by a factor, whether of 10^2 or $10,000^{52}$, by providing either more general or more specific commandments, and you've substituted both legal and social chaos for cosmic good order. Like trying to keep the peace (by treating only the symptoms of disorder) without any effort at peacemaking (by remedying and rectifying what's fundamentally wrong) and so also just try … try … trying to keep the peace by enforcing all the Ten Commandments (and even so many more spin-off commandments that make such a big and messy bird's nest out of any legal system) just can't be done.

Both these spiritual aspirations (peacemaking and peacekeeping) serve bilaterally related purposes at different stages or in different arenas of military operation. Their inherently two-valued logic equates more readily with the juristic recodification (through refined abstraction) of the Ten Commandments from ten to two. This recodification gives a deeper jurisprudential understanding of the fundamental integrity required of peacemaking in the heavenly vertical dimension and of peacekeeping in the earthly horizontal dimension. Sustainable peacekeeping on earth always relies on prior peacemaking in heaven, but sometimes this priority is pragmatically reversed (as a temporary measure) to allow those wrongs on earth to be righted and so to open heaven's doors to more permanent peacemaking. Nevertheless, heavenly peacemaking is always both our first and final priority, since, as *bogatyrs* (or heavenly warriors), our soul-catcher's calling is paramount.

Alas and alack, for the Pharisees, Sadducees, and teachers of the law (many of whom are still around today) in their continued lack of motivation to repair, remedy, and rectify this whole world's stock of rapidly disintegrating legal systems. It is on that same rapidly approaching nadir of decline in every still barely workable system of law and order that world peace is at present precariously poised. Indeed, the best-before date for undertaking such operations has long passed, and even the rapidly receding point of no return least remembered. [Bad-weather warning: When studying prophetic history up-close (which constitutes nine-tenths of this book), be sure to keep up your navigational dead reckoning throughout to ensure you *understand exactly where you stand in relation to where you're heading.* Otherwise— you'll fall!]

The process of both mindfully motivated and morally based abstraction (dealt with in these twelve books) when applied to demonic strongholds and worldly institutions is never popular with many professionals. Without any sense of professional vocation, those who substitute their own personal career for that vocation see themselves open to loss of status and income by reducing their institutionalised ways and means to no more than that required of any street-level understanding. Why, that's just like some whiskey priest who, for pickling his spritual calling in alcohol, somehow misses out on every last drop of mercifully fresh rain which still keeps falling on him from heaven.

The same refining (instead of brewing-up) process as applied to the Ten Commandments was somewhat experimentally suggested by Jesus Christ to the lawyers themselves (in response to one of their close-knit legal fraternitywho had snidely asked for our Lord's legal advice as to which of these Ten Commandments were the most important). Of course, for seeing Jesus (that upstart from Galilee, as they thought of him) only as a layman and not even a lawyer (and thinking even far less of him for his not being in the top-ten professional bracket as they were for being teachers of the law), they chose to stand on their professional pride.

Oh, don't tell us angels (who were there in person and shuddering at the enormity of this juristic confrontation) that these big-time Jerusalem lawyers didn't take the legal point that Jesus was making to themselves! Oh yes, they did (although not to heart) because that was the very last time on earth that they ever tried to trick him (that upstart from Galilee, as they saw him) by asking him for his legal advice!

After all, as even one of his own disciples had first referred to pride of place (so then the same rumour had got around), 'What good can come from Galilee?'

As well known, pride of face leads to pride of place and pride of place leads to pride of race. So then, instead of even just marvelling at the radical refinement to their concept of law suggested by this juristic wunderkind or whizz-kid from woe-betokened Galilee, this gaggle, cabal, and conglomerate of highfalutin yet professionally jealous law teachers just turned up their noses, pursed their lips, and stood sullenly silent.

There they stood, this cabal of law teachers, arms folded tightly across their chests, eyes glaring out from under beetle brows at this young preacher from Gallilee, as if themselves all turned to stone. It wouldn't have been any different had Jesus been teaching on the law from his own home patch in Gallilee—since no prophet makes any sense in his own home town. Jeez! (unless for being yourself a teacher of the law) how unbelievable!

Repudiating the radical law reform, this cabal of highfalutin law teachers would nevertheless still stone-wall this workable law reform no less than they would go on consistently repudiating the arrival of their own long-promised Messiah. Here's yet another (although in this case correlative) example of that best teaching practice generally so hated by the least committed of both teachers and students. Even as in this trick-or-treat case, when mercifully given the soft-hearted answer to the very hardest of those juristically posed problems, that messianic answer butters no parsnips (as the old saying goes) with those hardest of hard-hearted students who are still out to trip up their teacher.

Yes, there are very exceptional cases (especially when asked trick questions) in which to test the strength of those poseurs against their taking the trouble to learn by themselves. In any such exceptional case, the best teaching practices mentioned earlier may be judiciously sacrificed, whereby those who ask (as not always in good faith) for the answer to be given to them (often far sooner than they've come to grips with their own question) may be given the answer as to their own as yet uncomprehended question. As well as to test the strength of their opposition to self-learning, this is also done to measure their fealty to the questioning process in particular and as to the learning process in general. Like yesterday's Pharisees, Sadducees, and teachers of the law, today's poseurs would benefit from reading about the art and practice of the learning organisation in *The Fifth Discipline* as described (in his own terms)by Peter M. Senge. This reading (if not already done) must surely do no less than open both eyes and ears as well as to transform minds to vastly different ways of learning how differently to deal with otherwise impossible problems.

Have you ever gone through the gospels to count the number of controversies that our Lord stirred up? Well, as he said himself, 'Don't think I've come to bring peace on earth. No, I've come to cause divisions.' Our understanding of the pivotal place of peace (not as the world gives) in any understanding of the messianic evidence for the coming again of Jesus Christ is foundational to mankind's understanding of heaven's history, both that already fulfilled and as yet to be fulfilled. All history as to rightful origins is prophetically certain as to rightful outcomes. Repudiate the history of rightful origins (no less than the cult of constant human progress repudiates almost all it dislikes in being its own witness to the part it plays in human history) and you repudiate also the forthcoming history of rightful outcomes.

Yet both of these highly aspirational suggestions (both how to make peace and to keep peace) are becoming increasingly demanded (if not by many of those who deem them already impossible to perform) as both this world and whatever there may be of any next world draw closer to the advent of both a new heaven and a new earth. Still, just as so much of our even 'pure science' remains highly speculative (as shown by subsequently disproved 'proofs') so also a great deal of our deepest theology remains seriously conjectural (as shown by the rise and fall of so many religious denominations). That shared irony perceived between those whose sole faith rests in scientific proof and those whose supreme faith resides in heavenly truth surely provokes an ongoing paradox. As between every proof-reliant scientist and faith-reliant deist, the distinctions (whether false or valid) are still drawn no less credibly and cogently than are those still drawn between Jew and Gentile.

Why, even our Jewish brothers (both Orthodox and Messianic), who fixate their focus of faith more specifically on the Ten Commandments than do Christians and Gentiles, have no more success in keeping all these Ten Commandments (OT) today than do those (of whom much more may be expected) when persevering with only the 'Big Two Commandments' (NT). In any case, whether Old Testament (OT) or New Testament (NT) is barely now the point, since, with a new heaven and a new earth in the offing, we live (*nakanunye*) on the eve of their cosmic sublimation into their long-awaited 'Extra-Terrestrial Testament' (ET)

Woops—what a powerfully explosive sublimation of both OT and NT (by way of spiritual TNT) that will bring about! Alas, this is no more than a most general work of jurisprudence (or the science of law in relation to justice), so we shall leave the issue here at this point before risking any further blotting of our copybook (whether perceptibly shown or not) by discussing the apparent foolishness of having less law (rather than more law) to promote greater justice.

As demonstrated by the so-called march of civilisations (witnessed by so many still ongoing and technologically intensifying world wars), this present work in progress is concerned mostly with the historically determined hard facts experienced throughout human life. In yet other ways (as left to be decided by the discerning reader), it can be a principled work of prophetic insight (past or present) no less than of purely imaginative fiction (unconstrained by space or time).

The imaginative fiction (as if this were that) may be no more than personally promoted and privately imagined or else publicly promoted and extensively imagined. The imaginative fiction may be promoted by way of legal fiction, literary fiction, or any other sort of mythic fiction; or it may be expressed generally and influentially (as by standard practice, linguistic usage, peer review, or political correctness). As the subject of statistical survey, it may also be expressed and promoted by any public opinion, whether by way of moral opinion, religious opinion, professional opinion, or popular opinion. And it may be held both of scholarly and scientific conjecture, whether proven or as yet unproven.

The shared confluence of both hard facts and prophetic insight, together with the allegorical exercise of purely imaginative fiction, calls for some subtle demarcation and understanding (on behalf of both writer and reader). This is required between what it takes to represent the resulting amalgam from all these confluences not just as for any serious work of art but also as for some far more serious statement of truth. No character (whether factual, fictional, or figurative) represented in this book (of twelve books in one) is represented to his or her detriment for being in any way unreal; and every reported event (no less than any non-event reportedly omitted) can, or shortly will, be confirmed as having either taken place (or not) in the course of prophetic history.

This historical confirmation stands, despite whatever very different opinions may be held as to the religious status or proper place or spiritual space (other than merely geographical place) which these reported events (or non-events) may hold and mean to different mindsets. Whether they mean no more than what we mistake for being either their own good or else their own bad repute in our own very narrow understanding of this world's seriously contingent history is of no real matter. After all, the whole purpose of studying history is to widen the mind as to *what we don't know* rather than to narrow the mind as to *what we think we do know.* And that goes for both the history of science and the history of heaven.

Alas, we like to fixate our minds on what we think ourselves to know best. In the pitifully narrow and shallow context of what little that might be it thus becomes a huge challenge for us to admit to the inordinately enormous amount of what we don't have the least or slightest knowledge. One may proudly put one's pen to the writing of a book—called by God (or so one thinks)—only to find out that one really knows nothing at all about the subject matter. One can only pray, as one continues, that both God and the writer (since God alone is the author) both share the same sense of humour.

Accordingly, we put to you, dearest readers, a list of the most critical and pivotal points, which will as far as possible obviate every risk of causing unfortunate confusion: (1) because all spiritual relationships are pre-eminently personal, the God of this book may not be your God, nor his heaven your heaven; yet (2) as the writer of this book, I am just as interested in meeting with your God as I hope you will be also as interested in meeting with my God.

It also follows for the avoidance of further confusion: (3) that any resemblance of reported events to any other event (or non-event) than those humbly recorded in this history (whether engendered by prophetic proclamation, or by allegorical fiction) to the physicality of hard fact and whether as of heaven to hell or of hell to heaven or as of any mindset midway (whether capitalist or communist, democratic or republican) is stoutly disclaimed and denied.

Likewise (4) also stoutly denied, as to any character or lack of character (whether in the abstract or more specifically in the particular) when seen to be affecting any person (real or imaginary), that too is hereby declared to be seriously contingent on *what little we know and how much we don't know* and so then (5) to be no more than accidental, incidental, coincidental or at least contingent on what *nobody as yet knows for certain* to be the revealed truth.

Meanwhile, this prevailing level of contingent uncertainty remains to serve as a test of faith on all fronts (6) as to the advent of the promised new heaven and the new earth; whereupon (7) then the precise relationship of the absolute truth to our own very relativistic and humanistic measure of truth and falsity shall be either confirmed or denied or else amended and altered; and so by then (8) in whatsoever appropriate form (*also as yet faithfully believed although with full certainty still unknown*) shall be fully authenticated by the absolute and incontrovertible truth on which is founded the already given promise of all eternity.

We began rather pretentiously by claiming for this foreword less of a property right than that appreciation properly given to any honest yet however slight a work of angelic art. To honour God in those places (such as Kabul, Damascus, and Tehran) where some of the best high-flying carpets are traditionally handcrafted, there is a ritual fault or defect woven by the craftsman into each carpet by which to indicate the craftsman's humility before God. This process is to remind all who appreciate the artistry which goes into carpet making of how futile it is on earth for humans (despite being only a little lower than the angels) to seek perfection.

In the same mildly ritualistic way, the cover of this copybook (as to the practice of soul-catching as a divine calling) carries the very odd little inkblot here and there (all credit here due to the somewhat psychotic Swiss psychiatrist Rorschach—from whose name the word *rort* is possibly derived) lest the writer, reader, or reviewer could likewise be tempted to mistake this angelic work in full progress for aspiring to that level of heavenly perfection which has brought down many a demon to below ground level.

* * *

PREFACE
Encouraging a Prophetic Readership Far
Beyond 20/20 Vision for AD 2020

I
The Problem

Great fleas have little fleas upon their backs to bite 'em
And little fleas have lesser fleas, and so *ad infinitum*
And the great fleas themselves, in turn, have greater
fleas to go on
While these again have greater still, and greater still,
and so on.

Augustus De Morgan, *Siphonaptera*

'Is that a throwaway remark?' Novice-Angel Cora asked her Buddy-Angel Clara. 'I mean the one about the fleas?' Cora added, picking up on her buddy angel's startled expression of retro perplexity.

'You should know better than to ask a question like that!' answered her remarkably extravert buddy Clara. 'Whether up here in heaven or back down there on earth, there's no such thing as a throwaway remark.

It's true', thought the more introspective Cora, *that where all the world's a stage, many of the actors will mistake their own last line for being their opening first line and the above four lines of verse for being no more than a throwaway one-liner. It will take more than twelve books in one to explain what any novice might otherwise mistake for being a throwaway remark. Oh dear,* thought Cora, *what a little extrovert Buddy-Angel Cara can be sometimes for being so full in one's face... ...*

'Oh, sorry!' suddenly apologised Novice-Angel Cora to Cara [when feeling suitably chastened for her oversight]. *After all,* she rationalised, *during what little time we novice angels once spent on earth, the whole wide world could not provide what we needed for our infant souls to grow and thrive. Now all that remains of our tenuously shortened lifeline from earth is our barely memorable flight path of song first from and then back to heaven.* [From the very first instance of her soul-conception, Cora had so much wanted to be a teacher when she grew up. She had been relieved of that responsibility because where her own life was leading, there would soon be no more little children wanting to learn about how they came from heaven.

There's neither shortage of space nor lack of time nor lack of learning up here in heaven. It's so awesome the way in which every tiny jot and subsequent tittle of everyone's least word and smallest thought is made to count, thought Cora. *All the same it's going to take us all eternity to get our embryonic heads round the opening night of old earth's first creation! Just imagine, Buddy-Angel Cara insists that all we little angels were all there once, singing paeans (that's songs of praise) at the opening night of heaven's first creation! And here we are now,* mused Cora, *retro-learning new first lines for the opening up of some split new heaven as well as readying ourselves to look after some entirely new and so innocently virgin and untrodden earth.*

'So then, it's true, said little Cora to herself, and despite what all the biblical hackers say otherwise (as distinct from the biblical-backers)—that wonders will never cease! Who would have thought when back on dying earth that one's own so very little soul could yet be born again? Even for us angels there at the first opening night of God's creation, this is such a hard thought to get one's still embryonic head around! So then, how much harder it must be for grown-up humans to accept the need for a new heaven and a new earth—even if only by which to fulfil the promise of their own eternal salvation? But then again, as even any sort of angel, I myself have never known what it is to live on earth. Why, I've never known even what it is to be born! If grown-ups only knew what it felt like for themselves to die before their birth, they would be a very, very different kind of people!

'Yet had we been born on dying earth,' continued Cora, 'we would have been no more than actors on that world's tawdry stage. Now from here in heaven, we must learn to prompt God's already scripted guidelines as to what mortals must learn to expect during these last days of the dying earth. As novice angels, we too need a guidebook—a copybook, a safety net. Oh, I know we novice angels chatter a lot [as confirmed by the Holy Spirit] but sometimes we see things that other angels don't [as also confirmed by the Holy Spirit] which is exactly why I like to keep my journal [wrote Cora in her Journal].

'Learning, when done without any love of learning (a.k.a. philology), or without looking for wisdom (a.k.a. philosophy), is always counterproductive to the one way, the one truth, and the only one means of eternal life,' wrote Novice-Angel Cora in her journal. 'You can search out the reason for all things and so acquire the mundane science of knowledge and of power, but without looking for wisdom reached through your own love of learning, you can't live as you should for all eternity. No, you'll only trip yourself up by overlooking your one and only means of transcending both time and space to secure eternal life.

'We novice angels are not lost souls for never having been born as all other babies are born on earth. Learning to live as we should whilst on earth is as much a process of unlearning the ways of the world as it is a process of learning to live for all eternity. Why, that's the only one way (forever translational) by which anybody and everybody could or should seek to learn anything whilst on earth. Without that hallowed love of learning to motivate the translational process between heaven and earth, all else is but a vanity—which, in turn (as preached by Leading Agent Solomon, First Class), makes nothing worthwhile.

'There's a need here in this learning-unlearning process not only for exactitude but for absolute precision, not only in our thought but also in our doing. As to getting your head round such absolutes, think not just of absolute temperature or of absolute magnitude. Why, neither of these so-called absolutes can be any more than darkly seen by humans and as yet only in their rarefied physics. It's a funny thing, isn't it—that the more you persevere with earthly physics, then the less you persevere with heavenly metaphysics!

'So then, what's the score for ultimate reality (to be eternally realised in the promised new heaven) when humans are devoting themselves to more and more virtual reality on earth? Why, believe it or not, says Leading-Angel Ripley, but the score for ultimate reality in the new heaven is to do a better job of looking after the new earth!

'The more that humanity sees itself proudly prospering on the up and up, the sooner it gets scorched by the sun, which it mistakes (apart from the very odd meteorite) for being the source of all earthly matter.' *Who would it be in heaven then,* Cora wondered, *who plots the coordinates of passing (and not always passing) meteors? Surely not the task of fallen angels—unless perhaps in their own falling from heaven?*

'All the same, when we novice angels were make-do mortals on earth, we always ran scared of antimatter. Even now, antimatter can still appear to us novice angels as something no less scary. Realising its full abstract potential when called into being as substantive actuality is a process which remains near miraculous to us learners at the novice level. Perhaps, it's the nearest thing to what you mortals on earth marvel at for being your own three-dimensional scanning and design modelling. But then for you that's still always making something out of something (which in heaven is looked on as being a form of infinite regression).

'Making something out of nothing, that's basically the life on earth as it is in heaven of every author, every artist, and every composer; of every engineer, every designer, and every manufacturer; of every preacher, every teacher, and every reader; and of every statesman, leader, and administrator—no less than of every life-committed worker. It is the life of making something out of what otherwise would or might be shelved, overlooked, ignored, or dismissed for being nothing—and sometimes even lost for being less than nothing. Like so many of you human writers (Defoe, Dostoyevsky, Kafka, Woolf, Plath, Sand, and Steinbeck), it helps us angels also to keep a journal by which to ease our task of making something that matters out of antimatter. For some of us, as for every author, it's a very painful and long-suffering process.

'Sure, it helps us now to know that the antimatter, which we once mistook for the mythic void of all nothingnlessness on earth, is actually heaven's inexhaustible source of all matter throughout the cosmos. And as for proclamatory first-liners (largely prophetic promises) and last-liners (mostly bad-weather warnings), we haven't yet got to that bit in our study of heavenly linguistics, of which, for the purpose of transmitting messages between heaven and earth, we've still got so much to learn. Like so many of you novice humans, we novice angels have much still to learn about translation theory.

'And so, yes, like so many of you novice humans, we novice angels find it also helps to keep a journal. Mine's called *Ex Nihilo*, which means *Out of Nothing*. But as with *Ex Libris*, it sure helps to find out what other novice writers are journaling. To find out more about the painfulness of this most preliminary part of the creative process, be sure to read either Virginia Woolf's diary or else W. N. P. Barbellion's *Journal of a Disappointed Man.*'

Buddy-Angel Clara (once a novice herself and now an intern) smiled gently before blowing a kiss towards Novice-Angel Cora. 'That's okay in any language,' she said consolingly to little Cora, who had passed away to heaven before she could even be born on earth. For some earthly reason known only to the Supreme Command in heaven, little Cora's developing body on earth had ceased to engage in the heavenly journaling process. It had ceased to synthesise nutrients supernaturally from that inexhaustible void of antimatter, which gives rise to earthly living matter. Still a novice (and so prone to romantic crushes), little Cora, on coming to heaven so soon and sadly from earth, had rather unwisely developed her very first romantic crush, as so many writers do in journalism. She barracked for the journal (which she read religiously each night), celebrating the bravery of her journalistic hero, one W. N. P. Barbellion.

'Well, we're all born premature,' whispered Buddy-Angel Clara to Novice-Angel Cora. 'And that goes especially for those choosing to be born again and even far more for those babies never ever having first been born. No matter how intelligent or how powerful or how personable or how wise we may have seemed to be when on earth, these things don't matter a shrivelled fig when we get to heaven. [*Why a shrivelled fig?*' thought Cora, *since all the figs she had seen in heaven were fresh picked. And not just fresh picked, but always freshly picked, as befits the continued use of adverbs in heaven.*]

'Look, Cora, here's your own restored genealogy of perfectly reprocessed DNA. We'll pin it to your card of heavenly admission and attach it now to the bottom of your own little bassinet in heaven's recovery room. So then, sleep tight or rest in peace, or you can bawl your eyes out just like that beautiful little baby boy over there. Every single feeling or expression of feeling, from joy through anger to deep depression, is therapeutic up here in heaven. Consider this recovery room your heartfelt sanctuary.

'This recovery room (you can call it a rest room for the aged, a bedroom for those in midlife, or even a disciplined dormitory for adolescents, if you like) is only the first of many mansions in heaven. You can sleep as long as you like here (well, up until the last great day of judgement). Or you can walk and talk or get up and dance and play, or else—'

'What's all this about some last great day of judgement?' asked one stout old soul suddenly sitting up. 'I'll have you know I'm here … wherever I am … under duress and completely against my will … You may not know who I am, or else you wouldn't constrain me here … for my being the chief justice … the chief … the chief justice of … well, wherever I was chief justice … So what's all this about some last great day of judgement that could possibly apply to me?'

'Relax! You can come or go as you please,' piped up the shrill and by now shrunken voice of a soul which had once been embodied in the person of a stentorian court bailiff. 'As you know, m'lud,' he said, addressing the chief justice [obviously of somewhere long forgotten], now in a heavenly whisper, 'it's all a matter of jurisprudence, which is still the same as it always has been in trying to match up justice and mercy with the appropriate level of law. It's cosmic law up here, of course, but we won't go into that before you're ready for it. Whether or not you know where you are at present is also by now somewhat beside the point, but you're in the recovery ward of heaven here, where, after full recovery, you'll be assessed for being fit to plead your case.

'Don't worry. Never fear, m'lud! Not a jot or tittle of the law has been displaced, replaced, or in any way altered—as you'll find out when once you're fully restored and fit to plead your up-and-coming case. You may then, of course, either need to prepare or else want to prepare your own case, because there're no judges' clerks on call up here to come up with specious arguments or otherwise hold up proceedings. Never fear, the biggest offshore law library from earth is up here in heaven. We've got every law book here from Justinian's *Codex* to *Halsbury's Laws of England* as well as *Bullen & Leake & Jacob's Precedents of Pleadings.*

'You'll love flicking through all of dear old Halsbury's thirty-one volumes once again in hard copy first edition. As we say up here in heaven, "Virtual law is no law!" despite all that fuss over Brexit and dear old Halsbury himself in thirty-one volumes being now thrice extended to ingratiate Europe into his beloved England. Well, well, that's no doubt the outcome of his terminating that holiday he once took in Nice! But if you're offered counsel, m'lud, be sure to switch from your long-accustomed legal firm (the one that's by now administering your will). Instead, like Sir Walter Raleigh, be sure to ask for Jesus Christ to plead on your behalf when you yourself come to trial.

'We've all been born premature,' continued the former court bailiff in the same hushed heavenly whisper. 'Even for the purpose of being born again, we're all still very premature,' he insinuated into m'lud's judicial ear behind a conspiratorial hand. 'We've all been through this restoration process (even Jesus Christ himself, you know) so that every slightest choice we make as to the means of our recovery is freely chosen. Keep that well in mind. That's my advice to you, m'lud, since even on reaching here, we're all still souls in transition. [Word of warning, though, m'lud, don't sit at the high table (unless first asked) when you appear for dinner.]'

'Meanwhile, you must just relax,' said Angel-Intern Clara to the chief justice (whom she recognised from having once come before his lower court in criminal sessions on a charge of shoplifting). 'If you can't sleep,' she advised His Honour, 'just count up how many times the words "Never fear!" are to be found in the Bible.

'Nevertheless, you can still sleep as long as you need or like to sleep here (although, as said before, you're not likely to sleep through the last great day of judgement). Otherwise, you can simply walk and talk, sing, dance, and play. Or else you can choose to go to college (just as Cora has chosen to do, because she never got the chance of doing that before on earth), or else (as most souls in early transit do) you can lie in bed and read, read, and read.

'So then, call up Leading-Angel Alcuin, as once librarian to the emperor Charlemagne on earth, since he's now our chief librarian in heaven. No, you don't need a phone, neither landlines, here (as you may expect), nor even the most expensive of mobiles could excel our cosmic call-up prayer service whilst in heaven. And never mind if (apart from case notes) you've never ever before been any sort of reader. Why, in the non-readers' section, we've got the biggest selection of classic comics ever collected, either on earth or in heaven. For example, in the Scots' section (remember for what they call 'a mixed legal system'), we've got all past issues of *Oor Wullie* and *The Broons*. Or else you could watch film after film after film … Maybe you're of an age to watch *Back to Bounty*, or having never been there, then to watch *Forest Gump*, or else to learn from Sergei Bondarchuk's seven-hour-long adaptation of Tolstoy's three volumes on *War and Peace*.'

'Talking more of films, it seems to me,' said Samuel One to Samuel Two (both prophet-doctors on daily call to heaven's recovery room), 'that the overwhelming force of the film, for being full in your face although providing no more than a virtual reality, has come to oust the proclamatory power of the published word.'

'On which correlative decline in the fine art of readership,' interjected Leading-Angel Dan Needham, 'no better account has been given (as reported on the power of the prophetic voice by John Irving in his *A Prayer for Owen Meany*) than by Leading-Angel Harriet Wheelwright on her drawing the line at television.

'When thus deprived of grist to the reader's brain, films flourish, but books are remaindered, and even libraries begin to languish. The brain and the book are two of a kind, but the film relies alone on the heart (no less deprived than is the brain today of grist to the mill) and so feels free to manipulate the raw emotions. Without books, the human brain is becoming more and more depleted of serious thought. What then will happen to the book? It's the book that sustains the brain no less than the brain sustains the book.'

'Do you mean the Bible book?' boldly interrupted Samuel Two, who, for being a listener rather than a communicator, tended more towards thoughtful taciturnity than his colleague Samuel One. [The Quiet Souls, known familiarly now as the Backbenchers in heaven, were so often underestimated when amongst the Rowdy Souls on earth.] Yet all the while, Samuel Two still busily computed the veracity of what he heard, whether direct from earth or as heard in heaven. He did so according to a sideways scrolling system of truth tables he had devised, which would often stretch round and round earth's globe. Numeracy, rather than literacy, was Samuel Two's forte.

'No, no, I mean not just the Bible but also absolutely every other book,' snapped back Samuel One. 'You're not concentrating on reconceptualising my innermost thought,' he admonished Samuel Two. 'I mean that the power of every book, when faced by the auto-envisaging process of film, has fallen into desuetude. Well, yes, I know, I know … as the numerist you are and not a verbalist, you may never have heard of desuetude. But then again, why should I tell you what it means, since, as for any prophetic intern like yourself, you've been empowered for so long to conceive the inconceivable?

'So then, Samuel Two, put your truth accountancy at rest in trying to evaluate the contingency of what I'm saying. Instead of trying to perfect the 642 arguable aspects of numerical precision, both face up to and proclaim the plain truth that unless something near miraculous is done, all books on earth are in danger of dying from desuetude. They're being driven first to distraction and then to exhaustion, if you prefer that to desuetude, by the prevailing forcefulness of so often thoughtless and utterly mindless film. I know you scroll through truth tables, and that may well be your mission for all eternity, but have you never scrolled through all the world's television channels of an evening only to give up on finding any film worth watching?

'That's right, Samuel Two, it's just as you say, where even in medicine, *desuetude* simply means "use it or lose it". But primarily, it's a legal term denoting the state of dysfunction induced by fair wear and tear. No less than in medicine, it denotes the lack of bodily or mindful exertion required to keep both body and mind alive. And yes, now that you mention it, the problem of desuetude may well apply to the living Word of the Bible, because on earth right now, the Bible, as any well-worn book, is rapidly losing each and every one of its earthly bindings. Haven't you read the latest splash headline in *The Underground Daily Times*? The Counterfeit Command has resolved that each last earthly binding of the Bible to earth shall be cut, severed, and cauterised beyond all possibility of reconnection!

'So then, you're right enough, young Samuel Two. This proposition is neither self-referentially false nor self-referentially true but instead necessarily contingent. Well then, young fella, m'lud, what in heaven's name are we going to do about it? Not the same as down in the lower depths of hell, surely, where they're always cooking the books!

'Look at any library this way, Samuel Two, even although numeracy and not literacy is still your biggest forte. And if you can't hear what I'm telling you, then listen to Leading-Angel Alcuin, who is this heaven's chief treasurer of books. There's not always been a battle of the books, since the Koran only took to the offensive long after the Bible (with sixty-six books by forty or so different authors) had been both historically established and archeologically confirmed. In any case, the provenance of proclamation most nearly always looks for hard copy substantiation not only for sustenance and maintenance but also for ontological provenance and teleological fulfilment. Big words, sure, that's exactly why there are writing prophets—to whom one day it may be your angelic job not only to tell them what to say but also to tell them what to write.

'Long before God called this world into being—that God whom some souls even in recovery still call Yahweh or others Allah or yet others by as many different names as they bespeak their will to worship—the fatherhood of the one and only true God (although in the plural Elohim) would be the only coherent testament, in the face of outrageous human fortune, to the continuing love and kindness of this world's creator, however named. Yes, yes, I know that down on earth, fatherhood's no longer in fashion, but what else would you expect of a rapidly dying world? First contraception, then abortion, now euthanasia — and next it will be artificial insemination to cut down on the surplus population of needless fathers by which household peace-making and domestic peacekeeping can be united.

'All the same, this same loving provenance by which God so loved the world that on its behalf, he sacrificed his one and only Son, Jesus Christ, has been so sadly undercut—traduced, if you only knew what that word meant—by the terrifying triteness and unsustainability of human vision. And the result of mankind's failing vision (especially innermost vision) is that in the face of film's flickering flashback, flickering fast forward … and in general as determined by the transient flick, flick, flickering given over to superficial news, views, and the blues, then not only is the film foundering—but it's also taking down the book. Why, this is increasingly so for the lack of our 20/20 vision all around, and far more of a loss to every higher level of prophetic or artistic vision. Nowadays, everybody goes to church to watch the widest screen—but more rarely to read for oneself the underlying book

'Look on it this way—a book (any good book) is a boat (a cultural ark against all the storms of life, if you like) for which libraries (like churches) once provided harbours and secure safe-havens. Why, even if your best book were really a boat, and after a lifetime of film-going you could still clearly envision your boat to be sailing the storms of life, then let's face it, you'd have to admit this boat of yours to be now rapidly sinking!

'Whereas words are the key to thought, more and more films (although not by any means all films) are in the process of paving the way … flick … flick … flick … to thoughtlessness! Without books, literacy is on the way out, and without literacy, thoughtfulness is on the way out. And then when books, literacy, and thoughtfulness are all on the way out, then thoughtlessness is bound to be on the way in.'

'I can't believe all that!' said Samuel Two. 'But, as you say, whether worshipped as Yahweh or Allah or Jehovah or Jesus (and apart from the level of worship which is critical), there are as many different names for the one god of all things as there have been as many different gods once named for each individual thing. That's a matter of class calculus in logic no less than are both the Euclidean geometry and the non-Euclidian geometry that differentially exist in mathematics. And if you're going to become that much of an old-fashioned Unitarian, Samuel One, then what are you going to make of both Newtonian as well as of quantum physics as bedfellows? Look around. You'll find plenty examples of each bedding down together in this one-size-fits-all recovery room.' [Although the Quiet Ones, known in heaven as either the Backroom Boys or the Backbenchers, might have been given little enough to say, they were no less amongst those who visualise and envisage the dynamics of deep thinking.]

'Besides the dynamics of deep thinking, and even although faith comes by hearing,' Samuel Two continued, 'then surely vision further empowers the hearing! On earth, even with access to all four of the ten postulated dimensions, you'll never perceive more than two-fifths of the absolute truth. The issue for earth is one of matching form to function, and in turn, that more difficult match of the known to the unknown requires prophetic vision.'

'Whose vision?' probed Samuel One.

'Well, whoever wrote the book from which faith comes by hearing!' countered Samuel Two. 'Never mind for the moment whether book or film, or whether on earth or in heaven, but isn't it better to have those eyes that see as well as those ears that hear and so then, on both counts of sensory perception, to aim far beyond the earthly measure of only 20/20 vision?'

[Well again, what do you readers think—since that timeless question would be left hanging in timelessness by both prophet-doctors, Samuel One and Samuel Two, by their free-willed decision to leave every such deep epistemological question to its timely fruition in heaven]. Meanwhile, on their leaving the recovery room, Angel-Novice Cora, together with her Buddy-Angel Clara, would find themselves seconded from bibliographic administration (since volunteer librarians were very much a service provided to heaven's recovery room) on to a committee called by the Supreme Command to hold issue on whether to publish a forthcoming book (perhaps you've already telepathically heard of it) called *The Soul-Catcher.*

Cora had already thought twice (supra, supra) before raising a point of order at the opening of this meeting called by the whole heavenly host to air the issue. As things turned out, she was very glad she hadn't raised it. Her innermost thoughts might already be patent to all, because thought and speech were coterminous in heaven, but at least she wouldn't have to swallow her spoken words from off the written record.

The committee had been called together to confer on the substantive content for this much-needed handbook (or should it be sourcebook) on heavenly soul-catching. As yet, however, poor Cora couldn't get her head round the book's opening quotation from some surely irrelevant and perhaps even scurrilous verse on the zoological order of the *Siphonaptera*. The verse had been written by some obviously very minor poet named Augustus De Morgan.

'What's the point of proffering flea-ridden poetry on this highly sanctified subject of soul-catching?' she would have asked. 'And in any case, who is this Augustus De Morgan?' She felt she needed to know. 'From his name, he sounds more of a pirate than a poet! What then has he got to do with our decision whether or not to publish *The Soul-Catcher*—and if that title, then whether or not with a hyphen?'

As Cora now so clearly realised from the point of order she had intended to raise, although then all the while casually continuing to preen her newly fledged feathers and demonstrate her youthfully angelic wingspread (some secondary sources of this report substitute *wingspan* for *wingspread*), she had come perilously close (as might any novice) to committing another monstrously big boo-boo! *Yet God is so gracious,* she thought, whilst then quietly crossing and enfolding her wings. Had she not briefly glanced towards the convenor before raising her intended point of order, she would not have seen the convenor's name tag boldly proclaiming, 'Leading-Angel Augustus De Morgan'!

'Told you so!' said Samuel Two to Samuel One, nudging him playfully. 'What we need, even up here in heaven, is far beyond what humans perceive to be the maximum level for themselves of 20/20 vision. Without the prophetic vision encouraged by us of themselves, mortals must find themselves a lot lower in the heavenly scheme of things than are we angels! No wonder that their recovery period is so much longer than that of even the fallen angels.'

'Shh!' said Samuel One to Samuel Two. 'You risk muddying the current of both once unreformed thought and not yet entirely informed thought!'

As for Augustus himself, as the committee's convenor, he seemed highly amused. *Although many prophets speak darkly, all angels speak openly and frankly, but Cora speaks more frankly than most,* he, as the convenor, thought whilst smiling just as openly towards Cora as he did chuckle inwardly to himself. 'The fact that thought and utterance are coterminous concepts in heaven prevents long-windedness and, as once we would have said on earth, "cuts to the chase". Well, I guess that puts the onus on me,' continued the convenor, 'just as it lies on any author to explain himself!' Augustus chortled, holding up his once human genome card showing his former college calling to be that of logician and mathematician.

'Now, as we all know, it's an occupational hazard of long-retired teachers, preachers, and prophets to go on teaching, preaching, and prophesising perhaps long after their best-before date of active engagement has expired. Having been long ago retired from earth as an academic, it looked to most of the much younger members of the committee that from Augustus, we were in for a very long but surely needless lecture on the basics of soul-catching.'

Needless to everyone else perhaps, thought Leading-Angel Neil, *but never so to any long-ago retired academic.* At the subliminal transmission of this unvoiced (yet somewhat less than heavenly) thought, Augustus, with one bushy eyebrow raised well above the other, then turned slowly round to look rather quizzically at Neil.

But he's got quite a melliferous voice for an old fella, thought Neil, taking a second sight on what he had first thought. *And since he's thinking no faster than he's talking, it's a bonus to get the synchronous conjunction of both outer linguistic utterance and innermost mental conceptualisation. After all, you can read a person's mind, and you can read a person's lips. But they're not always precisely synchronised, not always completely congruent, and as so often on earth (and always so much worse in hell), each can be in outright conflict. Besides, it's considered good manners to voice your thoughts when in heaven—and that too is very different from more bluntly speaking your mind on earth.*

'So then, with the icebreaker out of the way, let's get serious enough to take ourselves seriously!' continued Augustus. 'For being only convenor of this committee, I'm dependent on you members to come up with your deepest of thoughts. This is your committee, not mine. And I know that in my saying that, you'll be thinking I'm passing the buck—just as deep down in hell they'll be thinking to congratulate themselves to have made me light the fuse of a bomb.'

'Most people on earth don't take themselves seriously because they've never been brought up to take themselves seriously.' *Thank you for that, Samuel One.* 'They've been brought up sometimes by inexperienced parents and hard-worked teachers, sometimes also by wayward priests and soft-soaping politicians, and even when brought before the most refined of judges in (at least the upper) courts, and otherwise compelled to obey the rough and ready rules and compendious regulations made by strangely idyllic legislators, it is then only to see themselves as mere appendages to an increasingly impersonal and mechanistic world. Instead of being brought up as one would hope wisely in their early life, their little souls have been put down (a statistical measure) more than once too often.' *Thank you for that, Samuel Two.* 'They have become the equivalent of displaced persons.' *Well, certainly on earth as much as that and, in some cases, far more than that. Thank you, Clara.*

Neil hoped that this introduction to the basics of soul-catching (a team sport if there ever was on) wasn't going to develop into one of heaven's infrequent yet sometimes very telling diatribes against humanity. What did Cora mean by her *not saying* (yet *still thinking*) that De Morgan sounded more like the name of a pirate than a poet? The brief look Neil then took around the committee members disclosed no obvious representative or known dignitary from the Counterfeit Command. That was odd, because whether covert or overt, as the Counterfeit Command liked to boast of itself in covering all contingencies, that false command disclosed of itself no coverage—no, not even in the usually dissident press gallery. Was there not anyone there, perhaps in top hat and tails (with an undercover plum in his mouth), representing *The Underground Daily Times?*

Who exactly was this De Morgan in the heavenly scheme of things? Another de Mandeville (that one who had caused such an uproar with his doggerel verse on *The Grumbling Hive*)? As Satan himself had confessed of himself before the council of heaven (recorded verbatim in the book of Job), he was prone to walk the universe, both forwards to and fro as well as backwards fro and to, as if to give the impression to everyone, everywhere, and by now even at every station of the cross, that he, Satan, himself was the father of all things and not instead, the father of all lies.

Augustus smiled. *You had to hand it to him,* thought Neil. *For an old fella who had spent all his earthly life in academia (where grumpiness can become even more endemic than academic), De Morgan could surely keep his cool! You can talk all you like about brainstorming on earth,* thought Neil (just as on this subject in action, read again the book of Job), *'but brainstorming there on earth is not a patch on brainstorming in heaven.*

Here in heaven is where you don't need to say what you think because what you think is already transmitted as if on a wall-to-wall magic carpet—technically speaking, the telepathic *samolyot* (as the ancients called it) of collectively interactive thought. Still, as said before, it's always considered good manners in heaven to front up to whatever one is thinking; and one does that by personally taking the trouble to voice one's even most innermost thoughts. What a brouhaha that would cause on earth (to bring about surely there a living hell), but then this is heaven!

During all this auto-interactive brainstorming (together with much more than could ever be recorded verbatim in this report), Augustus, as convenor of the committee, had gone soul-gathering amongst the various committee members as to their best means of harmonising, reconciling, and integrating the ever-growing tapestry of their mutually interactive thought. What he brought forth as convenor was by no means like any personally didactic lecture, sermon, speech, or oration as given individually from each committee member on earth who would frequently grandstand no more than on his or her own views.

This process of brainstorming in heaven (when based on *The Art and Practice of the Learning Organization* already mentioned) is particularly apt (as exemplified by Plato's *Dialogues*) for the writing or publishing of any book. Figuratively speaking, this process of harvesting thought is more akin to congregational carpet weaving. Earthlings, apart from those few exceptions such as Socrates (with his motherly maieutic) have yet to learn the difference on the one hand between their generally conflictive discussion (permeating and disrupting parliaments, legislatures, churches, colleges, and schools) and on the other hand their focussing on and following one and the same communicative flow of thought.

'As displaced persons from this so-called *Fifth Discipline* (although many have been brought up by parents and teachers to deny it), most persons on earth yearn inwardly for a life of their own.' *Thank you, Eli,* acknowledged Augustus. 'But by the time of this developed awareness, they've been programmed not to take themselves too seriously.' Augustus thanked Matthew.

'They've been taught to keep to their place, but unhappily for them, that's not always the place in which they can learn to be their own person but only the place (it may even be a transit camp) in which other people have gratuitously made space for them. And as often what little space can be given leaves the givers only less space, less room, and less time which the transients need to utilise the same small space already given.' [Excursus 2: 'Since by now this is the committee consensus, so long as we're following the same direction of travel, we'll leave aside the need for personal credits,' decided Leading-Angel Augustus De Morgan.]

'As we all know from the relatively recent concept of space-time, space by itself is of little consequence to humans. Parents to their offspring and teachers to their students give more and more space (a mistaken view of freedom) but instead give less and less time. More and more people thus occupy less and less space, yet at the same time (which is shrinking fast from the already miniscule space accorded to the present), this is the least measure of time in which fewer and fewer people are able to choose for themselves to occupy and utilise the space which they have been already given. Space without time is worthless to humans. It's only by spending time with anyone (together with all else that the profitable spending of time entails) that space becomes a place in the mind of any growing person. One's rightful place, as we all know from our own time spent on earth, is very precious to the person—and so in space-time is every bit as precious to the person as rightful time.

'Without finding one's own true place, every displaced person becomes at best a seeker, a pilgrim, or a serious traveller—but in these days, more often just a tourist in search of novelty, a vagrant in search of a job, a wanderer in search of some place in which to settle, and at worst, an émigré or refugee. As refugees, displaced people may often be sent right back to wherever it was they first came from. If worst comes to worst, which can also happen to the locals, their place is to sleep on the streets, to serve prison sentences, and to tweet and text without being literate enough to read and write.' ['Quite right,' said Augustus, congratulating everyone explicitly in precious words and not just by personal nods and smiles on having got the committee well underway.]

'Eventually, this highly mechanised, technologically savvy, yet increasingly impersonal world breaks down or wears out (this has all happened to the concept of civilisation many times before). The breakdown leaves thousands upon thousands of refugees without any place to go (other than some urban or suburban desert ironically called a transit camp), which even there, no refugee (unless so programmed by his or her basic needs) would ever think to call their own place, far less to consider it forever their home. Once again, this legally inflicted desuetude (here indicating the unforeseen consequences of having too many unworkable rules) has reduced rainforests to extinction and whole cities to exhaustion.

'The last times within living memory when this whole wide world (by now a flat-earthed cliché imported extravagantly from cyberspace) reached such levels of near exhaustion was immediately before World War I and, then again, immediately before World War II.' [Uncle Augie had fought in the spirit through both world wars, so like any old soldier, he was apt, as most lecturers were, to resort to his own war stories.] 'From the historical point of view, however, all such wars to end all war (whether avoidable or not) even when intended to do no more than to keep the peace (whatever the friendly fire, collateral damage, or unexpected consequences experienced) make of this no more than human twaddle.'

'Human twaddle'—the phrase struck Neil like a slap from some unseen teacher to the back of a small boy's head! Where, when, and for what slight misdemeanour had he heard, felt, and somehow survived that startlingly unforeseen and most miserable experience of his schooldays (kindy, primer, college, and even varsity) more than once before? In thinking himself to have got to heaven, he assumed he had long got over the misery of his schooldays on earth. In space-time, the cosmic distance between heaven and earth was greater than between heaven and anywhere else (except, of course, the distance between heaven and hell), but those cosmic distances were measured solely in space, which possibly was why so many souls needed all eternity in heaven to recover from their schooldays.

Possibly, and once again on the score of his schooling, Neil thought himself to be the exception proving the rule. Most souls that got to heaven (as if flying through life on a magic carpet) testified to their schooldays having been the happiest days of their life. Their heavenly destiny seemed assured from their very first day at school. Neil's first day at school had been spent looking after his gasmask so that he could get to heaven; and when, at the end of his long life, he finally got to heaven, he there woke up to find himself wearing his by then long-lost gasmask.

On this score, sometimes Neil began to feel that instead of getting into heaven (to which place he had never striven), he had been short-circuited back again to the headmaster's study in his own private hell. All his colleague angels went to their school reunions with the utmost of delight, upheld their former teachers without the least reserve, acted as unseen cheerleaders for every continuing sports fixture at their former schools, and just as miraculously, still slept soundly at nights! 'Feeling out of place on earth is bad enough,' mused Neil, 'but who, apart from Satan himself, could survive his feeling out of place in heaven?' *Oh, oh,* thought Neil, who suddenly felt very much out of place, as if he had yet an awful (but why not awe-full) lot to learn!

'Overcoming this difficulty'—[*What difficulty?* wondered Neil]—'is never insurmountable,' Neil heard Augustus say, and Neil then realised that instead of brainstorming, he, Neil, had been caught brain-napping. With a smile towards Neil, Augustus went on to 'admit that the difficulty of finding one's own privileged place on earth to pursue and investigate the difficulty of there being only limited space and not just fighting with or against others for a place in the sun is a tall order. What it takes'—[here, for some reason, Neil thought of a flea circus]—'to overcome such difficulties is made particularly difficult after a life of living in the excessively confrontational and so incredibly unstable place that others have made for you and everyone else.' [Neil thought here again of this same flea circus.] 'And this more often happens unwittingly than intentionally, by those others arranging things to suit only themselves.'[*The fallacy of unchecked upper management,* thought Neil of the long years when employed on earth, although still caught brain-napping.]

'This is [*What is?* wondered Neil, whether *unchecked upper management, the struggle for limited resouces, or fighting for a place in the sun, or perhaps ambiguously all three contributed to*] the first flea-bitten and subsequently typhus-ridden warring context'—(*Ra-ra-ra,* thought Neil, little realising that he was calling on the sun god)—'which is most likely to surpass any mere struggle for personal survival (however scientifically refined). In legal terms of an eye for an eye and a tooth for a tooth (or *lex talionis,* as one of those hidden-in-Latin school mottoes which embalm most institutions of higher education so declares), the immediate outcome (even amongst nations) is reversion to the primitive blood feud, before finally being superseded by the dog-eat-dog dilemma of outright terrorism and total war.'

Shit! thought Neil, although still in good company with both St Paul and Martin Luther for saying so—although the latter less emphatic for still awaiting formal recognition, at least on earth, of his sainthood. Of course, for being tempted to build an ivory tower (as did the true medieval church by establishing the falsely-mediaeval universities), the church encountered and brought down upon itself that same intellectual tide of modernist filth and shit (as the writer Flaubert wrote commiseratively in a letter to the writer Turgenev) which threatened to undermine both the gleaming spires and the ivory towers and so went on to undermine first the parental church and then its orphaned quibbling scholars and their quisling scientific offspring. There again, all writers are monsters (at least to non-writers), so who can trust Flaubert in his writing to Turgenev if not only those other writers who have learnt to know what it feels like to be seen as some sort of monster by readers and reviewers?

We're still in the best of company, however, with those who still call a spade a spade, thought Neil, *whether in their writing up ninety-five theses on the door of Wittenberg's Castle Church (although Luther must then have been as much out of his mind as so many still say also of the long-awaited Christ was for carrying his cross as far as would lead to his crucifixion). Yes, from Plato's Socrates to Turgenev's Bazarov and beyond we are privileged to live in the company of those whom the world has dismissed and despised for being so-called superfluous men. And we're still in the best of company when with any spade (for still being called a spade) we're busily shovelling away the same intellectual tide of shit which threatens to bring down both gleaming spires and ivory towers. Not much likely now a sainthood for Martin Luther,* thought Neil.

'Time's long moved on (far on) since both the Protestant and Catholic Reformations (with nothing much to show for it), and as for the Russian (yet to come) as distinct from the Greek Orthodox (which stood firm against the perceived idolatry of the Russian), there's even less likelihood of Lev-Leo Tolstoy's excommunication being rescinded any time soon whether by the professedly Orthodox in Kiev or by the professedly Orthodox in Moscow.'

As for any earthly institution (which, for lack of purposeful action, always becomes case-hardened), the ramifications for the church within the church tend to become always more important to the church than those same ramifications are for those outside of the church. As with every institution, especially when leaning always heavily towards a stable-state or steady-state institutional position, the church, as depicted by a boat to signify a place of refuge against the outer storms of life, is prone to be against anyone who rocks the boat—never mind anyone who might dream of ever walking on the surrounding water. Meanwhile, wisdom walks the streets, which, with today's ever-rising sea levels, are soon to suffer the biggest ever deluge since the flood.

In layman's terms (since there are no more than a very few physicist believers as against those who are believing physicists), of which there are no more than two, arguably three—stable, unstable, and neutral—states of equilibrium. A fourth, metastable equilibrium—which is by far the most exciting sort of equilibrium—tends to be denied by its steady-state opponents for being any sort of equilibrium at all. Metastatic equilibrium relies on the excited state of an atom (for argument's sake), although presumably in systems theory, it could be no more than that of a stray particle (of which there are more than a few of these in almost every viable church group or congregation) or, with very many more similarly stray particles, for their contributing to the excited (yet unstable) state of an entire system. Most churches have a lifetime (short or long), and their longevity is related to the excited state of their individual atoms, but a large number of excited atoms tend to accumulate only under a dynamic leadership (which may or may not always share the same longevity).

Most churches pride themselves these days on being steady state, looking only to longevity rather than productivity, so the dynamics of any church society are always further stabilised (sometimes to the point of irredeemable destruction) by the apparently safe option of fraternising with the profane and secular arm of any state-established religion (which could hardly then also live up to its full potential for being the incorruptible body of Christ). As for us angels, we are either like fighter aircraft (highly dynamic and so infinitely correctible to changing conditions) or else immensely stable, like trainers designed for and suited to novice angels for steady-state training conditions. All angels need to know their aeronautics (especially for soul-catching), but so also do churches (even if no more than to realise and maintain their potential for soul-training future generations for the very different times in which they shall live and still spiritually function).

A fortress citadel, even for an institution as dynamic as the Salvation Army, always poses problems in any era where the secular arm of the state is changing faster (whether in the ascendant or descendant) than is the spiritual arm of the church. Strange paradoxes accrue (as so they should to overly introspective and steady-state churches) by their oversight of literary, scientific, and anthropological expressions of concern, affecting their increasingly inward and entrenched oversight of the very signs which they should be reading regarding their own times in which they live and work.

Not only on historic but also on evangelical grounds, those filmic, stage, and musical reproductions (say, of Lev-Leo Tolstoy's *War and Peace*, Victor Hugo's *Les Misérables*, and Rice and Webber's *Joseph and the Amazing Technicolor Dreamcoat*) have come pretty close to toppling some of the so-called minor and now little-read prophets right out of the Bible. Maybe it's not before time to revisit the biblical canon, provided any such canon is not merely picked (although only a few of the picked—and fewer still of the pickled—are always chosen) for being redone by some fully paid-up member of the clergy.

King James (that so-called wisest fool in Christendom) did quite a magnificent job with his no-longer-regarded (and some now say retarded) Authorised Version.

In any case, are there any clergy here in heaven? Neil blithely wondered. 'They couldn't very well be blamed for avoiding what must surely be for them a busman's holiday! Sometimes the clergy get so close to God for the sake of others that they don't seem to see and hear him for themselves. Well, that's the preacher's dilemma, the teacher's dilemma, and the prophet's dilemma—the occupational hazard shared by all the professions. It's the same paradox by which at the grass-roots level, it's always the cobbler's household which turns out to be the worst shod. Please pardon the paradox, but for all the work of the clergy being done on earth, it wouldn't seem there's much room, far less free space, left for the clergy in heaven.

'Likewise, there's so much church politics unbelievably behind church history, whether arguing over the minutiae of icons and idolatry, over the minutiae of Quakerism and Methodism, or even over the minutiae of Catholicism and Protestantism (never mind the oldest bogey of Pentecostalism) that the future of the clergy seems increasingly bleak. That much of church politics hidden behind church history must be enough to give the church universal the creeps. Let's hope that the authorship of *The Soul-Catcher* won't be committed to any member of the clergy. If it looks like that, then committing it to the cautious hand of some completely unknown lay preacher might reach some sort of a compromise between the Vatican and ... and ... whoever has the effrontery (apart from Jesus Christ himself) to oppose his own vicar.

'Let's begin'—[*Perhaps begin again,* wondered Neil]—'by facing up to this difficulty right now!' reiterated Augustus. *What difficulty?* again wondered Neil, as Augustus took up once more on the committee's task of further advancing their spontaneously syncretic discussion. 'Perhaps the life of the warring human is not much different, in this very limited respect, from the life of the biting flea,' Neil suggested.

'Biting and warring are most assuredly related to biological functions,' postulated Angel-Apostolic Mungo of the warlike Celtic faction (whose priests once went into front-line battle against upstart

Romans and watered-down Proto-Anglicans). 'Perhaps if we could cure the human psyche of the backbiting that goes on amongst humans in peacetime (just as many secular psychologists manage to relieve their patients of all prayerful needs even in wartime), then we apostolic angels could cure humans of waging war for all time. That seems a far more sensible proposition than to think of waging some great war to end all war, since any great war to end all wars is just as likely to end all humans.'

'Hold on a moment there,' queried Junior-Angel Eli (aged nine earth years) with sudden insight. 'Could this dog-eat-dog dilemma demonstrated by humans when engaged in terrorism and total warfare be no more than an extreme variant of the flea-bitten-flea dilemma? In the absence of a common enemy, backbiting seems to come quite naturally to humans, and this as much in peacetime as at any other time. What we have described more directly, although in less loaded terms, is much the same lifestyle equation as our dear friend, the poet Augustus, relates to us more allegorically (that's to say, figuratively) by his hard-bitten homily (that's something that we should take to heart) on the lifestyle of the flea.'

'To resolve this difficulty, as with any apparently perennial problem identified with anger and violence or with evil and sin or with morality and metaphysics, is in itself difficult,' the meeting concluded, 'because it requires rectifying an injustice of such long standing. In this case, resolution entails going back at least to the time in which Abraham whetted his knife to sacrifice his younger son Isaac. It thus has to deal with a problem which has become deeply ingrained within the entire human race (especially for younger sons)—although hopefully no deeper (although see here Ivan Turgenev's novel on *Fathers and Sons* and Phillipa Gregory's novel entitled *Fallen Skies*) than for being mankind's seemingly innate propensity for backbiting.'

II
Towards Resolution

'Whoever seeks solely to save his or her own life,' said
Jesus, 'is as likely to lose it, but whoever is prepared

to give his or her life for my sake is most certainly assured of saving it.'

The Gospel of Matthew (paraphrased)

Well then, let's review the problematic outcome so far. Make no mistake, when talking about saving life (overtaken on earth by the so-called struggle for survival), we're really talking about saving souls. If you don't see that, then look for a closer encounter with your own ego, which you might find hard to do, for every ego hides behind a thousand and one alter egos. Strip to the soul, then, as if when bathing *po-ruskii* (both sexes and all ages, when only in the altogether, just as the Russians do when breaking the ice at each New Year on the Moscow River)! ['What did we tell you,' muttered Mungo and Ninian together, 'of this book's preface in serving as an icebreaker for AD 2020?']

This difficulty of self-identification is one reason why psychoanalysis exists in so many different shapes and forms, each itself fast-changing to suit what every psychologist (whether Socratic, Christian, or otherwise) would hope to encourage for being everyone's fast-maturing soul or psyche. So then, from psychoanalytic jurisprudence in the collective (for which see Carl Jung) back to the purely personal (for which see Sigmund Freud) then even if only when caught by the tail, the psyche is here on earth to learn (which may take as long as a lifetime) by which means to capture the somewhat dissociated and elusive id (standing for one's own still rapidly maturing and therefore fast-changing individual identity).

Intimately related to this search for individual identity (whether collectively of nations or individually of persons) is the problem (whether nationally or personally) of world security. The world problem of national security (both personal and collective), now capable of resolution only by transnational means, relies on the never-ending compilation and collation of small and often apparently insignificant items of data. These are to be shared amongst the participative members of various security forces wherever stationed.

So far, so good, as it seems to a sorely stretched mankind— although disasters, both big and small (9/11 in New York and 3/15 in Christchurch), are two a penny. Without knowing Jesus, and for being thus left destitute with nothing to lose, what other way could any poor mortal see of expressing his or her psychopathic feelings than to resort to this level of lawlessness giving rise to those many acts of suicidal terrorism by now gone feral? With every passing day, this question becomes more and more critical, since by such short-term transnational measures as these which do sorely stretch mankind, mortals doom themselves to their own freely chosen yet long-term outcome.

The heavenly kingdom's problem of security is in some ways very much the same as that of security on earth—since for more than the last two thousand years, the kingdom of heaven has been progressively promoting its presence on earth. Likewise also capable of resolution, although reinforced by a supranational means rather than relying solely on a transnational means, resolving this problem of heavenly security also depends on the never-ending collection, compilation, and collation of small (apparently minimalist) data to be shared, most often by prophetic insight, amongst the participative members of heaven's security forces wherever stationed.

The big difference between the short-term mortal process of dispute resolution (as if law were enough by itself to defeat lawlessness) and the long-term heavenly resolution process (by which lawlessness remains vulnerable to the faith factor) lies in the strength with which heaven alone has by far the greatest means (of any cosmic force) with which to tackle the underlying and unresolved conflict that gives rise to human lawlessness. Because this heavenly resolution process relies on the present way in which human beings now see things only as they seem to be, you can call this process one of psychoanalytic jurisprudence if you like, or else you can call it theological jurisprudence if you consider it according to the way that human beings were first made to see things as they really once were, but possibly now are no longer capable of seeing them (by reason of humanity's either apathetic lassitude or antagonistic aptitude).

Once again, the faith factor—which for mortals invariably entails a cost factor—needs to be employed here by humans to the fullest sacrificial measure. Otherwise for them, nothing can be revived, restored, and renewed to that promised position of such clarity that faith-filled humans will marvel (as in all innocence they have never done before) at the recreated *miraculousness*—a recently abstracted noun still overlooked even by the *OED*—of all creation.

Quite frankly, it's near to a logical impossiblity for mere mortals to give a head's up to their own so limited conception of God's most miraculous creation. For most humans the concept of their own *recreation* (as their casual misuse of that word now indicates) supplants for what they once conceived of divinely inspired creativity. What they now so indulgently seek by way of their own selfishly motivated recreation becomes a far more tempting substitute for their God-given calling to be no more than the instruments of his creativity. Their mistake is to think its both perfectly possible and eminently valid for themselves to supplant, usurp, and take over from God what is essentially his very own deistic process of creation. And if this essential distinction between the divine creator above and the mortal maker below doesn't make any sense in the saying, then read the metaphysical explanation given to the distinction by Dorothy A. Sayers in her divinely inspired *Mind of the Maker.*

Look on it this way: both a spanking new heaven and a spanking new earth are by now far harder things for humans even to imagine far less than to help achieve (never mind by thinking themselves single-handedly to resolve the world-problematique). This is particularly so since even to a wayward child a righteously administered spank has now been outlawed extensively on earth—a legislative mischief done strategically by Counterfeit Command to spoil the child—and so to mislead successive generations of children into giving their lives over to a tedious eternity of superficially unproductive recreation.

Earthlings are seriously all at sea in their conceiving of heaven— for example—as a paradise of delights, a happy hunting ground, or a little children's playground. They are so much a fallen people that, apart from their own sentimentally soporific longing for a settled home, they have no remembrance of the privileged security held out to them by their residence in Eden. Nevertheless, the Garden of Eden was never ever the paradise which humans later attributed to it—and which in any case they sacrificed by their own downfall in eating disobediently from the tree of knowledge.

So then (although not to change the subject of this world's increasing need for security) what about this need as required for the projected publication of *The Soul-Catcher*? The often tedious task of every security group so engaged in the provision of security (whether in heaven or on earth) as often relates to no more than the collection, compilation, and collation of what so often appears to be no more than the most trivial and insignificant of everyday data. When once collated, this data will be shared amongst the participative members of the group in the hope that their contributions will collectively integrate to provide a coherent, cogent, and comprehensive view of what action needs be taken. Of course, there are obvious issues of personal privacy and collective privacy involved. These issues beg a very serious question: are you prepared to assuage the injustice of everyone else (both believers and unbelievers and whether friends or foes) in order to resolve your own issues of injustice?

Any such task poses a perilous prospect. Then you too, like Moses, must open your eyes to look for your own equivalent of the strategic bush that burnt so brightly and to look also for your own tactical equivalent of the sacrificial lamb, which, for both Abraham and Isaac as well as for all the rest of us, was then caught fast in the adjoining thicket.

Like Elijah, it may be a fiery chariot instead of a burning bush which appears to the spiritly curious rather than some more every day but just as powerful sign. But like all signs and portents, however much related to their own time and place, these are also indexed for recognition intimately to whosoever takes the trouble to seek them out. Then you too, by reading and responding to those signs, will be following the way of the risen Christ so that signs and portents shall surely follow you. But first of all, you must find out who it is that you were really made to be and meant to be, which is something that you cannot find out by yourself but instead only by learning how to take yourself every bit as seriously as Jesus Christ so seriously takes you. Got that message—you're looking for yourself as a mirror image of the risen Christ; and nothing less than that will do!

The process of setting aright any wrong, especially when that wrong is so long established, is one of the most difficult issues of jurisprudence that any jurist knows. There is such a thing as poetic justice however, and without that sense of the poetic (akin to wisdom), there is no point to ascribing oneself to the search for justice (whether

1

psychological, sociological, or theological). This is something which the great jurist Solomon (anticipating the greater jurisprudence of Jesus Christ by his own experiential testimony given in the book of Ecclesiastes) also knows well. So then, to appreciate the hidden depth of De Morgan's seriousness on the lifestyle of fleas, let's consider his poem even still more seriously. As every wise scholar knows, there is only one way of dealing with difficulty, and that is going deeper and deeper into the difficulty until one sees the light shining behind, beyond, and even through from what by then is often the superficially paper-thin and rapidly dissolving difficulty.

So then, would you credit this prophetic poem (view it as a high-wire balancing act) for describing most accurately the celestial order of all things—whether in heaven, on earth, under the sun, within the universe, or throughout the cosmos? If you feel it apt to do so, you are, of course, crediting a monocular or one-eyed cosmic view (irrespective of whether calling it heavenly, earthly, hellish, or anything else) as perhaps you and other short-sighted or perversely determined humans may accredit it to your own single-minded concept of reality. If not fixated on the functionality of fleas, however, then perhaps you are fixated on the functionality of wealth, fame, reputation, or some other pursuit more tailor-made to suit your own individual personality. If all this sounds perplexing, then track back to the twelfth-century writer Maimonides, writing as he does for the perplexed in his *Guide for the Perplexed*.

For some people, this fixation (whether on fleas, no less than on fame and fortune) may be comically false; for others, tragically true; and for yet others, may provide for themselves (as much metaphysically as also metaphorically) an extremely accurate account of their own world view of what they pursue above and beyond anything and so also above everything else (but themselves). They may choose to keep their world view hidden, even from themselves, so that life for them is no more than a biological struggle for survival or no more than a sociological struggle for limited resources or even for life itself being no more than a wavering candle flame arbitrarily remaining alight amid the electromagnetic storms of this planet's solar wind.

On yet another view of it (since some humans try to ape either the all-seeing cherubim or else the all-doing six-winged seraphim), they may try to strengthen their own individual yet inherently pathetic and humanistic world view. They do so no less comically than tragically by aggregating or amalgamating with those holding to the same or similar monocular or one-eyed (mistakenly cosmic) view in order to enforce or compel a more collectively credible yet still only humanistic view of reality. Once, for having been sought through personal patronage, this same more collectively human impetus is now sought and maintained through promoting political correctness, enforcing standard practices, or ascribing to some collectively reinforced peer review—although all these processes can take humanity to the cringe-edge of totalitarian unreality (more on which later) rather than to confirm and reinforce the creative design of authentic reality. So then, beware—since not all those so engaged in enforcing a more collectively credible although only humanistic view of reality are able and ready to pull back from this cringe-edge of no return beyond which lies a less democratic and more totalitarian state of comparative unreality.

For those humans to whom this professionally specialist but monocular decision process, or any other one-size-fits-all envisioning process, comes as if quite naturally, the entire cosmos (of both earth and heaven as well as far beyond) eventually appears to them (although amongst their bitterest of disappointments) for being no more than a flea circus. Since every circus, even a flea circus, must have a ringmaster, however, these humans take this prestigious function upon themselves no matter how unthinkingly naive, youthfully inexperienced, or obscenely profane may be their own human thoughts and feelings. Alas, for their making the best of a bad job, this makeshift response (to make a circus or carnival out of life) becomes their first step in mistaking this world for being the best of all possible worlds!

By hiding behind fictions (whether legal, literary, scientific, religious, or otherwise), such profoundly let-down people often lose sight of all true signs and portents. They do so in favour of upholding this world's apparently unassailable facts. Thus, by such apparent profundity of thought, they so easily come to mistake proof for truth, information for knowledge, knowledge for wisdom, and eventually, the merely virtual for the ultimately real. Their whole life can be lived not in the real but instead in the surreal. All through history (for being the key to barely believable yet long-foretold prophetic outcomes), the descent of man is invariably mistaken by himself for being that of his own proudly self-determined ascent. It takes no more than common sense to tell you that (all other things being equal) the higher you climb this self-promotional ladder, then the harder you'll fall.

Once upon a time, winged cherubs (pint-sized cherubim) were all the fashion amongst human artists in their portrayal of all the saints in heaven. When pictured as surrounding the saints, somehow these childlike cherubs conveyed a sense of procreative stability to mix and match the beyond-all-time aura conveyed by every saint's iconic but very abstract halo. Even at any grass-roots village wedding level, these little cherubs would announce their appearance on invitations, if only to assert their right to appear much later whilst blowing their toy trumpets on bridal cakes. Sentimentality though all this may be, there's a history of increasingly lost sentimentality by which to explain the far greater seriousness of lost humanity.

Time has since moved on (for yes, that need be said), and fewer and fewer artists and still far fewer scientists and scholars either envision or seek to envision any of the saints, far less to assert even the false purpose of there being any winged cherubs. They were only humanly introduced (as even far worse beings were) to suggest the ongoing procreative stability of a long-lost heaven. Indeed, today's image of heaven (unless sentimentally so only imagined by wishful thinking at funerals) is one never even seen through closed-gate ramparts. Well, such a vision of today's gate-closed heaven could hardly be seen to conflict with today's corresponding vision of a wide-open gated hell!

Dear old Maimonides would put this reversal of vision simply down to the increasing lack of human imagination, but its seriousness may go far deeper than that. Its deepest, darkest demonstration in our own time may go towards our far greater loss (in comparison with Dante, Bunyan, Milton, and Goethe) of perhaps divine inspiration. Ours is a time (if any angel may be permitted to speak on behalf of the vast majority of nearly grounded humans) in which almost every form of human speech has lost its accustomed human profile, almost every form of human music has lost its accustomed metre or musical muscle, and almost every human word has lost its accustomed first meaning. In short, which seriously perturbs the heavenly host of angels very much, there are hardly any humans (as there once were) still left around. Meanwhile (that pregnant phrase again) the so-called law of entropy is fast claiming lost souls—hand-over-fist, as you humans would say!

Although the fullest extra-terrestrial measure of the heavenly kingdom (ETHK) may never have been nearer to earth than now, when viewed from earth, it seems that the distance between the two is far the greater, and not the lesser than ever before. Just possibly all these little cherubs have by now grown up, although by now the commonality on earth (apart from those voyeurs of art museums consigning them to artistic licence) would shrug them off (so too, with many another deity shrugged off) as anthropomorphisms that never were. What a lark—the biggest anthropomorphism that ever was is not God but that of man!

There's no point in our fixating on cherubs any more than our fixating on fleas or of arguing against both or either, since by means of reason alone, there is rarely enough lubrication to move the human mind. The needed faith factor (as often replaced by earthly and even sometimes demonic addictions) is missing from the motivational equation. Without the faith factor required to open any fearfully closed mind, then for lack of spiritual lubrication there's no moving forward—no, not for achieving anything of worth on any level. And for lack of lubrication (whether motivational, inspirational, or even just mechanical) then everyone's heavenly calling degenerates into a daily grind.

No matter how scholarly or scientific or businesslike any human may be, nevertheless for lack of minimalistic faith, that deprived human soul (whose only possible soul-food is faith) soon acquires the torpor of a cold fish. It is by such means that for many dead and dying souls, following Christ is deemed a lost cause. This comes about not for the lack of any good and sufficient reason but rather for the lack of whatever minimalistic level of faith would allow them to look for any reason. However minimalistic the level of faith required, the faith factor is the release factor by which to open doors and open minds in going through one's daily life on earth.

As the playwright Shakespeare (you'll have heard of him) says of every soul on the world stage, he or she may have their exits and entrances, just as Solomon says of everything there is a season. Sometimes one feels oneself to be like Shakespeare in being able to write one's own play, but at other times more like Solomon, to be like any other actor (pity the one with only a walk-on part) in having one's play written for him. This variable lifestyle requires discernment as to the closed doors and minds of others that as a preacher or playwright, one would open, as well as the self-discernment as to one's own doors and those portions of one's own mind which as yet remain closed to the exercise of one's ultimate calling.

Through faith itself, there is always much more to human life than just to keep lubricating and motivating one's physical body and intelligent mind as if the one were only a tractor or similar piece of hardware, and yet the other more elusive software were no more than the self-determined mind of the farmer in charge of the tractor. On the contrary, if you consider carefully the scriptures, you will find that there is no such thing as a self-sufficient purpose. And that's exactly why in exercising anyone's freely given volition, every human being needs also to exercise their maximum level of faith in daring to understand how wonderfully he or she has been wrought for the purpose-perfecting and, in turn, purpose-fulfilling of whatever may be their purposeful calling.

To move, direct, and activate any human soul in the making, much more than minimalist faith is needed. There is always that fearful temptation to tailor one's human faith to what (carrying less risk) will appear to be no more than minimally lower and so less miraculous outcomes. On the contrary, ask for the blessing of Jabez (one of the most overlooked of our 'honourable brothers' in the (OT) Bible) to suborn this temptation to be satisfied with less. So then, read Bruce Wilkinson on the subject of *The Prayer of Jabez* (if you will) in order to break through to the highest level of sainthood in this blessed life.

Oh yes, then for sure you'll be taking the greatest risk you could ever take with your life! Sadly, for thinking to take the less risk, then to realise the more certainty, and so then to reach the greater prospects of fulfillment, then you humans (because of your lowered levels of righteousness) shall reap all the less. On the contrary, the more risk, then the heightened certainty, and so the greatest prospects of fulfilment, think we angels. Righteousness of action alone provides the backing when investing in certainty of outcome. The keywords which open doors to the performance of miracles are those denoting that righteous recklessness when conveyed to humans by the Holy Spirit of everlasting life.

Listen! There is, already to hear a symphonic score long-ago faith written, however contingently the means may remain by which this score achieves the fulfilment of its eternally ongoing performance. Already scored, every human being has his or her own solo part to play. Faster than the cosmic speed of light, the faith factor is more than enough not only to lubricate and motivate but also to activate and move both angelic and human minds. But there is always the critical issue of keeping both human and angelic minds in symphonic harmony until the second coming of heaven to earth.

Together in tandem, both faith and reason can move mountains. What is being more and more called for, however, is an end-time harmonious action achieved together by both us angels, for whom faith is paramount, and you humans, for whom mostly fear and guilt still get in the way of both your own persuasively human rationality and faith. There will be some discordant notes at first, but these will get fewer and fewer the more that angels and humans see the narrowing gap between themselves draw ever closer, just as the kingdom of heaven draws ever closer to this already dying earth.

The human temporal mind, even when endowed with the maximum of rationality, can be motivated only for a brief time however. Nevertheless, when inspired by everlasting faith, the angelic mind can be moved throughout all eternity. Humans must learn to claim by faith their one and only prospect of all eternity. In all the different circumstances of their upbringing, teaching, and personal experience of life on earth, for humans to make that claim always requires some considerable courage. By way of breaking through human fear and guilt, however, no other way than by means of their own faith will open mortal eyes to see even where angels fear to tread in the ongoing battle.

This battle, going back long before humans were brought on to the battlefield, has been variously described through human history as between good and evil (often mistaken these days for between scientific fact and fabled fiction) or for justice against injustice (as often blamed now for failures in the legal system) or else in a thousand and one other different ways, each of which are only symptomatic of the last great conflict, which will be waged both there on earth as well as also here in heaven. It is this last great conflict, to which all true believers are enjoined, which we angels here refer to as that between the Supreme Command and the Counterfeit Command.

Let's reassess the odds. In all this preparation for eventually the greatest and ultimately final battle, strategically downplayed here to divert the machinations of the Counterfeit Command away from the preparations of the Supreme Command, much is yet to be done. Leading-Angel Augustus (himself a diversionary to midlifers and to novices, possibly even a piratical figure) is the one who has been appointed to convene and chair this first meeting of the angelic envisioning committee. As to the publication of someone or other's so-called book (author as yet undesignated), this is still only provisionally called *The Soul-Catcher.*

Well then, how much of a book is the author and how much of an author is the book? Presumably, there's no book without an author, but then whatever author there is (no less than whatever publisher there is) makes the book. And that's even the casebound book— although some books then remake or unmake the author (even in paperback) as if there had been no need for any author (or publisher) by which to make the book. Thus, *The Catcher in the Rye* would never have been a book without its author, but then without that book and its immediate sequels, their author would never have decided against writing another book.

The same goes for quite a few other authors (unless either called or addicted to writing and rewriting for a lifetime) who have had to be designated by either this envisioning committee (devoted to design and content) or by its subsequent editorial committee (devoted to form and function). For example, *Watership Down* got turned down by seven publishers (so it is said) before its chosen author was finally confirmed by heaven. And we could list so many more than those still deeply closeted in authors' studies. So too here, nothing appears on the authorial agenda apart from a few lines (by Uncle Augie himself) on the arcane subject of the *Siphonaptera*. The already distributed agenda for the book's envisioning process thus appears mysteriously blank (although Junior-Angel Eli is already holding his copy up to some sort of infrared light whilst Master-Angel Samuel One is busily brushing dilute ascorbic acid from a half-cut slice of lemon to try and extract a more meaningful message from it).

Despite all efforts by those who like to solve a mystery, the agenda still remains almost entirely blank. Indeed, there's no more than the above quotation from what seems to be the convener's own poem (published circa 1872). What follows by way of resolving this mystery, however heavenly inspired, may appeal only to those readers who enjoy the flea circus of the *Siphonaptera* on earth to reach for heaven in following any trivial pursuit. Nevertheless, there's more at stake for the extra-terrestrial creation (ETC) of a new heaven and a new earth.

We angels, so often mocked and scoffed at by the Counterfeit Command for our remaining steadfast to the Supreme Command, try to keep a straight face (OT model) whilst imagining the copious sweat and swearing which must now be going on in the lower depths of the Counterfeit Command, where, under severe duress (their NT response), they're all right now trying so hard to break the code by which to release the hidden extra-terrestrial message (ETM) of the *Siphonaptera*. Of course, breaking the code by them is not likely to happen (all other things remaining equal) because it is always a self-deceiving presentiment to those who are by their own choice in hell to mistake themselves for being in heaven.

So too, try your hand as codebreakers, all you readers still on earth who feel called on by us to do so. Remember always, however, that this is for real, and so nothing at all like the so-called *Da Vinci Code* (which turns history on its head). History on its head for being a spoof, although perpetrated very persuasively both by its author Dan Brown in his book and so also by Tom Hanks in the film of that same book, should never be discounted, however much for being a spoof. Why, *Gulliver's Travels* (for spoofing time and travel), *Alice in Wonderland* (for spoofing the ordinary and extraordinary), or

The Lion, the Witch, and the Wardrobe (for spoofing human power and heavenly politics) should never be discounted for being merely spoofs. Why, there are many otherwise highly intelligent people who dismiss the whole of Christianity for being just one big spoof!

On the other hand, you have to learn how to take spoofs seriously in order to explicate their carefully contrived codification. Goodness gracious, although many spoofs are engineered by the Counterfeit Command, the Supreme Command knows best how to deal with them! Nevertheless, serious spoofs are a much-overlooked literary genre. Treated by any author for being no more than a divertissement (that's ffrench, or Franko-English slang for creating a diversion), they may bring writers of books and enactors of films to engage in what, for them and others, goes a lot deeper than merely mythic fiction. Don't worry, dearest readers, we'll break the code for you before the end of this book is up for grabs. Ours is not just an allegory on the subject of soul-catching. There's a military operation (code-named the *Siphonaptera*) to back up this book! And at the same time, never fear, dearest readers, so long as you clearly understand that there's never any throwaway line (as Cora earlier discovered), especially any of those apparently incidental bylines that so often are let fall even although emanating from heaven.

Nevertheless, this present committee venue is most likely to be bugged and skyped (as all readers should remind themselves on reading this report). Remember that even the full council of heaven (as recorded in the stalwart book of Job) remains open to all. For Job, likewise for Scheherazade in the *Arabian Nights Entertainment*, these horrific nights of storytelling of which he (being Job) or she (being Scheherazade) were the narrators, were far more than any matter of mere entertainment.

So too, this brief military diversion (spoof or no spoof, as determined by the Counterfeit Command) must be judiciously allowed to go on. We accordingly rely on every reader of this ongoing report not to smile or laugh or otherwise give this diversionary game away to the Counterfeit Command. Our endeavours have a part to play (however small) in the overcoming of false arguments and in the destruction of spiritual strongholds. These just might otherwise get in the way of securing the strategic outcome, already promised and planned (with its operational password of ETH) of a new heaven and a new earth.

Just as the biggest of battles (think of World Wars I and II) begin with blustering before the fighting really starts, so does this one. Don't forget that our Uncle Augie (to the novices and now code-named Algie by the interns) fought through both these wars by battling hard in his steadfast spirit against every power, stronghold, and corrupt personality. So too, this present blustering (no less than the encrypted scoffing from the Counterfeit Command) must all be carefully and cautiously monitored. Remember, to respond to blustering with counterblustering no more answers blustering than counterscoffing answers scoffing. Without greater risk to one's own strategic outcome, the Counterfeit Command cannot be either mocked at, scoffed at, or even just ignored. This would do nothing more than overlook its counter-forcefulness in providing one of the most portentous and therefore God-given signs of our own troubled times.

So too, we warn readers off from their taking any of this committee's remarks on the subject of the *Siphonaptera* any less than seriously. You wouldn't want to wake up tomorrow and find your own widely grinning yet still incontrovertibly angelic face looking out of *The Underground Daily Times* (in many ways a pseudonym for much from hell you'll already find in Facebook and other forms of so-called social media).

So then, 'look after your honour in youth', as Russia's national poet, Alexander Pushkin, quotes from a well-known proverb by which to open his great historical novel *The Captain's Daughter*. There's no doubt (not even the deepest of Cartesian doubts, as later discussed with Leading-Agent Descartes in this book) that the *Siphonaptera* is as seriously sincere and as deeply a poetic measure as it is a military measure.

Philosophy has otherwise fallen into a deep academic hole (or else together with theology into a pit of despond) and not just been pushed to the wayside (together with the Socratic dialogues and even more so the Bible) ever since librarianship began to catalogue literary genres into exclusively watertight and unsinkable compartments. It behoves *The Captain's Daughter* not only in her own right but also for all those young readers who would otherwise never hear of honour, to have this proverb to look after their own honour drummed into their heads before being allowed any more romantic reading of what at best—until up to appreciating The Song of Solomon—could only be *The Captain's Daughter*.

And so too, not just for sickly romances, haggard horror stories, and the ongoing mayhem of action movies, there needs to be some moral line below which the action cannot be allowed to fall, since beneath such line, it loses all sense and sensibility. And that makes as much sense as does de Mandeville's much disrespected doggerel on *The Grumbling Hive*. Bad news prophecies are still bad news prophecies, which should not be let fall in their prophetic warnings. Let fall any prophesied reversal of not just moral but also all those other values, the loss of which produces today's sense of intellectual despair and spiritual depression and as a sign of the times these things come about.

Many of the same idiosyncratic and perplexing ways (think in their heyday of George Fox's Quakerism and John Wesley's Methodism) have been mistaken for being merely self-demonstrative measures or, worse still, for being no more than policies of self-promotion. Of course, at first there are both euphoric responses to those apparently novel and perplexingly idiosyncratic ways of worship as well as from others knee-jerk reactions. Nevertheless, every humanly professional, academic, trade, or ecclesiastical group has always demonstrated an extreme sensitivity towards safeguarding its own vocational calling. If it has need to do so, then it may seek to uphold that claim by trying to ensure the self-ordering of its own future by way of law societies, labour unions, and prostitutes collectives, as well as Wesleyan chapels, Salvation Army citadels, and the Society of Friends. The splintering schisms of divisions and denominations which have beset and divided the church universal have arisen for the most part from the failure to hear bad news prophecies for what they are and so then to put down or stone their prophets and then to suffer the consequences at length rather than to identify and repair the damage at the earliest.

On the legal front, the fear of every such self-ordering of any group's future is that of experiencing in first-instance initial burnout but, if surviving beyond that burnout, then succumbing to exhaustion and perhaps dying a lingering death in desuetude. Arguably, the aspiration is to break through the established order of the *Siphonaptera* to find for themselves a secure place of flealess refuge, where, all backs being of the same breadth, there are neither greater nor lesser fleas to go on biting ad infinitum.

The herding instinct of humans to go with the established ecclesiastical flow (or to go as with any other flow) is perhaps heaven's best way of letting both earthly institutions as well as those with heavenly missions find their own stable (preferably metastable) equilibrium. By and large, there are two groups of humans—those who are strongly attracted to what they see to be the security of stable equilibrium and, on the other hand, those attracted to the cut and thrust of unstable equilibrium. Both groups have reasons (sometimes no end of reasons) for their chosen or predilected state of equilibrium, but that does not mean that either or both groups actually *reason*. Quite frankly (which is always how we speak in heaven), reasoning can take place only within the level of faith required for maintaining within oneself the state of metastatic equilibrium.

Of course, the apparent lack of any given reason, far less lack of explanation for the quotation from De Morgan's *Siphonaptera* (designed to make each of the envisioning committee members think for themselves), caused (not unexpected) havoc among those novice angels as yet unfamiliar with the level of free volition called for by Supreme Command to be righteously exercised individually by them in coming to terms with their angelic duties. It will help to recall of *Siphonaptera*, that when published posthumously in *A Budget of Paradoxes* by the author's widow in 1872, many erstwhile academic reviewers (purveyors of reason rather than of faith) had privately been the first to dismiss, disparage, or laugh off this poem of human life as a flea circus. No less than earlier, however, they had burnt de Mandeville's book as they would have done with any sorely infected and grumbling beehive.

'Well, what's the point of proffering such flea-ridden poetry on the sanctified subject of soul-catching?' then asked latecomer Novice-Angel Chloe, unaware of the same point of order having been raised (although not earlier outspoken) by Novice-Angel Cora. Nevertheless, it was the thought that counted for more than the saying in heaven's standing orders, so when Cara went on to ask 'In any case, who is this Augustus De Morgan?' and 'What has he got to do with our decision whether or not to publish *The Soul-Catcher* (with or without a hyphen)?' both points of order were immediately elevated to the greater status of being seconded motions.

'What indeed?' Ancient-Angel (Shining First Class) Ninian good-naturedly laughed. Sometimes called Old Ninian, after the earliest patron saint of Scotland, here was the angel who brought the gospel to the ancient Picts, after that legendary saint once preached for four and a half hours at a stint where his cross still stands today (now on a traffic island halfway between the Battle of Stirling Bridge and the battlefield of Bannockburn).

'Maybe this poem on the *Siphonaptera* is what on earth has been called an icebreaker,' volunteered Old Ninian lightheartedly. 'Nevertheless, with climate change and global warming, there's not so much need nowadays for icebreakers. Indeed, quite the reverse, since both Arctic and Antarctica are now in dire need of angelic icemakers.' [Excursus 3: 'What—Ninian, and not Andrew, as proud patron of the Scottish Kingdom?' queried all the novice angels in chorus. 'No, not yet!' came the definitive reply. 'The hierarchic history of earth's patron saints is complex. St Andrew was by then still engaged in converting the Slavic tribes away from bear worship!']

'On the other hand,' suggested Leading-Angel Mungo, who had given his name to be patron saint of Glasgow and who had (despite the Scots winning both the battles of Stirling Bridge in 1297 and Bannockburn in 1314) prophesied not only the closure of Scottish shipyards, Scottish coal mines, and Scottish fisheries but also the termination of what had always been rightly famous for being a Scottish (and not an English) education, 'doubtless.' So Mungo concluded, 'This verse might be meant to serve as yet another severe weather warning.'

'Of course, Augustus (whether poet or pirate) could be posing no more than a somewhat perplexing parable on the proverbial lifestyle of the *Siphonaptera* ... or even of presenting an ingenious paradox,' Mungo then conceded. 'You can never really be sure with prophetic proclamations. Sometimes, even the prophet isn't aware of the prophetic message which he or she is giving. Possibly, this is a message meant for earth and not for heaven—although if the prophetic cap fits here in heaven, then it's ours for the wearing. In my opinion, this heads-up verse is best treated as a bad-weather warning.'

At least, not an icebreaker! thought Archangel Michael, despite being notoriously Anglican (as so seen by many dour Scottish Presbyterians) for his idealistic tendency towards wishful thinking. *There's many a good sermon gone to earth, many a fruitful lecture withered on the vine, just as many a serious discussion's been derailed, for the sake of raising a laugh by way of sending in an icebreaker. There's a point to every single particle, no matter however small in quantum physics, and yet on which every other particle in the cosmos is most miraculously pivoted.*

'Shake the elemental crystals of matter altogether, and you could get, unintended or not, an almighty explosion,' proffered Archangel Michael. 'There are hierarchies of the heavenly host in heaven who would be dismayed at that explosive substitution of chaos for cosmos, no less than there are hierarchies of humans on earth who would warmly welcome the same explosion. And of all certainty, the same explosion would heat the fires of hell—to kingdom come (although hell itself has not the slightest inkling of what is meant by that expression).' [After which, as confirmed later by the next meeting, there followed a short but very pregnant silence given over by several members to much listening.]

'All the same, dearest Chloe, whether Augustus intends to chair this committee either as a poet or as a pirate, you'll have to ask that question of Augustus himself,' Archangel Michael continued. 'He wasn't once called Augustus (if you know your Roman history) for nothing. Indeed, as first emperor of the Roman Republic (without whom the concept of *res publica* would never have prospered), he fulfilled an already six-hundred-year-old earlier prophecy by decreeing that a census should be taken of the entire Roman world. It was this decree of Emperor Augustus *in his own time* which obliged Mary and Joseph *in their own time* to journey out from Galilee and thereby bring about the birth of baby Jesus, as had been so much earlier and definitively foretold would be in Bethlehem.'

'He's quite a remarkable person, this Augustus, both in his own time and for all time,' Michael said, turning to both Mungo and Ninian (whom we, with everyone else, had dismissed for being none too young). 'Young men,' Augustus will tell you, "Hear an old man to whom old men hearkened when he once was young." Now that's quite a byline for young men to emulate, isn't it?'

'In his chairing this committee (the first of several deliberations on whether or not to publish an earthly version of the Supreme Command's report on *The Soul-Catcher*), that chair in which he at present sits'—here, at this point, Ninian nodded his head to where multi-tasking Augustus was both sitting and snoring—'is enough to justify his being here, never mind so much else. But as to whether Augustus chairs this committee either as a poet or a pirate (as well as being an exponent of heavenly disciplined dialectic)—why, that thought had never crossed my mind. What on earth is bugging you, dearest Chloe? What's bitten you and Cara so badly? Before you came here, there were thought to be no fleas up here in heaven!'

Why, surely not a pirate, mused Ninian to himself of Augustus, *at least not especially so or so that we'd know.*

In the publishing arena, as we all know, pirated editions are a big issue. It's true that the playwright Ben Jonson, in staging his play *Every Man in His Humour*, was amongst the first to write on the frolics of the flea family (to be ordered from all good booksellers who stock the *Siphonaptera*). Then a little later, along came the satirist Jonathan Swift (famed for his *Gulliver's Travels*), who pirated off the same but extended principle of flea-bitten poets to literature at large. So then, we have ample precedent (bitten to death by lawyers though it may be) for pirating the same good-humoured decision process to our own projected book on soul-catching (with a hyphen, as we would hope). There is a point (communicative at heart) to handling the most hard-bitten of subjects, just as they apply to human authors … but lightly … lightly … ever so lightly.

'Like any author, reader, and reviewer, we angels must also scratch where it itches—which is one way of finding out that every man's own humour, once for being heavenly directed, is the same good-hearted humour as we enjoy in heaven. There are storytellers and scientists (fictionalists and factualists, we would call them), but basically, every man's humour, when once heavenly directed, is much the same.' ['Well, not quite everyone's the same,' proffered a disembodied voice from earth. 'What *fictionalists*?' then text-messaged the *OED* (which likes concision), whereas H. C. Wyld's *Universal Dictionary of the English Language* is the last single-authored universal English dictionary (not of usage) to be consulted more prescriptively in heaven.]

'As our own Augustus knows, there's a mathematical theorem (once propounded for Imperial Rome) by which to demonstrate the means by which all apparently different directions (including even those traversing parallel straight lines) converge towards and meet at infinity. But we won't attempt to explicate that theorem (of non-Euclidean geometry) on earth from heaven just yet. Suffice to know that whereas there are so very many ways (possibly an infinite number of ways) of going wrong, each of which does no more than dead end itself in a cosmic void (as so often demonstrated in a court of law), there is only one way (not only exactly but also precisely) of doing right (as so often once demonstrated in any now defunct court of equity for administering its once well-known principles of justice).

'Thus (a favourite word of mathematicians), so also in both logic and mathematics, lies another answer to Novice-Angel Chloe's question concerning De Morgan's appointment to chair this committee meeting on whether to publish this report on soul-catching. In his own time, Augustus was a world-renowned logician and mathematician on earth. Indeed, if you read De Morgan's poem with angelic discernment, dearest Chloe (as you must later learn to discern those souls ready for soul-catching), you will pick up on why it was for his logical and mathematical bent that Augustus was appointed to chair this committee of envisioning.

'Keep in mind, dearest Chloe, that this is a committee of envisioning and not of editing (otherwise, how we got to where we're going would be cut from this present record kept for training and assessment purposes). That's exactly why so many of you novice angels are appointed to this envisioning committee. Your prophetic vision is youthfully clear. You may not altogether understand what you see so clearly, but that lack of understanding does not diminish the truthfulness of what it is which you see in this book. It is the clarity of youthful vision which constitutes true creativity, and for as long as you keep your youthfulness of heart, mind, and soul, you can maintain your creativity. Otherwise, both body and soul very quickly degenerate, first into confusion, and then into disorderliness.

'On earth, this envisioning power most usually fades with age, but for having always been a gift of heaven, this power never (unless contaminated by sin on earth) disappears entirely. Instead, it matures into the gift of appreciation—of which just one small part is that of the critical faculty. This most important yet so often disparaged critical faculty (prophets have been stoned and martyred for it) pivots on the gift of discernment (which is one of the longest and hardest of all gifts to acquire, develop, and mature).'

Meanwhile, understand this, dearest readers: that the essence of all creativity is always orderliness. Take care, since you may have to look hard enough to find it. No matter whether exercised synthetically by way of vision and appreciation or else analytically by way of critique, if there's true creativity, then there's always a certain kind of (usually innovative) orderliness. The best earthly examples of this innovative orderliness (for being at first often hidden) are to be found in everything from logic and mathematics to music and dancing and art and literature.

'Of course, of course, of course ... there's nothing new in soul-catching, as so many already written books show (even without today's later added hyphen), since, as we already know from our own time spent on earth (more on which later), there's nothing new under the sun. Whoops! Pay no attention to that sudden solar flare up! Just keep looking through the prismatic gospel of Jesus Christ! Then so far beyond this earth's already setting sun, you'll no longer be blinded by this solar centre's earthly light but instead seek only Christ's way, his truth, and his eternally cosmic radiance.'

'I can see why you'd appoint a poet to decide the pros and cons of a literary project,' persevered Chloe, 'but I still can't see why you'd appoint a maths logician (even with credentials in class calculus, with or without a hyphen) to chair a book committee! Why, if I were the author of this book on soul-catching, I'd be more than quite upset over the appointment of any logico-mathematician (for being another ffrench or Franko-English neologism!)'

'But you too are the author of this book on soul-catching,' responded Neil, with a gentle smile. 'You are one of the only visionaries who will promote the ideas behind this book. From where else do you think it is that authors get their (essentially divine) inspiration? Oh yes, I know, not always most directly from here in heaven, because often even the most divine of our heavenly ideas are either (1) contaminated in transmission or else (2) fell to the ground unheard of for lack of earthly reception.

'Besides such contamination and failure of reception, however, there are also huge factories and production lines on earth (schools, colleges, churches, and temples, amongst many other institutions) which counterfeit their own versions of our divine ideas. They devoid themselves of all divine initiative and of all divine originality. Worse still, they pass this plagiarised avoidance of serious thought on to their students, adherents, followers, and congregations.' ['This critique was obviously coming from the once-strongly Calvinist wing of the Celtic faction,' later argued *The Underground Daily Times*, 'some of whom are still martyred to the art of live flack gathering from the historic past.']

'We won't go too deeply into that,' responded Augustus, 'since one of the greatest of this world's authors, Lev (or Leo the Lion) Tolstoy, was excommunicated from the church (the body of Christ on Earth, no less) for daring to give something of our own heavenly views (however tainted by earthly transmission) on the subject of his book which he dared to entitle *Resurrection*. Kindly remember always that leadership on earth is always viewed from the top down (from president to toilet cleaner), whereas in the servant throne room of heaven, where God is no respecter of persons, it's always viewed as often from the bottom up (from hard-bitten sinner to the most gracious and godly of the Elohim).'

'Both capitalism and communism, however much extravagantly polarised, are each only aberrant forms of Christianity,' rebutted the Calvinist wing of the Celtic faction. 'Without the elemental ideas on which each of these apparently conflicting schemes is programmed, propagated, and enforced, neither could possibly work. Like many other belief systems contrived since Christ came down to earth, these are counterfeit forms of imperceptibly received and yet compulsorily enforced Christianity.'

'Maybe,' conceded Augustus. 'The consequent rise in lawlessness is hard to take, yet it also becomes harder and yet harder to right this fundamental wrong. The scholastic disciplines first and then the scientific disciplines later begin to fail because the words and terms they use then (1) fast begin to change their fundamental meaning, then (2) faster still will start to lose their substituted meaning, and then (3) eventually end by abusing every last shred of any remaining meaning.' [Here, unlike on earth, the heavenly envisioning committee convened a respectful period of silence to allow for every member's seriously prayerful thought.]

As Leading-Angel Augustus drew back from the blackboard (no whiteboards in heaven for toxic marker reasons), he looked ready to mount his hardly yet broken-in hobbyhorse of class calculus. At the moment, without the mathematics however, it might just pass for Neo-Aristotelianism—although that would depend on readers being able to distinguish their descriptions from prescriptions, their categorisations from predications, and their assumptions and presumptions from definitions. Alas, it is on earth! How many mortals think themselves to think without knowing anything at all of their everyday means of thought?

'All agreed!' called Augie of the committee. 'Then here goes!' he said, turning back to the autocleaning blackboard. 'We'll do this by way of invaginating (turning inside out) the long-accustomed way of every humanly employed means of thought … It's all very clumsy, as you must understand, but this is what goes on, subliminally if not also surreptitiously, in every human head … Look on human thought most mercifully this way, that every human would have a breakdown if he or she but only knew what went on in his or her head … Accordingly, there is no single human person immune from falling victim to his or her own means of thought … Bear with me a moment if we go through the process briefly … leaving specifics for your own investigation later …

'Even as a matter of *this* (usually spoken of as the subject) and/or of *that* (usually spoken of as the object), it becomes near impossible (in these latter days) to retain any clear concept of predication (*this* in relation to *that*). With the loss of definitive predication (as if subjectivity were everything and nothing were objective), the next clear concept to be defused by the Counterfeit Command has been that of categorisation. Without both predication and categorisation, nothing would be either true or false, good or evil, but instead everything would become entirely relative and permissibly contingent.' [On course, as this committee would expect from any retired academic, Augustus had made a good start to what eventually would become this book's Preface.]

'Discrimination then takes over from appreciative critique, from rightful classification, and from sustainable definition. There are no longer any justifiable criteria by which to support the necessary categorisation with which to record our progress in thought from predication to definition. Even dictionaries (pace *OED*) eventually default to every less than proper usage.' [Still on course, running well, and like any well-trained racehorse, Augustus had reached the first bend. As for most of the novice angels, however, most of them were left well behind.]

'Pejorative discrimination then runs amok. For lack of any discipline, it becomes impossible to keep discipline. Eventually, however, the polarities switch, the roles reverse, and then finally, might is not just right but becomes (first grammatically all right) then colloquially alright, and ultimately outright.' [Augustus was gaining as he came down the final straight and, in his reference to reversal of roles, more than hinted at De Mandeville having been prophetically right. Nevertheless, there was a bunch of committed angel interns coming up in their allotted interim.]

'Yet even then, when all is claimed as of right, there is no longer even the least exception left by which to prove any last, remaining, and vestigial concept of right, far less than to witness that there had ever been any rule of right. Instead of right being might, the exercise of might have become its own sole right.' [*It's going to be a photo finish,* Neil thought.]

'This is totalitarianism at its worst,' proffered Mungo, in an attempt to stem the former academic's verbal flow. [Too late. The photo finish shows Plato, riding Socrates as the best of nags in the Augean stable, to have won the day by a short head—from which we may presume the eternity of the soul to surpass both (1) the sophistic, substitutive solecism of the ego for the soul and (2) the transience of everyday science (whether 'pure' or 'social' or 'applied') over the incalculable eternity of the soul.]

'Scholastic terrorism (school bullying at the beginning) is always a prelude to physical terrorism (shooting in the schools and bombing in the streets),' contributed St Patrick to fill the void left by a breathless Augustus. 'For those who once postulated their descent from primal apes, today's humans begin now most persuasively to prove their point. It's a hard row to hoe to get to heaven, perhaps harder (save for the son of man) than any human being ever before, but as you're going to find out, dearest, sweetest Chloe, it's a far harder row you'll have to hoe when in heaven, now today, after all the trouble you think you've had to get here by crossing the Irish Sea in a coracle.'

'You too?' called out both Ninian and Mungo in chorus. 'Home and hosed is what most believers think of having hung up their hat on getting into heaven. What a shock it must give them to get here and find (1) someone else's hat and coat on the carefully credentialed hat peg they've chosen for themselves and (2) their own self-inflicted crown of thorns and self-calculated robe of righteousness not even on the floor. Now here in heaven, and looking back to where on earth you've come from and seeing now more clearly what's been going on all that time down below, it must sadden you no less than it saddens God to see the very same and worse things going on today!'

'Nevertheless, why yet another book on soul-catching?' plaintively enquires another novice angel (named Samuel Two— that information so whispered sideways to Ninian by Chloe, whose stars in her eyes never once left off taking in this Second Samuel sequel to Samuel One). 'And this projected book, not even the full report,' continues Samuel Two, 'but like so many of today's biblical translations, it was dumbed down for the less than serious reader. Why, to capture the market, we'll be doing the same thing here with *The Hyphenated Soul-Catcher*. Almighty God'—at which expression, Chloe flinched—'hardly anyone reads the Bible on earth any more, so how could more than a few readers take to heart any book on soul-catching?'

"Point of order!' quietly interjected Deacon Brodie (who served as clerk to Archangel Gabriel) after shooting an appreciative smile, which seemed not only to encompass both Chloe and Samuel Two (for whom Chloe still has stars in her eyes) but also to ripple outwards like shooting stars from the couple as if to engage everyone in Gabriel's own timeless appreciation of them both. 'But first of all, Leading-Angel Mungo, let me say on behalf of the archangel himself how much I admire the punctilious sense of awe with which you use such words as *Almighty God.*

"'So aptly put!" as Gabriel himself might say. These words most properly express our awe of and respect for our heavenly creator, whereas reverse the same words, as everyone knows when they hear *God Almighty*, and you've reversed their elemental values. So as for *God Almighty*, as coined in counterfeit) by the Counterfeit Command for use on earth by non-believers, that's invariably voiced as a dismissive expression to put down all awe and wonder.'

'But it wasn't Mungo at all who said this. It was actually Samuel Two,' whispered Chloe to Leading-Angel Neil.

'Never mind!' assured Neil to Chloe. 'As for Hansard or any other parliamentary record on earth, we're likewise able to reverse the values by correcting the prophetic transmission on the transcript. Our angel secretary will see to it. She's here in heaven on first-offence court diversion, which otherwise would have taken her straight to hell.'

'Next in order, I must confess to you, Mungo, that even we archangels,' said by Gabriel's clerk whilst all the time nervously fingering his own clerical collar, 'have mobilised ourselves (that's a military expression) from hard copy into text messaging these days. Nevertheless, if you're going to stick *de rigueur* (that's French for *rigorously*) to whatever your view may be of the one and only *Authorised Version* of a book that in any version is no longer brought by worshippers into church, you'll have to retreat (another military term) or resile (a legal term) also from its once generally authorised function.'

Admittedly, there are some such words still sufficiently alive to be projected on to what for many of this world's children would otherwise remain (but for their hearing them pronounced in faith) only dead letters on a dead wall. By now, alas for it, only one of this world's many stone walls remains wailing to the world for lack of the gospel truth, but you too will be obliged to abide by your own rules (a universal rule applicable to all lawgivers), including those who most certainly partake of the English grammar.

'Yes, on this subject, you might mistake me for speaking incomprehensibly as do some bishops (on this score, be so good as to read at least *The Warden* by Anthony Trollope), but you do understand that I'm speaking to you in parables, don't you, Mungo? It's the only sure way, whether they stone you or not, of proclaiming prophecies to dyed-in-the-wool formalists or to ritually habituated non-believers. You first have to stir them up—no less than did our beloved Socrates (who won the equivalent of the Grand National in Athens) as so also did our even more beloved Jesus Christ (who won the whole wide world by being crucified in Jerusalem).

'Think too that ours is the age of the disclaimer (to which statement, also terms and conditions apply). You may never even be told (in however much smaller the print) the terms and conditions which apply to your life. Despite your own little gold cross round your neck, you too might be hung out from some fossilised tree to drip-dry at your leisure or else, complete with full instructions as to its optimum effectiveness, still be publicly given some cup of fully fruit-flavoured hemlock … instead of being more surreptitiously hacked to death one dark night in the park.'

'On the other hand,' interposed Neil when nudged by heaven-sent recollections of his most unhappy schooldays, 'it may be with far more public school civility that you be put out to grass, blackballed from your club, or excommunicated from your church or even sent to Coventry (instead of Calvary) from wherever up the Amazon or any other lesser creek it is in which you're then found paddling. Nevertheless, we pride ourselves on having a civil society now, so you're not likely ever to be found out for having been burnt at the stake for misbelief, far less than for belief (and even far less likely now to be burnt for misbehaviour). On the other hand, you're more likely than ever before to be blown up in your own backyard or to be shot to ribbons whilst worshipping in some mosque or church—whilst the only sure thing that any so-called civil society can do will be to ban the record from Facebook.'

'So then,' argued Deacon Brodie, on picking up the fallen ball again, 'if you so insist on making sense only to the elderly, the infirm, and the long-accustomed, and this for no other reason than because you profess to stick with their strait-laced way of looking at things, your lack of a finite verb in your question of 'Why yet another book on soul-catching?' is going to seriously upset most of them.

'Accordingly, you yourself, without any knowledge of grammatical ellipsis (not a foreign word), are not going to carry the day in any convincing argument or discussion with them, whether over this point or over so many other points of what once so long ago was established to be the *summum bonum* (that's Latin for "the greatest good") of English grammar. What a paradox you've hit on—here's an age like ours when the English language has taken over from the once Classical Greek and thence to the once Golden Age of Latin in turn to become the whole wide world's *lingua franca* (that's bastard French, or Frankish, for "mutual understanding"). And none can speak it, write it, read it, teach it, or think it! Why, those who think themselves to have mutual understanding on the basis of the catastrophic breakdown in English grammar are sitting on a time bomb.

'A hit-or-miss grammarian (like any hit-or-miss lawyer) who *breaks* as many rules as he or she *keeps* is not much better at keeping others in good grammatical order (far less good legal order) than for anyone trying to keep any group of believers to orderly worship. You may think then to rely only on (1) any one-day-a-week and otherwise all-other-days-off worshipper or (2) any all-week but "never more than the most tepid of lukewarm" worshippers or (3) any "first swelteringly hot, then freezingly cold, and ultimately a merely token" worshipper. The sort of faith that moves mountains (which is that sort required for soul-catching) is far more than just covering one's clerical butt which otherwise might protrude from the pulpit or saying hello and goodbye to Jesus every Sabbath or Sunday from the pews. Instead, it's a life-and-death issue for both the believer and the unbeliever.'

'I'm not sure whether that view's altogether fair in the present circumstances,' then either apparently conceded (or possibly disputed) Archangel Michael. 'Sure, there's no shortage of books on the market, whether sacred or secular, already on the subject of soul-catching. However, very few of these books do confront the cosmic issues (whether explicitly or implicitly) since most of them are no more than merely cosmetic for their limited outlook.

'Such books of infotainment may provide a good read (in today's parlance) to someone who is looking for no more than a good read (also in today's parlance), but they employ the spiritual dynamics of soul-catching only fitfully for the author's own purely marketable purposes. Yesterday's ripping good yarn must now be embellished likewise with action, action, and more action, which, as in the context of today's increasingly gladiatorial sport, more than often evidences only a complete and utter paucity of thought (apart from narrating dirty deeds, dirtier deeds, and eventually the dirtiest of deeds).

'There is much in these matters, just as in life itself, which we must pass over. We may excuse ourselves for doing so by saying that these things, whether individually or in concert, are no big things. Nevertheless, our God is a god not just of very big things but also a god of very small things. He is a god of all magnitude in terms of his established creation, as well as a god of no needed magnitude whatsoever in terms of his requiring nothing but himself by which to bring about his own creation.

'From this most complete of all accounting points of view, just as there is no throwaway remark in heaven, so also for those in heaven, there is no throwaway remark on earth. From this point of view, every concept of there being a Passover is a positive one in its promise of redemption. Since what humans make of anything (whether miraculous, mystical, or just downright maddening) is always tested against their own concept of rationality (particularly by Westerners to which more and more Easterners conform) then this report allows for that—but not beyond the point at which miracles are miracles, mysticism is mysticism, and when seen from earth, God in heaven can seem downright maddening.'

III
Passover

> Get you into the city, where you'll meet a man carrying
> a pitcher of water. Follow that man! Whichever house
> he enters, ask the householder for the guestroom in
> which (for the last time round) I shall partake of the
> Passover with you.
>
> The Gospel of Mark (paraphrased)

'Every day's a Passover. Got that? Sure, yesterday's Passover could
be tomorrow's crucifixion, as every newspaper reporter knows
when passing over his or her copy to the editorial desk. Investigative
journalism (the sort that uncovers Watergate whatever the outcome) is
almost always a long haul, and the teamsters are not always on your
side. It's not before time, for this by now fully envisioned (although
yet to be fully authorised) report on soul-catching to be passed over
from the envisioning process to that same editing desk of the one and
only Supreme Command.

'Time moves on, at least on earth, where the timekeeping of
believers as well as the time-watching of unbelievers both serve as the
countdown to all eternity in heaven. Church festivals and lectionaries
have tended to subscribe, for example, Passover thought, Lenten
thought, crucifixion thought, resurrection thought, Pentecostal
thought, Nativity thought, and so on, to certain ritually determined
seasons and certain ritually determined days. However, the true
believer is mindful that every day may require penitence. The dawn
of every day is favoured with at least one more Passover, and yet that
last of one's days on earth may possibly open oneself to the terror of
one's own or of another's crucifixion.

'To every time, there is a season—to which precept of ancient
wisdom (if not called merely situational ethics) every true believer
is bound to have much recourse. By such means, even the darkest
of days may be replenished and restored over and over again by
the joyful prospect of yet another born-again nativity or yet by the
fulfilment of another joyful resurrection. Ever since the gospel came
down to earth from heaven, it's all good news. However, every true

believer may have to work very hard at not just seeing but also making it so. And there's already a fast-growing list of the same sort of tasks awaiting all true believers by way of the "busman's holiday" awaiting them in heaven.

'As writers and publishers, we all know what it feels like (on yet another busman's holiday) to read our own work. It may not live up to what we first imagined it to be. Worse still, it may be often sadly traduced (there's that word again) in a pirated, expurgated, or excessively edited edition. Sometimes we need either to run or fight. So then, let's change the subject.

'Before we adjourn prayerfully to our next meeting, unless someone else has anything to say, let us all congratulate Novice-Angel Chloe on drawing our attention to those who do exist to pirate and maraud the authentic provenance of divine ideas. These are as often filched to one's own earthly credit rather than rightfully attributed to the divine source of their heavenly inspiration. So here's an open acknowledgement to the one and only Supreme Command that whatever we think of, wherever it comes from, is not of our own. As to there being bad ideas, well at least in theory, we know where they come from. But they may well have once been good ideas before we made them our own.

'Well then, what happens next to what otherwise may have resulted from an extraordinarily good idea that didn't quite make it through from the Supreme Command? After all, these ideas are so often the very ones that simply refuse to fly. Did we catch them when they faltered, or did we just let them fall to some appointed place where good ideas go when there's no one around to catch them, and so either to let them or make them fly? This is a hard question (since there's not just heavenly soul-catching but also hellish soul-snatching) and so especially hard in the end for those who grab on to ideas as if these were all their own.

'Well, sometimes the self-accredited author gets clobbered. At other times, the author's purloined book or plagiarised speech or perhaps purloined plans or self-asserted invention or self-claimed newest idea gets clobbered. In the very same way that heaven's kingdom ideas can be so wilfully pirated, put down, hacked into, or remaindered off, it can be just as easy for those same kingdom ideas (once they reach earth) to be counterfeited. Instead of having been divined in heaven, they are passed off on earth, even as if they could have come out of the emptiest of human heads and the hardest of human hearts, which nevertheless still purport to promote them. For the sake of coming up with the goods, what then happens to those once perfect but now so often tainted, corrupted, and wrongfully ascribed ideas? Do they drop to hell where they are marketed off, whether for being rightfully or wrongfully remaindered?

'We all know what happens, because each of us at some time, inadvertently or not, has ascribed to ourselves something of the praise and glory which more properly accrues to another's name. Our forefathers on earth had a name for it—for shining in what they called reflected glory. The prime example of this happening to someone of great standing (which is exactly why this so often allows those of great standing to set a prime example) took place on that set day when King Herod was inspired to make a great oration to his subjects. Let's hear of it so that in following any path which may beset (stet) ourselves with fame and fortune (yes, beset ourselves with fame and fortune), we know the risks which can befall, and so take to perdition, this heavenly task of soul-catching.

'King Herod's subjects welcomed what he said as the voice of a god, and yet the self-proud Herod withheld from Almighty God his due praise and glory. It was there and then that one of the scariest of all our seraphim angels struck this king stone dead. His body, as everyone knows, went to the worms. Whether as the foremost or least of poets, politicians, priests, and prophets, we've all come to know (even if not at the time) what it has been to steal or pirate some of the greatest of God's ideas (either directly from God himself or indirectly from someone else).

'Ascribe divine ideas knowingly, or else when done too often ignorantly or negligently to our own vainglory, then unforeseen and unexpected things start to happen. As for Herod, even if it may not be yet exactly our own last moment on earth, theft (and even more so sequential theft) has its consequences. Whether knowingly or not, we all steal from God! But if you're a celebrity and, like Herod (or President Nixon), a front-line celebrity inured to fame and fortune, then like any other bright morning star who learns to love the limelight for being his very own light, have a care!

'We've all experienced this so-called moment of front-line truth, either when inspired to give a spontaneous word of encouragement (only apparently from us spoken or written) or else when inspired to give something to someone else (perhaps no more than our own listening ear), yet then we have taken (stolen) all the praise and glory for this God-given moment to ourselves. For stealing this moment that came not from within ourselves but instead from some source far beyond ourselves (yet from where or from whom we have withheld to ourselves all righteous credit more correctly given elsewhere) is a phenomenon of fallen man most disarming, debilitating, and in the end, so deadly to ourselves.

'Read of Herod—and yet fail to see yourself in him ... Read of Napoleon—and yet fail to see yourself in him ... Read of Hitler—and yet fail to see yourself in him ... Read of Stalin—and yet fail to see yourself in him. And although crossing a bottomless pit opening up in Afghanistan, in Iraq, or in Iran or Syria (or even just with Watergate in Washington D.C.) you may be walking a tightrope that is not of God's choosing or making. Either for walking that tightrope, or else through God's grace, you may never be put in the position of fighting for front-line truth. So then, you'll never be called to cut the mustard for soul-catching, or else for mistaking that to be your own personal calling, you'll then fall from the same height of responsibility mistaken by so many USSR and USA presidents, no less than by premiers of UK and NZ, as well as other leaders, for being what is no more than your own unhallowed source of power.

'This thieving urge which comes to steal another climber's moment of glory when he or she is climbing up the same cursus honorum or ladder of promotion up which you too are climbing we in heaven call by different names according to whether we are dealing with governmental climbing, academic climbing, commercial climbing, or simply social climbing. This thieving urge can come over any ideas-man so fast, frequently, and furiously, that, even before he begins to feel the slightest twinge of envy by which to register the innately debilitating influence on himself of anyone else's better idea than his own, this thieving urge in turn will lead whole nations to murder, mayhem, death and destruction. It is one which allows even popes and presidents (we're talking history here) to mistake some preposterously old and well-worn idea for being their own very new one. There's nothing ever been newer under the sun (so they think) than this, their own sudden thought, for being the most recent of their own positively brilliant ideas. Alas, a prophet without any sense of history commensurate with his or her call to prophesy is as likely to falsify the outcome as he or she is to lose their own vastly swollen head.

'Alas, for which sudden mind-blowing thought, and however most miraculously this could happen of their own making by coming out of what by then is the emptiest of their own chief executive, entrepreneurial, or presidential heads, they thereby attempt to trade in the credit and purloin the personal profit. Forgive us, Lord God Almighty, for our stealing, as we forgive others for exactly the same sin of stealing from you. What most properly has always belonged to you—and so to your name alone can be credited for being created or brought about by none other than you—could not possibly be of our own making!'

'Oh no, no, no … why then, surely not yet another book on soul-searching … and for that once more to masquerade as yet another book on soul-catching?' again asked Deacon Brodie, as he fingered his clerical collar nervously on behalf of Archangel Gabriel. With his own three-dimensional bushy eyebrows raised searchingly around the fast-gathering crowd of novice angels to hear from Uncle Augie's lecture, he asked this question as if it were an entirely new and once again original thought of his own. After all, these were all novices, none of whom would recognise that instead of being original, he had bodily snatched it from an old, much-loved, and now sadly interred angelic refrain. *God Almighty!* He might have been heard mistakenly to say (by way of widdershins for *Almighty God*) on his starting out once again to complain. 'No one reads the Bible any more, so how could they take to heart any book on soul-catching?'

Here, Tasha (short for Sasha, shorter still for Natasha, and even shorter still for her Russian saint's day name of Alexandra) dared to intervene. By now a well-known investigative journalist, she did so tellingly with a smile, as she hummed the tune to that once much-loved but now long-lost angelic refrain, from which the rather deadly Deacon Brodie had both filched and distorted the words. When speaking now as a well-known journalistic editor on behalf of the editorial (and soon to be no longer envisioning) committee appointed by the Supreme Command to see the projected work through the press, she too dared to change the topic in the cause of truth and justice by raising a point of order.

'Were the division of archangels now suggesting that books were already on the way out, seeing that it had been rumoured that the archangels amongst themselves had taken to text messaging and heaven itself had allowed so many once grand college libraries to be turned into pitiful IT centres? Could she be assured,' she asked, 'that such rumours were not true and that the division of archangels were still behind Leading-Angel Alcuin as chief librarian of heaven?'

'I'm sure it would profit us all, before I refer this point of order to open debate, to hear you explain yourself, Tasha, a little more on this subject,' rejoined Chairman Augustus to Tasha's point of order. 'I'm afraid for myself as a former lecturer—at which point Augustus bowed to Deacon Brodie—'that I talk more than I read or write these days. What exactly might you mean by an IT centre (the acknowledged hub or centre point of higher education nowadays) when technology is moving so fast that far apart from books, research, and technology, I can barely keep up with my own lectures? However, that's not just the state of each worldly nation but, as revealed by no less than Christ Jesus himself, the state of this present heaven and earth in their being about to be superseded by some promised new earth and promised new heaven. Now, Tasha, if that's not IT, then what's ET? Perhaps you'd care to write a serious paper (no spoofing allowed) on the extra-territorial technology required for implementing the promised new heaven and new earth? [As auto-recorded in the minutes of the meeting, a strange silence (of almost three-score of earth-hours) then accrued in heaven.]

'So then too, although for myself being already in heaven,' continued (surely no longer) Leading-Angel De Morgan (who for some unknown reason by now was wearing a pirate's fancy dress marked 'Property of Counterfeit Command') I too am looking forward, as we all can be presumed to be looking forward, to some new heaven.' (Hehehe, a haven from heaven, as the Counterfeit Command likes to put it!) 'Ever since coming to earth, this still present heaven's grown rather tattered and tawdry. And yes, ours is the age not solely of legal disclaimers against all claimers but also of as much restructuring as there is also destructuring. [For some reason (indicated by a red flashing light and the warning words 'insecure site') at this stage the auto-recording service had resorted to what it called 'ultimate heavenly narrative', just as in scripture that can be judiciously interspersed between prayerful conversations, sing-song psalms, prophetic outbursts, deistic opinions, and rebellious affronts. Obviously, the next paragraph would seek more objectivity by applying the same resort to 'ultimate heavenly narrative' as once devised by Leading-Angel William Caxton.]

'But then, if we look on the bright side of things (as in 'ultimate heavenly narrative'), just about everything all around is being restructured, if not reconstructed. Ever since the former Soviet Union went down through the process of perestroika, that's been the name of the game. We all think ourselves to know what ought to be meant by a library (but that's old hat now for as long as there's the web) no less than we take for granted that we know what ought to be meant by a dictionary (by now probably a lost cause), but what exactly do we mean (at least in heaven, if not in hell) by an IT centre?'

'Good question!' replied Leading-Agent Tasha. 'In actual fact (if facts *are* still facts), you yourself have answered your own question. I mean, a library that no longer has books but instead is packed with computers. I mean, often a world-class library whose librarians have been reduced to menial mechanics, student minders, and the lowest of service technicians. I mean, any library, large or small, whose building, once known as a library, is now known for being instead renamed an IT building … As exhibit A in any subsequent court action, I hereby table (without prejudice, because if needed I mean to institute court action) this worldwide map of all such former library buildings now housing (often stupidly smart) computers instead of (wondrously wise) books and so in consequence (pontifically renamed) IT buildings.'

An IT building … mused Archangel Gabriel, who had reappeared spontaneously to speak ruminatively into his flowing beard. *An IT building* ... he mused again, stroking his beard, pursing his lips, and then looking up into the ten-dimensional cosmos from which, quite casually, he squinted back down at the committee and gave a ten-dimensional wink as if that was no trouble at all to him whatsoever when ubiquitously he could fly through all ten dimensions of hyperspace and never be missed from any one situational space-time. Alas, like most archangels (as well as geeks and informational technicians), they were better practicians than theoreticians (and so couldn't always explain to others exactly what it was that they were doing).

Tasha knew that there wasn't all that much time left in the world for scholarly rumination and that Archangel Gabriel was of such a scholarly nature that left to himself, he might spend the earthly equivalent of several thousand years hobnobbing with the twelfth-century scholar Moses ben Nahman (colloquially known as Nachmanides), which would just as likely be on the subject of multidimensional architecture in the course of which both of them would most probably take a stopover to have another long historical look at reasons for the fire which took out the once Great Library of Alexandria.

And there, indeed, amid all the smoke, flames, and general bustle, once again debating between themselves the lengthy transition in communicative transmission (as both Nachmanides and Gabriel agreed to call the slowness of thought which beset humans deprived of all but four of heaven's ten-plus dimensions), they would take yet another look through what they liked to call their Museum of Modern Arts—that is, from cave art to catacombs (as they were prone to call their still early and by now legendry lectures on higher education).

And so then both Nachmanides and his Buddy-Archangel Gabriel (with Maimonides now going along for the ride) would once again revisit the now increasingly archaeological history of tagging early cave walls to writing curlicues on rough animal hide, from rawhide through to the finest and most expensive of parchments—'Here, feel this,' they would say to each other—then eventually to papyrus and from individual scrolls to books and even books like the Bible, which was the book of books. So possibly both to and through computers, before going back again to books (as everyone would, so they thought), but there, still on computers (until finally frozen by climate change), then ironically back once again to scrolling, no longer horizontally but now vertically (did that make a difference?). Who could tell? But prophetically speaking, they'd both know as they coupled each other through the streets first of Pompei and then to read about Brexit from walls in London and, from there, to find the latest on Trump being tweeted from Wall Street, now reconstructed in Washington (from previously in New York) as being the surest way of keeping up on current affairs (for which currency apply to the Dead Rabbit Grocery and Grog) by reading what the last and latest of big city taggers had written for posterity. They would always take the long way round (instead of the shortest wrong way round, as so many thankless people still took) on any and almost every such interesting issue of higher education.

Tasha (still short for Natasha and shorter still for Alexandra— unless itself shortened back to Alex) felt both exhausted and bemused, as she always did by the flashback and fast forward that always went on during any historical study taking place in heaven. On earth, it helped earthlings to focus on any present issue by relegating history to a barely relevant and always dry and dusty subject (which she felt intuitively was always wrong). Nevertheless, by thus denying themselves any prophetic insight into history, earthlings never seemed to learn from the past and so frequently made a terrible mess of things in the future.

As a child once on earth, Tasha had suffered a life-and-death experience in what was now mistakenly thought to be the former Soviet Union. Whilst later working in the West as a highly credentialed journalistic reporter, she thus still possessed a prophetic insight into the plain truth that may not otherwise have come to her but for her earlier suffering. She thus had a heavenly sensitivity to matters of the heart [thought Augustus] together with a lightness of communicative expression [thought both Ninian and Mungo, who discerned some allegiance to their Celtic faction], and these are just two of the many reasons why, as an investigative journalist of the most impeccable credentials, she had been secretively suborned by the Supreme Command [thought Augustus] to serve on the forthcoming editorial committee to look after this project. It was a project too readily dismissed by many non-soul-searchers to be yet just another book using soul-searching (possibly even soul-snatching) to masquerade as soul-catching. Don't forget—this was a military operation since all soul-catchers were up against soul-snatchers.

Archangel Gabriel, like any true scholastic, was still chewing on the fate of computers, which were so fast-changing that the world's limited resources to replace obsolescent hardware couldn't keep up with the brainstorming need for software. The worst result of computers, especially in higher education, had been to expect short, immediate answers to the deepest of quick-fire questions (as marked often by the dumbest of computers). He was glad to write, when he did still write, in cursive longhand. These questions sometimes do no more than skate across the surface of so many critically urgent and worldwide issues. Why, sometimes the most high-up and powerful people go for the answers before they've even been brought up properly to understand the questions.

Yet as even flash-in-the-pan students, scholastic skaters (there are millions in the world today) still pass (even doctoral exams) with the highest of grades for the lowest possible input of serious thought. Despite achieving the highest awards from their own era of credentialism, they retain the most mundane of hindbrain thought processes. Then, in turn, before you can say Jiminy Cricket (a figure of speech representing the declining academic conscience), such copycat scholastic skaters become the next generation of scholastic teachers.

After all, by now, even a doctoral degree is merely a wallpapered prerequisite for every university appointment. So then, these scholastic skaters, in turn, demand their own students to fulfil the same quick-fire expectation which had been inflicted on themselves. And by now, the academic process has degenerated to the point by which the students are required by management to assess the teachers. The result is to raise yet another generation of what were once known to be half-baked students, who, in turn, become pressure-cooked scholastics.

As yet, mere mortals on earth haven't got to what heaven has already foreseen to be 'the dynastic question'. As not yet posed on earth, the question is, which will encounter obsolescence first, man-made computers or divinely designed human brains? As a trick question asked of novice angels, the statistical likelihood (confirmed by today's novo maths) shows that, for being coterminous, both computers and brains shall become obsolete at one and the same moment of truth. Needless to say, this one and the same moment of truth will pass unnoticed by both the 'smartest' of computers and the 'smartest' of humans. So then, just in case you've never heard of 'the dynastic question', dearest reader, this is it.

Nevertheless, this moment of so-called truth (already claimed, engineered, and celebrated by the Counterfeit Command) is obviously not fail-safe, since there are a growing number of 'independent scholars' (as they call themselves) who, through Lilliput Libraries and other humble means, have taken upon themselves to maintain the world of books. Their steadfast hope is founded on the premise that the novo maths of today is not static and inert but instead is dynamic, reactive, and interactive; so that by the end of time, today's battle between hard copy books and virtual information (all done by smoke and mirrors) shall be won by books. Indeed, even in terms of today's, never mind tomorrow's highly interactive novo maths, the independent scholars are convinced that the battle for books has been already won by books.

Of course, there is more than one completely overlooked issue in this dynastic problem of replacing books with computers. Deeply dark for being a dynastic problem, yet for it being dismissed superficially as no more than cosmetic, the issue of replacing books with computers comes perilously close (as it does in terrorist operations) to replacing brains with computers. Indeed, the same imperilled matter of principle can routinely affect scholastic as well as both governmental and military situations.

This can happen because of the often simplistic way in which fast-moving information technology enables the operator (if not as often the 'smart' machine itself) to pose questions quite mechanically as if any operator can look for answers before needing to know the full nature of the questions asked. In consequence, a second issue (seriously compounding the felony of the first) is that (already said) of closing down libraries and doing away with professionally qualified librarians to replace them with janitors, technicians, and security officers to oversee IT buildings.

Don't mistake us angels (far less Tasha-Sasha) for being Luddites (that's to say, those who go around destroying or outlawing machines). Of course, we're not outlawing computers (on which this book may now being typed) any more than we're outlawing Kindle (on which this book may now being read). After all, when all is said and done (which on earth it never can be), IT buildings are perfectly fit for computers. This is true, despite all the risks computers present to serious scholarship when they are employed in sometimes the least literate of very powerful hands. You know, we keep a checklist in heaven of those scientists who think to teach science (including library science no less than information science) without themselves having ever read a work of fiction, far less the history (which is so often fiction) of their own science! Still with us—or have you abrogated yourselves from heaven? There's only one way out at the moment, and that's down—so avoid the one-way lift-shaft (since there's no lift)!

On this issue of computers versus books, Tasha-Sasha (a distant Slavic diminutive of the name Alexandra, owing allegiance to the fabled Alexander the Great) felt it too early to distinguish herself in print. As yet, for being a thoroughly committed investigative journalist, Tasha-Sasha was always amongst the first to come to the help and defence of others. All the same, this call to be another's defender (whether in law or in journalism) could often demand more of oneself than could be rightly given to many others. As said in heaven of military operations, 'Look to one's strength of cause to discover the source of that strength and so also to avoid the potential weakness of any unexpected consequences arising from that cause' (as attributed by Field Marshal Kutuzov to General Winter).

As time moves on, each seeded row on this world's earth becomes a harder and harder row to hoe (General Winter's coming). Out of Eden, all earth remains tainted by the blood of Cain. With every passing day, the task of hoeing whatever arable earth remains, so as to keep it free from weeds, thistles, and thorns by the sweat of one's brow, grows ever harder. The feeling of being not entirely squeaky clean, felt even by every angel when on earth's tainted ground, can become an everyday yet debilitating occurrence. Meanwhile, you earthlings are so inured to and injured by this earth's stinks and stinjins (stet) as not to notice General Winter's coming. [And this could be truer than you think, since (just as General Winter uses warming to warn of snow) then this earth's last Ice Age (as collectively remembered) was heralded in by global warming.]

To open one's heart, mind, and soul to the plight of this once wonderful planet Earth is to command of one's conscience a commensurate personal responsibility and vulnerability. Not everyone is aware of this relationship between conscience and conscientiousness, which thereby throws open the heart of the conscientious to sometimes an overwhelming level of responsibility and vulnerability (manifesting themselves in many unbelievers as guilt). Alas for them, the unbelievers, since there is no condemnation in Christ!

'Love your neighbour *as yourself*' is the scriptural commandment, but the words *as oneself* are as often overlooked by both preachers, prophets, and teachers, as well as by next-door neighbours. To those sensitive souls alone who hear this world's rising calls for help and justice, fairness and equity, right and righteousness, the task of living within one's earthly limits in these latter days becomes momentously stressful.

As said before, it becomes harder to hoe one's row. And as said before, a winter to beat all winters is coming! It can be as cold in the desert as it can be cold in the tundra. General Winter knows no limits!

So then, why not require more investigative journalism from Tasha-Sasha (although already carrying the burden of Alexander the Great) on these deeply prophetic issues? Well, with every prophetic gifting, there comes a contract (in reality, a covenant); and so then, no less than for prophecy than for contract, time is not yet the essence of either, until so made to be the essence of both. And yet for having been made the essence of both, that new dimension given to either of these relationships does not pre-empt but instead (both generally and particularly) requires waiting on one's partner to the contract, who, in the case of every covenant, is God.

Meanwhile, an apparently stray word (feelingly or unfeelingly given) or some changes in circumstances (whether apparently for better or for worse) can alter one's whole world outlook. Tasha-Sasha's mum on earth had been a wonderfully committed librarian to scholars, students, and books until one day, very suddenly, she had been made redundant from her college library. That was the day when computers came into vogue and took over from books to substitute (1) information for wisdom, (2) mechanistic button pushing for personal counselling, and (3) so-called distance learning for once personal lectures, for everyday mentoring of students, and for the giving of scholarly advice. Well, the sort of book-loss trauma which results from this loss of personal touch is the sort which can be passed on, either generically or specifically, to the detriment of others.

On the one hand, Tasha-Sasha had first-hand and inside knowledge of the library issue going back for centuries. Not for nothing had her own namesake, Alexander the Great, given his name also to the once world-famous Library of Alexandria. And as an investigative journalist with classical learning, she shared the same academic sense of trauma as well as of mystic regret and almost ongoing despair knowing always that one of the ancient world's greatest of libraries, to the disadvantage of thinkers and scholars like Aristotle (many of whose works were lost in the blaze), had gone up in one of the greatest fires of all time.

On the other hand, Tasha-Sasha also felt, as so many believers are made to feel, a certain conflict of personal with heavenly interest. You know, mortals (relying on their jingoistic RIP formula for death) go on mistaking heaven for being some sort of Rip Van Winkle's Sleepy Hollow! On this account, they overextend themselves, as if to make up for the respite they'll experience in heaven. In the new heaven, as on the new earth, however, there's going to be far more work for everyone (total employment as known to this world's politicians) as never before. A disappointment to some? Yes, but they can burn themselves out, and in living their spirit in the spirit, they can do this enough on earth to damage their soul before getting to heaven.

A disappointment to all? No, quite the contrary! Since heaven came to earth to resurrect a love that never dies in place of the deathly hollows and loopholes of the law, there's much to do. Heaven now increasingly exerts its dynamic domain for conflict resolution over all this yet still troubled earth. So if you're not interested in resolving conflict by heavenly means, then don't consider yourself to be any real believer in what you've heard of heaven having come to earth. There again, if you don't consider some part (whether the greater or the lesser part) of heaven having come to earth through the already accomplished ministry of Jesus Christ, then what's the point (to put it bluntly, as we always do in heaven) of your otherwise frittering away your remaining time on earth?

Rest in peace—(RIP) or the older formula of *requiescat in pace*? No, never ever at peace (and that's scriptural) ever since heaven through Jesus Christ came to earth! So then, don't befool yourself by hiding your still barely living soul, or under anyone else's still barely living soul, or yet behind any other solipsism (the most extreme form of scepticism that any dead language could bring) when derived from the 'deathly hallows' of the law. Sleepers awake. Keep your lamps burning. The stone's rolled away. There's no time any longer for any slumbering or sleeping spirits, far less for any already coffined souls.

Meanwhile, there was a grave likelihood (no pun intended) that Archangel Gabriel (who is one of the most anciently alive of angelic prototypes) might possibly misunderstand the urgency of the present earthly issue. As an ancient, he could become bemused by the way in which today's computers, by making something of a comeback to scrolling, had dared to adopt a vertical heavenly function instead of, as maintained more humbly by books, their earthly and thus horizontal function. For some reason or another (although in heaven, righteousness is righteousness without any need for reason), Gabriel felt that this was far too daring for any mere means of solely human communication.

Perhaps it was for that reason (although as said before, he didn't need any reason) Gabriel prophesised the need for some further transition or passover (although obviously not to any upper room and so not requiring any resort to upper case). By this prophetic recommendation, Augustus took Gabriel to mean that since all human knowledge of any further dimension or dimensions was being embargoed from earth and that earthlings were therefore being restricted to what they knew of the three spatial and one temporal dimension already known to them, he would decide that, on the basis of this embargo continuing to apply as it had ever since the fall of mankind, there was to be nothing new under the sun until the son of man should himself finally return to remove the embargo on all further means of acquiring human knowledge. Meanwhile (again that pregnant phrase) realise this: that until you've crossed the covenantal threshold, there's no real Passover, far less any real Pentecost; no, neither for you (and as that may mean, then also, neither through you for many others).

IV
Resurrection

> I commit you to stay silent of every supposed miracle that you've seen here (however much of a big ask this may be of every already wide-eyed communicator) until at least this son of man shall be resurrected from the dead to life to set you free.
>   The Gospel of Matthew (paraphrased)

Nocturn—itself for night-music, in bold black type, although we're translating here, through faded memories, from the configured conceptual curlicues of Chinese Mandarin to the increasingly required basic English of the New York times (no pun intended), so bear with us! At night, on the lake beneath the maple bridge, the sound of a lonely Chinese zither is also fading. The lyric fades most delicately up and away (like the first lark of morning) from the otherwise often stormy piano concerto of Wang Jianmin's immortal lakeside composition. The stone of darkest night has not yet fully rolled away, so we angels are still watching. The silence is golden … The silence is still golden … [Read three times subvocal, at no faster than a metronomic marking for Bach's 3/4 unusual alla breve of 60 to allow for ideogrammatic reconstruction of the still underlying Mandarin.]

Somewhere, in its upper harmonics, a flute is softly sounding to mark the break of dawn. A song without words—it's being played as if by someone whilst walking … no, by waltzing … incredibly to a slow 6/8 (not 3/4) rhythm … across water. Once again, like so many of the old classics (Bach, Handel, Purcell), it's a reconfigured dance tune. But which comes first, the not so much in the popular or pecking or biting order of man-made things or the truly creative order of existentially proclaimed and divinely created things—sight or sound, song or dance, rhyme or rhythm? Don't bother, says the deity, just dance and sing, just rhyme with rhythm—only theorists argue about it.

Reminiscent of William Walton's *Sur le Lac*, the player progresses through a number of heavenly variations, accompanied here and there by arpeggios on guitars, harps, viols, and zithers—even also by all sorts of penny whistles, hurdy-gurdies, mandolins, and other strings. The melody rises and falls just as other angels choose to join in this morning's theme song to open heavenly worship. Morning after morning, another newly improvised song will herald in yet another new day (yet one as never before) for those on earth.

'Who's the flute player?' asks Neil (not his heavenly name), who, as if again a child in the role of some father playing at happy families, would chair the editorial committee on *The Soul-Catcher*. What, not Tasha-Sasha? No, just like the Preface to this book comes first, Tasha-Sasha's entrance awaits a later introduction. It will be Neil's job at the moment to husband this book's already envisaged publication from heavenly ideas to earthbound print.

As on earth, the members of the editorial committee are quite an open-minded, seriously joyful, and yet immensely humble lot. And since acquiring humility carries a cost, this editorial section comprises more rejected authors on earth than there are famed reviewers reaching for heaven. Both three scions grafted to the same writing-reading stock, they each (as writers, readers, and reviewers) know to write as if they were a reader, to read as if they were a writer, and to review as if they were both a writer-reader as well as being a reader-writer.

'The flute player … judging from his upper harmonic improvisations on Walton's theme song … must be Marsyas,' opined Emma (also another unknown author, writing under the pen name Incognito whilst on earth). Emma's blithely standing in for her mum, Kirsty (also acting in her mothering capacity to the editorial committee), in this matter of the forthcoming publication of *The Soul-Catcher*. This is a breaking news novel before the committee on the arduous subject of how angels behave in front-line battle (from Kabul through Tehran to Baghdad) when both in and out of heaven.

'Let's listen … yes … it's the Phrygian flute player Marsyas,' confirmed Emma, after listening intently to the earliest of dance time improvisations, which so offended the once great god Apollo. They are being played most intricately by the famous flautist Marsyas in the Phrygian mode of flute playing,' Emma now elaborated for the benefit of the new editorial committee rather than for the former envisioning committee (can you pick the shift in genre from this prose?).

'Marsyas … alas, as you all know … was that fellow who was flayed alive (skinned alive, some sources say) for his audacity in presuming to contest Apollo's divine expertise in the Doric mode of flute playing,' quietly proffered Emma. A short earth-silence (of approximately eight earth-years overtakes the editorial committee, followed by a time of silent prayer, since striving for excellence, as did the highly competitive flautist Marsyas, was not something to be encouraged by the editorial committee either on earth or in heaven. It is written in many more places than one that none should test the Lord, who is one's own God, and that golden rule, for being one of pragmatic common sense (rather than emotive sensibility), surely applies to any and every deity.

Whereas books on earth are attributed directly to their authors, books coming from heaven to earth begin their unusually long life by being brainstormed before, first an envisaging committee, and then an editorial committee of kingdom publishers. This editorial, committee will both devise the book's direction of travel besides deliberating further on both its form and content. This is the way of things in heaven, where all the good ideas needed for every book are both first initiated and subsequently sponsored. This is heaven's first priority, no matter how much diluted downwards in value these ideas may become by those to whom such books (including all the very many different versions of the Bible) are entrusted. The first priority of all good publishing (upheld by all good booksellers) must initially proceed from heaven.

After all, where do all good books come from? Unless deceptively counterfeit, all authentic books come from heaven. Many are the books which begin by being devised in heaven and directed from heaven. But editing a book that has yet to be written is a very fine art indeed, despite how difficult it may be for any author to assemble, express, publish, and promote the ideas which have already been decided for that book from having been already brainstormed in heaven. [Nothing new in all this. When Christendom was Christendom, all books as far as Rome and even further still to Constantinople and yet further still to what was left of Alexandria came from being written and published in auld Ireland. And you'll mistake that, at your peril, for being Irish humour!]

Meanwhile (again a pregnant term), the result of this present writing is a team effort, both authorially and editorially, whereby the members of the editorial committee as often each cheerfully contribute whole passages to the sequentially written work (that adventuresome task being passed on by one member to the next member or back over to the sovereign author himself) in their contrapuntal writing of the work as a whole. It's true that, like the Bible (for being said to be sixty-six books by forty different authors, despite some wonderfully written books being left out), this radically alive team spirit tends to promote blockbusters—and even some Bible commentators have complained (in their book reviews of the Bible) that even the Bible could be a lot shorter than even heaven alone thinks it should be. [Well, now you know from which human mindset it is that catechisms, shorter catechisms, and shorthand creeds can emanate to deprive the Bible of all historical continuity, never mind also its narrative storyline.]

As you can see, since so much of heaven is to be found in books, then as much of this book about heaven needs to be about those books, just as most of this book about soul-catching needs also to be about that heaven. Sure, as with the Bible, this team effort can pose problems of continuity, as different members of the editorial committee brainstorm each other and the sovereign author too with the committee, since each, from either heaven or earth, have their very own and different ways of seeing things. Nevertheless, as pointed out by James Schulman and William Bowen (when writing of college sports and educational values) in their book *The Game of Life,* 'Writing can be a true team sport.'

Truth is multifaceted, however, and so on earth, it reflects the light into all the colours of the rainbow in different ways. As far as possible, it is left to the sovereign author to make a coherent whole in exercising his or her expertise as the earthly producer of any such editorially designated work, much of which has already been first designed, but not so designated before being given heavenly imprimatur following its review in heaven. To be sure, even in the taking of Holy Communion, there's many a slip between the earthly cup and the earthly lip, or as the old publishing adage goes up here, 'Heaven when seen from earth is nothing at all like the earth when seen from heaven.'

Today's authors must always look back to the authors of old—Job, Jonah, Jeremiah, David, Solomon, Elijah, Isaiah, Matthew, Mark, Luke, and John—without overlooking Paul's many epistles, and of course, the last and final word is given (although rarely preached or taught or talked about) to the Revelation of Jesus Christ. It's a long way back (so modernists think) to the book of Genesis, but we angels know that to find out just how to do everything quite properly in these very heady latter days, we need to talk with God, to think with God, to feel with God, and to walk with God. Like any very tiny toddler learning to walk with the Ancient of Days, that toddler still learns so whilst treasuring God's *rhema* (or spoken word) as to how properly his very own way of doing things should be done in these latter days.

As a generalissimo (pace *OED*), the temporal task for every fast-passing prophetic moment on earth is to assist the Supreme Command to keep heaven and earth for as long as possible in its first creatively designed holistic equilibrium. That means fighting every day and night against the Counterfeit Command, which would usurp the Supreme Command's first creative design, and so, for its own counterfeit and nefarious purposes, would seek to supplant its own Counterfeit Command for that of the Supreme Command.

As Leading-Angel Neil says, we are all—Emma, Zach, Luca, Malachi, Samuel, Eli, Matthew, and Kaia—new to this angelic process of contributory editing. And of course, many others shall spontaneously join in. Of course, the basic teamwork has been around a bit, since one book begets another, but never until these latter days of telescoped time has the need for editorial teamwork been felt to be so pressingly crucial as well as humanly critical to the earthly outcomes. Deadlines are deadlines, as they say, even of earth in timeless heaven. We are all novices, no matter how long-lived we may have been on earth before being set to undertake piecework to prepare ourselves for the homecoming of the promised second heaven.

So then, let's take the intro, passing on from one contributor to the other, piece by piece ... piece by piece ...

'Zach, you see, if you can find the right quotation for a headnote ... Eli, you next, expound on that headnote ... and so on ... and so on ... thereafter taking your appointed place ... as if you hear a pin drop by which you each ... like in any school of prophets ... keeping in good order ... are to tell the tale and continue the angelic story ... Any questions?'

'Yes, indeed, Samuel, and you too, Matthew, that's a good opening question by which to ask of any reader, what it is that the reader wants to get out of life? And yes, again, you're right, Eli and Zach, that's hardly a question which you'd ask of any angel. But then this is a book more for mortals who read rather than for angels like yourselves who've learnt to write, so that makes your question a fair enough one to ask of all readers on earth. And that's another reason why angels instruct mortals to act as their amanuensis (for which purpose any least-expecting mortal may be asked even to eat a book). Why, the Revelation of Jesus Christ (last book of the Bible shortly to be replaced by its already promised definitive action) is dictated by an angel to John and so to be written by him, another mere mortal on behalf of Jesus Christ.'

All the same, there's no shortage of books on—don't drop the hyphen from) soul-catching. Some books, such as *The Catcher in the Rye* or *The God Boy* or *A Prayer for Owen Meany*, can be as grotesquely misunderstood as *Heavens to Betsy* by earthly mortals. Those mortals who are tone-deaf frequently, but sadly fail to hear the always underlying spiritual voice—but then that's why even God sometimes rages and shouts. The Bible (sixty-six books by forty different authors—we'll take that number as standard rather than dispute it each time) is best. But even that number is more than grotesquely misunderstood. God still speaks, however, and just to prove so, even although the whole wide world is in the melting pot as never before, these twelve books (to constitute this present constellation) have been melded together as kingdom commentary (however contingent) on today's still ongoing current affairs.

Nevertheless, on all counts, the sixty-six books of the Bible for the price of one book is by far the best bargain. Nevertheless, we have managed to keep that principle of fair business dealing alive. In the same way, we market these twelve books to update the same multifaceted subject of soul-catching—all twelve books for the same price (without diminution) as one book. As said before, like the Bible, it's a team effort, whether by sovereign author, contributing angels, or earthling reporter in the front-line field of battle.

Indeed, that's exactly why we would entrust any such story as this one on the subject of angels to be told by any mere mortal! For their being on earth, mortals at least think they know better about what they want to get out of life than we angels in heaven could possibly know what's best for them—and it is exactly what mortals think is better for themselves (whether they're right or as often wrong) which we angels need to know most from mortals (for the present fact of their being so fallible).

It's a funny thing, although not always for the good, but most humans commit their souls to whatever they're most seeking to find and intend to pursue. So then, let's see, with some earthly reporter's help (however much from left field), whether we can gather our angelic wits together to pursue collectively, first, the envisioning of ideas and then, secondly, the writing up of those ideas, by way of what follows for being thirdly, *The Soul-Catcher's Chief Delight*.

Look at that now—in the course of this editing (but finally up to the sovereign author), we've already changed the title! Does any mortal really think that by learning to fly, whether by means of any magic carpet (or *samolyot,* as so described in so many ancient texts), he can learn to imitate the angels? This is going to be a very tragicomic book! Who did you say that fellow was, the one who got skinned alive for seeking to challenge the godly Apollo's flute-playing ability? That's right, Marsyas (or so you say), then pity any poor soul (or 'poor sod', as the macho unbelievers say) for thinking to keep up with any Apollo, far less to outclass what follows for being the heavenly fray!

Let's see now if our reporter in the field—let's say some leading agent of ours—no longer just in Minsk or in Moscow but now instead in a Baathist-afflicted Babylon, in a Taliban-afflicted Afghanistan, as well as in an Isis-infected Syria, can still be as lighthearted on earth when faced with decoding our editorial edicts from heaven! No nation on earth is by now left unafflicted. Let's see whether he or she, whose reports of the then fast-crumbling Soviet Union were once published as coming from our man in Minsk (1991) and later our man in Moscow (1993–1994), is still able to levitate (although not yet bodily unless first spiritually) and so by such strategic means to take off from planet Earth's now profusely ground-mined lower levels.

Who then kept score in 1991, 1993, 1994, and onwards? Well, by a series of his own now long-lost letters, he did so himself! There were letters from Lyubimova in the *New Zealand Tablet*, for those being then sent from 'their man in Minsk', and also letters from the law library in the *New Zealand Law Journal*, likewise for being also sent from 'their man in Minsk'. That's not all, since the so-called former Soviet Union was then disintegrating round everyone's bitterly cold ears. And so, whilst the USA was busily patting itself on the back for giving foreign aid to its Cold War loser (just as it had done to defeated Germany after World War II), the 'verra same fella' once nominated by the president of Belarus to be also 'his man in Minsk' then became the South Pacific's 'man in Moscow'.

Funny thing—it was another New Zealand reporter, Harold Williams (known undercover as the cheerful giver), who kept the score on behalf of the entire Western Front during that so-called Russian (but actually German-sponsored) Revolution of 1917. This probably explains why Dunedin became a UNESCO City of Literature—since Harold Williams, having family members in Dunedin but formerly a Methodist preacher who made no sense at all to his rural congregation in any one of the sixty or so languages he knew and spoke, became foreign correspondent for both *The Times* and, as back then, also *The Manchester Guardian*. [If you want to believe some but not all this biography, then read Ariadna Tyrkova-Williams's biography of her husband, *The Cheerful Giver*.]

Grundsheffer (this next New Zealander's undercover name as used in the *New Zealand Listener*) must be quite elderly now. And so, quite elderly he is—but in heaven's name, does that really matter? Some of his students are still convinced he was over there in Moscow busily drafting the new-styled constitution of the present Russian Federative Republic, but although that's just balderdash, every denial confirms it the more. At all such known times, as the dean of studies in the long-ago dissolved faculty of spurious studies can confirm, he (i.e. Grundsheffer) was busily planting spuds in his own back garden, surely as of now in Belleknowes, Dunedin.

Age and even also health are not everything. Even deans of studies (particularly those of spurious studies) can have demented memories. Everywhere you look in Kabul (as our man when once in Kabul will surely see), there are legless amputees pushing what's left of their torsos up and down the streets on either deconstructed skateboards or on horizontal hand trolleys. Their legless torsos are tired, their sometimes fingerless knuckles are raw, and their post-traumatic-disordered minds are either dementedly blank, or else overburdened from pushing what's left of their military-maligned and leg-amputated torsos around.

So too, can our hand-picked reporter remain undercover like any limbless one of them and, yet when heavenly need arises, still rise fast enough and take off far enough to traverse such pockmarked battle skies? We don't really know, since our sovereign author (who cannot really know (either way) what any one human will do) has extended to him (or will it be to her) his own sovereign volition by way of human free will. So then, like any angel (righteous and not counterfeit), will this undercover earthling still be able to fly and soar, as if on the wings of an eagle when less content to roar down ski slopes on Coronet Peak?

You remember, don't you, that the occupational hazard of every compassionate angel is to go bush or to turn native (as they used to describe the same phenomenon amongst earthlings when in the formerly colonial or now solely commercial rather than once highly cultured diplomatic service). Shucks (as they still say in rural USA) this world is now an open market for both terrorists and amputees, as well as being a closed market to most émigrés and refugees. Still, that's nothing new, since before the First World War, as before the Second World War, that's all happened before. And yet, as if never before, the same thing's now happening all over again.

We'll let the reporter, whoever he or she is, deal with that. Are you really sure that he or she is 'the man for us', as they say so often on earth of presidents, premiers, and other popularly elected politicians? Why, until he or she gets to places like Kabul, Tehran, Baghdad, and Damascus, our own poor soul (or sod) of an author hasn't the slightest idea with what turmoil this whole wide world is getting ready to face him …

'Hold on, hold on, here's breaking news—either something very, very old or else something very, very new! That's the trouble with investigative journalism—it outruns the short-term public memory faster than it can hope to break already historic headlines. Now here's something which could be either from this morning's *Underground Daily Times* or else from the remnants of Constantine's long-disbanded Praetorian Guard!'

'Poor sod, indeed, for being such a fall guy!' was heard coming over the airwaves, perhaps already from the Counterfeit Command. 'Hehehe—since he or she (whoever the fall guy) must learn to survive either (1) the ascetic loneliness of the desert experience, like Symeon the Stylite, when mocked at for his being atop the monastic column; or else (2) like Damascus of Rome when mocked at by political factions in the urban desert for his being atop the papal column—why then, since each must learn to cope also with the reciprocal market forces designed to promote the purposes of us in Counterfeit Command— then neither of these fall-guys is remotely likely... hehehe.... to make the grade.'

'There's not much to pick between either of the fall-guys, as the pagan Praetextatus would have roguishly said, "Who would not themselves be a Christian, whether ascetic or apostolic, for the sake of such reverential fame and indulgently selfish good fortune?" Why, he or she, just as any other highly aspirational reporter or author, will stand or fall according to Sod's law.

'Why, whether Sod's law or Murphy's law, call it what you will, but as long as we in Counterfeit Command are in charge of its administration (whereby if something can go wrong, it most certainly will go wrong), then we are the ones in Counterfeit Command who hold the keys to heaven. Don't let trivial dispute disarm you—this is what is meant between east and west (now lower case) as no less than Anselm of Canterbury put it, by being in "substantive agreement".

'Here, cross your fingers (of both hands, surely) for both heaven and hell now being in "substantive agreement". The pivotal issue, whether once between Jew or Gentile, Yahweh or Allah, or even now between East or West, is closed. As everyone now knows, there's no longer any distinction between heaven and hell in all this one great big cosmic sea of faith!

'So then, back off, you little bugger, before the same thing happens to you, as we made sure happened to Jesus Christ—that right royal bastard! We gave him all the opportunities, whether to rule the nations on our behalf or to feed the hungry on our behalf or to demonstrate in any other way his Father's heavenly power on our behalf. You don't know what it feels like to be usurped by your own father's smarty, smarmy, and always self-sufficient younger son. You don't know what it is to wake one morning to find yourself redundant and then be given short shrift from heaven. But as sure as hell, you'll find out—the higher you go, then the harder you'll fall. We'll make sure of that, and whatever you care to call us, by this false god or that false god, we'll be there—through scorching sun and stormy night at your very elbow and to every last syllable of unrecorded … unrecorded … unrecorded time!

'Don't forget, we make the rules, and we call the shots! We've known you from the very first moment you came into the world, and we've already got you more than covered. We know every single thing about you—from Nineveh to Baghdad, from Salt Lake City to Facebook, and from whatever may be your birthplace on earth (don't worry, we've got that sussed) to way, way, way … far, far, far … beyond in heaven. Not to stretch a point, we know you've already renounced the Lord your God more than 666 times! Google yourself on Facebook—we'll not only send you the data, but on your joining the ranks of the Counterfeit Command, we'll give you the app by which to make all that incriminating evidence against you disappear. We'll put you on the patrilineal payroll retrospectively as a lord lieutenant (either of back-owed dues or backbiting blues—the choice is yours to charge all indebtedness as you see fit).

'"Fair's fair!" as you always say! So then, come back home, if not yet to beautiful Babylon, then at least to Nineveh on whose banks of the River Tigris (not far from today's Mosul) you once lay down and wept! We've been killing Kurds there like flies in this, the second millennium—and the place is yours for a song as yet never sung. We're already working flat out on Kabul, Baghdad, Tehran, and Damascus. Haven't you heard God is dead? He abdicated from heaven to earth when his kingdom came to earth with his blue-eyed bastard, and for that being the gospel truth (no caps, please), the best proof is this presently fast-declining state of planet Earth!'

Like any Praetorian remaindered to the Roman colonies, this spokesman on behalf of the Counterfeit Command was apt to let his views run native. Picking up on a few Pictish views from across the remains of Hadrian's Wall and melding them with Yiddish views from here, there, and everywhere, he could be forgiven for not knowing how much he confused himself as well as others.

'Listen to him rant! Don't any longer be a fool for any God called Yahweh. He's long dead and gone, and so too is his soppy, although very stroppy henchman, one of the very many false prophets who proclaimed themselves to be Christ Jesus … the redeemer … the saviour … and so on … and so on … and so on … and so on … and so on!'

'What indeed? Oh, oh, oh.... ... ... Hold on there.... Find it hard to hear from hell, do you, whenever it happens that you really want to hear from heaven? Hell is all around us, don't you know... and often more so when we really need to hear from heaven... ... As for any boy-scout or young pioneer angel, this book will tell you how to be prepared... ...

'Well then, to hear more of heaven... then re-read *The Story of Christ*, written by Giovanni Papini, where in its best-selling tenth English Edition translated from the Italian by Mary Agnetti in 1923, his then renewed *Story of Christ* makes it clear that 'in the human and virile sense of re-making souls' our own evergreen *Story of*

Christ needs to be retold in its own way (without first having been 'de-fleshed by the knives of university professors') for each and every passing generation....

'Make no mistake about it! In these latter days when hell so closely wraps itself around us, we need to know (both us angels as well as you humans) as much as it will take to avoid going to hell as it shall take us to get us to heaven. That's exactly why, as part of your soul-catcher's calling, you humans must harden up your stomachs by way of learning to chew, like a dog on a bone, over any barebones history of hell, no less than to celebrate with us over even the briefest history of heaven.

'Well then... ... hold tight... as we fly over and into some of this world's worst hot-spots, sink-holes, and hell-holes... Syria, Iraq, and Iran are not so far away. Satan has only to flip his two-headed/two-tailed coin (don't trade your call or else you'll fall) by which 9/11 becomes 24/7, and all hell breaks out (from which there's no viable safe-haven) in your own backyard... .... Don't scoff, some of us angels once lived through the One Hundred Years War!

'What follows, like now, is a team effort. Of course, writing in heaven is always a team effort. Why the Bible itself (for being at least sixty-six books by forty different authors) is most assuredly a team effort. Were it not for its human input through this team effort of forty different human authors it would make no sense to humans for being God's own Living Word!

'Because outcomes depend on origins (as achieved by heavenly objectives) we'll let the introduction to each of the next twelve books on the subject of *The Soul-Catcher's Calling* be more explicitly rendered as a team effort according to the whims and fancies of each respective contributor than what follows by the concerted effort of us all together by way of reaching a more definitive outcome for each of these twelve books.

'Here goes, then... ... ... The whole point of this book (basically a history book) is to promote a 20/20 prophetic vision by which to foresee our calling as soul-catchers, not only for this next upcoming year of 2020 AD, but also for many more fruitful years on earth and far, far, far beyond... ... Then too, for the sake of all eternity... ... here goes!

'Oh, of course it goes without saying, that every one of you readers are most welcome to join in the heavenly discussion which follows. All our cosmic discussions are done by way of dialogue, and never just by way of heavenly monologue. Nevertheless, as one of heaven's rules for orderly and productive discussion, just remember this: that unless you can see *more than just any one way* of settling any outcome (whether that be your own way or someone else's way) then don't consider yourself either ready or qualified to join in the discussion. There are far too many closed-shop discussions held on earth (led by cabals, cliques, and coteries) in which the most powerful disputants come with their minds, hearts, and wills already made up (and sometimes also with trade-offs earlier negotiated, commitments already given, allegiances exchanged, and outcomes consequentially decided—all this to the benefit of a few yet to the detriment of all.

* * *

ACKNOWLEDGEMENTS

Thanks be given to all friends and family members, teachers and preachers, prophets and publishers—whether now in heaven, still on earth, in transit, or elsewhere in default of earthly life—who have contributed, whether directly or indirectly, discretely or indiscreetly, to the writing of this report on the current state of growing turmoil across all this now deeply groaning earth. Praise be also to those who, whether self-aware of their sponsored participation or not, have engaged themselves wholeheartedly in the divinely sponsored process of soul-catching—that much denigrated process whereby even the least of lost causes on earth may nevertheless reap the greatest harvest of winning consequences in heaven. Special thanks are likewise due to those very daring editors of this leading agent's associated work at different times and in different places, whether being that work published by the *New Zealand Tablet*, the *Harvest Field*, the *New Zealand Law Journal*, the *New Zealand Listener*, the *Victoria University of Wellington Law Review*, the *Otago Law Review*, and the *Otago Daily Times* (amongst sundry other domestic publications), as well as to those editors of the *Juridical Review*, the *Cambridge Law Journal*, the *Statute Law Review*, the *American Journal of Comparative Law*, together with the well-known journal of *Transnational Law and Contemporary Problems* (amongst many other worldwide publications), all of which have contributed greatly to the basis of this more allegorical report (all praise and thanks also to its own editors) on the subject of the world's sadly declining state of law and order. Likewise, the learning experience gained by the same leading agent's many arduous years—served whilst under heavy fire—in his contributing to the *Annuaire de Législation Française et Étrangère*, as quaintly published, despite quite a mouthful of his own jurisprudential views being edited out by the Service de Recherches Juridiques Comparatives du Centre National de la Recherche Scientifique sur L'évolution du Droit dans les Différents Pays (also quite a mouthful), must be gratefully acknowledged. This sad largesse (Franko-French for off-loading in *ffrench*) is given with gratitude, despite the graceless interregnum occasioned through the French bombing, causing grave loss of life in Auckland Harbour, of the scuppered Greenpeace flagship—the *Rainbow Warrior*—in itself an act of governmentally engineered terrorism done by France against New Zealand in retribution for Greenpeace's protests over the French government's release of radioactive material into the South Pacific. [Back translation from the church's Cyrillic script supplied earlier by the former Lenin Library [replete with conceptually viable but strenuously tacit breathing-point brain markers] by the London Institute for the hard copy preservation of English prose.]

Authorised First Edition
The Marsyas Press
Imprimatur 1.1.2020
nigel.j.jamieson@gmail.com

CONTENTS

The Cosmos Contrived in a Constellation of No Less Than Twelve Books

BOOK ONE

A Very Brief yet Also Overall Conception of All Things under the Sun

A Thousand and One Nights

Think you, that I put too high a price upon this carpet, my lord? Its properties are both unique and marvellous. You only have to sit on it, bid yourself in thought to be elsewhere, and no matter how near or how far or how otherwise difficult would be your predestined travel, in the twinkling of an eye, this carpet shall carry you there ...

The Arabian Nights of Unending Stories

Intro 1—Eli: Some souls come into this world as if on a magic carpet (in ancient texts, called the samolyot, or self-flying machine). For such free-flying souls, it's as if nothing ever goes wrong. It's as if some cosmic force goes with them. Do you begrudge such privileged people their forcefulness? Never mind, that's close to what lawyers call a leading question, so beware just yet of even asking that question, far less trying to answer it.

For any mere mortal, one can carry this process of *as-if* thinking too far. The heartfelt wonder which such apparently privileged persons evoke from others as to their forcefulness can provoke a corresponding vulnerability which everyone else shares. Sooner or later, the extreme positivity of as-if thinking engenders in mortals the negativity of *what-if* fear. We'll soon learn the universal equation— that to every particle of positive matter, there is a complementary particle of negative antimatter. There now, you know more about this existing heaven and earth, as well as about the new and shortly to be replaced heaven and earth, than you've ever known before.

This is the very point at which the battle—between right and wrong or good and evil or righteousness and unrighteousness—can come to the fore. The issue then becomes one of accepting public responsibility, both for one's own forcefulness and for the vulnerability it occasions both to oneself as well as to others.

From those often very forceful souls to whom much authority is given, much more is often required of them in the exercise of that authority. *What if* this magic carpet of their privileged authority, flying all the time so high in the public eye, then becomes for each of them a fearful and perilous tightrope on which they must learn to balance their own personal vulnerabilities against their public responsibilities? Each day and every day, on behalf of others, they must go on performing this collective balancing act in the public eye. They get tired, they get bored, they get blasé, and so down to earth, they come a cropper.

Intro 2—Daffyd the Welsh Songster: This is the high wire (frequently electrified) of public responsibility. That responsibility is as often socially and morally expected as it is professionally and governmentally imposed. It is the one on which the most celebrated persons of privileged authority and their followers—from heads of states down to members of the press—must learn most to walk their talk. As often sideways, backwards, or on their hands and knees, they do so all without a safety net. When always in the public eye, it's almost impossible to walk and talk as others do—more routinely straightforward. Have a care for those in public office—so often mistaken for celebrities.

Intro 3—Robert Miller, MA, BD: None in public office—from preachers and policemen to professors honoris and teachers of tiny tots—is/are exempt from this very often fearfully perilous balancing act. This is the expected equation of governmental equilibrium from those in high-wire authority that can be both hard to fulfil as well as hard to explain. It is an equation even still harder to enforce or to satisfy the expected well-balanced equation at the top of the high wire when maintaining the same privileged authority at the collective ground level.

All the same, it's as if the charmed lives of such apparently privileged people working beyond extrahigh voltage (and suitably salaried) levels on some of earth's highest and main grid wires are still enchanted. This is so despite their public lives being made so obviously dependent on either the grid stringers of those high wires or on the constant advertising of the magic carpet purveyors by which those privileged celebrities may be whisked away (with golden handshakes or by way of golden parachutes) whenever from and to wherever they would want to go.

From the ground level of a very mundane and still flat earth, it seems as if they live their celebrated lives, whether as legislators, judges, or police commissioners. For themselves, they live as if in a fairy tale, but as often, the fairy tale of their lives turns nasty—as nasty as a nightmare. For them, it's as if the whole wide world (as seen *as if* laid out flat from wherever they are) is an *Arabian Nights Entertainment*. Note well, these little words *as if* since a great deal hangs on them. And remember that in real life as well as in the *Arabian Nights Entertainment*, the daily miracle of each new dawning day depends on overcoming the scariest challenge of last night's nightmare. Life for many, whether at the top or at the bottom of the social ruckus, relies on the outcome of that nightly fairy tale told as by Scheherazade (the narrator survivor of those one thousand and one nights known for being the aforesaid *Arabian Nights Entertainment*).

Intro 4—Krystiana (sometimes shortened to Kirsty): There are some storytellers for whom these little words *as if* are part of their stock in trade. As everyone knows, it's the little words, like *love* and *hate*, *good* and *bad*, and *right* and *wrong*, which somehow have the most to say. They say most about the way things are—in this once strangely flat, now flat-out, and to be again soon completely flattened-out world. More importantly, however, are the ways in which we use these little words.

Love and hate, good and bad, and right and wrong—why, when employed in the right way, then such little words (and all they stand for) can have the most miraculous power to change things. We may have mined the earth of its coal, oil, and minerals, some say almost to extinction. With skyscrapers and the tallest of towers, we may have blocked out the sky. We may have drag-netted the seas of so many living creatures and polluted the oceans past the point of retaining what we need of them for our own lives. And by doing so, heedless and headless to the helplessness of our hands, we have case-hardened ourselves, through self-containment of our souls, against the far greater power of the living Word. And so, for being completely flat out ourselves in our toing and froing across what we have made of a completely flattened-out world, we fail to see anything of the far greater power than is ours by which this old world still goes round and around.

By the power of prophetic proclamation, when uttered in the right spirit, a single word (it may be no more than a *please*, *sorry*, or *thank you*) can change things from the way they are to the way they ought to be. By reason of its positivity, this is particularly the province of as-if thinking, without which one could not hope to navigate any magic carpet. On the other hand, the fearful negativity of what-if thinking demonstrates that contrary force which most often prevents as-if thinking from getting even just off the ground.

Intro 5—Malachi (for whom both Irish and Judaic spellings and pronunciations abound): Choose for yourself. We're talking either quantum physics, ethics, or metaphysics here. Take your pick, since you can't go wrong—they're all part of one and the same cosmos. And what's more, if you can't make sense of one, then you can't make sense of the others, which would be a great pity since, for missing the transition point at which the different phases of each discourse balance, you're most usually heading towards the ultimate chaos of today's increasingly disordered universe. More than obvious to most mortals on earth, there's already a need for both a new heaven and a new earth (on which account it is that misbelievers discount the old ones). This isn't the first and only book (by any means) to make that need for a new heaven and a new earth obvious—and there's nothing new in this book by which to make any more or less of that same cosmic need for a new creation.

As for the tightrope equation expressed by the forceful tension, we need to maintain between vulnerability and responsibility, so also there is this other tightrope equation expressed by the forceful tension that exists between things as they are and things as they ought to be. In each case, however, there needs to be a measure for the exaction of whatever tension is needed to maintain the balance. The tactical process by which to provide the means of motivation for getting off the ground is one thing, and the seriously strategic purpose to account for our walking out on any high wire or our hiring any magic carpet is very much another.

The tactical process is pursued by our actualising the potential of as-if thinking. This is a process which we all possess yet tend to squander. Either we misapply our forcefulness or else we overlook, if not dispute the rightfully strategic purpose of this forcefulness with which we are meant to resolve issues of vulnerability and responsibility. Without our better resolving these issues of personal vulnerability and public responsibility, we can't go on to determine the more strategic issues of how things ought to be better used, better employed, or better distributed in this world. Instead of our looking ahead we look backwards (well, some of us) telling ourselves it's good to grumble and preoccupy ourselves with the inferior ways in which these things are now being treated.

Intro 6—Neil (known biblically as Niger, but more colloquially as Nigger): What exactly is the power of proclamation that brought this world into being and which still holds this world in being? You know, many dispirited souls believe it follows from our God being all-powerful, all-knowing, and all-present, that he or she is then immune from all responsibility. That follows, so most mortals think, because of God being then able to do whatever he or she would like to do.

No, that just tells us what little responsibility most mortals would exercise were they all-powerful, all-knowing, and all-present deities. Quite frankly, they'd behave like fallen angels. So then, when mortals complain about God's irresponsibility (or unfairness, as they often call it), they're only saying that he or she doesn't do the things that they would like their God to do as they would have him do.

Our ultimate purpose on earth (for both angels and humans) is to harness all the power (together with every proper means of its control) which, when rightly exercised over the human heart, mind, body, and spirit, can translate all right thought into precisely the right words by which to fulfil every most precious vision of how things on earth ought to be.

That's the power of proclamation, which carries within itself a correlative responsibility! Many poets, prophets, orators, artists, and other visionaries are amongst those who experience most intimately this highly creative and inspirational process (but so often overlook its correlative responsibility); whilst many lawyers, teachers, preachers, scholars, and writers must struggle hard and long to experience the intimacy of this process because their more responsible outlook tends to inhibit this form of inspirational creativity.

Intro 7—Luca (once before or more again called Lucius): As everyone also knows, there are charms and spells as well as curses and blessings, just as there are grouses and grumbles as well as praises and celebrations. And just as there are histories by which to declaim our less-than-perfect past, and from which spring those hopes by which to enliven the ever-prevailing present, so also there are prophecies by which to proclaim the eminently foreseeable future. Meanwhile, the only way to avoid unwelcome certainties is to confront and deal with unwelcome possibilities.

After all, the prophetic future when revealed by as-if thinking is little more than the past turned inside out. But the trouble with the fearfulness of what-if thinking is that it reconverts the prophetic future (as revealed by as-if thinking) back into that staid, stick-in-the-mud, and self-perpetuating mindset with which we formerly processed our past actions. For the most part, those are the past actions which we now regret for being the ones which as often sprang from fearful thinking. What we truly seek is that cosmic transformation which can only be achieved through the spiritual renewal of our minds. And when that cosmic transformation comes, we'll know it's come by reason of our having no more regrets.

It is once again *as if* the tales themselves do tell themselves. They themselves are larger than life by reason of the power they hold to change our lives. By their charmed telling, the life too of the storyteller (or so we readers presume ourselves to think) is likewise both charmed and enchanted. It may even be the case that unless the storyteller is completely charmed and entranced by the words he or she uses, the storyteller has simply no story to tell. [Nevertheless, as believers it behoves us to find out exactly the source and origin of that charm.]

Intro 8—Neil again: Oh dear, but *what if* the fearful telling (made only sotto voce or said in a whisper) says of something so critically significant as to be that, say, of (1) Christ's nativity or, say, of (2) Christ's Second Coming or, no less positively, say, of (3) the fall of Babylon? Then would anything at all result of these promised prophecies (one way or the other) by reason of their lack of any more passionate level of communication? In short, with respect to the power of proclamation, is any low-key telling worse than useless, and any former passion even perhaps undone, until retold and restored with the same angelic passion given to its forerunner? That's exactly why those who are no more than lukewarm, themselves neither grieving nor celebrating over such things, cause great affront to the Supreme Command. So then, what's the force and power of all such passionate proclamation unless it be the passion to pursue the truth?

It is the case, therefore, that when we angels come from heaven to earth, we must be sufficiently charmed or inspired by our assignment from the Supreme Command (call it an assignment from heaven if you so prefer) to bring you earthlings the precise message which we have been entrusted to deliver to you by the Supreme Command. Yet most often, you humans find this communicative process highly scary, *as if* we were not indeed angels from heaven but perhaps instead were aliens from hell, and so you are not bound by our message from the Supreme Command to be altogether charmed or enchanted by our angelic presence. You have then mistaken our most positive as-if remark of proclamation for a negative what-if remark of counterproclamation.

More often than not, you mortals first panic on meeting us angels. You either scamper (like Jonah), simper (like Sara), wrestle (like Jacob), or else (like John) fall to the floor in a worshipful swoon. Otherwise, you grovel at our feet, doubt our word, or else hop up on your awfully high horse by which to dispute our message—before succumbing to your footloose feelings instead of holding staunchly to the steadfast position we have given you in this world's centre stage. You mortals have just no idea of how many times this situational comedy goes on by which you keep on missing out on the heavenly message. Why, of all those mortals who'll swear to never ever having met an angel, you lot who refuse to recognise us are amongst the greatest to deny us when we're so often really there!

For those reasons, we frequently appear to you *as if* not angels but rather (as from time to time throughout this book) only *as if* we were other humans. Now these as-if undercover operations of ours can get us into serious trouble (as they have done) in giving rise to a history of half-angelic and half-human creatures once inhabiting earth. If you really know your church history (as all believing humans should), you'll know that one of the last such creatures (as recorded by the explorer Abel Tasman in his ships' log) was seen standing on a clifftop in seventeenth-century New Zealand).

Intro 9—Emma (sometimes called Irmushka): Many mortals (mostly the unredeemed) who lack self-confidence in their own eternity tend to exaggerate and embellish what little perception they have of the eternal truth. One way of doing this is by telling themselves overly romantic fairy tales. They do so either in ways which try to belie their own feelings of guilt or else to exalt their own wishful thinking. Thus, they refuse to believe in hell or to admit that angels (if believable beings at all) could be any less than heavenly, upright, and thoroughly righteous creatures. The irony of this highly romantic idyll of theirs is that most of the angels they meet are fallen angels.

It is a sign of these increasingly terrible times (where terrorism appears to rule the global roost) to mistake and to prefer the saccharine sweetness of counterfeit angels pretending to bring good news as against the bitterness of bad news brought by the very best and most reliable of heaven's angels. Discern the spirits, whether clean or counterfeit, at every possible opportunity; and check their spiritual passports at every purported border crossing. Now that's the heavenly message as always, which so many of today's flat-out mortals prefer to ignore, because they can't be bothered to weigh up the life-or-death issues which like to hide behind what most flat-out mortals dismiss for being trivial details.

Let's now clear the air. There exist angels who are so far fallen from grace that it would be impossible for any mortal to exaggerate that perpetually chronic level of evil which saturates and defiles their whole being. Don't let's say any more than that about them here—except to acknowledge that (1) there's a far longer history of heaven by which to account for the far, far shorter history of hell and that (2) it's far, far more tempting to overlook and fail to see a chronic level of evil than it is to pick up on an everyday level of sin, besides which (3) it is part of the conjoint and overlapping histories of both heaven and hell on earth which gave rise to those half-angelic-half-human and sometimes hideously horrific creatures which we believe to be now extinct yet which still inhabit sometimes our nightmares and dreams. Meanwhile, don't hesitate to consult Dr Joe Ibojie on the subject of his book entitled *Dreams and Visions*, published by Destiny Image Europe, whose motto is for 'Changing the world, one book at a time.'

That half-angelic-half-human outcome on this earth (romantically misconstrued by some cultures to be heroic or even saintly) was most certainly never designed by the Supreme Command to have any sanctified place in the history of heaven. However, since all things work for the good of those who love God and who are called to implement his purpose, this once angelic misfortune can still be utilised by heaven (where thrift is a virtue, extravagance a vice, and where there is no wastage). Thus, for the sake of all creation, not even the worst of mistakes are totally discarded.

So too, there's a point (whether fact or fiction) to all horror stories (provided you see the point of them, take the point seriously, and don't discard it). Likewise, there's a point to catastrophe stories (such as of the fall and of the flood). Why, as everyone knows, fact is far stranger than fiction.

Why, even of your own time, dearest readers, there's so much more of a point to the rising tide of catastrophe stories (a spin-off from both the horror story and the action movie), but to explain that point right now might scare you to an otherwise preventable death, which, for the sake of this book, would be far too soon. All the same, bestselling author Dale Brown gives one of the clearest and most credible example of today's catastrophe novels, if one cares to prepare ahead for some of the perilous flying we're going to do, by your reading of his *Storming Heaven*.

Aside from such set homework, we'll leave a discussion (and demonstration) of this fast-rising tide of literary effort devoted to the genre of the catastrophe novel, of which there are also so many examples (prophesied, averted, and experienced) in the Bible, that this book too must reap the harvest of a similar catastrophic demonstration by which to explain and fulfil the strategic purpose of any soul-catching as a planned military operation. Meanwhile, back to the earlier well-known horror story of that Gruesome Goliath who challenged all Israel, and by whose defeat all Israel was in turn delivered from the catastrophe of being defeated by the Philistines. Now can you begin to see the developing relationship between the horror story and the catastrophe story? Very subtle, isn't it? And if you don't appreciate the pending catastrophe, then you don't see the point of the horror story!

As said before, then back to the horror story. Now Gruesome Goliath was one of the last of such unauthorised half-angelic and half-human figures on earth whose grotesque misshapenness was rightly put to death by Wee Davie Boy (whom you may learn about in the first book of Samuel, chapter 17, verses 12 to 58). Now, that was quite a long story for those days, when the fate of the entire nation of Israel hung in the balance, but all to the betterment of both earth and heaven forever after. In other words, the impending catastrophe to Israel, although against all odds, was averted. Unless you can see that, however, you've missed the point of Wee Davie versus Gruesome Goliath as a horror story. And you've also, in the process, missed out on the whole point of that horror story for being also history.

Intro 10—Kaia (also answering to Gaia): From this once ancient way of simple storytelling, *as if* all of any story could be told without non-fiction, there soon develops, although out of a very different sort of wonderment at the world, its scientific sequel. This development, although secondary in time to that of fiction, marks the birth of non-fiction. At first this was history (in itself no simple matter) out of which developed dialectic (the science of investigation) and, in turn, hermeneutics (the science of interpretation). Now that was the point at which all storytelling (to be known henceforth as narrative) came to that fork in the road where those who pursued non-fiction sought to part company from those who kept troth (i.e. kept faith) with fiction.

In the growth of both aural and literary communication, sometimes fiction would eclipse non-fiction, and at other times, non-fiction would eclipse fiction. Sometimes, the parent fiction would engender conflict with its offspring. The parental fiction would put down and abort non-fiction. At other times, the fully developed offspring, by way of being proudly non-fiction, would euthanise and so put down its parental fiction. Whereas military conflict took place physically on the battlefield, literary conflict took place on paper, but eventually, both forms of conflict coalesced into all-out conflict, sometimes into total war, and then into abject forms of communicative terrorism. All the same, both fiction and non-fiction rely for their communication, (not just on their still broadly shared road of bifurcated narrative) but also on sharing the same (both highly-imaginative and creatively-inspired) conjectural faculty. This is employed for non-fiction as a means to an end, and for fiction, either as an end in itself, or else as a stimulus towards advancing non-fiction.

Yet every scientifically sought-for non-fiction (although professedly at odds with fiction) is obviously poised on some explicit conjecture (or as-if fiction) as to this world being a different world than that initially thought of or generally first seen. Indeed, established science is therefore still more accurately and precisely poised on this now conjecturally specific but also parentally generic as-if fiction. It thus follows that unless the adventuresome scientist is likewise charmed or inspired by some ingenious and possibly incredulous *as if*, although entirely conjectural fiction, the scientist can have no non-fictional discovery by which to change the status of the former world by any means of proof, bringing about a non-fiction in place of a fiction (but in turn relegating the previous non-fiction on which the conjectural fiction hinged now to an established fiction).

In turn, this change of status relegates the previously held, but now disproved non-fiction (on which the subsequent conjectural fiction hinged) now to the level of an obsolete (but historically interesting) fiction. Such is the fictional fate of atoms (as no longer the smallest of physical particles), phlogiston (as a fictional element of chemical combustion), and the fictional traverse of the sun through the sky (instead of the earth around the sun).

Intro 10 (con.) — Saint Izaac (Newton): So much for facts, fictions, and non-fictions! But on this score (particularly on the relationship of physicality to spirituality) be sure to read, hear the voice, and not just look at my conversations with Michael Hoskin, on *The Mind of the Scientist*. All the same, because we are investigating the relationship of physicality to spirituality (for the long haul, as that subject has always been the prime consummation of my life) we must now take on the tough task of relating science (which is consummate) to everything else (which in turn either swallows up science (as a serpent swallows its tail) or else reversely leaves (as for law, logic, linguistics, and so on when all seen as sciences) not much! So, then, hold onto your hats!

Scientific non-fiction (as Kaia has shown) is thus but the child (and so often the rapidly changing child) of its parentally generated conjectural fiction. Thus, most obviously both the scientific fiction and the legal fiction (not to mention the philosophical fiction and the theological fiction) can be potential (sibling) rivals by virtue of their proven non-fictional claims to any commonly held fictional inheritance.

Every scientific non-fiction hinges or pivots on an as-if fiction. Likewise, the same goes for every adventuresome inventor, explorer, and would-be discoverer, as well as for every authentically adventuresome scientist. As already said, a great deal by way of faith and works, together with establishing the subtle identity, capacity for conjecture, and calling of one's own soul, hangs on these two words of *as if.*

Intro 11—Zachariah: From the point of view of philosophy (in its love of wisdom) which sometimes eclipses science (for being the love of knowledge) just as science (the love of knowledge) at other times eclipses philosophy (the love of wisdom), there is much to say in both of these disciplines of the as-if function. The development of the as-if fiction (with stories, tales, myths, prophecies, and visions) into the as-if non-fiction (with facts and figures) does not stop there.

As a highly prophetic form of communication, both disciplines come to benefit from the conjoint use of figurative expression. On the scientific side (through narrowing of meaning), this leads to paradoxes, puzzles, and problems, whereas on the literary side (through widening of meaning), this leads to poetry and parables, philosophy and theology, as well as to both history (in time) and geography (in space). Ultimately, however contingent (or conjectural) this may make our present heaven and earth, there's the promised prospect of all eternity (as an alternative reality) for both a new heaven and a new earth.

Those philosophers (i.e. lovers of wisdom) use figurative language for that being to them the most directly effective and scrupulously honest way of expressing the full gamut of reality (through parables, proverbs, prayers, prophecies, homilies, myths, stories, and fairy tales), whereas scientists (i.e. lovers of knowledge) insist on sticking strictly to what they more directly see to be the facts and figures (expressed more specifically in terms of surveys, reviews, graphs, equations, experiments, proofs, arguments, and conclusions). Scientists (in their dealing more directly with data) see themselves more honest than those who have a more literary bent. They see themselves more in touch with the elementary particles which go towards constituting the full gamut of reality (just as most lawyers, other than jurists, do stick to their primary sources of law contained in statutes and cases).

Intro 12—Matthew: Actually, there's no great difference between these two different kinds of searchers and researchers for their being either philosophers or scientists. Both of them—in their search after the truth, the whole truth, and nothing but the truth—pursue the same objective. However differently they pursue the truth as either philosophers or scientists is explained only by their concern for different sources and resources. The same goes for lawyers, jurists, historians, theologians, poets, preachers, and prophets—they pursue the same objective but are committed to different sources and resources.

Yes, their motivation or calling may also differ, insofar as the more reflective philosopher looks for wisdom (Solomon's choice) whereas a more impulsive person (like Moses) looks to learn, know, and discover through experience the ways and means by which to realise the same truth that both he as a scientist and the philosopher are each looking for to change the world. Nevertheless, personalities like Moses and Solomon (no less than Plato and Socrates) are multifaceted figures, and multifaceted figures have more than one personality between which they switch (much to the chagrin of monofacial personalities who, like themselves, look to types that stay singularly true). All the same, when once that earthly distance between science and philosophy (knowledge and wisdom) is drawn tightly together to constitute the one and only divine truth, then that new heaven (as promised) will have also truly come to (this new) earth.

Meanwhile, what may be seen of scientists and philosophers doing things differently is to be explained by no more than their adoption of different earthly means of pursuing that one and only divine truth. What we label facts as distinct from fictions (as if to discredit one from the other in many situations) is *as if* we disrupt the equation relating science to philosophy (i.e. knowledge ⇔ wisdom) no less ignorantly than were we to do the same with the biological equation between form and function (i.e. form ⇔ function).

Intro 12 (continuation)—Malachi: When here on earth, whether as angels or humans, it is wise to remember that truth here on earth is always at a premium—that's to say, always scarce and in (but not always available on) demand. Accordingly, the truth on earth can never be told exactly, far less precisely—which is the very reason that some of all those parties who search after the truth, the whole truth, and nothing but the truth will mistake heaven for being an incredulous make-believe instead of the incredibly true fairy tale that it is.

This paucity of truth on earth, to be briefly explained by the next eleven books in this series, accounts (amongst many other things) for the way in which many scientists despise almost every fictional and figurative form of attempting to reveal what is also some non-fictional truth. For them, in terms of their own knowledge, there are no two ways of expressing the full gamut of truth, so they are frequently disappointed to find out that the level of truth which they find out on earth does not hold true for very long and never ever equates with what they could only hope for in that heaven, which, in favour of this earth, they yet deny.

In consequence, that figurative or fictional form which others use on earth to express the truth, the whole truth, and nothing but the truth severely irritates them for being a fairy tale, a foible, or a fiction. What irritates those who seek only after facts, facts, and more facts is the way in which their search so often subliminally suggests to them that their own purportedly non-fictional research actually confirms that the way, the truth, and the life (which is really what they're looking for) has already come down to earth from heaven in the person of Jesus Christ.

It is this earthly irritation (as often expressed as an irritable response to heavenly unfairness, to heavenly injustice, and to heavenly mercilessness) which can make those who insist on sticking to none other than (as they say, the proven) facts most deeply irritated. As often as not, they so lose their cool as to demonstrate that for some reason or another, they cannot stick (as they say) to what they think to be their own proven set of facts. Instead, they spend as much of their lives haranguing those whom they see to perjure this earth's proof of their own truth as they do themselves search for their own elusive proof as to the non-existence of God and the nonsensicality of heaven. Their otherwise dynamic souls are deadlocked by demonic forces and grounded to this earth.

Intro 13 (moving on)—Samuel, Luca, and Eli: Besides being valued for its own sake, the love of wisdom (philosophy), for the sake of other disciplines, is also the science of abstraction. Now this topic of mindful (but never mindless) abstraction is one to which we must return to again and again throughout this series of twelve books (when at a bargain for the price of one). We must engage every reader in abstraction for the sake of (1) prophetically edging across any high wire above sheer hell below or for the sake of (2) flying physically across broad continents by any samolyot or apparent magic carpet, no less than for the sake of (3) finally learning how to walk on water.

Not everyone, for their differential leaning towards either the theoretical aspect of life or else towards the practical aspect of life, feels the same level of ease when called on to engage in abstraction (far less to have faith enough consciously to walk on water). This can remain the case no matter how meaningful and mindful may be those different levels of abstraction in which both highly practical people or highly theoretical people may be called to engage, aside from everything worldly or mundane, in this process of divine learning.

Yet anyone and everyone who prophesies—however minimally and however notionally and however subconsciously, subliminally, or unselfconsciously—has walked on water. And yet again, learning to walk, *as if* quite nonchalantly on water, requires everyone in the service of the Supreme Command to develop far beyond any mere mortal standard of 20/20 prophetic vision.

Intro 14 —Neil and Kirsty: If you're still reading thus far, you'll have already conceived some expectation of where you believe this book to be going. This expectation may or may not be fulfilled, because it is the author's own expectation throughout this book to prepare you, in more ways than one, for the entirely unexpected. Nevertheless, for making life so boring, unless when sometimes challenged by some measure of the unexpected, would be most counterproductive to our much-needed zest of life. This zest of life, which is also a zest for life and in life, comes from life being some sort of test, whether voiced as one of faith and pilgrimage, experiential exploration, or bodily survival. In the clinical sense, some may describe this zest as no more than that of any person being behaviourally motivated by his or her rightful level of stress—but that physiological description would fall far short of anyone who, in his or her spirit, knows what it feels like to have a real zest for life.

For life itself, as for choice of books, there are lots of options. At the simplest of writing levels as well as of reading levels, there are books with happy endings, and there are other books with unhappy endings. Likewise, there are some extremely uplifting books and films, just as there are some extremely disheartening books and films. How you choose to read life, like of any book, whether a chosen challenge or an arbitrary choice, so too is life.

At no more sophisticated a literary or filmic level than there are both uplifting and disheartening books and films, there are also both happily utopian as well as unhappily dystopian novels and films. Both genres of writing for books and films, whether right through from beginning to end, or in terms only of their respectively happy or unhappy endings, can be extremely polarised—as polarised (unexpectedly) as good may be from evil or as polarised (expectedly) as heaven may be from hell.

The pivotal point for all great literature or art (depending on its message) lies in some ratio of one extreme to another extreme—that is, for the sake of communicating that message to mortals on earth lies somewhere in between each such opposite extreme. This requires, even for no more than emulating the highest of literary standards, both the greatest of life experience (however painful) and the greatest of literary endeavour (however much falling short of the established standard) the work of the author may presume.

This book, for example, is neither a happy-go-lucky utopian novel nor a down-and-out dystopian novel. That much will be told to the reader, whose task will be to decide exactly (although not precisely) where the working ratio (whether between good and evil or between heaven and hell) lies. Nevertheless, there is no entirely right answer any more than there is any entirely wrong answer to this question, since the difficulty of communicating the message is (as usual) relative to the constantly changing relationship between writer and reader.

Once that ongoing relationship becomes static (whether through failure of the writer or of the reader or of both the writer and the reader), then until restarted by the introduction of some new dynamic (whether by the reader or by the writer), this book is then ended, however much longer the story may attempt to go on. On this account, the whole story told by this book is contingent: sometimes on facts as yet left uninformed; sometimes by a disparity of values, opinion, or humour between writer and reader; sometimes on the reading of other books referenced by this book as yet unread by the reader; sometimes by the reader choosing to overlook errors of either commission or omission or else infelicities of style committed by the author; and sometimes by the increasing irrelevance of this book to the reader's life.

Intro 14(continuation)—Emma and Kaia: As between the happy ending of any utopian novel and the unhappy prognosis of every dystopian novel, we two members of the editorial committee must confess to being not quite sure of just where this book is heading. We would expect more distinction to be drawn between the expected and the unexpected to resolve this question in terms of happy or unhappy endings. We beg to differ from the confidence of our colleagues that readers will have continued their reading of *The Soul-Catcher* thus far at all, far less with any great delight, and accordingly call for you to give the author of this report some instruction on this matter before *The Soul-Catcher* goes to press.

The pathos of today's cosmic situation almost entirely escapes all mortal recognition. Unfortunately for mortals, the word *pathetic*, when so ill-used by most of them, has undermined whatever possible perception of what *pathos* truly means. Only those rare scholars of classical literature who study 'the pathetic fallacy' can any longer come to grips with what pathos really means. Dedicated scholarship for the sake of scholarship (which entails so much else for the benefit of this planet Earth) is at a premium. The fast lane of thoughtless travel brings us face to face with fast-declining finances which oblige us environmentally to struggle on with the long-term impracticalities of an overwhelming technology as best we can. We have reached the point at which updating the software for one's computer renders one's computer obsolete to carry on! No longer than three years, say some, is the life of any computer. Compared to any computer, therefore, what a wonderful thing is man!

Pathos pervades whatever solely physical conception we can have of all things under the sun. It most particularly affects the pursuit of what humans have come to describe (both figuratively and literally) as even just the 'plain truth', never mind all the cover-ups required by which to prevaricate the 'naked truth'. Long before Galileo Galilei had entered the fray, the earliest of Christian cosmologists, Bishop Diodore of Tarsus (circa 378), had been questioning, 'How hot is the sun?'

In the face of the overwhelming political correctness which now pervades the most heavenly battlefields on earth, whatever naked truth can be any longer revealed on earth is almost immediately scorched by the sun. At best, it then withers, dries, and dies. Or else, at worst, it is perverted into something so horrendous that most mortals, even the most perceptive of them, would not dare to argue, far less fight for the naked truth.

Intro 15—Matthew and Samuel together with Malachi and Zachariah: Let's first say here that we second those earlier proposals of our angelic colleagues that whoever is appointed from heaven to author this report on earth be given some more definitive instruction than is already around on the histories of both heaven and hell. He or she requires to be instructed not only on the subject of both expected and unexpected happenings but also, and more so, on the subject of either happy or unhappy endings. So too, we would suggest the proposed incumbent be fully instructed on the related issue of literary postponement. Too many needless books just jog along towards already known literary outcomes. Perhaps the final pages should be left uncut.

Twelve books for the price of one—for being by now so much clichéd these days, that's barely a commercial conceit, far less a literary conceit! As we already decided in our Preface to this series of all twelve books, let's see whether our leading agent is still able to levitate, to take off from this planet's surface (since these antipersonnel battlefields in the Middle East are so profusely mined), and yet prove himself or herself still able to fly! This is obviously a military operation—requiring a level of front-line discipline when under fire and concerning which front line of battle. Then both night and day, we must constantly remind and counsel him. Why, until he gets to places like Kabul, Tehran, Baghdad, and Damascus, our own poor soul of an author has not the slightest idea of what huge turmoil this present whole wide world is facing!

Nevertheless, let's see whether he (for being no more than any mere mortal) can manage all this. Whilst yet a leading agent, although of only third class, nothing much on earth is to his favour. Yet whilst keeping all the time to the coordinates of thoughtful travel, wise reflection, personal fortitude, looked-for guidance, and acceptable good counsel, it just may be possible.

Intro 16—Melanchthon: What do you think are the heavenly odds? Unlike poor Job for being left all on his own, this fellow has family backing. And he's not likely to do a Jonah. Some folks on earth today would put his world at fifty times better than yesterday's world; other folks would put it fifty times worse. What would we say, perhaps both ways 50/50—but then it's far too early to judge, since it's people who make or break the world and not the world that makes or breaks people—well, isn't it? We'll take a heavenly punt on the earthly odds being 50/50! That might break the bank at Monte Carlo, but with all the kingdom mansions in heaven, where banking (and not just moneylending) is still an honourable profession, it's not going to break any bank in heaven.

So then, in harmony with the prophetic gifting with which we shall inspire him to look always both ways (especially when crossing any Roman roadway), we shall prophetically propel him both figuratively forward into the future-present as well as physically forward to secure the publication of this projected report and so editorially agree to cover his exploits wherever these take him (or maybe also her) and most certainly also us. We have already determined this project to be for every serious reader's delight, and this delight to be expressed through his or her following the angelic adventures to be reported on by way of this book called *The Soul-Catcher.*

Intro 17—Saint Martin (Luther): Nonetheless, as collectively requested of the envisioning committee by many of the novice angels here present, there is needed a handbook (call it a sourcebook, a workbook, or a copybook as you will) by which to instruct those novices on the subject of soul-catching. As any leading agent of the Supreme Command, the finally chosen author for this project shall be so instructed. Likewise, for being but only the leaven in the heavenly dough, he or she, as the duly appointed author of this book, shall then be the only (and so lonely) mortal amongst the heavenly host of angels to be thus engaged.

All the same, all protracted origins have their own protracted outcomes on earth. For this reason, every mortal's lack of life span is most frequently the determining factor of such solo engagements when undertaken by earthlings on earth. Whether authorially authenticated, editorially committed, or otherwise publicly commissioned from heaven, we would thus strenuously apprise the committee of appointment of the need to engage an authorial backup. After all, leaven has a much shorter shelf life than the seventy-plus allotted life span of most human authors. Of course, this is not to discount the ongoing input from the heavenly host, by which, through their total teamwork, *The Soul-Catcher's Handbook* (or *Copybook*, if so given the go-ahead) shall hope to serve every philosophic, scientific, and otherwise theological purpose as so determined by the Supreme Command.

* * *

All Things under the Sun
Part I

In the Era of President Saddam Hussein
Saddam Hussein had invited us to Iraq for a cultural
festival, to see the beauty of the new Babylon that was
rising from the ruins. Like the other visitors, I clapped
and smiled for my hosts at the appropriate times. But
something arose from within my soul—a feeling part
thrill, part chill.

Charles H. Dyer, *The Rise of Babylon*

The whole wide world is in turmoil—especially those portions of
the world that are built on sinking sands. The shifting centre point (a
solar symbol) of mankind's self-proclaimed civilisation moves rapidly
from ancient Babylon to modern Baghdad, both still in today's Iraq.
From there, largely as the result of Iraq losing the Iraqi–Iranian War
(initiated by Saddam Hussein against Iran), this same shifting centre
point soon moves to Tehran, the (literally fast-sinking) capital of
Khomeini's Islamic Republic of Iran.

At precisely this point of writing, warring factions fight over
the re-establishment of this centre point in Damascus, the capital
of Syria. No place or people are exempt, as shooting breaks the
prayerful silence of two mosques in the cathedral city of Christchurch
in faraway New Zealand. The shooting leaves more than fifty persons
dead, several others critically injured, and yet others seriously injured
and as many more bereft of family members, friends, and fellow
worshippers. As these very words are now being written, no more
than around the corner from the first-targeted Dunedin mosque (and
so not all that far from the carnage at Christchurch), this is a time of
national mourning all across New Zealand.

Yet all this military toing and froing is not entirely unforeseen.
Several months before the terrorist attack on the Christchurch
mosque, two correspondents to Dunedin's *Star* newspaper (Lachlan
Paterson, 31 January 2019, and Evan Sadler, 14 February 2019) are

arguing over the reasons for any such catastrophic happening here in New Zealand yet at the same time agreeing completely over the increasingly imminent likelihood of any such catastrophic happening taking place here, perhaps possibly in one's own hometown.

At any moment, the centre point of mankind's self-proclaimed civilisation (which ironically brings conquest, famine, disease, and death in its wake) can likewise spread its widening net. The late president Hussein of Iraq was not by any means the last of this world's bully boys—one who 'thinks in terms of circles' as reported by Prof. Amatzia Baram of Haifa University (*Newsweek*, 13 August 1990, p. 23). The encircling conflagration spreads, with sporadic outbursts erupting throughout not only those nations who compete to hold the shifting centre point of power but also through those nations and factions—Turkey, Lebanon, Israel, Jordan, Egypt, Sudan, Saudi Arabia, and Afghanistan—which, in some way or another (however precariously), still manage to keep a fingerhold (if not a trigger finger) on that supposedly human balance of power.

The fast-stretching circle (of death and destruction) by no means stops even there or even here. The entire Middle East is engulfed with uncertain rumours, confused conspiracies, and open conflict— and the whole wide world searches for whatever means (not always legitimate) by which to control the increasingly conflictive situation. Already profoundly deaf to cries of its own demise, this terrorist-torn planet Earth is rapidly losing all sense of that requisite balance by which to keep, maintain, distribute, and educate others in the orderly apportionment of political power.

The whole of Europe (as well as the greater part of the world which lies beyond) is flooded with displaced émigrés and often starving, disabled, and penniless refugees. Terrorism walks the quietude of what once were suburban streets in Greece, Italy, France, Holland, and Britain. The death knell of the latest empire in this world's long list of empires, that of the European Union (EU), is already sounding—if not for its own demise, then for that of the world (as we humans think to know it).

By no means the first, but perhaps the last of Europe's many empires, together with what was once its predecessor (then no more than the European Economic Community, or EEC), the mighty EU now looks towards raising a standing army to bolster up its present rapidly failing bureaucratic might. So too then, the tocsin begins to ring its alarm-like dirge of woe. Any standing army being first called up and then called in to deal with what cannot be considered civil situations runs the risk of breaking into either civil war or open warfare.

No nation, however distant from the most immediate field of battle—as for the USA on that infamous day of 9/11, when the Twin Towers of the World Trade Centre in New York were attacked by Islamic al-Qaeda terrorists—is immune. All this and much more by way of facts, figures, and responses (whether those of our sorrow and grief on the one hand or of gleeful jubilation on the other) are intimately known both to us angels and to the Supreme Command by whose authority this present investigation is authorised and for whom this report on the present state and standing of the whole wide world is requested. From the start, this is being done with the objective of sharing the findings of this investigation with all those on earth 'whom nothing may dismay'.

For this purpose, we are writing to you humans, who are not much lower in the heavenly scheme of things than are we angels, in ways which will accommodate our angelic vision to suit your more mundane ways of earthly understanding. Thus, whatever you have read so far from us angels in this report of today's turmoil extending throughout the whole wide world is written by us angels to you in the historic present (with which temporal aspect you are most familiar) rather than in that of the prophetic future. Alas, unless the message being brought to you humans, as you might expect on Christmas Day and Resurrection Sunday, is most likely to be one of good news (which these days cannot always be guaranteed) every other proclamation of today's prophetic future tends to scare you humans silly. This is especially the case in any time of approaching crisis (which is now) when our angelic task is to call on you (as we have so often called for your help in the past) for you humans being only a little lower than are we angels in the heavenly scheme of things.

Nevertheless, every explicit text, such as that of the above, is always written in a context which is so much less explicit to the human reader (and sometimes even also to the angelic author) that much, if not sometimes the whole purport of this text, in terms of its strategic plans and tactical methods, can be seriously misconstrued. For some reason that we ourselves can't fathom, the ongoing significance of seeing some burning bush or of keeping alive the vision of some ladder still extending between earth and heaven is too quickly relegated from the prophetic future to the historic past in the less than always more hopefully focussed human mindset.

Please pardon us for saying so, but it seems exceptionally hard for the human mindset to keep the redemptive past prophetically alive. Perhaps it's your fear of the future which erases your faith, both in the still living past as well as in the future-present. We must warn you, especially in this time of world crisis, that it is only by keeping redemptive faith alive that you will live to see your present hope fulfilled in the substance of so many things already prophesied but as yet unseen. Besides, you need this strength of spirit by which to stand witness to the way in which these prophecies can only be fulfilled—since nothing could be more unexpected, perplexing, and incredible (in both style and content) than will be the information which we shall pass on to you by way of this report.

And just as we angels will try to accommodate our angelic vision to your more human mindset (which always wants to know the reasons for everything before coming to any conclusion), then in the interests of attaining the clearest mutuality of understanding between us both (because we angels don't always know the reasons for those things which we tell you, nor even for many of those things which we ask you to do), we ask of you humans to extend a similar leeway towards our own more familiar means of angelic communication. We ask of you humans to share with us this mutuality of angelic understanding based more on faith and less on reason.

Because our path of heavenly travel is no more than a little higher than yours, we celestial beings also walk in faith (lest we too should fall into unrighteousness through sin). From the very first moment of your conception, one of us has been with you as your guardian angel. We know you better than you know yourselves.

Nevertheless, you humans will have much to learn from us before attempting to achieve and fulfil your heavenly calling to participate in the resolution of this world's crisis. You need to know so much more not only about the history of heaven but also about the history of hell. Don't back off. We angels have no illusions about the so-called 'milk of human kindness' on which you humans pride yourselves. Towards the homeless, the disabled, the deprived, and the powerless, whatever milk of human kindness which you first had is now fast drying up towards this last fag end of the earth's most woeful time.

In these dark days of governmental crisis (which, having gone so far, can only get worse), you lay the blame on limited resources or on the world for having gone on the warpath or for the seas being in an uproar or for the polar axis of the earth being about to switch its transit or for the entropic sun itself to demonstrate (whether with a final shrug, another big bang, or one last whimper) that it is in the nature of things that order should degenerate into disorder. Quite frankly (which is how we angels always are), your list of self-made woes is endless.

There's only one true light that can lift this darkness—and there's no point in joining the international merry-go-round (from Baghdad to Tehran to Damascus) by going from one illusive centre point to another (otherwise known as the game of thrones) in the same way as pagan sun worshippers once thought to worship their mistaken transit of the sun. *Thus Spake Zarathustra*, as some might say. Why no, not at all, since that was a spoof against all religions, as written by the atheistic Franz Kafka, no less than *The Game of Thrones* chose allegorically to morph the medieval romance (the equivalent of Tolkien's history of the search for the ring) into an upper-class, power-packed gang movie!

Why, like any Iranian Parsee (with his Persian roots deeply embedded in Zarathustra's mindset until later overtaken by the Muslim majority), would the West (through its efforts at peacemaking from Babylon to Kabul) begin to follow the same scorching sun in its mythical transit round these successive centre points of unholy power? *The Decline of the West* (written by Oswald Spengler) and *The Suicide of Reason—Radical Islam's Threat to the West* (written by Lee Harris) both testify to the academic reasons. Be mindful of reasoning, since with more than three good reasons for or against anything, any good lawyer will tell you that there's bound to be some element of distraction hidden in one of them, if not possibly in all of them.

Nevertheless, the darkness goes deeper. That the fiery sun, in its rising and falling, as well as in its mistaken trajectory across the sky and even by its reflected light from the similarly rising and falling moon, can bewitch not just the human senses but also the entire human mindset is something which we angels recognise most truly to beset the entire human race. There are tides of travel whereby people no more than follow the sun; there are tides of fashion whereby people (oblivious to the gathering darkness) no more than follow the moon. There are constellations of rising and falling stars (most mesmerising) by which some few people target their own personal fame and fortune to acquire for themselves that greater wealth and prosperity meant instead for those many impoverished people and many distraught nations from which such great wealth is withheld.

The sun, moon and stars were not placed in the sky to be revered for themselves. They were never put there to be the means of dividing one people from another people or one nation from another nation. They were put there to be for signs, for seasons, and to compute the passage of time. By dividing the light from darkness, they exert their respective rule over day and night. The space age (so aptly called for the growing space within the human heart, mind, and soul) has brought the human race to the cosmic edge of self-idolatry in what it believes itself to have done by conquering space. 'One small step for man, one giant leap for mankind,' profess the promoters of the space race. Don't you believe it—just don't you dare believe it! The space race has been no better than the armament race in depleting your dying world's best resources!

Now it is that whole nations mistake the sun, the moon, and the stars to be their own respective centre point of absolutely everything (from professed defence to overt threats of aggression) in the space race. Emblems of the sun or of the moon or of the stars—some or all of which—are sprinkled across the flags of so many differently competing nations. These nations think to decide the (so often conflicting) trajectories by which each may claim the monopolistic power by which to rule over others and, as often through conquest (whether military, commercial, cultural, or religious), to rule over all.

For the far longer haul, this account is not just to remind humanity what it first took to travel from the golden crescent of mankind's earliest civilisation (when Terah, father of Abram, left Ur amongst the Chaldees) to settle first in Haran. And from which, Abram left, on the Lord's command, for Canaan—which we now have before us the full Revelation of Jesus Christ. It is now this final Revelation, as much as any previously given *gospel*, which takes us further on the same continued pilgrimage begun in *Genesis*, right now until the end of time.

Most pilgrimages are begun and continued by those who are completely unaware of being in any way a pilgrim. The bigger picture is kept hidden, lest these proto-pilgrims tinker with its details or come to presuppose of themselves that they themselves are responsible for ordaining and fulfilling its outcome.

As the late pastor Peter Marshall once prayed in 1947 before the Eightieth Congress of the mighty USA, we too now likewise pray with faith 'that we shall be true to the pilgrim dream when we are true to the God they [these first pilgrims] worshipped' and so then 'to the extent that America honours thee, wilt thou bless America and keep her true, as thou has kept her free and make her good as thou hast made her rich. Amen.' And so say all of us, insofar as we each can say the same prayer for each of our own countries. Amen.

World history tells the world, notwithstanding that the world does not want to know its own history, that the military conflict between the Afghan, Iraqi, Iranian, and Syrian nations is doomed to failure. All, some, or none of these nations may survive—but none ever exactly in the same form as they have survived before. Their survival may be compromised by the peacekeeping efforts of the USSR, the USA, the UK, the UN, and with NZ from the outside, no less than their survival can be compromised by the efforts of the Arab League, Taliban, Isis, Hamas, Hezbollah, the Palestinian National Authority, and Khomeini's Islamic Republic from the inside.

In the very same way, the conflict between today's Israeli world (with its capital in Jerusalem) and today's Arab world (with its claimed capital also in Jerusalem) is doomed to failure, although each world is bound to survive that conflict in its own yet very different way. You humans fail to see forward because on these conflictive matters, you refuse first to look backward before you seek to look forward.

Even so, the future-present is before you always in the present-past. Look at how often your fast-dying sun or its reflective light given by always less than a full moon—together with anything from one star, through a sprinkle of stars, to a full constellation of stars—confronts you every time you raise your own (no less than our own) national flag. Whether you know it or not, the present-past *is* the future-present.

So then, look more carefully at the national flags to which you still salute. Would you not change them? Listen more carefully to the national hymns and anthems you sing. Would you not sing different hymns and anthems? Then with all other things being equal (which they never are), are you still happy to identify your own present-past with your future-present? If yes, then your present-future shall be precisely that which you more exactly see for being the result of your own present-past. If no, then your future indeterminate shall be as vastly different as you care to make it be.

The hope of all people and of all nations lies not in the horoscope you mortals make by which to read the stars and lies not in either the apparent traverse of the daily sun or in the phases of the nightly moon. The faith that promotes the assurance of all kingly and righteous power lies in the substance of things unseen.

So then, you'll think to know now why (for being angels) we angels are so seldom seen. Nevertheless, the word *why* is so often the counterfeit watchword by which history is made under the noses of distracted humans so busily engaged in looking for some non-negotiable answer to the substance of things unseen. Rationality, as a stand-alone concept, is the one that falls over soonest when faced with the irrevocable substance of things as yet unseen.

Nevertheless, everyone has a guardian angel. You must have felt his or her presence, whether unexpectedly or in some troublesome time of deep despair, or even felt the assurance of the whole heavenly host, either at first light of a summer's morning or in the first nip of frosty autumn's fall or in the first fresh snowfall of the winter season when families ski the slopes and, in the evenings, delight to gather round a roaring fire. Well then, if not in any of those seasons, who could not love the spring?

There's no contrived centre point (whether by solar, lunar, or other like luminary) or any semblance of light (released through intellect or other human artifice) which can be made to shine through something like the League of Nations or through the United Nations (or through any other institute, college, cathedral, church, or state) more assuredly than that released through faith in the one and only process by which things hoped for can be committed into true being. And it doesn't need any angel to tell you that Jesus Christ is the one and only true centre point at which faith and works do always meet. The evidence is all around you, however much your own little boat may be close to being swamped by the rising yet still complacent sea of warring faiths. Do you not know that by reason of seeing Jesus Christ as no more than a good teacher, there are more good Muslims amongst bad Christians than you can find anywhere else?

Nevertheless, the solar system (because it is, for mortals, their most familiar system and the one on which their bodily survival most obviously depends) has been exaggerated by all humanity, time and time again, to constitute the centre point of almost all human activity. Architecturally speaking (which is the best evidence possible in the face of the widening gap between those wealthy mortals who swank superficial lives in swish apartments whilst the destitute and homeless barely manage to sleep on the streets below), the basic truth of this disparity does not pass unnoticed from high heaven (as you humans may think) but instead (as we angels know with the prophets from our also having announced the coming of heaven to earth through song) our Supreme Command is already working here ever so hard at ground-zero level.

History is the key to prophecy no less than forgiveness of past failures is the key to their redemption. Now that's the good news (no less than the Supreme Command has always held possession of every ground zero (strictly speaking, the point on the earth's surface directly above or below the explosion of any nuclear bomb) since time ever began. Nevertheless, the bad news is that the world has little or no interest in the proclamation, far less in the fulfilment of any prophecy, because it cannot bear to look backwards into time to appreciate the fullness of its own mistakes. Once again, however, the world has not the slightest inclination to learn from its own history.

Lesson after lesson remains unlearnt (and so increasingly ignored). Who now still remembers the frightful collapse to ground zero of Nimrod's tall Tower of Babel (in emerging Babylonia, now Iraq)? Who now remembers the seventh wonder of the ancient world where once Nebuchadnezzar's Hanging Gardens (likewise then in Babylonia, now Iraq) testified to that country's upward climb before being scourged back again to ground zero by Cyrus of Persia (now Iran)? Well into the denigrated Middle Ages, these lessons as to human pride were told and retold by this world's greatest writers, were pictured and repictured by this world's greatest artists, but now are remembered no more.

To cut almost nearly to the present in this apparently never-ending and still ongoing saga of such ground-zero disasters (including those of Hiroshima and Nagasaki, whose inhabitants' mistaken reliance on the god-like transit of Nippon's own rising sun likewise had to be shortened), so too, by alien destruction of the Twin Towers of the World Trade Centre in New York, mankind has demonstrated the self-sown pride to choose and elevate its own centre points by which its own mortality makes every individual vulnerable.

By means of this falsely chosen centre point, which, whether in the professions or in the trades or whether in business or at pleasure, never stays stable, then the resulting fixation on physicality soon exhausts the human soul. Since all physically evident things require constant sensual substantiation, this ongoing search for past-present proof of their continuing identity soon exhausts the soul. By then, whether caught up in the Gulags, in the brothels, or in the prisons, none but a child can live by faith. This constant search for ongoing proof of identity (whether in the sciences, the arts, or in commerce and education) gradually eclipses all human hope and so undermines whatever faith and conviction humanity would have in the future perfectibility of things as yet unseen by every human outward eye.

The rot doesn't stop there. The human fixation on shallow physicality (to solace mankind's deeper loss of spirituality) gives rise to all sorts of false worships, adventitious fixations, and deep addictions, which gradually reduce mankind's spirituality to nought (despite any human scale from one to ten).

Because man is made to worship—literally made to worship—then in the absence of righteous worship, self-worship becomes the ultimate self-contradiction. Because the human need for worship seeks deep-rooted commitment, then in the absence of any physically obvious centre point and instead of undertaking whatever lifelong search it may take mankind to find out for itself life's one and only righteous centre point, mortals (conscious of their own mortality) tend to take a quick fix by following their own human herd instinct to the nearest drinking hole. All sorts of addictions (both humanly reputable and humanly disreputable) tend to follow from this humanistic herding instinct, and every war this world has ever known has introduced yet another means of human addiction.

For example, over centuries, and right up to the mistakenly eternal present, all sorts of cults, from the ancient Druidic to the modernistic theosophic, would seize and fixate themselves in all sorts of nooks and crannies of the world's surface. They would so long seize and fixate themselves on the solar modal (as if this earth had so obviously always been for them eternally flat and immutably fixed for the purpose of welcoming and farewelling the sun) that their resulting religiosity would become (in whatever shape or form) their primal motivating addiction. Through every day and in almost every way, the inverse circularity of thought inherent in that solely two-valued mindset would have severe consequences for human spirituality.

In short, whatever is false in that view of physicality (apart from the fairly large splinter of truth, it always takes to counterfeit an untruth) would transpose itself from that false view of outer physicality to express a constant circularity of inner thought, of inner feelings, and of inner worship. The foremost symptom of mistakenly solar religiosity is circularity—whether that be demonstrated by the circularity of humanly purposeless thought, the circularity of humanly purposeless behaviour, or the circularity of humanly purposeless worship. In no more than two words (or one when hyphenated), what we're talking about at all levels is self-referentiality.

Self-referentiality? Once this terrorist mindset permeates all the inner feelings as well as the outer expressions of humanity, there opens a monstrously huge void, a black hole in place of, at first, predicated objectivity and, in consequence, all-round rationality.

Nevertheless, the saving grace of rationality, as of mankind itself, is that both are fallible.

In some persons of extreme self-sensitivity, especially when confined solely to two-valued decision-making (for being either true or false, good or bad, but without leaving any room for contingency), self-referentiality leads swiftly to various disorders of the mind. At street level, these may manifest as indecisiveness or apathy or compromised complacency, but eventually to outright violence against oneself or against others or to falling victim to other versions of insanity.

Now this most severe and rigorous mindset of physicality can project itself into every humanly disputative process and particularly those of human judgement reaching and of human decision-making. It does so not only by way of evoking passing moods as to its rigor but also by way of intruding into and tainting almost every human argument as to the effect of its severity. By means of this rigorously two-valued mindset of physicality, it becomes largely overlooked that the sun rises as well as the rain falls both on the good and on the wicked and that in every lie, compromise, or expression of abject apathy, there is always a splinter of truth if one can but only find it.

Unfortunately, it's almost the universal temptation to which even the best-intentioned of human scholars and research scientists succumb when, in order to research the truth for oneself or to teach others by telling them the resultant truth, that one should facilitate both processes by exaggerating the truth in order to find it or in order to tell it. This happens most especially when for researching the truth or for teaching the truth, and we humans as well as angels have assumed combative positions, when from each of which positions, each participant assumes himself or herself to be in the right for opposing the corresponding wrong. Thus (through prideful self-categorisation of you-know-who) hell was born of a once-perfect heaven.

It is not for us angels to point any finger of blame or to pass judgement on any particular person, but as we, like the Supreme Command, are no respecter of persons (despite the institutions which afford them so much coverage for such sometimes horrendous mishaps), we would nevertheless look to the freedom of the popular press to rectify its own abuses. Alas, for this prevaricating process whereby one little white lie leads to another not-so-white lie and yet to another and yet another increasingly darker grey lie, this by then combative process leads finally, conclusively, and irrevocably to one really big black lie (whether then done for self-defensive protection or for self-promotional justification). Of course, embellishing the truth need not resort to lying—it can just as easily be done, as in the popular press or as in popular teaching or as in popular preaching, by a whole wide world of diversional info-entertainment.

The result, as often with the press, for example, is to demean the freedom of the press and of self-indulgent science and of anything less than seriously committed scholarship in general. Embellishing the truth most usually proves to be the undoing of all that is professedly impartial by way of search and research. The scourge soon spreads—from language to logic and from logic to law and from law to science and scholarship—until popularity takes over from political correctness for being the measure self-made by both men and women for everything from the profane and secular to the divine and spiritual.

The further result is to demean the universality of scholarship no matter from what quarter and to pour suspicion on any science failing to observe its own precept to observe, conform, acknowledge, and uphold the truth. Every embellishment (whether to make something less pleasant or more pleasant or to make something more unpleasant than it is pleasant) offends against the standard of proof with which in every quarter (from fantasy and fairy tale to pure science and good government), the truth must be upheld. And this standard applies no matter how radical, incredible, unpleasant, and even impossible that truth may first appear.

Regarding the process of conferring recognition to any apparently new way (or to any forgotten older way) of looking at things, whether that be exemplified by (1) the newly discovered forcefulness of prions or protein infective particles; or by (2) the return to uncertainty of much in genetics (as also in evolutionary theory) through the new science of epigenetics; or even by (3) the now more thoroughly investigated topic of bodily resurrection from the dead (of Jesus Christ), it must be accepted now that (4) academic peer review (in itself) is of no more use than of following the academic herd to any of its more accustomed watering holes.

We don't mean to single out any one group—whether the popular press, the no less popular research scientists, or the overly ardent yet ivory-towered scholars—in each of their respective propensities to embellish the truth. This human propensity for dialectic exaggeration falls so far short of heaven's passion for the truth as to be a stumbling block, which, once intrusive, subsequently extrudes itself through ongoing generations. The eventually lost cause of dialectic exaggeration (no less pervasive in the sciences than in the humanities) is a universally entertained temptation. It is one which can be carried out to demonic excess—and yes, this too by both upright angels as well as less-than-upright angels and as always (whether angelic or human) to the disadvantage of the elect.

Why, we angels have heard the same of so many erstwhile evangelists (until they face their own problems) by which they go on enticing their human listeners into the kingdom of heaven by telling them that once so admitted by confessing their sins to Jesus, all their problems will be well and truly over. Well (although aside from more than the splinter of truth in that enticement), you only have to look at the life of Christ (whose life in its entirety you commit yourselves to follow) and compare it with this present life (of which you may have experienced no more than a modicum of life's problems by comparison), and you'll realise that some of life's deepest problems awaiting your call to engage in their resolution are only just beginning to show their mettle whenever you commit or recommit your life to Jesus.

Besides (although for being on all sides and not just assumed from any academic centre point or standpoint), the presumed good in all this grand endeavour (as derived from any search and/or rescue operation of the real truth and before any first little exaggeration of or distraction from the ongoing pursuit of truth jeopardises the whole operation) has become, by reason of your going your own way about it, either incrementally or suddenly forfeited for breach of due process. Now this failure (the full effect of which, as disclosed by many of the saddest events in church history, may never be discovered until so much later) still goes on to affect most negatively the whole field (both human and angelic) of continued behaviour and of continued endeavour.

We might now like to assume (as a result of feeling disappointed within ourselves) as to what would have been the successful outcome of the preaching and teaching of what (once earlier but now no longer) might have been the legitimately reached truth to be told as proof of our endeavour. Nevertheless, the consequences may no longer permit of that backhanded way of reassuring either ourselves or others as to the still existing potential of that unrealised intent.

The imperfect realisation of that endeavour, when tainted by the uncertainty of due process, no longer carries any positive presumption (as to either the freedom of the press, the impartiality of science, or the universality of scholarship being responsibly administered in the examples mentioned). On the contrary, the failure (however slight) of that due process can often be seen to expose and vitiate not just (1) the particular trust attributable to our undertaking of the specific operation in question but also (2) whatever deeper, wider, and more general trust needed at the far more fundamental and metaphysical end of the trust spectrum, namely (2a) to undergird the entire systemic operation and notwithstanding (2b) whether that operation be political, legal, logical, linguistic, scientific, or social, insofar as (2c) the operation is one of pursuing the truth, the whole truth, and nothing but the truth.

In other words (as every lawyer so well knows) the merest whisper of untruth, whether by way of elaboration, exaggeration, or even when just left to be inferred from the equivocality of extraneous circumstances, can so estrange the legal process from its finding of the truth, the whole truth, and nothing but the truth as to completely invalidate the outcome. Indeed, the last man, James (Walter) Bolton, to be hanged for murder in New Zealand, provides just such a case in point. James Bolton was hanged in accordance with the law as it then stood as the result of a jury verdict given on the basis of entirely extraneous circumstances—on account of which defective outcome capital punishment was thereafter repealed).

Unless checked, whatever then was being specifically pursued (whether at law or in science or in the arts) for being the truth, the whole truth, and nothing but the truth then becomes increasingly buried beneath the resulting and ever-rising welter of untruth. The long-term effect is to take down with it the trust which not just the privileged few but also the whole of society had in pursuing the truth and the trust that one had in either passing on or inheriting the truth under any system of general education or of news reportage. Bolton's case did just that for taking down the entire system of criminal law in New Zealand—it took down first the truth, and then it took down the system. So then, just as it takes no more than a pinch of yeast to raise dough or to make wine, then conversely speaking, it takes no more than a little lie, an elaboration of the truth, or maybe no more than the suggestion of extraneous circumstances to overturn the whole handcart of human history as well as of future endeavour.

For one last look at the long-outdated solar model (which at the flight of a broomstick can move its centre point anywhere on earth to encompass any lunar, more luminary, or even cosmic model), let's consider how (when long past any expired best-before date for the solar model and its derivatives) the results can stand in the way of moving mountains, calming storms, and for the making of peace instead of just temporarily keeping the peace. If we were in Moscow right now, then to learn this lesson from the subject of the Stalinist era, we'd watch the film *Scorched by the Sun*.

For this last look at the solar model, whose many vestigial derivatives permeate not just each individual human mindset but also its superficially collective consciousness and socially deeper subconsciousness, then try to see this deeply dug-in propensity of the solar model to rule the roost. Try to see it, not as from the inside-out as you have grown to be so familiar with ascribing your worldly success to this model, and by which, from sunrise to sunset, you subconsciously account for the place you hold in the sun. Instead, try to see this sun-centred model from the outside-in as would almost every destitute hobo, unfortunate émigré, or disabled refugee see it, who, unlike you, is bereft of the place you hold in the sun. This process of cultural invagination (seeing something from the outside-in instead of from the inside-out) is critically important for your understanding of this solar model which for so many privileged people relies on their having a place in the sun.

You will find this reversal of roles hard to take because in the (circular rather than linear) course of your successful life on earth you will have come to claim, subconsciously as of right, your present place in the sun. By now, perhaps by reason of birth, intellect, health, education, employment status, social class, and all sorts of other credentials, you could not begin to see your vulnerability from the inside-out — for fear of your having so much to lose. Make no mistake, this solar model (subject to the same sunset clause as the sunrise clause by which you attribute your right to have your present place in the sun) is something entirely alien to what you perceive of your own cultural identity and quite possibly also to the present sunspace you attribute to yourself as of right. Empathise right now with all of those unfortunates (from the homeless to the hobo) because who knows when you too from rapidly dying earth will be one of them—and this possibly very soon.

Realise that you have fixated yourself for so long on this dying sun that you can only see it with the greatest difficulty for being anything other than any still rising sun, far less than to see it (surely, however laughable) for being any sort of (however slowly) dying sun. This apparently two-way travelling sun (now seen to be more settled than this just as rapidly spinning earth) may set exactly, if not precisely, before you die; or else it may more precisely die, most certainly from sight, as you yourself drop dead. Every system of no more than two-valued logic is bound to be faced with either problems or paradoxes of relativity, which is exactly why heaven and earth (without any intermediate hell) are insufficient by themselves to credibly explain the present (which in any case is fleetingly transient) until replaced by the eternity of a new heaven and a new earth. Meanwhile (for being another pregnant pause) if this to you sounds like hell, then maybe that's because you're now seeing hell for the first time!

Indeed, in all this, as if only of our conjectural imagining, then the law of entropy is neither any sort of help nor any sort of relief nor affords any sort of consolation. Indeed, when you so trouble yourself to see this sun as dying, you will find yourself headhunted (perhaps even demonically) so as to see yourself as no longer living, but instead as dying (like the sun). By then, the presently intense light of this noonday sun will for you have turned to darkness, the heat for you will have cooled, and your breath will have stilled. But still surely, for others, the same sun will shine on. The life span of the sun, as surely also the life span of the earth, is rejuvenatingly holistic, but yet if not, it is surely some small, if not indeed miniscule, consolation to the life of man.

Persevere and block out that demonic thought of yourself as dying—that's only one passing symptom of being scorched by the sun. Fight against it if you need to; otherwise, it will lead you into some desert, lunar, or similarly alien experience of abandonment. Beware of the desert jinn or spirit, since it is worshipped by some of the world's desert people who can thereby become, like the Bedouin, increasingly deserted and abandoned people. Consider carefully the extent to which even Westerners may be called more and more to face some similarly protracted experience—such as described in *The Long Walk* (as famously told by Slavomir Rawicz). In the collective subconscious, most people of the world have experienced similarly protracted experiences from which, through heatstroke, hunger, depression, and exhaustion, it can become increasingly difficult to extricate oneself. Indeed, as with the destitute and homeless, that can happen to anyone without leaving one's own city. So then, where is it and how is it that you now live?

Yet for others (as in an urban desert), the same experience may be very much worse. The djinn of an urban desert (such as that which passed over Minsk, the capital of Belarus from Chernobyl in the Ukraine), although not of the life-sadly-terminated variety (as some of those people most afflicted would have preferred to experience), instead becomes a stood-up, hung-up, held-up life of barely liveable experience. Yet nevertheless, as so many poor souls who have been consigned to some half-life hanging on a meathook have clearly proved by their fecundity of thought, their persistence of purpose, and by the clarity and credibility of their testimony, there is hardly any state of life that can be declared for being all time terminal.

Beware of the glib joke for being the devil's put-down. Beware of the clichéd consolatory remark for being a hired gun's stick-up job. Beware of the terminal diagnosis for being a slammed door. As you become more and more strategically fixated on the still blazing sun when tactically enforced by means of its still scorching heat, as well as by its darkening light (aptly named the dark night of the soul), one becomes increasingly convinced of there being nothing new under the sun by which to relieve you of its interminably scorching rays. The very air solidifies around you (freeze-drying your soul) as you attempt to break through the barrier of an obsolete yet still frightening mindset.

Persevere still further: you must get your already swimming head round the fact (completely mistaken as you will later see it) of there being nothing new by which to stop this by now interminable heat constantly emitted by this still always noonday sun. By now, this is that 'darkness at noon' as described of the Stalinist era by Arthur Koestler (which everyone at first dismissed for being a gross exaggeration). Keep up with *The Long Walk*, likewise dismissed for being a work of fiction. After all, this is only *One Day in the Life of Ivan Denisovich*, as narrated throughout that single day in Ivan's life by the writer Aleksandr Solzhenitsyn. Nevertheless, keep looking for *The Flame in the Darkness* as lit across so many nations by the Norwegian artist and writer Victor Sparre, who brought Solzhenitsyn and so many other *bogatyrs* (spiritual heroes) from East to West.

Persevere still more, for whatever flame can light up the dark night of the soul and so dispel the deepest sort of demonic darkness can itself testify to the falsity of asserting there to be nothing new under the sun. So likewise, it testifies against the first axiom of any self-sufficient solar system, namely that the sun is the source or first cause of everything. In this last stage, either of overcoming or of succumbing to physical death, whether in the Gulags or in the desert, the ambivalent outcome, like Dostoyevsky's *Notes from the Underground*, recedes further and further away from any desert pilgrim who is expectantly still moving forward.

In less than a millisecond, the fearful *what if* starts to substitute itself for the fearless *as if*. The translation time is often so incredibly short that under such desert or prison circumstances of last resort, the fierceness of the switch from *as if* to *what if* can hardly be gainsaid. As for Rex Warner's *The Professor*, no less than for that worn-down old Bolshevik, Rubashov, in Koestler's *Darkness at Noon*, the fearful-sounding *what if* has taken the place of any fearlessly alternative *as if.*

The outcome, exerting negativity instead of positivity, is practically determined by its outcome. So then, those who are fearless do triumph, but those who fall fearful go down. And that's exactly why those who seek against all odds to keep their life are those who lose what they most fear and why those who are unafraid to lose their life are all the more capable of keeping it. Of course, one way or another, it's always touch-and-go for the mindlessly apathetic, the determinedly stoic, or on the other hand, those who eat, drink, and are joyful, simply because tomorrow (which may not come any more than the sun will still rise) is no more for them than anyone else a forgone conclusion.

Once the as-if outlook is traded off for the what-if outlook, there is little room left to manoeuvre. With all other things remaining equal, the chosen outcome relentlessly proceeds. Whether we think ourselves travelling towards an unknown fate or by any other means towards an acceptably determined destination, nevertheless the die is cast. That present moment of no duration in which we made the trade-off, whether it be a millisecond (of earth-time) or a millennium (in heaven), is climacteric. Etymologically speaking (that's to say, doing something according to the inherent meaning of words), it decides the outcome, since that's the power of proclamation.

Nevertheless, for both that miniscule or millennial moment, the chosen climacteric effect remains contingently 'ladder-like'. This means that whether known or not, we have made a choice of destination either by looking up to climb up or by looking down to climb down. From this unequivocal 'looking up to climb up' point of view, don't forget what in the Foreword we emphasised in brutally black type— namely, that origins by themselves don't determine outcomes, but instead require the implementation of strategic objectives by which to determine and re-determine destinations. Meanwhile (that all so pregnant phrase again) keep-up your navigational dead-reckoning!

Let it be known here, dearest readers, that because some of you have fixated for so long on the dying sun of our universe for being the first cause and only source of all you could ever hope for or see fulfilled, you have been literally sunstruck out of every last hope of being rightly enabled any longer to make up your mind. For your subsequent failing to get your head round the fact (as you've seen it) of there being nothing new under that sun, which for you on earth is the ultimate resource of absolutely everything, you could hardly then hope, far less envisage (what then would be an absurdity, if not an outright blasphemy), of there being ever any need to create any new earth or new heaven.

But it is often only by then, when taking one's last gasp in the desert or in the Gulags or on the way towards one's own execution, that one finally sees, so surely by reason of the sun being not the only source for absolutely everything, that there's far more under the sun than one had ever before either seen or imagined. Thus said, the fallibility of mankind is offset by the grace given to mere mortals to learn from their wrongs.

What you then see, all of a sudden, is something so new and so precious that not only is one's own mind transformed by what one sees but also all that one had ever seen before is bound in consequence to be transformed. What one saw before, contingent for being no more than a matter of proof, will then become, if also consequentially transformed, not just a certainty but also in itself more than a certainty. Every revelation through faith—whether given of the law of entropy to Newton or of the periodic table to Mendeleev or of relativity to Einstein—is like that in its partaking of some first cause.

The moment of revelation may fade and may even be shattered, but the spirit in which the revelation was inspired and conceived still lives on. Nothing which we once thought to be impossible still holds to that exactly same level of ascertained impossibility we once determined of it. Thus, for any once unanimously held flat earth now to be proved round diminishes the level of credibility we would accord every other proposition which we adhered to before accepting the round earth now in place of the flat. Likewise, by the same domino forcefulness attributable to any such revelation, it becomes more than just eminently possible for some instantaneous creation to have happened in place of incremental evolution or for some wholly new heaven and wholly new earth to be waiting in the wings to take over from what we perceive to be the increasing obsolescence of the present earth and heaven.

Without the desert, Gulag, firing squad, or scaffold experience, however painful or perilous each of these may be, there is no other way by which to see the solar system finally freed from its occult capture by those djinns and demons who are set to profane and demean the true nature of things. Until then, however, humanity remains enthralled to a solar system, which it mistakes to be one entirely of its own making. Here obviously is a performance arena in which even the best of professional callings can so easily be mistaken for conveying the best of staged outcomes.

By way of demonstrating all such human self-accreditation, you only have to watch and to listen to ways in which weather forecasts are nowadays given. On the one hand, for this largely misunderstood solar system being seen to be the source of everything, so then do the most knowledgeable of humans expect of themselves to have both the first and last say.

Now that's a view which is all very so-so for expected happenings, but not so clear for any professedly omnipotent mortal (a contradiction in terms) in his or her dealing with those divinely or demonically unexpected happenings. These unexpected happenings could be storms (whether in life or in work or in faith or in spirit). They could be tempests (whether at sea or across the land or in the household or in the workplace). They could be floods, whether from the upper clouds, from deepest springs, from raging rivers, from tidal tsunamis, or from broken dams and overflowing watercourses.

Nothing is too minor, no small place is ever immune, no single mortal is either superhuman or completely invincible, but it is an established trend or temptation (choose whichever you will) of wishfully human thinking to pretend (at least to one's own family) to be superhuman and completely invincible. Like claiming complete veracity or complete infallibility, this is way off any humanly mortal target—and so when pretended, even in fun to one's friends or family (no less than to one's clients, patients, or students), this is a falsity both to them and to oneself. Like any enlargement or diminishment of the truth, whether by way of frolic or fantasy, fiction or fact, it carries with it the potential to implement the most serious of consequences. As for any war-ridden world, beset as earth now is with increasingly cosmic warfare, the seriousness of such false propensity is most likely to show up soon in irrecoverable proportions.

This first book then, as of this entire series of books on the subject of angelic soul-catching, presupposes not just a whole wide world view or even just a universal view but instead a completely cosmic view. This cosmic view (unlike any whole wide world view) is not just temporal or spatial or even spatio-temporal. On the contrary, it is a cosmic view of what eternity is divinely intended to mean to each and every human soul in terms of that soul's individual destiny. As never before, each individual soul is accountable in these latter days to the triune authority of the Supreme Command (as never before asked of any mortal soul). Each person's own soul-time on earth is given as a mark of their own exceptionality—so learn to read the signs of your own time!

* * *

All Things Still under the Sun
Part II

Conceiving of the Inconceivable
I was one of the many people taking care of the firemen
who were deconstructing the collapsed World Trade
Centre and carrying away the bodies—often bodies
of their own colleagues. ... At home again I couldn't
stop watching television coverage of Afghanistan and
the Taliban. I was especially struck by the footage of
the Taliban executing women in Kabul's Ghazi sports
stadium. ... There was nothing that anyone could
have done to stop me [going to Afghanistan].
Deborah Rodriguez, *The Kabul Beauty School*

Struck by some new thought? Let's see then, what could it be? Perhaps conceiving the inconceivable. Sure enough, this new thought, like any new thought, can be very startling. Its sudden and often unprovoked novelty can be thoroughly upsetting to one's existing mindset and heartfelt emotions. Why, if extreme enough, this radically new way of looking at things (which can either strike you down or lift you up or pull you each way alternatively) can become catastrophic to the person. It can even imperil someone's sanity by suddenly obliging that person to make decisions which will disestablish the routines of a lifetime. Well, that's nothing new—every writer experiences that correlative state of authorial disestablishment resulting from writing his or her book! What do you think God feels like by being authorially disestablished from his own creation?

It can be extremely disconcerting (to say the least) to be struck by even one's own most recent of thoughts. Perhaps it's not even one's *very own* new thought. But then would that be a relief, if not otherwise a disappointment, for anyone to find out that whatever one had mistaken for being the greatest and grandest of one's newest thoughts (perhaps by way of conceiving something which to oneself had been previously inconceivable) was merely someone else's very oldest of most routine thoughts?

For all one knows, conceiving the inconceivable might be something which every serious thinker—for being any poet, composer, or philosopher—does just every day. This handbook on soul-catching is about much more than whatever we mistake for being the sum total of everything under the sun. Yet the whole concept of there being any heaven apart from whatever's under the sun is one which scares off many people—sadly unto their ultimate death or else, sadder still, to their earlier demise! Nevertheless, in order to understand properly the kingdom of heaven, it is necessary also to give due regard, as did Christ Jesus, to everything under the sun and, so by this means, to render to Caesar that which is Caesar's, no less than to God that which is God's.

By reason of these modernist and fast-changing times, mortals are so much more at ease in ascribing creativity, novelty, originality, intellectuality, and innovativeness to themselves that they can also get adrenaline addicted to changing not just their own mood but also their own character. They see it to be a modernist sign of their own mental stability to be able to accommodate themselves to absolutely everything of whatever is going on (however fast-changing) under the sun. Yet by learning thus to accommodate themselves to these fast and fleeting changes of character, each such person just as quickly loses his or her own character. Make no mistake. This is a sign of these decadent times!

And yes, just as today's singer sings of these times, so too, it is true that 'they are a-changin''. Ah yes, but there's also a paradox here, and this pointed out by the ancient philosopher Heraclitus many centuries before today's singer Bob Dylan did so, since at the same time as the singer sings, these times of which he sings cannot keep up with the time the singer takes to sing them. So then, the times are so fast a-changin'; they are past before they can be sung about, which completely undercuts the whole point of anyone singing of their own specific times. Take that paradox seriously enough, as some followers of Heraclitus did, and by way of their communicative withdrawal, it renders all speech and song defunct. So then, in that sign of the times, there's nothing new—Heraclitus (although several thousand years ago) first sang the same song as Bob Dylan still sings—and perhaps, for the song sung by Heraclitus to have proved itself viable that long, he can claim to have sung it just as well as today's Bob Dylan.

For everything being in this state of constant flux, you might thus argue that none of us can read the signs of the times. Yet to be able to accommodate our mindset to constant change of whatsoever sort is no more indicative of mental stability than of mental instability. So instead of dealing with the root cause of the mental instability provoked by overextending one's own psychological capability, the collective reaction is to train up more psychologists, psychiatrists, and psychoanalysts. They at least can look after themselves in the course of earning their living by looking after others who are less psychologically capable of dealing with the fast-changing content of informational overload. [Exegesis 1: On this score, read the wonderfully written, well-balanced, and magnificently researched horror story not only conceived and composed but also performed so symphonically by its author Peter James on the psychiatric topic of denial.]

Mere mortals can get as much entrapped as they can become enrapt by this self-ascription to themselves of what at grass-roots reasoning is a manifestation of deistic power. To heal another soul, another suffering soul, is so much a manifestation of this deistic power that when attempted without any sense of calling or vocation, any mere mortal can so easily lose all sense of responsibility for its exercise.

Celebrities can then so easily become superproud (if not also mistakenly deistic for being also superhuman). What tempts would-be celebrities the most is the 'breaking-news character' of their own innovative attributes. They can fall victim to this temptation not always for its own sake or for any self-benefit arising from it but often for the dynamic release of adrenaline to which anyone can become addicted. Otherwise, although for one being just as unaware, one can also be tempted by some accompanied promise to promote personal fame and fortune (to which, both this promise and its fulfilment, one can likewise become addicted).

Once upon a time, all academics (especially scholars and scientists) believed in the universality of *scientia* (or knowledge). Because so much of soul-catching now pivots on science and technology, much of this *Soul-Catcher's Calling* must deal with most of the major sea changes (pirates are back) which have changed the routes of sea travel for science and technology (as well as for corporate commerce). That same *once upon a time* for science and technology would also have been a time in which no philosopher worth his salt (apart maybe from one or two of the lawyer-sophist philosophers) would have thought either to embargo or to place a price on his own *philosophia* (or love of wisdom). In many ways, the World Wide Web (today's equivalent of earlier Christendom) tried to reinstate that universally collective value, but neither capitalist nor communist economies could allow any more than its token survival from the earliest of mediaeval times.

There's a modernist run now on patents and intellectual property. Nevertheless, no patent, far less any claim to intellectual property, is ever completely watertight. If you have the time, money, and either street-legal expertise or engineering ingenuity, most of these rights can be sidewinded, self-defeated, hacked into, or traded off. This is a huge topic not just in terms of limited resources and stewardship of the environment but also in the way that the global market (by no means an open market) has devolved, first into a property market, secondly into a trading market, and finally into outright piracy and money-laundering.

In the context of the world's rapidly declining resources, every sort of property market (and not just that of intellectual property) has either reverted to or resulted in a fast-encroaching desert, a sadly polluted ocean, or else an overwhelming jungle. These default values or defunct situations are ones in which both protectionist and proprietorial powers passionately grapple against each other for those most credible ideas by which to contest their competing claims. They do so by way of ideas which appear to be so startlingly good or so startling new that to reinforce their claims, they personally identify their own hearts and minds proprietorially with those ideas.

Yet because the same resources they fight for are limited in the same way as each competitor acknowledges, they fight for possession of the very same things. Whether you call it a fight of faith to uphold capitalism and put down communism or to uphold communism and put down capitalism, it's still a fight for property. There are many subtle ironies by which to complicate the competition, the principal one (paradoxically of principle) being often that (as between the

USA and the USSR) both competitors strenuously profess to uphold democracy.

For exactly that reason, this handbook (if it is that to any *Soul-Catcher's Calling*), wherever possible, either attributes or contributes to the pool of shared, similar, and often identical ideas testified to by different writers, thinkers, inventors, explorers, and discoverers. This is done no matter how differently the conclusions of such differently committed people may be directed. Thus, many original thinkers may each discover for themselves, say, something of Darwin's theory of evolution or something of Jung's theory of acausal happenings, but then the fact that other intellectuals have each independently come to something of the same conclusion confirms at least the basic truth (however small or large) of the same discovery.

It is at least the same basic truth, no matter whatever different direction is given to the conclusions derived from that basic truth, which constitute the commonality. First, excise whatever exaggerated level of dialectic truth is used either to underlie the telling of that truth or to promote the credibility of the conclusions differently drawn from that truth, and you'll expose the mutuality. Why, in a very real sense, it is this collective process of gathering information (confirmed by scientific proof) which helps to establish, confirm, but yet also delimit the apparently speciously extended boundary at which there's (1) arguably nothing more under the sun (or cosmos) than what we see of the sun (or cosmos), just as there's (2) nothing ever entirely new under this sun (or cosmos) for that sun (or cosmos) being the first cause and sole source of everything. And that's exactly why we do keep libraries of books and exactly why so many other books have been referenced in this book by which to demonstrate that the so-called basic truths from which we derive such nihilistic conclusions are no more than earthbound assumptions.

Nevertheless, sometimes we mortals (who are only a little lower than are you angels) will try and block new thoughts. We may be afraid of creativity. We may run scared of being different. We may convince ourselves that because the sun is the source of practically everything physical that fills our mindset, then there is nothing new under the sun—and consequentially no room for anything new in our mindset. It scares us to think that there may be some way (far less many vastly different ways) of conceiving the inconceivable. Thus, in academia, you always have to find an authoritative citation (if not at least an often backhanded reason) for any proposition. There can be a point to that practice or process, which (for requiring a long treatise in itself) we won't go into now. But it can kill creativity, restrict the risk-taking required to reap the rewards of worthwhile innovation, and besmirch the whole concept of God-given creativity and thus humanistic originality of thought.

But of course, unless for being a newshound (or investigative journalist), one does not always want to hear the breaking news (far less groundbreaking news). Maybe if you only knew history as well as you should, you'd find that all groundbreaking news (no matter how bad or how good) is no more than prophetic history fulfilled. Could this conclusion be in itself a revelation? Now's the time, dearest readers, to find out how well you cope with revelation.

In this present age, when so many people, especially the very young and the very old, are first distracted and then distraught by their exposure to so much informational overload (which explains why this is also the age of denial and disclaimer), many highly stressed people (who in midlife may be more able to do so for their own protection) learn to shut themselves off or to shun what is always the trauma (however minimalist) of revelation.

Nevertheless, every real revelation alters the dynamic equation (emotional as well as intellectual) between the past conceivable, the presently inconceivable, and (as a result of real revelation) in turn, the future conceivable. To what extent, then, can you cope with the pace and content of further revelation? For the purposes of soul-catching, you'll cope better with your need for continued revelation by seriously self-assessing your capacity to cope with this question.

So then, coping with yet further revelation! Once again, just what does it take to conceptualise the inconceivable? To conceive the inconceivable differs markedly when trying to conceive either of the expected or of the unexpected. Of the expected, it is as often an exploratory experience which may or may not result in some discovery. Of the unexpected, there is always the element of surprise, if not also stress and trauma. We seek to conceive the inconceivable both to avoid trauma and to promote well-being.

It was on this day, Friday, the seventeenth day of March 2019, when this report sponsored by the Supreme Command was in course of its final revise for publication that an armed Aussie terrorist broke into two Muslim mosques in the Cathedral City of Christchurch, New Zealand. That's not very far away from Dunedin, the next biggest city (a small university town by world standards) from which the terrorist went to Christchurch to perpetrate perhaps the greatest of atrocities ever experienced in this hitherto safe haven of New Zealand. As the shooting in Christchurch began, this report sponsored by the Supreme Command was being written in Dunedin (more or less around the corner from the Dunedin mosque first targeted by that same terrorist operation).

It was in each of these two Christchurch mosques that, with a semi-automatic converted rifle, the terrorist broke in during prayer time and in total shot to death fifty-one unsuspecting worshippers, besides seriously injuring scores of their also innocent fellow worshippers. One may feel drawn to distance oneself from any and every sort of contretemps (for such distancing being the foremost indicator of an indifferent respectability). But whether domestic, cross-cultural, or cosmic, every such issue, whether in one's own backyard or elsewhere, is duty-bound to be confronted. So just what does it take (either post hoc or propter hoc) to conceptualise the inconceivable?

One thing's clear—we've now demolished the old-fashioned idea (derived from the Stoic philosophers of ancient Athens) that this is the best of all possible worlds. No, it's most certainly not the best of all possible worlds and, since mankind's fall from grace, has never been so! That's an idea which, on its coming up from down below (a shorthand expression by which to redact a far longer history coming later), would reduce earthlings to apathy and so evoke from heaven a full-on response to earthly non-action.

Take any upright angel's word for it. There's no upstairs policy of heavenly non-intervention in this world's affairs; otherwise, there'd be no need for us angels to be anywhere at all on earth, far less for us to daily trek up and down any Jacob's ladder. Still, it's a big kick in the bum to us upright angels still to hear this cosmic compromise still being proclaimed (even just by stoics) that this is the best of all possible worlds down here in these last days of planet Earth.

On the other hand, you humans should no longer attempt (like the titan Atlas of old, after whose Herculean task you once foolishly named the ill-fated ship the *Titanic*) to carry the weight of this whole wide yet already fast-dying world upon your narrow and rapidly aging shoulders. Let us angels impress upon you humans that there's a divine design for a far better world than this one. And with every passing day, this better design is made more clearly in the offing. You should learn more about this brand-new world which is already more than on the design board and whose design has already been revealed to you prophetically through the published word of the Supreme Command.

So then, this already fast-cooling and yet still possibly imploding or exploding solar system (as they might say who know that the devil is in the details) is not the be-all and end-all of what you humans like to credit yourselves for being either the progressive civilisation or the overripe fruit of many civilisations. This rapidly decaying solar system (indicated by this world's warring factions over their holding of conflicting centre points) is not (as the devil likes to make you think) the sole source of every resource needed for your continued survival on earth (as long as this old world holds out). Furthermore, this same rapidly decaying solar system is no resource at all for your transition to an ongoing life in all eternity (of which the devil himself has not an inkling of the details).

So then, you see (when both looking ahead as well as behind) that the more cosmic explanation of both heaven and hell is yet for this book (and for the next few books comprising this report) to thoughtfully explore and credibly explain. Nevertheless, much is clearly left for other resources (such as the biblical canon) together with the existing logistics (of prayer, prophecy, and preaching) to transmit these written pages into actuality. Step relaxedly back from all but your own human responsibility (remember what we said a moment ago about distancing oneself from any contretemps over deistic responsibility to shoulder any mistakenly *Titanic* task) when participating in any such divine programme of earthly as well as heavenly renewal. Remember, there's nothing to justify hanging on to any vestigial belief denying the possibility of a new world, far less a new heaven, which, in any case, the resources of this fast-failing solar system could never supply.

Admittedly, already within the war-torn and terrorist-afflicted portions of this world to some of which faraway portions we angels are briefly going to take you readers, there are many both conflicting and self-conflicting arguments against this great and grand design. Nevertheless, it is one of not just renovating and restoring the old creation but instead, just as it takes some new testament of truth to confirm the pre-existing truth of the old, it takes a new heaven and a new earth to reveal not just the continuity of what went before but also the existence of that selfsame youthful creativity by which to bring to fruition the old in the completely new.

Argument? Let's not argue, say many believers, but what they allow by way only of shallow discourse may contain many hidden arguments which perplex so many non-believers in their seeing any need for a new heaven (since for some, there's no present heaven) or any new earth, since this old one is most likely (so they think) to see them out. Well, even some of the greatest of evangelists shun argument (since that's their calling), but how else can any steel be sharpened (especially that which is blunted by unbelief) unless by being sharpened against some other believer's steel? There are certain evangelists (not usually angels, we admit) who nevertheless have a calling to cope with argument in sharing with others the sharpness of their steel for theological argument. All the same, that sort of sharpening is not our angelic purpose. Instead of sharpening, we shall be content with stirring the pot of evangelistic renewal, which is already on the boil.

Any other premises of argument than those we have used (no matter how much they may be impregnated with that level of academic detail which the devil delights to dote on) will lead to no other conclusion than one of argumentum ad absurdum (whereby the argument itself spells out its own absurdity). This is so since whatever satanic countermove could be promoted by any such devilish argument (say, to eat, drink, and be jolly, since tomorrow we die) will clearly try to prevent the establishment of this already designed new heaven and earth. But in the context of this clearly significant argument over whether this world is the best of all possible worlds, then consigning the promise of some new heaven and new earth to the fire (by giving oneself over to eating, drinking, and debauchery) and so turning one's back on this promise of a new creation is clearly an absurdity—both from the outside in (by way of the premises) as well as from the inside out (by way of the conclusion).

Never mind, say we angels to those who are both the stoically apathetic and the devilishly doubtful. Since psychoanalysis was invented by that most lovable Doctor Freud (which has both an upside-down pronation as well as a downside-up pronation), we can quite understand any mortal's feeling of being inconvenienced from whatever is your accustomed psychoanalytic pronation. Nevertheless, for a much quicker way of getting you up on your feet (through strengthening *yourself* in the Lord), we accept full responsibility for our call to you in this case to move house more away from earth and so to lay more explicit claim to inheriting your already bespoken mansion in heaven.

Of course, if you back off, then that's your Freudian ego that's involved, so you're already on course for developing a superego. And for every backing off, which is more and more likely to take you captive to carnal sexuality, then the more and more attention you do pay to sexuality instead of the attention which you once quite naturally paid as a child to your eternal soul. Let the heavenly host of angels remind you now (however much by way of understatement) that a sexual superego is not a very nice thing (either to witness or to suffer from). The satanic spirit of superman (unwittingly proliferated by the psychoanalyst Sigmund Freud and the atheistic author Friedrich Nietzsche) accounts for almost every murderous rape known to the Western world.

Nevertheless, there's always been far, far more to this admittedly mortal life of yours on earth than of lying on the beach baking in the sun—although that too is a perilous form of sun worship—and more and more so with the fast-thinning layer of ozone to protect you humans from the sun's ultraviolet radiation (UVR). You still need plenty of sunlight, of course, but don't either bake your bodies or tan your hides in the sun.

With tongue in cheek, we may say that Uncle Sol (the mythic sun god in Roman religion) has stood well disposed towards you humans who worshipped him (ra-ra-ra) for far longer than the two or so thousand years you've learnt of Jesus Christ, the Son of God. So then, don't poke fun at Sol or Ra or Surya or Helios now for each and all having been relegated to their proper place as amongst the earliest human perceptions of the mythic gods. Some of their earliest names are considered far too sacred to trip off any human tongue, so like the Tetragrammaton for Yahweh (YHWH) or the Abrahamic Allah, they would develop more common and everyday names, apparently from but as often creating the vernacular, like Elohim, Adonai, Jehovah (or even Kyrios, as in the Greek Septuagint).

The old gods (however named, renamed, regarded, or disregarded) are still too much around in human ways of thought for any mere mortal to take the singular risk of poking fun at them. You'd be surprised, as true believers, to know how many still rising numbers of world worshippers still profess allegiance by praying, as once did the Bedouin tribes, to the very oldest and most ancient god of the desert.

His name? Well, we don't want to call on him, since in these days, he's more than ever around. But who, for the sake of human survival amid the scorching sand of the desert (read again *The Long March*), would anyone call on but that god of the desert (known to and borrowed from the Bedouin) for being the deity (now brought up to date in Iraq) who is most obviously in cahoots with the sun god.

Nevertheless, as we angels warn you, the old gods (because that's what they still are to superstitious unbelievers) can still get really angry, and so they pull no punches when employed to promote the devil's wicked ways. [Excursus 1: As for the sun worship of King Sol, the vestigial remnants of which are still alive and kicking the whole world over, take special note of words such as *sole* (to mean the 'one and only one') or even as to the proper name of Saul in meaning the 'asked for one' or even more remotely the conceptually cognate words such as those of *soul* or *coal* (when relating to the primal bodily heat of any live human or to the apparent resurrection power of some dead but sun-warmed rock or to the potential of some still lit cinder to flare back into life again).

We all know in our hearts what is meant by the phrase 'in real life'. So too, when 'calling for his fiddlers three', then 'good King Cole can be a merry old soul'. And there's nothing like having a good cause for celebration, but don't underestimate the strength of his powers to distract more serious souls from seeing the already revealed need for some new heaven and new earth. In some places and for some people, real life knows no bounds where 'party, partied, partying' has become one of this world's most prevalent religions.

Likewise, don't underestimate the forcefulness of other apparently dead or self-indulgent religions, such as that of sun worship or of moon worship or of star worship, since you'll see the world very differently from the way in which many others see their own way of worship. You'll only hurt or grieve or anger others who don't yet know more positively for themselves what you're on about.]

Food for thought: perhaps (and so for more thought, both for and against it, since without more thought even false worship could come of it) but there is no allotted space or place for coincidence in either heaven or hell, unless amongst humans on earth (where the concept of coincidence often serves no more than as a ragbag in which to confine the humanly unknown). Nevertheless, don't despise fractals, for which (non-uniform structures demonstrating recurring patterns at a progressively smaller scale) you can consult any reputable dictionary of modern science. So then, without risking any further fractionation of thought, don't despise fractals any more than you would despise more conventional fractions (but then more people than ever before have come to despise both small change and conventional fractions).

Remember always, as any quantum physicist takes to heart whilst searching in his heaven for smaller and yet smaller particles, that, just as it took the life scientist more than four centuries to persuade his colleagues not only of the existence of tiny bacteria, tinier viruses, and now miniscule protein-infective particles as disease causative agents, yet both heaven and hell, each in its own way, have always recognised the often overwhelming significance of the small, smaller, and smallest of things to overcome the big, bigger, and biggest. Very roughly speaking, think small for getting into heaven (although being always aware that the devil is in the details), and so then stay collaterally beware of thinking big unless (by then so much bigger than your boots) you're aiming to get into hell.

So then, in more senses than one, there's more than one small splinter of truth to saying that there's nothing new under the sun because the sun is the source of everything, just as there's more than one small splinter of truth to saying that all is new, since even the sun as it is today is never quite the same sun as it was yesterday. Yet as said before, fractals do count—they really do—so don't dare (as you humans so often do dare) to overlook their consequences. Collateral damage is no more excuse for doing evil than is friendly fire, unforeseen circumstances, or unforeseen consequences.

Thus, when the Roman festival of *Dies Natalis Solis Invicti* (celebrating the rebirth of the unconquered sun each twenty-fifth day of December) was unexpectedly given over (on that very same date) to the celebration of the birth of some upstart (as some of these very old gods are enticed by the devil himself to still see Jesus), this anger gives rise to a great deal of the unholy revelry and mock worship of Jesus Christ that still takes place (commercially more than ever before) around Christmas. Now here again is a very difficult domestic as well as a very difficult national and international issue.

So then, for facing up to and confronting the issue of filching from Helios, the sun god, his rebirth at the winter solstice, what is little more now than the role of Santa Claus, then which role (if any) do you play in distinguishing our celebration of the good guys from putting down the bad guys around the time of Yuletide? Do we adopt the stiff-lipped role of the respectable stoic, or else do we front up like the Church of Scotland to play down Xmas? More openly confrontational (for which backhanded reason, confrontation by itself is never enough), Oliver Cromwell, as once protector of the English nation, once bit the bullet so hard (as did so often also the formalistic Pharisees in favour of law and order) as to break more than one front tooth by legislating to outlaw all celebration of Christmas.

Listen here now, for there being in Jesus Christ only one eternal source for everything, and that even for the milk of so-called 'human' kindness—which eternal source is neither worship of the sun nor of the moon nor of the stars (which many of you still sun-scorched, moon-mesmerised, or star-struck humans try to do by reading anything and everything from horoscopes to hands, heads, and even teacups). Instead, as can be correctly read from no other source than this through Jesus is the never-failing grace of God. [Exegesis 2: Every horoscope takes its name from Horus, one of the two mythic Egyptian gods of the sun. Quite frankly (and particularly when in Egypt or around any Egyptian artefacts in museums or wherever pyramids or sky-soaring Egyptian needles are scattered in streets or parks throughout the whole wide world), don't meddle with either Ra or Horus (which also means staying away from horoscopes) until you know you have our angelic backing to deal with them in the only way you should. We warn you of this because in these latter days, the old gods have their own way of using death to counterfeit life. Remember, anything not wholly 'in real life' partakes of death.]

Surely then, since that ever-flowing grace of God is the one source which can never run dry, then to explain the prevailing and increasing disorder of the world, someone (either celestial or otherwise) must have built walls, dug dungeons, blocked pipelines, or cut lifelines by which to sever that source of whatever defaulting species of mankind takes full credit for being its own milk of human kindness. [Exegesis 3: Well, that's exactly what we mean by both steering clear and staying clear of all such false deities (whether it's Tamerlane's tomb in Samarkand or Lenin's Mausoleum in Moscow) until you know you've got both a kingdom calling and our angelic backing.]

Before we angels begin to exercise the leeway of prophetic abstraction from these woes of the world by which to account to you for being that wisdom of heaven which demands the closest of attention to the least rather than to the most, to the one rather than to the many, and to the smallest rather than to the biggest, let us firmly reassure you again that the ever-flowing river of God's grace (sometimes known as that 'peace so like a river'), which can sometimes seem so walled out, buried deep, blocked off, diverted away, or distanced from wherever you might be searching for its true source, is never more than a hand's breadth away from relieving even the weariest of souls.

Bear in mind always that every such time of travel with us angels is not a tourist trip, nor yet an ego trip, but instead a soul-searching exercise. This soul-searching, as well as soul-testing, and as often soul-stretching exercise (as for Moses in being brought up as an Egyptian or as for Jesus during his time in the desert) can be undertaken by anyone anywhere. So too, as for Buddha (born more than 500 years before Christ), it would be undertaken under a Bodhi tree. Don't knock Buddha, don't knock Confucius, don't knock Zarathustra, don't knock Socrates—these are all protosearching types as much as are Moses, Abraham, and every other Old Testament patriarch and prophet.

Although more popularly called a banyan tree—which is a strangling fig and not a free-standing fig—a Bodhi tree is most certainly free-standing. The Buddha (or Enlightened One) left Hinduism because of its idolatry (although that hasn't stopped many Buddhists making little idols and also some huge ones, as were the Bamiyan Buddhas around the blue lakes of Band-e Amir in central Afghanistan. The Buddha is also known for giving a prophecy, subsequently fulfilled through the coming of Jesus Christ as the true God, who would be recognised by his walking on water.

Nevertheless, would-be Buddhists can get banyan-strangled in their search, no less than Christians can get banyan-strangled in their search, but since the kingdom of heaven came to earth through Jesus Christ, all the rules for any soul-searching (together with those for soul-testing and soul-stretching) have radically changed. Why, even the rules have changed their nature, to be replaced mostly by hints, hugs, nudges, and whispers, although in great moments of much significance, as that may pertain to someone, anyone, or everyone, then one or more or even a whole heavenly host of us angels may yet still appear to underline the significance of any auspiciously divine occasion. Never been there—no, not even to savour the flavour or to breathe in the presence, far less see the aurora, or feel the waft of anointing! Then take to heart Pascal's search (coming up later) for deeper abstraction.

Well, goodness gracious me (although it's still the heavenly host here speaking), but for us trying so hard to accommodate ourselves to the best models of your own human ways of thinking, talking, and writing, we angels (aside from the upper crust of archangels who are still largely loners) find ourselves so closely accommodating ourselves to your human company as to begin to feel like humans.

Well, if Jesus Christ managed to remain divine even whilst living on earth as one of you humans, we guess that's as equally a good model for us angels as it is for you humans.

Although we angels as often walk to exercise our legs (but more usually fly, because there really are some places still on earth where we angels would fear to tread), we do so along faith paths which are only a little higher (not much more than having our feet off the ground) than are those same faith paths taken by many of you humans. For any and every proper pilgrimage, however, be sure to think here of the perfect path, so much above us both, when so trodden by Jesus Christ, the Redeemer, whilst here on earth in human form.

We do now sometimes cause ourselves to smile (angelically, to be sure) at the way in which we are becoming less and less distinguishable from you humans. As mothers always tell their children, that's as much measured by the human company we keep for the purpose of this report, no less than by our fast-changing ways of linguistic expression (we hardly ever make proclamations now but instead resort to reasoned discourse) and as also evidenced from day-to-day by the increase in our more human sense of humour.

We find that, for not being human ourselves (although we've learnt to use human form as undercover) but all the same, always having been brought up to be angels, our increasing sense of humorousness for being more than remarkably human is also to us angels more than remarkably scary. *Just where will all this end?* we ask ourselves as angels for remembering all the time the great sadness of heaven when some of our angelic company sought to behave and think and feel (but always alone for their own greater good, as they thought) more as the humans they wanted to make of you than like us angels. Well, that was all part of the wicked ploy of the Counterfeit Command to inveigle humans into the ranks of fallen angels.

Oh, there's an immense amount of good humour in the Bible, and to enjoy it, you have to learn to marry the Hebraic sense of humour with the Greek sense of humour and then with each further translation of the Bible into almost every different tongue as spoken in this wonderfully wide world of so many different languages and cultures. Count it a privilege to read the Bible in each of its translated tongues and when complete with each of their correspondingly different senses of humour.

Why, you can't quite capture the folksy sense of the Hebraic Old Testament until you can begin to appreciate either the subtle punning sense or the fiercely oppositional sense of the Hebraic sense of humour. Neither can you begin to understand the interrelational yet also strongly conceptual sense of humour of the philosophic Greek until, even at the street level of Athens, you can begin to appreciate there the native sense of philosophic wonderment (in itself a translator's dream) by which Athenians like Socrates, Plato, and Aristotle play tag with the folksy sense of the Hebraic. Mark this well: that both (Greeks and Hebrews) are battlers; but (like Norman-French and Saxon-German) are of vastly different sorts. There again, aside from the miracle of cross-cultural communication whereby the whole wide world could change so radically as to unite these vastly different mindsets (both of which are really quite humorous, you know) the resulting mutuality between what is often very folksy, yet strangely wandering Hebrew with what is so often street-centred for being by then so very much less than classical yet by now cosmopolitan Greek, could and would shout 'open-sesame' to the even wider world of Anglo-American wonderment! Nevertheless, the last post is most likely to be sounded shortly in the South Pacific.

Well, what could separate us from the love of God, not surely for angels being angels and mortals being mortals, any more so for different cultures, for different languages, and even for having vastly different senses of humour? So too, there're pawky Scots (as you can find out by listening to Scots prayers), stiff upper-lipped English litanies, ironic Irish petitions, explosive and sometimes hot-headed Spanish inquisitions, temperamentally biased Italian, and sadly cynical Russian; but then some of these groups are so diverse within themselves (so Aberdeenshire humour differs so much from Glaswegian humour and both of these from Edinburgh humour) that there's more than any one devil in the details by which we are so pleased to simply praise God that nothing can separate us from his great love.

Well, let's hope for changing the substance of things as yet unseen, through each of us angels and humans adopting and accommodating to each other's means of expression, that the same change around not just from humans to angels but this time also vice versa, from angels to humans, may enable you humans to express yourselves in more than just one or two angelic forms of expression. We presume that all you readers too are conversant (mark well that choice of word) with glossolalia (better known to the divines as 'speaking in tongues').

And we angels will recognise with more particularity that change around in ourselves having happened when you humans begin more and more to proclaim and prophesy, especially for the sake of both a new heaven and a new earth, and less and less to grouse and grumble over the already revealed future (rather than fate) of this present heaven (which has already come to earth) and this present earth (of which so many portions and people have rejected and do so continue to reject not only what they think to know of but also what they know not of Jesus Christ. Praise the Lord! There are mighty things afoot for both you humans and us angels.

Why, if we're not careful, by the end of this report, whatever heavenly differences still exist between you humans and us angels may be pretty hard to pick on earth. Let's see next, however, whether you as humans can accommodate yourselves just as facilitatively to follow in our frequent paths of angelic abstraction. Blaise Pascal, this world's first statistical mathematician, managed it, and since then, the statistical measure of abstraction has both widened and deepened. Oh, and once again, there's a most practical reason, as for every piece of advice which we angels constantly give you humans, as in this case for you readers to learn to engage in abstraction.

Of course, there're proper abstraction and improper abstraction, just as there're proper ways of meditation and improper means of meditation. As for abstraction, you can call the process we recommend by way of relieving yourself from an issue (through abstracting yourself from that issue) to be 'waiting on God', if you like. In this case, however, if we're all going to take the risk of going to places like Moscow and Minsk—not to mention also Kabul, Baghdad, and Damascus—we've got a great deal of preparatory work still to get through to pick up on the higher levels of the most mindful abstraction. Don't confuse this level of abstraction with mindlessness, or else you won't get back from Moscow or Minsk, never mind even thinking to do so from Kabul, Baghdad, Tehran, or Damascus.

Nevertheless, getting through a great deal of preparatory work is nothing like either learning to abstract yourself from any issue or learning to wait on the Lord. Learning is always work, that's for sure, and hard learning is always hard work. But all learning always requires rest, and hard learning requires greater rest. So that both learning to abstract oneself from issues and learning to wait on the Lord can entail some considerably hard work—even although, after having learnt how to abstract oneself from those issues or having learnt how to wait on the Lord, both abstraction and waiting become the means of receiving rest. And rest is just as essential to the process of learning as is hard work.

The trouble with learning, which goes with any sort of learning (since all serious learning is significantly troublesome) is that making it playway rather than playful most often defeats the whole purpose of learning for which the means of learning was either divined, designed, or defined to achieve. The whole purpose of learning is that of learning what it takes to do the most with what you have been given. Doesn't sound much? Aha, then you haven't yet learnt how much you've already been given.

You may have been brought up or taught to suffice with less or even very much less than you've been given. This can happen no matter whether, like Huckleberry Finn, you are self-learnt, self-helped, or self-taught. You are thereby (unlike Huck) curtailing the potential to make the most of what you've been given. Once you fully understand the extent of what you've been given, what you've been given will never seem a little less than you deserve. Indeed, you will never begrudge again (however mistakenly) the little you've been given, because it will take all your time on earth and all your lifelong energy to make the most of it.

It may be, through any (formal or informal) process of learning, that this outcome is simply that of being able to do that which you have been taught or brought up to do. The task calls for exactitude, which, it may help you humans to know, need not yet aspire to angelic precision. Humans often fail in their tasks through the perfectionism that comes from their striving for precision. So then, be content for the present to do exactly (even if not always so precisely) what you have learnt to do or been brought up to do, just exactly as taught. *Nyet problema*—no problem! It's the qualitative exactitude that counts, not the quantitative precision—although you'll humanly profit from both if you're putting your back into making the most of the most of whatever you've been given.

This rather circular outcome nevertheless requires an intimate combination and intricate correlation of heart, mind, body, and soul, which, after having done all the learning work, then requires adequate rest for the purpose of translating that learning work into productive action. For harder work, then also add its equivalent of both adequate and sufficient rest for the same productive action.

In other words, learning is never ever done for its own sake (which may certainly impress the ego) but rather for its inherently practical purpose of well-integrated action combining heart, mind, body, and soul. In other words, learning to work well is the means of integrating the human troika (or triumvirate) of heart, mind, and body, together with the spirit or soul.

And so, whence from this sort of synergic input, whilst reaping the harvest from having learnt to work with the utmost concentration and meticulousness, the spirit-filled soul realises the opportunity to set that systemic learning into full-scale production. It is this sort of full employment (at whatever intellectual, moral, or other social level) that not only makes a nation but also makes every honest worker in that nation to be the noblest work of God.

It is the resultant integrity of both body and soul which produces for others the most social satisfaction, as well as to benefit ourselves with our own personal satisfaction. Both the human heart and the human mind are each (both individually and collectively) composite organs. They have both a collectively public as well as an individually private composite function. This is something that every prophet depends on for picking up on the rhema or spoken word of God.

You can deal with this process of theosophical integration from a number of different perspectives. There's the anatomical, physiological, and zoological perspective. There's the psychological, sociological, and anthropological perspective. But above all, since 'justice is mine,' says the Lord, there's the jurisprudential, theological, and metaphysical perspective. Let's leave it at that—we're on hallowed ground! [Exegesis 4: Don't trounce the very slight theosophical splinter of synoptic truth expressed by that earlier authentic search for the mystic soul by its theosophic progenitors, George Gurdjieff and Pyotr Ouspensky, whose search has been so badly derailed by theosophy's subsequent followers.]

Learning (never underestimate it for being easy work) requires you to reroute, redispose, or reopen your neural pathways or even to create new neural pathways. This process, as it is of all learning processes for being although a process of stretching your mind, is far more like stretching your soul rather than relaxing your soul, so you have to learn to look after your soul both ways, no less for being as often as you learn to look after your body (with rest as well as exercise), no less than to open (as well as to guard) both your heart and your mind.

Yet like stretching your soul through learning, you also have to learn how to relax your soul through every seventh day of rest. Abstracting the mind and relaxing the soul afford both the means of learning and also the means of resting the correlative functions of both mind and soul. We should also point out that the means of *earning from learning* (remember that phrase), although tactical in form, is strategic in function. Learning should never be ritualised— as it so often is for acquiring credentials from schools, colleges, and universities. Always use your extended mind, your extended spirit, and your extended soul to fulfil the advanced functions (whether in tandem or in triplicate) that either heart, mind, body, spirit, and soul have each been called to undertake.

Sometimes, for being more like telepathic communication (as if to fill the space between the written lines of this report to produce a palimpsest of further explanation), communication may proceed (without any words being used at all) by a process of completely abstract yet interactive conceptualisation. [Exegesis 5: Never fear. We won't leave you in the dark, since, as with our frequent exegeses, we'll provide you (as already here and there throughout this report) with explanations. Thus, a *palimpsest* is a document whose text is interlineated with another text or texts. That's simple enough, but to read a text as every text ought to be read must be something else you humans need to learn to do in order for you to know so much more than you already do about the closely interrelated histories of both heaven and hell. Oh, and for the kind of telepathic communication we're telling you about here, then whenever you feel the slightest nudge from the Lord to do, say, or write something for his sake, then that amounts to the telepathic communication which we're writing more explicitly to you readers about so that you may *earn by learning* from this report.]

So then, let's see if you can take the bull by the horns (as you humans might say, although we angels might think more of returning a demon to wherever he is bound to go when so told in the name of the Lord than of taking any bull by the horns). What we are asking you to do by encouraging you to follow our train of ongoing abstraction (more by heaven's way of telepathic non-thought than by your own mortal reasoning) is to meditate on the underlying meaning (which follows in the same way from that speaking in tongues) which from childhood upwards still underlies all overtly rational human language.

It is so often mortal reasoning (no less than overly liturgical prayer) which precludes heaven's own way of telepathic communication (especially) during any service of worship. Let's see then whether you can follow (by way of words being given here to aid your relaxed yet intrinsic spirit of meditation) what otherwise your human mind (but not your human soul) may still attribute to the most minimalistic form of merely mortal reasoning. Contra to human reasoning, this is the incredibly innate process of conceptualisation with which every person on earth is endowed by which to distinguish, in his or her own unique way, reality from unreality.

Rationality may enable us to put this process of conceptualisation into words, but the resulting rationalisation (or end result of this reasoning) is world's away from the inherent process of conceptualisation by which humans follow through the so many intricate processes of the body, mind, heart, spirit, and soul by which to arrive at those often very different conceptual conclusions of reality.

First of all (or so it may be as you mortals think it to be), there's a concept of first being. This concept of first being (unless dismissed for arbitrariness) is most usually associated with or even held to be generated by awareness of that first being's essential creativity. After all, there is far more to the world than this first being (whoever or whatever he or she may be) than just this first, only, and thus seemingly very lonely first being.

For this first concept (of anything or anyone) to be one of first being, however, there must be the process of conceptualisation by which to support it. So a concept is not just the result of the process of conceptualisation inherently present in and employed either directly or indirectly by every individual but is also related to and confirmed to exist by some quite precise moment of conception.

For this process of conceptualisation to be communicated, there must also be a process of rationalisation derived from a communal process of reasoning. If the social standard of this communal process is linguistic (for example), then for the sake of this process, words must keep, as we might say, to their proper meaning. This linguistic propriety may be monitored by various literary, as well as other social, legal, or political means.

When we angels look back on this little homily or meditation on the processes by which mortals may arrive at the point of what has become for many of them the problem of first being, we are anxious that you, dearest readers, do not mistake this exercise in abstract thinking to be any means of proof for what we're drawing to your attention. On the contrary, all we are concerned with is to establish the extent of your open-mindedness as humans to engage with us angels at this level of abstraction in dealing with any such problem as that which many of you may have not just as to the very existence of us angels but also with the reality of any first being.

Lest you feel hoodwinked by all the effort you have put into this exercise of engaging in abstraction by finding out that this homily or allegory or tall story (or whatever else you may care to call it) was never intended to afford you the slightest proof of there being any first being who can better account for today's so sadly demented world than you yourself see fit to do so, we offer some further remarks. These, given by way of the ongoing exegetical explanations which we earlier promised, are those which we hope in this case will help you to see the merits of your undertaking this further exercise when engaging in the subject of abstraction. [Exegesis 6: We warn you that this exercise on abstraction will require of you a higher level of abstraction (such is the accumulated result of continuing to exercise whatever level of abstraction you have earlier employed). Mindfully focussed abstraction will teach you to acquire still higher and higher powers of abstraction. Thus, you will continue to lessen whatever little difference there may yet remain between you readers and us angels by learning to engage in ever and ever-heightening powers of mindful abstraction. We'll have more to say about that process before we take flight on our soul-catching mission—probably first to Kabul (capital city of woefully long-invaded Afghanistan), although by then it might be Baghdad (capital city of woefully invaded Iraq) or, next in line, then Tehran (capital city of woefully invaded Iran) or else Damascus (capital city of woefully invaded Syria).]

This heightened level of mindful abstraction will be attempted by our dealing with some parallel issues intended to throw some light on the substantive issue of human proof (as distinguished from divine truth) the results of which you may have so eagerly looked forward to by way of advancing the credibility of any first being. The cosmic effect of advancing the earthly perception of this divine being's credibility will effectively diminish today's presently fast-increasing state of human dementia, and that shouldn't surprise you after comparing this world's different belief systems and the rising statistics for dementia.

What did you say—that to deny or falsify one's own creator leads to intensifying self-forgetfulness and eventually even to one of the many forms of dementia? No, you say (unless of course you have dementia). Why, for any such simplistic denial of dementia—you don't need any more than one first thought to denounce it by saying 'what rubbish!'

Yet think seriously on this proposition, and if also necessary, then (with sweet dreams) sleep on it. Remember also that the objective we pursue is to conceive the inconceivable. Most of the concepts we now have (such as the world might be round and not flat, or that there were once scoffed-at causative agents of disease which we now recognise for being infective bacteria—or perhaps even no more than just protein-infective particles) were once dismissed for being likewise inconceivable. So it's really only on first hearing that there's any relationship between human refusal to give credit to divine creation and the increasing rate of human dementia which afflicts this whole wide world, which could possibly surprise you.

Never fear, don't worry! It's only those who seek to save their life as any first priority who tend to lose it! Nevertheless, when you consider what might happen even if only in the earthly situation where some tenant (consider the parable of the vineyard) refuses to recognise his landlord's rightful claims, then just by the incremental loss of that tenant's mind (yet still preserving his life), the repudiated landlord were to afford the wilfully rebellious tenant more than enough time in which to change what remains of his demented mind, what do you think might be the outcome?

Surely this dementia is not an unfair consequence (mostly inflicted by the tenant upon himself) for failing to observe his landlord's rights. [Excursus 2: Before we do move on, however, we compliment you on the self-absorption with which you have so abstracted yourself from any outcome of this present exercise on abstraction as to be unaware (exactly but not always precisely) of all else but the means of proof, and so we apologise to you for incurring your earlier mentioned disappointment at what you mistook for being a sophistic hoodwink.]

The lesson to be learnt from any such disappointment is that by way of preserving objectivity, there is every advantage to pursuing any means of proof without substantively attaching oneself to either alternative outcome—valid, false, or contingent. For highlighting this purpose of attaining objectivity, we reiterate here that there can be no concept of any conception without some form of preconception. So too, there can be no concept of text without context (or context without text, for that matter) any more than there can be any concept of time without some correlative concept of timelessness.

Likewise, without some matter somewhere, there could hardly be any concept of what constitutes a void and, so presumably, also as of matter without at least non-matter if not also antimatter. This is not a matter (no pun intended) of Aristotelian metaphysics, although just as the idealistic Plato focussed on ethereal ideas, so then his former student, the rather mechanistic Aristotle, focussed more on scientific matter. It has been said in some philosophic circles that one is either a little platonic soul-thinker or else a little Aristotelian matter thinker—but no, neither is pre-empted from being a fully committed servant of the Supreme Command through Jesus Christ for being on balance a thoroughly platonic Aristotelian (or soul-body thinker).

Nevertheless, all argument is to some extent circular (or else it couldn't operate as argument), but once you have premises, then you make for conclusions. Just as every beginning must have an end, so this book must have an end. This is so, even if for no other reason (which is an end in itself) than this book having now made its own beginning could also be considered (for being more fiction than many readers would consider fact) thus also an end in itself—at least until the reader has got to the end of the book. Best wishes!

* * *

All Things Still under the Sun
Part III

In Search of Divine Abstraction
God of Abraham ... of Isaac ... and of Jacob ... yet not
of the philosophers and scholars ... Bringing certainty
out of certitude ... joy out of joyfulness ... peace out
of peacefulness ... feeling out of forlornness ... God
of Jesus Christ ... by whom 'Thy God shall be my
God' ... to bring forgetfulness of the world and of
everything ... save God ... save God ... save God ...
Blaise Pascal, *A Prayerful Poem on the Fire of
the Spirit* (paraphrased personal translation)

After our previous remarks on the possible causes of dementia,
you could be forgiven for thinking that Pascal's prayer 'to bring
forgetfulness of the world' was to continue our discussion on the
rising problem of dementia. Certainly not, although the search of that
state of divine abstraction in which nothing at all (save God) matters
to the human mind is as often (as it was to Pascal) a lifelong search
and, with his every day spent in lens grinding, a very long haul.

Everyone's day seems to entail a certain measure of lens grinding.
In the middle of lens grinding or stone breaking (read *The Road
Mender* by Michael Fairless, alias Margaret Barber), that's often
when and where the fire falls. Cultivating this degree of abstraction
(as often whilst working with one's hands) is one tactical measure by
which to let the fire of revival from heaven fall on earth by learning
to focus one's mind entirely on God. Besides, and on which account,
perhaps Pascal became both the father of statistics as well as of the
never-failing wager (for no one having anything to lose) by betting
on the divinity of Jesus Christ.

To take a punt on the divinity of God may thoroughly offend those
believers who recognise the divinity of Jesus Christ for his sake.
Never mind that. This punt is for the benefit of non-believers who
haven't got beyond doing things selfishly for their own benefit. No,

it's not even a punt to be taken for its own sake. In any case, readers will remember earlier when, for the lack of strategic commitment, we cautioned against their thinking to do things for their own sake. Without strategic commitment, long term tends to morph into short term, and effort grows lukewarm.

In any case (which, allowing for the exceptional case, is not every case), strategically minded mortals tend to shun every undertaking of things which seem to be an end in themselves. They don't like doing things for their own sake. This is because things which are done for their own sake (as an end in themselves) tend to remind mortals psychologically of their own approaching end on earth. Accordingly, all those unforeseen consequences of whatever things remain undone, because nobody on all of God's earth sees any point in doing them for their own sake, may sadly remain forever undone. And because we prefer to forget what we've left undone but should have done, then certainly we're still talking about wilfully induced forgetfulness (otherwise diagnosed as dementia).

This all contributes to the great sadness that permeates heavenly history (never mind to the disadvantage of human history, which has a mind mostly for making a bargain). It also brings great glee to those who tote up hell's history and who delight, by their well-developed Judas touch, to keep in hand their full commercial control of what (all other things being equal) it takes to make (as well as to break) the best of bargains. 'Such as purporting to sell twelve books for the price of one?' asks someone.

Well, 'all other things being equal' is something which on earth all other things never are. This is just a glib catch-all phrase which the sophist philosophers like to use to cover their big fat butts. All other things may be so equal as not to matter in the cosmos (where professors of philosophy like to think they stand intellectually at centre point), but when under the sun and on earth, no two things are ever quite the same. One can so clearly see that principle of singularity at work in quantum physics when giving any two sets of 'all other things' a closer scientific scrutiny, that one would never ever dream, far less think of giving equal wages for equal work on earth.

It's true that some things for certain purposes can be regarded as being equal on earth, but for the most part, that's a legal fiction, making no earthly difference to the facts. Arguably on earth, many things can be rendered down to be equivalent (as lard and dripping are rendered down in any butcher's shop), but just as human justice can never be more than an approximation to divine justice, so no two things can ever be entirely equal.

There are no two grains of sand, far less any two snowflakes, which are precisely identical. Put another way round, as in education, then every child is exceptional. Why, even if each of these propositions were to be proved so, that would only be a matter of proof and not of truth, since even the best of proofs is no more than an approximation to the truth. In this approximation of proof to truth lies the vulnerability of man in all his reasoning, whilst the immutability of truth lies in its comprehensive capability to account for the diversity and uniqueness of every single little thing. Thus, the Aristotelian metaphysics on which we rely for categorisation, predication, and classification is (relatively speaking) all at sea, as well known by both the early church (don't rock the boat) and today's quantum physicists (amongst which there's no end of rocking).

By the artifice of equating one thing with another or by the Procrustean means of cutting or stretching to define one thing to look like another, the appearance of things can be shown to be alike, but even this pragmatic similitude breaks down (in quantum physics, if nowhere else) under Heisenberg's principle of uncertainty. This is exactly where quantum physics and Christian metaphysics hold to the same stance in looking for reality not in the appearance of things but in things unseen.

Professor Heisenberg's principle of uncertainty (which possibly explains how and why he came to support Hitler's Third Reich) could just as easily be called the principle of extreme abnormality, since, in constantly changing space-time, no rock remains the same rock and no book remains the same book, far less than any person remains quite the same person. [Exegesis 1: Well, of course, whether in quantum physics or in any other sort of earthly physics, that's true enough. And this is simply so because there are no rock-solid absolutes, except either still held in heaven or through heaven having since come to earth. But if you know anything of Heisenberg's closeness to Hitler's National Socialism, you wouldn't find much room for any absolute in his principle of uncertainty. This so-called principle is really quite bizarre in any serious science, but not quite bizarre enough, obviously, to be laughed off the face of the earth (as when we angels point to the rising statistics there for both denying Christ and worrying over the cause of human dementia).]

You humans do so fear the great unknown (as heaven well knows—in being mistaken for it). Your captive psyche (or soul, except the psyche is not the soul, as psychologists well know) then backs off from all but the most obvious of earthly encounters. You'll run a mile (by no means any victory lap) to avoid us angels and so, in turn, more emphatically back off from acknowledging the remotest prospect of your having any Father in heaven.

Alas, the cop-out doesn't stop there, since you've then backed off from acquiring the means of faith by which to still your fear in what remains for you, instead of the great amen, the far greater unknown. Why then, by reason of your greater fear in the increasingly unknown, you can't even begin to fear the Lord, your God!

And so your initial fearfulness of this greater and greater unknown is raised to such dizzy, dizzier, and dizziest heights that you opt for every means to avoid the least encounter with heavenly persons and heavenly happenings. You mistake such meetings not to mark the beginning for you of any new life but instead, because of your ever-increasing fearfulness (which should diminish, not increase with age), only to presage the ultimate end of what little you know of your own life on earth.

Your place and name on the Book of Life can stop … stop … stop … just right here and now. This can happen no less than at just this same present moment. This page may be the last page which you read of this book (for being the last also of which the writer writes). You just have no idea of how far the life that is given to you is intended to stretch, stretch, and still to be more stretched … until … in choosing of your own rite of passage … it snaps, recoils, or is either finally wound down or wound up. Nevertheless, it is also the purpose of this book to tell you of how there is so much more to your own life than you at present think to know. And this is the case even if at present, you could know every last thing there is to know of all things under the sun (which, in any case, is no more than the twinkling of any furthest star in our ever-extending cosmos).

Why, if these twelve books in one book were any the less of a literary conceit for being as true an account as one could get of the cosmos, they'd go on forever … and forever … and forever … which is exactly why infinity, constancy, and eternity are characteristics of the eternally divine and not of as yet more than merely contingent of temporal humanity. [Exegesis 2: As the leading agent in the field for this report, we beg to report that these angelic representations on the subject of temporal humanity (recorded for training purposes) are being reported verbatim. We are led to believe that the as often didactic and sometimes abstruse style of this verbatim report is to be explained by many of the representations being made not from the field but by ivory-towered academics from heaven's foremost College of Angelology.]

You see, the concept of *ever*, especially when rhetorically raised to the concept of *all ever* as you humans are tempted to do by equating that which is *big* with that which is *beautiful*, then appears to be a far, far bigger concept (as you might be tempted to say for being something far, far more significant) than never. Put it this way. There could never be a concept of *never* (logically speaking) without a concept of *ever* (which the opponents of this argument try to deny). So just as it takes the concept of eternity to grasp the concept of anything less than eternity, so also it takes the concept of there being something forever to grasp the correlative concept of there being anything for less than ever.

Some say (mostly book reviewers, of which Bible commentators are an especially in-bread (*sic*) rather than an inbred class or more closely-cloned clan) that for any book left to make its own beginning (as if any such book were a text without context and so having been immaculately conceived of itself without any need for preconception), then such a book might be for all one knows (which in the human realm of things isn't very much) a world in itself without end. This jurisprudential variant on the argument of whether there will be any need for laws in heaven (far less than for the Bible itself, which of course puts the Bible commentators out of a job) is of course liable to escalate as to whether there will be any need for having God himself in heaven. Presumably like any other CEO in this rapidly declining world he (or she, preferably to save on the retirement fund) could be given a suitably munificent golden handshake out of the proceeds of his or her own androgynous creation.

They say, as so heard of the biblical canon (or when as often functioning as a cannon), that for never having had any preconception of its own birth, far less of initiating its own conception, it might just as easily lack any means of self-determination. Now the same may go for some timeless void, but that's not to say (although so said on earth often enough) that any such timeless void, from which all matter and life spontaneously erupts, is exactly that which is meant by all eternity.

Well, the trouble is (according to most of us angels) that most of you humans live your lives today on earth as if you have had no experience whatsoever of immortality. Why, for thousands and thousands of years, as even exposed (but barely, if ever revealed) to pagans, their gods were (an enviable, if also scary) part and parcel of everyday life on earth amongst people. For the most part, although with one very important exception, pagans would never have equated timelessness with eternity. They were, after all (as on any first contact with another civilisation) mere pagans or aliens or (as could be said of so many Christians) bloodthirsty barbarians.

Of course, for the purpose of exemplifying the end days, the Babylonians were and still are the exception. They were the earthly exception to prove the heavenly rule, we could say, whether from the days of Nimrod, the great hunter, through the days of Nebuchadnezzar and Belshazzar, and beyond to our own days. Witness now all the bricks being fired to build the new Babylon (as if to shame every concept of the New Jerusalem) with each brick being fired with the imprimatur of having been made in the era of Saddam Hussein.

Even to the Babylonians (and to the Iraqis who have succeeded them), Babylon is seen to have no beginning and therefore no end. In consequence, many Babylonians have simply no sense of history, no sense of time, and above all, no sense of eternity. Theirs is a day-to-day agenda, whose date of determination is already fixed.

It was Nimrod, the great empire builder, who sought to invade heaven by building the great Tower of Babel. It was Nebuchadnezzar who went insane, eating grass for seven years, as a result of the great self-pride he took in his building of Babylon. It was Belshazzar who feasted whilst his capital city of Babylon fell to the Medes and Persians. What we are called to witness today and every day is the fall of Babylon the Great. The days of this multimillennial city are already numbered.

It is (was and will be) the timelessness of Babylonian culture and its resulting ignorance of all eternity that over and over again trips up those who, whether in ancient Babylon or its successor (not far from Baghdad in modern Iraq), subscribe to the self-blinding culture of timelessness instead of humbling themselves to the prophetic promise of eternity. [Excursus 1: Sorry for the long sentences, but as in former times, only long sentences can once again make the most of what little remains of swiftly passing time.]

Overall, but still faster and faster with passing time, much has been written, rewritten, and overwritten on the wondrous subject of Babylonia (whose once-hanging gardens were indeed one of the Seven Wonders of the Ancient World. Nevertheless, it is the rebuilding of this Babylon the Great, lying destroyed for centuries by the invasion of Medes and Persians under Cyrus the Greater, that, like the prophesied rebuilding of the Temple in Jerusalem, this Babylon would be so recently and authentically restored by the late president Saddam Hussein. It's true that for many moderns, there's no point to antiquities, since the point so often escapes them. But here again, all in time for its ultimate and total demise, as so clearly and prophetically recorded twice over in the Bible, long-gone Babylon the Great would rise again from its former rubble to serve as one of the first and most significant approaching signs of the end times.

But then, although not to change the subject, can you hear when any prophetic pin (such as this one) drops to earth from heaven? It's not just a matter of having open ears and also open eyes (since what you see can affect what you hear) but also having an open heart as well as an open mind (since an open heart cannot survive a closed mind any more than an open mind can survive a closed heart). Some folks (especially mortals) neither see nor hear nor might even feel a pin drop from heaven to earth, and so whatever they may eventually experience of its magnetic effect (in terms of cause and consequence) is much too late (as for Saddam Hussein and many other self-inflated world leaders) to do anything about it.

So then, keep your increasingly angelic wits about you. At the same time (whilst keeping time), be on time (both synchronously all the time) as well as (with the softest and accompanying syncopation) consider how close we all are (both on-beat and offbeat) to the heartbeat (leading to this world's cosmic syncope) that marks the end of all past, present, and future time. So (then and when and where) get ready (both individually as well as collectively) to change cosmic gear when reaching that pivotal point that faces you all (each and every one of you) when reaching from in-this-time to out-of-all-time.

To participate in this last and heart-stopping syncope of all time, you must (like any poet or poetess) learn to multitask with both metre and melody. Not many of you humans, unless musically inclined— that's to say, drummers (for whom the contrapuntal beat is addictive) or lyricists or straight-lining songsters (running more in the melodic horizontal than in the harmonic vertical)—can master the cosmic syncopated heartbeat (in-time-out-of-time that leads eventually to all-the-time being out-of-time). That's the point (trashed, like that of the Beatles, so often in his or her or their own time) when every rap artist (from Bach to Beethoven to Mahler to Nyman) increasingly approaches the pivotal point ... of changing cosmic gear ... to leave this world ... with yet another message ... from beyond all time.

Take that rap ... most seriously to heart (from once beyond all time to being again beyond all time) say all ... of us angels (whom you know ... to be the leading rap artists ... both of your own time ... and of all time). And do so, not in any way of merely marking ... marking ... marking all time ... but instead ... by making the most ... of every demisemiquaver of remaining all time.

Do so indeed ... whether or not ... you know yourself ... for whom you are by reason of your complete and utter self-abstraction ... in waiting patiently for the return of the Lord, since ... by reason of that complete self-abstraction ... you wouldn't know yourself, whether to be in the heaven you'll then be in and no longer on earth or whether there is, or was, or will be any place ever called hell as once seen from this now dying earth. Don't you already know ... that to be asleep on earth … is simply to be … out of time … So then, sleepers, awake! This is your time!

It's a bad rap all round. Already the former USSR of thirty years ago is (by now almost forgotten) history. The United Soviet Socialist Republics (once feared for their fierceness) are almost all gone. Not even the CIS (representing the so-called Commonwealth of Independent States) could be said to be alive and well. These now comprise only ten (or is it now only nine, they say) of the formerly Soviet Republics. Those are only the few still willing or else still bound captive to their formerly communist roots to hold together. So then, it's a bad rap all round, and even for communism—although in China (apart from the hot-spot of Hong-Kong where old worlds still explicitly collide) a new world force emerges to which may be given the name of either capitalistic communism or communistic capitalism. Still, it's a bad rap all round, no matter what you call it!

No contender has quite (far less altogether) been able (even only as a face-saver) to take or maintain the former Soviet Union's place. Well, so what? Holy Mother Russia has always been piggy in the middle for being placed, both historically as well as geographically and both socially as well as spiritually, between the East and West. It's still a bad rap all round; with even Turkey (for so long the sick man of Europe) threatening the EU!

Empires are always under siege. It may not matter much whether that empire is administered as a monarchy of subjects (as in the British Empire) or as a federal republic of citizens (as in the USSR or in the USA) or is under the despotic and arbitrary rule of some tyrant or else is governed in accordance with some carefully hedged, wedged, and ringed-in democratic (although dysfunctional) constitution. The conclusion reached by every last commonwealth, as by every former empire, whether worshipped as divine from within and/or without (salute the flag, please), is still under siege (for no less long a time on earth than heaven is still up there under siege from hell or else has come down more to earth to do here front-line battle against hell on earth). It's still a bad rap all round!

Like celebrities at large, there's always someone (if not themselves from the inside, then someone else from the outside) ready to bring the greatest of empires down, down, down. Envy of others (whether from inside outwards or from outside inwards) is the most likely means of motivating imperial downfall. As Homer tells us in the *Odyssey*, it was so (between Greeks and Trojans on the inside outside) whilst on the field of Troy.

This is the so-called game of thrones (sometimes for some people just to sit on the throne without being seen to wear the crown and, at other times, by other people to wear the crown without sitting on the throne). It can be played on any field of earthly enterprise—whether on the stage, in the household, on the football field, on the cricket pitch, at the swimming pool, in the front line of some world war, in the local bingo hall, on a winning streak in some tall-towered casino, or by losing the toss to some seamless garment below Calvary's cross.

As empires become more renowned (and so more vulnerable to downfall from self-pride on the inside as well as from increasing envy from others on the outside), they build walls. These walls (whether spiked, wired, sapped, explosively mined, or plausibly, wall-papered) enhance that empire's sense of exclusivity, but of course, in any game of thrones versus thrones when waged from without those walls or in any game within those walls of which hero will wear the imperial crown, this exclusivity promotes a twofold (if not manifold) vulnerability.

As they say (with a loud ha-ha-ha from down in hell), uneasy lies the head (not yet in a basket or on a pikestaff) that wears a crown. The tumult grows, both from inside and outside the former empire (as to who shall wear that crown, command the army, or occupy the presidential chair) and from the outside (as to which empire shall seize the other's throne).

Encouraging exclusivity, whether by drawing lines, imposing and controlling borders, or building and manning walls, in the long run perpetrates a process of degeneration, not generation. The siege from the outside inwards (as felt most obviously to insiders) or from the inside outwards (as least obvious to insiders) is demonstrated by every single one of the world's great empires from Babylonia and onwards (although invariably downwards).

Draw lines—whether Hindenburg, Siegfried, or Maginot—and you may find them to be drawn no more than in the shifting sand. Consider yourself for too long being an island, and you may be either invaded by sea or from the air, picked off incrementally by those with more powerful resources, or be left marooned to starve on your own shores. Build walls, and the manpower exhausted in so doing may leave you with insufficient manpower to man those walls.

Instead, wherever possible, build bridges with your neighbours, not walls. But cut your neighbours (as Hitler did by first making and then breaking a peace treaty with the Soviets) and then you're in the liquid poo—not always right away, of course, since it takes some time for poo to accumulate, for cemeteries to fill, and for middens to overflow. Good heavens, but even great cities like London, Manchester, Glasgow, Edinburgh, and Aberdeen were once fast accumulating their own poo like that. Why, even to rectify the general mischief caused by cholera, typhoid and other insanitary deseases, Queen Victoria's consort, Prince Albert, had first to die of typhoid fever before anything like sanitary drainage would be dug and public health come into vogue.

Digging in (wherever, as at Stalingrad) or digging down (as once before, in the trenches at the Somme) won't help to resolve any hidden issue. All time, and not just your own time, is against you, and the outcome of not facing up to that prognosis of all time will be far more all the worse for seeing that even just your own time is against you. Not so long ago, as in this reporter's own lifetime (which is not yet history for being still current), open sewers ran alongside schools and houses, flowing openly underneath the very sour-smelling tenements in which whole families lived, and yet in those often fetid cesspools and open sewers, little children casually played before the same heavily polluted waters discharged into rivers, harbours, and the already dying sea. So that you may learn to care for others—to love your neighbour as you would yourself—then first learn to love yourself and so by such means to care for yourself in loving others.

Cut even just your enemies, and before you know where you are, you're cutting your friends. There's no saying where the exclusivity of hell will lead you by way of making more and more enemies of your fewer and fewer remaining friends. The acrimonious lawsuit of the *Montagues* v. *Capulets* is bound to overpower you—generationally if not personally, collectively if not individually, publicly if not also domestically, nationally if not locally—whenever you fail to foresee that those from whom you cut yourself off have still the potential to remain friends. Meanwhile, cast aside every mind-binding assumption, as the art and practice of every learning system requires you to do to open and free yourself up from every stagnant mindset.

Whilst time still remains, take to heart that tragically broken romance, as law reported so accurately by Shakespeare (both poet and playwright) of *Romeo and Juliet*. As of all young lovers who, through their love of each other, are made wards of heaven's own courts, the outcome, always so unhappy for that earlier generation which shelves their fate for being unforeseen circumstances (rather than unforeseen consequences), behoves on all human society to happen again … and again … and again.

So then, in every case, face up to not just all the so-called facts and fractals by which to constitute these facts but also to the ever-widening and ever-deepening space-time context of these facts (in which every fractal counts for playing its part). So too, instead of trying to avoid the causal issues, confront these causal issues—and not the symptomatic signs by which no matter how much it may hurt you to face up to them, you yourselves are so privileged to be able to read whatever may be brought to your attention by way of being the signs of your own most faltering times.

Even for the Russians (love or hate them as you will from as furthest West you can go before reaching the farthest East), they tend to fall into or swing from one to another of their different cultural factions—of Slavophiles who face East and of Westernisers who face West. [Excursus 2: By the way, CIS no longer means anything more to the decadent West than an acronym (CIS) by which to distinguish cisgender (as the still prevailing norm of human sexuality) from transgender (for thus now having become the deviant norm). So then, male and female are no longer complementarities, far less opposites. Instead, they now are (all other things being still as equal as they ever were) transferable contingencies subject to time and place.]

Hold on, don't you feel anything (we angels would ask, for there are many of us committed to the redemption of the Slavic nations) no less than to some measure of social androgyny between the sexes? So then, don't you humans feel exactly the same towards absolutely every single person (whether communist or anti-communist) who has suffered by this enormous upheaval in their lives?

Why, it's so easy to celebrate with those who, by reason of this upheaval, have finally made their way to freedom from their wrongful imprisonment in Gulags, mines, prisons, and places of false psychiatric detention. Nevertheless, consider the mammoth upset caused to society at large by this strange reversal of values whereby what was legally held wrongful before is now held legally rightful. The law in changing its values must always be seen to change its role. What affect will this reversal of political, moral, and social values previously enforced by the law now have on those previously considered to be normal, ordinary, law-abiding, and even heroic citizens? Well, as you might say when championing the legal change, then for the sake of previously saving their own skins, they've had it coming. By having given their support to these now frightfully obsolete values, they've surely had it coming. Hmm!

Yes, that's true—for the sake of saving their own skins, they've had it coming. But then (speaking as of you Western humans too) we've all had it coming and still have it coming! You must remember, even from what little you know of heaven's history by which there came to be a hell, then even heaven too (on your own by now broad view) once had it coming.

This world, as it is today, is still experiencing the aftermath of that first fall from heaven. As any human, don't think to hide either behind that first fall or behind its aftermath. To hide behind that fall from heaven or its aftermath (as you well know, because in some way or another, each of all humans, with only one exception, have tried it). Nevertheless, none get far until they come back out of that one-way closet or any other closet so long as they fail or refuse to see that it was by only their free choice (even in some indirect or very hidden way through lack of response) that they got into that dark hole of a closet (whether political, legal, moral, or otherwise) in the first place.

It's a funny thing about celebrities, you know, that for some reason (which may turn out in the long run to be for their own sake) that, as celebrities, they don't last, and so that heavenly downfall took out the greatest angelic celebrity of which heaven had ever known and of which earth had ever heard of down … down … and down, like a shooting star whilst burning not quite out on re-entry (perhaps amid the Siberian tundra) from the heavens.

One-third of heaven's angels then chose (there's always freedom of choice, you know, even in heaven) to splash down with their fallen leader. Don't, for one moment (if that's still left), mistake that heavenly fall for being any sort of comical event, nor that once bright star of the morning (still expressed on the flags of many nations) to stand for any sort of clown. Neither mistaking a heavenly tragedy for being a comedy nor a heavenly dignitary of Satan's stature for being a clown will get you very far in your own search for the way, the truth, and the life.

It's much the same for lesser splashdowns. It's a macho thing for humans (as well as for fallen angels of which most by now are demons) to make light of their own most painful splashdowns. By their clowning around, especially in times of critical stress, they try to divert other more serious searchers from their freely chosen and appointed tasks. The family Bible seems a very hefty book, but it can be explained more by human conduct and most particularly by parental conduct than by repetitiously repeating the divine word in the most mechanistic of theological or churchlike ways.

Learning (as so-called by heart, but most often by rote) before living the word for oneself in spirit and truth may build a thicket in which to catch a ram for the slaughter but yet still fail to light a fire by which to reveal the human soul. It may fail to reveal both the soul in need of attention (just as green or damp wood may refuse to light a fire) as well as fail to reveal the full glory of the human soul that has already been set alight and remains ready to stay alight by continued empowerment from the divine hand.

There's always some point (as often very sharp) to anything and everything if you could only choose to look for it, to listen for it, or to search for it. Hiding behind the heavenly downfall (temptingly to us angels) no less than behind every subsequent human fall (temptingly to you humans) gets us nowhere. If only you had been there (you say, whether at the building of the ark or at the crucifixion), how different you would have made things turn out to be. Why, even in hell, they laugh uproariously at that view for being the biggest joke of all time!

Still hiding beyond the heavenly downfall of errant angels, are you? Sorry, just as there's no room at the inn, there's also no room left behind the heavenly downfall, but (where disclaimers are made and terms and conditions apply) we can still offer you some stable room.

No, no, not at all … you're still entombed, perhaps more than ever before, this time in the closet of wishful thinking, and thus seriously mistaken in your human thinking. Never mind. No less mistaken than you were also Marx and Lenin, Stalin and Trotsky. It's very human failing to be mistaken, and the more you're mistaken, then the more right you feel you are in being less mistaken. That's the paradox of thinking yourself more qualified than anyone else to know yourself—when actually for being yourself you're bound to know less. Hey there, if you really want to break through this collectively imposed barrier prohibiting self-knowledge, then be sure to read *The Book* by Alan Watts—on the role of the book (i.e. books at large) in putting down the taboo against knowing who you really are.

Now, for the sake of learning more of yourself than you might think it could be, if Lenin's Tomb has been reopened we'll take you there. We'll do so only under our angelic cover, however; so then not today but yet sometime soon, you'll have time to be better prepared for that deeply bewitching experience (even under angelic cover) than you think yourselves ready and prepared for that experience now. Likewise, you'll have a great deal to catch up on before we ever think to guide you on a tour of military service. Yes, of course, angelic missions are more like military operations than you'll ever hope to find in any more humanly church service, so you'll have a very great deal to learn from the Supreme Command before you ever think to enlist with us in any battle corps.

So then, take things more seriously than ever before, since you may have to face even the risk of radioactive fallout from Chernobyl in our projected visit to Minsk—capital of White Russia or Belarus. This is the earliest geohistoric point at which communism entered the up-and-coming history (still undercover) of the swiftly developing Soviet Union. All the same, never mind little comrade Lenin here—he's a geopolitical diversion (as most front men and more so today's front ladies are in politics) from the real grass-roots history of cosmic genealogy. [Exegesis 3: But by then, you should know from your

Bible studies required for our future travel (particularly from the last book of the New Testament on the Revelation of Jesus Christ) that the Russian for *Chernobyl* means 'wormwood' in English.]

Chernobyl's been a painful experience for humanity all round, and you don't know an eighth (never mind a half) of what so bitterly happened at Chernobyl. Have you ever tasted of the herb wormwood? That prophetic herb (as mentioned in the Bible) has by no means a pleasant taste, and its pungent flavour takes a long time to leave the mouth.

So too, it was partly that bitter fallout—in botany as well as in medicine and theology, since wormwood is well known for being such a very bitter plant—from which the radioactive cloud (or djinn) passed over Minsk in its ongoing transit over Europe in 1986. Consult Live Science on this worst nuclear disaster ever seen by this world. Still hiding behind this cloud, world communism still survives, although (except for China) apparently gone into complete remission.

You wouldn't believe it even if we angels told you that the whole wide world is more Soviet (especially in the West) than ever before. And its apparent progress prospers because there's nary a scholar of Sovietology in the West who was able to keep his job after the apparent end to the Soviet Union in 1991. A clean sweep of those Western scholars who were most intimately knowledgeable of Soviet ways was made from colleges and universities all over the world— now beat that for being the most Soviet way of doing things!

That was the year when so many of us angels had been called into play (operation code-named Gorby). Our mission, if only to put an end to the coup that was designed to squeeze the last breath of life out from President Mikhail Gorbachev, didn't entirely fail. We did manage to save his life (by the skin of one's teeth, as we could foresee only in the east), but Gorby would by then be no more than the last president of the thereafter hidden but by no means completely defunct Soviet Union.

Learn never to fast-forward history before making sure of where you're going by taking each and every one of the most extensive flashbacks to be found explaining each of the prophetic fast forwards you would either think of making, far less hope to proclaim. This is the faster and faster filmic form of investigatory dialectic required in the context of today's increasingly telescoped space-time. It is only by thoroughly investigating and monitoring each and every one of these extensive flashbacks (in itself a cosmic exercise) before you can get the all-clear from the Supreme Command to fast-forward any prophetic proclamation. Go slow, often only painfully slow, on your flash-forwards (for once given, they cannot be recalled) and so even slower beforehand on processing what you make of your flashbacks.

As you construct or reconstruct your text, whether by prophetic fast forwards or by historic flashbacks, remember also that there is no text without context, just as there is no context without text. So also, it is the same basic but still more serious process for undertaking the history of heaven and its correlative history of hell. That's exactly why, for this first book being merely a very brief yet overall conception of the subject (although only when seen still under the scorching sun), this whole series of books is no more than a grass-roots introduction to Universal Theology 101 (as introduced to novices in any heavenly angels school).

For heaven's sake—always remembering how many such schools, advertising themselves for being set up to teach the angels, are merely demonic scams and commercially minded counterfeits—then be fully prepared to meet up with and to hold your own against some never before encountered djinn of the desert. It took Moses forty years and Jesus Christ forty days to be thus strengthened in the Great Amen. How long will it take you?

'Taste and see that the Lord is good.' Whereas every imposter will leave nothing but the bitter taste of wormwood in the mouth. Never go down the path of least resistance. Don't (like that much earlier, brightest, and most celebrated of morning stars) get shot out of heaven for being likewise so swollen-headed as he still is—he who still so much delights in himself to be the devil incarnate.

We nevertheless presume from your having lived as long as you have on this earth that you will have felt more than a little of the turbulence occasioned by this well-known angelic fall from heaven. You'll continue to feel more than a little of this ongoing turbulence, no less from its earthly aftermath giving rise to the flood (we presume you know about Noah) or from fire (since we also presume you know that volcanic and ground-shaking means of reprisal took out two huge cities, besides also leaving Lot a lonesome widower by turning his wife into a pillar of salt).

No, or perhaps upon sorry reflection, only somewhat? Well, in any case, there's more, very much more to the history of heaven, both presaging and after the flood than these two happenings. Later in this book, we angels shall begin to teach you humans (for being still so very backward in biblical ways) how to distinguish unexpected happenings from expected happenings. By means of such discernment, you shall learn at least to mitigate the impact of the unexpected. This text of our teaching, we'll teach not just theoretically, as so often theoretical texts are taught completely out of human context, but more practically in the proper context of your everyday human lives. Okay?

Meanwhile (which is a very significant word to indicate that there is room to believe of our having still time between this present now and some future then by which to alter outcomes that would otherwise remain fixed and allow of no alteration), we must point out to you that even the human tide, like so many other tides, is turning. The tumult's rising. Do you know what it's like when the winds rise, when the seas roar, when the rivers flood, when a twister comes, when a volcano blows, when a tsunami crashes through sea walls, when a nuclear reactor springs a leak, when a gunman runs amok, when mortgages foreclose, when a government goes down, when Wall Street shuts up shop, when small businesses then too shutter up, and when even the thriftiest of people (most often the most elderly) lose all their life savings? [*Aha, what's that you say—the loss of one's entire lifesavings? Not all of them, surely! Yes, all of them—every last cent! Well now—so then, out on the street, homeless in Seattle, and yet the stress of sleeping homeless hasn't even begun to tell!*]

Wow (exclaims the flashback human historian), since (to his knowledge, however limited) this was the very same question as first asked by Abraham of how many or how few (it's the same question) righteous inhabitants of any city it will take to save that city or, similarly, of how many (or how few) righteous citizens it will take to save a nation or (for being then still the very same question) how many or how few righteous persons it will take to swing the balance and so save the whole wide world. [Exegesis 4: Be sure to take each question seriously, since from one or more of the most important ways of looking at the same question, it's a trick question—since there's only one person by name (unless a needful triad, trinity, or team of three or more divine persons in collective concert) who can save the world. Look at it this way—if not for Ishmael, maybe Abraham could have saved the world!]

Nevertheless, if this Supreme Command of the Hebraic Elohim (in all their forms) or Adonai (in all their forms) or the Trinity (in all their forms) then so decides to enlist the help of more persons (perhaps both believers and even also unbelievers) to engage in this grand and final mission by which a new heaven shall be created to supplant the old heaven no less than this weary old world shall be supplanted by a bright and flourishing new world, then so be it (for whomsoever constitutes and gives rise to that then rightful calling from the Supreme Command). But isn't this by now the case that all believers have already been commissioned so to do by the Supreme Command? So then, for that being already the case, may the Great Amen himself honour this commitment!

This old world is in such a state of flux that not even the theologians (far less the lawyers, logicians, and linguists) can keep up with the increasing pace of change. Don't you have the slightest compassion in your heart for those who although they've asked for what they'll get (as we all ask for things yet not knowing for what it is we ask)? This is one of the most fundamental of questions we'll pursue with the best of human (as well as of angelic) intentions when asked of every field of politics, philosophy, science, scholarship, or any other serious discipline or profession.

So then, before we set off for Moscow or Minsk or Myanmar or Kabul or Baghdad or Tehran or Damascus (because that's the name of today's game of thrones, which require far more than ordinary tourist travel can provide these days), so there's much for us yet to do. We can view our task historically, geographically, commercially, culturally, educationally, theologically, or militarily—or a conglomerate of all these seven. So then, don't we have even the remotest drop of human kindness left by which to empathise with those, say, in the former Soviet Union (even although, by and large, the West is convinced that the brunt of most Middle East problems are to be laid at the

Russian Bear's back door)? In short, haven't we a responsibility (as required of any and every traveller) to reappraise, if not also change, our previously settled, static, and perhaps even stagnant mindset?

Let's change the political scene for a moment, however, if not indeed the political topic! On the eve of Brexit, let's take a flashback into that not-so-long-ago British history once so much and sometimes overly revered, and now in the doldrums both at home and abroad. For all its troubles over Brexit, the United Kingdom of (the now not-so-great) Great Britain is presently faced with survival problems as critical as when she (now reduced to it) reluctantly assumed responsibility for declaring, waging, and ending what became known (famously or infamously) for being World War II.

Alas, there is no stately Churchill now in these straightened circumstances to stand in the wings! Yet in that same historic flashback context, don't we have any reserve of that same milk of human kindness left by which to bolster up the depleted greatness of what was once Great Britain when now (like Poland and the rest of Europe before) Britain went to the aid of weaker nations? Yes, of course, nations come and nations go, so do we just stand on the sidelines and report on some going fast and others slow?

Aye, aye, aye ... but how now may it not be said for the UK to have called down upon itself not just the full-blown constitutional conundrum and associated legal difficulties it is facing but also all the other troubles which now perplex and lead the British people into an almost impossible stranglehold at both national and international legal levels? How now in their trying to leave (what began as the EEC and then morphed into the EU) are those Britons 'who never shall be slaves' again to assert their freedom? As seen from the inside, what remains of the so-called Commonwealth of Nations depends upon it!

From the outside (whether for being seen either from heaven or from hell), how much different is this perilous situation (in the West) from what's so recently happened (just as perilously but more to the East) in the snap dissolution in 1991 and even from the more incremental and more gradual yet ongoing demise of the now former Soviet Union? Ah, but perhaps for such huge issues as the survival of both once empires (the Eastern Bloc and the Western Bloc), their ongoing survival, if not revival, are both still very hidden issues.

Yet if you of other nations have absolutely no compassion for these huge upheavals resulting from radically reversed political, legal, moral, cultural, and social values, then we angels say yet again (most categorically) that wherever you came from and however you got where you are (which is wherever you find yourselves now), then perhaps you should be showing much more compassion than you do to those nations who are not much different from who you yourselves are. You know, there are pan-fried Slavs, just as there are pan-fried Scots, pan-fried Maori, and pan-fried Westerners. It takes a while to get your head round that universal concept by which, although all and each of us is uniquely different, nothing at all can separate us from the love of God.

So then, don't bother too much with those differences of face, place, or race. The Russian so-called Slavophiles (except far-eastern Slavophiles) and the Russian so-called Westernisers (except far-western Westernisers) are not much different from the way in which those American Democrats (in any present shape or form) are themselves not much different from those American Republicans (in any present shape or form). [Exegesis 5: And even if you don't think so, it might help you to consider this proposition more carefully by swallowing hard enough even if no more than just to say either okay or nitchevo!]

Both Russia of the historically downtrodden (but only recently and yet barely relieved) serf and peasant and America of the purportedly free (but only recently relieved) native tribes, coloured slaves, and Hispanic–Latinos subscribe to one and the same plainsman culture. It is for both these nations a culture of wide-open spaces (whether open range or taiga) and faraway horizons that can stretch from the highest point or zenith of the heavens as often down to the nadir (or ground zero) at grass-roots level. It is this one and the same plainsman ethos which encourages each—for one to look and go always eastwards and for the other to look and go west, ever westwards.

So then, for this world being as round as it is flat, both these much the same adventurous plainsmen are bound to meet (quite possibly sometime soon) perhaps quite conjecturally in the Kremlin for Russia rather than in the White House for America (since nothing's held back Trump having got thus far to Hanoi). Between East and West, Russia is more used and accustomed to being piggy in the middle of any big picture than is America. Despite secular appearances, Holy Mother Russia paradoxically goes on holding the reserve power (rather than before the default power held by the USSR) by which to call the shots. Meanwhile, each of these great nations are endeavouring to deal with one and the same problem—of each having its own version of one still monstrously frozen mammoth from the Ice Age slowly thawing out at room temperature in their corridors of power.

As with the demise of the former British Empire, no less than with the demise of the Russian Empire, it's hard for the former citizens and subjects of those empires (comprising all the many once red-coloured continents, subcontinents, and little islands on their own world maps) to make sense of their present far less extended yet once so extensive place in world affairs. And yet once again, so much like the more recent face-saving exit of the former Soviet Empire to negotiate the CIS, the creation of a commonwealth (quite a fall-away from any imperial way of looking at things) in many ways is the most logical as well as the most ethical choice. Thus, do utopian statesmen dream not of heaven but of humanly founding some great and grand cosmic commonwealth by which to subvert all earlier plans of a theocracy for planet Earth?

That same soft option of a commonwealth is now the one which appeals to both the fast-fading USSR (the 'last evil empire', as one former United States president has dared to call it) on which account USA has also dared to think that it has won the Cold War. But for the continued institutional prosperity of the EU as well as of the People's Republic of China, this might be thought of as the end of the era of empires.

Nonsense, already in terms of the world's fast-burgeoning bureaucracies, both the European Union and Chinese Communist Republic are but two of a kind. For each of those emerging empires, whether capitalism, communism, or democracy, that purely theoretical choice is of small moment. No, not precisely of the same identical kind but still very much two of a kind. Nevertheless, there are much harder and alternative options already waiting to take centre stage from where even these two mammoth bureaucracies still await their cue from the wings.

Nevertheless, for us to get to any place still called Syria or to any place still called Iran or to any place still called Iraq or to any place still called Afghanistan, there's still a lot of mind-blowing travel preparations for us yet to do. In the next few chapters, we'll prepare a checklist of everything you'll need for those intrepid journeys. That won't be an easy task, either to write, read, or implement into action, so bear with us for what each of us will first need to understand. The essence of all accomplished travel lies in the initial preparation, and since this requires of every traveller to be prepared for both the expected and the unexpected, then, apart from innocents abroad, very few people would dare to travel—and most certainly not to any of the war zones into which we're heading.

But don't expect (as would any Westerner) an all too simple shopping list. For this one you'll have to learn sweet-flow abstraction, swift-leap levitation, hard-case reasoning, and ruthless reconnoitring. Why, for travelling with us angels, you won't even need a passport— at least not any of this world's plush passports.These often cause more all-round trouble, both at borders and within borders, than they're worth. Why, we know a brave Britisher who was imprisoned for the night, left behind by his plane in the morning, all for having had his passport confiscated in the so-called City of the Angels— besides telling the customs officer who asked him what he proposed to do in the USA that 'he just wanted to get out of the friggin' airport and back to his British homeland as soon as he could'.

Travel, whether just down to your corner store (to discover that it's no longer there) or for a flight into Burma (to discover that a military coup has changed that nation's name back to Myanmar), has never been so precarious as ever before. Nevertheless (or so grumble those who would sacrifice their lives on any flight to hell for having flown on their own slightest whim), the all-time assassins and extraterritorial terrorists still get through. For security reasons, we won't even supply you with an itinerary. You'll just have to trust in the angels (as now) and go on relying on us for who we are and what we aren't. Still, that's no big deal for those who blithely sign the terms and conditions (read or unread) by which to download some update on their computer to keep it going.

Nevertheless, far ahead of the expected time of departure (despite all unexpected happenings, because this world is in a state of constant ferment), we'll prepare a comprehensive checklist of these requirements needed by you for your travels. [Excursus3: the same checklist of travel requirements will operate both as a checkout list and a check-in list (there and back) by which to qualify you for undertaking angelic travel.]

Take these checklists seriously, as you'll have to, because (as said before) they won't make for easy reading. Unless you qualify yourselves (which will take some serious study by way of thoughtful reflection, mindful meditation, and spiritual transformation), you will not be considered to have the required credentials (there's a minimum wingspan required for angelic flight and 100 per cent relaxed mindset required for levitation). As said before, these are not shopping lists. You cannot cadge a ride with us angels any more than you can buy your way into heaven with korus cards, bank statements, or academic credentials. So then, if you have the mind to explore how slight the difference is between you humans and us angels, don't let these check-in and checkout lists become an all over and out list.

Checking yourselves out from where we're leaving and into where we're going—a serious business in coming to terms with this world's conflictive cultures and one which many casual tourists never dream of, far less think of—will require of you a great deal of seriously scientific and open-minded study. The same heavenly rule applies to that requirement as it applies to every earthly travel experience or highly aspirational expedition—you won't get any more out of it than what you yourself put in. One can point to one's heart, one's mind, and one's soul; but as often as not, perseverance is the key concept (there and back) for this sort of demanding travel.

For one last look back at what you're leaving, you can do so now; but once we're (more than partially) on the bus, in the train, or on the plane or (for being angels) all together flying through the air (we'll show you how), then no matter how hard it gets (for buses breaking down in the desert sand of Rub' al Khali, for trains getting blown off the rails whilst crossing the Caucasus, for landing by Aeroflot in the middle of a howling snowstorm in Minsk, or for levitating without an aircraft far above the frozen River Lena in the hinterland of the

not-so-long-gone Soviet Russia), just don't look back any longer ...
just don't look back ... just don't look back! Since we're not going
any further forward just here but more hopefully shortly to go down,
then don't look back ... don't look back.

Woops... for hitting one of many air-pockets — since we're not
going to get any further forward across the tundra just here, but more
hopefully shortly to go down, then don't look back — don't look
back... but only straight ahead... straight ahead... ... and... without a
prayer both in your pocket and on your lips... since the undercarriage
is still tucked up... ... **DON'T LOOK DOWN... ... ... NO, NO, NO
— JUST DON'T LOOK DOWN!**

* * *

All Things Still under the Sun
Part IV

A Traveller's Checklist to There and Back
Ten beggars will quite willingly share the same single
blanket, but no two world leaders would ever deign to
share the same room, share the same travelling coach,
or ever think to share the same country.
Zahir-ud-Din Muhammad Babur, *The Memoirs
of Babur* (paraphrased angelic translation)

Stay humble. If only politicians would profess to be backpackers
when they travel, they'd get so much further in the cosmic peace
race (when globally mistaken to better themselves for that being only
their own rat race). We promised (contingent on those unexpected
events which will surely happen in these latter days to all space-time
travellers) to let you readers have a check-in and checkout list (not by
any means a shopping list) of needful requirements before our setting
off, which now suddenly looks as if all set for Syria and not as first
thought for Afghanistan.

That's a pity, since most of us in C company are more familiar
with the whirly gig descent we have to make when avoiding ground-
to-air missiles to land in Kabul. Well, as for any military operation,
be prepared both for the expected as well as for the unexpected. That
in itself is a tall order, since to prepare yourselves for the expected
tends to diminish your preparedness for the unexpected. It's as if
you're then trying to look round the same corner at the same time
from both sides.

For all this being more than just a military operation, however, it will
not be in any way straightforward. No form of soul-saving evangelism
should ever be mistaken for being in any way straightforward, but
in the most straightened of military circumstances in which we shall
soon be operating, soul-catching is in an evangelical league all on
its own.

Pardon me for saying so, but your face hereabouts looks peculiarly bloated. It's as if you've been trying to look round the same corner at the same time from both sides. Try to keep both sides of your face hinged on either side of your nose. After all, although you need two nostrils, you need only one nose. Nothing less than that would be my advice, until one of our very skilled surgeons (if still alive) can stitch you up. There's always a cost factor to soul-catching, but never fear, don't worry, our landing carriage is down (at least on this side) so at the very least we'll try to skate in. Let's just try to trim... whatever it is we trim... so it might help to jump... ... not ship (since we're on a plane) ... but a little more over to this side... ... there goes a wheel ... it's overtaking us at a rate of knots ... but don't worry ... it's come off from under the tailplane ... and we're up-front ... ... as they say, no worries!

For all this being more than just a military operation, however, it will not be in anyway straightforward ... since for every military operation, one must always consider (strategically or otherwise) the prospect (at least in retrospect) of retreat. No form of soul-saving evangelism should ever be mistaken for being in any way straightforward, but in the most straightened of military circumstances in which we shall soon be operating, soul-catching is in an evangelical league all of its own. We're a commando operation, as you may have picked, for none of us being any taller than 5feet too.

'Five feet two, sir?'

'No, mate, for a commando unit we're all one and the same five feet, too.'

The main trouble with most humans on these operations is that you think that implementing heavenly messages through miracles comes to angels all quite naturally. This experience of angelic evangelism in the field is going to completely change your human mindset (which, according to scripture, ought to be not much lower than the mindset of us angels, but then I can vouch for ours needing to be much higher).

You know, when you've carried out this operation, it ought to be as if you've never done it, since if you hold on to any successful ministry (as we pray it will be successful), the continued consequences of that ministry may well be interrupted or else fall flat on their face or achieve the opposite of their desired end. All of a sudden, things have turned critical in Syria, but that's not exactly true (as with any critical situation when commandeered by those off the field) since it takes a very long time, with often lots of yet entirely overlooked and yet entirely unexpected events, for any situation to turn from green to orange to red before being publicly recognised too late to have been critical on the field. They're all retired colonels back there, so it's always best to leave it to us lads in the field.

From both the military point of view as well as from the evangelical point of view, the great war to end all wars might have done its expected job (and never given rise to the Second World War) had the retired colonels from the so-called great war to end all wars not continued to hold rank in civvy street and to flaunt their medals in what came to be known as the period 'between the wars'. By so holding to their rank and continuing to flaunt their medals, they both denied what had begun as the great war to end all wars and so readied themselves and also everyone else (but the good guys) for the next one.

All of a sudden, despite cartoonists having a field day at the expense of those who continued to claim military rank, these retired colonels had become the upper class in Britain. Mere majors couldn't be blamed for following suit by their continuing to hold rank in name, if not by serial number, in Britain's post-war local government, and some even also continued to do so within the upper echelons of the civil service. The Second World War, as the continuation of the by now renamed First World War, was already in the making.

So also, by the time that the Second World War would be considered over, as soon throughout the Western world as that misapprehension had been celebrated, then eighteen-year-olds from schools would be drafted into military service against the Eastern world in places like Palestine, Korea, and Vietnam. Members of the judiciary in their royal red robes (signifying the spilt blood of Jesus Christ) would clank down the corridors of power to open parliaments in their military regalia. In like manner, the USA should have learnt to be more gracious in thinking itself to have won the Cold War against the Soviets—by which means, although a close finish, it has nearly lost the space race. We'll be off in the morning now. The next race for soul-catching (to which you're enjoined as observers and from which you'll hopefully be debriefed as survivors) is by now re-set for Syria! If we can believe what we're told, carpet-weaving is back in the streets of Kabul, the Taliban is ousted, Afghanistan has stabilised, and so we must move on... ... no time here for tiffin ... let's get a move on ...

So then, we're all now set for Damascus in Syria and not Kabul in Afghanistan. Whether post hoc (or propter hoc) whatever may be the apparently interruptive (although only associative and not causative) measure, we'll be off before first light. However unexpected to our plans, this change (still across several time zones as well as war zones) should not be seen to divert, disrupt, or interrupt our first projected programme. From start to finish, (as said before, from origins to outcomes) soul-catching (like any other evangelical engagement) is a military operation—so take off your pith helmet, throw away your brass hat, and wind your third-latest afghan-style turban round your head—no, round your head backside on..

In other words, despite every little change to our scheduled itinerary, keep your cool (although your also your right and proper turban on). Learn to be a Sikh-Arab-Afghan as if every little change in circumstances now being made has been programmed into our less than carefully planned operation from the start. There's no better survival advice than that which can be given for fast-changing military operations. Remember always, in your conceiving the inconceivable, that mortality, although a metaphysical abstraction, is not entirely the unexpected consequence of finding out that one is mortal.

In such cases, both for maintaining commercial confidence as for military confidence, focus on incorporating what's now behind you always *as if* needfully to alter what's before you. Sorry, but it's check-in time right now, and with no time to peruse any promised check-off list, that further change confirms this operation of soul-catching for being one most certainly required in the most critical of military situations! First of all, folks, and however belatedly, find a chute!

Although without your projected check-off list for any accompanying human endeavour (which often entails your mortal need, as in any war zone, to fly by the seat of your pants), look on the operation as having been already successfully accomplished.

We've already made it from there to here in Syria to complete our soul-saving operation, and from thence (although still amid a polyglot of different warring nations), it's already best to consider that we've also made it safely back home again. It's most often the only as-if way of looking at things, when all else you know of is up in the air, that pre-empts your being shot down.

Sleep on that advice before you discount it (without a single beer to swill it down). Refine your feelings on the plane, for that being the far less shonky way of feeling better than by stoking up on beer before your takeoff. Us military men are not always the best of angels when advised to engage in spiritual meditation! So then, open your heart and mind to the Lord to let him infill the resulting void in your wearied soul with strength. Fight your fear of failure, and fight hard, since most military losses are predilected by case-hardened hearts and slowly responding minds. Believe you me for my being no more than a corporal in the angelic host, but there's no army sergeant major that's more ruthless than any archangel in serving heaven!

Feel better now? Feelings count for much more than are usually recognised in the military. You can push them deep down (when aided by some bully boy sergeant major in dress array). You can have them hammered in flat (when in active service under heavy fire). You can even nail them down by yourself or else screw them in securely (whenever there's a really wicked war going on around you). Come peacetime, however, and the coffined casket you've built around yourself (forget the promised flag, the gun salute, and all the rest of the drapery) is going to spring open and fall apart. [Exegesis 1: There's a warring tension still within every fighting man (and far more frightening to any man when expressed by any fighting woman). It's that unrelieved tension, together with all like tensions (whether parentally inflicted, adolescently experienced, uxoriously expressed, or neighbourly or socially imposed), when buried deep within that person, which will break out from all still embattled people.]

When deeply confined and contained, it doesn't take much for this explosive tension in any individual to blast its way through the thin veneer of any engineered peace or else even more explosively to do battle in the next war. Peacekeeping is mostly worthless (except as a purely temporary measure) since it only tempers the stress-induced case-hardening of military action (by which to suppress still further the explosive force of raw emotions and to oppress every attempt at more rational thought). We're talking total war here or irrational terrorism or, when confined (but not long) to the individual, then whether by shoot-outs in schools, churches, and mosques or by drug-overdosed suicides or other acts of sacrificial immolation.

So then, when least expected, the funereal lid of any less than fully functional refuge will flip up, the casement sides explode outwards, and the floor propel you into an antisocial orbit over which you have no power to control. You can pick up the floor, reaffix the sides, replace the lid, and walk around for a while, going wherever you want to go, but all the energy and physical ability you have at your civic command will be employed in holding this whole wartime contraption of a walking foxhole together.

Still don't believe me as to the reality of this self-constructed coffin? Then talk to those imprisoned, whether for the purpose of reforming their criminal behaviour or else for the purpose of securing their psychiatric health, and they will know exactly what you're talking about. Waffling on, as if you know all there is to know about PTSD (or post-traumatic stress disorder) has nothing on it. [Exegesis 2: From one war to the next war, this is the conflictive spirit within you which maintains and builds up its warring tension throughout every false and fractious time of subversive peace. Beware of any nation, tribe, or person nursing his or her wrath to keep it warm. It takes but a gentle word to turn away wrath and yet also no more than some trivially offensive word to discharge a hugely wrathful explosion! Tread carefully. These days, everywhere you walk is heavily mined with high explosive! An anti-personnel mine—no, don't you believe any such euphemism—every such mine is intimately personal!]

Whether you're discharged (honourably or not) or peaceably put on reserve or retired (falsely or truly), then your repressed feelings will come roaring up like a volcano to take the roof off your mouth and your head off your shoulders. But then if, as you say, you're not on active service? Why, in total war, everybody is on active service, whether in the Boxer Uprising, the Clydeside Blitz, the Frankfurt bombing, the Zhawar Kili camp—the list is endless. In terrorism or total war (call it what you will), there's nothing new—not under yesterday's sun, not under today's sun, nor yet under tomorrow's sun—until that new day dawns as already checklisted to bring about both some new heaven and some new earth.

'Hold on, hold on, and keep your cool,' concur both our chaplain and our regimental sergeant major. Nothing's been lost without our own promised checklist, and perhaps something's even been gained, for in doing so (at least this once) without the accustomed check-in list (CIL) for transcontinental night-flying (TNF), we'll be in God's safe hands (GFH). Don't discount the forcefulness of acronyms, and YHHW himself was the first one! Oh yes, we'll be leaving before dawn, which will follow us for a little while right round the sky, but we'll have a lot of night-flying (TNF) also to do.

Try to get some shut-eye. Both deep sleep and spirit-filled prayer are vital to the military man. Don't forget to put your spiritual armour on. Despite some exceptionally close calls through continuingly changing war zones (you've yet to experience the chequered descent to Kabul in wartime, and yet this time, it's open slather in Damascus), the so-called fact (in reality, the fulfilment of faith) by which we survive (but many others do not) confirms the further extent of our continued travels through the Islamic Heartland.

We travel light, much as did also the author Christopher Kremmer when writing *The Carpet Wars*. Although all real authors (whether factualists or fictionalists) are adventurous explorers, the war-torn Christopher Kremmer was both particularly scholarly as well as highly adventurous in choosing to write his own true-life *Odyssey* of travelling through this fastest-spreading Islamic Heartland. Bone up as much as you can (to avoid culture shock) on the centuries-old history of the Islamic Heartland. You can't beat it, because it's written by an Aussie scholar! You can't beat it — because it's written by an Aussie scholar of whom, as we said of Monty in WWII, he knows his stuff!

Stripped of its history, hidden here is the former Golden Crescent, now the battleground (both internally and externally) of the Islamic nations, together with certain other regions. No heavenly check-in list (HCIL) can be signed off for human travel without several years of historical, prophetic, and cultural study being undertaken of this

Islamic Heartland. Your presence on this operation can thus be only post facto authorised, and so completion of the by now overdue HCIL will be required for any further conjoint angelic and humanistic travel (CAHT). Like all mortals who are military men, us flying angels (who transit at twice or more the speed of sound) need to communicate (if not telepathically) then in fast-flowing acronyms, but apart from critical scrambling of operational signals (CRISOP), as far as possible, we'll keep you novice observers (NOBS) informed without any resort to linguistic truncation (and its need for NOBS translation).

To these Islamic nations, we have now added a further complement of Western nations (including the since split Russian Federation, with Arkhangelsk as its centre point in this report's farthest north to New Zealand, with Dunedin as its centre point since 1848 in this report's deepest south. Likewise, from the European Union (like a fast-bolting horse across the European Plain from Brussels) especially when spooked both by Turkey and the fast-encroaching Islamic East, then across to the southern-challenged United States in the farthest west, (when spooked by the fast-encroaching Central American and South American South) then all points of this Earth's compass are covered. As said before, the whole wide world (very much in lower case) is in the gravest turmoil, never mind those hot-spots such as shell-shocked Syria and Hong-Kong.

All such coordinates (both cultural and geographical) are to be construed no less relative to the subject matter of the ensuing report than both this world's constantly changing context and the east-west angle to the solar system that the angelic authors (call them editors, if you will) hold as allowed by the presently prevailing axis of this globe known as planet Earth. [Exegesis 3: Note well that conditions apply to every unexpected contingency exercised by earthly means and that our every disclaimer is made to any demonic exercise of counterfeit power, unless our heavenly instructions, particularly over shell-shocked Syria, are followed to the divine letter.]

Here we are then, although by now for being *on route* to Syria (unrecognised by most US military men (unless in intelligence) for being an EU expression) is the beginning of the promised heavenly check-in list (HCIL). It shall serve as a military man's travel guide to take us through that previously Golden Crescent (now in its most sorry state of cultural decline) and yet to which has been for so long given the credit of giving birth to the entirety (subject to claimed centre points both east and west of Eden) of this by now almost defunct human civilisation.

Meanwhile (in itself, a constantly reductive expression), bone up fast on humanity's correlatively declining concept of civilisation. The remaining time you metaphysically mistake for being your very own time is finally at a cosmic premium for so many of you fast-lane, rough-riding earthlings. You hang up your architectural hard hats on conflictive centre points (whether in Athens, London, New York, Beijing, Brussels, or Washington), but each and all of such solar centre points are no more than plagiarised copies of this earth's first Babylonian centre point.

Whilst looking only for your own place in the sun, you convince yourselves that, for the sake of the sun being the supreme source of everything, there can be nothing new under the sun than the place you look for yourself in the sun. But what then of your eternal soul if you still stand in awe under any stations of the cross by which to understand such a question? Just what is your own metaphysical station or attitudinal standpoint?

So then, what worth or gain can come to any person even if he or she were able to gather up together all the wealth of resources which still remain under this old world's fast-setting sun? Surely nothing, if, in consequence of that gathering up of all the remaining resources (whether congregated towards any centre point in the name of any nation or on behalf of any person), all those authorising, implementing, or carrying out the gathering were to lose their eternal souls.

None of this world's chosen centre points would then bear close scrutiny. The statistical measure of the righteous to the unrighteous when sufficient to withhold the wrath of God was first enquired into by old father Abraham. On this score, we'll leave out the ALGEQ— the algorithmic equations! Nonetheless, the tightrope (or as often slack wire) stretched between today's centre-point motivation (not always stable) and the attitudinal standpoint (likewise unstable) is in no less a state of physical turmoil than are the pillars of assumed wisdom by which this world's leaders rule, direct, and control the rest of the world.

The final downfall of this world's mightiest Babylon, according to some intelligence officers in the Supreme Command, has been brought about by the same President Saddam Hussein, who would have raised it up to the heights of heaven in his own presidential name. More than once before, this same thing has been said of raising up Babylon only to see, likewise all over again, that great and mighty city come crashing down, likewise as more than once before. This ongoing rise and fall of (perhaps any and every) Babylon (whether ancient or modern) is given as a sign of the times. Like once before, raised and reduced again under Nim (already identified) or again raised and reduced under Nebu (likewise), it has again been raised up to the heights of heaven before being reduced to ground level again under Saddam Hussein. Its rise and fall, as a sign of the times, seems always to be in the offing.

Don't listen to those pocket philosophers who try to tell you that this blighted Babylon, which they know only as that mighty Babylon (which succours their commercial souls with fame and fortune), is only a figment of the whole wide world's imagination. They are not the ones who have fought in the Gulf War, the Iraqi War, the Iranian War, or in any other war. These pocket philosophers are, in thinking themselves to be above all, no more than the makeshift prophets of a false peace.

As a patriot of the USA (elsewhere rendered by draft dodgers as the disunited usa in lower case), see John Irving's summary of that country's military policy set out by his hero in *A Prayer for Owen Meany*. Now then, here's a literary question (given by courtesy of Owen Meany): what is the relationship between the USA and a stuffed armadillo?

Think of this question most carefully (and not yet of its answer) as we fly towards shell-shocked Syria. As we now head off into military operations in what we once thought was this very faroff Syria, it helps to keep some metaphysics in your head. Owen Meany, like the very best of teachers, only asked the question and never gave the answer. Here's a hint—don't lose your cool over the question, since that will only pre-empt your answer. So then, think of the question whilst we're in full flight over Syria. What's the difference (if any) between the USA (for others, the usa) and a stuffed armadillo? Take your time. We're not going down yet, far less bailing out.

The last vestiges of whatever mankind has claimed to its own credit from civilisation (despite the lesson to be learnt from the first and perhaps now last fall of Babylon) are all out on full display to be remaindered off in this world's last close-down sale. Still want to make a last-minute bargain by buying up the marked-down goods from this world's longest surviving empire of Babylonia? Then roll up … roll up … roll up … and place your bets—especially now that the mighty dollar has been so devalued as to make everything a gamble!

Meanwhile, for being a remarkably prophetic conjunction of this world's last two contingent vocables, there now comes here to you, from no less than the Supreme Command, for both your careful consideration, your intimate study, as well as for your most serious discussion amongst mates, cobbers, buddies, and friends the first two items of the checkout list. These are designed only to protect you throughout the fiercest of battles—whether that be in the mental field of the mind or in the physical field of the body or in the emotive field of the heart or in the spiritual field of the soul—and even although that fiercest of battles on all fronts and in all fields should be your ultimate and last.

Likewise (by virtue of two further vocables (namely, rise up … rise up … rise up…) when used to conflate two like worlds of conflictive wisdom for the same duration of your further transitory passage across this earth's ephemeral spatial-time), then don't hesitate to find the metaphysical means by which to refute, whatever of the first vocable or of the second vocable may seek to indenture what remains of your life on earth far beyond this presently fast-moving prophetic moment. In short, don't think to deny your further rites of passage even although these may be unknown to you at present.

Think carefully then on these prophetic whispers whilst you can, since once fulfilled in the future-present then the spatial-present is but an instant of no duration in itself. You might well ask God for more clarity (as we would all want) on this matter of the proclamatory vocables, but for this proclamation being itself a viable prophetic utterance (i.e. a well-formed-formula in terms of space and time—WFF) then short of its full fulfilment this will be as clear as it goes. Nevertheless, the future-present is an eternity beyond all time.

As said before, we are *on route* (in Anglo-American) rather than *en route* (European) to furthest Syria. After all, the final revival of all time will come through the South Pacific to all the Americas. If this seems nonsense, you have been stuck with the solar centre-point system for so long by yourself that you could not think to extricate yourself. The expected thus becomes more and more the unexpected. That's all there is to the fatalistic round, except for the reverse order, by which the poles switch to make you believe entirely in the unexpected order of things (which is chaos) and no longer in the expected order of things (which is cosmos). All the same (although on earth, since no two things are ever the same), the choice of engaging in this battle, as always until the end of time, is entirely up to you.

Everyone intimately conversant with institutional life knows something of the inner corruption which can beset centre-point administration so deeply within as to stand every outward profession of faith, mission statement, and written constitution of that institution on its head. Sometimes, the proffered key seems to lie outwardly through decentralisation, at other times inwardly (and so keeping to the institutional form only without). Thus MMP (or mixed member proportional representation) enables any parliament by name to keep that (no more than token name of parliament without) yet to operate even more disproportionately than ever before within.

Outwardly keeping to the earlier institutional form can be a worse feint to radical decentralisation (or restructuring) from within. This is achieved through inner delegation, and sometimes progressive redelegation (as if to decentralise solely within the institution rather than, as the institution is busily proclaiming to be the case, the decentralisation is being done as will be seen from without). Upper management (for being usually held captive by an exclusively modernist lower management) is mostly carried out by smoke and mirrors (more precisely by sending up smoke signals and removing all mirrors per se or by prohibiting their use). Needless to say, all other means of reflection (whether intellectual or else otherwise pro bono) are verboten.

Whether within or without any institution, we are all conversant with the restructuring process (or perestroika, as borrowed from the Soviets) which can do either nothing or enough to avoid, to assuage, or to remedy the innermost, most institutional, and corruptive rot. The trouble remains, no matter how persuasive the window dressing of perestroika may be, that there's been no change in the inner attitudinal standpoint by which to change the outer institutional viewpoint. A checklist in such matters is of no import whatsoever unless it reaffirms or changes our attitudinal standpoint. [Exegesis 4: The question for us here is whether we should stick to this world's more widely known solar centre-point system (so recently gone metric) despite nought or zero (when subject to any other plus or minus number) when the solar centre-point system is of so much less significance to heaven than the concept of infinity could be to all of us on earth.]

Alas, on earth we still remain so largely habituated to see the sun, moon, and stars as the arbiters of heaven. No, if we are to engage consistently in soul-catching, we have to take a different attitudinal standpoint (which is needed to match up and open sesame the safe haven of any functionally pivotal soul-point. By no other means can we remain true to ourselves and true to the call we hear to undertake soul-catching, as well as remain true to the process by which we each safeguard our own soul. From this point of view, we remind ourselves (through this check-in and checkout list for further travel) of all these intricately integrated issues in terms of our maintaining the correct attitudinal standpoint for the making of any soul-catch. Meanwhile, believe us when we say these fields are the ones ready for soul-harvest, for these are no longer pastoral green fields. Instead, they are by now bloody killing fields.

Attitudinal Standpoint 1—Be Prepared: There's a war on. So then, know exactly what to listen for, know exactly what to look for, know exactly both what and with whom to feel for, and thus know exactly what next to expect! But if not so prepared to hear, see, and feel for what happens when a pin (that's an allegorical expression to cover the widest multitude of meanings) is heard or seen or felt to drop from heaven (so it is asked, for the choice is completely yours), then how will you know exactly what to do—of course, whether on earth or in hell (since in heaven only the expected happens)—when on earth, the unexpected (and not the expected) happens (just as only the unexpected happens, as it does in hell)? Confused? But this is undergirded by the class calculus earlier explored, discovered, and proclaimed by our old friend Augustus De Morgan!

'Oh hell!' say most mortals (where only the unexpected happens) and leave it at that. 'Good heavens!' other more polite mortals may say. But likewise, they too leave it at that (for both sidestepping the same centre point as if it were dog's poo on an otherwise magic carpet). [Exegesis 5: Note the expressions *meanwhile*, *likewise*, and *otherwise* very carefully. These words, by now taken so much for granted, mean very much more than they are any longer thought to say or thought to mean.]

Otherwise, likewise, and meanwhile, it will take some far more seriously surgical situation by way of fulfilling the same dire need on earth to cover the same uncalled-for situation for anyone here on earth, won't it? But then what if there's no one here to satisfy the call (which has already gone out) to enquire any further into what exactly is meant by heaven and what exactly is meant by hell and what exactly is meant by earth to fulfil the strategic purpose of soul-catching? Until then, there's no point (is there)? The choice is yours in thinking about or talking about or envisioning how exactly any new heaven or any new earth is likely to apply to you, to us, or to them for this same purpose of soul-catching. Quite frankly (which is always how we speak in heaven), neither set of concerned or unconcerned mortals (again to use their own words) seems 'to care a damn'!

It's exactly the same when most mortals dare to speak openly of the immortals (although hardly ever speaking in church so frankly of their feelings, either for or against them). 'Oh, God!' say most mortals of the immortals, but only when caught out once again in the most serious of surgical situations. And then when their own part in the crisis has passed, most humans drop back to the rear of the fray by doing nought, thinking nought, and feeling nought—all exactly as they had not felt, not thought, and not done before.

All this apathetic lack of human action would be really quite disconcerting to us angels were we not already so accustomed to our hearing of such things by way of complaint from you humans. Nevertheless (although for us angels, verging on passive aggression to say so), we angels are never more disconcerted than we are by you humans for being yourselves so disconcerting. Whilst being no more than a little lower in military rank and saving function than are we angels, you mortals won't learn to levitate, far less learn to fly or trouble yourselves to walk on water. Well now, the sea-levels are rising—but that won't stop you drowning behind dykes and walls!

And so as you humans might care to imagine, that's exactly why we angels, although only marginally above you humans in the heavenly scheme of things, rest more easy to know for ourselves (much better than you humans do actually know yourselves) what it means to us angels for having been definitively designed to be angels. So also then, we angels look so much further forward (for knowing exactly where we stand) to our hearing from you humans where exactly you know yourselves to stand for being made to be human. [Excursus 1: Quite frankly, for both you humans and us angels being designed on one and the same double-helix model, we're no more than cousins apart in the heavenly family formula (HFF) creation model for both angels and humans. So on the score of having fallen through sin, there's not all that much of a difference between angelic celestial bodies and human earthly bodies, and it would help you humans to know where you stand to see that closeness more clearly. You know, the one thing which you unredeemed humans and those fallen angels have most in common is the assurance with which you both postulate yourselves free from all sin. So then, vulnerability is obviously a shared characteristic of both angels and humans.]

By 'sticking to the facts' (as you humans rarely do), we're only writing here descriptively and not prescriptively against such frankness of human expression. We choose to speak our minds, since most of these seriously surgical situations are permitted to pass under the heavenly radar (for which we immortals cop the blame and are made to take the flak from you humans for heaven being so 'unfair' as to hit you humans so far below the belt). Well, far worse things (as we remind you humans on earth) have happened to many of us angels who were shown to be quite unfit for any angelic function before the celestial fall when back in heaven.

At such peccadilloes (which word we're not going to translate for those who are continuing members of the European Union), we in heaven take no great offence. Well then, besides keeping your eyes and ears open, do you know what to look for, what to listen for, and what and whom to feel for when a pin drops from heaven? [Excursus 2: What, do you think that's occult? Well, wait long enough (for which purpose employ abstraction) until you find out (for which purpose look to inner vision) what it's like (for which purpose employ discernment) as if you're ever going to get to heaven! Got it? We're halfway to Damascus, but from the ubiquity of Afghanistan, back there in Kabul, can you, the reader, pick up on the telepathic vision?]

Look, there's the street preacher over there on Chicken Licken street, by the now-empty carpet shop in old Kabul. No, shut down your hindbrain for our being in an airbus on the way to Syria. We all know that ... But employ more your forebrain. That's right ... your frontal lobes ... more exactly now ... but a little to the left ... since there're no roadmaps any longer to Kabul (far less than to any frontal lobes remaining in my brain) and hardly any signposts now left standing there in my bombed-out lawyer's hindbrain. Never mind (although little Master Nevermind was made to mind) since over there—see, there's a street teacher over there, however, more exactly a little to the right ... beside the street prophet exactly midway and nearest to us here. Yes, yes, that's him, the elderly roast chestnut vendor who is wheeling his broken-down barrow towards us. You could surely ask one or more of them.

No, no, not at all. This is not an angelic setup, although all these three—preacher, teacher, and prophet—in their belonging to the heavenly host, are most certainly my Chicken Licken colleagues when altogether sent from heaven to spread the gospel most powerfully in this war-torn street. We just feel together that this one-man band of conflated battlers, as if all compounded out of no more than myself alone, are in need of contributing your own most considerable character augmentation by way of joining our battling band. Remember that we angels, as a born band of brothers and sisters constituting the angelic host, are never alone any more than you humans are ever alone for you being essentially social animals. But watch out ... watch out for him, the chestnut-vendor with his broken-down barrow (Caveat Vendor is his name, not Caveat Emptor) since this is one of the busiest of streets. Whoops! We're now in Dublin's fair city, where the girls are so pretty. What, do you think of angels as being all young men ... no, no ... that may suit all you young girls ... but that was a far earlier age ... there's many a solo mum today that's now an angel ... and with all earth in a ferment you can't very well expect all of heaven to stand stock-still.

Oh, oh, but there ... there ... there ... we angels forgot you humans have many gifts, but not (apart from the sanctified saints) any gift of ubiquity. Ubiquity? Well, that gift of ubiquity enables us angels to be able to turn up in whatever place we choose (and, of course, to be in more places than just one). We can switch from Kabul to Dublin (at the drop of a pin, whereas you humans must await the drop of a hat, and even then, for it being your own hat in the wind, you have to chase it down the street, and so for the sake of recovering your respectability (a vice no less) then either sacrifice or loose out on the gift of angelic ubiquity. Still, there're many humans far worse off, those who wouldn't admit to losing their hat, far less losing their head. So what would it take to bother such headless humans to confront the risk of losing their souls?

You humans must surely have felt the need of our gift of ubiquity to be in more places than just one, so you should ask for that gift of the Lord. There are some exceptional humans, you know, who have mastered the perils of human life, so as to receive and enjoy the gift of ubiquity. How do you think the old-time prophets managed— the ones like Moses and Abraham and Elijah or Elia, besides Jesus Christ himself, who were here, there, and everywhere? You might only get something like it (such as today by telephone, texting, or by Skyping), but still, in one way or another, the Lord never lets any praying person down.

Meanwhile, that's right, guys, that antique roast-chestnut vender from a far-off culture (what would you say, Italian, Greek, or Armenian—no, we're not being racist) might look like he's breathing his last. But you'll have more than enough time, lads, to rescue his soul, so then I'll leave him in your most capable of hands, lads. I've got to fly now and fast to keep up with yet another urgent appointment. This next one's in Syria.

So now you'll be thinking of me more of an Irish Catholic than I am, begorra to find me an angel now sitting in a bus (for being technically an airbus, a Boeing, or any other flight carrier, never mind you). We're flying fairly high (for being just an ornery old airbus), although across war-torn Syria, so there's nothing ornery about that. You'll be wondering how you got here. But look around … just look around …

I'm the only angel here, although dressed in battle fatigues, whereas you're the only human under my command. That makes you the only human being who's enlisted amongst the many US of A military personnel. (That's right, but don't take offence, since the military doesn't always count or consider its personnel for being strictly human.)

No, I'm not nervous, but don't pretend you're not, although you're in plenty of good company (C company, actually). All are getting ready to jump on command. No, don't ask me any more about this operation, but see that bloke over there, the only one whose knees are not knocking? That's the chaplain. Keep your eye on him, because we'll meet up with him when we jump.

Yes, yes, we know you've got no chute! And so that's exactly why so few of you humans have any gift of ubiquity. You'd all cause a melee by fleeing from one place to another to cause the most catastrophic of collisions in mid-air. It's bad enough for pigeon strikes in peacetime, although in wartime, as now over Syria, there's not enough pigeons left to go around the starving populace and fill every empty pot.

Just stick close when we come to do a little bit of angelic skydiving. Damn, and for saying so, there goes yet another case of beer. That's the trouble when speaking to any whuffo-non-jumper. Without keeping tabs on your own tongue, your mind picks up on the illogicality of every free-falling thought! And then the next thing you'll think yourself to be is a 100-jump wonder, and that's even before you've made your first jump!

Forget that it's already a war zone here, and then you're the one most likely to get shot! So then fix your eyes on the spirit-filled chaplain over there. That's the one and only fellow whose knees aren't knocking. Keep your eyes fixed firmly on him so that for the sake of your own knocking knees, they'll have a chance to stop. Don't take your eyes off him, because although he's the one seen to be jumping first, there's always Christ in front, and I'll be right behind you.

Right then, let's go! Of course, he's got a chute. Why else would he jump? But it's not going to open. So then stick close to us both and stop peppering your speech with profanities. Profanities at this higher altitude bounce back and put you off target. So then we won't be much above 35,000 feet (AGL)—that's classic hop 'n' pop. But you really ought to have been licensed for this. Well, well, never mind. There's always a first time (as well as a last time), so listen for the sound of heaven's falling pin. There you go. Join in the airborne shuffle. Watch the jump master and then jump … jump … jump …

Good heavens, the chaplain's chute is opening. Well, here's something of the unexpected. We must have pinned down this soul-saving operation on quite the wrong man. That's quite an unexpected turn of events. Should we have been in Kabul after all? I sometimes run for the wrong bus and get on the wrong train, but I've never before got on the wrong plane.

Never fear … no cause for panic … Look around. There's a greater need somewhere for someone else. All the same, stick close, keep flexing and fluttering your wings. But don't let anything ruffle your feathers. We don't want to land off target. Look, it must be that other military bloke. Look over … there he is. But that's the one who rubbished me earlier on the plane with a mild enough expletive in all the circumstances for pissing him off.

What a lark, he's going down like a stone. So much for his AOD. That's his auto-opening device. And his backup chute's packed up too. Bet you his altitude alarm (no, not attitude alarm) is either screaming it's head off or gone squat. So he's far beyond coping for what looks to be his last and fatal bounce. Well, well, well, even us angels can get caught short by having to face up to and deal with the unexpected. There's always the unexpected … the entirely unexpected … wherever humans are concerned. But never fear, never fear, since so long heaven's on our side (as always), there's nothing that can stop us. When God's with us, who can be against us? No, don't try to answer that. Like from the pulpit, it's only a rhetorical question. That's exactly and most precisely why it doesn't have an exclamation mark. Oh, oh well, never mind. Keep one up your sleeve. Here's two, so keep a spare one!

Here we are still free-falling ever faster. Never fear. Look for a favourable airstream sideways. Oh god, I need to pee right now. Don't worry. There's not the slightest need to shit. There's more than five of us angels up here right now, with just one lone human, the lone ranger, I think (at which half pi joke, my guardian angel winks). Thirty-two feet progressively per second. No, not for us. No speed limit for us. We'll catch up with that bloke without the chute in no time … in no time at all … for being out of time … so there's plenty of time …

That's the way it is. Whether skydiving, soul-searching, or soul-catching, you never know quite precisely (however exactly) how things can go in any brief slice of heaven's full history. Sure, already most nearly everything's all foreseen. But remember always, as on a pie graph of time, that every remaining slice is always short of that bingo moment in heaven's full history.

So here we are again, engaging in yet another very precise moment of making heaven's history, so then don't lose heart, even if, as any human, you've already lost your footing. So then be sure to keep your head … be sure to keep your head. As already said (once before but perhaps never again), there's a great deal of difference between historical exactitude and prophetic precision. So then keep going, therefore, and paddle your extended arms a bit more to the right. Try to share the same slipstream. And keep paddling … if you can paddle horizontally through the air at this height you can most certainly learn to walk on water … …

All the same, with the surgical seriousness required of this present assignment in hand (you know how talkative of their tasks are most surgeons), there's no time (literally) or place (left in space-time) for sermonising, although some sermonising in the future (if no other heavenly means at hand to satisfy my buddy's still present human need) is most certainly bound to come.

Funny fella, that chap, the one who's still hurtling earthwards. Don't worry. We've got loads and loads of gathering momentum taken from his own time with which to pass him. This is all part of the process allowing for anyone's final reflections. Still a very funny fella all the same. Why, when I asked him, travelling as he was on the airbus to Syria beside me, just as any angel would ask his brother in arms—we angels are warriors too, you know—as to what he thought of the possible differences between going to the devil in mortal combat instead of going up to heaven in peace. Wait … hold on … we'll forego the next three times plus 32 feet per second, because this needs to be written up in the report whilst falling.

Well, it was rather disappointing to find of him that (unlike most of the Irish with the gift of the gab, many of whom I'd got to know in Dublin) he was a closed-up Scots Presbyterian from Minnesota having nothing much to say—no, not even if only a few words to put on his own tombstone. Of course, the noise back then in these airbuses (never mind this slipstream) is really something quite demonic. So then I decided, seeing that our airbus had been rerouted to Damascus, to give my buddy in arms (we warriors look after each other's back, you know) the benefit of some further and final moments of spiritual reflection.

No less than before was my angelic disappointment, however, when my buddy then told me to pull my horn in—a phrase I hadn't last heard of since the Battle of the Little Bighorn (a.k.a. Custer's Last Stand), which was one big battle in which we angels had backed the Native Americans. All the same, our funny friend (the one in front whose chute's still not opening) turned out to be one of these blokes who mistakes every remark for one giving offence, which probably contributed a lot to his chute not opening.

All I'd asked him then was whether he hadn't heard the remotest tinkle of any heavenly pin dropping into his life (which I knew of his lifestyle to be a very wayward one) and hitherto very far from the kindly hand of his Father in heaven. In the end (which, of course, would turn out to be only his beginning), he told me either to shut up or to put his name down for a heavenly hearing aid. Of course, that was before (he being next in line to take the jump) he had readied himself to chute down into the desert wilderness that was then war-torn Syria.

Next in line, for being a soul-catcher by angelic trade and knowing more than he did about what happens (long term) if one's chute fails to open, I had already received the final call not only to engage in free fall but also, by every angelic means then, to draw abreast with him. Although this means now exceeding his constantly increasing speed (at compound interest) of 32 feet per second, there's probably time for a little digression here, since we stick to imperial in heaven's kingdom.

Well, as you can see—although for it being blacker than pitch here perhaps you can't—we angels have no problem whatsoever in exceeding the rapidly slowing speed of this dying sun's light (at last call, merely 186,000 to the nearest 1,000 miles per second). With my own fully opened eyes (which would be quite hard for any mere mortal like yourself in free fall), I see my future comrade in arms already in heaven forging far ahead yet on earth still going down like a stone, his parachute unopened. [Exegesis 6: As for us angels having enough ubiquity of self-expression to be in several places at once, so too, we can foresee from the present to the future not only for ourselves but also for most other persons.]

As once a street angel myself, I could see quite easily now far below us both, but when now caught up in each other's arms (that's all seven of us by now), neither the once quiet but apparently still cockle-strewn streets of Dublin's fair city (my own hometown made worldly famous by Molly Malone) nor even the deserted wilderness of today's war-torn Syria but instead the few last remaining Latin columns of the Via Recta once made Straight Street famous. Well, those columns can still be seen today, but of course, Straight Street is precisely (and so most exactly) remembered now by reason of the acts of the apostles in old-time Damascus. It's a funny old world, isn't it? But perhaps with all this wind whistling around your ears, you'll be finding my constant blethering quite tedious. No, okay, that's good. We'll be hitting ground zero in Straight Street pretty soon … just pretty soon.

So then, begorra and take a spell in free fall before you take the word of a committed soul-catcher on this, his latest of military assignments, that it was through the last-minute confession and repentance of his buddy in arms, given in the name of no less than his now other buddy in Jesus Christ, that changed the whole worldly order, as well as the whole heavenly order of things, before we both hit ground zero together.

Make no mistake over this, however, that in making the right sort of heavenly rebound from hitting ground zero is no less exhilarating for those who were once mere mortals than it is for us angels in our dedicated delight at our soul-catching from the perdition of all those humans who, at their last moment of earthly life, dedicate their eternal souls to Jesus Christ. Why, in less time than it took to flashback to ground zero for soul-saving in ancient Damascus, we're back in the airbus being fast-forwarded homewards after exiting from war-torn Syria.

There's snow blindness, as everyone in Minnesota knows about, but of soul-blindness, that's a humanly universal unknown (more or less for everyone on earth). We had hit ground zero as planned, therefore, at the very spot (or heavenly soul-collecting point, if you care to call it that) where a certain house belonging to a certain Judas (not Iscariot) once stood on Straight Street. But that was long before today's modernity (a.k.a. urban sprawl) took over from the ancient ways of yesterday's Damascus. [Exegesis 7: By way of another explanation, it was there at that pivotal soul-point in today's still surviving Straight Street that the redeemed Saul was delivered from blindness by Ananias (when still then Ananias was there before in his then earthly human form). Just as many apostles, preachers, teachers, healers, and prophets become saints incarnate, so many angels can reverse that process of heavenly incarnation to serve (incognito) also as saints incarnate.]

Well, we did promise you both practical as well as theoretical instruction in the fine art of soul-catching. We suppose, as of most mortals, you're not much impressed by the unseen measure of eternity, especially when left hidden by the more obvious measure of mortality. Well, on that score, we've barely scratched the checklist. There're a lot more learning of experiences as yet still to come before you become fully certified for the purpose of soul-catching. Meanwhile, mind the following inkblots (ritualised as asterisks) to remind ourselves that not even we angels are always exactly (far less precisely) on target.

* * *

All Things Still under the Sun
Part V

Checked Out Whilst Still Checked In
I indicated in the most circumspect manner that a
refusal to hand over the missionary could well place
a strain on Chinese trade relationships with foreign
powers, particularly if this trade continued to be
confined to Canton.

Erwin Wickert, *The Heavenly Mandate*
(translated from German by James Kirkup)

Shit, I'm fast asleep again. As Tolstoy says, the most free time that
any human being ever has in life is only when he's in the army. That's
just how wars are fought—one moment in the midst of life. Lots of
camaraderie, pretty girls, everyone loves ... loves ... Well, every
girl loves any front-line soldier surely. As much as for any war being
fought at sea, she'll love any roving sailor. Well, that's my experience
as a military man anyway. And then so suddenly ... the very next
minute ... one's pushing up the daisies ... pushing up the daisies, just
as fast as we were last reloading the guns. Love and war, eh? More
like death during war ... more like death during war ... and for most
of us, nothing at all to show for it.

Huh, well, there's not many daisies up here above the clouds.
They are clouds, aren't they? Very pretty ... very pretty ... much like
cotton wool ... woolly blankets ... plumped-up pillows ... with lots
of flowers ... lots of flowers ... I'd feel a lot better if I hadn't wet my
pants, but at least I'm still alive, although still very, very, very much
sound asleep.

How quiet it is ... very quiet it is ... quiet enough to hear a pin
drop, although the flak outside is like a hailstorm on a hot tin roof.
Never mind, although there's no telling ... although funny ... how
very funny it is ... why, now I've been left all alone on this airbus ...
still flying ... still flying ... yet still flying ...

It's all really quite pleasant, although I wish I hadn't … hadn't wet my breeks … This is not at all a funny business … not at all a funny business … Why love and death? Why not love and life? Why not love and life? I cannot make myself known to myself. That's something very serious, almost as if I've lost my soul … That's something seriously and surgically wrong with me …

So then still nowadays (as more than once before), it often takes at least one of these heavenly street functionaries, angels in disguise, to let you rather blasé humans know what to do when the unexpected happens. The rest of the trip for this, my new buddy's recently saved soul, is now (as once before for Saul) again up to my angelic colleague Ananias.

Right-e-o! And now for the debriefing, how do you, the reader, figure in all this? Well, by (1) refusing to panic (say, by closing the book on this programmatic novel) or by (2) otherwise copping out before hitting ground zero whilst on angelic free fall or by (3) refraining from assuming any more than one's authorised wing-support position (in this case, no more than that of a maintaining a lawyer's watching brief). Of course, one can either do or not do almost anything and everything, when done or not done out of panic. There's often not much to pick or choose (especially in space-time) between being either a hero or a coward.

Between one self-centred soul striving for apparently no good reason to take and hold centre stage or for another less self-centred soul running off and out of the same challenging arena, there may be not much difference. Each, as seen by others, may make either a wise or stupid, brave or cowardly, sensible or suicidal move in either taking centre stage or running offstage. So then how do you see yourself as staying with or giving up on this book? Relax, no matter what answer you, the reader, gives, you're no different from the author!

This book is not the same *as if* it were *Gulliver's Travels*, but then, as it once was, neither is *Gulliver's Travels* still *Gulliver's Travels*. Any book, once read personally and even more so when read collectively, is no longer ever the same book. This literary experience (once collectively augmented at the rate of 32 feet per second in free-fall reading) accounts not only for *Gulliver's Travels*, as that book once was, but also in the same way for any other well-read book. So too, then *Robinson Crusoe* is no longer *Robinson Crusoe*.

Oh dear, here's a hint for those who aspire literary appreciation (far less to any military operation) without engaging in metaphysics. The tip (before you trip) is always to search for the unseen spiritual point (like the significance of the stuffed armadillo to any patriotic American) and not the far more obvious centre point highlighted by our fast-decaying solar system. What, even on the stuffed armadillo question, you still need another clue. Well, because of its full body armour, every armadillo feels and functions as if it were invincible. But this one happens to be … well, this particular armadillo happens to be … Who knows, perhaps a mighty nation which, by reason of having relied on its past history (when not properly understood to confer invincibility) is now in process of realising its vulnerability.

Let's go abstract! All authorial messages (whether angelic or otherwise) change by their reading depending on whether they hit home, find their intended mark, or hit the author's prophetically foreseen or prophetically unseen target. Once the purpose of satire is served (as by *Gulliver's Travels*) or the allegory is understood (as in *Robinson Crusoe*) or the life-giving parable is taken to heart (as in the tale of *Jonah* or in the tale of *Ruth*), the message changes shape, form, and function either to the extent of its fulfilment or to the extent of its unfulfilment. Thus, except for the metaphysical conceptualist (or the high-wire acrobat, the highly speculative scientist, or the most successful spammer) each of whom cares most for the continuingly inconceivable, both *Gulliver's Travels* and *Robinson Crusoe* are rendered down (in words, thought, and action) to serve no more than as some child's pleasant goodnight story instead of every adult's strident wake-up call.

So then what does that make of the Bible? Well, there are many theologians who think (surprisingly) that the Bible (at best) is no more than long past history, which makes you wonder why they still bother to be theologians. Why, they're not even historians, since of all history itself, no more than a jot or tittle has yet been fulfilled of the epic still to continue. Of course, whether you stop to give them a leg-up after they've fallen amongst thieves and rascals on the theological road to Jericho will depend on what you too make of the

Bible. So far as we've gone, as by sticking as a reader or author with this book (which is neither *Robinson Crusoe* nor *Gulliver's Travels*, far less the Bible), then as a reader (which phrase Owen Meany would have written in all caps), you've passed with flying colours (likewise all caps). You're responding remarkably well to the military risk (theocratic version) of post-traumatic stress disorder (engendered as it always is by every test of faith) remarkably well.

Let's just say (since it's always heaven's policy to give encouragement) that you're still in the running by a short subliminal traumatic lead (STL). This result you will still need to process reflectively for the sake of your better understanding of this survey's later questions. Remember this: just as you were dreaming long before you were born, so also to process earthly experience when and after that dreamtime fades, you must learn to reflect on every iota of that grown-up earthly experience in order to read the signs of those times to which you were born and so also to read these still same but yet fast-changing signs with which you learn to live.

Understand this also clearly, although you may not like what you mistake for being our parental rather than angelic disposition, that the setting up of any viable life survey (such as this one) is designed only for your very own and no one else's life. As such, it is a unique work (no less than that of requiring the highest heavenly novo maths). It is not for us angels (as already said) to tell you (as if you were still preschoolers) what to think or what to say or what to do. These are your own life decision processes which take you into the same higher maths by you being the one to find out the answers for yourself. There are no answers (certainly not as you'll find for your own life in the back of any lower maths book), but instead, what you'll find out is only by yourself and for yourself and (even more importantly) what you choose to find out apart from yourself.

Once again, remember this life maxim of ongoing responsibility: that every exercise of freedom leaves you open to the consequences of your exercising that freedom. And because the exercise of every freedom incurs a responsibility, that's not always the minor trauma you might expect from exercising a claimed freedom. Most often, it's a major trauma when felt in the course of learning to live life. There's a paradox here too in exercising one's freedom, because the more and more you exercise your freedom, especially when making bigger and bigger decisions, then the less freedom you have as a result of all the consequences that flow from all those of your earlier decisions. That's exactly why every human being must learn as soon as possible to think *as if* always for the best. And putting that learning into play is most critical whenever the outlook appears to be the worst.

There's hope in that, but only when disposed to actualise the hope. There's far more to the concept of relying on hope than to linger on in the forlorn hope that something else or someone else will motivate the action. As likely as not, someone else (whether ostensibly in your best interests or otherwise) will try to preclude the action. And by then, all one's primal energy for action will have been spent in building up false hopes. Hope by itself is but a predispositional precursor to rightful action. Soured hopes (through timorousness or indecisiveness, postponement or prevarication) are always the result of failure to act, but only very rarely are ever the result of failed action.

And the next hard lesson to be learnt, because we angels do truly have a parental disposition to teach you to think and reason for yourselves (if possible) rather than to preach at you always to rely on us, is that through developing your own independence of thought (in itself a risky business), it leads on to still harder and harder lessons.

So then, the next hardest lesson is to actualise the heavenly expectation that you yourselves will *strengthen yourselves* in the Lord. Just as you can overindulge in hopes, so also you can overindulge in as-if thinking. Learn to recognise that as-if thinking for the best is worlds apart from hiding oneself behind your own best of intentions. Look around. Having the best of intentions (without the rigorousness of thought that goes into as-if thinking) condemns oneself to overlook the responsibilities which emanate from actualising those as-if thoughts.

After all is said and done, every issue of your own life is just that—an issue of your own life. Sure, as in geometry, most of your own life's geometry is given. Not even one's first breath is an axiom. No, it's only a response to the life that's already been given to you. We can't lay claim to our own conception any more than we can lay claim to our own preconception. So too, those mortals with less than 20/20 prophetic vision, those who claim the right to abort their unborn child, are often those who can't see beyond their own immediate bodies, which, in turn, blinds them to all else.

We have to learn to respect what's given to us and not to mistake what's been given for being something done by ourselves to which we're entitled to take the credit ourselves. We do so either for failing to recognise a ready-made geometry to which we mistakenly claim to be self-entitled by reason of our bodies or, worse still, by mistaking ourselves to have self-created our own geometry by way of our own bodily self-entitlement. Hey, almost every mortal at some time has played at being God (think even of holy Moses hitting the cliff so brutally with his staff instead of quite gently touching the cliff to source water). Whilst sometimes that's trivial enough to make God laugh out loud, at other times, it makes him raise the sea to near flood level with his tears!

Nevertheless, your own experiential undertaking of this checklist survey will help to demonstrate to you just how far (to the power of infinity) a wizard in maths is our Jehovah Jireh of the Supreme Command. This survey's first question (flashback here to attitudinal standpoint 1) which, were it the only question in this survey, would entitle you to exit earth right now (not that right now you should be wanting to take that exit) by which to enter heaven. But of course, for being just the first question in this checkout list, your result here determines only one of the preliminary heats in this race of life and not as yet anywhere near the victory lap. Believe it or not, there's still a long haul ahead of us, and that's even before we reach eternity (far less over to Kabul or back again to Baghdad).

Let's see how your level of responding to trauma (a sign of soul-maturity) bears to the further critical questions of this ongoing survey. The survey outcome could either close this book here and now or else open it still further and yet still further, as well as still faster and yet still faster, to engage both reader and author in either more of the same or else far different challenge. As reader and writer, we're both already on the seriously surgical list here. Our exit from earth by way of this victory lap is already booked. Since mankind only proposes, whereas God disposes, whether to exit entirely from this rapidly dying earth on target or else to extend this book of record to cover so much more than both reader and writer have yet to find out remains still in the unknown. Every truly prophetic history must be left to write itself.

For you humans being no more than a little lower than are we angels in the hierarchy of heavenly beings, this may facilitate you humans learning from us angels no less than (like teachers learning from their students) for us angels learning from you humans. No doubt that's part of the rationale for this report being sponsored by the Supreme Command. No less than for this the Messiah came to earth to find out for himself first-hand what it really means to be human. For sure, this is why we move right now to attitudinal standpoint 2 in our promised checkout list.

Attitudinal Standpoint 2—Relating to Coordinate Dimensions: As in music, with pitch rising and falling in the vertical y-axis and metred rhythm accounted for along the horizontal x-axis, so too, by taking up the cross of Jesus, the disciple must account for himself or herself both in the y-axis towards heaven as well as along the x-axis towards his or her neighbour. Thus, as coordinated by God (the overall conductor of every person's free-willed life song), the means of composing and performing his or her own uniquely beautiful life lyric is given to every disciple (as already left openly indicated for his or her own personal improvisation in the final celebration of creation's full score).

What happens to the non-disciple who has (as yet) no perception of his God-given score? What happens to the disciple who is so heavenly oriented and preoccupied with rising ever upwards in the vertical y-axis as to be no earthly use (or, worse still, the cause of great abuse) along the horizontal x-axis? On the other hand, what happens to the disciple who devotes all his or her time to giving neighbourly attention along the horizontal x-axis without paying any attention to his or her calling as indicated vertically by the rising and falling pitch on the y-axis of the God-given score? Consult the Bible, for the answers to these math equations are all there!

The Supreme Command, for being the creator of the full symphonic score, has his or her own way of dealing with the cacophony that can result from much more than just a misplaced note or from any small oversight that leads to a misplaced musical entry. There's uplift (which may be mistaken on earth for downfall), and there's downfall (which may be mistaken on earth for uplift), just as there's the slightest nudge (or fatherly hug) given from the great conductor of all things to any over-earnest disciple (which on earth can so easily be mistaken for signifying that disciple's dropout instead of his promotion). Didn't we all once mistake Christ himself for having been a human dropout when consigned to the cross instead of his having been given divine promotion?

Faith comes from hearing. If then you care to read and listen most carefully (in both head and heart) to the God-given score for all creation (especially the score so thoroughly revised after the angelic fall, the human fall, and the flood), you'll hear something that both comes and goes but still continues on from far beyond the sun (Ra), far beyond the moon (Thoth), and likewise, far beyond the stars (Shudyr-Shamich).

You can hear this symphony of creation resound through all the history of the patriarchs and prophets, rising higher than ever before on the vertical y-axis on to the coming to earth of the good news of Christ's gospel. Then for still closer listening, you'll most clearly hear a rapidly rising crescendo of sweet sound already heralding in the Second Coming to earth of Jesus Christ, which signifies most aptly for his own infinitely creative character, a symphony of salvation.

So then how will it be for you on the Pharisaic table of mutilated values, dearest reader—your overcoming of a misplaced note or of a wrongful entry, your heavenly uplift being mistaken on earth for being your divine downdraught or even downfall, your heavenly promotion for being mistaken for being your earthly downfall, your earthly rejection being regarded with the scorn to be rightly felt by any heavenly dropout? Whatever book of martyrs—whether ancient, mediaeval, or modern—you may consult, know that they have been redeemed for Christ or else, as for anyone else, let fall.

So much for achieving salvation through downfall (or, more accurately, resurrected downfall), as you will know of by our little episode of soul-catching earlier reported in relation to attitudinal standpoint 1. True, this sort of downfall doesn't always bring resurrection—neither to President Nixon over the Watergate scandal nor to President Reagan over the Contra scandal. It might have brought President Reagan's pants down, but without his impeachment, he had time to pull them up again. Likewise, to give President Nixon a pardon merely soft-soaped his soul by taking his presidential body off the devil's meathook. Saving one's soul demands more of one than just saving one's face!

Nevertheless, of any complete and irrefutably resurrected downfall, there are many examples known to the world. These are instances of this world's fallen celebrities, of whom the transformed Saul who became Paul is amongst those most widely known. Nevertheless, anyone already picked to have a new name like you in heaven can also, like you and through you, be just as widely known by both listening for as well as responding positively to his or her calling.

Those resurrected lives through downfall (which most usually happens wherever and whenever any soul-catcher steps in) as also every other resurrected life of each and every one of us (whether once known or never known) all testify to and solely point to the resurrected life of Christ. And whatever personal cost factor is called for from any of these celebrities through experiencing salvation by way of downfall is more than adequately recompensed by the resulting ease with which the renewed celebrity (think here of Paul) can keep pointing never to himself but solely to the risen Christ.

A similar point of order can be made here, and one of immense cosmic order, as it has to deal with, insofar as the real threat to the saints exists, of their introducing chaotic disorder. It is most unfortunate on earth that, through the misbegotten efforts of the Counterfeit Command, a great competition has been set up amongst the saints (just as amongst the disciples) by which to prove their worth (as if they themselves were celebrities) for their own sweet purpose (although not ruled out) of their getting into heaven. So although we angels in heaven celebrate every single soul saved (whether saved late in life or early), we do so just as profusely of any and every soul as any family would of any sibling at birth and even more so on their being born again and yet still more so on their bodily demise when gone to glory.

Then there are all this world's as yet earthly unknowns whose heavenly celebration of their resurrected downfall is yet to become more generally known. Of course, the paramount model for downfall evangelism, which both angels and humans celebrate worldwide on Christmas (although more so amongst believers on Easter), is that of Jesus Christ. So then, don't ever forget this—that he came down to earth from heaven for his Father's expressly prophesied purpose of saving the entire human race. And so then again (as also expressly and most clearly prophesied) every knee in heaven and on earth shall eventually bow to this same Jesus Christ this world's saviour before sharing in the general uplift of every single believer to all eternity.

The horizontal dimension (traditionally exercised by apostles, evangelists, and pastors) is every bit as important to every soul-catcher as the vertical dimension (traditionally exercised by angels and prophets). For being drawn by miraculous happenings to look more upwards than sideways, humans associate the vertical dimension (stretching between heaven and earth) with clearly angelic (and thus heavenly) properties, whilst desert-wandering prophets are seen to occupy a suspiciously no man's land, for being somewhere proverbially caught betwixt and between (as the quasi-redundant saying goes) for them being neither altogether on earth, nor being altogether in hell, nor as yet being altogether in heaven).

Yet despite their dynamic commitment to the vertical dimension of hearing every little whispered vocable (or pin) drop from heaven, for as long as they are engaged in fulfilling their horizontally expressed prophetic function, prophets are rarely seen to rise beyond the sometimes receptive and at other times non-receptive flat surface of this very mundane world. For over a hundred years before the birth of Christ, the prophetic word was in almost complete abeyance, and so shall it again prove to be in these latter days before Christ's Second Coming.

The Quaker or Shaker response (as perhaps also the terpsichorean response of the dancing dervish)—if one might so call the unqualified wonder with which some humans either quake, shake, or dance to express their awe of all creation—is yet another way (however exhausting this may be to others and eventually to themselves) of maintaining receptive contact between earth and heaven, no less than through constant prayer. However, in this space age (by reason of our temporal dimension becoming so prophetically compressed by the approach of eternity from above), the once traditional and almost terpsichorean toing and froing of this earth's wandering people (amongst them are Aztec, Romany, Bedouin, Jews, Chuckchi, and Australian Aboriginals) on the horizontal plane has been much corrupted by the Counterfeit Command's increased politicisation of all the planet Earth. And its resulting momentum (perpetuum mobile, as hell likes to think of it), afflicting émigrés, refugees, and other displaced persons, required both to express and fulfil their everyday needs.

Since this lateral movement is often sadly overlooked, certainly by today's less evangelical humans, it befalls us angels to stand in the gap (sometimes to the exasperation of those worldly powers, those who are not only building high walls, barricading open ports, and depersonalising people but who also have not the slightest regard to the other ways in which they denude the forests, rape the seas, and extend the deserts to depress, oppress, and supress what they see to be the world's 'surplus population').

Whilst all this destruction furiously takes place as much in the vertical dimension (if not more there than ever before for us angels), we also have so much more to account for in the horizontal or lateral direction. Rather than just the toing and froing of apostles and evangelists who once attended to the spreading of the gospel's good news across the 360 degrees of every horizontal dimension, we have the toing and froing of those homeless, hungry, and displaced persons also as never before over the widest and furthest possible surface of this Earth's globe. So then our angelic presence by now over all the earth is called into immediate action and likewise with a responsibility as never before.

From this added angelic engagement in world affairs, it happens that there are more and more miraculous happenings (however much unexpected) which are taking place on this much less humanly (than now demonically) oriented planet Earth. Yet all these miraculous happenings are more and more, both falsely and flatteringly, attributed to human progress by the Counterfeit Command.

At the same time (which nothing in space-time ever is), there is growing up (very aggressively) a far more flat-earthed yet skywards-soaring variant of human society. This proudly progressive yet fiercely retrogressive form of openly self-made society recognises less and less allegiance to the past. Education—the higher it thinks to climb— concerns itself more and more with dumbing down the hard-earned wisdom of the ages.

Need it be said, well not for believers (since in these latter days, we have been warned that there will be more evil done now on earth than ever before), that this proudly progressive yet fast-degenerating variant of once-human society is all set for having made its own come-down. Already, it is almost a complete counterfeit of originally created creation. This counterfeit, as now engineered by the Counterfeit Command with superhuman expertise (and so remarkably convincing to awestruck humans), is made to substitute for the authentic original as designed by the Supreme Command.

We could produce here an interesting graph (using the heavenly/earthly grid of vertical y-axis as against the horizontal x-axis) for these now latter days in the life of this already dying planet Earth. It is one, when compared with previous graphs, which would show this world's now rapidly shrinking yet once arable and highly productive surface. It is also a graph which once reflected more of a humanly concern for all eternity than, as now, it reflects more of a trend towards self-indulgent human satiety. On this score, there will be nothing truer than Darwin's much celebrated yet much misunderstood *Descent of Man*.

Like today's thoughtlessly high-rise architecture (accounting for so many less than heavenly aspirations to procreate the earth faster upwards, as well as to generate hellish conspiracies to take over both earth and heaven from the Supreme Command), this graph for the present would certainly demonstrate two critical needs for redeeming and resolving mankind's ever-present spiritual dilemma. The first critical need would be to offset and reverse that swiftly increasing rate of human regress upwards, upwards, and ever upwards towards achieving its inevitable opposite—the eventual downfall of human society through human satiety.

The second critical need goes towards emphasising the requirement for every human being, at every physical no less than spiritual level, to share in every life scientist's most intimate understanding of the primal form function equation from which is derived the only one way, the only one truth, and the only one means to eternal life. A deeper understanding of this abstraction, despite all scoffing from whatever source, would replenish mankind's critical need (through angels, apostles, and prophets) to engage more informedly in vertical as well as horizontal evangelism.

So too, without this most formal and most functional of life connections (on all physical and spiritual levels), the proof inherent simply in the way things are fails to influence even those who profess to be most struck by (their mistakenly irredeemable proof of) the facts. It would be this humanly vertical need, when once balanced against this world's critical need for more humanly carried-out horizontal evangelism, which would seek to pin its mistakenly solar centre point of Christ's cross of redemption even deeper into this already groaning earth.

The vertical piercing of that pin (from deep within the already groaning earth to utmost heaven) rises both formally (in this case, conveyed by the cruciform combination of both vertical and horizontal dimensions) as well as functionally (through the always open invitation to heavenly redemption and earthly restoration). Thus, even more today, does the tumultuous earth shriek to high heaven of the still fast-spreading blood of Cain just as it groans still ever deeper over mankind's ignored redemption through the blood of Jesus Christ?

So then, both in the vertical and horizontal dimensions, no less than in its temporal and spatial directions, this tired old earth shall quake and shake as never before seen, far less as prophesied before by any Quaker/Shaker. So too, shall the constantly rising sea level serve to remind the ever-faithful of Noah's flood? And so then these latter days, as yet still of the resurrection, shall continue (until finally time ended by the apocalypse). The horizontal plane of the earth's surface shall ripple, role, and fold, like waves across the surface of the sea. The poles of the globe shall switch, its axis shall shift, and the whole surface of the earth shall unroll like a scroll on which shall be written the whole history not just of this earth but also of this heaven first brought to earth.

Those who then live in fear of this world's ways shall fade. Nothing of them or of their fearful lives shall remain. Like the ocean's tide spreading across the sands of time, this by then past history of the earth shall be completely erased. The new shall be as if the old had never ever been hanging in the balance.

Meanwhile, throughout all the still groaning earth, as prophetically required be given to all tribes and nations by way of their more comprehensive understanding of the form function equation—both heavenwise as well as earthwise of the redemptive crucifixion—the last word on the subject of redemption to whatever few tribes and nations still outstanding shall soon be given. Until then, soul-catching still goes on with no less fervour in terms of the original equation.

Lest you readers find our angelic abstraction of thought hard to take on board (since without the myth of the falling apple, you humans find even Newtonian physics hard to take on board for being no more than a similar abstraction), we shall postpone all such abstract talk (still being recorded for training purposes in heaven) until after we deal more fully with this same topic of angelic abstraction later on in this checklist. Before returning more immediately to that 'urban distaste of the concrete' indulged in by *The Great Gatsby*, however, it may nevertheless help to assuage your present free-floating fears of abstraction to realise that even in the human realm of (persuasively concrete) communication, (1) no scientific paper begins without an abstract and (2) no scientific premise (however conjectural) could pursue, far less reach, any concrete conclusion without indulging in the human process (corresponding to the angelic process) of scientific abstraction.

So then, and having said so, we now climb down from upper-air abstract to return to the specificity of ground-level concrete. In doing so, however, we remind ourselves that long before mankind took to the upper air, the concept of human flight (unlike our own angelic flight) was no more than an *as-if* abstraction. [Exegesis 1: It may help you to envision this abstraction by looking into the Russian language, which has two alternative words (*samolyot* and *aeroplan*) for the modern aeroplane. *Samolyot* was borrowed from the Eastern conceptualisation of a magic carpet, whereas *aeroplan* is no more than a verbal retranscription from one language to another rather than conveying any deeper thought transference of a concept.]

Nevertheless, for those who are fixated on facts (as if facts were things and not themselves ideas), it may help to look on every kind of communication (whether of fixated facts or of abstracted ideas) as involving some kind of physical (but more likely mythical) road haulage. So whether you're carting the gospel by way of bringing good news (evangelistic haulage) or spreading lies and gossip (demonic haulage), the business of communication (carried out often by very different haulage companies) is still always a matter of haulage. And of course, the process of abstraction can reduce the need for heavy haulage to that of light haulage (which, in turn, explains why angels, unlike humans, have always been able to fly). They're not just light enough on their feet to levitate; they're light enough in their hearts and minds enough to fly.

By reason of moving long-distance haulage (if not straight up in the air) then from off rails on to roads, then lots of what once were unexpected happenings are taking us angels not just from John o' Groats to Land's End (in the UK) or from Archangel (in Russia) to Los Angeles (in the USA) or from North Cape to Oban (in New Zealand) but also to places (almost always of intense conflict) very much further afield. Will you then come with us at least on some of our apostolic long-haulage missions as well as on our faster and shorter airbus travels? There will be solemn sermons, unexpected prophecies, and perhaps even miraculous healings to contend with, so it won't always be (as you sometimes hope for) just one lifelong party to be eternally provided with beer and skittles!

So then we can at least tell you (dearest readers) that this search after the supreme truth (once known for being a sacred pilgrimage, but now regarded for being no more than a tawdry road novel) is going to be a very, very long haul indeed. Nevertheless, there's a point to slow starts as the author Mark Twain said of his hero Huck Finn. This makes sense by reason of the fact of our living for any length of mortal time on this earth (not always a fact but actually a reason) requires that everyone who does so is thereby bound (whether starting young or starting later) to stand in need of sure salvation. [Excursus

1: These two (relatively) short sentences (for all that jurisprudence or the science of justice often requires longer sentences to be given) could be mistaken for being a short sermon, but unfortunately, not all our sermons (or sentences, either linguistic or juristic) are so short.]

So then for not having said farewell to our cotton-picking folks back home (a common enough experience for migrants, émigrés, and refugees throughout this faster-moving planet), we ourselves can't even properly profess to be on the open road yet! No, indeed, for having a road novel still only in our otherwise empty heads (we angels need to go on vacation from our vocations, you know) and without having yet attended to whatever evil still adheres to our less than open hearts (we're speaking here as humans), we're no more prepared for what we intend to do (when faced with the unexpected) than to be found (as expected) still street lounging 24/7, far less 19/11, on the streets!

Well, we won't get very far along this less than open road (far less for writing a road novel, never mind for setting off on a pilgrimage) if we do no more than with perennially closed minds lounge around the streets. Never mind then (most literally, what's still closed up in our tortured mortal minds) if we really are any time soon to begin telling (although however prematurely) what will prove (even if no more than by way of literary postponement) to be a very, very long story. Well, we angels (whether on vacation or following more closely on or after our vocations) have all eternity, you know!

So then just as it's not out of the heavenly order of things for you humans to wait on the Lord, so also, it's not out of the heavenly order of things for us hard-working angels on earth to take a vacation from our vocations. So now here's something new, even if not novel enough to be a novel (by a reversal of roles). The streetwise teacher (earlier mentioned) is now looking to the page-turning preacher, and the page-turning preacher is looking to the fire-tending prophet, by which means of buck-passing along the clerical queue, so then it's the roast-chestnut vendor (you remember that one who fell under a bus) who is left to do the talking, although we can't rightly say he looks likely (unless being sooner reborn rather than later born-again) to start proclaiming the future any time soon through the streets.

Hold on … Hold on … for us intern-angels being both off on our annual angelic holiday and back again (no less this time—for to us all time is no time—since all your time, like one and the same sea tide is still both running and rising as well as ebbing and falling) so once again for us holidaying to Heimra, a heavenly holiday resort in the Scottish Hebrides, to which (as promised) we'll later go again where (as for this time spent—caveat emptor) we've been reading today's far-gone novels (*Harry Potter and the Philosopher's Stone* by J. K. Rowling and *Something Sinful* by Suzanne Enoch), together with watching plays (sometimes quite horrid stuff, like the *Death of a Salesman*, no less than *The Crucible*), still running on the world stage—so then (just like you humans after any holiday) now for us angels also (despite our ubiquitousness) back to this earth with a bump.

It's been a busman's holiday for us angels all the same, since we're expected to write book and film reviews on what we've read and seen for the benefit of the Supreme Command. [Excursus 2: We'd thought ourselves done with that reviewing work since graduating from novices to intern-angels. Nevertheless, heaven must enforce its own priorities, since yet another graph shows no more increase from our angelic efforts to encourage a widening level of horizontal evangelism by which to stimulate human understanding of the redemptive-restorative functionality of the no-quick-fix crucifixion.]

Nevertheless, here's a voiced-over model sermon from some stand-in for ourselves from still much further offstage. 'Ah well,' says the enlisted (but stand-in) literary reviewer, perchance from *The Underground Daily Times*, 'this is no novel (presumably *The Soul-Catcher*) exactly as we can expect such things as novels to be always done more unexpectedly here on earth, since it's always the least expected character, in this case, the deceased roast-chestnut vendor, who will turn out as entirely expected to take the principal lead (unless, of course, he is made up only to look the part and so confuse the reader) just as this clichéd technique of fudging the issues can be expected of any mediocre book, average film, or one-night play.

'This projected road novel then (for its lack of prophetic street vision) is not likely to encourage the making of any quirky, far less insightful, film (watch again Fellini's *La Strada*) whilst journeying exactly the same old road (read Bunyan's *The Pilgrim's Progress* and Lewis's *The Pilgrim's Regress*) so much already travelled before. So too (for its complete lack of any more telling or revealing words), this obviously only intended (or by now pretended) road novel (unless by chance also a programme novel) is not likely to produce any more than the most casually expected series of dull and depressing stories (watch *La Strada* again) by reason of today's average author never having yet got out (of his own street-closed mind) to make his own way on today's theoretically more open but also very chanciest of heavily congested roads.'

Poo! Now this present book (only one of twelve) is not, even by any (of the direst) means (which it would take to make), a dystopian novel. Indeed, the peak time of the novel on today's heavily congested literary roads is rapidly graduating (some say degenerating) towards semifactual science fiction. On earth, all last hopes (as well as the biggest bank balances—both offensive and defensive) are pinned, as in both *Star Wars* and the space race, on outer space. [Excursus 3: Indeed, the whole worldwide concept of the novel (apart from whoever it once was who first inspired Genesis) is flawed for there being nothing new under the sun, which, in turn, accounts for the very trying quality of every subsequent novel by its trying to prove otherwise.]

Nevertheless, there are lessons to be found in literature for those wise enough to wend their way through the cacophony of bells and whistles by which to find, follow, and learn from them. To do so, this same deepest urban (and as often suburban) darkness which is confirmed to exist by physicists now recognising different degrees of deep, deeper, and deepest darkness poses problems never experienced by humanity ever before. In these most modernist of scientific times when every manifestation of spirituality (whether for good or evil) is denigrated or dismissed in sole favour of physicality, then the Counterfeit Command has a field day (in which all the differing states of darkness are made all too real.

This is done by the Counterfeit Command at first presenting these differing states of darkness to be entertainingly surreal. Thus (at the level of prestigious infotainment) they fail to elicit humanity's explicit witnessing to its own lack of spiritual vision from which soon follows a correlative lack of spiritual hearing. Truly informed spiritual observers of this phenomenon are fewer than they've ever been. [Exegesis 2: Since when, if recorded anywhere, did anyone hear the last pin drop from heaven?]

What more could we say then (whilst still on our vocational vacation) unless to quote from the prophet Isaiah [at 60:1] when he proclaimed so long ago for all people of the world to 'arise up and shine, for the light is come, and the glory of the Lord is risen upon you'? Perhaps for the multitexting and multitasking people of today's more mechanistic and yet still power-crazy, money-money-moneyed, and so full-on world, we might dare to update the prophet's same message by reminding them once again of the same Isaiah's prophetic command for all time (more mechanically) *to change gear*. Still, for by now driving an auto-auto on an autobahn, you could hardly know how to change gears, far less double-declutch, or in any way even begin to experience what it really only once was to drive a car!

Take every care, and yet if you still find *changing gear* difficult for yourselves, then find out more of what it takes to *double-declutch* the most firmly closed of firmly fixed minds. Yet despite the very best of our shared messianic intentions, what difference will it make (says a very insinuating voice in our ear) since even the most modern means of breaking through the silence which seems to permeate today's still prevailing (and thus apparently both deeper and still deepening) darkness can startle even the most up to date and fully prepared of all current listeners for the sound of any pin dropping from the hand of our Father in heaven?

This most insinuating voice (which endeavours to intrude upon every closed mind) is most certainly not the same openly prophetic voice from the desert wilderness (out of which came John the Baptist) which brought the later good news of heaven's kingdom having come to earth. So then we on earth must come to know as much as we can of the history of heaven as well as of the history of hell (which is sometimes closer to church history than church history is as close as it ought to be (mea culpa) to the history of heaven).

So then once upon another time, begins the streetwise teacher (seizing the moment (carpe diem) before some other just as insidious voice takes over), there was a time in the history of both church and man, which was long before the street wariness of scouting came in (and then just as soon unfortunately went out of fashion), when for all that short time, you humans were all still little children, then all of you could hear a pin—even the very smallest pin—drop from the hand of your Father in heaven.

Yet still alas and alack, for there are still beings around called Old Father Time (known to the Greeks as Chronus), Mother Nature (known to the Maori as Papatuanuku), Father Christmas (or Santa Claus, as also so known from Alaska to Barbados), and so many other carnival figures, most of whom are only stand-ins for the Supreme Command that holds everything together. And yet by such pleasant but faintly improper means, these carnival and even more carnal figures (icons of hipsters, rock stars, rap stars, and drag queens), when pinned up on even nursery walls (begin to serve as prototypes for parental icons of further fame and fortune), all of whom can so easily divert every growing child's attention away from the reality of his or her (or androgenous—no, surely not) Father in heaven!

Well now, that puts an end to our vacation! But by now, you've all become so grown up (a miracle in itself, or so your parents say) that you feel now proudly impregnable. *Impregnable*—a new word to you? All right, but nothing at all to do with birth control!

Your grown-up pride (not much fast forwards from the previously rebellious, independent youth) is now made complete with flashy cars and smart wives and also by having yourselves such cool children and grandchildren, which I'm now speaking (whether or not for being heard as an angel by anyone at all) only to respectable midlifers and to others far older but actually no more responsible for mistaking themselves to be completely grown up. For heaven's sake, as humans, you're pulling my leg, aren't you, for thinking at this point on the stage of life to take for yourselves a bow? [Exegesis 4: No, we're not here drawing a long bow, far less taking a short bow. Instead, it's all you humans who, from the waist up (imitating short-arsed Zacchaeus), are taking a mighty big and self-celebratory sycamore bough (stet—presumably short for any cowboy wearing a Stetson, which stands for 'leave well alone').]

Let me remind you humans (since everything said here is being recorded for teaching or training purposes in heaven) that none

138

(but any fallen angel) will, for any reason (or lack of reason), allow you to make any sort of reverential bow (from the waist) or bough (from the tree)! You can be severely startled, as many humans are on encountering an angel, but you risk being clobbered (like that two-timing Balaam in the Bible) or being rubbed out for being sneakily supercilious (like bad King John in Magna Carta), which is what you risk right now in your trying to pull my leg by taking for yourself a self-reverential bow. So then stop shuffling around like an idiot, will you, since bowing to any angel (whether by way of pretence or for real) is simply not on the heavenly pack of cards (even if you thought long enough to do so).

Instead, take a good long look at where you stand (as a supercilious smart aleck) in this increasingly smart-aleck world. Despite overloading yourselves with extra vitamins and food supplements, you humans have grown so very, very, very tired. Why, even the young have grown so sedentary (almost geriatric) by their being auto-driven to and from school.

And just as both fallen angels and fallen humans grow so excessively tired in trying to maintain their sham respectability (by which to hide their lack of real life), then over countless generations, you've even given up on looking for the fabled fountain (or so-called elixir) of eternal life. Why, you've even got to the stage of legislating, well, first for abortion (since why start what you'll stop) and then for assisted suicide (since why continue what you wish you'd never started)!

In consequence, how prematurely old have now grown up all the world's little children? In all the Wildest West of this once wide world, the West has depleted itself of all its once little children! Why, nonsense, say us angels of all of you who are no more than midlife mortals. Why, despite everyone considering themselves so grown up, you're each still a little child! It's true that you've all become so very hard of hearing, by which you're as stone deaf to any heavenly pin dropping as you are also soul-blinded now to the light of truth still shining. Despite all appearances, however, we angels sit not in judgement of you for being only a little lower (whatever that means) than us angels.

Nevertheless, all causes have consequences. You no longer hear the everyday directions (which us angels still keep on giving you) as to where, when, how, and why you're never ever so grown up as to stop searching for that way, that truth, and that life which underpins the counterfeit fountain (or so-called elixir) by which you've been falsely promised to become every bit as powerful as the gods. Quite frankly, it's only this ongoing search for the way, the truth, and the life that keeps you mortals (who do so still search) everlastingly young.

Listen carefully! Can't you hear—no, not even the faintest tinkle—when a pin drops on to earth from heaven? No, no, instead, you're looking for a falling star on which to pin all your already crashed hopes to make a career, to find a mate, or to inherit a fortune; but you won't ever see a falling star (far less a shooting star) in such a deeply clouded-over sky, so you'll just have to learn to listen most carefully and to hear exactly when it is that a pin precisely drops for you from heaven.

You know, us angels (who are heavenly messengers through the stars and not just worldly passengers in some phantasmagorical starship) don't back off and stop talking just because you midlifers on earth stop your ears from hearing what we say. When we want to keep you (as well as ourselves) on the one and only true path—that one path which is so often perilously hard going and yet still the only path by which to reach our still mutually sought-for destination—we'll still keep talking. The big question, of course, is whether you still hear us.

Even if you do not see or hear us (since the human eye is not satisfied with just seeing, nor is the human ear satisfied with just hearing), then we straightforward angels will be still full in your face, because otherwise you'll have to stretch yourselves or else face the unpleasantness of being sorely stretched. Faith in the future then will arise only from the measure of your suffering. Why suffer the imposition of a challenge when you could be accredited with enjoying its acceptance?

What misery then awaits you from any such imposition from the hound of heaven! You'll be forced to take down most of today's many iconic pin-ups (those in favour of counterfeit fame and counterfeit fortune) by which all your present work is no more than this world's vanity. Did you not paste up those false icons by which to advertise your lives as painted sepulchres?

And from one generation to the next, didn't you pass on these misfortunate prototypes, allowing them to be pinned up to advertise the same sort of serial hoodwink on nursery walls? You think us angels to preach against these things *prescriptively*, but (from cause to consequence) we warn of these things *descriptively*.

So like any other angel on behalf of our Father in heaven, what more can we say now to you midlifers and other long-ago grown-ups when, as said once before (by Ecclesiastes, the preacher in King Solomon's time), 'all is vanity, all is vanity'. All is vanity (now most surely) for you now have no real remembrance of your former greatness. You have lost or mislaid your inheritance, trading it in for a mess of pottage and exchanging heartfelt significance for the superficiality of relatively mindless things.

Look here, when everything seems new to you, as even under this old and fast-waning sun, there is (as a matter of logic) no new thing! These things, as they say, have reached a pretty pass (the point of no return), so just as little children must learn to sit still, you too must learn once again to look and listen in waiting for the Word of the Lord. It's as if, like long before you ever thought about it, this Word was a pin, a very precious pin, to be dropped to earth from the hand of one's own Father in heaven.

Look at this exercise of waiting on the Lord in this way, because for being all now long grown up, we all have to learn to exercise all our gifts of sight and hearing (both inner sight and outer sight as well as inner hearing and outer hearing) in order to both see and hear from our most faithful Father in heaven. He has always something to say. He has always something to show you. And until you see the Father's face through that of Jesus Christ and hear the Father's voice through that of Jesus Christ, the desert shall not bloom as you hope it to bloom wherever you walk.

That's enough of this checkout list for now. Like any street evangelist, we've lathered ourselves into a good old Pentecostal sweat hardly in keeping with the Bible, far less in keeping up with the Bible. It was that backhanded book review from (presumably) *The*

Underground Daily Times which (just as presumably) got under our angelic skin to take us unawares whilst yet all set to go on our annual angelic vacation (now postponed to a much later book).

We dare say (when reading again from between the lines of *The Screwtape Letters*) that's the thing always most likely to happen, especially whilst on vacation, when one's defences are down. [Excursus 5: Beware of this especially when travelling on vacation and highlight this vulnerability with the most special care whenever you prepare to leave or to arrive at any intended destination. It is never any sort of superstition (despite being scoffed at for seeking such a blessing) to gather round together and sit prayerfully at the table before leaving on a journey.]

Having finished this exposition of attitudinal standpoint 2 as yet not even nearly halfway through our checkout list (presently expected to cover no less than nine points of preparedness), nevertheless, for the sake of our further travelling (and having just demonstrated by our own failure, when under demonic attack, to keep our angelic cool), we here take (not a spell, which is an ambiguously occult expression) rather a time out (when construed as some sort of strategic retreat if you will).

At this most pregnant point, therefore, we shall spend our time out in listening for, until we hear that elusive pin drop (if not otherwise a big explosion) before going on to tackle what follows which is the attitudinal standpoint 3. Thus, by keeping good time (under the sun, if not by the sun), we shall continue this checklist in the next part of this very brief conceptualisation of all things, remembering as always that this report (whatever its shortcomings) is both sponsored and authorised by the Supreme Command.

* * *

All Things Still under the Sun
Part VI

A Continued Checklist for Cosmic Travel
He wished he hadn't said anything. If there was one thing the Dursleys hated even more than his asking questions, it was talking about anything acting in a way it shouldn't, no matter if it was in a dream or even a cartoon—they seemed to think he might have dangerous ideas.

J. K. Rowling, *Harry Potter and the Philosopher's Stone*

Having long ago blasted off from attitudinal standpoint 2 (but nowhere near midway to where we're heading) we're now getting ready for vertical takeoff from attitudinal standpoint 3 (no further identification needed), although we still have the longest haul through fourth-dimensional space-time to complete the purpose of learning always to confront and never to avoid what would then otherwise remain for us the fearful void. This we do, always *as if* to actualise our dearest hopes, whilst always remembering that desires, as distinct from both hopes and wishful thinking, can serve either to fulfil or else to undermine very different functions than we think they do.

What awaits our extraterrestrial touchdown is a lesson on confrontation, for which the prescribed reading (preferably in the original) is *The Day Lasts More Than a Hundred Years* by the Kyrgyz author Chingiz Aitmatov. [Excursus 1: If a voyage for that length of time seems too far-fetched, then try for a long weekend with J. K. Rowling's *Harry Potter and the Philosopher's Stone*, whilst being guided (more particularly on breaking through the barrier of Cartesian doubt) as by any standard history on the philosophy of doubting.]

We now take time out for this serious reading (by no means any sort of quick-fix magic spell) having left roughly from that by now long-embattled attitudinal standpoint 2 (from where whatever once scorching sun could be seen quietly setting in the west). It now remains for us to hear and see a pin drop (figuratively making touchdown) before our checklisted re-entry to tackle this up-and-coming attitudinal standpoint 3. On this point, we have no illusions as to literary fame (or as to any other sort of ephemeral fame) since one never encounters the same world as one may have only so recently left, even if only to confront another world in its passing. And make no mistake about it—on all fronts, where legal, logical, and linguistic fronts stand for the Big Three in any Rule of Three required by all humans for the sake of their limited understanding, this world is the one which is fast-passing!

Take our word, nevertheless, that this pin drop we have both seen and heard and by which we now go on to execute by that apostolic power of proclamation next-one-up from prophesying is already under action. Accordingly, we irrevocably declare and proclaim (despite the purely temporal, and so far contingent fact of its earthly registration illegitimately relied on by the Counterfeit Command as if for its own bomb disposal) that this so proclaimed pin drop (both seen and heard) is irrevocably set down for heavenly fulfilment. And by such means of exercising earth's largely overlooked power of proclamation, we do so further actualise this checklist by means of the attitudinal standpoint 3 to follow.

This outcome we intern-angels will execute as part of our standard learning practice for heaven's soul-catching process. We do so most humbly by way of continuing our very brief conceptualisation not just of all things under the sun but also of all things in the heavenlies as these signs of the times have been both sponsored and authorised for this process by the Supreme Command. We shall keep to as short an account as possible (however long we may spend for global observational purposes of this planet Earth in outer space-time). And we shall do so whilst still also keeping in mind the preaching excesses of the previous part required for learning and instructional purposes with which to round off this still critically important checklist for all our further travels. Oh yes, and since you mortals never move your minds without some sort of reason, although one could never say the same for your emotions, it is only by compliance with all these nine attitudinal criteria for soul-catching (held out to all those promised eternity) on which all your continued travels still remain only contingently expressed. As said before and again of both this project and this book, every reader may pull out whenever so liked.

Attitudinal Standpoint 3—Discerning Prophecy: Meanwhile (for being still so much of a contingent expression of passing time rather than of present time) then so much also for the bad news of those who have never heard a fourth-dimensional pin drop to earth from heaven. Nevertheless still for them who've never heard a heavenly pin drop here's also the good news. So then shut your ears, then you mortals who can hear a single pin drop, even when in the desert, because here and now (unless you don noise-cancelling headphones) there's going to be such a shower of end-time heavy rain that the sound of falling pins on the hard-surfaced streets and roads of worldwide cities is going to drive the faithless deaf, the sightless blind, and many, many of those who still remain unbelievers completely insane! So then, good news, no, unless … unless … unless believed in, operated on, and fulfilled by those whose lives are thereby called to be redeemed—but then worse news then too for those who most willingly refuse to believe.

Oh yes, this prophesy (as of most others in this scientific age) looks (without proof) to be entirely equivocal; seems to be most ambiguous (unless for at least its excessive if not extravagant width of meaning, then maybe); downright irrational (and so blighted for expressing no more than purely personal opinion, then perhaps); and so for its lack of needful interpretation, both then unsure and unclear; while for the lack of all certainty (both statistical and otherwise) then surely even as a test of faith also grossly unfair. Nevertheless, for this prophecy that's as clear as it gets—although, since there are both bad prophets (who go on making mistakes) as well as false prophets (in the ploy of the Counterfeit Command), then who can say whether this (or any other prophecy) can be attributed to the voice of the Lord?

To every promise made (and there are hundreds of thousands such promises divinely made), there's an expectation of fulfilment, but so also a trial of faith (the cost factor) by which to realise that expectation of fulfilment. That promise and expectation of realised fulfilment already exists for being implanted at birth in the mind and heart of every (even fallen and still most vulnerable) human soul. That's exactly what you need to know about what you need to do whenever anything unexpected happens. So as already said, be prepared!

Yet don't mistake this friendly warning for being a fearsome threat. No authentic angel, in being authorised by the Supreme Command, will motivate anyone on earth (far less in heaven) through fear. Fear is the domain of the demonic—that false authority assumed by those fallen angels who serve their very own completely false, utterly satanic, and yet still so-called bright morning star, as they still do under the purloined power of the Counterfeit Command. The question at issue here is simple, do you recognise a scam when you see one, and if not, then why not?

Nevertheless, you humans must somehow learn to understand that when a pin, no matter how precious, drops from heaven (although itself no bigger than a mustard seed), it does so not randomly but with a purpose. So in its falling to earth (by which it may express the heavenly Father's tear, the Father's song, his feeling, or his thought), this tiny seed (for its future growth) relies on making communicative contact with those who otherwise would not know their Father's determined need, expressed desire, kindly wish, or preferred choice.

The Father's message relies on sound, since faith comes from hearing. Besides the need for open ears, it relies for sight on there being open eyes, just as for thought, it relies on there being open minds, and for feelings, on there being open hearts. Each of these open doors into the eternal life force of the soul is needed to receive and respond to whatever may be the heavenly Father's message. Human receptivity? Of course, there's the pH factor (standing for one's sense of humour), but we won't get into that right now any more than into the wintering or vernalisation process (as often for others a scorching experience) by which, since God is a gardener and you are his chosen and carefully planted people, vernalisation is needed for the germination of any idea (no less than for the smallest of mustard seeds).

Yes, we angels are sometimes the powerful proclaimers and soul messengers of God's will, no less than of his Word, but at other times, we are only the incidental interpreters, as often merely the scholastic translators, or perhaps no more than the academic transporters of

146

his heavenly message. In all this, there's a great deal of heavenly technology involved, besides which (as with the lessening speed of light and the consequential speeding up of time) the cosmic context is fast changing.

Nevertheless, despite the battle being already won (the big picture overall), there are still thousands of individual souls to be redeemed (in the particular) throughout this rapidly disintegrating world. For the saving of such souls (whether on the killing fields, in the academies, in the refugee camps, or on the streets) is where the angelic hosts are nowadays most employed. Those souls who are saved may fall away, but by and large, the individual choice is always personally given. The race is on, and the mopping-up operation (a military one) is where we are employed by the Supreme Command on operational soul-catching. You can call us counterterrorists if you like, since you humans are so often scared off (rather than brought on) when meeting up with us angels.

But what happens when all the angelic avenues (or neural pathways) of heavenly communication are closed (ostensibly for repair, as so often said by those who would block the way)? Oh, don't believe in that most monstrous expression of devilish deceit, since all heavenly roads, pathways, and ley lines are open for all those whose eyes, ears, minds, and hearts are also opened to receiving divine instruction. Accordingly, besides giving you a very brief history of heaven (as in Book 2 of this report), we'll also tell you more (in Book 3) about such demonic barriers between earth and heaven which block interactive communication and give you also (in Book 4) a bare-bones history of hell.

Attitudinal Standpoint 4—Don't Blame the Designer: How many contrapuntal standpoints can you have before losing all point to having any heavenly centre point? Face up here to the rising level of fourth- versus third-dimensional confusion! Consider the whole point of having any heavenly centre point before you take a fix on any such centre point—whether it be that of Buddha, Confucius, Yahweh, Allah, Jesus—or any other purportedly multidimensional figure.

There's a paradox of belief (for some, the paradox of doubt or unbelief) which has been incorporated into every human concept of heaven or hell ever since the fall of mankind (out of idyllic Eden's baby basket and by way of one's own freely chosen free fall) on to this either concrete-grounded or bitumen-surfaced, or else weed-strewn Earth). Believe it or not, but what we'll tell you briefly about heaven in Book 2 of this report is already seen to be the truth by many earthly humans who as yet do not believe in heaven! This is just so, however perplexingly, no less than what we'll tell you in Book 4 of this report by way of a bare-bones history of hell that already resounds throughout every place on earth by those humans who believe all of which it says to be true but as yet surprisingly don't believe in hell.

Let's just say this, that when this falling pin (say one which represents a heavenly thought and yet is no bigger than the smallest mustard seed) cannot reach the earth because human ears, eyes, minds, and hearts on earth are closed, then there's always something big that's about to happen. Yes, indeed, there's always a big bang as the little pin let fall from the hand of God hits the barrier of human unbelief. Sometimes then, there's a big enough bang to take away all power of hearing from closed human ears, to take away all power of sight from closed human eyes, to take away all power of thought from closed human minds, or to take away all power of feeling from closed human hearts.

Sometimes the biggest bang may become so explosive (allowably so for the sake of saving human souls) as to take away human lives. In every such disaster, Satan himself is always the hitman, but he couldn't save a single soul no matter however much he tried. On the contrary, for the battle of the heavenly host against him, Satan and his still powerful cohorts would take every last human soul to perdition.

Who do you think, then, becomes the proverbial catcher in the rye? Stand up and be counted! Don't you yet know that the heavenly host needs you? Don't you yet know that under the Counterfeit Command, the wages of sin are death? Don't you yet know that the battle against sin and death is already won, that you have nothing to lose, and that your place in heaven is secured by you taking up your inheritance?

Oh, oh, oh! You pride yourselves on being completely grown up! You no longer believe in the beauty of earth (far less than in even the greater beauty of heaven)! Until disaster strikes—perhaps with some tsunami, the oceans roar, the earth shakes, the mountains tumble, the tallest of buildings fall, the climate changes. But yet until then, your stiff upper lips still curl back in disdain at all mention of any saviour. Oh my god, you don't even know just how close this tired old world is to the point of extinction. And without transforming your mind, without confessing your heart, without releasing your worldly baubles of fame and fortune, then like any old dinosaur that's lived out its era, you're fast on the way to extinction too!

Until you grown-ups who are perplexed by the paradox of disbelieving in both heaven and hell learn to open both minds and hearts to acknowledge the existence of both (by which means human eyes and ears are also opened so as to hear and see the precious pins of wisdom that are let fall from the hands of their Father in heaven), then without hearing the sound of the Father's voice or without seeing his fatherly face through that of his one and only Son, the already dying world of the human race will continue to be consumed by the proliferation of many big bangs (signifying an outraged heaven).

Meanwhile (which by now won't be for so very long), since (for being the cause of time more rapidly speeding up) the speed of light is now more rapidly slowing down; but for this having now become the way of the world then what are we to do because some of our world leaders say slow down, while other of our world leaders say speed up? So then, don't dare laugh and don't dare scoff at today's apparent frailty, elderliness, and obsolescence of our Father in heaven (the once long-aforesaid Ancient of Days). This Ancient of Days, through his field agents of both David and Solomon (for which read in their reports, first sung in Psalms, and then proclaimed by Proverbs), has much to say by way of warning us all (both angels and humans) against scoffers.

So then don't abuse the Ancient of Days for having lost his marbles (as put about by those who so regularly abuse the elderly on earth). Likewise, don't abuse him for bringing about wars, storms, tempests, or other big bangs (done not divinely by him but instead through demonic interference) or for dropping his pins (which, were they only to be heard by opened ears, would otherwise effectuate his fatherly promises) since all the intensifying confusion on earth, between the outrageously demonic and the righteously divine, is bound by universal law to increase from day-to-day before this by then stone-deaf, increasingly sightless, and rapidly dying world ultimately experiences the biggest bang (since that of before time) now of all time.

Again, likewise, don't dare doubt me, an angel of the Lord God Almighty (even if only second class, although up for promotion), for what I'm transmitting now to you humans directly from your Father in heaven! No, indeed, for in my exhorting you to open your eyes and ears, I'm saying nothing new (at least not since the crucifixion). Oh, of course, I forgot that in these days now of dynamic discovery (as if *scientia* or merely human science were the only kind of knowledge and near-miraculous technology were the only proof of scholarship), it is newness and no longer oldness (far less any continuing form of respectful address) which has become the sine qua non (ha-ha-ha, caught you out there) of low (and no longer high) fashion!

So also, don't mistake me, an angel (still only second class), for lacking any sense of humour, although humour (the pH factor again) is never usually this acidic (except on earth) and perhaps for this same pH factor being more strangely always alkaline (whenever in heaven). Thus, don't dare me any more than mistake me as to the big bang theory (as seen from heaven), because isn't it the case that some of your own scientists, as well as many of your own astrophysicists, astrologists, and other skywatchers have the same big bang theory by which to explain the very first pin dropped by our Father in heaven? [Author's note: We already warned you, didn't we, dearest readers, that you, even for being perhaps unbelieving humans and us for being completely committed angels, would eventually agree (as now both so many physicists and theologians do so agree) on the phenomenon (whether physical or metaphysical) whereby this old earth has survived so many big bangs!]

After all, wasn't it this very first pin which gave rise to the very first big bang (coming rapidly after the satanic fall) which created this still present earth (then out of absolutely nothing) and which, in turn, would be corrupted by your own human fall into this present and increasingly confused world? [So for our agreeing already on so many very big things, then take seriously the possibility of our coming to agree on so many other both very big and very small things over which we might at present disagree.]

Attitudinal Standpoint 5—Relating to One's World Leaders:

You're not going to like this multifactorial lesson on multitudinous standpoints, are you, because once you go from three to however more there may be of further dimensions, you're going to have to break through the surrounding darkness that comes from having more standpoints to your life than can be permitted by the ultimate, omniscient, and supremely all-powerful one.

You don't like where we appear to be taking you by way of this foreword, do you, gentle readers? You'd rather read whatever pleases you rather than read what the Supreme Command (of whom we warned you that this was a military operation) wants you not only to read and hear but also to respond in every way by following the one and only (very narrow) way by which to reach eternity. There's a limit to how many times a warning may be given before it becomes a threat, however, so then let's make this a last warning.

Let's then tell you (exactly if not yet quite precisely) who they are, those world leaders who are today's most misguided persons. [Weather warning: *Precisely* is not quite the same as *exactly* any more than *precision* is the same as *exactitude*. If you as yet fail to detect the exact difference between the two concepts, then make a closer study of Thompson and Thomson's linguistic profile (for being exactly 'the same two profiled peas in the one pod' yet less than precisely so, both namewise and personwise, for one being Thompson spelt with a *P* and the other without a *P*) in Georges Remi's comic book *The Adventures of Tintin* series.]

Amongst many of today's most misguided persons as to the existence of any Supreme Command (call it heaven if you will) are many of the world's most powerful political leaders and supranational businessmen. They belong to no nation, conform to no culture, respect no religion, and observe no conventions. Completely powerless in themselves, they are but only clones of the immensely powerful underworld. Professing to be global, they pretend to be cosmic—both as the creators of the cosmos as well as the maintainers of the cosmos (but in reality, they do no more than bring about the destruction of this world in preparation for the new heaven and earth to follow). The supreme irony of their existence is that what they do and what they say prophetically proclaims the advent of both the new heaven and the new earth, which they so ardently dispute.

Frequently, the fall guys—those who serve neither father on earth nor any father in heaven but who, for being more obviously always in the public eye, are thereby seen to carry the status of transnational world leaders—are no more than clones (not creatures) who are impotent in themselves. By their running round the earth, toing and froing from pillar to post in ever-diminishing circles, they convey the impression of being couriers serving the Supreme Command. Yet believe it or not, these clones of the Counterfeit Command, by misrepresenting themselves to be the highest and most righteous of archangels, serve as nothing but a cover-up for the present world order of false prophets, false teachers, and false healers. These are the ones who promote every most plausible form of witchcraft or prestigious conjuring tricks in place of the one and only divine truth. Look here, what do you think it cost such clones to get them into such places of apparently high command?

* * *

All Things Still under the Sun
Part VII

On the Ticklish Subject of the Unexpected
Be prepared ... A Scout is never taken by surprise: he
knows exactly what to do when anything unexpected
happens ...

Robert Baden-Powell, *Scouting for Boys*

Oh well, here's a question for not-so-trivial pursuit! What was the
subtitle to Robert Baden-Powell's book entitled *Scouting for Boys*?
Well, Baden-Powell's book entitled *Scouting for Boys* was subtitled
A Handbook for Instruction in Good Citizenship! "So what?" some
of our dearest readers may ask, for their not looking any deeper than
they usually do into their every trivial pursuit. "What's the odds,
where's the trick, how goes the punchline?" they enquire; whereas
other readers (no less well loved), may respond with an, "Oh my
golly!"... and... so then "Goodness to Betsy, how intriguing!" Which
one of these readers are you?

Take heed of just how little different from each other may be
angelic and human beings. By standing not much higher in the
heavenly scheme of things than you earthlings, we angels can just
as easily fall from grace by striving for promotion. How else do you
think it is that so many amongst the most gifted of us angels are so
far fallen from grace? Disturbing, isn't it—one out of every three
angels is fallen! How would you then put the stakes, perhaps at two
fallen out of three, for humans?

On earth, this fall may be buffered by you taking early retirement,
redundancy with a golden handshake, or demotion (if not sideways
then into top management). All these concepts integrate, disintegrate,
and reintegrate with each other with varying degrees of complexity.
Thus, never mix up *management* with *administration*. These are
poles apart, unless when closely knit as they should be for the
purpose of management facilitating the 'ministry' of spirit-filled
administration. But alas, now the executant roles have been reversed,

as on earth, by which administration (a spiritual gift) is made to serve the mechanics of management. Satan's downfall, from his position of CEO of heaven, should be a warning to all who attempt to manage instead of to facilitate the ministry of administration.

For this process of 'getting on', as it is called on earth, you have to know 'on which side your bread is buttered'. Indeed, earth is the only place in the universe where 'to stay on your feet' (as another saying goes), you have to learn how to fall upwards. For this, it helps for any CEO (from president to prime minister) to be seen as God. See, there's not really all that much difference between any fallen angel and successful human! As human history shows, most of those promoted to top-flight positions of power and prestige on earth turn out to be fall guys (as once again the saying goes) for the real rulers of society.

There is no similar system of promotion in heaven, except for those with a mind to plummet downwards in the course of their striving upwards. 'Getting on with it' (however rarely heard of in heaven) gives us angels more and more real work to do instead of to avoid. We angels are called more and more to be on earth (in consequence of heaven having come to earth), so our promotion entails more angelic commitment to more and more exacting work rather than as for so many of you humans, on the basis of having attracted fame and fortune, your promotion counts for less and less. Why, as for libraries, schools, polytechnics, banks, postal services, welfare, and community services—your sinecure appointment may simply be to close them down and wind them up!

This angelic work advancement, so far as we can comprehend, is to acknowledge how we angels are constantly discovering ways (despite being knocked by you so often sideways) to give you humans every last chance. Oh yes, we still have every authority from our Father Yahweh to pull the plug on you or the carpet from under you, whichever we prefer, for your point-blank refusal to open your eyes and ears to the existential precariousness of your present world! Take heed then, for unless you have prepared yourselves to scout the universe (as did Scout and her family in *To Kill a Mockingbird*), what you least expect for being the most unexpected is very soon about to happen!

The unexpected may be good or bad—or apparently good but really bad or else apparently bad but really good—to which contingent alternatives, most people (imbued with a gambling or grumbling mindset) prefer to roll a dice or to close their eyes. So then please open your eyes, but first put on these prophetic glasses, since there's a brilliant revelation coming, which may as often come by way of filmic flashback (as in *Back to Bounty*) as by fast-forwarding (as in *Back to the Future*). When the signs of the times are all around, there is no sign so little as to be overlooked for being one of the most significant signs of the times.

None but the prophet knows more intimately of this than does any other physicist, physician, or metaphysician, that the history (of time backwards) and the prophecy (of time forwards) are but two aspects of one and the same divine time management mechanism. It may take the most powerful of filmic flashbacks to harvest the fruits of an earlier generation—a historical flashback (say, to the founding fathers or back further to the Ten Commandments or even further back as made to Abraham as the founder of all nations) by which to resolve those metaphysical (or life-and-death) issues for this present time.

Without the resolution of such life-or-death issues, this present generation cannot know exactly what to do today. Consequentially, the next generation of mankind is going to be significantly, if not permanently, panic-stricken. Just as for the going down of the mistakenly unsinkable *Titanic* in the North Atlantic or for the collapse of the ill-built Tay Bridge between England and Scotland or for the Tangiwai disaster in New Zealand (each taking place through lack of prophetic preparedness), then avoiding that same resulting panic (on the even larger cosmic scale of unexpected consequences) will shortly prove to be the only means of providing for the generic welfare of all humans tomorrow.

So when mindful of this earth's now excessively slippery slope (prophetically proclaimed by spiritual text and confirmed from day-to-day by rapidly spreading environmental context), some things necessarily follow from this world being still 'the same in kind' (for being a legal term). Thus, yesterday's world and today's world have the same slope in kind (although not before with the same now increasing tilt). So too, yesterday's world and today's world have the same oceans in kind (although not before with the same now rising tides). So too, yesterday's world and today's world have the same winds still blowing in kind (although not before with the same now increasing storms and tempests). We could continue further with our catalogue of environmental woes, and sometimes we need to, because unless we reintegrate the swiftly moving and miniscule fractals of earthly disintegration, there's no big picture, however scary, of how close we are to ultimate disaster.

Oh, but there again, do you know what a fractal is? It's not until you know what a fractal is that you begin to understand what we mean (but don't yet truly understand what it is that we really mean) by being a fact. Sounds odd, doesn't it (and it is odd, isn't it) to think that we don't really know what we mean by a fact. But then, even more mysteriously, we don't even know what a fractal is (far less of anything else which we suppose to be in the physical world) until we know a lot more about what we ought to mean by being a fact.

The fact is (pardon the usage) that every big body of a fact (the 'bigger picture', as we like to call it) can be shown (figuratively in the same way as all is shown) to be comprised of far smaller (much, much smaller) fractals. As a matter of fact (beg pardon) every fact (although for only being a human construct) is far, far more than whatever we can physically see. On the other hand, a fractal (very roughly speaking) is only one of those very little fractional portions that together go towards constituting that much bigger (but still incomplete) picture of what we believe to be a fact. As another matter of fact (beg pardon) the however much smaller picture, which is really always only what little we see of any 'bigger picture'is comprised of only these fractals we can see. Once again, we rely for reality on the substance of our faith in things unseen.

It is of such portents of disaster, when partially conveyed by the fractals contributing to the making of any such prophetic big picture that we learn—for the purposes, first of interpretation, and then to the upholding and maintaining of the prophecy, and finally to our contributing towards the prophecy's fulfilment—to take on board each small fractal of the bigger, and possibly biggest picture slowly. We believers do so without panic, so that the rising wind of the always lively Holy Spirit, which in its way of now warning us may be already shrieking to high heaven, can still be heard and pragmatically actioned by us in our making whatever response the Spirit calls for us humans to undertake on earth. This is done by humans no less than when seen or unseen, heard or unheard, felt or unfelt by all other living things.

Of this by now self-evident truth that all continued life and travel on earth (whether in terms of either fitful progress through space-time continuum or by insistent regress in what can be sadly mistaken for being each person's own time) pivots on the implementation of more than their own freely chosen and insightful means. These means, when righteously employed through Jesus Christ to reach each believer's own motivationally foreseeable ends and prophetically understood destinations will enable them to secure these ends and so reach their own appropriate destinations. [Exegesis 1: Yes, we very well know how much of a prophetic mouthful this big picture can pose both for us angels to deliver as well as for you mortals to receive! Alas, you've never been taught to engage in the spontaneous comprehension of either *continua scripta* (a.k.a. *scriptio continua*), far less engage in glossolalia, or the speaking of tongues.]

Why, you've never even learnt to read, far less to write, by way of *scriptio continua* (where all the unspaced words, paragraphs, chapters, and verses of the Bible are conjoined together as close as possible to the space-time continuum required to sustain any living Word)! So then we'll cut to the chase so that you can chew on this relatively trivial text message in the privacy of your own biblical preschool. Until what follows by way of being our next standpoint, which, together with our included punctuation, is yet another concession to your lack of reading skills, so we'll thus remainder to that standpoint (if by then still standing) what has been known to prophets for more than half a century as the *world problematique*. There now, for those who deal today only in one-line text messages, there's an equation by which to wrap up the entire big picture. Of course, once upon a time, panoramic pictures (of historic wars like that of the Fall of Kiev to the Mongols and biggest of battles like that of Waterloo) were all the rage, but now the fashion hemline has fallen to that of taking selfies.

Did you get the trivial text message to which the answer is WP (or *world problematique*)? [Excursus 1: All the same, please excuse the literary long-windedness of these sentences (perdition to every current reader who is no longer a deep breather and, worse still, to any non-reader of that scriptio continua whereby all words are made to conjoin and console each other in mutual harmony by way of communicating their clearly coherent and eternally living Word relationship to each other). Do you realise how far words lost their meaning, narrative text its continuity, and associative conceptualisation its inherent integrity, when *scriptio continua* was chopped into particles?

On the same topic of hemline fashion and selfies, this present angelic editor (shortly to be relinquished through redundancy by being put out to pastures green) must now say to all you readers of this very difficult book a fond farewell. She got into Bible school long before the preceding centuries of scriptio continua had begun to consider chipping away its continuous text into individual words (prophetically forewarning the rise of individualism) and, from there, clipping off entire blocks of its holistic message and bedding them down into severed chapters (which so frequently gave rise to religious or clerical factions) and then more so into little verses (to operate no more than as lay fractals).

We thought that by then, it surely would be the end of all this messing about with the biblical message, but no, to reduce the resulting void would be inserted commas, colons, semicolons, and even full stops. And this is done by way of often very equivocal and opposing views of punctuation. And despite all the formal full stops so introduced into the message, neither would that be the end of dabbling with the primary-sourced message. From altering the biblical form, the would-be reformers moved next to biblical content. Instead of the traditionally presumed source translation from Hebrew, Koine Greek, and Aramaic, radical translators came up with what they called target translation.

Through today's good news versions, international versions, revised authorised versions, contemporary versions, and the most modern of message versions, we travelled very quickly into Anglo-Americano, Esperanto, basic English, and even Geek (*sic*) versions. However, all of us who live or work in time (then until out of time) are made, if not actually forced and compelled, to travel. So then God bless and a fond farewell from your angelic editor who now retires from this exceedingly temporal issue.

This editorial farewell then enhanced the view that God's Living Word could mean whatever readers made of it. By this means of handing full control of scripture from heavenly proclamtion to earthly interpretation, soul-saving would be put on hold (except for DIY, or do-it-yourself ministry). This reformist view (with great cost-saving) might eventually lead (so thought both clergy and laity with some degree of thoughtful self-importance) to heaven being declared redundant. From hell below, the *Underground Daily Times* came out with great splash headings—***HEAVEN ON HOLD***.

To many mortals, this outcome was entirely expected, and yet to others, completely unexpected. To the ever-expectant and evangelically-expectorant denomination of Christians (EDC's, as they were called) they, with good grace, gave their now redundant heaven a great farewell feast, together with a most memorable golden handshake to their retiring clergy. On the other hand, the unexpectorant denomination of Christians (the Non-E's, or Nonentities, as popularly so-called) were so stunned and traumatised, that they didn't even have the good grace to give their now redundant heaven any sort of feast, nor even the least tepid handshake to their clergy. On the other hand, the unexpectant denomination of Christians (DCnonEs, or meanies, as they became to be known) were so stunned and traumatised that they didn't even have the good grace to bid heaven a civil goodbye far less lay their communion table for a farewell feast (or extend more than three fingers in fellowship to their departing clergy).

Meanwhile (now seven days overdue until born again) we have now heard that there are to be no flights from earth to heaven, at least for today—although some reports (possibly counterfeit) do say, '*from* today" instead of '*for* today'. As again reported by the *Underground Daily Views* (a 17 glossy-paged Sabbatarian version of the *Underground Daily Times*) all the steps (save one) have now been pulled up heavenwards from where once stood Jacob's Ladder. And a fast-moving, non-stopping, razor-edged escalator has been installed from earth to wherever indicated by the sign (manned by a crude threesome of two nude mannikins) saying **BYO PARTYING BELOW**.

Without any need to prepare for our continued travel of any sort today, none of us can avert the already instituted, although less than constitutional means by which the unexpected will happen; and if not happening today, then to the least suspecting of those to whom it could happen tomorrow. That's simply so because without both historical insight and prophetic foresight, only the expected can be explained for being bound to happen; and this event may be so boring to those who live only for the prospect (however good or however bad) of experiencing the novelty of constant surprises, that they'll engage with drugs, disease, and even death itself, just to experience what it feels like to have turned one's back on life.

Turn your back on the kingdom of heaven (as so many great and exceptionally gifted people have done) and it's as if there's nothing more to this earth than the kingdom of hell. Without insight, without foresight and so then without hindsight (and thence, for being without hope, left hopeless by your own act of self-abandonment) all that's left to you for being the entirely unexpected is no more than what's more and more clearly bound to happen to you if not today, then perhaps tonight, if not more certainly tomorrow. Yet still meanwhile (for being by now years overdue to measure up to whatever it costs greatly to be born again) all hell itself cannot stand in the way of your last and only remaining freedom of choice).

From this not entirely nefarious point of view, that is to say, when arising from the withheld view of the completely unexpected, we therefore disclaim all responsibility (both legalwise, streetwise, and otherwise) for blowing the gaffe on the advent of the completely unexpected. Is that clear? Because from the very beginning, this comprehensive report on the state of affairs pertaining to both heaven and hell (as well as to this increasingly misshapen earth) is being implemented as a full-scale military operation.

Meanwhile, don't laugh, don't scoff, or else the pin or person (yours be the choice) that holds this world together might well be pulled or prayed for (if not from high above, then from down on earth below) to bring about the biggest bang of all ever imagined. Why, what could be more startling than to bring an earlier end to this already dying world (the ultimate choice of every terrorist than when even less unexpected than ever before. With one's back to the wall and against the kingdom of heaven, not even logic holds good. This is a military operation—so then, face-about (a.k.a. about-face)!

Attitudinal Standpoint 6—Relating to the World Problematique:
We earlier promised you an attitudinal means (see previous attitudinal standpoint 5) of resolving this and other metaphysical (or life-and-death) issues that perplex those who have been led to recognise this present *world problematique.*

'Hey there,' you say, 'what are you talking about? What do you really mean by this *world problematique*? We don't find all that much wrong with the world to make a fuss about!'

'World problematique? Well, that's one of the perhaps highfalutin terms for a world that can't resolve its own problems. One reason for this world's failure to find this resolution is because it's so confused by its very own self-created plethora of conflicting solar centre points. And if you think this whole wide world can accommodate all of them by bowing down to all or any one, two, or three of these conflicting centre points, then you've got a far bigger world problematique coming!'

Most people find the world problematique altogether too scary to confront, far less than to suggest or attempt its resolution. For those readers curious to take the challenge of finding out more, then read *The First Global Revolution* (the result of a spiritual retreat held by the council of the Club of Rome held at Petrovo-Dalneye near Moscow in 1990) as carried through by authors Alexander King and Bertrand Schneider of the council's sanctioned report.

Right then, back to basics! Here then, to begin with, is the intergenerational (or historical) flashback to a time when so much of urbanised Britain (as well as urbanised Russia) were nothing but fetid slums, when the British were fighting the Boer for the sovereignty (amongst other things) of a future South Africa, and when the liberation of the Russian serfs, the resulting famines, the ensuing revolutions, and the assassination of Russian royalty brought pogroms against the peasants (although first squeezing the kulaks financially dry to be sure) and the overthrow of Adam Smith's capitalism in favour of Karl Marx's communism.

Okay then! [Exegesis 2: It may help you here (and anywhere else in your reading of this report) to remember that every history of heaven, however brief, is a living history (as recorded of ideas in heaven) and not a half-dead history (as recorded of events on earth). For such matters as the world problematique, those who are intellectually curious enough to refer to the Club of Rome's reports may well be shattered to find how far this present world has already expired its use by deadline.]

Accordingly, can all mankind congruently cope with all such great cosmic events within the limitations of any all-alone little human head, or do you (as Adam did in blaming Eve) still default by passing the buck to whoever is nearest or dearest before defaulting completely by passing the proverbial buck all the way back to make God himself answer for his design fault in asking too much of his own creation?

Hey there, then, Dear Daddy of All Mankind (being but a target do-it-yourself translation of the Aramaic *Abba*), but isn't it you who, ostensibly on account of all mankind's apparent faults, must accept responsibility upon yourself as creator of all things, both the living and the dead, for being mankind's exceedingly deficient designer? Yet there's more than a suggestion here (no less than here, there, and everywhere) that the Counterfeit Command has somehow squeezed its way into even this most personal and familial of heavenly conversations. Then 'take a flying fugit, Satan', which, alas for being another target do-it-yourself translation instead of a source translation for 'get behind me', does no justice to that same lawless one (now snidely smirking) who is nevertheless still one of heaven's great dignitaries. 'Gee, sorry, Satan', I unwittingly follow up with yet another target-oriented do-it-yourself translation.

'Pardon me then,' I hear from somewhere, 'you little defaulting man, for disputing your disclaimer of cosmic responsibility, but it's no less the devil (than any other dignitary) who resides entirely for his own purposes in the details of world history. Yet we angels recognise that by your own human means of slicing up world history (and most nearly everything else) into various specialisms (since out of each smaller, less generalist, and more specialist slice you specialists might mistake yourselves for knowing less to earn more kudos). Instead, you've made it harder for yourselves as mere humans who look only for kudos (if not also for dollar signs) to see the full cosmic picture.'

Nevertheless, in almost all that world and also increasingly in cosmic history, both what's for the good and what's for the bad, is made or brought about by yourselves for being so often only money-minded humans. It's really of no use blaming God for what goes wrong in world history any more than it's right to pass the buck back to God (or, worse still, to rant and rave at him) for being an incompetent craftsman, never mind also a deficient designer.

'Look at the cosmic issue this other way,' proclaims the very young and as yet 'upstart preacher' (the opposite of Samuel Rutherford's 'stickit minister') whose first and as yet untouched task, since Noah and his sons beat down the first great flood, is to be fruitful, multiply, and replenish the earth. From his high-above street-level pulpit, far from both the maddening crowds and the rising sea levels, he points out from this rather coldly celibate and exclusive vantage point that the stewardship of the world was handed over to mankind, both male and female, and so to both of you, manly Adam, and you, womanly Eve, who grabbed it up with your all four hands, you can't very well blame God for being such an incompetent craftsman or deficient designer. [Excursus 2: By any 'upstart preacher', according to the as often upstart presbyters of the long-ago Church of Scotland, they would mean one who preached from the head but not from the heart, which as often gave rise to a headbutting contest between Scots presbyters and Anglified clergy.]

'Look too at the same cosmic issue yet still another way,' says the often arid academic from his ivory tower. 'History is not so much a matter of events as it is a matter of abstract ideas, to which the idealistic Plato says amen and the mechanistic Aristotle shrugs off for being no more than a speculative abstraction. Between them both and their supporters (science versus the humanities) more often than not develops an intellectual battle, if not a physical fight, against one's own colleagues for possession of these selfsame ideas.'

Well now, isn't this what so often happens when one wants (by way of ensuring peace for our own time — and to hell with others) for us to revert to continuous narrative from fiercely interactive conversation? The objective (to mitigate conflict) we believe is all for the best by way of suppressing controversy and enforcing neutrality — and yet live long enough to find out that all this sort of intellectual suppression does, is to provoke open, and often bloody revolution!

This fierce ivory-towered or pulpit battle (or underground attempt at managerial overthrow) at best makes history more a matter of personal aggrandisement (whether of events or of ideas) than of ongoing cosmic communication; and this even with successful scholarship to have no more outcome than the career objective of individual gratification. Nevertheless, the whole concept of history (however insightful it may be in itself) is consistently downplayed by its own human makers (in order to keep all competitors off established claims to their own innermost ideas) and so on the outside to be a dry, dusty, and mechanistic matter of record—that of no more than keeping a tally (not even an accounting record of profit and loss) but of what is made out to be no more than a tally of settled past events.

'So then that's history, is it not?' say most of those ardent, and top-spot students who have listened to some arid and ivory-towered academic yet still left to themselves (without the slightest notion of having lived through their own birthright) without understanding one word of it (except perhaps the likelihood of the best possible reference to get a job—who says patronage is dead) and if not aiming for the most public acclaim by which to get the coveted peace-price (sorry, peace-prize) at any price!'

No, it's not like that at all, since history speaks almost all the time, and when listened to with a cautiously discerning ear by humans, those discerning ears are as likely to hear God speak through history, either directly or else indirectly, through the signs of the fast-changing times. History is made as much (and more so) by those who respond to events, as it can be made the other bully boy sort of way by those who—like Tamerlane, Genghis Khan, and Napoleon or like Vladimir Lenin, Josef Stalin, and Adolf Hitler—think themselves to be in full control of world events. No, quite frankly, it's the other way around insofar as these world events are in control of all such bully boy people. First, learn to bite the bullet before you're made to bite the dust.

Of course, thanks to all these bully boys, that's all human history—the fallen correlative of human destiny—turned upside down and arse-for-elbow, as more than one truly prophetic historian (take your pick of Carlyle, Tolstoy, Spengler, Korzybski, et al.) have pointed out. The true life force of history (whether past, present, or prophetic future) and however much maligned for turning human destiny upside down) lies not in the so-called events but in the communicative responses made to those events. The lesson to be learnt from that, since the tongue is but a little member that boasts of many things, is always to bite the historical bullet before firing off your open mouth in prophecy.

You don't believe me? Hey, then let's look back (this here paragraph's a flashback to an earlier paragraph) to some of the responses already made to the world's most fetid slums, to the world's most unrighteous wars, and to the anarchic ousting of one culture or system of government or of religious faith by another. So then flick back a few pages (if you can't yet flashback on your computer) to the three examples already given when so much of urbanised Britain (as well as of urbanised Russia) was nothing but fetid slums, when the British were fighting the Boer for the sovereignty (amongst other things) of a future South Africa, and when the liberation of the Russian serfs, the resulting famines, the ensuing revolutions, and the assassination of Russian royalty brought pogroms against the peasants (although squeezing the last buck out of the kulaks beforehand to be sure) and the overthrow of Adam Smith's (still tepid) capitalism in favour of Karl Marx's (more than ever rabid) communism.

Consider then the responsive counsel given at that time of revolution to the slums of Britain, which came through William Smith's Boys' Brigade, the same responsive counsel brought to international youth through Baden-Powell's *Scouting for Boys*, and even to Comrade Lenin's counterfeit organisation of Soviet Young Pioneers as a means of caring for youth in the Soviet Union. By such responses (to which all through world history, many more could be enjoined), the offensive as well as defensive positions for the ensuing warfare are always clear and incontrovertible.

As also for any military operation, the primary exhortation to the troops (as cribbed by Comrade Lenin from Lord Baden-Powell) is always that of *vsegda gotov*—the need to be prepared. So then in looking far forward now than this homiletic report, be prepared for a bigger cosmic bang (if indeed, the first time round, it did take any physicist's proverbial big bang to create this by now dying world). Still, no offence is intended by our saying so, since big bangs are so beloved by both nuclear physicists and most small boys.

Likewise, don't be caught with your feet up (like former President Nixon when he has had to explain the Watergate scandal) or with your pants down (like former President Reagan when he has to explain the Contra scandal) as may well come about after the last and final trump sounds (no reference to any later president intended here). If you do, then for you being no more than merely lukewarm to the signs of these rapidly deteriorating times, the end of this already groaning world will be less of the big bang required from you (to help prime the recreative process) than the dismal whimper that results from your being hit by the recreative recoil. Hey, if you don't go with this flow, then you'll have to wait until you hear what you hear in the next part of the already promised pH factor.

* * *

All Things Still under the Sun
Part VIII

Every Traveller's Now Terminal Checklist
Ten beggars will quite willingly share the same single
blanket, but no two world leaders would ever deign
to share the same room, to share the same travelling
coach, and far less would they ever think of sharing
the same country.

Zahir-ud-Din Muhammad Babur, *The Memoirs
of Babur* (paraphrased angelic translation)

So too, when you know more about us angels (as you will do by
reading to the end of this report), you will have learnt that (for the
sake of maintaining our everyday level of joy) we are endowed with
an unparalleled sense of humour—the aforesaid pH factor. Believe it
or not, but this hire-wire, yet hard-wired sense of humour (startlingly
unexpected to the earthbound) is the only means (by way of laughter
through tears) of making this geriatric old world go round, round,
and still go further round (which mathematicians for centuries have
referred to as being their task and not our task—as might otherwise
be left to wordsmiths—of miraculously squaring the circle).

Nevertheless, for both mathematically and spiritually squaring
the circle (together with other near miracles) see mathematician Anne
(Annie) Hamilton's series of truly inspired poetry books, especially
those entitled *The Listening Land, The Singing Silence,* and *The
Winging Word.* [Weather warning: This prophetic task of squaring
the circle between prose and poetry is not anywhere as miraculous
as it mathematically sounds since (aside from the calling to engage in
the endeavour) it otherwise requires only the exercise of that angelic
sense of servant humour, which is so often increasingly required
by those who care for those who are driven near-demented by the
vicissitudes of this world. On this score, remember that all true
miracles (as pointed out by both Jesus Christ and Annie Hamilton)

are done for a heavenly purpose, and none (unless falsely conjured up for earthly power) are done solely for their own sake.]

If already suffering from informational overload (as you now claim) and you still can't get your head round either the Boys' Brigade or *Scouting for Boys* (far less Lenin's atheistic but now disbanded Young Pioneers), then you can either sign off here or else (for the sake of your own lost heritage) seek the help of General Booth's still hard-fighting Salvation Army.

Attitudinal Standpoint 7—Relating to Open-Textured Communication: Without revelatory flashback, although we could go back to the beginning again, as we've so often been allowed didactically to do (*did*, or in the didactic plural *diddums*), nevertheless, let's try revelatory fast forward. In the beginning (Genesis 1:1), as required for any scientific report, comes the abstract (John 1:1), which some of you, being non-scientists and so thus amongst the more literary-minded of experienced readers, may avoid for being as big a poetical void as can often be found in any phishing scam (or publishing blurb).

No, no, no, surely not, because there's an attitudinal point to publishing blurbs (apart from the counterpoint of phishing scams)! But be serious, because it was out of such a void that ex nihilo (out of absolutely nothing), this once perfectly precious and wholly wonderful world was first created. [Editor's note: Don't quibble; we're all scientists here, both writers and readers, both angels and humans. And this even for some of us scientific deadheads not knowing that we were once created to be scientists at heart and not just for being so self-defined in only one's own mind.]

So then we shall follow this (alternatively legal) due process of scientific reporting (prophetically fast forward instead of only (as before by means of historic flashback) for the purposes of completing this largely military operation. And we shall do so (whatever the odds) as commissioned (even although often arguing reductio ad absurdum) as authorised by the Supreme Command. [Exegesis 1: No academic apologies required here, despite reductio ad absurdum being in Latin, since arguing from the assumed truth of any proposition to prove its absurdity is the most common yet still valid way of disproving the assumed truth of that proposition.]

For all you readers being thus fully prepared, we can then rely on your being able to distinguish the whole point of reducing to absurdity all but our most serious of non-reducible arguments. Nevertheless, as a concession to those less curiously colloidal human readers of today, many of whom (even if remaining grammatical) wouldn't read a preface any more than they would consult an instruction manual, what would otherwise inordinately lengthen this abstract has not been shortened but instead both strategically abstracted and differentially diffused. [Exegesis 2: Scientists may argue over its resultingly colloidal form, but all life, as we know it to have been created, is not merely colloidal (by chance) but instead (for being very much more than merely colloidal) infused with purpose.]

Abstracted and diffused as the various portions of this abstract now then appear to introduce all twelve books of this report (so then twelve books for the price of one), these various portions are wedged interstitially (as seriously substantive matters are so often prophetically secreted for enquiring minds alone) within the already decaying formalities of the human communicative process. The result (as lawyers describe all those loopholes by which they make their money in the law) is a non-legal form of open-textured communication—in this case, a theological form as open-textured, for having both heavenly loopholes (to and from earth) and demonic funk-holes (to and from hell) as open-textured as is space itself. [Exegesis 3: All colloidal creatures, especially those with souls, are created to be curious creatures, but this does not make their creator responsible for the results of their freely chosen investigations.]

Even if, as a curious reader, you have never been aware of this world's increasing decay (since at the same rate as the speed of light slows down, not only do days, years, decades, centuries, and even millennia shorten through the speeding up of time but also the humanly communicative elements of law, logic, and language break down under the resulting stress), so too, this report will make you aware of this increasingly distressed world. This will be done not only directly (which would depress you to death by way of informational overload) but rather in a cautiously chosen yet reciprocal fashion, by introducing you to the blinding light of revelation.

Thus, be prepared (as said before) for unexpected consequences, remembering always of the historic past that future consequences always have past causes. In this age of denial and disclaimer, not even the angels can accept responsibility for all the midlife crises and breakdowns (at individual, national, international, transnational, supranational, and global levels) that result from mankind's unpreparedness to accept the future consequences of its own past thoughts and actions. So bully for you, but don't pass the buck back to your creator (even although as creator he's been reduced now to lower case)!

Consequently, wedged tightly (as would be any adverb these days) between the different parts of this report (as being done right now, both historically as well as prophetically for these first few books) will be diffused (since diffused light has far different properties than concentrated light) the appropriate portions of what otherwise would remain unread today for being a lengthy abstract, prophetic preface, fulsome foreword, or unread instruction manual on as indifferently-understood ancient affairs as are indifferently-understood current affairs. [Exegesis 4: What 'otherwise would remain unread' thus means, in the context of affording any such abstract or manual an obviously human reason for remaining unread, then a reasonable recognition of this situation arising out of the highly stressed state of this fast-declining world in which people cannot bear to be told where they are heading. Oh, and as for an exegesis (which term, unless for being a theologian, you might never have encountered before), then if you still must know of its meaning (without any enforced need to be a theologian), an *exegesis* is merely a comment accompanying any text by way of excuse or explanation. Every aforesaid excuse or explanation nevertheless remains merely a secondary source and so is not to be substituted (as secondary sources so often are mistakenly substituted) for the primary source of the original (and thus more authentic) text in question.] Okay?

Nonetheless, as for any preface, foreword, or instruction manual, there are no shortcuts to the reading of this abstract (however much diffused throughout the primary text), unless unavoidably dead-ending all further attempts to grapple with the significance of that primary and all-important text (to which all else, but the abstract is no more than theological commentary on the primary source). [Exegesis 5: So as for any biblical commentary, scientific research, or literary classic, don't hang your hat on any exegesis or commentary, scientific abstract, or legal headnote; but as with Darwin's *On the Origin of Species* (a sci-fi fantasy provoked by *The Voyage of the Beagle*) or the book of Genesis (as a prelude to Leviticus) by Moses or the *Magna Carta* (devised in 1215 by the emerging Anglican Church to keep secular government on the rails), then always go, at least searching for the primary source.]

Attitudinal Standpoint 8—Relating to Multiplied Abstraction:
So again for starters and/or restarters (referring back to Genesis 1:1 as the proclamatory text and to John 1:1 again as the continuingly prophetic context), how are you now disposed towards our last exercise on abstraction? Yes, we know, those of you readers who mistake heaven for being only one huge hole of abstraction are none too keen to face up to abstractions. Instead, you go for matter, molecules, atoms (once impossibly divisible parts) before … no, no, no, we're not dealing with infinity here. [Exegesis 6: There's abstraction in everything, and unless you use the thinking grey matter—typified by the wrinkled whorls that (within their protective integument) cover the predominantly unthinking white matter of your brain—then your entire mind will remain blank (even when reading this report) and so be reduced pathologically to a grievous coma (not comma) of absolute abstraction. No, what we mean by *abstraction* here is 'the optimum height of abstraction', but we've taken this opportunity to introduce yet another exegetical explanation so that the wrinkled grey matter of your brain won't be unnecessarily whorled to hit the low ceiling of radical thought whenever you encounter yet another exegesis.]

So now we've got this far, it's time (which is still moving faster and yet faster) to get personal. After all, whether in playing Bach's baroque or in teaching Mendel's genetics or introducing the Bible ('Oh no,' you say, 'not the Bible again!'), it's always the personal touch that counts, because that's the way we're made, whether by the three persons of the Trinity or for us writers being similarly triad-angels (if not teamsters) or for you, still following readers, being humans (although dismissed by you know whom in hell as yuk!). Nevertheless, we're still all persons and so neither machines nor aliens nor clones nor demons can separate us from the love of God.

So likewise, the question (person to person) is this, do you shun abstract thought in favour of accumulating data-driven particulars, or do you embrace the more sweeping strokes of any artist or wordsmith by which to portray and communicate the far bigger cosmic picture? For example, many people are ill-disposed towards the concept of heaven for being the ultimate absurdity and the silliest form of abstraction there could be, but only as a result of their mistakenly thinking heaven to be pie in the sky. No, heaven to the hungry is soup on the stove, stew in the slow cooker, and pie in the oven.

Now that's not scientific (to think of heaven being pie in the sky), so let's be scientific, both in our thought and talk (T&T, although sometimes known as D for dialectic) whilst we are together investigating the most serious side of this deeply scientific question. Okay (or not, please say so)!

Well, admittedly for any such serious investigation of what it takes to be scientific, your answer depends on whether you can recognise a lighthearted academic spoof (for which spoof's seriously scientific side consult Sokal's hoax) on the allegorical subject of academic pretence (already declaimed for scholarship at large by Swift's *The Battle of the Books* and for people in particular by the same author's *Gulliver's Travels*). Contra, you have to be able to recognise that Defoe's *Robinson Crusoe* (instead of being just a young person's adventure story) was instead a scientific treatise on the economics of time (for which, see Fuller's *The Morality of Law*).

Such strongly secular (although faithfully scientific) folks as we were last talking about before diverting ourselves with great works of literature (a popular diversion of retired scholars) are hardly persons but maybe folk persons, although also amongst them are many great minds (GM). Nevertheless, they cannot accommodate their static thinking (ST) to get their heads round the multidimensional means (MDM) by which heaven, as substantiated by so many nitty-gritty particulars (NGP), has already come to earth. Thus, the purpose of this present abstract (PA[1]) is to employ the catalytic function (CF) designed by the Supreme Command to bring static minds round to the exercise of their own rightfully more open and dynamic human function. [Exegesis 7: CF (catalytic function) = T&T (thought and talk, a.k.a. D for dialectic.]

In other words, the Supreme Command needs not only you but also as many other great minds (GMs) as it can get. Nevertheless, as scientists of the supernatural, don't get taken in, either by algorithms (such as $E = mc^2$) or by acronyms (such as GMs or PMs or MDMs). Instead, stay always totally colloidal. Quite frankly (and we, the authorial WE), as your guardian angels (GM), we should be the *one* at least first in line to know that it's only the truly alive (TA) and not the patently dead (PD) that get to heaven. So however abstract may be our abstract (AA), don't turn off (TO), but stay colloidal (SC).

Not only is the literary form of the scientific abstract instituted by the operational need for both communicative exactitude and scientific creativity but it is also hallowed by the inherent ability of the abstract to encompass past, present, and future dimensions. Of course, past, present, and future temporal dimensions are no more than a few of the many more heavenly dimensions. To borrow from a grammatical rather than a temporal model by way of illustrating a fuller range of humanly perceived dimensions (expressed as much, although differentially, by way of Slavonic aspects as Germanic tenses), there are, at least as denoted figuratively in English grammar, more than twelve temporal dimensions.

These twelve (we may consider them as if they were the twelve apostles) are past imperfective, past perfective, past continuous, and past perfective continuous, just as there are present imperfective, present perfective, present continuous, and present perfective continuous, no less than there are also future imperfective, future perfective, future continuous, and future perfective continuous tenses (which indicate different temporal dimensions for human action). Of course, some languages will have more, and others less, and each language usually introduces its own subtle nuances (as by way of Slavonic aspects) in expressing its own differentially employed temporal dimensions.

Nevertheless, in heaven, there's a continuity of time (the space-time continuum, or STC, not to be mistaken for the concept of eternity) which has escaped all human notice until recently on earth. This temporal continuity (detached and disconnected on earth) is that of the eternal present. What this eternal present means, so far as anything can be seen or said of it on earth, is that past history, present prophecy, and future fulfilment are merged into one and the same point of singularity at which they integrate to constitute many more than the accustomed five dimensions (nine, or maybe twelve, would be by now a good guess) experienced on earth.

Thus, as seen from heaven's eternal now, both the past flood and yet even the future fire of the spirit, as prophesised for the final days of this earth, presage even the beginning of creation. Thus, you could also say (as best that Leading-Agent Einstein could explain) that past, present, and future are relative (but that's very far from the heavenly truth, although as near to the earthly truth as we are as yet authorised to tell it). [Exegesis 8: Relax! Never fear! No further exegesis at this point of singularity would explain either the eternal present (ET) or its accompanying correlative of the future interminable (FI).]

By way of extending the accustomed past, present, and future to at least nine further tenses, we are not only multiplying the humanly perceptive number of temporal dimensions but we are also rapidly moving along the earthly communicative plane from generality to specificity (i.e. from abstraction to particularity). In doing so, we are also running parallel in a different plane between the macroscopic and the microscopic (i.e. nominally between maximum and minimum or behaviourally between maximising and minimising or else between the very big and the very small—and so ultimately as the ancient Greeks expressed the ultimate ratio, between the one and the many.

Look at the problem of communicative expression this way: since every well-formed abstract (ABA) transcends time by telescoping the *topos* (or topic) of its scientific research into the smallest of communicative spaces (SCS), then there is no alternative but to take the reader on time travel. The coordinates for both liftoff and subsequent re-entry of this ongoing abstract are thus dynamically determined (both spatially and temporally) by their need to introduce different parts (constituting the forewords of books 1–12) of this report.

The least serious of intellectual readers (IR, but also including IT) may take offence to this level of abstraction to which they are called both to commute and to commit (C&C). That is one reason why the least serious of readers of this report, without any appreciation of their own present life being an abstract for the fulfilment of their future life, are most usually restricted to the preschool level of learning which requires only their obedience to legal command.

No matter how unhappy this restricted situation (RS) may appear to such preschoolers, their level of learnt abstraction (LA) is as yet insufficient for their being commissioned for time travel (TT) as hallowed by the Supreme Command. And until themselves committed to time travel (for which lack of learning, they usually plead their own very pedestrian lack of toddling time), they cannot commit themselves to space travel. Stuck in this preschool arena of legal command, they fail to see that their own personal need for their own higher education in life (particularly in the life of the spirit) is also a cosmic issue. Yet this is only one of very many alternative ways of seeing the already mentioned world problematique.

Attitudinal Standpoint 9—Obedience versus Commitment: Our presently submitted scientific abstract (according to the traditional formula for storytelling) thus begins with an overall account of past and present generalities. It preps an already stretched but not overly time-bound canvas, outlines the intended composition (both historic and prophetic) of our ongoing research, clarifies the future focus of our travel (from legal compulsion to personal commitment), sets the present tone (literary rather than legal), and otherwise engages the scientific reader with a greater exactitude (no more humanistic than scientific) of ongoing vision. As for humans being only a little lower than the angels, then the level of abstraction accordingly required of human readers will be no more spiritual than that of coming to terms with the angelic.

Yet as said before, this is a stout military operation and not just an arid academic operation. At the heart of this equally historic and prophetic (as well as colloquially colloidal) matter is the readiness of every human reader for space-age travel, as distinct from just his or her everyday entertainment by way of space-age fiction.

Nevertheless, this distinction between space-age travel and space-age fiction is not so definitive (for being so pre-eminently colloidal) as once first thought. [Exegesis 9: The reason for this exercise in ubiquity, much to the chagrin of imaginative metaphysicians and biochemists, is that ubiquitous colloids are no longer thought of as being independent states of matter. 'Och aye, it's aye change, forbye,' as the Scottish biochemists now more independently say in the UK when north of their own Bonnie Scots Border—the English never before having had to recognise that selfsame border for being any bother to their own border far less than to anyone else's border.]

'Sae, it's aye change!' (Or 'plus ça change', as they'd say at most French borders.) Nevertheless, who would have once thought that planes would fly any more than that pigs could fly (and now even both pigs and people can fly thanks to their flying in the planes that fly)! Thence, what are the odds (say, 5000:1) for flying angels being a good deal more verifiable than most Xmas advertising if it's well established that pigs, people, as well as planes can fly nowadays? 'An' pit that in yer pipe, an' smoke it,' as they still say north o' the border i' Bonnie Scotland, whaur as like as no' they still say 'nooadays' fur 'nowadays'!

On the other hand, the faith of many resolutely firm believers has plummeted as if to outlaw flying angels (presumably under the rules of civil aviation) in the face of mere humans now being able to book seats for space-age travel. The trouble is that so many of these lapsed believers have had their feet (and their minds) so firmly pegged into the terra-so-called-firma (as distinct from their airy-fairy notion of heaven) that they don't find it possible to believe in either angels or heaven any more because they've been told that it has been only one very short step for mankind to lift off his feet to the moon. [Exegesis 10: Pray earnestly for the fast return of such lapsed believers to the sheepfold in Bethlehem, since their spiritual minds have calcified instead of remaining colloquially colloidal.]

To do no more than obey commands (even for a lifetime) is a relatively passive pursuit. So also in these increasingly telescoped end times, unthinking obedience is just as risky (relatively speaking in terms of $E = mc^2$), by way of bringing any merely lukewarm reader under and subject to a Counterfeit Command. On the other hand, learning to exercise one's personal commitment to the Supreme Command effects a transformation of mind, heart, body, and soul into the active arena of a space-age cosmos from which humans are no longer debarred.

Indeed, it is into this space-age cosmos (effected by a New Testament of personal commitment) that humans are increasingly called to commit themselves personally to the Supreme Command. Henceforth, all passive and unthinking obedience to the Supreme Command will be of no more worth than passive and unthinking obedience to the Counterfeit Command. By this New Testament of personal commitment to the Supreme Command, the pin (and not the proverbial penny as counted and quoted by the Counterfeit Command) has dropped (hopefully into our now open minds) that the reading of this report will require a seriously thoughtful as well as a seriously practical and, of course, also a seriously spiritual response.

By this time as well as by your own effort, dearest readers, you should be fully prepared (for what is no longer the entirely unexpected) by way of what follows for being a very brief history of heaven. It's all a battle still for every true and even every fully prepared believer, so be fully armed for fighting in the very front line.

Make sure too, as would any accomplished scout or spy, of being on the right side, which is that of the Supreme Command. In these latter days, there are many counterfeiters—false priests, false prophets, false preachers, false teachers, and even false angels—so watch your every step. For 'the times they are [still all] a-changin', just as Leading-Agent Bob Dylan once so prophetically sang (of the world problematique as far back as 1964). [Exegesis 11: The world problematique (as so coined by the Club of Rome) still stands (unchanging in its generality) for all the remaining woes of the world.]

Get to know your enemy—particularly for what great evil your enemy perpetrates as the Counterfeit Command. Every foreword (except for strategic retreat) should lead forward, but stay humble, and just remember that sometimes you also have to go backward (as far back as even first beginnings) just to move on.

If in serious doubt as to the direction of your travel, apply for leave, go on a retreat, take counsel from your commanding officer, even take a vacation from your acknowledged vocation; but otherwise, at least stay standing. The front line of the Supreme Command never wavers, and just as often, instead of travelling, your vocation may simply be to stand still. All twelve books of this report are travel books, but they, like the sixty-six books by forty leading agents who wrote the Bible, did almost all their own travelling (and all on your account). So if it's your vocation to hold the front line, hold firm, wait on the Lord, and prepare for the ensuing battle. Nevertheless, until then, hold your fire, both lads and lasses, hold your fire! There's still a great deal of the history of heaven (especially in the use of heavy artillery) that you have to learn to understand!

* * *

BOOK TWO

A Very Brief History of Heaven Presaging Both Past Flood and Future Fire

> On the Seafront
> It was said that a new person had appeared on the seafront: a lady with a little dog … 'If she is here without a husband or friends, it wouldn't be amiss to make her acquaintance,' Gurov reflected … He was under forty, but he had a daughter already twelve years old and two sons at school …
>
> Anton Chekhov, *The Lady with the Dog*

Intro 1—Neil: Why the seafront? Which freeboard (eastern or western) will it be? Will we look to port or starboard or simply out to sea? There is a sea of faith these days which purports to transcend both national and international boundaries, whereby (so-called) freedom of religion (as often at the expense of each individual soul) aspires to supranational significance.

Will the giving of supranational significance to this already stormy sea of faith work, or will it ultimately provoke a breakdown of cosmic communication at every storm-level. Everyone, apart from the homeless and the jobless (but not the thoughtless) now flies from domestic through international, transnational, and so then back up to supranational levels. They do so just as they now drive, instead of walking, to the nearest corner dairy. So far so good (as the fast-and-faster falling steeplejack reported on passing what by then would leave no more than four further floors of wide-open, and yet fully communicative windows. Head-on, by then, however, loomed what could only remain of the same conflictive, but also ultimately conclusive communication.

The Golden Crescent, situated between the Tigris and Euphrates Rivers, was once thought to be the cradle or solar centre of mankind's civilisation. Now that once Golden Crescent is given over to air strikes, and even the swiftly flowing Tigris can be clogged with bloated bodies.

It's only at the level of cosmic communication that there's something meaningful for everyone who has ears to hear and eyes to see that source of the truth, the way, and the life from which any hope emanates of true cosmic significance. The sea of faith seems endless, but look, there's a lighthouse, and here's an anchor. And out there on the sea, there's even a boat. We'll walk out to it across the water and surprise its passengers by our saying hello!

Meanwhile, hear now a question: what prophecy worth its salt leaves nothing to the recipient's imagination, leaves nothing to his interpretation? The aforesaid sea of faith can thus seem endless, especially to those when all at sea. So why the seafront, if not somewhere on land, yet open to the sea of faith, on which perhaps to do no more than to walk one's dog? Well, if any dog that follows its master can walk on water, then so can any human. The question is, as always, who is the master?

Intro 2—Kirsty: To one person, the privilege of walking out her dog may be the highest heaven. To another person—lonely, sad, and ill-matched in marriage (as was Chekhov's *The Lady with the Dog*)— the chore of walking out her dog may take that lady into the depths of hell. It is not always clear to humans which is heaven and which is hell. There's often no saying by which to resolve these heartfelt issues, but as by Chekhov, it is by telling a story. Even then, however, there are those people who insist on facts, facts, and only the facts but for themselves won't even read a story, far less try to tell a story, or even learn how to tell a story. If such people have children, then like Hansel and Gretel, these children must learn to cope with being held captive in a cage.

The distinction between heaven and hell, especially for those who are in default of storytelling, even if only by way of expressing fine distinctions between right and wrong, good and bad, fair and unfair, is not only very hard to define (but completely impossible for mere humans by themselves to define and so then refine). And people of whatever age who are in default of the requisite means of figurative expression by which to conjecture up their own more hopeful stories than their present lives admit of, or are unaware of, by way of their insistence on the fullest possible plenitude of facts, only more facts, and still only more facts, are also very hard to redefine.

Intro 3—Sasha: This is not a journalistic justification for storytelling, but it could be. For some relatively straightforward issues, you need the facts, but for many other and more subtle issues of life, you need to listen most acutely to the stories and to tell your own stories by way of personal testimony to these subtle issues. This is certainly so when such stories need to be told to those who would not otherwise listen to the facts as well as to yet still others who would not otherwise listen to the stories. You must know, as well as every angel knows, that most humans (both very young and very old, as well as every middle-aged for still being in between) are in the most mortal danger if they do not have a story to tell by reason of which they can relate to themselves and by which they can learn to relate to other people's stories.

In default of either external inspiration or internal imagination, such people are in danger either (1) of drawing up hard and fast rules (which may be legal, moral, religious, scientific, or social) by which the subtle differences between heaven and hell pass unnoticed under their spiritual radar or else (2) fall victim to whatever scam story, hoodwink, or counterfeit tale from hell that may be told to them. Some souls are so often fast asleep, because so often as children, they have been simply sent to bed (perhaps even without a hug or a kiss or without supper) and so also made to go to sleep. Next morning, their little bodies may wake up, yet their little souls remain fast asleep. Sometimes, for all the rest of their lives, their impoverished little souls remain fast asleep.

Other little minds, without a story to comfort their daytime rigours, remain too much wide awake. Without a story either told or read to them, their unwrapped souls remain at the mercy of their wakeful minds, so that by mid-morning, then both soul and mind reverse their wakeful and sleeping roles so that for the rest of the day, until perhaps nightfall, these souls too are fast asleep.

Intro 4—Tracey: The sleeping spirit, at home or in school, at work or in play, is either deeply dulled or easily distracted. Where winters are long and summers are short or where one lives cluttered together in cities and not in small towns, villages, or open country, the sleeping or slumbering spirit can pass for years quite unnoticed. One can live through one's whole life thus fast asleep. Thankfully, I am now completely awakened — otherwise I could not discourse now on what it once felt as any grown-up human being to be still fast asleep.

In such a state of slumber or sleep, differences between right and wrong, fair or unfair, just or unjust, or even just good or bad, may pass unnoticed. That's life—or so we think, with a slumbering soul and even more so with one that's fast asleep. We have no motive or incentive to move our feelings, our thoughts, our wills, our minds, or our hearts to do things differently, although, for the lack of all motive or incentive to take action, much of what little output we have is distorted and distraught by fear.

Generally speaking, when we are caught up in this non-conjectural state of mind, specific alternatives pose decision problems. We are held captive by the fear of what might happen if we dared to action what vestige of hope remains in our lives to live, even just a dream. Our fear dispels that dream by predisposing us to live out our present nightmare. By that fear of what might happen, we are thus made vulnerable, for what we most fear will happen.

Intro 5—Luther: Don't you remember the story of what happens through self-indulging one's fear, as it can happen to even the most righteous man in all the great country of Uz? That story is told as a gambling boast between God and Satan for the soul of Job. What was the already existing means by which to provoke the allowable catastrophe on which the decisive outcome of the gamble between Satan and God would hinge? Don't you remember that what befell Job was, as he himself said, 'his own greatest fear having come to pass'?

On the other hand, any awakening of a deeply sleeping spirit (which some folks might say also befell Job) may be both rude and crude, as well as also highly demanding. There is no saying what life itself, by means of either heaven or hell, will then substitute for the lost years of any so long fast-sleeping soul. The breaking away of one household to another (as through marriage) is often the pivotal point for either awakening or downfall, and it may take years of marital confrontation and restoration to determine which is which. Redemption, by its very nature, is an uphill battle.

In all this, of course, I am not speaking of your human self or of my angelic self but rather voicing my own angelic opinions at an altogether abstract level of how sleeping souls can appear in general. Job's soul was fast asleep, even to his everyday, deepest, and ongoing fears. So then, as if awakened out of this earth's anaesthetic cover over all bedspread of sense-derived superficiality (but for the fact that you've been talking in your sleep again), then we say, as once, twice before, and now thrice again—awake, awake, awake!

In these latter days, there is nothing short of the eternal vigilance required to make and again to maintain the peace of one's own immortal soul. Look what it took to wake up the soul of Job! He had to come to terms with his greatest fear. It didn't matter how prosperous he was or how righteous he was. For the sake of all eternity, as typified by this heavenly wager, he was called to recognise his vulnerability and so, by strengthening himself in the Lord, to overcome his deepest and most personal fear.

Intro 6—Marcus: It's a hard road, a narrow way, and as often a dark tunnel through a bright fairground of counterfeit diversions. As with Job, one's false comforters can be all around. Waking up to reality can be the most gruesome experience for those who, by God's grace alone, have managed to survive through darkest fear. Meanwhile, make no mistake about this—the really bad guys in the story of Job are his false comforters!

As the most prosperous and righteous man in the whole land of Uz will tell you, Job was called to overcome his greatest fear. To do so, he was called into painful self-awareness. Such is the way since this awakening process—(1) to the apparently plain (but as often illegally concealed) truth, (2) to the true (but so often falsified) way, and (3) to the real (and yet so always genuine and never surreal) life—can only properly be done through the voice of the Supreme Command. So then don't dare turn over and go back to sleep. To be caught napping is bad enough, but to fall asleep when on fourth-dimensional guard duty in these dark and dismal times means that you may not be alive to wake up!

After all, it was the Supreme Command that gave you birth and brought you into space and time (even although today's only rapidly decreasing space-time). Then it was that your angel chauffeur sang to none but yourself what would become your very own (and no one else's) soul-song. Heard that song of others before, if not yet aware of your own? Oh yes, you have, for first having heard that of others, if not already yet of your own! You can still hear that soul-song of Bach, thanks to the lovingkindness of his wife, dear Anna Magdalena, who notated so many of her husband's compositions. Would Beethoven's romantic soul-song have ever sounded but for the inspiration given by his 'immortal beloved'? There were many women in the life of Victor Hugo, from his childhood sweetheart and wife, Adele Foucher, to his companion of fifty years, Juliette Drouet. Who is fit to judge either another's earthly prosperity or state of righteousness, far less the soul-song with which he or she expresses every subtle nuance of his or her life?

Intro 7—Callum-John: Hi there, don't suppose you ever expected to find me here, and perhaps neither did I myself. What would you say it takes to constitute a crowd of witnesses? I dare say that's a legal question, but then most legal questions begin more creatively as deistic or divine issues, then decline into theological issues and then further still, having lost all their procreative forcefulness, degenerate into legal issues—much in the same way as plutonium decays into lead. Well, whether as a matter of nuclear physics or not, a crowd of witnesses takes all sorts (as well as some may say non-sorts). And that's exactly why we have three syncretic or lookalike gospels (for being those of Brothers Matthew, Mark, and Luke) and one stand-alone (for being that of Brother John). I guess I identify most with John, for being myself also a stand-alone! As much as uniformity, so also diversity is a needful criterion for constituting any crowd of witnesses, and that goes on all fronts, whether from deistic or divine, through theological to legal, before being resurrected once more to the procreative forcefulness of the divine.There's more to physics than just Newtonian physics (and dear old dad never got much further than that in physics) just as Sir Isaac (Newton) stayed a layman 'for the sake of the church'.

Intro 8—Neil: So then right now, seek to rouse yourselves (like Moses, Elijah, Ezekiel, Isaiah, and so many other patriarchs and prophets)! Shake off the torpor of these very difficult times (as often the product of self-important individualism as of both ruthlessly and collectively imposed socialism). These are the very times in which human mindsets become filled to overflowing with successive catalogues of cataclysmic events.

There's WWI in the past, WWII still ongoing, and with WWIII already in the making. There's Korea in the past-present, Vietnam in the present-past, and both the Middle East and the Far East in the future-present. There's no help in sight unless from the Supreme Command breathing life into your war-weary and as often broken bones. 'Dem dry bones' are not yet dry enough (not by a long shot) to be returned to life, far less (we would hope) than to fire up yet another living hell.

There's amputated limbs and severed heads spread through Afghanistan, Kurdistan, Pakistan, Iraq, Iran, Syria, Ukraine, and into Europe. Prepare to break with the never-ending flow of this thoughtlessly unfeeling present. It masquerades most persuasively for being all eternity in hell, not heaven. As the Supreme Command, we're speaking here to both the angelic host as well as to all humanity. Sure, although that break with the present may not make much sense to those humans who stand so much overawed by all the heavenly host—including both those fallen angels as well as those still upright—the whole point of breaking with the present (as by undertaking some deeper study of the past) is to learn how to discriminate between ongoing good and evil.

Intro 9—Tristan-David: When we cease to wonder at the world, *then* bad things seem to happen. We grow morose, apathetic, and lack motivation. Maintaining the right level of wonderment (for mortals a case study in itself from earliest infancy to extreme elderliness) looks to be the master key by which to open and reopen each successive aspect of every earthling's fast-changing and ongoing life. 'Wellness is wonderment' is what we angels would tell you still searching humans. 'Wellness is wonderment!'

The first paradigm for wonderment in the developing child is simply the human voice. You've no idea how awesome that can sound to any child en ventre sa mère (whilst in the belly of its mother)! The next paradigm—and this throughout one's entire human life— is the fairy tale! Without developing any fairy-tale quality to life, there is no receptivity to inspiration, no inducement to aspiration, no encouragement to motivation.

Right through all of one's human life, fairy tales are the fundamental key to wellness. Why, the two best-known and bestselling English writers to survive soldiering in WWI and yet still retain most positivity in their literary work were J. R. R. Tolkien and C. S. Lewis. And as everyone knows, they still wrote the very best of fairy tales!

Of course, as you'd expect from fairyland, there are fairytales, fairy-tales, and yet even faerie and faery tales. Yet from the singular science fiction of heavenly astrophysics to the more mundane task of environmental engineering, it's still the fairy tales which are designed to engage our sense of wonder. To be sure, some fairy tales are for children, and others are for grown-ups. And it is not always clear which is which, since some children never seem to grow out of hearing fairy tales whilst many grown-ups (perhaps those who have been denied their childhood either (1) despise fairy tales altogether; or else (2) entrap themselves in fairy-tale situations to appease their earlier sense of deprivation. In these singular days of standardisation where one size fits all, we shall follow the Procrustian formula of reducing all pre-existent permutations derived from the fast-declining fairytale to the modernist fairy tail.

Intro 9 (con.) — Neil again: Chekhov's *The Lady with the Dog* (essentially an urban fairy tale) is definitely for grown-ups. You can teach maths and physics to most teenagers, but the substantive kernel or content of great literature means less than nothing to midlifers. Likewise, some fairy tales afford a reprieve from reality, whilst others confront and reveal a reality on behalf of those who could not front up to such reality for themselves.

Not every tale of any sleeping beauty has a prince—no, not even a frog prince by which to confer a happy ending. It's not easy, as every angel knows, to be a prince. There are a lot of counterfeit princes around. They do a lot of damage. But even for any true prince, the prospect of a sleeping beauty is less risky than being married off to anyone else wide awake enough to the prospect of inheriting a kingdom by means of marrying its prince.

In any case, not every woman needs a prince. Nevertheless, every sleeping beauty needs a prince—a real prince—to wake her up and bring her completely to life. That's not a task suited to everyone. On the other hand, every counterfeit prince makes for a dysfunctional family unless either brought to heel or, more preferably, for the counterfeit to be cleansed of all muck-metal, and so to be coined anew.

That's not the end of the matter, however, because all princes are born to be priests and kings—at the very least within their own families. And the same goes for any apparently successful family and even, as history shows time and time again—from Babylon to Britain—for any prosperous empire. Read once more, from possibly the earliest-told, first-written, and most thought-provoking scripture in the Bible, that of the book of Job. And as you read, then lay again your bets (with or without the same or different reasons than those you held for your previous readings) on the outcome of the boastful gamble between Satan and God for the soul of Job.

Intro 10—Callum-John again: There's another well-known story. It's open-ended, just like the tale first told of Job must have been open-ended when it first began and might, but for the persistence of Job, have been still left open-ended. For all that, you can't have an ending without a beginning, a closure without an opening, or even a creation without the risk of desecration. One way or the other, the only finite form of closure this world knows comes through God. At the moment, however, the alternative all-open ending is not the popular choice.

You should reread *The Lady with the Dog.* Reread it anew (and not just again) as you might think Anton Chekhov, its author, cared enough to write it. Nevertheless, what it means to you is more important than what it means to anyone else (including even the human author). It surely lies in this overall conjunction of mind, heart, body, and soul to hear the best possible story from whatever source.

The epitome of truth is to be found at the heart of every authentic fairy tale. That's wherein lies the fundamental freedom, through the evocation of inspiration, aspiration, and imagination, to make up your very own mind about its message. Likewise, there is a story, a narrative at least, if not also an embryonic fairy tale, in everything. Its welfare of wonderment stretches from fairy tale to myth, from myth to history, from history to science, and from science to law, to logic, to language, to morals, to theology, and from whatever then still remains of wonderment to God himself. It can survive through even death by our love of life for absolutely everything.

Learn to pick for yourself the best of all possible stories. You might care to call it a novel, a satire, a work of science, or of art or of music; but at its very heart, it all began with and still holds to being itself a fairy tale. For me, it's the fairy tale of physics (of both hardware and software) but for whatever is your fairy tale, as of my fairy tale in physics, don't doubt its life-purpose, even although space-time may change the way the same story is told. Before closing off on fairy tales, it might be helpful to consult both J. R. R. Tolkein and C. S. Lewis, who as the only romantic writers to survive the so-called 'great war to end all wars' were each so passionate about the concept of 'faerie' from which in turn sprang their fairy tales.

* * *

188

A Very Brief History of Heaven
Part I

On the Subject of Angels

Cradled in the arms of an angel who sings to the glory of God with unfeigned praise as he or she flies through the midnight sky is every young soul destined for this world of sorrow and tears; and the sound of this angelic song, remaining unique to each earthbound child, shall fill the soul of that child with a wonderful longing, which, resounding with life for as long as this newly destined soul remains youthful in spirit, shall never be replaced by the tedious songs of this world.

> Mikhail Lermontov, 'The Angel'
> (paraphrased translation into prose)

Since asking a question is one way of eliciting a response, we shall begin this very brief history of heaven (in itself a long haul) by asking you readers to answer a question. It's a nine-month-old yet still pregnant question on the status of the unborn child. Here is a deeply metaphysical issue whose continued perplexity poses for the entire human race a huge learning curve. It's not a rising curve, as it once was, but by now posing an almost straight decline on that much misunderstood topic of human procreation. Are you in for the long haul, or are you happy enough to accept (with a shrug of the shoulders) or happier still to scoff (with a great big grin on your face) whatever you either collectively fear or individually ignore of man's mortality?

The acknowledged human life span is around three score and ten years, but in our reminding you of that life span, are you still with us angels on the related status of the unborn child to this thereafter dormant life span? As angels commissioned to look after the souls of as yet unborn children, we don't think you adult humans quite measure up. Indeed, your concept of human procreation is so both undervalued and devalued (as it seems to us angels) that you couldn't possibly think to understand the concept of divine creation. Your conception of divine creation is being steadily undermined by your own preconception of procreation.

Procreation and creation are but two aspects of the same heavenly design. How can we angels help you humans to conceive of what for so many of you is inconceivable? Haven't you ever heard of the child being father of the man? So then too, what do you make of Lermontov's poem on the subject of angels? What do you think both of the unborn child and of the intimately related human life span to that unborn child? What you come up with after some considerably serious thought will have a great deal of input into what you think of Lermontov's poem on the subject of us angels.

Of course, what you make of angels in their transporting of souls will also depend on what you make of souls being transported by angels. Yet on the subject of souls, many humans have not the slightest notion of souls at all, unless and until for having first met up with an angel, which, of course, may be the angel who brought your soul to earth. Perhaps the chief purpose of this entire book (twelve hits for the price of one) is to introduce you to your soul.

Don't throw away this opportunity, since souls can wither away and die unless properly cared for, and they can't be properly cared for, either directly or indirectly, unless for their being nourished by that precious body which from before birth has been appointed to serve as the temple to that spiritual soul. It's true that some people get rather soulish over caring for their souls, either selfishly for their own soul or parentally for the souls of their children, but that's because they don't have the right relationship with their own guardian angel whose first priority is to look out for the welfare of their soul.

Consider closeness as a measure of intimacy. Chances are these days—we put the Western ratio at one in twelve (some say one in twenty-four)—for any human being able to get any closer relationship than 500 metres to their soul, far less than to acknowledge the partnership which they have with their own guardian angel (at, say, no less than 5,000 metres). Of course, as you can guess from the measure of choice these days—whether in metres, pascals, or megabytes—the measure is always one of physicality. Accordingly, the above formula for spiritual intimacy is not going to make much sense to anyone at all. And so then, as an alternative measure consider the after-effects of this growing distance between angelic spirit and human spirit— no less than this is deletariously affected by the increasing rate of divorce of the human body from the human soul. Without spiritual intimacy, the human soul, which ought to have remained youthful in spirit by remaining true to the angelic song with which that young soul was first brought into this world instead falls victim to the tedious songs of this world.

Of course, soul-relationships take a great deal of careful nurturing—and angelic relationships with humans even more so. [Nevertheless, a brief word of whispered warning here: don't become so self-centred (a common affliction of celebrities both angelic and human) as to be tempted to revere and then worship your own soul! Why, some folk seem to do so well on that self-worship while on earth that they never get to heaven!]

Of course, it took more than a whole heavenly host of singing angels to bring Christ, the long-prophesised Messiah, into this sinful world. There was Mary, his blessed mother, for example, as well as John the Baptist (who lost his head to Herod over the outcome) for another. Most mortals wouldn't now give a fig (whether ripe or unripe) for that vision of any saviour-redeemer—save (no pun intended) commercially at Christmas. Meanwhile, both up-close and far away, the whole wide world is being given over to scenes of the utmost terror. Still, there's nothing new under the sun, as they say, for didn't the same thing once happen with the massacre of the innocents just after the birth of baby Jesus?

Yet each day and every day, that angelic singing still goes on, sometimes a straight lyric by a single unaccompanied voice and at other times by a huge contrapuntal chorus of symphonic sound. That symphonic soul-music will never die, although for anyone lacking that youthfulness of spirit by which to recognise how exactly now is the state of his or her own soul, that person may gradually cease, even at Christmastide, to hear the sound of those same angelic voices. People think only of how to buy their way into Christmas these days, and there's hardly one of them any longer tempted to put a penny down on getting into heaven.

So then how well is your soul, dear reader? Let the text of that angelic question be to the individual as if it were strike a bass, tenor, contralto, alto, or soprano note on heaven's audio-spiritual thermometer. Moreover, let the context of the whole wide world, as questioned by this report on the state of the individual soul, be equal to evoking a global resonance from heaven's audio-spiritual barometer. Listen well, will you, since faith comes from hearing, and you can't very well be hearing without listening.

Each question of the soul, asked and answered both individually and collectively, first temperamentally of the personal reader then read barometrically of the whole wide world, is so momentous at this very moment of space-time that it cannot be more than very roughly approximated to what should already be prophetically known of the expected outcome. Nevertheless, the final outcome—as we know it to be—is already assured.

After all, it is only by making one's own personal response (which will determine the entire course of one's life thereafter) that we angels can be sure of your having heard the question. Of course, we presume that even whilst en ventre sa mère (within the womb), you are listening.

It won't be a rhetorical question (so beloved by our friends the preachers from their pulpits) as if we street angels alone know the answer (in which case, that would be a sermon), so all of you, dear readers, ought to be both wide awake and listening (since this is no sermon). Because in order to answer the question as to what you make of your own soul, and so to make an individually authentic response, only each of you readers will know what you each like, and so we have chosen to ask of each of you a purely personal question.

For being a purely personal question with a purely personal answer, this makes every answer you give to be itself a fail-safe answer. But you don't even need to give that answer to us. For even conversing with your very own guardian angel, it's enough for him or her that you discuss it with your soul. You do talk to your soul now, don't you?

You do, don't you, talk to your soul—whatever the problems that may reveal; because most males have feminine souls, just as most females have masculine souls; but often the troubles start when males

192

mistake their souls for being more masculine than feminine (the problem of macho-mateship); and so too, when females mistake their souls to be correlatively more feminine then masculine (presumably the lesser of these two mixed-macho problems for not being yet known by name to psychoanalytic jurisprudence) then strange things begin to happen. Now we all know the problems of macho-males in their being unable (through an excess of macho-mateship) to relate adequately as they should to women; but the correlative problem of virago-mateship (resulting from women over-compensating for the misdeeds of macho-males) is still very much overdue (although still outlawed by most viragos) for psychoanalytic study.

Likewise, to help you know where we angels stand, then from time to time, we'll explain ourselves if not directly to your soul, then sometimes by some such exegetical remark that follows or by an excursus in our relating to your soul what seems to us to be a missed point of earthly contact between us. [Exegesis 1: We remind you again (as once before) that all interactive communications between heaven and earth are being monitored for the purposes of teaching, preaching, and training services. Well, 'what about the intellectual property in our remarks', you ask? Well, as with all so-called original ideas, the intellectual property remains as always vested in heaven (and this, despite every counterclaim processed through hell from earth) since nothing ever really new comes to earth, no matter how much abused it may be there, except originally from heaven.]

We think yours is a fair enough response (for being a humanly indicative response), but the purely personal question goes deeper, as it does in the spiritual when asked in the context of Lermontov's world-famous poem 'The Angel'. For being every bit supra (that pun from 'above' intended), then that is so, since the inspiration for 'The Angel' most obviously comes down from above in heaven. It is so uncontrived that none but some demon from hell would dare to dispute its authenticity (whether only as a work of art or of deeper metaphysics).

Whether you like the concept of the human soul or not and whether you can identify yourself with what you've just read about your already much-travelled soul (although expressed here only in English rather than also in the Arabic, Persian, Hindi, or any other translation of the holy Russian Orthodox original), it still remains that anything other than by way of being your very own response is completely beside the point. It's a corollary of their allotted freedom that from time to time, humans will choose to take the wrong way; but all we'll do as angels is to help you rediscover the right way.

We angels are quite at ease with that, however much it makes our task harder. You see, just as you may never discover God until you bear the cost of denying God, so also you may never find your soul until you bear the cost of denying your soul. Learning processes are all so very peculiar to the personality. Some people have enchanted personalities (maybe even wrongly so) from which they must first be disenchanted in order to find themselves. Other people (whose either greater or lesser task is to remain enchanted) are rightly enchanted from the start. What then do you make of Lermontov's poem telling of both souls and of angels?

None can tell you more of this matter than is already recorded by the short-term poet Mikhail Lermontov (1814–1841). Don't scoff. It takes a brave soul to be a short-term poet! Maintaining one's youthfulness of spirit can be a very exhausting process, and most of the romantic poets (Burns, Byron, Pushkin, or Lermontov) either die young or become realists from having outlived their more youthful souls on earth.

In much the same way, the Bible affords no shortcut. For being mistaken by many dunderhead preachers and deadhead teachers to afford any sort of shortcut to heaven, the Bible itself proves to be a dead end to most (but not all those) who believe in the efficacy of this shortcut. But don't take offence at this issue of short-term poets any more than at dunderhead preachers and deadhead teachers. Take no offence either in the literal sense or in the literary sense of taking offence, since most poets (contrapoetesses) burn out fast and so (apart from such macho exceptions as Moses, Shakespeare, and Milton) are short-term poets. Oh yes, quite true, you yourself may have long forgotten what it is to be 'youthful in spirit', but as a reader, you must nevertheless still 'try to recapture that first [heavenly] note of careless rapture'.

Of course, nothing (but the facts of life) hang on the gerontology of growing old. [Elderly editor's note: Not quite true, gerontology (the study of the aged) also hangs on angelology (the study of the immortal angels) in ways that by this report to the Supreme Command (or as a riposte to you humans), we angels shall try to make better known.]

The guardian angels ministering to short-term poets (who are often—like Burns, Byron, and Rimbaud—rebellious cod-wallopers) get off with short stints of earthly service. But we angels who minister to long-lived rascals like Moses (first a murderer, but then arguing day and night with the Pharaoh before leading his flock on a forty-year circular tour through the Middle East) or Wee Davie Boy (another murderer, although the world's longest living rock star) have to hang around on earth (sometimes for as long as their human charges or spiritual clients) and may be vouchsafed very lengthy lifetimes. We're not complaining, all the same, since if you claim to keep company with the angels, you're bound to live in very exciting (although strenuously exhausting) times.

And yet for those poets who do live long lives (Longfellow, for being such a fellow both by name and nature) or perhaps in different ways (Walt Whitman or Robert Frost or even more so Voltaire, when once divested and disillusioned of his earlier so-called enlightenment as recorded in his best work, *Candide*), their task from the inside out is very different from that which you see from the outside in. You lesser mortals so often fail to see what it takes to maintain such great gifts, as often foam-wrapped and bubble-wrapped as they need to be, and even more so what it also takes to keep such great gifts under the strictest of human controls.

Such level of genius as the greatest of human minds have can so easily either exhaust their gifts or else bore themselves to tears. The exceptions, for being exceptions, are so easily overlooked (unless, like Longfellow, for keeping his gift of poesy alive by working through until his "day is done") that we fail to provide the extra care that must be given to the lives of such poetic and romantic celebrities.

Yet people generally love to point the finger of blame at fallen celebrities. They point at presidents, popes, and pastors, no less than at monarchs, missionaries, and ministers—all of whom are seen to be fair game for a come-down. This is especially so for those often fall guys who have gotten so far up themselves not to foresee their own downfall or who, for some other perhaps more private reason, have just gone off the tracks. It can be quite a fall from off some high-up monorail, private jet, or company directorship, which they mistook to be running entirely for themselves alone.

Populist justice, as one might call it—and as often that's fair enough for being so-called—although (apart from the catchcry of how the mighty have fallen) the jurists have not yet come up with any theory of justice by which to explain the downfall. You could say, particularly in any democracy, that those who express most affront at the downfall of any celebrity are expressing little more than self-condemnation for not having sufficiently looked after their leaders.

Genius (as once thought, but now largely forgotten) is a human universal. Now it's so rare that we angels on earth like to mollycoddle it (and so ruin it) before it matures to full fruition. We did that with Elvis, and we did that with the Beatles. But we also did it with Samson, with Alexander the (so-called) Great, and with Frederick (another so-called) Great. We gave them too much leeway.

In any case, it's otherwise with so often envious mortals, who are as often out to decapitate whoever stands higher than themselves. Like captive crabs in a pot or fleas on each other's backs to bite them or like the prettiest of tall poppies in a field of corn, they can't stand what we angels see for being exceptional to the ornery run (as we see it) of the human mill. Instead of other mortals emulating each other's pursuit of genius, they stultify their own potential. They can't withstand another's celebrity status without cutting tall poppies down to size or else preventing other captive crabs from escaping from the same pot in which they feel themselves to be imprisoned (poor, poor dears) by their unacknowledged genius. Of course, there's no more lost cause than that lost through envy.

Genius (although a human universal) is rarely recognised by humans in other humans, unless (through poetry, prophecy, science, music, or the arts) that genius (or tutelary spirit) is then most clearly seen for having been estranged from its accompanying soul. Then, instead of the accustomed colloidal amalgam of tutelary spirit and soul, the resulting brokenness of spirit, for being seen to pervade the whole person—whether personably of some Bach or Beethoven or of some Galileo or Darwin or of some Hegel or Solzhenitsyn—becomes so much more acceptable to those who have never put themselves through the ornery human mill of sacrifice or sufficient suffering required to fulfil such genius.

For this pitiable state of brokenness, the once enviable genius (as of Hans Christian Andersen or Tusitala Stevenson, as tellers of tales, or of Alexander Cruden, who wrote the greatest of biblical concordances) becomes less enviable since each such genius in their own way becomes a tragicomic or idiosyncratic figure. Likewise, each such genius is drawn towards being more accommodating of others and so, in turn, more acceptable to others, without which its true celebratory values would probably never be recognised. Alas, for the whole humanistic process, however, since the genius thus made more acceptable to others as often becomes less acceptable to himself or herself!

However, for becoming more obviously acceptable to others, this gives rise to the whole (mistaken) concept of what constitutes a genius, for that concept being allowed only by way of being the exceptional case. On the contrary, unless each and every mortal (by reason of the uniqueness of his or her soul) can be regarded on earth as in heaven for being an exceptional case, then (for the very same reason) each and every person must be admitted to have his or her own genius.

Thus, in all it says and does, humanity looks for brokenness and so, in consequence, produces brokenness instead of developing the universal potential of each individual person to be nurtured by the colloidal amalgam of tutelary spirit (or genius) and constantly searching soul. There is much in all this which we either take or mistake for the brokenness of the as yet unresurrected Christ (whose body as if still hangs on the cross).

In consequence, our notion of what it takes to constitute the human soul, the human spirit, and in turn, the genius of a person is all at odds with what it produces by way of grim reality. Our every systematic endeavour—whether by way of upbringing, education, law, religion, or morality—is out to produce the brokenness by which we may celebrate the genius of a favoured few rather than the genius of the many. And that's one reason, in turn, why the many who are thwarted in the development of their full potential to demonstrate their genius can turn so nasty by demonstrating first their envy of celebrities and then their spiteful glee at the downfall of celebrities.

Brokenness promotes brokenness. It's fear of that brokenness which distances so many self-striving souls from Christ. Yet a pin dropping from heaven will often not get through to earth without a broken humanity to hear its fall. Nevertheless, all things still work for the good of those who love God and who are called according to his purpose.

At the same time, however, unredeemed mankind falls so far short of understanding the genius of Jesus Christ that, for humanity being focussed solely on its own brokenness and not on the brokenness of Christ, it fails to understand the Christian genius which it shares with Christ. Because of being focussed so exclusively on its own sinful brokenness, humanity fails to make the right response to this very different brokenness which Christ in his humanity went through for the sake of restoring the wholeness of soul and spirit to all humanity on earth. It is this wholeness of an otherwise fractured human relationship between soul and spirit which is healed and redeemed through all which has been achieved through the genius (or cosmic consciousness) of Jesus Christ, and by which, both before all time and beyond all time, Jesus Christ remains Jesus Christ.

Otherwise, in every case, the human brokenness persists. This brokenness is brokered by falsely equating personality and character (through life and works) to account for inherent genius. No, the genius of Jesus Christ is far more than the very little that either we angels or you humans could conceive of what it means to be Jesus Christ. Likewise, for the poet Lermontov, as for any other person, whether human or angelic, they each have a genius far greater for their being unique than we could ever categorise in terms of personality or character.

We get nowhere close to that for those reasons given above. We get nowhere close to that even in thinking of the genius of a Shakespeare or of a Milton or of a Chekhov or of a Dostoyevsky. As for the genius of that less-known Lermontov, he was a Scots-generated Russian whose namesake ocean-going liner went down in the Marlborough Sounds whilst that ship went sailing the South Pacific Seas surrounding New Zealand. Being Scots, by descent from the family of Learmonth (and, in turn, much earlier from Thomas the Rhymer), he cuts the traditionally tragicomic literary figure encompassing three literary continents (Scotland, in terms of

James Macpherson and Walter Scott; Europe, in terms of Mikhail Lermontov and Alexander Pushkin; and the South Seas, in terms of R. A. K. Mason and James K. Baxter). [Exegesis 2: As Oswald Spengler remarks in his introduction to *Decline of the West*, 'Today we think in terms of continents ...' [to which today we could likewise add oceans].]

With the earlier warning as to a long haul begun by this however brief history of heaven, we also boldly sound another weather warning. It's a bad-weather warning, so don't be surprised, dear friends, to discover how much of this history of heaven is already being worked out right now (with all you souls) whilst still on earth. You may have been led (or misled) to think that when the long-awaited kingdom of heaven finally pods down on earth for all eternity (what a big cosmic splashdown that will be), it will herald in an apostolic sitcom of beer and skittles for all believers! [Exegesis 3: There're better things (pardon the rapidly declining grammar of this age) than beer and skittles, so don't you believe it.]

But that big cosmic splashdown (as if never heralded already by way of personal water baptism) happened more than two thousand years ago (without any beer and skittles), and the far bigger baptism by fire (already long lit and brightly burning) is not the more likely to bring about any happier-go-luckier sitcom of beer and skittles. [Exegesis 4: In other words, this is one of the most seriously final of weather warnings of which any serious reader (either angelic or humanistic) could ever conceive.]

This fundamentally humanistic misconception of Christendom (or whatever else you care to call it) of being still pie in the sky ought by now to be way beyond any serious believer's seriously believable belief. Far too many believers still hang up their hats on a heaven that is no more than pie in the sky. [Exegesis 5: Think of the resulting quandary this misconception causes to personalities such as the little artillery captain Touschine in Tolstoy's *War and Peace*. There, the little captain says, 'It's all very well to say that the soul goes up to heaven. We know very well that there's no such thing as heaven, since there's nothing above us but empty space.']

Remember, little Touschine is an artillery captain who relies on empty space through which to plot the coordinates for the explosive missiles he fires, so he's an expert on the subject of earthly ballistics and the mayhem they cause to life and limb. As to plotting coordinates for the purpose of heavenly ballistics, however, this little artillery captain is more than a little confused for being both nearly right and nearly wrong about the location of heaven. He's so nearly right since it was more than two thousand years before his own time when (without any beer and skittles) heaven came to earth. And he's so nearly wrong because his earthly coordinates are so much at odds with his own pie-in-the-sky concept of heaven.

Nevertheless, it's often still pie in the sky for you humans to go on thinking that souls still go skywards to exactly that same pie-in-the-sky sort of heaven. [Exegesis 6: Reciprocally speaking, when humans took (deistic) pride in themselves (as many did) for having conquered space in their having gone to the moon (don't laugh at this, you other angels), many of humanity's most ardent believers likewise lost their faith for there being no more pie-in-the-sky sort of heaven.]

Far too many humans have hung up their hats on a heaven that for them was once no more than pie in the sky. But then they lost their hats (together with their heavenly crowns) when space was conquered, as if to show them that no such pie-in-the-sky heaven existed up there in the sky. Nevertheless, the loss of their hats (or golden crowns) was sufficient enough to dissuade many of them from every last vestige of a belief in heaven. What they had mistaken for pie in the sky was a heaven which didn't even have a cloakroom (however high in the sky) from which they could pick up their long-promised golden crowns.

Look here, a cloakroom in any building is most usually by the entrance on the ground floor of the building! Whatever golden crowns are awarded in heaven are awarded on the strength of what's achieved on earth where the front line of heavenly action is most usually on the ground floor. Besides, the kingdom of heaven had come to earth with Christ nearly two millennia before men learnt how to walk on the moon.

By refusing to recognise so much of the heavenly kingdom that is already here on earth, your human commitment to heaven is thus made so much more contingent on only after you've gone to glory (so to speak) that you miss out on almost all of heaven on earth in the here and now. This so-called fallacy of prevarication has got to be corrected, or else (we are speaking not only with you humans here as the closest of buddies but also of ourselves as fallible angels) none of us … no, not any of us so mistaken … will ever get to see the coming glory.

Despite all our wishful thinking for this to be a better world, the kingdom of heaven is present in the pain of the here and now, no less than in the bright hereafter. Much of this report (published now with the authority of the Supreme Command) is about this present pain—the pain that needfully prefaces and accompanies what it takes to redeem every mortal person from their often confused, if not openly rejected, concept of what will be demanded of every single believer to bring about our promised new heaven and our promised new earth.

This continuing pain, which is still present in what remains of our prevailing darkness, is basically that which comes either through those greatly corpuscular faults of human ignorance or else in wave after wave of human rebelliousness, each by way of refusing to acknowledge the divinely authorised and prescriptive forcefulness of the deontic (or rightful) crucifixion. Yet unless as the closest of buddies, both we (for being angels) and you (for being spirit-filled humans) will die where we lie … will die where we lie for the lack of our doing together what now needs to be done to dispel what remains of the prevailing darkness.

You can stand and watch, or even play dice at the foot of the cross as dismissively as you like, but unless you too are prepared in the here and now to catch something of the divine soul by taking into your cleansed hearts and also into your transformed minds the life, death, and resurrection of the still living Christ (the one who came to earth as Jesus of Nazareth), you are nothing at all to the creator of all things, who, perhaps for this present purpose alone of transforming your mind, took the trouble to make you—yes, you—the measure of his power and glory. [Exegesis 7: Don't think it was just for your own benefit that you were most wonderfully made, will you? We wouldn't want to shame you into heaven (even if that could be done, although some old-time preachers have tried hard that way) by making out what would then become a fearfully tear-jerking film of your already continuing life.]

So then, who knows, maybe this is to be your freely chosen last chance to relieve and redeem the continued sufferings of Christ. So then let's be buddies in this final fray—that's the message that we angels (who are no less fallible than are you humans) would bring to you. Our military objective is to unite forces, as close cobbers together, for the purposes of this mopping-up operation on earth. You humans may opt out for each having only but one mortal life to lose, but we angels know otherwise for witnessing those of our once complete angelic contingent, some of whom mistakenly felt themselves free to fall from heaven.

It may be, or maybe not, depending on your interpretation of your heavenly Father's living Word, to see your own calling to take part in this spiritually disciplined operation for being a readily recognisable military one. The scriptural text of that living Word remains exactly the same, yet the earthly context is fast changing. The speed of light is rapidly slowing down; time is growing increasingly short. The powers of darkness coalesce for their last and final fling.

There's passive as well as active resistance to every interim or final awakening, but the trouble with passivity is most often that it doesn't register at all. That passivity of human spirit explains why we angels give you so many of the same reminders. If your souls were fully alive and awake (so as not to nod off again), then you wouldn't need to hear, far less want to hear, the same things more than once.

Indeed, you may or may not immediately want to accept what you see to be a military commission to serve in the forces of the Supreme Command. Nevertheless, if you want to see heaven from earth, then don't any longer look up, around, or down (as a light-blinded person does when suddenly shocked to see how much remains of the prevailing darkness) but instead look to yourselves, as now fallible humans, to see for yourselves what it takes to be already commissioned for heavenly service.

We're not preaching here. No, not even teaching here. We're hammering on the door of your heart. We're not a press gang or even an enlistment team but instead only travel guides. Your task as humans on earth is not just to enlist as passive observers of heavenly ways but to relieve and redeem the sufferings of Christ as still promoted and experienced through the ignorance and rebelliousness of those who profess to be merely civil citizens and not militant citizens of heaven. [Exegesis 8: Remember, (1) civility is a vice and not a virtue, as held by John Bunyan in *The Pilgrim's Progress*; and (2) soul-catching is run from heaven's kingdom now on earth with all the much-needed discipline of a military operation.]

The remaining time for enlistment is short. We angels on earth are only the messengers of this kingdom message, but because you humans are only a little lower than are us angels, then so much of this task of implementing and maintaining this kingdom of heaven on earth is already clearly allotted to you humans. On this score, your task will become clearer only if you choose to accept it, since the discipline of discipleship which many of you humans already profess (often sadly without practicing it) is in itself not unlike the exercise of a military commission. [Exegesis 9: As Tolstoy will tell you in his monumental military manual on *War and Peace*, the most frequent trouble with any militia is that it has more time than it rightly knows what to do with.]

Perhaps, you're already more than a little tired or jaded that Jesus hasn't yet fulfilled his promise of coming back to earth. Maybe you're rapidly in process of joining the league of those who least expect and who thus so overlook this most specific sign of the nearness of the Messiah's Second Coming. You're no longer looking forward to hobnobbing upstairs with Moses and Elijah, besides giving the finger downstairs to Marx and Lenin, and you might even have reached the point (of no return) by thinking it more enjoyable now to place your bets on capturing as much of this world's limited resources before joining the barbecue of non-believers being fired up for feeding those already downstairs. It sure would surprise and shock you, we would hope, for you to find yourself fried, fricasseed, and served up from hell's dinner menu. *Fried Green Tomatoes* at the Whistle Stop Cafe (by the author Fannie Flagg) would have nothing on it.

Possibly, you reconcile these two commercially sensitive views of heaven and hell (those who least expect and those who most expect Christ's Second Coming) by rationalising that people get what they deserve (which is just what they would get were it not for God's grace). No, as a matter of heavenly ergonomics, the rationale is rather different. By the grace of God, nothing is wasted, or to put the same ergonomic equation more brutally into Afghanese, 'goat meat makes for good tucker no less than lamb'. The trouble is that people will try ever so hard to avoid their own pain, even to the point of inflicting what would otherwise be their own pain on others. They do this rather than to admit to the painful consequence of their own actions.

Make no mistake. The pain you see, hear, and feel for this dying world of today (and for which pain you may even blame Almighty God) is most certainly your own continuing pain for the way in which all humans are still a party to Christ's ongoing crucifixion. Nevertheless, there's not much room (in space-time) left either here or there to party, party, party. Yet even as a seriously situational comedy (or sitcom), the exceedingly plain truth (which hurts every feeling person so much more now on earth) isn't going to be anything like what we fear it's going to be like (for those whose lamps have been left unattended) when the new earth and the new heaven are wonderfully renewed as one.

Love ousts all fear. The new heaven (like the new earth) is not going to be a cut-and-paste job of whatever escapes the holocaust of this old world. We mistake that for being the outcome just because we are by now completely blinded by our attachment to this old world. Our present blindness disables us from appreciating and accepting what it takes to create (or recreate) some entirely new heaven and new earth.

But don't worry. Never fear. The Lord is still as good and as constant as ever. Your mind may well falter on your finding out from this report just how much more is expected of you than you earlier believed of yourselves in these end days, dearest readers, but keep your hearts intact. Yes, indeed, more than ever before will you ever need to guard your hearts.

Remember always that the transformed mind is translocated in both space and time (the space-time continuum, as the physicists call it). There is so much of heavenly history already played out on earth that you cannot be unduly surprised (surely) for even more of what has been already so intimately prophesised on earth to be also fulfilled on earth. There is nothing new here (unless new to you) but to read the signs of the times and to implement your prophetic calling.

Just how much lies in your having been chosen to be the principal protagonists for the working out right now of this very same history of heaven on earth has already been revealed on earth. In these latter days, heaven is no more pie in the sky than it ever was in any former days. The greater part of heaven's final kingdom fulfilment lies already in every believer's heart and hands. From the solely human viewpoint, the history of heaven (apart from whatever else remains as yet unknown to man) is made up as follows: first, the compiled personal history of each individual human soul; and secondly, the more collective history of all mankind in relation to the promised eternity of all those individual souls; when thirdly, as each believing soul already knows, the born-again creation comes about of this blissfully awaited new earth and new heaven.

So it's no longer just in heaven (where the battle between good and evil is already won) but still on this deeply groaning earth that the last remaining phases of this great cosmic battle are being fought (for right against wrong, for justice against injustice, and for righteousness against unrighteousness). This heavenly battle will be hardest fought by you, dearest readers, now on earth. It will be fought to the death in every last nook and cranny of this already dying planet, and it is no exaggeration to say that the earthly outcome of this once heavenly onslaught rests entirely in your human hands.

So then we write to you, our dearest readers of the living Word, not only to warn you of physical storms, rising tides, and tempests in the offing (for the very earth itself is in a ferment) but also to encourage you to persevere in the fine art of prayerful proclamation. We beg of you to soak yourselves in every subtle nuance of the living Word, as if you yourselves were that word's best advocate throughout every last moment of this final fray.

Be brave, be bold, and yet be temperate. Stay humble, settled both in mind and spirit, so to be always content yet never just passively introvert (far less inert). Instead, through every right form of action, exert what it takes, whenever so-called to be responsively, responsibly, and righteously extrovert. Consult every day how goes your own soul, and both look for and listen to your very own guardian angel. All these are not commands. Between your own soul and yourself (or psyche), they are personal commitments.

* * *

A Very Brief History of Heaven
Part II

On the Subject of Friendship
A sweet friendship refreshes the soul.
From the wisdom of Solomon, popularly
known as the Proverbs (27:9)

Dearest friends, these sweet words (now much abused) still ought to sing their own song of a good-natured comity between serious readers and serious writers. There was never a writer who wrote anything without first being a reader and never a reader who wouldn't be a better reader for becoming more of a writer. Nevertheless, friendship for its own sake (and not for any selfishly ulterior motive) now rarely configures to rise above the disfigured bass of this now greatly groaning earth.

By getting back to basics, we could try to reconfigure also back to that once concordant figured bass (both a musical and a mathematical term) by which to harmonise today's now discordant and declining continuo under which, for being weighed down by all the woes of this world, this old earth continues to creak at the poles, crack towards its epicentre, and groan more or less continually as it comes closer and closer to the end of all time. From baroque to classical, through rock and roll towards the world's final last rap, we've nearly got there. No, there's no turning back, since the reconfiguring of today's discordant bass by unwinding today's continuo back to baroque would be an epic task far beyond our angelic capabilities by which to manifest our heavenly calling.

We have earlier looked at some of the problems which arise from fixating on individual genius, but many humans look beyond the individual to see mankind more collectively as a social organism. At one extreme is psychosomatic individualism (giving rise to capitalism), and at the other extreme is psychosomatic collectivism (giving rise to communism).

Midway, there turns out to be not much difference, say, between capitalism and communism apart from the strategically religious conflict, increasingly to defeat the ends of each, in their seeking to win and occupy the same solar centre point. Nevertheless, the individual and the collective need not be conflictive since, to a greater or lesser extent, personal and societal values are generally shared except by isolated (and isolationist) individuals on the one hand and by the most collectively secured and excessively insulated societies on the other hand. Once again, read Daniel Defoe's *Robinson Crusoe* on the trials and tribulations of extreme individualism and Samuel Butler's *Erewhon* on the trials and tribulations of extreme collectivism.

Very roughly speaking, since not even paradigms are perfect in practice, the human individual projects a bilateral (front-side and bum-side) symmetry, whereas humanity as a collective organism projects a radial symmetry that looks all ways. [In other words, bipedal individuals move definitively on two legs, whereas the amoebic society of collective mankind greases along on as many pseudopods as it can think to manage for locomotion.]

Even more roughly, since the bilateral symmetry of the individual reflects two tangentially opposite yet composite portions of the radial symmetry projected by humanity as a collective organism, both the individual and the collective can be seen to be intimately related by their sharing parts of the same logical domain. Envision this, and we could go on to apply and extend the class calculus developed by our mentor Augustus De Morgan to the different levels (both functional and dysfunctional) of psychosomatic individualism and psychosomatic collectivism, but not this for now, except to propose the need for finding and maintaining some means of balance between the humanly individual and the humanly collective.

The most obvious and conformist way of maintaining this orderly balance between individualism and collectivism is by law—some swearing by Justinian, others by Bentham and Blackstone, and yet others by Newton, Einstein, and Hocking—but there are many very different legal systems by which to do so, and in any case, none of these are forever self-sustaining. Up here in heaven, we are told by Jesus not to swear at all — but 'Jeez', down there on earth, everybody swears like troopers.

Yet another very different key to maintaining this orderly balance (in the legal domain) at more than one level of relationship is friendship (in the social domain). Of course, there are many other domains of discourse, such as political, moral, aesthetic, religious, and military (together with logic itself), which both individuals and societies will employ to resolve their differences of mindset and behaviour. Each domain of dispute resolution promotes its own sense of discipline, and the way in which each domain works and interrelates for the promotion of justice confers on the universality of jurisprudence, one of the widest and deepest measures of discipline required for domain discernment.

To many, if not all these logical domains, in extending to and diversifying amongst many different cultures, languages, and mindsets, most of us will claim some kind of limited or unlimited fellowship. Our fellowship may be token and conformist or seriously thoughtful or else dismissed and rejected because of being seen to conflict with other domains to which we are already affiliated. We might be locked into a fixation for the sciences which, in the way we process that fixation, makes us spurn the arts and humanities. We might be locked into a fixation for religious worship which makes us trivialise many or most or even all other domains of discourse.

The question here, as with other key questions to this conundrum of jurisprudence, which is essentially the same conundrum as that of the one and the many postulated by the ancient Greeks, is very much part of any effort to solve today's universal conundrum already defined to be that still under the sun of the world problematique. And that's exactly why, in the face of today's widening and deepening global problems (such as those of starvation, invasion, disease, terrorism, and warring), we angels choose to focus on the rather humble domain of friendship rather than on anything so monstrously beyond our calling as world government (which you will hear so much about, with lots of hoo-ha, from the Counterfeit Command).

Nevertheless, can you ever make of any one of these domains a certainty, ask our opponents whose own views on one-world government are none too clear? Could we say of our own freely chosen friendship (as any domain for its own sake might be so easily dismissed for being the lowliest domain of all by those who are so much higher up in this world than are we both ourselves) for being in this day and age of ours any more than yet another uncertainty?

To be certain of anything, one first needs an absolute. For such an absolute, psychology looks inwards to the individual, whereas sociology looks outwards to society. Then for the sake of itself as an absolute, can friendship be a certainty? If not, then by what other absolute can we see friendship either as an absolute certainty or, for being in relation to some other absolute, more or less of a certainty?

Friendship for its own sake can be voiced in all sorts of different ways, in all sorts of different cultures, and in all sorts of different situations. Try voicing friendship for its own sake in as many different languages as you can muster. Starting from ancient Hebrew if you like and working your way through Koine Greek, Arabic, classical Latin, Church Slavonic, Russian, and pidgin English, there's not a great deal of difference to be found for those who dare to conceptualise what otherwise would remain inconceivable for anyone. You can always at a pinch fill in any linguistic void by spreading your angelic wings to their fullest wingspan with glossolalia. The main thing as always is to keep open lines of heavenly communication with those whom you would establish friendship for its own sake.

Remember that friendship for its own sake (a song in itself) is but only the second-highest level of friendship established in the kingdom of God. Nevertheless, you have to reach that second-highest level before you can top it. Those who mistake this second-highest level of friendship for being the highest level usually come a cropper. They are aspiring to fly solo before they have learnt to fly under more constant and personal supervision.

This is all part of preparing to enter no more than the novitiate of soul-catching. Be content, more and more, until you reach the breakthrough barrier (for both sound and sight) to do the right things for their own sake without worrying about fulfilling their strategic purposes. This is the key to early learning in all disciplines—first, learn the technical tactics for their own sake before thinking to apply those tactics for strategic purposes. This is the same in science as it is in music, the same in the exercise of lovingkindness as it is in the exercise of friendship, each for their own sake; otherwise, you'll never ever learn to forgive, far less to love, your enemies.

Such is the decline in expressions of national, international, transnational, or supranational friendship that often neither friendship nor lovingkindness can any longer hold to their own still hopefully melodic part. Nevertheless, as for writing and reading, so also words without any semblance of a song are always deficient for their lack of a lyric. True, one must listen for the tune, even although the words may falter, since whether in reading or writing or singing or speaking, there's always a sense of loss (either perceived or unperceived) for the lack of a song.

Does that not make sense? If not, then you must learn to sing or to play or to dream or to dance or else to speculate in science or to explore the domain of human relationships in detail or to study the dialectic of argument (each for their own sake), for this very first purpose is of both extending the depth and strengthening the width of your own individual mind. It takes as much strength of purpose to engage in soul-catching as it takes to walk on water, so don't cut corners or fall by the wayside.

Remember always that by individually employed tactics are all strategically collective outcomes reached, fought, and won. The present calling of the heavenly host is to raise humans by the power of one (whatever that means in novo maths) by which to work in tandem with heaven's angels. Now hell's angels scoff at this, which is very much a good sign as to the outcome, but let's perfect the tactics before we even think about, far less celebrate, whatever may be the strategic outcome.

As will be often said, this is as much a matter of keeping military discipline as it is a matter of keeping spiritual discipline. But then, not to change the subject, have you ever wondered how it is that the best and longest-lasting songs, from foot-slogging troop songs to heavenly oratorios and symphonic overtures, are born out of matching the metre of military discipline to the righteous inspiration by which relatively unknown strategic purposes are, in the midst of life and death, still being set to song?

The song may either be sentimentally sad or else be bright and cheerful and sometimes even both sad and bright (and so bittersweet both to the songster and to the listener) all at one and the same time. There's no saying when the sound of the song may change, whether from pidgin English to classical Latin or from Church Slavonic back into classical Greek. Both writer and reader, as well as singer and listener, must keep their wits about them, for although the incidentals are always in continuous change, the verities are forever constant.

So as for any would-be writer or would-be reader, take your pick between centring yourself, either on or wherever in between the gamut of continuous change and the constant verities, that you would choose to position yourself. And do so, picking your way with caution, since some folks settle for what others see to be the routine constancy of the humdrum (not always for everyone a poor choice) whilst yet many others forego that chronological constant (in classical terms, whereby truth gives birth to virtue) in favour of making the most out of what may be no more to most (unthinking persons) than (the nonsense of) only continuously changing incidentals. Consider, but cautiously we warn you, when you next see and hear singers, those who sing with their souls and those who sing with less than their souls, as well as for those whose souls are asleep, so too those who barely sing at all!

All the same, like most preschoolers, we're still looking at least for constants but more preferably for absolutes. That's exactly why we so often get fixated on strategic purposes before having mastered the tactics by which to reach them or even having begun to establish the boundaries of our strategic calling. So too, we fail to establish those boundaries that determine and define the authorised domain of our discourse. Consider the case of today's often linguistically deprived adolescent whose conceptual vocabulary ricochets between *awesome* and *gruesome* whilst all the rest (apart from swear words) mindlessly qualifies for acceptance *absolutely*. In such ways, doesn't everyone, whether knowingly or not, admit to feeling the loss of absolutes and express that loss by way of overcompensation.

Adolescence is the pivotal time for homing in on our life absolutes. How then do we balance such adolescent mood swings from *awesome* down to *gruesome* and from *gruesome* back up to *awesome*? The short DIY answer to that question is to deal first directly with the *awesome* because that's more controllable and easier to deflate than it is to elevate the reciprocal cycle from *gruesome* to *awesome*. Underneath every such mood swing, however, there's always a linguistic issue, since everyone's world view is determined and held in place by the way they use words (in this case, such swinging alternatives as *gruesome* and *awesome*) in their search for equanimity.

It's not the words themselves which are at fault but the irrationality of thought and the resulting misuse of extreme alternatives. Allowing for most alternatives, however, one constant cannot make sense without either having (1) some other constant by way of comparison or else at least (2) another constant by way of stark contrast. And that other constant in stark contrast may extend to something (or to everything else) by which the contrast is stark enough to make some or all other constants utterly inconsistent with it. [Excursus 1: For example, *love*, however constant in any specific case, makes not enough generic sense to serve as a cosmic constant. *Unconditional love* may be a cosmic constant, not in itself an absolute without being (not just predicated of some other constant) but actually equated with some other constant (say our constant God) who is in himself or herself the supreme cosmic absolute. Thus, 'God is love' by which this existential copula (more forcefully expressed in some languages than others) indicates a conjoint absolute. Alas for this two-valued predication of subject with object, however, since the fracture between the related fractals hides the underlying reality of the conjoint singularity by which God and Love are one and the same constant, both in name and nature.]

Of course, for there to be any conceptualisation of a constant, there has to be some preconception of what it takes to be a concept. Consequentially, some folks cautiously withhold their choice or else impetuously decide their own outcome by diving head first into the maelstrom of this life's conflicting opposites. And so through fear, apathy, or impulsiveness, they avoid every opportunity of becoming great minds (GMs) by aligning themselves with whatever conventional constant (as it seems to them) makes sense (once again as makes sense to them) of any or of all other constants. If this proposition lacks clarity, as we angels think it does, then for remembering that kings and priests have the right to investigate what may be a mistaken, misunderstood, witheld, or even embargoed lack of clarity, then as both priests and kings, we readers have the right to make that investigation.

Needless to say, still take your pick (as much of objectives as of outcomes), since even the commonly continuous colloquialisation of today's speech may suddenly assume tomorrow's status of the classic constant. It may do so whilst devolving from standard English down to the lowest levels of largely illiterate nonsense (not witheld from this book) or else up to whatever either officially or politically correct form of communication comes into vogue (whether for being yet another kind of nonsense or else making good sense).

Life and language, no less than thinking and vocalising, are so intimately intertwined that one in flux makes for both in flux. And just as yesterday's continuous colloquial (whether plainsong or baroque) may assume tomorrow's revered status of this classic constant (and today's classic constant be then reduced to the status of yesterday's continuous colloquial), so too the seemingly eternal verities of today may be relegated (either nicely, exactly, or more precisely) to the level of tomorrow's seemingly gratuitous incidentals. [Exegesis 1: For the full forcefulness of atonic incidentals (although far less of transient passing notes, yet together with the means of modulating between key constants in the context of the changing continuous colloquial), don't overlook your study at least of musicality (appreciation being the reader's choice), if not also of musical improvisation (composition being the author's choice), although both by now are once again notoriously minimalistic instead of once gratuitously symphonic. Got the message? No? Then go back at least to Book 1 and read the abstract on abstraction!]

Meanwhile, be prepared to be spoofed, seriously spoofed, since we all as friends must learn to tease as well as to take a tease, if only (1) to sustain our friendship and (2) to break new ground in conceptual thought. Without ears to hear and eyes to see, how otherwise than by a friendly tease can even the dearest of staunchly believing readers be sure of holding to their faith in the veritable substance of those things still relatively unseen, far less also of those things also still relatively unheard? The same theoretical relativity (TR) that reinvested physical science (PS) with faith-based credibility (FBC) has yet to recognise, far less to reinvest, theology with that same credibility from which it sprang. [Excursus 2: We'll shorten our stylistic flow (SF) as scientists do, by our recourse to acronyms here, before bouncing back to FUC (fully understood content).]

Some say (by way of friendly tease) that the faith factor (even for the speed of light) has gone completely relative when viewed in today's continuously colloquial conversation of quantum mechanics. So if the speed of light is no longer the constant it first was before it began slowing down (and thus also before time consequentially speeded up), then what was that very first constant when this world was first proclaimed prophetically into being?

What indeed was this constant when so proclaimed by the creative driving force of the words 'Let there be light!'? So if the faith factor (even for the speed of light) has gone completely relative, what tokens this for relativity if the whole notion of relativity is founded on a mistaken constant (MC) for the speed of light? Well, as for each and every hypothetical constant (such as the formulaic speed of light utilised in $E = mc^2$), these conjectural fictions are subject to refutable proof and disproof according to the credibility we ascribe to their resulting non-fictions)!

It follows (as lawyers say when sticking steadfastly to their case) that fidelity itself has fearfully imploded (apparently all on its own accord) into one and the same black hole of what seems to be both the relatively big as well as of the relatively small. In this report, we shall stick as far as possible (not so very far in these days of rapidly decreasing possibilities) to conventional metaphysics (i.e. the metaphysics of causation, predication, categorisation, classification, and, above all, definition), otherwise known as Aristotelian. We shall stay glued or fixated to this species of inherited Aristotelianism before trying to square the quantum physics of today's existentially spreading academic circle (ESAC). Yet already, according to the new choreography provided by today's quantum physics, this exercise is not greatly different from deciding (at *minus 273.15* degrees Celsius) just how many mediaeval angels can dance (more when medieval) on the head of some (by now 18/8) stainless steel pin.

Meanwhile, tempus fugit (or time flies), as we once said with the classic status of borrowed concepts incorporated into standard English instead of coping with the glottal stops of today's more cosmopolitan pidgin, since time still flies (and yet flies even more so for flying so very much faster). In short, we may well ask which aspect (as with the Russian verbs of relatively instrumental motion) is the authentic and which is the counterfeit when both relatively unseen opposites brand themselves and purport to trade as the one and only Supreme Command. What's the answer (which is bound to be different, surely, whether depending on the different coordinates of liftoff and touchdown for either source translation or target translation of the biblical and otherwise existential question)?

In other words (to find out which other words would once constitute a primary school exercise in recombinative conceptual comprehension), the same identical question may still be asked, namely, with what pitch, timbre, and changing intonation does it take to sing something prayerfully into being—so as to bring any imperilled ship into port out of the turbulent waves of the sea in the overwhelming sound of a storm or as to the bleat of some lost lamb in its race to find its one and only rightful ewe or as to whatever first words of endearment may be wooed from a man to assuage the fears of his intended or much younger wife?

There are no short answers to these questions. The sounds made by the words by themselves are rarely sufficient to redeem any situation by themselves until transformed into some more continuous song. The litterateur (or bookman) knows of this, but not so often the physical researcher (or scientist). So too, the lawbreaker knows more vividly of what it means for his being made to sing than does any ivory-towered academic when invited to be heard no more than for his supper; and likewise even more vividly still will that song of ongoing life be heard of any woman when forced to sing in her pain of maternal labour.

Yet don't boggle at any such preliminary attempt as this to determine the pitch, key, and metre of what may be only a precursive attempt to edge closer to the ultimate song of all life (whether a little offkey like that of Charles Darwin or less so like that of Gregor Mendel). Nevertheless, in each such case, unless you can already hear at least a little something of that ultimate song which permeates the whole universe and presumably the entire cosmos, you must first be resurrected from the tomb or from the grave in which your sleeping soul mistakes for your present songless life.

Listen here, and always closely, not only to the words either as they may be of kindly wisdom or of crude absurdity—in one case of revelatory proclamation and in the other case of judgemental accusation—but just as closely to the timbre, pitch, metre, and tonality of the inherently creative or inherently counterfeit and substitutive song. The commonly accepted form of most things—whether the commonality of law or of morals or of any culture, civilisation, system of education, or what is thought to be the best form of government—can disappear completely from sight (as if overnight) for the lack of it ever being transposed into song. [Exegesis 2: The key to nationality (listen for it) lies in any nation's national anthem (i.e. KN = NA)]

The perceived commonality of all things can thus fail (1) so rapidly and (2) happen so suddenly, as did the fall of (1) those rebellious angels once from heaven or as did (2) that later dispossession of mankind from Eden. Thus too, the former Soviet Union was struck so speechless by the sudden collapse of communism that all it could do for several years was to hum the old tune whilst trying to find the new words to go with its former national anthem. Know as much as you can about the history of music (both righteously angelic as well as disgustingly demonic), which is so much the key to world history, before you opt for this or for that way of assessing this very public and revelatory report now being commissioned for release by the Supreme Command.

What any nation (whether proudly or reluctantly) sings is far more telling than whatever is said (unless humorously against itself by or on behalf of that nation by one or another of its very own comedians). For example, whether from the historic 'Scots Wha Hae' to the current 'God Save the Queen' or from the chequered career of the present 'Russian National Anthem' to the many versions of 'The Battle Hymn of the Republic', consider the forcefulness (whether purportedly official or not) of your very own national anthem. Take your own time to consider (although keep to the musical measure) and sing each national anthem in different circumstances (both sadly at funerals and joyfully at coronations and inaugurations) whilst pursuing your own sought-for answer.

Then after having given your sought-for answer some considerable reflection, consider this: whether with the national anthem that you have for your own nation, would you make any treaty of union, treaty of peace, or even just a transnational trade agreement with another nation (far less than consider going to war against that nation or any other nation) in each case whose national anthem you had not already most carefully assessed and compared with your own national anthem? 'Shit!' you may say—as also apostolically exclaimed both by St Paul and Martin Luther—since each national anthem of any nation is a scientific abstract (see earlier) for what you can expect to experience from the behaviour of that nation!

We dare say that any such firm advice herein offered (unless received from some better-known Delphic oracle than this angelic host) first to consult every country's song and dance routines (no less than to consult what makes folks laugh at themselves) will occasion great mirth at most of this world's consulates, embassies, and ministries of foreign affairs. But how much did either the former USSR and the former USA know most intimately of their own national anthems, far less of the national anthems of those other countries— amongst them most recently those nations of Afghanistan, Kurdistan, Iraq, Iran, Turkey, and Syria—with whom they either consorted, financed, supplied, opposed, betrayed, or fought (for or against)— with weapons or else simply walked in, marched in, or flew in, to effect some sort of military invasion?

'Shit!' said here again without apologies to both St Paul (formerly Saul of Tarsus) and St Martin (formerly Luther of Wittenberg) for once more borrowing from them their seriously scatological invective. Unless justified by a lowered pH factor (for the measure of acidic as well as alkaline humour), this invective of the saints both affirms as well as confirms humans to be even more than just a little lower than first thought of the angels. Alas, such is the pervasive affliction (to take oneself overseriously) of these increasingly modern times!

Now it's the case that any and every nation can bray (*sic*) for peace, peace, peace, as much as it likes (at this point, learn off by heart (both tune and words) of the well-known English folk song

'The Vicar of Bray'); but unless that nation has a clean enough heart close to the one and only source of righteousness, every single one of its proclamations is likely to be counterproductive. This may be the first time, but by no means the last time, that we refer all our seriously scientific readers (solely social scientists are exempted from that description) to accept responsibility for all these political hotspots of both civil and military unrest where all sorts of atrocities are perpetrated in the name of peace, order, and good government.

It may seem here to be very strange (albeit for this report being very much a military operation) by which we have (metaphorically but not metaphysically) extended our tent pegs so much further out than they were before from just these three little islands of New Zealand. Why would it be, from such a small solar centre as this one is, that we would dare to take such pre-emptive action to encircle those political hotspots of the world by way of soul-catching from this once apparently safe haven? They're nothing in the world's eyes, these shortly-to-be-disappearing islands (due to climate change) within this so-called Ring of Fire in the South Pacific. But here (or there) again, from where else would you expect this report commissioned by the Supreme Command to emanate if not from what's so long ago been codified as 'God's own country'?

The strangeness of history in the making does not stop there. Why else do you think (in favour of one-world management over heavenly administration) that the humanities are being dumbed down throughout the western world (by now lower case) in the name of purportedly big business, purportedly pure science, and purportedly progressive technology? And the fastest place for all this dumbing down being done is in the backblocks and boondocks of the South Pacific—at the centre of which (offshore of Australia) still lies the uncracked code of 'God's own country'! Can we have got our geographical constants or, worse still, our heavenly absolutes wrong?

This is where the panic sets in (concurrently with the once EEC (now EU) going down the perilous YouTube by its treatment of the UK). The aim also of the Counterfeit Command is to justify the bringing into full effect the earlier negotiated Trans-Tasman and South Pacific trade treaties. These things sound like nothing (either too good or too bad) by themselves, since (unsurprisingly) all the rest of the information is embargoed. Nevertheless, they all testify to the rapid rise of global warming (if not outright conflagration) in the commercial sector.

Likewise, the prophetic writing 'mene mene tekel upharsin' is once more up again on the already multitagged global wall, but the issue, now again as then, is as to what this writing means— unless just put up again (as Confucius so frequently recommends) for further historical reflection. Alas, we are all too much at risk of disregarding prophecies when once fulfilled as being no longer capable of being stilll further fulfilled. So then just as Napoleon decreed (1) every army to march on its (as often empty) stomach; and nutritionists more recently went the whole hog to rehash the far earlier adage—the one which warns *you are what you think*—now to mean (2) that *you are what you eat*; which is all very well unless (3) as in the retreat of Napoleon's army from Moscow you have nothing at all to eat; then (4) the same historic tagline of 'mene mene tekel upharsin' at Belshazzar's feast surely means the same today as it did yesterday, namely (5) that *you have been found wanting*; thus again proving (6) that there's nothing new under the sun. Fair enough; (7) history repeats itself—but (8) it doesn't stop there; since (9) the military decree to walk on one's stomach after having eaten that rehashed adage from the nutritionists is bound to pose (10) at least a nutritional problem; if not also (12) a cosmic quandary.

If no more than a nutritional problem, then you readers (for being also kings and priests, as said before) are fully capable of working it out for yourselves. If also a cosmic quandary as well as a nutritional problem, however, then angelic help comes right now; since to escape from this quandary without this needed help brings first individual nations, then (the as with the desertifying dustbowl of the mid-western USA, and the loss of moujik farmlands in the emerging USSR) the cosmic quandary brings whole continents to the point of famine and starvation.

As a solely secular answer to this cosmic quandary—(1)politicians devised the welfare state; whilst (2) social psychologists thought to save the day (3) by declaring that (you are who you think you are (even if you're not who you think). Since then (4) there has been an assiduous effort in all primary producing countries to save the world by diverting resources well away from wherever they are produced; and so to maintain the uncracked code (despite the counterfeit surveillance) of what exactly it still could possibly mean for small but still essentially self-sufficient countries like New Zealand to be 'God's own country'.

Nevertheless, the fast-food trade has put an end to thoughtful rumination evermore, even in God's own country, where producing ruminants (both humanly intellectual and pragmatically otherwise) has for long been the nation's primary industry. At the risk then of suffering intellectual indigestion and committing moral misfeasance, don't think too fixedly of the arts or of the humanities for being so much threatened by any big brother (whether in the person of Cyrus the Great, the European Union, or any other lawless one).

Yet why else would the Taliban outlaw all forms of music from the areas it purported to control if not to further and maintain its own exclusively bully boy administration? For the sake of maintaining peace, order, and good government throughout this rapidly failing world (where the humanities have been reduced by western management to their lowest ebb), there ought to be experienced musicologists (as well as choreographers) in every ministry of foreign affairs, no less than in every consulate and embassy.

Laugh (if you like) at this bare-bones account of musicology (for being no more any national anthem than it is any song and dance routine, as the commonality may for a time pretend to see it). But the general level of absurdity (together with today's commensurate rise in general sea level) throughout the world has reached such a feverishly political pitch (1) as to cover the screams of this world's own war-torn, impoverished, and dislocated victims that (2) what is now universally laughed at (by way of being the so-called supranational sense of humour) is more often the sober, serious, and tragic truth (put down by presidents and prime ministers the world over) by which (3) the world's self-indulgent rich mercilessly rape, plunder, and prey on the world's more and more limited resources to account (ironically) for what more and more will become merely their own very brute but delimited days of survival. The conflicting philosophies of both John Calvin (the faithful one) and Thomas Hobbes (the doubting one) will by then (here a loud *hahaha* is heard from the Counterfeit Command) have each come into their own.

Nevertheless, what counts for so much more than the historic words of any nation's national anthem in declaring either its message of *pax aut bellum* (if not peace then war) is as often conveyed only by the whole song being sung (and so its lyric message is just as much rendered by the anthem's frequently only borrowed tune). Thus, those words of the anthem (as for any other hymn) may be no more than senselessly sung (devoid of any intellectual, far less spiritual, rumination) than as for any other act of worship, the same words (without the appropriate musical backing) may not always be sensibly understood. Nevertheless, many songs (whether ostensibly of love but really of war or ostensibly of war but really of love) and not just national anthems (which can have an international mission as well as that of self-administration) are hymns (both ancient and modern) of interrelationally human as well as of divine (but sometimes no less than demonic) worship. The trouble is that all anthems (deistic or demonic) are intended, at best to be soul-catching, or at worst to be soul-snatching.

This is as much a military operation (pivoting on power) as it is a jurisprudential operation (pivoting on justice) as we shall find out later (whilst under fire in the field) when engaging in combat. We shall target such military hotspots as Kabul, Baghdad, Damascus, and Tehran later in this report. For being only a little lower than us angels, however, you humans are going to be mightily surprised in the field of battle to find out that mortal combat has a forcefulness that far outstrips the forcefulness of our own angelic yet immortal means of combat. It is often exactly (but not always precisely) because of that differential forcefulness between ourselves when combating together against the Counterfeit Command that we angels not only want but do really need the military help of mortals in the field of every spiritual battle.

Towards our seeking your human help—here is a lesson on our mutual understanding. Learn to understand (by means most literally of that precious *understanding*) which can never be gained solely by academic study (but only by experiential *understudy*) of whatever it is we wish, want, or need to understand. Just as our every conception is based on one or (usually many) more underlying preconceptions, so also the standing or status of anything we wish to know relies on our *understanding* of both where that thing stands and where we ourselves stand in relation to that thing. To gain that mutual understanding we have to learn not just how to study, but more thoroughly how to understudy both that thing as well as ourselves which (at the same time but often unknowing of this needful mutuality) we are striving to understand.

Standing—in relation to understanding—is as often acquired by standing down as by standing up. Think here of Mstislav Rostropovich who remained seated while others stood up to acknowledge Stalin's favourite national hymn tune. Understanding—by its *lying under*, and always for the deepest of understandings *lying well under*—what is often no more than the most superficially human perception of any global, far less cosmic issue either is generally undervalued, or else is passed over for being completely unseen. That's exactly how wars are fomented. Satan hasn't the slightest inkling of the depth of God's mind.

For example, consider once again the not-so-plain fact (constituting a complex contributed to by the many multitudes of complicating and apparently arbitrary fractals) that most national anthems are songs of worship. These anthems are either explicitly or more often inexplicitly understood for being their own declaration of either divine or demonic worship both by those who listen to them as well as by those who sing them. Of course, this accommodation or aclimatisation process more commonly takes place—as at most academic, sports, and electoral meetings, or at most evangelical, church, mission, and cabinet meetings—where one's own individual views (whether right or wrong) are so easily and effectively compromised, conceded, or accommodated to the collective views of others—since numbers do count. We dare to say that the generality of this processs (since mankind is manifestly a social animal) as well as the conciliatory forcefulness of this accommodation (providing often no more than peace for our time) would be immediately rebuted (for not being either widely or deeply enough understood by those most affected by it.

The resulting lack of innocence, whereby the human spirit thinks to know as much as it needs to know about itself, is the stumbling block to all future learning. Once it happens, whether consciously or unconsciously, that you distance yourself from children, for whom this world is never like it seems (as it does seem to be to those who are proudly professing adults), then you lose your learning capacity. One only has to open and reread the best of children's books for any adult to recover one's childhood innocence.

The truth is this—that to the true believer, no less than to the true scientist or true scholar, this earthly life is nothing like it seems. Read Laura Ingalls Wilder's account of travelling ever westward in her series of early settler stories, known best for her book *Little House on the Prairie*! There, you may so easily mistake each of the Wilder family, perhaps Laura especially, or the whole family collectively, for being the principal characters in this pioneering travelogue.

Well (despite being deeply mistaken), that's still true on the face of it, but the face of it is so far from the full truth as to leave the hidden depth of our understanding very much mistaken. It's not until near the end of Wilder's pioneering days, when we come to read of the death of their long-suffering bulldog Jack, that we begin to realise, if only upon our own serious reflection (i.e. rumination) on all the 'incidents' in which Jack played a leading role, that nothing of this pioneering account which required combating wolves, warding off horse thieves, meeting up with Indians, and surviving not only deadly blizzards but also swarms of locusts and failed harvests could have happened without the unswerving loyalty of Jack, their family watchdog. What—you don't like, nor read children's books! Then hold on! Instead, read Tolstoi's criticism of Chekov's short story, 'The Darling'.

So too, for just as deeply therapeutic purposes, reread Dostoyevsky's epic novel on the subject of crime and punishment! When read either as a picaresque novel or as a detective story, the chief criminal character is obviously the ex-law student Raskolnikov, but that is by no means the sum total of jurisprudence (in relating law to justice and justice to law) with which this far, far greater epic novel is concerned.

If all it took to be a criminal (even when augmented by a persevering detective) were all there was to *Crime and Punishment*, that deeply thoughtful book might, by being turned into a ripping yarn (and short-term bestseller), just manage to hold the reader's diversionary attention. On such grounds that might very well be so whilst reading *Crime and Punishment* mistakenly for relaxation at the beach or as a diversion whilst waiting for a train or whilst disappointed by the weather when on holiday. No, the storyline in Dostoyevsky's *Crime and Punishment* is only that means by which the far, far deeper message of personal sacrifice, redemption, and spiritual salvation can be conveyed. And that's exactly where the angel that is Sonya (in the person of Mary Magdalena) comes into the narrative to play the redeeming part of the soul-catcher.

Without there being any possible doubt here of Dostoyevsky's far, far greater talent to plumb the depths as well as to climb the heights, Sonya is the principal character. And although the radical character of Raskolnikov provides some remarkable insight into the psychology of the criminal mind, Raskolnikov's role is very much a supporting one and nowhere goes as deep as does the principal role, which is that of the sacrificial redeemer as demonstrated by Sonya.

So much for stories and storytelling (as any casual reader might say of Laura Wilder's *Little House on the Prairie* no less than of Fyodor Dostoyevsky's *Crime and Punishment*). Nevertheless, in the same way as many data-driven academics have dared to remind us angels of fairy tales and storytelling (as if we angels were of no more than the same fictitious standing), then (as the same academics may ask) what of the so-called real life? Well now then, as an issue of real life, how much do you humans really know of how Mount Everest was really conquered?

Press-button technology has undercut (and continues to undercut, sometimes eventually to shreds) almost all our under-standing (stet) of epic endeavour. Instead of being the classical historian that he then was (of such troublesome cities as Troy), Homer came to be dismissed for being no more (say the factualists) than a storyteller for centuries! Well, now then, how much do you really know of how Mount Everest came to be climbed and conquered in these more modern times?

Human life here on earth is not always precisely understood exactly as it happens. It cannot be accurately accounted for on earth, from which it follows that it cannot be exactly recorded. Instead, all human history of any earthly event can be recorded by humans only as it seems on earth to happen. The whole truth and nothing but the truth frequently escapes not only mankind's immediate senses but also even man's most honest attempts at truthful telling. This poses grave problems for heaven on earth.

The as often pivotal issue of who's first and who's last in the human race for recognition and even far more so for accrediting both fame and fortune (think of the Nobel Prize list) can quickly become a very messy and self-defeating competition. There's no point in blaming God for the very often most unfair outcomes by which the world's last in line becomes the world's first when first and last are viewed differently from the respectively human and divine perspectives.

As to the highest physical peak of human endeavour, unclimbed Mount Everest (although then no more than a figurative token for mankind's physical endeavour) has long been held by humanity to be first and foremost in the climbing stakes. We angels, who were obviously there when both Hillary and Tenzing 'knocked the bastard off', were there to see Everest conquered by Hillary and Tenzing not only for their being the favoured first but also for them being the (lucky) last to do so.

That's by now the thoroughly inbred way of manifesting either psychosomatic individualism (at the personally heroic level) or its correlative of psychosomatic collectivism (at the nationalistic or as often racist level) on earth. The race is on when competing to be first up the highest mountain, to be first to reach the South Pole, to be first to run under the four-minute mile, or to be the first achiever in doing whatever else remains undone on earth. Some countries—often little countries like Scotland, Switzerland, or New Zealand—despite the risk of their internal burnout, show themselves to be pretty good at producing heroes or at coming up collectively with grand ideas. Their good fortune is to be born small; otherwise they'd be waging cold wars or engaging in space races whilst on the road to their own and other's extinction.

That first time for any one person or for any one nation leaves little or no time for the same thing to be done (unless either imitatively or for its own sake) by any other nation or person. You could say as with many mountains once climbed for their first time, then that becomes their last time. Aha, but the competitive streak to excel does not stop there, since the Counterfeit Command comes up with the self-contradictory concept of sustainable excellence by which all of mankind puts itself at risk of driving itself (with other lifelong species) into the ground.

So then for being the favoured first, Hillary and Tenzing were also the lucky last because once conquered, the same token peak of physical endeavour couldn't be conquered any more. Hillary was a New Zealander, and when New Zealanders climb mountains the mountains usually groan and grumble. They may throw avalanches like Mitre Peak; they may sacrifice their sides to keep their tops like Saddle Hill; they may shed their tops like Mount Cook or (possibly out of peek) bow their heads, sulk, slide, or slip; or else more volcanically blow their tops like once Tongariro, sometime Rangitoto, or even right now, Whakaari or White Island. Meanwhile, what's the present height of Everest? Still rising, so is there still room for sustainable excellence? Fact or fiction, not even we angels can say, because once climbed, it's no longer the same Everest, so we haven't since bothered to climb it.

Not even the intrepid George Lowe, who, amongst so many other climbers, had contributed so much to Everest's conquest and who had made it so much more possible for Ed Hillary and Tenzing Norgay to climb it, could any longer be in the run to compete with others against Everest. Competition is so often, and so much, of a worldly gamble that it's left often for only the losers to win. That's exactly why to right so many apparent wrongs and even non-apparent wrongs, the first shall be last and the last shall be first.

In any case, competitions—whether athletic, academic, or artistic—are notoriously arbitrary, if not also unjust affairs. Sometimes, as with Newton fighting against Leibniz to be recognised as the first discoverer of calculus or for some of the dirty tricks that fate appears to play in the Nobel's sweepstakes, the fray for first place appears hideously like a poker game from hell rather than the holding and playing of any hand divinely dealt by heaven.

Sometimes one must (even as an angel) get down on one's hands and knees to understudy the finer (tactical) points at issue for resolving any problem. Ground-level tactics come first before trying to find the bigger (for being also the deeper, wider, and higher) strategic view. After all, this present report, as much made for informing humans as for reporting to the Supreme Command, is at least a diplomatic mission, if not also a military operation.

Nevertheless, we have relational decisions, decisions, and more decisions to make as between or amongst (1) diplomatic missions or military operations; (2) reporting to the Supreme Command in heaven or publishing for humans on earth; and (3) between the wider, deeper, and higher strategic views or else the finer tactical points, as both are required for successful military implementation. So that's life, as you humans often rather dismissively say (at which humanistic remark, we angels simply smile at what so often determines earthly outcomes 'in the midst of life').

So here, whether in the case of successfully (but competitively) climbing Everest (for example, climbers versus guides) or disastrously flying into a whiteout over Erebus (for example, pilots versus management, as in the all-out Erebus disaster), we have problematic situations which are at least complex, if not indeed compound, but hardly ever capable of any simple solution. Our first order of reaching any reasonably objective solution is to reduce the concrete issue (RCF) to the absolutely infinitive abstract (AIA)—which, of course, would be an even infinitely harder reduction were the concrete issue that of Hillary versus Tenzing, for example, or of Hillary versus Lowe, for example, even if all were not already decisively determined by the as yet unknown fate or achievement of Mallory.

Unless you go highest-mountain-climbing or furthest-foot-tramping or widest-ocean-sailing, or deepest-sea-fishing, you may not have the slightest notion of what we angels are on about by discussing the risks of pursuing sustainable excellence (or any other sort of metaphysically unsustainable competition), especially when in the context of your increasingly limited resources. From the spiritual point of view, we're trying to draw your attention both to what you see as well as to what you don't see, since then you'll know what to look for by way of increasing your faith in the substance of things unseen *since faith itself is the substance of those things unseen.*

But first answer this related yet more fundamental question (when couched by digging even deeper into the unseen although far more substantial realm of the abstract). The question is this, namely, which of these situations—the simple, the complex, or the compound—is really the easiest for humans to understand? The specialist (because of being a reductionist) says the simple, the generalist (because of being an existentialist) says the compound, whilst the professed expert (qualified by width and depth of experience) opts for the complex as being somewhere in between the simple and the compound. [Exegesis 3: Nevertheless, every musician knows most accurately of any apparently simple piece of music that it is the simple piece (and not the technically most difficult piece) which requires and exacts the most by way of the virtuoso performance (required from the musician to 'knock the bastard off')!]

Looking back again at the climbing of Everest, which, if not at first sight a compound situation, is most certainly complex (unless *from first to last* indeed a compound) and so is surely not a simple situation. This requires you humans (who, for being more personally involved than philosophically motivated) to engage in a critical analysis for which you may not be overly qualified, so by way of taking a first step in pursuing that analysis, you must be prepared to see what appears to be one and the same problem in different ways. At the outset, this involves both a microscopic as well as a macroscopic examination of its history.

For example, it is more fitting that Hillary (as a New Zealander) be allowed to conquer Everest and not Lowe (as an Englishman). This is so, for the sake of the wider view, because, in the short term, the British Empire has just given way to the Commonwealth of Nations. Consequently, the message of hope in the continued order of things should come from that wider commonwealth and not from any closer and more leading representative of the former empire.

Secondly, there is a responsibility that comes from accreditation, and in the longer term, Hillary has obviously been the divinely appointed one to exercise that self-recognised shepherding responsibility (yet to be developed) towards his Sherpa people in Kathmandu. Thirdly, there is also a cost factor (invariably suffered) in any divinely accredited (or trialling) process (by which to bring to the attention of the accredited person the responsibility of his or her duly appointed office). In Ed Hillary's case, it will be altitude sickness, which, however ironically, will go on plaguing Hillary ever since his triumphant conquering of Everest. Read the finer detail of conquering Everest and discern the hand of God at every point of decision-making towards the completion of this laconic, ironic, as well as iconic endeavour. The substance of the humanly unseen is invariably tragicomic—acquire a feeling for the angelic pH factor.

Look at the conquering of Everest then not just in hard-slogging human terms but also in some other less earthly and more heavenly way. But for all that, you may not agree that humans pay less attention to those people (like Lowe) who enable heroic things to happen or who have made it possible for them to happen (and less attention still to those who prevent or prohibit things from happening that would get in the way of what others need or want to happen). We're dealing with the way in which heroic psychosomatic individualism interacts with the so-called greater good of psychosomatic collectivism here on earth. The required critical analysis of that complex, if not compound, situation (ideally a commensal one) is extremely hard going by which to realise that in heaven, the first on earth shall so often be the last and the last on earth shall so often be the first in heaven.

Those people who personally fulfil their own heroic dreams have had those dreams so often long nurtured, developed, and built on by others that they are barely identifiable beside those others who themselves have been the first to realise and develop the only possibility of such heroic dreams being fulfilled. The same human psychology (or multifactorial metaphysics of individually and collectively related commensalism versus mutualism) also works reciprocally, the other way around (prophetic clockwise, historic anticlockwise), by which the heroic and historic deeds of Odysseus would not be remembered but for Homer's divinely prophetic gift of storytelling.

Just as the storyteller is as much of the story as the singer is as much of the song, so we come to recognise the friendly mutualism in place of the competitive commensalism which highlights the individual hero by relegating the collective contribution to the shadowy background. This is the global arena of all-in wrestling in which the worst aspects of psychosomatic individualism (otherwise known as capitalism) and of psychosomatic collectivism (otherwise known as communism) are likely to bring about the death of each other, unless we can identify, coordinate, and amalgamate the best aspects of each. All the same, it's always the individual heroes who we've always been brought up to emulate, extol, and celebrate.

You may not care enough about the hidden truth to throw a chair at some pontificating preacher (as did the fishwife Jennie Geddes in Edinburgh's St Giles' Cathedral), but you may care enough (as did the world-famous cellist and conductor Mstislav Rostropovich) to remain always seated during the restored state-rendering of Stalin's hymn when this was chosen to serve as the national anthem for the new Russian Federation. It takes a great deal of personal courage, even with the help, backing, and authority of the Supreme Command, to make any such deeply personal (yet also publicly prophetic) statement.

As with any rationalist or formalist, you may dismissively argue against the disturbance of ritual that necessarily follows from throwing a chair at some pontifying preacher or from remaining seated in a reconvened republic whatever may be the source of its former national anthem. What's in any such totem anyway, whether benefit of clergy, reconstituted republic, or reinstituted national anthem? There's surely much more to a totem than merely a token.

Why then is our Father in heaven so emphatically against graven images and all other such totems? Surely it is that he or she who makes such an image is bound to worship himself or herself as the maker of it. Reconsider the parts played by Jennie Geddes, Mstislav Rostropovich, and all other such iconoclasts! Would you seriously believe God's presence to have been in any way diminished on account of either of their deeply personal, although also collectively disturbing, testimonies to the truth? Would you not instead conclude from the immediate electrification of each issue that there was more of God's presence now surrounding each of these issues?

In such critically electrifying circumstances, the testimonial to hidden truth may be more vitally at stake than any merely mortal person then perceives; in which case, for lack of any solely secular (or mundane) explanation of an already extremely polarised situation, the spiritual issue as to truth or falsity, already complex and confused, becomes even more incredibly complicated for its lack of that solely secular explanation. Put this way, both the human faith factor and the human communicative factor then come to the fore, both to pose problems for human decision-making no less than to present the prophetic paradigm for the resolution of those problems.

The same prophetic paradigm may be expressed in innumerable other ways, since the human soul, even when unbeknown to the human body, is in constant contact with truth and falsity. Thus, the issue of truth or falsity, whether real or imagined, will present itself either to the advantage or to the disadvantage of the human person.

Telling lies, for example, is not just bad for the human conscience. Telling lies is bad for the eyes (as also for the hearing, for the balance, and for almost every other physiological function). This physiological phenomenon can be clearly proved for sight by a retinal examination of the human eye. So then don't fool around, you humans, when attempting to tell the truth, the whole truth, and nothing but the truth. There're better men than you are who have lost their voice (Zacharias, father of John the Baptist), lost their sight (Saul of Tarsus), or lost their life (Samson amongst the Philistines).

Pursuing the truth, whether within or without of any court of law, is an immensely serious business. Why, believe it or not, but as presented to the as yet unrighteous human mind, even the plain truth can so often belie belief. Why, believe it or not again, but within every human believer's most ardent belief, there is deeply embedded (as in each of these words used themselves to tell this truth) at least the very littlest of lies. Unfortunately, the human propensity (attributable to the ongoing state of fallen mankind) is always, either consciously or unconsciously, to tell (even if only through exaggerating the truth) some sort of only little white lie.

Nevertheless, when any such lie is told whilst occupied in that process of visual accommodation required of the otherwise healthy eye, there is always an error of refraction resulting from telling any lie. It may be an error of refraction gross enough to prevent one person looking into another's eyes. People may minimally lose their sight (grow short-sighted) as they often do in adolescence, either from telling lies or even from thinking to tell lies (whether told to themselves or to others). 'Would you tell lies to God', asks Job, the earliest of the Old Testament patriarchs, 'in the same way as one man tells lies to another?' [Exegesis 4: Read the book of Job, the man from Uz, chapters 12–14].

So too, the inner eye has a similarly affected refractive index, distinguishing between truth and falsity, no less than accommodating to the (physical) contrast between light and darkness or to the (spiritual) contrast between righteousness and unrighteousness. Opening the inner eyes of one's heart to the light of truth (sometimes in itself a scorching experience) as often requires first a transformation of mind with which to withstand the resulting fire.

Yet to change one's mind is as often a choice. It can be an extreme choice—say, between renewing one's mind or when faced with demonic dementia of losing one's mind—and, in very extreme cases, for a time losing one's mind to renew one's mind (like St Paul on the road to Damascus or Prince Andrei on the field of Austerlitz). Both human dementia and demonic dementia are frequently self-inflicted by the failure to face up to the falsity of one's previous thoughts, to one's wilfully entrenched wrongful beliefs, and to continue with one's unrighteous or irreligious actions.

Outlawing our own bad memories takes with them a lot more of our memory by default than we are then capable of retaining. Many memory problems which we ascribe to the dementia of old age or Alzheimer's disease arise either from deeply ingrained childhood trauma and/or our perpetuated failure in later life to confront and expose this hidden reality. We become 'old crocs' when bad memories are pushed from the front to the back of our increasingly crocodilian brain. The physiological task of maintaining this divide of the present from the unpleasant past eventually takes all of one's mental life force to keep them there. We then dare not move on for the sake of coming face to face with the still present reality.

Thus, without any coherent means of recollection, we're left in that grey area of limbo (literally 'on the edge of things'). This edginess, explained by way of our partial brain death, corresponds quite accurately to that defined limbo in the once Christian catechism.

Of course, there's no need now of this concept of limbo with premature senility all around and before us. Still, apart from the trauma of affliction which at the beginning besets the still aware sufferer, the now obsolete catechistic definition of *limbo* serves just as good a definition of *dementia* for being that 'state or place of natural happiness free from suffering or pain but without a share in the eternal life God promises to those who die in grace'.

What will work for everybody, whether in mind or in body, is for all of us to work through the false darkness of this world in search of the true light. Since for this purpose, there is no condemnation in Christ—oh then, what a friend we have in Jesus!

* * *

A Very Brief History of Heaven
Part III

Sound Sight and Insightful Sound

A person may have good vision when he is telling the truth; but if he states what is not true, even with no intent to deceive or if he imagines what is not true, an error of refraction will be produced, because it is impossible to state or imagine what is not true without an effort.

W. H. Bates, *Better Eyesight without Glasses*

'Seeing is believing,' goes one old adage. Ah yes, but then another and perhaps older adage says, 'There's more to seeing than meets the eye!' It pays always to remember that the certitude of faith relies on the substance of things assuredly promised but as yet unseen. But can you say yes to that whilst still looking me straight in the eye?

These unseen things are evidenced only by the faithful hope we mortals keep alive in the promised reality of such assurances being fulfilled. Yet it will be through those already present things, which to mortals remain as yet still unseen or else by God's grace through mortal oversight then pass for being unrecognised or ignored, that these promises shall still be faithfully fulfilled. That parents ceasing to exist for not being seen is at first torture to the infant's mind. That's exactly why (to develop infantile faith in the substance of the unseen) parents play peekaboo to reassure their child of their continued existence and return.

Common sense amongst humans (although varying markedly from one cultural context to another) is largely based (whether rightly or wrongly) on autonomic (or non-volitional) behaviour. By force of thought, discipline, or discernment, the class calculus to which common sense belongs may be experientially changed or challenged. Since this is the age of rationalism run wild and with sensualism set to overtake it, common sense is neither now so common nor yet so sensible. On the one hand, this outcome (the opposite of autistic withdrawal) persuades us to rely for everything on science (as confirmed commercially in the marketplace for those who can afford the fruits of technology) and to commit ourselves more and more both to searching as well as stretching the limits of humanly self-indulgent sensation. The polarised outcome, either through different degrees of autistic withdrawal or else insatiate and often drug-induced searching after sensation, means that the increasingly commonplace (however deviant) substitutes for what was once common sense by way of being accustomed behaviour.

Be sure to keep your eyes and ears fully open to the signs of the times! Yet be careful since every professional (whether philosopher, poet, preacher, or any other sort of committed professional) gets caught up (sooner or later) in his or her own predilections for both sound and sight as well as for silence. The secret of staying professionally relaxed (however much this may irritate every otherwise committed professional) is to keep yourself clinically open-minded. As Galileo says (in the case of that natural philosophy of his to which the closed-minded clerics of his time took offence), all 'is written in this grand book of the universe, which stands continually open to our enquiring gaze'.

Since sound and sight afford significant windows (although maybe not on your computer) into both this world and the next world, heaven's history frequently pivots on differently authorised versions of employing sight and sound. Both these senses require sound ears to hear and sound eyes to see, but even with or without this assurance of bodily sight and bodily hearing, then employing one's innermost ears and innermost eyes makes for a surer means of developing one's insightful hearing and insightful vision.

There's no room here for either idle eavesdroppers or lascivious peeping Toms, since by such means as aiding the development of your inner hearing and inner vision, we angels are out to close the gap (already much less than you can imagine) between you mortals and us angels. That gap is so much less than you mortals can already imagine that in our writing of this report, we shall most often use the inclusive 'we' for both of us.

Without both insightful sound and insightful vision, not even 20/20 sight and perfect bodily hearing (enhanced by 20/20 listening and 20/20 looking) will see you safely through these latter days of intensifying spiritual conflict. [Exegesis 1: Nevertheless, this account of heaven is written not just for all those with 20/20 sensual perception but also for all those with anything less than this world's standard.]

To the musician, both the receiving and communicating of sound is of vital significance. This is true on every intellectual, emotional, and cultural level, as well as on the spiritual level. Every little 'white lie' (notice the figurative amalgam of sight with sound) is a 'bum note' sounded in the ongoing performance of creation's symphonic score.

Indeed, how and what one likes to hear, hates to hear, cannot hear, or is left unmoved to hear operates either communicatively or countercommunicatively. This is so not just for all professed musicians but also for absolutely everyone. We are all actively engaged musicians (or else sadly disengaged musicians) as testified by the spiritual need for music in our natures.

We are talking here about both outer ears and inner ears—and also about something even more extraordinary—although little talked about or recognised openly except by musicians. The outer human ear is extraordinary, and so also is the inner ear, but the innermost ear is the most extraordinary of all. It is the innermost ear of any person that has been divinely designed to be most receptive to insightful sound. To quote the profoundly deaf Helen Keller, it is the innermost ear which senses the deistic presence of immortal life always around and this to those not even knowing the deity's name.

The profoundly deaf person (like the composer Beethoven, when so stricken down with deafness in later life) may hear and compose a near-celestial music that is hard, if not impossible, for more ordinary ears to hear, far less humanly to understand. God speaks (either directly or indirectly) to the innermost ear of many disabled people, especially those who are profoundly deaf, devoid of speech, and totally blind. To many of them, as then to others, their silence is truly golden. From their divine source, gifted people (like the author Helen Keller) develop a level of insightful sound that both exceeds and supersedes what so-called normal people may never learn to listen for, to look for, or to search for and so may never either see the innermost vision or hear the innermost sound.

As for the spoken tongue, it can also be the same, sometimes visually and sometimes aurally, but always conceptually, and so also for the written languages. Thus, every phonetically written language not only makes for a substantive sound (even when written to be read) but (through the poetry of its form, style, inflection, and metre) also sings a song. And yes, many wordsmiths who proclaim creation solely on the printed page are also sound musicians, no less than are those other wordsmiths (especially in the non-phonetically written languages) who seek to paint visual pictures (quite literally) with words.

When carried along on the wind of the prophetic spirit, the power of proclamation (whether spoken, written, or envisioned) has a creative capacity which cannot be gainsaid in the lives of both angels and men. Evolution (for being only a dragged-out, ever-so-slow, partially true text in a fast-changing, somewhat arbitrary, and overly contingent context of scientific proof) is by now a rather tired, dry, and boring concept when compared with the percussive yet divinely engineered big bang that accompanies every albeit rejected act of creation.

To the visual artist, however, it is soundness of sight (as well as soundness of light) that surpasses in significance whatever the aurally prophetic musician holds to be more vitally communicative to advance the aurally prophetic musician's promotion and reception of sound. For many people (especially preschoolers) this distinction drawn between sight and sound can be a critically communicative one. Yet in all this, we are still only talking (or phonetically writing) about the soundness of (what bodily we mistake for being) primary sight and primary sound. We haven't yet begun to enquire seriously into what makes for, say, second sight (or prophetic foresight) or for insightful sound (by which even mountains can be moved by the forcefulness of verbal proclamation).

Massive mountains are moved (as now every day in the sciences) for which scientists must formulate the right equations and learn to pronounce the right words (which may vary from 'thank you, Lord' to that of some more scientific 'open sesame'). At the start, whether in terms of phlogiston theory or of wave theory or of light theory, scientists (and even increasingly women scientists) are typically like highly interactive small boys. Their strength lies in their sense of wonder—their persistent and continuing sense of wonder—without which miracles (even scientific miracles) simply do not happen.

One of the reasons why so many ultraserious people (for the most part deadpan technologists rather than uplifted scientists) cannot get their heads round the Genesis account of creation is that they cannot conceive of God himself (the so-called Ancient of Days) for ever having been a typically small boy. In basic form (since the DNA helix is the experimental prototype for all this earth's manifold life forms), the creator of the universe is also just that little bit more of an experimentalist (on the cosmic scale) than we can ever imagine of any small boy. We marvel at the miracles of modern science but forget (atheistically) that every human scientist has been made most wonderfully in the image of God.

Look at all the wonder of this world's diverse genetic creation, which is existentially linguistic in every conceptual aspect of its coded communication! In this same intimately encrypted way, the microscopic double helix of DNA is essentially a linguistic model. It has been microscopically written with the solvent yet sovereignly designated power to proclaim creation.

So too, as a matter of physics, because every beginning is destined to end, this dying planet has been birthed into every macroscopic aspect of its materially entropic resolution by similar processes of linguistic proclamation. And in the same deistic although humorously ironic way, most sunrise pronouncements for this planet Earth, whenever and however encrypted, whether into science (through laws of entropy) or into scripture (through divine revelation), are also sunset provisions (as were also the evening and morning which constituted the very first day).

Consider also, the measure of almost divine judgement required of any scientist, entailing both *sophia* (or wisdom) as well as *scientia* (or knowledge), in assessing the validity, viability, and reliability of the (often statistical) conclusions reached (especially in the social sciences) either to establish, refute, redefine or modify the original conjectures giving rise to the first, and sometimes strings of following experiments. In terms of the initial conjectures, there may be clearly positive, clearly negative, or clearly contingent outcomes, with differently perceived levels of validity, viability, and reliability, which in the wider context of this experimentation may look to prove to be of greater or lesser significance, or else to be proving little or nothing at all.

In view of these statistics, we might dare to say that scientists, as against prophets, are not much good at conjecturing—in itself a conclusion requiring more than to be just lightly tweaked for correction—since none but false prophets are engaged in conjecturing. As like as not, however, even the processs of peer review (whether scientific or literary) will pose as many problems (unless at the highest level of deciding between alternative realities) as it affords academic advantages.

Besides, too many ultraserious people (in this case, often informationally overloaded academics who have lost their sense of childlike wonder) will have only their own narrow view of both scientific and scriptural interpretation (not to mention even more narrowly of prophetic revelation) at their command. With no more than their own time-tuned tunnel vision, such academic dunderheads (no offence intended) will accordingly think to read the specific text but still omit to read or else intentionally ignore the generic and so often rapidly changing cosmic context.

The resulting cherry-picking clarity (like tax-driven charity) is less real than virtual. And since in the main, such dunderheads are reading both programmed science and programmed scripture from different versions and in various translations, they will completely overlook the translation theory by which source translations have remarkably different objectives from target translations. The first nails the trinity to the (ontological) source, whilst the second nails the trinity (teleologically) to the target and so sometimes leaves aside everything instrumentally in between by way of being what otherwise would be the means of uniting source (Genesis) and target (Revelation).

So then by way of connecting defined text with indefinite context, consider the cosmos at the time of creation to be then possibly very, very small (although correspondingly very, very dense) and not as now so apparently very, very large (although for having been so far stretched out between now and then (through space) by the passage (not always constant) of intervening time). In other words (i.e. cosmologically speaking), we've come a long, long way, although perhaps like any piece of cosmic elastic when stretched to its final limits, more clearly subject to the law of entropy and inevitable breakdown, and so now reaching almost to breaking point.

In short (as of remaining time), even universal laws, once so dense and immutable, have taken on the less than solid appearance of our human laws for being just as contingent, just as confused, and just as retractable. All laws (as humans think to know them) then become increasingly open-textured and semipermeable (in allowing humans to do their own thing), and so without the help of some further and extradimensional measure to be made available on this now rapidly declining earth, these once dense and immutable laws become completely unsustainable.

When all was once measured by depth and density (as so then also were *scientia* and scholarship), the state of being big was not thought to be so beautiful (as it is now with the world's competing tall towers, three main meals a day, SUVs, and total life insurance), but as the cosmos became less and less dense and laws became more refractive, then big, bigger, and biggest became increasingly mistaken by humans for being beautiful, more beautiful, and most beautiful. Then extending his outstretched arm (not the left one imprinted *Favour* but the right one imprinted *Grace*), our Divine Experimentalist experimented with also extending space and so creating distance that consequentially heightened heaven from fallen earth.

To fill this ever-extending space (achieved by squeezing more and more light out of the timeless darkness which interstitially still pervades time), our Divine Experimentalist had not just created great dinosaurs (as an experiment in stretching their DNA to compare its viability with that of tiny voles) but also had a further creative fling with giant dragonflies (a.k.a. the Protodonata) in giving them (for their being not yet metric) a two-and-a-half-foot wingspan as a result of polyploidy (or a doubling of their chromosomes). This was not always the successful experiment it once was, yet it was demonstrated eventually between Wee Davie Boy (later to reap a harvest as King David) and Gruesome Goliath to be put down for bombast against already the Lord's annointed. As shown over centuries in dealing with giants (as well as in gaming with dungeons and dragons) or as in a still much later case by the throwback to King Kong, winning any sort of battle at all requires more and more of the outstretched arm of *Grace*.

So too, the divine experimentalist of all creation (in those days a small boy at heart) went with his own idea of creating (as small boys do just for fun) the largest ever known lobster. This was Pterygotus (as Adam called it whilst himself still a lad), which reached a length of more than nine feet (also premetric) before it ran out of food. Well, for the lack of what it took to feed a nine-foot lobster (never mind what any child finds out what it takes to feed a bunny), that experiment (as with the dinosaurs and dragonflies) also failed, leaving poor Pterygotus to turn cannibalistic towards the end of the Paleozoic Age.

Likewise, since all things big, bigger, and biggest were now being marketed (under a policy of 'think big') for being beautiful (although not for the nine-foot lobsters which had eaten themselves to excess, and were now facing the fate of looking for alternative food resources) then books too, like the Bible had to be blockbusters to become bestsellers. Accordingly, lots of little books—from Job to Jonah and the minor prophets (the so-called little writers)—had to be rounded up and collected together so as to compete against all the other blockbusters. So then this was done, even for the Bible, before being shot out of a canonical cannon (in the course of which reformative explosion, readers lost a lot of the so-called lesser books) to become the one big book (which became known (for all time) as the Authorised Version).

It was only then, after it became obvious (first to the Bantam Neanderthals—not a soccer team) that the biggest of creatures (to which mankind collectively conspires to supersede for being in his own turn the biggest of all Cro-Magnon creatures—definitely a rugby-football team) would consume more of the planet than the limited resources of creation could possibly provide, that the other arm of the Almighty (the one imprinted with *Favour*) began to favour the small. Thank goodness (in itself a sly artifice by which to avoid thanking God), this was the point of belated time at which a certain suspicion arose (implanted by some renegade artificer) that the Cro-Magnons were killing off all the Neanderthals. This then was the point at which the grand designer of all things turned the world right round (a reversal of values marked by several Ice Ages by which thereafter to maximise the small and minimise the big).

Soon, the smallest of things—'Go to the ant, thou sluggard,' he said—would take over from the mythic monsters of leviathan and behemoth, before he allowed the descendants of the humble field vole to reap the harvest of the world's very smallest of things. In time, which then was so plentiful, this harvest of incidentals (krill, aphids, ants, and bees) would become increasingly more significant than what hitherto had been the apparent mainstream of those vastly bigger things depending on the smaller. Thus, the human ascendant would quickly become the descendent and human progress regress into recess, which meant that (1) devolution would shortly be mistaken for evolution; and (2) the feudal order would degenerate into disorder; before then (3) aspiring back again into social order; and in such ways (4) the pendulum would swing; and (5) keep on swinging; until (6) eventually it would stop.

It was there and then (if you can pardon that anthropomorphic anachronism before space-time had been explained to non-comprehending humans) when the first would become the last and the least would become the greatest. It followed (as heaven's lawyers surely pleaded) that those who went without would become those to reap the fullest possible harvest, and likewise, only those who mourned would have the propensity for being comforted.

There is a heavenly logic (as well as a biological practicality) by which all these biblical beatitudes and blessings make sense. It is only by virtue of this biologic that those who hunger and thirst after righteousness can be replenished, no less than only those who are impoverished enough in their humanistic spirit can (without any bodily bravado) dare to squeeze through the exceedingly narrow gates of heaven. Biologically then (of course, since spirituality is as much a life science as for mortals entailing a death science), the biggest omnipotent particle would depend on the littlest particle, the cosmic macrosphere would rely on the minimalist microsphere, no less than even the still incomplete biblical canon would remind every human being that 'all flesh is grass'.

Once you've captured this pyramidical construct for all creation (consult the one US dollar bill) or, as for Mayan step-up-to-heaven-stairs or Egyptian all-seeing pyramids, or even just Russian matroyshka nesting-dolls, then you've got the message (with many systemic variants for law, logic, or language) never mind the flea-circus by which to account for human relationships, whereby big, bigger, and biggest becomes beautiful to some, while instead others look to the smallest possible particle by which to explain the significance of the overall entirety. Then, either way you can think yourself to have a handle (occult or otherwise) on the hidden mysteries of all creation. Alas, for thinking yourself to have the answer without beginning to understand the question, is bound to be occult.

The most self-serious (and as often prestigious, but least percipient) of scientists thus began to conjecture that the great designer's grand design for making life began with (something like) protein-infective particles. These speculatively set up a woof-waffle chain reaction (a precursor to the World Wide Web) resulting in viruses, bacteria, and other low, lower, and finally the lowest forms of life. 'Ha-ha-ha,' scoffed the theologians (before being made to cry), 'but it wasn't, isn't, and wouldn't be that way round at all.' Meanwhile, with the great apes absconding from any hint of their being tainted with human culture, Darwin's *Descent of Man* (as the leading text in the diminishing context of its very own time) would hit world headlines in the rapidly warring context of church–state relations.

One needs to read Kierkegaard *On the Concept of Irony* by which to realise how Darwin's *Descent of Man* is so very accurate an account of man's *descent*. As for any happily ending novel, therefore no less for the same author's earlier *On the Origin of Species* whose happiest ending is no more read than that of Tolstoy's epilogue to his sixteen books on *War and Peace*, then without reading to the very end of each great work, neither can ever be said to have been truly read.

Such great books, whose writing we relive by our reading (as often backwards from reviews and so in reverse order rather than forwards in the right order of their writing), ought to teach even the most backward of human readers not to repeat the same mistakes of history whose learning they have foregone by their wrong-way-round reading, even when of the right books. The entire history of the world can be read in books (since the history of books is the history of the world) in ways which cannot be replicated any more than by a virtual shadow of itself on the World Wide Web.

You will have cherry-picked from all such lighthearted sing-songs of creation (from yesterday's baroque to modern minimalist) that sound and sight have each a refractive index which, when expressed relationally to each other, become common knowledge amongst educational psychologists. It is with this common knowledge that these psychologists classify people into being either primarily aural or primarily visual in both their learning capacity as well as in their means of communicative expression.

Nevertheless, for a musically minded visual artist, one and the same person may look to be equally sound in both of these sources of sense perception and communicative expression, no less than each human overall looks towards, strives, and searches to be equally sound in body as well as to be sound in mind. Looking and listening (certainly when aspiring to the heights of communicative expression) both have to be experientially learnt in order to see and hear to the best heavenly advantage. Besides, this experiential learning (as an experience in itself) is built into the eventual outcome and cannot be left out of it.

The human scientist may be brought up or taught to reject all such talk of 'insightful sound' or of 'innermost vision' (instead of his relying, more soulishly than he thinks to know himself, on his own sound sight or on his own sound hearing). Focussing all his faith and powers of reasoning on these bodily means of proof achieved experimentally through his own organs of sense perception—primarily those, however much technologically enhanced, of his own seeing and hearing—he thus seeks every means of avoiding and eliminating all figurative in favour of solely literal expression. This he seeks to achieve by what he attributes to his very own powers of objective reasoning. Unless and until aware of all such gifts of human understanding being God-given, however, all his own awareness lacks deistic competence for its successful implementation. This loss of competence results from his having excised every last hint of deistic poetry from his human prose.

The way words work when used by both angels and humans says a great deal about the different significance each attribute to the work of prose and poetry. Why, most of the world's greatest scientists are at heart poetic songsters. The scientific genre of poetic communication they see to be the reverse of that stiff-lipped prose reportage which they attribute to themselves by way of fulfilling their own fictionalised objectivity. Nevertheless, even when singing symphonically the best of scientists will still demean themselves to be no more than descriptive prose writers. Thus, they will either fail to see, or else take offence at any of these great lyrics being more properly attributed to their looking and listening.

In their own times, both Ernst Haeckel and J. Arthur Thomson (each with different worldviews) brought their own bio-poetic to lighten up the post-Darwinian darkness. So too, did J.Z. Young with his *Life of Vertebrates* and J.Z. Young with his *Memory System of the Brain*. Yet to conceive of scientific feats as anything less than an answer to where great songs come from (however imperfectly heard and sung by humans) is to mistake human incredulity for deistic credibility.

Some of the greatest lyricists in science (including those singing songs of nature, including human nature) attributed to Bacon, Newton, Darwin, Freud, and Marx may nevertheless be based on no more than observational reportage, which sooner or later in each case turns out to be scientifically wrong and sometimes all wrong (and not just scientifically wrong). This paradox (as of *philosophia* serving one's love of wisdom no less than of *scientia* serving one's love of knowledge) is always present when, for seeing or for hearing or for every other sort of professedly scientific but solely mundane observation, people profess to rely solely on their own sensory perception (or that of others) as a purely physical, bodily, and material function. In such ways of doing things, mankind has simply no claim to the level it exerts, however partially, of acting with deistic omniscience.

All the same, many humans (when not always walking with the angels) do still admit to walking out on thin ice here (the nearest they can ever get to walking on water). This ice is as thin or as broken through now as it once was when, in those near final days of WWII, the Baltic and Ladoga Seas would nevertheless freeze over sufficiently to allow food, medical supplies, and munitions to be transported from the Allies (via the Road of Life over Lake Ladoga) to those beleaguered citizens explicitly doomed to extinction by the Axis powers during the Nazi siege of Leningrad (now once again St Petersburg). During those days of worldly crisis, angels then abounded on earth, as shown by the flourishing aurora borealis (or northern lights).

Now today, it is the last humanly unsettled continent of Antarctica (where the aurora australis reigns over the southernmost oceans) that the current battle rages. The unhappy battle over the Falkland Islands was not fought defensively for nothing. In such ways, despite the wrongfulness of man, Father God may still extend his grace and favour. Nevertheless, in these more and more worrisome times of unexpected happenings, be prepared, as we first warned, so that with constant prayer, you humans may know what to do and not be caught napping (or worse still, kidnapped in this age of human trafficking).

We angels are therefore going to end this brief part 3 of our history of heaven with a whole wide world weather warning. It will tell something of what's going to happen once the increasingly burdensome weight of human technology fails to be supported by the less than complete perceptive sensory infrastructure of which you humans are so proud of for having self-created.

There's nothing worse than self-pride (oh, but there is, you know) by which to close both human and angelic eyes to all this suffering in the world. As already prophetically foretold, however, humans will rely more and more on their own self-confidence by which to assume adequate support for their rapidly failing world.

Despite the world's rapidly melting reserves of both Arctic and Antarctic ice, humans will, by reason of their own self-pride, fail to pick up on the parallel meltdown in the concept of what they mistake for being their own infinitely ongoing and immutable science. We will thus (whilst risking the metonymy by which 'hell-bent people' can so easily give rise to 'hell-bent books') devote what later follows by way of being Book 3 of this report towards achieving a breakthrough of those anthropomorphic circumstances which seriously afflict what ought to be the righteously upright stance of science. Crediting yourselves with all of God's good grace and favour must be reckoned with, since so many areas of scientific endeavour are already afflicted with problems (such as that of singularity and uncertainty) which are metaphysical rather than physical and yet which you attribute to lack of *scientia* (or knowledge).

It is this tall tower (of sometimes no more than self-praise expressed through pseudoscientific babble) by which you mortals, for being still so far fallen humans (especially in the social sciences), think to attribute deistic omniscience to your own human self-knowledge. Know first more of yourselves, as we angels now counsel you mortals, before thinking yourselves to know more through science of this rapidly shrinking and disappearing world.

* * *

A Very Brief History of Heaven
Part IV

The Fragility of First Causes
Elizabeth Ann had a wonderful plan: She
would run round the world ... Till she found a
man ... Who knew *exactly* how God began ...
A. A. Milne, *The Christopher Robin Verse Book*

What do you aim for in poetry—a warm fuzzy feeling, the pin-point accuracy of surgical expression, a latitudinous width of meaning, or just another run around the block? Unsure —then we'll try for the lot—although that tactic usually muddles everyone up to please no one (which, for the purpose of finding out where you stand, is still sometimes the very thing you have to do)!

Aha—but what about God's poetry. Believe it or not, but the verse or verses written especially for you are already encoded into your name! Nevertheless, as if you couldn't possibly believe that, even of anyone known to Christopher Robin as Elizabeth Ann (or Anne), then read of *God's Poetry* by Anne (Annie) Hamilton who writes of the way in which your very own identity and destiny is already divinely encoded into your name. What does your name stand for; Anne stands for 'dedication'; and Annie Hamilton stands for one of this world's most dedicated writers (coupled also with a surname of great historical fame).

Look here, even if you don't like your own name's poetic standing, whether as a writer, a fighter, a preacher, or a teacher, you can find out more of what you don't know about your name's far greater width of meaning before you dare to make a change. Why, even as a writer like Annie Hamilton, already words, letters, and numbers (all of which you don't yet know about) may partake of the destiny already woven into your codified name. Whether you now just toddle as a child, lounge around like an adolescent, run in midlife aimlessly like an adult, amble or even just totter as an elderly person, then get into your stride, make up for lost time, decode your code by which to cross the threshold of your already established destiny!

Once you get into your stride (at least until you trip-up) it's rather like jogging; but even when you trip-up, you can always pretend, as with today's increasingly irregular verse, that you're still going with the (at least intermittent) flow. Nevertheless, poetry, like breathing, is nothing like it once was. Unless you disagree with that, please excuse the asthmatic breathing resorted to keep this part (on the fragility of first causes) of our very brief history of heaven alive.

Without changing the issue, then here's the same question, although less abstract and more specific. What woman, like Elizabeth Ann, does not run round the world until she finds a man? And blessed is she who finds a man who can tell her at least something when humbly inferred from God's own creation of how God himself began, but even should Elizabeth Ann not find any such man who can tell her *exactly* how God began, she shall learn in the process of not asking too much from any mere man.

Apart from this wonderful fantasy but impossible plan, as devised by more than one (little theosophist) Elizabeth Ann, to run round the world until she finds some man who can tell her *exactly* how it was that God began when not even the angels—please forego any mere man—are authorised to tell her how *exactly* it was when her very own life began. Yet never mind, so they tell her. She can ask the same question at any old time of her own heavenly Father, who reigns over all for being the supreme over all and in constant command, in which case there need be no risk of any little Elizabeth Ann asking too much from any mere man.

'Shucks!' say us mortals to Elizabeth Ann. 'We never knew that we could when we can. As earthbound humans, we are prone to witness both Christmas and Pentecost only from our severely limited and earthly point of view. None on earth can yet know with any *exactitude* about how the eternally living triumvirate of the Supreme Command [Father, Son, and Holy Spirit] came about.'

Let's face it—first causes are acausal! They could not be otherwise since, for being first causes, they must be beyond all causal explanation. Yet some dreamers are boldly given to dream, and some seers are boldly given to envision. Yet other humans are boldly given to preach, to teach, to heal, to prophesy, and to have wise words of knowledge. So too, still yet other humans may learn to speak coherently in tongues and to interpret and to translate clearly and meaningfully for others from whom such gifts are not presently held or functioning. So then for all such serendipitous and synchronous happenings, how far can one go to legitimate the so-called first cause beyond all such happenings?

Why, for whatever 'first cause' there must be for all such phenomena, there is no first cause capable of rational explanation except our faith in their being such 'first cause' by which to account for the reality of all such happenings. On such account, some mortals, such as Elizabeth Ann, base their ongoing search for God, and other mortals shrug off their experience with happenstance. Nevertheless, as must be said over and over again, especially in these most perilous times, you humans (speaking generically) are only a little lower in the heavenly scheme of things than are us angels. [Exegesis 1: But for all that, it needs also be said that no Elizabeth Ann should ever mistake any mere man for being an angel or yet any angel for being a mere man.]

All the same, for any Elizabeth Ann being only a little lower than the angels, this position is even much less than you can imagine when viewed in the light of Jesus Christ, who took human form as a test required of his Father's creation to find out what it means for all humans to be human. This Son of the Father, born both of God and of woman, took that supreme test on behalf of all you humans to prove that you too can pass every test you might face in life with flying colours.

Of course, it takes much more than any mere man always to come to the Lord, and so the Lord has both first and final choice, although that is operable only after being confirmed by the freely given assent of the previously picked out individual. So too, the experience of coming to the Lord always takes much more than the exercise of merely human inclination, although in bringing any man to the Lord, a good woman may demonstrate a level of heavenly persuasion (beyond that of any mere man) on behalf of the Lord that may catalyse that man's rightful choice in favour of his freely given confirmation.

Apart from this wonderful fantasy but impossible plan, as devised by more than one little Elizabeth Ann, none but us angels, for our being only a little higher than you humans, as you know, can ourselves know with certainty and in the sight of our Lord God Almighty, the most ancient of all days yet to come, what most assuredly is yet to come.

We were there at the critical moment of the world's first conception, you understand—as near to the preconception of all things as any heavenly being can come—yet as now, with the already prophesied climax of all creation awaiting he who has come ... still yet again ... to come ... just as ... he has already promised to come ... is assured.

We still singing angels know that the end of all things (as we know them, like Beethoven's Eighth) will be greater by far than the beginning triad (with which Beethoven's Fifth) once began, no less than that eternal One, the creator of all things with the mindset of caring for the many, who, after the fall, faced up on our behalf to the onslaught of the Counterfeit Command, will most assuredly face up also to that final onslaught from whatever forces then still remain of the Counterfeit Command.

Lost the metre ... have you ... perhaps gone with the flow of thought? Yet what's the price paid by which to cost the loss of our once so many brilliant angels and then (when downed like dominoes) to cost the correlative price paid by Jesus even although what he paid counts for nothing amongst the vast bulk of just as brilliant unbelievers who still constitute mankind? This is a hard accounting task—although we hear that the Counterfeit Command runs summer courses (Costing 101) in this subject.

We remaining angels (as well as more than just a few of you humans), already still arrayed in front-line battle, now recognise for having over us not just the threats of the Counterfeit Command but, still with the resounding hammer blows of Beethoven's Fifth, that robe of righteousness over the full-body armour (from hopeful head to peaceable toe) by which to provide the full care and protection of the same Supreme Command. So then we will sound the last trump—*ta-ta-ta-TUM* ... *ta-ta-ta-TUM* ... *ta-ta-ta TUM*—played on the fullest range of all horns. [Exegesis 2: But then unless you lived through and survived the Second World War (which is still continuing in its ever-widening space-age phases), you wouldn't have the slightest notion of this token tribute to the ultimate victory as fought for by all Britons—first to the cost of the king (Edward VIII, yet another (the last) of England's long line of playboy kings), then by way of more serious aftermath, sacrificing the country (through repaying war loans to the USA) and finally the empire (in favour of a passive commonwealth) all later to be laid at the feet of the tiny and about to be (once again) war-torn Poland. You think yourself, as do most nearly every pacifically professing Christian, to remain mindlessly neutral, then quite shortly, in the ultimate conflict of all time, you've got another thing coming!]

Stuck for discerning the key... major, no ... minor, no ... atonal, perhaps... That's all at the very beginning, you know, at the very first pre-conceiving moment of first conception of creation, as it most surely was, which began with 'the sudden spread of stars [some wisdom-books think of them being angels] across the void'. Then later (as it must surely have been in spatial-time), when all the stars sang songs to light up the sky ... and when (according to the poets) 'the shape of music'—[yes, of course, music has a shape, or form (either demonic or divine) as every musician well knows]—while, back to the poets 'out of stillness grew cold clay of silence moulded, filled with breath' ... and when, look will you ... with eyes to see ... where 'a great glory [lights up] the mind's dark walls like torchlight gleaming in the house of death ...'

Ah yes, for being so long ago it's all a bit clouded with stardust now, but it takes a poet ... a very great poet to recapture the crystal-clear concept (the very first *magnificat*) of creation now. For being ourselves in the South Pacific and under the Southern Cross we've chosen a poet no less than the now relatively unknown A. R. D. Fairburn. Back in his own time he was described as 'the most vital person' who any man might ever meet. His whakapapa (or genealogy) credits his descent from a lay missionary in New Zealand who married a daughter there of Bishop Colenso. And so (with his own poetic words above) it has been given to him to recreate that critical moment of first conception by which to recreate what happened not long after, when the first light of Jesus Christ began to light up also the dawn of human time. [Exegesis 3: A. R. D. 'Rex' Fairburn (1904–1957) could be held to be the founder of New Zealand poetry.]

Because you humans may be needlessly misled in this part of our report by some of the apparent diversions it contains—whether that be on the earlier search for some mere man by Elizabeth Ann, on the ongoing Darwinian struggle for human survival, or on the by now historical debate between Newton and Leibniz over which of them was the first to invent calculus—for your own lives, you must learn to distinguish, quicker than ever before, the public from private, the societal from personal, and the comic from tragic. So too, there is so much else which we must disregard for being space trash in today's astrophysics than that indicated by its current and all-consuming search for aliens.

Why search for aliens? According to CIS (in this case, the Cosmic Intelligence Service) there's a big embargo placed over the whole of planet Earth. 'Please keep away!' it says, since the inhabitants (particularly the rich and powerful) are all unstable. Consequently, there's not the least likelihood of youse humans (pardon the space-travel patois) meeting up with any aliens.

This sort of thing (like many other sorts of thing) all happen by reason of your now having the responsibility incurred by every freedom of choice to think more deeply of the state of yourselves, the state of the world, and the state of the cosmos than ever before. Besides, it will help every earthbound reader firmly to grasp that the purpose of all such apparent diversions is more specifically to demonstrate that it always takes much more than any one mere man (no matter whether a Genghis Khan, a Napoleon Bonaparte, or a Benito Mussolini) to come to the Lord.

In other words, when speaking to scientists and other military men, you cannot rule out life's every other dimension than that of the purely physical just because by now, they have become so accustomed to withholding every last iota of credibility from all but that upheld by the most physical of proofs. Alas, such scientists (for being lovers of knowledge but not always of wisdom) fail to recognise their own heightened faith factor (however fallible) when so heavily and solely invested in physical proofs. Never overlook anyone's faith factor (whether or not restricted to the finding of scientific proof) just because it differs from your own, however.

All the same (apart from aliens), there are three (not just two) views of the world (uprightly angelic, midway human, or downright demonic) as seen differently when either grounded by this life on earth or else inspirited from the heights of heaven or whilst still held captive in continuing free fall. We upright angels still soar like eagles on creation's heavenly updraught, whereas those rebellious spirits, still angels (although sadly fallen), remain as often caught in their own spiralling downdraught as they do when groping for a hold on human souls.

The soaring updraught (as if for being conveyed on some magic carpet) is one of rock-solid hope, faith, and promise, whilst the spiralling downdraught, already rapidly nearing rock bottom, is one of fast-diminishing space and of faster-expiring time. Yes, even space and time—like this earthly oil and coal, this earthly wood and water, this earthly thought and feeling—are increasingly limited resources. And when these increasingly limited resources eventually extinguish themselves for having hit rock bottom, there shall not be much difference experienced by you humans already physically confined in those end times, between joy and sorrow, between pain and pleasure, or between faith and action.

No, instead of the accustomed conflict between opposites, which you humans have for so long assumed to be fundamental to your lives, then however much the earth may shake and however much the seas shall roar, that accustomed conflict between order and disorder shall be thrown wide open to the confusion of all but a chosen remnant. Then the very poles of the earth shall switch to confound the worldly wise as to what is good and what is bad, as to what is right and what is wrong, and as to what is real and what is unreal.

Why, this is already the age of the surreal, where what is still only theoretically virtual has been made to masquerade as practical reality. So too, this dying world still moves on to further close the gap between what is real and what is unreal. Eventually, the rapidly narrowing distinction between order and disorder shall be categorically closed, at least until the day of absolute judgement resolves every diminishing difference in increasingly relativistic human values.

Prepare yourselves now for that very day of absolute judgement. Build on whatever real difference you can still see between the conflicting opposites of good and evil, right and wrong, truth and falsity, righteousness and unrighteousness. Pay more attention to what is only for now your own very human and fallible perception of what stands for being either undistorted good or undistorted evil. Remember, 'woe unto those who call evil good and good evil'.

There is a difference, nevertheless, between the days of the end and the end of days, which most of you humans not only overlook but also try to overlook. Instead of focussing on the hope, faith, and promise of eternity, old-time preachers have so often focussed on our being caught up on the spiralling downdraught of fast-diminishing space and ever faster expiring time. Such old-time preaching wants to promote that 'shocking stillness for an instant', which follows from uttering the word (so supernatural is its effect) or (so scary is our response to it) of our reflecting on death (especially when encountered in the midst of life).

Well, sometimes the results of old-time preaching can be equivocal, which some of us hold sufficiently excusable for the way in which it drives some oversensitive souls away from the divine ruthlessness instead of drawing them towards the divine kindliness, of any such god as we might mistake for projecting only our own image. [Exegesis 4: No, hold on. It is our human task to project God's image, and that's exactly why we humans are made in the image of God. But by such a demonic reversal of divine and humanistic values, we can be misled into mistaking God for being made in the image of man—yuck, yuck, yuck—instead of man being made in the image of God.

Our own human image is bifurcated, both physically and morally, by which Yahweh himself knows both the evil that taints, as well as the search for redemption which inherently motivates the fallen human soul. All the same, we are not always allowed to keep to the earliest of our Sunday school callings, whereby we are brought up to focus only on the 'gentle Jesus, meek and mild' myth, which, when so divorced from reality, can cut short our more adult calling to go into the world (unfair though we may think that world to be) for the rest of our days on earth. [Exegesis 5: Read R. C. Zaehner on the subject of our savage god.]

Death, to every unredeemed soul, still remains a fearsome word. Some souls batten down the fear and so think themselves to carry on regardless; others batten down their lives to repress their constantly growing fear. G. K. Chesterton (called the Great Gilbert when undercover) points this out in one of his *Father Brown Stories* [the story entitled *The Queer Feet*] by which 'so supernatural is the word *death*' that even for the idlest of men, it can cause 'him to look for a moment at his soul' and to see it 'as a small dried pea'. And not even the most secular of scientists, given the chance, is exempt from confronting the Gregorian (or Mendelian) state of his unshriven soul (however apparently smooth or wrinkled) in this way—for it being no more than a shrivelled pea (instead of a cup filled to running over with the heavenly spirit).

Meanwhile (since time is still in the offing), 'we beg to interrupt' (as the good soldier Schweik would gently rebuke his superiors) to say that Stephen Hawking, author of *A Brief History of Time: From the Big Bang to Black Holes*, has just passed on (and as to the recent passage of his soul, the Supreme Command will already have determined). We know that for sure since his bodily remains (although not those of an Anglican, far less than of any other identifiable denomination) have been interred (as now thought permissible for all, even secular celebrities) in Westminster Cathedral. We beg also to report (also as heartbreaking news) that religious space for the passing on of still more famous men (with nary a woman in sight) is at an increasing premium in these holiest of cathedral precincts. Even for Stephen having been consigned to embers, it was an increasingly tight squeeze between those of Isaac Newton (still experiencing free fall for his onslaught on poor little Gottfried Leibniz) and Charles Darwin (at present being made to rewrite most of his memoirs in heaven).

Well, we are all still inspirited battlers as are these three (altogether six with their guardian angels), for Sir Zak is still remembered for being a very grumpy and ungracious old man, whilst as for the far more stoic, much-travelled, and relatively undecorated Chas D. (*D* for Darwin—better known as the fellow who gave his name to the

Darwinian debacle). The whole wide world, even with genetics now far out and epigenetics now well in, could hardly be the same as they left it.

Poor old Chas, they say, is having a hard time rewriting his *Descent of Man* (unlike the Bible, for so long being out of authorised print, but now, as only some sort of intellectual curiosity, being back in publication). But that's the trouble with science, since with the next big bang, all that went before falls into the resultant void of the latest black hole for then being sadly out of date. Just as it takes cholesterol to go from basic need to incidental no-no and thence back to basic need, so also in the end, it takes a BA to understand the historical development of the BSc and a BD to understand the implications of that historical development for the underlying metaphysics of both the fast-outgoing BA and the even faster bulrush of so many incoming BScs. [Exegesis 6: There is room for a thesis here (since epistles have long gone out of fashion). So too, it's become fashionable to down-score wisdom for being found to be reversely proportionate (at mean sea level atmospheric pressure) to the weight of academic credentials.]

Poor old Chas, but what a preacher, what a teacher, and what a successful polemicist of the revealed need for the BSc (Londinium), although now driven so sadly out of date in redbrick universities by the BCom (commerce, not communism) and the MBA. Authors, beware: having written so very much over his long lifetime, the designer of the Darwinian mindset has now himself a mammoth task (no pun on 'mammoth' intended) to undertake his whole life's rewriting—from coral reefs (now also in climatic decline) to his present trouble with finches (apologies to Lamarck)—besides that of owning up to the effect of his own poetic licence (privately admitted to the forcefulness of childish imagination in his rather wonderful autobiography on the vicissitudes of growing up). As the motto of the Royal Society says (still in Latin), 'Stick to the facts!'

If only the Darwinian debacle could have been avoided—but it's even said now that the Father of Genetics, Gregor Mendel, cooked the books to make a savoury soup out of both sets of smooth and wrinkled peas (left over from his experiment). And it was that soup (no longer savoury but secular) which finally force-fed opponents of Darwinian thought to go with the flow, which by that time had become a mischievously secular flood.

You would have thought that the designer of Darwinism, for being some sort of independent scholar yet with only a modest BA (the prerequisite at Cambridge, which, but for his gap year on the *Beagle*, should have led the said Chas to become a clergyman), might have dropped out of the race (no pun intended). But that humble BA never stopped him (as it did many others before the introduction of the BSc at (by then) again Londinium, the once commercial centre in Roman Britain). It is of course a great shame, explained by the increasing shortage of religious space, that the late professor Stephen (so much addicted to outer space) should be somewhat squeezed between or alongside these other two battlers in both space and time, besides being also so compressed in company with an even greater host of bonnie battlers from all sides. But then such is the price of fame and fortune. Such too, is the increasing density of celebrity-remains buried here, there, and everywhere on earth, that this fast-dying world is rapidly reaching implosive breakdown. Isn't there anyone on earth (knock-knock-knock) to realise that the limit (when once reached) to human progress is (for all but the chosen remnant of a spiritual few) that of human regress?

Still, *requiescant in pace* to all three (for being also still in Latin). It's a good place for all battling bodies eventually to be (with now all three at relative rest within nodding distance of the Herschel astronomers (father and son), James Clerk Maxwell (the Scot who discovered radio waves as a result of his racking a stick, like *wid onnie ither bairn dae*, along some palings), Howard Florey (an Aussie pioneer of penicillin, long after the Scots bacteriologist Alexander Fleming discovered the same), and not far from Michael Faraday (one of those unsettling polymaths whose free spirit probably still wanders round the cathedral precincts). As the Anglican Book of Common Prayer (if not also the Episcopalian and Catholic Books of Common Prayer) so often remind us (even if only a smattering of believers on earth any longer read the Bible), let us now praise famous men (and our fathers that begat us).

As you read this report, now being released to all by the Supreme Command, the speed of light (at least in this fast-cooling universe) is unhesitatingly slowing down. In consequence, we have a fast-approaching deadline denoting the demise of time. You as reader (if this book ever gets that far) may have (without you already knowing it) an ever-diminishing deadline (not just with your own death, which, as Euclid would say, is 'a given', but with what you now choose to forgo forever as an alternative destiny for being home and hosed—quod erat demonstrandum).

It's one thing conceiving of a book, whereas the birthing of a book is very much another thing. And it's still yet another and vastly different thing to bring any book to readership. *Publication* is what they call birthing a book into readership, but at any stage, from conception onwards, the book may be stillborn or, worse yet, stifled by reviewers and aborted.

How long do you really think, in terms of human cost, far less heavenly cost, it took for the heavens to open wide enough to write the book of Revelation? Oh yes, written as it was on the Lord's Day—but each and every day to those that walk in the way of the Lord is the Lord's Day—and on the island of Patmos, where John the Divine was kept prisoner, the prophetic measure of time can be as much as the longest of lifetimes and more. Some say (even from the pulpit) that the same John of Patmos was somewhat out of his head; but perhaps from that high above the rough and tumble of any maddening congregation, pulpit-preaching would immunise you against partaking of alternate realities.

What—as between pulpit and pew (never mind between courtship and marriage, or between reader and writer) you've never experienced anything of alternate realities! My goodness then, but you must read the hard-to-find book (or better still watch the four-star film) called *Heavens to Betsy*! Oh—and be sure to take the film seriously, because although it's a comedy (of manners) it befuddles those few film-watchers who can't see any point to distinguishing between alternative realities. Taking things just as they are (the stoic extreme) they see no point to kicking up a fuss by distinguishing right from wrong, peace from war, or even hell from heaven.

Alternative realities (both major and minor) as they exist between solid and liquid (in the physical) between good and evil (in the moral) between lawful and unlawful (in the legal) between valid and invalid (in the logical) between true and false (in the metaphysical) between righteous and unrighteous (in the theological) and between heaven and hell (in the categorical) are all around us. Sometimes the linguistic mindset (absent from the Russian and increasingly from the English language) which requires us to explicitly express their copulative existence either overtly together or through predication by means of some finite verb, smudges both the conflictive contrast and our quandary over their defined relationships.

Thus, it takes a writer of alternative realities, like Kristina Olsson in *Shell*, to expose the nakedness of their relationship by omitting finite verbs and so avoiding predicating one of the other. As an example of her broken sentence structure serving this purpose, 'The contrast, the ambiguity, of two opposing states [say, heaven and hell] held within the one idea. Two ways of seeing reality [perhaps, good and evil, right and wrong] the deep truths [perhaps, validity and invalidity] within each.' It will become obvious that lawyers need coached up to be masters of alternative realities, and judges likewise to be the masters of their resolution, whereas others are left often confused by the problem; and so then often defaulting to legislation for 'something to be done about it' by way of wiping the cruddy slate clean.

Stoics apart, we all feel the squeeze —although for being a decision process, the legal system revels in its administration (which in turn makes stoics out of lawyers, legislators, judges, and law enforcers). Probably this tight squeeze on earth being increasingly felt in time (no less than that on earth through increasingly restricted space) explains why something also so increasingly uncertain as modern physics has reversed its more cautious role of explaining what once would have been more stoutly proved (like an apple simply falling to the ground) by way of some more straightforward (yet still fallible) observation. And don't dare tell us angels, whether from any genesis to any final revelation, that fallen humanity, any more than any fallen apple, is nothing but a myth. [Exegesis 7: So too was Homer's Troy mistaken for being only a ripping good yarn until along came archaeology to confirm the account as serious history.]

From the po-faced pragmatic mindset (with which Newton so bludgeoned Hooke and so upset the gentle Leibniz) to that of the highly conjectural, philosophically speculative, and adventurously otherworldly outlook begun by a romantically disappointed Charles Darwin (and carried back into astrophysics by Stephen Hawking), the burden of scientific proof has degenerated into the fantasy of as often slipshod conjecture (as often theological as astrophysical). Many of today's scientists, when tempted into philosophy by their own highly introverted technology, have turned their back on whatever quod erat demonstrandum can be attributed to the certainty of their professedly acknowledged facts.

Why, even as philosophers, so many of today's scientists (like so many of the sophists) have simply lost the philosophic plot. And if you mistake us angels here for having lost the plot by reverberating here from time to time on the good soldier Schweik, Stephen Hawking, Charles Darwin, and Gregor Mendel—well no, since we are only demonstrating at greater length just how it always takes more than any mere man to come to the Lord.

Take astrophysics, for example, which has given up (except in terms of finance) most nearly everything else, except looking for aliens! Well, that just proves the point that whenever our own backyard is most at risk, everyone remotely responsible will take off looking for novelty by way of some grandiose human diversion.

So too, scholarship no less than science has given up on whatever once was the search for immutable truth in the by now obsessive hunt (through the dead lands) for no more than popular recognition. Like pop art, pop music, and now pop science (all taken most seriously now amongst the highest academic circles), so too, perhaps pop theology is just the same old geriatric search (as was once the adolescent craving for motorcycle maintenance still a subterfuge) for seeking personal fame and fortune.

Despite their hunt for aliens, most astrophysicists wouldn't recognise an angel (whether straight or demonic) if they saw one. They are not up to that level of discernment any more than they are up to assessing the brute facts of their stargazing, which for years they have dismissively relegated to their made-captive-women star counters. No less than the professions have all turned academic (the same complaint once made of doctoral-seeking theologians by Martin Luther), scientists now seek to cultivate their public press, impress their sponsors, and enhance their private reputation by becoming theoreticians and so, like the sophists, in their desire to provoke paradoxes, to deal out disconcerting dilemmas. And by engaging themselves otherwise in no more than airy-fairy conjectures, followed by either down-to-earth or even subterranean refutations, they popularise (to wide applause) the uncertainty rather than the certainty of their subject.

What exactly is their subject? Well, as often as not, they profess to pontificate on the whole wide world—from ethics to aesthetics and from morality to legality—and all this and much more from no more than their relatively shaky stance on the narrowest of specialisms. For example, Darwin is still the world's leading taxonomic expert on barnacles, but from there and his wide-world travels (epitomised by his work on coral islands and his account of the *Voyage of the Beagle*), he conjectured on the life sciences at large (*On the Origin of Species*) and on the social sciences in particular (*The Descent of Man*). And from the life sciences at large, he took over the whole realm of theology (which his father had already planned for Darwin to do by advising him so much earlier to pursue a clerical career).

The purport of Darwin's increasingly anticlerical conclusions carried increasing sway, which soon seemed to carry the day. They did so through a process not unlike that of evangelism. His resulting profession of a faith which ran completely counter to that of the established faith of his own country still most credibly pursued that limitless love of wisdom identified by the ancients (whatever the cost to self-sacrificing Socrates and other patrons) as *philosophia*—in the true sense of that once hallowed word.

Both Darwin's staunchly scientific work, together with his highly speculative quasi-scientific work, when enhanced by the anticlerical disposition of his most ardent supporters, rapidly produced a counterfaith, which, by its end result, when once deprived of all the love of wisdom for its motive forcefulness, became the same hollow shell or lukewarm sea of faith which had, in its own way, allowed the entry and establishment of Darwin's counterfaith. This point of entry, once confirmed by Gregor Mendel's not altogether honest foray into the new science of genetics, was, in turn, to offset mankind's pursuit of wisdom, which is so much less expected of data-collecting scholars and scientists today.

What both scholars and scientists are expected to pursue for a lifetime and profess for posterity rather than any history of traditional wisdom is today rather the profession of radical and quick-fix knowledge (which, judging from many high-flying credentials awarded by today's universities and colleges, is less the pursuit of *scientia* in the true sense than in the collection, management, and implementation of data to the best possible advantage of its own institution in the trivial sense). [Exegesis 8: For example, take the motto of Britain's Royal Society—the clubbable equivalent of Rossiskaya Akademia Nauk in Russia or of the National Academy of Sciences in the USA—whose equivocal Latin motto *Nullius in Verba* (whether or not wrongly mistaken for *Nihil in Verba*) translates to mean 'nothing in words' or 'stick to the facts' or 'take nobody's word for it'. Oh boy, this topic wouldn't need to go under the exegetical microscope of a PhD thesis to contradict every institutionalised reliance on its own attempts to proclaim the naked truth!]

Instead of ruthless scholarship, it can be increasingly decided by some witches' brew of personal opinion, presidential preference, academic reference, bureaucratic survey, committee decision, or peer review that such fellowships or other honours in science and the arts can be extended. Aha, but here, under the rubric of its own disguise, we can have an example of employing the classical disguise by which to disavow the classics! *Sapere aude*—'dare to be wise', proudly proclaims one institutional motto, but then the same institution sets out to diminish the status of the arts by heightening that of the sciences and to do away with much of its internationally recognised excellence in the teaching of many literary classics in several languages.

When ironically donned (every pun intended) by the most professedly radical of modernist institutions to exact the most kudos from the highest flying of classical mottoes, then this can be temptingly done or ignorantly misused merely to hide behind the conventions of established tradition of that selfsame institution's most daringly radical modern manoeuvres. Apart from its history going back to the Greeks and the Arabs, the style and content of fast-changing modern science is one of the least permanent to ape and counterfeit the expected stability of mindset and steadfast permanence of the classics.

Unsurprisingly, it is this hidden depth of academic misapprehension which in the end brings about the end of many great educational and scientific institutions. For the sake of counterfeiting the permanence of the classics by keeping up to date with no more than the mindset of the present, not even the biggest and greatest of institutions can serve two masters. Ironically, the best-intentioned and most-enlightened will to serve both the wisdom of the ages whilst pursuing the transience of the contingent present introduces an ambiguousness and equivocality which, without constant and unremitting attention, may shake the stoutest of apparently unshakable foundations!

Well, academic mottos, least of all as scientists working algorithmically in sterile laboratories, are never as precise as might be expected of wordsmiths working heuristically in ivory towers. Likewise, after an angelic lifetime in the courts listening to lawyer's Latin (not a good recommendation for clarity of expression, far less for classical pronunciation), we would say as before (although still maintaining our upright inscrutability of angelic expression) that the Royal Society's motto of *Nullius in Verba* must be taken [by semantic entailment at least] to mean most clearly 'stick to the facts', which, in turn, outlaws from science passing off most of today's fanciful conjecturing as proven facts.

There's a warning here [as well as an encouragement] being given to scientists by means of the Royal Society's bipolar motto to 'stick to the facts'. When fanciful conjecturing oversteps pragmatic boundaries [like small-boy scientists building bigger and bigger cyclotrons or boring deeper and deeper down into the earth's magma just to see what might very well happen to the rest of the earth], we could be looking at the ways in which not only do words lose their meaning but also whatever of the earth still remains might just have reached the point of losing all its people.

The existing facts related to our survival [both of words, thoughts, and people] in the face of the world's increasing pollution and climate change can be attributed to this same relatively upstart and so highly disturbing role of theoretical and overly experimental science. Together with its wizard technology, this limitless experimentation (of which both Hiroshima and Nagasaki were prototypes) increasingly wagers all that remains of this world (which is less and less) against there being anything else to follow. So rampant has this addictive search (and research) for the experimental become that a so-called new science has been resurrected out of primal religion to be renamed experimental theology (or else as parapsychology or extrasensory perception)—the respective claimants of whichever often differ only in their degree of cynicism.

Well, all of us already know from the signs of the times that this old world down here with you is dying, and on any day soon (as already long biblically advertised in Revelation), this world shall be superseded not just by a spanking new world but also by a spanking new heaven. Nevertheless, secular science [perhaps for being already so very far up itself] is least aware, far less convinced, of such perilously bad news prophecies; and this is likely to remain so for as long as science can foresee its own continued funding. Love of one's own resources, since everyone steals from God, remains mankind's chief motivation. [Exegesis 9: Be sure to look out that already mentioned book *Everybody Steals from God* on the subject of communication as worship by Edward Fischer.]

Nevertheless, almost everyone, just as a matter of brute common sense and whether personally aware of doing so or not, still sets out (sooner or later and in some extreme cases only very much later) to find a first cause or fundamental explanation for absolutely everything. As for absolutely everything, most of us are happy enough (unless lawyers or accountants) to restrict this to whatever we are able to sense (when sober) or as now, even (in our heads) only to imagine.

Meanwhile, don't worry over the highly abstract level of our presently rarefied conversation. This is a technique taught in the first year of our School of Righteousness (Current Affairs 101) by which to enjoin complete strangers in whatever level of small talk might lead on to some larger level of more significant talk and therefore to far more informative real talk for being classical dialogue. Thus, onwards and upwards (or excelsior, as we might once have said when the classics were still around) without giving cause to offend those whom we know more about than they do know about themselves, when telling them of their own more specific (and occasionally scandalous) particulars.

Basically, we angels (at still only first grade) are no more than novice messengers, so it would be only in the most extreme of cases, either to get a hearing or to imprint a long-term message, that we would either startle or move to mirth, says an Abram or a Sara, or likewise threaten fire on those who took their time or chose to look behind on leaving Sodom. As said before, never fear and don't worry. You humans are but only a little lower than are us angels, and although we might know a little more (and in some cases, a good deal more) than you know of yourselves, still take seriously what we bring to your attention and take heed for your own good what also we require of you.

Talking of angels might discountenance some readers of this report, but there are more angels, both combatants and civilians (yes, true, there are also soulless zombies), who are now walking the earth in these latter days than there are humans. For instance, every human being has a guardian angel, although most folks keep their distance; and so by falling down open manholes or by going to sea in leaky boats or by picking up the wrong woman or by marrying the wrong husband, the vast majority of people take years off their lives by choosing the road most travelled rather than the road least travelled. As for all the rest of us angels, you only have to look for us, and you'll find us.

Yet as always with prophecies and prayers, so also with good counsel and spiritual advice. A lot depends on how long you can keep alive in your minds and hearts the living Word with which that word is given or else the looked-for message you receive by way of answered prayer, and for both, of course, you need to learn to read the signs of the times (Current Affairs 302). For any presence of an angel always posing a test of faith (without which test their presence would be worthless to humans), angels rarely appear as such (in full angelic regalia) unless on those most momentous of occasions which are employed publicly to separate sheep from goats (i.e. the good guys for being the wise men and the shepherds from bad King Herod and those others responsible for the slaughter of the innocents).

Seeing angels is like hearing directly from the Supreme Command. It is often just as scary, just as upsetting, and often just as demanding (especially for those in high-powered positions) as to be suddenly converted whilst dawdling along (when thinking of how many Christians one could stone to death) whilst on the main road to Damascus. So too, one minute you think you've got Watergate all sewn up fine and dandy (for having the best of cronies as well as the best of technology), and the next minute you're reflecting in prison on what all went wrong whilst everything was going so well in Washington's White House. As for so many personal conversions and spiritual revelations—whether revealed in Patmos, Moscow, or Rome—it can be a privilege to find oneself in prison. Chuck Colson went to prison (together with his guardian angel), and so his soul was saved for all the part he played in Watergate. But President Nixon sadly went scot-free, so we angels sadly missed the big catch.

This all might seem like a rort to you readers by way of what it takes to implant so much new information in so little time to expand your already so far shrunken mindsets, but to think of saving one small soul, never mind to engage oneself more extensively in supranational soul-catching, requires no less than a whole wide world mission. You can't very well fly just by the seat of your pants to places like Kabul, Baghdad, Tehran, or Damascus (at least not at the present time). You'll need to grow wings. Don't worry. We angels can make the most of everything, which is why you need to know as much as you can about how to grow wings.

People try to get their head round the way in which the Supreme Command can make the most of everything. Well, trying to get your head round that equation (without your heart) is usually the way of the godless (or as believing Russians say, the *bezboshniki*). For true believers (or *veruyeshchi*), it's far more a matter of faith that the Supreme Command can turn wrong to right; and that only happens because everything, whether good or allowably bad, has been either made or redeemed by the Supreme Command to serve a godly purpose.

The trouble then is that people try to impose their own strategies on the will of the Supreme Command and so think to effectuate these strategies (which are entirely of their own making) according to what they then presume will be the tactics of the Supreme Command that will best fulfil them. No, we need to learn to read the signs of the times, for these times being also allowably made as much by mortals as by angels to be these very same signs of our own time. And as for reading the signs of the times, then in the next part of this report, we shall examine what reading and writing mean to you. But as for reading anything written, although your reading of the living Word is second to none, learning to read the signs of the times is still essential for your reading of the living Word.

So then, we don't mean here to engage in the philosophy of existentialism—the same sort of thing by which French culture became so effete between the wars—but in just searching for or even finding for this eventuality of some final cause, this search or finding soon becomes either this person's idée fixe (or psychological preoccupation) or else, when implanted more deeply into the human personality, becomes instead another person's raison d'être (or sole reason for being). Of course, this kind of highly abstract although somewhat pettifogging thought is not generally encouraged in our heavenly School of Righteousness. Nevertheless, it's still required for the purposes of enabling everyday conversation between those ascending and those descending on Jacob's ladder established to maintain completely open and highly interactive communication between an upstairs heaven and a downstairs earth. Meanwhile (a most pregnant expression), don't forget that there is yet also a much lower existential basement which underlies this apparently free-floating and still solar-circling earth. It is from the many underground levels of this existential basement (which once held all the springs of this earth) that a rising damp of demonic depravity still pervades the earth.

However differently this first cause or fundamental explanation to account for everything may appear to each person who seeks for it, nevertheless the extent to which almost everyone sooner or later seeks such first cause (by way of fundamental explanation) indicates—at least the great likelihood if not the complete certainty—that to search for such first cause (or fundamental explanation) for the existence of everything is in itself a valid first cause. All the same, and as said before, there is very little that you as humans can yet know with certainty about whatever happened before the dawn of time and the beginning of creation.

Not even from us angels (a third of whom once fell from heaven, so be sure at all times to test the spirit appearing to sponsor your thought) is your own human uncertainty derived. It is derived more directly from the fact that (whether angelic or human) we are both imperfect beings and then, secondly, from the chaotic lawlessness that for some reason begins to permeate and disorder our sense of a once orderly cosmos of creation. Nonetheless, not all of us are born with an innate sense of that divine orderliness, and even if we still have such sense for that being our birthright of righteousness, then more than just a few of us still seem disposed to trade it in for the more instant gratification of the proverbial mess of pottage.

The prophetic fact of our continued existence, whether on earth as either fallen mortals or fallen angels, is that we have long forgotten our own very fallible shared history. The history of mankind is only a little lower than that of the angels and so most probably rests now on par with that of the fallen angels. And yet having forgotten our mutually shared history as a consequence of this fall from grace, we have each become case-hardened and oblivious to every prophetic promise of redemption. Hence, if we see anything of ourselves at all (which at all costs we try to avoid), then we fail to see ourselves as anything other than irredeemably lost (most usually for failing to see anything of ourselves at all). This is a fallacy.

For those of us whose birthright of righteousness is still lost in the wilderness, it is another fallacy for us to search in that wilderness for any still lost first cause that will explain, far less rectify, anything of our present historic instance, far less of our future perfect existence. There is a universal logic in this, although at odds with that logic relied on by most of mankind. Any first cause, as proved by the human history of our already lost righteousness, although demonstrating that we are no longer at risk of losing what we have once lost, tends now only to hide or minimise how much we are at risk from our failing to redeem its recovery. Without availing ourselves of that act of redemption (don't mistake this for being a sales gimmick), there can be no revelation of the final consequence entailed by losing any first cause and no point to searching in the wilderness for any lost cause whose continued purpose can only be found through claiming our redemption.

Without redemption, nothing for having once been absolute seems now to be any more than merely relative. Alas, there's nothing like the lack of absolutes to discourage anyone from absolution! So then if God is love and love is relative, then God is relative. It also follows that instead of God being constant and immutable, he becomes entirely mutable and inconstant.

Worse still, from our loss of righteousness and despite the greater our adult (or academic) level of informational knowledge, then the lesser becomes our childhood understanding. What, for being the worst of all, then swiftly follows is, first, from our loss of innocence and, secondly, from the overwhelming confusion that results from our lengthy failure to distinguish right from wrong, cause from consequence, fact from fiction, truth from falsity, and justice from injustice grows the increasing passivity of our old age. Yet this outgoing passivity, as if having seen everything become nothing, serves only to hide an inner torment that besets unredeemed old age.

Meanwhile, some of you humans (for being only a little lower than are we angels) have been bright enough to formulate a law of entropy by which to explain this increasing degeneration of our once-upon-a-time more orderly created cosmos. To the physical scientists, this disorderly degeneration, principled by an increasing lack of certainty, is simply the natural consequence of what was once an orderly cosmic generation. Every building up must be followed by a reciprocal breaking down.

It follows from this once-upon-a-time inclination towards generation in terms of developmental genesis that our present lack of any stable state is now destined to decline in the absence of any further revelation. So too, in terms of natural philosophy, just as there is a time to be born, there is also a time to die; a time to increase, so also a time to decrease; a time to think big, so also a time to think small. Short of any further revelation, it might seem as if both physicists and theologians have reached the same predestined dead end by accepting their own situational ethics of non-participative passivity. The world, as we now know of it in its old age, is firmly set for destruction, say some, whilst others plump for regeneration or renewal, resulting from what we attribute to its present course of entropic decline.

Short of having any far bigger picture of cosmic creation than that of the descriptively historic, one may be forgiven for thus thinking that all is vanity, always has been vanity, and always will be vanity. None, since Solomon, have ever more been aware of that—vanity, vanity, all is vanity. Fortunately for both angels and humans, however, that programme has been radically changed.

Without the prescriptively prophetic as well as the descriptively historic pictures, however, there is no bigger picture. Without this united field theory required for a bigger picture by which to integrate both past history and already foretold prophecy, there is absolutely no room for any further revelation. The historic past, as we choose to know it, has already predestined the prophetic future. For those whose sins have been redeemed, however, that's just where the far bigger picture appears, for which all to see, then look to the shortly coming filmic programme as revealed through the prophetic vision already given by Jesus Christ.

Some others of us still speculate over some sort of cataclysmic rebellion having already gone wrong in the heavenly realm. We think to assuage rather than redeem our fears by which to explain the introduction of this increasing lawlessness, disorder, and confusion, which we experience in the earthly realm from day-to-day. We think, that through the perestroika of continual restructuring and the conjured-up transparency of hoodwinked righteousness, we can see this dying world through either without or before running out of our own allotted time. *Thus Spake Zarathustra* (according to Zarathustra's protégé Friedrich Nietzsche), but only for as long as this dying world still lasts will these, his own last words, be mistaken for living much longer on.

As imperfect people (although don't mistake us for angels, since they're not all perfect either), we are not entirely sure when this heavenly cataclysm happened. Whether it happened before or after any conception of our own creation had entered into the strategic design and tactical administration of the heavenly realm, we really don't know. It might be helpful for us to know more of this history, or it might not, since academic knowledge so often pre-empts the right sort of intuitive understanding of what is right or wrong, as well as the faith to undertake what is more obviously and clearly right.

Yet others of us (take your pick between angels or people—you can't go wrong), for being less aware of there being any Supreme Command, will dare to pride ourselves on the constancy of our own human (or angelic) progress. By means of this 'progressive' process (narrowing the gap between both the angelic and humanistic fallen), we hope to tame (and take the credit for so taming) the chaotic lawlessness that increasingly permeates and disorders the original cosmos of our no longer presumably divine (if otherwise unexplained) creation.

Pride (both human and demonic) seeks power by which to implement its own self-promotional objectives and so misjudges the only source of power by which these objectives could ever be achieved and held. Its celebrity status, when infrequently achieved, is increasingly short-lived. And on that note (which like the first repeated note of Beethoven's Fifth could be either in E flat major or C minor), we shall cut short this fourth part of our brief history of heaven (on the subject of both human and angelic pride) before we find ourselves heading (intellectual pun intended) for yet another angelic downfall.

* * *

A Very Brief History of Heaven
Part V

Finding One's Own Voice
When a native of the temperate north first lands in
the tropics, his feelings resemble, in some respects,
those feelings which the first man may have had on
his entrance to the Garden of Eden ...
David Livingstone, on exploring the
Zambesi and its tributaries

Life is a song. If you're either a botanist (familiar with the magic
carpetweeds of genus Lithops) or a theologist familiar with the
encouragement given to humans by the living Word, you'll also
relate to life as a living stone.

This is so, whatever the song, and even although to many suffering
souls still singing (until by their executioners reduced to swinging)
from prisons in the Soviet Union or in Somalia or in Yemen or in
Sudan or whilst trying to survive a famine in darkest Africa) their
life-songs seem grotesquely unfair. Yet even there in the darkness,
where these poor displaced souls can still find breath to sing, there is
hope expressed in their song even though it be only a sorry lament for
their own day-to-day survival. 'Save your breath,'say their gaolers,
knowing all the time that their captives are barely surviving in a hell
of their own world's making. The earthly odds are all against such
captives, but the heavenly odds are all against their gaolers.

Whether the life-song of one's soul be short or long, be major
or minor, or be martial or missionary, it usually takes never less
than a lifetime to learn all the subtle nuances, changes of key, and
more than permissible modulations, of one's often fugal soul-song.
Don't plead your own tone-deafness, but instead listen to your own
life-song constantly. It's part of your self-identification encoded into
your name.

Break the code to find the song, or else find the song to break
the code. Otherwise, you'll stay sadly undercover, and your destiny

remain less than completely fulfilled until you can either find the song or break the code. But when you find your song, then you'll be amazed to hear what you first heard sung ... so joyfully ... by the angel who first brought your soul to earth. For the very first time in all your earthly life, then you'll begin to truly recognise who you truly are and what your destiny exactly is in life. It may help you to know here that the soul-catcher's calling is also the song-catcher's calling.

Some souls (and your's, like that of little David Livingstone who went to darkest Africa from the little village of Blantyre in Scotland, may yet be one of them) arrive already on earth with a soul-song firmly embedded in their hearts. It's as if such songsters have been through this song-learning experience already once before, or else in all innocence, they have no need to be put through life's mill to find out or relearn their own always immensely personable soul-song.

There's an etymology of the soul no less than there's an etymology of song. From *vox, vocis*, to mean 'voice' in Latin, there are many things (the professions amongst them) never to be attempted without this song-calling or soul-voiced vocation. Nevertheless, some of these already very accomplished and professional souls either just sit back without giving voice or else perhaps give up on voicing their soul when they can no longer enjoy the sound of their own voice. Thank goodness then for others who, for the sake of filling the hole in their hearts which they sense is there for the lack of some more song, nevertheless hit the ground running and don't stop until the day they're carried off (most usually still singing their only then newfound soul-song).

If you're any sort of singer (and we're all born singers), you'll know what it takes to work through the task of finding your own voice. It's not just what voice you're given (which can be near-ruined by lethargy or overwork) but what you choose to make or remake of it that counts. And remember this, that every gift from God comes gift-wrapped. When you find your own voice, if you care just enough to listen, then you'll hear also God's voice. And that's because God personally gift-wrapped every single syllable of your voice in his voice.

But don't just sit back to marvel at the pretty gift wrap. Yes, that gift wrap is still God's own voice, but the gift of your own voice, since God chose it for you, is always far prettier still for being your very own voice. [Excursus 1: On the subject of voice profiles, read both Aleksandr Solzhenitsyn's *In the First Circle* and John Irving's *A Prayer for Owen Meany*.]

All the same, it most usually takes a great deal of worldly effort and spiritual patience and persistent commitment to unwrap any divinely chosen and spiritually authentic gift. And if you have more than a few such gifts, you may also have a long life (in itself a further gift) to engage in the correlative responsibility of unwrapping them, including all those gifts you may not even right now know about.

Likewise, the joyful but disciplined exercise of unwrapping any divine gift (invariably incurring a rigorous responsibility) is yet always a form of grateful worship expressed towards the giver. The unwrapping, which is not to be hurried or squandered or yet overlooked, is the greatest of learning experiences by which to come to terms with one's gifting and so, in turn, to get to know the giver.

One's gift may be to preach, to teach, to prophesy, to heal, or else as some apostle, (like a travelling salesman on heaven's behalf) to take the good news of God's gifts to others who as yet may be not even aware of their gifts. Nevertheless, each or all of such gifts (although not withheld from even the very young for their exercise) may take even longer than a lifetime (think of Moses, Abraham, David, Paul, and Christ himself). In each such case, that process points in its own way to the immortality which comes from learning on earth to exercise and attain one's proper place in heaven.

There's some sort of logic to all this, but it's not the animistic one by which God saves time, energy, and his other resources by authorising the transmigration of souls from, say, a poisonous centipede to a fawning politician or from a bone-lazy academic to a busy housewife. But there is some sort of logic, or call it psychologic if you will, by which to coordinate what happened before, even long before, one's own time began with what happens in one's own time and, even after, with what happens after one's time. Prophets are always born before and sometimes well ahead of their own time (so therefore, their prophecies often bear fruit only long after their own time).

On the other hand, historians are always born after and often well after their own time (so they are more likely to live long enough to witness their work bearing at least some fruit, even if no more than first fruit already prophetically tithed from them towards ongoing history). Last, however (for not being the least), there are of course the prophet-historians (although exceedingly rare) who, like Job and Jeremiah and Elijah and Elisha, are always born into all time as well as both into and also out of their own time. [Exegesis 1: As you can guess (on standby), there's a great providential need for preaching in hell, but besides this great providential need, there's also a great providential provision (although not always generally recognised or acted on by humans) for their securing providential implementation. In consequence, the alternative realities of hell and heaven are not so distanced from each other, either in time or space, as each seems to be when viewed by those on earth and particularly by those who fail to recognise the providential provision of heaven (required through human action) to meet this providential need of hell.]

Likewise, call it multiparental inheritance, generational learning, conditioned learning, or imitative learning if you like, by which to allow for the subconscious or for the extrasensory perception or for the forcefulness of subliminal experience, if that phrase suits you better. But sooner or later, you begin to learn that some sort of either harmonic or discordant relationship exists between one's own soul-song and the soul-songs of others and that this relationship just as surely exists between one's own soul-song and the songs of both those long past and those ever present and perhaps even of those many more who are yet to come.

Ah yes, you say, but why not since man is a social animal. And so for his being (biologically placed) amongst the animals, this (perhaps only token) placement can be taken to cover both every humanly behavioural need for explanation as well as a multitude of many other sins. [Exegesis 2: Rather than point to man (with his very own indicative finger) for being a social animal, however, it might be better to recognise every person as having, besides an ear for melody, another ear by which to express an innate harmonic sense. Of course, this harmonic sense might be witlessly battered out of many people, no less than for all of us, the task of developing and fulfilling its immense social potential requires greater listening powers.]

So many of us more discordant humans (especially men) take what they mistake for being the easier way out by either excusing themselves for being tone-deaf (which they couldn't possibly be and yet still talk) or else by their keeping a tight-lipped stoic silence (which will not disclose, as from their speech, that they're not tone-deaf). Nevertheless, at the level of abstract ideas (of which formal logic is one level and semantic entailment another), how can you ever begin to understand the notion of a paradise lost (far less that of any paradise regained) without ever having first felt and known what it was to have lived in some once perfect or almost perfect paradise? In short, without first having lost what you're looking for, how can you be looking for what you don't know is lost?

It does not take a Bach (who lost his sight) or a Beethoven (who lost his hearing) to realise that the search for life as a song—as one's own song—can take up one's entire lifetime and that although one may go blind or deaf in the process, there is a logic behind the giving of all one's heart, mind, and soul to the process of living one's life to the fullest in searching for and finding one's own voice and so, through one's own self-recognition, being able to give all of one's voice to the ongoing song. Nevertheless, it can take more than a lifetime for many people just to find their own voice, by which time many may be martyred either for their newfound voice or else recalled for giving up on what was once their authentic voice or else substituting for that a counterfeit voice.

Finding the song, finding the singer, and finding one's own voice, whether as the singer to sing the song or as needed to engage another singer (or a whole choir of singers) in the singing of that same song, are all three aspects of one and the same collective enterprise. The search to find one's own voice and to keep to one's own part in the collective enterprise of glorifying the sound of all creation evokes either intimations of mortality when wrongly sought or intimations of immortality when rightly sought. The choice of voice, the choice of song, and the choice of the collective enterprise are entirely ours, whether for us being humans or for us being angels. Neither angels nor humans are immortal, except by their own freedom of choice (otherwise, it could not be said that you humans are only a little less than are angels).

We could have headed up this fifth part of explaining the history of heaven as intimations of immortality. Instead of more collectively speaking, however, we have simply called it that of individually finding one's own voice. In music, as in politics, as in economics, or as in heaven itself (but not in hell), the collective (whether the Elohim, the Trinity, the choir of angels, or the symphony of instruments) is each very much more than the sum of the individual parts.

We could have continued the rapidly rising history of heaven for that being the only living history by which to explain the rapidly declining history of hell, but this rapidly declining history of hell (which unbelievers fail to notice) is testified to by the increasing closeness of hell (however conflictive) to heaven. For their lack of understanding on both sides, this will anger more than a few undiscerning believers as well as many unbelievers—that the triumph of heaven over hell in our own times should restore historic hell to looking like some more prophetic heaven. Face the music, however unpleasant may be the song, however, since the closer that people and nations come together, then because of their differences (a phenomenon observed not only among conflicting cultures, as with surveys of war brides, religious fellowships, political parties, and domestic households), then the more conflictive the members become in expressing their attachment to alternative realities.

Nevertheless, the collective enterprise of both heaven and hell (however apparently abstracted from each of their individual enterprises) is only the obverse aspect of each individual enterprise, since both aspects share most intimately in each other for being (non-coincidentally) coincident. That there is nothing coincidental about immortality means that there is nothing coincidental about anything (although ultimately everything will be shown to be coincident in working out for the best). If you would see through and not just run from paradoxes and parables, then listen closely as much to the brazen voice of hellish history, if you would seek to hear far above and beyond it, as to the often no more than whispered voice of heavenly prophecy for both.

Take Abe Lincoln, for example, the backwoods lawyer who resurrected the United States of America from a bloody civil war— what was his voice? Take Ulysses Grant who led the North into victory in that war, who became president, and who, when financially destitute and fighting terminal cancer, recouped his family's impoverished finances and restored their besmirched reputation by writing a blockbuster of a book (a literary masterpiece and the most significant work of American non-fiction) to be completed but a few days before his own death. This was a book to be published only post-mortem, yet what was Grant's voice, to be heard resoundingly throughout the reading of this book? Take also Wee Davie (Livingstone, no less) who, as a child, walked six miles every day to school and back from school, eventually to explore, discover, and take the gospel to darkest Africa—what was his voice?

The human voice, each with its own unique personal profile (distinguishable to every listening musician who hears it and not to be copied or counterfeited by any other voice without detriment to an authentic voice), conveys an intimation of personal immortality which is either reinforced or else supressed by the life of the speaker or singer or instrumentalist who proclaims it. It echoes down the ages, whether to and from Pericles of ancient Greece, to and from Gorbachev of the former USSR, or to and from Oscar Natzka, Inia Te Wiata, and Ed Hillary in New Zealand. But the collective endeavour is still coincident with the personal endeavour however, since, as in the case of David Livingstone and many other Scots who searched to find their voice in Africa, there are few who could have survived those early African treks without having been first brought up in an impoverished country to walk, walk, and walk for days, days, and days and live on nothing at all but porridge, porridge, porridge, and for some days, even for some many days without porridge.

Every voice, whether human or angelic, and when developed to its full potential, is prophetic until the end of time. It tells a story or sings a song or springs a tune that is not just of past and present but also, whether of mortality or immortality, speaks of a future which is either capable of being fulfilled (whether sooner or later) or else lost completely—as often for being never tackled, as for being either put down or left unfulfilled. To find one's voice is hard enough, but to keep one's voice is harder still.

There are lots of such soul-songs, but many are often missed or discounted for being let fall or let pass as if unheard and so allowed to remain unremembered. Without a clear, open, and uncluttered mind, there is no prospect of hearing, far less acting, at least through prayer, either in support of or against a prophecy. All prophecies (but beware of false prophecies)—whether given by way of warnings, threats, or encouragement—are given for the purpose of being acted on. Fulfilment is sometimes said to be the acid test of any prophecy, but that's not quite so, since even many false prophecies (which are different from wicked prophecies) are allowed (through grace and favour) to receive their own sort of quasi-fulfilment.

So then, what's prophecy? This question is such a very good question that even if remaining unanswered, so much good comes from simply asking it (that may be missed by our trying to answer it) that it's more worthwhile to leave the question unanswered. So then, we shall do just that (which academics find so hard to do) by leaving their own questions unanswered.

The question itself breaks through spiritual barriers, behind which so many believers as well as unbelievers hold themselves back from hearing from heaven. Here's a very famous soul-song or prophecy, for example. It was first given in 1911 (in tsarist days before the Russian Revolution of 1921) and, for its authenticity, is attributed by many in the Russian Orthodox Church (which is only one of the many churches—whether Greek, Slavic, Coptic, Asian, or Western (in which we angels *are seen* to worship)—to the Russian monk Seraphim:

> *An evil will shortly overtake Russia, and wherever this evil comes, rivers of blood will flow because of it. It is not the Russian soul, but an imposition on the Russian soul. It is not an ideology, or a philosophy, but a spirit from hell. In the last days Germany will be divided in two. France will be just nothing. Italy will be judged by natural disasters. Britain will lose her empire and all her colonies, and will come to almost total ruin, but will be saved by praying women. America will feed the world but will finally collapse. Russia and China will destroy each other. Finally, Russia will be free, and from her believers will go forth and turn many from the nations to God.*

What you make of this prophecy in your own voice, whether true or false or whether to be prayed in or out, is vitally important, since, whether for being dismissed as a curio or else clung to as an authentic *rhema* (for that being a validly spoken heavenly word), this proclamation of yours is vital. Listen with your inner ear; look with your inner eye. Faith comes from hearing, so sometimes reading the notation gets in the way of even the musician's outer ear (and more so of his inner ear), just as the overly familiar shape of things gets in the way of the artist's outer eye (and more so of his inner eye).

For being thoroughly vital and alive to every aspect of your life (which is just what vital means), your own least response, whether to affirm or deny what you hear, will affect your deepest feelings, as well as often having the potential to turn or transform your mind. As for your own emotions, remember that the heart can be a most deceitful thing (ask those who philander their emotions) just as the mind can be severely closed by guilt or trauma (no less than by overreasoning or by faintness of heart).

Fear—both of the known and of the unknown or of the expected, no less than of the unexpected—prohibits both inner feeling and inner sight. Do you think we angels never fear where we're called to tread? Do you think we angels never fear to reason against what we're called to do? Do you think we angels never fear to fear? We're only angels, you know, not those so-called supermen and superwomen who would divert us from expressing God's grace.

Where do you think the concept of superman came from? Like any Gruesome Goliath brought down to hit the earth by a stone from the kingly slingshot of Wee Davie Boy, it's a genetically modified, unauthorised half-breed concept. By substituting pseudo miracles for divine mechanics, it diverts and distracts our attention from what such characters as Clark Kent and Lois Lane were themselves being called to undertake. Through a perverted sense of pathos and an exaggerated view of justice being at our personal command, it's very easy to cultivate the required empathy to follow suit, which, in turn, explains the rise of the picaresque novel, the crime novel, the pornographic novel, the gothic novel, the catastrophic novel, and the dystopian novel and, in turn, therefore, the action movie, the pornographic movie, and the horror movie—none of which are in any way novel at all.

There is a point to fear, a point to reasoning, a point to feeling, and a point even to forgetting one's fearfulness. Yet this fear of the unexpected blinds us to the expected, just as fear of the expected blinds us to the unexpected. Fear, both of the known and unknown, typified by our fear both of the expected and of the unexpected is the biggest subliminally subconscious reason why people generally do not want to hear the prophetic word, since it is too testing of oneself (even just to hear the slightest particle or pinprick of the coming truth ahead of time).

Perhaps without some introduction to the Church Slavonic of Holy Mother Russia, in terms of both her faith, language, and culture, this testing of the overly familiar is too much of a trial to one's own faith, language, and culture, so let's take the trial both closer to our more accustomed home (which is the body of Christ inhabited by the third person of the Trinity, namely, the Holy Spirit). We have thus abstracted the prophetic words out of every semblance of hell, by which even every true prophecy can be mistaken for being the victim of merely a religious (and not a purely spiritual) setting.

You humans are so predisposed to your own feelings of right and wrong—as to what is *kulturni* (respectable) and what is *nyekulturni* (unrespectable)—that you fail to realise that through the multicultural understanding of the Supreme Command, then just as the rain falls on both the good and on the bad, on the righteous and on the unrighteous, so too, the prophetic word is given to everyone and for everyone, not just to the righteous to the exclusion of the unrighteous. God's gifts, grace, and favour are never the human trade-offs (that you humans would expect of them—otherwise, Christ, for example, would never have come to Paul (far less than to us) on any road leading to his or our Damascus).

Coming closer to home in New Zealand, therefore, couldn't be any closer than coming to Tom Scott (of *Listener* fame) and Ed Hillary (of Everest fame), even although at that particular time, both of these New Zealanders were isolated by bad weather in the little village of Kunde (adjacent to its neighbouring village of Khumjung) in Tibet. There, Hillary, already conqueror of Everest, is rapidly succumbing to one of his increasingly serious and by then critical bouts of altitude sickness, to which sickness he has been prone ever since his triumph over the climbing of Everest. On account of the worsening weather, oxygen supplies cannot be replenished, which will happen only hours later, after he is literally reduced to the last gasp and yet from which he shall be restored to life as by a resurrection miracle.

Tom Scott (unaffected by the altitude) steps outside the cabin for some fresh air and away from his own and others' suppressed grief over Hillary's impending death, as Ed's face turns grey and his lips turn blue. There outside, Tom experiences a vision of his best friend (dead from cancer five years before) 'in full colour and three-quarter profile … still smiling his old, familiar, and knowing smile … and with a celestial wind ruffling his fine hair'.

Heading back inside the shack where Ed (if not already dead) is dying, Scott (not this time that same Scott of the Antarctic) spontaneously blurts out something that again he has no premonition, understanding, or explanation for his saying. It is this: 'My father has just died, but Ed will live!' The saying hangs in the oxygen-depleted air and stays hanging in the oxygen-depleted air and is neither let fall or put down by any voice of dismissal.

Hillary, conqueror of Everest, recovers from the altitude sickness which has taken him to the last breath of life. Much later, after everyone getting picked up by helicopter, Tom is challenged by a fellow traveller, 'So your dad has died?'

'Yes,' replies Tom stubbornly. 'And as soon as we arrive, the manager of the hotel will walk across the hotel foyer and hand me a fax confirming that!' he concludes with an unaccustomed and prophetic force.

And so as exactly prophesied, it precisely happens: 'The manager in a tuxedo [comes] dashing across, bowing apologetically. "So sorry, Mr Tom, so sorry …" And he hand[s] me a fax. The fax say[s] that my father ha[s] died.' Of course, the other climbers, those who heard his earlier prophecies, are as stunned as usually anyone is when a predictive prophecy is so clearly and so shortly fulfilled after its proclamation.

If each and every one of us humans thought hard enough about the issue, we would have similar prophetic testimonies. Every spiritual gift first experienced is a calling to its greater development and sanctification.

The memory system of the human brain—especially through its aging, informational overload, and continuing burden of unresolved conflict—is very susceptible (like any computer) to connotative afflictions. It is especially susceptible (like an aging yet constantly updated computer) to those neural susceptibilities arising from the repression, suppression, and oppression of uncommunicated and, more so by then, of uncommunicable data. For being itself an artefact of the human brain, the computer models each frailty of the human brain. Like any aging computer, the human brain needs to undertake 'compatibility checks' between origins and outcomes, past forms and present functions, old and new ways of working, as each of these are represented and expressed by earlier hardware and current software.

It takes art, music, dancing, science, scholarship, and literature to break down built-up neural barriers and to create new neural pathways, no less than for the provision and enjoyment of the prophetic word. As for the collective practice and exercise of prophecy, this is required to identify positive potentialities as well as negative frailties to withhold and fence in susceptibilities, as well as to point out, correct, and repair misdoings. In short, the whole point of prophecy (whether directly as such or in the course of any other ministry) is to afford the best possible means of collective communication. Indeed, all of mankind's divinely sanctioned pathways (together with those trod by our more everyday professions of faith) hinge on the profession of the prophetic. This is a must for every ministry for being the only means of learning to recognise, manage, and apply the sanctified use of divine inspiration.

How very different things could have been (perhaps) had the more wilful West, and not just also Holy Mother Russia, chosen to listen to the prophecy given by Seraphim in 1911! Responding to the prophetic utterance, after learning to discern the authentic voice from every taint of the counterfeit, is one way of testing your own voice in the context of other voices and in the context of the world's collective voice, for this is a prophecy which has been proclaimed and reproclaimed many times and in many different situations. Yet because Mistress History is left alone to repeat herself (to the extent that this whole wide world thus suffers from the spiritual debilitation effected by her chronic indigestion), then no good comes from the repetitiousness with which the same things go wrong, go further wrong, and as if doomed (from lack of learning to take her lessons to heart), then go always further wrong.

We angels wouldn't want to coerce your feelings (although someday, there will be a book written about who did), but your reasoning may be more openly extended if you know that when the Berlin Wall came down and a split Germany was reunited, the last days came to many university academics all over the world—from Aberdeen in the north-east of Scotland to Otago in the deep south of New Zealand—since almost all those academics who had staked their lives on sharing the treasures of Russian language, literature, and scholarship to the decadent West [on which subject of the declining occident read the commissioned report to the Supreme Command of Oswald Spengler, 1918] suddenly lost their jobs. They (together with their students) lost their positions overnight because of the false surmise, reached by those who flattered themselves to have won the Cold War in the West, that Holy Mother Russia had finally, completely, and irrevocably lost her bearings and that, ironically, by her turning from communism to democracy, there was no further point in sustaining what they had always sought to get out of the earlier Cold War conflict.

But you, dearest readers, for being amongst the most eminently *respectable* of humans (*kulturny* rather than *nyekulturny* in Slavic culture) may well find this argument hard to understand. Nevertheless, since not even the proponents of this pogrom of university academics could understand their own motivation to rape, ravish, and cut down their colleagues' years, decades, and centuries of established scholarship, how could others who hadn't even been through that academic mill understand the loss thereby being suffered to Western culture, never mind the resulting vulnerability accruing to Western defence?

Sometimes, for the heaviest of weighed-down academics (those who carry a weight of respectability that grounds them from even the shortest of scholarly flights), it will need a spoof or hoax (of which there are many in this report) to unburden them. Don't hold your breath for long to await their recovery from being spoofed or hoaxed, however, since it may take many of them at least a generation to recover, and many don't or won't ever recover sufficiently for even minimal takeoff. All the same (since this conversation is being recorded for assessment and training purposes), be sure to remember the much quoted Great Gilbert (not Gilbert Ryle, for being the philosopher putting down what he was pleased to call *the myth of the mind*, but rather the inimitable Chesterton, writing on the righteousness of mind) by which to conclude that 'angels can fly because they can take themselves lightly'.

The key to lightening up is, of course, to lose weight (although always at risk of losing one's respectability), but with academic success, most academics become first heavy-footed and then flat-footed, until eventually, they may remain grounded for good in their professorial chairs. As for Einstein's professor of physics, so also for many other professors, they never learn from what their students are trying so hard to teach them. If there's one rule that angels would legislate for humans, it would be one to ensure that all humans were kept in their rightful place by being hoaxed (as by Thomas Carlyle's most celebrated *Sartor Resartus* or *The Patched-Up Tailor*) from time to time.

What do angels mean then by any spoof or a hoax? Well, that's an increasingly difficult question these days to answer, since, with so much spam and so many scams around, it might seem (maybe for being true) that almost everything on earth (not just from breaking news on television to commercial advertising) is by now some sort of a spoof or a hoax. We won't risk pursuing this point of view much further since it possibly explains why humans these days are so psychotic. For a current example of a serious scholastic hoax sponsored by the Supreme Command, however, one cannot do better than cite Sokal's hoax (taking in science, philosophy, education, and every other manifestation of culture) to reach its 'only solution'.

What is this solution? It's not just proffered as a sneaky spoof. Instead, it's a carefully contrived and seriously minded academic hoax (along the lines of Lewis Carroll's *Alice's Adventures in Wonderland* or Samuel Butler's *Erewhon*) by which its outcome is both explained and redeemed by its suggested solutions. Amongst those, so Leading-Agent Sokal suggests, is that of '[of paying] less attention to [academic] credentials and more attention—*critical* attention—to the [substantive] content of what is [being] said'. Of course, of course, of course … that's entirely the opposite of most exam-marking these days, where the student is marked not on his or her own substantive content (of which there may be almost none contributed at all) but instead on the citations and credentials going towards the support of the examiner's views.

We angels could give a long list of what to us are highly comical hoaxes ranging from the oddest and oldest of missing links to the rejection of the most obvious evidence. The intelligentsia are no more immune from wishful thinking, whether in courts of law or in white-coated laboratories, than are those persons who are without any academic credentials for critical thought. It was Leading-Agent Carlyle (known to us for being so long undercover as simply Tommy) who came up with *Sartor Resartus* (literally *The Patched-Up Tailor*), which spoofed the leading academics of his age into thinking his own most fanciful flight was absolutely serious (as for those academics whom he took to their graves, it most certainly was).

Of course, apart from those individuals searching for their own voice, there are many singers and musicians and writers, as well as those dedicated to working in other artistic fields who have never come to explore or to discover the need to find their own voice. This part of heaven's prophetic history, written from the angelic point of view, is about the need for both angels and humans to find their own prophetic voice.

We are apt, even if neither the composer nor the singer of any song, to focus overly on our own part in the musical process. As for just sitting in the pews only fragmentally to hear the sermon, so also that may be mistaken for just sitting (not even listening) in some music hall to hear (even far less than fragmentally) what is programmed for being a symphony. As every experienced soloist knows, he is not alone. Even as an accompanist (whether or not symphonic for a concerto) or as an impresario (whether or not for a single concert or for a lifetime), these roles of accompanist and impresario are at least fundamental, if not critical, to every musician's life and livelihood. Both accompanist and impresario may help every soloist to find their own true voice.

So then (well-before your own last swansong forces you to retire from stage and screen) seek right now to recover what will be your lasting soul-song. Everyone, as testified to by one of the greatest sopranos of all time, Renée Fleming, has been given one's own inner voice, which must be discovered for the making of every great singer (and even for any not-so-great singer)—but this uniquely personal voice must first be identified before being developed. It's embedded in your DNA (to find which gene go along the main line of your double helix, then first on the right, before last on the left). Now, although your relevant genes for hearing and singing (bass, contralto, merely alto, tenor, or soprano, even coloratura and countertenor are all there (nobody's tone-deaf, you know), this most unique of all love songs may have been switched off for some time. Yet these genes (for both staying in pitch and keeping to time) can—we solemnly promise you (on money-back guarantee, although terms and conditions apply)— be switched back on again. Word of warning—this sort of gene-switching (in both major and minor keys) requires both patience and perseverence. You can't expect to jump from bass to countertenor all of an instant. So, if you really do want to join the Don Cossack Choir be prepared to make some effort.

These then most musical genes, even if by now long ago switched off, are most intimately your own genes, so the first step in switching them on again, as we warn you now, will be to realise the ongoing cost (apparently hellish to both yourself and others at the outset) of your own lost self-awareness. Nevertheless, don't be fearful and don't be frightened. We're not spinning yarns, although what we say is (here in hell) but a very small part of the best story (as told in heaven) of all time and for all time—and further and better by far (as even we angels down here in hell have to admit) of any humanly known superlative (forgive us, Caruso) in its ability to transcend all space-time.

It's true that some of you/youse still quite youthful readers will feel needlessly stressed by this warning, but some levels of stress are needful for taking up all transformational challenges. We'll stick with the biblical (lower case, *OED*) standards for what are often the military operations required by these end times. Remember, all the same, that the vast bulk of the Bible (still upper case, although cobbled together by the wisest fools in Christendom from at least sixty-six books by forty different authors) is in itself a barbarously bare-bones book (whereas this one here, seen by many reviewers possibly to come from hell, although hopefully expurgated through heaven, is still only a flesh-and-blood account).

Every flesh-and-blood account requires every human reader to read for himself or herself the signs of the times and to balance carefully the tension between body and soul (as between Old Testament and New Testament—both now in lower case) for these fast-changing times in which each of you/youse very youthful readers live. [Exegesis 3: So then what about catch-23 for coming after catch-22? No problem—or *nyet problyema*—since it's when dividing twenty-two (and not twenty-three) by seven that pi delivers a constantly ongoing lack of conclusion.Well then, likewise *nyet problyema*, since reading the signs of the times is as often done by reading between the biblical lines (a Bible college trick); and by remembering that, although the Bible (of whatsoever version, but not the Wormwood Bible) is divided into the Old and the New Testaments. Nevertheless, these are really only the older and newer parts of one and the same continuous story as deeply breathed by the Supreme Command into our (both human and angelic) respiratory systems. No secret as to when this happened. Don't you remember that first great gulp of freshest air we took when first we committed ourselves to Jesus Christ? But yet (apart from all those self-professed infallible theologians—who are not likely to read this book) we must all most cautiously tend to our own very fallible lives.

Meanwhile, the role of the entrepreneurial impresario has been extended far beyond that of music and the arts, to curators of museums, to conference organisers, and to others who have leading roles in organising events. Jacques-Yves Cousteau held himself out as an impresario to scientists. The lifeline held out by impresarios, in many cases mere managers and minders (as when holding out so-called lifelines as to the Beatles), is unfortunately so often no more than a hoax (and in many other cases, more obviously a scam).

Heaven has many leading impresarios on its both humanist and angelic lists, but of course, there are lots of counterfeiters working hard for the opposition. James D. Watson and E. O. Wilson have been described as the impresarios of Charles Darwin's works, but have they (or you) read enough of Charles Darwin to know for whom he, Charles himself, was the impresario? Many of us angels have yet to meet an evolutionary-believing scientist who has read much of anything (if anything at all) written directly by Charles Darwin (who himself wrote tomes). As all Anglo-American common lawyers know, it's the primary sources (and not commentaries) that count.

Marry honest words to uplifting music, and through spiritual song, you have the means to open hearts and stir up sleeping souls to more lively and positive participation in greater and greater deeds of heroic action. Through the formal disciplines of well-founded science and serious scholarship, you can, by opening categorically closed minds as well as clearing doubt away from any half-open but still clouded minds, thus liberate not only the same investigative scientists and studious scholars but also the more profane and less disciplined of mankind from public prejudice and private partiality.

Yet again, throughout all the diverse ways we sing of life—whether in science, sport, scholarship, or arts—it follows from exchanging one's blind faith for visionary faith that something (for then being only truly miraculous) begins to happen. With envisioned faith, every slightest thing we say or do, however apparently trivial or insignificant, acquires a distinctively spiritual and thus immensely empowering value. With envisioned faith (as said before, so then let's try again), we can learn to move mountains.

Nevertheless, any faith, however strong, that is merely cold, hard, and grasping is of no account whatsoever. Faith, however tenacious, that is merely complacent, compromising, and compliant is of little account, except perhaps for a limited time to safeguard the peace of the person. Faith, however widely shared, that is merely shallow, no more than socially satisfying to the person, and basically conformist to the collective is of even less account than are those previous forms of faith to the collective, insofar as by keeping the peace of the collective that (as often spurious) peace can imprison the spirit of the individual person and so, in turn, imprison the spirit of the collective.

Based on the mistaken premise of allowing the scriptural admonition that 'sufficient unto the day is the evil thereof' to be one which both sanctions and allows us to overlook the evil of this very same day, then these corrupted, impoverished, and disempowered levels of faith are nevertheless upheld for being 'pragmatic'. The little good they can do is temporal and transient, and the far greater evil they can do, without the need for human reform and God's grace, often scares the observer away (as far as he or she can go) for having found himself or herself being so obviously near to (being part of) what scares them for being eternal.

Aside from this often wishy-washy, indecisive, purposeless, and as often excessively pragmatic yet no more than hold-the-fort level of faith is formalist faith. Formalist faith deals in (for being no more than their own sake) repetitive mantras, established formulae, introspective rituals, clichéd prayers, and strict adherence to lectionaries, as well as to orders of service and as much also sometimes to the holding of excessive celebration of festivals, fetes, and performance of pageants—which serve often no more than as memory aids and mnemonics.

All such three degrees of worldly pragmatic faith, together with the many, many more forms of that increasingly formalist faith which indicates the decline of the church, the demise of the temple, and even the subversion of the substitutive lodge, are of no real account until each pragmatic degree or each of the many pervasive forms of formalist faith is reformed. This can be done only by satisfying their requisitely critical need for deeper forms of more closely communicative worship. Without these deeper forms of prophetic prayer, enlightened vision, personal testimonies, informed interpretation, and the collective encouragement of dreams, visions, prophecies, deliverance ministry, healing, and miracles, together with likewise deeper levels of spiritual experience (as for being slain outright in the spirit or for being taken timelessly up to heaven or for the dead being resurrected to life), the church and other congregational worship stays static and, short of divine intervention, becomes stagnant.

In all this discussion of signs and miracles, we are overapt to arrange them in some exclusively human order of their significance— say, to denigrate prayer and vision (for being every day) and to dismiss testimonies (for being mostly personal) and (on the other hand) to elevate bringing the dead back to life as being an example of the ultimate miracle. No, the realm of signs and wonders is nothing like that at all. Jesus, when speaking for himself, was not all that happy with those who desired the raising of the three-day-dead Lazarus. Major miracles may pass unnoticed, just as the most significant signs of the times and other wonders of the divine hand may pass beneath our human notice, and so also the least spiritually significant of events (such as washing the feet of one's servants) be elevated to the highest of not only human heights because of our own bodily needs, mental afflictions, and wilful desires.

Oh, and by the way, it may help here to see that the history of heaven (however offensive that phrase may seem to those caught short of seeing heaven thus far having been brought down to earth) is primarily one of ideas. Heaven's history is not like world history, most certainly not as taught on earth where heavily burdened little souls have become schooled and accustomed to associate their own human history only with reams of dates, names, and events.

No wonder it is, then, that even adults still shudder over the history both in and out of their schooling (although all history, for its required reflection, is most fittingly only understood when taught by gentle-minded grandfathers). For any adult human being to learn anything sure of the history of heaven, one must be prepared to climb up, as would a little child, once again to seat himself or herself on the generous knees of the Ancient of Days.

No wonder too, with today's earthly emphasis on data, data, and on yet more data, how devoid of understanding your human minds become without your least concern for values, values, and more values. Of course, such is your human way of thought on earth that more often than sometimes (but justified surely for the purposes of our mutual conversation), we angels too must learn to converse with you humans as you humans would expect to converse with us angels. It can be a very sad and disquieting state of affairs, nevertheless, when even for the purposes of reaching spiritual communion, there has to be so much increasing need for compromise in the differing processes of heavenly and earthly communication.

Thus, because of the radically different processes of angelic and human communication, much of the Bible is misread by most of you humans. You misread the Bible by mistaking it for being one of your own human history books and not one of our heavenly history books. The same goes, albeit the other way round, for church history. Ooh-la-la, since on the basis of being of the body of Christ, church history is so often mistaken for being heavenly history—instead of more accurately being a branch of human history. Alas, for that same body of Christ being so unmistakably human, how then could humans come to mistake church history for being heavenly history?

Perhaps, it's because church history—so quick to indulge in its own concepts of the clergy, the trinity, never mind the church (itself unmentioned but for the ecclesia), is likewise so close to provoking schisms and heresies (no different in kind from pogroms, wars, and acts of terrorism) that humans can think themselves the better to understand heavenly history (as well as church history) as belonging to human history. Here, not unlike the catch 22 paradox, is the church paradox, where the figurative body of the resurrected Christ gets trodden over until sat on by—and as often buried under the physical body of the church.

Here's a clue to rectifying both these humanistic misapprehensions. Unlike the history of the world, which is always written as if backwards about the past, the history of heaven is always written forwards for the future. Indeed, for being written in the future perfect of its own fulfilment, the history of heaven lives also eternally in the prophetic present. Once again, if you prefer a formulaic paradox to beleaguer yourself into a closer understanding of both past and present, then history and prophecy must again be seen as one.

Nevertheless, as near to your own human thought patterns as we angels are authorised to give it now to you, then every present moment is made nonetheless momentous for being the still living reincarnation of some single past moment or conglomerate of past momenta. In the words of yet another song, we live entirely in the past whenever we choose to live in no more than the present, and we live in no more than the present when we think to live without any thought or hope or feeling for the future.

Present time (as we angels see it) is then nothing but an aggrandisement of all past time. That's what makes it so hard, whether by way of ethics or reason, to found either of them on any such history of heaven. This is so for each of them affecting to be a political mission so protracted far beyond both past and present, as to either fast-track or shock-treat the ever-changing present into reformulating the immediate and foreseeable future. Nevertheless, there are limits to the principle of ever-ongoing informational aggrandisement of which the future, when, alas, overloaded by the unrequited pressure of the past, can no longer stand the stress of stretching the present required to process and incorporate further change. Thus, has Alvin Toffler's once prophetic *Future Shock* by now become past history in the process of incorporating its long ago foretold and yet by now largely fulfilled series of once startling but by now blasé changes?

We all feel increasingly stretched, especially those in early childhood and those in second childhood, by the increasing tension exerted by this temporal and kaleidoscopic process of aggrandised incorporation of both the trivial and the not so trivial in our search for constant change by which perhaps to hide from ourselves our lack of any absolutes. The eventual outcome, so some say, each in their own very diverse and often conflicting ways—through exceeding limited resources, the consequences of climate change, the effects of increasing pollution, or environmental collapse—is that in one way or another, the end (already exceeding the point of no return) must come soon. On such matters, we angels make no comment. The coming apocalypse of both heaven and earth couldn't be made clearer than by that revelation already foretold.

Nevertheless, there are so many of you believers, for being otherwise extremely well-informed humans, who cannot come to terms with the concept that all the past there ever was is still all around us, if only for being reconstituted in the present. So then as if still on earth, we then happily go on living through the Babylonian captivity (although unaware of it, except perhaps until we are retuned and reminded of it by the Iraqi wars). Likewise, we go on living through the Thirty Years' War and the Peace of Westphalia of 1648, and yet how could we forget that treaty which, because of failed government within the body of Christ, the responsibility of conducting good government was passed from that failed body of a forgotten Christ to that of the newly instituted secular state? Wow, how so much of our very recent history has been let fall into the pit of preferred oblivion?

The concept of the eternal present (for being in reality our eternal past) is not a pleasant one for earth's inhabitants, especially once awakened to the reality of their living completely in that most familiar and ongoing past, which they yet, for lack of any secured future, continue to sleepily inhabit. This failure of awareness, arising from humans choosing what they mistake for being the lesser of two evils, in most cases, unless rectified, compromises all they can ever hope of eternity. As of all confusion over past and present, the key to clearing up that confusion concerns clarifying the closely related concepts of space and time.

It is only because of there being no apparent lack of or end to space in heaven and no apparent lack of time by way of substituting eternity for time in heaven that we angels can, with the help of humans, generate sufficient space and time by which to maximise the redemption of souls in what still remains of time and space on earth. Under the false leadership of Satan, it is the ploy of his Counterfeit Command, as fast as can be made possible by disobeying all the universal rules of space and likewise by subverting all the universal principles of time, to eat up all earthly space and time and so to reduce all otherwise available opportunities for the fullness of human redemption.

Needless to say, this evil ploy of the Counterfeit Command won't work. By way of the victory already won, the full measure of redemption will not compromise the harvest quota already sown and tended by the Supreme Command. The divine stage is already set in ways that cannot be upset, but we, who are still upright angels, need all your humanly help to have it turn out that way. In no uncertain time, but far less than during any certain time, the curtain of our final and greatest war (already long started behind this and that lesser curtain of continuing hostilities) will finally go up on the ultimate outcome. So why be couch potatoes sitting back to blow your brains suicidally on televised action movies when you may learn to lead others, be commissioned in, and take command in helping to decide the angelic outcome of this world's biggest and greatest final fray?

* * *

A Very Brief History of Heaven
Part VI

Where All Ideas Come From

> There are composers [the greater composers] who
> have given to the world great thoughts imperfectly
> expressed: in others [the lesser composers] technical
> perfection is made to compensate for paucity of ideas.
>
> A. F. Barnes, *Practice in Modern Harmony*

Remember, great thoughts (whether in the arts or in the sciences) are
often imperfectly first expressed. Don't let it startle you, but because
you mortals have thought to devise, revise, and authorise what you
each deem to be your very own Bible, that also goes for the Bible.
Once again, the devil himself is in the details of biblical compilation.
Poor Tobias and poor Susanna, and look what might have happened
even to poor Esther (as stand-in for our God unseen) and even to
James (the supplanter)!

The Bible (in any shape or form) is not by any means a complete
code. Or else by fulfilment of all its remaining prophesies, including
that of a new heaven and a new earth, we might not even *need* a Bible!
Don't always be looking out (especially at first sight or on first night)
for technical perfection in everything we say or do. On the least as
on the greatest of apparently the brightest and the newest of ideas,
the best advice that can be given is to sleep on them. And yet having
slept on them, be also prepared to nurture the biggest and best of
them over the nights and days of many years.

Likewise (although on the other side of things), watch out, so as
to be always on the qui vive (the military alert) for any (often well-
disguised) paucity (or lack) of ideas. You may be searching for and be
in need of some great thought (or new idea), but in these end times,
the pins that drop from your Father's hand in heaven convey as many
warnings as they give cause for celebration. Be patient, since many
clear warnings, when acted on, pave the way to clearer thinking from

which can come unexpectedly new ideas and, when given time for reflection, even the very greatest of thoughts.

Great thoughts—as of open government, freedom of the press, and democratic suffrage—need careful guarding. Now it's so often the paucity (or lack) of ideas (whether great or small) that comes ribbon-wrapped or bubble-wrapped (and mind too, the entrapment posed by plastic bags, sophisticated seals, redeemable discounts, and other professedly 'hidden treasures'). Today's commercial confidence is often maintained by means of hidden minefields sustained by money laundering and tax evasion, as it is enforced by the ballistic threat of intercontinental projectiles and the sale of other armaments. Watch your step wherever you go, but don't stop going wherever you have the Supreme Command's calling.

Look on every business proposition (from downsizing your house to upsizing your business) as a learning experience. The world's great thoughts don't always come most obviously gift-wrapped to technical perfection or even bubble-wrapped with technical precision. And because this is the age of gift-wrapping with the populism of today's higher education (where formal credentials come first before fulfilment of function) or else are accompanied with the mystifying freebies of cutting-edge technologies, then know, first, exactly who you are and, secondly, the terms of reference given to you by the Supreme Command for you to pursue your committed calling. And for you readers having got as far as this, we angels by now presume your committed calling to be that of soul-catching.

For those of this present age who know now a little more about how much the long-expected Messiah changed the world, none can doubt that the Messiah Jesus Christ introduced some radically new ideas. Why, even in hell, nobody doubts those ideas for a millisecond, so where do you think those ideas of Jesus Christ being the Messiah came from? [Exegesis 1: Once you accept Jesus for being your saviour from sin, it's only rebelliousness against his Father in heaven that can make you believe that every new idea coming to you is entirely of your own creation.]

So then keep your head down whenever you think you're the only one to have had a new idea. Examine that proposition most carefully. You may have borrowed it, eventually to receive the Nobel Prize (that happens all too often) from someone who for years has been working in your adjoining lab or who has opened her heart to you during a moment of personal anguish when she has been your next-door neighbour. Oh yeah, on the basic idea that there were molecules of emotion, you did all the macho work, and after all, chemistry (forget the bio bit for the moment) is a man's job. You can't get the Nobel Prize (whether for discovering the double helix or for any work of literature (whether as between Pasternak or Nabokov)) once you're dead and gone, so then since 'all is vanity', as Solomon says, what's the problem? None whatsoever, which explains why the so highly competitive Nobel Prize was introduced only long after King Solomon had passed away! Why do you think candidates have seen fit to withdraw their names from consideration?

Then only when you dare to raise your resurrected head (it took J. S. Bach a hundred years and more to live down his more fashionable compatriot G. P. Telemann), look both ways—first to the Supreme Command, then once fully armed by the Supreme Command, towards the Counterfeit Command and then back again to the Supreme Command, by which cautionary process you'll then know not only whether your idea is either very new or very old but also, far more importantly, where exactly it was your idea came from and how long it's likely to last. Self-promotion is no more than a wilful wile of the unwise.

Stop here to think. Speed-reading (a device of the devil) is no substitute for personal reflection, and the technical perfection (behind which the unreflective world thinks to hide its own deficient personality) will prove not the slightest compensation for its paucity of new ideas. Learn to see where all ideas come from. Why even all the bad ideas that come from hell are counterfeited from all those good ideas that come from heaven! And yes, once again there is the limbo of the lukie-warm-ers (the limbo-lukies) who swither and dither by trying to get the best of both worlds from fraternising with both hell and heaven.

So then, is your place of worship a church of conflicting realities, where you actively recognise, say the ongoing battle between good and evil, truth and falsity, or life and death) or else (as a conglomeration of all alternative realities) between the warring kingdoms of heaven and hell? To recognise only one (whichever) of these conflicting realities renders you openly vulnerable to all the others. Like any lawyer, you'll have to learn how to deal with all alternative realities—but of course without selling your soul to the devil by trading in your calling for a career to become stoic!

There are good ideas (all ideas are basically good), but some become corrupted, either in their passage or by their reception (and so prove to be bad ideas, even thoroughly bad ideas). To the extent that even the best of ideas can become disastrously corrupted, it pays to be sure of one's own ideas (in terms of how, why, and from where these ideas originated or were borrowed). The only thing you can do as a human is to nurture ideas, and to do so, you may have to strip down and rebuild what has been tainted in passage or corrupted by its reception into what will remain (until its eventual redemption through your or someone else's effort) a bad and sometimes even thoroughly bad idea.

All ideas, being basically good, are born of the Supreme Command. That's exactly how it can happen, when, after a good idea has been corrupted by the Counterfeit Command, the Supreme Command (as creator of the originally good idea) can still resurrect that corrupted idea and so make the best out of its own fallen first creation. Thus, despite every level of corruption, which, through the Counterfeit Command, can befall the best ideas of the Supreme Command, what then looks like a very bad idea (for example, the crucifixion) is redeemed to serve the very best of otherwise unobtainable results. The very worst of all ideas (so corrupted by the Counterfeit Command) still has in it some element of truth or virtue (however slight) by which to justify it being born again through the process of redemption. God never gives up on his creation!

Do you think the Messiah Jesus Christ fabricated all these radically new ideas which he introduced into the world when all alone by himself in his stepfather's joinery shop or else perhaps after being baptised by his cousin that he nurtured them from nought to fruition by fasting for forty days and forty nights in the desert? No, all that Jesus said and did, however much explained by his own divine obedience to the Supreme Command, fulfilled not his own design but instead that of the Supreme Command.

Admittedly these new ideas were seen by those around him for being very much newer than they really were, for so many of those people who had opposed his teaching, decried his calling, and scoffed at his miracles had forgotten their own prophetic history from which, and to fulfil which, these apparently novel ideas had sprung. Despite every last jot and tittle of Hebraic history in his favour leading up to the so-called Orthodox Judaic faith of today, Jesus Christ (until being known for whom and for what he is) remains to be seen by those disposed to go on crucifying him as the biggest ever of this world's fraudsters. By these same people, he goes on to be seen as the greatest ever of the heretics to be held responsible for bringing down those so many different and conflicting forms of institutionalised religion which have been so widely proliferated by the Counterfeit Command to confuse both believers and unbelievers alike.

As time moves on (faster and ever faster), humans struggle more and more to keep up with their own history. As already time-bound (rather than time-honoured) by their own history, they are less and less inclined to look to where they're heading. Once again, as proclaimed by the prophet, woe to those who call good evil and evil good!

Every history of heavenly ideas is far more prophetic than any world history could be time-bound by mere events. These mere time-bound events (until placed in prophetic hands) render life—1066, 1215, and 1314—only dryly historic. These dry bones of history (of this world) sprang back into life when Jesus Christ was born again into this world (the same world for being the one which he had helped his Father to make at the moment of first creation). Unless you sense the resurgent liveliness of these once dry bones of world history and thus the prophetic calling of every would-be historian, you have no right, far less any claim, to dabble in the dry data of what you mistake for being world history (far less that of world prophecy).

For being prophetic, every history of heavenly ideas is therefore more open-textured and perhaps (until finally concluded) even always contingently equivocal, but self-sufficient humanity prefers the sort of history where the causal flow of events is continuous, where the events themselves are clearly ascertainable for being conclusively concrete, where the persons responsible can be clearly identifiable by reason of their characteristic responsibilities, and where the means of motion through time and space for all such events (in terms of both their eventful entrances and eventful exits) are highly credible for being pre-eminently rational. For God's sake (and here we're speaking literally and not figuratively), real life's not at all like that!

Well, all the same, it can be made so by self-sufficient humans for self-sufficient humans, and although humans are only a little lower than the angels, then who knows how much lower humans are than are the fallen angels. And this poses quite a quandary, since it provokes the worrisome conjecture that some, if not all, humans are no higher (but even perhaps lower) than are the fallen angels. For God's sake (again speaking literally and not figuratively), surely a lot of our human living is just like that, and as both vulnerable humans and vulnerable angels, we're not even dignitaries in our doing so!

For the sake of relying solely on its own human history, struggling humanity loves all things to be cut (even though it takes a thousand cuts) and dried (so deep to the bone as to be DNA deprived). In this respect, science (overlooking for the sake of science our prerequisite faith in science) is the epitome of today's human secular society. For the Arabs, the place on which they took their stance was algebra; for the Egyptians (if not also the earlier Babylonians), their stance was on geometry; for the Greeks (if not also Euclid's geometry, as we still remember it), it was general philosophy; and for the Hebrews (especially today's Messianic Hebrews), it is on our fully informed faith.

The irony of each such prevailingly human stance, however, lies in its first cause and initial source (which is rarely ever as viable as where it finally flourishes). Thus, as with each such initial attempt to cut, dry, and preserve (if not finally mummify) all viable ideas, so too humans as with all their wall-hung trophies (and most particularly this one celebrating their humanly self-accomplished scientific mindset) lies the second irony, no less than in the still subsisting ironies (such as might is right, or a tooth for a tooth) of their earlier self-deceptive mindsets..

Consider not only the pyramids but how the architecture of almost every dying empire and civilisation flourishes to peak before its fall. Without everything being reducible to being cut and dried and so preservable through time, then mankind would not feel itself to be master of all things. The third irony is, however, those who cut, dry, and mummify what once were viable ideas are themselves, in turn, cut, dried, and mummified as token wall-hung trophies when the tables are turned.

There are humans (and humanists) of all sorts—historians, scientists, novelists, storytellers, preachers and teachers, as well as poets and prophets—who have tried to write or tell of the history of ideas. Frequently, it takes entertaining fiction to express a hard fact, a fanciful conjecture to evoke a means of valid proof, and an allegory on angels to change an already hard-set opinion on the ways of the world.

Thus, *Uncle Tom's Cabin* changed the whole history not just of the USA but also of the whole wide world. *One Day in the Life of Ivan Denisovich* changed the whole history not just of the USSR but also of the whole wide world. Sure, straight-talking academics like Copernicus on *De Revolutionibus Orbium Coelestium*, Spengler on *The Decline of the West*, Toynbee with his twelve volumes simply and humbly on *A Study of History*, the default engineer Korzybski on the general semantics of *Science and Sanity* (like Descartes, ostensibly on thinking and knowing but actually on the process of doubting from which to take a leap of faith) find non-fiction a harder task than those storytellers who take the purposefully fictional approach of Homer or of Harriet Beecher Stowe.

'How so', it may be asked, 'that a story can tell so much more than a whole heap of facts and figures?' Well, a story can move hearts, whereas facts and figures usually move no more than minds. And once both hearts and minds are moved, then through their effect on the soul, the soul can more readily move mountains.

These more ruthlessly innocent, if not also brutally passionate, tales and stories of a different heartfelt reality than those generally perceived to account for no more than the mind usually provoke and excite an instantaneous and inflammatory response, no less than Beecher Stowe enflamed the most of a whole continent into civil war. But then as Christ says, he came not to promote peace, any more than did Martin Luther, Beecher Stowe, or Martin Luther King!

The history of ideas—particularly the history of still viable ideas—promotes, evokes, and reveals so many of this life's little ironies that most human historians prefer to deal with the data-laden history of events rather than with the rather vaporous although more forward-looking history of viable ideas. You humans have been brought up to be more comfortable with hard facts than with the thoughts that go into constructing those hard facts, and you are happier to rely on the assurance of other humans for your conclusions rather than you would rely for them on angels, far less work through them (either with angels or from scripture) for yourselves.

In human terms, today's standard work on the history of ideas is probably the four volumes of *Ideas: A History* by Peter Watson. As good as it gets on this subject of still viable ideas, beginning with *Fire to Freud* and ending with *From Wittgenstein to the World Wide Web*, this still wonderfully encyclopaedic work still nevertheless suffers, both explicitly and implicitly, from presuming mankind (once again, as of so many histories written before) to be the one and only measure of reality. What a pity then that to look up the worldwide index, we find Jesus Christ gets little more personal mention than Scott Joplin and that the Holy Spirit gets no direct mention at all, but then one has only to read the author's account of Christianity to realise how the least Cartesian doubt about anything at all can permeate and dissolve all claim to academic objectivity.

Well, after all, sometimes for man mistaking himself (however unfortunately) to be the one and only and ultimate measure of everything then, insofar as he measures the present world crisis (climatic, environmental, economic, and governmental) most accurately to be brought about by himself and thus to be entirely of his own making then, however tautologous may be his argument, he has reached the right (although not logically correct) conclusion! And as for 'man is the measure' (a Greek concept), that idea is going to have to front up very shortly to the four horsemen of the apocalypse (on which it may take more than one misguided Hail Mary to avoid these fast-approaching horsemen signifying conquest, war, famine, and death).

From the angelic point of view, Watson's work commits and extols many human shortcomings (but those could not very well be avoided if the whole history is premised purely on the idea of constant human progress). This false premise promotes anachronistic human causes by which to mistake views, values, and opinions (mostly current and conjectural) for being age-old ideas. The result is to ascribe to dried-out datelines and dispirited chronologies, first, a spurious rationality and, secondly, a spurious secularity. So then by substituting human rationality for divine design, the forcefulness of the so-called secularity manages to absolve the human race from its responsibility for all the cosmic downside emanating from so many of its shadowy, stumbling, shambling, and fumbling research into alternative beginnings.

Indeed, the ideological paradox is that so many events (from *Fire to Freud* and *From Wittgenstein to the World Wide Web*) take place in history without even the most well-informed of their human protagonists (from Moses to Muhammad or from Descartes to Leeuwenhoek) having the slightest idea of what, by way of their increasingly anthropomorphic outlook, turns out to be one of the most catastrophic results for mankind. This essentially counterfeit notion whereby man pats himself on the back for the making of every step taken by mankind as if each such step has been made towards the progress of all mankind leads eventually only to the cliff-edged downfall of all mankind.

Whether by way of conquest, war, famine, or death, these logical consequences of wrongful human action may once again provide the only means for so many humans being taken captive in their sole search for personal as well as public good fortune. Unfortunately, in each of these accustomed processes which begin so often with a back-slapping self-aggrandisement by way of first premise, there is no further premise by which to consolidate any resulting self-credit by way of conclusion. From first to last, the arrant tautology only begs the question.

On this score both the first premise of self-aggrandisement as well as the self-accreditative conclusion of mankind's own self-worth count for nothing at all. 'Good try!' we may encourage those sophistic, but highly intellectual and deepest of thinkers employed by the Counterfeit Command. Their self-serving argument is void by reason of the circularity and subjectivity of their own tautologous argument (an offshoot of self-fulfilling prophecy). When proceding from no more than this single premise of human self-aggrandisement, the argument's conclusion by which self-accredited humanity puffs out its chest with self-pride is rendered void, not only for irrationality (which so offends every humanly proud intellectual) but also for human presumption (which like satanic presumption) more usually than not passes under all earthly systems of diagnostic radar.

Oh dear! From off this unexpected cliff-edged precipice— whether symbolised by mankind's threatened downfall from (1) some steepled church or turreted temple or from (2) some self-sufficient state or nation or by judgement of (3) some highly elevated juristic court or by decree of (4) some sovereignly constituted legislature or by (5) graduating from some studiously self-promotional academy of scholarship or by means of any (6) other sort of institution or alter ego (featured figuratively or otherwise as in so many of the temptations of Christ)—it's a very long drop down to the reality by which the credit for good ideas is claimed by those *to whom* those ideas come and not to those *from whom* they came.

One would have thought that if ideas were humanly self-induced, self-made, or self-fabricated, their progenitors would have better insights into the outcome of their own ideas. The fault is not to be found with the shadowy beginnings (any more than with many of today's even shadier of new beginnings) but with the risk of giving spurious structural and architectural credibility to 'so-called events' and, worse still, for the lack of scientific evidence to non-events. But throughout Watson's work (a.k.a. his magnum opus on the subject of ideas), then as with his chapter on the ideas of Israel and the ideas of Jesus, what we are reading of is an almost entirely human history of events and non-events.

The fundamental setup is blatantly humanistic. It concerns itself solely with whatever values most enhance the claim of humans to credit themselves with their own progress rather than with a history of ideas either for their own sake or for heaven's sake. This produces a most humanly self-idolatrous work affording no more than a saccharine self-satisfaction. In short, that kind of history (especially when professed of ideas) fails for its lack of discerning the existence of alternative realities. What we have by way of the resulting irony is a remarkable history of human failure, instead of human progress, in terms of mankind's failing to adequately discern and realise its human potential.

Nevertheless, where ideas come from, whether instrumentally shot straight from the shoulder or bowled underarm, is bound sooner or later to blow your mind! It will not only blow the average mind (which is very adverse at all times to being blown) but will also blow up the greatest of minds (for being never adverse at any time to being blown apart by thoughts which are so much greater than their own). It was Beethoven (so the story goes) who, on listening to some of his earliest music, remarked on what an ass Beethoven had been!

The same explosive equation applies to science and scholarship, no less than to music and the arts. The human mind by itself is miniscule, and it doesn't take the whole wide universe by way of comparison to prove that point. On the contrary, the inherently miraculous nature of the human mind is not so miniscule as to overlook that point, which becomes pitifully self-evident when left to be decided by the human mind alone. Giving oneself the credit for great thoughts that come to mind (even for those great thoughts that come secondhand through other human minds) is the greatest sole explanation for those who sooner or later suffer abject failure of thought.

For this reason, many of those folks who are taught solely to think for themselves come a cropper for their becoming unable to distinguish not just good thoughts from bad thoughts but also the great from the greater as well as the greater from the greatest of thoughts. So having come a cropper all by themselves or as near to that as to scare themselves witless from engaging in all further human thought, they retire from all further attempts at self-creation and devote themselves to the review and criticism of what they ascribe solely to the inferior output of other human minds. Without the calling of the Supreme Command, there can be neither seriously creative thought nor seriously thoughtful criticism.

As merely armchair critics, and not only of those only self-motivated creators (like, as once yourself, you may have been swayed by the pursuit of personal fame and fortune) but also of those whose creative ideas are implanted by reason of their obviously divine calling, a cosy armchair (however much empowered by past respect and ongoing popular opinion) is substituted for the personal breakthrough required by their still heavenly but as yet unheard calling. For the sake of this poor substitute gleaned from the respectability of public opinion, the fate of go-it-alone thinkers is most often (as retirees from active service) inclined to revert to the status of grandfatherly couch potatoes.

Indeed, why be couch potatoes sitting back to blow your brains on televised action movies, situational comedies, and all the other non-news of so-called world affairs when you have far more fundamental and even still truly self-rewarding options at your command? By reason of your already worldly but relatively non-rewarding of worldly experiences (governmental, academic, or professional), you may even now learn from all your failures what it really takes to lead and take command of others. So then don't let personal pride get in the way of active service. Instead, just remember this: the meek shall inherit the earth in this world's biggest, greatest, and ultimately final fray!

If you (otherwise so intellectually well-informed) humans could only come to terms with this most exciting idea (which poses the ongoing issue of human receptivity to our angelic presence constantly on earth), then you humans, for being then so much better informed, would find the adventuresome present a most exciting challenge towards reordering the cosmic future for both heaven and earth. This is a calling for your human contribution towards establishing one and the same shared presence together, with you having attained your humanly intended heaven at one with our angelically intended earth.

But the presently determinative fact of this critically cosmic matter is this: you humans will more easily believe in aliens than in angels and, at the highest of intellectual levels, behave more like mediaeval bogles, wizards, and witch doctors than like more fully informed and enlightened scientists of any once ordered (but increasingly disordered) universe. But then again, whether as scholar, poet, or prophet, you can still only make sense of any angelic message if you can make sense of your own calling.

Of course, prophetically speaking (which accounts for our being able to commune both in and out of time), all such pagan and barbarically profane behaviour will be wiped away, first, by opening up the inner springs of the world (which would, in turn, release rain from heaven) and, secondly, by opening up the earth's inner inferno (which would, in turn, elicit lightning from the same heavenly source as the rain. Both these heavenly responses to those world events—when the earth cries out and the seas roar—are jurisprudential responses made on nature's own homeostatic autopilot to the signs of the times, as conveyed both to and from the Supreme Command by such as these reports.

Nevertheless, the resulting flood of water, more now from melting ice and climate change than from inner springs (and although serving both its immediate purpose as well as adding a later and long-enduring warning (although that lasts only for as long as the resultant rain continues to water the increasingly dried-up earth), are all continuing signs of both former and present and no less than of still future times. The admonition to read the signs of the times is generic and so is not by any means restricted to one's present time. So then in reading the signs of the times, remember always that the key to prophecy is history.

So too, when (likewise speaking now prophetically before the dawn) the past is brushed aside, as it is so often by humans, for being either dry and dusty history or mythic fantasy or else to forget your own so many human failures, as well as our own angelic failures (both in and out of time), then there is not much hope for the future that can be generated by humans out of your own motivational failure to deal with the present. We say this not reservedly of the past but encouragingly of a far different future.

The trouble is this: humans largely programme themselves to think not always of right and wrong (and so of righteousness) but more frequently of merely good and bad. This is no more than the mechanistic means by which every action (or cause) promotes a reaction (or consequence) which Buddha postulated as the rule of karma, a rule rendered obsolete five hundred years later by the rule of righteousness as brought, taught, and explained by Jesus Christ under the grace and favour of the Supreme Command.

Of course, every cause has a consequence; otherwise, it couldn't then become yet another cause! So then any cause, as distinct from an event (which may also be a cause if it has a consequence but is no more than an event if without a consequence), is still the source of that event (*be-cause*) being the consequence (*con-sequence*) of that cause.

The later move from karma to righteousness is a move away from the physical (so beloved by algorithmic scientists, manufacturing mechanics, and modern miracle-making technologists) to the metaphysical (beloved by heuristic historians, speculative philosophers, and prophetic theologians). The prevailing irony of our own highly technological age (apart from being stunned by discovered parallels between theology and quantum physics or by witnessing the reverse sweep of epigenetics back from the genetics which seemed to confirm Darwin and deflate Lamarck) is then to find out that for the most part, humans (more especially those who pride themselves on being up to date) are still religiously stuck in the now more than two-and-a-half-thousand-year-old mindset of physical causation.

According to this humanistic mindset, the shortcut semaphore of good and bad ideas allows them to be differentiated from each other in terms of causation. As you might expect them to do, good ideas produce good consequences; whereas also as you might expect them to do, bad ideas produce bad consequences. But who is to say, apart from getting whatever it is you first wanted from good ideas, that these consequences are truly good any more than not getting what you wanted from what you thought was a good idea was enough to write that off for being a truly bad idea. The point at issue is that good and bad are only relative measures. The proof of any pudding may most certainly lie in its eating, but the likes and dislikes of those eating the pudding must most certainly be taken into account in proving the pudding.

There are two or three ways by which we may give the humanistic mindset of causation more clout. One is to regard the causative process of differentiating between good and bad as an ethical one (a little more difficult) to be judged more accurately in terms of good and evil (or, as some say, right and wrong). Another (more difficult still) is to evaluate (rather than just compare each side with the other) the holistic righteousness of the entire equation.

Oh yes, and the third process, which is more critical to the operation of soul-catching, is less definable for being a catalytic interaction when conducted through Christ of kindred souls. It is this third process, always verging on the miraculous, which requires the most discernment of the critical circumstances and which, in turn, makes it the most difficult process to accomplish of all.

In this third process (a freeing process so often counterfeited as one of capture by the Counterfeit Command), the process of categorical soul-differentiation is purely pragmatic in terms of applying tactical causes to promote and obtain strategic conclusions. Since each of these humanistic ways has its own set of significantly spiritual overtones, these overtones evoke greater and greater discussion, but we shall cut to the critical point of this discussion by considering the tonality of righteousness in its ability to differentiate and judge between right and wrong.

In the case of any idea, the cutting edge between right and wrong, according to the tonality of a supervening (or fully symphonic) concept of righteousness is thus decided by the source of the idea. As of any speech or song, where does the song or speech come from? How does it make its way? How qualified are those to recognise its source to understand its content, to hear and appreciate its melody? And in what context, or out of context, is it received or dismissed or ignored? The human soul speaks most clearly through the human voice, whether transmitted directly or instrumentally or whether through speech, song, or in writing. As one might also expect, the human soul—when so expressed in song, speech, or writing—is intimately impacted by the ideas which either inspire upwards or deflate downwards its either beneficent or pathological expression.

Well then, where do your ideas come from, like lawyers (surely not, you say, when thinking of backward-thinking reptilians or dry-as-dust historians) who so proverbially work from their crocodilian hindbrain, like politicians (or so others say) then proverbially from their pragmatic midbrain, or like philosophers (or so yet others say) then proverbially from their prophetic forebrain? No room for the likes of you within the human cranium? Don't worry, since even by eliciting backward-thinking reptilians, this is what lawyers would call a leading question (as if that idea were generated by a counterfeit proboscis instead of relying on an authentic prognosis reached by the forebrain).

In any case, how could you answer this question as to your own ideas, unless you knew where all ideas and not just your own ideas come from? Oh no, you say they come from outer space (well, that's better than from inner hell, we angels would suppose, but why not cut to the fray and allow them to come from heaven, just as they came to Jesus through the Supreme Command?).

Facts and figures, however valuable when even only contingently proven valid (as they are when only premised on the perceived facts), and even fictions (when authorised by the presumed purpose of their function) are still no fair exchange for any absolute truth when perceived through the highly spiritual process of discerning and negotiating ideas. Every empire rises to fill what would otherwise remain a void in the world for the strength of its ideas to fill that void, but then it falls back to ground zero as the result of its failure to put those professed ideas into continued practice.

Histories of ideas are very different from histories of events, so you must not be disappointed by the absence of accustomed names, accustomed dates, and accustomed events from this very brief history of heaven. You should also refrain from being affronted by our correspondingly chummy lack of capitals and our use of lower case, as well as by our absence of figures and formulae and equations, because we are more qualitative than we are quantitative thinkers here in heaven.

The only key to deliverance from either the corruptly pragmatic or the corruptly formalist services of would-be praise and worship is personal vision. There is actually no praise or worship that is humanly possible without some conjoint heavenly with humanistic vision. And just as there is no real faith held by the excessively pragmatic or formalist worshipper, neither is there any real faith to be gained by either the purely intellectual worshipper or the entirely abstract academic worshipper. It takes envisioned faith to open the already impassioned (and often already corrupted) heart, envisioned faith to open the wilfully determined (but as often already corrupted mind), and envisioned faith to motivate the slumbering soul to fervent action. Without any envisioned faith, the human soul has no truly spiritual, far less heavenly, motivation.

But what of those believers who, without any introduction to the envisioning process, apart from their purely physical vision (which is then prone to physical deterioration from their lack of any more multidimensional participation) have no sense of spiritual vision? Their souls may thus be slumbering or even somewhat dead to sunsets;

to landscapes; to music and song; to sport, dancing, and gymnastics; to poetry and literature; and even to sociable relationships with other humans (and so they feel particularly estranged from those who are more inspirited than they are themselves).

So then what is this envisioning process, without resorting to which everything—from the history of heaven to the fantasy of fairyland—becomes as dry as dust? If we, as the angelic heavenly host (of whom you know from your gossiping of both scripture and myth are amongst the most passionate of singers and musicians) were to explain this envisioning process to other musicians, we might perhaps make the need for envisioning better known. We then would point to the way in which those who improvise and compose so vividly in the spirit can be withheld from communicating their compositions and improvisations to others (otherwise than by themselves in the flesh). They can be held back from ever going forward (for example) by their inability or disability to notate their compositions on the written page.

Think of Beethoven's most soul-filled *Moonlight Sonata*, as first improvised by the composer (so we are told) on one, now forever memorable, glorious moonlight night and with which Beethoven chose to beguile his near neighbours. What if that now immensely well-loved sonata had never been notated by musical manuscript, far less made and shared to so many others on the subsequently printed page? Why, even composers and especially prolific composers may forget their own work or, like Telemann, be disparaged for its plenitude.

There are many musical improvisers and potentially great composers who cannot envision their music on manuscript, far less on the printed page. They may be good readers of music (just as there are many good readers of literature who, for their lack of any envisioning process, cannot marry their own thoughts with words to fulfil their innermost desire to write the book of their dreams). What are they to do?

Well, through constant practice (as through constant praying), one may learn to envision more than just the physical relationship of one's instrumental hands with the sound emanating from the keyboard (and if you think seriously of every human instrument from the closeness of the human voice to the sound of very distant organ pipes, you will realise that also from flutes to double bass, every instrument has a keyboard or the spatial equivalent of a keyboard). It follows just as by coordinating sound with fingering, so also that when one improvises or plays from memory, one should at the same time learn to envision also the notation of those same sounds as they would appear on any printed page.

Likewise, if we as the angelic heavenly host (of whom you know from your gossiping of both scripture and myth are amongst the most passionate of proclaimers) were not ourselves also convinced of the need to have our most visionary proclamations written down, we would not demand the same of such writers as John of Patmos to write them. Ironically, were our messages not written down by our own spiritually instructed writers, you humans would not know so much about our angelic heavenly host.

Nevertheless, just because some soul on earth can read and be well-read and even very well-read does not by itself qualify that same soul to write. Sure, it takes a visionary process to read (which is one reason why the most perceptive of preschool teachers once objected to overly illustrated children's books), but to envision oneself or to be envisioned as a writer is a vastly different envisioning process for being one that carries very different risks from the reader. When once thoroughly envisioned as a writer, that writer will never again read merely as a reader. No, not ever, since when having learnt then to read as a writer, he or she shall be reading at least a hundred times better (i.e. more intensively) than would or could a non-writing reader. This is one reason why every thoroughly well-read reader should always be something of a writer.

In all our angelic talk about the envisioning process, we angels hope you realise that we are not just talking about learning, not just talking about encouraging visionaries, and not just talking about increasing one's life experience (by itself often no more than another barren variant of existentialism). No, dearest readers, we angels are still talking about one of the most important ways of increasing, maintaining, and safeguarding human faith levels. Faith requires forward vision because without any forward vision, there is no motivation, and without constantly ongoing motivation, most humans lose faith and fall by the wayside or even into a ditch and from thence back into the pit from whichever it was that they may have first climbed out.

Of course, in this often tedious, tiresome, and troublesome world, it can be as hard to maintain one's constant vision as it can be as hard for any adult (thus far from his or her own birth) to still believe in miracles. The most exuberant of one's earliest faith beginnings (if by old age still blessed for surviving through one midlife crisis after another) may yet be resurrected from one new day to the next new day by constant prayer. So does every believer defeat the grave risk (every pun intended) of his or her envisioned faith becoming dimmer and dimmer as it becomes more historically distant from any diminishing hope (as often induced by unrelieved memory loss) in its prophetic fulfilment.

For scientists, artists, and scholars, no less than for farmers, parents, and householders, it follows that maintaining one's envisioned faith may take one's whole lifetime. This is where the test of faith counts for more and more, since faith is worthless until put to the test, and surely for any human being, no test could be harder than maintaining one's faith for a lifetime. By and large, as for founding or healing nations or for making discoveries through exploring the unknown, the wider, deeper, and more intense the envisioned faith, then the more protracted (as may be evidenced by the work of so many artists, composers, writers, and statesmen) will be the fulfilment of that vision.

None with a truly envisioned faith will escape scoffers, cynics, flatterers, and do-gooders. Promoting and implementing one's envisioned faith excites the most intense of opposition. So many visions have been blown to smithereens by apparently friendly fire. So many faiths have been undermined, the fulfilment of prophecies postponed, or the most righteous of expectations deferred, likewise by the most obvious of overlooked consequences or by the least unforeseen of obvious contingencies.

Look to Sara's expression of scorn, to Eli's slumbering spirit, and to the priestly Zacharias for his expression of disbelief, and what do you see? Learn from each of their failures of faith what can happen, both to them and to all others whose lives hinge on keeping faith with angelic proclamations. Look what happened to the whole world order when Abraham and Sara set out to self-fulfil a prophetically given angelic proclamation. It was Lot's wife who also tempted providence, wasn't it, when she looked back for herself as if to confirm the truth of the specific warning which had been given to her against looking back to the catastrophe from which she had been favoured with deliverance?

Was it really so much out of the question that Lot's wife should turn into that same pillar of salt which is just as likely to afflict all who look back to where they were before being saved? As already said, every empire (good or bad) rises to fill what would otherwise remain a void in the world. Nevertheless, but for the strength of whatever ideas it will take every rising empire to fill that void, it will fall back to ground zero as the result of its failure to put those ideas into continued practice.

* * *

A Very Brief History of Heaven
Part VII

The Symphonic Form of Life
Satan and the fallen angels and demons under his
control must submit to every Disciple of Jesus Christ
who has the indwelling Holy Spirit and who knows
and uses the delegated authority given by Jesus.
          Selwyn Stevens, *Dealing with Demons*

It's no less required for every human being than it is for us angels to
see and appreciate that every slightest thing, whether said or done,
has for itself a hugely spiritual and overencompassing dimension.
Beyond human ken is also the extent to which this hugely significant
spiritual dimension closely impinges on the correlative areas of other
hugely spiritual dimensions. This is something more of what the
prophet Isaiah means by his saying of the Christ child that 'the
government shall be on his shoulders'.

Without human recognition accorded to the potential of these
further spiritual dimensions, the full symphonic form of life in which
both angels and humans engage is at present truncated for humans
to no more than four out of ten or sometimes twelve dimensions
with which heaven is accustomed to both govern and administer the
cosmos. As between four and ten dimensions, the power differential
between the two (human and heavenly) is that of no more than a
human string or wind quartet as measured against the Wagnerian
forcefulness of a full symphonic orchestra.

Here then, in that constantly extending spiritual dimension
(which Satan would have us dismiss for being no more than earth's
constantly increasing secular dimension) lies the lesson that also you
humans and not just us angels need most prophetically to engage
ourselves in both our study and practice. Through whatever we
envision of ourselves to be saying or doing, then so for this vision
to prosper, we need not only to envisage of ourselves succeeding
but also of others succeeding through our promoting this mutual

fulfilment of whatever we may be called upon to engage by way of our own envisioned faith.

By way of first asking a question (sometimes repeated and even again repeated) and thereafter by that same question (whether by then having become implicit in the continued process of questioning or else for that particular question having been made forcibly explicit by its own constant repetition), not just the superficial questioning (but preferably the more metphysical questing) process then goes on. Whether then and there or at least eventually this questioning evokes or provokes some responsive answer is more beside the point than that it institutes the questing mindset.

This is an example, by way of question and answer, rather than of telling and repeating back to the teller, of one of the simplest, earliest, and purposively interactive forms of communicative expression. Of course, you are completely free to respond here, either by raising the questionability or else by denying the efficacy of this questing process. You may thus proclaim your reservations as to this process, even although as yet we angels have not posed any more explicit or specific question of you humans.

By such human questing, however, whether achieved formally with words (as in science or scholarship) or socially in dance or feelingly in art or by song or by any other human means, a collective symphony is gradually built up by which to testify to the wondrous diversity of human life. Accordingly, we angels (whether or not you believe in us) shall begin our own questing of you humans, although warningly of our question's seriousness, by asking of you humans a simple question as to where exactly you stand in the midst of all this wondrous diversity of human life.

Thus then we ask, which comes first … But take your time and tread cautiously and lovingly and self-reflectively before beginning to answer what we shall ask of you as to where you stand in the midst of this wondrous but now, alas, sadly declining diversity which so increasingly seems to disadvantage all remaining life forms—all those which survive the little that remains of our fast-shrinking time. This once wondrous diversity (in all both known and unknown dimensions) now rapidly narrows, making for a tunnel vision in the narrowing lives of not just all the remaining animals and plants but also in the narrowing lives of all remaining humankind. Take special care then since this question, for being not just a global question but also a cosmic question, is bound to be a loaded question, the answer to which tells more about whoever answers the question, as some people insist on doing on behalf of all humankind than it does in any way resolve the cosmic question through all eternity for all mankind.

This cosmic and thus universal question will best be couched, musically speaking, in terms of both cheerfully major modalities as well as of sadly minor modalities, since such questions (however diversely asked and answered in symphonic form) are all part of the ongoing song of life. But by now, we are in full voice and so already singing and not just speaking, since to sing of some new life (rather than just to grouse or grumble about this present life) makes most sense to those who, already searching for their very own song of some new life, require the utmost encouragement before taking flight, at least like eagles if not yet angels.

We angels most earnestly endeavour to explain (to those earthbound souls still grounded) our angelic task (in bidding even those humans now so sorely grounded eventually to take heavenly flight). So then we angels sing to them from on high, always of new life, although for many older souls, for having been exposed more and more to the woes of the world, these older souls become increasingly tone-deaf to our tuneful entreaties and so either miss or else soon lose the message of redemption.

We angels persevere, even although for us to accomplish angelic communion in ways that will be meaningful to the wondrous diversity of human life requires humans to recognise (1) not only the fallen history of their own humankind; but also (2) the fast-rising history of a kindred new heaven as well as that of a kindred new earth. At present, most humans (even many committed believers) are prepared to mock or scoff, far less to believe in, or even just open-mindedly look for angels. What remaining hope can they have then of witnessing to any new heaven or to any new earth?

At present, so many earthly woes pretend to stand in the way of all heavenly flight that almost all of humanly attempted liftoffs, if done without any angelic help, either (1) entrap many already deep-grounded souls; or else (2) entail their unredeemed exposure to a fate worse than that which most humans would mistake for bodily death. This slow shrivelling of any entrapped soul can take place (1) in close enough quarters for such victims to be one's next-door neighbours; or else (2) thence where (more comfortably as would seem to most humans) could be considered to be far and distant places. Do you need any longer to be told, however, just how fast it is happening that all these once far and distant places are (surely not by happenstance) closely coalescing, more and more closely closing in?

By reason of this worldwide entrapment of souls and their unredeemed and premature exposure to bodily death, however, we angels are now being tasked not only for the once Far East (as you shall soon discover in this report) but increasingly also for the next-door and rapidly growing wilderness of the increasingly Wilder West. It is in this rapidly intensifying situation of everyone on the move (so common to the beginning of many major wars, earthquakes, and fiery conflagrations) that many other once firmer souls nevertheless opt out from their human responsibilities to the Supreme Command.

Whew! These once so much firmer and stronger souls do now so opt out of the heightening battle! Many of them, older and more passive, are going now absent without leave, by hanging their hats up on (procrastinating) prayers for the Second Coming of their Supreme Commander! They set their own very bad example not only to midlifers but also to even still younger souls (who still have some leftover notes from their hard-earned song of life in their otherwise hardened hearts) yet who nevertheless grow edgy and, for lack of the requisite spiritual stamina, lose what little is left of their envisioned faith.

Then for lack of this envisioned faith, only but a few humans, even those whose faith in the heavenly future has been redeemed, can hold on strenuously to their least inkling of how they themselves are each responsible for their bringing about the conjugation of this new heaven in its prophesied descent towards earth. Pity them for holding to this no more than earthly way of looking at things; since this near to final outcome (seen by them for being no more than a single unconnected event) shall bring us all, both angels and humans, closer conjugally than ever before on earth, besides relieving us, both angels and humans, from so many of our present responsibilities by virtue of our already proclaimed new heaven and new earth.

This is the one big strategic reason of our writing this report, which is simply to promote a new awakening amongst humankind of their spiritual responsibilities. What is presently at stake by reason of any human failure to do so is why we angels have not only been called to prepare this report but have also been commissioned to reveal its findings, more publicly now to humankind at large, both believers and unbelievers.

It is, for example, a source of great present sadness in heaven that so many humans pay more attention to their personal rights than to their public rights and to their conjugal rights than to their conjugal responsibilities. We say so most particularly in the context of their called-for contribution (often withheld) to recreating this conjugal enterprise by way of implementing this new heaven and new earth when each shall finally come to proclaim their togetherness for all eternity. The creation of such new soul-ties to a kindred heaven and earth will, of course, necessitate the dissolution of old soul-ties, but this is also part of our prophetic song of preparing the way towards eternal life.

Whatever errant soul-ties are already being released from believers here on earth means that these same soul-ties shall be released from these believers also in heaven. It is part of our angelic task to encourage believers to hear more clearly their own song of eternal life through listening to the whole heavenly host singing their songs of redemption and salvation. Implementing the release of such errant soul-ties on earth and so saving souls in the here and now, at whatever point of the earth's compass that this can be done still in both space and time, is already one of the largest parts of our angelic task, and the reason for this priority is that there are increasing deadlines in both space and time.

So just because human life is so wondrously diverse, we angels do so try to commune with humans in all of many, many exceedingly diverse ways by which all humans (however diverse they may feel themselves to be) can always hear and feel and testify to the same promise being given to each of them of new life. Unfortunately, however, it is one failing of all humankind to draw false distinctions where none do truly exist and another failing of humankind to overlook true distinctions where they truly do exist.

The resulting confusion caused by such human failures to perceive the supervening universality of cosmic truth means that not all humans hear, accept, or even recognise the true prophetic promise of renewed life in this earthly life, far less of heavenly eternity in their next life. So once again, of you the human reader, we angels (perhaps now irritatingly) again pose the universal question (in song) of where it is that you now stand in your answering the question of which comes first in your present reckoning. But then again, as once before, we sing so that you will take your time treading again cautiously and lovingly and self-reflectively before beginning to answer what we have already asked of you, and although however openly asked before, as to where you would now stand to still sing yet in the midst of what we have shared with you of this wondrous but sadly declining diversity which affects all living things and not just mankind during all that remains of this present earth's fast-shrinking space and just as fast-shrinking time.

You humans have always fought for place and space. You've done so in the mistaken belief that more space given to your place in this universe (which you regard for being your very own solar centre point) must surely generate more time. Such has never been the case. On the contrary, your warring over place and space has always sadly narrowed down your time. There never has been any free market on earth (since there's always a cost factor on earth), far less any earthly or heavenly trade-off in space or place for time, and this is no more for angels any more than for humans on earth!

In more specific, if less demanding, terms by way of eliciting the answers to which these same questions may induce some more general understanding as to your own individual stance, we now more particularly ask which counts more for you—the singer or the song, the words or the music, the rhythmic beat or the melodic line? Or to put the same question in yet another way—the dance or the dancer? Or yet, in still another way, then, which comes first, either the maker of life or the life of the maker?

Once again, take your time, tread gently, dare to sing to yourself, at least a little of life for yourself. Perhaps at first softly, empathise closely with your own feelings. There are so many different forms of this fundamental question that we can so easily be hoodwinked by drawing false distinctions into seeing them as vastly different questions and, in consequence, different questions to which we must thus give vastly different and as often incongruent answers.

So then tell us again, what is the most significant answer you can give to the most significant form of what is fundamentally the same question as all the other incidental versions of the same question, since the fullest measure of this greatest cosmic question of all time is what comes first in counting for most in this life—the maker of life or the life of the maker? Well, which is it do you say by way of your given answer to this heavily loaded question, or are you still now hoodwinked by your own false distinction between the maker of life and the life of the maker?

Despite our angelic wonderment at this great diversity of human life, your diversity as humans is but only a little less than our diversity as angels. Nevertheless, because your diversity as humans is largely dysfunctional, we angels experience often the utmost difficulty in communicating with you humans.

Indeed, you humans put us angels on trial at every turn, because we are forced to recognise, as with your own earthly use of the word *dysfunctional*, that you barely know what the heavenly concept of *dysfunctional* means. You have no idea what trials and tribulations you humans have caused us angels in getting us to the point of our being able to convey to you humans the message of this book, compiled from many an angelic report as to affairs on earth, as we angels have been now commissioned by the Supreme Command to reveal to you.

For example, you seem to use words—especially those words denoting soul, angel, life, and death, not to mention also those denoting the notions of sin, redemption, justice, and righteousness [far more also those common code words of good and evil, of crime and punishment, and of law and order]—in the most extraordinary of earthbound ways. And of course, as for the true meaning of almost any word at all—even when you cry for peace, peace, and more peace—then, as in this case, the same goes for your own dyslectic concept of diversity itself—as if you're already so sure of yourself that without war you'll still be perfectly able to both recognise and enjoy living eternally at peace. Sure enough—so then, you're already one up on the angels (whom you'll remember once went to war)? Then since God is love, should God (hypothetically) be gone, nevertheless you'll still be able to live in love?

Accordingly, you make it very hard for us angels to hear your prayers, far less to answer them, and likewise, you make it very hard for us angels to convey messages from heaven to earth, just as also to convey your messages from earth to heaven. All angelic as well as humanist communication thus become inconsolably scrambled. As already said, because your human diversity is largely dysfunctional [being blighted by plagues, wars, and internecine arguments amongst yourselves], your diversity appears no more than miniscule to yourselves when compared with that far more functional diversity amongst us angels. Not so, however, not so. Don't pride yourselves on being so much better than these sadly fallen angels!

Nevertheless, because this almost great diversity amongst you humans [as amongst us angels] is written off by yourselves for being dysfunctional, you humans also write off the even greater although fully functional diversity amongst us angels. Whenever will it be short of you ever reaching heaven that you humans will ever come to realise that diversity is not per se [in itself] dysfunctional? No, indeed, in the grandest scheme ever devised by the Supreme Command. Diversity is not, as it may humanly seem to be, a demonic diversion.

On the contrary, diversity is made to fulfil all this (most natural part of the) divinely providential process of redemption. The strategic purpose of this tactically redemptive process is to ensure the correcting and remedying not only of mankind's fall (with which so many humans selfishly preoccupy themselves) but also with the fall of Satan (for which mankind, on account of its freely enjoined participation, also bears its own full and ongoing responsibility). Accordingly, as put particularly to those who hold to the unfairness of the Supreme Command, there cannot very well be salvation being pursued for only one, quite without holding out the same promise of salvation to the other. Can there … well, can there be?

Accordingly, when we talk to you (as of your souls, for example, or of ourselves as angels by way of being another semantic example), for the sake so far as possible of reaching communion in our communication, we shall employ your understanding of such words. After all, these are the words which you use in your own human way (yet as so often used when confusing soul with spirit and spirit with soul or righteousness with respectability and respectability with righteousness), so perhaps some sort of communicative compromise (surely at your expense since for your benefit) is in order. Nevertheless, unless for the sake of reaching communicative communion, we would not mislead you over this, since to go along entirely with whatever human conception you may have of such things, unless for our reaching full communion [even whether with kings, presidents, and other monarchs], would require your most severe correction.

Be well informed, therefore, that all communication between heaven and earth (including this end time and possibly last attempt at communion from us angels) can be heavily compromised. And as between any two political protagonists on earth (say between Gorbachev and Yeltsin), there's an awful lot of RF hash or broadband noise (by which to secrete or hide the text in context), and this is no less than by the false comforters of Job, likewise by any other means of earthly misinterpretation.

And on such matters, human unanimity is as often dysfunctional (as when reached by democratic compromise, corrupt bargaining, or dictatorial imposition). For such reasons, the Sanhedrin bound itself to hold unanimous verdicts invalid. Both functional as well as dysfunctional forms of professed unanimity are always vulnerable to the slightest whiff of diversity, however, as proved by the Sanhedrin's breaking of its own legal protocols against unanimity in the trial of Christ. The Sanhedrin self-justified its own unanimous and therefore invalid decision which allowed the so often prophesied Messiah (the one scapegoat to suit the many sinners) to bear the brunt of more than twenty failures of due legal process (including that of holding the trial at night). By doing so, the Sanhedrin perpetrated one of the greatest scams of all time by which to give its invalid verdict the appearance of due legal authorisation. More than just a little unorthodox, wouldn't you hold of that trial of Jesus Christ, when viewed against the profession of faith espoused by Orthodox Judaism?

Alas, for the Sanhedrin, since it's not seen-appearances that count (whether in court or out of court) but the substance of whatever's unseen that counts for most! There's no informed lawyer (as proved by the legal research of both Jew and Gentile) who could hold the verdict of the Sanhedrin valid. On well over twenty counts, its blatant breach of its own rules (both evidentiary and substantive) prevent any credibility being given to any other juristic outcome. Indeed, on behalf of the Sanhedrin, it is also near impossible to make any plea in mitigation.

Yet as still so often heard in those tragic miscarriages of justice which continue, it's still so often said by way of exculpation that hard cases make for hard law. That may be so, but those hard cases which make for hard law do not justify the breaking of the best of rules by which to uphold and apply any patently just and clearly applicable law that will resolve any disputable situation. Alas, the priesthood of the law and the prophetic voice of justice don't always mesh in together, as we shall see shortly when we look at the hidden history of hell-bent people.

* * *

A Very Brief History of Heaven
Part VIII

The Substance of Things Unseen
Just what goes on in those tumescent whorls of grey
[yet supremely superficial] matter in the human brain?
One thinks to know everything about far-distant
spiral nebulae, but about all these much nearer whorls
of grey matter [for being so much a part, themselves
of ourselves] that we know virtually nothing. This is
probably the reason that distant history is so much
more of an oracle than the [less superficial] *scientia*
[for being more than just apparently out there] by
which we worship for being [so much human] science.
                    Arthur Koestler, *Darkness at Noon*
                              (paraphrased translation)

We angels, partly for the purposes of translating the above quotation
to move with the times, have paraphrased [as above in closed brackets]
what Leading-Agent Arthur Koestler (first class) reported over fifty
years ago to be the crucially experienced phenomenon of 'darkness
at noon'. When this report to the Supreme Command was first read
by humans, it was mistaken by many readers for being no more than
a ripping good yarn. And so it is—and even more so than just that
for being also so notoriously true.

It took until news of the Soviet experience would break worldwide
(particularly of the pogroms and Gulags under Stalin—our favourite
Uncle Joe during WWII) to demonstrate the crudely inhuman reality
of this experience. Yet across this same old earth's increasingly
troubled crust, the same old evils are still being perpetuated over and
over again. So then what goes on in these tumescent whorls of grey
matter in the human brain? And will the presentient cleft between the
human brain's two hemispheres foretell the way in which this tired
old earth will finally split apart?

Don't think we're pointing any angelic finger of blame at the divinely designed brain. We angels (no less the unfallen than the fallen) are no less vulnerable to demonic afflictions. The trouble with humans, for the way in which they denigrate Satan (still a dignitary of heaven no less), is that in the same way as they extol Michael and Gabriel for being invincible, they never dream that for every heavenly archangel, there is a counterfeit imposter. Make sure, by testing the spirits, that you have not just whom you think is the right angel but as always the righteous angel. So then what more goes on in these whorls of grey, sometimes very grey, yet frequently also tumescent matter in the human brain?

Maybe nothing, since most of what humans take pride on (colloquially giving rise to a swollen head) may be no more than the result of brief electric charges skating superficially over the grey matter's surface rather than what we would hope to discover by probing much deeper into the heartwood of the human mind, of which the brain is more often a brake on thought than a powerhouse for thinking. Quite frankly, human thinking doesn't seem to go much deeper than that, which is probably demonstrated by the frequency with which humans change their mind. You have to make up your mind before you can change your mind, you see; so then, what's so often mistaken for a change of mind is that lack of decisiveness (indicative of a well-thought-through mind) which is first needed to make up one's mind to account for there being any change of mind. What so often passes for brilliance of mind by way of footling changes of strategical plan and tactical direction by someone said to be 'on the ball' is almost always the result of indecisiveness.

The fact is (if you're still looking for facts, however) that humans so seldom change their minds for the very fact of never having seriously made up their minds. This leaves the human brain to be one of the least used of all human organs (and therefore the most vulnerable to use and abuse and so also to conquest, conspiracy, espionage, and subversion). As already universally known (and shortly to be confirmed for its own algorithmically quantifiable equation), nature abhors a vacuum, and there's usually much more than an adequate vacuum in everyone's little-used or ill-used brain.

But despite superficial appearances, human thinking does go both deeper and higher than that, which is why the answers to this question as to the functions of the brain's grey matter demand some understanding of both the history of heaven (as so very briefly outlined in this book) and the history of hell (as outlined even more briefly in the next-but-one book). Most probably, the grey matter of the human brain is grey because, although commissioned by an open heaven, it has also been tainted by the darkness of hell.

The human being (both anatomically and physiologically as well as both psychologically and sociologically) has been defined, refined, and redefined to explain its progress in so many different ways—from pedal feet to bearing hips, to crafting hand, to speaking tongue—and now it's the turn of the brain to leave the mystique of human evolution far behind. Technology has superseded every need for humans to rely on their own evolution. Believe it or not, but the doctrine of evolution has served its day.

The next great techno craze, marked by the ease with which computers oust books, will be towards neural implants in humans. These will control human behaviour as directed by the mastermind of one centrally located, institutionally corporate, and excessively swollen big brain. Clinical trials (known worldwide, when read upside down, as the 999 Project) are already underway in every technologically supportive country. Just as the outcome of the secret Manhattan Project for the building of the atomic bomb was called Little Boy, the preferred name for the outcome of the 999 Project (when read upside down) is Big Brain.

What will it be next—we ask ourselves in heaven—since, through psychoanalysis, you humans have already substituted the self-made ego by which to dispose of the divinely created soul? Yet this bad news of the self-made ego is not by itself the worst of the bad news. The leftover vacuum (or less than voidable void barely taken over by the 250 terabytes of self-made ego) gives enough leverage or legroom to allow for invasion by 675 terabytes of super self-made ego.

The result of this further egotistic invasion is to delete every least and last recollection of there ever having been anything remotely identifiable as the human soul on earth. Well, the Counterfeit Command is already more than halfway there with its mass production of what it calls the steady-state soul (Mark LVI). It has been calculated (already by Proto-Big-Brain (PBB) that by the year 2050 (NE^{2050}) every single human (automaton) will have at least 15 known electronic implants controlling what was once his-or-her human brain. Look out for the still-pending *Report from the Underworld* on neural-implant surgery—for which purpose you must bone-up (no pun intended) on the expected four-dimensional circuitry by which to reform and regulate (amongst all other things) praying and proselytising, soul-catching and soul-snatching, and in general, by restricting all forms of ecclesiastical raving by the introduction of soul-time rationing. Secularist password for money-laundered edition: 'Warzone'!

As already forewarned in the previous part of this book on the history of heaven, this part of the same book, now on the substance of things unseen (when conceived of so confusedly by humans from earth upwards rather than angelically from heaven downwards) deals with the downside (rather than with the upside) of relying exclusively on purely sensory perception. One of the worst inducements to do so (like so many scientists who really ought to know better than their students) is to stick to the facts when the facts are no more than seen for what they are in a world where so much more depends on the reality of the unseen.

Thus, as with the reality to humans of the multidimensional symphonic and so also cosmic measure of life, you have to open both your inner eyes and inner ears to the substance of things that will otherwise remain completely unseen. On this score, don't scoff like Sara or be struck dumb like Zacharias or be turned to stone like Lot's wife, but instead, pick up your bed and walk—and so eventually learn to carry your cross with Christ!

Explicably of the reverse, almost all you humans have been brought up to look more to yourselves for being the measure of all things (in terms of proof as well as in terms of truth) than you even bother to listen (far less hear) and look (far less see) the angels who (so we are both reliably told from above) are no more than a little above you humans. Of course, even scientists have faith (otherwise, they couldn't be scientists), but when sensory perception is satisfied by means of only scientific proof, most scientists sweep the personal faith by which they were first motivated to discover truth securely under the most public of secular carpets. Nevertheless, when the credits start to roll in, then it's very hard not to count the cost and recoup expenses.

Successful human proof all too quickly gets converted into an appearance of deistic truth (at the risk of convening demonic untruth); at the upper level of which, the proof-makers (not a few of who have been proved to be charlatans) are revered beyond all measure on the basis of being the most modern of magicians. Beyond this point, there is no going back, since that would disrupt the advance of science and so provoke the dissolution of that business confidence on which the search for scientific proof (not truth) is founded.

At this pivotal point, by equating proof with truth, scientists often get very angry when the secular carpet is lifted (as it often later needs to be lifted to separate the grain of deistic truth from the chaff of scientific proof) to show what has been their earlier faith and commitment to the Supreme Command. Nevertheless, for having been their earlier faith in and commitment to the Supreme Command, this same faith becomes less than shit to the Counterfeit Command. Lifting this scientific secular carpet (to sweep their old faith under it as if it were shit) is then in danger of becoming shit to the Supreme Command by signifying the scientist's greater commitment to the Counterfeit Command.

The resulting hierarchy of swollen heads (like the swollen stomachs of De Morgan's *Siphonaptera*) is not much different than the psychoanalytic hierarchy of Freud's id, ego, and superego. The swollen head of the scientific fraternity (by no means an abstraction) is then no more tolerable to heaven than is the swollen head of the legal fraternity or the swollen head of the mathematical fraternity or the swollen head of the ecclesiastical fraternity. Indeed, if you look carefully at most icons in the Church Slavonic, you will see that the true saints, but for their correspondingly heightened halos, have quaintly unswollen heads.

How can one resolve or control this problem of swollen heads without resorting to neural implants? The whole point of abstraction (whether in language, logic, law, or science) is that (for the purposes of judging, assessing, or evaluating any task) humans have a means of sidelining their own participation in the concrete particularity of that task. In turn, this can enable them to break the bondage by which they can so easily be induced to equate proof with truth and thus still go so wrong as to presume themselves to be the measure of all things—whether from just hat size (for braggart swollen heads) and halo size (for more modestly shrunken heads).

Further then for still going backwards, further back than that of the self-made man being the self-made measure of all things, these self-made mortals then commit the ultimate mistake of thinking themselves to have made all things—from which wrongful presumption, they run the risk of destroying what another has so rightfully and righteously created. Look at their intellectual and moral decline this way. First, they crib the creative capacity, and then they mistake that crib for being their own creativity. And then having cribbed their own creativity, they think themselves to have the right to pontificate over that creativity or to substitute for it their own very different measure of creativity.

Why, even amongst the legal fraternity, there's this saying amongst many of its members (whether legislative or judicial) that because we made the law, then we can change the law! Well, that may not be totalitarianism in caps and bold type, but it sure is its own kind of totalitarianism! Alas, there's always something either comic or tragic or both about so rapidly going downhill—we angels would suppose it's the force of gravity which humans mistake (so often catastrophically) for being their own source of power. Alas, like some swollen-headed beginner snowboarding down a steep mountain, once you've exceeded your speed and skill for turning, there's little hope of restraining your momentum.

Earlier on, we posed the question of whether you, our dearest of readers, related more intimately to abstractions than to constructions (which in any case are as often mere constrictions). At one level of intimacy (the communicative level), abstractions seem more figurative than real, whereas constructions seem more literal than figurative. At another level of intimacy (the spiritual level), communicative constructions seem to be more this-world-oriented (or worldly), whereas abstractions seem more mystical, mythic (or heavenly), and so otherworldly.

In other words, do you deal with the world more easily for seeing it all laid out on the flat for yourselves (whether figuratively or literally), or do you see it (either literally or figuratively) for the world being less readily coalesced collectively (and not only selfishly for yourselves alone but for others too) into a sphere? The question is a complex one, since this critical analysis is predicated not just on levels of abstraction but also on levels of intimacy. In yet other words, what exactly is going on (can you honestly say) within those whorls of tumescent grey matter in your human brain (unless we try to deduce what it is, either rightly or wrongly) from the way you humans behave as a result of thinking with not all your grey-mattered whorls?

At today's most modern (and progressive) of moments (for which you humans take all the credit to yourselves), popular science is tops (bully for you), whereas faith in there being any heaven at all serves only to take the piss of the populace in a pardon-me context in which by now even Santa Claus is losing the last vestige of credibility. [Exegesis 1: Pardon the piss, since what we typed was *pits*, but our smart-aleck computer (without Windows) substituted *piss* and won't retract its own misspelling. So sorry!]

Nevertheless, you have to remember that the council of heaven (being given more than a passing mention in the book of Job) is open to all-comers (both the fallen and the elect). So, as said earlier, it was not a good idea to filch, from Sol (the sun god), his name day of the 25th day of December in each year, for the purpose of celebrating the birth of Baby Jesus. Make no mistake, sun worship (giving rise to more than melanoma) is still very much around.

Many of your churches, especially those of the Druidic-Scots persuasion, which compromise the attitudinal standpoint of the cross with an encircling sun, find it very hard to cope (especially in the hot summer of the southern hemisphere) with such a solar compromise. Well, instead of honouring the solar eclipse marking the moment of Christ's crucifixion, then once a compromise, always a compromise, and once a sneaky theft, forever after (until final redemption) an ongoing series of sneaky thefts. So too, just as the pagan Wheel of the Year from Yule to Alban Eilir would still keep turning, then just as Christmas gives way to Easter, the Easter bunny (a pagan fertility symbol) would take over to proliferate so many more editions of

Santa Claus by which to propagate the same cycle for each successive year.

Compromises bring about confusion. From earthwards upwards (as if by means of another tall tower by which to reach heaven), this perpetuum mobile of confused worship wends its ancient and often weary way. The physicality of what can be felt and seen by way of solstice and equinox settles the score for most in favour of the sun, moon, and stars against the mystique of the spiritually unseen. The temptation is to bolster up one's flagging faith in the substance of the unseen by having recourse to more and more of what was once unseen but yet through science and technology can now be seen. Choose between your options carefully—since what you see is not always what you get!

This further compromise to close the gap between physicality and spirituality allowably proceeds on the apparently humanistic but increasingly formalistic basis that scientific method—and now also increasingly logical method, linguistic method, and legal method— are the only sure means of reaching unassailable conclusions. [Exegesis 2: Remember, just as the ancients saw that height and depth were only two different aspects of one and the same vertical dimension, then be sure to keep your pecker up! Otherwise, the professedly unassailable conclusions of this sorry world will take you only to the lower depths or, worse still, for being inadvertently inconclusive and deprived of hope, keep you caught in the limbo of the in-between.]

Face the music (or else learn to lip-read our angelic choir)! What it is you see is not always what you get, because (1) what you see isn't always there and (2) hope lies not in what is seen but in the substance of things unseen. Look to yourselves in the unseen, therefore, and not in the seen (which, however hard to believe, isn't always there).

Like any kosher (although mediaeval, and not medieval) friar, one should always look to being suspicious of tall towers, whether on churches, monasteries, mosques, temples, colleges, or other propertied institutions. At first, church spires were intended to draw human eyes, ears, and minds away from earth to heavenly things; but increasingly they draw human minds, ears, and eyes away from heaven to earthly things—and for being so once redrawn even to fix themselves on housing bingo, and even gambling halls (besides places of worse repute) so begin to impersonate those tall towers purposely designed to suck good souls downwards instead of drawing them upwards.

Tall towers (with a history of their own since the days of their first CEO, the great hunter Nimrod, and his empire-building Tower of Babel) now tend to counterfeit versions of the first angelic ladder seen in a night vision by the patriarch Jacob, on whose behalf is coined the phrase 'Jacob's ladder'. And instead of looking towards heaven (whether figuratively or literally), people now scale tall corporate towers (to make room for themselves at the top) no less than they compete to conquer space (likewise to claim for themselves the heavenly view from the top) as if that were every bit as good as getting to heaven.

Without any spiritual song to sing (try 'John Brown's Body' since his soul still goes marching on), then earthly sight and sound can ground us (no less than can any other bodily sense) to pin us fast to this sadly groaning earth. Without that or any other spiritual song (try here 'Lord of the Dance', 'Jesus Loves Me', or 'Amazing Grace') to sing to or march with or march against, whatever one sees or hears (when sleeping homeless in the streets or in and out of prisons or to queue for months to be seen in hospitals, then whatever can be understood of this already deeply groaning world is no better than Koestler's description of 'darkness at noon'.)

So then, pick up your bed, if not also at the same time pick up your cross, and simply set off like any Shaker or Quaker to walk across the desert. The spirit alone—if not already made holy like that of the saints and martyrs, then even just human like whoever may turn out to be my good neighbour wherever next door—can free us from being captured by this blood-drenched planet Earth.

Dear friend, you ask (as did the ancients ask by the phrase *unde ubique*) now where you'll go, how you'll travel, and when you'll begin to take your leave, then both look carefully from where you'll leave and keep on reading this and other seriously written travel books, because it's from where and how and why you choose to leave where you are at present that will answer all these other questions about the future. The success or failure of whatever travel we each undertake (whether as angels or as mortals) depends on whatever preparations we make to travel.

The travel or pilgrimage which we each undertake in life is no different for us angels than it can be for you humans. This life or engagement, however short right now for humans, is in preparation for whatever eternally follows. This life of yours on earth—whether spent as an Isaac Newton or as a Paul Bunyan, as a David Livingstone or as an Albert Einstein—will determine not only whatever sort of life you next shall live but shall also serve for a far higher and wider purpose than you have any present *philosophia* by which to theorise or any present *scientia* by which to know. From us angels, who are only very little higher in the scheme of things than are you humans, our advice (attained from our experience of observing those angels who lost their footing in the satanic fall) is to stay humble.

When masquerading as all-righteous angels (a notoriously common disguise assumed on their travels by do-gooding but self-deceiving humans), those of you who see yourselves to be so well intentioned are nevertheless prone to overlook the fallen condition to which humans generically belong. For example, the communicative significance which you humans observationally attach to other people's words is often no more than your very own value judgement or personal (and sometimes excessively personal) opinion. Neither human philosophy nor human science (any more than human law or human reasoning) can render obsolete the role of prophetic revelation.

Thus, what literally would be 'insightful sound' to a thoroughly experienced musician might be completely meaningless to a non-musician. In such matters, we need to use words as best we can. In such circumstances, we need to evoke, however figuratively from their 'insightful sound', what otherwise cannot be derived from their socially case-hardened, often etymologically depleted, and merely accustomed routine use. We must accordingly relearn (from the forgotten classics) the meaning of such words as were once used poetically, precisely, and exactly to communicate and share (without being afflicted any longer by today's prevailing ambiguity, equivocality, and increasing inconsistency) what once then strengthened, rather than weakened, the minds, hearts, and motivations of righteously kindred spirits.

As already said, face the music! Face the music, because the prevailing war waged right across this world's now fast-cracking crust (in whatever sphere of politics, science, religion, and good government the cracks appear) is that very same war of words that precedes every war of action. So accept that wherever there is a lack of sufficient human derring-do (i.e. risk-taking) to bring about the revelation of any perceived untruth (or of any hidden truth which may in turn offset the as yet unperceived and so hidden untruth), then the humanly collective temptation is towards blissfully ignoring the entire situation. So then, sleepers, awake!

Still sleeping or slumbering? Then the most likely result (as with the failure to deal with any aspect of this world problematique, such as that of prioritising fast-declining resources or of preventing the increasing spate of political crises) is either of any truth (1) to convert that ignored level of truth into an even lower level of less obvious and so more deeply concealed truth or of an untruth then (2) to convert that ignored level of untruth into a more deeply concealed and therefore less obvious level of untruth. For heaven's sake, wake up! Your day of either destiny or doom approaches!

Despite their prophetic responsibility to tell the truth, it is on this score of the humanly declining faith factor that prophets come (at least to be disregarded in their own backyard), if not also (as more generally throughout the whole wide world) to be held more completely in disrepute. For telling those truths that other humans feel should not be told, and so opening the eyes of the profane (who, by no more than their own measure, profess to lead the world), then prophecy, when so disdained or disputed, rapidly (through lack of faith) becomes unproductive, then counterproductive, and finally, altogether withheld. [Exegesis 3: It will thus become increasingly obvious in all this that (instead of being any earthly absolute) telling the truth varies according to the communicative level of intimacy (short of the spiritual absolute) enjoined by and shared amongst the communicants.]

Responsibility for telling the truth then bears on the visual acuity with which we see. It also bears on the aural acuity with which we hear, no less than it bears on the tactile sensitivity with which we feel. Don't forget that at least one-third of all the angels you meet, for being fallen angels, are by now pathological liars, and it's sad to say that most humans (for still being at least fibbers) on that account run shy of meeting those angels who have much to say to them (just as elders have much to say to youth). And this no less than priests, prophets, poets, and teachers remain spiritually responsible to both man and God for their remaining staunch to the truth.

The pity of all this entropic decline in the proclaimed faith (evidenced in those gifted or called to bear responsibility by their own declining eyesight, hearing, and life span) is that many otherwise grown-up humans have never been told their mission in life. Many may even have renounced their own guardian angel, and so they run or send others (by proxy rather than by going themselves) to faraway places like Damascus, Baghdad, or Kabul. Most wars, at all levels, are fought by proxy; and just as (doubting Thomas) Carlyle pointed out so truly that most hanging judges wouldn't convict if they themselves had to place the noose or pull the trap or slice the neck, so too, most wars wouldn't happen if those bigwigs backstage who called the shots had to front up to the front lines from which to fire at those rapidly moving targets who, in turn, are disposed to fire at them.

Whatever the battle cry—whether favourably in terms of liberty, equality, fraternity, democracy, or simply peace and prosperity or unfavourably against irreligion, slavery, or taxation without representation—it's as often the impoverished, the jobless, the ne'er-do-wells, and the riff-raff who carry the can. They are the ones who are either enlisted to do the dirty work of waging warfare or who are promoted to the apparent safe haven of keeping faith alive. Don't you know enough of heaven to realise that right now there's a war on?

Meanwhile, all the time, those who keep their hands scrupulously washed and squeaky clean (as once required by courts of equity) are those who manage now to keep their bank balances soaring into never-before heights of solvency. The collective result (since the blind follow the blind) is to fabricate a new set of so-called moral values by which whatever dirty washing they may have made for themselves through investing in the manufacture of land mines, toxic gases, and other prohibited munitions stays extremely well hidden behind their enormous bank balances. Nevertheless, don't give up on your grey matter if you would want to keep your sanity!

Exactly one-half of this world's irreligion is mistaken by its irreligious proponents for being their sanctified fight for democracy. These are mostly the Western nations, but there's no need to specify either which nations or who are the mistakenly irreligious proponents. Meanwhile, the other and almost exact half of this world's irreligion is mistaken by its irreligious proponents (likewise unspecified, but mostly Eastern nations) for being their sanctified fight against democracy. Give up on your grey matter at this point, and you'll be scheduled for a neural transplant!

The naked truth of this otherwise carefully concealed and irreligious misapprehension (afflicting both sides) rests on the implied premise that if either were truly religious, there would be no such fight at all. So likewise, just as if neither were mistakenly irreligious, so also there would be no such fight at all. Instead, the typical misfortune of this present world (strategically endorsed by the Counterfeit Command) is to mistake politics (of whatever sort, good or bad) for being true religion.

This mistake most usually arises from people substituting their own brand of (often mistaken) democracy for the ultimate truth. From the collateral damage they themselves then mistakenly cause, most of them either fight or run away, or else by opposing another's brand of democracy (under whatever name) for not being precisely their own brand of democracy, they then irreligiously oppose it. On this score, neural transplants can be done merely by watching television. There's now no licence required to watch whatever channel of substitutive neurology you choose!

None of these wars (first of words and then of action) are true wars anyway, which is why those believers who are truly religious are clearly warned by the spirit of truth not to be swayed by the way in which counterfeit wars so often manifest the most extreme elements of irreligion. Such irreligious wars only counterfeit the true spiritual battles being fought all the time on earth both for and against the kingdom of heaven. To misunderstand the spiritual nature of those truly religious battles leaves every human spirit vulnerable to being drawn into counterfeit battles (so many of which deform the thinking and debilitate the minds of true believers). If not by television, the (so-called) social media (as upheld by the Counterfeit Command) is the next best means of receiving a negatory neural transplant (NNT), by which, in comparison with this fiercely warring earth, you'd never know that even in heaven, there's a far greater war going on!

Spiritual battles are very rarely (if ever) fought with big, bigger, and yet even bigger threats, far less than with big, bigger, and the very biggest guns. Believe this with the heavenly host, as testified to by the constancy of their behaviour, that the power of the pen and the proclamation of the word are a far, far more powerful explosive by their action, if not by now to redeem the world but at least to save souls, than is the impact of any bomb or gun. And if you don't believe us in our proclaiming the power of words, then why bother to read on? So then it's got to that point, has it, where, without being bothered to read on, you say there's no war on!

Perhaps your ears have been overlong blocked and your eyes have been overlong closed to the everyday sight and sound of so many, many professedly spiritual things. [Exegesis 4: You would have been in a coma by now, however, had you been closed off to absolutely everything beyond the veil. Don't panic over yourself or over anyone else for being in a coma, however, since many who have been in a coma for all their life have been resurrected out of that purely physical condition into everlasting life. And likewise, don't mistake the purely physical material (or bodily) dimension (in which you've still managed to survive) for being entirely secular, far less for it being in any way non-spiritual. That mistake is most usually induced by the Counterfeit Command whilst you've been in some sort of physical coma.]

Nevertheless, there are more as yet untold dimensions than you humans have been already told of by which no more than a very few of you have already learnt to navigate. By reaching the requisite level of righteousness through divine grace and so learning to navigate these extramural dimensions with the counsel and backing of that paramilitary paraclete (the one who buddies one's back in spiritual battle), some of you humans have nevertheless been already anointed. So then what's your anointing if not to see and hear more clearly than most humans want to see and hear of reality (or to allow themselves to perceive of such personal potential to perceive of or of any preparedness to participate in that reality)? Aha, but then you may run shy of allowing yourselves to perceive of such personal potential, since you would then have to participate in that reality.

But even many humans (as artists, poets, and musicians) have neural pathways better developed than those other humans who are less inclined to hear and see, as do seers (who are visionaries) and prophets (who are proclaimers), what lies beyond the already torn veil. [Exegesis 5: A seer or visionary is someone who, by some means whether divinely sanctified or demonically blacklisted, can see or envision beyond the temporal dimension of the physically present].

Indeed, it would have been much too soon before in this report for us angels to have reminded you humans that the whole point of our publishing this report to you humans is to encourage your eyes to see and your ears to hear in hitherto undiscovered dimensions and, in short, to extend, deepen, and improve both your hearing and seeing far beyond your existing limits of belief. As you can surely already guess from what you have already read, we angels are not just talking here about hearing and seeing in the bodily sense. Those who are bodily deaf or bodily blind, whether from birth or through aging, often have far more acute spiritual perception than those persons with both 20/20 hearing and 20/20 vision in midlife.

The whole truth, when frankly speaking, is that telling a lie bears on every intellectual, moral, and metaphysical appetite we human beings have for being able to taste every truth and distinguish it from falsity. This lie-detector test (now officially applied at every border crossing) operates regardless of whatever little we know at all known levels of law, language, and logic. Be well prepared whenever you're called to cross the border between any two disciplines, between any two nations, between any two cultures, and between any two countries to be faced with every such test.

It follows (as said before, but we'll say so again because every copybook is a teaching book) that clarity of vision and clarity of hearing, especially in the spiritually withheld dimensions, is accentuated and intensified throughout the entire body, mind, and soul ever so simply by telling the truth and being prepared always to tell the truth. And the proverbial buck doesn't even begin to stop there, although there's a danger that even what began here as a lyric on telling the truth can itself rapidly become a lecture (or a need for a lecture or, worse still, a need for a sermon) against telling lies. Be even better prepared when you're called to cross the border between past and present, between present and future, and even more especially, between the historic past and the prophetic future—that it is (so it is) but a very faint line that marks the border between hell and heaven. And in most cases, you'll never know till you've crossed it.

What we angels (as well as you mortals) witness on such occasions of mistaking ourselves to be upholding the truth with the big, bigger, and biggest guns (which include unlicensed law, unlicensed language, and unlicensed logic) then bids us to exercise with even more care for the very personal way in which we choose to believe ourselves to be rightly doing so. Trusting ourselves by virtue of the love song we sing to be acting on behalf of the Supreme Command, we will then choose either to contribute or else to dedicate more or less of our own souls (wittingly or unwittingly) to upholding the only spiritual measure of authentic forcefulness on whose behalf we thereby pray for others. And so by worshiping only the truth, the way, and life that sets all mankind free, then by such means we shall be free ourselves.

Living that universal love song, by which this world's captives can be set free, nevertheless remains a tall order, since complex contexts should make us forever cautious of construing apparently simple texts. Even the best informed and best intended of this world's *bogomiles* (literally God's own warriors) can get sucked down into the softest of body-snatching quicksands or caught up into the worst of bog mires (as did the parliamentary speaker of one small near republic in the South Pacific) by thinking to prove his nation's inclusivity by excluding the name of Jesus Christ from parliamentary prayers.

We should *take five*, if not *ten*, or else a longer break, before blazing a new trail through the jungle of lost hopes and broken promises here, but time is pressing as the speed of light further and further declines. Look again at the worldly context of your own lives in this way, and at this international level once again (as already done), compare the complexity of that context with the apparent simplicity of each nation's national anthem! The whole wide world (henceforth abbreviated to www throughout this commissioned report) is by now rendered as much oblivious to the worshipful nature of this world's every anthem as it is rendered even more oblivious to the prophetic forebodings of this world's every supposedly secular song. [Exegesis 5: Since the veil has been torn, the naked truth is not withheld from anyone. No, not even from Napoleon. No, not even from Stalin. No, not even from Hitler. No, not even from anyone at all. But yet there's nothing like a nation's national anthem by which to prove it.]

One reason for the gargantuan oversight of this world's secular prophets (apart from the great number of human souls taken captive by individual egos) is that so many mortals have been rendered oblivious to the level of self-worship which commits them (like dumb waiters) to their own nation's national anthem. We've been here before, we know, but then people will go on singing what they mistake for being their own divinely sanctioned national anthem, and we can't always not hear what they still sing.

They sing their own brand of militaristic song, if at all, either under demonic duress (because they have collegially foresworn the song's professed principles) or else because they expect titularly to serve two masters. This is attempted (although, as you know, cannot be done) by means of the hollow word as ensured by either their completely absent spirit or else when deeply drugged by their still slumbering spirit. [Exegesis 6: Alas, the more serious sequel to the tragicomic *Dead Souls* on this point of resurrecting the slumbering spirit was unfortunately destroyed by its author, Maxim Gorky, but in lieu thereof, read John and Paula Sandford's *Healing the Wounded Spirit*.]

It is by means of this hollow word—do you recall hearing the speech profile possessed by the hollow word when spoken by any slumbering spirit?—which is unacceptable to the Supreme Command (yet made so acceptable to the Counterfeit Command). You can't do better here than to construct in your copybook a catalogue of speech profiles by which to discern this hollow word on whose account an exceedingly but imperceptibly slippery slope can be made to extend from the Supreme Command to the Counterfeit Command. It is by means of this imperceptibly slippery slope of slumber that the hollow word depletes countless believers from fighting against the Counterfeit Command from the front-line ranks of the Supreme

Command. What can you do to help them, for the slippery slope of slumber is exceeding slippery to the slumbering spirit of the already taken-captive soul?

We angels (musicians in our own right) have become very much aware that for the sake of a catchy tune, most people (without a thought for what they're singing) can be made to sing what they otherwise wouldn't be prepared to say. They'll sing 'God Defend New Zealand' whether or not they admit to believing in any god at all (or whether they can identify where any need for their requested defence lies). At a pinch (no pun intended), they'll accept a knighthood from the reigning monarch whom they swore once to uphold and defend, although with much the same breath as they shortly before sang 'God Save the Queen', they'll still seriously argue for a republic to be instituted on the present monarch's imminent death.

Why, predicating anything of this sort on any sovereign's death (be he or she president, king, or queen) is tantamount to treason! All the same (which it never is), the www (for being by now almost a republican nonentity) is very different from today's groaning (non-pc entity) of an almost worn-out earth. If you think otherwise (as inculcated by pc programming), then turn right round to face the increasingly cosmic music.

There now, when facing increasingly westwards and no longer eastwards, you'll discover that this aforesaid www is one that is becoming increasingly tone-deaf to the difference between right and wrong, good and evil, and even justice and injustice. More than a hundred years ago, the prophet-historian Oswald Spengler (who was pilloried for the same idea) first discerned humanity's about-change of purposeful direction by what he diagnosed for you, now to be read again in *The Decline of the West*.

Take a breather. Take a breather here, since the full force of mankind's eventually complete fall from both Eastern and Western cultures is yet to be experienced. The spiritual impact of more than any mature adult's continued disgrace (as for the world's still ancient Israel) differs vastly from the everyday gracelessness of (the still ancient Arab's) still avidly learning child. Nevertheless, no matter how hard one tries to avoid carrying one's own cross (far less anyone else's cross), the human respectability which one looks for by way of return can be just as much a burden to the lowliest of humble people as the holding of status can be a burden to the proudest of high-born people—with neither burden being heavier than the other in its carrying off many an otherwise bright spirit to an early grave.

Today's monumental changes, both in the direction and intensity of mankind's moral momentum (with its loss of human motivation to engage in the still fundamentally moral although increasingly jurisprudential, ecological, and environmental issues), has gone so far as to divorce logic from language (and so also language from logic), law from rule (and so also both rule from law as well as rule by law); and this is no less than to excise both tonality from musicality (and so musicality from tonality) and so (hold on, hold on, and still hold on) to reduce love as any sort of constant to an ever-increasing pantheon of very confusing and apparently conflicting relativities. And that's surely enough for now (literally speaking) since the more known of enough right now serves only to indicate (however prematurely) the end of whatever time you have left in which to take action.

* * *

A Very Brief History of Heaven
Part IX

The Suffering Servant in Man
Psychiatrists and psychoanalysts might well be described as modern magicians. If they called themselves in plain English 'physicians of the soul' no one would believe them. How could they, since our humanist and pseudo-scientific *élites* have told them they have no soul?

R. C. Zaehner, *Our Savage God*

'Tell me now', asks my guardian angel, 'who is speaking to you through these words of Zaehner on the subject of "our savage God"? Do these words of wisdom come from some human being or from some angelic being?'

'No,' my own answer (if it is my own answer) comes, 'wisdom is not a divine prerogative. In some shape or form (whether artistic, philosophic, scientific, or governmental), it has to be asked for, searched for, and followed through. If it comes, it doesn't come quietly. If it settles, it has to be maintained rigorously. And even if a given (as in geometry), it still isn't held in perpetuity. On the contrary, it can be undone by some momentary act of the utmost folly. So then who dares to speak on the subject of "our savage god"? Who dares to speak wisely on any such subject?

'Well, I don't really know,' I myself conclude, 'because just as humans may sometimes fearlessly walk where angels fear to tread and so then keep so close company with those angels who accompany them that they too behave like angels, there is good cause to believe that the reverse process may operate for angels in their keeping close company with humans. Indeed, from the history of heaven, we know that this is so, because certain angels were so captivated by their love for humans that they forsook their commission with the Supreme Command and so fell from heaven. Once again, however, the biological offspring of these forbidden relationships testifies to how little lower us humans are (in terms of our functional DNA) to you angels.'

The closeness of this relationship between angels and humans on both sides raises the greatest need for caution. This is especially so because to be mistaken for being human is a tactic so often required of angels (both those fallen and those still upright) for the fulfilling of some strategically divine or demonic plan that the semblance of another identity can promote self-identical confusion. Likewise, then also humans, from having advantaged themselves through keeping company with (even the upright) angels, may increasingly appear both to themselves and other humans to be themselves as angels. Besides, for children who still remain so close to those ministering angels who brought their little souls to life on earth, this explains with more particularity how so many infants and young children are many times seen and described (without the slightest hyperbole) for being themselves little angels.

The sheer diversity of the human condition remains humanly indescribable, since every single human being is truly unique, but even if your own personal individuality is truly unique in the generic context of the human condition, the uniqueness of our own personal individuality in the generic context of the angelic condition exceeds and excels all human conception of what it can be to be truly amazing. [Exegesis 1: But just remember that if the truth that sets us free were more adequately known, we would all be vicars of Christ, and wouldn't that, despite the extent of our continuingly different diversities, be even more truly amazing!]

Nevertheless, it is the shortcoming of the human mind, especially when faced with infinite diversity, to generalise all things—whether snowflakes or grains of sand, no less than men and women, or even all of us angelic beings—to be pretty much all the same. By this barely logical means, humans then tend towards lumping so many 'renegade diversities' together (into the killing fields of Cambodia, Guadalcanal, and Vietnam or into the gas-chambers of Dachau, Treblinka, or Auschwitz) by arguing in favour of 'the exceptional case'. This allows for such diversities to be herded together and made subject to 'the most exceptional means' of reducing all such diversities to something that (least of all) we could wish to be all much the same. Overcoming this urge to conform (whether by way of placid confirmation or outright rebelliousness) takes its toll on two-year-old infants as well as on adolescents and all the way upwards.

This societal small-mindedness resulting from the effort to impose 'conformity' on 'diversity' in the name of 'equality' is one of the most explosive of charges laid under professedly civil societies. The harm it causes, as much through overcompensation as otherwise, leads to much invalidity of argument—in itself producing as much arrant capitalism as arrant communism, as much arrant socialism as arrant individualism, as much arrant fascism as arrant sovietism, and as much arrant chauvinism as arrant tokenism. At its bottom line, it will not confront the consequences so often of 'the most exceptional means of applying the exceptional case' to all men (and as often women) being rendered equal to each other, whereas whether in the political or moral or even biophysical sphere, it would be truer to say that in their yet unique, diverse, and combinative equivalence (not equality), every individual is more rightly appreciated (and with much less risk) for being both complementary and complimentary to each other. Likewise, the same tension applies to the relationship of the individual to the collective, from which we derive our concept of the 'civil society'.

The key is one of combinative valency and not one of enforced equality. The fact is (where facts are paramount) that the secular mind increasingly gets its algorithmic equations in a twist for its failure of spiritual awareness by which to accord significance to the smaller print as well as to the bigger imprint) of human diversity. So then what hope is there of humans recognising the far vaster realm of angelic diversity? Not much hope at all, which is why so few humans ever see even their own guardian angels. We're back into class calculus again—the class calculus to which many humans have never got closer than to recognise that 'big fleas have little fleas upon their backs to bite them ... and little fleas have lesser fleas ...' and so ad infinitum. Indeed, most humans would as soon turn their backs on their own guardian angel as they would crush an aphid, pick off a caterpillar, or squash a flea.

This failure of spiritual awareness to recognise diversity is pertinent not only to the algorithmic (and so mechanistic) mind of many humans but also to the (increasingly mechanistic) mind of so many otherwise heuristic angels. It explains not only the fall of mankind from Eden but also the fall of Satan from heaven (both of which are increasingly mistaken for being only mythically mechanistic equations instead of altogether heuristic happenings). In more abstract terms, this same failure explains every act of antagonistic confrontation, every threat or act of violence, every call to battle, and every war or act of terrorism.

The very same lack of spiritual awareness goes even further in (1) its failure to explain the existence of laws and other logical means by which to suppress or repress unwarranted conflict; (2) its failure to explain the allowance, encouragement, and also promotion of excessively competitive and gladiatorial sport; together with (3) its failure to redeem all other psychorecognisant means by which the better to supervise, sublimate, or resolve those issues giving rise to unwarranted conflict. Human society without benefit of law and its resultant social order would be no better than the heavenly kingdom without the spirit of creation having moved upon the face of the waters and given constant counsel as to the continuing forcefulness of creation.

For the most part, the human condition is open to recognise us angels as being either bearers of blessing or being bearers of woes. But likewise, and also for the most part, whether for being either a blessing or being a woe, this is determined not so much by what sort of news it is we bring or bear but rather by how (or in what spirit) humanity receives or rejects what news we bear. By and large (because not all of us are upright angels), we don't bring down deficient souls from heaven, nor from the moment of any person's unique foundation are there any such things as evil souls.

It is true that some fallen angels seem to have placed themselves quite beyond redemption, but although we other angels still stand upright, such things are not for us to say. Indeed, were we to exercise any such unauthorised judgement, we, in turn, would be held responsible to the Supreme Command for thus far exceeding our angelic commission. As for you humans, however, many of you are so naive as to think that because you only praise and encourage, therefore you never judge. Alas, for false encouragement and false praise, *you do so very often wrongly judge*! And you do so as much for mistaking whom you judge as for mistaking the judgement by which you judge.

The law of legitimate authority counts for as much in the upper heavens as it does either on middle earth or in what we perceive for being lower hell. In many ways, observing legitimate authority (no less on earth than in heaven) provides a touchstone for one's loyalty to the Supreme Command, whilst in other ways, it becomes the touchpaper by which to set off a firework display of still falling angels by which to demonstrate its legitimate authority visually across the heavens. Let us be content to remind you, as very vulnerable human beings, that there is hardly any fallen angel who does not consider himself or herself to be now standing far above and beyond the lawful authority of all those who are more humbly upright.

That surprises you? Well then, perhaps that's a good sign for you. All temporal signs must be verified (most usually done against the (slowing) speed of light), and since this verification is required most particularly for the signs of the times, we (still the angelic 'we') can only here speak contingently. As with distinguishing good signs from bad signs, friends from foes, and us angels (but whether good or bad—a more difficult issue) from you humans (for us easier and easier, but for you harder and harder), there are many, many books on the subject, although as can usually be said of such a subject, the devil is in the detail.

Let's leave it (the demonic, no less) for the moment at this point. As a prophylactic measure, however, it can be beneficially pointed out that in all such matters, it behoves the spiritual investigator to go to the source—always the source—and not just the target. This particularly applies to issues of good and evil (mistakenly thought of as morality instead of as metaphysics), issues of injustice (casually mistaken for matters of morality), and curses and blessings (customarily dismissed for being matters of profit and loss).

In each of these areas of fierce dispute where the issues (all either jurisprudential or metaphysical) are so often engaged in gladiatorial combat, then once again, go to the source, the source, the source and don't be diverted by the target. And this advice applies most particularly whenever you yourself feel yourself to be the target.

In eighty out of a hundred cases (sometimes ending in death and destruction), folks who mistake themselves for being the target (and so feel victimised or martyred or incurably hard done by) are nowise the target at all; they just happen (by reason of their ignoring the signs of the times) to get in the way of the target.

Oh, of course, sometimes hard-done folks will learn to target themselves or target their progenitors, and so to evoke sympathy for themselves, they will use their own friendly fire to shoot themselves in the foot or, worse still, through the heart or head. Nevertheless, for the devil being always in the nitty-gritty of these domestic details, we must here stick to the basic principles for living a good life (which the devil avoids, just as he would avert every cure for his own many plagues).

Above all, look to the only reliable source of this life's redeeming love instead of devoting yourself to any stifling blanket of self-pity. So too, either in finding yourself under a curse (that's not the source, that's just the instrument of woe) or else crediting yourself for being worthy of a blessing (no, self-credit is the least source of any blessing), you may unwittingly compound the curse or bar the blessing. Most frequently, there's a test of faith before any blessing. And even amongst the angels, there are too many complex temptations masquerading as rewards.

But if you doubt us (the angelic predicative case) for what we say on the subject of rewards, then, however briefly we deal with that subject on this scratch-card introduction to source and target interpretation, first get your heads round the book of Job for being an introduction to reading the signs of the times. [Exegesis 2: Meanwhile, there are so many communicative enterprises (including both angelic and humanistic evangelism) which are so intimately involved with translation theory (although every act of communication, even with thinking or talking to oneself, involves translation theory) that even those engaging in the highest of levels cannot avoid the issue as to whether the translation being made is, for the purposes of the conveyed communication, being done either more true to its source or else more true to its target.]

Thus, in one of two ways, the communicant may depart from the true source either (1) for the sake of his own telling or else (2) for the sake of the recipient's limited understanding, and so (3) the communicant may exaggerate or diminish the gospel source in order to make it easier for himself to understand, explain, or believe in that source or else (4) to exaggerate or diminish the gospel source to make it easier for the recipient to understand, accept, or believe in what is being presented to the recipient for being the source. Nevertheless, these are only two of the many possible fractals associated with presenting the truth by way of translation theory. [Exegesis 3: For source- and target-oriented translation in comparative law (or in any other discipline where comparisons are drawn), then see as previously reported in the *American Journal of Comparative Law*, Volume XLIV, Winter 1996, No. 1]

Hear ye this then that all angels, both the fallen and the unfallen, are dignitaries of heaven; and it is not our place (at least of those still standing) to sit in judgement on one another. In our own sight, there can be no such angelic difference made by us between the fallen and the unfallen any more than as for all humans on earth, since both the saved and the unsaved are equivalently loved by their heavenly Father.

We (not the authorial 'we' but the angelic 'we) now leave to some later account where the boundaries more accurately lie between you humans as you serve the Supreme Command on earth and ourselves as angels who serve the Supreme Command amongst the heavenly host, but in this brief preface about ourselves as angels, we do take this final opportunity of communicating our deepest concern at the way in which humans remain so unaware of their pivotal position in achieving the already decided outcome of our present cosmic conflict.

Much of the cosmic responsibility for achieving that already determined outcome of this conflict now rests with you humans alone, to be waged with your every spiritual gift from the Supreme Command against the cosmic machinations of its opposing the Counterfeit Command. So then begin right now to bolster up all your human willpower to fight the good fight. Faith does not exist in the abstract (over which there is much misunderstanding). It only exists after being put to the test to learn what each and every word of faith actually means, so by being put to the test of faith, then stand your ground, and thereby come to know what is required of you (and in this case, none other than you) to distinguish friend from foe.

Love for the law does not outlaw the law of love (copy that maxim into your copybook whilst all the time meditating on its meaning), and just as every lawyer learns (often the hard way) to draw distinctions, every would-be lover must learn (as also often the hard way) to distinguish potential friend from potential foe. So many human relationships falter on this simple precept, giving rise to broken souls and thence to misguided wars and outright terrorism. And yet if you know the metaphysics by which, without attempting to give any quick-fix for the moment, even a severely fractured soul can be forever redeemed, then you too can be vested with a confidence in all creation and not just in your own salvation. As always, like any minimalist musician, do the most with the least, and then you may well find yourself doing far more than you could ever do with the most.

Your own self-worth (but not for the sake of yourself, which is a common misunderstanding, but rather self-worth for the sake of being engaged in collective soul-catching) is near to being paramount for anyone going into battle. There is no weapon formed against anyone called into the front line to do battle on behalf of the Supreme Command that, given the right choice by way of hallowed response to that weapon, cannot be deflected. If you only knew it, every love song is a battle song; and if you only knew that, how many false courtships would be deflected, how many broken marriages could be repaired, how many fractious families could be restored, and how many nations could be redeemed? The Supreme Command operates best in battle zones, whereas the Counterfeit Command promotes only a false peace by which to pursue its own nefarious ends.

Think of a love song—an authentic love song—and review it as a military operation in terms of both strategy and tactics. You'll discover, for the lack of finding many genuine love songs today, that so many of the tedious sounds of this earth promote only a false dawn in the enlightenment of love. It is so easy in this world to get hooked on a false dawn, no less than to get distracted by a mistaken love song. Like Odysseus, tie yourself to the mast or put wax in your ears to avoid every false love song!

Homer's *Odyssey* is not just an ancient battle song but also an eternal love song. As authentic as this love song is for lasting this long out from Homer's epic age, it is too seriously a long-term love song to appeal to the most tedious of today's short-term lovers. Thus, the Broadway musical of *Home Sweet Homer* proved a flop, and even Max Bruch's greatest choral work, *Odysseus*, has by now fallen into oblivion.

Every epic tale of love has been reduced to the level of a one-night stand. Nevertheless, Homer's *Odyssey* still operates, at the very least, as this world's greatest proto-love song. And with the exception of the book of Ruth (which is streets ahead in proclaiming the music of human courtship), so also are so many of the Old Testament books no more than proto-love songs. And on this score of courtship shall remain so until the relatively neglected *Song of Solomon* is more generally recognised.

Once again, as at the start of any angelic or heavenly song, we can now more explicitly ask, what's in a song? So many people—whether teachers, preachers, prophets, and even apostles—seem to be tone-deaf to the ongoing continuum of heavenly sound. If not their ears, then have their hearing aids also gone dead? Why, even the angels can deafen themselves to scripture in song. Nevertheless, the fallen angels are not, as you might think, tone-deaf but instead are obliged by their Counterfeit Command to wear not noise-cancelling earphones but instead music-cancelling earphones. Accordingly, they soon lose their sense of angelic wonderment by listening only to the hash of counterfeit scripture and to the perpetuum mobile of counterfeit sound.

Wonderment is conveyed best by the sound of a song. Of course, there are no words without their music (although you may have songs without words). Not just with the sound of the Psalms but so also with each book of the Bible, you have a song book—sometimes slow and sad, at other times quick and joyful. And yet still the whole Bible, from creation to revelation, sings of an eternal symphony of sound! But if you can't as yet identify with this sound, then for starters, listen to Handel's *Messiah*, Haydn's *Creation*, or Mendelssohn's *Elijah*.

The trouble with our lives (as with so many of the attempts we make to communicate our love) is that we don't know how to woo or even how to be wooed! We stammer through a courtship. We fall silent with our spouse when, after the honeymoon is sometimes sadly over (as can happen long before the wedding service begins), what were once mistaken for being the stoutest of marriages begin to break down. [Exegesis 4: Poets generally, for being the best of theoreticians, usually make the most mess of their falling in love. But read of the poet Longfellow's life. His biographer, Oliver Smeaton, of George Herriot's College in Edinburgh, provides the most reliable guide as to Longfellow's courtship and marriage. And as always in love and marriage, take the blessing of Tobias (by whose book, his blessing should never have been excised from the Protestant Bible) for the sake of every married couple both looking forward to their growing old together.]

Every husband of choice, no matter how much younger or older may be his wife, will always see his wife to be in years younger and in wisdom far older than others may see her as she is to him or to them. Life is replete with trials of faith, and since faith untested is worthless, any marriage for a lifetime (as every marriage is for life) is one of the best of trials of faith. So in marriage counselling [which also falls within the angelic province of saving souls], we angels [who, after all is said and done, are only minimally higher in our heavenly attributes than are you humans] need to learn how to woo, when, and to whom, as so described in one of the earliest handbooks to courtship, first published in 1855. On the other hand, if you feel the need to be a little more up to date, then read Stephanie Dowrick's *The Universal Heart* (2000).

You see, knowing how to woo, when, where, and with whom (rather than to whom) is the essence of every act of communication. At every level, despite whatever block or barrier that the Counterfeit Command may put in the way, the objective of all communication— whether to reach a decision, resolve a problem, come to an agreement, or to air one's feelings—is to establish an instance of true communion at that level. And as often as not, the ways of the world are of no great help to achieve this undertaking.

For example, take the level of communion required for marriage. Is this, as with Shakespeare's *Romeo and Juliet*, either a personal or a familial relationship or both? So too, how near or far from each other should the prospective spouses be in age? In *Future Shock* by Alvin Toffler, the author prophesises that the relationship of marriage would henceforth be less concerned with the relative ages of the prospective spouses but instead settled and determined more by their stage in life. *How to Woo* has its own point to make about this age/stage formula: those intending to marry should be more immature than mature, since mature people find themselves less accommodating to each other and so harder for themselves to meld and mould themselves to each other than when they are younger. Well, learning to meld and mould can take some lengthy life-experience too, and very often far beyond accomplishment by the romantic mindset of the still immature and overly young.

Of course, all such formula for securing marital compatibility (if it is that which we are talking about) depends on how one defines maturity, and as often, this is defined either merely on subjective appearances (commonly as to age) or from the relativity of one's own standpoint (as to stage). Nevertheless, for being an investment in the close communion of communication, then continued courtship is not only part of the marriage continuum; it is the essence of even the most trivial and transient of conversations and the province of communication (to which both serious courtship and passing the time of day belong).

With the simplest of pastoral songs, David, the shepherd boy who, in turn, became king, solaced the broken soul of King Saul. Even many of us angels now seem to lack for the simplest of songs. So many see-through songs are counterfeit these days that we too, although amongst the heavenly host, are in danger of becoming tone-deaf. None of you down on earth seems any longer to believe in the music of the spheres, and so we angels in heaven miss out on the prophetic power of your songs, pretty much as we also miss out on the prophetic power of your prayers.

Let it be known now, as never before, that just as he whom we know as Jesus Christ is not only lord of the dance, so too he is the lord of all songs. Rap, ragtime, rock, plainsong, baroque, jazz (multitudinously of all sorts), minimalist, or symphonic—the genre (or brand name) doesn't matter. The lord of dance and song (no less than of any song and dance) is lord of all.

Yes, indeed, and needless to say, although for some good reasons that even many musicians fail to understand, Jesus Christ, the great redeemer of things gone wrong, is bound to be lord of all songs—both of the bad and of the good, as well as of the in-between. He is lord both of the sad song and of the cheerful song, no less than he is lord of both harmony and counterpoint, as well as of the loneliest lyric.

How could it be otherwise, because, whether mankind or even all the angels know it or not, our lord of both dance and song is also the lord of all things—all things both great and small!

The lord of all things both great and small (both so great that you cannot see them, as well as so small that you likewise cannot see them) is lord both also of the authentic and of the counterfeit—he is not only lord over all the truth but over all the ways of falsifying the truth. You may therefore thoughtlessly ascribe to him another but grossly mistaken identity—as if pertaining to the one-eyed Cyclopes in Homer's *Odyssey*. No, our Father in heaven does not have the so-called all-seeing eye of God—as may even be pictured in all ignorance on the ceilings of some churches and cathedrals. Let me clearly warn you that this is a counterfeit concept dreamed up by the Counterfeit Command to scare, threaten, and terrorise all but the saints and true believers. The only true eye of God is already in one's inner eye, already in one's spiritual consciousness opened up by God in one's own heart, and so done in answer to one's own request, and as implanted there by the will of Father God through the ministry of the Holy Spirit. Hmm—for picturing so well any one-eyed Cyclopes, one might well be drawn into doing battle against that one-eyed Cyclopes.

The all-seeing eye (on this, read Tolkien who knew his classics), whether of some big brother god or through the dictatorship of some big brother man, is a counterfeit abomination, which, through the so-called brotherhood of man movement (without any other god than man) or through corrupting the concept of god more directly to reach the same end through the abuse of technology, incrementally builds up distrust between man and man and so, consequentially, between man and God. [Exegesis 5: As a mere matter of military tactics, you see, the Counterfeit Command lacks the full angelic personnel to do the rounds of earth in reporting back to the full council of heaven [as noted in the book of Job] by having only one-third of the angelic host to implement its Counterfeit Command. And that's just one big reason (i.e. shortage of personnel) why press gangs from Counterfeit Command engage both day and night in all-out, no-holds-barred, soul-snatching.]

Continue to look up to heaven, by all means, but always far beyond the ceiling of any place of earthly worship [whether low church or highest cathedral]. And always, avoiding judgement of the lower sort, stick to your calling—just as firmly as any scientist should stick to what he proves for as long he believes in that proof (in itself a matter of faith) to substantiate whatever are the facts. [Exegesis 6: But here, after saying so, let this infinitely limitless issue reconciling quantification (in space) with qualification (in time) now contingently terminate with one of the earliest questions from quantum physics: how many angels do you say can stand on the point of a pin?]

Let it be known now also by these presents that it is as if from the start of all creation yet then still in that dreamtime long before the coming dawn so long ago proclaimed that we too both once lived. Yes, it is from such a time as both that and this that your human spirit looks and yearns for this strategic outcome of our cosmic conflict. As if it were already expressed as heaven's most holy and angelic love song, that battle song has been most strongly implanted not only deep within each of your own human hearts but also like a prophetic revelation to be duly fulfilled within each of your own human heads.

By this tactical means, this long dormant revelation from the Supreme Command is made personally to you through your own human strength of will, through your own human power of prayer, and through your own human persistence of faith. So too, in turn, may your human hands also be hallowed both by the shield of faith and by the sword of scripture. And so it is that we angels pray both for the prior purpose of your being sufficiently prepared and able to take up and play your expected part in the fray, as well as being also further hallowed by the part you play in what may still unexpectedly follow of and from that ongoing fray.

* * *

A Very Brief History of Heaven
Part X

A Little Lower Than the Angels
'I am quite sure that we were angels once ...
somewhere perhaps far beyond ... or maybe even
here ... and that's the reason why we remember a
previous existence ... After all, since the soul is
immortal, and I am to live forever in the future, I
must have existed in the past ... so I have eternity
behind me, as well too ... as eternity also before me.'
Lev Tolstoy, *War and Peace*

That's Natasha Rostova speaking from Lev (Leo-the-Lion) Tolstoy's
War and Peace. She's speaking from earth on the subject of angels in
heaven. But beware, she is still no more than a romantically inclined
teenager. She is of an age when, on first falling into love (which she
mistakes for being herself in love), it is as if heaven has just come
down to earth.

From Natasha's point of view (however much mistaken), heaven
and earth have coalesced, as if for all eternity, she and the angels shall
partake of the same heavenly history. Her mistake is one commonly
made for all sorts of reasons by mortals, which is why the gates of
heaven are opened wide to afford the consolation of its own heavenly
history to what thereafter befalls so many heartbroken humans.

As for any *krasavitsa* (amongst young Russian girls), Natasha
is wonderfully attractive (certainly to every *krasavits*, or handsome
young Russian man) for her high-spirited innocence. Would you (like
every other person who encounters her sparkling personality) not
also give her a high five or the thumbs up by way of affirming the
favourable life that lies ahead of her?

Nevertheless, listen most attentively here since the high-spirited
Natasha is speaking now of herself as being an angel and so having
already had an eternity both behind and before of herself. But
take heed ... take heed since she is proclaiming this eternity not

much sooner than she will think to elope before breaking off her engagement with her long-standing fiancé and to run off with the rascally Dolgorukov (just as can happen in any Jane Austen novel). So what would you now think of her own postulated identification with the angels?

We angels couldn't hold her back from this nefarious affair any more than could then any closer member of her earthly family. [Exegesis 1: Beware, not even we angels are invincible! So also, every single human person (unless or until called to account) can become no more than the sum of unexpected happenings. Be prepared!]

Alas, it's no less perilous for any human being (however powerful his or her own personality may be) to inflate their own human status to being that of an angel. And once mistaken on this score is more than enough to be only thus so mistaken than it is to mix one's metaphors, as between what is so seldom all fact but is so often made to share also the spice of maudlin fiction. [Excursus 1: Given (as in geometry) so that you may receive (as in theology), do you get the message (as in psychology) so that you may be saved from the statistics (as in mathematics) of those who fall victim (as in metaphysics) to the counterfeit fruits of unexpected happenings?]

Likewise, as in our everyday battle between right and wrong, so also it can be perilous (without as much serious prayer as serious thought) to hold steadfastly to one's position (as between outright war and/ or tendentious peace). The ingenuity (whether heavenly or demonic) with which the human heart overrules the human mind to precipitate either the most heavenly flight or else (even after the stoutest of fights) to suffer the hardest of earthly falls never ceases to amaze us upright angels. Big businesses go down like ninepins, office blocks lie shut and empty, banks close up their counters, and secure investment falters. If you can't see this admittedly complex connection between fall, failure, fulfilment, and success, then study it both generally and in as many as you can find of its most prolific demonstrations!

So then do you know how (even if not enough of why) to keep your place? If it's anywhere in the South Pacific, you may already from there (once here) have lost your long-established place to stand (known now there as turangawaewae) for its submersion under the world's fast-rising sea level. Perhaps by now your long-lost place to stand is no more than *Erewhon* (which, according to the émigré writer Samuel Butler (when once a settler here in New Zealand) stands for 'nowhere' when, as now, spelt backwards).

So now also, perhaps it's some such turangawaewae (or place to stand) that you (unlike Sam Butler) have been overencouraged to keep. It's all the craze these days, preferably in relation to your own place or property, to have at least a space, if not preferably a place, in which to stand. If you're well-off, you might even manage to buy a place in the sun. Of course, for this purpose, you have to have some legal grounds (preferably also by way of curtilage or garden) on which to make, place, or lay your claim.

You may have rights (real or presumptive) for being the first to discover and claim your place of standing, but who can truly say? You may be a native or indigene (real or presumptive), but then likewise, who can truly say? In relation to the places and properties already sequestered (at least historically) by those who, as native folks, can make a better claim than can others (on grounds of their indigeneity), you may have that better claim, but once again, who can say?

Who can say, since, like the issue of $E = mc^2$, this is a very relative issue; and so is one perhaps without any probity (for affording any trustworthy indication of each and every individual's not so much *personal stance* as it does their propertied *circumstance*)? [Exegesis 2: Nevertheless, a person's place (as often as not) is indicated by their personal stance (which may be a mixture of how they see their status (upright, skewed, or fallen) as portrayed (as much in court by the way they take the stand) as how (outside the court) they are seen by others to stand in court.]

The first life principle or precept of social priority, as held by humans to accord with their lives together (the so-called civil society), is said by some folks to be people themselves; thus, 'he tangata, he tangata, he tangata', as they say —unless for being when all at sea— in the South Pacific. However, other folks (and sometimes the same folks) attach themselves to place or property (and preferably to both) and so swear by location, location, location (which may be some designated river, mountain, or other alma mater or marae).

Then by which precept of social priority do you abide, either swearing by location or else living in your own right as a person or else simply swithering indiscriminately, first one way then the other, or (as if caught in a limbo or whirlpool at the foot of some waterfall) swithering between the most likely, desirably, or contingently rewarding of the two? For most people, acquiring status (whether static by means of social position or dynamic by means of personality) is more than a bit of a gamble!

Feeling caught? At the bottom of some human whirlpool and as if for keeps? Never mind. Look around! You might be caught up in some glory hole. In gold-bearing country (try the Karori Hills), the gold nuggets carried along by streams in spate often get cached (by reason of gold's heavier weight) in those glory holes that develop at the bottom of the waterfalls. Still, if you're still struggling to find out where (in terms of place) or on whom (in terms of person) to place (no pun intended) your bets (still got your scratch card for finding a husband), you can't do better than to lay them all on following Christ!

Who knows, for being like some poor soul caught up in the whirlpool of a glory hole, you might yet turn out to be a very rich man! You really only have to look for the gifts of God, which are so often hidden in the depths of every glory hole! And as every wise man knows of every dark cloud (from which falls the rain to fill the whirling glory holes with nuggets of pure gold), there is of each dark cloud, besides the promise of rain, also a silver lining. Look for it, if not right now even whilst rivers of rain still pelt down to fill the glory holes yet at least later when the sun begins again to shine.

Meanwhile (which won't be for long), then (after such fast-falling rain has peeled back the darkness) we return to research the lowered glory holes for clearer precepts of social priority. You now know something of these precepts (or principles) even when caught swithering between restful location, location, location (according to the precepts of place and space) or else of more dynamic elevation, elevation, elevation (according to the precepts of constant change, continual advancement, and spiritual transformation). The question is, as always, that of what makes a poor man rich, no less than of what makes a rich man poor.

Perhaps, for thinking yourself to be such a rich man (a Croesus, no less) and in every possible way a wealthy person, you have merely elevated your claimed right to inhabit whatever space or place, which (on account of your gifted intellect, your gifted work ethic, or your gifted indigeneity) you feel yourself to have most rightly earned. Alas, there are so many false priests, false prophets, false teachers, and false scholars that you fail to see how very near to starving you are of real wealth and so how very, very poor you humans all are!

And so you strut your stuff with the other stinking rich before the multitude of much poorer men to claim your reward (not award) of self-elevation (by which you obviously enjoy a universal and thence heavenly feeling of elevation, not levitation), and in turn, you (as one of the filthy rich) feel you have every right to do. Alas, this is fool's gold (only iron pyrites, FeS_2) which you have claimed to have found in some false glory hole, which has been salted deviously by the Counterfeit Command!

And so (in some such self-rewarding way or another) you have laid claim to hold a high-ranking social status, either as a preaching person, a teaching person, or even merely (for being Scots, Irish, English, or other fast-lessening minority) a native person, whether on the basis of personal gifting, gifting, gifting or else of location, location, location. In either event, it pays to know yourself very well before accepting the least award, far less the claiming of any reward, whether for being (an even just relatively) a native person or perhaps for being no more than the solely monied victim of location, location, location. [Exegesis 3: Solving the predicament of the solely monied victim of location, location, location is easy. Simply cash in your investments and give away your cash! Meanwhile, to know more about yourself (a lifelong task, indeed), most people are happy enough these days to leave that cosmic task (still open to negotiation between heaven and earth for as long as they live) to learn what they can from their more mundane Fitbit!]

From this bifurcated point of view (although applying differentially across the same www.com), there are two very different kinds (or species) of humans. First, there are those humans (thought to be inferior by others) who prioritise *he tangata* for being simply people in themselves. Then secondly, there are the propertied class of persons who, by place or space or status, consider that 'quality' (which they elevate to an essence) by which they accord to themselves, as people of 'quality', the first principle of life.

According to this critical analysis (which may be valid or invalid as well as right or wrong), such self-elevated persons self-satisfy the leading precept of social priority (by which they themselves, as people of quality, are elevated in all other dimensions of which the spiritual or metaphysical is paramount) by reason likewise (so they say) of their individual essence. [Exegesis 4: On this score, we angels have absolutely nothing to say.]

Nevertheless, if you find all this anthropological talk of social priorities to be still confusing, this finding probably indicates that you still swither (either sometimes or interminably) from location in space and place, as one criterion of social standing, to the other conflicting criterion occupied by persons of quality (whether self-identified with either of those or other alternatives either faintly or strongly). Some people elevate their pride of face, others elevate their pride of place, and yet others elevate their pride of race. Once again, as Socrates says, know yourself!

And if believing yourself to have gone as far as you can with the task of knowing yourself yet only to find yourself still swithering between who you are and where you think others are, then (for such a time and place in space as this) still seek to know yourself more fully. There are those whose lives are caught up in a glory hole of pure-gold nuggets yet whilst still trying hard to satisfy both conflicting criteria (rich man/poor man) for the precepts of social priorities! It's never a struggle to find out for yourself whether you'd be happier rich or poor, well-known or unknown, so long as you're sure of your innermost priorities.

If still confused, then (even-now-then) listen to whatever songs you're singing and focus on the lyrics for precisely (and not just exactly) what they tell you. You might have to change your song (from rap to rock and roll and upwards to baroque or vice versa) before becoming more confident of who you are and who you want to be. Don't allow yourselves to be shocked into becoming tone-deaf to the apparent distancing (but really the more closely drawn) differential between then and now any more than between now and then.

Yet you may very well miss hearing the classic message here today, unless you care to listen to each day's never-before-heard song, which is bound by today's temporal shrinkage of space and telescoping of tonality. On both counts, the shrinkage turns out to be vastly more discordant (think once again as much of the romantic Ludwig (a.k.a. Beethoven) as of the modernist Michael (a.k.a. Nyman) than ever heard before. But don't swither here over still emerging dissonance (whether a cappella or symphonic) or think to dismiss the previously so-called modernists for their apparent lack of dissonance, because these things, like all things, are all a'changin'.

There is an ambiguity here that is made much of by the Counterfeit Command, between the then-before and the after-then. The inference to be drawn from this ambiguity is that there is no less time in the world (now-then) than there has ever been (before-then) or that there will ever be (after-then). We thus have all the time in the world (now-then) with which to right wrongs, which is, of course, not the case (on account of the rapidly pending now-after-then). That there's 'all the time in the world' tells us nothing about how much time there is, any more than for it being 'as long as a length of a string'.

Accusations (brute accusations as distinct from legitimately investigative accusations) always depend on the then-before having gone wrong in ways that will not only implement but also consequentially institute a categorically dependent outcome that cannot be denied (possibly for all time). On the other hand, proclamations (which are either future-perfect for being prophetic or else present indicative in which case retrospectivity is both prohibited on earth and made impossible in heaven) cannot bind time in the way that brute accusations pretend to do then-before or even-now-then, as well as for-all-time. Got that, no? Then until then, on the spot, mark time!

There's bad news here, nevertheless, unless the expression 'for all time' can be clearly understood by all believers to be a dangerously limited expression. Many mortals mistake only 'their own time' for being 'all time', and so in itself, time becomes a purely personal commodity—like houses, cars, and bank balances—each of which they think themselves to privately own. Anyone's time (even when charged for) is not at all like that, and neither at all is the largesse of living space which so many mortals mistake for being entirely their own 'real property'.

What else (apart from mere mortals mistakenly claiming personal ownership of even just all their own time) makes 'for all time' to be such a dangerously limiting as well as limited expression? Well, for one thing, it curtails having that 'time of one's life' which could otherwise be enjoyed right now by so many otherwise deeply suffering mortals. These are folks who unnecessarily constrict all extensions (both past and future) of their own time.

Thus, there are folks (including academics who profess to be adult) who still childishly think (their maturity being put to the test in the most advanced of history classes) that all history (through obsolescence) came to a sudden stop upon the existential present starting from the very moment (day, hour, minute, and to the second) of their own personal birth (or of any other relatively incidental happening). They are dismissive of all world history, aside from their revering the very specific and domestic exclusivity of their own history. [Exegesis 5: They have yet to feel the full force of history either as a cosmic steamroller or hellish juggernaut, and when they do, it will either flatten them to ground zero or else raise them to heroic heights. The choice of response is theirs.]

Yet there are other folks (professing themselves to be adult, although not so academic) who still childishly think (professing themselves to be head and shoulders above all other men and women of historical action) that all world history sprang into life only from that very same and very precise moment of their own personal birth. They live (if they can be said at all to live) likewise with a history whose exclusivity (like that of any Napoleon, Lenin, or Hitler) is restricted to that of being only their very own (and thus so self-limited) time. Yet each of these (for being still either somewhat academic or non-academic) are only two possible extremes of the many different variants of historicism.

The trouble with us humans—think back to Natasha's problem in *War and Peace*—lies so often with our sentimental (and largely self-indulgent) upbringings. So many of us have been so sweetly and gently brought up (for lack of exposure to that severe history by which we must learn to appreciate the sad songs of former times) that we have no realistic idea of how contingent on our overcoming of humanity's sad generic past may be the prospects of our enjoying what we assume unthinkingly to be our own personal right to some more idealistic future.

Without our historic recognition of our own humanly generic sadness, we have no understanding of the way in which prophecy (the more joyful song with which we learn to look forward to future times of humanly fulfilment) is yet so intimately requisite to our overcoming so much of that generic sadness which is carried forward from our historic past. We can have no real appreciation of how bright our future might be (which we mistakenly equate with so-called human progress) without the divine means (which we mistake for the difficulty of growing up) of our having overcome that fierce turmoil of the past. Indeed, the closer we come to the prophetically final outcome of this world's events, the more it is that we need to rely on information that can come only from the prophetically historic past.

The prophetic process (when sanctified by due historic process) so pivots on generic history that just as there can be no jurisprudence (or perception of justice) without history, neither can there be any prophetic perception of the future without prophetic perception of the past. More often than not, our jurisprudential perception of the future is no more than that of the historic past, which (by the prophetic process of temporal invagination) is simply that of the past turned inside out. [Exegesis 6: Refer to surgical and post-mortem techniques of invagination (say, by turning the body of a giant squid inside out by which to effectuate its internal examination). In a similar way, we come to grips with reality through applying historic-prophetic techniques of temporal invagination. Thus, the future-past of WWII is simply the same past-future of WWI when turned inside out. You must therefore telescope out of WWI into WWII to understand anything of either, besides being also more than something of both.]

It follows (according to the mathematics of time) that prophecy is always given to be deeply prayed over, whether into reality or out of reality (according to the metaphysics of space-time). The future-present may be prayed into being for its understanding, interpretation, and fulfilment or else held at arm's length for confirmation or else let fall until so confirmed and sanctified or even prayed right out until supported by exegesis, confirmation or correction, recognition, and acceptance.

Without prayerful reception, prophecy is worthless, just as without any testing, faith is also worthless. But alas, despite this risk of rendering any prophecy worthless, most prophecy, at best, is no more than humanly entertained. On the other hand, what sort of music would you allowably sing or play to assuage the souls of those entering the gas chambers at Auschwitz? What sort of prayers would you pray against the same sort of thing which happened at Auschwitz ever happening again?

Well, prayer too is often no more than humanly entertained, so what is to be done, either to raise the seriousness of prayer and prophecy or else to raise the seriousness with which almost all humans (although at vastly different levels) pursue (even prayer and prophecy) as some sort of entertainment. The key to seriousness (especially of the lighthearted and yet most seriously intellectual sort) is faith.

Now, in itself, the prophetic process is always a test of faith, and the more it is a test of faith not just to the prophet but also to those who hear the message, then also the worthier becomes their expression of that faith. If prophecy is avoided, as so often the fulfilment of a prophetic warning is through prayer avoided, then so also can the submission of faith to prophetic testing be avoided (in which case the same test of faith is achieved through faithful prayer. Oh, and so are those themselves avoided (for being of such little faith) who on their own behalf try to avoid the test of faith without submitting the expected test to faithful prayer.

If you want (without making errors) to foretaste the future and look ahead, then be sure first to look back, further back, and still further back. And until then, don't think to look forward, far less move forward, as you might otherwise do more impulsively in the present. Know your own history most intimately before thinking to avoid and dismiss both your own past and your own future on the foundations of which the prophecy you might at first seek to avoid is that on which your future is or should be built.

No mere man, although apparently a man disposed beneficently towards the outcome of many seasons, can literally be a man for all seasons or for all time. Jesus Christ, as proved by those facts of history (which by themselves confirm the already prophetic future), is therefore no mere man. Beyond those merely historical facts, however, it takes the prophetic witness of every believer in those historic facts to fulfil the full design of this already prophetically proclaimed future.

This is exactly where, beyond those historic facts, the forcefulness of faith comes in. It comes, often sometimes and in certain places, at still great personal risk, to join in the historic proclamation of that already existent yet prophetically ongoing future where every iota of personal faith is primed to advance still further the kingdom of heaven and, yes, the disciplined engagement of each and every believer to his or her calling within this kingdom (which has already come to earth) in what is still very much a military operation.

No mere mortal can rely on either his own standing or understanding (both literally and figuratively) for more than a very short while. And sometimes all mortals have to fall, perhaps once or twice and very hard or else both also very hard as well as also many, many times, before the testing and tempering of one's mortal faith is held fit to last for all eternity. [Exegesis 7: Hey, hold on for our butting in here again, but to reinforce our personal standing, we humans are often tempted to generate a very different sort of standing. We'll seize instead on professional standing, social standing, civic standing, national standing, international standing, and almost every other kind of standing. In our efforts to create the illusion of our own 'good standing', we'll then find to our cost that these misguided efforts, although often securing personal fame, fortune, and a certain kind of respectability, do no more than heighten the self-deceptive illusion of our own 'good standing'. When done without any sense of our vocational calling, we're always engaged in this kind of social self-deception.

All of us sadly fallen mortals share the same propensity for doing wrong as that still demonstrated by Angel Satan. Like Natasha in *War and Peace*, all of us can hoodwink ourselves that we too are angels. Without knowing ourselves for whom we truly are, then as either innocents like Natasha or else con men like that rascally Dolgorukov in his dealings with the fair sex, most of us in some way or another fall victims to our own self-deception.]

* * *

368

A Very Brief History of Heaven
Part XI

Yesterday
Yesterday I remember thinking I was the happiest
person in the whole earth, in the whole galaxy, in all
of God's creation. Could that only have been yesterday
or was it [then] endless light-years ago?
                          Author Anonymous, *Go Ask Alice*

No, this is not Natasha Rostova still speaking here (however much
it could have been that same Natasha from *War and Peace*). Nor
perhaps is it even the tragic Fantine speaking (as it could have been
from *Les Misérables*). No, instead it's Alice speaking, although not
any more as once the little girl in *Alice in Wonderland* but here more
tragically from her own journal, published now more anonymously
under its title *Go Ask Alice*.

It's Alice who tells us, through her journal, that it is now endless
light years ago when once she thought she was 'the happiest person
in the whole earth, in the whole galaxy, in all of God's creation'. In
the end, her subsequent unhappiness (brought on by drug addiction)
is too great for her to bear, and sadly, she takes her own life. As said
before, gifts of grace and favour are not to be misunderstood for
their being held in perpetuity. Every lively yesterday (for lack of due
recognition) may be exposed to the rigor mortis of tomorrow.

The real faith factor (so you humans think) looks towards things
which can be seen in the flesh. Physicists call it matter, and sure
enough, this matter seems to matter most of all to mortals. Call it
carnal, if you like, although that's only another euphemistic expression
(a hilltop hideout) for this life's gruelling body factor.

Got a pretty face? You'll marry well. Your fortune is obviously
already made! Got a lively soul, a forward spirit? You'll do so well
in business—insurance, banking, finance. As a secretary, you'll be
sweet and neat, and (for all ongoing directorships) you'll never need
to retire! Got a head on your shoulders? You'll get the highest of

credentials by which to appear the wisest person wherever you go! Chock-full and gushing over with self-expression? Perhaps you'll found a global corporation and be forever in the public eye or else write a picaresque bestseller from the viewpoint of the lowest private eye. No? Well, maybe for being filled instead with self-compassion, then you'll rise to a bishopric long before you even know who you are or where you are (or who it is that's with you and pulling your most compassionate strings for you to flow along solely in their own firm direction)!

What is this flesh, this carnal flesh, in every shape and form, that it should even tempt the angels to have intercourse with humans, to tempt them to take over both heaven and earth, as well as to assail the entirety of all creation and so also of mankind (in being only a little lower than the angels) to compromise their eternal souls? For what reason, and by what means, *does matter so much matter*? How is it so that by means of matter, and of almost any kind of matter, that mankind will be drawn to trade off from all eternity so many of their own very precious and often hard-won souls?

What, don't you know how hard we angels fight for your souls? Have you never felt the flow of that angelic battle going on all around you? It may have been in a pub, at a party, on the beach, in the schoolroom, or on the concert platform. Sometimes, the push and pull between the elect and the damned for possession of your soul is no more than a heartbeat away both from your own demise and the greatest (for being as yet unknown) of public disasters. Without seeing it, without feeling it, you are, in the sight of us angels, so often completely irresponsible as humans.

Oh yes, we angels know very well how in these latter days, the eternal soul is being downplayed—ever always downplayed—in exchange for being some wishy-washy, slumbering, if not fast-asleep human spirit. And for those who won't trade, then they're offered in exchange for the soul, the ego (as if this is some supernew creation). And to those who want or need an upgrade on the ego, then lo and behold, there's an upgrade to the superego! And before you know where you are (since little egos, like little fleas, love to suck sustenance from the backs of bigger egos), you'll be surrounded, hemmed in for life, by hundreds and thousands of not-so-little alter egos. By that time, who you are (in terms of who you once were) is pretty well done for, unless you can retrace your steps and retrieve your soul from the trash can—or for those who suffer a far greater and more painful public fall—from the dumpster.

History is full of super-super-superegos, although you'll find none in heaven, some always on earth, and many more may perhaps have already gone to hell. Don't just think of Napoleon or of Mussolini or of Stalin or of Hitler. There was always some counterfeit and embittered or otherwise highly motivated character who played and performed a most critical yet often hidden role in the superhero equation. Most usually, this counterfeiter of souls is a speaker. He may be a statesman or a politician; or he may be a writer, a poet, or a musician. He or she is almost always a communicator, and if not by word, then in deed (indeed).

It was he or she (the hidden undercover agent, however explicitly and more obviously otherwise) who contributed to what and to whom these superegotistical heroes became (although always through their own choice) in the last resort to fulfil the role of superheroes. In world history, they are like crabs in a bucket, climbing on top of each other and yet getting pulled back by others in their efforts to get out to the heaven they've barely heard of yet earlier most nearly always strenuously repudiated.

Every second man's an alpha male, a macho superman these days, and so he most certainly has, if to become so, traded in his soul! So just what's the going rate these days for a soul? Need one ask? The exchange rate for the soul these days is the very lowest it's ever been! The soul-traders will look after you (in the recovery room, or so they say). For starters, they'll give you a drink and drugs (with suicidal depression thrown in). These devious analgesics will offset the resulting void felt by the surgical excision of your eternal soul.

Oh, make no mistake about it. This surgical excision process by which to falsely redeem your sinful soul is just as touch and go a surgical process for these demonic soul-surgeons as it is for you. You will be hooked up to demonic soul-support for most of the operation. Your DNA will never be quite the same, even if you were still to meet Jesus (which by then after any such trade-off operation, although not impossible, is still very hard). By then you would sadly bear the demonic scars of this tragic soul-excision, just as Jesus still bears the heavenly scars of his correlatively joyful crucifixion.

As for the soul-excision operation, well, this might take no more than a microsecond for any wishy-washy soul. This invariably washed-out soul is one which has been brainwashed into believing itself to be no more than some exceedingly polite, supremely cultured, eminently civil, and passive spirit. Every such already washed-out soul is almost always demonically implicated and as likely as not, during the operation, to relieve and express this counterfeit civility, passivity, and politeness by going on the rampage).

On the other hand, this extremely delicate operation of soul-excision may take hours, days, weeks, months, and even years, because unless the surgical void left by your excised soul is fully and completely refabricated, there's always a hopeful possibility (however remote, say these nefarious soul-surgeons) that something of the heavenly presence might descend to implant some seed of the Holy Spirit in what remains of their operational and still open soul-void.

To lose your soul, yet for the victim never to miss its loss, requires one of the most delicate and demanding of neurosurgical as well as of spiritual operations. On account of such hellish difficulties, the heavenly prognosis is painfully poor, since once gone (for the victim by then being a captive subject of hell), that entirely lost soul becomes exceedingly hard to catch, capture, and redeem. Likewise, although the trade-off cost of the operation (as can be carried out only in hell) is hellishly high to the victim, the cost both to the victim as well as to the heavenly host is eternally extortionate. You have to remember that for being put on demonic soul-support (for however long required to complete the operation), the cost of this support extinguishes demonic spirits (admittedly of hell's most lowly sort) at the rate of roughly $666 per millisecond.

We angels cannot always be as clear about dystopian (or nihilistic) outcomes as we can be about utopian (or idealistic) outcomes. We can as angels, of course, be clearer than humans as to what constitutes the absolute truth. Since the absolute truth is neither nihilistic nor idealistic (as most outcomes are so often polarised towards either of these two extremes on earth), the absolute truth by itself tends to remain beyond the understanding of most human beings. Indeed, most humans are encouraged to regard the absolute truth as an abstraction for what lies far beyond human comprehension. Not so, not so (although the task of comprehension, as once taught for its own sake in schools and colleges, has almost entirely lost its meaning).

Without drawing comparisons (most of which are odious in the face of any absolute truth), most humans are thus at a loss in trying to discern any inherently absolute truth. For that very reason, many unbelievers buck at the promise of believing in God (unless so driven by their fear of the devil). Even when trying to testify to the existence of any absolute truth, that truth is, so they say ... well then, whatever they say or don't say, they then find themselves doing no more than drawing a comparison. All humanistic explanations (whether by recourse to reason or emotions) are hunkered deep down (either explicitly or implicitly) in comparisons.

So then without exaggerating some rigorously two-valued system of conflicting opposites (take your pick—good or evil, right or wrong, up or down, in or out, light or dark, or rough or smooth) by which to express, represent, accommodate, and then define what they mistake for being the inherent relativity of (even absolute) truth, they then fall into the box-thinking mode of proffering their own categorical generalities (once again—good or bad, sensible or nonsensical, wise or stupid, credentialed or uncredentialed, rich or poor) by which the same no-ending list of conflictive opposites serves only to mask the fact that they are still drawing only comparisons.

This may well be the point (beyond which they'll never be able to return) at which they decide (as between hell and heaven or as between the counterfeit and the authentic) that there is no absolute truth whatsoever, but that instead, everything is either comparatively relative or else relatively comparative. Conflictive though the choice may be (as between heaven and hell), it's no real cliffhanger for being seen by them (yesterday as merely mythic, today to be merely virtual), so then they either pull back from the unseen cliff edge, step out self-confidently into outer space, or eventually fall over the cliff—either to be saved by us angels or to fall into the yawning pit of fire and brimstone which they themselves have lit.

By being allowed to participate most fully (i.e. mature) in this life, despite all that's said at many funerals, there's no mere 'passing on' (whether from this place to the next place, whether from this life to another life, whether by this soul in this body to the same soul in another body). No, there's no such euphemistic 'passing on' any more than this sojourn on earth has been any merely 'passing through'. At some point in one's own time (the earlier for most of us humans, the better because none of us know how long we have on earth), there has to be some leap of faith. For some humans, it may be no more than a hop, skip, and a jump into heaven. For others, it may need a pole vault. And for others, it may be a long and arduous obstacle race. One thing is for sure on this earth, that there's no more 'just passing on' than there's any 'just passing through'. This so-called mortal coil we most joyfully bear through this life on earth is the rough fabric out of which is woven the robe of righteousness we inherit from Jesus Christ in heaven.

Without this leap of faith (big or little though it be), it becomes impossible for us earthlings to make the best of all the most difficult space-time decisions we have to make in real life on earth. 'Keep your cool,' we say to encourage each other during the present time of climate change in which the whole wide world is rapidly heating up. In no other way is the difference between us angels and you hot-headed humans more obviously demonstrated than in our widely differentiated senses of angelic and humanistic humour. For these reasons, keeping a balance between your own often astringently acidic humanistic humour and our own far kindlier (for being always slightly alkaline) angelic humour (with roughly 6.5 as its going pH factor) is essentially our foremostly communicative measure.

As you humans already know so well, both from the book of Job in scripture as well as from so many, if not all, of your own human problems, our both fallen angels as well as upright angels, although each remaining as dignitaries entitled to be seated in the council of heaven, are not all squeaky clean and upright in the service of our Lord God. Just like many humans, there are angels with one good foot in one camp and their other foot (look out for any club foot) in another camp and who therefore think themselves to be capable of serving two masters. That's just not possible, but their ongoing equivocality can make it difficult for humans to discern not just the authentic upright angel from the counterfeit upright but also the authentic upright from the slightly counterfeit and no more than slightly bent. You won't find any overly categorical or determinist box-thinking in heaven (whether for sinful humans or for fallen angels), so you must allow for such difficulties of interpretation and discernment to test your faith.

Yet again, since demonic humour is vastly different from heavenly humour (although each shared by fallen and counterfeit angels as distinct from upright and authentic angels), it can help to test the level of angelic humour (and so by means of the crucial pH factor) to distinguish the acidic from the alkaline and again to discern the upright from the fallen, the upright from the bent, and the upright from the badly bent. And of course, as with humanistic gossip and humanistic rumour and also with humanistic humour (by means of the same pH factor), then you can most usually distinguish the level of uprightness in humans, at least from those whose minds have been taken captive or made counterfeit by either increasing the acidity or reducing the alkalinity of their humour. That would require a whole treatise for itself on discerning humour (say, demonic scoffing from serious satire or scholarly hoax from academically pulling a fast one), so we'll leave the subject there, except to say that every pH factor test for humour must be applied and measured most righteously in the prophetic spirit.

Yes, of course, applying the prophetic spirit (especially to law and order) is in itself a very tall order and, in many cases, produces also a tragicomic legal order from those who don't have the requisite measure of prophetic spirit for relating law to justice. It can be one which provokes the seriously impatient person, the seriously irrational psychiatric patient, the highly committed tribal patriarch and national patriot, and both the seriously incredulous no less than the excessively committed scholar (each or altogether) to first personal outrage and then social outrage. As often as not, the responsively social outrage produced by this tragicomic legal order, if instituted severely enough and applied more and more intimately, will produce first professional unrest, then trade unrest, then civil unrest, then civil protest, and ultimately, either outright war or terrorist action.

Now it's a tall order (as demonstrated by first the brief success and then the eventual failure of most nations) to develop and keep faith with the requisite level of prophetic spirit to sustain law and order. Without this level of prophetic spirit, it will prove either impossible to found or else to develop and sustain any legal order both sufficient and adequate to keep law and justice both securely and intimately related. As a case study of such a challenge, one has only to consider both the long history and consistent prophecy needed both to sustain and learn from what are now known (no more than colloquially) as the Ten Commandments.

As we all know from the secret infighting between the sad Sadducees and the relatively happier Pharisees, these Ten Commandments have the potential (so long as they're allowed to keep going) to proliferate as fast and furiously as profligate humans have misunderstood what it means to procreate. Now there is no surer way of bringing down any legal system (legislating for those proud enough to pay a tax on mint, anise, and cumin) than to proliferate the laws to and far, far beyond the first, second, third, and every ongoing point of overregulation. It doesn't then take much of a jurist (concerned not just with enforcing the law but also with the administration of justice), far less a fully fledged prophet, to discern that there's far more than a token disaster on all fronts looming.

Aha, but then again, who are the real rulers of society? The scribes (or teachers of the law) or the prophetically blind Pharisees? They both (and not the Sadducees) are the ones, are they not, who now sit most comfortably in the seat of Moses, the lawgiver? Then are they not the ones we've been all the while looking for in their being 'the real rulers of society'?

Is this not their profession of faith in the law to be required of them? Is their own admission of responsibility to uphold the law not to be held of them? Are they themselves not to be bound by that same rule of law which these professional lawyers enforce on every poor and witless layperson? Nevertheless, all sounds good, looks good, and feels good to the lawyers, to whom, perhaps once again, the end justifies the means. So then, as the Hebraic Sanhedrin says of itself, no need to read the runes or test the spirits as to the substance of things unseen, since Caiaphas, the chief priest of the Sanhedrin, has the simplest of all possible solutions to the deepest of all metaphysical problems!

And so like the cutting of the Gordian knot by Alexander the Great, the Hebraic solution reached by the Sanhedrin to the Greek problem of the one and the many is simple—let one be taken for the sake of the many! Just meditate on that maxim for more than a moment before you copy it into your copybooks. Its deeper two-edged meaning for both Jews and Gentiles (as fighting still continues between them in the streets) shall be revealed all too soon by the final fulfilment of that maxim.

Look here, these Ten Commandments of the Old Testament (reduced to but two commandments for the most practical of reasons given in the New Testament) have been given to both youse sinners (pardon the street parlance, since by now we're on the street) as also to us profligate angels. Just as all ten of them were given to youse sinners earlier (under the Mosaic Law) for your specific and most immediate safety, so also now these remaining two can be more clearly seen to apply not just to all earthlings but also to all angels. Notice also that the earlier Mosaic Law of Ten Commandments (don't do this and don't do that) was mostly prohibitive and negatory, whereas the reduced format of these two, just as encompassing of commandments, is more positive and enabling.

See here, first by the higher level of abstraction generated by showing those 'big two' commandments to take care of all the eight others, the former exclusivity between human beings and angelic beings is lessened, and so also in consequence, the distance and differentiation is narrowed between heaven and earth. This affects the legal compliance factor, since it has been pretty near impossible for humans to keep all ten commandments as so drafted, but more humanly possible to keep (at least the spirit of) the two commandments as redrafted. It can also be seen from the logico-mathematical shift in the equation of low compliance attributable to the ten commandments (as once drafted) to the higher compliance ratio for the reformulated two commandments (as redrafted) that there's now more available room for a providential shift coming into play. The reformulation and redefinition of divine providence then allows not just for one's human lifetime on earth but also for all eternity in heaven.

This divine grace and providential favour of eternal life, prophetically and messianically proclaimed by Christ himself whilst here in the flesh, came before there had been any real understanding by any of youse sinners (here again, pardon the street parlance) before being introduced more fully to the heartfelt concept of eternal salvation. Until then, salvation was providentially restricted only to this earth's temporal and transient safety, although it may have taken by that time all 'ten by ten by ten' proliferated commandments to have seen youse sinners safely through the forty years it took (by then no more than a remnant of those who had set out) for youse to cross the desert.

In comparison with this Old Testament view of temporal and yet transient safety (which so many of youse humans, until put to the test, by now take for granted), the providential extension of life insurance is cosmic. Why, the New Testament revelation of eternal salvation is not just equivalent (in modern minds) to the discovery of some unified field theory in physics. It surpasses every possible significance of there being the need for any unified field theory in physics.

Unified field theories in comparative religion (witness the ongoing crises of faith for theosophy as well as for Christian Science or the attempted unification of Methodism and Presbyterianism or all the horrors effectuated in the name of one united Christendom) are generally as elusive in attaining their objectives as are attempts to reconcile and integrate conflicting geometries, opposing schools of art, contrary systems of thought, and different modes of music. Perhaps the human spirit is willing, and yet the flesh is weak, but often, all that results (which could also be the case for continued attempts to reconcile quantum physics with traditional physics) is to bog ourselves down in that unsustainable state of unrelieved endeavour (which can fixate even the mind of an Einstein) and so divert both scientific research and religious worship away from wider fields of contemplative wonder. The upshot might be to restrict both our physical and spiritual resources from engaging more productively in each field of endeavour, besides running the risk of our losing hold on both sorts of physics as well as on the invigorating diversity employed to suit different mindsets in their often apparently conflictive forms of worship, whether that be in their expression of faith in science or as expressed in their science of faith.

Less, rather than more, dependent on the key or means by which the less is redacted from the more frequently provides the prophetic insight by which to unite different fields of diverse faith in science, which, if successful in its unification, may then go on to extend that same science of faith. Thus, in chemistry, Mendeleev's periodic table (although having the enormous potential to deal with so much more than ever before had been understood of chemistry) would be revealed by looking for less rather than looking for more. Indeed, the prophetic revelation in Mendeleev's case would be prompted by no more than a night vision he received in a dream).

The resulting periodic table (which Mendeleev wrote up on his awakening) provided the rarefied clarity, revealed simplicity, and in turn, the touchstone of certainty for chemistry, which as a chemist, Mendeleev had been looking for to explain his subject. And so, from this slightest prompt (akin to the magic moment of thought which later inspired Einstein in physics) came the prophetic insight resolving the biggest ever problematic field at that time for the subject of chemistry, and this is done (as by Einstein) in looking for less rather than for more. The key, as always, is to focus on the essence of any subject, which, in the case of mankind, means always focussing on the human soul.

As for the Ten Commandments, it would be a refined redaction (a publisher's term) as well as for being a recodified reduction (a chemist's term) from these first formulated ten commandments (in two tables) down to only two commandments (testified to by the rapidly changing signs for this vastly different time in human history) which would reveal the essence of these ten commandments with a rarefied clarity, a renewed simplicity, and a touchstone of certainty as had never before been understood. Ironically, as demonstrated in some way by every suffering soul, this breakthrough by Jesus Christ in his pursuing the science of faith would bring this world's greatest ever legal teacher nearer to his already appointed time of crucifixion.

To already fully open minds, looking for less will always demonstrate more potential for the resolution of any problem or dispute than the same resolution is likely to eventuate in looking for more. As often as not, to seek for that much more will only serve further to hide what is already hidden and unseen. That's exactly why faith must always focus on the substance of things as yet unseen. On the other hand, the less than open mind (whether human or demonic) looks only for more by which to hide his or her less than open mind.

In the case of the Ten Commandments, the near miraculous simplification given to them by Jesus Christ should have been so positively upheld above all by the teachers of the law that the underlying message (explosive in itself by which to open minds) could conceivably have resolved most existing jurisprudential problems. Alas, however, all academic minds were not only closed but resolutely determined to become still more closed. The result would be to increase the containment by which the same message would become still more highly explosive. Not for nothing does the gospel preach woe to all such lawyers!

In terms of their own messianic incredulity, that collective, conflictive, and otherwise very mixed-up bunch of excessively legally minded people (known to the already up-and-coming Gentiles as the Pharisees, Sadducees, and teachers of the law) would, under the aegis of the greatly feared Sanhedrin, bring themselves face to face with carrying out that one and only so clearly prophesied event, which would be so precisely singled out, reliably confirmed, and so positively identified by reference to so many other congruent, concurrent, and foretold happenings, each of which would make an irrefutably unique event of this crucifixion. For being carried out by the Sanhedrin completely illegally (at odds with their own court protocols, evidentiary rules, and legal process), that unique event of the crucifixion would thereafter change the moral, legal, and religious face of the whole wide world.

The effect of disobeying so many of their own court protocols and of taking responsibility for this illegality explicitly upon their own heads would reduce themselves to an unworkable exclusivity. Their attempted adherence to the human impossibility of fulfilling such a task as complying with those Ten Commandments in their originally unworkable form would push and coerce others into their own unavoidable disobedience and resulting depression of spirit.

Whereas the whole theory of legal command poses the practical problem of obedience (Old Testament jurisprudence), the alternative legal theory of commission (New Testament jurisprudence) poses the practical problem of commitment. And in any case, both obedience and commitment pose problems of universal communication as also do the giving of commands and the appointment of commissions.

Since these are practical problems—as are all communicative problems of composition and interpretation (when required of every military command and even of every military commission)—we shall reserve the theoretical issues of both, until after discussing the practical issues affecting each in the historic context now of specific cases. The first and most momentous case is that of Professor Bruno Baer, formerly of Tübingen in Germany. The second is that of Professor Lloyd Geering, formerly of Dunedin in New Zealand. Both professors experienced a crisis of faith (a common enough crisis amongst all sorts of professors) to which in different ways they each succumbed.

Likewise, each professor (by then professing apostasy instead of faith) provoked a national decline of faith amongst both young and old (of all denominations) in each of their countries. This decline in turn sapped the strength and spiritual commitment of both church and state in the worshipful religion of each of their respective nations, as well as then fast stretching outwards from these centre points of apostasy far across the globe.

But for Professor Bruno Baer's contribution to cosmic confusion spreading out from Tübingen in Germany, neither the Soviet Union may have taken over from the Russian monarchy nor the First and Second World Wars thereupon chanced to happen. The torchlight history of ideas—by spreading sparks, lighting fires, and particularly when resorting to cosmic flame-throwing—is nothing like the far more mundane history of dusty dates and foregone events taught by sedate, although as often non-professing professors in schools and colleges. Yet there's always at least one, if not two or more professors of uncertain beliefs (stirrers usually), to account for some apparently novel, but not always new, far less always any proved-to-be-good idea.

As for the just as popular apostasy of Professor Lloyd Geering, which so much confused the tattered remnants of the Free Church Settlement in New Zealand, the South Pacific (still far beyond the spreading conflagration as yet to follow) will sooner or later (like all Germany and the Soviet Union as a result of Papa Baer's apostasy) have to bear the full brunt of Papa Geering's still faster-growing apostasy. After all, as for any sheep who lose their shepherd (far less find their shepherd revealing himself to be a wolf in sheep's clothing), what more is likely to happen to the sheep when any such shepherd (whether preacher, prophet, teacher, or even Sunday school teacher), far less the moderator or president of any church assembly (nay, nay, however unlikely, say, even the Pope himself), should he (however unthinkable) become apostate instead of remaining apostolic?

What is there left to say of all this, since, as a first reader of any such military report as this, you may never have heard of outright apostasy (for being the renunciation of one's faith)? Let it be known that it was faith in the power of the redeemer that drove Napoleon out of Russia and not merely (as the history books profess) that Napoleon caught a head cold! Let it be known that it was faith (in the power of he who keeps to his word) that drove Hitler out of Russia and not merely that Hitler lost his nerve! And although it may have seemed very different so many centuries before, it was actually his fate to succumb to hard liquor that drove Genghis Khan also out of Russia since, as the poet says, 'there is a destiny that shapes our ends rough-hew them as we will'.

Yes, it is true (as the logician Augustus De Morgan has long maintained) that in one very limited sense (for being primarily the renunciation of one's own faith), apostasy is a private matter. Nevertheless, how one presents that private matter to the public—especially if one holds a public office as defender of his or her own renounced faith—can make a public matter out of a private matter. It is on account of the celebratory status held by any apostate thinker that he or she becomes accountable both for the extent to which and for the means by which he or she has made their own private matter (whether one of morals or of politics or of religion), in turn, a public matter.

So much for us angels lecturing you in the abstract, but this message is even more telling in the concrete. So then by emphasising the same abstract message by pricking your hard hide, if need be, with even sharper tungsten-hardened facts, then let us then tell you all over again how the theoretical formula for faith in the substance of things unseen works with complete practicality in the concrete measure which so many humans mistake for being the cold, hard facts which alone explain this often unforgiving world.

Faith has its own praxis or practicality by which to explain its relationship to the apparent reality of the cold, hard facts of this world. Certainly you can catch a cold (as Napoleon did) or lose your nerve (as Hitler did) or lose your motivational will (as Khan did) or commit a sin (as we can all do), but in terms of origins, objectives, and outcomes (as foretold in the foreword to this book), to decide which is which of these are either origins, objectives, and outcomes is itself a moot point (no less than it is to distinguish causes from consequences).

Almost all origins (righteous or unrighteous) are attributable to the exercise or lapse of spiritual faith, just as all outcomes (past, present, or future) are consequential upon some exercise or lapse of spiritual faith. In each such case, however, the steadfast faith that, for example, drove out both Napoleon and Hitler from Holy Mother Russia or had driven anyone else (such as Tamerlane or Genghis Khan) also from Holy Mother Russia, is both real and verifiable in terms of the cold, hard facts which befell Tamerlane, Genghis Khan, Napoleon, and Hitler. To be sure, no origins, objectives, outcomes, causes, or consequences operate in a vacuum (any more than whole nations can evade the cost of choosing leaders such as Stalin, Mussolini, and Hitler), but then these leaders are so often chosen without any prophetic insight and when completely oblivious to the substantive presence of things as yet unseen.

Whatever may be the historic or prophetic destiny of any nation or of any individual (whether angelic or human) is no more assured than is their possession of prophetic insight. Whatever may be manifested in their loss of nerve, motivation, or in any other aspect of their health or ill health must be accounted for amongst the signs of the times. If Holy Mother Russia still has her historic destiny as saviour of the West (once having stood in the gap against invading Scythian, Mongol, Napoleonic, or Nazi horde), it is surely to save but not to impose upon, far less to aggrandise, or overwhelm the West.

In principle, that's really no different than the responsibility of anyone and everyone for what may be the consequences to the world at large of that person changing his or her mind. Teaching (never a vocation for the very young) is a most serious business, and the older one gets as a teacher or preacher, then the more and more serious becomes the business of teaching and preaching. This is one reason why every teaching and preaching body (including the body of Christ) should avoid becoming overly institutionalised in the ways of its own present world. That only risks every educational institution mistaking worldly order for heavenly order.

Nevertheless, merely despoiling public confidence in anything (for example, commercial confidence under capitalism or moral confidence under communism or scientific confidence under modernism) when done (almost always demonically if without good and adequately communicated reason) is always a no-no. Otherwise, for dismissing the phlogiston theory or for substituting this round earth for that earlier flat one (or even for the need at any time for human enlightenment or for religious reformation) comes often close (as testified to by the martyrs) to being considered a capital crime.

Well, the late professor Bruno Bauer of Tübingen in Germany— close friend of both Karl Marx and Friedrich Engels and one who lost his professorial chair for the sort of heresy which later became the cornerstone of communist apostasy—led one such spiritual example eastwards (known for being demonic even to himself) in the name of the proverbial Antichrist. The outcome of that apostate origin is documented in the hard facts of WWII and long thereafter.

The other example of Professor Lloyd Geering (a so-called prophet of modernity) concerns outcomes in the South Pacific already felt but for which the full force is yet to come. Modernity (debating neither communism nor capitalism or any other controversy which might get in the way) is part of the *Cult of Progress* (for which read the works of historian David Olusoga). Modernism, founded on the cult of progress, attempts to transcend the future by falsely rewriting the past. Modernism thus takes advantage of the hard fact that history is a closed and unpopular subject to those who are uninterested and unmoved by their own origins or who are more moved by having their own way by force of outcomes.

This cult of superior human progress is an offshoot of the worldly superego at the expense of the eternal soul. When led by Geering, this cult began in the heartland of New Zealand's Free Church Settlement of Otago (which it brought to its knees). In terms of origins, this was a Christian settlement situated at the opposite end of the earth from its former home near to the Heart of Midlothian in what had once been Presbyterian Edinburgh.

This cult of the superego went on to undermine the faith of so many rightly believing presbyters (and in consequence, so many others of lesser faith around the world). These innocents abroad were won over by Papa Geering's just as preposterous claims as were those innocents abroad of Papa Bauer's preposterous claims. Make no mistake, the foremost desire of those who falsely cultivate progress is always to reform and set right the faithful in this South Pacific case by resorting to Geering's own apostate ways of thought.

'Well, that's all history now,' say Papa Geering's still apostate supporters (who so characteristically set out to transcend the future by their continuing to misrepresent the past). Likewise, we can be told no less convincingly of this planned and projected outcome by reading as lawyers and jurists of New Zealand's first ever heresy trial on the same subject, which, if you have the hard-lined legal stomach for it, you should also be sure to read as laypersons. Nevertheless, be sure to read, as we angels have read, all the many other books, reports, and articles on this most perilous of subjects—the difference between personal belief and collective faith, as well as between past history and the prophetic future, and so no less than between inherited origins and diverted outcomes.

Thus, if you have the strength of mind (but not if you lack the requisite faith or otherwise suffer from a weak heart), read the books (by now Sir Lloyd Geering, OM) *God in the New World* as well as *Christianity without God*—in itself a giveaway title. Nevertheless, don't dare read these fundamentally demonic works (as proved by their physical outcomes) without also seriously considering *Layman's Answer* (written to dear old Lloyd) by Professor E. M. Blaiklock. Likewise, as further proof of where modernism and the cult of progress misleads many nations and people (as if you could still possibly have any remaining doubts), be sure to read *Secular Christianity and God Who Acts* written by Robert J. Blaikie (together with his many other books and articles touching on the same subject). Nevertheless, we angels will have more to say on this cultic mismanagement of human progress by its corrupt process of rewriting history.

Yet in all this theological fracas, stay well under spiritual cover. What you are witnessing, even from well under this protective cover, is no less than a demonic onslaught. There may, or may not, be weapons of mass destruction in the physical offing, although for a preventive strike, that strike only requires some certitude in exercise of the potential. Nevertheless, that lack of the physical doesn't lessen the destructive forcefulness mounting in the spiritual. There's a science of warfare, but we won't—not here—get into some of these militaristic equations which can be found in manuals of military warfare.

Meanwhile (however temporally short-changed you may feel yourselves to be), keep your spiritual powder dry and your spiritual lamps well lit, since you may have to wait for years on the Lord before being given your command (always command and never demand) to join in the battle by your being called to engage in fully authorised military action under the Supreme Command. After all, for any resurgence of Babylon (wherever felt throughout the www.com), it takes far more than even just Saddam Hussein to blow the whistle, sound the bugle, or call the troops.

As said before, it is an extremely tall order (for which taking a law degree works to disadvantage as well as to advantage and so both ways) in learning to distinguish the goodies (whom we think are going to heaven to advantage us on earth) from those baddies (whom everyone is convinced are going to disadvantage us from hell). There's the element of self-deception (one's own self-deception as well as theirs) that has to be cautiously considered, as well as the apparent fact (since we credit most of this world's appearances for being fact) that most world leaders either artificially enthuse, invigorate, enliven, and inflate their human personalities to substitute for what would otherwise be more obvious to all and sundry for being their character deficiencies. That's one demonic strategy.

Another of their demonic strategies (not restricted to world leaders) is to activate and nurture both mood swings and memory losses (both temper tantrums as well as hugs and back slaps) by which to manage and manipulate what quite often/frequently turn out to be their own multiple split personalities—for which extremely compounded affliction refer back to this book's Preface for the strange case of Chris Christopherson[34]. The most obvious male (but now increasingly female) dysfunctional split is between home and work (between domestic home life and the need or temptation to increase one's employment earnings). But of course, for public figures, especially celebrities such as prime ministers, presidents, school principals, and chancellors of well-endowed colleges, there's simply no saying when and where they're going to split, successively continue to split, split and resplit, and eventually either completely fracture or else coenjoin.

Yes, indeed, as said before, it's an extremely tall order, whether with or without a law degree (or any other degree), to learn how to separate the world's goodies from the world's baddies. As representatives of the entire heavenly host, let us tell you that it's not going to get any easier to learn that lesson soon. So even if you may not already have picked up from this most seriously commissioned report (for not being any novel) that what we're reporting to you of the cosmos (which is vastly more than the dog-patch state of your own particular nation) is very much something that is bound to put yourself on trial to find out where you stand, then don't take fright of where you may find yourself standing.

So many protocols of standing or sitting are associated with recognising status or exercising authority as to be quite frightening. By such worldly means, superficial appearances are given more clout than the substance of the unseen. It's very much the same for what you hear, since idle chatter and gossip are once again given more clout than the substance of the unseen. Yet when once seen, it is only this substance of the unseen which will enable you to relegate that idle chatter and gossip to its proper place.

Likewise for the substance of the unseen being conveyed, perhaps without due deference to the hearer or when given in the vernacular replete with infelicities of speech, mistakes of grammar, and non sequiturs of reasoning, then what's left unseen can be denied the respect and authority which could have been given to the substantive content of the communication once searched for and seen. Here's a little test, then, if you'll pardon our miniscule use of the vernacular, to see whether you can strain the substantive content of the unseen from the appearances which prevent it being seen.

So then although you won't be asked to take the witness stand in any court, any more than in any court of common law, you'll risk being put in Stevenson and Osbourne's *Wrong Box*. Nevertheless, your duty will still be to remain prepared for the unexpected. This requires you to reappraise yourself right here and now and so for possibly reprioritising your presently existing bucket list—yes, be prepared for even that—in the task of forever after searching seriously for the unseen! [Exegesis 1: So if you don't already have a bucket list, then your first step is to make one, but for this bucket list (which is all your own), you're already all on your own. So also then, for this little test, you won't need one of this world's so-called holy books (whether the *Communist Manifesto* or Mao's *Little Red Book*), far less any other religious factor, such as transcendental meditation or occult practices or any one of today's so very many false messianic leaders or whoever else purports to decide such matters for you—apart from the Supreme Command.]

As at all inter-trans-supranational levels, youse humans (pardon the continuously changing parlance between cafe culture and street argot) must learn to flatter yourselves as having gone (from your own backyard in Dogpatch or Dunedin) to being completely global. Friendship by itself (whatever the personal trade-off) eventually gives way first to the competitive hurly-burly of big business and then, by getting rid of the locals, to the eventual disappointment of having waved (for perhaps the second-last small-time) the formerly big-time banner of free trade.

Alas, alas, alas, for youse humans (nichevo, yeshto na ulitse) now brought to a commercial standstill over the formerly global concept of there ever having been (even only once upon a time) any such workable thing, since once a weekly local market as then a legislatively implemented common market, far less now any longer hopefully a global market! Brexit now, but then for being also in a global turmoil, Glexit next—and yet this progression being never more sure of itself, whether for being declared already sure or (as many of youse humans say) maybe all avoidable for being only prophetically splenetic.

Youse humans (again pardonnez-moi, for still being in the street-scene) but youse humans have made things so much worse for youse-selves by finding out that the once flat world is now no longer flat but now instead is being rounded up before being finally taken down. Still, you've yet to find out what makes this earth still spin (subject to polar switching) on its present axis. And this know-how (as of once United Nations and, before that, League of Nations—for neither of which definite articles now apply) ain't any longer what most of youse sinners nowadays think them are (or, as more respectable and responsible people than we are would say whilst completng their comparatives, 'would think them to be'. What hope have you of knowing so who've never even heard of us folks from heaven now operating in the Supreme Command? Meanwhile (as first not so meanly said), be prepared!

To all such most plausible accusations, nothing needs to be said, but much must be done. So then look ahead and stay prepared! Nations rely on locals, and locals rely on nations. Get rid of the locals, and you've done away with nations. That's what it means to think global, but it won't work, except to make for war, more war, and yet more war. These days are by now the latter days (when coming in first then means going out last, when going good means feeling bad, and when feeling flat for being flat out means being unable to avoid every merry-go-round, carousel, and round about). The last days (rather than these latter days) are yet to come, in which almost every last and as often lustful measure of human accord gives way to rampant discord.

As for humanity's once regular heartbeat, every beat is now regularly offbeat. Even musicality has reversed its rhythmic role. Those who follow today's band of so-called song leaders are expected to clap offbeat so that the maddening crowd, when divorced from on-beat leadership, will mistake themselves for having a mind of their own. This weary and war-torn world is about to suffer its long foreseen and final syncope, and this final feinting, fainting fit has already long begun.

For being still the overflowing measure of God's grace as first designed by the Supreme Command, these once strangely simple for being on-the-beat lyrics pledging eternal friendship become less and less recognised by the offbeat maniacally clapping crowd. How then can one dispel the long-foreseen doom and gloom of this world's rapidly redescending darkness, especially now when this darkness misleads so much of mankind to mistake its own dark encroachment for being this world's first resurgently creative light?

For this purpose, some brave souls (pardon the church speech) point to their own light switch, whether of law and order or of economics or of genetic engineering or of space exploration or even of giving oneself over to as much entertainment as many try to make for themselves out of this world's rapidly prevailing downturn. We could use here the word *demise* instead of *downturn* just as before. We should have written perhaps of this world's 'last fling' instead of 'final syncope', since us angels are obliged to target the locals as closely as possible to their own (as often as not) rapidly declining forms of colloquial expression (i.e. street argot, koine, patois, or pidgin). Keep learning to stay prepared!

Unfortunately, despite the well-meaningfulness of all such switched-on means of human enlightenment, there are no such authentic light switches, far less authentic human searchlights with sufficient power loading, to stand in the way of this weary world's already prophesised demise. Those who have put themselves forward (in itself a giveaway as to their unsuitability) have only to look at those people—like Tamerlane, Alexander the Great, Napoleon, Stalin, and Adolf Hitler—each of whom claimed to be saviours of the world, to ascertain their complete lack of authenticity. And even just their pH factor from their very start is bitterly acerbic. The fact remains that no man can redeem himself, so how can he redeem the whole wide weary world when that man seeking to do so, either in full or in part, is himself in so much in need of redemption? So then all that can be said (as Baden-Powell first said) is still be prepared!

Far, far different (but not in kind) from Baden-Powell's given advice was the prophetic act of proclaimed creation by which the Supreme Command first floodlit the world. Here was employed a source of supreme power by which to translate darkness into light. It was not light that is shone into the darkness, as youse humans think of in terms of being 'your very own' artificial light. Instead, this far higher and steadier source of light came from turning *darkness into light* in terms of *authentically sourced light.*

Indeed, it was one of the Supreme Command's leading agents of light, Matthew Luckiesh, whilst in his capacity as director of the Lighting Research Laboratory for the General Electric Company of the USA, who wrote in his report *Light, Vision, and Seeing* (1944) to remind us all (from highest to lowest) in the Supreme Command of something which youse humans (to the detriment of your own now sadly depleted night vision) sadly forget, namely, that the 'proper function and objective of artificial light is to compete [perhaps, as we'd now say, 'compute'] with daylight, not with darkness'. [Exegesis 1: In his own day (which still triumphantly continues), Dr Luckiesh became known as the Father of the Science of Seeing.

Here's a hint—buy a UPS (an uninterrupted power source) to ward off darkness these days and from which to share with others your own personal enlightenment. There's no more reliable source of power for maintaining light these modernist days than still from your well-read Bible. You won't need a surge protector because you can expect always to enjoy the ever-incrementally increasing surge of spiritual power.

So too, both from your constant and continued reading of this uninterrupted power source (brand-named for all eternity as the living Word), you will for always (and always) be both sourced and resourced under the constant and continued counsel of the Holy Spirit. This constant counsel (beyond even the best of in-house lawyers) will do the most for you to stay prepared for every unexpected as well as for any prophetically expected happening.

Don't leave your Bible (UPS Version) behind for anything, as we now conclude this much-needed brief history of heaven (in Book 2) before deep-sea diving into the apparently shallow and still coastal waters (yes, still coastal waters) of Book 3 to life-save hell-bent people. Only thereafter, looking further ahead to Book 4, shall we pursue an anatomical analysis of those (by now bare, but not yet by any means dry) bones which many modernists mistake for requiring nothing more than a summer's archaeological dig in hell.

All the same, don't mistake hell for being the counterpart of heaven. That's but a pagan and solely three-dimensional sort of both heaven as well as of hell. We've got a lot more dimensions (than merely three) and gazillions of aspects (never before yet encountered) for you to learn. There's simply no end to any real narrative once you have a UPS (or uninterrupted power source) by way then of the living Word to decode the story of all creation.

Fear not then (since this deliverance from all fear through the expulsion of every last shred of demonic influence is the antidote to your now gloriously expunged but once so strongly held and mortal mindset of humanistic thinking). Focussed as that mortal fear once was to provoke only confusion and ambiguity, it would prevent all foresight of any great and glorious future, but instead fixate its victim's attention only on the most humanistic of sadly human 'meanwhiles'. But now, thank heavens, the demonic meanness of that mortal mindset is now forever broken. So then fear not, say us steadfast angels. And yet for the third time again fear not, still saying the same. But yet still stay prepared for every happening, both the expected and the unexpected, whilst still keep to reading the living Word in the heavenly light of its own uninterrupted power source (UPS)!

Before we move on (from this already long haul despite being only a brief history of heaven, however), we'll let you into a little secret. If you've found this first book on the history of heaven hard going, then relax, because even the greatest of human minds, such as already said of England's greatest poet John Milton, have always found the history of paradise lost (for being a potted history of heaven) to be far easier for sinful human minds to understand and explain than the far more prophetic history of that lost paradise regained. But this is just yet another one of life's little paradoxes (so watch that panda punctuation, whether a comma here or a semicolon there) perhaps for your being born human (although not just all) but never less than human!

So too, it has been the same for all those (both celebrated and non-celebrated) authors who have given their own hand to the trialling tale of, say, *Doctor Faustus* (for being as intricate a topic in the history of literature (both non-fiction as well as fiction) as that of *Doctor Frankenstein*). [Exegesis 2: Mustn't go down that path of the gothic novel now, which would be just a diversion. Still, in non-fiction, the original Dr Faustus was known, either rightly or wrongly, to be a necromancer, which gave rise to (both very credible and incredible) literature from Goethe (amongst many other writers, as well as an opera by Gounod).]

All the same (as we must say) for those readers who find this brief history of heaven hard going, then in the same way as writers find the treatment of hell far easier to write about (examples abound from Dante to Milton) and likewise more credible for readers to read about, it is (perhaps because of their own sins) that mere mortals find the concept of hell easier to understand than the concept of heaven, which is the one main reason why the Counterfeit Command so often can have a field day.

So then our angelic compliments to all you human readers (both young and old and in-between) for having got the hardest part of our worldwide travels over. It's been for us angels too a very long haul. And for being ourselves heavenly creatures, we angels (still unsuccumbed to the temptations now befalling you humans) are still steadfast to the plan of creation to avoid indulging ourselves, as you humans do so very often nowadays, in self-promotion. To the same tune (as sung by the Volga Boatmen), then keep on hauling!

It is not yet time for celebrations, for none of us serious readers would think of visiting hell in a celebratory mood. And in any case, before you get there, we must first clearly establish from your level of human vulnerability that you are not in any way a hell-bent person, so we angels have still some preliminary investigations still to do.

Nevertheless, as historically trained students already of eternity, we angelic authors, as well as now also you humanist readers, are all up to proclaiming our full measure of spiritual positivity. So then keep praying and prophesying (for the somewhat clandestine purpose, as this may seem so from earth, of obtaining student visas to open the gates of hell). Nevertheless, such are also the real risks of pursuing any so-called higher education (especially down below) for us all to maintain extreme caution. So then be very much aware (as after watching the film of John Grisham's *The Firm*) of any person to whom you may later be required to present your personal profile when applying for a job (particularly in any law firm).

Likewise, for once having encompassed that fundamental notion of an open-doored heaven, even you humanist readers will also facilitate your own further understanding of that funk-hole of fear (we're shortly about to visit) called hell. We dare say that for our even just figuratively leaving heaven, you'd perhaps fear then going straight to hell.

Fear not! There's no limbo in between, as once such a place of purgatory was thought to exist after death. Apart from those dear souls who seek to sleep or read or who otherwise need to relax or desire to rest, there's RIP, which might well be purgatory for authors who want to go on writing, plumbers who want to go on plumbing, and apostles who want to go on spreading the good word.

Nevertheless, whilst still alive and kicking (even if only like Dostoyevsky's little dream horse in *Crime and Punishment*), there are those in the queue for heaven who *seem quite frankly* to be hell-bound (and even admit to being so) as well as those also in the queue, less sure of themselves perhaps, who *seem only* to be hell-bent. All the same, there are yet others in this same queue for what they maintain is the heavenly airbus to which (although without any tickets, maps, or any other means of preparation than their hearing a last-minute rumour of this airbus leaving) are still so cocksure of their claim as to persuade everyone else that their far-distant tail end of the queue is actually the head of the queue from which this heavenly airbus starts. Needless to say, on account of all the screaming and yelling, the vast majority of heavily laden yet would-be passengers on this airbus flit from one end of the queue to the other in their trying to establish which is the head of the queue from which the heavenly airbus leaves.

Meanwhile (although this airbus to heaven is not likely to be around on earth for very much longer in the heavenly scheme of things), we sign off this very brief, to you perhaps incredulous, yet always open-ended history of heaven by repeating Baden-Powell's advice to all still serious Scouts on earth, 'Be prepared!'

Nevertheless, if you find this brief history of heaven about to end now in the anticlimax that you fear it could, then don't despair—you haven't got there yet!. '*Vous comprenez*', you haven't got there yet!

* * *

BOOK THREE

The Hidden History of Hell-Bent People while Still Caught in Darkness and Before the Dawn

God's Awesome Gift
Beyond the mysteries associated with the 'sovereignty of God,' there emerges what is to many of us an even more troubling mystery—the *sovereignty of man* and the awesome gift God has given us: our own free volition!

Dr Chuck Missler, *Cosmic Codes: Hidden Messages from the Edge of Eternity*

Intro 1—Samuel Two: Volition! Well, what's volition? Volition is an exercise of the will and, in your own case, of the human will. When we angels bring heavenly news to you humans—most usually good news (since bad news of your own doing is best brought by your own prophets)—you are free to accept or reject that good news. The reason for this—because we angels have learnt how much you humans rely so much on reasons to facilitate your willingness—is one of the first principles of heavenly jurisprudence (in this case, the science of justice).

We've discovered this about you humans—that bringing even good news to you invariably backfires whenever seen to be enforced by compulsion. So that's exactly why the whole of mankind, no matter whether good or bad, is given God's great and awesome gift of free volition. By God's grace, this gift of free volition helps you humans to recognise, understand, and accept our every tiding of good news.

Yet something even more awesome follows on from God's gift of free volition to all humankind. In order to enlist and safeguard that freedom of volition, God sacrifices as much of his own sovereignty as will safeguard all human exercise of that free volition from which is derived the sovereignty of mankind. God does so by making his own sovereignty contingent on mankind's free volition.

The resulting vulnerability of God to man turns every least communication between God and man into a close encounter. Through self-imposed vulnerability, our infallible God thus chooses to partner himself with all fallible humankind. Jurisprudentially speaking, the eternal and infallible lawmaker considers himself bound by his own laws to his own subjects whether they be in his own kingdom of infinite light or else in what looks to be the other kingdom of ultimate darkness.

As for even the biblical Samuel, the exercise of free volition must often be taught. There's no willingness without an exercise of will, and that willing exercise of will, if as yet unlearnt, then must be taught. It was the biblical Eli who taught the biblical Samuel how most willingly to exercise his free will. That's what we angels mean by learning to exercise God's awesome gift of free volition. It's an exercise in discipline that, if not yet rudely learnt, must then be finely taught. But yet beware, for there are as many counterfeit copies of hell-bent free will as there are hell-bent counterfeits challenging God's awesome gift to mankind of free volition.

Intro 2—Eli: The difference between hell-bent people and hell-bound people is quite a subtle difference. That subtle difference between the bent and the bound makes for a very hidden history. Right now, almost the whole wide world is remarkably hell-bent, but not yet categorically hell-bound. The subtle difference is as yet apparently slight. For many mortals, this subtle difference is therefore hard to discern. So then realise this right now—that there's been no one ever made (whether in heaven or on earth) who is bound (whether on paper or pigskin) to be bent, bent, bent—and so forever bent.

Without being yet hell-bound, however, there's always the leeway to be redirectionally straightened out. Whatever's been bent, then with the right reverse thrust, can almost always be straightened. Mechanics and metaphysics are not so far apart.

Likewise, morality and legality are far closer than either moralists or legalists give them credit for in the class calculus of jurisprudential thought. So then despite whatever negativity may be expressed on earth by the rapidly deteriorating signs of these most challenging times, the remaining positivity exerts a clarion call to remind each other that whatever's been bent can almost always be straightened when given the right reverse thrust. The problem is to find the right-minded people, no matter how far hell-bent, who will respond to the right reverse thrust.

Intro 3—Matthew: The whole point of this book (Book 3) on hell-bent people, therefore, is to develop for their benefit this right reverse thrust. As a physical exercise, you may mistake this thrust for being delivered in a bodily sport like boxing—no, that is a right feint, so look out for the coming left hook—but it's a reverse thrust, remember, so as for any military operation, it's more like learning to keep your own self-control in unarmed combat.

The whole objective of this first lesson to be learnt is to get to know your enemies so that you may better recognise whom you may rely on for being your friends. Even you novice angels, and not just you mortals, may think learning first from enemies before friends to be the wrong way round; but no, even although you'll be kept on a short heavenly leash, you'll find that almost all of heaven's heroes have been put through the mill of meeting up with their enemies so that they could learn to distinguish most clearly whom they could rely on for being their friends. Thus, did the Wee Davie Boy first meet up with the Mad King Saul and the Gruesome Goliath of Gath?

Intro 4—Emma: Long before hell (and so before even hell's angels), there were hell-bent angels, but then before too long, there were also hell-bent people. That's the essence of history. It either trickles down like the gentle rain from heaven above, or else it throws itself up as did once all the earth's hidden springs volcanically as if from all hell below. There's nothing like a falsified history of one's first beginnings to defeat one's already long destined outcomes, so think more than twice before you disagree.

You will understand, therefore, that for this book having been so long begun before history ever surfaced, much of the prophetic past is hidden from the present by hellish storms which rent the heavens as well as by heaven-sent floods which rent the earth. By now, for this history to reveal itself in terms of time, and place, and person (which same cut-and-dried clarity you, our dearest readers, expect from the Bible), that history already revealed is not about to be superseded by this or any other third- or fourth-rate book on what the Bible means. Better than any book before or after, it is the Bible which speaks to everyone who has ears to hear, eyes to see, and an open mind to listen; and it speaks most clearly of what it means to everyone who dares search both the mind of God as well as their own soul when enlivened by the Holy Spirit for the Bible's clearest meaning. This is merely a copybook by which, in the course of our writing to let mankind know our most intimate of angelic thoughts, you will have the opportunity to meditate on how you would think to copy them into action.

Intro 5—Luke (alias Luca): From your reading of the Bible as this world's yardstick of historical clarity, then learn to read all the promises and prophecies given by it with your own corresponding faith, or else risk going back more religiously to that father of lies who delights to conjure up details by which to split hairs and develop arguments! He'll confuse you still further with dates and data all prestigiously conjured up to bring you to the utmost level of counterfeit clarity.

This is the means (including as often the theological means) by which he who first fathered lies can finally confuse you, as he designs to do so beyond all further hope of your eternal redemption. And he'll do so even as to what you mean by the confusion you mistake for being his very own brand of counterfeit clarity. It's a human failing (that of perfectionism) to mistake oneself for being precisely right when one could have been more exactly right had one not gone more precisely wrong.

This third book—bound to be loose-leafed, subjectively mixed-up, and objectively muddled—when focussing on hell-bent people (most of whom are still open to redemption), cannot avoid being more than a very mixed bag. As any sort of history at all, it's still a largely hidden history (as all history of redemption is somewhat hidden) by what most muddling humans mistake for what they think to know most precisely of people, places, space, and time. Most of today's readers now read the Bible (if still reading it at all) as a do-it-yourself manual for the purpose of doing away with all need for God.

Every hell-bent person is either caught in the lingering darkness of every predawn or else is blinded by the carnival lights of this world calling himself or herself to ephemeral fame and fortune. In terms of earthly place and personal position, none is immune either in terms of time or place. As said before, therefore, scout out every situation, scout out every single person, scout out every apparent happenstance, and scout out, most particularly, everyone who claims to be in anyway expert or professional. Laymen are only a little lower than the angels, so it is the occupational hazard of professionals to consider themselves somewhat above us angels. Historically speaking (so much to the detriment of clergy), this half-baked concept came to be known as 'benefit of clergy', by which even in the law courts, they couldn't be wronged.

Intro 6—John (alias Neil): Every history of heaven is one of ideas, which, without grace, is really too virtual and not concrete enough (as needed to be enforced with fire and sword) by which to penetrate any thick-hided human understanding of what history is all about. For just that reason, the history of hell-bent people remains until now a largely hidden history. And that's one deeply penetrating reason why prophets speak in parables, figures of speech, and other deep, dark sayings, since anything more direct would only ricochet off from what, in exchange for the naked truth, their father of lies sought to cover his own backside by showing them how to develop their own humanly thick hide!

So far as thick-hided humans are concerned, history is all about happenings—and preferably about past happenings, because, unlike prophecies, past happenings can be proved (so humans like to think of themselves) by facts and with figures. For this purpose, most histories are carried on the back of false chronologies. Humanity (in itself a false concept and, for so many people, a visa, if not a passport to hell) mistakes itself for having created time, and in the same way as the judges think themselves to have the right to change the law for having been the ones who made the law, so too, then false humanity mistakes itself for being the arbiter of all time. It is no wonder, therefore, that every history of any hell-bent person (so he or she thinks) is kept so well-hidden from the heavenlies.

Facts and figures—well, there's plenty of them—so much of each (in fact) that there's very little room left for any sort of wisdom in the mind of man (except expressed through parables, homilies, and fiction). Now wisdom is not something that we miss (for having been already given to us) when young. Indeed, its sense of early loss (mistaken at first for false maturity) is something which really only comes with age.

You see, the trouble with facts and figures is that they are not even humanly constant. They vary with the quantum seasons for being subject to the world's far wider statistical measure. Woe then to anyone who believes himself or herself to be the one and only measure of them! And woe even more so to any collective humanity so thick-hided as to think man to be the ultimate measure, either of all things under the sun or far less of all things in heaven or on earth!

Those facts and figures on which mankind most relies are no more than his own means of proof (and so always subject to disproof even although when mistaken for proof). Nevertheless, their apparent continuity (despite their often inconsistency and inconstancy) affords some sort of security to those in all walks of life—more especially to those who limp (but who fail to recognise their limp), those who are blind (yet fail to see what they cannot see), and those who are deaf (even to the sound and songs of creation all around).

Intro 7—Tasha (alias Masha): Indeed, the senses are nowise secular; they are God-given! All the same, most people opt for sensuality rather than for spirituality, and so they take an irreligious stand on sense perception rather than admit of spiritual perception. They do so under the misapprehension that they are supporting principles of non-religious secularism. Alas, they miss that peculiar point of quantitative transition by which purportedly non-religious secularism threatens to become one of the world's biggest of irreligious religions!

'No, we're not' they say, 'because instead of relying, as you do on the supernatural, we're not departing from the non-religious natural!' Yet to ignore the creative forcefulness that is supernaturally all around in the so-called natural is one of the greatest blasphemies (an issue in itself) not just (1) against God but also (2) against one's own creative mind and so (3) against one's own creative heart and thus all told (4) against one's own creative soul.

Mankind was made in mind, heart, soul, and body to copy its creator. Without engaging in some minimal level of cosmic creativity, mankind possesses only self-awareness. That's exactly why, by withholding oneself from God, one fails to see anything of oneself in God and so also anything of God in oneself. The result is to completely immobilise oneself in both mind and spirit and so also (for the lack of being true to oneself) in power and in authority. Aha, but it's exactly at that point of quantitative transition where the counterfeit challenge to true creativity comes in and the irreligious religiosity of secularism takes over.

Intro 7 (continuation)—Nigger (a.k.a. Nigel): Woe to those who mistake themselves, on account of this world being the best of all possible worlds, to be secure in themselves (at least for all time). Woe to those who, after the end of all time, when there is no such world as this one still around to solace them for being the best of all possible worlds, find out that there is nothing more by which they are capable of doing to rectify it. Then there shall be no leeway or loophole left in the grand scheme of things by which this present world (as they see it) should give way to any new earth, far less than to any new heaven. Out of time, as many of them already are, figuratively speaking, is not much different from being out of one's mind, literally speaking, and yet still far short of the point of transition from earth to heaven, spiritually speaking.

Many (not all) of today's thick-hided humans are hell-bent people, and if you think yourself secure for not being one of them, then consider yourself most seriously to be a hell-bent person. This is no more than a weather warning—who knows, perhaps the last bad-weather warning you'll get before the end of time.

As said before, this old world is in a ferment. The process of fermentation has been long in the making. By now, although most of the world's well-off people either ignore or refuse to recognise their predicament, the fact remains that every single person, whether rich or poor or young or old, is in the same sort of long-fermented pickle.

The ways not just of mankind but of every kind and kindred are in a turmoil. If you cannot hear the voice from heaven, then open your eyes, open your ears, open your hearts, and open your minds, because the security of this present world which you rely on is a false security that bids you be hell-bent (rather than heavenwards-looking).

Intro 7 (continuation)—John (alias Zacharia): Rather than you should face the shock (and sometimes the everlasting trauma) of going straight to hell, we angels propose to introduce you readers more gradually to the concept of hell. And to those many lovely people who have never heard of hell or seriously considered the implications of that often soul-shredding concept, we angels shall try to reveal the soft underbelly of hell just as once before in *The Screwtape Letters* so lightly, gently, and even humorously the author C. S. Lewis did so.

Perhaps those most contented people who have never heard of hell have led lives which have been so accommodating to this world's mischief that (even when for their own good) they've never been told often enough to go to hell. There are many dynamic souls whose misplaced travel to hell needs redirection, but there are also souls, either slumbering or so deeply asleep, who, without any enlivening of their hibernating souls, might not make it to heaven. We angels shall try to enliven the deeply slumbering souls of such mortals gently, but as you, our dearest readers, know from scripture, that isn't always possible.

Sometimes, you need to disable a priest (Zacharias) by letting him lose his voice, sometimes you need to deny a strong man (Samson) his eyesight by letting him forego his hair, and sometimes (as for Job) you must let a rich man's worst fear come to pass before he can surpass and overcome that fear. Of course, all these little incidents are backed by universal law, on which account most mortals complain of heaven's unfairness or allege that instead of being ruled by a loving father, we are more than put upon by a very savage god.

Intro 7 (continuation)—Ariadne: Accordingly, we shall endeavour to be as gentle as heaven's universal laws allow. Unfortunately, with the prevailing singularity of today's all-consuming relativity in quantum physics, this situation (provoked both by Heisenberg and Einstein) makes for hard cases requiring hard laws (as the lawyers say). Still, we shall try to be as gentle as we angels can possibly be with such uncomprehending mortals as so many of you dear readers are, although we doubt whether you'll comprehend the specificity with which to this end, we'll apply the principality of principles (both those generally specific and those specifically general) which attempt to expound all-out relativity (in post-dated pop physics denoted by the formula $E = mc^2$) for being as yet in the (relatively shortest) possible history of fallible science, the most impracticable of absolute non-absolutes.

Likewise, in short (since so many readers today are looking for every possible shortcut), we shall, by taking an angelic observer's neutral stance along the perimeter of supposedly heaven's barbed-wire fence (between this earth's declared no man's land and the categorically demonic), there and then engage with you (in the field) in some discourse (very generally) for a (very short and specific) space-time on the (vaguely mischievous) subject of hell-bent people. However, beware of mistaking whatever (apparently legal) loopholes may appear in this fence, as if (1) to afford some rewarding shortcut over no man's land or else (2) to afford some more kindly entrance (allowing for your slumming, smuggling, and spying by way of making a profit from the deterministic rule of hell). Rather than being any rule of law at all, this rule of hell is one which always pushes its luck (always at every potential intruder's expense) to its own highest profit.

Intro 7 (continuation)—Alcuin: Without going into the counterfeit economics of hell by which the real wealth of nations is thereby circumvented, this demonic turnover is extracted not just from hell's own non-absolutes but also by short-changing the rather more open-textured (for being the merciful rather than merciless) and more kindly absolutes of heaven. As said before, we shall heighten your awareness of the demonic power of the Counterfeit Command (even when exerted over every appearance of no man's land) most gently, kindly, and unobtrusively rather than to risk rocketing you into the heart of hell (on which point, read Conrad's *The Heart of Darkness*).

Remember that (1) the first axiom of mortality (still implemented and enforced as far as possible by the Counterfeit Command) is that every mortal is vulnerable, and (2) the correlative proposition derived from that first axiom of mortality is that every mortal's vulnerability should never allowably be reduced but instead always be increased to the maximum level possible of human vulnerability. And yet whether you humans see yourselves here to be either hell-bent, hell-bound, or heaven-bound, you are still in no man's land right now and are so immensely vulnerable. Consider how it might be then when, on some dark night, you might need to swerve to avoid running into where all hell has broken loose; and so when finding yourself on the run, as you mistake yourself for being still in no man's land, you then simply panic as so many uncommitted souls do panic when forced to go on the run for finding themselves then trying to run the wrong way from heaven to hell instead of the right way from hell to heaven.

Intro 7 (continuation)—Callum: That no-man's land is any man's land (even to the disparagement of indigenes) has long been the sadly presumed principle of land settlement. So-called civil societies prevailed upon their expectancy of exploration through which to claim discovery, possession, and ownership, no less than the most powerful of peoples, tribes, and nations relied on the element of unexpectedness to exact military conquest. Of all such things, there is nothing new in no-man's land, since the same human engagements still go on—from resettling Tartar and Kurdish tribes far from their homeland to building islands in the China Sea—although the criteria for exploration (or exploitation) as for military conquest with its resulting demographic dilution and fragmentation (versus consolidation and absorption) of different races and cultures are now, as a sign of these present times, defined differently. The ongoing relationship between the expected and the unexpected (which was the fulcrum on which Baden-Powell built his need for preparedness in his *Handbook for Instruction in Good Citizenship* (*Scouting for Boys*) is now far less sure. Despite $E=mc^2$, genocide is still around.

Any book (particularly for this one in being only the third of twelve books) which, instead of allowing only for the unexpected (as once did Baden-Powell) attempts to deal with both the expected *and* the unexpected (one up on Baden-Powell, surely there) as many might then mistake for being today's dystopian novel *Brave New World* by Aldous Huxley (who filched the concept from Shakespeare's *Tempest*) and so to prove a failure (like George Orwell's *Nineteen Eighty-Four*) in its attempt to avert disaster. This must make our own by now long expected and overdue series of twelve books (at least since Pirsig's *Zen and the Art of Motorcycle Maintenance*) one of the literary world's most unexpected happenings. [Exegesis 1: No comment, except that on any first reading of Pirsig's ultimate meditation on the maintaining of any motorcycle (when compared with Burt Munro's aspiration to be "the world's fastest Indian"), then, whether it be Zen or any less abstract form of meditation, neither makes much sense to anyone (except perhaps to some Southern man) riding a machine of under 50 cc at a top speed of 75 mph (and that on a rocky road round and round the Catlins before thence to Invercargill) and all without experiencing unexpected consequences.]

Very roughly writing (as always, but not roughly speaking), we have come to the halfway point (of no return for casual readers, but not for ongoing angels) in this very fractious and near-miraculous by now third-hand book. As usual, in realising any project so prodigiously apostolic as this present project has become (with a cosmic significance beyond all previous earthly conception), we too (like Pirsig) refuse to shut the door on truth by telling truth to go away (as we too might think to do so because we too believe we're looking for the truth).

On the contrary, we angels celebrate reaching this less than halfway point (for both the overly meditative Robert M. Pirsig as well as the eminently practical Herbert 'Burt' Munro) by our throwing out to earthly readers (those both casually minded as well as those even less so) a largesse of helpful hints as to life in general, besides also decoding those equations (leading far beyond the stultifying relativity of $E = mc^2$) by which to reveal the transcendent existence of each human soul in particular. And on this score, we point to Pirsig's celebrated *Motorcycle Maintenance* for several reasons: (1) to establish that this present book both confirms and conforms to a genre of writing already long established for being nothing new under the sun and in turn (2) to confirm and conform that rough-riding as well as rough writing are each as much of a fine art as are motorcycle maintenance and Zen Buddhism.

Intro 8—First Peter: To the unchurched as well as to the churched, this book may seem a very unchurchy way of stating today's reality and this even more so to the scientifically churched as well as to the scientifically unchurched. The key to this conundrum lies first in our recognition of both the fictional status of fact as well as the factual status of fiction—the result of which is to generate what smaller minds fail to comprehend for being the two-way interchange of fact and fiction (fact⇌fiction).

This project, reaching far beyond the earthbound technology required by which to prove that the eternal truth of Einstein's equation of $E = mc^2$ (or thereabouts) could (or could not) be realised by more (or no more) than one extra (half or whole) dimension when added to the latest fourth dimension (which as yet goes only so far as to account for time in space but not yet space in time), is not just cutting-edge technology (at lower than the required ground level for human understanding) but also at the heavenly faith level required for field theory (whose forcefulness equates with splitting the atom). Likewise, it is also that same heavenly faith level (not far below the scientific faith level) which seeks to merge the three-grade interactions of particle physics into the long-sought-for grand unified theory of soul-abstraction. Hallelujah!

In all this, it would help your mortal as well as moral understanding of the above paragraph here (1) to know more of the Arabic language expressing the concept of 'whole health for all eternity' and likewise (2) to know more of the Latin language for the way in which ad infinitum first expressed the concept by which the end of a pretty bow or rainbow (in place of a plethora of successive fleabites) always recedes endlessly away from any approaching observer. And since both of these concepts, whole health and infinity, are part of the grand cosmic order pivoting on eternity, then for each of us (3) to pursue and enquire into (a) the likes of any still burning bush or (b) the likes of any ram still caught in a thicket or (c) the likes, say, of learning more of mankind's still largely hidden histories, whether these be revealed by way of (i) mathematics, (ii) logic, (iii) linguistics, (iv) legality, (v) equity, or (vi) jurisprudence. Then we find each of these critically significant enquiries revolve around and incur the same faith level required for realising the sought-for field theory by which all things are made relevant to the pursued outcome. Meanwhile, bear this in mind—that the lemniscate-shaped symbol for infinity (∞), as adopted by the English mathematician John Wallis in 1657, stands for a set figure far more powerful than any mortal has ever yet been able to see, say, or achieve by way of configuring the absolute truth.

Intro 8 (continuation)—Second Peter: So then, 'the Word of the Lord endures for ever (*in aeternum*)', as we mortals may glibly say (by way of the motto of the Lutheran Reformation). Nevertheless, we still remain short in our faith as to what we can truly and with all seriousness conceive of infinity (ad infinitum). Nevertheless, for daring to proceed in faith (however presently incomprehensible in practice), here's still a clue. When you find those two still parallel lines (of whole health and infinity) already designed to meet *in aeternum*, you shall by then—whether ready or not—have your sought-for conclusion. 'What of it?' say some scoffers. But this angelic largesse from the stars will explain and reveal so clearly (as if by returning to the lost writings of Euclid) the means by which each helpful hint (by way of being a given) may promote (most punctually in time and most precisely in space) the exegetical interpretation required of each successive book in this series of twelve books.

'But what of that?' say the same scoffers (not themselves being mathematicians or logicians or of any other like sort who know what it means to run the extra mile) and yet others again who (for being legalists) would just as soon outlaw such endeavours and exploits (as well they might say 'to keep the peace'). Well, the twelve books (five more than the seven pillars of wisdom and so needless if only we had that wisdom) stand for each (respectively) of the nine gifts and nine fruits of today's living, breathing, and faster-moving-than-ever-before heavenly spirit. Whereas the remaining three books (not quite surplus to all these eighteen gifts and fruits) for which (the last shall be first and the least endowed shall be the most fulfilled) you must wait on the Lord until the end of all twelve books for yourselves to evaluate the outcome.

Meanwhile (a still pregnant term), don't mistake the increased lightness and humour of this aforesaid heavenly spirit (a person of both scientific precision as well as of heavenly exactitude) for being anything less than (1) a sign of these increasingly terrible times and (2) a means when needed and when applied as the Supreme Command so lovingly directs, one which has the potential of saving the seriously enquiring souls of otherwise hell-bent people. We talk here seriously, as we do everywhere else, of soul-catching, so then as of any closely ciphered palimpsest, be sure to read what's written between the lines. After all, this is a military operation whose ultimate codebreaker is to be found only in the very best of books.

Intro 9—Jeremiah: Perhaps (like the Sadducees) you don't believe in the existence of souls. Then you'll slip through the soul-catcher's safety net. Perhaps (also still like the Sadducees) you don't believe in the existence of angels. Then you'll have no use for this soul-catcher's copybook. Perhaps (also again like the Sadducees) you believe that God's lost his tongue! Then for your own lack of listening, you'll hear no reply. [Excursus 1: we did warn you, did we not, that in any hidden history of the hell-bent, you could likewise be hell-bound by the close company you keep and so find yourself in the same very mixed bag.]

Well, we never thought to make it here. But then our God is so compassionate! Our God is so both loving and lovable! And above all, our God is gloriously communicative, especially to those who seek to hear his voice and to listen and marvel at the many different ways in which he speaks (through all the arts and sciences, as well as through all the storms and catastrophes of life), and so you (like all who hear his voice) are open to change your mind or to change your minds (by upholding whatever you hear him say)!

So then even already (although more towards the end of this bittersweet book on hell-bent people) you may think to change your mind, but until then (for your own continued and more secular of purposes), you may still know this book not as *The Soul-Catcher* but instead as *The Safety Net* (and this before you treat it for yourselves as any sort of *copybook*) For reasons of safety and security (which were some of the same reasons that appealed to the non-risk-taking Pharisees and Sadducees), these same reasons may allowably appeal to you—but yet with this most fatherly of (fisherman's) warnings by which to weigh in your catch—then be sure to do so before inviting your guests to barbecue groper steaks for breakfast on the beach!

Intro 10—John (alias Callum): Every net (including even the blessedInternet) is full of holes—spongiform or open-textured (as either the biologist or legalist might each care to describe it)—and so too are all books (otherwise, as in watching a film, you'd be given no space to think or feel, far less than to turn the page). Of course, the same trauma can be experienced (an old English public school kind of punishment) from being hit overhard on the head with a book.

There's no point to being hit on the head, no matter however hard, with a book—no, not even the Bible. Now if the Bible were a bare-bones book, it might be otherwise. But no, for being a living 'incidents' book, it goes on being written and rewritten as fast as it's being read. So then you can't put your own mind and heart on hold whilst reading a book as you can when watching a film, which, even for the actors, projects no more than a virtual view of the world and very little, if anything, of real life.

The Bible is, or ought to be, some sort of a safety net and not a hangman's noose! Nevertheless, sometimes on walking into some high-vaulted church or even into some ancient but low-life cathedral, you can feel yourself walking into a hangman's noose. Who knows how that happens but for trying it! Sometimes it's just a feeling of being cold-shouldered; at other times, the floor is just too red-hot to think of taking off one's shoes, as one would for being in any holy place. Instead, not even the thickest soles will insulate one's feet from the subterranean heat.

Now not every book's a safety net. Some books, not mentioned here, are not for the hell-bent. That's for sure, as sure as misusing the Bible to hit either yourself or anyone else over the head with what you mistake for being the living Word. That won't work, except on yourself by way of rebound. And don't try it, unless experimentally by way of evaluating the strength of biblical rebound.

No, hold every book the right way up. Every safety net, like also every fisherman's net, has far more holes than any net. If you are looking for a safe, secular alternative (in the slow lane) to the calling you've been given to a spiritual life in the fast lane—no, for having been given any calling at all, no matter how small—then you're not going to find that calling bearing fruit fast enough for one short life to learn all about what you'll need for your next everlasting life. You'll just never get there, for travelling no faster than you can in this slow, safe, and stagnantly gridlocked lane, which is what you mistake for this world's most secular and fastest lane just short of you ending your own as well as this earth's limited life.

For being ever such a little chap, however, you can think yourself able to squeeze unnoticed through the least of microscopic holes in any so-called safety net. On the other hand, for thinking yourself to be the biggest and swiftest of pelagic fish, you can blow up (like any prickly pufferfish), whereby you're bound to get caught up for good (or for bad) in the strongest of any fisherman's net.

Well, there's sporting (or righteous) fishermen and unsporting (or unrighteous) fishermen. And yes, such subtle distinctions as these exist all around. They exist as between those who make and those who break, those who construct and those who destruct, those who create and those who desecrate, just as they exist between both soul-catchers and soul-snatchers. And all these subtle differences can be hard to discern. For now, when still in process of developing one's soul-awareness, it may still help to see this book not yet as *The Soul-Catcher* but instead more relaxedly as *The Safety Net*.

Intro 10 (continuation)—Nigger again: Bear this in mind whenever in any neverland or no-man's land: it's hard to tell the difference between prophets and pirates. After all, from where and by what means do prophets get their ideas from? Perhaps from other prophets, you might suggest. Well now, that's not untrue (unless by way of pirating), but in itself, it poses both an infinite regression (in terms of historic origins) as well as an infinite succession (in terms of prophetic outcomes).

Hey there, it's not even the prophet's own idea that he or she is communicating. But there again, who knows what's his or her own idea? As first said, if it's hard for one, then it's hard for all. So then it's often hard to tell the difference between a pirate and a prophet, between a scholar and a plagiarist, between a copywriter and a creator, or between a priest and a publican.

Nevertheless, rest assured, since as you might expect, there's a very great difference between each of these communicators. It's simply this—that all prophecy, together with every other form of inspired communication, comes from outside the field of human discourse. The answer isn't even in terms of what the prophet, copywriter, or composer means or even thinks himself or herself to mean. Instead, the answer lies in what the original inceptor of the message means it to mean. And that's exactly why, instead of engaging in mere human discourse between earth and heaven, it's preferable always to reach the source, which can only be reached by engaging in prophetic dialogue.

* * *

Hell-Bent People—a Hidden History
Part I

When Words Lose Their Meaning
When words lose their meaning, then people lose
their freedom.
Confucius, *On Language and Freedom*

What happens when words lose their meaning? Answering that
question in a neutral setting requires no more than three whispered
words—hell breaks loose. Nevertheless, when words lose their
meaning in a front-line military setting, *all* hell breaks loose! Today's
whole wide world is in a front-line military setting. The latest of
many world empires (the EU) pushes for a standing army and already
passes all sorts of (even extraterritorial) legislation affecting not only
its own member nations but also every other nation.

Peace is neither induced nor upheld by a welter of laws and
regulations. Why not, since the Ten Commandments prove our Father
God to be a most succinct yet telling writer, but not an overly jealous
writer, since he allowed his Son, Jesus Christ, to edit and erase from
these, the Father's Ten Commandments, the surplus eight which
had no more meaning than the two, which, with their heightened
meaning, then still remained to mean far, far more than all the many
more commandments apparently lost.

There're lots of different ways by which words may lose their
meaning, as often by saying too much as by saying too little. This
loss of meaning doesn't happen all at once. It would take more than
twelve books just to outline today's almost complete breakdown in
cosmic communication. And as if by demonstrating the paradox of
publication, these twelve books pointing to this complete breakdown
might then do something both to stifle the breakdown and to reassert
and recapture the pristine beauty of whatever remains of authentic
language. Never mind newspapers, pamphlets, and journals which
are obliged to go with the tidal flow of the tongue, but books alone

(for as long as there are librarians and libraries) constitute the lapidary bulwarks of authentic expression.

In no less than the time it takes to outline this breakdown in the required twelve books, however, hosts of writers from hell are flooding the market with ten thousand books extolling the merits, say, of the English language (the new lingua franca), whilst that same language is going down the tubes to be interred alive with classical Greek, Latin, Maori, Erse, and broad Scots. [Excursus 1: It's a funny thing about all the classics, but if ever interred, then they're always interred fully alive.]

The still relatively hidden history of hell-bent people (remaindered off in Book 3) demonstrates not only (1) the grace of God in his making it so hard for many sinners to go straight to hell and (2) just how far off hell can appear to be (for being substantively unseen), even although just only round each next corner. Sure, the supportive culture for any language (take Norman-French) may disappear (and be absorbed into Anglo-Saxon). Likewise, political correctness is nothing new (just as Anglo-Saxon is now preferentially called Old English).

Besides, for as long as civility is seen to be a virtue and not a vice, there will always be unethical advertising and a lack of straight-talking. Flattery is providential to getting ahead (observes the Counterfeit Command). And hard copy (to those who still believe in a biblical heaven) will always be preferable to virtual mishmash. Linguistically speaking, the suspicion we all have that a polyglot hell is just round the next corner is probably a curb on our tongue and a cramp/clamp on our writing style. The Lord of Hosts didn't bring down the Tower of Babel for nothing—however long it took the Supreme Command to backfill the resulting void in cosmic communication with glossolalia.

It requires more than a move of the human spirit to discern heaven from hell (of which speaking in tongues can be one of many indicators of heaven at work); otherwise, revivals can so easily be mistaken for breakdowns in cosmic communication and the sanctified reforms in worship required by the Supreme Command dismissed as the devilish work of Satan's foremost counterfeiters. In the beginning and from the beginning of all things, words have always been much more than mere tokens. Dismiss any thought for being no more than a matter of semantics (in itself the science of meaning), and you are halfway (by now three-quarters way) to hell.

Before we are more than halfway to hell, Confucius [he say, *sic*] that when words lose their meaning, then people lose their freedom. So far, so good, since whatever words are being used by way of answer (whether substantively true or substantively false) seem to make some minimalist sense of whatever words are being used. No? Well, as in this case, since whenever we ask a question, we do so by way of expecting some answer, which is what in logic is called semantic entailment. [Exegesis 1: Yes, that's true, since at its most trivial of hind-brained levels, this reasoning operates by way of semantic (and sometimes also, as in this case, syntactic) entailment. This linguistic rather than logical process is given to back up any question and answer (both ways) by the syntactic appropriateness which we are accustomed (whether validly or invalidly) to expect from our own use of language. In its most extreme form, it can be taken to mean that there will always be an answer even to the most unexpected and even unanswerable of questions. Hind-brained lawyers, by their further probing, just love to apply this process to discount someone else's witness in cross-examination.]

This is exactly why, at the lowest of educational levels (long after the preschooler has stopped asking why, why, why to account for every answer given to his successively asked previous question), the same format continues to operate (hiddenly) at almost every higher educational level. The primary student, the secondary student, and the university student have each accustomed themselves to the process of trusting someone else (if not teacher, then through teacher) to answer all the questions, including even every unasked question (of which most will never be asked). It can become the same too for the churchgoer, the medical patient, and the law-abiding citizen. They accommodate themselves to those answers, of whatsoever sort, which they (unlike the curious preschool child) have never asked of themselves, far less begun to formulate the question (to which *unasked question* the answer is to be taken on trust).

In other words, they are first told the answer to the question of which in itself they might have not the slightest knowledge and to which (for never having been in any way perplexed by the question) they are then told the just as empty (exam) answer. Here apparently— apart from the questing Luther, the questing Newton, the questing Thoreau, and the questing Einstein—is an academic shortcut (no matter how anaemic) first to exam success, then perhaps to a most comfortable professorial chair, or to the most populist pulpit or, worse still, for those who follow the academic herd, to the teaching, preaching, and the perpetuation of the same rigmarole to successive generations of would-be scientists and would-be scholars. [Exegesis 2: From their own personal experience, both Martin Luther and Sir Thomas More would most certainly have agreed with Confucius, and so also each in their own way, Newton, Thoreau, and Einstein would most surely do the same. Reconsider here also what it takes to promote and perpetuate a bare-bones Bible, where one is content to do no more than skate across the superficial slickness of the case-hardened surface, below which is hidden the deeper spiritual content of what have become no more than superficial words.]

Let's seemingly change the subject from seeded words to harvested books. Do you really still know (after having watched so many films and having listened to so many rock bands) how it is (or would be or might be or once was) to read a book? That's not something that's still done much nowadays. The trouble is that we've lost the knack of safeguarding our seeds of thought (since we're no longer concerned with the etymology, or deep meaning, of words), and so we've given up on the harvesting of anything more profound by way of that far deeper thought which can only come from carefully constructed books.

Books are not just hard copy as distinct from virtual constructs. They are bound—sometimes even case-bound—to prohibit trifling with their contents and go through various refining processes of drafting, redrafting, editing, re-editing, publishing, and reviewing to assess both their validity and credibility. [Exegesis 3: No, the point at issue, by which words so rapidly lose their meaning and so result in the loss of human freedom, is exactly (although not precisely) the same as when the freedom to think is curtailed by those who tell you the answers to unasked questions and who insist on those being the only answers to questions which are far wider or deeper than they themselves understand.]

For even any would-be author (perish the thought), the task of writing (never mind just of reading) a book—for being nothing at all like that of having once learnt forever to ride a bike—is like learning (all over again) how to disarticulate a fully clothed, fully fleshed, and still living, walking, talking, and proudly authorial skeleton (by taking him or her right back down to preschool ground level! Now that's a seriously surgical task, but more so for bringing back to life the disarticulated dry bones of the once walking, talking, and still writing authorial skeleton (from heaven to hell and back) to come out with a book! [Exegesis 4: No, we're not talking here, neither figuratively nor factually, about the former Soviet Union (of the USSR) any more than we're writing (either fretfully or fancifully) about the trauma still affecting the failed Confederacy (of the Southern states) of the CSA/USA.]

Take heart! Possibly even by now, the book (whichever in question) is deeply entombed in literary reviews or alternatively entombed as by political, legal, evangelical, or even military reviews, just as the four fat volumes (sometimes in three fatter volumes or else in five slimmer volumes) of little comrade Lenin's *Collected Works* are also entombed by being so often run over, again over, and yet over again by various military march-pasts—eyes hard left or is it now hard right—on passing Lenin's Tomb in Red Square almost every year, wet or shine, in Moscow. [Editorial Errata: (1) Keep your eyes well peeled when in Red Square, but don't peel your cucumbers, or in Russia you'll always be mistaken for being an English spy (anathema to both all Scots and Southern Irish). (2) Always remember the *krasnyi kvadrat* (better referred to for being the *krasnaya ploshad*, unless you risk being mistaken for being yet another English spy) since the *krasnaya ploshad* of Red Square is more historically, according to the deep etymology of the Russian language, 'the beautiful square' and so has nothing to do with little comrade Lenin at all (any more than to do with George Washington, George Bush, Abraham Lincoln, or Donald Trump).

What, since most people don't and thus won't ever learn to disarticulate until they can learn to rearticulate any still living book (try Genesis through Exodus and Leviticus all the way until the end of Revelation), you still want to learn to do the most you can in life by learning (exactly, no less) than how (precisely) to read (always at the double) any long book (far less long books)! Shortcuts, eh! Shucks, still taking shortcuts, eh! Well, as they say, although not yet on the short list (of the world's 100 best books), you'd still be in the offing (but for the fact that most of those 100 best books (like Tolstoy's *War and Peace*, Rousseau's *Emile*, and Hugo's *Les Misérables*) are (each in themselves) mighty long books.

So then (for being amongst the fellowship of would-be authors as all great readers are) we can take for granted that you or youse (pardon me) have already planted words (seeds, so to speak) by learning the alphabet—although for planting words, seeds, or even just learning the alphabet, some folks never do—and thence, by attending to the tree of knowledge, slither up that little shrub to go on to graduate to the taller tree of higher things and then perhaps by having got a degree to bring up other people's children (than your own, which is a chore) or in some other way than that (because marriage is now strangely out of fashion) to try by some other means to grow your very own family tree. But still, you say, for having the want/need (as being the better to write than merely being only just proficient to read), you need to know what it takes to bear that figuratively very polished apple of desire for being only a lookalike or something like a papier mâché (or already otherwise chewed-up) fruit.

Well, a one-sentence answer (even if by no means a prison sentence) is simple. To bear fruit, eat fruit (although for being put into such a small nutshell, when you crack the shell of this simple sentence (in itself a hard enough task), you're most likely to find a nut (instead of the desired-for fruit) and still something else entirely if you mistook your daughter's favourite matryoshka doll for being an unopened pistachio nut and a pistachio nut for being a groundnut and a groundnut for being a fruit.

Ah, but then, after all this, comes the moment (the exact moment) of (precisely perfect) revelation. It's at this point, when absolutely worn out to find the right word to describe this infinitely regressive task, that only then can you or youse (pardon the parlance again) put aside the false humility of eating only the humble pie that you mistake for being that pie in the sky (by which such perspicaciously false thought) many ornery folks appear to opt out of heaven and into hell!

So then by taking this big book (although infinitely smaller than the biggest Bible, and not just any little bare-bones Bible for being brought to church only once a week), you think … you think … you think to think (we've got a full-blown intellectual here) that all by yourself (a blue-stockinged female intellectual is by far the worst), you can teach yourself the Bible and so be fit (all by yourself—first-class honours) to write without first learning to write. [Exegesis 5: No, pardon me, not the Bible, since not a single person since Jesus Christ has learnt how, entirely by themselves and without the aid of the Holy Spirit, to read that most wonderful book. No, not even Moses, for his writing of the Pentateuch (the first five books of the Bible), since not even then (when all days stretched even far longer than they do today) that every learnt author learnt how to read 'his own book', far less to write 'his own book', when he or she is obviously not the only author of what is primarily someone else's book.]

Take a long look at as many authors as you can before even ever thinking of learning to write a book (in order to read a book). Now, for example, Leading-Agent Thoreau (whose books never sold in his lifetime) has written much for every reader to read on the subject of reading books (and thus even more on the writing of books). He never stopped writing, you know, simply because he knew his calling; and he remained committed to finding and perfecting his voice, even although in his own short time, very few (of the very few readers he had) understood what he chose to write about and so understood far less of why he wrote, which tends to indicate that he wrote not just with his own voice (which never is prophetic solely to oneself) but also (for being prophetic to others as well as oneself) is also always someone else's voice.

Now until you understand why any fellow (guy or gal, although some guys are gals now just as some gals are guys) wants to write (which revelation comes to the reader often only after the writer is dead and gone), then you won't really understand what he or she writes about, since there's nothing like death to bare the writer's soul (which, until the writer's death, is often hidden from the reader behind the book, the book, and yet again the book). To many writers and readers, that protocol of more complete communication seems unfair, but it's the only prophetic way (as proved by the history of books) to produce (through the melding of authorship and readership) whatever will mature to become amongst the best of books. Oh, and as for the rest, why, the rest is chaff—chaff blown away in the wind—unless and until taken up by what comes next when blown towards any other intended destination by the Holy Spirit.

A lonely man, therefore—although not by choice, since solitude is the basic need of every great writer—Thoreau would row out into the middle of Walden Pond late on a summer's evening, where, instead of thinking to launch yet another great unread book, he would play his flute to the late summer evening rise of freshwater fish. [Exegesis 6: Beware, since saltwater fish (as the writer well knows from his saltwater fluting) won't rise to the flute, and besides, no flute will survive a saltwater rinse.]

If that exegetical explanation makes no sense to you for never having been a fisher (whether of words or of fish or of folk), then you should first learn to write a book (when not written just to be sold but instead, like Thoreau's *Walden*, written primarily to be read). What it takes to fish for words, and far more for the souls of hell-bent readers, takes only a writer who can also read the signs of the times to know. To learn the measure of fast-changing times by which any such book can be written, then every such wordsmith (at the risk of losing his own soul) must learn to hammer white-hot words upon this world's anvil of life experience to find out how even just to read, far less to write, such a book. It may be a book written of those hell-bent fisherfolk who empower no more than this present world or else more importantly of those deep-sea fisherfolk empowered from heaven despite this world.

Who has not learnt to write whilst yet in hell has not yet learnt to write whilst not in hell! This is the case no matter whether aiming to write (as leaven) either in heaven or else even just about heaven (also as leaven)! Writing about heaven whilst in hell is providentially sanctioned by the Supreme Command as writing whilst undercover, of which there are three levels: (1) under sheets, whether of rain or lightning; (2) under blankets, whether of snow or frost; or (3) under the thickest of counterpanes, whether of fictions purporting to be non-fictions or of non-fictions purporting to be fictions.

'Meanwhile, see that notice?' queries a disembodied voice, which, given in the absence of further identification, we would nevertheless hope to be that of the Lord! 'What does it say?' then asks the same disembodied voice most obviously by way of a rhetorical question, since as for so many preaching-teaching prophecies, the selfsame voice goes on to answer its own question. Without a certain measure of trauma required of us, whether by facing up to what we hear of the perplexed, the ridiculous, or the unbelievable, there will be no breakthrough.

In such circumstances, we can expect to be startled, even shocked, and thrown off balance (as a test of our faith) by the incongruity of what we're about to be told. 'It says, 'Duvets don't count!' Under which, in very small print, someone (surely hell-bent, if not yet already sponsored by hell) has tagged this message: 'Well, whoever thought that duvets could count!'

'Uh-oh! Change channels—from the deeply dark prophetic to the see-through transparency of the proclamatory,' we plead when preferring to be told (what we ourselves think to be) the plain truth rather than be left to puzzle things out for ourselves. As humans, we flatter ourselves always to get our heads round the blatantly unbelievable, but we hate being hit so hard on the head by the ridiculousness of the unexpected! All the same, there's nothing like being made to feel ridiculous to put down self-pride!

As so often turns out to be the case when teased by the Lord with some such deeply dark and hiddenly prophetic saying, we find ourselves presented with not much more than the incomprehensible farce of our own humanity. That lonely Thoreau of Walden Pond, very much his own writer and pre-eminently a naturalist by privileged occupation, never referred more than once or twice to that Supreme Command which had commissioned him to write of what he wrote. Presumably, like so many other naturalistic writers, he was writing undercover.

It's hard to figure out how some folks—especially the most romantic of poets, writers, composers, and other creative artists—experience death as this life's final deluge of creative output, yet for other just as creative folks, death is no more than a feather duvet, a soft quilt, or an intricately patterned counterpane, counting for no more than a thin veneer or veil between this world and the next, on it being gently drawn up and over and so to cover their heads. Yet since every strongly prophetic communicator of the next world depends on death to act as the ultimate editor of his or her by then retrospectively bared soul, that same Thoreau sings still today ever more strongly than before.

Now Thoreau's simple song (never heard to resound in his own time) is heard all the louder by the most secular of environmentalists and all to the glory of what was once God's bountiful creation. That simple song of stewardship, perfected through Thoreau's own recreation in the wilderness of his then lonely and unrecognised writing, now makes Thoreau famous for his prophetically environmental treatise on *Walden*. That treatise was so far ahead of its time, although written during the USA's earliest and most euphoric period of railroaded industrialisation that it was bound (on account of loose couplings) never again to entrain (after being so long diverted on to a siding) from what had been then read by so few of his own contemporary readers. On which disastrous subject of American railroading, be sure to read more both as reported by *Tintin in America* and *Little House on the Prairie*.

Likewise, Thoreau's later piece on *Civil Disobedience*, written in defence of the slave abolitionist John Brown (executed illegitimately for treason), would have to wait many years after Thoreau's death before being taken up by so many civil protestors such as Mahatma Gandhi (another well-known great soul). Just as to the tune of John Brown's body lies a-mouldering in the grave, Brown's great soul is still marching on to the same tune as later sung with the words of Leading-Agent Julia Howe's 'The Battle Hymn of the Republic'.

Perhaps, just barely … just barely … we still do know how to read, as we might say (both by the authors as well as the readers of this book) in our still being perplexed enough to pick up on the whys and wherefores illuminated by the signs of the times picked up and portrayed by this book! Sure enough, sometimes it's a battle, a regular battle against time and place, and sometimes even against people just to read a book. Its first reader is of course the author, and by the end of its writing, it's bound (no pun intended) to be an already well-read book.

There's a lovely little five-starred book called most simply *Henry*, which the Supreme Command commissioned from the writer Leading-Agent Elizabeth Yandell. Writing *Henry*, through several of her most diligent drafts, took Elizabeth all her lifetime (because it's all about her life). It's also a loving treatise on her gardener friend and lifelong soulmate Henry, who gives his name posthumously to Elizabeth's book. Having herself serendipitously reached into her eighties and just a few days before the good news came to her from the book's publishers of *Henry* having been accepted for publication, Elizabeth quite quietly and unobtrusively died.

In other words, that intricately patterned counterpane of Elizabeth Yandell's life, counting for no more than the thin veil or veneer between this world and the next one, was most gently drawn over Elizabeth's head. Read of her life's work in her little book, *Henry*, to find out how some writers make their own heaven out of a situation which would be sheer hell for other writers. In many a hellish situation some life-long readers will turn to writing, some long-term writers will abandon their writing and gratefully relax to take up reading, yet other writers feel called to go on writing. Those who go on writing, do so sometimes more passionately than ever before for now being privileged, either to report on hell, to escape from hell, or to escape from hell by reporting on hell. You have to read what they write (if they do still write) to determine the exact means of their motivation—and in each case, whether currently writing (humorously or otherwise) directly about the closeness of hell or (with the same identical motivation) then contrariwise about a very remote and distant heaven, in each case—as with John Bunyan, Elizabeth Yandell, Miguel De Cervantes, or a thousand others—it is by the grace of God.

Well, in that case, as for both Thoreau's and Yandell's life stories being of their same constant battle with time and place, that's an extrinsic battle (from the outside in) which is one way in which (from the inside out) it can take a whole life's battle just to learn to read, far less to learn what it takes to write a book. So too, try Tolstoy's *Resurrection*, Darwin's *On the Origin of Species*, or Churchill's

History of the English-Speaking Peoples, just to read a book, far less than to write a book. On the other hand, however, the battle can be from the inside out rather than from the outside in [an intrinsic battle] to read and far more to write a very different book.

This intrinsic battle may be waged (1) from within oneself against reading the book or (2) from within the book itself against whatever one does not want to read that's in the book. Most usually, any intrinsic battle has elements both (1) from within oneself as also (2) from within the book. And on either account, we may either (1) slate ourselves or (2) slate the book but (3) most usually both.

There are books (1) slated in the short term but revered in the long term, just as there are books (2) revered in the short term but slated in the long term, but the outcomes differ according to whether one reveres (3) no book more than oneself or (4) some book more than oneself. There are also many other books (like the classics of Greece and Rome) that take aeons just to fall into their pride of place. Indeed, most great books, like most great music and great films, have to go through a period of slating, as if their composers, artists, and writers have to be discounted, disparaged, or slated before being recognised for whom they really are.

We've already talked (a figurative expression used by many writers who need first to hear voiced, whether from themselves or from God or from others, what they only then, and also then only, have gained the requisite clarity to write). What they may have to hear before they write or else write in order to hear or, as for others, a mixture of both may be about what others say or about what others write or about what others hear (since we are all different about how and what we hear, about how and what we say, and about how and what we write.

This need for hearing a voice is no less than when we all have different views about the meaning of words and about what happens when words lose their meaning. Right here, we're going to talk about the way in which the resulting loss of freedom brings down entire languages, entire cultures, whole nations, and eventually, the widest extent of human society in general. This happens even for anyone who goes on believing in what they say, write, report, legislate, promise, or judge and even to think for themselves about whether they can seriously go on meaning what they say. You see, if dear old Confucius is right about the loss of freedom resulting from what happens when words lose their meaning, then we've lost that freedom of volition (or personal free will) with which we use these words not only to communicate to others but also to think for ourselves.

Well, don't blame us angels but rather you/youse humans for that, since we'll plead, what we know we can prove by all the powers in heaven, that the English language, for claiming the same universality that was once claimed by so much of the Greek and then of the Latin and what later was being incrementally built into the Germanic language too (from which, like any jack-in-the-box, out popped English), is now so much imperilled like its own linguistic forebears. In their own day, each have claimed its own universality and now wore itself out just like, first, the claimed universality of the Greek and then, after that, by way of the Latin language following suit (by devaluing its first golden age to silver, then devaluing its silver age to the leaden clichés of the streets), each to wear out much exactly (although not precisely the same way) as first did the classical Greek to streetwise koine.

Why, it looks as if Greek, Latin, and next Hebrew and English are now failing, as did once every dead and dying language, head first, by falling into universal favour! As we angels surely say in heaven, pride goes before a fall (and for us angels, as you know, that fall for those that fell to this planet Earth was this planet's longest long drop. And there's a sure formula for the formalists here—for pride of face gives way to pride of place and pride of place gives way to pride of race, and pride of race is usually reached when that level of pride (whether Slavic, Germanic, Hebraic, Turkish, Babylonian, Anglo-Irish, Scots, Aussie, Kiwi, or French) is usually of the most likely sort to lead that nation to the linguistic long drop.

So then for all of us in these pretentiously pretending times, we angels ask once again, as might any remaining librarian ask on earth, far less than one from heaven, do you still know how to read a book? That's the question, and one for you as any reader to think deeply about and ponder over rather than to be told a purported answer long before you've ever thought to formulate the question. We'll give you just a hint or nudge as to the direction in which you might go to find the answer, which will be measured by the extent to which you still care for and safeguard your heartfelt love of words.

We dare say that you are possibly puzzled by us angels being thus so bookish about books, but insofar as it has been promised on earth that all things shall be revealed to us when once in heaven, most of our first year of internship as angels is spent in heaven's library reading up not only on the science of librarianship and on the art of caring for books, together with the cataloguing and classifying of books, but also to perfect ourselves, through the reading of books, on the reading of the souls who wrote them. Try to do the same with information technology (IT to youse) and then youse (quite literally will have another thing coming).

It was Jonathan Swift, now more famous for his *Gulliver's Travels*, who wrote *The Battle of the Books* (no less than he wrote 'to vex the world rather than divert it' on the warring typology between Lilliputians, Brobdingnagians, Yahoos, and Houyhnhnms), and such also is the most fundamental and cosmic character of this great conflict that consumes both heaven and earth that we are brought up (as well as being bound personally and individually to our own dynamic present no less than publicly to the collectively dynamic present). And so it goes without saying, both as readers and authors (however funny it sounds to say what goes without saying), on what it takes in learning both how to read as well as how to write a book is that which becomes the combined essence of both the writer and of the reader by which to constitute the essence of the book. In other words, it takes both the soul of the writer and the soul of the reader (as guardian angels together of any book) to bring into birth the essence of that book.

Never mind for our saying so, because we often get our mouths into gear before we've got the rest of our heads into gear, so we say many, many things that are most needless to say. Yet perhaps that's yet only one more thing by way of telling you humans of what it means to be humans. At any rate, the angels say it means nothing to them, although it does mean everything to them that humans truly know what it truly means to be human, and that matters most particularly to those humans who profess to be the people of any book.

Nevertheless, you can read in any book (if you studiously look for it) exactly what it takes to write that book, then when once you know not only exactly but also precisely what it takes, you cannot even just read that book for your very own lack [even just then as a reader] of not knowing how it comes to be written. In other words [by way of interpretative exegesis as well as of soul-searching excursus], you always need a certain level of commensurate life experience in order to make sense of what is meant by the written word that you are reading. And that very sense of meaning is often clouded and at other times clarified by the rising smoke and prevailing fumes from the always surrounding, always immediate, and never intermittent, but almost constantly ongoing battle. [Exegesis 7: Take five (as they say here) for having some time out. You may have to catch your breath before facing another catch-22 situation or until you can pick up on replenishing and restoring your already lost or else fast-diminishing sense of humour.]

As already said, take five here, for its been a long haul from Confucius to here to figure out not just how much meaning we've already lost from the words we use but also how much more meaning from those words that we're still losing. In most cases, the hard copy of this world's greatest books are the only real measure, and the paradox (of our own making) by which we attempt to bring those classics up to date, in most cases (apart from proving the point), serves only (by those greater ambiguities and doubtful meanings introduced by those alternative versions) to demean that same classic measure. Want proof? Why, that's easy, since how often do you hear now of anyone either speaking of or thinking of, far less troubling, themselves over the state of their soul?

* * *

426

Hell-Bent People—a Hidden History
Part II

The Battle for the Soul

Each man's soul is a battlefield in which God and the
Devil contend for [their] supremacy.

> Arthur Blessitt with Walter
> Wagner, *Turned on to Jesus*

In your coming to understand what it takes for the making of any evangelist, prophet, or apostle, then 'each man's soul is a battlefield'— as said by Walter Wagner of the evangelist Arthur Blessitt—'in which both the Supreme Command [or God] and the Counterfeit Command [or the devil] contend for supremacy'. Yet also, both the source and the instrumental process as well as the decisive result of this battle (over books, as some may dismiss it) is far more significant than may be thought of for being any merely academic or bookish battle. Apart from books, how does one hope to measure the ebb and flow of any battle, especially as so many books about battles (including the Bible itself) either dissolve or heighten into battles over books?

Well (unless discounted by you for being no more than a matter of mere semantics, in which case you neither care nor are concerned for the meaning of words) then here, for once being sold at half a crown, is a little book (with no author named in it responsible for its writing but instead inscribed and dedicated to the British Rifle Volunteers of 1860) which carries the title of *The Twelve Great Battles of England.* But before even opening such a little-known book, however, then what's *your* measure? Maybe you're not even qualified to read such a book until you've given some serious thought to measuring the greatness perhaps not just of books and battles but also of everything else.

Of course, quite conventionally (as might be given *simpliciter* in the lower schoolroom), the first great battle of England (aside from considering any far earlier Beaker invasion) would be (as said by any

Englishman) that of the Battle of Hastings in 1066. Of course, in the upper schoolroom, one might learn of those earlier battles with the Vikings versus the ancient Britons or with the Romans likewise or by the Scots from Ireland versus the so-called Picts. And some other battles (such as the Battle of Britain in 1940) might be even greater according to a different scale of values.

Nevertheless, were *you* to say what these twelve great battles of England were (as judged by your own scale of values), then what would you say? Perhaps, as proved by still existing monuments, it could have been that depicted by Christian crosses all over England, Ireland, and Scotland when these were first employed to mark the introduction of Christianity? Some say the gospel came first to the Picts and thence to both Brythonic and Celtic Britain before England, whilst others have a different scale of values. No, some others might say, without any more need to argue, according to our present scale of greatness, England is no more a Christian nation. Thus, the battle for or against Christianity no longer features in our scale for greatness!

The last named battle in the list of *twelve* is that of Waterloo, but there have been many more and perhaps even greater battles since then. Then what of all the everyday little but highly significant battles both before and since? How do you judge—by what's at stake, by what's the cost, by what's the loss, or by what's the gain? What did it cost or gain for the Druids to fight or retreat from the introduction of Christianity? What was gained or lost for the Ancient British Church (hardly known of at all now in church history) to battle over different forms of Christianity, both prereformation as well as postreformation?

Well, what you once have read by way of being your first book may well determine what you next read by way of being your last book. Indeed, your first book and your last book may, or may not, be that one and the same book. For being either the book you never ever wanted to read or else for being that one you always wanted to read before reading any other book (for the first being last and the last being first) both may be one and the same book. Do you understand the question any better, or is it the case that words for you have truly lost their meaning?

Of course, as voiced above, on many counts, it's a heuristic question and not an algorithmic question. So let's reformulate the philosophical question for scientifically driven logico-mathematicians in the form of an equation. There may well be one since, of course, there is always a heuristic (or substance of meaning) basis to all formal issues (since you can't have form without substance nor substance without form). Likewise, there may well be a due process by which to relate each of them to the other for being different forms of the equation (since both logicians and mathematicians, together with pure scientists, argue (worse than even lawyers) over matters of form as to whether no more than communicative clarity equals true understanding).

Why, maybe you don't even understand the question. Let me give you (rather than just drop) a hint. First, as that long-ago lover of wisdom, Confucius say (*sic*), 'It doesn't matter how slowly you go.' Secondly, as the same Confucius still say (*sic*), 'What you are looking for is learning.' And thirdly, as to the learning of wisdom, Confucius points out the three means by which this wisdom may be attained: first, by reflection, which he says 'is the noblest means' (and so is never attained by speed-reading); secondly, 'by never cutting corners' (which as any college student should know cuts out copying); and thirdly, 'by life experience' (which can never be acquired without the deepest reflection).

[Voice from offstage] On account of philosophy having so recently gone to ground (as explained by the rapid rise in speculative science from what was once science fiction), you will note from the previous paragraph, if you're really still reading this book, that we (again the angelic and not the authorial 'we') no longer denote lovers of wisdom for being the literal equivalent of philosophers (who are likewise scripturally grounded for substituting theological argument for their love of wisdom) since these words, both *philosophy* and *philosopher*, are examples of words which have lost their original meaning by which to connote their 'love of wisdom' and to substitute at best 'a love of reasoning' and at worst 'a love of argument'.

So [when back on stage] do you know any better now how to read a book? That's a harder and harder task today with your reading of every passing author. And that's because it's a harder and harder task for any author to write a book. And the reason for that, if you can forebear complaining about two sequential sentences starting with the same conjunction, is that (except for the by now utterly dead languages like classical Greek and classical Latin) all words in all other languages (but more especially in the English language for its claim to be the world's last and ultimate universal language) are more and more readily losing their essential meaning. And the consequence (besides again using the same sequent conjunction) is, as the ancient Chinese lover of wisdom, Confucius, pointed out, the user's loss of freedom.

By now, without a single proverb to our name in today's so-called English language by which to demonstrate that words still keep their essential meaning, we have long forgotten that pride breeds nothing but conflict and contention. When words say no more than what we ourselves think them to mean, then we have lost the power to express their meaning, no less than having lost all our remaining power to think alternatively. We have then begun arbitrarily to usurp the power of words irrevocably towards our own personal purposes and to abuse them increasingly towards our own favour.

'I *will* ascend to heaven,' said Lucifer, the light bearer, speaking of the celebratory status of his own divine person in the imperative voice. 'I *will* seat myself above all the angels. I *will* be the most high [i.e. in the Supreme Command]!' [This self-promotional way of looking at one's entitlement to short-lived celebrity status has become so strongly established in today's institutional life that one must read Leading-Agent Elijah's earlier report in the book of Kings, as well as Agent Tolkien's preparatory portions of his earliest *Silmarillion* (precursor to his epic *Lord of the Rings*). Both these readings will refresh one's mind as to its presumptive enormity of the light bearer's imperious declarations.]

The saddest thing about Lucifer—once the wisest, most handsome, and most perfect of all divine creations (until iniquity outstripped all his moral, artistic, legal, and jurisprudential faculties)—literally lies everywhere in his fallacious choice of words. He cannot help lying, both in his own self-imperative choice of words as to his own capabilities as well as in his self-accusatory denunciation of all others. Once again, there is a universal logic to all this, since you cannot fallaciously promote yourself [since all self-promotion is fallacious] without demoting others.

With this preposterously presumptuous promotional as to his own self-worth, Lucifer demonstrates not the slightest idea of what is meant by the words he uses of himself, nor of the accusatory implications by which he denounces others. The only thing sadder than such self-deceit is when the same bombast deceives others, as it did when Lucifer misled one-third of the heavenly angels to follow him in waging war against heaven. And now the lying tongue of Lucifer seeks to heighten the odds in his own favour (always in his own favour) by advertising the same self-promotional process (for cut-rate cannon fodder) to humans.

Were we now engaged (subjunctively) on writing a work of fiction or, better still, an outright allegory on righteous authority instead of this account for being a straightforward report on historical events, we would draw attention to the fiendish way in which the self-promotional approach has laid claim through sycophantic patronage, self-sown credentials, and honorific trade-offs to take over almost every traditional promotional or appointment process. How often is it now that we are led to think that it is by ourselves or by our work or by our insight or by our wisdom that we have climbed the cursus honorum or ladder of promotion only then to find out that we have been appointed or promoted (sometimes even as a fall guy or scapegoat) for the very worst of reasons? In any case, what do we think to achieve when climbing up the ladder by ourselves, as we might think of our powers of persuasion, when then in consequence we are required to live and work so very far off the ground?

It might be wise then to warn of the occupational hazard by which those in high command sooner or later aspire to be in the Supreme Command and by what means they will endeavour to seat themselves on the throne of the Supreme Command to which they have not the slightest claim by due process of authoritative appointment or promotion. In such ways, those financiers and treasurers exercise the power of the purse over those authorised or equipped to engage in its meaningful expense and distribution. Likewise, instead of merely executing, implementing, and carrying out decisions, as executives were once appointed to do, these so-called chief executive officers become self-empowered to make those very decisions of which, when made by others better qualified, they were once appointed merely to fulfil, implement, execute, and carry out.

Not even sport is exempt from the same self-promotional hype, by which on scoring a goal or making a try, the player immediately sets off on a self-congratulatory victory lap (which for the betterment of the game at large, someone from the same side should swiftly intercept or tackle), but the extreme level of competitiveness blinds players to many such breach of ethics of gamesmanship, promotes bullying of those who don't conform to this same breach of ethics, and edges its way towards that state of corruption where those doing the most wrong are so completely entranced by their own personal power as to be completely oblivious to their own wrongdoing.

The scandalous state into which so much sport has fallen—through the trading off of players, the hazing of newcomers, the drug taking, the betting, and the gambling—has reduced sport to the level of internecine warfare, exactly the opposite role which it professes to perform. By going so far as to be openly professional (even in the Olympics), sport has also subjected itself to the paradox of professionalism by which so many of the professions cannot even appear to be fulfilling the role which they profess without in practice actually subverting that same openly professed role. The big winners have then become the little losers because there is no way left systemically open for them to do right.

But how could it be otherwise in sport when exactly the same problem is being faced in education? How long ago was it said, no less constitutionally in an Australian speech from the throne, that 'a competitive model in tertiary education has led to unsatisfactory outcomes in terms of both the quality and the appropriateness of the skills produced'? So long ago, especially in the context of our ever-increasing competitiveness in the so-called higher education, both the source and the outcome of our educational shortcomings by now pass completely unnoticed. For as long now as education survives for being seen to be immune from criticism for being a big (dollar-earning) business (which may not be all that much longer), the fact that this big business subverts its own educational ideals is bound, if continued, to bring about both internal and external collapse.

Roles then are more and more openly reverse, and rules more and more revert to non-rules; strategies stagnate and tactics conflict with mission statements. In the same way, management and administration take over substantive production, no less than party coalitions and cabals may capture elective parliaments, just as day-to-day managers may overrule and suborn the work and lives of teachers, doctors, lawyers, and other (professedly self-governing) professionals. The demonic fallout is enormous, but then, by solely human hands, this is not heaven brought down but hell brought up to earth.

It was long before even the creation of the world, or so we are told of this most reliably by the Supreme Command, that we humans (only a little lower than the angels) were then already a work in progress towards perfection. That is harder now for us even to imagine, because all such epic stories have fallen out of favour. Technology has long since usurped the human imagination, and we think to work our own man-made miracles by having machines undertake the tasks on our own behalf.

To overlook our continued state of imperfection—since we are, by our own choice, no longer a work in progress—we prefer today's narrowly abridged version of life whereby, so far as possible, we are content to eat, drink, and be merry today because tomorrow we die. Nevertheless, for that shortest of short stories, being too much abridged for those who increasingly find themselves overwhelmingly bored whilst still in the midst of what could still be an epic life, then we start accommodating ourselves towards years of no more than self-indulgent retirement.

Epic stories—whether of the Red Sea opening up or of Agent Elijah being fed by ravens in the wilderness or of the wedding between widowed Ruth and gentleman Boaz (never mind the subsequent accounts of Christ's crucifixion, the Messianic resurrection, and the Commissioning Day of Pentecost)—have most certainly fallen out of favour. The biggest, longest, and so far most continuous epic story— from Genesis to Revelation—is, of course, that of the creation. But of course, we mortals as well as angels like to put our own slant on things, especially on the beginning of things, as if we too, like Lucifer the light bearer, were ourselves the most high.

This is the point, long before the midlife of any prospective book, at which most authors begin to lose the plot. Of course, the midlife crisis of any book, no less than of any person, can come at any age. Some ultrasensitive people [mostly artists, musicians, and authors] have at least two or three midlife crises every week [besides the most creative, at no less than one a day].

Think too of statesmen—real statesmen like Pericles, like Caesar Augustus, like Churchill. And think too of those people who are in a permanent state of midlife crisis 24/7—people like Tamerlane, Genghis Khan, William the Conqueror, Napoleon, Adolf Hitler, Benito Mussolini. They most usually mistake their own lives for being always called to be in free flight. But oh, what pain and disappointment they suffer when their balloon of personal fantasy ruptures or, when in the end, they are shot down for all their crimes or, on their deathbed, when, like William the Conqueror, they are faced with all their sins and are drawn to freely confess that they had no rightful claim to what they conquered.

Oh my goodness, what great gifts those poor yet largely unforgiving people had been given, and what a grave misfortune to the whole wide world that the great gifts of these so greatly gifted people were never realised. God cries through his prophets for such lost souls. Perhaps you never met, as I did, Stalin's mum? Oh, how she prayed for her own dear little Sozo!

But then alas, for mankind being so much the talking animal, since when words lose their meaning, so also do people lose their sense of that once reliable meaning, because not even those who use such meaningless words (far less others) can trust themselves to say what they mean or to mean what they say. Social decline always begins with linguistic decline, leading next to moral decline, then to legal decline, and finally, to physical decline. Why, for the lack of anything authentic to say or even just mean to say, you can't even counterfeit what once was the real meaning of life.

Some people (including authors who try to substitute the clearly written for the more commonly misspoken word) never get over their midlife crisis. They may be highly gifted people, but they do not listen for, far less hope to hear, their true calling. Like Virginia Woolf [well, who's afraid of her—but they ought to be], Katherine Mansfield, James Barrie, Rudyard Kipling, or Mark Twain, they have breakdowns. And these breakdowns get in the way of their calling—so that in the end, their callings get in the way of their broken lives and their broken lives either get in the way of other lives or else break up their own relationships.

The trouble is that this listening … this constant listening … just to hear the least whisper of one's calling … of one's true calling … may take a lifetime—a whole long lifetime and thereafter. Once heard, all the rest of one's lifetime, as that may be so allowed, is just taken up to perfect one's calling. Read Victor Hugo's *Les Misérables* in any language [for the moment, never mind the musical, far less any of the many filmic versions].

Yes, we know, Victor Hugo's *Les Misérables* is a long lifetime's work—it's 1,900 pages long—which explains just why, also as a musical, Victor Hugo's *Les Misérables* means so much to so many more people who would never have got around to read the book. Of course, the artistic worth of *Les Misérables* lies not just in its quantity of work (which, as for many authors such as Dickens, Scott, or Galsworthy, is important to their art and their own need to keep moving) but also foremost in its quality of work (which is paramount for any work of art). Nevertheless, it is this underpinning of true virtue which explains how the more momentary musical (as of *Les Misérables*) can become one of the most celebrated musicals of all time. Thus, despite all critical rebuffs and reviews made of turning any classic writing into a film, the successful transformation from one medium to another, in the course of extending its audience, can confirm and/or verify the true worth of the original as a work of art.

In this vastly communicable way, a work of art—a true work of art—is of infinite [and not just linguistic or cultural] dimensions. It knows no human limits. For being divinely inspired and implemented through one's calling, it also extends its eternal inspiration, transmuting through space and time, and transformational through apparently otherwise definitive genres of communication from one person's calling to another person's calling—from literature to law and from law to literature, from music to dancing and from dancing to music, from fact to fiction and back again to fact, from the humanities to science and from science back to spiritual to physical and back again to the spiritual.

For you, being the scientific reader and so possibly a box-thinking, case-hardened specialist, you won't readily believe me, will you? Then read Isaac Asimov's *The End of Eternity*, but read it backside foremost, and then, contrary to his own more conventionally scientific but completely problematic and paradoxical conclusion, you will have found not only the algorithmic end of this counterfeit eternity but instead the heuristic source of authentic eternity, which is where, despite all the changed values given to old words, those old words keep their authentically ascribed meanings.

The spirit of any true work of art is thus not only multidimensional in a space-time continuum; it is also truly multitransformative [both of the work's original calling and of its ultimate completion]. This widely transformational potential is exercised by any true work of art. Yes, of course, this transformational aspect poses problems to the scholar, to the scientist, to the reviewer, as well as to the librarian, to the academician, and of course, also to every level of everyday classifier as well as to the specialist taxonomer.

So then here's a test case to match your angelic wits! We'll deliver it in the form of this next year's graduation question. You've got five months from now in terms of sidereal time to answer it. Here goes: exactly how, and more precisely by what specific means, would you classify Giovanni Guareschi's *The Little World of Don Camillo*? Would you catalogue that so-called little world to be either a work of literature (whether of fact or of fiction) or else of theology (or else of both)?

Don't panic! From your close reading and perhaps third or fourth rereading (don't pull any punches from further readings), would you classify this work—in the whole context of the well-known Camillo Saga (not unlike Galsworthy's Forsyte Saga or Turgenev's Fathers and Sons Saga)—either as a work of popular fiction or classical fiction or serious theology or popular theology? Or would you skip the specifics (as not everyone can do for being a bookish librarian or a high-tech barbarian) by crediting it towards a work of the most general jurisprudence rather than having any more specific (or particularist) leaning?

Would it help you to know, for the purposes of your classification of the Camillo Saga, that the author's father didn't think much of his son's writing? [In flagrante delicto (or caught in the act of spilling the beans about exam questions which nobody as yet ought to know), then reconsider whether Guareschi's Don Camillo books make for apt compulsory reading in Church History 101 by which to examine first-year angelic interns to qualify for passing out into the field of battle, as later taught by Professor Cornelius Guareschi-Gibson by distance learning from heaven.]

This taxonomic [or classificatory] question of, say, librarianship [as well as of biology, geology, law, or jurisprudence] is deeper by far than any or all these disciplines. This is so since the same question also arises over, say, classifying the social sciences as apart from the pure sciences or the pure sciences apart from the applied sciences. It also arises internally, say, of law as a science (as so it can be classified in many continental and federal systems) or for interdisciplinary subjects (such as biochemistry, bioanthropology, astrophysics) or (for being no longer any sort of buzzwords) any other cross-disciplinary or cross-dressing academic pursuit. Nevertheless, all such rapidly changing, critically provocative, and often definitively unanswerable questions of taxonomy (transfusing the lifeblood of the librarian) are apt to provoke a series of midlife crises (of a generalist nature) in the working lives of many specialist academicians. So then how goes your academic funding?

As a sign of one's own time (see Signs and Insignia 201 as taught to angelic interns), any midlife crisis demands a clear response to one's calling. It may be a communicative calling (for which read Spengler's battle to communicate to the West in his *Decline of the West*). It may be a caring calling (for which personal battle, read C. S. Lewis's *Pilgrim's Regress*). It may be an exploratory or research calling (for which academic battle to promote general semantics, read Korzybski's *Science and Sanity*). As already asked by us once before, as also must be asked by any angel of an academician (see here, when writing on the subject of higher education, Simon Leys's book *The Angel and the Octopus*), so then how's the 'soft money' going, you know, that finance [by way of grants instead of salaried employment] which makes up your scientific funding? Meanwhile, here's the question for you, dearest readers to find the answer—is the extent to which higher education relies on 'soft money' either funny or phoney?

* * *

Hell-Bent People—a Hidden History
Part III

Witness to an Execution

Oh, what a terrible day … They executed him. His head bounced off, and so continued to bounce across the public square like a handball. People swerved into one another in their trying to avoid it. Nonchalantly, the executioner wiped the blood from his arm with a towel. Then they moved in to dismantle the scaffold as quick as they could … Oh, what a terrible day, what a terrible day …

Konstantin Sluchevsky, 'After Witnessing an Execution in Geneva' (prose paraphrase)

Although first starting off with a rapidly bouncing and bound-to-be-brief history of heaven, before then moving over to a hidden history of hell-bent people (since there are always two sides to every algebraic equation), this book does not subscribe to a bare-bones writing style. The reason for this should be obvious—that in every angelic relationship (whether by the provision of a burning bush, an edible scroll, or the dictation of some last and final word), there should always be sufficient incentive given to the recipient to scratch his or her head as to what the angelic author really means.

It follows from this head-scratching formula that every worthwhile book (whether fiction, non-fiction, or mixed fiction) should entail a fairly serious measure of head-scratching. Thus, anyone who sees the vision or reads the word without submitting himself or herself to any self-administered measure of head-scratching (formerly known as soul-searching) ought to be put out to pasture. Wherever sheep may safely graze (as did also King Nebu) is as good a mode of recovering one's spiritual senses as any other.

Today's production line system (of so-called higher education) is all against this baptismal immersion into the life of the scholar, however, since, when once under the control of the Counterfeit

Command, the time and trouble spent on this educational immersion fails to squeeze the last buck (which indeed may be the very last buck) out of education. Why is it so much the fate of institutional life—whether in ancient Athens, modern Moscow, or lively London—to be so completely taken over by the Counterfeit Command?

Providential soul-food (crack the shell first to find the kernel) rarely comes on a silver platter. Soft-selling any prophecy (don't try it) whether to Abraham, Jonah, John the Baptist, or Jesus Christ is unlikely to bear the smallest fig of righteous fruit. At the very least, what's foretold must be put on the world market (nothing less) at a high enough cost to the purchaser to set him or her back on their heels. Think what that very first Hail Mary given by the angels cost to Mary and at what little cost it's passed on to you!

Marketing the heavenly creation is bound to set the whole wide world back on its heels. Bringing heaven to earth (it's already here, you know) or replacing both with some new earth and new heaven is no soft-sell transaction either. The cost factor prohibits any more stylistic soft sell. But then perhaps you/youse mere mortals (apart from the odd author, dancer, and musician) are not too fussed about stylistic matters. You'd like a straight pitch as expected from the shoulder of the Supreme Command rather than a queasy underarm from the Counterfeit Command. Non-stylistic scientists say likewise, since Einstein also claimed to be no more fussed about matters of style (than he mistook other matters for being non-matters), although God still saw fit to savour his style.

From what began, entitled simply as *The Soul-Catcher*, this same *Soul-Catcher's Handbook* or perhaps even *Soul-Catcher's Safety Net* could, with more positivity, develop into what we angels think would be more revered for being *The Soul-Catcher's Delight*. But then again on earth, you mortals are often hell-bent on either form or function (and so on account of this somewhat hellish and falsely exclusive disjunction between these two so closely coupled non-integers of form and function (neither of which is complete in itself), then this disjunction gives rise to warring factions). That's not so in heaven, however, where we focus more relaxedly on style (as part of the unified field theory by which to balance and integrate both all life forms (upwards from the smallest protein particle) and all life functions (from myth and fairy tale to metaphysics and all eternity (∞) beyond).

Yet from its increasingly introduced negativity (contra *The Soul-Catcher's Delight*), this book which began as a military report (entitled simply *The Soul-Catcher*) could already be backtracking to find itself remarkably reduced to being no more than *The Sadducee's Fright*. That too, for being something of a hellish compromise between positivity and negativity (instead of their heavenly resolution as expected by the Supreme Command), might well, from the unexpected turn then taken by this report, give even the Supreme Command at least something of a little unexpected fright. [Exegesis 1: It has been proven (by five concurring universities and only four against) that at least a modicum of stress is not only beneficial to all of us but is also most critically needed for those to function at their best in high command.]

Since time moves on faster (and not just on and on) and so faster and faster than most mortals can find enough space to keep up with its increasing pace, we angels might recommend preserving our own neutrality (instead of positivity or negativity). We further recommend that this neutrality might be maintained (as angelically supported by us) by ourselves staying static on the sidelines (as mere reporters of both the expected as well as of the unexpected). We think that this neutrality could be achieved more simply than ever before (since simplicity is an attribute of style, although not always of function) by renaming this book *The Safety Net*. No, let's be more specific—*The Soul-Catcher's Safety Net*!

You may think (don't stress) that we've been through this issue of naming (such is part of every birthing process even of a book) many times before. Why not, since to call Jesus instead as Jacob (for some 'respectable' reasons, the obvious choice) and/or to call John who would become John the Baptist instead of Zacharias the Baptist (also at the time the most obvious and respectable of reasons) would cause some critically serious problems later.

As already first said, however, it is not our angelic intention (nor our angelic objective) to pursue a bare-bones writing style; nor would (1) that style suffice for any howsoever brief history already given of heaven, far less than (2) expose any more succinctly the already dried-up bones we have already exhumed as required of any bare-bones history of hell. Nevertheless, it must still remain our angelic mission (however improbable this must appear to mortal minds) not to sacrifice the detailed smallness, say, of protein particles (as viable life forms) from our ongoing description any more than to sacrifice the overall stylistic function (by which we could best communicate the conjoint forcefulness of both form and function) when, without such heavenly understanding by humans themselves of the formal forcefulness of stylistic functions, neither heaven itself nor earth itself nor hell itself would make the slightest sense at all to mortals (which reads to us angels for being a hell-bent suggestion coming out of the Counterfeit Command at the highest satanic level).

Do you like equations—and not just the easiest of earthly equations but those most perplexing heavenly equations (such as the first shall be last)—for so often being the reverse of earthly equations? Trick question, since, like reading books, they can be either exceedingly hard or very hard to decipher in terms of the eternal truth or else fairly easy or even very easy to decipher in terms of this world's apparent truth.

Likewise, you need a certain stylistic understanding by which to realise that neither heaven nor hell are the stand-alone entities you case-hardened humans would like to find them (for their being so much easier to think of them to be). And they are even less stand-alone entities than they have ever been since Jesus Christ brought the kingdom of heaven down to earth, so they require a good deal more caution exercised for the purpose of their deciphering.

It's as if ever since the advent of Jesus Christ in his coming to earth, all the clergy have been done out of their jobs (and that would look to be even more of the case if all believers took up their prescribed earthly calling of being priests, prophets, and kings). And yet the deciphering process (so intriguing to those with a logico-mathematical bent) is still exactly the same (however much more precisely different). In other words, since the advent of Jesus on earth, Moses is no less of a holy moly than he was before the advent—and as we shall again witness shortly before the end of time, when the figures of both Moses and Elijah return to resume and fulfil their end-time roles according to the book of Revelation.

That's exactly why we angels will show ourselves not only to heavenwards-looking humans (who can be just as case-hardened as any other sort of human) but also regularly show ourselves to hell-bent humans as often with no earthly holds barred. As already said, this book (with both Moses and Elijah as well as Jesus amidst the hell-bent) is a very mixed bag (but for saying so, that doesn't curtail different deciphering responses, since Jesus also was hell-bent for the purpose of redeeming those in hell).

Neither heaven nor hell can make any further sense whether here, there, or anywhere else without first accepting the historical authenticity of Christ's advent to earth, his death and resurrection, his hell-bent mission to redeem souls from hell, and his reiterated promise of his own apocalyptic return to earth, as well as of his already fulfilled promise to send a constant counsellor to guide those on earth until his return. This is the substantive text (some of which still unseen) to which any stylistic context must conform by which to maximise every attempt at angelic communication. Quite frankly, it's of more communicative worth to hard-sell than to soft-sell any earthly closing-down sale, where almost every last shopper is fighting over the last of this earth's limited resources, which shortly won't be worth a penny (far less a dime).

Paradoxically speaking, it may take more of an atheist (such as Franz Kafka, who wrote on the topic of queueing for heaven) than it falls to many believers to understand more accurately (if never precisely) just what is required for admission to heaven. For the sake of two abstractions, as if chemically combined to produce the most intimately integrated of non-integers (for each being neither complete in itself), this combination is indecipherable from earth, except step by step, according to the already highly detailed formula expressed by Jesus Christ himself in his own book of Revelation. To this most logically and mathematically complete equation, nothing less will do, nor anything more can or dared be added.

The combination (as for most equations, no matter whether of an earthly or heavenly nature) relies for its expression and understanding on a matter of faith. Call it intellectual faith if you like, whether for its holistic expression on all levels (whether the logical, legal, or linguistic or whether the aesthetic, artistic, or scientific or whether the physical, metaphysical, or spiritual), to express (stylistically or functionally) the essence of life itself, without which both stylistic understanding (compare the faith with which we accept the double helix of the DNA equation), neither heaven nor hell could make any sense at all.

It's not a matter of breaking the encryption; since there's no saying where that may take us. Instead, it's a matter of first comprehending the full significance of the encryption. Accordingly, our pursuit of worshipful comprehension is most cautiously based on our humanly limited capacity for intellectual, moral, and jurisprudential understanding.

It will be our angelic (as well as apostolic) intention to retain each and all these alternative life forms (the logical no less than the linguistic, the historic no less than the prophetic, the intuitive no less than the rational, the poetic no less than the prosaic) for the sake of each contributing to their cumulative literary function). This is done, even although likely to be dismissed for not subscribing to what otherwise (for being arithmetic rather than algebraic and for being arthritically immobilised rather than dynamically evocative) would serve many less than serious readers (worse in the long run) for being a bare-bones writing style. Their turn will come with what follows in the next fourth book of this series to which, unless straightened out, they are already hell-bent to enjoin for contributing to that bare-bones history of hell.

On the other side of this same stylistic equation, however, neither is the algebraic series (of these twelve books in one for the cost of one) more corpulent than any such series of these books needs to be. This is so, even although the anorexic bare-bones of the next book (on what it could already mean to the hell-bent for any present lack of awareness in their heading to hell) may be for them to so mistake the midlife corpulence of this book for being either grotesquely overweight and/or functionless, that they never graduate to heaven from either being already hell-bent as to distinguish that personal choice from its next stage of being hell-sent.

Yet big and small (like first and last) are not just relative but also (like heaven and hell) reciprocal equations (either authentic or counterfeit) of the same reality. This cosmic relativity (as between the angelic and the humanistic, for instance) nevertheless affects the cosmic reciprocity (as seen by humans) to counteract rather than to implement the worldly reciprocity (for instance, of good and evil or of male and female or of odd and even or, as in the case of this book, big or small).

Sometimes (as throughout this book) it can be very difficult (whether going from heaven to hell or coming back from hell to heaven) to see where we are going, and of course, it's the same with every very big (and often unexpected issue) and even the same for every very small (and yet apparently expected issue) in life. This sometimes paradox, sometimes problem, sometimes paradigm, and sometimes even whatever excruciating dilemma any of these may present evokes the very same humanistic relativity which perplexes human sense perception, as it does whenever we are coming out from what has been to oneself consolatory darkness but then suddenly, startlingly, and most unexpectedly as if into the searing pain of blinding light. What's small (like any little baby at first instance) can grow into the one and only Jesus Christ (for being in cosmic terms the biggest figure in any history, whether of what we see of there being any heaven or hell or of any other possible and/or impossible configuration at all).

The first thing one sees on first coming into the light (which point of entry may be through the light of teaching or of preaching) is very often abject darkness. That's why the first part of this report on the prevailing darkness is so much longer than will account for the far shorter fulfilment of its breakthrough. This breakthrough, whether slow or fast, invariably comes through revelation. [Exegesis 2: The human lifetime is by now quite short, so even if the revelation takes—or, as for any Abraham or Moses or Esther or Christ, long exceeds that person's earthly lifetime—the breakthrough, whenever it comes, is always sudden for being by then least expected and, as a test of faith for others, crucial to fulfilling their part in the ongoing paradigm, pilgrimage, or narrative plot.]

As to fulfilling the ongoing plot, humanity (take Machiavelli as an extreme example, so also Haman, and perhaps so too Samson, for not even the strongest of men is invincible) invariably gets caught up on the tactical means at the expense of the strategic mission. The strategic mission, whether seen to be a marathon or a short sprint (in whichever direction) is not just determined by the short-term or long-term runner but by either the Supreme Command or the Counterfeit Command, as the freely chosen sponsors of the runners. Defeating the darkness can be a long-term mission, no less than training to break the record for a short sprint can be a long-term mission. Don't talk here or think here about fairness until you can be sure (never usually in the short-term present) as to what exactly are the stakes.

Indeed, one's soul can be blinded by first light (whether instantaneously for a fast learner or incrementally for a slow learner) to see nothing at first (or at last) but deep darkness. Sure, it may take a slow learner longer to retrace his or her steps (by self-reflection) from any such state of first blindness and then yet to travel far further (and yet far further still) than it takes for a fast learner (initially) to jump a fault line (as it opens), to brave the breakers (to save a child), to brave the sea swell (to catch up with one's wayward yacht), or even to raise a family (which can be sadly mistaken for travelling far less).

Here's a constant nightmare. 'Stalin [may have] died yesterday,' as the poet Robinson Jeffers proclaimed the day after his death. But then 'watch how soon blood will bleach [especially when covered over with fast-falling snow]' and so let 'gross horror become [these] words in a book'. Do you get the point, or must you also read Aleksandr Blok's poem *The Twelve* (on which these twelve books are modelled) to find out how much of the history of heaven (focussed on the pilgrimage of the human soul) is fought not up in heaven and not down in hell but here on earth? Neither heaven nor hell nor even earth are matters of location, location, location.

Let us pose a riddle. Whenever people (who themselves are in the dark) are drawn to search for any heaven (known to be in the light), that is not at all the same sort of (space-time) situation as when people (who themselves are in the light) go searching for an unknown heaven (which is in the dark). The (space-time) distinction is a subtle one, since each sort of people (by their own respectively different mission) risk mistaking counterfeit lights for the one and only righteously real light, which is the one, through Jesus Christ, that came only with first light. We can call a lot of people baba (for being often a baby's first word to mean daddy), but whether known or unknown, the only one way to the ultimate Father in heaven is through brotherhood with Jesus Christ, who brought his and our Father's kingdom to earth. For some people, even for many people, this is not any sweet dream, far less glorious reality, but rather for them, it is a nightmare, a nightmare, a nightmare! This is no place for psychoanalytic jurisprudence, but for the very long haul, that's often the only thing that can help.

We make all sorts of allowances for dreamtime, but not even the name, far less the concept of dreamtime, is accurate; for there is no time, as such, before first light—no time at all to be sure of the way, the truth, and the life without first light. So don't go into the dark without a good guide—whether to Geneva or to Paris or to Montreal or to any other end of this now loose-ended world—since not even the most faithful Jew in Jerusalem is immune by reason of his or her own time, his or her own space, or his or her own place. It's a proven fact of this life right now that time, space, and place have never been more up for grabs.

'His head bounced off and so continued to bounce across the public square like a handball.' That was in Geneva, but the same thing goes on day after day, even in the little places like the deep south of Palmerston North or when touched by the cold shoulder of Stonehaven or Glensaugh in Kincardineshire and even in the midst of each day's solitary Slavic struggle for life along the length of Lenin Prospect in one of a thousand former Soviet cities. Here, in the foothills of some police state, tread carefully, since the prisons are housed as often barely below the main street, and even passing footfalls in the snow are monitored 24/7 from beneath the footpath.

On any less than Lyubimova Avenue in Minsk (the equivalent of Straight Street in Damascus) to reach the seventh-floor apartment where you might then live, always use the lift. Don't climb the stairs. When people sleep, they've learnt to sleep only lightly here. You'll waken those lightly sleeping citizens and those frightened, sleepless citizens, since only those personnel from KGB once used the stairs to block the stairs. Most of these big executions, which can happen anywhere—and at all hours of both day and night in big places like London, Washington, Edinburgh, Moscow, or Wellington—are done as unbidden as they may be unexpected, but of course, you may never pick them for happening (according to the most successful of subversive tactics) since as far as possible, they are perpetrated as long-term strategies against the youthfully innocent by giving them exactly what they want (and nothing more) by way of playschool education.

Those who grumble against God for such unexpected happenings (and there's both a righteous as well as an unrighteous way of doing this) complain that from all such mind-boggling events God is not even standing in the wings. The Supreme Command (following the example of MI5, CIA, KGB, SIS, NZSIS, etc.) does its best to keep itself out of the big picture. Those who grumble against God can vary from those who try to keep the lid on things through faint-hearted prayer as well as those who advocate turning the other cheek to those more passionate radicals who, like Simon the Zealot and John Brown, see the need to start a civil war. There's surely a thin ice here, which, of course, is the most terrifying of reasons (although untroubling to whistle-blowers) for explaining why, without doing any righteous grumbling, most people wouldn't think of grumbling to God any more than of grumbling to MI5, CIA, KGB, SIS, NZSIS, etc. about either his absence or his presence.

But then the trouble is—and it makes for a lot of trouble too—that on their own account of doing nothing, the non-grumblers then write off God for doing nothing, and then before they know it, voila, they've written off God for good! There are, of course, like the prophets of old, a few persistent grumblers; and for some reason or another, even when unknown to themselves, they won't give in. And so by means of their own apparent irrationality, they testify to the presence of God both by fiercely disputing his presence and their own refusal to shut up.

For the most part, this is the self-appointed prerogative of many atheistic physicists (of which Stephen Hawking was one), of many atheistic biologists (of which Richard Dawkins was another), and of many atheistic logicians (of which Bertrand Russell is the last we'll bother to mention), each to testify to the presence of God by so avidly disputing his presence. Is that their God-given mission? Because, otherwise, they don't seem to serve any sensible purpose than that of flailing the grain and winnowing the chaff.

* * *

Hell-Bent People—a Hidden History
Part IV

The Lord of Hosts *ats* Richard Dawkins
Once it is put together, a clock has no reason to fear, to respect, or to obey its maker. It must then be the purpose of science to exhibit the continuing and immediate supervision of divine Providence.
Charles Coulston Gillispie, *Genesis and Geology*

'What in hell is meant by *ats*?' asked Wormwood of his Uncle Screwtape on his suddenly bursting into Screwtape's boudoir for his uncle's long-accustomed advice and guidance as to how to confound believers. He did so, as usual without even knocking, but then struck dumb, although still replete with a snide smile, as if to find his uncle unceremoniously engaged in dishevelling the undergarments off a very minor minor.

'Frig off, will you, coming in here at this time of night, and that only to ask yet another bloody question! As like as not, *ats* is a typo misnomer for *ants*. Take a punt at whatsoever odds youse likes on *ants*! As you ought to well know (for being down here in hell amongst split infinitives), all our allotted time is at an unholy premium!'

'Hell's teeth, as you might well have guessed from being in hell, it's a legal term!' said Screwtape on consulting his *Legal Dictionary for Lynching Laymen Lawmen*. Of this *Legal Dictionary*, Screwtape prided himself on being its editor-in-chief, although, of course, he left all the lesser work of its compilation to be carried on by those who did his legal devilling. Nevertheless, as he often boasted of this lynching law book for being his very own magnum opus, it had been frequently cited (almost always by himself) when pleading before the council of heaven.

Never hard-copied (which might prove to constitute evidence against him), Screwtape nevertheless carried the virtual forcefulness of lynch law wherever he went on his more than mildly satanic state-of-the-art e-phone. 'Why, *ats* stands for *at the suit of*, as in this clear case when the Lord of Hosts himself is being brought before the courts on a charge, such as that of the present,' he said in his giving the finger to heaven, 'of perpetrating what we all know in hell to be the same as ever unholy and irreligious nonsense.

'Hey, lads, then at the double, we've got a law case once more on our hands. Let's make the most of it!' Screwtape called to his minions, one of whom crawled out from under the bed and another from behind the wardrobe door, as he threw a robe to his dishevelled daughter-in-law. Alas, this is just one more of these all too ugly scenes becoming more and more common amongst hell-bent people. All the same, don't even begin to worry, for there's none so hell-bent, which, by virtue of the right reverse thrust from heaven, can't be straightened. Even over that mechanistic thinking by which the bent is bent is bent, the openly metaphysical exerts first priority through prayer.

'Nevertheless, and it's not so hard to see [that, for the benefit of his nephew Wormwood, his Uncle Screwtape is going to continue giving his party piece of imitating God] that even on account of one's own persistent ignorance, anyone (at least from earth) should sometimes risk seeking to chew God's ear. At the worst, he'll say'— whilst still speaking in his accustomed most fatherly way—'"Stop tickling, will you ... I'm trying hard to concentrate on this very big and precious problem of how you physicists on earth regard quantum mechanics, and at this most precious moment, although I've got all the wherewithal, which you on earth don't have down there, you're only getting yourself (as *you* would say) in *my* goddamn way!"

'So then head off, will you,' as any good shepherd would say to his sheep (although 'piss off' is what, like any backbiting flea, you're still as likely to say to me, your sergeant-major). 'Believe me, you're not only by now too big for your boots—take them off soldier—but also by now, according to your own short-sighted way of blowing up yet a bigger and bigger military operation (once code-named Desert Storm), you're not even in your own eyes big enough (when the tide of war turns, as it always will turn) either then or now to stick up for yourself! You haven't learnt much from your time in Vietnam, have you, and yet despite all the ancient history of Afghan, Arab, Pashtun, and more and the prevailing geography of the Khyber and of the Bolan, you're still wading into what remains of the same old problem of the North-West Frontier!

'So then go and levitate to the likes of "giant lumbering robots" like Richard Dawkins, who hasn't yet learnt to control his "selfish genes". So then too, head off please into the wilderness of this world's fifty thousand ardent atheists (who, amongst themselves in their self-interest to be amongst this world's most famous fifty, have learnt only to count as far as being no more than the most famous fifty).' As you can guess from this riposte (after his own quick and not altogether honest count), Uncle Screwtape didn't make it into the most famous 500,000 atheists.

'Will you then [although not sure right now who's speaking] not back off from heaven (since theology is a poor substitute for this world's more direct action)? Besides, learning to deal with the default position in world affairs is not mine any longer but actually now yours. [Be sure to test the spirits, won't you!]

'Think then too, won't you, to do a bit of whistle-blowing for yourselves if you like, or else learn Urdu for the benefit of those who speak Urdu. Or perhaps even eavesdrop in on the military leadership in Myanmar (formerly Burma, I believe). Well, will you, or won't you, if, as it seems to us in the Supreme Command, that you're so stuck for being at such a loose end around this house of heaven right now as to be invading my inner temple of intellectual, moral, legal, logical, and political repose—but all to no good purpose but relieving yourself of responsibility—in the outer courts where it lies—so it seems.

'Meanwhile, the choice [whose choice?] either to sit on my divine hands (which the Supreme Command wouldn't enjoy) or else to do the job yourselves is precisely yours. For goodness' sake, that job is one given by us in the Supreme Command to youse humans (*Chto-to, chto-to*—again pardon the parlance), or haven't you heard? Why else would we in the Supreme Command have invested free will in any otherwise "gigantic lumbering robots"—do you think (or not think)?—and more especially in any gigantic lumbering idiots, sorry, robots who were 'controlled by [selfishly stupid] genes'? Much good may it do to suggest, but any such professor of much little understanding needs his head read!'

It's not all that hard (which is why most folks wouldn't want to go 'up') in order to get 'sent down' from Oxford or Cambridge, or as the humourist Tom Scott did to relieve himself from Palmerston North Veterinary School (somewhere in the North Island of the South Pacific). In poor Tom's case (the case of *Muldoon* v. *Scott*, as overly reported but never set down), prime ministerial passion had risen to the highest of journalistic levels (as frequently happens in the most apathetic of countries) where whenever the flat ground shakes, only the mountains are left to blow their tops. Presumably, instead of his being needed to look after mere animals in the course of studying veterinary science, the Supreme Command had something more in mind by way of political preferment for poor Tom (for his being the least of anyone like the Vicar of Bray) in giving him over to the tending of parliamentarians.

Why, even from churches and other places of sanctuary, old hands to the spiritual plough get picked off suddenly (as did poor Tom). They say (what they say, let them say) that such bad happenings are always done by the Counterfeit Command, but those who grumble against God for such bad happenings can have their doubts, which is one terrifying reason for so many of the best guys being dispatched from politically active service. They are heard of no more, as if for them to have disappeared just as suddenly from the face of the earth and into the Gulags, and stands for their having become non-persons. Sovietism has spread all around since the fall of the Wall and the demise of the former Soviet Union.

Nobody really quite knows what happens to such non-persons, but everybody knows not to ask. In tsarist Russia, you'd be sent to Siberia; in the Stalinist Soviets, you'd be made to serve time in the Gulags; whilst in much-the-merrier England, you'd be either sent to Coventry (to rebuild the cathedral) or deported to the Colonies (to work the sugar plantations). That's how great empires are built—on the principle of spreading thin and conquering greatly—which also explains how Gypsies, Jews, and Arabic-speaking strangers are held so suspect to those who consider themselves considerably the 'greater for having their own more masterfully able powers'.

Nobody gets an invitation to any of those executions. Just as often, however, they are promoted as farewell celebrations (but not funereal celebrations)—to which everyone goes just to show their complete lack of self-condemnation. There may be a golden handshake here and there, even for a parachute drop (instead of a free fall), and the last to know may be the leader of things, like some dean of arts, law, or science or else some football hero or even some chancellor of the exchequer (especially if he or she is the one to be dropped from such a great height). Once upon a time, scapegoats were despatched to wander the wilderness, but now the preferred method of public dispatch (which serves to keep minions in order) is first to be promoted by general acclamation and thence to be dropped from that earlier mentioned greatest of heights.

Beware too of false humility! If, even at the gates of heaven, you put yourself down, you might not quite measure up to paying the admission fee, so it helps to remember that the fellow who asks you to grease his palm on this side of eternity is an imposter. No, for the sake of your false modesty in putting yourself down, you are likely only to be complimented on your self-awareness by all the others trying to push past you through the gates of heaven.

Nevertheless, the resultant drop may not always be downwards, as you may find out when you get to heaven and ask some of the popes who got there. But be gentle with them, and don't ask them why they're then dressed in rags and no longer in riches. Most of them would testify to the almost unbearable responsibility of being Vicar of Christ on earth (whether or not their learning from that office was the last straw in qualifying them to enter heaven). And that's the way promotion in this life should be understood—as an expression of being entrusted with greater responsibility.

Nevertheless, most people, on looking for personal promotion or asking for advancement, are really asking for trouble. If they haven't been promoted as of right, then they're not likely to benefit from being promoted as of wrong. Instead, they need a shake-up, which they may well get from being promoted (which sooner or later turns out to be the trouble they've been looking for) instead of their biting the bullet by deciding to find another job. You should know by now, surely, that the Supreme Command runs the biggest employment agency both in heaven or on earth and that the Counterfeit Command has no show of doing so except by doing away with all work in hell.

Nothing personal, you understand, although some people have to drop office (from a very great height) just to enter heaven. It helps to understand all promotion—whether of someone to professor, to prison manager, to attorney general, or to chief justice or of anyone else just from scullery maid to kitchen maid—as providing a trap or drop beneath one's feet to be opened or taken away at one's time of execution.

Unless seen as something that heightens and not lessens one's responsibility, the promoted result of mistaken advancement can be disastrous. Most people, if they knew what was behind their proffered promotion, would unhesitatingly turn it down. They would read the signs of the times for that so-called advancement in their career being the first cut (whether academic, political, legal, moral, or social) as leading to their death by a thousand cuts.

This sort of execution (slow, fast, or intermediate) invariably takes place (as for the leading agent reporting Sluchevsky's case in Geneva) just as you've come to misbelieve your own place in the sun to be impregnable. Some folks pray for a fast death; others would like to postpone the inevitable to the interminable. Does it matter much whether it is by the axe (Mary, Queen of Scots) or by the rope (John Brown) or by the book (William Tyndale) or by any other means, including 'death by a thousand cuts', since for China alone, as this world's only remaining communist nation, it too can be treated as 'the exceptional case'?

In any other more ordinary case, aren't all such sorts of execution legal? Well, a great deal of Book 3 is bound to be about the law. This is because we profess to be bound and governed by the rule of law (and not by the rule of conquest), although sometimes we can profess to be bound by values that turn out to be false, no less than we can falsely profess true values. All the same, because we profess ourselves to be bound and governed by the rule of law, a great deal of this book (and too much for many, if not most), readers, is going to be about the law.

The price of peace (even if no more than that of enjoying domestic comfort) is, as they say, that of eternal vigilance. The trouble with just keeping the peace, however, is that to the most successful peacekeepers, no less than to all their minions, the situation becomes intolerably soporific. The best intentioned of us all (RIP) can mistake heaven for Sleepy Hollow and Sleepy Hollow for heaven!

Even domestic situations need a bit of stirring up from time to time, whilst for huge nations (not to mention mammoth confederations and fast-shrinking commonwealths), well, they can't do without an Ivan the Terrible, a Margaret Thatcher, a Nikita Khrushchev, or a Donald Trump. People like to think that they themselves pull all the strings. They forget that everything—absolutely everything—lies in either one or other of two places. All things lie snugly in the open palm of the Supreme Command or, if not lying snugly there, then are held together, all ready for action, in the tightly closed fist of just the same yet slow-to-anger Supreme Creator.

There's nothing wishy-washy about the Supreme Command, although if you overstay your time in some Sunday school, you'll never matriculate to any discipleship with Jesus Christ as he really is—*Sye Chelovek*—in terms of your need for a higher and more heavenly as well as closer-big-brotherly and yet down-to-earth relationship.

No, they (the real rulers of society, as they think of themselves) don't make for this world a very happy place, but until you get to heaven, you'll never see the fully funny side of life. That's one good reason—amongst many more—for avoiding the other, opposite, and very dismal place. Believe me, you wouldn't want to see that resting place or cooling-off chamber called by some as Sheol, by others Gehenna, and by yet others hell or Hades.

'Yet likewise for that toffy-nosed Supreme Command in its conquest of earth—*veni, vidi, vecum,*' (as so said in hell), 'then here now too for that same insufferable supremacy of command by reversing its roles (again batting back upon our own heads) one of our very own and best conceived of strategic policies) so that this self-same mantra of *veni, vidi, vecum* (as we first so blithely generated) now wings all the way back (albeit in fierce descent) to roost on our very own Sheol, Gehenna, and Hades! 'And so—yet with no holds barred—*he* (you know whom we mean) once again broke down all our precious strongholds,' expostulated that same now nerve-wracked but yet still self-postulating titulary head of the Counterfeit Command.

'Oh, woe is me (but don't either say, far less think of *mea culpa* down here). Thus did *he* decommission our own prohibited entry to all of the above (yet deeply-rooted-down) places—and executed every such highly deleterious home invasion for no more than his own inane purpose' here again scoffed the same titulary head (of whom there are more than one-and-a-half thousand of the same such genetically cloned satans in hell) still in strictest servitude and belonging to this now down-sized Counterfeit Command. 'And all for the inane purpose,' so this highly hay-fevered titulary satan chose (by way of compulsive confession) to continue, 'of pulling up Confucius, Buddha, Socrates, and all the other pre-Christian heroes into the everlasting light of that blue-eyed bastard, Jesus Christ.

'Never mind, we can always fix things up with a neutron bomb. It only kills people, but doesn't harm property,' rationalised another titulary satan, with his one fat finger already on five small buttons ...

'Meanwhile, however, just as every last stone was once rolled away, so also no lesser stone has been left unturned now by that stupid one-eyed Supreme Command,' snidely snuffled yet another, this time highly hay-fevered and defeatest titulary satan— but such is their hellish persuasiveness of both intellect and rhetoric, that, in this report (as picked up on earth only third-hand from hell and transmitted heavenwards by agents in the field who are no more than mortal) we angels have no way at present of extracting, far less conveying the slightest splinter of underlying truth.

So shalom, or peace be with you, say the still wandering Jews whilst holding back their tears (although those firmly settled ones— for reasons best not told—are silent); and this policy of holding back the tears whilst caught out in the midst of yet another pogrom will at least help you, a benighted goy (although wearing your biggest of bigwigs instead of your shortest of side locks), to at least try whilst even still on earth to see always, even through your copious tears, also the funny side of life. This funny side of life, although so sad (the *smeshno-grustno* equation for the Russians performing bears), is the best indication of what it takes for you humans to get to heaven.

But as it stands, you humans have (what to us angels) very unfunny (*nyesmeshnye*) ideas of heaven and so, in consequence, very non-sad (*nyegrustnye*) ideas of what it actually takes to get to heaven. Any herring (no more than the size of some headless Baltic sardine) would have a better idea (even when smoked and salted) than most humans have of heaven. To quote Lermontov (since it takes thus a Scots-Russian poet) to sum up this pathetic equation of *smeshno-grustno*, since 'this life would have been all so funny had it not been also so sad!'

Laugh off this life, as you may do, to avoid seeing anything of this life's sad, seamy side, and yes, you may very well choose to eat, drink, and be merry until you die. But don't you know, especially you stiff-lipped lot of macho males (as so extended by the learnt ruthlessness of today's now self-liberated females), that the Supreme Command collects up every single tear that's shed on earth? There's a purpose to everything, as you'll find out why, if only when you get to heaven, and that's where the question mark on your life, whether as a writer or reader, expresses a profound truth and not a scurrilous lie.

This is one reason why the world's celebrities should always be aware of self-inflicted celebrations—the equivalent of masochistic self-flagellations. Celebrating their life and work, even when given by their lesser lights, very soon gives way to a funeral service to accompany every celebrity's future or present internment. The world turnover of celebrities is extremely fast—on which subject read Danielle Steel's *Amazing Grace*—and with the daily slowing in the speed of light to explain the quickening passage of time, that turnover becomes as much a meteoric burnout in their descent (as did that of another leading light) as this can be so often mistaken for the bright morning star in their ascent.

But unless, like the poet Konstantin Sluchevsky (forget for the moment that he's a Russian Jew in Geneva), you have anywhere witnessed a physical execution, you won't know, unless by reason of transformational metaphysics, just how close to one another are both the figurative and the physical dimensions. [Here's room surely for another exegesis, this time on metaphysics, since—apart from Aristotle, the founder of metaphysics—there's so much rabbiting on by metaphysicians far removed from physics, and by physicists so far removed from metaphysics, the transformational awareness from one to the other is lost by boxing up their static separation apart from one another. Rather than recognising their dynamic, interactive, and transformational potential for each other, their functionality is thus imprisoned.]

456

We couldn't do better, here then, than to quote Marianne Williamson, who, when writing on work, money, and miracles in her book *The Law of Divine Compensation*, would remind us that since *meta* means 'beyond', the key to us humans on earth who are so often trapped in the physical is to look beyond the physical and so into the metaphysical. Quite frankly, there's not much [more than from any other life-or-death issue] to pick between the physical and the metaphysical, as in the case of executions, where there's a bit of blood, a bouncing head, a botched injection, a blunt axe, a mistaken identity, a power failure, a mislaid reprieve, a frayed rope, a stuck trap, a wrong knot, a wrong jury, a wrong judge—there is so much extraneous detail to divert us from the fundamental life-or-death issue.

Quite frankly, the enormity of the Christian crucifixion lies in the figurative dimension of that transcendentally cosmic event rather than in its mundanely physical, earthly, and solely static dimension. Exaggerate the commonplace horrors of the purely physical, and you will miss entirely the transformational power of the metaphysical message. Don't you understand that God so loved the world … so loved the world … so loved the world … that … that … that … he would thereby set in motion not just the half-measured recreation of what went before, but instead of that recreation (which for mortals to their own way of thinking has become nothing more than an earthly soft-option for more serious living), but instead the entirely new creation of his promised new earth and promised new heaven.

We're all believers, but the question is (as always) that of exactly what it is in which we believe. Every believer (and we are all, like Scarlett O'Hara in *Gone With the Wind*, believers in something), even the most atheistic of scientists (no names here please), will be a steadfast believer in his or her own figurative expressions of a non-transcendental reality that leaves no room for more than man himself in responding to any other than his own expression of any different version of a figurative reality.

There's a need for another sermon here (as indicated by the Supreme Command) so we'll move (keep yourself covered) from whichever state is (ambiguously) nearest to Georgia—whether in the Deep South either of the USA or (to employ an inclusive disjunction) then also, of the USSR—now to McDonald's in Moscow (try Tverskaya), where our itinerant and ubiquitous preacher (able to be in so many places at once) is boldly haranguing the queues (now much shorter than before he began) on the need for heavenly aspirations (under the watchful eye of the local *militzia* (whether civil, military, or (in whatever name and nature) the more scary security—take your pick). [Editorial correction: There *is* still a need for another, and much longer sermon here, so 'keep your patience' as our Scots sergeant-major always tells us instead of 'hold your fire'. We'll move from whichever state—whether formerly Soviet and/or still continuingly American—making no difference to us angels for being nearest to Georgia (in the Deep South either of the presumably continued USA and/or of the former USSR). And now then, for a trip first to McDonald's in Moscow (as said before, try Tverskaya), where (under the watchful eye of the local militzia) our itinerant preacher is haranguing the queues (now still again much shorter than before he began) on the earthly need ('dire' he said, and still 'says') for heavenly aspirations.]

Hey, this preacher looks uncommonly like the young Stalin— the very young Stalin—before he was expelled from the religious seminary and so reverted, like the Antichrist to world politics, instead of following his first calling towards heavenly righteousness. On this score, be sure to read Simon Sebag Montefiore on the subject of the young Stalin. Even if without time to read this detailed biography (in which the devil appears over and over again in the details) at least look at the pictures, each of which will grab you as to what it takes for any younger Stalin to grow into a much older Stalin. Alas, but to quote from my colleague Connor's farewell to our one-time Uncle Joe, 'few men by their death can have given such deep satisfaction to so many.' But then—and not at all to change the subject—have you ever met Stalin's mother—the delightful Ekaterina Dzhugashvili— who is still indeed, such a wonderful old lady? For that, as said before, we must visit a different and 'often-neglected Georgia' (this time in the Russian Vice-Royalty of the Caucasus (brought to an end—long before McDonald's took over the world—way back in 1917)

I met Ekaterina on a much earlier mission in 1936, as the guardian angel of the author Eileen Bigland, then on her heroic and fantastic journey which took her from Moscow (where she met Stalin, then reported to the West by John Gunther for being the greatest *single* personality in the world and who was about to begin his political purging of the Soviet military). Eileen's trip took both of us across the mountains of the moon in her *Laughing Odyssey* and thence to Tiflis at the tail end of Europe, where it was that 'unexpectedly' we both met up with Stalin's mum.

'She was a darling,' we both decided of Ekaterina Dzhugashvali, Stalin's mum. 'Listening to her, I saw Stalin not as the towering figure in peaked cap, greatcoat, and high boots (like most self-inflicted world leaders, he was closer to being a midget) but as the little barefooted boy who had run errands for his mother through Tiflis streets and always brought her back a wild flower.'

Nevertheless, she worried so much (like any mother) about her younger son—Little Sozo, she still called him—for his being now so far away from his mother's tender care and for herself now remaindered helplessly so much further away from him in the benighted Caucasus. And so once more, she was praying for the same Little Sozo, whom she said would be stuck for a good night's sleep without his mother's goodnight story—stuck so firmly as he now would be behind the sleepless battlements of the world's only second-biggest armoury.

Nevertheless, just what's he talking about, this man of steel, this Great Helmsman of Holy Mother Russia? What does he mean (literally, when standing on the bare earth of the Gulags soaked by the blood of Cain)? What does he mean behind the fortified walls of the Moscow Kremlin when he talks in Old Testament terms so glibly about the priesthood of the law? He'd better look out (which is why he cannot get a good night's sleep) since there will up and come some President Kluchikov—stands to reason—who, with the Supreme Command's permission, will knock the man of steel off his Kremlin perch and replace him with ... with ... with ... perhaps no more than another and another and yet another talking parrot.

Oh, in the West, of course, with benefit of parallel translation, the priesthood of the law is called the rule of law, just as when left to the Jews still untranslated, it is called the love of law; and yet to the Christians, likewise with parallel translation, it's called the curse of the law. And to us Jews (pardon that obscene reference to ourselves as if you'd know, unless from what it means to be a chosen race), it's been so watered down by the Talmud that to the Ashkenazi (or Akkadian) Jews, the Hasidic (or lovingkindness) Jews, not to mention the German Jews, the Forfar-Bridie Jews, as well as the British Israelites, it means something as different to each of us as are the days of the week.

Quite … quite … quite obviously (as the English would say), this excessively itinerant preacher's son is not Orthodox (whether Judaic, Slavic, Greek, Catholic, or Presbyterian), nor yet is he of any Congregationalist, Adventist, or much earlier persuasion. But he could be Lutheran or maybe Luthran (as some folks might mistake this for being a different denomination—so we wouldn't want to leave the devil in the details for lack of the fullest explication. So too, possibly even Church Lutheran (as in Chekhov's short story of The Fat and the Lean—so forget Roman Polanski here, who surely borrowed his book's title from Chekhov). But then perhaps (on having checked to find Chekhov the author of the short story and not, as first thought Gogol) so then by now not excessively Church Luthern for the fact that he (meaning by now the excessively itinerant preacher's son) takes his coat off to preach rather than do many more Orthodox avail themselves of orthodoxy (Genesis 3:10–11) by putting more clothes on.

Everyone on the scaffold (unless when seated whilst heavily sedated in some electric chair) is entitled to the utmost benefit of clergy—before his or her life is concluded with a sermon. Preferably this sermon should be on the responsibilities of mankind rather than on the rights of man; otherwise, any such sermon on the rights might well reduce both clergyman and executioner either to tears on the topic of capital punishment or else to boredom on the alternative rights of this man to that man and of that other man to no other man. So here on the scaffold, whilst the traps and ropes and knots are being provisionally inspected, what follows is a little less moving (for being a slighty more academic) sermon on the far more subtle subject of the priesthood of the law.

* * *

Hell-Bent People—a Hidden History
Part V

The Priesthood of the Law
I'm well aware that I'm speaking to those who think
themselves to know the law—but the law is limited
to this poor excuse for our present life; so then surely
something else is needed right here and now to waken
up the living-dead.

Apostle Paul, Letter to the Romans (7:1)

Since the devil is in the details (a once well-known maxim of now
long defunct equity), it has been left to the devil to liven up the law.
This he does first by juristic default and then by electrifying the legal
process with the capacitance of spurious regulatory detail. He thus
so deadens down the main grid of the legal system by doing away
with straightforward principle. This the devil also achieves by juristic
default, since dealing now with all the legal details most usually
makes it far too costly to go to law.

A recent jurisprudential survey conducted by a mid-western
university (of no little repute) has shown that in every court judgement
of more than 100 pages (the higher the court, the more the pages), the
more frequent the case (at odds of 500:1) to be decided (if decided
at all), then it will (or will not, as the case may require) be decided
on some very small hitherto unforeseen matter of the utmost detail.
By fixating on some hitherto entirely unforeseen and never before
judicially noticed detail (instead of grand-standing on some already
strongly established principle of law), many small-time judges have
learnt to cover their butts and thus avoid what might otherwise result
in a disparaging appeal.

Thus, the devil (in some courts both wigged and gowned
whilst in other courts both shaved and tonsured) is said to be in
the details (unless at common law instead of in equity) when the
case is unanimously held by law practitioners all around (unless
going on appeal) to be mainstream. Whether mainstream, upstream,

downstream, side stream, or subterranean, this is what is meant (mostly by jurists) in their constant debate as to whether the concept of law (in itself a moot point) is close-woven in texture, wide-open in flexure, or else so wave-like, corpuscular, or dendritic as to be more formal than functional (in applying only to lawbreakers at the lower levels) than more exclusively textured (to suit only the upper levels) in its task all round (as St Paul says) of wakening up the living dead.

Those who think themselves to know the law (far less than professing to practise the law as they themselves think to know it in any of the world's fast-proliferating legal systems) are invariably hell-bent people. The law, especially in its highly refined, most subtly concentrated, and universally cosmic form, can be extremely corrosive to the unrepentant human mind. And it is only the unrepentant person, whether lawyer or layman, who would flatter himself or herself to know, far less keep to, the law. But as for the judges, well, they flatter themselves (even openly in the law reports) to be either above the law or else by reason of dotage (a legal term) to be well beyond the law.

Besides, that's not all, since debating the efficacy of the universal law can be particularly toxic, if not downright deadly, to those who, with their inordinate pride, think themselves to know and thus always be able to administer the law. Nevertheless, a lawyer without humility is nothing but a Pharisee. Yet never fear, since even the proudest of Pharisees can be redeemed, although not always without their unredeemed (examples charitably withheld) from taking the mightiest of falls.

See here, it's a very funny view that humans project of themselves, since they erect so many more memorials to the fallen than they do to the redeemed. That's the biggest and most obvious difference between heavenly values and earthly values—that whether through the consequences of their own human actions or else through what they otherwise call natural disasters, mankind erects huge memorials to those who have fallen rather than, apart from their often vastly belated and token lip service, they do honour the efforts of the redeemed.

The history of heaven, when you come to think of it and when seen from above and beyond and not just as it seems from earth far below, is not just of the historical past but also of the prophetic future. Of course, for any prophet on earth, the past is never quite buried beneath the future than it seems buried so deeply beneath the present to those without any prophetic foresight. Of course, this is not what you humans are taught by your historians [so boringly] of your human history on earth—you know, the history of the world as you think it to be—which is the world you celebrate [or as often abuse, by your trying to hide behind your own humanly imagined world from heaven].

Alas again, then, for the human condition! There's only one sure thing that results from trying to hide one's own history from heaven, and that's hiding from yourselves what you try so well to hide from heaven. Why, by now you've so long ago forgotten one of the strangest controversies you humans could ever have engaged in—no, it wasn't how many of us angels could stand (far less dance) on the point of a pin [the answer to which song and dance is pg^2, where g stands for grace and not gravitas], but instead rather whether there are any laws in heaven!

Well, why should you not know the answer to that perplexing question now, since so many lawyers stand arguing on the forecourt of heaven without aspiring to enter—no, not even just the first court of heaven—and that the outer gates of heaven may close for them at any moment and so leave them outside for as long as there is still any forecourt? The first court of heaven is that of the Supreme Command, which is bound to require laws, since the rule of command requires reciprocal rules of obedience to command. [Exegesis 1: In earthly terms, what little of this is understood (despite being much misunderstood) is enforced on earth (and likewise in hell) for being known as the command theory of law. The command theory of law proliferates law to the point of the legal system's dysfunctionality, whereas the commonality of heaven (whether in heaven or on earth) most intimately integrates responsibility (both in terms of command and obedience) to the strategic purpose of its either completely or sufficiently understood functionality.]

Still in earthly terms, you might think that all lawyers would be intimately familiar with the command theory of law—if for no other reason than to exact their obedience to the law—but such is not the case, so an increasing multitude of lawyers go no further than the forecourt of heaven in their arguing over what is meant by requiring their obedience to the law.

Never mind, it's too early in the scheme of things to move on from the command theory of law whilst we're still arguing the toss with those lawyers in the forecourt (mostly Yids) as to what exactly is meant by obedience to the law. It's typically a Yiddish (or Old Testament) argument, so it could go on forever. But for some reason or another, if not only to decide the outcome, the non-Yids, despite their present penchant (or inclination towards) non-law, have a reluctance to participate in the command theory argument, which may well decide the outcome.

Well, once again, there is more than ample spiritual authority for wishing all the woes of the world on to lawyers, but at the same time, you humanists (so us angels contend) freely choose and profess to be ruled under the rule of law. Nevertheless, the law is such an ass, and most legal systems in such an international mess, if not already all in one and the same supranational morass, that non-lawyers might surely be forgiven (without even having any practicing certificate by which to give their legal counsel) nevertheless to advocate most strenuously against there being any laws in heaven.

Well, goodness gracious me, then from where do you think it is that both laws as well as all the best of lawyers come from? [It takes Comps 606 to learn that us heavenly hosts can sometimes get away with saying some things our own way provided we use an exclamation mark and then, like any stand-up comic, quickly change the subject.]

Why, even church history [in terms of what church historians mistake for being only facts and figures] would be just as boring as secular history were church history not so much out of touch with heaven. Instead, it is rather in terms of heaven's future-present (which comprises both the past imperfective as well as both the future perfect and the present indicative), which distinguishes the earth's present indicative from that of heaven. What we're pointing out here is really that most of what we [both the angelic host and humanistic society] identify for being hell on earth is man-made and not heavenly made and that there is some [more than slight] cause to believe [as all the historians in hell believe] that the fallen angels were infected with more than a sufficient humanly pride by which to excuse their angelic fall.

Alas, the logic of language, once taught for being the grammar on which communication and, in turn, the communion of like minds depends, is now so seldom taught and, in consequence, becomes so much abused for being imbued with non sequiturs [conclusions drawn falsely from their premises] as well as countless other invalidities that both such cause [linguistic abuse] and consequence [notional misapprehension] probably render the preceding paragraph irrecoverably incomprehensible to humans. Accordingly [because persistence is not just a human virtue but also a heavenly gift] we, in our angelic capacity, shall endeavour here [by taking a page out of the theologian's book] to exegete [or explain] where that first [leading paragraph] on distinguishing heaven's truly future [and so prophetic] present from earth's so truly false yet still presently here indicative.

Now the same present indicative on earth [where relativity rather than universal law now rules] can so easily be mistaken by today's humans for being either their own past perfective (the casual mistake of the sinful conservative) or else relying on rampant technology for their very own future perfect (the more purposeful mistake of the radical but still immensely sinful neo-liberal). Human history, rather than heavenly history, thus affords not much human choice, which tends to doom mankind towards experiencing his (and increasingly her) very own kind of self-imposed predestination.

It must be seen [before being able to be felt] that for human salvation from every concept of sin, there can be no allowably self-imposed predestination of the sort that is now so rife on earth. This very notion of human predestination is nothing but a throwback from hell, a recriminatory payoff for the [probably mythic] blame attached to humans for the way in which the Counterfeit Command claims to excuse itself from its heavenly fall by its historians pointing to the infective pride from which it suffers having been disseminated to them by first-afflicted humans.

It must be realised [in itself a compulsive expression so redolent of the Counterfeit Command] that despite all past data on the descent of man, those so sinful humans [for being so judgemental an expression, not one likely to be employed by the Supreme Command] therefore employ their own science fiction to espouse and proclaim the legal fiction by which their history teachers [most often so boringly in terms of the dates and figures] affirm the theological principle [rather than heavenly principle] of humanistic predestination.

Sadly, this principle of humanistic predestination is as often expressly, as it is implicitly, applied throughout all fields of human upbringing—from teaching to preaching, from judging to legislating, and from birthing to burying. *Sooner or later*, for being its own self-fulfilling prophecy, such humanistic predestination may well reap its own rotten harvest, unless by the fatherly grace of God, one hears with ears to hear and sees with open eyes that dare to look, by which to realise that any such humanistic doctrine can only be a device (usually intellectual) of some slightly sneaky devil under the aegis [Take in Higher Education 401] of the Counterfeit Command.

You feel yourself put down, spiritually asleep, deeply depressed, shut in or shut out, left all alone, completely abandoned, utterly doomed, or significantly suicidal—these are more than just the first signs of falling under the humanistic spell of predestination. So wake up, rise up, get up, move up, and keep moving. And don't exaggerate your past predicament by giving any mention, far less testimony or credit, to Satan; he probably hasn't even heard of you until (when at least halfway to heaven) you really start to bother him. He has more minions than you're ever likely to know about before you ever meet him.

Meanwhile, don't go AOL [absent without leave] from this book, before looking more closely to heaven, for seeing heaven itself this way—as a stand-alone concept, quite independently of either hell itself or of however much of hell may be on earth. You have no business to think of heaven and hell duplicitously. That will only split your mind, confuse your heart, and fragment your personality. Fix your sight by focussing entirely on heaven. Don't swither in maintaining your most determined heavenly focus! It doesn't help to give credence to Satan when, unless you're like Dr Faustus, you may never meet him! The Counterfeit Command is itself a counterfeit, which you can best recognise as such by maintaining your sole focus on heaven.

Let me tell you this [when caught in the act of looking from the top down (like any bigwig) rather than (as any novice) from the bottom up—that we are all born forever to look up. So then, from the start we are all quite naturally brought up from our birth to look up. So then, don't go off the rails like dear old Uncle Joe, who, by ensconcing himself way-high-up in the Kremlin, brought everything down he could bring down by his persistently looking down instead of persistently looking up. Why, even although heaven itself (reduced now to being printed all in lower case) is less like any (OT) mountain than the (NT) mini mustard seed which we must all learn to tend in order to perpetuate that seed of generic faith as well as our own seed of specific faith throughout the process of our growing up, we never look down unless for either our own, or someone else's specific purpose of growing up]!

So then, look into whatever minimalist metaphor best suits you to ensure your seeing the highest and broadest vista of heaven to be seen at all. But as even then far earlier foretold, just as the mustard seed grows and grows and grows, then still can you. The kingdom of heaven is not static. With every breath you take, with every song you sing, the kingdom of heaven just keeps on growing—and for as long as you live, it is exactly the very same issue for you (no matter how old you live to be) to keep on growing up.

Even right now [although that, for the sake of earth thinking, is purely a temporal expression], the kingdom of God is no small kingdom. The kingdom of heaven [a spatial or locative expression] tends [except for the constantly expanding universe of the astrophysicist] to denote a static circumstance. Sure, it stretches further than any human eye can ever see. It stretches far further than even the human mind can either ever tell or foretell. But the kingdom of God is a personal and thus highly dynamic expression.

You see, it takes supernatural wisdom and not just human wisdom for none other than the creator of this cosmos to know, feel, and understand its creation intimately enough to maintain and sustain this cosmos, which can only be done by the same universal laws of creation when applied to its sustenance, to its maintenance, and even to its suppression and supersedure, no less than this Old World [Mark

1] is heading into oblivion for the purposes of resurrecting its new model [Mark 2].

On this score, some unbelievers [or nyebogdyeny, printed as pronounced (both in lower case and without benefit of italics), to indicate the hell-bent destination of such unbelievers] are those who find most fault with *Yahweh*. This purposely unpronounceable name some believers have added to the names we angels often give to the Lord of Hosts and the most Ancient of Days for his having given us the word of both Old and New Testaments (as well as of much more besides).

In their finding fault with Yahweh, these unbelievers (the aforesaid *nyebogdyeny*) complain bitterly against his being unfair. This is no more than their rather watered-down way of complaining of his ruthlessness, his savagery, and as of in every other way, his poor record of fatherhood. Well, aside from every (male) patriarch (because there are also patriarchal solo mums) being most savagely called to account for their lack of husbandry these days, there's not really much more truth than that in this proclamation of divine savagery [although yet once again, reread Zaehner on the subject of our savage God].

What, you mistake this rambling lecture (your description) for what you dismiss for being tinnitus in the head! Well, there's a street preacher over there by which to distinguish that same street preaching (over there) from street teaching (over here), but to distinguish preaching (there) from teaching (here) is not going to ease or cure (what you choose to dismiss) for being tinnitus in the head. What's noise to you may well be news to others and still always noise to those who refuse or care not enough to listen and yet still be the best of news to those who care enough to go on trying to listen.

What you need to do is to find the faith by which to distinguish both street preaching and street teaching (whether here or there) from the tinnitus (using your own description again) by which you choose to denote (pick here the musical pun) or else dismiss outright the ongoing voice of God which you already hear (however distorted) within your head. Likewise, don't bother to deny that God speaks to you just because you haven't heard more identifiably from him any more than to wonder why you've got a loose connection that gives you (again your own description) only tinnitus in the head. Instead, look on the continuing privilege of your space-time situation when all this time, there's still plenty of the already redeemed around (without even earphones on) to swear and testify not just as to the presence of God but also to tell you what God says when received quite clearly through the hi-fi stereo in the inner ears of both their open hearts and heads.

It's true that for every one of this world's nations, both big and small, being right now stretched out to their furthest limits, both east and west, as if once again hung on the barbed wire of some no man's land, there seems again no hope. Nevertheless, for this being a report (although neither on street preaching nor on street teaching) instead on reading the signs of the times (and so with every nation stressed out to breaking point on every possible front), then this is most certainly the widest of all possible global reports. Paradoxes abound, but the absolute truth will soon be out.

Sooner or later, this world-wandering teacher or peripatetic preacher tentatively begins (but by now speaking through his teeth to the multitude here *in italics*). Then *sooner or later* is at least the message to which (whether sounding powerfully titanic or else feebly tintinnabulate) all must learn to respond. It may be preached in street argot or taught for a time with a genteel plum tightly plugging some far more highly educated mouth. It may come unpleasantly to some as the corollary to their worthless fame and fortune no less than more pleasantly to others to redeem them from their present poverty and powerlessness.

From those to whom much advantage is given—governmental power, professional calling, commercial success, creative composition, prophetic foresight, and insightful wisdom—then much more than from the less advantaged is that which is both divinely discerned and logically demanded. Witness every single one of the world's great revolutions (agrarian, industrial, moral, intellectual, political, and governmental), and you can account for both the originating misery and the ultimate sense of satisfaction (whether righteous or unrighteous) of the outcomes.

To be held accountable and to enjoy being held accountable for who and what we humans are and hope to be becomes one the greatest of (privileged) challenges we can learn to manage in both human and later life. Whatever we humans do and however each of us may be seen, this self-evidencing of accountability (although at odds with what we more usually claim as of right) puts each of us on heaven's front battle line.

So then from the big chip on someone's broad proletarian yet democratic shoulder, to assert that *every lawyer* (no less than every citizen) *is called to account for the complexity of law* is a view (however excusable) that then attitudinally fails to address one of the most critical of educational issues as well as of governmental issues of all time. [Oh yes, for this novice angel to think that I too, as once a struck-off lawyer, have been there before whilst on earth is chastening. And that even after only nine years through law school, to have felt the deep foreboding of the legal profession long before it happened of being struck off, without notice or warning, by a passing statute is, when it happens, more comically liberating than tragically depressing.]

To be struck off by some passing statute now for any lawyer (as some of our novice angels once were), that there is (if you can pardon the parlance) a very professional form of execution! Watch out, look right, and look left before you step off the kerb. This is Museum Street, so also look up, but not down, because that's straight into the abyss! As they said to investigative journalist Tom Scott (sotto voce via one of parliament's security personnel), 'Watch your step! They're out to get you!'

Things are moving so fast in time and space now (with the speed of light constantly slowing down and climate change rabbiting up) that not even Google Maps can keep up with the foreplay. One minute (like Martin Luther), here we stand (pillars of the legal community, no less than of the church) apparently still strongly upright in court (perhaps even in the High Court of Parliament, although never now so-called), and yet the next minute (perhaps because there's a spanking new Supreme Court now and no longer a Privy Council elsewhere), we're in the legal dogbox. And just like some very big law firms—read Anthony Molloy's *Thirty Pieces of Silver*—I'm speaking here not hearsay but instead firsthand.

There's always a surfeit of legal history making (a.k.a. Trumpism) when the law moves too fast for society to catch up. Legal historians (both of Cavaliers and Roundheads, no less than of Democrats and Republicans) get themselves smothered in personal trivia (just like the legislators) and thence burdened by legal detail (just like the judges). What's left of the once workable legal system then quickly goes to pot (by thinking to legalise marijuana and introduce euthanasia). Severe storm warnings take over, royal garden parties are cancelled, and birthday honour lists curtailed.

Just as Henry VIII (the Eighth, for those without Law Latin) died after a surfeit of lampreys (or back then, when legal 'thingummies' were moving slower, wasn't it only Henry I (the First) who was then still only in the process of dying?), so also a surfeit of legal history can be fatal for the legal system being made to go faster, faster, and ever faster. Sooner or later, then, the (surely not) Latin (but instead Aramaic) words *mene mene tekel upharsin* are bound to come up on every nation's legal screen. [Riddle-me-ree: Believe us implicitly at the Counterfeit Command, please do (since we're the ones who've already synchronised the next following great scene), but when you're sitting banqueting in some great hall, the Assyrians are already knocking hard on that hall's front door.]

The trouble is (as always) that everything is still done these 24/7 days by faster and faster statute (unless more and more so on 7/24 alternate days by under-the-table regulation or ministerial decree). It's all now up (unless down) on the World Wide Web, so there's no need for lawyers to worry any longer about keeping up to date. We can even get struck off from lawyering (without being called to overloaded courts) and just like any other criminal when done all within our own heads.

Given the new technology perfected by means of our radical 666 neural implantation of law, we'll all soon have every last bit of the law for everything literally implanted (by machine code) into our fast-shrinking yet faster-emptying heads. Hold on, if you're updated already with the latest 'app', you'll have the most recent Resource Mismanagement Act coming through right now. Got enough neural space left (frontal lobes no longer need)? This is yet another biggie in our programme (all rights reserved) of implementing law for laymen (where even pea-sized forebrains qualify)!

If you want another name for this process of downloading the law directly into every citizen's head, it's called bending the law. This is done by a process of (one-size-fits-all) neural transplant. By doing away with all the bother of exercising free will, this resulting 'bent law' instead of case or statute 'bound law' does away with all forms of lawbreaking. That leaves no need for courts, no need for judges, no need for police, no need for lawyers, nor (of course) even any need for law schools.

The entire legal system (and from there on the entire educational system) is then administered by means of electronic technocrats, whose further project of law reform (in the absence of anyone's remaining free volition) is to download all religions into one massive machine code. This will not only do away with all this world's troublesome clerics, pastors, preachers, professors, teachers, prophets, and theologians but also do away with all their conflicting belief systems. This is what the old-time prophets really and truly meant by saying 'peace on earth to all men of goodwill'. [Riddle-me-ree 3: And to which St Tristram Shandy once said 'Pish!' and twice said 'Pish!' and thrice said 'Pish!', although we at the Counterfeit Command have no more scholarly obligation than this to quote with chapter and verse from any such scatological novels as Laurence Sterne's *The Life and Opinions of Tristram Shandy, Gentleman*!]

Now the code name for this military operation (by which to clear away all churches, cathedrals, temples, and other places of fractious worship and so ultimately to do away with heaven itself) is called the Great Amen. You can download an 'app' for that right now from the Counterfeit Command—or else do the same and more so when you come to this book's orgiastic book launch.

On this score, don't listen to the so-called Supreme Command. This whole nihilistic process of listening leaves no time for troublesome reflection. There's no longer any slower Anglo-American common law (that's the second once troublesome problem now out of the way) as there once was when upheld of every Englishman's castle by Eddie Coke (before women's lib, brave fellow) and Abe Lincoln (afterwards assassinated, poor sucker) to be of the people, by the

472

people, and for the people. A bit delayed (as all case law and statute law is for being always delayed and not out of the question as justice always is on earth) but here now is the long deferred absolutism of George Orwell's dystopic novel *1984*, now directly implanted by way of machine code into every citizen's otherwise empty head!

The fourth (estate) trouble is (because troubles, like prophecies, always come in threes) that commissions are set up to reform and thereby simplify existing law. Politicians who promise to reduce the confusing output of new laws are chosen. Both those who reform old laws and those who draft new ones are expected to satisfy the clear standard of legislative composition expressed by the Ten Commandments, but surely not the same entire ten with which Apostle Paul (ahead of his time like most reformers) raised such a dust by apparently sweeping most of them under the by then obsolete religious carpet.

Many law reformers and legislative draftsmen are driven to distraction by what is expected of them. Why should they get so uptight when their work today is compared with centuries-old commandments? Does their response testify to the truth of the Ten Commandments' divine origin and man's failure to live up to God's creative composition?

The point of the comparison is that laws are made for lawbreakers and laymen. There are two ways of dealing badly with this. The first Pharisaical way is to tempt lawyers to think themselves above the law. The second correlative (and just as Pharisaical) way is that for thinking themselves above the law, lawyers begin to think that the law is made exclusively for lawyers.

Lawyers are tempted to forget this first principle of jurisprudence— that laws are made for those who otherwise would not or could not keep to the social order. Sometimes, lawyers talk about lawyers' law, and so the law becomes increasingly lawyers' law. At other times, they talk as if all the law (increasingly lawyers' law) were thus made most obviously for lawyers.

The law, when made not so much for laymen but instead then more and more for lawyers, lifts lawyers high above the law to give them a spurious social status. Through this pretence, lawyers become the real rulers rather than the real servants of society. Nevertheless, the sheer simplicity of the Ten Commandments brings everyone down to earth. 'Thou shalt not kill nor commit adultery, nor steal, nor bear false witness against thy neighbour, nor covet whatever belongs to him.'

Why do most of us remember and recite the last five of the Ten Commandments first and leave off the abstract generalities (by which the specifics make sense) until last? Is it because (1) these are the specific commandments that get in the way of what we would otherwise do: and so (2) we are made most conscious of them; or is it (3) because we break the other five commandments more frequently (and perhaps unknowingly) than these last; and so (4) would prefer to forget them as coming first; or is it (5) what we least want to recall, remember, and recite is that from which our biggest burden of guilt springs? All explanations could be valid. 'Honour your parents, sanctify your days of rest and recreation, don't demean God's name, abjure idolatry, and worship the one and only living God before all else.'None can claim, far less swear to be squeaky clean!

The Ten Commandments are quite simple. They come in two tablets. Lawyers recognise the force of these at least in their legal attire by wearing what they sometimes call 'tabs' and at other times 'weepers'. It is probably more truthful for lawyers to call them 'weepers' because lawyers have forgotten what they mean and why they wear them. This is the clerical tie that binds the legal profession to the clergy and so makes out of lawyers the priesthood of law. So then what's the problem for lawyers with the Ten Commandments continuing to serve as a standard for legislative composition?

The trouble with the Ten Commandments is that they are lapidary law. They are engraved on stone. Sure, they are simple and to the point—simply because nobody is ever verbose who writes on stone. Sure, they are clear and certain, because when they were first handed down, they had to be clearly cut into the stony surface of a backsliding reality. It is true too that they are complete because nobody conceives a task of that magnitude without completely considering its end result. And they are also long-lasting because they were first made to work without any prospect of amendment. Where lapidary laws fall down, as even the longest standing stones eventually fall, is in their administration. When lawyers divorce lapidary laws from the

474

life of the spirit that created them, the hearts of the people to whom the laws are applied then soon turn to stone.

Lapidary law may be primitive, but it is still all around. Our traffic law is almost entirely lapidary. It depends on signs sometimes painted on the stony ground, sometimes hung on posts, and sometimes flashed in coloured lights. In some countries, the sensate simplicity of the sign has supplanted the intellectual simplicity of what once called for (as in observing the right-hand rule) the self-awareness required of rules.That too, thanks to the plethora of signs (from advertising signs to road signs) corrupts the context (in one sense) to constitute the text (in another sense) of what makes for the signs of the times.

A three-tiered, if not four- or five-tiered, system of lapidary law now controls traffic on the roads. Once just local (and at risk of being equivocally parochial), now for tourists and foreign travellers, traffic signs have had to become at least international. They now face the task of almost global communication.

There are signs to warn us of ice in Cumberland, wild horses at Rotorua, sudden dips on the Kilmog, or to tell us where we can go either to Land's End or to Coromandel. These signs are purely informative. There are others such as 'Please let the bus go first', which seem to plead for some sort of privilege for public transport in Melbourne or in Dunedin. (It is not really clear what these signs signify or mean, but they are big business for bus companies.)

Then there are rules of courtesy as with two drivers each turning right at an uncontrolled intersection. Finally, there are rules of law, but conflict between road users still goes on and is even intensified as when pedestrians are permitted and encouraged to 'cross now' into a stream of turning traffic. Opting for the initial simplicity, clarity, and concrete strength of lapidary law to regulate transport has divorced us from the original purpose of traffic legislation. Roads and railways, motorways and cycleways can end up keeping individuals and communities apart rather than bringing them together. It is at this point of diversification and isolation that lapidary law breaks down.

The fact is that lapidary law soon dilapidates. It does so once the original purpose of law to soften men's hearts is misidentified with hardening them into monuments of stone. The spirit of the law then evaporates as fast as paint peels off the roadway, vandals rip up road markers, whilst wood rots, steel rusts, and alloy corrodes.

So too, speed limits can reversely discriminate against slower drivers. These slower drivers (like slower legislatures) are seen to be holding up those who always drive at or above full speed. Likewise, blood alcohol levels can be taken to permit and even encourage anything less than the limit for being a legally and therefore socially acceptable level of alcohol in any driver's blood.

A courtcancelled driver's licence for drunk driving may be reinstated for restricted purposes within days of its original cancellation. A criminal first charge brought against a defendant, even for burglary, may be administratively shelved and discretely diverted. In all these ways, the legal fiction by which paper substitutes for stone in any modem legal system itself disintegrates just as surely (beyond a certain point of uncertain computation) as the last stone of what had before been a lapidary system crumbles and turns into dust.

It is the same with the lapidary law of the Ten Commandments. They soon dilapidate once the heart of Israel has turned to stone. In laymen's terms, the province of law is taken to uphold the Ten Commandments. In lawyers' terms, the province of law is to uphold the traffic regulations and the criminal code. Many lawyers (especially legislators) think that this can best be done in a masonic way, that is to say, by turning the hearts of the people into stone. Petrified people, so many public in-house lawyers believe, won't break the law. Instead, petrified people will break themselves against the law. Fear of the law rather than freedom from the law then soon becomes the chief weapon in the lawyer's armoury.

Amongst themselves, lawyers deal with the law differently. They deal with it as if it were a will-o'-the-wisp and something altogether airy-fairy that can be both modelled and remodelled and even changed at legal will. When applied to laymen, however, the law becomes as hard as prestressed concrete. It entombs folks in concrete overcoats instead of freeing up their lives.

Lawyers are mistaken when they like to think that the law can be upheld and enforced in a masonic way. Fear works only so far in the service of the law, and once legal systems become nightmares, they break down as people wake up to their misery. Even if the law were lapidary and lawyers were masons, it would be their task to free up the law for laymen, not petrify society through hard-hearted and as often unenforceable legislation. Lawyers may profess to be free masons of the law, but they cannot claim to practise that legal profession by turning the hearts of the people to stone through enforcing the blackest of black letter law.

How does all this come about? First and foremost, we are looking at the results of a decadent priesthood. Lawyers have lost faith with the law. That is why they spend so much of their lives shoring up a structure that would otherwise fall down. Secondly, the dispirited house of our legal system, left empty and no longer a home for law-abiding people, becomes a house haunted by spirits that serve only as substitutes for law. These are the spirits of rebelliousness, of indecision and disorder, and of strife and confusion. Arrant chauvinism (whether of the male or female variety) abounds. Arrant humanism conflicts with arrant legalism, no less than arrant capitalism conflicts with arrant communism. Euphemistic social welfare in place of self-disciplined employment turns workers into slaves of the state. False freedoms beget anarchy out of the arbitrariness of law. Society then loses its essentially collective symmetry—at which point deprived individuals seek to eject themselves from the previously binding force of the law.

What makes lawyers mistake the stony form of the abandoned castle of the law for the sweetness of its spiritual strength? These lawyers may assault the by now empty and haunted house of the legal system. They repossess in the name of legality, but yet themselves behave as robber barons. Once lawyers again regain the abandoned castle of the legal system, they may claim the so-called right of 'finders keepers' to keep it entirely for themselves. Sweet Mistress Legality then wanders the world homeless, and the concept of law becomes identified with hired gunmen and self-seeking thieves.

What so turns lawyers into robber barons? The answer (although not the only one) lies in their legal education. The same hard-hearted masonic mistake runs right through both legal education and legal practice. The first principle of all this world's legal teaching, as of almost all professional education (for the purposes of teaching, healing, administering, and governing), is to harden the human heart.

And one of the foremost risks to case-hardening the human heart is that the softest and most romantic of human hearts have the potential to become the hardest of hearts as a result of their ruthless reaction. Between the passionate romantic and the aggressive realist is but a very fine and almost imperceptible line over to switch or cross, no visa or passport is required.

The first thing the law student is taught to do in almost every law school is to forget about justice. The second thing he faces is to forget his social service calling. He can no longer afford to indulge in that vocational calling when compelled by the enforced competition with his peers to turn all his attention upon the law. To get from fresher first year into second year has a statistical probability of only one in four. This produces a tunnel vision that excludes not only language and logic but, eventually by reason of that intensifying tunnel vision, produces an intellectual contempt for life at large by which to assuage also the loss of first moral, then ethical, and finally, all jurisprudential feelings.

It is possible for the finer feelings of human nature, besides also the law (when full in your own face), and morals (when confined only to the schoolroom) to survive a legal education, but the survivors are nearly always scarred. And sometimes these survivors are very badly scarred (both legally and morally) when taught to forget about justice. In the end, only those who have themselves robbed the law can tell anything of who the real crooks are amongst the more obvious gunmen and robber barons, since they are by then invariably the big heavies who openly promote their wares rather than the small gangs who hide out amongst the nooks and crannies of the ruined castle of the legal system.

So much for some of the more figurative generalities concerning law and society! Nevertheless, what about the real specifics—nerve gas murders in quiet country towns, big business sequestering their profits in corrupt tax havens, adolescents running amok with guns amongst their classmates, and terrorists so distraught for having nothing left in life to lose by their committing mayhem? Without specifics, we have no way of knowing whether what is seen for being general is either true or false, nor have we any way of rectifying a legal system gone so far wrong as to be in the hands of highwaymen and robber barons.

A legal education is by now almost entirely academic. This is the case the whole world over, even though this academic focus still remains a very new thing for the law. There is no way into the legal profession anywhere on earth today except through law school. In less than a generation, this has come to be not just the accepted norm but also the rule of law. Nothing by way of taking articles or serving an apprenticeship can ever substitute for academic examination; but even there, the bigger the law firm, no less than the bigger the law school, the bigger the carcinogenic fallout for society at large and the more so in particular for small towns, struggling families, and the homeless.

One of the peculiarities of academic life is that you can say anything you like, nonsense or not, so long as you can either cite or preferably footnote a reference to someone else (preferably held in the highest regard) for having said the same nonsense all before. If you want a citation for that, then look at Judge Abner Mikva's 'Goodbye to Footnotes'. But we (the authorial *we*, in this case) don't allow footnotes any more than we allow citations (whether citations for bravery under fire or for any other kind of infantile impulsiveness, adolescent arrogance, or midlife bravado).

So then bravery under fire is expected of any military operation when led by the Holy Spirit. We don't promote much more senile nonsense in our writing. Stand or Fall—that's not our motto, but instead it's simply to remind you that whenever led by the Holy Spirit, you stand always on holy ground.

What's that you say, that Judge Abner Mikva's 'Goodbye to Footnotes' deserves at least a judicial citation? So now here, in the body of this text, [1985] 56 University of Colorado Law Review pp. 647–653 now appears what otherwise would be the footnoted citation to Judge Abner Mikva's 'Goodbye to Footnotes'. So then, also now, both there (as well as here), Judge Abner describes how 'the abomination of footnotes' has 'spread like fungus' through all legal writing. Of course, Professor Fred Rodell was saying the same thing some fifty years earlier. He called footnotes 'phony excrescences' and made the point that 'every legal writer is presumed to be a liar until he proves himself otherwise with a flock of footnotes'.

So too, the surest way of making the worse appear the better cause is to do so (surreptitiously) with a legal footnote. Judges have taken to legal footnotes and even illegal footnotes, like dead ducks do for lack of water, and even dying legislatures have dabbled in the resulting deadly muck by giving illustrations and examples of what they think themselves to mean in their otherwise more lucid texts. In no time at all, the real law (whether by way of two commandments or ten commandments or ten thousand and ten commandments) becomes no more than a commentary on a commentary on a commentary on a commentary—so that nobody can find the law (as for the law on scooters, skateboards, and similar contrivances) far less obey the law.

There is no need to give you the citation for Rodell's 'Goodbye to Law Reviews', which, after all, is cited (surely also by way of footnote) in Mikva's 'Goodbye to Footnotes'. Lawyers look to citations not just because they don't trust each other but also because they can't trust themselves. Most footnotes, references, citations, and even precedents of pleading and conveyancing forms are the means by which lawyers have come to hide behind rather than reveal the law. Magna Carta is but more so, being drafted by feudal barons and the declaration of human rights no less, drafted by one who was a substantial slave owner. Computers are only going to intensify the legal paradox by providing yet another screen between the law and laymen. It is, after all, the *cancelli* (or set of curtains hiding the chancellor) that makes the chancellor and not the other way around.

What all this preoccupation with detail does for academic work at large is to make it very arbitrary, relative, and impractical—exactly the reverse of what's intended. Apart from modern science—and even that is already fast succumbing to the conjoined assaults of its own history and philosophy—we have lost faith for the lack of there being any philosophia perennis or eternal wisdom of scholarship. The form, as well as the function, of academic activity likewise becomes affected. The text of academic discourse becomes completely case hardened, surrounded as it is with countertexts of references, footnotes, and citations. The gloss supplants the mainline text, and the exercise overshadows the performance. No wonder the priesthood of the law declines and degenerates in this context as also would (in their healing, teaching, and preaching) the faith-driven priesthood of any other profession.

Legal education exaggerates all these difficulties (to make them more recognisable to students). Lawyers rely on precedent more than principle, so what has gone before is more prone to clog up and get in the way of when and what could follow. The increasing palimpsest of precedents (one on top of the other) bends and binds one's juristic mindset (concerned with factual truth, ecclesiastical equity, and heavenly justice) to the ground. Thereupon, the arbitrariness of academic activity in being more concerned with temporal issues and established interests rather than with the absolutes of truth and righteousness likewise builds these ephemeral interests and issues into legal scholarship. This results in the relativity of all legal discourse, because none can any longer agree on there being any absolute legal values.

We can discern this arbitrariness of legal scholarship in the present impracticality of legal education. Legal training is concerned almost exclusively with keeping up to date or at least maintaining the appearance of doing so in company with most of the other professions. Bar the odd legal historian; however, no one reads, far less teaches, from the classics of legal writing any longer. Blackstone on the common law is considered an artefact. Dicey on the constitution is dead. Equity has gone the same way of all flesh as Maitland. Anson on contracts is unheard of. Salmond on torts is regarded as being barely relevant. The result is that none knows what it takes to read, far less to study, or even learn to write the likes of Maine or Maitland. The case method of legal teaching whereby students keep up with (if not head off) the latest bills before the legislature and the most recent and as yet often unreported decisions of the courts has taken its toll. Legislation is at its lowest ebb. Nothing but constant change (in the name of so-called law reform) is any longer held sacred to the law.

Of course, the intention behind getting away from a classical legal education was quite the reverse of what actually happened. With humans who rely entirely on their own strength, aims are reversed by results. What some lawyers would do to return our legal system to its rightful strength is to find out and formulate the system's once fundamental law.

What is fundamental to our legal system is a question that has been asked often before. 'What is the greatest of the law's commandments,' tempted the lapidary lawyers of Jesus Christ.

And Jesus said unto the lawyer who tempted him, 'Thou shalt love the Lord thy God with all thy heart and with all thy soul and with all thy mind.' This is the first and great commandment. And the second is likened unto it, 'Thou shalt love thy neighbour as thyself.' On these two commandments hang all the law and the prophets (Matthew 22:35–40).

It is made clear by its absence that the spirit (or kernel) of all law, both secular and divine, is love, but the legal form of love when given in the fallible human context case-hardens the human heart with such a tough integument that often the human spirit must itself be broken to reach the loving kernel. Nothing other than love can melt the heart and transform the mind of those who profess to practise the law, profess to administer the law, and profess to make the law. For already having done all this on behalf of those who have ears to hear and eyes to see, Jesus Christ (yes, the same disparaged prophet who came from once benighted Nazareth) is the supreme jurist... ... ... is the supreme jurist.

[At which point of the sermon, for which the self-appointed guardians of society had been hanging in to hear, it must be reported that the state police (*Gosudarstvenaya Militzia*) intervened to carry off the now no longer peripatetic (or in any way still mobile) preacher.]

* * *

482

Hell-Bent People—a Hidden History
Part VI

The Prophetic Voice of Justice

> The very considerations, which judges most rarely mention, and always with an apology, are the secret root from which the law draws all the juices of life.
>
> Oliver Wendell Holmes, *The Common Law*

The secret root of the law—eh, well, there's a shrewd saying! Besides being also a brave conception—and that even when only superciliously thought! But what would it really be like (whether writer or reader) for some legal archaeologist (another Maine or Maitland, Blackstone or Bentham) to dig deep enough down—right down through the book of Leviticus, to find the deep taproot of the law?

That task would surely require some great, almighty, and heroic endeavour. Even just to garner all the diverse concepts of law (sometimes mighty boughs and otherwise tiny twigs) that spring from that secret root (no less than those adventitious roots which serve the root itself) would be a task to out-Maine Maine, to out-Maitland Maitland, to out-Blackstone Blackstone, and to out-Bentham Bentham. Nevertheless, perhaps one need not dig that far down as that ancient lawbook of *Leviticus* still delves beneath today's adventitious grassroots to find the secret taproot of the law. Indeed, for all its sound and fury, the overwhelming ubiquitousness of modernist law conveys an over-communicative sense of superficiality; and as that sound and fury intensifies, so also does this sense of the law's superficiality increasingly pervade the context of these latter days.

Nevertheless, how can one determine the way in which 'the law draws all the juices of life' from the secret root of considerations 'which judges most rarely mention' without our coming to grips with 'the secret root of the law'? Well, even just from the study of tree-rings, the previously mentioned science of dendro-chrono-logic can tell us the history of every tree's growth, lack of growth, and (and inferentially the organism's salubrious wellbeing or otherwise insalubrious ill-health as generated in terms of its own biological text in situational context)—so also there are similarly inferential means of testing for the epidemiology of law gone wrong.

Meanwhile, just keep well in mind the above key given by which to unlock the secret life of our now much less than deeply rooted Common Law, as explained by one of the most dedicated of Anglo-American law-teachers, the jurist, Oliver Wendell Holmes (Junior). Likewise, keep all your wits about you, for, in some way or another it happens to all hell-bent people for whom everything under the sun is everything there is, that there is nevertheless much, much more to the deeply-rooted underground life of the law which to those sun-only-worshippers must remain still always a hidden history. In other words (those of Baden-Powell, again) 'Be prepared!' And as always, stay prepared—both for the expected as well as the unexpected (which for both together is a very tall order) but remembering always, that for history being prophetic of the future, the present is always decided by what happens next. So then, 'Be prepared to be decisive (well-informedly-decisive) about all things both past-present as well as future-perfect!'

Meanwhile, as heard now to intervene, in the accustomed form of barely decipherable below-ground muttering (projected from the same soured-grapes literary-funded underground) as used so many times before to demean such epic writers as once A. A. Milne, again Enid Blyton, and yet again Katharine Tozer (not to mention Thomas Carlyle and countless others) here the same muttering arose all over again now to attack those once sacred writings of Oliver Wendell Holes (Junior), on the serious subject of our shared Anglo-American Common Law—possibly the very last of this world's fast declining legal systems.

Listen closely for clarity to such mutterings as follow, because the prevalent s-s-s-speech profile (which we also advise you closely to analyse and discern) is excessively heightened by s-s-s-sibilants. Thus, 'the s-s-secret root caus-s-s-se (con-c-c-c-cerning those very con-s-s-s-siderations, heh-heh-heh, which judges-s-s-s most rarely mention, heh-heh, and yet always with an apology when mentioned), and from which, heh-heh, the law draws (or withdraws-s-s) all the juic-c-ces of life!' Sounds masonic, doesn't it, but perhaps, given benefit of clergy, then no more than an extreme attack of tinnitus provoked by the tintinnabulum (a bronze phallic figure) taken over from pagan Rome and crowned with the papal tiara and keys of heaven to signify the papal authority over even the counterfeit church.

But as to what mystically mentioned considerations, heh-heh-heh, does dear Oliver Wendell (foremost lawyer of the Anglo-American common law) then refer? What secret root of the law, heh-heh? Sounds deeper to go-go (pardon here again the prevailing street patois) than any merely masonic root, but if not, then in being so beholden to Uncle Screwtape in the *Screwtape Letters*, to be also utterly and uncompromisingly demonic (as in Screwtape's advice given to his nephew Wormwood).

Hold on here (since said in a different tone of voice), since even angels can be disguised as bums, prostitutes, insurance salesmen, whiskey priests, and struck-off lawyers (for being one of the 'very [many] considerations which judges most rarely mention'), then perhaps such angels in disguise are really 'the secret root from which the law draws all the juices of life'! For centuries, we've given the benefit of law to the clergy, but wasn't the law made to benefit those who, without benefit of law, would otherwise commit a crime? [Exegesis 1: Besides Barbara Kingsolver's *Poisonwood Bible* on the subject of overseas missions, God-bothering theologians should be sure to read Anthony Trollope's *The Warden* on the subject of home missions.]

No doubt this proletarian suggestion deeply surprises you, but that's the way it is, just as it was for Leading-Agent Sonya in Dostoyevsky's epic novel on *Crime and Punishment*. Of course, you may baulk at any book (ostensibly of fiction) deciding any such serious issue, although New Testament parables (unlike Old Testament hard facts) are surely an extension of God's communicative grace.

It should cause you no surprise by now (conjecturally as a reader) how often it is that you humans also mistake so many really bad guys for being the best of good angels (although that really does surprise even the least of us good angels), so why should it cause either of us any surprise that you so often mistake the utterly good for being the utterly bad?

Likewise, here it is all over again, since the Supreme Command commits me here—at first thought, to be a defrocked priest; at second (since all the professions today are under fierce attack), to be a struck-off lawyer—to be proclaiming on behalf of the Supreme Command the prophetic voice of justice. We angels are like spies in being masters of our disguise, which is one of the many explanations for the currently increasing disbelief in the existence of angels.

So now, on behalf of the Supreme Command, here's an angelic sermon in the making when standing here all homeless in the street; yet whilst preaching and teaching outside the courts (obviously an embarassment to those who walk on faster when walking past me) I must realise that for no longer being credited with, or even just discredited by being any sort of lawyer, then (unless for being a struck-off sort of lawyer) I can no longer be your sort of lawyer far less anyone else's sort of lawyer.

Likewise, no more than any defrocked priest can still claim to be a priest, then here's my legal disclaimer now being given by me to you, by which it is both hereinbefore and hereinafter denied, that the aforesaid prophetic voice of justice so about to be proclaimed on behalf of the Supreme Command could be either construed or misconstrued anywhere on earth, whether under the Lawyers and Conveyancers Act notoriously of New Zealand or of any other similarly notarised nation, for that aforesaid prophetic voice of justice so proclaimed, whether for free or for a fee, to be giving any sort of legal counsel or advice.

So then and what then is legal counsel or advice, if not that which is illegal for any but a legal lawyer to give, which then cuts out most of that which could otherwise be perfectly legal for anyone other than any legal lawyer to give? There's nothing by way of any sensible advice that could not also be legal advice for any lawyer to give without thereby victimising any layperson to give for that being also legal counsel and advice. Of course, for carrying its own burden of tautological argument that the law is an ass … the law is an ass … and the law is an ass—but don't mistake that for being legal advice, since there's none but a few lawyers who'll give that advice for themselves (without a hefty fee) for being jurists instead of just lawyers.

So then, listen to this, you transnational and supranational big bodies that trample on the needy and try to destroy the poor! You think that you can hide yourselves behind political correctness? By such means, you demote employment to extend investors' profit margins and to extract the last cent from the world's increasingly limited resources! You engage yourselves in all sorts of sharp practices—inflating prices, dumping produce, squeezing competitors, hiding profits, and evading taxes. The small flies get caught in the net, but the big boys barge their way through.

You think that the Lord God of Israel is bollocks? Well, don't you ... don't you think just that ... that the Lord God of Israel is bollocks! But believe me, the King of heaven (to whom you have already turned your back) is not going to overlook your devilish deeds. The time will come, and it's not just as before, when time was once the steady constant, which you think of being your own time, always to suit your own nefarious purposes that you can play around with but, on the contrary, when least expected, although always as promised, is faster and ever faster and with every day yet still approaching. The day of reckoning for everyone, and not just for you, is always ... always ... always ever so increasingly near.

Believe me, the earth itself shall then shake to its roots. Everyone, and not just you, shall be then the most distressed. The fact is that so many of you big-business people hate anyone who challenges injustice and who speaks the whole truth in court. You have oppressed the poor, even the most indigent poor, and stolen their food (sometimes right out of their mouths) and put worthless substitutes like breakfast cereals or processed meats in its place.

Likewise, you introduce new technologies and destroy age-old livelihoods. You substitute this wheat for that wheat, this potato for that potato, this rice for that rice, and this corn for that corn—and you yourselves know not what you do. Yet you do all this with great pride in your own accomplishments but with no compunction for the lives and livelihoods you reduce to rubble. I tell you now—that the day is coming someday soon when it shall be the most technologically advanced nations that shall be amongst the first reduced to rubble.

You have no compunction in persecuting good men, in taking bribes, and in keeping the poor—through long delays, high costs, and fast practices—from getting their day of justice in the courts. I dare say that keeping quiet in such evil times as are these present times is the smart thing to do, but the day will come when they, the so-long oppressed, will drag you away to be hung on meathooks. Yes, every one of you, unless hanging dead from their very own meathook, will be dragged off like a hard-struggling fish on their very own gaff hook.

There's nothing new in all this, even although it may seem to you that you've never heard or read about it. So prophesied old Amos about eight centuries before the birth of Christ—and this even in a time when Israel enjoyed great prosperity and political security. So then there's nothing new in all this. So also, you can be tempted to say, 'What of it?' We've all heard something of the same (like of climate change and of falling birth rates and of famines, floods, and other fearful fantasies) going on long before this in time. But look here, every empire falls just after a time when the rich grow richer and the poor grow poorer—just like today.

From the time of mankind's first great fall from the creator's closest friendship, when illicit power (also just like today) first began to concentrate itself in the hands of a few, then some great catastrophe— like a worldwide flood, a worldwide war or a conquest, a spate of earthquakes, or a plague of diseases—took place. Will mankind never learn? we angels ask ourselves. Will mankind never learn?

Meanwhile, as the still ongoing speed of light slows down and time moves faster, governments grow more and more inhuman and so corrupt—again just like today. And so then injustice too becomes commonplace—again just like today. Finally, everything becomes entirely relative, or worse still, values reverse their accustomed roles—so that evil is pursued as if for the common good, and what was once objectively good is denied now to all as if for being uncommonly bad.

You're altogether right—there's nothing new in all this. Old Amos (he was actually then a very young man) was amongst the first to ask you whether broken horses can manage to run up the steepest of cliffs or the oldest of grandfathers can plough the sea with exhausted oxen. No! Yet you humans persist in turning the concept of justice into the most toxic of nerve poisons and so make what's right come out as if wrong and what's wrong come out as if all right.

You also brag about your conquests—taking control of this city or of that city, of this company or of that company, or of this woman or of that woman. You then like to lie down on your couches, paying others to compose rude and as often crude songs about your grand conquests and accompanying yourselves with the best of background music played by underpaid yokels on pseudo harps, guitars, and zithers. Yes, you may even hear the same (although the drummers wear earmuffs) in places of worship!

So too, you swig the most expensive of Chardonnay by the flagon and put on the finest perfumes for all your worshipful performances, yet you fail to be moved by the fate of your homeland. And so you pride yourselves on being citizens of the world—on being true cosmopolitans—but without ever first knowing what is meant by that cosmos by which chaos is kept in check, which is what it takes by way of knowing what in any sense it is to be a true cosmopolitan.

Believe me, you counterfeit cosmopolitans, how terrible it will be for you when you will find yourselves amongst the first to be forced to leave home. Then when your feasts and banquets come to an end, you will be forced to face famine. You are doomed, for sure, all of you who twist justice and cheat people of their rightful heritage.

Believe me when I say of olden times that old Amos still even then cried for justice. He compared it to an ever-flowing stream, and even when seemingly run dry, he still had the prophetic strength and willpower to go on proclaiming it to be an ever-flowing stream.

So too, old Amos (even then whilst still a young man in spirit but old in wisdom) went on crying out for this ever-running spring of righteousness as well as for this ever-flowing stream of justice. He went on comparing what he and others needed to this eternal river that would never run dry. Did his own folks hear him? Did his own folks hear him any more than today's young folks hear the old wisdom of old Amos today? So then what happened to them? Why is it that we now hear only of old Amos but not of the folks to whom he preached and prophesied?

Punishment had to come, for justice and righteousness are absolutes, but Amos also pleaded with God for mercy. Perhaps God would be merciful to those who remained after punishing the nation for its iniquities. Now that's a tall order, because, as even every maker of the smallest thing knows, there's nearly always some wastage. Are you going to be saved, or are you going to be wasted?

The equation for salvation is truly simple, not intriguingly complex. The erudite love to puzzle the uneducated and the ignorant, to puzzle those excessively simple folks whom the erudite can thus label for being the unenlightened, and so dismiss them and keep them apart from themselves, for the fact of the matter as the erudite so mistake them to qualify for being amongst the illiterately profane, then so the illiterately profane shall swallow up the mistakenly erudite. Do you follow the switch, the switch of values? Then sooner or later you'll be feeling its forcefulness upon your own bare back! Terrorists are not born—terrorists are made.

By nothing more so simple than a complete reversal of values, the plain truth is entirely the other way around. Nevertheless, the erudite like to puzzle the so-called unenlightened with equations that are apparently simple yet hard to explain, but the equation for salvation is so excessively simple that it excludes from its operation the erudite who are put off both by its simplicity as well as the obviousness by which, as the truth of the matter at present stands, they themselves don't qualify for having what they don't have.

The equation for salvation, as prophesied by Old Amos (to distinguish him from Amos the Younger), requires everyone to work for what is right, not for what is evil, so that everyone can have the same opportunity to live in harmony. Then the Lord God Almighty really will be with us, just as we angels claim he can be for all who humble themselves and serve his purpose. So we learn to hate all evil, to love everything good, and to see that justice prevails in the courts. And then perhaps the Lord will be merciful to the people of any such nation who are still left alive, because, yes, for those who do and think otherwise than to live with the simplest of equations for seeking salvation, then even with the most merciful of lords, there is bound to be some (at least apparent) wastage from what it takes to qualify and fit within the formula for salvation.

It may therefore help to know something more about our friend old Amos. Even only as a little shepherd with something to say, yet also as for any angry young man with lots more to say, his role, as for all developing prophets, grew quite perilous. Some prophecies are let fall to the ground, the prophets may be stoned to death, and the collective consequences tragic to almost everyone. Other people to whom the Supreme Command speaks (because the Supreme Command speaks to each and every one of us if we care to listen) may run away or block their ears, exit or eject themselves from taking up the prophetic challenge.

As said before, Old Amos (however old in wisdom but young in spirit) was just a small-time shepherd from the little village of Tekoa in the Judaean Desert, but everything that he prophesied came about to fulfil its historic as well as prophetic truth. Born some five miles south of Bethlehem, Amos was the first spokesman for the Supreme Command whose message is recorded at length in the Bible. He spoke out against the establishment—the corruption of commerce, the boisterousness of big business, and the indolence of rich folks lying on luxurious beds, stretching their limbs out on couches and feasting every day on veal and lamb.

Old Amos was nothing as a young man—if not fully forthright and if not fully honest. Listen to what he said to the women of Samaria! Well, are there any men at all today, any men anywhere at all today, who would, in our own present day and age, dare to attack the women's lobby, as Amos then attacked the women's lobby?

'Tell me this, you women of Samaria,' he challenged them. 'Yes, it's to you women of Samaria who grow fat like well-fed cows that I'm speaking. Yes, that's right. So don't pretend it's otherwise ... and not you same women who grow fat like well-fed cows whilst mistreating the weak, oppressing the poor, and ordering your henpecked husbands to cart you round the fast-diminishing commonwealth. Pooh! What sort of husbands are these for being all the time required to feed you up like pigs for slaughter and to bring you salacious drinks and other alcoholic beverages to still your social conscience?

'Yes, you refuse to admit that a day of disaster is coming, but your everyday actions encourage the most gross and retaliatory violence. And as often as not, you already experience that very same sort of retaliatory violence—without you yourselves having the slightest inkling that you yourselves bring it about.

'Take another look again at the monstrous crimes being committed in our own little sun-burnt-up Samaria. You wash your hands of such crimes, yet you oblige your cuckolded husbands to turn a blind eye to the consequences of your own scandalous behaviour. Why, you crap in your own nest, just as you defile your own country, and you infect others with your scandalous behaviour as if your own place in the sun were no more than someone else's long deserted and completed vacated village.

'Don't you see the great disorder created by people who fill their mansions with things taken by crime and violence? Such people, even as children, don't even begin to know how to be honest!'

Let us angels tell you, since you won't read for yourselves, what Amos forewarned his own countrymen and countrywomen.

'Your land will be surrounded, your boundary defenses destroyed, and your mansions plundered by your enemies. Just as a lion leaves only one leg and an ear of a lamb for the shepherd, so only a few oddments of Samaria's luxury-loving people will survive. The rest shall be as dogs, waiting on scraps thrown from someone else's table, and finally, with fleas upon all their backs to bite them, they shall succumb to their very own dog-eat-dog kind of world.'

Then from being a struck-off litigant preacher-teacher, the Supreme Command commissioned Amos to become, at first thought, a caregiver-nurse to his own country but then, more recently, no more than a struck-off itinerant teacher plying his writings outside of the courts, outside of the colleges, and outside even of his own home country of Samaria. Alas, no prophet makes any sense within his own four walls, far less within his own home country, until either his warnings are heard for what they are or else his prophecies are most surely fulfilled.

Old Amos was not alone in pointing out what had gone wrong with his country's legal system. The prophet Hosea, who preached in the north, did so only a few years after the prophet Amos had spoken out against the root causes of corrupt government and the inevitability of divine judgement. Hosea prophesied against the priests of the law.

'Listen to this, you priests! Pay attention, people of Israel. Listen, you that belong to the royal family! You are supposed to judge with justice—judgement will fall on you for not doing so.'

Hosea did not mince God's words. He spoke out against the crown for refusing to recognise their royal responsibility for the administration of justice and the maintenance of law and order. We are doing the same today, with criminal law becoming, on the one hand, more and more like private law (negotiated through plea bargaining and entrapment) and, on the other hand, more like a tribal blood feud in which the victims state and expect their case to be enforced against the culprits. Once upon a time, every crime was committed against the crown, which took the responsibility for enforcing the law and administering justice. Now as often as not, the trial is held and as often decided by social media.

'It's the leaders of the law that are at fault. Don't let me hear any one of them accuse the people. Let none of the leaders pass the buck, for my complaint is against them. Day and night, they blunder on, growing fat in the priesthood of the law, and the prophets of the law do no better. The more of you priests there are, the more you sin against me. I'll turn whatever remains of your honour into abject disgrace. You grow rich as a result of others going wrong and, instead of putting a stop to wrongdoing, encourage it as a means of making yourselves all the more richer.'

Not much more is known of the young prophet Micah, who supported what God was saying through Amos and Hosea about law and justice, than we can gather from his prophecies of catastrophe for the corrupt government of the southern kingdom of Judah in which he lived.

'How frightful it will be for those of you who still lie lazily in bed whilst planning evil! When morning comes, you'll carry out your evil plans as soon as you're given the chance. When you want a field, you'll ease the way (stopping the water course) by which to take it. When you desire to obtain a housing estate, you'll make yourselves a nuisance to the neighbourhood until you get zoning permission. You'll either tempt, bribe, or coerce the authorities. Binge drinking and illicit drugs take you far beyond the limits of rational communication. It's perilous to even think of talking with you.

'No smallholder's home, family, or livestock is safe in such circumstances. Listen, you bigtime rulers of Israel! You're supposed to be concerned about justice, but you wouldn't recognise justice— no, not even if you saw it come down from the skies. You don't even obey your own rules. Local government is a travesty of justice. You'll encourage money laundering by bringing in big business from overseas. You'll build a stadium the size of a football field and sell off its naming rights without regard to those whose established businesses you put out of business.

'You've come to hate what's good and, instead of what's good, learnt to love what's evil. You flay my own folks alive, and as if by a thousand cuts, you tear the flesh off their scrawny bones. You behave like cannibals to those whom you have a duty to protect, stripping off their skin, breaking their bare bones, and chopping them up like meat for the pot.

'Soon, you'll cry out to the Lord, but he won't answer you nor even listen to you because of what you've done and keep on doing to maintain such evil ways. And when called to account, you'll say that's progress, and all must change by giving way to the new. And besides all else, what you say of past traditions is by now no more than all just history. Very, very shortly, all such history is about to catch up with you.'

All three prophets—Amos, Hosea, and Micah—predicted what became a history of lamentation over human disobedience to God's law. In 734 BC–732 BC, the Assyrians came down 'like the wolf on the fold, and his cohorts were gleaming in purple and gold. And the sheen of their spears was like stars on the sea, when the blue wave rolls nightly on deep Galilee.'

So too, Ashkelon and Gaza were defeated. Judah, Ammon, Edom, and Moab paid tribute; and Israel lost almost all of Gilead and most of Galilee. Damascus fell in 732 BC and was annexed to the Assyrian Empire. Samaria fell in 721 BC and was likewise annexed to the Assyrian Empire. Samaria fell in 721 BC, and Judah was defeated by Sennacherib in 701 BC. So then what is most likely to happen to you?

These same three prophets of the law—Amos, Hosea, and Micah (the so-called minor prophets in Hebraic jurisprudence)—also provide a record of God's grace, the divine response of fatherly forgiveness after due discipline has been administered. Thus, is the prophetic voice of justice fulfilled but not silenced from giving praise and thanksgiving in accordance with the law?

'I will bring my people back to me,' sings the Lord through Hosea. 'I will love them with all my heart. I am no longer angry with them. I will be to my people of Israel like rain in a dry land. They will blossom like flowers. They will be firmly rooted like the trees of Lebanon.'

We can compare the prophetic function of these old-time people who spoke out on behalf of justice and righteousness with the role of today's most professional lawyers. This is particularly the case with Hosea, Amos, and Micah, whose lamentations against injustice and prayers for mercy in righting that injustice can be read through the twenty-eight centuries of jurisprudence that developed from them. Human history records their prophecies fulfilled. Scriptural authority foretells the woeful fate befalling lawyers who back off from accepting the lesson to be learnt from them.

Even if we treat these cries from the Old Testament prophets as fit only for anthropological jurisprudence, we are struck by the fact that our notion of justice has survived in a way that makes most of our modern values slight and superficial by comparison. The fact that when we cry for justice today and we cry in much the same way as Hosea, Amos, and Micah cried out against injustice demonstrates that we belong to and share the same single living heritage of jurisprudence. 'Justice is', as Amos says, 'an ever-flowing stream, and righteousness is a river that will never run dry.' Without recognising these eternal verities, there is no prospect of mankind ever having a philosophia perennis (a complete record of legal development), far less a history of justice. Worse still, there is no prospect of humanity ever enjoying justice now.

The fact that it is by now only our rarely recognised Hebraic heritage of jurisprudence—which has survived Egyptian, Assyrian, Babylonian, Carthaginian, Greek, Roman, Soviet, and more recently British notions of justice (to mention but a few)—is an awesome testimony in merely secular terms, never mind on its own intrinsically spiritual terms. The surviving Hebraic heritage of jurisprudence, however, is not just a secular but a spiritual one. Indeed, that is the secret of its survival.

Mankind's search for justice is thus not just secular (whatever is meant by that) but demonstrably divine. There is no lawyer (of the many, many lawyers who set out to disprove Christianity) who has not thereby been converted to the way, to the truth, and to the life of Jesus Christ. It is really the Lord, after all, and not merely Amos who says, 'Stop your noisy songs. I don't want to listen to your harps. Let justice flow like a stream and righteousness like a river that never runs dry.'

The overly secular and exclusively humanist anthropologist may still read this record of divine justice as one of merely human survival, which should give (if not himself) then also the psychologist and the sociologist grave cause for thought. From their wider and deeper studies, both the archaeologist and the historian should more rightly know better that the overly secularised anthropologist is at risk of being drawn by his own profession, but even both historian and archaeologist are as often constrained by the humanly poised camaraderie of their own professions to ignore or dispute both the proof and the truth.

For a certain length of time, one can precariously poise oneself on the boundary between the fact that in the Darwinian struggle for survival, the fittest are those who go on surviving through their faith in God and in the biological value of survival inherently expressed in that fact. One is thereby faced with taking the quantum leap from humanistic secular theories of justice to God-given theological jurisprudence, since nothing more than that, when measured in even just brute terms of survival, has ever either more won out over contrary conflict or won over other more contrary souls.

It is by taking this quantum leap that enables an anthropologist of law such as Max Weber to consider our history of human survival to be explicable only in the context of God's covenant with man. In his work on ancient Judaism, Weber wrote, 'The God of the prophets based his frightful threats of disaster (which actually came about) on the violation of the contractual good faith sworn personally to him as a contracting partner.' So then, thus it is that Amos asks (3:3), 'Do two men start travelling together without first arranging to meet?' And Micah (7:20) even reminds God of 'his solemn promise to show his faithfulness and constant love to his people'. What a grand jurisprudential basis on which to begin studying the law of contract by which to account for the faithfulness and constancy of God!

* * *

Hell-Bent People—a Hidden History
Part VII

The Transformational Power of Prayer
Writing is a form of prayer.
Franz Kafka writing to Max Brod

'Writing is a form of prayer.' So wrote the (albeit atheistic) writer, Franz Kafka, while writing to his best friend, Max Brod. Maybe we all have an atheistic streak of unbelief in ourselves, or else we wouldn't need to pray... ... So then, let's pray!

Writing ... writing ... writing ... when so seriously undertaken, with all one's heart and with all one's mind and with all one's strength and with all one's soul, is most certainly a prayer. It is a prayer, which, like no other prayer, so deeply bares the soul—in itself the substance of things which, but for remaining unwritten, would also remain unseen. So then, after such a prayerful peroration... or merely an icebreaker... let's pray... ... but no, the prevailing mood is one of continued peroration... or perhaps, even prophetic proclamation... ...

It brings the substance of those things unseen to light. It's part of the process of conceiving of the unconceivable. It breaks bonds and barriers for being no longer time-bound to the present, because it can both preserve the past and proclaim the future. Left unwritten, but otherwise not only to oneself but also confessedly first pledged before one's own creator, there is no reader or reviewer of more moment than one's own paternally hallowed God.

We are his people. We are his handiwork. And so we write. Yet it matters not what we say, since we confess (whether we know it or not or whether we ignorantly refute his handiwork or not) with our own epistolary hand. However scratchy be our pens, however obsolete our technology, however wayward our thoughts, he is our first and foremost constant reader.

Isn't it strange, and yet so paradoxically true, that so many non-believers are writers and so many purported atheists (from Franz Kafka to Bertrand Russell and Stephen Hawking) are not only writers but also compulsive writers? If you ever wonder how God finds the time to hear all our prayers, you must wonder still more where God finds all the time to do all the reading we call on him to do, since writing is (as even the atheistic Kafka admits) a form of prayer.

Look here, all of you humans, the whole creation, as conceived with the mind of God and as proclaimed into being from the mouth of God, is also written with the same handiwork of God. God reads not just what we write with our hand but what we think with our innermost mind, because with his own handiwork, God is both a reader and writer too. What he proclaims into being, he confirms by his own written handiwork, for which he does not withhold from us either the design or, through his handbook, the means of its implementation or, for that matter, the means of his assessing our participation.

Alas, ever since the subject of handwriting (with a good hand) ceased to be taught most seriously in schools, the whole concept of handiwork (together with that of writing and reading for its own sake) has fallen into oblivion and, in consequence, also likewise the concept of God. [Excursus 1: Already with the passage of the whole creation being increasingly credited to your own human hands, dearest readers, it has become a hundred times more plausible to credit the entire creation to your own minds, from which serious thought, with all its many prayerful implications, you pass over first to prayer and worry beads and from these to the largely thoughtless manipulation of man-made machines. Don't you realise that writing, as a form of confessional prayer, is on the way out, since you have no concept any longer of there being any heavenly reader?]

This is all the ploy of the Counterfeit Command who would have us (both angels and mortals) counterfeit ourselves to read and counterfeit ourselves to write what the Counterfeit Command would have us read, write, think, say, and do. The continued existence of this divine creation, in terms of its rapidly decreasing resources (including those of people, no less than property), is perilously close to that default position of apostasy, which, for many centuries ago, was clearly prophesied. Can't you already feel in your dried-up bones how much of this humanly accepted default position is an abomination to the creator of creation who entrusted the stewardship of his handiwork to be coterminate with our own survival?

The continued existence of this divine creation, just as of your own continuingly human creation, depends both on the power of prayer that brought both into being as well as on the power of prayer that promotes and upholds their continued existence. [Excursus 2: Remember always that your present appearance on earth—however virtual and temporal, for being mortal, as that may be—is no more than a reflection of your continued potential by which to update the realisation of your eternity in heaven.]

For those of you going forward, there's no going back. This entire creation, from chaos to cosmos, is written entirely in his hand; and the resulting scroll of his handwritten creation is still being still stretched out across all the heavens. It is a scroll on which every written iota is the work of his hand and to be held tightly in his hand, within a grasp that will not let go. The creator of this world is not only this world's creator, maintainer, and sustainer. He is also this world's executor. And just as when he says to let go, he'll catch you in his arms to convey you from the old to the new! Father God, through Jesus Christ, and the Holy Spirit is the one and only fail-safe soul-catcher!

As previously indicated, this short part written on the transformational power of prayer is itself written as a form of prayer on the power of prayer. [Excursus 3: In scripture, we are told that short, brief prayers (the ones that hit the offending nail precisely on the head) carry far more powerful sanction than do those circuitous, long-winded, and cumbersome long prayers. These somehow hit so much else in the cosmic process as to make little folks fearful as to their function.]

Nevertheless, it's often a long haul to remedy things gone wrong or even to preserve and maintain something of the former status quo to allow for the most rightful of new beginnings. And that's exactly why so many mortals (for being themselves divorced from all prospect of a new creation) find the Bible to be this world's most boring book. For lack of reflection (as Confucius says), they haven't learnt to read between the lines. Without thought, they'll happily recite the lines—any lines—but between the lines, they'll expend not even a modicum of thought.

On earth (but not as we do in heaven), we angels must report that most folks tend to formalise prayer, and so then, contrary to scripture (which reminds us to pray constantly), even the staunchest of Christians compartmentalise prayer, as evidenced by their very common but rather startling supplication to say 'Let's pray' (which is a complete giveaway that instead of praying constantly, they haven't even yet begun to pray).

One is then led by this, as often priestly, supplication to 'let's pray', to wonder what indeed it is that people have already been doing, sometimes even in the course of praise and worship, as if these and so many other activities could be possibly attempted, far less achieved, without prayer. The result of this earthly compartmentalisation is that prayer is squeezed more and more into the default position by way of keeping the peace, not righting wrongs by instead avoiding wrongs, promoting wish lists, settling nerves, and generally maintaining not even the status quo but the sad and dynamic decline towards the lowest default position.

The big squeeze that comes with the constantly slowing speed of light is felt by us older ones (including us angels) most strongly in terms of time and most strongly in terms of younger ones (for the most part, vulnerable children and animals) in terms of space. The big squeeze, at present typified by increasingly rising temperatures and rising sea levels, might yet (as in times before) go through another big freeze. None can accurately predict the seasons in these latter days.

Then the struggle for survival, as predicted by all the evolutionists, will never again be encountered as once conceived of by them for being so naturally a part of their lives as ever before. Children will then compete with parents and parents then with grandparents for what remains of this earth's increasingly limited resources. Free trade shall no longer then be debatable; it shall by then, even with the mark of the beast on one's forehead, become a tragic joke.

People shall then literally eat shit rather than suffer from an empty stomach. Even those shit-eaters who, like the writer Flaubert wrote prophetically to Turgenev about this experience of eating shit, for themselves had always, as a means of escape, tried to live in an intellectually environed tower (or clerically whitened sepulchre) shall find a tide of shit beating at that tower's wall and threating to undermine it. What is worse (because after, there's nothing more than shit to read, shit to wear, and shit to eat) is that the intellectually starving, the morally starving, and the spiritually starving millions— sooner than you'd ever dream to think—will come to learn to like it.

'Jesus!' (but no more) say most people (on hearing this) and so leave it at that. But some few (like the writer Flaubert to the writer Turgenev) will have something more to say about it. By then, prayer, apart from the fragmental residue of a chosen few, perhaps only that's left behind in writing, shall be at a premium. Commercial competition shall be so rife then as to be indistinguishable from civil protest, self-defence from outright violence, civic violence from military war, and military war from universal terrorism.

No wonder that so many compartmentalised prayers, simply by their own default, fail to make it into heaven. How could they make it into heaven when they're not even prayers? We beg to report that on this score, something needs to be done, but we'd rather not say so, because it's going to take quite a lot of explosive force to break down the present compartmentalisation of prayer. And already the Counterfeit Command is wrecking worldwide havoc as a result of increasingly disempowered prayer.

It is so little understood now that whatever calling one may have— whether to teach, preach, heal, make peace or keep the peace, run a business, mind a household, or govern a college, city, or kingdom— unless done prayerfully, none of these things can any longer be done. Not only that but the power of prayer runs ever deeper—whether pruning trees or keeping bees or restoring cars or cooking stew or baking a cake or resigning from office or accepting a commission. All these things as if every other things need to be done prayerfully. And it's not enough to have one's prayerfulness as second nature. No, prayerfulness must be one's first nature.

What then do *you* make of reading and writing? Or should we not more accurately ask writing or reading, since without writing, there would be nothing to read, although we usually learn to read contemporaneously by our learning how to write? Nevertheless, what you make, whether of reading and writing or of anything else, is a most serious question, since value may be added to or subtracted from anything by whatever we make of it. Whatever we make of something is not just an interpretative act; it can also be a creative act.

This equation of added or subtracted value is particularly true of the world's great books whose value may be either augmented or diminished according to the seriousness with which they are read. It is as often the reader who brings the word to life and so life to the word, as much as the living Word brings life to the reader. This mutual process is as often proved by both writer and reader bringing each to life.

How many writers you know (and not just know of) is usually determined by how many books you have (seriously) read? You may think to read a book (any book) purely for its subject matter, but unless you have thought to meet the author in so doing, you have not read the book. And should you dare to judge a book, you're then judging the life of the writer, so beware of what it may take by way of life's experience to write that book.

Beginnings generally entail endings, and first causes generally implement final outcomes, but unless from Genesis in the beginning until the very end of Revelation, you can read all that's in between without ever finding out from where exactly you've come and thus to where exactly you're going, then you haven't read that book. There are no shortcuts, unless for being cut short on our travels, so let's pick up and study well our travel plans from beginning to end.

Our first angelic placement, as will possibly be also our last placement in the heavenly realm, is most usually in the prayer brigade. We begin there, as do most beginners, with very little appreciation for the power of prayer, but instead we look forward to more active service in the front line of the heavenly battle and go on hankering after this greater spiritual command until about midway in our military service, when we begin to realise that we are already fighting in the front line of the heavenly battle and that we could not be doing any more anywhere else but for our appreciating far more than we do of the greater power of prayer.

This is a humbling experience for most of us novice angels to realise that the outcome of the battle in which we have already been so long engaged has so far hinged on what we have so long overlooked as the infinite and unlimited power of prayer. A good sermon may last for as long as it's given—a very good sermon for the length of a day—but a prayer, well, that touches on infinity and so may, by hitting the mark (which requires some expertise), last as long as forever. We are all prayer warriors in the prayer brigade, and the only advancement in our lifelong order of service is achieved functionally in our acquiring an ever-greater appreciation for the power of prayer.

How then do we gain this largely pragmatic appreciation for the power of prayer, unless through humbling ourselves in that military command where we mistook ourselves for being already so powerfully and successfully engaged? One way is simply to extend our personal appetite for prayer and to realise that prayer always transcends the accustomed forms by which sometimes others, if not only ourselves, would seek to limit our understanding of its reach.

There is nothing more ineffectual than the accustomed prayer by which the mob will try to coerce the carpenter's son into remaining the carpenter's son. Prayer is either prophetic—breaking through barriers, giving insight, releasing revelations, proclaiming rightful over wrongful ways of doing things—or else, without any cutting edge whatsoever, it is simply putting a plaster on a gangrenous wound.

Music, art, science, and literature, together with the humanities— all these engagements of the human mind and heart and soul are capable of communicating the fullest power of prayer. Of course, all these completely permissible forms of prayer can be tainted, usurped, and abused, no less than the Counterfeit Command will strive to traduce every least remaining power of prayer.

Unless you can discern the darkness of the soul that gives rise to Dickens's *Nicholas Nickleby*, to Eliot's *Waste Land*, or to Orwell's *Animal Farm*, you have completely missed the prayerful communiqué of these and most other writers. There is literally no other way of teaching literature—or science or music or law or commerce or dancing—except as through the power of prayer. Likewise, unless you can read the Word of God as prophetic prayer, you have not only missed the point of prayer; you have also missed the point of God's Word.

There is nothing you can say or do, as said or done by any prayer warrior, that will exculpate you from the consequences of being engaged constantly in prayer. Whether you know it or not, you are already now praying constantly, since there is absolutely no way of getting away from the multidimensional power of prayer. Scoff at this description of yourself, if you so will, but in doing so, whether as a professedly secular scientist or as a worldly wise lawyer or as a wheeling-dealing entrepreneur, you are simply cursing yourself through your own freely chosen form of scoffing prayer.

Our first job in the prayer brigade is to keep tabs on world prayer. It may surprise many on earth to know that for this purpose in heaven, we have no dumpsters, trash cans, wastepaper baskets, or quarantined spam messages by which to sift out unwanted or unworthy prayer. Everything eventually gets through, although there are some more direct prayer routes than there are others. Thus, anything marked for the attention of our supreme translator in the name of Jesus Christ is promised to have first preference, although what is meant by first preference in relation to the many barriers which can be erected by the Counterfeit Commission will have considerable bearing on the eventual action.

There's nothing said or done (and sometimes even just thought or hinted at) that we don't know about. Some people (the common ground claimed by them today is that of personal privacy, with state security a close second at the public level) find this kind of spiritual surveillance immensely terrifying, but anybody and everybody could read the signs of the times if they so choose to cope with the otherwise prevailing fear of our times.

The signs of the times are given to make us wonder. This applies to both you humans as much as to us angels. Without wonder, there is no respite from fear, and so nothing worthwhile happens. If you don't wonder about these signs and if you don't wonder about these times in which you've learnt to wonder about these times, then it follows that you haven't read the signs of the times. Recall yourselves to wonder—that's something always to be done before we pray.

If you haven't yet wondered about these times into which you are born, then you may have missed your calling. The trouble is that without having any well-developed gift of prophetic insight, most people would suffer (as they do already today) from the affliction of informational overload. They lose their sense of wonder and so compromise their lives.

You can always ask for wisdom (but that's a tall order in these troubled times). Likewise, you can ask for understanding (likewise not always a very pleasant task when applied to understanding oneself). Nonetheless, no one with either a modicum of wit, wisdom, or understanding would ask, like Elisha, for more than anyone else's share of prophetic insight in these changed times—or would they?.

Oh yes, at first one's prophetic insight (in its early learning phase) is no more than a minimalist calling. It may be into music or into art or into law or into preaching or into teaching, before being into absolutely everything, but then, whether quite suddenly or incrementally, the prophetic score changes. On reaching fulfilment, the prophetic score changes from the learning (or philological) phase into the praxis of the performative phase.

The one-line lyric gradually extends more and more vertically when it can no longer do so horizontally to reach, when commensurate with one's calling, into what then seems to others to be an individually extended overreach. It touches on the more limited or unheard calling of others and therefore begins to intrude into, however uninvited, the mainstream of their lives. Suddenly and startlingly, it is out there in the public arena—the prophetic calling of a Beethoven, a Prokofiev, a Dickens, a Pasternak, or a Nabokov—without cause, enquiring into and so upsetting and unsettling the securely established and self-ordered lives of others.

People still pray, but the cutting edge of prayer is lost to a passive and apathetic population. People still prophesy, but the prophetic words have likewise lost their meaning to that same passive population. Everything hangs fire, as if on the eve of some monstrously huge battle. Some people lose their nerve—throw away their weapons, switch sides, prefer captivity, sometimes even choosing to end their lives. The front line, whatever the ministry, is still the front line. So then, until our further engagement we'll say, '*Nakanunye*'—meaning 'on the eve' (a Slavic expression used whenever the deeply groaning world holds its breath before reaching some crucial crossroads, coming crisis, or approaching cataclysm!

* * *

BOOK FOUR

A Bare-Bones History of Hell From Prior-Flood to Future Fire

Through Darkness to Light
You have to go through the darkness before you can get to the light.

Haruki Murakami

Intro 1—Katrina (also known as Kate, sometimes Kat, and with the proper Scots Gaelic pronunciation, Catriona): When did you poor benighted souls first hear that mixed message about darkness and light? At first, so we are told, there was a void, with darkness (presumably pitch darkness) upon the face of the deep. So then presumably the cosmic light came later? Well, not exactly later, since any time later, just as of any time earlier, would surely anticipate whatever could be rightly said of anything before time began. It was in the beginning—in the very beginning—that God created the heaven and the earth, so this is not one of your accustomed fairy tales which begins with 'once upon a time'.

Maybe as with the birthing process, you then first experienced that contrasting but purely sensory relationship of coming out of the darkness and into the light. The trouble is that we're not there yet—out into the light—but to get there, then there must be some sort of hope (however subconscious) to take oneself through the darkness to get to the light. On this less than full score (although provided with a figured bass), then in treating of the subject of cross-cultural conception, be sure to read Judi Picoult's *Plain Truth*.

Intro 2—Neil (commonly known to his mates as Nigger): Without some sort of primal preconception, surely there is no possibility of conscious conception, although we note that there are still some primitive people around who have their very own preconception (in most cases, a deistic process) of what it is for someone to conceive and so then hope to bring a child to birth. Indeed, that's one of the last bastions of conceptual freedom from which to abhor abortion. Certainly, it's a tall order to put yourself in place of any as yet unborn child—but you as a child were there once, you know, so resurrect your own prenatal feelings of what it once was to fight for your as yet unborn life in the womb.

Alas, however, since that once defensive bastion of freedom has been now so undermined by the loss of the fortress it was designed to protect—the freedom of the soul. Indeed, we ourselves would be dismissed, in this day and age, for being still so egotistically in the dark as to conceive of ourselves as still having souls. Why, so many of the Bible's soul-references (as once in the Authorised Version) have been expurgated from scripture by target-translated modern versions.

Some of these modernisations do no more than appease our sense of loss for having traded in our souls. Very soon, Chancellor Mephistopheles (who ousted both Plato and Socrates from the classical curriculum) is going to call on every Dr Faustus (including the one and only Dr Freud) to account for his having either sponsored or promoted the human ego by way of trade-off for the human soul. Watch carefully. When that happens, you are very likely to see Freudian psychology go down the plughole for having done as much harm as good!

Intro 3—Kirsty: Nevertheless, there are several good grounds, however much these may be dismissed by secular reasoning, that we all, both angels and humans, share in some extrasensory experience that we possess a soul. It is from this extrasensory experience, possibly long before even we humans are born, that we humans can infer some primal preconception that not only do we possess a soul but that there are angels of darkness no less than there are angels of light. These oppositional angelic forces either fight to keep free that soul in the light or else to smother it for the sake of their own prevailing darkness.

So then this light of the soul is fundamental to life. So lighten up you readers there who feel disposed to dispute this light, but instead try to understand also the darkest world in which many of you humans have lived as often as those rats who, for having lived so long down a dark hole in fear and trembling, then begin to shun the faintest glimmer of light from any open heaven above. Down this funk-hole of fear, bright order becomes rank disorder, with the result that all life forms there mistake the darkest night for being the brightest light—a most remarkable phenomenon in itself, but one which is also paralleled in the biosphere as well as in the cosmosphere, where alien life forms exist (both aerobic and anaerobic, both microscopic and macroscopic), by their avoiding whatever we others have learnt to seek and have been brought up to revere for being the true light.

Intro 4—Callum-John: Hi there again. And for my being still an independent thinker, John's Gospel (exceedingly abstract, exceptionally figurative, and yet still all straight as a die and full in your face) is still my very own stand-alone sort of book. No safety net as yet, of course—either full-on or full-off—just like quantum physics.

Well now, what a shock it is to find out that the little God Almighty of all Good Samaritans is yet another quantum physicist! Almighty Lord—not just another Gregor Mendel cooking up a mess of pottage out of split peas or yet another Dmitri Mendeleev dreaming of yet another white Christmas in the steppes of rural Russia, but a fair dinkum quantum physicist with a belief system that transcends all others!

You don't hear that at all from any pulpit these days. The clergy used to be up—far, far up—in all the sciences. Why, these days, they're still fawning after Sir Isaac Newton! They've never heard of Max Planck, far less of Werner Heisenberg! No wonder that the church has fallen on such hard times! The poor old clergy have got trapped in their own little struggle for church survival and so have finally given up on the hard facts! Why, even Einstein is barely up to Father God's knobbly knees right now, never mind up to what were once his father's sweaty armpits!

For the further hard facts, then—just as some microbes, like those causative agents for lockjaw or tetanus—avoid both light and oxygen, so too, there are many people (still loved for whom they ought to be and were made to be) who yet are drawn down, day by day, into this anaerobic darkness of the lower depths. In many more ways than one, these drawn-down ones come to inflict this same darkness on other people, besides infecting and afflicting yet others with this same darkness (all these again are remarkably real phenomena), so every single person must quickly learn enough true discernment not only to seek the true light but to avoid whatever false and counterfeit light appears to be shining through the same prevailing darkness.

Intro 5—Tristan-David: You may hear the message of true light in all sorts of authorised and unauthorised forms. Today, you can hear that message about light and darkness from the poet and author Haruki Murakami. Why would he, the preferred choice for an earlier award of the Nobel Prize (for literature), appear to put himself down by withdrawing himself from competing against other authors? We don't like to tell you, because the best of teachers don't give the answers to their own otherwise unasked questions, but well, we hope you are curious enough in your seeking to find out.

So then did you hear Murakami's message resonating in your very own avidly listening ear, to hear with all the dulcet tones, overtones, and undertones of your once unimpaired hearing? Before you can get to the light, you'll have to work your way in faith through this world's rapidly descending darkness. There are no shortcuts—no shortcuts at all open to you in your going through the darkness (least of all for the already high-born, filthy rich, and even the immensely famous) since, without working one's own way in faith through the darkness, one may short-change one's already appointed process of redemption to receive less than one's full measure of light.

Perplexed? Well, so you should be, just as humans always are first time round when they find themselves in the presence of angels of light! If we need to tell you something which you could never find out for yourself, well then, we'll tell you. Otherwise, you need to find out, just like the reader of any other worthwhile book, for yourselves. Sure, learning the Scottish Shorter Catechism for a bare-bones Bible may (but with no guarantees) keep you on the straight and narrow, but the dire straits you face may be a lifetime long, and they'll narrow to the point that you may never feel the wind in your sails, however much you may be forced to motor on. As ongoing readers, you may get used to it. But let's be charitable and change the subject here, from the intensely personal to the intensely public.

For some people, the supernatural is all one—with no distinction drawn between the Supreme Command and the Counterfeit Command. In one way (but so very limited in sense), the supernatural is all one, but the spiritual is most certainly not. Get this straight—the kingdom of heaven (with the King of kings as its head) is very different (literally a world apart) from the republic of hell (with all its members in some way or another competing to the death against each other to be president).

Intro 6—Callum-John again: Learn to know on which side your spiritual bread is buttered—whether on the side of heaven or on the other side of heaven (which learners know as hell). You may mistake that question (hell or heaven) for being an easy one to decide, in which case, you're very likely to be on the wrong side of the tracks from heaven. Indeed, for any human to mistake these different tracks for being obviously distinguishable—between good and evil, righteous and unrighteous, or just and unjust—is one of the most fundamental of mistakes (at the highest of metaphysical levels) that any such (very fallible) human being could ever make. Not since Lucifer paved the way is there any bigger drop between heaven and hell, far less between heaven and earth (before going over the edge to hell), since God extended his kingdom from heaven to earth through Jesus Christ. What, you've never heard of heaven having come to earth and yet all you Good Samaritans go on praying for that day by day?

You'll have heard already about big bangs, and in the bare-bones history of hell that follows, you'll learn more about where these big bangs come from. If all neural pathways between heaven and earth were wedged securely open (a sci-fi fantasy, if there ever was one), there'd be no big bangs, but unfortunately, all hell (mostly a man-made category for innocents abroad) frequently gets in the way of those on earth to wedge heaven shut. Nevertheless, to understand hell one needs to know as much as one can about the human race on earth.

All hell (especially when breaking loose) poses huge problems hard to handle by humans until all hell is once again enchained. In the context of the so-called struggle for survival (a misnomer for the still ongoing struggle between the forces of good and evil) what you humans make of your own human race (another misnomer unless waged by humans against all hell broken loose) is yet mischievous in the way it presumes to be naturally and acceptablely ordained—(1) for this so-called struggle for survival to be ethically acceptable when waged all out by the so-called human race against all other races of living things for each other's increasingly limited resources; and likewise—(2) for humans to compete all out and against each other for their own increasingly limited resources.

The truth (not the whole truth, but still the truth) of this great cosmic and metaphysical matter is that (unlike rats and other life forms designed, or descending to serve as scavenging creatures) humans were never made to race (as in the so-called struggle for survival either against themselves or against other life forms) as indeed are so many of those scavenging life forms which can so deletriously affect and infect humans. Thus, as vectors once traditionally pigs, sometimes cattle, even dogs, but also rodents, and now opposums, but always typically rats can turn what was once called natural history into a cosmic nightmare of struggle for brute survival at every step.

Yet you humans (presumably for seeing yourselves for being so much higher up the pyramid by which to represent ascending forms of life) are so much know-alls about proud place held (ironically on the so-called evolutionary tree) as to bring up your own offspring to compete with other offspring and so to compete as adults with other adults, and then—win or lose, but always lose—to compete against yourselves. As you humans say—most truly when judging of the rats (and so consequentially judging also of yourselves)—it's a friggin' freakin' rat race out there! It might just help to end this nightmare by reading Prince Pyotyr Kropotkin's 1901 essay republished in book form many times, now under its present title of *Mutual Aid:A Factor of Evolution.*

Intro 7—Katrina (or Kate or Kat or whatever): There's really no point in us angels hammering you humans about such things when most of you readers are midlife humans who know so much more about this world's rat race than do we angels. We angels can't know as much, far less know any more than you humans, for youse having been so long already adapted or adopted (mostly by default) into the human-rat race. And this is the case, whether for you humans being raised or being made or being adopted (by parents or teachers), to first race with and then race against each other (and even ultimately against all parents, teachers, and mentors). That's exactly (but not of course precisely) where rebelliousness first begins! The closer the competition (sports, scholastic, artistic, trade, professional, or whatever), then the more the soul is likely to be warped by that competition.

Intro 8—Chloe: The idea (false to the core) that close competition is good for the soul is anathema (like husbands to housewives by pissing in the kitchen sink). It is anathema both to any searching soul and to every heavenly soul. It works by way of putting out whatever vestige of any true light may remain, besides buggering up every argument against the still prevailing darkness. As said before, us angels are nothing if not forthright.

Of course, the same goes for any close competition for souls between churches, as well as between guardian angels or between soul-catchers. Look around (on the road to hell), and you'll see joggers competing against themselves, like midlife drag roadsters, out on the main strip, until, for their trying to do the ton (on their already clogged-up vascular circuit), they'll flip the lid with a subdural big bang or else keel right over with a blown-out abdominal aortic aneurysm. Sorry, still running … still running … still running … still running … still … still … still … running. Yes, indeed, the closely competitive streak, whether competing against just yourself in chess or against just yourself in fishing or against just yourself in fluting or against just yourself in bagpiping, can be monstrously self-inflicted.

Intro 9—Clara: Sure! So then slow down … slow down … slow down … as we're always told in studying for Exegesis 101. Breaking the speed limit (at all ages) is nothing but a vanity, a vanity, a vanity. Well, all very well, but what could that mean for Values 203? And it's nowhere at all (except for being always in hell) that all is such a vanity. So then, in what kind of private hell do you think King Solomon was when he sat down to write Ecclesiastes?

There are no tickets for tours to hell, but just stand in the most disorderly queue. You might find that oddly strange, but there's every point to irony, as pointed out by more than one of earth's famous philosophers (the one who never got married as a result of spending his whole life on earth trying to make up his mind whether to or not). Don't scoff, at least he had a mind! Indeed, he had so much more of a mind than most (much more than Descartes, for example) that he couldn't find the requisite method by which to keep to whatever he had decided. And who was he? you do ask. Well, I'll only tell you if you promise to read what Kierkegaard has to say on the subject of irony.

Nevertheless, those routes to hell are engaged in the tourist trade (with so many folks slumming on board, you'll be lucky to get a seat), so that's one of the twenty-four reasons why we commit you to stand in the most disorderly queue. You see, what may seem to you mortals to be disorderly on earth is not in the least disorderly to us in heaven. Once you know the reasons for any doggone or flea-bitten disorder, then it's no longer a disorderly situation but just a different kind of order. Ironic, isn't it? Well, not in heaven and not in hell and possibly not even if you're hell-bent, but only if you're like any other sinner on earth!

No, there's no timetables—that's not likely. You could risk taking a *marshrutniye taksi*, if you're in Moscow, but they might just put you on the wrong plane for Samarkand! Those buses, trains, and planes run continuously 24/7 (since there's no rest in hell for the wicked), so all you have to do is to behave exactly like all the rest by pushing to the front and elbowing your way on either the phantom plane, the phantom train, or the phantom flier. And don't try to pay the conductor (unless by bribe), or else you'll get thrown off whilst crossing the Bering Sea.

So then on your next day of rest, your task is to front up here at the bus stop for hell, but be sure, most exactly, to get in the right queue since not all routes are circular (in their screwing only down to hell with no way back). And most of the linear routes (of which there are many, some most curiously supplied with airbags and lots of stopovers) as well as Mickey Mouse biplane routes, decidedly and determinedly, flying across the Andes, which are still routine. But here's where we come to pass the parcel by way of our having finished with sharing our souls. Guess, for the lack of our good grace, we'll be stuck for the course (if not already far off course) for another three books at least as novice angels!

Intro 10—Emma: The straight-to-hell routes (rocky road, they're called) are rocket-powered. Never mind, you don't need to be a rocket scientist to fly them yourself; any sort of scientist (apart from a social scientist) will be good enough. From these fast-forward downward routes (by rocket propulsion adapted from WWII cross-channel doodlebugs, as youse, for being an air force man, will know), we angels thus warn all youse interns that none of you—we repeat—none of you will have any right of return, so then if any of you interns have the least reason to doubt your calling or vocation—whether as priests, prophets, pastors, preachers, or prophets again (yes, prophets get more than one chance to back off)—so then we repeat … there's absolutely no return, except sometimes for apostles, that's been known. But we don't call them apostles ever again … no, no … most certainly not as apostles from hell. So don't be hoodwinked there. Also, no slumming please, since no slumming tourist has ever been known to return from hell. It's not on their cards any more than apparently on our cards. Don't know why … don't know when …

So then, all phones off. It's the world's last airbus after all. How else do you think we'd fit everybody on by road? Excuse me, please, lady, but is this your Fitbit? Then … no, no, no … the pleasure's all mine. I've just transferred all your data—lungs a little peaky, heart rate above normal, a little leakage in the right ventricle—but (as yet) no major problem. My privilege, ma'am … my privilege. Have a nice flight. Dinner on the hoof. No, don't look down, lady. We'll be landing 18.50. Follow me, as your co-pilot, through customs … and so to bedding down in hell's back room, say, about 19.50 … No, it's now all on your database—there's now no backtracking … so then don't lose your Fitbit!

Seat belts, no … we don't need to bother with them on this route. The turbulence is all down below on earth, because that's exactly where all we fallen angels from hell chose to make it … Right then, if you're all quite ready, tickets please … tickets please … return tickets only please … only with returns, as already explained. Is it true? Can tickets be accepted from interns on this queue? But don't run … don't run, sir …

No, youse won't get on this bus (nor on any other airbus) if you choose to run after any bus to hell, sir. For some as yet unknown reason, it's against the rules (the 666 rules made in hell) for passengers from heaven … causes some sort of disturbance, sir. That's all we can say … some sort of unforeseen disturbance, which makes the point, punctiliously, that for legislating from hell to keep heaven in its place … says something about the limited resources of hell … But we're not supposed to talk about that—even when as now we're already halfway to hell.

Intro 11—Tristan: Just remember, whilst all the time you're travelling, to keep in constant touch with your embassy in heaven. Remember that even in your travelling to hell, you are still heaven's ambassadors. We'll warn you from heaven again and again (whether or not the message is blockaded or corrupted by static) that halfway to hell is far, far less than would be halfway to anywhere else. So also for being more than halfway to hell and so working on earth 24/7 (since there's no rest for the wicked), you're less and less likely to find any turn-off that takes you all the rest of the way to hell.

Respectability affords earmuffs (which old age now bids us wear to hear rather than to censor sound) by which to avoid hearing big bangs (which in themselves denote the bad news of there being no news of any sort). If you can't hear when a pin drops in heaven (or see the lightning flash), then you should listen for the resulting big bang, which follows as close as thunder does to any lightning flash. But instead of looking for lightning flashes and listening for big bangs, most humans (by now barely in any state of being) go around wearing dark glasses to avoid the light and their ears plugged with Bluetooth transmissions to earbuds with noise-cancelling to pre-empt what they define to be extraneous sound.

Intro 12—Augustus: As you can guess, Leading-Angel Tristan is a much-travelled soul-catcher on several continents. And his speciality in these times of rising sea levels is environmental hydrology. If you want to keep your head above water, then consult Tristan.

Nevertheless, in terms of our own impending travel, let's immediately get down to basics! This (once clarion call) is really again to recommence revision of the already much-revised modernist version of heaven's brief history. We could leave this task (of going back to basics) to the capable hands (since 'vanity, vanity, all is vanity') of both geologists and biologists (but any angel with zoology in his or her degree would rather be a drag queen or even just an aphid for being engaged in vegetative reproduction than do just that).

It's better to know the hard facts by which the biogeologist who goes in for billions and trillions of years by which to explain what he couldn't expect to happen overnight, far less over a week of days or even over a year of days, doesn't know because (1) he can't believe in, what for him as a scientist, is the unexpected and because (2) as a scientist (and so a drag queen, when dressing himself in divine drag), he can't find any way, other than procrastinate for billions and trillions of years, of reducing the unexpected to the expected.

Intro 13—Callum (John Three): Well, of course, quantum physics is barely back to basics (at which point, it does a half somersault through the so-called higher education to reach the lower depths). There are both human beings (very limited in cosmic outlook) and divine beings (pre-eminently of cosmic outlook) with yet also a bastard offshoot from the still divine. This bastard offshoot makes them demonic beings (of whose business on earth we know about only too well), but because many human beings (with one foot off the planet into outer space) consider themselves to be the highest sort of cosmic being (and as often seeing themselves to be the only sort of cosmic being), then they're the ones who see themselves (whether in space drag or out of space drag) as only through an environmentally disturbed glass very darkly.

Intro 14—Little Comrade Lenin: 'Row, row, row the boat gently down the stream. / Merrily, merrily, merrily, merrily, life is but a dream … Row, row, row the boat gently down the stream. / Merrily, merrily, merrily, merrily, life is but a dream … Row, row, row the boat gently down the stream. / Merrily, merrily, merrily, merrily, life is but a dream.'

* * *

A Bare-Bones History of Hell
Part I

By Overstating the Heavenly Case
Never was anything so well accoutred, so brilliantly
presented, and so finely disposed by any two armies
[each of which thought the other evil and of no
account]. The trumpets, fifes, hautboys, drums, and
cannons made such harmony as had never before
been heard in hell itself. The entertainment these two
armies gave to all mankind began with a discharge of
cannon, which, in less than the twinkling of an eye,
laid flat about six thousand persons on each side.
François-Marie Arouet de Voltaire, *Candide*

For the first part of this bare-bones history of hell, we are going on
a little holiday (angelically supervised from heaven) to undertake an
archaeological dig in greater hell. [Exegesis 1: In hell, greatness is
measured proprietorially in terms of territory—and the greater too,
in terms of conquered territory. Once upon a time, as in Imperial
Russia, property was measured in terms of souls, but now, almost all
over the world, souls are measured proprietorially in terms of their
owned (and preferably conquered) property.]

On our rapidly shrinking earth, the same universally metric
measure is proudly followed, as by Greater Glasgow or by Greater
London, to champion local government's urban conquest of the rural
countryside. Our greatest triumphal conquest can be measured by
the little and once country town of Dunedin in New Zealand, whose
population of little more than one hundred thousand souls inhabits a
conquered countryside greater than either of the nation's competing
capitals of Greater Auckland or of Greater Wellington.

Digging up a midden on earth (despite everything from condoms
and drug syringes to fully charged two-ampere cadmium batteries
and still live 8mm ammunition) is one thing. Digging up mass graves

in greater hell of aborted babies, suicide victims, victims of sexual attack, and death by a thousand still fresh cuts is quite another thing.

Yet whereas on earth, the worst of life seeks either to hide or else allowably to be pushed underground, in hell the worst of life walks as if upright to make every dislocated claim it has with which to occupy each last breath of air and shard of viable surface. Apart from the US dollar (with its paraphernalia of pyramids, all-seeing eyes, and other occult objects), hell's souveniring archaeology is in its heyday. As in Athens, do as the Romans do, and join the dig!

Dig in then, all you little heavenly gophers, by which we all hope to disinter the long-ago disarticulated backbone (of this world's still suppurating spine). Confirmed date of death: long before the twenty-first millennium (DT—Darwinian timekeeping). That's long before even sin was sin. Nowadays, sin is sin—mostly human self-inoculated sin—which still (like the blood of Cain) lies buried deep in the darkness of this now not-so-naked earth. And that's where this still treacherous flow of human blood continues to saturate a great deal of this world's both ancient (BC) and now also modern (AD) history. Hold on, you gophers. Take a deep breath here before we risk releasing more deadly fumes from more deep digging!

We unashamedly use the terms BC (before the birth of Christ into this sinful world) and AD (after that glorious day in which our Lord came into our lives on earth) rather than the spiffy (OE, which tries to substitute overseas experience for old era and NE, or new era, for the humdrum lives we live after living down the furlough of our overseas experience). Yet the bare-boned version of greater hell (in this, the writer's quarter) has the world's greatest library of both ambiguous and unambiguous acronyms and initialisms (besides—with all devilish details to consenting adults on demand— the likewise ambiguous, but yet unaccustomed collections of both soft-born-soft-porn humanistic situations as well as of hard-born-hard-porn satanic situations); so then don't hesitate (so we are told, although the mechanically extended invitation is somewhat quizzical for being written (as they always do in old-style Cyrillic) still upside down and back to front) to pay (as also into Lenin's Tomb) as many as you like of heavily discounted midnight visits.

Meanwhile (evidencing always the meanness factor) move on, move on! Don't be mistaken for the walking dead when shuffling past the sleeping dead, while worshipping the immense time and effort that goes into the earthly task of ensuring we'll be remembered for always and always (on closed-circuit television) for our pilgrimage [no exegetical note supplied] to Lucky Lenin's Tomb!

As you may have already picked up (since finders keepers down here), we speak a lot of flutter-gutter by way of soft-sell price reductions (for which you don't always need to pay) down here in hard-sell hell. Besides which, there's always a lot of confusion over persons (whether first person, second person, or third person) for anyone or everyone in their deciding exactly (with not a hope of their conclusion being precise) as to who the real speaker is. Well, as with angelic telepathic communication as well as with angelic teletransportation, both are common to heaven and hell, so as we've said before, don't let technology fool you when as usual, we each throw our voice. Ventriloquism (carried to the level of an esoteric art) is all the rage down here. Appraise each voice both by tone (A440) and content (divine, demonic, secular, or sacred).

There's no smoke without a fire, of course, and so the whole purpose of the hellish smoke always all around these here parts (with magnifying mirrors so often on the side) is to make it absurdly clear as to where the real fire of hell never is. It's really quite remarkable (as close to a miracle as anything can ever get down here in hell) that whenever anyone (usually the most recent novice) cries out (mostly under the greatest of self-induced pain) 'Fire! Fire! Fire!' how so rarely, except by further subterfuge, the least spark of any fire can be found. Of course, we prosecute very heavily in hell for all such false alarms.

There's always a splinter of truth (by itself invariably unseen) in every counterfeit you see. That's the devilish dodge by which we accentuate the positive by which to make the unseen seen. Every best-before and hell-produced counterfeit (where barely read terms and conditions still apply) can thus be made to hold its own. This enables a concession to be granted (in every case relying on the modicum of splinted truth by which to negate the far greater measure of untruth arising from this devilish dodge). This, in turn, satisfies the purpose of open markets to further the purpose of free trade (for whatever lost cause) against the truth, the whole truth, and nothing but the truth. Consequently, we take much hellish pride in our being defenders of every last splinter of what otherwise would prove to be a lost truth.

Our archaeological dig (you should be relieved to know—no, not here, the latrines are over there) is fully commissioned by false agents of the Supreme Command (despite youse hoi polloi being here in hell). That heavenly upper crust of the Supreme Command (all double agents disguised as trade commissioners and military attaches in place of diplomats) are all on hell's payroll. According to our own way of looking at things (from far below upwards), we 'hopes' thereby to account for the way in which 'youse humans' (on whose behalf we'll speak the lingo-orongo-tongo, the counterfeit form of glossolalia) may be heard as uttered in this dark place below. As best we can, this lingo-orongo-tongo will be used for communicating with youse otherwise grammatically correct (but so often morally abject) upper-crust humans. So then stick strictly to hell's firebreaks (rule 231). We're obliged to tell youse (rule 513) to take off your fancy, fiery footwear before entering the sleeping quarters (rule 117), and likewise, don't cook (far less attempt to bathe, except nude) in hell's so stylish, hot mud pools (rule 631), or else (for being subjected to severe self-reprimand) you'll fry your tits and bollock your balls!

You're here now in hell (without working visas, of course) even where angels (despite the long-ago idiot exodus from heaven) have previously feared to tread. Meanwhile, youse humans owe us! Consider how (before we twist your arm, whether both or individually) us angels have so far fallen from being amongst the highest of upper-crust dignitaries by our employing the humour of hell to hide the extreme gravity of youse humans further contributing to the follies which have so beset the upper crust of this sin-saturated world, eh?

Over and over again, us little demons, with our devilish sense of humour, have let youse humans off the heavenly meathook. And here's the paradox of this saving grace (however much counterfeited it is here by us in hell) which, meanwhile, so much more it is youse owe us, since youse humans have thereby achieved (although at the instigation of us in hell) what we here in hell could never do, and this mostly by your overstating the seriousness of the awe which you profess to hold (but do not attempt for yourselves to do) for all those heavenly miracles which can be done only under an open heaven.

With their *ha-ha-ha*, as well as with more of our non-provocative but instead courteous reply of *ho-ho-ho*, we'll then think to simply *go, go, go*, in getting on with our *dig, dig, dig*. [Excursus 1: Together with such mutual pleasantries of sharing this same lingo-orongo-tongo means of expression, please overlook, and don't think to track down, either the reasons or lack of reason for the peals of cacophonic laughter, which, at the oddest of intervals, punctuate everyone's everyday conversations when holidaying (or partying) in hell.]

As unexpectedly funny as some of youse humans may have been brought up to find this part of hell's history—oh, here's another missing vertebra (tail end it is)—our hard-working holiday, for the most serious purpose of digging into and unearthing human sin, is also (down here) likely to prove the blackest and therefore least funniest part of this otherwise exceedingly serious subject of sin. Funny, ha-ha—no, not funny at all! Meanwhile (another pregnant pause), take a big, big, big breath here, because we're about to exhume the next big coffin of a dead sentence as delivered in court (or as more usually on earth confined to victims of the debilitating St Vitus's dance of legislation).

So then to the breathless tune of bureaucratic legalese, prepare yourselves to survive either the unreasoned onslaught of perfunctory legislation or else the overly reasoned and self-justificatory onslaught of judicial reasoning. Either of these (take a deep breath now), when thus used in any hellish context, is no more than verbally hyperventilated (for being hyperhyphenated) so as to allow wheresoever in hell, howsoever in hell, and so also, as we're told, with whomsoever in hell. But not more closely coupled as to be mistaken any further upstairs for conferring any rights of marital covenant when made in heaven, then we angels (although expressing our reluctance at being so unsettled by this unexpected happening) won't further presume to disturb (without our hearing a pin drop by way of our otherwise expected calling) the enjoyment either of our much lesser angelic colleagues or of our far more secular of human interns who may thus expect (subject to their guaranteed disappointment) an even greater level of human enjoyment from their downstairs experience of sharing in something so privileged as this working holiday, to be completely paid for by the Counterfeit Command on completion of the course (although fully acknowledged now that this payment, on behalf of lesser colleagues and intern students, is still only promised orally). And as all this is declared to be true (as already said—somewhere, somewhat, and somehow, the same as before)—it is therefore in consideration of all souls (both of the lost, the found, and the mislaid) made subject to the abovementioned disappointment to be administered most fully in hell. There, there, relax completely and have a good day. It's now (so we're told by deed poll) all street-legal!

'Look at whatever outcome you've signed up for this way,' says hell's in-house counsel, Dr Faustus, LLD. 'All this is no more (nor less) risky than taking out a student loan or else going on a three- or four-year extended lap gap around the disintegrating EU on some very personal OE. As promised before (despite all promises in hell being voidable) no green cards, work visas, tax numbers, or welfare cards are required down here for either work or play. All kosher work (as undefined) and undertaken down here by them (i.e. the student interns, of course) will be guaranteed (likewise voidable) without the slightest need for their being indemnified (likewise, of course) for the far deeper out-of-pocket purposes (construed disjuctively) of the wider public's higher education arising out of any intern's more than accidental death. Well, well, now then, that's all—in accordance with our mission statement—as clear as hell!

'All that remains for me now then—*ha-ha-ha … ha-ha-ha*—is to tie up (reef or clove-hitch) some very loose ends. In accordance with whatever meaningful meaning of meanwhile still remains to console any erstwhile victim of unintended consequences, then whatever costs (minimalist) are likely to be incurred (unlikely) will be offset (or money laundered) by way of unsuspecting charitable donations than more perceptibly would occasion from selling off whatever treasures (unlikely) may be retrieved (just as unlikely) from no more than this great archaeological dig (gunrunning excepted) to rediscover (mind the minefield) the root causes of sin.'

'Are you all then (all of youse still on the street) still with me? Good, then raise your right hands (no need to detach them from either your arms or your armaments), and so *voila*, your autoelectronic signatures have been already auto-obtained. So then have another good day, everyone!

First and foremost, a word (and a very new word it is) on wellness! Whenever holidaying in hell (which is wherever this happens to be on earth), but hold on, always be discrete here as to where exactly on earth it is that you're going to take this holiday in hell, since you must always be prepared for the hitherto expected to turn out to be completely unexpected. Every sort of hell (where there are thousands of sinkholes, slush ponds, and scamper farms) has the perverse propensity (for at least a little while unless for one's entire lifetime) of making itself appear as utmost heaven. For that very reason, we angels won't (indeed, can't) exempt you, young student interns, from your OE (sorry OT) experience of learning to live through the worst.

For one thing, whilst unthinkingly (a predisposition to disaster whilst holidaying in hell), you may be disposed to believe yourself (for all eternity) to be holidaying in heaven, since the barest of bones (besides being rightfully brought back to life in other OT circumstances by the Supreme Command) can also be deceptively returned to only a semblance of life by the occult and demonic forces of the Counterfeit Command. Get the message—the deepest darkness almost always chooses to express itself as the brightest source of virgin white! [Ellipsis 1: For exactly that reason (although more precisely to avoid self-deception), it is best (without any more ado) to advise every young bride (unless still in purdah) to get married in off-white].

Some say that to visit hell (especially on any tourist visa, far less on any slumming permit), you must first be blindfolded. Chances are that if already blindfolded, you're already in hell. So no blindfolds please, but if you're already wearing one, we'll help you out of it.

On the other hand, don't go touring, tramping, slumming, or even just gratuitously exploring any part of hell, especially if only to satisfy your picaresque and slumming curiosity; or else, when it comes to leaving hell, the powers that be in charge down there may never let you out. Be advised that 'down there' for hell and 'up there' for heaven are always figurative expressions, because (especially when being pulled 'sideways', the histories of both these 'places' (another figurative expression) make all such figurative expressions more pertinent to histories of ideas than are the dates, times, places, and names of persons more pertinent to histories of events.

Other voices (to which shut your ears), likewise other sights (to which shut your eyes), since you don't really want to see or hear the sorrows of hell—so then, simply do as you're told—or else for more than one very good reason (of which, being scandalised doesn't count) then don't! So just tightly shut your eyes (so these mocking voices say) to all such hellish sorrows in the very same way as you so readily shut your eyes and ears to all those sorrows which still prevail on earth.

We advise you never to mind such people, unless they're the same sort of folks who, when you fall under a bus, tell you to 'have a good day'. If truth be told (which rarely happens unless by accident down here), they're most likely to be infant demons (twerps, they're called) who haven't learnt to don any divine disguise! Likewise, when visiting hell, you too will have to pass by many of those same people who, like that once rich man Lazarus who never thought to relieve the thirst of others whilst upstairs on earth and now thirsts sorely for the living waters to relieve his own thirst when now downstairs in hell. We warn you not to give him any more time of day than you'd give to any similarly beleaguered beggar on the street.

We'll also warn you right now, before we all enter hell (along this widest of main streets and straight ahead to pass under the arch which says, 'Work will make you free'), that getting out (by simply losing consciousness or passing out on the way in) simply won't work. It simply won't work since for your getting here, you don't have that level of consciousness to lose. Likewise, any other form of exit, which (on passing by) can so easily be mistaken for being the quickest of exits by which to get out, is by no means the most desirable (although the most dependable) of ways (whatever the consequences) by which to try to make a break for it. But then we give you such good advice only because we know you won't believe it.

Nevertheless, on any way out (whether only another dead end or not), don't look back (as did both Orpheus, who thus lost Eurydice, and Lot's wife, who in consequence of ignoring that angelic warning, turned immediately into a pillar of salt). Tiresome, ain't it?

All the same, you'll be constantly ministered to around the clock (which in hell alternately drags through wakeful nights for being allowed to get very rundown, then euphorically speeds up by whizzing through the day on strong coffees and sugar highs). You'll be ministered to (24/7, as the common expression goes) by us angels in hell (as we're more familiarly known to the Supreme Command). Nevertheless, this most intimate of family support applies only if you're meant to endure that desert experience by taking (every seventh year) as your sabbatical (whilst undercover) in hell.

Yes, for the sake of your soul, you may be meant to be there in hell, where (for the sake of the kingdom, since hell's the most restrictive of republics) most angels have done more than a few stints (not just in Kabul under fire or in Tehran under fire or in Damascus under fire but also under the hottest fires of hell). Yet once again, as after every successful time of spiritual ministry, don't look back … don't look back … don't look back!

Lot, as we/they say, way down here in hell, was some sort of a funny bugger. It was not for that but rather for the disobedience of his wife that she was turned into a pillar of salt. Ever seen a pillar of salt? Yes, we angels have during WWII, when salt was cut, carried, and sold in long rectangular blocks to save space in transit, which reminded the Allies not to look back on good times when the going forward got so mighty tough.

So then stay together (like preschoolers on their first field trip) when called (but never when told) to go to hell. Watch out for each other, don't trip on the kerb, and keep your eyes always open for the unexpected sinkhole. And besides keeping your cool in the midst of the fire, keep all your wits about you when you're also under fire. So then stay calm, relax always, and never risk losing your faith through fear.

First thing to notice on entering hell is that the signposts are all reversed. Look, they would have you believe that instead of just entering hell from heaven, we've just entered heaven from hell. No, no, don't look back … don't look back … don't look back!

You'll get used to it here in hell, or so you think you will, but just don't you dare to do so. Just as west is west and east is east (ignore that notice in neon lights which says 'West is east and east is west'), you'll thereby be tempted to think that neither the twain shall meet and so shall it always be with heaven and hell (until perhaps on that great day of judiciously negotiated compromise bringing about our ultimate reconciliation). Whoops! But we have no more time right now for speculative theology than for speculative jurisprudence. In this dark and dismal place, we are where we are, just as we are who we are and going where we're going.

Get this straight—which for some folks mean for them to stop smoking weed and for others to give up the drink and for yet others to humour their wives. Where were we … ah yes, for going cold turkey and getting things straight … that in life we've all suffered the severest of traumas … of traumas … of traumas … in just having crossed over from heaven to hell (and it may well be a worse trauma which we experience in trying to pass back eventually from hell to heaven). Either way, some folks go blind, go deaf, go dumb, turn psychotic, become paralytic, or like Bad King John after signing Magna Carta, fall on the floor in front of his not-so-loyal subjects, and chew … chew … chew the carpet …

From the ensuing silence at this point, it sounds as if you more serious readers are in need of some exegetical explanation as to Magna Carta (buried as it lies under a welter of other classic comics in the libraries of hell on earth). To this most serious of subjects and at the further risk of extending (any more from heaven to hell) this already runaway book, we shall devote a whole separate paragraph to the topic of what has been always consistently swept under the carpet in any history of signing Magna Carta. So then hallelujah (as they say down here) with knobs on!

Well, well, well, here's a historic exegesis of Magna Cart all on its own! [Exegesis 2: It helps us all to understand the transformational situation here (whether at Runnymead, the foremost pub in hell, as it advertises itself to be, or else at Runnymede, its competitor along the street for the privilege of going cold turkey) to realise that it's not bad King John himself who, after signing Magna Carta, shocked all hell for appearing to have been slain in the spirit before his falling to the floor and giving himself over to chewing the carpet but instead that he is manifesting a demonic carpet-chewing spirit (afflicting many

CEOs) who, like Bad King John, still today remain in much need of further ministry.

On such score, then read Leading-Agent Jamieson's supplementary report entitled 'Magna Carta in a Handcart, from 1215 to 2015 and Far Beyond'. You'll find it in the *Otago Law Review* volume 14, no. 1 (2015), pp. 91–2015—if you can find the *Otago Law Review*. So then are you still closely following the fierceness of this present military action being devoted (unlike that of the Turks on Constantinople, any more than the same Turks on the Armenians or more recently on the Kurds) to our assault on hell? Then for all being okay (at least on the formerly Western Front), keep to orders and still carry on!

* * *

A Bare-Bones History of Hell
Part II

By Understating the Hellish Case
'Oh hell!'—as an interjection—when serving as an
exclamation of surprise or annoyance.
                        Oxford English Reference Dictionary

Let's get this straight. Whether as an interjection in lower case or as
a proclamation in upper case, never underestimate the forcefulness
of the slightest call-up signal however inadvertently made to hell.
Damn it, for allowing myself to get completely tied up to drafting
this document, then by letting my own defences down, so likewise
my computer's gone down! Don't follow us down, dearest readers.
Switch off your Kindle, if that's what you're reading from now. With
hell so much into top technology these days, it's always much safer
to read from hard copy. Buy the book!

For this second phase of our archaeological dig into hell, more
caution will be required than for the first hard-digging-down phase.
The risks we'll face to extricate ourselves from the hole we've dug
for ourselves to reach this place (remember, ours is still a military
operation) will remain exceptionally difficult (even although
sanctioned by highest heaven). The only one person who has ever
done anything remotely like this ever before was Christ Jesus. Take
heart, he has promised that we should do even greater things than
he did!

We're not grave robbers, you know—although they won't believe
that down here where all the graves are already robbed! So then for
the purpose of confirming and fulfilling prophecy (as said before), be
sure to bone up on your history. The outcome of every archaeological
dig (as for that which broke into Tutankhamun's tomb or which
rediscovered Troy or which later opened Tamerlane's tomb) depends
on far more than the morally informed meticulousness of our digging.
No more than by boring into our own earth's molten plasma would

we want to bring more than we could manage (whether of Troy, Carthage, or Sparta) to this earth's surface.

Bear in mind that after the Second Trojan War, the Greeks tore down the city of Troy, and after the Second Punic War, the Romans burnt and salted the ground of Carthage. It was to put an end to the evil in those cities (as done more directly by our Lord God for Sodom and Gomorrah). The divine objective was neither solely punitive nor simply recriminative, nor even more mercifully jurisprudential, but instead to prevent the restoration of those warring cities, both for every good reason as well as for all time to come.

Nothing (not even the spoils and treasures left there) was to be redeemed, and for anyone to look back on what was left would incur outrageous disaster. Yes, for every good reason, our God is self-bound by the laws of his own creation to be (in your less than all-seeing human eyes) a most ruthless god. Believe us angels for what we say in our having seen so many of you humans kill both yourselves and other humans through your acts of mistaken kindness.

Now that youse humans have learnt to fly and so have come to think of yourselves as the real rulers of whatever measure of the heavenly kingdom has yet to come to earth, the archaeological dig into history has been humanly replaced by such events as rocket launching, gun and drug running, and air bombing. This is now a whole wide world phenomenon, whether the targets be New York, Washington, Christchurch, Kabul, Baghdad, Tehran, Dumfries, Dunedin, or Damascus. Be prepared for further furies—the existing momentum is intense.

'Cool winds shall [no longer] fan the glade', as they once did for Semele in Handel's famous oratorio of that name, since land mines are often 'where'er you walk'. And as for peacekeeping forces, when exposed to their being bombed in Beirut or of citizens in countless cafes throughout Europe, terrorists are no further away than round the corner. For the fierceness of our own continued assault on hell (where still innocent laughter, however canned, can achieve far more than threats, tears, or fears), youse more and more need to know exactly (but not precisely, which would only bug youse for being beyond even us) why we first have had to work through a brief history of heaven before we could risk visiting hell. Yet this 'dare look back to heaven' function (when close to panic under heavy fire) serves the very opposite of what we do whenever we 'dare look back to hell'.

A word of advice here, since hell never seems the same to any two people. Hell is unique to almost every single person—the only exception being that of Jesus Christ, who came down here to hell for the weekend to see how each and every one of hell's inhabitants (having arrived here before him) would feel about shifting off upstairs or else for staying on down here more permanently despite his crucifixion. One and all of hell's inhabitants (apart from those very odd ones whose souls felt strongly otherwise) reassured him, whilst thanking him profusely, that they couldn't see any point to following his policy of resurrection (far less the possibility of their own crucifixion). From the top down (as it always is in hell), they all felt very much at home there, where they promised to stay (or so they said) until they'd made more permanent arrangements to take over heaven.

For having dropped only so recently into hell, we're still in recovery mode now, so take things easy (and don't step off the straight and narrow path). Look hard—no, no, no, not to the right and not to the left but only straight ahead where you'll see the footprints of our Lord's one and only way still glistening on the floor of this Sheol, Hades, or Gehenna. [Exegesis 1: Just as there once were three parts to ancient Gaul (made famous by Julius Caesar), there are also (as for the local government of almost every one of this earth's nations) these three parts (the rich, the poor, and the in-between) to what we know altogether for being hell on earth.]

Eyes ahead, don't look down, walk in faith, and (as with the Irish blessing) 'the road will rise up to meet you'. This is the same path (remarkably like that which when printed on the uncarpeted floor of any hospital) that guides patients through sanctuaries, havens, hospitals, and other places of respite and refuge that Jesus took on coming down to (what in caps for being more important then than now) what was once up-marketed for being Sheol, Hades, Gehenna, or now no more than just plain old hell. Look around, and you'll find the names of some very famous people who once were here (Buddha, Socrates, and Confucius amongst them), although there's plenty more even more famous in their own time that you'd never believe for being still left behind here.

Take care. We're still in recovery mode. All the same, although by giving you readers now a bare-bones history of hell (instead of augmenting what, after all, has been no more than a very brief history of heaven), it may not seem so. The trouble is that the greater your commission to the Supreme Command, then the more you need to know for your own protection against the Counterfeit Command, which is out to get you not only in every way you might first think possible but also in every other way it can. This it always does by such brilliant means of counterfeiting that you'd never have thought of that level of technological expertise as being in any way possible at all. [Word of warning 1: When down here, don't get caught up in the technology of counterfeiting (which can be extremely captivating) any more than in the technology of hacking, hoodwinking, scamming, prevarication, and lying—through the teeth (whether or not lying on the ground). Once you're really caught up in even the very least of these hellish measures, it's very hard to break free.]

At first you may not think so, because the Counterfeit Command will lull you into a feeling of false security by reason of your own assumed commission to the Supreme Command. Indeed, your commission has not even been actioned yet, since your loyalty to the Supreme Command has to be put to the test of faith. Yet the closer you relate to the Supreme Command, the more vulnerable you will be to be taken out by the Counterfeit Command. The emphasis throughout this test of faith is on your learning of spiritual discernment.

The second phase of your first (but not earliest) introduction to the Counterfeit Command is that you will only begin to experience the very least of counterfeit pressure—and yes, your initial urge to answer to the Supreme Command may lead you to mistake this counterfeit pressure for being that of the Supreme Command. And yet this is only the very beginning of your ongoing test of faith, which will never be complete on this present earth (far less in your field of duty in hell against hell) for as long as you remain vigorously committed (avoid apathy) to the Supreme Command.

Indeed, this test of faith will continue for as long as your commission continues, either on earth or in hell, to be actioned by you on behalf of the Supreme Command. Beware always of this very narrow and sometimes very unpleasant learning road, especially when it gets so much wider, apparently so much shorter, even just a little less uphill, and so much easier to travel. Read always the signs of the times, therefore, and ignore the counterfeit signposts (which you may often find as much, if not more misleading, on earth than they are here in hell).

We accordingly begin again here and now (which is so often only the past all over again) by raising a point of order (which is why parliaments have rules of order and Presbyterians have whole Books of Order. It is that hell (as described above for being a counterpart to heaven) is not a heavenly construct. On the contrary, for the most part, mankind makes its own hell. This may be seen especially by that level of hell as raised by mankind to so often apparently heavenly heights. Of course, this concept of there being any heavenly hell is a counterfeit concept especially when it is achieved so extensively by today's deeply bewitched (and sometimes even demonically possessed) mankind.

Our advice then is to look (but not directly, or else the searing heat of hell might blind you) at the continuing history of hell this way: once upon a time, heavenly heights were measured (however fortuitously) by every city's tallest steeples and foremost college spires, but now the heavenly heights are measured by soaring sky towers, crowded gambling casinos, and student pubs. But don't prevaricate from the gospel truth by holding any great architect of the universe to be responsible for anything like that by way of being today's great architectural outcome. Just because Jesus Christ came down to Sheol, Hades, and Gehenna or any greater hell (now, like greater London, reduced by Brexit (or any other means of Procrustian persuasion) to no more than hell), it doesn't in any way sanction Satan, far less his cohorts of demons, any more than it sanctions the place (whatever place we think to know of) by calling it hell.

Nevertheless, for each of (*youse*—don't say 'believers' for needing to keeping *youse* incognito here) being in any way human, you need to come to grips (although in the most minimalist of ways) with some far, far shorter history of hell (no more for the moment than by this bare-bones version) in order to qualify you for reaching a far, far greater human understanding (than you already do have) of heaven. Your present concept of heaven, alas, is often only that one which you humans mistake for being no more than contentedly and apathetically human. Well, what do you suppose we angels would have to sing about for being just that! No, you've still got so much more to learn about heaven, which is why you're on this trip to hell!

Meanwhile, relax, heaven is no mean city, although it is every small town's aim (if not to gobble up its neighbour) at least to raise its head (even just a fraction) higher than its every other smaller neighbour. This competitive mindset on the brutish basis that big is beautiful certainly promotes the tourist trade, which, in turn, operates (sometimes to hellish depths) as today's greatest leveller.

Big business (at which point we may mourn the loss of the once corner store or family farm as much as we may mourn the loss of the family doctor or the family lawyer), in turn, promotes 'economy of scale', as often as not a self-contradiction, whose only purpose is to postpone the biggest of economic meltdowns. [Word of warning 2: But woe is me (as well as woe is you) if you humans should mistake this apostolic message for being yet only another instance of overstating the heavenly case. Believe you me, but we angels still of heaven keep our feet firmly on the ground of heavenly understatement, whereas the key to understanding hell (as in horse trading, car selling, and land selling) is that of discerning overstatement. And that's exactly why you should never underestimate or understate the case for hell.]

This raising of hell on earth by humans (otherwise known as raising Cain) is done always at the direction of the Counterfeit Command. Its false objective is always to disparage the efforts of the Supreme Command. These efforts of the Supreme Command are to straighten what's crooked and to keep all already straight things still straight on earth as they are for still being straight and to the point (mind out for that presently falling pin) in heaven.

The due process of the Supreme Command is thus always that of restoration and so to keep all things from going so sadly and badly crooked that they can't be repaired or restored. There's no more point (though you won't want to see or feel it) to the new Adam blaming Satan and his cohort of fallen angels for this world's escalating state of corruption than there is to the new Adam blaming the old Adam (say, for not keeping tabs on his wayward wife) than there is to next blaming the divine giver and creator of Adam's helpmate, Eve, for his not keeping (probably the requisite genetic) tabs on what he thought he (the Almighty) was doing to mismatch the hitherto upright Adam with any such senselessly unthinking and so utterly wayward wife. And even if you can't recognise that carousel of blame for being a merry-go-round going nowhere, ditch it fast before it takes you so fast you can't get off.

Nevertheless, this world's hell (as you may not like to hear of it) is almost entirely constructed by humans. Satan is simply sitting back in his easy chair—very likely a professorial chair—with no other aim than to run off with the academic credits won by his burgeoning minions. He is the foremost exponent of production line presidents, production line politics, production line welfare, production line education, and even production line prayer groups. Yet his foremost vulnerability—mark this vulnerability well, all youse hell-bound humans—is that (for his being almost entirely egocentric) Satan is always a short-term thinker. Having renounced all long-term prophecy in favour of such ephemeral things as political correctness and business confidence, he thinks, as does any politically correct and self-confident but still unsound politician, that he has only to keep himself well seated to cover his butt.

Actually, most such heavenly constructs (more accurately misconstructions than reconstructions) are anthropomorphisms (now there's a big word for mistaking an angel of the Lord, far less mistaking a brick or a stone or a car or a ship for being that of any angel) in his making his angelic appearance resemble some notoriously defaulting simpleton. Anthropomorphisms are mostly the result of human theologians in their thinking and so not more like God but still even more like humans. [Excursus 1: As the theologian Barth reminded us, by our being made in the image of God, we're all theologians. True in essence, but alas, for that divine image once given to man for being so often extremely falsified.]

Actually again, for Satan being predominately a short-term but very fast thinker, he has learnt so much from youse fast-buck humans. It takes a great deal of time, usually for us angels (actually as long as any human lifetime), to teach any theologian to think like a divine, and in the course of this lifelong learning experience (which many more worldly theologians mistake for negotiating or arbitrating between heaven and earth), many, many (otherwise very nice) theologians run completely off the biblical rails. [Excursus 2: As you can see from all us angels of the Lord belonging to the heavenly host, we tend towards the generic fault of congregationalism in our 'sticking together'.]

'Now let's get this straight,' interjects the Lord. 'Idolatry is a human mindset brilliantly worked out in the superlative brain of the Counterfeit Command. Its military objective is to effectuate a strategic onslaught at all levels against the kingdom of heaven. Why, one of the most common, most extreme, and most provocative forms of idolatry to us in heaven is for humans to idolise one or the other (either Father, Son, or Holy Spirit) as if he or she alone were the entirety of the triune equation. That matters very, very much to the resulting outcome.

'Of course, it doesn't matter a tinker's damn to those in heaven (to use the only words which they in hell can understand) that this kingdom of heaven has now come to earth through the supreme sacrifice of both Jesus Christ and myself as Father God as well as of herself, the Holy Spirit. Make no mistake for all creation being the work of all three persons as one and the same celestial being when functioning *a cappella* in the Supreme Command. Yet anything— literally *anything* (or *things*) or *anyone* (or *ones*) *at all*—by the perverse mind of any human can be made idolatrous.

'Law and order can be made idolatrous (as so often brought about by church and state). Health and welfare can become idolatrous (by relying on the hollow promises of well-meaning politicians). And even praise and worship can be made idolatrous (as so insinuated by no less well-meaning false priests, false prophets, and false teachers of the law). It's a hard road to heaven, although not impossible when closely following that same road of suffering taken by Jesus Christ.'

* * *

535

A Bare-Bones History of Hell
Part III

Making the Most of a Very Mixed Bag
'Funny place, this, don't you think? Pilgrims and
rogues, rascals and saints all mixed up together. It's
not easy to tell them apart, I may say; for some fellow
praying may be a bigger scoundrel than any of us ...'
Pär Lagerkvist, *The Death of Ahasuerus*

What does it entail to make the best of a very mixed bag? Without
knowing it, could we have gone to heaven, or are we still on earth, or
(heaven forbid), might we have already gone to hell? Placement, as
we are told in our youth, depends on deportment. What then prevents
'a bigger scoundrel than any of us' from praying the most? Nothing
at all, surely, because in hell that makes a bigger scoundral than most
of us. Why then, when all's said and done, there's no bigger scoundrel
than me?

'Why me?' you might well ask—since there's no bigger scoundral
than *I am*. Obviously, the respective cases for the first person pronoun
(now me-me-me, instead of I-I-I) have gone all to hell in changing
their allegiance from classical grammar as spoken in heaven to
modernist grammar as muttered in hell. So what, you might say
by yet only another reversal of roles to keep pace with reversing
roles in everything from virtues to vices and vices to virtues, from
conservatives to radicals and radicals to conservatives. So then too,
since grammar schools have now been done to death, then why not
the same reversal of roles for grammar?

Quite right, without change where would we be without the
spice of life! So then, what once was ungrammatical has now
become grammatical, and what once was grammatical has become
ungrammatical. And yet (without considering every possible
permutation) what would you say of me, for my being the biggest
scoundral in heaven although praying the most, as of me in hell for
being the least of scoundrals there, and yet never thinking of praying

at all? So then, as some may think, there's nothing left in either heaven or hell (although we've no more than scratched the lower surface of heaven than we have scratched the upper surface of hell) by which to make the most of it!

'Whoa … whoa …,' as you might think to say here to halt an unruly horse like Guareschi's real-live priest who sponsored *Don Camillo*! But think on this apparently preposterous paradox allowed even to evildoers as by my 'grace and favour', points out the Lord! How else then could the divinely appointed crucifixion of my one and only Son have taken place, unless by my allowing the idolatrous worship of law and order to bring about his death? Yet when so insinuated by false priests, false prophets, and false teachers of the law, then what can you know of my ways, that I should think anything at all of yours?' thus asks the Lord.

'Then too, having thought both hard and long about your answer to this first critical question concerning the apparently insanitary disposal of my very own grace and favour, then let me ask you also this second critical question,' more quietly requests the Lord. 'Just how idolatrous is your own personal worship of me', he asks, 'if you will not consider seeking the answer (whether sought or reposing in either heaven or hell) to such apparently preposterous questions? So then, my dearly departed Don Camillo and my dearly departed Pär Lagerkvist and my dearly departed François-Marie Arouet de Voltaire, what's the point of us seeking the way, the truth, and the life if we cannot cope with those critical questions about life and death, far less coming to grips in this life with my own critical answers?'

[Bad-weather warning 1: The voice changes, so test the spirit (not just in terms of time and place, but also in terms of truth or falsity). Do this most carefully before you take for granted that the voice which you first heard, is the same voice which still continues. And since you explicitly ask for the gift of discernment in all such things, then okay, but this gift (which requires an annointing) doesn't come, as with the crack of a whip or the shot of a gun, but as the result of experience gathered more gradually. As to discernment then, see here as to what might be meant by the full width of meaning to be attached to the text of the above quotation or headnote to this third part of this bare-bones history of hell.

Remember that every quoted text has a context which is pertinent to the text, just as the aptness of quoting that text (as embedded in its own context) extends the full measure of its own particular context further outwards (like a pebble thrown into a pond) to cause a continuingly extending context of further and wider texts in even greater context. In general, you could ask what do Lagerkvist's Ahaseurus, Voltaire's Candide, and Guareschi's Camillo have in common. Be prepared, at the risk of losing perfect clarity, to look for mixed messages. Mixed messages are usually conveyed in (not always discernably different) mixed voices. For example, refer back here to Voltaire's own earlier way of putting things during his enlightenment, as against 'such harmony as never before heard in hell' described in his *Candide*. And as for making some sense of the widest possible context as heard from the utmost diversity of voices, remember that all the various voices quoted are being accredited to the earliest phase of this archaeological dig of hell's history.

Voices … voices … voices … You will realise from our earlier quotation from naughty old Voltaire, don't you, that in writing *Candide* (for being a philosophic tale, much as this philosophic tale is about soul-catching), the born-again Voltaire is no longer the Western world's (correct to lower case) well-known Father of Enlightenment but is by then writing (in that old age with which the Supreme Command chose to favour him) about his own now deep doubts over the whole notion of human progress. Likewise, his once youthful enthusiasm, which continued far into his early old age over the whole notion of worldwide enlightenment, has given way to an even deeper sense of disappointment. Alas, by then the Father of Enlightenment is not at all a happy soul.

Indeed, not just for Voltaire alone but for the entire www.com outlook of his time (1694–1778), the prevailing mindset of his age has suddenly and startlingly changed. From having faith in that feeling of human progress which had been promised to result from ongoing enlightenment, it has morphed into a feeling of great dread of the humanly unknown. [Exegesis 1: Such a violent mood swing from the enlightenment (fast falling into academic disrepute at the ongoing rate of thirty-two feet per second as then experienced by Voltaire and expressed in *Candide*) might be attributed by today's psychologists to overcompensation for his previously euphoric view of human progress.]

This massive change, for the moment bringing an end to the so-called enlightened mindset of mankind (in both its socially collective as well as its psychologically personal aspects), had jarringly come about by the catastrophic destruction of Portugal's great capital city of Lisbon in 1755. The complete destruction of this great European centre of learning and culture came in the night, as if howling out of nowhere, by the fiercest and most sudden of earthquakes.

This then felt (as if godsent) catastrophe (a natural disaster, as we'd call it now) gave rise to the same real sense of fate as Voltaire had more entertainingly portrayed in his previously philosophic tale of *Zadig* (written in 1747). What took Lisbon to the ground in 1755 went on to shake every one of Europe's other great capital cities off their hitherto complacently humanistic foundations. Nevertheless, we who have lived through the hellish destruction of the Twin Towers in 2001 haven't as yet felt any such lessening of our enlightenment and immense sense of having made great human progress, as once in 1755 put an end to the Enlightenment.

Such harmony as had never been heard before in hell might not exclude having been already heard [although this is still before the fall] in heaven. It has been said that 'the harmonic sense is born in a person, although there is no doubt that any type of harmonic idiom [for being merely idiom] can be acquired, yet what cannot be acquired is its appropriate application in expressing thought [since] this [we think also for being the supreme force behind every great musical composer] is the composer's sphere'.

Does this figurative explanation suffice? Well, obviously not for the still more enlightened scientist, since in many ways the unreformed Voltaire made up many of his very own (rather discordant) harmonies to highlight the greater governmental discord of an effete civil system. By such personal means, his promoted enlightenment came in turn to shatter the Ancien Régime (both all the good as well as only some of the bad that went before). It did so by promoting the same bloody forms of war and discordant revolution which Voltaire held not up to the transcendent light but more just to measure comparatively the remaining strength of his own will against the still prevailing darkness.

Even one's own human enlightenment (whether on this point or on any other point, when pursued without any authentic calling from the Supreme Command to do so) can be mischievously idolatrous both to oneself and others. Why, even the (merely philosophic or academic) pursuit of justice (for 'Justice is mine,' says the Lord), when humanly pursued by someone who can so easily overstate the case for justice through his or her lack of juristic understanding (literally *understanding*) of heaven's as often military operations against the kingdom of darkness, can soon become hugely idolatrous of humanity, which, in turn, can promote so much worse injustice. And so then the cult of human progress still serves to undermine the true soul of struggling humanity.

One of the troubles (at least of the many in hell) is that there are (as in any company of so-called colleagues or even of soldiers called to arms) many uncoordinated voices. The resulting compromise (on earth) of the so-called secular jurisprudence, as if justice can be administered by solely human means (since 'Justice is mine,' says the Lord), thus becomes something, although none but the Lord can say how much that something is, of an abomination.

As with both the League of Nations and United Nations [dissolute voices] and even with the World Council of Churches [still more dissolute voices] and most certainly by any more fractious movement as the Sea of Faith [yet still more dissolute voices], every attempt at any solely secular jurisprudence becomes jurisprudentially counterproductive to the institutionally professed objectives of their progenitors. ['Ha-ha-ha,' came a sudden peal of laughter from down below.]

Likewise, all so-called religions, through their corporate temptation to overstate the heavenly case, are idolatrous by their substitution of themselves, as often by their preference for their own ritualistic law and order, and as much for that purely personal relationship between each still struggling being who does not commit wholeheartedly to the authority of the Supreme Command. That's exactly how—by grossly overstating the heavenly case for justice—it comes about that religious wars begin (but then all wars are at heart religious, says who if not the Lord?).

'Voices … voices … voices … Why is it that to those with all-open ears, the world is so full of voices?' warns the Supreme Command. 'They all proclaim so many conflicting messages that two ears are not enough with which to hear them. Listen carefully, and eventually, you may hear the truth, because sooner or later, every scoffing tongue trips itself up!'

'One of the many troubles which plagues all youse human beans', begins to scoff the Counterfeit Command, thinking itself to have achieved some military advantage, 'is that youse has-beens measure light against darkness (no less than youse measure most things against darkness) instead of measuring them against the one and only … ha-ha … authentic first light. Why, half the time you think you're getting the nod from God'—at which point, the Counterfeit Command launches a flurry of cruise missiles into the steppes of Turkistan and lets go of a flood of napalm into Vietnam—'whereas in reality, you're getting the nod from me.

'Basically speaking … ha-ha-ha … ha-ha-ha (wear your beanie over your nose on reading this), youse human beans (infarct-fart-fart) are more afraid of the light than youse same human beans are afraid of the dark. Here, I'm reading verbatim from a classic hell comic, so you end up computing and accounting for both forms of light (daylight as well as artificial light) in terms of this world's presently growing darkness. And that fundamental fear … of the light … ha-ha-ha … in turn … ha-ha-ha … gives youse human beans (fart-fart) a very much infarcted … ha-ha-ha (again) … opinion (again fart-fart) of your own extremely artificial intelligence or anything else that youse human beans might mistake … ha-ha-ha … for being your very own first light.' [Bad-weather warning 2: It may help to confirm your own growing powers of divine discernment here to understand that just as the Supreme Command is known for being the Great Amen, so too the Counterfeit Command is known (most often for its scoffing) for being the Great Lord Ha-Ha.]

'On the contrary, the measure of light is light, not darkness,' corrected he who is lord over every form of debate no less than over every other known form of dance. 'Every flickering measure of candlelight should be computed not against darkness (as humans so often do) but only against the one and only true and first authentic source of light. Then you'll never ever be afraid of the dark, because there's always some authentic measure of first light by which to discern, distinguish, and cope with the darkest measure of the void—that void, when the earth was without form, whilst yet the most mysterious form of darkness (deep darkness, scientists now call it), was upon the face of the deep.'

'Ha-ha-ha … ho-ho-ho …,' came a resounding laugh from the lower depths (being yet another figurative expression of the very many figurative expressions) of hell. Whatever such secondary source of artificial light may be, whether resulting from turbines translated into hydropower or from fossil fuel translated into motor power or from photoelectric cells translated into artificial light or from chemicals translated into luminescence (there's no end to technology), these are no more than variants of a far more fundamental equation.

In the all-silent and deeply pervading darkness, little lights flickered before great bolts of lightning flashed, and a deeper and darker silence supervened whilst waiting for the greatest clap of thunder overhead, which never ever came—no, not even to shake the ground beneath all the quaking feet of all (but one) of the little divinity interns. Except, most suddenly and unexpectedly, as transmitted through the sound of an almighty Bluetooth speaker (brand-named Goddamn Mister Speaker), came the only one word that can never be uttered, far less repeated. [Bad-weather warning 3: 'It could have been *myedvyed*,' proffered the geek, as he was known by other interns in his class. 'If so, then you shouldn't have said that!' they told the geek, as they rolled him up tight in the floor carpet, pinning it between six chairs, a communion table, and a pulpit lectern, stopping their victim from releasing himself by unrolling the carpet back across the floor.]

Oh dear, shivered all the little divinity interns, foretasting an up-and-coming question in their final divinity exams. 'Is *goddamn* a good word in hell, an only impolite word on earth, and either only barely, or else a thoroughly, thoroughly bad word only in heaven?' they buzzed amongst themselves—yes, all the little still shivering interns. One buzzed to all, and all buzzed to one. And also each buzzed to one and so buzzed to another as 'Ha-ah-ah-ha-ha-ha' roared out again from the Goddam Mister Speaker!

'And what about this other forbidden word? Look here, we won't try to repronounce it, but *myed-vyed* was what, now on paper, it sounded like when reproduced asexually on paper, as closely as it could be reproduced when only once geekly, geekly voiced. We'll have to find out,' they decided, at least in time for finals. Professor Twinkley-Toes (not his real name) has a banned book (we know, because we've seen it) entitled *Banned Words Both Heavenly and Hellish Vol. 666* which he keeps under lock and key. But the Geek— short for Greek (although not Koine Greek)—can pick it, as he can pick all locks, and so get himself both in and out of anyone's bottom drawer.

So then in turn, another voice came, 'For the commonality of mankind to mistake the historic source of its own present blindness, however much a self-induced blindness even to this first light, but'—interrupted here by the greatest and longest postponed peal of thunder, which appears to set off church bells ringing—'is far more wonderful (than is) what we do in Counterfeit Command—'

'Stop, hold it right there, to decide who is right now ... ha-ha-ha-ha ... now speaking ... in youse humans (beans), giving youse-selves all credit for technology ... to youse human beans ... thus we too (we too?) have a truly resurgent light still expounded by us and at all levels ... both human and angelic ... of resurgent creativity ... and yet still so massively mistaken by mankind for being no more than its own obsolete, although by now entirely self-dispelled offbeat darkness.'

Make no mistake, for being a cacophony of offbeat, off-key spirits, this is (upper case) truly hell! So then we ask you, most seriously, just how could mankind by itself manage to dispel this long foreseen yet rapidly descending second and final darkness of our now greatly groaning earth? How so, unless by some complete reversal of values, whether attempted at the level of the angelic fall or else at the level of the human fall, whereby the lower order of things illegitimately aspires to be the upper order (last shall be first, so say them. But then so can the devil (lower case) quote the Bible (upper case, we said *upper case*)—no, upper case for the Bible (that's right)—or the last to fulfil all unauthorised claims to be first? But where's that coming from? Nothing now seems to fill that once primeval and yet now returning void of darkest days, which again threaten to quench the spirit and to snuff out every last candle of redeeming light—no, hold on—that's for sure not (well, maybe not precisely) right!

Dearest readers (even far dearest by now for having become dear friends), we must in all conscience remind you (since, still as usual, this continuing conversation of ours is being recorded for training and psychological assessment purposes). Nevertheless—and whatever happens—we must still hold fast to our mutual faith, like kindred spirits, as in *Anne of Green Gables*, forever keeping alive our supervening faith in eternal friendship!

Hello … hello … hello! Hell! Shit! Donner and Blitzen, are you still there?

Oh, right-eo … right-eo … thought we'd lost our heavenly connection with you, dearest readers! We in the Supreme Command lovingly salute you with these once authentic words of genuine friendship. But listen always beyond every word of welcome for the author angel's underlying soul-song, since this once lyrical expression of our dearest regard for you, although now rendered almost obsolete on earth by the obverse (or 'hail fellow well met' tactic) to be no more than a signal given there of these most perfunctory times, is still authentically sung (at least by all of us who still stand upright in the heavenly host) for the salutary benefit of your preternaturally living soul.

Do you then still follow—follow what we're both saying and singing, since learning to follow is the first prerequisite for belonging to the priesthood of all true believers, and this of all true believers as later required of them by their leading others to follow? Learn a lesson here too, even from the rock bands (despite the best ones) who themselves strenuously pound your ears with their own perverse beat, by way of reinforcing their own exclusive leadership, yet all done to divert the crowd from following their own on-beat lead by expecting all of them to clap offbeat. Learn to pick the on-beat/ offbeat difference between hell and heaven.

544

The much so-called music is made (but rarely inspired) at all levels—from the warlike 2/4 martial level up to the waltzing 3/4 missionary level and down again to rock—by which to divert, disavow, disempower, displace, and deflower the purported text and content. But beware of false prophets, false priests, false poets, and false prayer givers, since for the sake of capturing your soul, they too occupy front lines (either as ravening wolves in sheep's clothing or in some other more modernist disguise). Yet from true believers, these counterfeit followers may readily be distinguished by their own demonic policy of reducing to ranks all other more proper and potential leaders than they are themselves. [What makes this irreversible advice reversible for all situations, however, is the way that with vastly different mindsets ('headsets', we call these in hell) it can be made to be played, pretty nearly word for word, in both hell and heaven.]

Huh? you say. But don't we ourselves always follow and so lead others to follow what we always follow, whether we're following the sleazy fashions, following today's woeful news, following the leading bands, following the latest porno films, following the winning odds or else for ourselves being no more than blind to what we're following, then for ourselves, also likewise, to be following the blind? Quite so, this is exactly what we mean in hell, both by mankind having been divinely made to follow as well as by the demonic policy of reducing to ranks all others than themselves!

Exactly, that's both exactly (but not precisely—remember Thompson and Thomson (for being the one with a *p* and the other without a *p*), which is both what we mean as well as what we want to warn you of the blind leading the blind, by our saying that mankind is made to follow! So then don't either ho-hum or ha-ha at what's so significant for being either (1) deadly whenever misunderstood or as well as being (2) beneficent when more righteously understood. But shucks, as so many of you say after spending a night (not to mention night after night) at the pub, since talking about such things without doing something about them (stopped smoking pot yet?) is just too much trouble. So here (youse are all so apt to say), let's share a joint with each other in our trying to be so good!

Nevertheless, let's get real (relatively so on earth, not even relatively so in hell, and realistically so only in heaven)! Alcoholics Anonymous might work—there's a thought. Moral Re-Armament might work—there's another thought. Plucking out your own eye (an extreme remedy) or cutting off your dick (or else, not to be sexist, buying a dildo) will somewhat work, but just for the present, both of these (the former certainly so, but the latter maybe not) seem too extreme.

Never mind all that—no, no, never mind—since obviously, we're still not out of hell. The hard sell about heaven, which is exactly why we're here and now in hell, is that sooner or later (preferably sooner), since it's only when open-eyed, open-minded, and likewise open-hearted (besides being also stone-cold sober and off the weed), mankind is both rightly and fully made (since most of us are as yet only half made) to follow. Meanwhile, what's happened to all youse (still grammar in default) critters? Not a lot (if you'll pardon the fact of being overweight but undernourished, always tired but forever half-asleep, overexcited but strangely apathetic, always hungry but conversely stuffed—yes, stuffed with what all youse grammar-in-default lot (whilst still in hell) still mistake for being healthy food).

Now none of youse grammar-in-default lot don't now sing (triple negative, must be lower-case slavic spy app) nor don't now whistle (nor even don't now hum) in the openhearted, open-minded, and openly aware way you once did when ever-so-strictly, strictly following your everyday prayerful objectives. Are you now all so smitten in hell by slumbering spirits (even in the grundies) as to have become now chronic sleepwalkers through life? If so, you'll sleepwalk throughout all the day (in deep depression) for fear of losing your way (a common personality disorder) or for having already lost your way (much more than for suffering any mild neurosis), then in each such case (of which any two previously mentioned, take your pick and we'll psychoanalyse your choice), you'll succumb to the ultimate necrosis (shortly after your by then soulless, last-and-final visit to any hell-run funeral parlour).

Then as for now, since every horror story (you call them action movies now) carries (for both singular and plural as the hell-bent lawyers say) some sort of deeply embalmed (if not long since mummified) moral message, then let's face the music now. We'll do so whilst playing either Wagner's 'Ride of the Valkyries' or Mendelssohn's 'Wedding March' (same price for either choice), and we'll do so whilst considering whether (to a greater or lesser extent) your already slumbering spirits have become so surreptitiously enthralled as to require a replacement hard disc (or better still, electronic implant) for which we await your every command.

If then, so surreptitiously enthralled (in lieu of your once steadfast obedience to the righteousness of the Supreme Command), now you're given over to the wrongfulness of the Counterfeit Command. At such point, as at every point, the theo-low-gians (catch up here on the pun, however low and below the belt, as here in hell always intended) express their right as divines to take command. [Worst-weather warning 1: This is not the place in which to debate the divine place of (even hellish) theo-low-gy. As said before, everyone is a theo-low-gian, according to the theologian Karl Barth. So there's nothing personal (far less impersonal) for Barth to concede his own rank of theologian (in some shape or form) to absolutely everyone (even all in hell) since most such theologians (for whom these exegetical or explanatory remarks are intended, even if only to divert their quasi-academic minds away from their own interminable arguments over the nature of the divine) can learn to distinguish the Counterfeit Command from the Supreme Command (to be completed in less than three easy lessons, available on demand if you purchase any printer from hell) by which the Supreme Command always affords humans some clearly discernible measure of truly free choice.]

Here for you, whilst still in hell (at no extra cost), begins the difficult question of divine destiny (or predestination, as some would have it) to triumph over free choice. But alas, for free choice, since so often all youse (still in default lot humans) are so keen to follow what seems to youse to be the only way (for being your own way) that youse can see no other way than that for being your very own way, to all of which youse exclaim in chorus, 'Choice!'

We forgive all such defaulters (each and every one of them, of course) for their being without the rudiments of logic, by which they wouldn't recognise a tautology (or solely self-professing truth) if they ever were redeemed enough to see one (which, without their satisfying all heavenly criteria for genuine, heartfelt atonement, couldn't very well be done), and even less so in their hearing of any self-made act of purported redemption (to be purchased as at leaving from this book launch in hell) for being a solely self-professing truth. [Worst-weather warning 2: You'll notice that every purported dialogue in hell (as this one is) substitutes for every attempt at rational argument only on ongoing verbal merry-go-round.]

Let's now hope you're still enjoying every moment of your subterranean trip to hell. The humour is purposely weak (no more than 28 per cent proof) because the poet Milton in his *Paradise Lost* and the poet Goethe in his *Faustus*, each by overstating the heavenly case, gave far too much literary credence to hell. Thus, for *Paradise Lost* being so credibly and persuasively lost, it became hardly possible for Milton to write just as credibly of any *Paradise Regained*.

Don't despair! This fully guided, although much downplayed, tour (incurring travel reimbursements open to recoupment by double-dipping instead of the sexual skinny-dipping in course of travel which no longer passes on earth for sin) has yet to pass through customs. [Worst-weather warning 3: One of the giveaway signs of being still down here in hell is that of being faced with the need to cover one's otherwise bare-boned butt. Down here, we do that with the full quota of exegetical, excursive, excusive, and discursive comments which one has to make in order to justify one's every least thought, lest it be taken captive upstairs by the Supreme Command.]

* * *

A Bare-Bones History of Hell
Part IV

In Free Fall from Heaven to Hell
An uair bha Gàilig aig na h-eòn—when once all the
birds in Gaelic sang ...
William Black, *Donald Ross of Heimra*

It's a free country (so they still glibly say and even still sing of it), although practising one's freely chosen profession of faith (without free will) is always a much harder matter these days. Once also in free fall, as for almost every nation also these days, then there's no saying where the free fall may, can, must, will also lead to—or end. The most you can do is to hold on to your hat, if you still have one.

All the same, which country and whose country really is any country which can be so glibly proclaimed in these days to be the land of the free? There's no country these days that is in anyway free, and for living in your car whilst homeless, you're most likely to be taken captive for presuming yourself to be any vigilante, vagrant, or other relatively unfree person.

No country can be proclaimed to be free, surely, for being any country of the present where the homeless sleep down and out in the streets! No country, surely, from which many are withheld the requisite permit or visa to work as the only means by which they can legitimately survive! No country, surely, whose borders are walled in for no other reason than to wall out the so much woefully worse afflicted! Then as already asked of every country (whether of the USA, EU, UK, NZ, or CIS), whose country, purportedly of the free, really is it?

Meanwhile, it's a bright spring morning whilst still here in Heimra, in the Gàilig-speaking Hebrides. So then once again—God's in his heaven, and *an uair bha Gàilig aig na h-eòn*—the birds are still singing to him in their originally God-given voice. Unaware of this being a catch-22 situation, however, you feel most free to develop (but not indulge) your personality (yes, you can do so even allowably, so we are most reliably told, whilst still in the heavenly haven of this little-known isle of Heimra).

There's the beginning of a Scottish Odyssey here. So then the timorous spirits choose to free-fall e-v-e-r s-o s-l-o-w-l-y, whilst those who think themselves to feel (or need to demonstrate) more freedom of spirit decide to do things differently (and so very often impulsively). Of course, feelings alone are no criteria by which either to develop, to constrain, or to indulge one's personality. Fixing on whatever the spirit may be by which to exercise one's openly chosen carnival choice (that of picking life's final outcome) is no small thing (when mistaken for being today's biggest tourist bullshit).

This freebie of deciding on one's own final send-off is a small consolation for delegating downstairs the responsibility of determining one's own final destination (which you can pretty well cherry-pick from the ethos of the send-off, which for being either slow or fast or sad or jolly) has not the slightest effect on the eventual destination. All a little ambiguous you may say (and *pettifogging* would be the legal word by which to describe such demonic tactics as well as their description), but the ruthless logic of causal choice (however freely chosen for being either heaven or hell) decides all determinative and still prevailing outcomes.

Can you believe it (from still looking on the bright side of things)? But once upon a time (and there is testimony of the saints to prove it), the animals all spoke in accents understood by humans. And even after those first tall towers reaching up to heaven collapsed and the tongues of men were distorted into conflicting languages and different dialects, some saints (of whom St Francis, the first ecologist, was such a one) to whom the birds and beasts still spoke as clearly as once did Balaam's ass. It pays still to listen, both to birdsong and to the songs of other animals (think of a whale's song, of a monkey's chatter, and of bees humming), because Balaam would not himself have lived but for the angelic utterance given to him from Balaam's ass.

Today's free-falling history, whether that of much-acclaimed heaven (to which we aspire for being this life's final safe haven) or of unknown Heimra (a heavenly holiday resort in the Scottish Hebrides much frequented by both fallen and upright angels), becomes less clearly heard as spoken by our birds and animals of today. Yet what remains of this interspecific communication is nowise disadvantaged by the myths and stories told around snug firesides and roaring campfires than it is disadvantaged by the academic theorising, whether about the hound of heaven or about any other aspect of the character of Jesus Christ, that preoccupies those of a more theological bent in ivory towers. Nevertheless, the history of human opinion is every bit as important to the Supreme Command as the heavenly history of ideas which stirs up so much (and as often conflicting) human opinion.

In the Supreme Command, we are also so often mystified by the length of time it takes for one of our own and brightest of ideas—whether conveyed by sight or by sound or in song—to strike up even the slightest of (even contrary) human opinions. And far longer still does it take for popular opinion to acknowledge its own authentic and more complete reception. It took the whole lifetime of our servant-poet Francis Thompson (1859–1907) for his poem 'The Hound of Heaven', even just to be recognised as one of the greatest lyric poems in the English language. What a shame it is that nobody's written the music to match that lyric yet. Perhaps the time's not come yet. Indeed, sometimes—as with the Greek and Roman civilisations—it takes not just their lengthy development but also their often far lengthier decline and ultimate fall and the more difficult passing of their refined ideas on to subsequent civilisations before human opinion is stirred into active reception.

Then again, the harder and longer it takes to learn something, then accordingly, often the greater is the commitment to whatever is learnt from one's devotion to the task. This is one explanation of why we in the Supreme Command challenge lives not only by their allowed hardship but also by the length of life demanded of their learning and why also, as between races and nations, some rise and fall with tremendous rapidity, whereas others birth only with great difficulty, develop incrementally, and hang in there against all odds. Slow off the mark, individuals, races, and nations are chosen by us in the Supreme Command for their pertinacity. The real race in life is rarely won by the swiftest. But the responsibilities of any slow yet long-lived learner, as of any chosen race or as of any preferred nation, are not those either understood or eagerly sought after by popular opinion.

In the early days of the apostles (now often institutionalised unrecognisably into humanist church history), an understanding of the beatitudes consumed so much of the slow learning and hardship required by their common practice that by now, without their practice, the church has lost all sense of its own history and so, in consequence, lost also the cutting edge which comes from being fully aware of one's purpose in life. Substituting political correctness for such paradoxical purpose as the early church once wholeheartedly pursued on earth by its living the heavenly beatitudes sounded the death knell of the church. That lost purpose which the beatitudes gave to life is now missed more by those who oppose the church than it is missed by church adherents.

Thus, as well said (but least understood) by the secularist writer John Gray in his magnificent résumé of church history in his *Black Mass: Apocalyptic Religion and the Death of Utopia*: 'Modern politics is a chapter in the history of religion.' Alas, how often it is that the best of prophets can be tempted to mistake their own fallible interpretations for the future outcomes of their prophetically true insights. However true it may be that 'modern politics [has become] a chapter in the history of religion', far worse it is that the by now defunct history of religion has become no more than a chapter in modern politics.

Over more than two millennia since Christ was born in Bethlehem, the Counterfeit Command has made every day a field day in shelving aside the collective core value of the beatitudes—as much to the detriment of the individual soul as to the breakdown of human society at large. As every jurist knows, not only are there those rights, more rights, and still more rights on behalf of which every lawyer claims in court but also privileges, immunities, and powers and yet more powers and yet still yet more powers by which to entice every claim, both in and out of court, as of right ... as of right ... as of right.

Learn this, dearest readers, that more of what nearly every human wants to have (as of right) for being more personal power (and no less even of spiritual power) turns out to be so much more less than they could possibly exert! How so? Why so? Well, because humans ask the most for what they literally least know—namely, that for them to have more power would entail of them that reciprocal measure of responsibility which as yet they don't have the least capacity to fulfil!

Shelve aside all understanding of the beatitudes (however puzzling they are intended to be to worldly ways of thought), and the church is back to legal formalism, both with the Ten Commandments as well as with the Lord's Prayer. Lose sight of life's great mysteries—whether of law, logic, and language (when worldly values are stood on their head by the reversal conveyed by those otherworldly beatitudes)—and you've lost not just the beatitudes but also the entire cosmic plot of heavenly salvation in which you profess to participate.

As for the disciples perplexed by Christ's Sermon on the Mount, which preached the practicing of these same beatitudes for the scriptural prime focus once taught, held, and practised, their human successors today (without seeking to surmount the hardship of slow learning) now mistake their own merely human commitment to accord themselves the same pride of place as the early apostles more humbly held in putting those beatitudes into everyday practice. What do you say to this, then dearest readers, of the same scriptural study being made of these beatitudes today, when this purely academic study is humanly seen to be accomplished without putting them into their fullest and most common practice?

'Whoa then!' as said to a runaway horse (and not 'wow', as might be said to some more disciplined disciple of miracles)—get ready for yet another full fall from grace or whatever else it takes to precipitate yet some further reformation. If the time is ripe for revival, it will take first the fullest reformation of church practice. People pray passionately for revival, yet all the while heedlessly overlook the need for their own reformation.

Confront the truth. There's never been a revival without first a reformation! In this sad and sorry state of the world, any church which still considers itself to be doing well is completely out of order! Let it be seen that your human reverence for these apostles as the early church fathers is a reverence which now hides the hardship by which their faith and devotion to the cause of learning actually moved mountains. Christ preached his Sermon on the Mount *from* the mount, but for even the most professing Christians in these latter days, that sermon is no more than still on the mount for having never left the mount.

Until the Sermon on the Mount comes to earth from off the mount, it cannot be truly said that the kingdom of heaven has really, truly, and irrevocably come to earth. And no less than the law is encapsulated in the severity of the commandments (by way of drawing attention to the severely deleterious significance of sin), so too the heavenly kingdom is encapsulated in the blessed softness of the beatitudes. These eight states of blessedness (but look also for a ninth) carry rewards by which to explicate their corresponding states of blessedness, so don't stop short of receiving your reward in heaven for experiencing the ninth. Besides, no less than human history evokes a divinely prophetic response, so also heavenly history evokes a prophetic fulfilment of that divine response as contributed through its needful recognition in the human history of purposeful action.

There are two different ways of looking at most of the nine beatitudes. At first sight, some of these provoke humanistic problems by apparently turning the expected heavenly virtues on their heads and thereby proclaiming puzzling paradoxes. Each beatitude, both formally and functionally, is of two parts. The first is that of an accredited responsibility, which, when carried out, implemented, or practised constantly enough to constitute a character trait, by way of the second part, carries or entails a blessing.

Each of the nine beatitudes is to be understood comprehensively in both of two ways—one with the Hebraic mindset and the other with the Greek mindset. The Hebraic mindset is pragmatic, whereas the Greek is philosophic. The Hebraic is functional, whereas the Greek is formal. The Hebraic has to be practised in order for the beatitude to be understood, but the Greek needs be no more than intellectually discursive to be understood. The Hebraic is concrete, whereas the Greek is intellectually abstract. The Hebraic is purposively motivational and dynamic, whereas the Greek is passively static and permissively inactive.

We humans miss the message of heavenly history when we read it as if it were world history. In that sense, the 'historical Christ', as conveyed by and to world historians, is a misnomer. In the same way, some of the greatest feats achieved or catastrophic falls suffered throughout the throes of time have either not yet made their way into horn-bound history books or else have by now slipped out from between their pages. Indeed, the whole point of all history is to keep the past alive and to bring it constantly before the present, since without the hindsight of history, there can be no prospect of prophetic foresight. Thus, no less than for us all being encouraged to prophesy, we must for that purpose also serve to keep the past alive.

'So how now are you, Lucifer the light bearer (for so long my nearest next-door neighbour, although not of my own mind's creation, as so many of his own minions think of him)? So then how now are you, dear brother at law, for being still the bright son of every day's once long protracted dawning? But for now, alas, even as we so gently ask of you, how do you feel when cut down to the barest ground, after having fallen all the way from heaven, you who laid the nations low, you who proclaimed in your heart, in your mind, and through all the rest of your ways that you would ascend to the highest heaven, far above the stars of any Supreme Command, there to set your own throne on high, to sit on the mount of assembly to the farthest north, to climb above the highest clouds, and so to make yourself out for being the most high?

'Can this be the one who once made all the earth to tremble; who made to totter whole kingdoms, commonwealths, and vast republics; who turned the greenest of pastures into the driest of deserts and brought down proud cities to the very depths of their dungeons? How does it feel, we again ask you ever so gently, to be brought down to the lowest depths of the everlasting pit? So then have you changed, Lucifer, son of every day's now increasingly dismal dawn, when you are now cut down to Sheol, where those who see you there, those who once relied on your great conceit, will stare at you and ponder over your plight?

'No, you have not changed, Lucifer. Your extreme self-pride prevents it. You, who are by now your own lord and your own god, cannot see any way of changing it. You have made yourself immutable to all self-change. You, who amongst all the angels were picked to have the greatest of all callings, sacrificed that calling by your attempt to usurp the giver of that calling. You outbid the exercise of your own greatest power in the service of none but yourself. By busting yourself in the service of self, you cannot have the slightest insight to see yourself as you really are, although we pray that by the infinite grace of our own Lord and Redeemer, if it were possible for you to see another light than that of your own, then that light of Christ's world would become so much more visible to you.'

There are no trade-offs here, no compromises here, no privileges here, no preferences here—in terms of universal law. The chips are down! The proverbial fall from heaven is not anything like the proverbial fall from Eden, although they still share much in common. To whomsoever much is given, much shall be required no less than from one to whom much has been entrusted, and even more shall be expected by which to fulfil that trust.

Humanity, by reason of its own downfall and continuing default, has little spiritual largesse to extend as yet by way of heavenly distribution. The reason that the Son of God appeared was to destroy the works of the devil, and this even greater task is the one to which you humans are more and more enjoined. If it took seventy disciples to return with joy to Jesus, saying, 'Lord, even the demons are subject to us in your name', then how much more is expected of you so many millions more to hear Jesus say for the last and final time, 'I saw Satan fall like lightning from heaven!'

Yet still like fallen humanity, this remains a fallen world. There is a greater need in this fallen world than ever before, as the renowned musician Dr Barnes of Oxford once pointed out as far back now as in 1937 (the year before the Second World War broke out) for what he called modern harmony.

Some folks seem to have harmony built in, whilst other folks seem full of discord. Harmony is not as it seems, however, since it can often take a long life for a seriously struggling individual to resolve what has been for him or her actually a passed-on generational discord. From an angelic to any mortal musician, we would say watch most carefully your passing notes!

It is the same for harmonic and discordant nations. As said of so many different and increasingly difficult international situations, there ought to be a musicologist in charge of every international situation. There is, of course, a history of harmony no less than there is a history of heaven, and the two histories are so inextricably intertwined in the history of both heaven and of the church that there would literally be no harmony, as we know it, without the church having developed the harmonies we now take so much for granted. Can you hold to a tune on your own by which to lead others, or do you have to strum on a guitar or fine-fiddle a flute or else bow down to a keyboard or commit all one's four limbs (like the four horsemen of the apocalypse) to extracting the maximum level of worship from a pipe organ?

No less than a tune may rise or fall, anything like that which may allowably develop may likewise also allowably decline and possibly even degenerate to sink below all possibilities of generic recognition, and so then the harmonies of our forefathers do not always remain constant. 'Forty years ago [as Dr Barnes wrote in 1937], a connection between a chord of E flat major and A minor would have been regarded as a sign of incipient lunacy, but times have changed. Justification is found [as we expect now to find it for almost anything in the infrastructure] in the contrapuntal framework.'

There is a great need, as never before amongst people, to come to grips with the principles of change, insofar as change (in the purely physical) may reflect development, decline, or even degeneracy (in the metaphysical). Take the development of musical harmony (for instance), which may be described as the art (or science, as some scholars have held) of combining different sounds. Listen (not all that carefully) to find out that (as never before) almost anything goes.

What happened to harmony? Why is it that now almost anything goes? Well, the answer to both questions is simple. Satan, before his fall, was the foremost of Father God's musicians. Music has never been the same since Satan's downfall. What passes for much music today in the ears and minds and hearts of unbelieving youth is often a passport brought on by drugs and disease to hell.

Melody (in the horizontal time frame) combines different sounds sequentially, but harmony combines different sounds conjunctively (in the vertical time frame). A further development from harmony via melody is to combine different melodic lines contrapuntally (according to both melodic and harmonic principles when integrating both vertical time frames as well as horizontal time frames together).

This requires some considerable ingenuity, from which may be developed, on the one hand, eventually the acme of symphonic expression or, on the other hand, the gradual degeneracy produced by that overly ornamented and elaborative musical expression which (until outlawed by the church in 1322) nearly killed off plainsong.

Harmony's first cause, or prime source, was in the very early Christian church. Unknown to Greek or Hebraic worship, the principles of musical harmony evolved from what had previously been congregational singing. When the Holy Spirit breathed into individual lives, those individual lives tended to express themselves in collective harmonies, reflecting not only their own parts but also those in relation to what they heard of other parts as being sung by other worshippers. Can you do it? It's not much different from speaking in tongues, but then that too requires the same level of spiritual relaxation as required of spontaneous harmonising.

For some people, the rate of change (in many, if not all things) both would be and is simply too fast and furious to accommodate both old and new. And in many other cases, there are so many missing links between the old and the new that, despite every human effort to maintain the past whilst advancing the present, both old and new seem irreconcilable. Yet, without one being blessed with the required transformational musicology, this reconciliation of the apparently irreconcilable can be achieved only by accommodating to both old and new at the most minimalist of levels.

Then even the great composers suffer, so we lose almost all sense of their innovative and creative talents. 'It is a curious fact [again writes Barnes] that when we think of and listen to the masterpieces of such giants as Bach, Beethoven, Brahms, and Elgar, we are never conscious of their ingenuity.' Why, without at least some academic awareness of all history (musical or otherwise), we would then be left without any sense of the loss we at present suffer without there having been any contribution of past to fulfil the present.

The same fast and somewhat illicit move from novelty to cliché not only robs history of our inspirited engagement but also overloads the history of everything with dry and dusty details that mean nothing until resurrected from their dry and dusty historical tomb. Nevertheless, music is a powerful tool by which either to excite or pacify the emotions, and a songless citizen is no citizen whether of earth or of heaven (but by then more usually caught up in some mob, gang, or political faction).

Angels sang at the creation and, again with the birth of Jesus Christ, at that long-appointed recreation. Good news betokens a song as much as a song betokens good news. Silence (by itself sometimes so suspect) is never as golden as when punctuated by song or accompanied with song. Well, that's one reason for being doubly suspicious of that notorious silence, wherever and whenever encountered, which is masked by idle chatter, widespread gossip, or even just blaring noise. Listening to what shouldn't be said, far less heard, is one of least detectable yet most avoidable ways of going deaf.

Which is worse, falling from heaven for being the far greater height or falling from Eden (since you humans are only but a little lower than us angels)? Why should salvation be held out only to you humans but not also to those of us angels who are fallen? The height of the fall and the status of the participants in each of such falls would seem to both parties to be much of a muchness. But remember this throughout: even fallen angels are still dignitaries who, as described in scripture, still sit in the council of heaven.

Whatever answer lies to this question, whether in the premises of any subsequent argument or in the conclusion to which all such premises would lead, seems largely beyond both the angelic host as much as their human counterparts; but the issue of fairness is one which, more for worldly reasons than for heavenly reasons, seems to perplex humanity rather than us angels. One proffered reason for this difference of outlook seems to lie in the way that you humans have tried to excuse yourselves by taking shelter behind the fact of satanic temptation, as if your human sin is to be explained—as perhaps it could be—by the existence of the satanic initiative. No, for the fact of having your own free will, you have no lesser responsibility, despite every temptation, to exercise your own initiative.

Once again, we are probing the inescapable concept of diversity as if it poses only a problem, yet in truth, it may pose a problem to the decision process, which is never one that can remain unremittingly in human hands. Ultimately, the issue of life-or-death supervenes, by which the Supreme Command determines the outcome for humans through all eternity.

Nevertheless, none would doubt that the sheer diversity of the human condition, although only a little lower than that of the angels, verges on being humanly indescribable; but the far greater diversity of the angelic condition is beyond all human reckoning. From your own human point of view, we angels can be numbered one-third fallen and the other two-thirds still standing upright, but we too of the angelic host are no less vulnerable to losing our salvation than are all you humans still capable of redemption.

Because you humans are only a little lower than us angels, for the looked-for communion in communication sought by this book, we (the angelic *we*) shall sometimes be speaking in the first-person (authorial) plural (that's us angels) and at other times in the second person (sometimes plural as well as singular) for you humans. This may prove at times confusing, but English grammar is itself a rapidly disappearing convention. And it is better by far to indicate the truth, insofar as many humans are closer to the angels than one who is not an angel might think; and likewise, just as there are both upright angels and fallen angels, so too some humans are ra-ra-rapidly going down, down, and down, whilst others are just as ra-ra-rapidly going up, up, and up. And yet the vast ma-ma-majority of humans (until they read the signs of their times) are still caught fast in … in … in be-be-be-betwixt and between, between, between.

As time moves faster on, the unequal conflict [of 2:1 between righteousness and wrongfulness] intensifies. Earthbound humanity considers it more fitting to be delighted by its own purely secular equations. Nevertheless, in searching for such solely secular and humanistic solutions, the algorithmic [a.k.a. mechanistic] mind of earthbound humanity so often overlooks its own heuristic [or heartfelt] basis as to believe that even angels can be thwarted. [Exegesis 1: The unredeemed human heart, when stuffed with those superficial and worldly affectations which, when left to themselves, so rapidly develop into deep-seated afflictions, infections, and affectations, can be no less passionately evil even when professing itself to be most passionately good.]

It follows from this algorithmic [a.k.a. mechanistic] mindset that even when a soul is being cradled to earth and there to be implanted within the womb (en ventre sa mère) by his or her own guardian angel, then there too, even the newly conceived child, despite the divine calling of its guardian angel, may still be thought by humans to be permissibly put down [a.k.a. humanely aborted]. And even though the soul of this so-called foetus may survive this barbaric assault, nevertheless, after its more natural immersion into this woeful world, the resulting baby is then [as commonly expressed] made to feel unwelcome [and so disregarded or abandoned sometimes psychologically, sometimes physiologically, sometimes spiritually, for the rest of its life].

The result of this aberrant and abhorrent process is to falsify the truthfulness of the ongoing secular equation by which the empty cradle is mistaken for the absence of angels, and the tedious songs of this world are substituted for the lack of all human feeling over the loss of a child [either bodily or in spirit]. Yes, there really are ghosts which wander this earth looking for their proper placement, and because of the way in which they have been bodily put down, there is only one way of raising them heavenwards.

Perhaps you're still stumbling (as we all do) over the psychological differential, as well as over the logical differential, between the aforesaid algorithmic (or formulaic) and heuristic (or intuitional) reasoning. We hope not, for leaving that issue to be preferably picked up on by yourselves, dearest readers, rather than by our satifying the need to have you programmed to avoid experiencing for yourselves the difficulty. Then now look at the difference more reflectively this way—namely, through the means of an academic exegesis or explanation [as indicated by square brackets here and elsewhere in this book] even although this formal academic condescension may only compound the felony [perceived by the reader against the reader] of the writer speaking over his or her head. So then leave this discourtesy to be felt only by the writer, which is felt even more so by him or her wherever an exegesis [or explanation] is felt unneeded by the reader.

Yes, even look at the same issue another way again. As if when engaging in an algorithmic (or formulaic) endeavour, man proposes his own outcome, but yet God, in his own heuristic (or intuitive) way, intervenes on behalf of man to dispose his own divine outcome. Thus, although originally proposed algorithmically by means of humanly academic formulae and scientific equations (as often only to pursue mankind's perceived needs and fallible aspirations), then the more heuristic outcome is divinely disposed whereby all things work together for the good of those who love God and do his calling.

Through redemption, humans travel largely in faith by engaging in a more intuitively heuristic (or intuitive) endeavour. But don't mistake this present exegetical analysis for being that which deprecates either of these two modes of intellectual versus intuitive travel. The two modes—one prevailingly masculine, the other prevailingly feminine—are made to complement each other. The intellectual (for being proof-bound) versus the intuitive (for being truth-bound) closely complement each other not only for worldwide travel (which can so easily become the addictive preoccupation of the tourist culture) but also, in the heavenly sphere of serious action, for all angelic travel. Both modes, as for the angelic and the humanistic, each have a necessarily shared and increasing arena of mutual participation.

* * *

A Bare-Bones History of Hell
Part V

Counterfeit Angels
We are men, and our lot in life is to learn, and to be
hurled into inconceivable new worlds.
Carlos Castaneda, *The Teachings of Don Juan*

Hi there! Can you recognise a programme novel when you see one? As taught by Castenada's Don Joan, 'our lot in life is to learn, and [so] to be hurled into inconceivable new worlds'. Well then, here is what you've been both looking for and asking for—an exercise in discernment. Your task is to evaluate the different speakers of mixed messages in this dialogue, and, as far as possible, giving reasons, to ascertain their either heavenly, earthly, or hellish origins. Any two minimally congruant evaluations shall be presumed plagiarised—so don't come back 'wearing drag' to your reading groups with anything like the same ways of doing this exercise far less having anything like the same reasons for having the same answers! [Terms and conditions: (1) it won't be worth your while just to allot the names of different speakers arbitrarily to different voices in this exercise; so you may either use already established literary characters or else create and develop your own literary characters by which to discern, develop, and discriminate the different voices; (2)] From Descartes to Goebbals, then on to J. Alfred Prufrock and Elizabeth Taylor and far beyond, no names already used in the text for this exercise in learning discernement when being unexpectedly 'hurled into inconceivable new worlds' are eligible for re-employment.

'Hi there, again! Ye've sure goat a nerve. Whaur in hell do ye think ye are, sayin' prayers oan behalf o' the condemned? Whaur's yer licence? If nae tae preach, then tae teach, but if nae to teach, then at least to grovel wi' me in worshipful prayer.

'Doon oan your knees, doag, doon oan yer knees. Yer no' the son of God. No, nae even his wee kid brother! No, laddie, dinae talk tae me o' prophecy. That's nae likely tae be heird in hell. Why mon, ye dinae even hiv benefit of clergy! As already asked, whae in hell dae ye think ye are? Do you really think ye can use the word (forbye the name) of Yahweh? Ye're no' a rabbi—thaat a' kin tell … nae a mullah … thaat a' kin tell … sae bob's yer uncle … Sae whit wae did ye geit here?

'How's the digging going? Six feet deep, eight feet long, three feet wide—standard specifications—guaranteed (without undue subsidence) to carry a heavy headstone … epitaph (if desired, cost extra)—Consider if this is a man …

'Doesn't matter whether prospecting for gold, for oil, or for uranium or even for writing a book (but you didn't say for righting a wrong, did you) or (since this is nae mair than a bare-bones history of hell) for stalking a woman or for seducing a man …'

'Shouldn't be telling you this, but then that's the way down here— we always do what we shouldn't. So you won't have the least hope of paying any attention to what I say. So then here's a weather warning for down here—steer clear of the women. They're far worse than the men … far worse than the men …

'Down here … in hell, where else? They talk all the time about equal rights for women, but all the time, they're far, far worse than the men. Yes, far, far worse than the men … But of course, you won't believe me down here. Nobody believes anyone else down here … so everybody finds out for themselves, including the women, that when they're really bad (as they all are down here), they're really far, far worse than the men …'

'Let me tell you (sotto voce, you know, although down here in hell, what you whisper is heard the loudest (apart from what you ponder) and what you shout or yell or scream is never heard at all. So then let me tell you, for having misspent all one's life upstairs chasing after women, when you finally get down here, you'll find you've wasted your entire life upstairs … Yes, your entire life upstairs completely wasted, which is why down here, all these religiously celibate old men now keep sodomising young boys … No, it's not pretty, but that doesn't get in the way of the tourist trade down here any more than it does up on earth. So then make the most of it …

'And yet for some reason unknown down here, because all the really tough jobs are entrusted to shag-ridden women, it makes us old wankers really wild down here, but all the same (as it never ever is for being all the same down here), who can dispute this fact-ridden hell (informational overload down here, and not just the electric chairs upstairs is always blowing the fuses) that for some reason or another (which possibly isn't any reason at all but instead a deeply submerged and half-drowned sense of value), the women down here are far, far worse than are the men ...

'But then what would you know ... fur bein' no-think mair than some mere man ... since Li'l Goebbels got his tongue cut out a week back for speculatin' that all them women wis wursen i' hell, because they wis aye better'n than men when up in heave ... stop heaving ... stop heaving, will you? Didn't say that ... didn't think that ... didn't do nuthink ... the dropping voltage down here ... has no-think to do wif wot ... a' juist heerd ma' frien heer fur saaayin' ... that's right ... no wrong ... wrong, wrong, wrong ... always wrong ... so then take him ... take him ... take anyone ... but not meeeeeeee!

'Lookee here, there's no end of ways going wrong. So they've promised me on coming into hell ... where every most boring day is spent, as it should be, in the deepest of induced sleep, and every night is wakeful until dawn with something new ... with someone new ... both put together for a night ... and taken apart before dawn ... as both never before and so never since ... will ever be ... will ever be ...

'They do tell us down here'—said with a chuckle—'that there's only one way of doing right ... of thinking aright ... of being all right. Good God, what a bloody farce that would be ... Jeez, what a bore! Boring as hell, we'd say ... that's what we say ... if we want to get a push off the sidewalk in front of a bus (the equivalent of a golden handshake on earth or a golden crown for those sots who strive to get into) ... stop heav-heav-heav ... stop heaving, will you? Stop hea-hea-heaving, will you, and get down on your hands and knees to lick up that heav-heav-heaving mess on the floor.

'We don't even have any books ... not real books ... down here. We only have reviews and commentaries, but none of the actual books, same for films. Well, no real films ... only film reviews—all the best film reviews and all the best book reviews ... but none of them films reviewed and none of them books reviewed ...

'Just now and then, we're given a scrap of news from the outside world, which we pin up on the wall. We specialise in walls down here … electrified, of course … won't kill you, because nobody ever dies down here, although attempted suicides (quite a lark, they are) take place by the lorryload every day—*nyet problyema* (no problem), *nyet problyema* (no problem), *nyet problyema* (no problem)—so take your time (although time's never yours) to read the wallpaper. That too is electrified, so don't touch it, or else your suicide will be presumed (and you'll be given a bad doze of the clap from which you'll take a long time to never recover).

'See here, for being yet another voice although unplainly heard and written. Although nothing new, so we'll deadline rather than headline its mixed message—in Latin (not Aramaic) for being *Dubito Ergo Sum*. This barefaced mantra seemingly saying *I Doubt therefore I am* to those who believe themselves to know what this mantra means likewise presents nothing new—although among academics (both in their practice and profession) it carries a wide following. This is the underlying alternative reality to what, according to some once well-known fellow called Descartes, who, although for being himself a military engineer, knew no better than to shut himself up for a whole day in a funk-hole without an air hole, in what he called a one-stove back room. There, in danger of being asphyxiated, he remained fixated on finding what he called a system of method.

At first, endowed with adequate ventilation—but it was a charcoal fire, you know—Descartes' first thought was to stake his fame and fortune on the alternatively mixed message of *Cogito Ergo Sum* (a.k.a. by thinking I am), but as the stove began to asphyxiate more and more oxygen from the room, his thinking grew less and less sound and soon had him, also more or less on the carpet, for his being taken to mean "by doubting I am" instead of *Cogito Ergo Sum* for his not knowing any longer who he was.

'If you can follow Descartes's lack of reasoning (not all that clear, but then neither was anyone else's at the time), you'll learn (like the Royal Society) to doubt pretty well nearly everything, according to their motto of *Nihil in Verba* (look, there it is, although some say it should be *Nihil in Verbis*, others say *Nullius in Verba*, yet others *Nullius in Verba*, and some even (apart from one retired medic opting for *Nullius vertebrata* (sp. Smith)) that it should be *Verbissima Verbis* (there's a lot of academics gone underground down here) to compete with the Royal Society).'

Always remember, but what's the point, since you can't believe whatever you see or hear down here—no, not even for being the *anti-Christian truth*. That's one of our whole wide world newspapers—no, not down here, since there wouldn't be any point to that—but published in Washington, where it competes (suburb by suburb) with the *Washington Post*.

Nevertheless, it's a good (a.k.a. bad) exercise—every bit as any bad (a.k.a. good) as to ladies is *Amor Est Titillatio* (a.k.a. 'love is but a tickle') as old man Spinoza said to Alice, once when just out of kindy wonderland and thence into Lawrence's *White Peacock* (as read by J. Alfred Prufrock (a.k.a. a prude in a frock), but always known for his love song to be notable amongst women).

That's the trouble with the human midden—there's not much to discover that isn't bad. Tedious, isn't it (like the thought of spending all eternity in heaven)? Perish the thought, we'd say, when we've got something to lose, but just suppose we have nothing, absolutely nothing … absolutely nothing to lose … There's not many whose spirits survive with nothing to lose. Take away a man's house (or horse), his work (or wife), his hands (or land), his laws (or cause), his drink (or drugs), and with absolutely nothing left to occupy his mind or to fill his heart, then his soul is ours to do with as we will to fill in every last worthless instant of remaining time.

The trouble with being bad, however ticklish it may feel at the time, is that there's always worse, very much worse, and yet still very much worse which you could ever possibly imagine … inevitably to follow … Tedious, isn't it? but perhaps there's some way of preventing the bad from going completely rotten.

Now anthropology (mankind's study of mankind) can give a bit of spice to life, especially when mankind graduates (through adolescence) from naval gazing to womanising. There's nothing in a naughty weekend, surely, when you compare it with the tediousness of spending all eternity in heaven. Enjoy your adolescence with *The Captain's Daughter* (sired by Pushkin) whilst you can. You're young only once, you know.

What's that, you say, there's a bad-weather warning tucked up in the opening proverb to that story? Well, it couldn't possibly be 'you're young only once, you know', since Pushkin (although never living beyond midlife) died in a dual. What's that, you say, Puskin's bad-weather warning is merely that which parentally advises every young reader to 'look after one's honour whilst young'? Oh, that's just a spoof—Pushkin was no more than a young adolescent when he met up with 'the captain's daughter'. Besides, no woman, least of all Elizabeth Taylor in Tennessee Williams's play, forgets what it feels like to be a 'cat on a hot tin roof'. Here, let's cuddle up-close and watch the film and like the music … It's 'Lost in a Summer Night' by Andre Previn and Milton Raskin.

You're right, the weather's changing. Besides, apart from Maggie, the film's more serious than either first seen or last remembered … that's the trouble with adolescence—it never lasts. And now the rain's just pissing down, like packets of pins on any hot tin roof … Anthropology's all a scam … Adolescence is all a bad dream … And growing up is worse … far worse … than anything one ever first thought …

Everything's a fight … Two elderly anthropologists on top of a dung heap fighting to be king or queen of the castle—the well-known game of crowns—to see who it will be as the dirty wee rascal for not getting to the top of the castle … Behold, this time, it's the *Freeman* v. *Mead* controversy over Margaret Mead's so-called *Coming of Age in Samoa*. Of course, that's not something we read down here, nor do we read any other book, since all we've got and all we need down here are all the reviews and commentaries—online, down-line, along-line, and offline. We have a saying down here: 'Save the trees or fall to your knees', which means you'll never fall to your knees for trying to save the trees and you'll never save the trees either for failing to fall to your knees. Look there, it's up on the wall, the wall, the wall—it's up on the Wall Street wall, since the *Wall Street Journal* never gets here until the month after the latest slump. But tell us do … have you ever read the review (not in the *Wall Street Journal*) for that book called *When the Dollar Dies*? Not much point in reading it now (some say) since the mighty dollar's almost dead.

And not only that, but we're known far and wide for it not only in literature (when our libraries (copied from wee Andrew Carnegie) are crammed with student crammers reading bare-bones histories of absolutely everything) but also in law (where acts of parliament and decisions of supreme courts (all in lower case) give way to commentaries, commentaries, and more commentaries), in science (where abstracts are more telling than articles and reviews are more significant than proofs), in newspaper journalism (where editorial headlines and second-rate opinions clinch conclusive outcomes rather than eyewitness reporting), and where all across the academic board, peer reviews, testimonials, and upper-crust referees deciding peace-or-war issues over policies, promotions, dismissals, and appointments. As some third-rate reviewer has already said, 'This world is in a tumult', and there's none but us down here in hell that can take the credit for that—so don't you try (without first wanting to die)!

We're really quite proud of that not just down here in hell (where we've got consummate self-pride) but by now all over the earth that we don't even need a cover by which to judge a book, far less the book itself, since we can judge it entirely by all the reviews and commentaries. Down here in hell, we've got the biggest library— both repository and research—for all the world's reviews and commentaries. It's our proudest boast down here in hell that with every single gospel review and Bible commentary ever written, we can do down here what no one else can anywhere do without a Bible.

The whole wide world read Homer for being a fairy tale, until along came an archaeologist (doesn't matter who, he's served his purpose) who dug up Troy. That's our model for the Bible—a fairy tale—to bed you down until it's all too late to raise you up from where you'll drown ... So then earth to earth and ground to ground, I practise all the circus acts, you know, ringmaster, clown, prima donna, impresario, strongman, professor, maestro, animal tamer, king of kings, lord of lords ... I am all things to all people. There is not the heaviest headstone in this whole wide world that can hold me down.

So then what's the price of fame? It's all a game, you know. So what good fortune will you pay for some worse fortune made? You've looked forward to holidaying in hell—a cheap option at reduced rates.

There's nothing like slumming around to see how much worse all others are. Once under the ground, there's so many ways of digging your own grave down here that you'll never be able to choose, but take your pick. You can be anything ... be anyone ... do anything ... do nothing ... for as long as you like ...

So then tell me, how's the digging going—whether for oil to grease the way, whether for gold to pave the way, whether for steel to win the day? What's your way, just what's your way? Oh yes, you may think to run away, but overall, I have my sway. Choose which ... Don't delay ... don't delay ... don't ever think to leave it for another day. You've come down here. Don't say, don't say ... We know you've come down here to suss your way ... to suss out your way ...

Anthropological investigations (however risky to one's reputation, as for Margaret Mead in her *Coming of Age in Samoa*) can take you far, far, far further in academic circles than you could ever go yourself. You'll have our backing all the way. All you have to do is to discover, and we'll help you there ... Is some new way ... for some new day ... by which we'll give you full-world sway ... It's all play, you know, it's all play ... it's all play down here every day ...

Don't mourn for dear Margaret— she's had her day, she's had her day—and Freeman too for joining in the fray to make his own day. Of course, each is right, in his or her own way. There's really no such thing as adolescence (except as a pathological condition, or didn't you know?). On our behalf, dear Margaret took the adolescent construct (by way of a cargo cult, you know) to Samoa. Like measles and chickenpox, cowpox, and every other kind of pox, together with every other affliction of heavily urbanised and industrialised societies, adolescence had never been heard of there before.

Of course, to Margaret's leading questions (about sex and the city, well, the city where she came from—she was a lonely old lady, you know) the answers are provoking. We girls would pinch each other and tell her we were out with the boys. We were only joking, pulling her leg, you know, but she took it seriously (which made it funnier still). As you know, Samoan girls are terrific liars (well, not really, we just like to tell the stories that others in need of a good (or bad) story like to hear), and we tease and make fun of each other no less than we make fun of other people (especially to their face). But because this was what poor Margaret wanted to hear, poor Margaret thought it was all true. And of course, as we all know, whether down here in hell or even more so on earth, there's nothing quite like believing something to be true (especially something scandalous) to make it come true. Well, on that score too, Dr Freud got his due.

Lacks security, or so you say, the search for truth, at least when undertaken in academic life. People then pull back from confronting the naked truth, whether in a court of law or under strictly regulated lab conditions or from the dizzying heights of intellectual endeavour— yes, they do pull back, don't they, in their moving from teaching, professing, and preaching (and more especially from prophesying, crying, and advising) into the humdrum bureaucratic of college management (where there's no *as if*, far less any magic carpet).

Okay, then go for discovering yet another missing link. Ever since the Piltdown man (what, with a jawbone like that and him not even a woman), that's the ultimate search for security. Don't think of searching for the truth as being some sort of spoof. Be creative— something new (any novel will do), something borrowed (begged is best), something old (stolen to rue), something blue (a stocking will do)—but best of all is having much more than just sixpence in your shoe! [Exegesis 1: As you've guessed, they send all the bad poets down here.]

* * *

A Bare-Bones History of Hell
Part VI

More Counterfeit Angels

See this sword—the prince of darkness sold it to
me ... and though I bring the world to ruins ... when
the world will dumbly pass away ... that [for me at
least] would be really living ... So then thus it is, that
heaven I've forfeited—I know this full well ... since
my soul once true to God—is now chosen for hell ...

Compiled from the early poetry of Karl Marx,
Oulanem, The Fiddler, and *The Pale Maiden*

In terms of Sokal's hoax—a scholarly sting perpetrated against
academics by Professor Alan Sokal—everything is (or could be or
probably is) a spoof these days. Collegial security is at a premium,
and nothing can be relied on. Nothing too new and written seriously
(not even just quite yet on protein-infective particles, please) gets
published—lest, like Sokal's sting, what goes into print turns out to
be the biggest academic hoax since Thomas Carlyle wrote *Sartor
Resartus* (a.k.a. in English as *The Patched-Up Taylor*).

The Greek cynic Diogenes, the fellow who in broad daylight
shone a lantern into the faces of his fellow Athenians looking for
an honest man, was the first to seize the moment (carpe diem) by
which to get his head round any such scholarly sting as this one.
Coming across a philosopher who discoursed on theological matters
(no less than does this book), then Diogenes, evincing some degree of
surprise, asked him when it was that he had come back from heaven!
[Exegesis 1: Not just yet ... for being still in hell!]

So then let's just go on again searching for the missing link,
and so please today's politically correct multitude by showing it to
be the jawbone not again of a man (far less of an ape or of a bear)
but (aside from the argument over virgin birth) something better by
reason of its large cranial capacity (ignore the massive jawbone) to
uphold today's remarkably overlooked status of women. Meanwhile,

ad astra still shout the astronauts in their hard-won attempts (*per aspera*) to conquer the stars, no less than in the ongoing space race, the cosmonauts struggle (once again *per aspera*) to keep their place and maintain their pace.

Meanwhile, keep digging then, since we're not just blowing the gaff about both celestial as well as earthly matters but instead serving our time in hell by engaging wholeheartedly in this second last of archaeological digs. So then by way of discovering this dislocated second phalanx (of the nominally indicative first human person) whilst we are holidaying in hell on this most privileged of archaeological digs, we begin to shudder at the implications for the future of mankind on earth. [Excursus 1: For some lack of good reason in hell, every attempt of mankind to steal a march (which it does) on any other still surviving species drives it to extinction. Now that's what we call black humour in hell.]

Whilst on this earth (upstairs—quick) people like to cover the odds (as when a point spread line is available to gamblers) by their keeping one foot firmly in heaven and the other foot just as firmly in hell. As between heaven and hell, however, the odds (however equal they can be made to look from earth) are never equal enough to constitute a point spread line from heaven to hell. Accordingly, every gambler from hell always feels the downward draw more than the upward lift in his or her trying to cover such unequal odds, which is exactly why—to offset the down draught—casino architects design tall towers. And this seems a certitude to the non-gambler, however much this downward draw may pass unfelt or unnoticed by the one who is mistaken enough to bet on equal odds. [Excursus 2: In gambling as in everything else, there're those who punt according to form and those who punt more intuitively according to function. Take your pick, then, form or function—but don't bet on eithyer by itself!]

In somewhat the same way, half of humanity (and maybe more than half) wants to hear more about hell, whereas the other half (or possibly much less than half) wants to hear only about heaven. Such is the conflict of opposites on earth—between right and wrong, odd and even, justice and injustice—and this inbuilt conflict is so greatly misunderstood that there could hardly be any concept of heaven (far more misunderstood even than to be minimally understood) without there being also for humans to understand heaven (however much also misunderstood) also a correspondingly conflictive concept of hell.

The trouble (as always) is humanly constructive (either in the intellectual or in the propertied sense) rather than divinely creative (in the deistic sense) or humanly responsive to one's calling (in the servant sense). And it is the humanly constructive way of doing things (either in the intellectual or propertied sense) which largely explains why there is so much hell on earth. [Exegesis 2: The key to the failure of so many human attempts at construction (or reconstruction) lies in mistaking the constrictive for being constructive. For example, most attempts at restructuring (done to save time, to save labour, to save costs, or to save face) are constrictive in consequence and so only rarely result in constructive events.]

Propertied sense … propertied sense … what in hell, you may ask, is propertied sense? Well, everyone steals from God, just as Eve first stole the apple. And intellectual sense … intellectual sense … what makes for intellectual sense? Well, it means as often mostly intellectual nonsense just as any unrepentant Adam will still pass the buck, either back to Eve or on to God, for allowing himself to be tempted by Eve, his own soulmate, who was made and given to him by what in Adam's view is by then a deficient deity.

The trouble is that [as humans like to pontificate], even although otherwise made so clear and obvious by the history of the first human fall, people who don't know where their ideas come from (as with the temptation of Eve first and then Adam) or who don't know who or what empowers them (for being either the Supreme Command or the Counterfeit Command) are the ones who go on bringing about most of this world's woes by their causing so much needless trouble to themselves and others. Get this straight (although never so in hell, where the crooked appear straight and the straight appear crooked)—that the trouble with many both far-off and near-at-hand intellectuals is that, whether in defence of capitalism or communism, democracy or autocracy, or else republicanism or monarchy, they are each only attempting to rewrite their own version of the Bible.

Humans generally veer between expressing a pathological curiosity in hell or else a perverse belief in its non-existence. There is a middle ground, but that's not limbo (where folks don't know where they are or where they stand or what it is they're doing or what it is they're feeling), for having had their lives surreptitiously put on hold by the Counterfeit Command.

Dearest readers (once again, although this time from hell, so you mightn't believe me), this is not a novel. There's nothing novel about giving readers only what they want to read. There are bookshops (chock-full to the gills) of long-remaindered novels because they are written about only what inconstant readers once wanted to read but now no longer want to read. For reasons of commercial sensitivity in the publishing field, we look here to the plain truth as needfully written, which is the only way to avoid saying anything more than needed about publishing anything that need no more be read.

What is written that readers most need to read so often pisses readers off that they leave entirely unread what is then left for shit (by all such inconstant readers), although it is that so long-ago written book—guess what we dug up from a midden in our archaeological dig—which most inconstant readers constantly need to read. No, we can't tell you the name of that once so novel book—no, not here, whilst holidaying in hell (back downstairs—quick), or else we'd shatter the glass through which we now see things (otherwise unseen) but although only so darkly.

It may be possible to write an undercover novel about what youse readers constantly need to read; but every sort of subterfuge as that one, dearest readers, seems to smack (most openly) of the demonic. It is exactly that demonic temptation to exceed our terms of angelic reference (back upstairs—the trap's open) which makes all of us, still righteous angels, shudder of our doing wrong.

Without the express authority of the Supreme Command just now to open anything else more explicitly than that top drawer of your bedside table—here, well, look here, just *who are* the Gideons?— would take us back right now to where all, but not those less than righteous angels, would still fear to tread. Close the drawer. You might not know exactly of what book that's there, but at least you now know, quite precisely, of that book being there. And as for ourselves, besides being as innocent as doves, with good cause, we angels can also be as wily as serpents (and more especially when in hell).

For lack of further insight (when blocked by hell), then like any human being, we angels must therefore resort to rationality. It thus follows from our exposing the plain truth of this report for being a non-novel and so (1) not the sort of book to be taken on any holiday in hell and yet so also (2) for not being an undercover novel (like that book still secreted in the bedside table, dearest readers) that (3) we angels rely entirely on our spiritual status as angels during this mission (as we do on any other angelic mission) no less than to rely entirely on your faithfulness and trust.

There is no need to change the subject of your faith and trust, which is always put to the test by resorting to rationality, since for every virtue, there is a vice—first of counterfeiting the virtue and so then, in consequence, using the counterfeit virtue (which is really a vice)—to undermine the inherent validity of that first assaulted virtue. Thus, for modesty, there is a false modesty; for steadfast courage, there is an impulsive foolhardiness; for frankness of speech, there is a wilful and prejudicial outspokenness; for peace of heart amongst individual persons, there is a slumbering spirit; and for peacemaking amongst the nations, there is no more than a superficial and counterfeit role of peacekeeping. [Excursus 3: A foot in each camp—down here as well as up there—that's our motto both ways.]

This is precisely the point of systemic disintegration (and, eventually, systemic demise) where fear creeps in and confusion abounds. All these counterfeit virtues do no more than spawn the fruits of vice and yet are so easily confused with the virtue they so subtly simulate that in these times of great cosmic stress (hold on, as we said before, love is but a tickle), they carry away souls that otherwise might discern the wrongness of the road down which they are travelling.

The sure sign of decline in any empire (whether human or angelic, civil or military) is the reversal of verities. By this sure sign (what could be clearer), then the wrong way is upheld for being the right way, and the one and only truth is put down for being yesterday's prevailing falsity. On account of this reversal (what could be simpler), falsity acquires a spurious validity, whilst injustice is made successfully to masquerade as justice.

This reversal of core values working both upwards and downwards is then bound to express itself most flagrantly through already strongly established institutions. None but a few of these institutions are exempt from the resulting confusion. Moving downwards especially from the higher courts of justice (who in both name and function consider themselves supreme) as well as moving upwards from the commonality elected (often corruptly) to parliaments and legislatures where justice itself is scoffed at and deplored for being unjust or impracticable or mythic or unsustainable, then the whole of individualistic society (whether civil, military, spiritual, criminal, vagrant, or terrorist) is drawn into participating as principals in this reversal of core values.

In the end, living becomes dying and dying becomes living. But this is nothing new, for today being known by a few and followed by most throughout the world as 'doublespeak'. As the linguist, Leading-Agent Don Watson pointed out to the Supreme Command on his report (2003, Knopf) *The Decay of Public Language*, for any government with the responsibility for maintaining law and order, this is a 'death sentence'.

Relax, don't worry, and never fear. There is absolutely nothing happening now that has not been most accurately foretold (however long ago) by those in the Supreme Command. We have leading agents everywhere, writers and reporters, like G. K. (Chesterton, the Great Gilbert), C. S. Lewis (just plain Jack to us all), J. R. R. Tolkien (by now made known to mankind (through film) as the Foremost Inkling). Besides, these include many, many others who, for the most part, don't even know (and many of whom wouldn't even want to recognise) that their work is sponsored (however incongruously as this may appear to themselves and others) by the Supreme Command.

If you don't understand this paradox of life by which you can so easily be grounded by the Counterfeit Command, then learn to levitate. As the Great Gilbert once wrote in his report on *Orthodoxy* to the Supreme Command, 'Angels can fly because they can take themselves lightly.' So then learn to take yourself lightly, and don't disparage others who take you lightly, or else you'll lose the lighthearted power of levitation and never learn to fly.

This is precisely why this present book (being actually four books (so far) thrown out as largesse instead of one), by writing itself on the exacting subject of soul-catching, turns out (with apologies to both Carlyle's *Sartor Resartus* and Gogol's *Dead Souls*) to be one of the funniest and yet most serious of history books ever written. We say so, of course, apart from the Bible, which, for the gambling man at sixty-six books for the price of one, is the only book, as pointed out by the philosopher Blaise Pascal, to offer the best gambling odds ever underwritten.

Life today, to coin a smile, need no longer be all that was once before (BC) deadly serious, since the Supreme Command runs flying schools for those to learn the principles of flying lightly, whereby Christian life (despite all the dull and boring sermons dumped down from high church pulpits) is the least deadly serious of all ways of our living life. So then dispel all last vestige of gloom in the body of the risen Lord in his preference for our renewed life being taken lightly so that we may soar now with the angels, just as once we sought to soar with the eagles. [Ellipsis 1: 'How so for still holidaying in hell?' asks a lone voice whilst growing fainter ... fainter ... and ever fainter ...]

The truth is that there are times, even deep down in hell, when you just can't stop heaven from coming online. As for Radio Free Europe during WWII (continued through the Cold War), you just have to listen (in Russian if you like) even if you don't want to hear, more than that, as in any language, the voice of the Lord.

So even in hell, we still hear that the only authentic way, the only validly affirmed truth, and the only completely fulfilled and genuinely accomplished life—being all the means to that end which has always been so gently yet so persuasively communicated many times before—are no more at stake now than these same widely proclaimed means ever were at stake in the first place. The counterfeiting with which those who know more of what they're doing yet who are, by their own self-pride, so vehemently opposed to be followers rather than leaders nevertheless remains completely counterproductive to their own counterfeit measure.

That these counterfeiters presume, by force of arms throughout the world if necessary, to substitute their own demonic alternative, for being an entirely counterfeit version of heaven brought down to earth, will nevertheless do nothing of the sort. Instead of undermining the battle for heaven and earth already won by the followers of the Supreme Command, this device, by way of diverting off those unable to withstand the increased spiritual pace of these end times [perceived by all as the demonic heat in the kitchen], will only affirm the earlier-won victory—that victory over death for which Christ the Messiah died on the cross and which cannot ever be undone. [Editorial note: We presume you angels to be sleepwalking in hell whilst sleep-talking of heaven and yet all the whilst still possibly bedded down on earth, but please make your positions clearer to your readers.]

Dearest readers (from heaven, hell, earth, and all surrounding suburbs), the choice, as in all things, is still yours. You may choose to be an authentic creation, to live as never before even whilst still on earth or else to be counterfeit for as long as you're allowed to live. If the latter, then unless and until your counterfeit character is redeemed, you may pass into near oblivion for never being heard of again.

Look at it this way—those of you readers who think yourselves to be sleepwalking with angels on earth. Some folks, snubbing their noses at all and any promise of grace and favour, say they look forward to whatever is meant by whatever form of eternal solitude, which, without their suffering any unexpected surprise, strikes them down. Yet there are other folks who, scouting beyond the three most obvious dimensions of past, present, and future in the less obvious and most recently discovered fourth dimension of time, think to prepare themselves not only for the expected but also for further and unexpected dimensions of space and time as yet undiscovered.

Nakanune, meaning 'on the eve', is a pregnant expression signifying the evening before some momentous event, the cosmic outcome of which, whether known or not, still hangs in the earthly balance for most of us. So before going into what is now no more than a mopping-up operation, think deeply and meditate now as never before [since there's no more spatial room in which to ruminate and no more temporal room in which to procrastinate] on the remaining military operation on the eve of which all you believers, for being the staunchest of followers of Christ the Messiah, will shortly be called into front-line action against the counterfeiters of cosmic law and order by the Supreme Command.

Be prepared! And as already said so many times before, don't focus on this world's woes of warfare, terrorism, and natural disasters. These will only keep you awake at nights. Instead, relax, don't worry, and never fear. There's nothing happening now that has not been most accurately foretold long ago by those in the Supreme Command.

So then learn to deliberate most carefully all you hear (since faith comes from hearing) and all you see (which for being seen as yet still hides and evidences the substance of things hoped for but as yet unseen). Listen to all the songs you hear sung and to all the words you hear made to resound, each with alternative views of heaven and of earth. Consider carefully both of what persons and of what views you would choose to follow. Beware of false prophets, and so dare yourselves to prophesy what's only true!

And where you're given responsibility to lead [for which you're lost without the prophetic gift], don't give up either on the responsibility which underpins true leadership or on your continued following of the Supreme Command. Do so faithfully follow that you may learn to discern and, if necessary, discriminate between the way and the non-way, between the truth and the non-truth, and between the life that leads to life, more life, and yet still more life as distinct from that counterfeit limbo-like life which leads ultimately to final death.

Coming soon [and there's no doubt about it] is the death, burial, and resurrection of this rapidly aging world, which event will, if you so choose, give you a leadership role [without any disclaimers or conditions in small print] to live on and flourish in the world to come. And don't tell us, for being the widest awake of angels, that, for being old dogs, you can't learn new tricks, because there's also going to be a new heaven—one with very many different mansions, with many different tasks, and yet still with all the very best of the by then supplanted old heaven. Well now, are you excited or else depressed? Are you saddened or else angry? And are you going to fight for this cosmic restoration or else run away?

So far (if you've come thus far), this report on the signs of these times may sound to many of the world's most respectable people (for the main part very rational, intelligent, and well-intentioned people) like utter nonsense. That's quite understandable, especially when you begin to understand the extent to which so many once reliable words have not just lost their authentic meanings but have been put down by being made to assume their contrameanings.

Thus, if you read the small print put out on earth [but not in heaven] by many of the wealthiest of banks and finance houses, an *investment* now means (written most explicitly) that you have no right to get back any of your money (whether of interest or capital). And that disclaimer, however much full in your face, doesn't even begin to cover or exonerate all the frauds and scams that some of the most leading banks practise in putting their profits ahead of looking after their clients' accounts.

Some 'investment', huh? But the same goes for most words that percolate from humans through to the heavenlies (computers have been taught not to like that plural noun; the plural form of *heavenlies* frightens them sufficiently to freeze their hard drives). The fact is (although all facts are more fragile than you think they are) that there's not much of any worthwhile moment that percolates through to us in the Supreme Command from your so fast-moving, high-tech, and smart-arsed-phoned earth talk today! [Exegesis 3: You may not have noticed, but Facebook is far enough out, in its very own way, to outdo the Bible.]

We in the Supreme Command are not just speaking about hell's recent survey on the rising tide of the world's spam (first etymologically designed to denote those canned shoulders of pork and meat from the USA without which Britain may never have survived WWII). No, we too in the Supreme Command are also talking about our own survey of the widening extent of scams (on whose origin our etymologists are as yet disagreed). These self-proliferating scams (in finance, banking, education, economics, welfare, literature, and everyday nutrition) are so rapidly overtaking yesterday's old-fashioned spam, no less than the word *prestigious* so rapidly changed sides (surreptitiously by a reversal of established values), namely from its first meaning of a cheap conjuring trick to signal instead the conferring of the highest academic accolade.

Hold on a minute, you're just not listening to whoever's preaching on self-proliferating scams, and that's because you readers on earth think of us in Supreme Command to be not just airy-fairy but also, even as for now jet-age angels and even rocket-propelled angels who levitate without wings, flying much too high! But just who do you think you are, down there on earth, already in fast descent?

'Come down from the clouds,' you readers on earth again dare to wheedle and entice us! 'Do some miracles! Show yourself once more to our naked eyes, then we'll have every [lost] cause [once again] to [dis]believe in you!'

Well, well, well, we in turn from heaven would ask you, 'Where exactly and precisely does that temptation come from?

'Well, we all know what happened last time, whether on Mount Zion or on Golgotha, when we in Supreme Command came down from the clouds! Third time's final—that's the rule of three—although you can't even count up to three for mistaking next round for being just our Supreme Command's Second Coming.

'Look around, we keep on telling you, and read the signs of the times! You're not yet cleared on earth for what will require our instrument landing! At thirty-two feet per second, per further second, and per even further second (don't dare to talk to the Supreme Command in terms of metrics; there have been more air accidents through converting from analogue, so then computers don't like that word either) to digital and from so-called imperial to metric (false French Imperial), there's a limit to how far you can free-fall before making ground contact (unless you want to go straight to heaven), so pull out fast from this nosedive of yours lest you want to avail yourself of this kamikaze alternative posed to you by the Counterfeit Command. [Exegesis 4: Whenever the kamikaze option or any like option insinuates itself to mind, you can be sure it comes from the Counterfeit Command, but as to who monitors the monitor, whether in hell or heaven, that's already long been settled in favour of the Supreme Command.]'

Well, once again, it's the same age-old and infinitively regressive question of who watches the watchers, minds the minders, rules the rulers, judges the judges, or cares for the caregivers. Just how would you answer this question (infinitively progressive, not regressive, say its proponents) after watching *Star Trek XIV* for the twenty-third time or more quietly whilst reading Dr Seuss for not being 'a Hawtch-Watcher in his own hometown of Hawtch-Hawtch)' whilst watching all the other Hawtch-Watchers in watching that town's lazy town bee—how lucky you are you to see like Seuss (what this means)? Of course, if you're a big boy now, you can go to the classics and read Juvenal's Latin of *quis custodiet ipsos custodes?* Which means 'if so the guardians, then who guards the guardians?'

We're not trying to let you know how raw and wet behind the ears you may be as any youthful reader (never having served in Vietnam, far less Korea, or tried to keep the peace in Iraq or Afghanistan). Instead, we'd rather like to emphasise our message to you that the apparent persistency of certain questions (which the Counterfeit Command, in its own favour, would prefer to present for being perennially unanswerable instead of just contingently persistent) have almost just as long ago all been conclusively answered in favour of the Supreme Command. These days, intelligence (including that of MI6, SIS, and CIA) is all the rage (which, in itself, is not a very intelligent thing in which to engage), since rocket scientists have faulty takeoffs and meltdowns (no less than farmers have storm-swept field days) whilst brain surgeons, from Faust to Frankenstein, have far less trouble repairing the brain than they have to mend the mind.

But never mind the mind. We can do without the mind these days since it's the brain alone (so we are told) that counts, so then once again, never mind the mind. By now, despite our brilliant brains, however, most of us are mindless. Nevertheless, let's just see if, as persistently retroprogressive readers, we can still (to the accustomed acclamation) follow (either the clues or the chaos) to answering this question of *quis custodes*. [Exegesis 5: Marijuana memory blank for *quis custodes*? Consult second-last paragraph on *quis custodiet*!]

As further revealed by this report (written in this instance from hell and confirmed by psychological assessment of our continued heavenly conversation by lip-reading aliens), the current situation of heaven on earth, although safe as houses to all retaining their faith (even whilst now sleeping in the streets before being eventually housed in heaven), does not ameliorate the lack of heavenly mansions there in heaven to house those who are of little faith on earth. Instead, it rather now indicates that for those of little faith who now live in earthly mansions, a most perilous housing situation is now pending for them should they ever choose to get to heaven.

To all others, for their lack of faith in places as far removed from where we are (actually, heaven's not more than round the cockney's *jolly horner* from anywhere), the housing situation everywhere is perilous. Likewise, whether in Bangladesh, Damascus, Moscow, Syria, Turkey, Paris, and even in Washington (USA) as in Auckland (NZ), the survival situation is just as perilous as the housing situation. Paradoxically, however, the housing situation on earth is most perilous of all for those of little faith who live in earthly mansions. Just as all these places are no more than a stone's throw apart from each other, we too are no more than just round the cockney corner (in rhyming slang, the jolly horner) from each of these places by also being no more than a stone's throw from heaven to hell and for that same throw from heaven being by now not much less of a throw to earth.

Meanwhile, for being the rightful custodians of the custodians (check back to *quis custodiet ipsos custodes* on this recorded message for training purposes) to find that the brainy but all too bossy intellectuals are given most credence by the non-intellectuals (since amongst non-intellectuals, the overweening self-confidence of the know-all intellectuals can be so much more easily mistaken for instilling the confidence of others in their favour). Nevertheless, many of the most brilliant brains remain enthralled by the horror of their own most terrifyingly terrible minds. What sense does that make to either the mindless intellectual or to the brainiest of non-intellectuals?

The horror of the so-called intellect is not over yet, since the most prestigious of academics can be so prestigiously sucked in by such prestigious spam in their own most prestigious favour. Then what earthly hope can remain for the hoi polloi (meaning by now the downtrodden masses of some bigger brother's proletariat)—except perhaps to bless the truly meek, for they shall inherit the earth—although whether that means the earth of this old worn-out world or of the next new one is apt to appear a complete scam to those who have accommodated their minds, hearts, and lives to this present age of scams?

There was a time, not so very long ago, when to belong to any self-governing profession exacted a responsibility equated with not a hell-bent career but literally a heavenly vocation. Note for the record, not *vacation* but *vocation*, which denotes nothing less than a spiritual calling. You 'take a vacation' when you take time out from your 'vocation', but if you've never been called to a vocation, then all you may be doing is interrupting your hell-bent career.

Teaching the young, at whatever level from preschool to so-called higher education, exacted some degree of self-sacrifice for the sake, at least of explaining the temporal continuity of past, present, and future, to those younger than oneself. Now whether for being a teacher, preacher, lawyer, banker, healer, or any other professional (for the professional bandwagon is bursting at the seams), these are seen, for each member being once explicitly called and choosing to follow and now for merely being in the business of education, merely opting for a church career or for self-serving in the banking or finance industry. So far as any remaining basis for commercial and professional trust is concerned, here too a fast-changing venue ('errors and omissions excepted', as on any lawyer's bill, whether the client understands the acronym EOE by which this is meant or not) is the age of all-round disclaimer.

Besides this being the age of the all-round disclaimer, the age of all-round spam, and the age of the all-round scam, this is also the age of the less than serious song. But then it is also the age of the less than serious book, the less than serious dance, the less than serious letter, the less than serious film, the less than serious legislation, and the less than serious court decision. These are all counterfeits for the lack of that lighthearted levitation of the human spirit, by which not only are we angels able to fly but also by which you spirit-filled Christians can take to the streets (as well as to the skies).

We could go on ad infinitum (a figure of speech for not knowing when and where to stop). Nevertheless, the conflictive seriousness (of both the angelic and humanistic situations) might then reduce most of you to tears, unless for you readers (already reduced to tears) being by then no longer amongst so many of your still dry-eyed peers. So it's the time to change the tune, for more of this same one tune is not going to move many more of your still dry-eyed peers to tears. [Exegesis 6: On the biblical basis of the blessing by which those who mourn shall be comforted, we could continue, but by what means and to what end we leave to those theologians just back from holidaying in heaven (whilst we've been holidaying in hell) to whom we address this and every such exegesis for being the only readers who know not what to do, except to argue with any such exegesis as this one so freshly dug from hell. Meanwhile — take five!]

* * *

BOOK FIVE

The First Fully Opened History of First Light Morning Has Broken

When the Angel Comes Down
Went with my wife to the King's House to see *The Virgin Martyr*, which is a mighty pleasant play ... But that which did please me beyond anything in the whole wide world was the wind music when the angel comes down, which is so sweet it ravished me, and indeed, in a word, did wrap up my soul ... just as I have formerly been when making love to my wife ...
Diary of Samuel Pepys (27 February 1668)

Intro 1—Samuel One: What does it mean to any human 'when the angel comes down'? What does it mean to any preacher (whether street or pulpit preacher) when he or she finally hears the sought-for message (given by that illusive pin falling from heaven)? It may be far more than as to what, even when rightly heard from the Lord, should be preached, proclaimed, or even no more than just quietly whispered. Likewise, what does it really mean to be pleased 'beyond anything in the whole wide world' and this when pleased by something 'so sweet it ravished me and, indeed, in a word, did wrap up my soul'? In other words, for never having yet found one's love and made love to her, what yet awaits you to be blinded by first light? Then, sleepers, awake—morning has broken!

Intro 2—Samuel Two: But how could any morning ever be thought to be broken (which presumably required fixing for having been broken in either the process or purpose of making that first ever morning)? There are many (even staunch believers) who still struggle with a belief in their bones that somehow God is either neither altogether there nor altogether here or (if otherwise both here and there) then not altogether fair. Accordingly, their belief in an all-powerful, omniscient, and all-present God never gets beyond giving him, as they say, the benefit of their own self-doubt.

On the face of his every living Word (which admittedly was far more believable for humans when written in and testified to by their own hand than now when machine printed on paper or conveyed by any merely virtual image), the most Ancient of Days nevertheless leaves no room for doubt. Likewise, his every word, no matter how ruthlessly expressed, is still that same message of divine love, which so ravishes the soul (by conflagrating and melding both thought and emotions as one together) as to leave no room for human doubt. When put yet another way, it was no other than his first and only begotten Son (whose majesty by itself gives rise to many imposters by which to prove that point) who first opened and then reopened the by then still hidden history of first light.

When the Ancient of Days says something is good, like he said of the very first day of creation, then it is good forever. If it ain't broke in his opinion, then there's no call to fix it. In the history of heaven, there will always be remembered the goodness of that very first day, and no matter that by reason of wars, famines, plagues, conquests, and death, most memories of that very first day would thereafter be spoiled, counterfeited, not just once, but also over and over again in the most deformed, anguished, and outlandish of ways, so many otherwise believing people cease to celebrate each passing day for being whatever now remains (despite the historic flood and the near fulfilment of a final fire) of that very first day having been irrevocably broken.

Intro 3—Augustus: The great creator may be an experimentalist, but like all great experimentalists, the creator does nothing without a clear objective. So what of that void and formless earth when darkness lay upon the face of the deep and when light was divided from that darkness by which to distinguish day from night and by which both that first evening and first morning would constitute the first day? Both angels and humans look to that first daybreak as a cause of great celebration and which they still share in the general delight which almost all living things give to each new day's dawning.

But oh dear, here begins the great problem between different cultures, different systems, different measures, different means, and different calendars for the measurement of time. Here is a subject so perplexing in itself and so prone to resulting in confusion that both all history and all prophecy (both biblical and otherwise) pivot on its true understanding.

Once, days began at sunset or at midnight and not at sunrise. Once, there was a twelve-hour day (with four night watches in the night) and not a twenty-four-hour day. Once, there was an eight-day week and not a seven-day week. Once, there was a thirteenth-month calendar and not a twelve-month calendar. And these are just some of the more obvious differences—most of which, by way of political, cultural, and scriptural compromises (as between Hebraic, Greek, Roman, and Anglo-American for being the most obvious), give rise to major misunderstandings in the computation of biblical measures. Why, not even the Authorised Version of 1611 has Genesis right, although its convenor (James, First of England and Sixth of Scotland) would have personally experienced something of the same general diversion by reason of Scotland and England having different calendars in force in their respective countries in 1603 when he became their conjoint king.

So then if morning has broken, there may well be much to do to fix our understanding of what we mean by it. 'From one new moon to another and from one Sabbath to another', as proclaimed by the prophet Isaiah, meant to him not what we now misunderstand him to mean by it. This is but a small still specific indicator of how diversely different measures of time (from once phases of the moon to phases of the sun to accord with Roman sun worship and thence to change from an eight-day to a seven-day weekly cycle) can throw out our present means of computing time for both past and present, as well as for future events.

Intro 4—Samuel One: Arguably, by birthing light out of darkness rather than by dispelling, pushing back, or breaking darkness to bring out the light, the creation was entirely a synthetic process by way of bringing things to fruition. Indeed, there are still some pockets of coalescing darkness, since creation, although well underway, is still very much, as always intended to be, a work in progress.

Nevertheless, there was something both determinatively explosive as well as evaluatively assertive about each such sequential step in the proclamatory process of creation. What then the divine voice drew forth, day by day from the still surrounding darkness, were things so unique in their conception (pristine states of being, unclouded and untrammelled in their original state of glory) that (for our being so long accustomed to them) we cannot any longer conceive of their originality.

When mortals think of an explosion, they first focus on the explosive, but it is not the explosive alone that brings about the explosion. The explosive has to be contained in order to set off an explosion. It may be contained by packing the sticks of explosive into holes drilled for that purpose into rock, or the explosive may be contained by being filled and packed into a steel casing. Apart from some sort of fireworks display, no explosion will take place without containment. Nothing can exceed the density of that void out of whose containment this world's creation was called into being.

Intro 5—Novice-Angel Chloe: What are the various stages of awakening in the passage of the human soul through life? What, please tell me again, is the slumbering spirit? Once awakened, will the awakened spirit always stay awake or could it just as easily fall back to sleep again?

So too then, what happens to the soul when the spirit starts to slumber, fall asleep, and perhaps, as every infant so often fears, never wake up again? By the same token, what then is wakefulness, especially spiritual wakefulness (or awareness)? It so often takes a lifetime on earth (or longer) to learn that bodily rest comes only from being at spiritual rest.

We are told that just as prayer enlivens every soul for spiritual rest, physical exercise enlivens the body—and this *both* for bodily rest *and* for spiritual rest. It's not a matter (no pun intended) of mind over matter. On the contrary, it's a matter (pun intended) of making every single iota (of matter) matter. It is this sort of spiritual chain reaction which makes the whole realm of matter to every iota of matter and, in turn, every iota of matter to matter to the entire realm of matter. Now this is the angelic acme or height of wakefulness which comes through self-awareness of sharing as one soul in the cosmic context of all souls (whether as the heavenly host of angels or as mankind when still in the making and passing through its stages of increasingly spiritual awareness).

Look at it this way—souls were never made to sleep. In fact, they're more awake when you're bodily asleep than when you're bodily awake. That's when young men hear how it is to prophesy and when old men are given to envision great dreams. So then awake my soul and sing, to allow for my having a very different way of looking at things, no less than when bodily asleep and dreaming than when bodily wide awake. This is the state of being not just individually self-aware but of being also collectively soul-aware.

* * *

Blinded by First Light
Part I

In the Beginning …
God created the heaven and the earth. And the earth
was without form, and void; and darkness was upon
the face of the deep …
The first book of Moses on beginnings,
commonly called Genesis

You boast of your tupuna (or predecessors)—a South Pacific failing
(boasting, that is) and common to both Pakeha and Maori (much
of a muchness, as they are). As a third-generation Christian, you
think yourself to have no need of first light. With the milk of human
kindness, within your own whanau (or family), you believe it's
generationally passed on. Why, the first light of each new day's
dawning is first (well, runner-up, at least) to strike these shores. So
you've never been blinded (needlessly as this would appear to be) by
any first light?

Be well prepared for the unexpected happening, then when and
next to come. You may yet be blinded by last light, if already too late
for first light. Although with 20/20 prophetic vision and never having
been blinded at all, you may yet be given something to think about.
Often, the greatest must fall … fall heavily … just as that Paul (who
once was Saul) was given so much to think about on the road, as you
now are, to meet your destiny in Damascus!

Some babies are born whilst stifling a yawn (although you,
like them, may not hear or by now may have forgotten to listen
for whatever pin is falling from heaven) whilst they, perhaps still
like you, are stifling a yawn. Of course, and again like you, these
babies may yet go on to create a great havoc in the course of their
growing up.

Other babies will come into this world with no more than a
whimper and go out with cries of great joy, whilst yet others will
come in to set off a great hue and cry and still happily go out, even as

592

great kings and queens themselves will go to the scaffold or guillotine without the slightest murmur. Life on earth (even when trademarked or branded with a fish, a boat, or a cross) is just like that (for being no different—apart from one's own response—than from being branded (rightly or wrongly) like any criminal with a wolf's head).

There's no accounting, apparently, for either beginnings and ends or origins and outcomes, or if there is, then perhaps only on account of what takes place in between. Yet whilst it's a cliché to think of that life in between as being exceedingly full of the utmost surprises, it's also a cliché beloved by those who are never surprised for themselves to think that to be taken so by even the slightest surprise is inversely proportional to one's level of intelligence. Yet for all that, the world is chock-full of unintelligent stoics who spend all their lives repressing their utmost surprise. They fail to see that the expected provokes the unexpected, which is why they succumb to the unexpected (irrespective of stifling their surprise).

So however it was (speculatively speaking) that we first began (and we each have a uniquely different generational path from which to review our differential beginnings), from there on, we travel to reach our collective destiny yet still uniquely personal end. There is no foretelling of exactly how it is that we each shall learn to travel our path, nor of how exactly we shall each end our travel. Nevertheless, without our first learning the most we can about how we first began, since prophecy both pivots as well as hinges on history, then there is no foretelling of how and where we shall end—but first of all, a word from our sponsor of first light!

This may be a very ordinary book (in the affairs of heaven), but this first word from our sponsor in the Supreme Command (very shortly to be recommissioned in the history of first light as the Supreme Commission) is no ordinary word. On the contrary, every word commissioned by us from the Supreme Command is the measure of every word that has ever been uttered in time and space and of every event since to have happened in time and in space. Accordingly, we look to hear and to read of this commissioning word from the Supreme Command in keeping with the faith given to us, no less than we began our lives in faith, went on to travel in faith, and go on all the time by looking forward to whatever will end this present life of ours in faith.

This faith now of ours in the living Word of the Supreme Command is unconstrained by time or space, since both time and space are in the hands of the Supreme Command. Hence, the Word of the Supreme Command is the only authentic measure of this faith, although, just as there are many false prophets, so also there are as many counterfeiters of this living Word.

These false prophets and counterfeiters of the living Word owe allegiance to the Counterfeit Command (which no longer has the forcefulness in this fray to recommission itself as anything other than it still is as the Counterfeit Command). These counterfeiters misbelieve themselves to be unconstrained by time and space, and this is the material source of their self-deception by which they mistake themselves able, by their seceding from the Supreme Command, to authenticate their own counterfeit kingdom by usurping the authority and power of the Supreme Command. Secession (without any prospect of recommission) is a very perilous road to travel, giving rise to civil wars (as in the USA), conquests, invasions, and bloody revolutions. In 1830, the kingdom of Belgium seceded from the Netherlands, and has been under constant attack through two world wars and their aftermath then ever since. Now, what does that bode for the so-called European Union when today ensconced in the Belgian capital of Brussels?

Nevertheless, the authority of the Supreme Command transcends all time and all measure of time, in whose hands of the Supreme Command, a day may be as a thousand years and a thousand years may be as a day. On the other hand, the Counterfeit Command, by attempting to manhandle time in its own demonic way, is always pressed for time. It deals in deadlines by which to enforce its own instant action and so allows for no leeway in the breach of these deadlines.

Moreover, on the basis that the Counterfeit Command made these same deadlines, the Counterfeit Command claims the right of the Maker (as if it were creator) to break its own deadlines. Of course, this is only another version of that same lawlessness by which lawgivers who make the rules believe that they themselves have the right and power to break the rules. Indeed, none can trust the Counterfeit Command to abide by its word. Consequently, the power of any word when transacted by the Counterfeit Command is in such constant decline as to trip up and confuse its own followers.

Because the Counterfeit Command does not abide by its own word, it cannot believe in its own word, unless by self-deception. When words thus break down, then thought gives way. When thought thus gives way, then whatever attempts to sustain thought gives way. When whatever is attempted, even for the good, happens to give way, then even whatever is done breaks down by reason of the ongoing self-deception. That is exactly why, as the Presbyterians say, so much damage is done by those ('the unco-guid') who credit themselves with the best of intentions.

First language, then logic, and finally the law, then all else (domino fashion) falls by the wayside. For the command theory of law to hold sway, words must hold firmly to their prescriptive meaning, which is not an easy thing for them to do when, as nowadays, all prescriptive meaning has faded away.

Prescriptive law requires prescriptive language, both for its maintenance and enforcement as well as for its prescriptively informed administration. These different modes of prescriptively informed operation also require prescriptively informed legislators, prescriptively informed judges, and prescriptively informed lawyers.

Weeds of the wayside, subtly sown into these fields of authentic endeavour by the Counterfeit Command, soon spring up to cover the commanded counterfeiting. False language abounds to discredit the propriety of prescriptive meaning, false arguments take over from the truth of syllogistic reasoning, and wayward jurists seek to prove the worse for being the better cause.

Every clear concept of communication then becomes more and more clouded. Whatever conclusions can still be reached then rapidly become counterproductive to whatever merited their first design. Good intentions become increasingly thwarted. Morality becomes an archaic mismatch for mortality. Hope no longer springs eternal—no, not even in the most heroic of human breasts.

Deep dismay, depressive disappointment, together with the anger of disillusionment, set in. The victims of such apparently universal counterfeiting now see themselves to be privileged persons amongst the still walking dead. At first, they look for no more than rational closure. When without this closure, then as deeply rebellious and antisocial terrorists who have nothing to lose, they give themselves over to irrational and intensifying acts of death, destruction, and arbitrary acts of violence. We're here describing a systemic affliction, so don't make yourself even more vulnerable for mistaking yourself to be immune.

What was once a living word for the Counterfeit Command then becomes a dying word that sucks and depletes goodness from all the world, and this no less than it does the same and more so for the Counterfeit Command. This dying word breathes death and destruction over all to whom, for the sake of its own limited survival, this Counterfeit Command most flatteringly speaks of grace and favour.

That original cosmos of law and order once safeguarded by the truly spoken and truly written word then turns to chaos and disorder for the Counterfeit Command. Not until we see and understand the reality of the Supreme Command for being our Supreme Commission, however, will we truly understand the Counterfeit Command for being a commandeered command.

The brevity of first light does not detract from its brilliance. History [as a rule] tends to be long, dry, and tedious—at least to those readers who are either unready or ill-informed as to its purpose—whereas revelation [as a rule] is straight to the point, which is as often the jugular. We shall not compromise the fleetness of our travels, whether to the furthest, as always east is from the west, by mistakenly trying either to quantify or to qualify the diversity between east and west (which, to the detriment of both, would suit only one at the expense of the other).

Instead, throughout this part of our report on the dawn of first light, we shall rely on that brilliance itself to shine out, whether as by the first rays from the first rising of the sun in the morning or from the last diminishing gleam of the same daylight or from the reassuring beam to shipping of some lighthouse or even, as for the military, the same reassuring tracking searchlight during the no longer supervening darkness, so expect these accompanying revelations as to the first piercing light of creation to be staccato short.

Righteous revelation is implosive (working within) as well as explosive (working without). From without, it may send a blinding rush of blood from the heart to the head, which, without more absorption from within, may do no more than strike a fellow dead. Righteous revelation is never less given than by first light (but never ever of last light, unless the fellow marks himself down for death instead of transformation.

This is the so-called Damascus experience. Through both carotid (once mistakenly thought to be stupefying) arteries, the revelatory message is carried directly from the heart to the long stultified and calcified portions of the human brain. It is vitally important on all fronts to get the transformational formula unique to each person (whether for a Moses, an Elijah, a Zacharias, or a Paul) just right. Raw and refined emotions have vastly different molecular structures, you know. This is not just brain surgery, but also mind surgery, and so in turn soul surgery, with brain, mind, and soul being all transfigured with the same single stroke of first creative light with which to transform the unruly, and so often unrighteous human mind.

* * *

Blinded by First Light
Part II

Cosmic Communication

One can imagine that God created the universe at literally any time in the past. On the other hand, if the universe is expanding … an expanding universe … does place limits on when he might have carried out his job!

Stephen Hawking, *A Brief History of Time: From the Big Bang to Black Holes*

Everyone believes in cosmic communication, but hardly anyone believes in hearing from God. Radio telescopes (as often as not now manned by atheists and agnostics) search the universe for signs of extraterrestrial life, but not all astronomers believe in their hearing from God. Philosophers like Plato can spend most of their lives wondering where ideas come from, but not more than a few philosophers today believe in their hearing from God. Oh dear, it's not just science which equates evidence with proof, and thence proof with truth, but philosophy has also come to the same wimpish dead-end!

We are told that faith comes by hearing, so for anyone to believe in God obviously comes by his or her hearing from God. Otherwise, if faith comes from hearing, those who have faith only in themselves hear from none but themselves. Of course, if we chatter all the time, we can't very well be listening, so what's the point of radio telescopes when all the time, it's only you humans that do the talking? There's no point then in looking or listening for aliens, because, no matter how hard we try to make him so, God is simply not an alien.

In his introduction to Stephen Hawking's celebrated *Brief History of Time: From the Big Bang to Black Holes*, the physicist Carl Sagan introduces Hawking's book 'on the frontiers of physics, astronomy, cosmology, and courage', as being 'also a book about God … or perhaps about the absence of God'. Now that's a fair enough summation, since any book about the absence of God (as Hawking's book most certainly is) is also most certainly bound to be about God.

Indeed, most books written about the absence of God are more about God than are many of those books written about the presence of God. One way or another, when being pursued by the hound of heaven, even to the very end of the 'universe with no edge in space' there's just no getting away from the presence of God

According to Sagan, 'Hawking is attempting, as he explicitly states, to understand the mind of God', but the unexpected conclusion of Hawking's effort is to arrive at a 'universe with no edge in space, no beginning or end in time, and nothing for a creator to do'. Well, it's such a tall order for any mere man to know his own mind, that perhaps this leaves a great deal for one's own creator yet to do!

So then, how real is Hawking's universe, because everywhere one looks and whether or not one believes in God, one finds that there is more than plenty for any God to do? In fact, there are far more disbelievers in God whose main reason for there being no God is that either he's doing so little (in the context of so much to do) so he couldn't be here or else what little he's doing (in the same context of so much to do) is not worth the doing. Hawking is very much out on a limb, both by way of his own faulty logic as well as his own atheistic peer review and by way of deciding that there's no God anywhere for the lack of anything for any god to do. Perhaps Hawking should take another look from where he now is (even if having got no further in his present travels than Westminster Cathedral) to see and confirm his earlier view that there's nothing on earth for any god to do.

This half pi but extremely explosive conclusion (by which every spiritual dimension to reality is denied) most certainly sets off a monstrously big bang in the minds of all believers claiming to have heard from God and so, to the credulous, creates both a huge void in their lives no less than for them to find that they have been hearing from a do-nothing god living within a great black hole which they have mistaken for heaven's own extremely dynamic and divinely created universe.

Nevertheless, on any such matter as conjuring up the counterfeit of a do-nothing god, our Supreme Command remains completely unperturbed. This very same mistaken apprehension of a do-nothing god emanates most forcefully from seeing the crucifixion no more than as a catastrophe, during that moment of utmost despair to the disciples when it was not yet in man's mind to know intimately the miraculous mind of God. Of course, the Supreme Command could still give Stephen Hawking the Damascus experience, but only if, like an earlier Stephen, he is truly set on knowing the divine mind of God.

But for the sake of speaking to the credulous, those who might come to believe in the mistaken physics or philosophy that would promote a do-nothing god, then let it be clearly understood that it could never be 'the ultimate triumph of *human* reason', as Stephen postulates in his final conclusion 'to know the mind of God'. To believe no more than in 'the ultimate triumph of human reason' would be one of the principal barriers to both listening for and hearing from God in whatever one does and wherever one goes. It would also be one of the most cogent of security barriers in the history of science by which to instil the necessary humility to make one's rightful beginnings as well as to secure the necessary persistence to pursue these beginnings to their rightful end.

All the same, whether concerned more about the presence or absence of God, everyone, including both believers and unbelievers, go on believing in their own brand of cosmic communication. Not just physicists and philosophers but so too, psychologists pursue research into extrasensory perception with no less avidity than parsons pray for their parishioners. And after working on no more than a hunch for almost all their lives, physicists and biologists overcome whatever stands in the way of their foremost discoveries. Likewise, parents will pray as often beneath each daily breath as steadfastly during each night for the welfare of their children.

Testifying to their own brand of belief in cosmic communication, some people feel called to light candles in cathedrals, others to turn prayer wheels or to tell beads, and yet others to worship at wailing walls, in verdant groves, or at sacrificial altars. It is most often in our very own unique way, however, that each of us makes most sense of whatever belief we hold in our receiving communication from the otherworldly cosmos. And instead of resolving the collective consciousness of all conflicting beliefs as to there being a universal Creator, the secular and as often satanic state, as heaven's usurper, is invited into the arena of worship to distance one believing soul from another believing soul through an unworkable system of purely personal, secular, and inherently conflicting rights. There are of course two and more ways of thinking about the Universal Declaration of Human Rights, but only one is sound.

It is as if the strongest sense of cosmic communication must be felt personally, individually, and directly for that experience to be most fully fulfilled and appreciated by any person. This need for individuality of experience (explained by the uniqueness of each person to the Supreme Command) still remains the case, even although the strength and sanctity of that personal experience may well be socially initiated, accentuated, and confirmed for these same people predominantly through their family upbringing, work ethic, group support, or congregational participation. Nevertheless, the question then next asked by the Supreme Command is whether each person then still seeking for the strongest sense of cosmic communication will choose to go on searching for what he or she is tempted by the ongoing struggle to dismiss for being either the unobtainable or else for being never more than part-filled.

Then will the astronomer still go on searching for signs of extraterritorial life? Then will the philosopher go on wondering where ideas come from? Then will the scientist still pursue his lifelong hunch? Then will parsons and parents go on praying for their parishioners and children? And then will people still light candles, still turn prayer wheels, and still tell beads if by then they think themselves to have reached the highest level of cosmic communication which they might mistake for being divine communion? This is a huge question, but then all such cosmic questions, when asked, even if not yet already answered down the ages, have been tackled only by overcomers.

For many other searchers and researchers, however, this same level of attaining cosmic communication seems achievable only by their being reduced to the personal loneliness of some desert experience. Their philosophy of ideas may be denigrated, their psychic research into the paranormal may be laughed at, their worship whether at wailing walls or in verdant groves or at sacrificial altars may be completely misunderstood. As with the scientist who discovers his hunch verified by final revelation after years of painful exploration, he or she is apt to find themselves in the minority of one or else, adding insult to injury, their work attributed to someone else.

Without there being some sufficient theory of translation between different perceptions of reality, however, it seems that unity of both mind and heart on the subject of cosmic communication is beyond all human capability. To appreciate one's own calling to communicate and to be sure of its verification and confirmation for oneself, then the sense of social deprivation derived from the desert experience as well as the sense of social belonging generated from sharing our own experiences with similar believers both need to be felt and undergone by each individual. The fact of our being more like social animals instead of individual clones, as proven over and over again to the satisfaction of the Supreme Command, shows that faith, until put to the test, is worthless. And none is more worthless for being our faith in human society until put to the test of finding ourselves all alone in its midst.

The sense that we ourselves are engaging in cosmic communication cannot be conventionalised, cannot be formalised, and so cannot be legitimated or verified (unless by crediting ourselves with that experience and so disqualifying ourselves). Thus, the strongly hunch-led physicist may poke fun at the quietly praying parson, who, in turn, may anger the pragmatic psychologist and the incredulous radio astronomer, just as the praying parent may anger the secular educationalist, no less than those who dare to conjure up their dearly departed by way of a séance may be called to pay the price of their own sleep for thinking to have disturbed the sleep of their loved one.

All the same, when left to their own way, most people generally believe in cosmic communication. This is true, and often even more so, of those who remain relatively unaware of the spiritual similitude—as between the professedly secular scientist and his professedly spiritual adversary—when shared by their very different ways of relating cosmic beliefs. It then follows that often the most ardent opponents of cosmological communication are also the most ardent practitioners, in their own way, of that extrasensory, highly intuitive, and often mystifying art of cosmic interpretation.

Likewise, the follow-through of any eureka moment given by some creative hunch or of encountering some previously unthought-of idea is often overwhelmed—as by Edison's pursuit of the incandescent filament for electric lighting—by the immense amount of often arduous and painful work it takes the inventor or discoverer to implement his or her first inspiration. For this sort of reason, one's celebratory status (as for Herod in his kingly oration impressing his neighbours from Tyre and Sidon) is most usually short-lived.

In the same way, as by reinvesting our deliverance with the demonic, we can so easily return like the proverbial dog to its vomit. What we focus on by way of any spiritual sacrifice—as by overemphasising the morbid details of the crucifixion—may again so overwhelm our merely mortal senses as to take away and reduce to nothing our ability to undertake and build on all that has been achieved and overcome by that same sacrificial and immortal spirit.

Even the cross, at one extreme when trivialised around our necks for being a talisman and at another extreme exaggerated beyond all physical measure to still allow for spiritual resurrection, is not beyond the wiles of the Counterfeit Command when entrusted to the hands of fallible humans. So it is not for nothing that all graven images are outlawed—yes, even what we are tempted to think of the rugged beauty of the old wooden cross, says the Supreme Command—since the graven forcefulness of all such images on the human mindset tends to backtrack on the deliverance ministry we have received and so risks reinvesting our sense of salvation with the demonic, which by that deliverance had been then so stoutly overcome. For such a reason, it is the Lord himself speaking when the Supreme Command says, 'Look forward!'

Yet thus, by being tempted always to look backwards, do so-called spiritualists call up unclean spirits, who, even as to kings, are most usually imposters and counterfeiters of the dead, in their being called up from their privileged rest? So too, round their secure firesides, do grandfathers scare as much themselves as they do scare youngsters by reading fearful tales and ghost stories to their grandchildren? By which time to come, then bored adolescents will have learnt to do the same to themselves by reading even more scary books about ghouls and vampires and by watching films of witches and warlocks, all of which, unless sanctioned by the Supreme Command, can open entry to the then intriguing realm of the Counterfeit Command.

Thus, even demure young ladies shall on the one hand think it fit to pray and then on the other hand cast the runes on Halloween for some right hunk of a husband to romanticise their lives. Down the same track, those left desolate by some loved one's death shall dare to hold séances, even most minimally, as these false callings of the Counterfeit Command may so subtly insinuate themselves into a survivor's tortured mind by which to ease their grief by conferring or relating themselves backwards to the will of their departed one. In each such counterproductive case, says the Supreme Command, we are called on to strengthen ourselves and to strengthen ourselves in the Lord.

There are far better ways of dealing with loss, including that first primordial loss of innocence for which a fallen humanity was expelled from paradise, than to persist and so perpetuate one's life through grieving over one's loss. This perpetuation of penitential grief (where the joy of the Lord is imprisoned and confined) gives rise to all those forms of asceticism and self-denial (both personal and public) which so much play into the hands of the Counterfeit Command.

There is certainly always a time, no more than in the transient present, for expressing one's grief, but this never by way of prolonged indulgence at the expense of the perfective future. Instead, one must look always forward to see and do the will of the Supreme Command.

Despite the forcefulness of Stephen Hawking's secularist mindset in the physical sciences and despite the same secularist mindset of Richard Dawkins in the life sciences, there is no shortage of their own given evidence for that highest level of cosmic communication which both their secularist mindsets so strongly deny. As Shakespeare would say (as in *Hamlet*) they 'protest too much' or (as he said of Cassius in *Julius Caesar*) they 'have a lean and hungry look' (as all humans can express when fixating on their own powerlessness to the point of dangerous dissatisfaction). So too, thanks to the carried-away fans of J. K. Rowling at no different a narrative level, the evidence of committed mindset to some sort of cosmic communication is likewise overwhelming. Pretty nearly everyone who bothers to read, who bothers to pray, or who bothers to believe wholeheartedly in anything, unequivocally affirms cosmic communication, whether done each in his or her own way, either through the forcefulness of their negative denial or the forcefulness of their positive affirmation.

Likewise, for being the study of the cosmos, cosmology is all the rage nowadays; and why not, since everyone believes in cosmic communication. For being the study of absolutely everything (in the time and space continuum, as the physicist might say), there's no brief account which we can give, whether accounting separately for time or space and much, much less in our trying to account cosmologically for both of them. [Exegesis 1: Cosmology has become the rage nowadays particularly amongst those persons (mostly physical scientists, social scientists, and similar academics) who have become addicted to the gathering of provable information and who thus measure their own worth only in terms of proving brute facts.]

The cosmic picture, even when limited to what we think ourselves to know of the purely physical, remains far beyond our ability to depict or envision its extent or even our own position in it. Our own global picture of the cosmos is therefore miniscule, and that's not even half of the problem we have, on a starry night or during a solar flare-up or during a tropical cyclone, of thinking ourselves to know what all the rest means by way of being the unknown cosmos.

The other half of the problem of our accounting for the cosmos lies in the different ways we see of ourselves on earth. We have seen that in the very beginning, when the earth was void and without form, then the Supreme Command created the cosmos of law and order which we now know of generically as heaven and earth. Because we humans were, either directly or indirectly, made from the dust of the earth, we tend to remain earthbound and so focus on the earth from which we were made and on the earthly affairs with which we were entrusted, together with the earthly tasks we were commissioned to undertake. And in that sense, even just sun-worship (however false) was a big breakthrough from considering ourselves forever totally grounded.

Nevertheless, for any cosmology to undertake and attain its divinely appointed purpose of communicating between the divinity of heaven and the humanity of earth (a purpose seen as only through a heavy mist by seers, prophets, shamans, tohunga, and others in primeval religions), the cosmology and its cosmologists must be sanctified. Unless sanctified, then the orderliness of the cosmos declines and degenerates into the disorderliness of chaos.

Unless sanctified into orderliness and maintained in orderliness, every bridge of communication between heaven and earth will either collapse through disuse or be a scene of continued conflict or else shall be commandeered by counterfeit forces. We end this military review on the subject of continued cosmic communication by which Jacob, one of the patriarchs (or early fathers) of ancient Israel, went on a journey from Beersheba to find a wife in Haran, and on the way, he lay down to sleep at a place called Luz, which, because of a dream that he dreamed there, he renamed Bethel.

This then was the dream of Jacob, son of Isaac, grandson of Abraham, which Jacob dreamed whilst lying down to sleep on the stony ground, with no more than stones for his pillow there, one night whilst on the way to his uncle Laban, his mother's brother, whilst journeying eastwards from Beersheba in search of a wife at Haran. As of any story that is told, told, and retold, it is a true story.

Whilst Jacob dreamed of his night at Bethel, he saw a huge ladder set up on the earth and stretching towards heaven, to which the ladder reached, so that all the time he dreamed, he saw in this, his dream, the angels of God who ascended and descended from earth to heaven and, in turn, also from heaven to earth; and at the top of the ladder stood the Lord his God who said to him many, many things.

First of all, Jacob's God introduced himself, saying, 'I am the Lord God of Abraham, your father, and the God of Isaac.' Secondly, he promised to Jacob, 'The land on which you lie I give to you and to your generations, through which all the earth's families shall be blessed ...'

Now that this true story which could not be contrived is proved by the countless times, it has been told in its original form and by the countless places in which it has been retold in its original form, as well as by the fulfilment of the vow that Jacob made with the Lord his God ... then that the Lord God at the top of the ladder should be his God.

This lasting quality, whether of ideas or of things—and in itself the authentic classical measure of worthiness in time and space—is that which has been regularly honoured by the study of the classics (whether biblical or pagan) until our present age. Now our own age, however, for having been consumed with a passion for purely human progress but yet for being completely ignorant of its own history measures quality by its apparent newness and novelty and so, by the inbuilt obsolescence of all its own works, foretells the end of all things.

The wicked irony, by which this classical formula (constancy amid inconstancy) for assessing worthiness has been stood on its head, so also becomes the reverse formula also for our own passing. Instead of, as once before, imbued with a passion for our own persistence. Following and becoming absorbed into the context of constant change, we become reluctant to pursue this same stolid mindset of persistence. Whether we know it or not or whether we like it or not, we ourselves have categorically decided against our own survival. These end times, whether couched in terms of limited resources and environmental failure or of human ingenuity and constantly resurgent human progress, are entirely of our own making.

This reversal of what were once seen to be universal values in time and space gives rise to increasing anomalies or antimonies between these classical and modern measures of worthiness. By now, in scientific terms, we have come to worship the continuum of time and space by which to explore the universe, yet at the same time, we bow down to relativity in our having ceased to revere the continuum of time and space by which we once assessed worthiness.

By now, also in social terms, the exuberance of youth no longer gives way to the wisdom of age, but rather, more experienced age is expected to give way to less experienced youth. And once again, this upending of a long-established formula foretells the end of the world as we know it, since what is being handed on by way of responsibility to youth presages a state of affairs that is far more critical than ever before experienced. It is increasingly one in which humanity is content to pass on no more than brute information in place of life-learnt wisdom. Besides this, as a result of our present consumer age, we have now come to revere obsolescence, for which in readiness for the next most crucially reached age of an increasingly passive humanity, many of those well-off elderly have, by their refusal to foresee this crisis, already rendered themselves reverentially obsolete from their task of bridging generations with prudence and wisdom.

However surprising it may be, nevertheless counterfeits serve a purpose. Because there can be no counterfeit without an original, therfore every counterfeit confirms the existence of its original. Thus, by the presence of Satan counterfeiting the presence of God, then the presence of Satan confirms the presence of God. So too then, that ladder of angelic communication which Jacob dreamed of as extending between heaven and earth is also confirmed by those counterfeit ladders promising easier access to heaven (but in reality often leading straight from earth to hell).

Likewise, for that cursus honorum or ladder of self-promotion by way of affording fame, fortune, and personal advancement in the course of one's own selfish striving, that ladder too (although just as countefeit) in turn confirms the reality of Jacob's ladder. Such counterfeit ladders are typified by today's sequential promise of institutional offices or appointments, say, in the career of a politician, the advancement of a professional, or the achievements of a businessman or commercial trader. Rarely if ever nowadays, as so often once before, is there any Lord God identified as there was to the patriarch Jacob when he lay asleep and so dreamed of heavenly things at the bottom of the original ascending and descending ladder of cosmic communication between heaven and earth. Most earthly ladders these days, whether promoting personal success, or purporting to open avenues of communication between heaven and earth are sadly counterfeit. Learn to discern and distinguish them from those which are valid for being both original and authentic.

* * *

Blinded by First Light
Part III

Cosmic Conflict
Does it ever give thee pause that men used to have a
soul—not by hearsay alone, or as a figure of speech;
but as a truth that they knew and acted upon!
Thomas Carlyle, *Past and Present*

We'll have a lot more to say about all sorts of conflict later on. For the
moment, we're speaking more generally about cosmic conflict. This
is as often expressed by different worlds in orbital collision, whether
or not represented by different elements (such as hydrogen and
oxygen), different compounds (such as acids and alkalis), different
formulations (such as those of sea and sky), different processes
(generation and degeneration), and different aspects (individual
and societal), together with different longevities (such as that of the
eternal soul instead of the mortal body).

Much here is generalist and so focusses (very roughly and thus
inexactly) on the metaphysics of conflict. It is vital to realise that
the angelic mind, like the prophetic mind, is generalist. The only
person to whom any generalist thinker can make sense (often any
sense at all) is to another generalist thinker. There are most obviously
vastly different levels of generalist thinkers, as there are of specialist
thinkers. It will be even more obvious that divine persons who are
omniscient, omnipotent, and omnipresent have no other option than
to be the most generalist (as well as the most specialist) of thinkers.

This is one explanation why specialists (even those who as
theologians specialise in their study of the divine) have considerable
difficulty with more generalist (and often lay) thinkers. Thus, the
generalists (whether or not amongst the theologians and clergy) like
Tyndale, Luther, Foxe, Bunyan, Knox, and Wesley are the stuff of
whom Christian martyrs are made of, and one could add acres of
unknown names to *Foxe's Book of Martyrs* of those who were shipped
out to the colonies to pursue their own worshipful predilections.

Nevertheless, at the human level (although only a little lower than the angelic level), the generalist thinker is always at odds in any profession, whether of faith and/or works with the specialist thinker. To the specialist, the vertical text may be all, whereas the horizontal context is nothing. To the generalist, even where the vertical text is everything, so also the horizontal context is everything, and neither could have the same significance without the other.

Even the generalist, when speaking to the specialist on one or more of their mutually owned specialisms, may make no sense or so much less than sense to the specialist as to be dismissed for a fool by the specialist. The vertical and horizontal—as with text and context, public and private, individual and collective—tend to be fixedly oppositional and fractiously fixative.

Thus, the generalist context, in trying to account for both heaven and hell, appears antithetical, heretical, and even apostate to everyone and anyone who focusses or fixates exclusively on heaven. But then any mere mortal with a heaven-only fixation can be perilously disadvantaged by mistaking that exclusivity for being a heaven-sent calling. His mission, no matter how much heaven-sent, may be seriously disadvantaged from his looking round every next corner into what he would see for being the seething masses of those in hell or bent for hell.

Then again, that sort of categorical exclusivity is most certainly not shared, enjoyed, or imposed by heaven. As either angels or mortals, we are most surely told by the book of Job that even Satan himself (presumably with voting rights) still sits on the council of heaven.

Much, if not all of human philosophy and more especially natural philosophy, focusses on conflict; and, particularly in philosophy and among human philosophers the conflict, both procedural and substantive, is more open, more personal, and more extreme than experienced anywhere else on earth. Of course, this level of almost personal antagonism amongst philosophers passes almost unnoticed these days, because classical philosophy is now so rarely taught, or even is no longer taught, as part of the core curriculum in philosophy.

For example, the four basic elements propounded by the philosopher-scientist Empedocles were fire, air, earth and water, of which the philosopher-scientist Thales proposed water to be more fundamental in explaining the others. All are, in different measures, conflictive.

The more extensive Pythagorean opposites (than those of Thales or Empedocles), when taken over by the metaphysician Aristotle, are likewise even more conflictive; but by way of being a life scientist, Aristotle comes up with generation and degeneration to afford some more structured principle by which to integrate their generalised interaction.

'War is the father of all things,' presumed one of the forthright sayings of the philosopher Heraclitus, summing up this generally fractious outlook. Until the coming of Jesus Christ, apart from the principles of deductive reasoning as applied to geometry, there was little structured process devised and devoted to the reconciliation of such opposites as the first and the last, the righteous and the unrighteous, the poor and the rich.

Likewise, for our loss of faith, on account of which we excuse ourselves by gaining science, we count not the cost of losing faith but rather credit to ourselves the self-invention of reason. By means of this shoe-strap device to lift ourselves heavenwards (particularly when assisted by technology), we can so easily make the worse appear the better cause and so befuddle ourselves to deprive ourselves of any sense of loss as to believe infallibly in our worship of inevitable human progress. It is a sorry tale, but this no less than for most people today, as then too, the literally genetic period of our paradise, which was lost so long ago, remains at best a puzzle.

As a matter of professed fact, it may be an evolutionary puzzle—a cosmology of physics, chemistry, and biology—by which grown-ups try to secure their hold on life for as long as they think to know of it. Otherwise, when seen to be a mythic tale of Troy or of Star Wars or of some long and drawn-out search for a very significant ring, it may be told as a never-ending story to little children with the object of reassuring them that in their own little world, all is safe, sound, and secure.

As these little children grow older, their fears may be further diverted by tales of the tooth fairy, of Santa Claus, and of countless heroes, both real and imaginary, such as Spiderman and Superman,

Jack the Giant Killer, and Jesus Christ. Nevertheless, there are problems with both the scientific puzzle and the never-ending story, but not so much difference as between these different sorts of problems, since the scientific puzzle may be retold as a never-ending and constantly changing story whilst the never-ending story (as with the archaeological rediscovery of Troy, no less than of Sodom and Gomorrah) may be told no less for being a constantly changing scientific puzzle.

Likewise, there can be a religiosity (no less than a corresponding fickleness) that overtakes and ousts our faith in science, no less than it can overtake and oust our faith in recorded history, in communicable language, in logical reasoning, and in law as well as literature, besides also in every other means we have of still trying to tell the truth, the whole truth, and nothing but the truth and thus testify to the existence of some immutable level of universal truth. What we continue to search for is the immutable answer to many questions, each of which we as yet don't profess to understand which lack of assurance makes us, in turn, as unsure of ourselves as we are unsure of our search and as we are unsure of our answers.

This is clearly the case, since we cannot get clear answers without as clearly knowing of what exactly it is that we ask, so whether in science or in any other discipline, there is this faith factor without which there is really no point of persisting in our search for the universal and immutable truth. Therefore, in the context of our continuing search for immutable truth, the current concept of 'relativity' is a cop-out. Remember, that if you can't see of more than one way of dealing with this problem, you are not ready or qualified to discuss, far less deal with it.

Nevertheless, there are many very different ways of searching for answers, whether concerning professedly factual or professedly fictional matters, as to throw light on to all these apparently very different questions of beginnings and ends. As a matter (1) of professed fiction by way of a tale to be told to credulous children; or (2) as told by anthropologists to other anthropologists as a sentient account; yet (3) in telling more of whosoever tells the tale than of which the tale is told; whilst yet (4) somehow inextricably interbound each to tell of the other; then (5) these matters are all intertwined like text and context. So in searching for some clarity, some revelation of the end of things by which to explain more than we can testify to our personal experience of their beginning, this is bound to remain such a multifactorial puzzle to the puzzled, at least for so long as they remain without having any prophetic revelation made known to them of this same lost paradise of theirs having been already regained.

In this book, we add nothing to that prophetic revelation of all time, which in itself puzzles so many of its would-be readers by transcending all time. Nor shall we take anything away from that revelation of all time, by which to further explain how all that first great loss of life from the presently perplexed shall be regained to resolve the puzzle of all time. Nor do we add or subtract anything to or from the puzzle itself that brings an end to all time or add or subtract anything away from that same revelation of all time to explain how much more gain than that just regained shall surely accrue from making amends for the way in which such deeply puzzled people instigated their own first great loss.

Hanging in the balance for such deeply puzzled people, between their understanding of genesis at the beginning and their experiencing the fulfilment of revelation at the end, lies a crisis of faith, the vital key to which is held by someone very special. He is the one (the supreme translator of time and space) who effectively translates and transmits every communication from heaven to earth and so back again from earth to heaven by his reporting to heaven in accordance with the Supreme Command.

It is only by this telegraphic key to the kingdom of light (as yet still appearing to many only dimly in the lower case) that the present puzzle of paradise once so painfully lost can eventually be resolved and regained. For such deeply puzzled people—stoics, cynics, and unbelievers in general—much still hangs in the balance or measure by which all puzzles shall be resolved.

The puzzle is not principally a legal one, as first generally thought and as still many deeply puzzled people who believe in the law of rights (based on rewards) and in the commission of punishable wrongs may still think. The puzzle is not principally a moral puzzle, as also first thought and as still many deeply puzzled people who believe in the attribution of good (as often to themselves) and the ascription of evil (as often to others) may also still think. Likewise, the puzzle is neither principally a logical puzzle nor principally a linguistic puzzle or even an economic or environmental or political or governmental puzzle. Instead, for being inclusive of all things and exclusive of none, it is something of each, for any reader who cares enough to make the journey.

For those who need a name for this journeying—although naming is wearing and so can defile the person as much as the person can defile the name—the objective is not first, if ever, to define the unseen. This naming process, for being no more than a linguistic action to muzzle the puzzle, in peremptory fashion is then likely to kill hope in the metaphysical womb by pre-empting faith in the substance of the unseen. Whether named or not, this journeying process is more metaphysical than physical, more mental than sensual, and more figurative than literal and so, for being more exploratory than definitive, would thus be dismissed by many readers for being more hypothetical (and imaginary) than factual (for being real).

This copybook (like most copybooks) is thus for both thinkers and doers alike. It's for those who meditate and reflect on where they've come from no less than on where they now are, and so too by reflecting on where they've been, this is to assess where they're likely or unlikely to go in terms of their differently begun beginnings and differently determined ends. So then if this copybook is not for you, just as your eye or ear or tongue might otherwise defile you, then just throw this book away. It is, after all, a very ordinary book for not telling you in what to believe, for not telling you what to say, and for not telling you what to do; and it's very much your own mistake for thinking otherwise if you think so.

You can go to almost any college of higher education these days and, by having been told there what to think, thereby gain the highest of credentials by which you too will be qualified to teach others not how to think but only what to think. If you think otherwise than badly of such extraordinary colleges, as of this very ordinary instead of extraordinary book, then you have not learnt to think of what little authentic teaching you receive for being told no more than only what to think. Why else, therefore, would the Supreme Command allow agents provocateur to still go about their business of paining both angels and humans to pay more attention to how they themselves might learn how to think instead of being subjected to those 'thought doctors' who tell them only what to think?

Unfortunately for those who expect instant insight into the eventual outcome of their own worldly predicament by being told only what to think, this cut-down, propagandistic type of non-teaching has a stultifying effect, first, on the exercise of free-willed volition; secondly, on imaginative and conjectural creativity; thirdly, on independence of thought, feeling, and expression; fourthly, on the entire physiological learning process; fifthly, on character and personality (both angelic and human); and finally, on the welfare of the soul. Believe it or not, but many angels as well as humans have fallen under the spell of this counterfeit process of propagating the collective propaganda which passes so often for the so-called higher education.

Having been once so programmed, as if they could be thus enlightened by the flick of a switch under their own command, instead, their own perpetual struggle for brute survival (however limited its objectives) thus preoccupies, perpetuates, and eventually exhausts most of any sadly institutionalised academic's vital energy. Otherwise, instead of being preoccupied with their own brute survival, they would be engaged in researching their own truly eternal salvation by following their own professional calling. Meanwhile, their very transient struggle for self-seeking survival (the mantra which substitutes for true praise and worship for a future yet to come) defeats its own purpose, since it blinds their eyes and stops their ears to an outcome, far more metaphysical than merely physical, that has already been won.

Many similarly perplexed people eventually give up on trying to resolve their own worldly predicament, whether in searching for instant enlightenment or even for having been caught up in the brute struggle for their own self-survival. They do so because they rationalise that it is better by far simply to eat, drink, and be merry, for tomorrow they die. They thereby give up on life, since their battle (if engaged in at all and not just copied from others or counterfeited by themselves to conform with others) has been levelled largely but needlessly against death and destruction rather than, as they mistakenly believe, in any real struggle for their own more authentic survival.

Nevertheless, that battle against death and destruction, which many perplexed people mistake for securing their own survival, has already been won. And it has been won not just in this world's terms of limited survival (since even the survival of this world is limited) but on the far greater terms of eternal salvation (brought about by the recreation of a new heaven and a new earth). Then with the even greater brilliance derived from cosmic unity, that first light of an earlier genesis shall most certainly be restored and yet go on to shine, both above and below, to a level of fulfilled revelation far exceeding even that earlier light which first shone with such prophetic brilliance.

Yes, this restoration of world's first light shall be most certainly restored to a level of even greater brilliance than ever experienced before. With an unconditional certainty and recalculated speed of travel, this renewed light shall search out every last corner of our then superlative kingdom, which even every last corner shall not just reflect but shine out instead with its own contributed light, and this, whether on earth or in heaven, as part of its inherited light from the Supreme Command.

This then shall be the light of eternal life, which not only so far exceeds the little of light that allowably could pierce the prevailing darkness of what went before, but when once endowed (both physically and spiritually) with a speed renewed to the ultimate level of all light, it is destined to redeem all eternity. It is this light of eternal life which not only overtakes but also redeems the previous unwisdom of earth's predecessors, both those human and those celestial, who have taken and still tempt others to take their own demonic shortcut towards fulfilling their own destiny, instead of their following the straight, narrow, and sometimes exceedingly unpleasant path towards eternal life as proclaimed by the Supreme Command.

Yet this soon-to-be-fulfilled outcome of eternal life still appears so much more contingent than certain to all those who remain puzzled by, perplexed by, and as often also openly rebellious to the constant guidance of the Supreme Command. This is because, so often as an explicit sign of these most tortured times, such likewise tortured people prefer to look for closure—almost any sort of closure—rather than to search for and acknowledge the need for an increasing openness on all fronts, including both their view of heaven as well as their view of earth and so also of themselves. Like Raskolnikov (in Dostoevski's *Crime and Punishment*) or like Nekhlyudov (in Tolstoi's *Resurrection*) or like Jacob (in Moses' *Genesis*) we are all in need of redemption and reformation.

For the sake of closing off this, that, or another troubled view, it comes about that the very limited view, with which the most perplexed of people are happy to identify themselves (even unto their own death), reduces their need, like that of Gollum in Tolkien's book *The Hobbit*, for sharing in any higher (however disconcerting) level of light. So long as they possess their own talisman of security—it may be material, it may be social, it may be intellectual, it may be emotional, it may even be spiritual—which they equate with their search for closure, then they receive no more than a very limited and transient relief (which stoic philosophers may lead them to mistake for passive contentment) instead of answering their call to action which comes through the awakening of their physical, intellectual, emotional, and spiritual response to any perceived false closure of their troubled minds.

Nevertheless, by their successful search for closure, especially in their search for the most mundane things in life, such seriously perplexed people become addicted to lower and lower degrees of comfort, which has taken addicts far enough down (as in Gollum's case) to lower and lower degrees of discomfort (in the way that polarised values eventually reverse themselves) in their increasing avoidance of the light. By then, of course, the same prevailing darkness that one so earnestly sought to relieve by closure (whether by the application of law, morals, or religion) has become mistaken (like physics for metaphysics, peacekeeping for peacemaking, or a career for a calling) for the first dawning of renewed light.

This all happens because the power of closure is something that can so incrementally increase its power and so perpetrate its exacting cost in perpetuity that in everything mundane—from logic, law, and language, never mind one's own total mindset and, in turn, the mindsets of many others (especially those minds of deeply programmed leaders)—it closes down whole nations, entire empires, whole realms of temples, synagogues, and churches and, in the end, even also every broad avenue of sincere and authentic learning that will lead to the still greater and greater light of both a renewed heaven and a renewed earth.

Closure versus openness—which then of these values is the counterfeit of the Supreme Command and by which other yet only one means does the Supreme Command light up its ongoing straight and narrow path towards realising the explosiveness of long contained truth, which, in this earth's final sunburst of spiritual light and fulfilled revelation, will burn up all untruth? There is truly only one authentic way towards realising this eternal truth, since transparency, for being no more than a see-through and virtual image of man's wishful thinking, is most usually but only a political compromise; and most attempts to restructure the present (as with every historic attempt at perestroika or glasnost) are no more than last-ditch attempts to perpetuate the present (by foregoing the future). Originating with the best of intentions to introduce both governmental transparency and strategic restructuring to the eastern world, both perestroika and glasnost have made the western world more Soviet than ever before; and this even although that in the eastern world, both perestroika and glasnost brought down The Wall, imploded the once Soviet Union, and so provided the catalytic reaction by which both the USSR and the USA terminated their Space Race and disestablished their Cold War.

What so often puzzles today's still perplexed people, however, is that so much work, obviously needed to restore that first light, still remains to be done. Their mistake, since self-credit exacts self-responsibility, is to attribute that task entirely to themselves. So, in turn, they are dismayed, depressed, and distraught; and if not made so by, with, or at others who are as powerless as they are themselves, then they are most angry with themselves. No, theirs is not by any means the sole responsibility. That conclusion is tragicomic, but they still do need to hear their calling to enjoin the task commensurate with their gifts and calling.

So the predicament of today's very puzzled people during this present darkness remains as if they have not yet learnt to decipher the binary logic of this codified message, whether couched in terms of good and evil, legality and illegality, justice and injustice, or righteousness and unrighteousness. In short, they have either both closed eyes and closed ears to the signs of the times or else they have never met for themselves the translator of this strangely universal, metaphysical, and cosmic equivalent of Morse code.

What Morse code is this, you may ask (typified by which the first shall be last whilst the last shall be first and, so too, by which it shall be the impoverished rather than the worldly rich who are destined to inherit the earth)? Do you capture the urgency of this message in Morse, • • • _ _ _ • • •, no less than the more universally translated one by which it seems that between heaven and earth, the 'dits' (or dots) on earth become 'dahs' in heaven and the 'dahs' (or dashes) in heaven become increasingly mistranslated on earth as 'dits'?

Some sort of reversal of values accounts for an upside-down kingdom of heaven (which offends so many who consider themselves doing so well on earth when compared with the upside-down scale of values operating in the kingdom of heaven). The increasing contrast in cosmic values (between heaven and earth) becomes exceptionally troubling when measured against today's ongoing reversal of even just worldly values whereby traditional virtues (such as personal thrift, the inviolability of the person, and public stewardship) are supplanted and given over to what were once clearly vices (personal indulgence, abortion, and euthanasia on demand and capital gains derived from environmental mismanagement).

The present puzzling predicament is prophetic (particularly at the cosmic level), and the liveliness of this puzzlement to those who no longer experience any sense of loss is vital to the resolution of this puzzle as well as to the fulfilment of the prophecy. There are those who do not like puzzles, however, and these are usually the same sort of people who do not like prophecies. They prefer all things to be cut and dried, for which purpose they make rules, rules, and still more rules and so hide from themselves the fact that most of these rules are inconsistent not only with themselves but thus also with reality.

The point is then reached where it is impossible for the rule-makers to abide by their own rules. Then the rule-makers say (as some judges already do as never before) that because they make the rules, they can therefore change the rules. They have reached the precarious point of any rule-making system when, to avoid admitting to their own failures of lawmaking, they say that they are then (so close to heaven as to be) above the law. This signifies the complete breakdown of any man-made legal system because of its inability to correlate law not only with justice (which is the object of jurisprudence) but also with righteousness (which is as much a matter of logic and morality as it is a matter of metaphysics).

This is all tiresome talk to many people and most tiresome of all to those people who live only in and for the present moment. They don't mind how many rules they are obliged to observe so long as they themselves are powerful enough to ensure that those rules which affect themselves can be subtly or surreptitiously broken. Likewise, jurisprudence (the province of correlating law with justice) poses no problem to such people, so long as they themselves (whether stoic or case-hardened to their own misfortunes and oblivious to the misfortunes of others) are inured to injustice. The law is the law is the law, so they say, and they have absolutely no feeling of loss (either specific or generic) that *once upon a time*, all things were really radically and completely different.

By their use of all such mythic or fairy-tale expressions (extended generically to almost all the arts but most particularly to poetry, scripture, and other forms of what they shrug off for being mere opinion, figurative language, or creative expression), many memory-deprived people dismiss all remembrance of *once upon a time* when all things were really quite different. They have thus no sense of loss, even of their own lost childhood, and out of this (most often self-inflicted) failure to deal with some traumatic memory, there develops a second-order dementia.

We shall leave for our next part of this report to be made in the military service of the Supreme Command an account of this second-order dementia, which at present carries off the mindfulness of the aged and, by this loss reflected in their resulting mindlessness, confirms the obsolescence of the elderly to the youthful who are thereby so much more easily induced to reverse the roles of respect between parent and child, as once commanded by the Supreme

Command (and on the grounds of giving the elderly a better quality of life, to promote their euthanasia).

To foretell the future of this account of second-order dementia in the next part of our report, you must learn to keep in mind (however hard at first you may find it) that the human brain is created to engineer its own hardware for the soul (by now an obsolete word to represent the human ego or will) which you will need to know before you can understand how the human heart has been created (however much tainted by the Counterfeit Command) to manage the human software.

* * *

Blinded by First Light
Part IV

Human Twaddle versus Divine Truth
Did any of you ever think that around the time that the
notion of a SOUL disappeared, Freud popped up with
the EGO to take its place? The timing of the man! Did
he not pause to reflect? Irresponsible old coot! It is my
belief that men must spout this twaddle about egos
because they fear they have no souls! Think upon it!
Thomson Stubbins, former member
of the Sigmund Freud society

Just as most of the longest-lasting songs and verses are often
anonymous, so also the longest-lasting records of who said what
are often better remembered for being dismissed as apocryphal.
Perhaps this is because such apocryphal fables, tales, and stories, like
anonymous songs and verses, are better remembered for their own
sake rather than for their artificial status, whether for their being real,
imagined, or in any other way more memorable for being attributable
to their often more than fallible human authors.

In the same way, the cautionary tale (because, like any fable, this
too is a cautionary tale) is told (and retold by Stephen Hawking to
open his *Brief History of Time*) of some little old lady (here comes
the caution) getting up from the back of the room at the end of some
prestigious lecture on astronomy to say, 'What you have told us is
rubbish. The world is really a flat plate supported on the back of a
giant tortoise.' [Excursus 1: As said before, unless you can consider
two or more alternative views of reality then don't dare to discuss, far
less deal with their resolution or of any problem posed by them. This
little old lady, possibly a diversionary plant by Counterfeit Command,
nevertheless serves the same purpose (reductio ad absurdum) of
debating souls versus egos (on appeal from egos versus souls).

If it is indeed true that the science lecturer with a superior smile
to this little old lady then condescended to ask most dismissively of

her interesting observation, 'Well then, what is the tortoise standing on?' then he missed the moral with which the same fable could be told of his superior smile. On this score, there is many an angel disguised as some grumpy old man or little old lady who plays the scapegoat by retorting, 'You're very clever young man, very clever—but it's turtles all the way down!'

Besides, Stephen Hawking himself takes the cautionary point, as we all have to take the cautionary point of every fable, when he says to us, 'Most people would find the picture of our universe as an infinite tower of tortoises rather ridiculous, but why do we think we know better? What do we know about the universe, and how do we know it? Where did the universe come from, and where is it going?'

Likewise, when we dare to talk or write about the most intimately known of our own personal beliefs, whether as some grumpy old man (as Sir Isaac Newton became) or as some little old lady who maybe had come to the wrong place at the wrong time to hear the wrong lecture, then maybe, because when outside of the space-time continuum that we claim to be our own, then (like Einstein's professor and so many other professors of the truth) we don't hear the cautionary message. Then again, maybe because the most eminent of scientists or scholars can completely spoof not only themselves but also nearly everyone else with their own most intimate and personal attachments to the belief systems in which they are immersed, how can one not relate to this little old lady, as if she were one of ourselves, for being taken completely out of her depth?

This fable, by now developed into a parable, has yet still a deeper meaning, by which, although being somehow so much more misunderstood by the successful, the accomplished, and the celebrated in this world, nevertheless the Supreme Command chooses to speak through the suffering, the broken-hearted, the rejected, the poverty-stricken, the lonesome, and the disempowered rather than more directly at present to those who least understand. Here is a form of teaching, belonging to the highest of all educations, which for only those who know how it feels to belong amongst the lowest can be truly understood.

So then consider this final case for being a no-left-brainer: this little but argumentative old lady—she could be an angel-astronomer in disguise—had been called and commissioned by the Supreme Command to represent at this science lecture on astrophysics all those so many lady astronomers who for so long had been consigned to menial work far below their passion for astronomy, their commitment to astronomy, and their credentials for astronomy (a case of turtles buried under the welter of a giant tortoise) with possibly under them, if it be known, an even greater overlooked welter of buried terrapins.

The left-brained intellectual (roughly speaking) may experience this trauma (as often as not expressing conflict between thought and feeling) by finding life overwhelmingly comic, yet the right-brained and highly artistic individual (once again roughly speaking) may experience the same trauma by finding life overwhelmingly tragic. Nevertheless, a bigger picture is coming through here, because whenever we start talking and thinking even just about right-brained and left-brained people, the ease with which we slip into our own cleanly categorised, exclusively compartmentalised, and self-chosen means of using our own brains to box-think their own cleanly compartmentalised form and functions not only raises certain doubts as to subjectivity and lack of objectivity arising from the lack of any means of independent predication but also raises a sense of caution over relying or applying our subjective results to the same subject (and not object) of our own investigation.

Of course, as always—whether in the pursuit of pure science, social science, or any other means of scholarship—this is still the 'anthropologist's dilemma', since in such cases, the fallible man is always the one making the move no matter whatever may be his means of proof and whenever subject to his own assessment and evaluation regarding the credibility of the origins, objectives, and outcomes of his own investigation. A word of caution is thus always needed when the study of man is man (and even more so when the study of man is being made by man himself of man).

In other words, every human self-analysis, whether individually or collectively done, cannot derive objectivity from its inherent subjectivity; nor can we angels find any reason (no matter how much reasoning appeals to humans) that it should. Self-reasoning is so prone to self-justification (see again Tolstoy's excruciatingly detailed self-analysis throughout the entire thesis of *Resurrection* on this human condition) that every serious reader is literally 'beside oneself' to find some more credible alternative. And as for science or law or church or state—each of which Tolstoy so rightly lambasts in this book the same largely overlooked subjectivity applies, much to the horror of those few who seriously read the book. Remember this also when you read the psychoanalytic jurisprudence of Tolstoy's greatest work on the human conscience: that it was written, dedicated, and published to support the Doukhobors, a Christian group (persecuted by both church and state), a spirit-filled group who opposed military conscription, yet who took the bad-mouthed name of 'spiritual-fighters' given to them disparagingly by the Russian clergy to signify their own spiritual battle to uphold God's command.

Both psychology and sociology are thus inherently subjective by reason of their own human self-analyses. Accordingly, for the sake of acquiring the least objectivity in anything and everything we humans say or do, then mankind not only needs God, but to be as close to God and in his presence as mankind can come. In such a way, as we angels say, you mortals shall learn, not only to think but also to reason more and more as do we angels.

Arguably, the human brain in search of itself and without any more external and objective measure by which to evaluate its own form and function (as seen only by itself) is prone to birthing only half-truths and tautologies. Likewise, by seizing on solely naturalistic rather than on metaphysical measures (such as on today's increasing use of the biological measure) to explain its own existence, the human brain likewise comes to purely naturalistic conclusions as to its own existential form and function. In the long run, these solely naturalistic conclusions pose more metaphysical problems to account for human existence than do the naturalistic problems that they more apparently resolve. This is because of the perilously short run of intellectual experience it can take for the human brain, by self-promoting, self-praising, and then self-worshiping its own far less than fully comprehended form and functions, then to regard itself as some sort of self-created god or demigod.]

Nevertheless, even when investigated on no more than any naturalistic measure, everyone is both more or less a right-brained as well as being more or less a left-brained individual, and for the individual to be more or less equally so for both hemispheres is such, surely, to promote the well-balanced individual. Thus, on any purely biological investigation, humans, having pretty nearly two of everything (two arms, two legs, except only one head, one heart, and other exceptional organs, to which uniqueness they thus attribute considerable sanctity of form and reverential worship of its various sensory, intellectual, and linguistic functions) would classify themselves (again very roughly) as being bilaterally symmetrical and so attribute to themselves the bilateral model of a beam balance (even in psychology) by which to evaluate (again very roughly speaking) the well-balanced human mind.

No, once again, that's possibly only still the smaller very flat-earthed picture, whose very much larger and projected picture poses once again an extraordinary need for caution in our relying on the smaller picture's application. Conjecturally speaking, the larger, more metaphysical picture, when seen and given, is that of a supervening radial symmetry, which comes into full play, as witnessed even by the single human brain when engaged with other brains in their projects of both creative as well as communicative thought, since man is not just individually knowing (or psychic), any more than for being just bodily alike (somatic), but instead shares the same life force (or zoe) with other humans through the same means of life (or pneuma), which makes each and every human individual, at whatever earthly or heavenly level of metaphysics we care to describe it, pre-eminently a social organism.]

All the same, we humans frequently take all sorts of shortcuts, using as it were a microtome to take the small thin-sliced (microscopic) picture (say, of private health) rather than the bigger macroscopic picture (say, of public health), just as we may debate the primacy of either sociology or psychology (to accord a different balance for either the individual or society). Complementary ideas (such as those of heaven and earth) can be bilaterally expressed and understood to constitute one single cosmos (although the asymmetry either of hell or of purgatory poses problems to the more pristine clarity of this purely bilateral thought). The brain itself, when considering itself to be a construct of two bilateral hemispheres, likewise leans to the same polarity of bilateral expression, and this no less than it may take the introduction of a radial symmetry (as in literature to allow both tragedies as well as comedies to balance the ongoing trauma for both intellectuals and creative artists in their earthly life), so also for different nations in their international relations.

To overcome both apparently alternative and apparently irreconcilable expressions of this same trauma as being either comic or tragic, the well-balanced brain (again roughly speaking, since there are not just neurological hemispheres but also neurological pathways as well as fore, middle, and hind fields of neurological activity) will seek to expurgate the trauma through (at least) two-way communication, just as the holistic individual both lives to communicate as well as communicates to live. Thus, to resolve both the comic and tragic aspects of life—although for the most part (since epic journeys like Homer's *Odyssey* and Tolstoy's *War and Peace* are few and far between)—then readers and filmgoers like to choose between conflicting genres of comedy or tragedy rather than to resolve the impasse provoked by the mixed messages between the two. They do this to resolve ambiguity and reach clarity, and they do so (no less than there are happy clowns and sad-sack clowns) more according to their own mood of the moment or to their prevailing psyche. All the same, this life on earth is as tragicomic as it is comically tragic, and the looked-for clarity cannot be reached by either the Procrustean process nor by the Pythagorean process. Mixed messages cannot be resolved by either of these means any more than by box-thinking, compartmentalisation, or arbitrary definition.

Sanity or insanity (as between the symmetry of balanced brains or the asymmetry of unbalanced brains, both in form and function) are not only big issues of psychiatry; but for being also huge issues of general semantics, basic metaphysics, criminology, and general jurisprudence at large, they cannot be isolated from every other issue of everyday life. [Academic sidekick: Compare Gogol's *Dead Souls* (taking into account that Gogol destroyed what he could no longer bear of what was probably the most and best of his book) and the seriousness of Carroll's *Alice in Wonderland* (reminding yourself that Carroll was primarily a logician), or else compare the even more seriously black comedy (particularly to those bereaved) of Stevenson and Osbourne's *Wrong Box* with Nabokov's *Lolita* (which evoked such mixed reception of its intended seriousness). Consider also Heller's *Catch-22* (either dismissed for being black comedy or else revered for Heller's anti-war seriousness for being now no more than a vintage classic). And perhaps also for that same reason (like the *Wrong Box*) could Heller's *Catch-22* be just as easily dismissed as either the book of Job or the book of Jonah.]

Bear in mind (for that being always an example of carrying your own cross) that the whole point of receiving any brachiating sidekick from the Supreme Command—whether seriously academic, seriously prophetic, or seriously metaphysical—is most often to demonstrate that, besides having our own innate sense of seriousness, we also have our own correspondingly innate sense of humour. So then this continuing puzzle of prophetic revelation (whose explication for your benefit we are presently engaged in) shall sooner or later be resolved not only for such wayward or damaged people like yourselves (since so many of you have by now forgotten your own once deep sense of loss) but also shall be needfully resolved through prophetic fulfilment for advancing the good of the kingdom. This mutuality (although posing a paradox of powerlessness to unbelievers yet in keeping with our own recursive kingdom metaphysics) is because the kingdom itself needs (as it has so often decreed) the recovered awareness of such deeply puzzled and wayward people as you are yourselves.

Without the sanctification of such a wayward and uncomprehending people, the kingdom of heaven itself goes on suffering your loss; and this innate sense of loss continues until by your recovery, through deliverance from what besets you or by some other means, your loss from us can be restored or recovered for the sake of the kingdom. The frailty of the kingdom (although so saying will be offensive to formalists who overlook their own power to advance the kingdom, together with their own responsibility to make amends), as invested in them by the Supreme Command, is something that functionalists look forward to and, when entrusted to its members to fulfil, in no way belittles but instead extends and advances the kingdom. As the Supreme Command, we are not in the least sorry but only sad in all this, that we have to persuade and convince you of the only way in which you can be empowered to extricate yourselves from your present and extremely perplexing predicament.

So too (although for being much more than we can at present understand), the fulfilment of this prophetic revelation by the means of which paradise shall not only be regained but also (through both transformation and transubstantiation) shall be completely superseded in both form and substance is something that will become more and more part of your commission under your growing and continuing allegiance to the Supreme Command. And had the kingdom (however infallible) not made itself frail, fragile, and dependent on humanity playing its part, then humanity would not be qualified (as already confirmed by the ruthlessness of kingdom history) for your admission to the kingdom. There are no pro forma admissions to the kingdom but only functional admissions, for all being both kinship admissions in kind.

Hanging in this balance, by which paradise lost can be more than just regained, is also the commission (take more and yet more note of that word) entrusted to all people of goodwill and of firm faith, by which the victory, already won by he who holds the keys to the kingdom, nevertheless needs to be implemented and enforced by those of both goodwill and firm faith. Only then by your committed participation (even unto death) will all realise the greater gain to the kingdom of light that results from this kingdom task being entrusted by the Supreme Command to a once wayward people.

For the sake of the human motivation required by those commissioned to effectuate this greater outcome, it follows that the vital sense of a paradise previously lost must be maintained by those commissioned to this kingdom task of proclaiming the coming presence of an entirely new kingdom. This most vital and ongoing sense of loss is required in order that (all previously wayward) people comprehend the full import of their helping to fulfil the prophetic revelation of this new kingdom of heaven on earth far beyond their realising just their own lost paradise regained. [Prophetic sidekick: The expression 'kingdom of heaven' (with by then capitals or as now without capitals) is just a recommissioned expression for the Supreme Command (which will by then be reduced, however paradoxically, to lower case.]

Meanwhile, things by now have gone too far, both in heaven and on earth, to deconstruct the present state of affairs and to reconstruct the past. That last forlorn expression of wishful thinking is the professedly secular pretence by which to avoid facing the ever-emerging truth. One cannot merely turn the clock back to the first moment of genesis and so flash back through human history away from the present and thus away from all need to fulfil every last word of prophetic revelation by which to redeem the still so seriously fractured past. Let's face it—the past was fractured beyond all prospect of quick-fix redemption and beyond all prospect of manipulative reconstruction by what happened on the cross. There is a battle, although already won, which is still to be fought for the sake of those who would otherwise still be lost, and this despite the greater victory for others being already won.

From Berlin to Baghdad, from Mogadishu to Kabul, and from Tehran to Damascus (often via London, Washington, and Moscow), this world-shattering and ever-extending fracture of a cosmic sinkhole is often all that now remains of the first created world, which the Supreme Command so first loved. And for which purpose to redeem its people, the Supreme Command sent its Supreme Translator to stem the tide of both ongoing death and destruction. Death he defeated, as shown by his own resurrection, but the battle still goes on for the redemption of those contributory souls without which there is little prospect of fulfilling the grand design of the Supreme Command for the fulfilment of a new heaven and a new earth.

To this soon-to-be-accomplished end, the same cosmic sinkhole then further opened up not only to disclose a greater distance between good and evil (as between also justice and injustice) but also between righteousness and unrighteousness. So too, it also opened up new and limitless dimensions of metaphysical revelation (through the ongoing spirit of prophecy) by which to contemplate the increasing incongruence between (1) these once very much closer of traditional opposites and (2) this revelation of the Supreme Translator to believers who might even think otherwise. And so then just go on complacently sitting, as academic observers of death and destruction, on this old world's already overloaded observational fence.

And yet still happily on this platitudinous fence, many (including the most gifted) of believers still sit, especially those who think to be in no fear of their own lives, and so to see themselves remaining there by virtue of their own faith (yet without executing any works) until the prophesied Second Coming of the Supreme Command. Meanwhile, however disorderly all things are when down in hell, even down there right now, the Counterfeit Command has already gone out (accompanied with a tot of gin) to demand those who are by now Lieutenant Wormwood's minions 'to get off their chuff!'

But for what other purpose could there be for the centuries of persecutions suffered by those selfsame believers than to heighten every believer's awareness of his or her ongoing task to participate in the ongoing battle to fulfil this Second Coming of the Supreme Command? And so in these last days, the call goes out for more and more translators—angels, apostles, prophets, preachers, teachers, and prayer partners. That same commitment for continuing translation of the same message from heaven to earth still goes out, though the risk of commitment still be to suffer, as did Jesus Christ, the kingdom's greatest translator of heaven to earth, the same means of sacrifice it took for him to proclaim the same truth.

This then is the supreme sacrifice of the supreme translator of all truth, as once done (but never ever needed again to defeat death), and although to the dismay then of all those believers who, until his confirmed resurrection, remained then still stuck in the shadowy valley of death, this remains even a myth to many believers today who, without their commitment to resurrection with their own same confirmed conviction, also still remain then still stuck in the shadowy valley of death.

That's one more explanation (apart from the greater distance now stretched between such things as good and evil, even so far as to switch their roles) for there being so much professed faith around these days without any corresponding execution of works. Alas, for those earliest of disciples, there was very little of any viable comprehension for them of what that first fracture of their previous reality entailed for redemption of their own sin and death, except as later revealed by their own need to join in the task of both proclaiming and implementing an entirely new heaven and earth.

That contrary temptation of many people merely to bolster up the present by misrepresenting the past would only risk perpetuating the same old human cycle of holding on to the best of intentions when similarly bolstered by their least will to act on them. Only the keys to the kingdom, when employed by the Supreme Command, can unlock the means to resolve this soon-to-be-experienced crisis of faith, which many of those formally committed over many years to the enterprise of professing their faith yet still remain relatively unaware of their critical part in fulfilling the prophetic revelation of which, despite the blessing of the Supreme Command, they rarely read.

How then could this present word be any ordinary word and one as if for some very ordinary event, when here instead we have a prophetic proclamation foretelling the future of our completely recreated life, which would then be lived to the fullest, on what then would also be a completely recreated earth? Herein also lies a warning as to the many, many counterfeit claims (through such hoodwinking devices of our own age as restructuring and transparency—glasnost and perestroika) by which we could be given only humanly reconstructed rather than divinely recreated futures. There is no semblance of lack whatsoever any more than there is any perceived lack of the truth, the way, and the life whenever there is a plenitude of false prophets. So read for your own selves, in this very ordinary (not extraordinary) copybook, of the signs of the times which in all ways provide the most unusual and extraordinary of portents for a future lying no more than just around the corner.

The renewed light of this most remarkable event (by which this dying world shall be shattered and yet still be redeemed by a vastly new heaven and a vastly new earth) shall be resurrected (not just reconstructed) from the void (black hole or, as in the Tatar tongue of that place known to the ancients as Tartary, the *t'ma*) left by this present darkness. Today's darkness is a darkness so deep and presently prevailing, but for this prophetic proclamation, many tortured souls would see themselves doomed to forego their earlier gift of first light. Rejoice, therefore, in the saving grace of our Supreme Command, and grieve not over the present prevailing darkness of this heavenly extended time!

Meanwhile, look towards this new heaven and this new earth with every fibre of your first being, for the first heaven and the first earth will shortly pass away. And although by no ordinary event but one most amazing to all mariners, likewise there shall be no more sea, for

632

the sea, when properly understood, is but a vestige of the flood that for a time was sent to cleanse the first earth. But there shall then be no more need of any cleansing on the second earth, which shall be completely redeemed to the purity of the original when conceived in that very first light of all creation, which was then long before there was any need for any flood. So then rejoice again in the saving grace of our Supreme Command, and look ahead not only to the end of time but also, for being not just readers but also doers and not just doers but also overcomers, dare to look beyond all time! What, you boggle at this phrase 'beyond all time'! Well, that's only because as yet you know not what is meant by time!

By not knowing yet what is meant by time, you humans cannot even begin to account for time. You may have heard by now of the molecules of emotion, but of subtle differences not just in their constituent atoms but also in the diversity of their molecular relationships, you are as ignorant of such things as you ever were— and the very same goes for the particulate structure (with both fast-forward, flash-back, and hold-fast tabulations) of time. Have you really any idea (even in slow motion) of what it takes to receive or write down a prophecy, or of how many very different lives a person may live in his-or-own time?

Then indeed, as long foretold through John the Divine by an angel of the Holy Spirit sent by Jesus Christ to be revealed to all people through his same servant John, as he was then imprisoned in Patmos (that John who was the first disciple of the Lord to write most explicitly of these things which must shortly come to pass), there shall then be, not far away in either time or space, a holy city called the New Jerusalem. And believe it or not, that New Jerusalem shall be either for all time, or beyond all time, however you choose to see or not see it in your own time.

This holy city shall descend down to earth from up in heaven; and in this holy city, Father God, with his entire family of adopted sons and daughters, each of whose lives have been magnified to righteousness through the work of his Son, Jesus Christ, (already seated at his right hand) and together with all the angels who, like the holy prophets, are also the fellow servants of the same Lord God of prophecy, shall live altogether in this New Jerusalem where all former pain and suffering are completely passed away.

So then yet again and for the third time, rejoice in this saving grace of our Supreme Command, and looking not only beyond the ever-darkening present towards this revelation of our glorious future, we can thereby (by the prophetic uniting of past, present, and future) see also with renewed faith what needs to be done by ourselves, still as very active overcomers, when, by means of this glorious vision, we no longer feel trapped in the deepening dungeons of this ever-darkening present.

Accordingly, for as long as there is light enough to see, there is also much work to be done and yet so very little time left in which to do it. Prophecies do not fulfil themselves but, at the very least, need to be prayed into reality. Just as for eggs to hatch, they also need careful incubation. Blessings in the wind may land and even find space to root on earth, but just as prophecies may be left to fall (and so to fail in their making), so also blessings need their own firm attachment by holding fast to whomsoever on which they land. And for this period of blissful incubation, such blessings need to be held tight to the person, perhaps for many years, so as to survive and achieve their own end, as it may be for that person or for that city or for that nation, instead of being blown away again in the wind. So also the faith, which we so often sing and pray for, may often rise (no less than sung and prayed for); but likewise, as faith itself, it won't go far without our own most active participation to uphold its flight.

Nevertheless, put now all your faith in that when all former things pass away and thus are superseded by what comes later in their place, so too will this Supreme Command both change its form and substance and so have a new name no less than you, as reader or listener to this prophetic proclamation, shall have new names (which as yet are known only to the Supreme Command), because by then, in the New Jerusalem, by reason of all our most intimate love, we shall have no need either to make, to heed, to enforce, or to carry out the least command. So what (here's a puzzle for priests and kings) shall our new name be if we shall no longer be known to you, as now, by the name of the Supreme Command?

And here's a clue as to what will happen when we, now known to most of you as the Supreme Command, then break cover, for none of us then in that new heaven will still be as lawyers concerned with making rules, as judges concerned with passing judgements on those who break those rules, or as military men in fighting battles to enforce the rules. So there's no way in which we can then retain the title of the Supreme Command. But for the moment, we shall continue to be known as the Supreme Command, since that is basically still the concept you, as deeply disciplined military men and women, have of us angels. The trouble is that you've all been so badly brought up for so long that in both form and substance, you have still so much to fear, if not revere, of us.

So too then, we may ask of you, how will the spirit of prophecy behave once all known and unknown prophecies have been fulfilled? Well, perhaps then, all our real work will have only just begun; and all our present tasks are but preparation for our future responsibilities, which we are as yet unqualified to take over. By faith alone, not works, you shall be saved. But in the meantime, you shall be judged by works, so don't expect that all you'll have to do is laze around, playing harps and singing songs, in that new heaven of eternal life.

Saving seeds and sowing potent seeds is hard enough, tending seedlings amongst thorns and thistles is harder still, and bringing in the harvest from the burgeoning fields is thought to be the most difficult and demanding of all tasks and in all times (and your work in this present darkness shall bear that out). But as yet you have not the slightest notion of what great adventures shall befall you in the brilliant light shone by the Supreme Command's new dawning for the soon-to-become eternity beyond all time. Don't despair, for all your hard-learnt lessons have prepared you for the final onslaught.

Risks, however great, are commensurate with rewards. The way is narrow, as you know, but it is also one which, as the way nears its destination, is ever rapidly narrowing. It leads to a gate (or so it looked from afar) yet which, now up-close and still on this side of it, appears so infinitesimally small as to be mistaken by merely passers-by for being no more than a hole in the wall or perhaps, for being now so low, only a rabbit hole. Why, by the end of our continued approach to heaven, this once no more than a hole in the wall has shrunk to no more than a peephole.

This often lengthening but also rapidly narrowing way is also severely straight, as you already well know, and this is so despite the many self-indulgent temptations to divert ourselves, both angels and humans, away from the rapidly increasing incline of its still severely straight yet by now otherwise unmarked path. These diverticular temptations amass themselves into seemingly incontrovertible obstacles lying across by now on this almost completely hidden narrow path; all of which obstacles make the slightest advance towards the hidden kingdom beyond more and more demanding. Don't despair, all your hard-learnt lessons have prepared you for the ongoing fiercest of battles ever next to be fought.

* * *

Blinded by First Light
Part V

The One and the Many ...
Christian was a rare soul, and he detested what his
country was doing, but the same cannot be true for
many Germans, who believed in the dream of the
Thousand-Year Reich.

Mary Ann Shaffer, *The Guernsey*
Literary and Potato Peel Pie Society

Dream or nightmare? Could there be any doubt of the Thousand-Year
Reich being any less of a dream for being more of a nightmare? The
universities (with only some exceptions) supported that nightmare.
The churches (with only some exceptions) not only supported but
also enhanced that nightmare. The biggest of businesses and the
greatest of professions (with only some exceptions) both supported
and even applauded that nightmare. Indeed, the whole country (apart
from some few and vigorous exceptions) not only supported but also
participated in that nightmare.

Such was the case, otherwise, quite frankly, that same nightmare
could never have come about—no, not even if all such dreams
were no more than nightmares. Collective participation in such
nightmares by popular default is actually far more irresponsible
than participating by fault at the individual level. Soft-soaping the
populace who supported and followed their leaders after the whole
affair was over (and holding only the leaders to account as if the
populace were completely exempt) betrays the soft underbelly of
pseudo-democratic reasoning.

If all ideas come from heaven (irrespective of how received
by humans), then where do all dreams come from (irrespective of
their human reception)? Both dreams and ideas can be corrupted
in transmission and even more so corrupted on reception. What
corrupted the dream of the little corporal to set the warring factions
of Italy aright and, when having done so, would make him then

conceive of enforcing his own vision of Napoleonic grandeur over all Europe? What corrupted little Adolf's dream of rescuing Germany from its economic depression after WWI by means of his promoting der Führer's Thousand-Year Reich? More anciently of all, what corrupted the dream of the great hunter Nimrod to reach heaven by his building earth's first tall tower designed to effect heaven's first physical conquest?

History by itself, having chosen to imitate the sciences, has no more than arrived at a series of conjectural questions (as one may expect of a half-pi science). The answers to those questions lie not in science, although they may be better understood through the means of psychology and sociology and then still more thoroughly understood in terms of metaphysics, jurisprudence, and the phenomena of religion, before any near readiness presents itself for the examination of scripture.

The present darkness of this present world is still fast descending, yet the still surviving promise of a glorious future in the next world yet to come is still more propitious. Look always towards the dawn, where the promise of great things to come is now more propitious than ever before. And yet, all the while reflecting on the as yet unlearned lessons of human history, make sure on all sides that your screwed-on head of human reasoning, however stoutly fastened, is facing right way round.

You can still read that cosmic promise of a glorious future, now most clearly seen in fiery, starlit letters, each passionately aflame against the reverse impression given by this presently descending darkness. By now, both this passion for life aflame as well as the stifling darkness that bodes of death and despair are felt to be equally matched not just in one's still passionate heart but also in one's still thoughtfully serious head, the likes of which has never been experienced before.

This presently fading light shall all the time yet grow stronger, although in this gathering darkness, it shall soon be made most apparently to disappear. It will be given the most prestigious appearance ever made before of its ultimate disappearance, which is something the Counterfeit Command can barely muster and so never sustain. Nevertheless, what we mistake for our having no more than the best of reasons we can find in the past to promote communism, socialism, fascism, and even Zionism (together with so many other isms) have often been no more than prior attempts to substitute some form of the counterfeit Christianity.

Yet many will be fooled, literally hoodwinked into misbelieving that this eternal light has forever been extinguished, no less than the Counterfeit Command would seek to do just that for evermore and evermore. It is as if all eternity hangs in the balance over this impending battle, the last and final conflict between rightful and wrongful authority, so that even time itself, of that solar measure authoritatively designated to allow for the proverbial outcome of this great cosmic conflict, simply backs off into a cul-de-sac of hitherto unaccounted-for and sidereal space.

On the contrary, this unaccounted-for cul-de-sac of sidereal space has always been accounted for no less than it has been utilised to hold up the passage of solar time more than once before. Thus, by its disallowance of any progress being made by the passage of any intervening event through solar space, then solar time stands mute, silent, and sentinel, as if, entirely of its own accord (instead of under the Supreme Command), what we choose to understand of time on earth were, for being itself once more non-committal and insentient of this great conflict's outcome, to exert no more than its own will in standing still.

Nevertheless, as human beings who still desire to be told rather than to be made to think and feel for ourselves, we have this counterfeit gift (given and taken at our fall) of expecting everything we ask of the Supreme Command to be made completely comprehensible. 'Spit it out!' we say even to the longest-suffering prophets. 'We have had more than enough of your dark sayings. Tell us most exactly and most precisely what you truly mean!' [Translator's note: In other words, 'speak clearly as would any God, and we shall give you all the praise and glory and not just when spoken so unclearly, as to be most obviously only yourself (even if on behalf of God) from which lack of clarity we shall give you no credit at all, for you then doing, as we see it, no more than half your job!']

No, it takes two to translate (and also many more) just as it takes many more than even just two to create a language, grow a culture, found a nation, establish a family, or even, over the many generations it may take, conceive heaven's most awaited child. Only a truly disciplined military man, woman, or child—since none with any prophetic gifting is exempt of their proclaimed allegiance to the Supreme Command—can make any sense of this hiatus in time (or *nakanunye*, as so said by those who read the signs of the times) in that passage of time, known as 'on the eve', that precedes every great and momentous battle for those already called to be on the front line.

Nevertheless, with Satan now on the rampage as never before (since at this moment, he is most excited to hear the mistaken report given to him of the Supreme Command stepping down from its command), this presently renewed prophetic proclamation of our glorious future (as much the shared future of the Supreme Command as of its many saints who have freely harnessed themselves to the Supreme Command) is no more than a reminder to all our presently extended time, long ago promised and explicitly foretold, without the saving grace of which many souls (no less in number than once were lost as were once so many angels lost) would now once again be lost to grief and despair. For this reason, it is vitally important that all overcomers take enough of their remaining time to read the signs of the times towards their overcoming all fear of this most pervasive darkness.

This presently pervasive darkness is nothing new in kind from previous periods of pervasive darkness, but in the width of its present pervasiveness as well as in the depth of its intensity, it accords a heightened significance to our disciplined reading of these signs of the times. Trivially, it has something to do with the once common but basically fraudulent catch cry of new lamps for old. Less trivially and in faster pursuit of its still demonic strategy, it employs the tactics of, first, continual restructuring to wear down the overcommitted workforce and, secondly, the prestigious transparency by which to delude the highly intellectual and artistic idealists. Both of these spurious tactics, wrought by secular idealists highly misapprehensive of the future, brought down (through the restructuring of perestroika and the transparency of glasnost) the once mighty Soviet Union, and they continue to threaten the biggest of empires and wealthiest of nations, not to mention also the biggest of churches and the wealthiest of religions, so that these, by taking their own gargantuan size and strength for granted, strenuously persist in growing too big for their own fast-diminishing size in footwear.

Once again, however, this present reiteration of that very first prophetic proclamation from Patmos bids the Supreme Command (together with all the saints) to recreate the future as boldly, as powerfully, and as surely as it once was given to everyone with eyes to see and ears to hear of that first hope and promise of his or her eternal life. To all scoffers, cynics, and other sinners alike, this first hope and promise of eternal life, even when accepted at their own dawning of first light and with their faith publicly confessed through Jesus Christ, is yet for all remaining unbelievers (together with those who may more quietly disenfranchise themselves from the divine Word of the Lord Jesus) a most ridiculous notion. So too, therefore, this by now deeply darkening world is likewise destined to be born again, although this redemptive labour to resurrect a new world out of the rapidly descending void, like that of redeeming one's very own miniscule labour during this extended period of time, will be extremely hard.

Although this reiteration of that first prophetic proclamation from Patmos now being heard reaches to no more than a whisper above the hubbub of today's broadcasting (by now the universal medium of all news, views, and opinions at every personal and public level), the commandeered airwaves (reinforced by radio waves and filmic representations) marginalise this straightforward message of hope and promise by means of projecting today's scenes of deepest darkness (invariably towards the highest and ever hopeful heavens) most times by way of only simulating a counterfeit light. So never fear the prevailing darkness—the Counterfeit Command can do no more on its own behalf with all its subterfuges and cheap conjuring tricks than to counterfeit the one and only true light in Jesus Christ, the Saviour of the world. [Translator's note: And if that explanation by now still makes no sense to you, then consult the Supreme Paraclete, or Holy Spirit, for what follows.]

By this reciprocal means of inducing counterfeit light to dispel its own darkness, informational overload perplexes the mind, upsets the emotions, and stresses the heart. Political correctness compromises the real issues at stake for the world by first sedating the mind and then compelling us to look for closure. Meanwhile, the button-pushing mentality induced by an unthinking over-reliance on technology (the successor to box-ticking bureaucracy) sets the stage for the lowest ever compliance factor of today's citizenry in serious thought. Both a dumbed-down acceptance of diversity and a conciliatory drive towards a heavily compromised sense of unity—said to be for the good of all because present teaching (so wrongly) presumes that we are all for the good—so quenches the spirit (both human and divine) by relieving ourselves of responsibility for our own future inaction.

This sort of counterfeit light (the sign of the times showing how little oil is left in that counterfeit lamp) is given by the Counterfeit Command to enable these vanities—whereas the preacher says all is vanity—shine brightest at the highest of humanly mistaken virtues. This is the process (by falsely equating verities with vanities) by which humanity thinks to hide itself behind itself (an obviously lost cause) as if none other than humanity were its own god. Don't worry—though avoid being drawn into the initially comfortable but fundamentally false light—at the expense of which unprofitable diversion you may overlook so little oil being left in one's own unattended lamp!

There in the counterfeit light (brought about by producing lots of smoke, by applying the most expensive spin-doctoring of limited resources, and by deriving a virtual reality from the high-powered manipulation of the most convincing labyrinth of distorting mirrors), the demonic self-confidence of the Counterfeit Command surreptitiously intends to divert humanity from its supremely commissioned task. At first (perhaps given as a test of our faith, since untested faith is worthless), this task was once simply one of pastoral stewardship. But by now, most people on earth cannot even remember exactly what that task of pastoral stewardship was. Something to do with … perhaps first a garden … and a little later perhaps … of looking after sheep …

So then perhaps at least, as some lone voice will tentatively say, it was then first as gardeners that we looked after the garden of our Lord God, and it was then, in the cool of the evening, we would walk and talk with him. And it was good for us to do so then, for we still breathed the one and the same breath (or pneuma) by which our Lord God had given us life. So also by the exercise of that same breath that gave us life, we would freely converse together with our Lord God, because that same breath of life so given to us, either directly to me or through me, from the Lord to my helpmate—called woo-man, was she not? Yes, just as I was then first called man and so is also that same first breath of the Lord which enables us, for my being Adam, the first of men, and my helpmate, Eve, the first of women, most freely to talk and this both as freely with each other and so us as freely with the Lord.

The recollection grows. So too, in that same still of the evening, as of many a pleasant end to the day, just as our Lord God had once been so interested in what names the first man, Adam, should give to all the animals, so also our Lord God would remain immensely interested, as would any kindly father, in whatever, no matter however little thing, his children would think to say. This is the first testimony as to our interactive human conversations with our Father God, and for the future sake of our continuing purpose and for our ability to hear, however distantly the voice of our Father despite our intervening fallen status until redeemed by Jesus Christ, it is vitally important to understand the closeness of this exercise of naming the animals by the first Adam when alone with Father God in Eden.

The significance of this naming exercise is as double-edged in the same sense as the cutting process of the Holy Spirit is also double-edged, and also as this naming exercise is as mutually productive by way of God's delegation of the exercise to Adam (first agent of the Supreme Command), as it is to God to hear and sanction the results, either as described or as prescribed by Adam. There is a vital lesson to be learnt of this exercise as to what Father God expects of us by way of us sharing intimately in both the process of creation, no less than through Jesus Christ in the process of redemption. We cannot always be source takers of grace and favour without also being target givers of that same grace and favour.

If you were Adam, in that very first innocent exercise of naming the animals, how would you fulfil the exercise? Would you have judged by their already decided looks, personality, and character—a roaring lion, a loathsome toad, a charging rhino, a monstrous leviathan, a cumbersome hippo, a changeable chameleon, a fleeting hind, a sneaky crocodile, a footloose horse, or even for being then the seven-headed behemoth—or would you have given them names that actually invested these roaring, loathsome, charging, monstrous, cumbersome, changeable, fleeting, sneaky, footloose, seven-headed characteristics on their bearers?

In other words, is this testing of Adam an exercise in discernment as to whether he correctly understands the character and temperament of these animals, or is Adam given the greater creative task of determining what their awaiting character and temperament shall be? What do you think? Would you either welcome or shrink from the more participative task of sharing in the design of creation?

Both tasks are creative, the one of correctly naming, but the other also of predetermining the character, behaviour, and temperament of the animal to be named. Once again, what do you think—remembering that this process of name-calling, however discerning at the very least or determinative of present design and future outcomes at the most, will have critical consequences for almost every one of your as yet unknown descendants—of Noah (leading agent of the first recreation) who is called upon to build an ark and Jonah (agent under training) who will travel in the belly of a great whale, all of whom, as yet unknown to you, will still come after you to be dependent on your decisions? Well, in one way or another, that's nothing new—our descendants are always made dependent (like it or lump it) on the decisions of their forebears—so don't get indecisive over this one!

It's not such a straight question as it first appears. Much depends, linguistically, on the power of names. Give a dog a bad name, and it may well stick to what then becomes a bad dog. Tag a child with being slow, clumsy, backward, bad, or being a thief, and the statistical probability for the child may well veer towards the same result as he or she has been so named and so identified. Naming is not as if a rose by any other name would always be a rose; otherwise, there's little hope of any lion ever lying down with any lamb. Misunderstandings in linguistic philosophy over the inherent power of naming (as with Ogden and Richards in their very misleading book *The Meaning of Meaning*) have led to the confusion and breakdown in communication and thence spread throughout the world and into almost every branch of science and scholarship.

Some readers may dismiss this discussion for being trivial and so chit-chit-chatting about nothing of any significance at all (as if words in themselves were devoid of all but their own very arbitrary meaning)—and this in the worst sense of this chit-chit-chattering being ambiguously philosophical (and so unscientific) or for being equivocally theological (and so no more than mythopoeic) or for being so anthropological or psychological or sociological (as to have no independent objectivity whatsoever apart from the one-eyed way that humans are tempted to see themselves when looking only at themselves). But biological form and function (no less than anatomy and physiology) have an interactive intimacy in deciding character, personality, temperament, and behaviour, and so also does naming, as every parent who takes parenting seriously knows.

In due course, Adam's first exercise in naming was the most seriously pursued (in the interests of scientific taxonomy or the art of naming and classification) by Carl Linnaeus in his proposing a binomial nomenclature whose principles of taxonomy and classification are those which still apply today. Librarians, no less than any other specialist (from lawyers and logicians to philosophers, psychologists, and theologians) in their own areas of taxonomy and classification, will know of the difficulties of classification and the perils of misclassification and of the ensuing degrees of systemic disorder that may be perpetrated both within any system and amongst related systems when these difficulties are overlooked, ignored, or abused.

As once newcomers into this most amazing and divine creation, then we once spoke to each other with childlike innocence and prophetic wonderment with which, thanks to our heavenly Father's own breath of life remaining in our bodies, sounded even to us (for our being then little more than his infant children) and so nevertheless still basically sounding like only smaller versions of very much their Lord God's voice. So surely it still must be for those who dare, again as little children, to speak and write and teach and preach still with the voice or still by the hand of their own acknowledged Father in heaven.

Of course, until something terrible happened, our eyes had never been opened to good and evil, so we didn't then know that all this freedom we enjoyed and most especially that complete freedom of speech to converse with the Lord (as also no less freely to converse with each other) comes to us only from the Lord, nor did we know, until sensing its loss, that this freedom of speech could continue with us only so long as we still shared in that first breath of life given to us by our Lord God. We had not yet begun to learn the power of the word that had brought this whole wide world into being, nor yet did we know of the terrible war that had already broken out amongst the angels in heaven and yet from the same terror of which treason this garden of Eden gave us safe sanctuary. Only by our own future disobedience were we yet to learn of the strangeness and of the fear and sometimes of the abject terror to others of what it means for us to be considered an outsider.

Until that most terrible day of our being put to the test whilst we were still there in Eden, we freely talked with the Lord, we freely walked with the Lord, and we freely ate the fruit of all the trees there in Eden, but one (although later we were told there were two), since of that first forbidden tree, we had been warned by Our Lord God that, even if we merely touched that tree (as we later most surely did and also ate of its forbidden fruit on that terrible, terrible day of first temptation), we would surely die. The rest is world history, which, for the sake of prophecy, is best not forgotten.

To the human eye, which still yet is never fully open, this history of creation may appear inordinately long; but to the prophetic eye, which is always more fully open to the incorporation of both past and future in the present, this history of creation is incredibly short. Alas, for ourselves, through our eating of the tree of knowledge by which we would think to discern good and evil, we humans still presume themselves to be the measure of all things and so, as if we too were the angels, to be both immortal and eternal for always!

Thus, for our ever-present guidance, as well as for being a constant remembrance of how that terrible day came about by which our freedom to talk and our freedom to walk with our Lord God became sadly curtailed, we have our Lord God's written word as to the consequences of our own disobedience. Before thorns and thistles took over the earth and before we thus became obliged to survive on sowing and reaping and binding and grinding the grain we would grow and then baking the bread that we managed to make from the grain (and this bread, although in truth made more by the sweat of our brow than by any toil of the grain), we then ate that providential bread, instead of what once grew so much more plentifully and easily as fruit, and we did so for the rest of our lives by the sweat of our brow until, exactly as earlier warned, we each fell victim to our prophesied death.

* * *

Blinded by First Light
Part VI

Fact, Fiction, or Fallacy
It is remarkable that what we call the world, which is
so very credulous in what professes to be true, is most
incredulous in what professes to be imaginary ...
Charles Dickens, in his Preface to
his novel *Nicholas Nickleby*

Bear with us a little while. We angels need to point out to you the means by which both the credulity and incredulity of the world in which you live is not so remarkable as it first appears. What is remarkable to you mortals for what you call the world by reason of its inability to distinguish either the true from the false or that which professes only to be imaginary from what masquerades as reality is not in the least remarkable to us angels. It may help you to penetrate that first credulous appearance of things (which instead to us angels is one of incredulity) to realise that the greatest works of imagined fiction (whether by Dickens, Scott, Shakespeare, Milton, Tolstoy, or Hugo or by any other great author of fiction you may care yourselves to imagine) are always based on hard fact.

So then bear with our own angelic, yet to you incredulous, way of looking at things a little further. Whether by helping to bring any universe into cosmic existence by the power of the word or by taking that or any other universe out of existence by the same power of the word (in each case supported so strongly by the forcefulness of our angelic song), you need to raise your level of faith to accept on earth our angelic commitment to the Supreme Command for the sake of such events. It is not only our own angelic task which we ask you mortals most credibly to recognise but also for the sake of what follows from your own credible recognition of our task that matters most to the Supreme Command.

By virtue of your enjoining in what for you mortals then becomes a mutually angelic-mortal endeavour towards the establishment of a new heaven and earth for all eternity, you will be demonstrating by your then heightened level of faith your complete commitment to the Supreme Command. We already know the extent to which today's incredulous world regards such credible levels of often self-sacrificing faith, so as we angels most credibly ask you mortals to bear with us, so we too angels most credibly bear with you.

We know too just how many of you mortals shy clear of what appears to be the most catastrophic of outcomes concerning this fast-declining earth. Never mind, that is no more no less than what is already foretold by the Supreme Command. Why, even if you mortals cannot as yet understand how and why we angels trouble ourselves for the sake of the love we hold towards your incredibly well-imagined and first created world, that is beside the point. What's now at stake is for you now to enjoin in all such things as matter to Supreme Command. now for yourselves to enjoin such things at the Supreme Command, Then this will raise your faith level to support the only means by which your switch from time to eternity can ever come about.

Don't worry, we're not breaking any confidences by telling you any more than you could already know and for your having been already most credibly told about all such things. All you need to do right now is to look around at your own fast-dying world. So learn to read the highly credible signs of your own fast-diminishing time. But know exactly where you stand; that's of the highest importance when increasing your level of faith in any belief system. Believe it or not, but although by very different means, that's exactly what the Counterfeit Command is also doing right now.

Suppressing the truth long-term gives rise to second-order dementia (in one or the other of all its many forms). We angels know what it can take from both ourselves and you humans to confront the truth. You're crossing often a very scary threshold of pain to reach the other side. Step aside or hold back, and you may never get the same chance to confront that particular truth again. Time moves on. Meanwhile, so too does the oppression that led to your suppression, and from which that suppression leads most likely to depression, and from where depression then leads to a succession of afflictions you'd most prefer to forget, which is exactly where forgetfulness first sets in.

Whatever the consequences, you must learn always to face up to the truth. The signs of these present times vary from heightening oppression to deepening depression coupled with a rising level of dementia from a failure at all levels (local, regional, national, international, transnational, supranational, and global) to face the God's honest truth. First-stage dementia is physical (caught early enough, the willing patient can be helped, healed, and even cured); second-stage dementia is demonic (harder to help, more difficult to treat, and hardest ever to heal); whereas third-stage dementia is satanic (almost impossible to diagnose humanly by reason of the plausibility it manages to confer on an alternative (although completely counterfeit reality).

Reading the signs (once known as reading the runes) won't make for pleasant reading. Nevertheless, you have more and more need to know where you stand in relation to the dizzying rate at which your own yet by now threadbare universe is as fast expanding as this present world (of both heaven and earth) is fast going down. By faith alone, keep your balance, since what you have been brought up from infancy to regard as the slow march of time has rapidly become a fast scherzo (which for all unbelievers will end in a frenzy of unbelief).

This frenzy of unbelief, typified by the 'suicide of reason' as some percipient scholars already recognise, will continue to intensify and widen the presently increasing epidemic of lawlessness on earth. This will serve by which to discount not only heaven (already largely come to earth) but also hell and so, both self-referentially as well as finally, all sense of that earthly order by which any longer to maintain planet Earth.

As an exercise in abstraction, we need here to distinguish credibility from incredibility, credulity from incredulity, and the credulous from the incredulous. It will be obvious that to exercise the power of the word, whether it be the spoken word or the written word, one must first painfully learn, next come most intimately to know, and then dare prophetically to proclaim the power of the word, whether it be to move hearts or to move minds or to move mountains.

There is no great difference here between the supposedly secular and the supposedly divine, since all gifts to exert the power of the word, especially any word that moves mountains, come from the Supreme Command. Hence, the gift might just as likely be given to a Charles Dickens as to a John Calvin, to a Virginia Woolf as to a Mother Teresa, to a Karl Marx as to an Adam Smith, or to an Adolf Hitler no less than to a Winston Churchill. Yet to each one of these people—no matter how bright, no matter how gifted, and no matter how credibly or incredibly empowered—the full picture of their life in context is always hidden, and on that largely self-hidden basis, each person's life constitutes a freely chosen work of faith.

Certainly, by reason of their own free will, what these recipients do with this gift of the Supreme Command to move mountains depends entirely on their own responses. So we are not only vitally interested in these radically different responses but also highly intrigued to see how these responses, whether authentic or counterfeit, invariably fulfil our own strategic outcome—the one that was long ago prophetically predetermined by our planning at Patmos under the aegis of the Supreme Command. The supreme irony of this free-willed interlocking, as some might mistake of good and evil in their reaching the same outcome, is just as startling at our seeing how many great mountain chains are able to be moved around the world by this power of the word before the end of all things as we now know them as clearly in sight.

Of course, there are also many other very gifted persons than those who manage to move mountains, let alone cast them into the sea, but generally, these persons are of the very lukewarm nature to which state of lethargy they have been reduced by the Counterfeit Command. They pay no more than lip service to the existential power of the word. So it is by this lip service of theirs that the power of the word never passes further than their lips. Instead, it either hangs on their lips or else drools down their front and so slips between their legs, as does any let-fallen prophecy to earth.

Such persons mutter prayers to themselves and as often to none other than themselves, so that whatever little faith they have in prayer is misdirected to form rather than function. How incredulous of, rather than most incredible they might then find their answered prayers—but by the grace of God that most surely happens. To them their answered prayers are not even imagined far less imaginary, and of what they remain most credulous is only what they see and hear for already being the credulousness with which they regard the established truth. If only they were to move forward, into the realm of prophetic proclamation, then what wonders could be achieved.

There are—very roughly speaking—facts, fictions, and fallacies. Each may be qualified in various ways, as for logical fallacies, legal fictions, and proven facts. They each may be employed prescriptively, as by outlawing a logical or grammatical fallacy, or else dealt with descriptively, as by merely enumerating different genres of literary fiction or different kinds of legal fictions or different classes of logical fallacy. They each may declare generally held values (as to this or that being a fallacy) or else express mere matters of opinion (as to this or that being a proven fact).

The facts are most usually taken or mistaken for expressing matters of truth, fictions for matters of untruth, and fallacies for matters in one way or another mistaken. In consequence, our perception of the truth is frequently restricted to matters of fact, our perception of untruth is so often equated with the telling of fictions, and fallacies are equated with mistaken perceptions.

We are writing here of fact versus fiction; and we are writing here, as sponsored by the Supreme Command, to reduce the forcefulness of this perceived distinction, which, when so much exaggerated as it tends to become, tends to obliterate our sense of fundamental values and also to distract us from our sense of universal truth.

This is one of the fiercest of conflicts (not just in literature, as between the forcefulness of fiction compared with that of non-fiction) but also in the world at large (as between science and the arts or as between law and morality or as to the efficacy of algorithmic quantification over heuristic qualification or as to some of the impasses that suck or segregate scientific confidence away from righteous confirmation through its rightful sharing in religious faith). Let's remember that this can be one of the fiercest of conflicts in the reality of human life on earth; and so too, let's not forget that the fierceness of this conflict (whether expressed in the physical, in the mental, or in the spiritual) is rapidly heating up.

Thus, serious readers of non-fiction may discountenance relaxed readers of fiction, committed physicists may discountenance non-physical chemists, pragmatic legalists may discountenance theoretical jurists, straightforward judges may discountenance convoluted legislators, evolutionary biologists may discountenance just as deeply thinking theologians, and those who write research papers may discountenance those who write academic books no less than both may discountenance mere journalists. It is surely unremarkable that this one huge arena for these many different areas of conflict hinges entirely on issues of credibility, and this especially since it does not affect the sentient truth of any proposition—no, not a whit—as to whether it professes to be fact or fiction or is shown to be more believable in biology than could be in physical chemistry or as a precept of morality or as an article of religious faith confirmed by revelation. What it purports to be, by way of any proposition's alleged status, cannot affect the fundamental issue of the proposition's truth or of its falsity.

At the heart of credibility is some credo of faith or belief system. The credo, as for most of us who rely for everything on our sensory perception, may only be conditioned and so merely assumed. Or as in the case of those who seriously pursue scientific investigation, then, on the basis of experimental proof, the credo may then be at least presumed, conventionalised, or even codified. Or as in the case of religious faith, it may rely on what seems, to all others without that religious faith, to be no more than some unhinged revelation.

At the outset, therefore, the issue between being a fact or a fiction most certainly seems to be one of belief or credibility, which, in turn, makes it so very remarkable (in the literal sense) that the world at large can be so credulous of what we profess (as a fact) to be true and so incredulous of what we profess (as a fiction) to be imagined. Of course, in our professing this present formula to be true (on its face value), we are putting our formula to the test—the test not only of its rectitude but also of its correctitude. And so we present something of a paradox, since, apart from those readers who find in this formula nothing remarkable about it (for being in any way incredible), there will be other readers who are neither credulous nor incredulous of what we profess to be true and yet others who will be most incredulous that we can profess to be true what surely can be no more than speculatively or conjecturally imagined.

Yet think on this paradox, which is one so suggestive of the old acrimony in educational circles between the classics and moderns, that, on this score at any rate, there is obviously nothing new to give grounds by which to wage war under the sun. On the one hand, the ancient poet Homer, although for so long given credence only as a fictional storyteller of the *Odyssey*, is no more than the recognised champion of storytelling. Aha, but then suddenly, many centuries later, with the advent of archaeology which rediscovers the ruins of Troy, that same storytelling champion of fiction turns out to be an unassailable historian of the facts. Once again, the very best of fiction shows itself to be founded on hard facts!

So too, Stanley Prusiner, with the more modern discovery of proteinaceous infective particles, is redeemed from the scientific oblivion of academic ostracism to receive the Nobel Prize in physiology and medicine in 1998. For his now having become a hero of science, Prusiner is now rendered immune to 'the slings and arrows of outrageous fortune'. No longer will he be hounded out of scientific conventions for being either a madman or a charlatan.

Both these and many other cases of credulity versus incredulity (as Dickens describes the paradox) demonstrate the viability of a universal truth which so often goes far beyond the merely arbitrary status of peer-reviewed opinion. The level of credibility which we accord those facts, fictions, and opinions from and into which we both derive and invest our own transient form of authority as often as not depend on propositions which transcend our accustomed view of what could be anything new under the sun. They simply do not fit into our existing criteria of credibility, and the bigger the default value between established values and that of the universal truth, then often the greater is the trauma of warfare and adversity by which our perception of that universal truth is regained.

As a source of the widest and gravest conflict, this arena of hostilities impacts upon both believers and unbelievers, as well as upon whole belief systems, and on believer and unbeliever, each systemically from the top down to the bottom up. Consequently, as between heaven and earth, this is seen by the Supreme Command to be one of its most battle-ridden war zones throughout the world. It is one currently being fought between faith (often quite rationally) and reason (not always quite so rationally).

As one of the fiercest and therefore widest of epistemological conflicts, the search for reality pervades almost every category and discipline of science and almost every branch and division of scholarship. It provokes as many unholy alliances as it can promote any holy alliance, and neither philosophers nor theologians can keep out of the arena of contesting reality without being stood up by others to answer for their patent unreality.

Yes, indeed, here we are writing of fact versus fiction. As Charles Dickens describes the paradox, it is quite remarkable that what we choose to call the world can be so very credulous by being drawn so easily into believing in what we profess to be true, and this credulity about what we believe to be true made even more remarkable when we consider that this same world can then be so incredulous about what we profess to be imaginary. Some folks, being right-brained people, have more imagination (roughly speaking) in their serving as poets, prophets, musicians, and artists than left-brained people who are endowed with imagination (again roughly speaking) as priests, professors, policemen, teachers, lecturers, and lawyers.

We are speaking here only of the run-of-the-mill ways in which different groups of people somehow seem to sort themselves out so as all to share the same mindsets and thus never themselves mind that those of different mindsets are somehow excluded from their own group. Likewise, we are talking here only of the resulting representativeness that groups acquire from this exclusivity and of the typical character and personality that we come to expect, most usually for the worse, from each member of any group.

As to the different and often very different warring classes, groups, and factions, can you pick up here on the class calculus by which to identify the human flea circus promoted by the allegorical *Siphonaptera*? Of course, Dean Swift, perhaps in his own capacity as the biggest flea riding on the backs of lesser fleas, has already been here before in his biting satire touching on mankind in general in his *Gulliver's Travels*. Likewise, so also in *The Way of All Flesh* has been Samuel Butler.

Yes, amongst earthbound mortals, there are greater fleas and lesser fleas as if for all eternity on each other's backs to bite, bite, and still further bite each other ad infinitum. Indeed, it is often all the same whether the group is that of journalists or of celebrities, of leading statesmen or of local politicians, of preschool-teachers or of family lawyers—their character and personality becomes more and more defined by their own self-generated exclusiveness.

What we angels are describing here is the human disorder of the cosmic class calculus. It will take nothing less than the righteousness of heaven to redeem this already catastrophic level of worldly disorder, for which the present level of conflict between chaos and cosmos requires nothing less than a new heaven and a new earth. Never mind, never worry, and don't fear. As already long-ago promised, this Second Coming is already at hand.

In his Preface to *Nicholas Nickleby*, Dickens has something again to say on this subject, in his dealing with a certain class of teachers and on the subject of education. What he writes is this: 'Where imposture, ignorance, and brutal cupidity are the stock in trade of a small body of men, and one is described by these characteristics, all his fellows [surely, as a result of their ongoing exclusivity] will recognise something belonging to themselves [whether by way of their trade, profession, labour, or calling], and each will have a misgiving that the portrait is his own.'

We could also just as imaginatively apply this generic process more particularly to literature in distinguishing the different responses made to fictional literature on the one hand and to non-fictional literature on the other. So then what makes the comparative rarity of right-brained imagination so suspect to the generality of mankind and, on the other hand, the left-brain concern for orderliness and management so respectable to the same generality? The answer to that leading question is already foretold in your having read thus far in this book.

Meanwhile, the days are ever shortening, just as these histories are ever shortening, because the speed of light is constantly slowing. And the latter days are ever and ever faster approaching, and there's less and less both time and tide, both day and night by which to change one's own direction of travel.

Calculate your own momentum. Just as for any catcher in the rye that goes also for any soul-catcher. Assess and reassess your own position. Don't forget from where you left, and in which direction you chose to travel. No matter how sure you may feel of where you are, always beware of the unexpected. What's been expected may unexpectedly never happen as so expected. Meanwhile, time and tide wait for no man (nor for any woman either). Keep up your daily log of every day's dead reckoning. If not always you at the helm, then who's your helmsman?

* * *

Blinded by First Light
Part VII

The Hidden Cost

So painfully felt by one's nearly breaking heartstrings
is interminably deferred hope, and so wearing to one's
soul is the fear that our every last expression of hope's
fulfilment shall be irrevocably postponed, that we
lose all heart to wager any longer on securing our
objectives ... and so are left to rely solely on our
strength of will ...

> From the wisdom of Solomon, popularly known
> as the Proverbs (13:12) (as now paraphrased)

We have seen that to the seriously thoughtful intellectual, the trauma of life can appear comic (since to that intellectual, pure thought prioritises rationality and so comes before feelings). Just as to the highly artistic and creative thinker (for whom feelings are paramount), the same trauma of life can appear deeply tragic. The clue to sustaining one's own survival, whether between the emotions and the intellect, lies in the communicative response by which equalise and balance both, and certainly when no less to and from the Supreme Command than interstitially amongst one's fellow human beings.

So do you hear from the Supreme Command? And if not, then why not, if you, by putting in your reports as to the state of affairs in the field to the Supreme Command, must then surely expect some response from the Supreme Command? But then what's your calling? What exactly is your calling from the Supreme Command—to be openly in the field or to be foremost in the front line or as yet to be still completely undercover? Take care as usual here, remembering as always, that without alternatives to discuss (whether within oneself or abroad) then there's no fit room in any place for productive discussion).

Without a calling, you can't very well make reports, so you might very well be writing nonsense rhymes or begging questions or making impossible requests for an arsenal of arms and munitions that couldn't possibly be administered by the Supreme Command. So are you sure enough of your calling as to be most properly in the pay of the Supreme Command? It wouldn't be the first time that we in the Supreme Command have received requests to blow up cities and take out the most important of our adversaries. Maybe, just maybe, your reports, however conscientiously prepared and formulated with the best of intentions, are going into a different drop site and so falling into the hands of some Counterfeit Command.

Perhaps it's long past time to call up your calling with the Counterfeit Command. We, at the Supreme Command, always acknowledge receipt of reports from our leaders (even those of third class and even much lower) in the field. If not that, however, since you're so sure of your present calling from the Supreme Command— whether as some angel, apostle, prophet, teacher, preacher, or prayer partner and beyond—then you'd better clean out your ears or else learn to read the signs of the times more closely with your more widely open eyes.

We ourselves, although the epitome of kindliness in the Supreme Command, have also to come clean as to how things stand between heaven and earth and so to speak clearly and too often also ruthlessly; and this on so many things because there is a counterfeit romance that denies the need for ruthlessness in love and so dons idealistic and chivalric disguises by which to compromise the most important of kingdom outcomes. Oh, and by the way, from angels and apostles to preachers, prayer partners, and beyond—all these are also translators commissioned as communicators by the Supreme Command and so are responsible to the Supreme Translator himself.

For this most practical purpose of continuing communication (especially between heaven and earth and earth and heaven), we all need to know something of translation theory, which requires us to distinguish between source translation (construed according to the textual source or emanation) and target translation (construed according to the context of transmitted reception). Thus, for prayers to reach heaven, they must be targeted towards the context of their transmitted reception; just as for responses to prayers to be picked up on earth, these must be sourced from the context of their heavenly emanation.

As far as humans contribute to making communication possible, then the Supreme Translator keeps all heavenly lines of communication open. Likewise, the reciprocal responsibility of humanity by means of their contribution to keeping interactive communication between heaven and earth open is to remain immune to the wiles of the Counterfeit Command. These wiles are not few, nor are they always self-apparent.

Residual mortality still remains for those on earth—although the mere appearance of death is now only a vestigial remnant of what was once the real thing. This by now token wedge between heaven and earth is still one of the greatest obstacles to open communication that the Counterfeit Command chooses to employ. It is for this reason we are told that he who struggles solely towards securing his own survival, then to that extent, will surely not survive, but instead, by his own misdirected travel, he will risk losing every prospect of salvation through his diminished potential for eternal life.

So we say this same thing once again, although said as a warning and not as a threat: the clue to sustaining one's own survival (in whatever one does) as well as to overcoming whatever opposition or conflictive lack of response one's calling evokes lies in the efficacy of our communicative employment. Whether between the emotions and the intellect or as between obedient or disobedient response to acknowledged command, the efficacy of our human survival lies in one's ongoing communicative employment and certainly no less to and from the Supreme Command than amongst one's fellow human beings. It takes two or more to enter into a relationship, and no relationship—no, not even under the Supreme Command—can, however awkwardly expressed, exist by one or the other going it alone. In other words, we live to communicate, no less than we communicate to live; and communication is always more than just one way.

Thus, there are writers and readers, speakers and hearers, priests and prophets, preachers and teachers, no less than there are light comedies and dark comedies, both long stories and short stories (some even telling tall stories), besides serious histories no less than serious novels, deeply dark tragedies and maudlin romances, as well as kiddies comics competing with soft porn and hard porn.

So also, as with songs, there are sad songs and there are happy songs; and the two are destined to meet at various points of crisis, sometimes within one and the same song (more often, symphony) of life. Likewise, there are serious songs of all sorts just as there are frivolous songs of all sorts. So singing the blues in their own sphere are every bit as important to the Supreme Command as are our classical anthems of praise and worship, and this no less than *The Beggar's Opera* by Gay and Bizet's once much-despised *Carmen* can become as much loved and appreciated for their own sake and their own work done as can Handel's pontifical *Messiah* or Mendelssohn's prophetic *Elijah*.

It could not be otherwise, especially for us strongly temperamental folks in our need to remain authentic (i.e. true to ourselves and true to each other), since, without any (sometimes even conflictive) contrast in our lives, the hidden cost of our having only happy songs to share with each other on this earth would mean that their resulting banality of merely assumed happiness (without our experiencing this world's grief) could never be fully heard or accurately shared. It can take a sad song, even the very saddest of sad songs, by which to allow a truly joyful peon of praise to hit its rightful mark.

Besides, without the need to retune one's voice or flute or harp to a different key throughout this rapidly changing world, each major or minor change of key could never be properly understood. Speaking both literally as well as figuratively, these different keys, whether of sadness and suffering or else of jollity and jubilation, are also amongst the different sets of keys to the promised kingdom held by the Supreme Command. It is only by mastering those different major and minor keys that we can modulate between them whenever we are called to cry with those who are mourning (it may be the loss of a loved one), no less than to dance with those who are celebrating (say, a wedding or the birth of a child).

Thus, we have no more excuse to be tone-deaf to those who are mourning than we have from being tone-deaf to those celebrating a wedding. And this requires as much sensitivity as to distinguish the piercing *khalil* of the flute at a funeral from the very different piercing sound of the same *khalil* or flute at a wedding. Likewise in our need to prepare for our transition to the promised new world in which our supreme joy supplants our present transient happiness in its going far beyond all constraints of time and place, we would be laid back (like the *lotophagoi* of this world) by our lack of all present motivation were we unprepared for our future mission.

So although this last hope of ours be interminably deferred and every trace of its eventual fulfilment be continually postponed, both even so far as to seriously sadden and even to sicken the human heart (which expects instant results), we are also promised that our continued desire and longing for the fulfilment of this long deferred hope will be a tree that we can rightfully begin to climb (even now) into our new life. We are thereby called (by way of our own overcoming) to strengthen ourselves in the Lord and not just to revel (partywise) in the bombast we are tempted to preach from pulpits, proclaim from pews, and publish from books as to our being little more than just the possessor (rather than the actioner) of these great gifts. On the contrary, these gifts have a dynamic purpose, which falls to the ground unless for us being also the priests and kings appointed to enquire into their function, and yet without which dynamic sense of our own purpose, we shall let lie fallow and so defeat their purpose.

* * *

Blinded by First Light
Part VIII

Making Mouth Music
If anyone speaks or writes, let whatever he or she says
be as the sound of music heard of any message when
given by Supreme Command.
Apostle Peter, his first open letter to believers
in Asia, Pontus, and other diverse places

There's a lot about music in this copybook, since words without
lyrics rarely speak to the heart. You will have already gathered from
our sponsor's word—spoken for this purpose into our very own
soul by this copybook—that our Supreme Command is like no other
command. In the first place, like the best of all great music—here,
think of your favourite love song—it is a minimalist command, as
often as not first heard as a whisper either when falling asleep as a
child or when fast asleep as a child.

To appreciate its minimalist message, therefore, we often need
to close our ears and shut our eyes to the otherwise overwhelming
hubbub of counterforces in this world. Then only do we hear the full
power of the divine proclamation that brought this world of ours into
being and yet again experience the divine breath (or pneuma) that
first filled our lungs and brought life to ourselves on earth. The stars
sing all the time, you know, otherwise your own planet wouldn't keep
going around. They sing songs of light at night, you know, by which
the whole cosmos stays in tune.

For this apparently minimalist purpose (of maximising what
would otherwise be for us the overlooked message), the written record
tells us that sometimes (to break the barrier of our own hubbub) we
need to hear music (and so open our inner ears) before we can listen to
the spoken word. By means of this overture or entr'acte, we are given
the musical means to allow always for that far less listening effort
required by any musically metred word that's sweetly sung. Was it

not the prophet Elisha, as recorded in the 2 Kings 3:15, who called, 'Now bring me a minstrel so that I may hear the voice of the Lord!'

We are not told of what the minstrel sang or played any more than we are prohibited from thinking that Elijah plainchanted the Lord's command for a minstrel. One test (not infallible) of a person's readiness to hear the prophetic word is whether they are awake to what's usually called a rather roughly (or even crudely) mood music or soaking music. The music most appropriate for this purpose is also most difficult if not in each case impossible to define. Any born-again musician gifted with prophecy might describe it as playing or singing in the Holy Spirit. It may turn out to be compositional in its own right, but that depends, as does its prophetic purpose, also on the inspirational and improvisational forcefulness of its awakening power. So whether for the unsanctified bad or the sanctified good, do you not agree as to first the prophetic power, and then to the productive power of music?

No, you still don't think so? Then listen again to Debussy's *L'après-midi d'un faune* or to Dvořák's New World Symphony. (Of course, you may be more visually rather than aurally inspired, then look at John Martin's painting (rather than Rembrandt's painting) of *Belshazzar's Feast*. The key—no prophetic pun intended, although as with Belshazzar's feast, our Lord of the prophets is very much a punning prophet—to appreciating the prophetic quality of music (or minstrelsy) is to accept the fact that in its ability to evoke moods and to switch mindsets, the language (or more accurately the message) of that music is more likely to be that given by poetry and less like that given by prose, in its more methodical search for precision and accuracy of expression.

From harpists to songsters, the written record of the prophetic spirit is replete with singers and musicians to break down barriers and lift up those who struggle to hear the voice of the Lord and sometimes, as even with kings and rulers, to heal those afflicted who suffer from tortured and demonic spirits. This maximising of the gospel message through music is no concession, because without some sense of song (and the need for its maintenance and development), we could not savour the corresponding poesy conveyed by prose.

664

Whether descriptively of good or evil, all music is prophetic in its own right—and therapeutic when ministered in the name of achieving wholeness and wellness of the soul. So no matter whether our favourite love song is Bach's *Sheep May Safely Graze* or Beethoven's *Für Elise* or Fred Weatherly's *Danny Boy* or Jamie Yorkston's *Sweet Molly Malone* or Rabbie Burns's *A Red, Red Rose*, we then need more of such love songs to break through the frigid ice that hardens and calcifies broken hearts and to overcome the steep barriers that seek to close up and isolate so many troubled minds.

These steep barriers that seek to close up and isolate so many troubled minds themselves are many. [Excursus 1: The written record of the prophetic word tells us that apart from the truly creative breath, that now fallen angel, Satan (a.k.a. the father of lies), who was once charged with music and worship under the Supreme Command, is still lord of the air (without whose airwaves, there could be neither words nor song). So as we are prophetically warned, we are to be extremely careful of what we say, and such is the power of music to infiltrate the mind, even more especially of what we sing and, presumably also, even more of what we read and write.]

Nevertheless, as already said, even our Supreme Command is very much a minimalist command. And even if you dare think of this minimalist command as being as many as there could be of Ten Commandments (of which even just ten are impossible to keep), nevertheless by pondering deeply and with help and guidance on these ten, a touch (however fearful) from the Supreme Command will tell you that they can be encapsulated into no more than two commandments. The first (encapsulating five of the previous ten) is to learn to love the voice or calling of your Supreme Command, and the second (encapsulating the remaining five of the ten) is to learn to love whoever happens to be your neighbour in song every bit as much as you love yourself.

Note how closely the minimalistic message of the Supreme Command relates to learning. We are called to learn to love, and this is our calling, just as our calling is for us to go on learning to love. We are not expected to know all about loving; otherwise, we would not be called to learn about loving. But we are expected to listen to the voice of our calling to learn as much as we can about loving. So then there is no condemnation even when we mistake our calling to both love the Lord our God and our neighbour as ourselves.

What was once the command theory of ruthless law (so much enforced by threat of dire consequences for its breach) has now been melted down and refined by sacrificial fire into a paternal/maternal relationship of love. We thereby discover that we're all a family—one of brothers and sisters—not just under command but by then also collectively within the Supreme Command, which, by our calling to learn love, is given also to reside in us for the purpose of overflowing into others. This transformation process from whom and what we once thought ourselves to be (so distant from who and what we now are) can often be severely traumatic.

Nevertheless, from this trauma resulting from our exchanging law for love and no matter how joyfully motivated we may feel towards this process of transformation from death towards life, we are given time to rest and recover (which may itself be a test of faith) until we are faced (sooner or later) with the further challenge (still arising from our initial trauma of joyful transformation) that we have a still serious although also surprising (if not shocking) discovery to make, namely, that no matter how differently our lively means and purposeful motivation have become, we have still always been born to bear arms.

The victory is ours, but the fight still goes on. And it is by engaging in the fight against counterfeit love that we find we have so much to learn about real love. There is thus a shared purpose to the fight both for helping others and for helping ourselves to learn the art of loving not just family, neighbours, outsiders, strangers, and even enemies but also, for being sometimes the hardest task, in learning to love ourselves. We may not really know what this means—unconditional love—but we have a call to learn, and because victories are won only after a fight, we have to be prepared to fight for what this means.

It just so happens for us, all the same, that, for our having changed sides (so often such a hard thing to do) from upholding the curse of the law (which threatens death) to that of being blessed by unconditional love (which gives us life), our fighting methods (both tactical and strategic) have completely reversed not only our own personal history but also (although in ways that we cannot always foretell) another's history and perhaps even (because we don't know but act often only in faith) the entire course of human history. For the first time (perhaps since early childhood), we are consciously fighting for a cause that is both far, far beyond ourselves, yet by reason of our personal calling from now within the Supreme Command, we are still inextricably committed to securing our own eternal destiny.

Almost all the new arms—patience, lovingkindness, truthfulness, peacefulness—we wield in this renewed battle engagement against the side on which we first enlisted will now be defensive, however, instead of those which we formerly used for being almost entirely offensive. Nevertheless, there is still one, which, for being although no more than the word of our collective calling, has itself a cutting edge which, by the power of that word, cuts right through the flesh and penetrates straight to the soul. All the same, in most situations, patience and perseverance (for being far more than just virtues) can be far more effective (by their avoiding explosions) than can land mines, barbed wire, or trinitroglycerine in any military action.

This is one of the many military reasons by which, as agents of the Supreme Command when recognised by the fulfilment of our calling, we can be considered to be only a little less than the angels in the fulfilment of their calling. Whereas before our transformation from death to life, we sought only to change the world (a task far beyond our calling) and we sought only to change ourselves (so leaving our formerly mistaken task now collectively to the Supreme Command in which we function) instead of, as before, thinking to create or support some alternatively human empire by which, we as gods, would presume to try and change the world. Ours (at least for a while) then seems to be an upside-down world, therefore, which will take a little bit of getting used to before we get used to reading signs and recognising orders.

So call what next follows a preface or introduction, if you like, but for the lack of any sure beginning, there is no confirmed direction of travel. How a book begins says a great deal about how that book will end, since every beginning presupposes some sort of ending. From beginning to end, however, the inherent direction of travel (aside from wrong turnings, discontinuities, and diversions) is always clearly settled. You might not like to hear that right now that every starting-off point, however experimentally undertaken, carries within itself its own inherent direction of travel. But such is the case, so consider most carefully, especially when not a beginning made by your own choice, the nature of every first beginning as reflected by its own inherent direction of travel.

For those of you humans who are born again, the exercise of greater freedom will be far more complex than you've ever barely understood or been called to deal with before. Whereas before you were always no more than bilaterally symmetrical in thought, feelings, and action (deistic or demonic, introvert or extrovert, socially or selfishly minded, either on the make or else relinquishing the world and letting go) you will now possess a radial symmetry in all you say and do. Your domain of discourse as well as your sphere of action and span of influence will have been extended in all directions. Extra freedom entails extra responsibility—and that is the price to pay for what so many humans mistake for being fame, fortune, and (above all) power.

Nevertheless, don't mistake your own personal destiny—whether as reader, writer, or any other sort of fighter—for being in any way predetermined. You may be in the army by now, but the ever-prevailing choice, even that of whether to run away or else fight this day, is always yours. And that's not written deviously in infinitesimally small print but always clearly written in big, bold, and barefaced capitals. It's called FREEDOM OF CHOICE. Now that's the very sort of thing—requiring brazen faith and forthright action—that most offends the enemy.

Let's be clear here, that FREEDOM OF CHOICE, when freed from the curse of the law, by no means allows for any continuance of that counterfeit freedom of choice, which the world means to convey, however ambiguously by its own mismeasured freedom of choice. To be clear about this, it helps to realise that when we exercise any FREEDOM OF CHOICE consciously chosen in accordance with our calling, then that exercise, although subject to every test of faith, (1)will be confirmed by what we do to carry it through in ways that go far beyond what we would otherwise do when under compulsion, coercion, or by any other threat of reprisal or legal sanction; and (2) although our composite FREEDOM OF CHOICE is a spiritual gift derived from peace, joy, patience, lovingkindness, and perseverance, its exercise within the range of other chosen freedoms actually restricts our still prevailing width of choice, and so (3) incurs a responsibility in the exercise of our own choice to confirm their calling. In short, FREEDOM entails RESPONSIBILITY. It helps us to keep this in mind when we truly realise that every freedom, when once exercised, then determines and limits our almost every future action, and this notwithstanding that its exercise may also open other and hitherto closed avenues to further action.

For sure, once committed to the arms of Christ, one may still always run away or choose to fight the day, but depend upon it no less than for the one and only hound of heaven he shall surely follow. So then it is written, 'As the hound follows the hare, never ceasing in its running, ever drawing nearer in the chase, with unhurrying and unperturbed pace, so does God follow the fleeing soul by his divine grace.'

For most of us still trapped in the primeval darkness, this promise of everlasting grace may seem no more than a pocketful of rye, and there are many of us who would turn to drink, drugs, or overwork to escape our calling or to escape experiencing this grace and so to engulf ourselves in an even greater measure of this overwhelming darkness. Once committed to the arms of Christ, however, there is no turning back, no turning back, simply no turning back. And the presence of God, whether with or without dire consequences, will surely follow us—whether turned, unturned, or returned—through space and time to the ends of this earth.

What then does it mean to be clearly settled in the beginning? Clearly settled in the beginning—however much opposed by any reader, writer, or reviewer—does not mean predestined, although unrequited wrong turnings, discontinuities, and diversions can always produce outcomes that differ from that inherent direction of travel once clearly settled (but never ever programmed) from the beginning. So that leeway does not mean, as for writing any book or living any life (since, as for any writer, these two tasks are always lived in parallel), that their inherent directions (or ley lines) of travel will always end where first clearly settled. [Author's note: As in following a compass, ley lines may be magnetic or, as in following one's calling, ley lines may be redemptive or, as in following military orders, ley lines may be transformational.]

Many of the saints have once been scallywags, and more than a few of them have even been complete scoundrels for most of their lives. Sure, some of these fellows (before their hearing from the Supreme Command) we would have thought doomed always to be the bad guys. But as said before, the FREEDOM OF CHOICE, whether to run or fight or to pitch in or to have fun or to help out or to turn aside or to eat, drink, and be merry because tomorrow we die, is always given.

There are so very many different ways of going wrong that it's not surprising for us to find out that there's only one way of going right. In our thinking to make our own way, we all go wrong in our own way and often very far wrong, although without realising it, when judging others to be so much worse than we are ourselves. Unsurprisingly, it is so often by judging others and so being judged ourselves that we find out that we are so much worse than those others whom we judged.

Some of the biggest bad guys were born to be good guys, but somehow, they never seemed to make the grade. On the other hand, some of the greatest good guys lose their way, hit the broad road with everyone else in their heading off somewhere, and so fall off the lonely trail that leads to the only place worthwhile to be. Potentially the least promising of people can turn out to realise the most from life. Potentially the most promising can turn out to realise the least. Those who lose out here now can win out elsewhere for all time, and those who think to win here now can lose everything wherever else they get to be when their time runs out.

For those who think all this toing and froing quite unfair, they may only have the wrong world view (now gone global) as they search the geophysics and technoeconomics (not that these words are bad in themselves) by which to decide and resolve the so-called world problematique, which is only today's flash term for yesterday's 'woes of the world'. That too seems even a bigger pretence at truth, and so it is because such words often provide no more than academic fronts behind which to hide our own total lack of understanding of ourselves. But this isn't just a matter of logistics (a.k.a. failure of reason) or of situational ethics (a.k.a. misunderstanding of morals) or of limited resources (as if divine providence on God's behalf had finally been declared bankrupt) but also of fundamentally universal laws. But of course, to discern these laws for what they are and to distinguish them from the mere contingencies we mistake them to be take open hearts and open minds.

Accordingly, it is not by our gifts but by their fruits that we are finally and so also divinely assessed. Wrong turnings in our travels can be righted, interruptive discontinuities can be reconnected, and misleading diversions can be straightened out—in each case by way of returning to what was once clearly settled. And if we turn out to be the bad guys, that is only because we decide on the means by which to settle our own doom. You may think to hide behind genetics, for all your life blaming the parents that begat you, but then all your cover is blown with the discovery of epigenetics. You should have honoured your parents rather than disowning them.

Consequently, the available permutations of chosen travel (which broadens the mind, although often only trivialises the soul) become increasingly infinite (stet) in numberless number (stet) as time speeds up and light slows down. More and more, by means of the machines, we have made to replicate our own thought, and we let those machines decide for ourselves by the same means (technoeconomics and geophysics being only two of the many means) by which we have allowed machines to make up our own fast-shrinking (instead of fast-growing) minds.

In this machine age, we already worship the machine and, in turn, worship ourselves by worshipping the maker of the machine that is so much programmed to think and feel like ourselves. And so unsurprisingly, we feel completely distraught (as if facing a death in the family) when computers go down, or else we celebrate the wake of our own personal computer by replacing the lost one (as if it were a spouse) with the newest model. We don't think any longer to replace parts so long as we can go on proliferating new machines to simulate our fast-shrinking patterns of thought.

Only the increasing levels of future shock, when experienced by ourselves, at the results of letting machines make up our own minds (thus generating a closed system of solely human thought) bear increasing witness to our flight, both from faith and reason, instead of our fight to maintain both faith in reason and reason in faith. This, yet once again, is the way in which we see our own thought, when self-confirmed by our own mechanistic thinking (idolised by us through our worship of computers, calculators, and other humanly programmed machines) to be the answer to our own far closer, self-created, and self-integrated 'predicament of mankind'.

Of course, there may be consequences of being allowed to choose our own path, since the broad path is frequently the hardest road on which to travel, just as the seemingly shortest path is often the longest way around to one's inherently settled outcome. Keeping faith with that first promise of one's earliest beginning requires persistence of purpose in sticking to one's first confirmed direction of travel, which came intuitively with the first breath one took on being given birth. Yet alas, there's machine thinking now (which means that we humans don't need to think for ourselves; so too there's machine logic now (which means that we humans don't need to think logically for ourselves); and there's machine grammar now (one of many offshoots of machine language by which we humans don't need to pay the slightest attention to how we speak, what we say, any more than to what others think of what we say and how we speak—since it's hardly likely that they know any better than we ourselves know of what we mean by what we say and how we speak.

Here then is a further word from our superlative sponsor—the one and only sponsor of life in all its many forms—both earthly and heavenly. His Supreme Command for continued creation goes out into the void throughout every least part of his own constantly expanding universe. He himself, who fathers both writer and reader, is also father to both priest and prophet, to both preacher and teacher. By breathing into us the breath of life, he himself fathers also every mother and child. He alone knows how many stars there are in the sky, as well as how many grains of sand there are on the shore. He alone (when worshipped as Father, Son, and Spirit) is the only one throughout all our both known and unknown world and the only one who will never let us down.

Because we quantify knowledge, as if information were all the same quality, we suffer from informational overload, expose our elderly to dementia, and deprive our youth from founding their faith in values. Knowledge thus loses its power, and information loses its significance. The key to good health is good speech; the best speech therapy is through constant communication; and the key to human survival in this already fast-dying world lies in the highest and most heavenly form of prayerful communion.

We humans are thus in sharp decline at every level—the arts, the humanities, the sciences, as well as in professional, governmental, managerial, and administrative services. Overloaded with apparent trivia, we know not what to do, which is another reason why we hand over our own human predicament to be resolved by machines. Sorry, but for all the handing over of humanity to machines, that sort of metaphysical and transformational resolution just won't happen. Aha, but hold on, no matter how much collateral damage may be caused and unforeseen consequences eventuate, the ultimate outcome must hinge on what for most humans will be entirely unexpected!

We can programme all of ourselves into machines (perhaps), but we can't programme into any machine what we haven't got within ourselves to programme. There is thus no human predicament whatsoever, except that which we make of ourselves by considering ourselves to be limitless in power, limitless in personality, limitless in experience, limitless in character, limitless in knowledge, limitless in wisdom, and limitless in progress. 'He tangata, he tangata, he tangata'—whether voicing the limitless sovereignty and supremacy of mankind over all the universe and in whatsoever language of Latin, German, Russian, Greek, Finnish, or Maori—is simply bullshit in each and every way that could possibly be fulfilled by man alone, and this despite whatever credit we give to our own computers and other ingenious machines or to any other means of lifting ourselves up by our bootstraps.

Without some superlative sponsorship, we are nothing—as nothing in a wilderness of nothing—and with every passing moment, we subject ourselves to such self-deception, making ourselves increasingly vulnerable to being declared void; and this not merely for all time (for we are all tempted to make a mark for ourselves to outlast our own time) but instead vulnerable for all eternity in our being reduced to that presumed state of nothinglessness, exactly as if we had never been born. And for those of us, of which there are many immersed in their own means of seeking this world's salvation, who ask for themselves no more than this state of nothinglessness to succeed to what little they've known of themselves in this world, then they have been promised under the universal law of 'ask and receive' the fulfilment of that request whereby they shall be rendered to nothinglessness as if they had never been born. Why, you can't have a bilateral foot in each conflicting camp and still aspire to the full width, height, and depth of radial symmetry. All time and space (never mind all of the other dimensions) is against you.

Nevertheless, to those of us who do not yet know how to answer as military men to this Supreme Command, then today's world, with all its constant warfare and no more than plausible peacekeeping, must surely present itself to be one of the most brutal and scariest of places. Surely this is so, especially when our awareness is self-limited to no more than thinking to know its physical dimensions.

No, we are buffered by our own personal pride, we are beset by our own personal power, we are uplifted both by the acclaim of others and by our own self-acclaim, and we are providentially sheltered from recognising so many of what would otherwise be the increasingly limited necessaries for our own day-to-day survival. What we have made of this world to counterfeit the real world is thus one of the scariest places in all the universe. It has become so because we ourselves are opting more and more to take the credit for the real world's creation rather than for its disintegration. In the same way that FREEDOM entails RESPONSIBILITY, so also PROVIDENCE entails STEWARDSHIP.

In today's fastest-moving but rapidly disintegrating world where substantive content is press-ganged into the boldest of editorial headlines, our compulsive speed-reading of **FREEDOM entails RESPONSIBILITY.** Alas, for our untold lack of these attributes (being more than a sufficient evil unto this day) serves only to allow tomorrow's freed-up front page being just as boldly headlined for tomorrow's greater evil. Then, by the corresponding huzza-headline of **PROVIDENCE entails STEWARDSHIP** we speed-readers shall most comfortably fail to notice the loss of these further attributes tomorrow.

At the same spacetime, since headlines can be reduced still further down to more clinical formulae to suit and promote the mystique of popular science (in the same way as $E=mc^2$ can be made to hit the front covers of the tabloids) then $F \vdash R$ and $P \vdash S$ more than confirms the ongoing loss of these same attributes without any need for expressing it. Using such equivocal means of governmental sloganeering, the soft-selling Soviets for some relatively small splinter of their own time excelled; and for our own moment, under the rubric of **SUSTAINABLE EXCELLENCE** there also appears to be 'peace in our time'.

We can reverse the transformational equation from pie in the sky to pie here on earth as much as we like, but it's not going to work any more than by trying to pull ourselves up by our own bootstraps—and this whether in trying to get to heaven by our own work credentials or by bringing heaven to earth likewise by our own work credentials (with both more and more of this work being left to machines). Learning to love (although in itself a loving work) belongs to a far different level of work than looking for the highest return from learning to work.

This is not to say that our exit from this physical dimension and entry into other dimensions is devoid of risks. On the contrary, how we exit the physical dimensions of height, breadth, width, and temporal space to entertain or augment the supervening spiritual dimensions of reality within the limitations of our purely human awareness is so fraught with risks that this gateway, either to heaven or to hell, holds back those fraught with fear, fraught with worldly success, fraught with counterauthoritative power, and fraught with every other form of self-indulgence.

Besides our need for a transformed mind, we have a need for a universal metaphysics. We are all too often motivated only by physics—the physics of finance, the physics of welfare, the physics of influence, and even by the physics of failure, by reason of which it is our fear of failure that drives us to partake of what we would most seek to avoid. On the contrary, there is a metaphysics of fulfilment—a transcendental metaphysics of fulfilment that opens hearts, strengthens willpower, and transforms minds—that drives out from us all fear of failure. Of this transcendental process, we have not the faintest notion until we hear our calling from the Supreme Command.

This is a calling like no other calling; this is a command like no other command. And we receive it often only in escrow—as the lawyers call it—long, long before we are even aware of it, for it begins to operate only when we begin to act on it. Most usually, this supreme calling, even when given anticipatory in escrow, is heard by us only after a life-or-death experience. It may be the death not of our own life but of another's life. It may be the death of what we ourselves have mistaken for being that of our own life. It may be a desert experience—the death or abandonment by a spouse, the loss of a child, or of our falling victim to a grave injustice or to some other turn of (what we may mistake for the throw of) a dice.

The paradox is this: those who see heaven have, besides their great gift of spiritual awareness, comparatively little (in terms of the perceived health, wealth, and transient happiness of this world) to lose in making their choice. And that FREEDOM OF CHOICE, as so often exercised between either heaven or else hell, is exercised either in response or in reaction to the Word of the Supreme Command.

The Word of the Supreme Command, if we listen for it, is spoken directly by himself into our lives. It is not sponsored, as by that echo (amongst the many echoes of other voices), when heard by us only more indirectly (and as often falsely) about how our lives should be lived. Instead, we learn to recognise his voice, appreciate his advice, and so willingly learn to obey whatever may be decided under the Supreme Command. And the paradox of our freely accepting allegiance to this Supreme Command is that we shall be thereby set free from every form of counterfeit allegiance like never before.

He who is most laid captive to this world is also the most blinded by that experience to think himself also the most completely free, so this breaking-away process that must be undertaken by every captive spirit is usually one of apparent turmoil. To be sanctified through the universal laws of metaphysics is no easy process. A long life within prison walls, especially after having climbed to the top rungs of this life's cursus honorum (or ladder of self-promotion) to become, perhaps on behalf of other prisoners, no more than a governor of that prison, does not make for much less than a fall from that topmost rung in order to see and appreciate the freedom that pertains to belonging to the other side and being on the other side.

Thus, writers, by exercising either their own hard-learnt effort or alternatively their own vivid imagination (or else a combination of both), frequently see themselves to be in full command of their own literary endeavour (and so, in turn, imprison their readers in their own false command). Without the Supreme Command, even although inspired by the creator of all things, almost every writer's work is still destructively tainted. They may have the best of human intentions, but without having heard their true calling and put that calling into action, their resulting work contradicts their own best of intentions.

That which is strategically evil so often assumes the tactical role of whoever would purport to do the most good. The do-gooder (himself an expendable fall guy who often ends up being a bully boy, a hatchet man, or a world dictator) is foremost in the ranks of the destroyer of all good things. We waste our energy, first, on promoting such people to positions of counterfeit authority and then, secondly, on lambasting them and ourselves for having rendered ourselves powerless by putting them there. Thus, counterfeit champions of democracy bring despots to power, and counterfeit champions of morality reduce societies to libertarian lookalikes.

People like specifics; they like to point to other people, either to blame or praise, instead of looking to themselves. We could do so, but each of those we blame or praise through history, whether revered or despised by us, is not entirely a self-made man. Likewise, neither our own process of blaming or of praising them, since we too are people of the same sort, can be entirely objective. They too, like us, can fall victim to powers and principalities. We all have a tendency to overextend our very limited powers of judgement, as if good and evil were completely within our own cognisance and as if we were so authorised to do so by the Supreme Command.

But this sort of encouragement towards those whom we revere, as well as our disparagement of those whom we despise, is only to fight, as often against ourselves, in the purely physical (which is just as often the moral or intellectual) dimension. In that physical dimension, we choose our own leaders, either by this political means or by that political means, and then for their failure (most often as fall guys) to fulfil our expectations, we invite ourselves and others to witness their imprisonment in places such as St Helena and Spandau Prison or their beheadings (with others) as in the football stadium in Kabul.

'Allahu akba!' nearly everyone shouts to such an execution, as severed limbs and then the victims' heads hit the field, before (believe it or not) the same game of death by a hundred cuts plays on in so many of the world's war zones as well as games arenas. Like so many of ourselves, these scapegoats or fall guys lack the metaphysics of fulfilment, that metaphysics of fulfilment which opens the heart, transforms the mind, steels the will to persevere, and drives out all fear. And so then their work falls to the ground through the collateral damage they cause, the unforeseen consequences they give rise to, and above all, the immense pain to themselves and to others that they bring about (not always straight away) through their own friendly fire.

But what of the writers and journalists themselves? Are they up to mark? We don't like bad news, so to get our heads round the message, we first deprecate the messenger. And it wouldn't matter whether the message really were (stet for being a subjugating subjunctive) that one of bringing good news of the gospel. No, instead of being received as good news, that's increasingly seen as bad news by many who either don't want to hear or else who openly deplore the gospel. None want to know how bad they are before hearing for themselves the call to be good.

Nevertheless, not even divine news is always good news. The prophets have a harder time of it than the priests, since nothing, absolutely nothing (whether for evil or for good), ever happens without having been first foretold. The trouble is that most folks keep their ears only to the ground (where rumours abound) rather than looking and listening for the signs (good or bad) of the times.

Meanwhile, there's never been a prophet—no, not even the greatest far less the merest novice—who, during his life (before being stoned to death or crucified), has been held to be up to any good in his own hometown! Aha—but thereafter in that town's central business sector, he-or-she (whether Malusha Malkova, Joan of Arc, John Knox, or John Wesley) soon become the biggest of tourist attractions. Aha again, but no jurist, for his-or-her needing to be both prophet and historian, can afford to be so blasé.

The historical fact is that nothing, whether for good or bad, ever happens without having been first foretold in the divine, and that is what it means to be truly divine (punning intended). The voice of the Supreme Command always speaks androgynously through his or her continuing creation and as often into the soul of the earliest believer as if what's heard were no more than the whisper of his or her own voice or as a vision of his or her own mind, whether during daylight hours or seen when fast asleep as either a night vision or else as a dream. Around these things, myths and legends are told and woven, monuments are raised, heroes and heroines are raised to places of respect and even worship, because people would like to forget how, way back in their own time, their own forefathers stoned, slayed, and crucified the prophets.

* * *

BOOK SIX

Second Thoughts
This Recurrent Darkness Called Night

A More Certain Guide
The only light in this dark night is that which burns
in the soul: and that burning is a more certain guide
than could be afforded by the mid-day sun.
St John of the Cross, *Noche Oscura*

Intro 1—Augustus (still steadfast): This twelve-book series (already only halfway through completion) began as a report commissioned by the Supreme Command into the state of all human tribes and of all human nations. These make up what mankind (forgetful of the ant, the flea, the bee, and the bison) is so proud as to constitute itself the supreme ruler of (1) this whole wide world and, from there on, (2) all this still expanding universe and, thence far beyond both these, to lay claim to (3) all that constitutes the cosmos.

Intro 2—Kingston-Braybrook (classical scholar in an age of self-indulgent libertarianism): The earth's deadline is already defined mostly in terms of encroaching darkness, because wherever there is darkness, it is that darkness which is the more obviously illuminated and thus most intimately revealed by the increasing intensity (power transferred per unit area) that results from any diminution in the cosmic speed of light. Thus, evil appears to have its fling in these latter days, but only because it is being searched out by the one true light. Nevertheless, because of this highlighting of evil by the one true light, mortals shun the relatively unseen good, and just as moths are perilously attracted to any and every sort of light and so to their death on any dark night, then mortals indulge themselves more and more in their own form of dicing with death because they cannot distinguish between darkness and light.

Intro 3—Samuel One: There are different gradations of humanly discernible darkness (morbid, corrupt, pitch, deep, midway, shallow, and superficial), no less than for the human visual spectrum, there is the multicoloured rainbow of colours for light. Indeed, there are evil forces to counterfeit the entire spectrum of light, just as there are also differing wavelengths (with their different amplitudes relating to intensity) for true light. The spectroscopy of good and evil (for being only a small part of the entire electromagnetic spectrum) is studied as an applied science in heaven (although grotesquely overlooked for lack of the requisitely sterile lab conditions both on earth and in hell).

Intro 4—Walter-Walters (a Scots-Polish émigré musician): In the phenomenology of spiritual matters, especially concerned with the contrast between darkness and light, recognition must be paid to the dark night of the soul. One encounters a season of spiritual desolation devoid of all consolation. It is a desert experience, either induced to test one's faith or else encountered, some say naturally as a learning experience, as one travels along the spiritual way. It may pose as physical burnout, deep depression, overwhelming oppression, or as feelings of utterly forsaken abandonment.

Intro 5—Leading-Agent Emma: Like very young children, we so often mistake darkness for night and night for darkness. For a long time, in our growing up (and not all adults are completely immune), we may remain scared of the darkness and even afraid of the night. Yes, there are such things as ghosts and bogles (no less than witches and wizards), but then maybe you've never journeyed across Scotland's blasted heath or walked along the shoreline of the Karori Hills or travelled through some parts of the New Zealand bush or walked the deserted streets of Minsk, each at dead of night.

Intro 6—Leading-Angel Ninian: Nevertheless, whatever the process for you—whether short and to the point or long, drawn out, and lengthy—there were once two women, Dorothy Doanne and Allene Brumbach, who clearly saw beyond the physical. We know this because, as retold by Demos Shakarian in his autobiography about *The Happiest People on Earth*, they each (or at least when both together) had that 'rare and wonderful faculty of being able to sense the invisible angelic host which the Bible [the Full Gospel Believer's edition, where every word counts] tells us [of that heavenly host which] sometimes visits the earth'.

But of course, we know of all that very well already because of what we celebrate by way of joining with the heavenly host every Christmas to celebrate the coming of the Christ child, Jesus Christ. Besides, here I am, and so also, here right now are many other angels doing something of the same sort of thing (and more so) every Christmas for you. Believe you me, says Jesus Christ himself, that to be born again is far more important to the individual person than just the fact of having been already born.

On this score, whether looking back (regressive) to go forward (which often is the case) or else going forward to find oneself looking back (progressive) can each be—in terms of contrasting light with darkness—the precursory (or preliminary) phase to being born again. For example, Nicodemus (as many others like him) took advantage of the darkness (simply because he was less afraid of the darkest night than he was of the mind of man) to visit Jesus by night. 'And unless you're born-again,' Jesus told him, 'you'll remain unfit for the kingdom of heaven.'

Intro 7—Leading-Agent Alcuin (as always, a librarian): You want a word of knowledge? Here's more than one such word: 'God speaks through books!' Why, the Bible itself (at least sixty-six books by forty different authors) is a whole library in itself. Nevertheless, many of us, especially unbelievers, remain afraid, sometimes scared, and even occasionally petrified with fear and turned to stone and not just always because of the dark but yet for so many other good reasons that it would require yet another whole book to be written about them. The nightingale apart, we retain some presentiment of nightbirds such as owls and of bats, frogs, fleas, worms, wolves, and other creatures that live and hunt by night. We label scholars bookworms, because very often they are the only ones who have taught themselves to see in the dark, and for some reason (which would take yet another book to explain it), this scares the proverbial 'living daylights out of them'. This is one reason why true scholarship is so much avoided, particularly amongst colleges of higher learning.

Intro 8—George Barton (once and forever Queen's Counsel): There's not much joy in pleading before any court of justice which is blind to the light. The blindness may be temporary, or it may be permanent, but wriggling round the law to advance the course of justice may neither demonstrate the blindness nor expose the truth. On this score, the blindness may remain transient and temporary, or else it may become systemically permanent. So then on the difficulty of distinguishing between the transient and the permanent, there is a very presentient (or insightful) short story about a man, blind from birth, who suddenly recovered his sight. Alone by himself during all that first day of his restored sight, he understandably became overcome with fear that as evening approached and darkness fell, yet again he had become blind. Now that's a scary story (of which there are many different versions), but the one to which I'd refer you to has (as I hope you'd prefer) a very happy ending. [Exegesis 1: Beware of every ghost or haunted house story that has a mischievously unhappy ending. Remember that even Charles Dickens was forced by popular opinion to change his first intended ending of *Great Expectations* to a happier outcome.]

* * *

The History of Recurrent Darkness
Part I

> Back to the Beginning …
> I needed to start school … In order to protect myself
> and the other students I would use a different name.
> In August of 1986, the embassy hostage crisis had not
> been forgotten, and the Iran Contra Affair was about
> to capture the world's attention.
>
> Mahtob Mahmoody, *My Name Is Mahtob*

'Suffer the little children to come unto me,' said Jesus Christ (much to the amazement of his closest and not quite grown-up disciples). Perhaps, for being yourself a little girl yet for being caught up in the sorry affairs of this world which no longer allow you to go to school, then as well reading of little Mahtob, you should read also of a little girl called Malala Yousafzai. She too has written of herself in her book *I Am Malala*. Here she tells her own true story of how her steadfastness to the point of death in standing up for the rights of women to receive an education has changed the hearts and minds of all humanity across the whole wide world.

Where do you stand, dearest readers, on this subject of universal education? How would you explain this subject, both in terms of what is meant by *education* and in terms of what is meant by *universal*? So then how would you implement universal education? Do you think that boys and girls are so very different that each should be segregated from the other in their education? If yes, then why yes? If no, then why no and not yes? Exactly, if not quite precisely, because both boys and girls belong to one and the same human universal yet still differ in many, many most delightful aspects of their shared complementarity.

Take time for sufficient thought, but for the moment, back to little Mahtob as well as to little Malala, for each being children having much more than grown-up initiative, influence, and worldwide impact and all this, as any educationalist would say, 'for the good'.

Meanwhile, how do you relate the concept of *education* to the concept of *freedom* in such a way that those who are free to receive an education won't take that fought-for freedom for granted or rebel against the responsibility that every exercise of freedom entails or start to classify, categorise, and accredit to themselves and to others frequently false levels of learning by which what was once a freedom is so far taken away that thence through intellectual snobbery, excessive competition, and class consciousness, the old primeval darkness afflicting both thought and feeling fast falls again?

Darkness, even in the physical (when quite often the darkest hour comes before the dawn), comes even more often when the Counterfeit Command (for being then the closest it can get to the Godhead) pretends to be the backside of God. Believe me—even when speaking to humans (as if I too were human and not an angel)—even then, dear readers, still believe me when I proclaim that kind of darkness to be nothing at all like whatever Moses may have glimpsed (or thought himself to have glimpsed) for being the backside of God. [Exegesis 1: It may help life scientists to think of God (for being radially symmetrical instead of bilaterally symmetrical) thus looking the same (without any backside far less front side) the whole way around.]

The trouble with recurrent darkness (as conjured up by the Counterfeit Command) is that it projects itself into almost every human activity, where it masquerades itself either as the true light, or else for failing to secure credibility in so doing, it then purports to be either prevailing darkness, persistent darkness, continual darkness or even that constant darkness by which it hopes for itself to be mistaken for the real creator of this much put-upon aging world.

You know, sometimes this whole wide world (www) seems like no more than one great, big, and frightful scam. But don't you believe it, because that's just what the Counterfeit Command wants you to think. Remember this: evil purports to triumph wherever there is light. And sometimes, those who see the extent to which the Counterfeit Command (purportedly in the name of the Supreme Command) has caused this whole wide world (www) to appear as if it were no more than one huge scam is seen more clearly for being so by those who are thereby held deprived of their full mental, emotional, and motivational faculties, so as to be labelled—at least the deprived, if not the disabled.

These poor souls—described so specifically in the great works of both fiction and non-fiction and so generally experienced by all people, either of themselves or of others in their personal relationships—are so seen by yet others who deem themselves (a legalistic phrase) either to be completely normal or so superior or so privileged by birth, class, wealth, or intelligence as to be exempt and immune from all the wiles of the Counterfeit Command, then of those disabled to be in need (as they may well be) of medical attention or social welfare or spiritual ministry for being deprived of their human faculties. The ultimate consequence of their dismissal (on account of their assumed deprivation or disability) is to be rejected as unworthy of the human race—as have been the Jews, the Slavs, the Eskimos, the Negroid, the Romany, the Maori, the Australian Aborigine, and even down to the Irish, the Scots, the Polacks, and anyone else who appears off the chart for standard shape and standard practice. Yet every single human person, just by the very slightest change in the flow (however strongly established) of history (whether it be that of heaven or of hell), is vulnerable.

If you want to know more of how this wholesale disparagement and dismisal of many different peoples comes about, then read *The Pedagogy of the Oppressed* by the international educationalist, Paulo Friere—although until you read also his *Pedagogy of Hope: Reliving 'Pedagogy of the Oppressed'*, then his earlier work won't make for pretty reading. Of course, there's nothing new in all this, whether in Imperialist Russia or in politically fractured Brazil, as those readers of Tolstoy's *Resurrection* will recognise. Those poor disabled and socially ostracised souls seen to be in need (as they may well be in need) of medical attention, or social welfare, or spiritual ministry, for having been (at least pedagogically) deprived of their human faculties, are a worldwide force for righteous freedom (but only when coupled with a corresponding forcefulness for accepting righteous responsibility).

For as long as this rapidly aging world lasts, the darkness is recurrent, and yet as the force of battle between this outgoing world and the incoming world strengthens, the recurrent darkness (as a sign of the times) grows more and more evident. The disparity (most obvious between the haves and the have-nots) grows exponentially (as apparently unlimited resources become more stringently and severely limited). None but those made aware by the signs of the rapidly changing times are in any way invincible, except by their faith in a future already long foretold; yet by reason of that faith, they shall be shunned, made a fool of, and even martyred for what may seem to be their hollow faith, all done by their self-styled superiors on the basis of what lies, deceptions, and delusions put about by the Counterfeit Command.

Sure, there can be a counterfeit enlightenment by which evil is enticed to show its hand, but wherever there is any sort of light, then evil will purport to triumph. It helps here to discern true revelation from false enlightenment. To do so, most times you need to go right back [like Huckleberry Finn or Mahtob Mahmoody] to reassess the source or start.

Whether theologian or scientist, you may not like what you read here about prophets, mystics, and magicians [but we were all mystics once], so in this front-line report from the field of battle, I shall preach about prophets neither to the pulpit nor to the pews, not even to the professedly pure scientist stuck in his clinically clean laboratory (who, for the sake of evincing his own need for popularity to fund his increasingly expensive research, no longer wears a white coat (if he can help it) by which to provoke the white coat syndrome of scientific exclusivity).

No, instead of preaching anything to anyone at all, we shall prophesy here, in this part devoted to explaining as well as to dispelling the resurgence of darkness, only to those who are for themselves in dire need of prophecy. They are in dire need, whatever the cause, for their being amongst the abject homeless—the abject homeless who steal from dumpsters to ensure their own survival; the abject homeless who have no other place to sleep but on the streets; the abject homeless who, as the old Anglo-Saxon Chronicle from long ago affirms, have no family.

And yet it is this oldest, most closely integrated, yet least exclusive and most publicly beneficial of all human institutions, which this woeful world has ever witnessed, which, all over the western world, by such policies as the recognition of so-called 'independent youth', the family is being sadly oppressed, suppressed, depressed, and politically undermined by secular governments (as in New Zealand right now). With the end of the family, our own era may well realise into actuality what previously would have been regarded as the downside of some highly imaginary but dystopian novel.

You may mistake that prophetic proclamation of dire need for being only one of hollow rhetoric, but where there is a dire need, there is almost always a valid logic—however much that remains hidden to the switched-off brain—by which to justify (through authenticity) the passionate rhetoric. Indeed, for doing every slightest thing with all of one's heart, with all of one's mind, and with all of one's might, there is no possibility of remaining passionless, whilst by those who favour such a passionless state of the sleeping soul (mistakenly rebuked by the professional for being unprofessional and a dirty slur on the valid logic of both properly impassioned rhetoricians and properly impassioned politicians), the Counterfeit Command moves to dispense with all but the most counterfeit forms of passionate preaching, passionate teaching, and passionate prophecy. Besides, in these end days, there shall be (and not just will be) Old Testament prophets who, like those present at the time of the transfiguration of Jesus Christ, shall rise again to prophesy with passion as if from their graves.

Besides, if you, as true philosophers who love to know the Lord (and not as the stoics, cynics, and scoffers whom the Counterfeit Command uplifts to fame and fortune and the Supreme Command still loves but turns away from what they say and do) are truly in tune with the eternal truth of my word, then besides all logic, all morality, and similar rules of law, you will learn to know my voice and to recognise not just true prophecy for what it is but to know all things, more by the gut feeling for the truth that I give you according to my way, and for the truly spiritual instinct you are given for hearing my voice (that is to say, the voice of your Lord Jesus Christ) to recognise that besides my being both the truth and the way, I am also the veritable spirit of prophecy that joins us both together for the sake of eternal life.

Let me tell you this about the mischief that can come through academic overthought, says the Lord: that if my servant Martin Luther (who, in his youth, was like most people a typical academic in relation to logic, to law, and to language and so also to philosophy at large and then likewise to theology) had thought (as he was prone to do to excess when I so allowed him) even just a little more seriously about hammering up his ninety-five theses on the door of the Castle Church in Wittenberg, then, like most others who let a prophecy fall to the ground before ever being proclaimed, he most certainly wouldn't have so proclaimed them by tacking them up to the door. As said before, a prophecy comes, whether at night or during the day or over a week or over a month or over a lifetime, like a great gut feeling for the truth, and that even when the Holy Spirit may sit unforeseen and even for years all unseen, like a dove on one's shoulder for as long as the proclaimed prophecy remains unfulfilled.

'So what are you going to do about all this?' asks the Supreme Command. 'Because a prophecy … is not a prophecy … is not a prophecy at all, unless and until you do something about it … do something about it … do something about it,' continues the Supreme Command. 'You haven't pinned it up, so you can hardly let it fall … let it fall … Or if you do let it fall, I'll give it to someone else … Here, don't let the pin fall … for the purpose of pinning it up … to hammer up, if need be … And what will you think of yourself then? I simply don't need to guess, but the dove that now rests on your shoulder might well then constitute for you an unbearable load even when passed on to another … But I don't think I'm going to let you get away from this … so I'm telling you now … that it's most unlikely that I'll pass it on … So what are you going to do about it?

'You could write a book about it,' proffered the Supreme Command. 'You've been writing books all your life—some published, others never published, and many others, both already written and still to be written, as yet to be published … So then what do you say, what do you say, what do you say? Okay, well then just remember that books are for keeps, whereas virtual reality is never more than virtual. Indeed, for lacking true virtue, virtual reality is often so much less virtual than it looks. Having no virtuous claim to any sort of reality at all, from one day only to the next, it pretends to exist for being yet no longer around the day after.

'Come on, mate ... make a move! This is not a game of chess ... nor even of the North-West Frontier. We've both already long begun, and you don't even know it ...

'Look here, I too have written books,' said the Supreme Command, continuing rather modestly with a smile. 'So I know what it's like,' confessed the Supreme Command. 'And not all published ... but countless, countless, countless more books ... as many, many, many books as there are grains of sand on the shore ... both books written and books published, sometimes by me directly but mostly by me through others ... sometimes here and sometimes there ... once as by a moving finger (that was fun, but also rather sad) on a palace wall ... once as by my son, your brother, whilst he doodled in the dust ... And I can do the same for you, although it won't ever carry the same clout as once on Patmos, so let me know when you've made up your mind to take me up on my offer ...

'I can't wait too long. These are the signs of the times ... Central Asia, now post-Soviet Central Asia is once again in almost complete turmoil ... And I said complete t-u-r-m-*oil* because (whether real or imagined makes no difference) there are huge oil, gas, and energy reserves over there in that part of the world, and the impending decision whether to flow the oil east or to flow the oil west makes for problems which are not even known about outside the post-Soviet Caspian countries of Azerbaijan, Kazakhstan, Uzbekistan, and Turkmenistan. What is clear is that we are back into the power politics of an earlier age, which you, as some sort of Sovietologist, as far back as of the North-West Frontier, already know something about.'

So do you think that for being only tokens of the past, only historical replicas from the days of Moses and Elijah but not in any way again true prophets of the present, they too shall not speak again? Do you think that for being only these token prophets from the past but not again true prophets of the present, they shall compromise the severity of what they have to say about things of today? And do you likewise think, although it takes them to the very point and then beyond that very point of their death, they shall speak to please the rulers of that day, those who dismiss them for being Old Testament prophets who by now, in these days of mass information and almost instant communication, are obsolete in both mind and body and yet again in both heart and soul without all measure? Don't you recall reading from Georg Hegel's *Phenomenology of Mind* that until someone has truly faced a life or death issue for him-or-herself he is short of being a proper person... ...

So too, if you think so today of Moses and Elijah for being obsolete and out of date in this present day of la-di-da new reasoning, in this present day of la-di-da new science, and in this present day of la-di-da new technology, your prophetic sense (if you so prefer to call the spirit a sense) of authentic science, your prophetic sense (as you will) of scholarship, and your prophetic sense of life itself is each and all going to be, first, severely endangered and, secondly, severely remaindered, and thirdly retributively retired.

This, as in the days of Moses and Elijah, although you may not know what it feels like today until the danger itself falls—although not by flood this time but by fire—is today's prophetic message from the Supreme Command. It is not a threat; it is not a promise. It is instead a prophetic warning. Although as always before and mistaken for never before, this prophetic warning can be confirmed again today by the signs of the times.

A prophet, as distinct from a priest, is someone special. He or she is made special by reason of their prophetic calling. Read closely the Word of the Supreme Command, and you will find that nothing happens—whether sooner or later, whether sought or unsought, and whether righteous or unrighteous—until first prophesised to happen.

No less than this whole world was brought into existence by the power of the word, this same power of the word, whether proclaimed scientifically (by way of proof) or intuitively (by way of insight) or in any other way (as by divine inspiration), forecasts every little or slightest subtle change (whether perceived or not) in the way we live. Read the signs—they all have subtitles, footnotes, and endnotes—for without the prophetic gift in all of us to read the signs of the times, we would not still be around to revel (as we are all encouraged to do) in the present power of prophetic revelation.

Explorers, inventors, and research scientists, as well as the most creative of writers, composers, and artists, tend towards being not priests but prophets, whereas teachers, ministers, managers, accountants, and lawyers tend towards being not prophets but priests. So you will see that we are not just talking about what (we assume) happens still only in churches, temples, and great cathedrals (although these days may happen there no more often than not) but also of what (these days more obviously happens) by way of open worship, committed prayer, and prophetic proclamation in football grounds, race tracks, political meetings, parliaments, polytechnics, and universities.

We are not writing here (as if sitting in judgement) of what is righteous or unrighteous but of the spontaneous (and sometimes even autonomic) exercise of worshipful, prayerful, and prophetic functions and roles. Like curses and blessings, all these functions and roles may be exercised either seriously and significantly or else trivially and insignificantly, and although the respective outcomes may differ enormously between each level of employment, both levels operate (sometimes interchangeably for a weak blessing to effect a curse or for a trivial curse to effect a blessing) so that their forms, functions, and roles are constrained by many other different factors. And this happens no matter whether these forms, functions, and roles are either understood or not understood as such by those who exercise them.

We acknowledge that this new view of the old ways of looking at things (to see, for example, that we pray more for miracles on the football field, in the law courts, and on the surgeon's table than we assume ourselves to do when only in the churches and in the great cathedrals) may be highly controversial. But then most new ways of looking at very old and long-established things are far more controversial than when we are content (without any serious macroconsideration of microcauses and microconsequences) to promote or proclaim the novelty (especially the technonovelty) of some just very new thing.

As for the very old and long-established ways of seeing things, however, we tend to get trapped into the temporality of space and time—the logistics of place, the role of person, the formal aspect of function, and the functional aspect of form—to lose track of the basic fundamentals by which history and prophecy are but two correlative aspects of the same phenomenon whose severance from each other in any field of study promotes false prophecies resulting in counterfeit science and governmental mismanagement bringing about social disorder, together with the curiously overlapping of yet false and often contrary specialisms and the (sometimes explicit and very obvious) refusal to learn from our own mistakes.

Indeed, absolutely everywhere—in each case, where people are gathered together or are collectively engaged in some common pursuit—in terms of the basic metaphysics of their human personality, they are praying and worshipping, preaching, teaching, and prophetically promoting whatever in their own case may be their own profession of faith, whether in work, science, sport, politics, the arts and humanities, or teaching and education. Indeed, they do so even in the professedly secular institutions (often in themselves the fiercest hotbeds of praise and worship (although for being professedly secular, then mostly couched in self-praise and self-worship) where, whether or not aware of their inherent religiosity, (1) they seek either stoutly to hold to the way things are by way of their priestlike, pastoral ministry or else, as prophets of change, (2) they declaim or proclaim the things they see that should be other than the way things are or else, as most usually the case, (3) they either try to amalgamate both pastoral and prophetic gifts or, as in the case of church–state separation or of legislative, judicial, and executive limbs of government, institute and operate by way of separate powers and divisions of labour.

We may not be able to say where all this universal engagement in today's increasing religiosity (comprising often highly conflicting praise, prayer, worship, and welfare) is going (some say uphill with a righteous blessing, and others downhill as damnably accursed), but it may help to profile this increasing religiosity (rising as never before amongst professedly secular institutions whose several religiosities— as between departments of state, no less than between church and state—come increasingly into conflict). It is this once again religious conflict, in terms only of the primordial relationship between conservative priest and radical prophet, which we are examining. [In the *Little World of Don Camillo*, these traditional and radical roles of priest (Don Camillo) and prophet (God himself) are for the most part suitably reversed.]

Every culture—Hebraic, Greek, Roman, Slavic, and Goidelic, to mention but a few—have their priests and prophets. What follows is but a scratch list (comprise your own) of priests and prophets. Amongst the most radical prophets (take your pick) are from Elijah, Socrates, and Jesus Christ to Darwin, Marx, and Newton, together with (amongst the moderns) Spengler for his *Decline of the West*, Einstein for his general theory of relativity, and Toffler for his *Future Shock*. Amongst the conservative priests (again take your pick), there's a scratch list of Alexander the Great, Pericles, Napoleon, George Washington, Abraham Lincoln, Winston Churchill, as well as rogues like Joseph Stalin and Adolf Hitler. As said before, we are not writing here (as if sitting in judgement) of what is righteous or unrighteous but rather of priestly and prophetic roles, forms, and functions. [Author's note: And remember that the counterfeit priest, like the false prophet, is, to our very fallible hearts and minds, most often the most persuasively convincing.]

The conservative role of the priest, particularly of the pastoral priest, is [often strangely] static, whereas the more radical role, particularly of the fervent prophet, is [often startlingly] dynamic. They clash—the conservative and the radical, the settler and the pioneer, the prophet and the priest. [Author's note: For the churches and universities in Germany being strangely static explains how so many of them so unthinkingly came to support Adolf Hitler during WWII, just as the radical forebodings of the otherwise conservative Winston Churchill would be dismissed until, on account of those forebodings being fulfilled, Churchill would be 'elevated' to the priesthood of premiership.]

Priest and prophet may have different seasons, drawing close or moving distant, but by and large and by reason of their different callings, both pastoral priests and futuristic prophets tend to diverge from one another rather than converge towards each other in their respective roles. They work best in tandem, but as for past, present, and future, each in different temporal and spatial dimensions. So just as truth (as well as every form of scientific and legal proof) needs a sustainable and relatively static context for its acceptance, teaching, and promulgation, so also social change needs a sustainable and relatively static context for the acceptance, teaching, and promulgation of that same dynamic change.

It follows that the future still remains always contingent on the present indicative as that is only apparently settled by the past (without further exercising our freedom of action) to promote the future perfect. Most prophesies, for their fulfilment or avoidance, are still open to being prayed in or prayed out or simply acted on to promote their fulfilment or avoidance. That is exactly why, without every need (according to its season) for such divergence between the static and the dynamic (between priests and prophets) to be righteously accommodated in every place of prayer and worship (which fails not just in one season by having too many priests without prophets as also in another season by having too many prophets without priests), this demographic imbalance will exaggerate the respective differences between and so reduce to or else promote or sustain a wrongful or unseasonal balance of the static and dynamic.

This happens by force of his or her anointed role, whether one likes it or not, and this role, whether one likes it or not (and many priests do not like this distinction, which, in turn, makes them less of a prophet), happens by force of his or her prophetic calling. Indeed, it is still extremely difficult, although not unknown to be both a priest and prophet. Nevertheless, prophets have a proclamatory (and sometimes also a declamatory) role that does not sit at ease with the pastoral role of a priest. And of course, there are false priests and completely false or counterfeit prophets whose objective is to falsify the truth, invalidate the way, and destroy the life. And of these alien priests and prophets to the cause of life, the more pastoral priests, often tripping over their garments in haste, don't confront but instead run off most comically in fear and trepidation.

A lot may depend on the times, so there may have been seasons (sometimes a hundred and more of years) without a prophet. And at other times, there may be no more than a single prophet, or yet at other times, there may be a whole host of prophets. Moreover, there are prophets who speak but do not write, just as there are prophets who write but do not speak. A prophet may be told to write because none listens to what he says; or a prophet may be told to speak because none reads whatever he is told to write. And yet again, for the sake of a certain situation, it may be a season in which, perhaps for utmost urgency, a prophet may be told to both speak and write.

All prophets need to be severely schooled. Having the gift of prophecy (which is far more common than generally recognised) does not by itself sanctify the gift, and the greater the gift, the more the need for sanctification, the wider the life experience required, and the deeper and longer the schooling. As already said, all prophets need to be schooled most usually in suffering as well as for being sanctified (through faith and works). They must have a lightness of spirit—a sense of humour even—to deal with life's (so often bitter) ironies.

Like every committed writer or reporter or journalist, however, these prophets are messengers from beyond—it may even be just from next door (because with every passing day, the kingdom of heaven is nearer to hand), or it may be from some far country, like from Afghanistan or Iraq or Iran—of which we need to know. Of every such smallest thing, even the direst prophet needs the lightest touch. It follows from every prophet's need for a pastoral ministry with words that he too is a priest, but it does not thus follow that every priest is a prophet any more than every priest needs to have a ministry with signs and words.

Instead of receiving and passing on the lightest of touches received from the creator of all things, some writers (and prophets too) worry themselves to death over the way to put (what they think are their own) words, words, words and especially as to the influence these same words, words, words may have (whether so sought or not) to their own favour as seen by others. Like publishers and editors, authors also may be seeking (often unbeknown to themselves) only intellectual or artistic influence (as often affording only yeast to the flesh), no less than far more mundane means of acquiring fame and fortune. In this way (as yeast to the flesh), such writers suborn their Supreme Command by letting the reading public command for themselves what in all creation shall be written to be the most popularly read.

What is most popularly read is most popularly thought, so the rising of this earthly yeast to satisfy the flesh is taken over by governments, no matter whether those of church or of state (since none is immune). A book requires a patron—a person of influence (whether intellectual, moral, or financial) to promote the writer's book—then a publisher (likewise having such promotional influence) by way of undertaking its promotion. And in a reverse way, some state and church governments devise systems of censorship and/or authorisation by way of encouraging or withholding publication. Each of these ways of promoting and determining what is popularly read and popularly thought has strengths and weaknesses—but as often (even for the most spiritual of texts and (Bible commentaries) substituting a humanistic system of cultural, moral, legal, and sometimes even political values merely clouds rather than clarifies the communication of the Supreme Command.

If we take seriously whatever may be the least word of the Supreme Command for us even when that word (at any time yet for all time) is no more than whispered into our lives, soon, under his constant counselling, we shall have our own whole life story transformed and made complete to be finally and irrevocably confirmed in his sight. His lifelong sponsorship, once accepted and held to by our faith in the Father's concern for our lives, cannot be faulted.

He alone is the supreme tactician of ways and means, as well as being the supreme strategist of purposive action. Privileged by his sponsorship, we have his everyday presence, which we humans need, lest in our own more casual and less committed minds, we mistake the tactical process for the strategic purpose and so, in turn, mistake the everyday means of our own due process for our own life's ultimate end. It is only through his Supreme Command that we can unify our own human form (made in his own image) to serve its ultimately divine function and so transmute the means by which we live first to secure and eventually to reveal our own divine end.

So then before fighting any battle, even that battle for birth (since even before the birth from which we need to be born again, we are all potentially men and women prospectively engaged in military action), we are already engaged in warring against those forces that would still further limit the range of choices we could make, although perhaps still unaware that our own exercise of any existing freedom logically must limit the range of all related further choice.

We explain that process to ourselves in terms of cause and effect (and as often consequence) and, later in terms, as often of unforeseen consequences, as if mistaking the element of the unforeseen as having nothing to do with us. Our life stories thus logically proceed from freedom to self-curtailment. This happens by means of our own responsive freedom through the risks we take, the rewards we seek, the choices we make, the challenges we accept, until we experience closure of that freedom-seeking process by facing the consequences of our most ultimate choice.

This life itself is then a multifactorial complex expressed in an equation unique to each person of his or her freely given responses to a multitudinous series of causal situations which eventually culminate in a consequence by which the effect of all these choices bring closure to that individual's life history—of which we ourselves, even of our own life story, can know so little until the full multifactorial complex of all our human lives culminates in its own fully collective and situational closure—at which point the secular and the spiritual once again recombine.

In both form and function (as much biological as physical, as well as being metaphysically spiritual), we are thus describing a process of soul-searching of which some of us still know nothing about, of which others fear to the point of their own death, of which others repudiate in favour of fate or else stonewall because of hate, and of which yet others embrace with all their hearts, with all their minds, and with all their souls.

For those who seek to hit this soul-searching mark whereby the divine and the secular metaphysically recombine, our Supreme Command gives constant guidance as to our hitting the mark, lest for our lack of soul-searching, we wander off track and so, instead of evaluating the struggle solely by the rectitude of our own responses, get bogged down completely in cause and effect or else confuse ourselves in terms of statistical likelihood and unlikelihood or in any of the many other ways by which we mistake order for disorder and disorder for order.

Lest we miss the mark by which this 'divinity shapes our ends, rough-hew them as we will', this Supreme Command may pose questions, relate parables, give us proclamations or counsel or words of knowledge or visions or insights or revelations or dreams. We may be shocked by the suddenness of the proclamation or struck by the apparent incongruity of the revelation or by the perplexity of the parable or by the intensity of the vision or left distraught by the discipline required of ourselves by the counsel or upset by the apparent meaninglessness of the word of knowledge that we require help to clarify the message.

By reason of our own self-induced discomfort, we are often too close for comfort to the message to unravel its meaning for ourselves. Thus, the parable or prophecy from on high may speak too personally into our own low lives that we should be able to hear its high-minded message. The task is therefore a collective one that we who are privileged to receive it should also need an interpreter.

Once, perhaps when children, we thought ourselves free enough to hear the Word of the Supreme Command, as this would be spoken directly into our lives, and we thought ourselves purified enough by our passion to hear this word given directly to ourselves to understand its revelation and to apply that revelation to our own not always high but yet often increasingly low lives.

Where priests failed, the Supreme Command sent prophets; where prophets failed, the Supreme Command then deputised his one and only Son; where the Word of the Supreme Command still failed to be heard, the Supreme Command sent the Spirit of the Word he had already given then to open hearts and ears still further to the message of the Word. Then even once more, he chose to speak directly into the hearts and minds of humans to open those hearts and to transform those minds that were otherwise so besieged by their own trivial wants (for personal power, prestige, and influence) that, even if then only to their own eternal damnation, they might still refuse even to hear the voice—not even the personal voice—of the Supreme Command.

There are those rebellious spirits who will not suborn themselves to military command. How then are we to deal with these defaulters? That is one of the biggest of many big questions in relating the enforcement of law to the administration of justice. It is so big a question that it can divide lawyers from jurists and so also lawyers from lawyers and, in turn, jurists from jurists. It can cause even law schools to outlaw jurisprudence from the study of law, and it can cause whole countries to abrogate from upholding their own law.

Lawyers divide legal systems into those that enforce the command theory of law and those others who operate under a far different rule of law. The difference between these two systems lies in the relationship between law (as a force) and love (as a means). One legal system (for lack of any better short description typified by Pharisaic, Roman, or Napoleonic forms of law), says most emphatically you *shall* or *must* obey the law. Whether by threat or fear of the consequences or not, the citizen is left without the least vestige of personal freedom by which to disobey. Instead, the law *compels* the subject's obedience outright. For example, under the Emperor Justinian's code of Roman law, the emperor's mere will has the force of law, whereas under the other great system of law (typified by the Anglo-American common law) the law merely points out the consequences of disobedience (and so actively allows for civil protest).

This relationship between law and love is intricate; the full expression of the universal equation is far beyond our present expression. It is not like any scientific or legal equation, which we as yet think to know, such as Kepler's three laws of planetary motion or Newton's law of gravitation or Einstein's law of relativity. These equations too, for all their apparent exactitude—whether by $F = G \times [(m_1 m_2) / r^2]$ to express what we think to observe as gravitational force or for $E = mc^2$ to express the principle of relativity—are not as logically or mathematically or scientifically or legally accurate as we think they are. They are no more than the approximations to reality, which our level of love and commitment to the pursuit of truth allows.

Certainly, it is expressly open in the scriptural dimension for any king or queen, whether of science or of law or of life, to enquire into such approximations and, through their earnest and academic endeavours, to seek answers to their questions. Without the full complement of love which we require for such earnest and often lifelong endeavours, however, these rough approximations are no more for the present than are the most apt (but least accurate) of legal fictions.

Nevertheless, on the one hand, there is the law of love, and on the other hand, there is our love for the law. And these different expressions of love (manifesting in the most righteous pursuit of every human discipline in the course of revealing greater and more accurate truths) are bound by the law of love to reveal more of themselves. They will not suborn themselves to those more totalitarian views of human conduct by thinking to do away with righteousness in their administration of legal rights or of jurisprudence in their administration of the law.

Through the law of love, we eventually come to recognise that the whole concept of love, like our concept of science or of the law or of language or of logic, is but at present no more than a legal fiction in our committedly loving pursuit of righteousness and justice through a legal or ruling framework. It once perplexed earlier thinkers to worry over whether there were laws in heaven. If you care to see it that way, then both yes and no or neither (as the angel replied to Jacob who asked the angel whether he was for or against him), because in heaven, there is no longer (since the fall of Satan and the triumph of Christ) a default position.

* * *

The History of Recurrent Darkness
Part II

Seven Emerging Woes
Woe to you who think yourselves so worldly wise
St Matthew, the seven woes of the Pharisees

Never mind your name (whether Matt, Cliff, Tim, or Tom) for the moment! Personal privacy, once having been wiped with the public bumf of political correctness, becomes now two of a kind with public notoriety. And although celebrity status has a short shelf life these days ... well, as we all know, even in the criminal courts, public anonymity can be enforced by means of personal name suppression. [Don't worry, that's all about to change!]

Thus, for so many of the rich, the famous, and the professionally well-known, as well as those upper-class persons (that they know themselves to be), well, they can come out of court chuckling as to their anonymity having become for them an almost human right. Yet how close have these anonymous persons now become to the Soviet non-person for having kept and not lost their celebrity status in the no less Wild West? [Never fear, things have gotten as low as they can go before they show!]

After all, as you say for yourselves (unless when seeking fame or for finding a fortune), what's in a name? So although before the dawn, we're dealing with fame and fortune right now (as fitting representatives of the false dawn) so that the correlative question of what's in a name (the ultimate issue) can be considered when we get to the end of this book. [Make a name for yourself, so they say, but then without fame and fortune, what's in a name?]

Well then, what's your work or line of calling? That's right, what do you do for a living, you who delight to answer this selfsame question when asked by others of yourselves? I know you're not beef boners or fish filleters any more than you are beekeepers or dustmen (not a job for women), because you hold yourselves apart as being so different from other men (and women). [Then fear not, since for being made in the image of God (so we're told), we're all made the same!]

You are obviously not amongst the ranks of the homeless or of the unemployed, since by now, you're walking past me all the faster. You are like three wise monkeys all in one, since you pretend to be unseeing, unhearing, and unfeeling. So then, mister, since there's no point in asking you, please to drop me ... just a dime!

Please mister ... just a dime ... But no, that only makes you walk faster. Nice shoes ... smart suit ... flashy hairstyle ... once there myself ... but now there no longer ... couldn't see ... what's coming ... what's still coming ... couldn't read the signs ... those same signs still there ... now all back here again ... yet not as once of distant things all afire any more ... but of all the same things up-close, yet tinder-dry and filled with fury ... yet all still the same old signs of these new times ...

Indeed, that increased pace—of nice legs, as even lawyers have nowadays—in passing by your professional predecessors tells me most emphatically both who you are and to where you're heartlessly heading. You are today's accountants, bankers, businessmen, doctors, lawyers, teachers, and priests of high finance. Well then, listen to this, because God has given to me, for having been not so long ago a most successful lawyer and business mogul in the making, the task now of breaking news far worse than you can professionally imagine.

Of course, you're not going to like what God (whether my god or your own god or his or her god) has got to say. So too, just as you treat me, so you also treat him—as a bummer. On the basis of my own military experience in the front line, let me assure you that it's not very streetwise to treat any Supreme Commander as a bummer. And let me further assure you that once you have seen our Lord God dressed in battle fatigues, you are not likely to forget either his power or authority or ever again to mistake him for being a bummer.

Nevertheless... spare me a dime, mister ... one can preach, teach, and prophesy as much as one likes to think of doing ...thanks, missus, bless you ... no less than one can pray as earnestly as one likes to a wailing wall or to a voodoo doll or to the church universal... bless you, kiddo ... but without the Spirit of the Lord over the prophet or over the preacher or over the teacher or over whoever lifts up the prayer, at best there's no breakthrough and at worst ... fuck me for a florin, would you lady, because that's a foreign coin ... eliciting a demonic response. So then take heed. Very soon, most of you are going to find life very hard (on cold, hard ground) and excruciatingly bumpy (even when up in the air), and what you feel of this when on your backside gets caught up in some counterfeit slipstream won't be a contrived joyride down Disneyland's Splash Mountain.

Now thanks to the technology by which most of us live off the fat of our predecessors, it's as if we're walking on the miraculously laid-out surface of the moon. We only have to take one gigantic step of our own for all mankind to praise our name and glorify our works. Nevertheless (single negative, rather like an orphaned or widowed preacher's page), most of us are going to be out of work very soon because of the changing way in which the law relates to our kind of society.

When rendered down (as of all worthwhile fat), what we think of as being our own kind of society (under its rule of law) will have become by then no longer any sort of fact but instead a very distasteful fiction. This is one reason why this book (sponsored by the Supreme Command and so predominately about love) is also bound, in more human terms, to be about our rapidly disintegrating law.

Yes, right now, this forewarning of a distasteful future seems so shocking to you humans that you would like to laugh it off as being ridiculous. You are too proud of your own prowess even to feel afraid. Yet why should the possibility of our being unemployed appear so absurd when all around us, there are lots of other folks without jobs, without work, and even without the remotest of aspirations?

'Oh, but these are just factory workers', you say, 'manual labourers and adolescents fresh from school.' There, see now, how far apart you hold yourselves from all such other folks! How can you be so sure that being an accountant, banker, businessman, doctor, lawyer, teacher, or priest entitles you to work? [Since tomorrow's not going to be the same!]

Let me tell you something even more unpleasant! This present threat has all come about because of our mistaken upbringing. Most of us have been bribed into education by the promise of worldly rewards. [You say, how come?]

Well, in many cases, parents simply wanted us youngsters off their hands. For this to happen, we had to become financially independent. We too wanted our own kind of freedom. So then we allowed ourselves to be corrupted by the prospect of a worldly return from education. We trained ourselves up to be our own boss just to get away from the bossiness of parents. Unfortunately, this is the bossiness in dealing with other people that still comes through in the professions. We are haunted by the ghosts of our parents who viewed children as an infringement of their adult freedom and who planned our professional lives as a bid to get us off their hands.

'Of course, we have credentials by which to follow our calling,' you say. 'In most cases, they cost quite a lot, as you know. Often, we never know at what cost they have been obtained until long after we have acquired them.' [Is this why the majority of well-educated people become a self-seeking and thoroughly discontented lot?]

At heart, we are still hurt children who have been misled into believing that to suffer on someone else's behalf entitles us to a reward. Our credentials seem to promise some return for our suffering. They enable us to practise law or medicine, to run a bank, to teach a class, to give financial advice, or to pastor a church; but most of us do none of these things for their own sake. No, we have some other end in sight.

Practising law or leading worship, so we have been brought up or taught to believe, are not ends in themselves but merely means to an end. Consequently, we go through our professional lives alternately fearing that our promised reward will be perpetually withheld or else by being bitterly disappointed by the way in which it falls far short of what we have been led to expect.

There is no point in putting this proposition of professional entrapment to parents. Most of them would deny it because they don't know how glad they would be to have their children off their hands. And this is why so many actually fear for their children, that they should fall out of their hands in unplanned ways. If they hadn't already planned for their own adult freedom by programming their children's lives, then they wouldn't be afraid.

'Historically speaking, sacrificing one's children to the professions is just a vestigial remnant of the mediaeval custom of sacrificing one's children to the church, or even much earlier, as it was before, the Lord spoke to Abraham and put an end to the ancient ritual of infanticide. Alas, yesterday's ritualistic infanticide has been replaced by routine abortion. Today's infanticide by way of abortion sacrifices one's children to the sort of society we live in. As evidence of the way in which we self-worship our own human society of today, there is no difference between the ritualistic infanticide of pagan tribes and the routine abortion of so-called civilised societies.

'So don't bother, all you discontented professional people, to blame your parents. That only self-perpetuates the problem. No, if you really want to break the genetic chain of servitude, you must begin by setting your own children free.

'How? Well, that's easily said but hard to do. Because this false security obtained by sacrificing freedom has been ingrained over countless generations and because all sorts of institutions such as public schools and parliamentarians living away from home are founded on it, rooting it out can't always be achieved in one single move. Until all bitter-root expectations are rooted out, they merely metamorphose into different forms of just as deeply demonic and counterfeit growths.

'Some people will lead you to believe otherwise, but this is only to substitute one for another kind of disappointment. On the contrary, as Kutuzov said of throwing Napoleon out of Holy Mother Russia, it takes time and patience, patience and time—in this case, to deal with bitter-root problems. Let's make sure we can deal with the problem of our own probable unemployment first before we try to solve it for our children.

'You still smile at the concept of someone with credentials being out of work. Look here! Things are changing. Can you continue to rely on your outmoded credentials to provide you with work? This really depends on whether your credentials were designed to do that in the first place. How something ends is always determined by how it began.

'You may have always viewed your credentials as a means of securing your livelihood. Some of you may even have seen them as the means of securing the best of all possible livelihoods. Thus, accountant competes against accountant, banker against banker, teacher against teacher, as well as each priest against his own priesthood. Yet look here now, things are going to change!

'Yes, some of you've always wanted to pastor the biggest flock, to govern the biggest bank, to preside over the most prestigious university, or to be renowned as the capital's leading lawyer. What disappointments lie in store for you when you find out that you actually feel for those you trample on and disparage?

'We forget that degrees and diplomas were devised for something quite different. They signify a state of passing out rather than of entering in. Had they been meal tickets, these fancy degrees would have said so. Academic aspirations have always been to fulfil the mind, not to fill the stomach.

'What brought about this devious diversion whereby a purely physical result is seen to substitute for and satisfy an entirely intellectual endeavour? Can one comprehend the extremes exerted by the substitution of the physical for the mental, moral, and even spiritual planes?

'The average university graduate these days can barely supplant the physical with the mental way of looking at things. No more than a bare few are privileged to reach the level of intellectuality, and fewer still reach any point of correlating intellectuality with spirituality.' [Yet look here now, things are going to change!]

'The width of a lawyer's waistcoat establishes him as a faithful father figure in the courts. What judge would not feel the dignity of the law best upheld, all other things being equal, by deciding in favour of the senior practitioner's claims?' [Yet look here now, things are going to change!]

'Have you never, as a newly fledged practitioner, heard senior counsel answer your case with the words "In all my fortytwo years of pleading before the courts, I have never heard such nonsense", and did not the judge then take you both into chambers after your indignant objection to remind you that the counsel on the other side was much your senior and so knew more about the case than both of you put together?

'Such things happen, don't they? But not always in exactly that way. When once a young lad in the courts, it was thus in open court and not in chambers that the judge thus shamed not just me but also himself and so, in consequence, the court and, were (subjugated subjunctive) he only able to recognise it, also the opposing counsel.

'It can take nearly a year or more to win the appeal from such a decision, and the surest way of winning the appeal is to substitute a bigger waistcoat for the appellant (that's worn by one's senior partner) than could be carried by yourself as a new practitioner. Court cases are as often won by the width of the counsel's waistcoat as they can be lost as a result of the judge's indigestion.' [Yet look here now, things are going to change!]

'The other professions are no different. Pastoral care is measured by a smiling solicitude of pleasantries. Woe to any priest, say all men of the world, who dares to challenge the right to change money within the temple. Though half his congregation should engage in adultery and the other half in fornication, their vicar is expected to keep on smiling and go no further during baptism than to smack the resulting bastards' bottoms.' [Yet look here now, things are going to change!]

'What, indeed, brought about this disgraceful degeneracy amongst those who profess to serve the public? Until we can discover, accept, and atone for our own shortcomings, we shall be at the mercy of what is going to happen. Because we assume that we have every right to feel secure, we don't realise how insecure we really are. What is going to happen when our whole world, as we now know it, suddenly falls apart?

'At the moment the world is found, like an apple, and all puffed up with our professional pride, what will happen when we find ourselves out of work? It will deflate as we ourselves fall flat. That is going to happen very soon, and because we have, as professional people, been misled into believing that we have more right to work than do others, this makes us, not them, more vulnerable.

'An accountant without accounts, like a barrister without a brief, turns out to be a far more fragile person than is any factory worker without an assembly line. This is because the professional person has been taught to listen for a call, if need be, even if that does mean whistle up a wind. Once established, all his training and experience leads him to identify himself with his job. Without accounts, the accountant is nothing. Without pupils, the teacher is nobody. Without clients, then what use is a lawyer? Without a congregation, what point is there to preaching?

'How adaptable is the accountant? Can he cut his losses once his credentials prove uneconomic? How quick can the teacher learn a new lesson? Quick enough to take up market gardening? Will the lawyer without a case to plead just sit twiddling his surplus thumbs? Can he analyse the justice of his unforeseen unemployment sufficient to reform the law of employment, or will he give up the law and turn to crime?

'On the other hand, the factory worker is only out of a job. He has never misled himself into believing that what he put of himself into his job preferentially entitled him to its continuance. Having less to lose, he could prove more adaptable. That has already been foreseen by those who put labourers before professional men, for labourers being amongst the first to go on the dole.' [Yet look here now, things are going to change!]

'Therein lies a different and far graver danger to democracy, that those who have not realised their fullest potential in choosing to be free to serve others as doctors, lawyers, teachers, and accountants are more amenable to being dealt with as slaves of the state. Freedom exists only to the extent of its exercise, and otherwise, atrophies away.

'There are always those on the lookout for some poor man who cannot pay his debts, not even the price of a pair of sandals, so that they can buy him as a slave. They may even bring him into debt for the very purpose of exacting his servitude. Meanwhile, should we pity more the poor professional man who is likely to lose his job even though he has exercised his freedom in choosing to serve others?' [Yet look here now, things are going to change!]

'No! After all, look at what has happened to the professions. For example, what has become of banking? Before, bankers considered it a professional privilege to take care of clients' money. Now they charge them a fee for lending their client's money to other folks as often to big commercial traders of their choice. Banking has degenerated into moneylending. There are, as once were formerly, now no banks any more.' [Yet look here now, things are going to change!]

'Before, bankers encouraged thrift, now they encourage spending, borrowing, and more spending. Governments do the same. Bankers tempt young people to begin a life of borrowing by extending them interest-free loans. They tempt elderly people to invest so that they win a prize in some raffle or draw.' [Yet look here now, things are going to change!]

'Can anyone tell the difference now between a casino and a bank? No, the swing doors, plush carpets, chrome and stainless steel fittings all testify to the fact that even the architects can't tell the difference. The bank clerks all dressed to look alike in black sleezy dresses don't differ much from croupiers. Is that why the banking system still stands, because like any gambling den, the only people who can't lose are the management?

'Look at lawyers! Consider how courts have become like casinos. Legal aid has become a lottery that lets lawyers grow rich by defending the most hardened criminals—sometimes over and over again. Legal aid, which means what it says, lets lawyers pursue the most trivial claim. Litigation has increased threefold since legal aid was introduced. The initial aim was of allowing poor folks to take their case to court.

'The reverse has come about because the tail of legal aid has wagged the legal dog. Lawyers are wealthier, and the rest of the country, poorer, as the result of the lottery of legal aid, as the result of the lottery of law reform, and as the result of the lottery of legal education. If Shakespeare were around today, he would claim that all the world was a casino and not a stage, although for watching television, it is more than frequently a lottery on stage, although all the men and women are still "merely players".

'What then shall I say about this nation of lawyers? Nothing pleases you! Everything you do is dispirited and self-destructive. When they are playing your tune, you expect everyone else to dance to it, but when someone else's tune is played, you immediately put a stop to it.

'So too, the great cities of the world go their own way as if the legal system were established by their own command rather than what they owe for their existence to the legal system. Woe to those who, from high towers and behind city walls, misuse the law to laud themselves over the humble countryside. They join one property to the next—as once prophetically foretold—so that nothing is left sacrosanct.

'O Father of heaven and of earth, thank you for hiding the truth of your law from those who think themselves so wise, and instead of revealing it to the wilfully wise, you reveal it only to little children. You yourself alone know how much more of a mess the wilfully wise would have made of the law had its truth been revealed to them.'

* * *

The History of Recurrent Darkness
Part III

Yet Again a New Beginning …
Mother heard [Little Isaac] out and said: [Dearest
duckling] 'they only need an excuse to fight. Today
they fight over oil; tomorrow, it'll be over soap or
cream of tartar. The fact is that they are evildoers,
and [it is a well-known fact of modern psychology]
that the evildoer feels the need to do evil. All they
need is an excuse.'
Isaac Bashevis Singer, *A Little Boy in Search of God*

A great many people (in these latter days of declining empires) want
to do things although they're not entirely sure of what they want to
do). They want to have things, and they want to get things, and they
want to have things (although they're not always sure of what things
they really want to get, or what things they really want to have, or
even why they really want to have and get what they want).

"It would be nice to have a boat," or so they think without really
knowing what it takes to maintain a boat, or else to have a bigger
car, without knowing what it costs to run a bigger car. Bigness across
the board (particularly the corporate board) becomes mistaken for
beauty, but eventually the mistakenly broad board (not just national
but also transnational and supranational) of apparently limitless
resources is bound to give way. This is a sign, not only of the bigness
we attribute to our own time, but of that reciprocal measure of sorrow
which is bound to follow, and which will be felt most fiercely at all
local and personal levels.

Most often, it's the process of acquisition rather than the fact of
acquisition which first attracts would-be purchasers (providing retail
therapy, so they rationalise) which then enthuses or obliges them (to
become either squanderers or hoarders), which finally augments
their acquisitive addiction (to the point over which they have no
control). And since the purchase of goods and services are taxed

by governments, then, instead of encouraging thrift, governments (to uphold business confidence, so they say) advise us openly to "spend, spend, spend!" Apart from the issue of personal debt (which many governments encourage in lieu of their own public debt) this is bad news in the long run for everybody (both governments and individuals) on all fronts.

Most of those material things (not dark in their own right) which many people persuade themselves to possess (but through indebtedness may never come to own) rarely do more than proclaim the fashion of their otherwise dysfunctional lives. Rarely are such acquisitions put to any relevant use which would advance their objective in the long run or which would secure their best possible outcome when credit ceases to be measured (as it is today) by debt.

Possession secured by debt is no security at all. The virtual ownership (at all private and public levels) which proverbially mistakes possession to be nine-tenths of the law will be reduced to one-tenth or less overnight by what may take little more than the slightest spin (up or down) in the already fast-fracturing global economy.

In extremely dysfunctional cases of misapprehended reality (which is what acquisition-fever is all about) where possession (at whatever public or private level) is pursued beyond the point at which available resources permit the presumed fulfilment of functional ownership, those parties (on both sides of the exchange equation) who have been afflicted by, or who have become addicted to pursuing the superficial appearance of things (now evidenced by the unavailability of resources required for the functioning of the exchange equation) the economic outcome is critical. This is so because the commercial factors can no longer hold to their presumed market value (at whatever public or private level the exchange had been presumptively engaged). The big question then is who benefits from any presumptive market falling apart? And the next and even bigger question is who brings about that breakdown for the purpose of benefiting from it?

By their own wants (not needs), they have been taken captive by the material world, and so then they fall risk to being consumed by the bonfire of the vanities being fast built up by the materialist world. What a void they have created for themselves, by their choice not to fulfil their appointed destiny! Which of them, big moguls all, shall be the first to be engulfed by flames whenever the least expected of all of them, for being far outside their approaching ring of fire, is the first to strike the match which, in turn, will light up the now darkening night sky from their already gathered bonfire with then its searing flames?

Without there being more to life than their own so superficial and thus selfishly inclined contentment, the prognosis for these committed seekers after their own masses of matter (whether real property, intellectual property, or just not-so-plain money-laundered cash) would, for all and others, be decidedly bad. How many righteous men and women (asked Abraham, the father of nations) will it take to save a small town, far more a city, far more a nation?

Seeking contentment only in the physical dimension, these great moguls (should they live long enough) end up by being amongst the most discontented of individuals. And since this discontentment of theirs is felt and expressed so deeply only in the spiritual dimension, whereas they are so intensely preoccupied with seeking contentment only in the physical dimension, this experience of finding the reverse of what they are looking for is something that is always disconsolately hard for them to take. In such situation, it takes a great deal of life experience to know whether you should pray for their fall in order to rise again, since spiritually, they'll be too far gone to benefit from their physical fall.

One can tell them (as kindly as possible) to look elsewhere for what they seek, but they are so committed to their present search that they fail to hear. Besides, as Tolstoy points out in his epic account of all things (and not just of *War and Peace*), they possess the worldly power (which they often use) to make a mess of whatever moves the lives of those who would humbly help them.

What profit (we ask them) can it be to anyone in seeking to be thus contented, seeking for something like the right thing in the wrong place, and time after time after time, still seeking somewhat of the right thing but still in the wrong place and, by this time, when long past midlife (and the point of no return), still so often in the wrong space? They have exercised a freedom of will to the point at which they have committed themselves to choose a far different set

714

of responsibilities from those responsibilities whose exercise will reap contentment.

Beware, we say, not only because what we say is being recorded for assessment and training purposes but also what we say is true to the book of life. It is true not only as measured by the living Word of that book, but also by that further truth and that further way as demonstrated by the life of Jesus Christ! We angels do so humbly warn you (just as we spoke through Balaam's ass) that your seeking of personal contentment without finding it puts you at great risk of becoming stoic or cynical about your search and so provokes you (through discontent instead of thankfulness) to turn your backs not just on where and how and why you and by what means you have so fallibly searched but on life itself, and so in some way or another (although you still vociferously deny it), you have chosen what you (both then and now) may little realise for being the path of death.

Mere wants, for their lack of passion (to get back to the underlying issue of their continuing discontent), are very different from our expression of desires. Indeed, we are encouraged to satisfy our wants (as well as our needs) without engaging our desires, and the result is that once having satisfied our wants (as if wants were needs, which they're not), we have no longer any desire by which to express even the most minimum level of our self-satisfaction, far less to express our ongoing passion (without which we cannot express even our thankfulness).

Wants are satisfied—most usually only self-satisfied (and so eventually dissatisfied)—whereas every true desire is most assuredly fulfilled. Most catch-22 situations arise out of conflicting wants. They are not even true dilemmas; they are merely parables, which may take whole books or entire lives to resolve. Yet when our most passionate of true desires are fulfilled, they lift our spirits to the next level of passionate aspiration. Especially in times of indulgence, we have few real needs, an excess of wants, and a dissatisfaction with both ourselves as well as with most others, including all those who, instead of encouraging our most passionate of desires, have diverted our passions to the pursuit of the most self-indulgent of personal wants.

Now true wants—no matter how much we crave their self-satisfaction—are never true necessities. Our addictive pursuit of this self-satisfaction (when satisfied) quickly turns ourselves into the most passionless of self-satisfied but completely unfulfilled people, often madly competing against each other for the increasingly limited resources by which to satisfy our needless wants.

Without enough passion for soul-searching, many less than serious folks give up on the search for meaning (a.k.a. significance, which some other more serious folks may ascribe to the search for God). Sometimes the word of knowledge and even its interpretation is so very exactly and accurately and precisely given that it requires further pondering. Yet it may take further prophecy, another parable, and more intense interpretation for the eyes of our heart to open wide enough for us to see, sense, and understand what it will take for us to recognise the target aimed at by this word of knowledge, far less (or more) than even feel it hit the bullseye.

Words (whether of knowledge or not), whilst both at large in their changing context of usage as well as by themselves etymologically understood according to their history of modified derivation, have various and varied levels of meaning. Words like *niqab*, *desuetude*, *logical*, *logistical*, *algebraic*, *algorithmic*, and *metaphysical* each have lengthy conceptual as well as experiential histories built into their present confirmed but increasingly confused understanding. Without the slightest hint of prophetic history in our human makeup, we will dismiss all such talk of linguistic confusion from our present conversation and change from that confused topic to the next confused topic to be discussed not with any word of knowledge (unless from hell) with the supercilious but commonly heard phrase (categorically enough, when heard from hell) of 'that's history!'

Truly enough, even when uttered from the yawning mouth of hell itself, that phrase, when uttered knowledgeably as it can be heard often made from heaven, then means what it says according to its heavenly level (although categorically dismissed by hell) of prophetic history. So although time may move on and the way in which we fight over the meanings of words, appropriating and disappropriating them for sometimes opposing purposes, the living Word of the Supreme Command is everlasting, insofar as the sole purpose of different renditions is to regenerate and communicate their unmistakably and initially true meanings as well as their true values.

As well as keeping tabs on how well enough poised is our concept of the balance between means and ends, process and purpose, tactics and strategy, the task of holding fast to the eternal word in its eternal meaning is one of the strategic concerns of theology in its pursuit of divinity. As well as that of employing the linguistic expertise and historical knowledge amongst the many other due theological processes by which this strategic outcome can be achieved, this pursuit cannot be achieved any more in theology than in law, logic, and language and in both moral and natural philosophy without keeping faith, collectively as well as individually, with the words we use.

Very much mistaken (in metaphysics) is any person (as many people are today at almost every level) who believes (like Humpty Dumpty) that words can be given whatever meaning he or she (whether judge or jury) chooses to give to them. Thus, for the sake of accuracy and exactitude, the Supreme Command has no hesitation in making this report for what often will prove to be difficult reading, difficult hearing, and difficult understanding. Dearest readers (both friends and foes), it is not the Supreme Command which has made these increasing difficulties but you yourselves, our dearest readers.

That's exactly why, for everything the Supreme Command says or writes, he or she (or it, for being the tactical and thus triangular Trinity on earth or the full, already triumphant triumvirate in heaven) always provides a fighting buddy—the Paraclete, to borrow from the Greek language, the most significant name for that personal fighting partner who will look after your back in any military fray. So then fear not (as the master of tactical theology frequently says) since all facets and aspects (both plain and parabolic) as well as all tactics and strategies (both of infrastructure and superstructure) are under our Supreme Command's full control of this merely mopping-up military operation whose success is already assured.

Whether told factually as in a description, fictionally as in a story, reportedly as in a historical narrative, figuratively told as in an allegory, or passionately as with preaching, one must learn under the Supreme Command to ponder on our sponsor's every whispered syllable. However differently we may be led—sometimes in the arts, sometimes in the sciences, sometimes in each of the professions, or alternatively in one of the trades—it can pain us how differentially we each hear the same words of the Supreme Command. Nevertheless, the key to such diversity on earth is not the common law of conventionality.

Instead of conventionality (instilled by brute and often unthinking obedience to command), the key to diversity on earth is again (our already mentioned but rarely studied) jurisprudence. As already said, jurisprudence stands for the relationship of law (even universal law, as well as that of all earthly legal systems) to justice. Hallelujah!

But of course, what we angels mean here by jurisprudence is theological jurisprudence, as commonly studied by us intern angels in heaven as Laws 101. This theological jurisprudence (where justice is mine, says the Lord) is hardly ever studied if at all on earth, but wherever so studied is bound by its nature to produce both strange and explosive consequences. It can provoke a spiritual ferment by which to stand previous teaching on its head (for which purpose read Gonzalo Arias on the subject of the poster people (or encartelados), or Ivan Illich on the subject of deschooling society, or Paulo Fiore on the pedagogy of the oppressed. It can exile or outlaw its proponents from their convivial colleagues, conformist colleges, and comfortable countries (as it did the present leading agent responsible for writing this report). It may exile them (whether in the spirit or in the flesh) to Afghanistan (that was hell), then to Myanmar (that likewise was hell), as well as to Syria (that too was hell), no less than to many other *stans* (or nations) before called back again to Afghanistan, and there again to teach the same old jurisprudence, but only of the faintest theological nature (in what was once reportedly a private law school somewhere in the sticks of, say Allalabad, Dar-es-Sallam, or once again Jerusalem). Again, hallelujah!

In case you haven't already picked on the tune to which we're singing the praises of this book sponsored by the Supreme Command and called *The Soul-Catcher* (although snidely renamed and caricatured by the Counterfeit Command for being *The Soul-Snatcher*, thereby mocking its chosen marketing mode of soft-selling (although not in hard covers), seven (or eight, at last count) separately identifiable books for just the price of one)—a snip, as they say, in bibliographic circles—this still remains (according to the completely independent assessment of our marketing managers) a unique work of twentieth-century theological jurisprudence.

In other words, this *Soul-Catcher* has no time for the hanky-panky of institutional life, which relies on reducing or seducing the life of the professions no less than the life of the proletariat (for being merely Adam and Eve and Pinchme) to live on by no more than institutional proxy. Aha, but that won't be living for long, as the old nursery rhyme tells us; since on all going down to the river to bathe, not you and me (for being Adam and Eve who drowned) but then saving only Pinchme (to starve to his death on K rations) will give no greater consolation to the proxy-professions or to the proxy-proletariat, than to Pinchme.

Alas, we live only by proxy, whether under the conventions of any professedly secular, professedly communist, professedly democratic, or professedly religious life. We think of the Supreme Command to be conveyed only through another's long-buried dead bones (brought back to life) and his long-ago shared blood (by which every day is a remembrance). We ourselves are brought back to glorious life and not by our own dead bones and stagnant blood, left for dead on the field of battle.

Likewise, as a work of the utmost theological jurisprudence, this account of the Supreme Command, even when ministering to 'the lower depths', has no time for the equivocal grandeur of constitutional life by which everything moves by clockwork on the outside. This ever so expected happening on the outside only happens to happen because every inmate within the constitutional facade is quite unexpectedly called to spend all his or her time and energy winding up this world's increasingly rundown clock on the inside.

Well, that's a clock, which, by reason of its fast-failing mechanism, can only be repaired on the outside; whereas we, by reading the signs of the times, have a clock which can be both adjusted and even repaired from the inside. Better to be with the Supreme Command in the front line of the lower depths, therefore, than to serve the upper echelons of earthly power when they are being fast overtaken, on the outside by both telescoping time and stretching space, to advance the inevitable outcome of the last and final conflict.

One (but by no means last) word right now from our sponsor to those already in the front line and prepared to do battle straight away on behalf of the Supreme Command. Some people talk mysteriously in whispers (most usually, it's the mysterious mathematicians, but now also the logistical logicians) about the above so-called higher powers. Yes, no doubt that is somewhat the case, especially when considered in the rough-and-ready (and oh so relative) way of speaking which prevails in these increasingly uncertain times. Certainly, there are higher powers and lower powers—no less than there are the empowered and the powerless—but absolute (rather than just relative) power is held only by our Supreme Command, and our understanding of this absolute power not only enables our obedience to it but also enables us to participate in its exercise.

To state the extreme case arising from our obedient participation—yet that which is by no means an uncommon case—our exercise of this absolute power through our obedient response to the Supreme Command *empowers the powerless*. That is exactly why those searchers after truth, like the theosophists who think to mix and match what they see as the strong points of all the world's religions (and so constitute that perilous 'sea of faith' which the poet and prophet Malcolm Arnold so accurately denounced), render themselves so utterly powerless by distancing themselves from participating in the absolute power of the Supreme Command.

* * *

The History of Recurrent Darkness
Part IV

If Taken Lightly
You can be arrested and threatened with death if
someone reports you for converting to Christianity
in Afghanistan. It's not something to be taken lightly.
Deborah Rodriguez, *The Kabul Beauty School*

What is it like to be a leading agent in the field of war? Well, that is what this book is all about. And that's why it's written by a leading agent to the Supreme Command. Most folks might think any such writer overly self-centred for even thinking to being sponsored by the Supreme Command. Never mind, for once having been a leading agent fighting for the Supreme Command in the front line of its many battles, why hide one's light under a bushel by not speaking out on behalf of the Supreme Command?

Never mind, such critics (in a crisis, which is the only valid place for criticism) wouldn't object to calling themselves Christian any more than they would object to me calling myself Christian. And I guess, for myself being still undercover, even when as a leading agent of the Supreme Command, they don't know the full facts, as they might say, for my claiming to be now no more than a leading agent on behalf of the Supreme Command.

Most people don't see themselves as any sort of agent, unless thinking to lead for themselves, in which case, they presume themselves to be a principal and so not any sort of agent in receipt of superior orders to serve any other person, far less all other people. Leadership and agency are intricately related to each other in terms of the Supreme Command, so this book will have a lot to say not just about agency but also about leadership.

Leadership tends to be something to which we all aspire, although sometimes we mistake a want for a need, and self-promotion for divine appointment. There is the hardware of the soul (which you'll have already heard and read about, but we too easily equate with the physical brain) that often needs healing before there could be any prospect of divinely appointed leadership. And likewise, there is a regime of maintenance we need to learn by which to keep our software free of bugs and in good working order if we are of the mind to process those military orders which we are called upon to execute by the Supreme Command. As in the movies, we are so often stand-ins, including stand-ins even for the Christ we crucified, and there is a logic to this process of atonement for our sins, as well as a divine irony in our privilege now to be Christ's stand-in.

Wherever we look, we tend to see the broad easy-going way and not the hard narrow way—sometimes trying to bring up our own children to be perfect angels when that is not at all the extremely hard and narrow way (for their own good) that they should go. We're trying too hard (as often motivated by our own needs and wants) to make things easy for them. We do the same for ourselves, setting ourselves impossible tasks, as if we ourselves were so much higher than instead of only a little lower than the angels.

Sometimes, the Supreme Command has the mind to allow us our own mind to determine how, when, and through whom of his agents in the field we are to be saved. If there are fallen angels as well as fallen agents (who, for being agents, are still only a little lower than the angels), then surely, if fallen agents can be saved, then just possibly so also fallen angels can be saved.

Then again, we may apparently do all things right, as if like the anointed kings of Judah, we too were royalty. And then so it is that we make a reputation for ourselves, which soars beyond the ken of mortal men, until, through self-pride and incautious encouragement, we blow the gaffe and fall to earth in flaming tatters. We look for gifts—gifts of leadership, such as those exercised by those who, through their personal fame and fortune, generate a following—without realising that gifts, especially those gifts which generate a following of those who want to share in the same largesse of leadership, are really responsibilities.

To understand and so hopefully avoid this default position from whatever fame and fortune accrues to us, we must read of those princes of Judah and Jerusalem in the days of Uzziah, Jotham, Ahaz, and Hezekiah, the kings of Judah when the prophet Isaiah (agent first class) ruled both Judah and Jerusalem through his prophetic vision from the Supreme Command and when great was the anger of that command (owing to the kings chosen and obeyed by the people) in being kindled supremely against his own people. The nearer to the monarch or president, then often the more vulnerable may be the subject or citizen; just as the nearer to the pulpit (for the preacher) or the nearer to the academic chair (for the professor), the further may one be from God.

Through Christ, we are all priests and kings, but most usually priests, kings, and prophets are vastly different persons—as vastly different as most usually are pulpits from pews, parents from children, and professors from students. Since it takes the desert experience to make any full-scale prophet (although all believers should expect of themselves to prophesy), the priests who pontificate and the prophets who prophesy each see things, one from the inside of a pastoral ministry and the other, if not from the outside with the hunger and thirst of a desert dervish, at least looking outwards as a nightwatchman from the city wall.

Here is no matter of contention but rather of the utmost attention. Thus, the whole concept of being a leading agent (whether in peace or war) poses intricate issues of free will, the exercise of personal initiative when committed to serve some principal other than oneself, as well as that of keeping faith with the Supreme Command on whose behalf one has been already chosen to serve as a leading agent. Peculiarly enough, most of these issues (of free will and keeping faith) are resolved when one realises that the relationship of leading agent to the Supreme Command is one that is always held in time of war.

Every freely committed leading agent of the Supreme Command in whatever field of war he is called to serve—whether as teacher, preacher, nurse, scholar, or medical man—is thus called to be also a military man, however much that may be no more than to fight undercover to promote peace, which, considering his everyday call to do battle not on his own behalf but on behalf of the Supreme Command, may surpass even his own present understanding. Accordingly, until his cover is fully blown and he goes to glory, no leading agent is ever out of the field of war.

So much for the field of war and of the military discipline required when working as an agent of the Supreme Command in any of the many fields of war. It is a matter of traditionally human logic (now much denigrated by the shock tactics of full-in-your-face headlines, the evocation of deep-seated emotions when often triggered by no more than free-floating feelings (if not inducements to indulgence, then principally those triggers evoking fears), yet all accompanied by an almost total lack of reasoning) to work one's way (as once was the norm) from the general to the particular. So here now, only after such principled generalities have been exposed, are some specifics.

Afghanistan—where as an angel of hope I am at the moment and where I will be for some time—is a very big country. You may not think so when you look for Afghanistan on the map, but then maps, for being drawn solely to their own scale of significance, tell you at most the physical size but never the interactional significance of a country. Besides, not many of those Pashtuns, Tajiks, and Uzbeks, each of whom contribute their own ethnic and religious woes to the interactional significance of Afghanistan (apart also from the Pakistani militants trained by the Taliban on Afghan territory), would recognise Afghanistan on the map, far less be able to tell you from the map what were the surrounding countries.

You can pay me a visit whilst I'm there, if you like, but it will mean hard work, seriously hard work, so no time there for sightseeing, far less for slumming. No, not allowably that, any more than is this a picaresque novel through which one slums the whole wide wicked world within one's own head. The forcefulness of the picaresque and the pornographic never fail to fortify each other.

And I'll take you out myself (in the military sense) should you come over here for slumming, and no less for sightseeing (in the very same military sense of being taken out for that), since, whether with or without a niqab, you'll be forced, sooner or later, to face up to witnessing some unfortunate Afghan's beheading. And this is exactly why this story of mine doesn't make for easy reading, since tourism is for the effete, and there's no room for the effete in Afghanistan.

That same ruthlessness of purpose applies as much to me as it does to you, since the delegated authority I have under the Supreme Command to take you out applies to me as an author as much as it does to you as a reader. Don't mistake this level of legitimate ruthlessness under the Supreme Command, which, by reason of its purpose—as by the bombing of the turncoat French Navy by the British during World War II—falls far short of that peacetime ruthlessness applied by many so-called civil governments (and their lackeys) to their own citizens. You might not like what you hear or believe that you're hearing from God when you do so, but to distinguish wishful thinking from prayer, we all need to be ready to chew God's ear.

If you can't understand the instructions from the Supreme Command, then there's no point in saying 'Yes, sir. No, sir. Three bags full, sir' before carrying out orders. That's what gave rise to the charge of the notorious Light Brigade—'Canons to right of them, cannons to left of them'—when they all went down at the Battle of Balaclava. Sometimes you have to chew the ear of the Supreme Command. Yes, indeed, sometimes like Father Abraham, you just have to chew God's ear.

I'm a military man myself (at least until I break cover), so when I tell you that one very small drone on behalf of the world's mightiest nation happens to be targeting some remote village in the goat-grazing backblocks of Afghanistan right now, there's no denying that, in terms of interactional significance, the war in Afghanistan suddenly acquires a site specificity to fill world headlines. International significance and not brute size is what counts nowadays no less than it did in the time of David and Goliath.

You might never have heard of theological jurisprudence, where the battle for souls is more often now fought by the Congregationalists than the clergy. And there's a reason for this spiritual imbalance between crowded pews and lonesome pulpit that has case-hardened the growing distance between the clergy and their congregations—whether professedly Baptist, Presbyterian, Episcopalian, Congregationalist, or denominationally belonging to any other sort of church government. This is because the church, itself always a sanctuary, more often only serves now as a hospital than a strategic command post and, more recently than even that, often only as a hospice.

The fighting spirit of the church (when denuded of its Old Testament origins as well as faith in fulfilling its ultimate revelation) has gone into remission throughout the Western world. The clergy have never quite grasped their continued need for grass-roots reformation. How different is this world today from that when every ordinary fellow was made extraordinary by his preaching the Word of the Supreme Command from every market cross! We angels wait with baited breath and bleed with righteous desire to hear from the Supreme Command through the next John Bunyan, the next Malcolm Muggeridge, and the next C. S. Lewis.

How extraordinarily unique was once then every individual—whether writer or reader, preacher or teacher, speaker or listener—considered to the kingdom of God! The key to dealing with such diversity is not institutional conformity (in itself the sign of false religions). That sort of institutionally cloned conformity imprisons the mind, closes the heart, and quenches the spirit. Look here, I tell you as a fighting man (okay then, as any undercover angel) so that you, the reader, may see how different all the regiments are of fighting men (and angels)—why, as different as are all the nations—and, even within one and the same fighting nation, how different from each other regiment are the Scots Greys, the Gordon Highlanders, the Black Watch, and the Highland Light Infantry!

As much in going to war as in winning a war, whoever has moral ascendancy holds the trump card, but only for as long as that cardholder, both before and after the war, manages to stay in the moral ascendant. Holding on to moral ascendancy is a hard task, both in military action and when out of action, and one that requires of every military man to be schooled in the ethics of warfare.

Oh yes, the laws of warfare may be long gone, but hang in there for as long as the ethics of warfare survive the conventions by which another's terrorism acquires the legal status to sanction the insurgency with which we blithely choose to reciprocate that terrorism. By trying to outlaw war, first, by the laissez-faire of the wimpish League of Nations and, secondly, by the impish disunity of our own United Nations, we have done so much more than just reduce the laws of warfare to desuetude. Instead, by provoking what has become outright terrorism to fill the vacuum and so thereby sanction our own insurgency, we have undercut and overwhelmed whatever justification could once be given under international law to our maintaining any balance of power under the recognised rules of warfare by which to keep the peace.

Despite the present level of almost complete disorder amongst what were once independent nations (none of which is any longer a nation for lack of that needful independence), there's still as much statesmanship required in time of peace as needed in time of war. Accordingly, all statesmen (as much as military men) need to be commissioned as military officers to serve in both peace and war, and this as much for them to keep the peace by winning wars as these same wars may take to keep the peace.

Meanwhile, here's a tactical diversion from the present Anglo-American bombing of Iraq, Iran, and Afghanistan when tracked back to at least the Second World War. This tactical diversion is thus more apparent from fiction than from hard fact since, when extracted only from records of past action, it relies solely on what so many readers (including the foremost of general historians) will never read for being merely military history.

Thus, the Second World War could have been fought and won (if any such need to fight still arose) by reading Liddell Hart on the First World War (much prophetic forecasting of which seemed then like fiction). Likewise, without any understanding of how this present war (wherever waged) is still being fought (as often by drones, now from far further away than ever before from the field of actual conflict), we have not the remotest idea (far less understanding) of how the Anglo-Americans still come to be waging war in places like Afghanistan. It's a cliché (however false) that history comes to be written by the victors, since none can be sure of knowing the victors (far less their victims), and in most cases, as in the continuing aftermath of the Cold War (no less than so much earlier of the Peloponnesian War), it becomes increasingly evident that all leading parties to every such engagement have lost every such thing as every such war was ever fought over.

Likewise, every such military campaign (from Nimrod to Tamerlane, from Genghis Khan to Napoleon, and from Kaiser Bill to Li'l Adolf) produces its own crop (as so seen from the opposing lower ranks) of tragicomic leading figures—from the sleepless Stalin to the dithering Chamberlain, to the farcical clowning of a Khrushchev, and thence far beyond the stagnating self-preoccupation of a Brezhnev to the insouciant seriousness of a catastrophic reformist such as Gorbachev. If not a man for all seasons, most surely a man of all seasons, since Khrushchev (here borrowing from historian Robert Service's *History of Twentieth-Century Russia*)—'at once a Stalinist and an anti-Stalinist, a Bolshevik believer and a Menshevik cynic, a self-publicising poltroon and a crusty philanthropist, a prodigious troublemaker and a cheerful peacemaker, a stimulating colleague and a domineering boor, a strategic statesman and a cheap politicker who was far out of his intellectual depth'—still remains, together with Brezhnev, the most popular Soviet statesman (even this long after the demise of the Soviet Union).

Yet the quasireligion of militarism, especially when convened in cahoots with land-grabbing imperialism, quickly develops a sense of mission by way of trading off obsolete weapons in the arms market, getting rid of surplus weapons by opening up new war zones, and testing out new weapons ostensibly to maintain the preferred balance of power.

But at the risk of breaking my own cover as a military man, let me tell you that without the so-called North-West Frontier (and its widely related territories) being exploited for as long as Britain and Russia and other empires have gone to war (as much against each other as against the locals), the continuing hostilities (including 9/11 against the USA in 2001), as well as what will surely follow, remain completely inexplicable. In the same way, but for certain breaches of faith by the Allies in the Second World War, there might never have been any Cold War.

* * *

The History of Recurrent Darkness
Part V

Winning World War II
Old Joe in the Kremlin is feeling pretty aggrieved of
late. Look at it from his point of view: we have broken
off the convoys; got bogged down in North Africa and
let the Red Army do the brunt of the winter fighting
in Europe; we've even got him to forswear the cause
of world revolution, even though he had sworn over
Lenin's dead body never to abandon the concept ...
All that and still no Second Front.

Eileen Townsend, *In Love and War*

Call it folklore and not history, if you like, but it takes a considerable
degree of abstraction (never mind for the moment, Ivan the Terrible)
to get one's head round what's still going on in the Kremlin. It's there
still, where the dispirited ghost of old Joe is still trying to forgive
himself for swearing over Lenin's dead body never to abandon the
concept of world revolution. It's the same in Scots history (still
folklore also, if you like), where the dispirited ghost of Macbeth,
or is it that of Robert the Bruce or of William Wallace, who still
fiercely yet sadly roams the moors or walks Auld Reekie's Royal
Mile, searching for their country's elusive freedom of thought and
independence of action.

England's Tower of London too has seen many deeds no less dark
than those committed both within and without the Kremlin. No great
nation, whether for declaring its own rightful independence or for
engaging in the bloodiest of any civil wars or for surviving through
the fiercest of any revolutions, is ever yet immune (until going through
the full redemptive process and making reparation) of the subtle and
continuing influence of its own past and often darkest history.

Most ordinary folks (unless authentically academic) don't pay
much attention to cause and effect (whose circularity they mistake
for carnival swings and roundabouts). As in their own more linear

lives, so also in the greater circularity of public life, they give all their attention to sowing, tending, and then reaping what they mistake for being the vertical harvest of their own purely personal desires.

These personal desires (producing whirlpools of circularity) are almost always counterfeit yet from which ordinary folks may go on to reap accolades of both specific and generic satisfaction. This is almost always an addictive self-satisfaction, because (apart from philosophers, poets, and prophets) most ordinary folks don't pay much attention to the finer details of the ongoing cause and effect (the singularity of which in personal lives produces the collective circularity experienced in public life). Nevertheless, at both personal and public levels, the ultimate effect of every such whirlpool of circularity is to confirm, for those who can cultivate the requisite level of self-awareness through abstraction by which to see it, that they may have spent their entire lives no more no less than as little children on swings and roundabouts.

So then have a care all you greater bigwigs in high places (as well as all you avidly listening little earwigs in the lower depths), since this psychometric equation (however contingent) carries greater consequences. These relate to (1) sowing purely personal desires in the name of collectively advantaged outcomes, as well as (2) managing to do so only by overlooking their causal effect, since (3) both causes with their consequences express only a very partial sociometric truth.

Too abstract, for you? Go on, bite the leaden bullet! You'll never get very far as a military man without learning to bite the bullet! It takes a skilled theoretician in the headquarters of the Supreme Command to distinguish the present means from future ends to discern today's back room strategy from tomorrow's front-line tactics and to draw up whatever ley lines need to be drawn without overlooking the contingency of the above psychometric equation to produce no more than a very partial sociometric truth.

Since most folks fall short of being genuinely academic, however, then look to specifics and learn from mistakes. Mingle with Machiavelli, say hello to Uncle Joe, make friends with Mussolini, shake hands with Richard Nixon, and rely on 'peace for our time' from Adolf Hitler, no less than learn congruent lessons from Tamerlane and Genghis Khan. In other words, study prophetic history.

But just remember that in our thinking to learn from mistakes—like (1) Watergate (which sent Nixon's minions to jail but largely absolved the president); or like (2) the Great Patriotic War (in which Holy Mother Russia lost more than five million of its citizens to the Nazis); or like (3) Machiavelli (who first spawned the notion that ends could justify their means); and so (4) in turn sanctioned what the Nazis in WWII meant by being 'the exceptional case' to justify their extermination of more than two million Jews and many more Slavs—we don't learn fast enough nor remember long enough. Yet neither quantitatively nor qualitatively could Machiavelli's maxim be restricted to any 'exceptional case'. Just remember that the devil is always in the details (i.e. in the particulars rather than in the generalities).

For all that, there's nothing wrong with specifics. As our CO used to say in the USMC (United States Marine Corps), 'You can learn a hell of a lot about military tactics from poker and cribbage.' Just remember that the bigger the picture, the more need for abstraction, which is exactly why the prophets speak in riddles, the teachers teach in parables, and the preachers (if each entitled to their role) preach in homilies and allegories. Why, sometimes the height of abstraction takes you so high, as it took Apostle John on the Island of Patmos, that very, very few, if any of us—not living in a cave or alone when all at sea in a small boat or trudging through the desert when half-dead from thirst in some godforsaken continent—could imagine the aforesaid apostle for being anything else than out of his mind. No indeed, not out of his mind at all, for our dear brother John of Patmos, being then in the mind of God, was then (where so few of us have ever been) in the supreme state of divine abstraction.

As always with the divine, however, there's a counterfeit, so beware too of every counterfeit abstraction. The higher you go (here take a deep breath because the air is rarefied) in the prevailing hegemony of advancement (i.e. the ladder of personal promotion to share in the limited store of generic satisfaction), the least likely it is that you are able (from within this hegemony of advancement) to observe that already mentioned still only partial sociometric truth.

Here (again take another and deeper breath), since the full truth—to be seen only from without the hegemony—is needed to complete our understanding of the two-way passage both up and down the ladder. Understanding this passage is in itself complicated by a large number of variables, since both personal progress can bring about social regress just as social progress can bring about personal regress. Yet by such means—of still taking an ever deeper and deeper prophetic breath (or pneuma)—and with each breath devotedly followed to its ultimately ascendent outcome then the full picture is usually made visible. It can be seen by those in the ascendant either through personal, private, and individual default (as from rags to riches but then so back again to rags) or else (as by natural disaster, outbreak of war, revolution, or international terrorism) through public default to those who have been hitherto in the descendent but who are now (at least potentially) in the ascendant.

Bite again the bullet! Most of us, for sitting pretty, thus fail to see ourselves as sitting pretty, and so for expressing to ourselves only the partiality of the psychometric equation, we fail to appreciate the sociometric side of the equation. That's exactly why, instead of pursuing the sociometric side of the equation to go out and spread the good news to all and sundry, some of us cut meals, privately wear hair shirts, publicly climb up high poles, sojourn in deep caves, take monastic retreats, and languish in so-called sanctuaries to avoid every slight modicum of comfort.

Nevertheless, it is a fetishism to identify divinity with discomfort, especially when something very much worse than discomfort may well be on the way to you without being sought by you. As you can see, we're still dealing with the circularity of cause and effect, since there's no getting away from cause and effect, although we tend to mistake laws of association for being laws of generation and so put our own imprimatur of cause on some very different source of effect.

Scientists, for the most part, focus objectively on cause and effect yet, unless until now in their trying to resolve quantum physics, have come to relegate origins and outcomes (the metaphysics of existence) to the outmoded theologians. For these multifactorial kinds of reasons (although so briefly stated as to overlook cosmology as a science as also the partiality of even pure scientists in pursuing their personal careers), hardly anyone is brought to realise that for the sake of the kingdom of heaven, it was the USSR who won World War II.

That it was the USSR who won World War II still seems like arrant nonsense to the arrogant West. If this conclusion is arrant nonsense for you too, then hold on there, since you may be missing the point of this very complex and theocratic argument if you think that for the sake of the kingdom of heaven, winning World War II by the USSR can be attributed directly to the virtue of communism.

On the contrary, it has always been the explicit mission of Holy Mother Russia (not to be confused with the so-called Soviets) to sacrifice herself as saviour of the West. It is on this account that Holy Mother Russia, all through World War II, as well as throughout the continuation of hostilities known as the so-called Cold War, took the brunt (faced up to the Soviets) of East–West relations. Holy Mother Russia—believe it or not—is still bleeding to save the West, no less than the West is now bleeding itself to death to save the East.

Holy Mother Russia bled the red USSR white, no less than by doing so, it also exposed the historic bones of serfdom and rebellious revolution to the light of a new dawn in each of these two East–West world empires. HMR (for being His Majesty's most royal Holy Mother Russia) did so through prophet-preacher visionaries like Martin Luther King (in the name of Jesus Christ) by turning the white–black confrontational USA into its present recovery mode of geriatric grey. So then you see—although only in a very roundabout and circuitous fashion and at the interactive level of both the demonic and the divine, the full details of which God only knows—communism (no less than capitalism) has most certainly had a part to play in almost every aspect of this outcome.

The West is still trapped in the resulting doldrums of thinking itself to have won World War II. The Anglo-Saxon nations (both Allies and Axis) still hide behind the spectre of producing yet another Napoleon, if not also another Hitler. Little Adolf does not, by any means, secure any such great end any more than Kaiser Bill did in World War I for his sordid bullying of the nations, from which Holy Mother Russia retired to promote the vacuum by which to introduce the Soviet Union. Talk with the present inhabitants of Frankfurt and Dresden, Berlin and Hamburg, and little of them have the slightest inkling of how World War II began, was fought, lost, or won. You might be surprised by their antagonism towards Britain.

Talk with inhabitants of London, Liverpool, Glasgow, Coventry, and Hull and likewise to Axis countries; most inhabitants of Allied countries have little inkling of how World War II began, was fought, lost, or won. The British likewise still hide behind little Adolf, no less than the West during the resulting Cold War would hide behind Stalin (that man of cold steel) and his like successors who once, to fill a wartime need, had been slapped on the back as Uncle Joe but then betrayed before being renounced (behind the security of what was believed to be a one-way Iron Curtain) as leader of the evil empire.

This is no place to survey the rise and fall of empires as the result of what have been, relatively speaking since the world's first empire, a resounding number of world wars. Ask the average British schoolboy whether Hitler led the Axis or the Allies, but don't be surprised by the unexpected answers you get. Like the West, having fought through so many self-made wars after World War II, the UK (still fighting in India, still fighting in Ireland, still fighting in Palestine) went down first—its lifeblood drained to repair war loans to the USA (whilst the USA meanwhile played Father Christmas by airlifting food and fuel to Berlin).

An issue in itself, the airlift to lift the Soviet blockade on traffic into West Berlin would have been needless had West Berlin agreed to more Soviet input into governing Berlin and likewise to refrain from floating the Deutsche mark. But then unlike the Soviet Union, the United States had not yet been invaded (until the indignity of 21/11), and neither had Britain been invaded (although seriously threatened several times) since 1066. And in terms of how much the Soviet Union had been ravaged by Hitler's blitzkrieg [here we are hiding behind little Adolf again], the Soviet Union had more excuse for the brutality of its reprisals and more reason by which to justify its claim to more involvement in the outcome of deciding the fate of Berlin and of the German nation than had any of the other nations who were still purportedly Allied with the Soviets.

History (with hindsight) is still as speculative as the prophecy (with foresight), which, by reason of both effectual cause and causal effect, must always circuitously precede it. Yet for as long as it would take for both the USSR and then the USA to go down under the Cold War of Attrition (with both capitalism and communism being buried together in a common grave), as most world empires decline, descend, or die eventually, most usually through the bravado of thinking themselves superior, they do so by enjoining themselves against those others in these same wars of attrition.

World history (at least to the professedly secular historian of only facts, figures, events, and happenings) is little more than a graveyard. Without prophetic input (whether that of a Churchill or of a Hitler), there is no obviously living spirit or rhyme or reason by way of explaining expected happenings, far less unexpected happenings. And so despite all the sowing of personal desires and the reaping of accolades of generic satisfaction from both the high and mighty on which the lowly depend (and so also reflected back from the lowly on which the high and mighty, in turn, depend), the beginnings and ends (origins and outcomes) are as intimately related to each other (through objectives) as are the tactical means related to the strategic purposes, in their own terms of origins and outcomes.

The moral is that despite all the subtlety of diplomacy (which often isn't very much evident in the declining art of statesmanship), despite all the intricacy of international law (which seems so paradigmatically ousted by the blatant irrelevancy of transnational law and the self-superior airs and graces of supranational law), and despite all the tricky entrapment and wheeling and dealing behind global law (by which nations shed their civil and municipal responsibility), the closest to obtaining metaphysical closure by way of righteous law and order is to take one's jurisprudential stand on morality. In other words, to find a moral, you must first be moral enough to have what it takes to conceive of morality.

As already said, wars are lost, although not always right away or even outright, by first loosening one's hold, then next losing one's hold on first the moral, then on the mental, and ultimately the spiritual ascendancy (to which the politics of pleasing the people most often gets in the way) required for decision-making. [Author's note: All right then, every one of you by now deeply gentrified readers who've never known what it is to fight a war. Here's the Second Front. Make the most of it, because in the midst of life, there's death. And no one knows, least of all old Uncle Joe (formerly Great Helmsman of the late) and not always lamented Soviet Union, when and from quarter the winds of war may spring. And our past life, even as we little knew it, may very shortly all be swept away.]

For sure, sometimes the moral ascendancy (as exemplified for a while between communism and capitalism) is equally matched. It is equally matched in both communist and capitalist countries by the presence of the proletariat of both countries, each of which is needed both to keep the peace and to fight the wars. The checks and balances may be as different as the latest edition of the USA is from the last known version of the USSR, but there's a commonality shared in the pragmatism of their respective proletariats as well as in their respective avowals of democracy, however differently these most major of components may interlock in order, by way of corresponding outcomes, to produce, what can often be the case with huge federations, almost a complete match.

No, you might say and likewise you might not think so for any so-called autocracy or so-called democracy until you've felt the outcome, which is pretty much the same sort of bureaucracy for each failure of these apparently different instruments of governmental power. The balance of power principle (dynamic in its function, but static in its outcome), as quaintly polarised between USA and USSR during the Cold War, passed momentarily (as by some alternating reversal of polarity) between these Big Two (as they thought of themselves with no other for being the survivors of the Big Three in WWII).

Baiting each other by the race for space as much as by the weapons race, the so-called Cold War would bleed each of these protagonists near to death until whatever remained of both in maintaining the balance of power would pass on, as perhaps now already done, to some rank outsider. [Exegesis 1: As a military man, let me remind you that the tactic of baiting and bleeding is employed in almost every such war of attrition. Nothing new—it has always been applied from the time the Mongols took out Baghdad, through the Cold War between the USA and USSR, no less than by al-Qaeda's baiting and bleeding the USA by its 9/11 attack on New York City in 2001.]

The beginning of al-Qaeda has been tracked back only so far—delicately done mostly by the USA as the self-appointed champion of Western democracy—to begin with the Soviet Union's invasion of Afghanistan. Now listen to this: designed to let all the

Western-invading Allies off the hook, this military fairy tale is merely political self-correctness (a common tactical manoeuvre) promoting itself no further than to disguise itself under the considerable cover afforded by historical bullshit.

Unless as comparative historians, we can relate to Boadicea's Britain being overcome by Caesar's Roman legion, and then when those la-di-da legions pulled out, the remains of ancient Britain being overtaken by Hengist and Horsa's seven Anglo-Saxon kingdoms, we won't then firmly enough grasp the stinging nettle. No, we won't understand how, after all these (by even then already one United Kingdom), they must feel on falling victim to the catastrophic Norman–French invasion of William the Bastard in 1066, and so then likewise, we've no idea how Afghanistan must feel for itself today for having been so often an imperially invaded country.

The trouble is that feelings count for more than reasons in any area of international relations, which is one reason (but no more than a reason) why, without interactive statesmanship and cross-cultural diplomacy (both which are now at the lowest ebb in the continually rising tide of militarism since WWII), the whole wide world is now ruled by raw emotions, in which case, what we witness for being the loss of all our remaining hope in rational resolution is (as the writer Lee Harris puts the issue) 'the suicide of reason—radical Islam's threat to the West'.

By itself, however, that's only the Western defence, which the East, without the rationale of Aristotelian logic (think of syllogistic reasoning) or the experience of the Christian Reformation and its focus (on individual freedom of belief and expression), interprets as aggressive to itself (and to what the West would consider to be Islamic commandeering). On the other hand, however, as argued by the lawyer and independent academic James Kalb in his book *The Tyranny of Liberalism: Understanding and Overcoming Administered Freedom, Inquisitorial Tolerance, and Equality by Command*, the weaknesses of Western liberalism are seen to pose a threat to Islamic solidarity and its administration of freedom at the level of collective rather than of individual self-interest.

Allowing for several intervening centuries of insight into the history of religious thought, there is a perplexing parallel between papal command and Islamic command that awaits the rational resolution of its conflict between each other with the Supreme Command. But then no less than the potential for still simmering conflict still existing between papal command and the Supreme Command, there's no less than the similar conflict between Jew and Christian likewise awaiting resolution under the Supreme Command. And as for any military man from whom is required the exercise of personal obedience to any command, the Supreme Command also refuses to commandeer the strength of will required to dispute any illegal command.

Of course, as frequently palmed off to excuse such failures of international law allowing 9/11 to take place (since there's no point to any war, whether cold or otherwise, without an outcome), it has often been and as still often said (mostly by lawyers with a tongue in each cheek) that 'the real rulers of society are undiscoverable'. Nevertheless, our own Western world history, not just of invasion and infiltration but also by way of invitation, should make us, who are rank outsiders of the east (for us still in lower case, unlike the West), mighty cautious of infiltrating, far less invading, little, fragile, and relatively unknown war zones like Korea, Vietnam, Iraq, Iran, and of course, Afghanistan. [Author's note: Despite your being the most discerning of readers, you are most probably in danger of losing the plot behind this military action by now (code-named Operation Soul-Snatching), but for myself, as one of the most disciplined of military men when engaged in baiting and bleeding the reader, I have not the slightest intention as yet of blowing my cover.]

Nevertheless, as seen so often before, when moral ascendancy once again falls victim to yet another retributive attempt at international law (say, by legislating retrospectively against individuals for war crimes in WWII instead of requiring fair and just reparations against offending nations), 'the real rulers of society are rendered undiscoverable'. On the contrary, the real rulers of our society are pre-eminently discoverable; we just choose not to recognise these 'real rulers' for being no more than ourselves. And that is exactly why the real rulers of society are undiscoverable.

Recognising terrorism as the work only of individuals exculpates nations from international law, so when the president of Iran pleads with Britain's foreign secretary Jack Straw in 2001 that 'nations should not be punished in place of terrorists', he is denying the responsibility of nations for what happens as a result of their harbouring terrorists within their territories and even possibly for their own citizens who commit acts of terrorism.

Despite the pragmatic power of every proletariat—and this especially in every purported democracy—we are the ones who are each called as priests and prophets to lead against, for the most part, counterfeit autocracies or stultifying bureaucracies, if not also against outright dictatorships, each of which lay claim to counterfeit authority over ourselves. But look just here, we don't have much success in doing just this [although never before attempted by anything as all-out as Operation Soul-Snatching], even just over the petty dictators and officious bureaucrats within our own small towns. [Exegesis 2: Although a most successful pre-emptive strike was once made against the small town of Dunderisimus in Operation Big Dogs and Little Dogs way far back as 2016.]

On the basis of this most successful pre-emptive strike (which changed the configuration of dog parks throughout the Western world), we may here go so far as to say that fewer wars are fought in the field nowadays than are fought on paper, so don't be taken by surprise (the first principle of defensive warfare) to find out how far beyond civilian reckoning us military men have become more academic than are the armchair academics. Strategic planning (of warfare, no less than of moral philosophy) requires a clearer conscience now than ever before (especially when tested in the field of an increasingly global context of fast-diminishing resources).

As with the human conscience, how small are the things that most matter! For example, this is but a beginner's book, since there's no end to it, but since there's no end to it, it could hardly be a beginner's book. [Exegesis 3: Nevertheless, when still from over in Afghanistan as a military man, you're still not going to tempt me to break cover. Just take it on trust that for there being no end to a beginner's book, this is a programme novel by which you'll come to know how to end it.]

* * *

The History of Recurrent Darkness
Part VI

Simplicity and Complexity
Was not life exciting when every simple act acquired
the complexity of a dangerous secret mission?
Azar Nafisi, *Reading Lolita in Tehran*

How slight, small, frail, and fragile are the things that matter most! A pin, but for just being a pin, perhaps dropped on the ground, we humans heed it not. Why, even for its falling from heaven, we heed not the falling of this tiny pin. For umpteen times, we heed it not, and so eventually and thus finally, we hear it never. And that's not all, of course, since we then go on to dispute the possibility of there being any pin whatsoever that could ever fall from heaven and then, even more so, that there could be any heaven from which the pin could fall.

Why no, of course, it couldn't—no pin could ever fall from heaven—by which time we have begun to doubt, when even a sparrow falls, its fall from flight could be felt by then in any non-existent heaven. No, the fall of an eagle may be or could be felt (by such warriors as we are) from some such purely conjectural heaven, but hardly a sparrow and most certainly not a pin. By this time, there's nothing to see, nothing to hear, and nothing to tell about anything that matters, whether from the fall of a sparrow, from the fall of an eagle, or from the fall of a pin from heaven. Alas, we once were warriors, but hardly now for being without a cause!

Yet how slight, small, frail, and fragile are the things that matter most! Of course, that's the very reverse of how humans (for whom big is beautiful) and so many of the scientists who have gone beyond being even just global have accustomed themselves to think of matter and, in turn, to think of heaven. After all, if it's only of matter we're talking about, then the more of it there is, it surely follows that the more it matters.

Big is beautiful, and the bigger, the better, or so we think, for the bigger being even more beautiful than could be anything smaller.

Nevertheless, we are drawn in two apparently contrary directions; and whether we like the resultant feeling of paradox or not, we are eventually forced to recognise that the cosmological macrocosm of the whole universe, of countless galaxies as we think to know them, is underpinned by the cosmological microcosm, as we think to know it, of atomic particles. And so just as the little old lady in Stephen Hawking's *Brief History of Time* pointed out, 'It's turtles all the way down!'

As a matter of interest here, dearest readers, which of the two are you—an analytic separatist (who believes in turtles all the way down) or a synthetic cosmologist (who believes in protons, electrons, atoms, molecules and, from thence, in stars and stripes and union jacks, all the way up)? Your taste in cooking (as much in the cooking of food as in the cooking up of anything else) is probably the simplest way of deciphering your personal code. Do you go for composite flavours whereby your ultimate culinary endeavour (as with devising your own recipe for pumpkin soup) is to coordinate an entirely new composite flavour out of quite specific, relatively unrelated, and distinctively different flavours (let's here add a little coconut milk), or does your separatist appetite (in looking for pie, peas, and chips or oysters *au naturale*) hope and intend, so far as possible, to keep separate flavours separate?

For high cuisine, it's usually composite flavours (to make turtle soup) all the way up, and for low cuisine, it's usually separate flavours (to care for little turtles—or pies, peas, and chips) all the way down. So then are you an analytic separatist (for avoiding soups, stews, and fricassees) all the way down or a synthetic cosmologist for avoiding particularist dishes (like liver and bacon, ham and eggs, and sardines on toast) all the way up?

Alas, for the ages of paradox and parable being by now so far bygone! The Greeks, with their flair for armchair philosophy, produced the paradox; and the Hebrews, with their flair for nomadic survival and storytelling, produced the parable. Pondering on the paradox halted the Greeks in their scientific tracks until the Hebrews came along with their stories of the miraculous, whereupon the paradox and the parable provided a unified field theory, however perilous to passive bystanders, by which we all learnt to think twice, if not thrice, before doing what the religious priests, scientific pundits, and political powers would tell us what to think and what to do.

Nevertheless, even as to the holding of our most intimate of personal beliefs, there are many unthinking people who would prefer to be told what to say and to be told what to do. Unlike the way that non-fiction has become the principal vehicle for that process of delegating thought to others, both the scientific paradox and the priestly parable were designed to make us think for ourselves. So apart from the challenge which space fiction issues to scripture, we are very soon induced by smart technology or quickly drowned in the rising informational overload or else either to forget or to dismiss the paradox by which it was out of a formless void or conjectural black hole or of apparent nothinglessness that the Supreme Command created the material world we still now live in.

There are magnetic ley lines (if you care to call them that) which the smallest of countries in size—think of Scotland, Switzerland, Israel, Madagascar, or even New Zealand—still seem to exert a disproportionate influence over the largest of countries. And if you don't believe in ley lines, then don't think to talk of the beelines that bees use to plot their flight trajectories or to use the expression 'as the crow flies' any more than to learn how to lay a gun, far less plot the trajectory of a missile to the moon.

Once again, how slight, small, frail, and fragile are the things that most matter! It's the same for the history of ideas as for the history of events and even more particularly for warring nations. It's often the merest whisper of an idea (like thinking to turn a war of attrition, whether already good or bad, into a war of outright annihilation or *vernichtungskrieg* (whether done to Troy by the Greeks or to Carthage by the Romans or as attempted by the Nazis towards the Jews and Slavic nations) that changes the whole face of human history forever after.

Yet still for some reason (as curious for our lack of recognition as for our lack of understanding), these smallest of countries exert themselves along such (perhaps telepathic) ley lines, each of which release an energy—perhaps magnetic—in inverse proportion to the limits of their apparent physicality. For instance, three of the world's seven continents—Asia, Africa, and Europe—still meet

742

today (with all sorts of geophysical, geobiological, geopolitical, geo-religious, and sundry other consequences) in the tiny, ancient, and still deeply troubled nation of Israel. Likewise, it took the impetus of MacPherson's Ossian from the backblocks of ancient Scotland to trigger off the Napoleonic Wars across Europe and so then far beyond from not so Bonnie Scotland. How slight, small, frail, and fragile are the things that most matter!

Whole books could be written academically on the history of thought, politically on the history of conflict and warfare, and biologically on the prevalence of species, by which to demonstrate these spiritual and as often fiercely fought-over ley lines. Alas, like the lawmaking, film-making, music making, and book writing of these, our own days, such things are made to sell—and as often made, written, and sold—not to the highest of bidders (in terms of their spiritual quality) but to the lowest of bidders (in terms of their commercial quantity).

From all such talk of deep data troubles, most couch potato folks, when relying on 'peace for our time', lazily excuse themselves. Spiritually asleep, they do so by accrediting this inversion of geodesic values more to the more active intellectuality and human ingenuity of the people in those places than to any ley lines. The choice here taken is between secularity and sanctity, and at present, the process of sanctification, whether by ley-line prayer or by ley-line pilgrimage, is no longer in the ascendant.

Likewise, landscape and seascape are always concomitant or alternative factors by which (not only allegorically) we express relationships between the different dimensions of the physical with the moral, the intellectual, and spiritual dimensions of our life. Similarly, the personalities, both individually and collectively, of our leaders and followers—as in the case of Cuthbert or Thatcher, Scots or English, Maori or Pakeha, Stalin or Roosevelt, Churchill or Hitler—each contribute to or impact on the most intricate of multifactorial outcomes.

Had someone else instead of Stalin taken over the USSR from Lenin or had Edward VIII continued to rule Britain for the Second World War instead of George VI, we may pose the 'what if' of history otherwise, since with hindsight, we can see something now of what historically then lay round corners but not of what we could see at the time. Thus, what we mistake for established ley lines in science, no less than in the humanities, may fracture themselves and distance themselves from each other.

The ascendant and the descendant (whether in physical, intellectual, moral, or spiritual matters) afford the most stable of directional ley lines that permeate most of the means (whether heuristic or algorithmic) by which we make decisions. We strive for factual integrity and moral integrity (or jurisprudential righteousness) in each of these dimensions, as we do for both rational integrity and righteousness in the spiritual dimension, which obliges us to strive for integrity in each of the other dimensions.

It is significant that the biblical vision of Jacob's ladder affords two-way communication between heaven and earth; other visions, such as water opening a doorway to the underworld in both Greek and Gaelic mythology, are for the most part only one way, although for the Greeks, the heights of Mount Olympus are also the two-way military headquarters by which to explain their vision of the Supreme Command.

Nowadays, most people mistake the cursus honorum (or ladder of personal promotion) for the biblically recorded Jacob's ladder—the meeting point where angels once ascended and descended between heaven and earth (Genesis 28:12). For the same lack of impartiality, secular anthropologists (as also many religious apologists) jettison every notion of ley lines (although the forcefulness of magnetism acquires a come back through quantum mechanics). They jettison the notion of ley lines (rediscovered in the physical by Alfred Watkins in his book *The Old Straight Track*), whether or not the magi or wise men chose by their pilgrimage to follow the ley line traversed by the Star of David in order to get to Bethlehem and irrespective of the New Zealand Maori who navigated by the Matariki (*mata ariki*, the eyes of God) for their sailing back and forth across the most turbulent South Pacific.

Nevertheless, to those who recognise, go on to experience, and personally research such counterintuitive relationships (as every military man of action should always do to avoid being taken by surprise), it seems more likely to be otherwise. History tells us that for those big and mighty empires trying to swallow up the smaller and very fragile communities whose ley lines in both time and space seem magnetically to attract and provoke the antagonism of the bigger nations, the truth as to the lack of the moral ascendancy by which the bigger allow themselves to grow parasitically upon the smaller will eventually bring down the biggest—just as this policy of 'dog eat dog' or 'flea bite flea' seems to suggest—and the very last of this world's great global empires.

That empires (whether trans-Australian, trans-Pacific, or trans-European) try to swallow up every last crevice of the earth's crust (often first picking off those little communities with long histories of warfare against the mightiest of nations) is, for being a fact of history, likewise also a foretaste of prophecy, which no military man can afford to overlook. The spirit of creation still hovers over these hotspots by which to promote, either no more (so say the surveyed majority) or else much more (so say the statistical few) than a possible return to the tohubohu (or state of utter disorder) that pertained before the first creation of these small but often also very ancient countries—of which Iraq and Afghanistan are amongst this world's most ancient.

As a second-order sightseer (or only armchair tourist), you scoff, and this despite my warning of what open action I would take were you here with me when faced with a difficult read. As already admitted, this is not only a difficult read in terms of words which will express exactitude but also in terms of concepts that once were clear but now are clouded. For example, the whole concept of war at international law (and not just the concept of war but, in consequence, also the whole concept of international law) has been clouded by the present inability of nations to deal with terrorism.

This existential transition of nations and their empires from ex nihilo and back again can happen only through the reverse psychology of drawing a bead on what—let's hope only for the merest of moments—will be (historically once again) this world's biggest other country. There's nothing new in all this, so we don't need to rely any longer on there being any weapons of mass destruction in Afghanistan, as in Iraq. In any case, we still, so we rationalise as military men, have Infinite Reach.

As said once before (at which remark you fell silent), you can pay me a visit (if you like) whilst I'm here in Afghanistan, but it will be hard work keeping up with me and not for the purpose of sightseeing. Us military angels, like military men, are primed to join up and see the world, but that kind of sightseeing (call it peacekeeping if you will) is no more than my cover for soul-catching, which means far more critical work for me to do (although your lesser calling would be nonetheless important). And you never know, you too may then be called to undertake the same precarious work that I do once you see the need for it.

For you, the work from the start would be a bit like looking after refugees. Not all countries and cultures hear that call. Sometimes the most self-indulgent of cultures despise even their own poor and their own homeless. As another military man, General Booth of the Salvation Army, once called that 'crying scandal of our age' in his book on *In Darkest England, and the Way Out*. We glibly talk of 'saving darkest Africa' but ignore our own fellow citizens whose 'inexorable destiny' and resulting 'fatalism of despair' brutalises them into worse than beasts by the condition of their environment. Nevertheless, for me (now being an angel all alone whilst undercover and serving the Supreme Command in Afghanistan), the endeavour of soul-catching goes far deeper into metaphysics than merely looking after refugees.

So then and as said before, there are ley lines, if you still care to recognise them for what they are, which the smallest of countries in size—think of Switzerland, Scotland, Israel, Mozambique, or even faraway New Zealand—seem to exert over the largest of countries. For some reason, or perhaps for many reasons, the smallest of these countries exert these greatest of influences in inverse proportions to their apparently limited physicality.

This same startling inversion of significance pertains also to the constituent states of great federations, of vast commonwealths of independent nations, and of huge conglomerate empires of vastly different people, no less than the same inversion exists within the vastly different factions of the smallest states, in the one country between the citizens of closely competing cities, and between the very different households within one and the same warring family.

Thus, it is surely so, that some Orthodox Jews will hiss through their teeth at Messianic Christians as they pass and repass each other on the streets of Jerusalem. And Sunni and Shia Muslims covet each other's preferential claim, politically expressed by the Kingdom of Saudi Arabia versus the Islamic Republic of Iran, for each being the only one of Islam's seventy-three sects, according to the Hadith of Muhammad, to escape consumption by final hellfire.

Beyond a certain size of city (whereupon the collective consciousness grows, at first uncertain, next confused, and thence fractious), urban dwellers soon become a race apart from rural dwellers—although by now urbanisation is almost a universal—leaving aside only the resultant wake of increasing desertification. But just as great countries and great cities compete (with each other and ultimately against each other) for constant growth—Glasgow with Edinburgh, Auckland with Wellington, Moscow with St Petersburg, and London, as if, for being the world's megacity, it can compete with no other city than itself—this is often done (as can be plotted on a graph) to the greater detriment of all other cities and many smaller towns and, as in the case of many capital cities, to the complete detriment of the countries of which those cities are the capital.

But which is the greater or lesser, the bigger or smaller, the worthier or the worthless almost always entails, as modelled both by the arts and sciences, some sort of reversal of the obvious. So as with Nathanael, that fella who would be led to ask Philip that leading question regarding Jesus, 'What good can come out of Nazareth?' (John 1:43–46), we tend to dismiss the trivial, to uphold strongly established values, and to correlate power with might, authority with recognition, and familiar values with personal security.

We are taught to presume from appearances that big is powerful, might is right, and big is beautiful. And even if, in his asking this question, Nathanael already had Bethlehem in mind instead of Nazareth for the prophesied birthplace of the Messiah (Micah 5:2), nevertheless, the basic question is still one of at least prophetic foresight or of metaphysical understanding, if not also of mystical and perhaps miraculous significance (all of which values are increasingly incredulous to the modern mind).

This reverse (to many perverse) relationships of size and function in our evaluation of Afghanistan surprises the casual onlooker of world events—that the least should be more forceful than the greatest—but we're not talking of physical mapping here. Unless these ley lines (often legally or jurisprudentially expressed) can be seen as some sort of moral, metaphysical, or even spiritual mapping to accord with still hidden dimensions perhaps disclosed only by metaphysical or even spiritual mapping, then their real significance remains hidden. As in economics, the biggest return received by any capitalist consumer is often the least beautiful, whilst instead the smallest contribution made to that return made by the most menial of wage earners turns out to be the most beautiful. But that principle, even just in the economics of limited resources, takes a lot of getting used to.

Most folks would attribute this reversal of geodesic values whereby the high and mighty are humbled to human intellectuality or to human ingenuity, but it seems more likely that in some small places of the earth's crust (often those with long histories of warring attrition), the spirit of creation still hovers over them by which to promote either a possible return to the tohubohu (or state of utter disorder) that pertained before these countries were first created.

To explain this phenomenon, the New Zealand Maori would call on the cutting edge of the *Wairua Tapu* (or Holy Spirit), and the Scots would call on the prophetic gift of second sight held by their *Sennachie* (or seer), by which to explain our still very limited understanding of these interactional relationships. It is hard, apart from their recognising the spiritual dimension, for many humans to accept the reversal of values by which our physicality in this world is ultimately suborned to the spirituality of the next world. And it is even harder for those many to accept that this is done by eventually promoting the power of the least over that of the most, the power of the last over that of the first, and the ultimate authority of the utterly powerless over that of the presently most powerful. As a matter of metaphysics rather than of theology, however, this reversal of present worth for future worth (little different from literary postponement) is no more revolutionary than to substitute quantum physics for classical physics.

For the moment, until you get to know me as any prophet better (as some say, for my being in real life the author of bad local news and global misfortune), we'll stick for just a little bit longer to classical physics (with all land measurements authenticated by *The Times World Atlas*). With Afghanistan at 251,825 square miles (be the same a little more or less), then that's nothing to the size (at its height) of the Russian Federation (6,592,849 square miles) or, at roughly half of that, then the size of the USA (3,787,422 square miles and allowing for nothing less since the election of President Trump) or even just looking (as any everyday Afghan would have done) at the size of Saddam Hussein's Iraq (168,754 square miles, but before seizing and being expelled from Kuwait) or Ayatollah Khomeini's Iran (at just 636,296 square miles), then what's the point of saying (if any point there is to anyone saying) that Afghanistan, which is where I am for the moment and where I shall most probably remain for some considerable time, is such a very big country?

Well, for being mostly a matter of quantum physics rather than of the so-called classical physics that is still taught to us in schools, it's very much like this: maps merely show places (as often no more than those hidden and to us still unknown spaces within our own heads), whereas full-in-your-face public history outreaches geography every time and, for some still far and unforeseen places, even beyond all time. That's exactly why someone, like any president, who can dare to tell all the world (as if his presidency is that of all the world) that the USA is sending another 4,000 additional troops into Afghanistan is surely, as with Vietnam, still out of line. We're still talking single-photon emission computed tomography (SPECT scans) here, which should surely be a compulsory credential of brain function (whether for moving into the Far East from the Far West or into the Far West from Far East) before standing for any sort of presidential or monarchical office.

Not until it was when we were told of there being heaven and hell (the most categorical of all metaphysically mistaken distinctions) did place-based identification redefine good and evil for being the critically place-based outcomes of our previously indeterminable travels—from which this finite outcome of the present for all infinity makes us very suspicious of the homeless wanderer, the refugee, and even of the itinerant preacher—as such, on all counts, as I most surely am.

There's no surprise here, since time and space (despite the closely coordinated hug to them both as given by the greatest Albert of our own time) were never ever that close coordinates (as the hug given to them and the square mileage of mountainous countries is no more taken into account, even in the Himalayas) than mapping can ever quite get its head round the laying out of any globe on the flat. The fact of the matter (if ever matter is a fact) is that the world we live on has a very rough surface (which we prefer to the simplistic smooth)—and this roughness being the case (for being a matter of fact) in far many more ways than we would like to think of it for being just one level playing field or billiard table of unsurpassed perfect smoothness on which humans choose to think that they can play the game of thrones.

Of course (since we don't have to set any course for being permissibly all at sea in this landlocked country), none of us here in Afghanistan is likely to go overboard on any such cosmic explanation, since today's world accords more practical value to the geography of space and to the status or significance of one's place in that space than it does to the eternity of infinity which we more negatively refer to (according to the law of entropy in classical physics) for being the end of time.

Meanwhile, please follow these codified instructions closely, because we are shortly to leave the airport, to which we just arrived, not this time from Dubai but instead from Islamabad in Pakistan, and through which gunshot-pockmarked airport we have walked, each with two suitcases, in fear and trembling of imminent arrest. In case of your being held for either smuggling diamonds or for your shirt hanging out, simply offer 500 afghanis, together with (to any woman official) 'Pardon, ma'am, but your cleavage is showing', and if to a man, then the alternative password of 'red city alert'. So too, despite all provocation, keep a straight face.

Maps and tour guides mean nothing here, since the streets have no names, but instead they are known solely (as in some singularly photon emission scan) by their function—such as Chicken Alley or Lamb's Fry Avenue, or Gold Street. Whether or not you wander down

Gold Street is no matter. Dressed as a Westerner, you'll be known for being filthy rich, at least a kilometre ahead before you appear. But be careful. You'll have to live up to your reputation of being wealthy with good grace, so don't shame the locals into thinking themselves poor. Remember always that in getting here to Afghanistan (unless as a peacekeeper who doesn't count for anything here), you're walking along the outstretched arm of entrenched history, which is sometimes a tight wire and at others a slack.

Don't pay any attention to the geography (not even to the open sewers that border the Afghan pavements), but learn your history to the point that you know it (as Victor Hugo got to know the sewers of La Belle Paris) inside out. We have a straight, linear (lack of) concept of embroidered time in the West, but history (as always in the rough) is ever far more convoluted (although exaggeratedly so) in the East. It doesn't just shuttle backwards and forwards as in the West, but as already said before, when in the East, it twists and turns, oscillates, reverberates, explodes in your face, and implodes in your belly, as well as leaves runnels of raw sewage in your trouser cuffs after walking the streets of war-torn Afghanistan.

* * *

BOOK SEVEN

East and West of Eden A Pivotal History of East–West Relations Back to the Future

Come Back to Mandalay
By the old Moulmein Pagoda, lookin' lazy at the sea,
There's a Burma girl a-settin', and I know she thinks
o' me;
For the wind is in the palm-trees, and the temple-bells
they say:
'Come you back, you British soldier; come you back
to Mandalay!'

Rudyard Kipling, 'Mandalay'

Intro 1—Zakariah: Why ever did the West (Britain, Russia, and Germany, to name but a few of the insurgent nations) wage war on the already long-beleaguered Afghanistan? Why especially did those least ever invaded countries of the West (Britain, USA, and New Zealand) seek to invade Iran, to invade Iraq, and more than once again to invade Afghanistan? Ah yes, of course, to keep the peace, and still yes again, even if keeping the peace meant waging war!

No, it's not as simple as that. *Pax aut bellum* (as usually put in the strict disjunctive afforded by any proffered choice between peace or war) is hugely complex. On the subject of peace in particular, read Lieutenant Colonel Bailey's *Mission to Tashkent* and Fitzroy Maclean's *Eastern Approaches*. And on the subject of war in general, don't miss out on Special Correspondent William Russell's eyewitness reports to *The Times* on the Crimean War, the American Civil War, and the Franco-Prussian War.

Intro 2—Malachai: These are not new questions. On the contrary, these are very, very old questions. They are as old as the Egyptians, as old as the Babylonians, as old as the Assyrians, as old as the Medes and Persians, as old as the Scythians, as old as the Mongols, as old as the Vikings—as old as the dawn of the so-called civilisation.

Intro 3—Gideon: The Huns invaded Christendom no less than the Belgians the Congo, the French Africa, the Russians the Caucasus, and the Italians Abyssinia. Given time, invaders can become settlers, just as the Vikings, after invading France, so became the Normans of Normandy. Yet once having settled there, these by then Norman-French set off in 1066 to invade England. By then, of course, the Germanic tribes of the Angles, the Saxons, and the Jutes had already long overstayed their welcome from the Ancient Britons, who had earlier invited them home to Britain to defeat the invading Romans. Fighting for their new homes in Merrie England against the invading Norman-French, the losing Anglo-Saxons then fled north to settle in the Scottish Lowlands, where, caught between the borderers of the Southern Uplands just traversed, with the impenetrable mountainous Gaelic-speaking Highlands to the north-west, and with the cold shoulder of Doric-speaking Scotland to the north-east, they then became more English than the English.

So then what of the so much later resurrected Ancient Britons, at least the few who managed to retain their identity against those stiff-lipped Norman-French who, after winning the Battle of Hastings over the tired and worn-out Anglo-Saxons in 1066, would masquerade with the utmost brutality for centuries against the Scots and the Irish in their trying so unsuccessfully to convince all comers that they were forever English? Well, after invading Afghanistan, once again to lose the play (and after giving up the plot to others in what they would then forlornly call the Great Game), they would bring up their future generations to be what they called 'good losers'. It would be by this self-inflicted concept of what had once been *perfidious Albion* that the Norman-French-English nation would eventually lose their entire empire in the West, both politically to the EU whilst also culturally to the USA, both whilst in the process of funding peacekeeping economically to the East. Meanwhile, the outcome otherwise would be pretty near exactly as prophesied by the far-seeing classical scholar, army brigadier, and maverick politician Enoch Powell.

Be sure to read *Who Killed Enoch Powell*, a novel by Arthur Wise; and *Museum Street* by Michael Wall for 'dirty tricks writing at its best'; together with *The Man Who Shot Rob Muldoon* (written by the fellow who wouldn't own up to it). Without any novelist-diplomat-statesmen such as John Buchan (famous for *The Thirty-Nine Steps* and *Greenmantle*) still around we have to make do, as best we can, with many writers who are but observers of the fray.

Intro 4—Zakariah: We talk of East–West relations as we talk of science at odds with the humanities or religion at odds with science or politics at odds with morality. Why, we can't get on within ourselves in the West (read *Decision at Dawn: New Zealand and the EEC* by Michael Robson) so how does the West expect to get on with the East? "I can see those New Zealanders now, coming over the trenches. I hope nothing happens to them," said French President Pompidou to New Zealand's Prime Minister Holyoake (sometime before the *Rainbow Warrior* incident, when the French blew up that ship with loss of life in Auckland Harbour).

Intro 5—Eli: So then, but not to change the subject, what constitutes the so-called *Soul-Catcher's Delight*, because that's what I've copied into my copybook? Is it travelling as so many of today's tourists do, simply for the sake of enjoying experiential novelties or for the sake of eluding the demands of household and homeland responsibilities or for just making a show of oneself (whether by way of exporting cutting-edge technology or giving prestigious performances), as once engaged natives, equivalent to their performance of the ancient Indian rope trick or the still surviving Buddhist lotus position or else demonstrating the English Acts of Union, the United States Declaration of Independence, the European Economic Community, or the so-called United Kingdom? In other words, what are the tricks of the tourist trade, both the trivial and entertaining, as well as those seriously associated with soul-saving? For one's first and earliest understanding of such baptismal full immersion into transnational relations, read Baroness Orczy's *The Scarlet Pimpernel*, or for any second baptismal full immersion, read Thomas Keneally's *Bring*

Larks and Heroes, then followed by that same author's *Schindler's Ark* (filmed as *Schindler's List*).

The real trick, in each case, is to bring two conflicting opposites together (whether male and female, east and west, or north and south, or Catholic and Protestant, or continental and insular) without provoking one almighty explosion. Sometimes, whole continents depend on little islands (as did Europe depend on the British Isles during the early years of WWII); at other times, little islands are scavenged by large continents (as were the British Isles by their repaying war loans by way of transferring intellectual property to the USA after WWII). Sometimes, there's no alternative to what there is—in which case, there's no comparison by which to decide whether that one and only is either right or wrong. As for Baroness Orczy, writing *The Scarlet Pimpernel* because 'it was God's will that she should', so also it is God's will that we angels should engage in the delight of soul-catching.

Intro 6—Zakariah: Perhaps the so-called *Soul-Catcher's Delight* goes (or for being but a work in progress, ought to go) far deeper. For this, I now need at least intaglio (in this case, a deeply inscribed design). Perhaps, still with its provided safety net, this inscribed intaglio can penetrate all the way into the fiery magna of chaotic hell. Perhaps, likewise still with its provided safety net, this deeply inscribed intaglio flies far higher up than ever before into cosmic heaven.

These are two things far beyond what any mere tourist alone can possibly hope of doing and far less conceive alone of undertaking. At a trivial level, every tourist may choose to bungee jump, to hang-glide, to free-fall, and to queue up in order to zip down some Splash Mountain. Alas, for their being satisfied with superficial novelties, however, tourists very rarely study the history or look to the language or consider the culture of wherever they take and carry with them their own brand of tourism.

Without a Big Mac and chips in Moscow, they feel deprived. When faced with escargot in their posh Paris Hotel, they turn pale, lose their appetite, and indelicately puke. In Archangel, their stomachs heave on being served Baltic sardines with ... look, will you ... their heads are still on! It's more than obvious from all this recidivist travel that tourists could not cope with any military operation (far less keep their cover to engage in any needful spying operation)!

Intro 7—Walter-Walters: Nevertheless, touring through the countryside of other countries whilst feeling free as a cloud, even the most superficial tourist can get jolted from his flight path or dislodged from his high horse. If not falling amongst thieves, then by falling for some native girl or for some exotic culture hitherto unknown to him, he can be stopped in his tracks.

As between mere tourism and even just wayfaring or exploring, it is often survival (through the element of personal risk) that is at stake. Most tourists return home; yet some wayfarers may sojourn, settle, and never return. On the other hand, for never being a mere tourist and always being far more than any mere wayfarer, the soul-catcher, like that Maori demigod Maui, is a shape changer, a time changer, and a space changer.

Wherever the soul-catcher goes, he or she does so always as an evangelist of the good news which brings the prophetic future into the present. He or she therefore seeks to unite conflicting opposites, non-intrusively and non-ostentatiously, in the only way they could be united for their better understanding and future function. Wherever two things conflict, the hunt is on by which to find some third thing (or tertium quid) by which either to moderate that conflict or else to resolve it.

Intro 8—Marsyas: In any system of two-valued logic (typically Western), if one alternative way of doing things is wholly right, then we tend to presume (or, worse still, assume) its commensurate opposite to be wholly wrong. Either way, deducing good from what's bad or bad from what's good, we can also read the converse signs. There are more subtle problems when relating to any system of more than two-valued logic (typically Eastern) where no such clear conclusion follows—as from the Slavic state of *nitchevo* or from the *mokosatsu* in Japanese.

Intro 9—Augustus: The history of human thought demonstrates the same sort of difficulties in our acceptance of alternative geometries and set calculi. Our default position in the West (no thanks to the ancient Greeks by their reliance on two-valued logic) is to fall back on the conflict of warring opposites. It was the typically three-valued and Eastern response of the Japanese by way of their reply of *mokosatsu* to the Potsdam Declaration that the West decided to drop atomic bombs on Hiroshima and Nagasaki to confirm its own two-valued outcome. Be sure, in every situation, always to consider *how apposite are opposites.*

Intro 10—Patricia Ralph: In turn, the fixity of classical logic (when re-examined) opens up the Pandora's box of the social sciences. By way of answer in this age of individualism, psychology takes it into its head to lord itself first over logic (by way of psychologic) and then, from there, by which to leapfrog over anthropology, sociology, and all the remainder (including the humanities) of the so-called social sciences. The trouble then is that by psychology aping the physical sciences instead of retaining its own sense of philosophic wonder as to the human mind, it introduces its own fixity both of form and purpose.

The Napoleonic response (by way of resolving any conflict of opposites, such as fixity or flexibility, no less than peace or war, male or female, or right or wrong) is never far from the wide-open arena of human temptation either to denigrate, put down, swallow up, or else to get rid of whichever conflicting opposite gives most offence to the other instead of trying simply to explain, moderate, or resolve their mutual conflict. Sometimes, all that's missing to resolve or rectify a thing gone wrong is a credible explanation of that thing gone wrong.

Would it be too much to leave the life sciences (which most certainly include the wisdom of scripture in action) to have the last word? It takes great wisdom to read even just *Ecclesiastes* (never mind the *Song of Solomon*, and the *Revelation of Jesus Christ to Saint John*) and yet there are many people in the highest positions of earthly power who dismiss it, even just *Ecclesiastes* out of hand, as being (in their own words) 'utter rubbish'.

* * *

A Pivotal History of East–West Relations
Part I

A Traveller's Tale
To meet regulatory oversight standards of the EU all air carriers of Afghanistan airlines are banned from entering into the airspace of any member state of the EU.

List of air carriers banned in the European
Union at 30 November 2017

First, when having a mind to travel, whether east to west or west to east, find your present bearings. So then for one moving pin being pivoted almost miraculously on another static pin, here's a compass from which to deduce not only north from south but also east from west. What do you think it cost, in terms of no more than the originally charitable trust set up in heaven (long before self-indulgent tourism took over), to let this particular pin fall (for better or worse) into human hands from heaven?

First time, is it? And even for you now, dear readers, in your coming to the Far East? You won't ever get further east (at least not by road) these days than Afghanistan. There's the Khyber Pass (both ways) to contend with, and never mind just yet the Bolan Pass, infested as it is by the Kakurs, who still live by daylight robbery.

There too, through the Kyber Pass (both ways) as everywhere else, history will continue to come down like a flood. As through the Grand Canyon, history will continue to surge, even through that most historic and almost perpendicular Bolan Pass, which winds through the Toba Kakar the mountains. As an almost vertical flood, it shall sweep away almost all this presently remaining history amongst these mountains—all before it—just as in the past it swept away the once famed North-Western Railway. Yes, indeed, all before it, just as once before, the Assyrians too swept down 'like a wolf on the fold'.

History is like that—once the heat of human history reaches a certain peak, then history (like a self-cleaning oven) becomes self-cleansing. There's no holding it back, neither in the physical nor in the spiritual, since a combination of both have triggered off the self-cleansing process by which history in the short term repeats itself in the fulfilling of its final end. Humanity mistakes the strategic impulse of history for being mere tactics and accordingly thinks both to divine and determine the historic final end. No, history is not like that at all; it is history's strategic impulse that will determine its final end, just as it is humanity's own strategic impulse which will determine its own final end. And human tactics have little input to other than advance its own strategic end.

But before that flood-like cleansing process of history comes about, you should have gone first to the Soviet Union or else then to the Caucasus, and so by winding yourself backwards through the history books, you should have realised what it once took to be British or Russian or German on the North-West Frontier. Never too late, as they say (when learning to recover one's lost love for time), since not only does history repeat itself as in the West but it also oscillates, reverberates, and either explodes in your face or else implodes deep down in your belly or else reverberates constantly in your mind as it does in the East.

What, you don't like travelling by airbus, not even on a samolyot or magic carpet? [Editor's note: Until recently, you'd scrabble for seats on Aeroflot after entering the passenger cabin, since no seats would be allotted passengers beforehand, but don't scoff, since American Airlines would frequently book more passengers on any flight than there were seats and then encourage passengers to ballot amongst themselves for preferential stand-downs. The Far East and the Far West, as with the former USSR and the former USA, have more in common with each other than they have with the EU for being any Eden.]

It's never too hard to rewind history, because the historic past is always with us until dealt with by the present to forego the so far settled outcome of that past for the future. Thus, and a good deal more than just allegorically speaking, the gung-ho North-West Frontier was catastrophically replaced by the Western Front for the British in the First World War, whilst the withholding of any Second Front from the Russians by the British took the place left by the North-West Frontier for the Russians in the Second World War. So too, it has been much the same for the Frontiersman American as for all the rest of his Western Allies in their ever constant bid to westernise the East, as witnessed by their catastrophic loss of face in Korea, Vietnam, Iraq, Iran, and Afghanistan by their frontiersman policies of Westward Ho!

Think to hold history down ... No, you won't, not even by doing away with every Timur-the-Lame, with every Saddam Hussein, and with every Osama bin Laden any more than in the West, you may think to do away with every Napoleon Bonaparte, Adolf Hitler, or Benito Mussolini. History, unbeknown to every little upstart dictator for being metaphysically founded as it is on the continuity of causes and consequences and no less unbeknown to each collectively mightier dictatorial institution (think here of the Scythians, the Golden Horde, or the Wehrmacht), is always far, far more forceful than people.

Causes have consequences. And the older causes, for still being the entrenched historical causes, then, for the sake of this more continuously present, become in turn the consequences, until, for the sake of lessons unlearnt, this still continuous past will regurgitate itself back into your mouth from which to spew forth—yes, then spew forth from your own mouth—with renewed arrogance in warfare, insurgency, and worldwide terrorism.

As they say, history repeats itself (which fact, as for revising our views (although in different formats), we shall employ through the teaching technique of repetition). This is especially valuable for time travellers (as we all are) who as yet have never learnt to stomach its lessons. History's always here; there's no getting rid of history. And to prove that point, there's no better place to come to than Afghanistan—although you should have gone to the Soviet Union first—since the great Golden Horde got through there long before you and were eventually repelled, although that event never held back those infidels until the world's greatest cavalry charge led by John Sobieski against the Ottomans under Kara Mustafa Pasha, who, once again with the Tartar hordes, got as far through to the West as Vienna.

So it is, for both those lessons learnt, as in Sobieski's words on winning the Battle of Vienna, 'Veni, vidi, Deus vicit' (I came, I saw, and God won the battle), as well as for those lessons that can remain unlearnt. That greatest cavalry charge known to history, of the Polish hussars to relieve Vienna in 1683, would engender a national pride amongst the Poles—at odds with Sobieski's attribution of their victory to the divine hand—that could not possibly prevail when the same hussars with drawn swords would later charge against Nazi tanks in World War II.

So it also is, but only because of the outstretched arm of world history, that this Afghanistan, paradoxically situated on the North-West Frontier of the British Empire and on the South-East Frontier of the Russian Empire, would turn out to be a far bigger place by reason of such conflicting imperial histories than can ever be shown geographically by the space allotted to Afghanistan, whatever may be the scale on any map. Nevertheless (for being so much more), the paradox of its situational status in Afghani space does not end there any more than there is any end to the history of East and West until the end of space-time.

Here again, the Battle of Vienna in 1683 affords a remarkable lesson in world history by which that battle, one of the most important by which to define the respective terms of conflict and conquest between the East and West, was won by a spiritual coalition of like minds, which, whatever its painful drawbacks and ungainly downsides, saw itself to be blessed, as in both later world wars, by a spirit of defensive rather than of offensive action. The fact is that unresolved conflict engenders further conflict—and, as often, conflict from quarters that seek to reconcile and resolve the earlier conflict to which, unwittingly, they add their strength.

Thus, the Second World War is but a continuation of the First World War, the Cold War is a continuation of the Second World War, and so on for almost every war thereafter, because the USA, as one of the last of this world's great empires, has assumed the imperial role of umpire not only in all the world's wars, whether in Korea or in Vietnam, in Iraq or in Iran, or in Afghanistan (which is where we are now), but as if the USA were the appointed arbiter of democracy everywhere (without any need of the holy coalition of like minds and hearts that presumably saved the West for some bigger purpose than merely for itself).

It is as if Washington were bigger than all the United States of America (which it is) and as if bigger than all the rest of the world combined (which it isn't) in its trying (as always with the very best of intentions, like those of Britain) to resolve all the world's problems as best as it can. But (despite United Nations being already on the North American continent no less than the League of Nations was once on the European continent) this universal reconciliation is something which has never before been achieved between East and West—no, not even by Holy Mother Russia which stands midway like piggy-in-the-middle. Forever tried, both by those nations which have simply failed most miserably in the way they've gone about this self-appointed task, or else, if not already gone mostly bad in the process, but sometimes also completely mad in this continued pursuit to unite East with West, most of them, for once having so tried, eventually give up on their process of trying.

Nevertheless, neither the political paradox of status and space nor the situational paradox of position and place enables us to stop there at any point in our process of trying any more than we ourselves can slow down the speed of light by which time speeds up and so for ourselves to spend as long as we like in sorting out the affairs of Afghanistan. The point is that (for being no more than a pinprick on a map to denote either London, Washington, Paris, or Wellington) no matter however big or small Afghanistan may be, by reason of the outstretched arm of world history, there's so much more at stake.

Oh, we can't wait before beginning to spill the beans, but it so happens that Kabul, the capital of Afghanistan, is bigger by far than that very same country of which Kabul is the capital. Indeed, Kabul may prove in the end to be bigger than London, Washington, Paris, and Wellington in achieving, against all political odds, the sought-for breakthrough which others, whether in the name of democracy or of communism or of capitalism (or of any other of this world's political beliefs), would seek to impose on (and thus fail to secure for) Afghanistan.

Behind this largely speculative enquiry into resolving the present impasse for Afghanistan (as arduous as the Khyber forces its way through the Hindu Kush) lies the basic yet still largely unknown question of what constitutes the Afghan. This is as much a matter, as Aristotle would say, of knowing as much about other than Afghans than we might otherwise mistake for being Afghans. Like the Greeks (as was Aristotle, the philosopher-logician) or like the Maori (as was Kupe the explorer-discoverer) or like the Scots (as was King James for being the wisest fool in Christendom), are not also (for being so unique) the Afghans?

Don't also the Afghans have that proverbial union of tenderness and severity which so shocks the unserious? That kindly union so startles those who will refuse to compromise their own terms of self-reference. For their own part, why can they not think of reconciling the truth (as they see it) with what it takes (at one and the same time) for them to be both tough and kind? We could leave this for being still an open question, although (despite all sorts of conflicting academic opinions, each of which may hit the same target although shot from vastly different directions) etymologically, the Hindu Kush, formerly Caucasus Indicus, is no more Afghan for having been corrupted from the ancient Greek.

And so ... and so ... Kabul remained a well-ordered conundrum under Russian rule, until, as for any capital city besieged by its own countrymen from its hinterland (like Pétain's Vichy France under the Nazis, although in Kabul's case, by so many of the mullahs, the mujahideen, and the Taliban), it could be seen to have had all by itself 'a jolly good war'. Such then, as by this irony of fate, would Kabul, as capital city of Afghanistan, be seen to merit both *the best of times* as well as *the worst of times*?

Such is the fate of capital cities to share both their country's best of times as well as worst of times. Just as Londoners and heads of state during the London Blitz, as British Royalty opted to remain there during the Blitz, or of Moscow's minions as Hitler's shock troops reached the suburbs, the good and the bad are equally shared. The proverbial Dick Whittington, made lord mayor of London, bears no resemblance to the hard facts. It remains extremely hard to count the cost (as often earlier promoted during good times in terms of prestigiously making one's way to personal power through fame and fortune) of what it takes to exercise those correlatively continued responsibilities that risk their brute survival during bad times.

But then what are bad times? Once again, as compared with those we think to be good times, the equation is so relative as to make no sense than to be derived from the comparison. Thus, once again, as from *A Tale of Two Cities* (whether Kabul and Washington or Tehran and Baghdad), we quote the 'closure' with which Charles Dickens began his assessment of both London and Paris during the revolutions of that time. We'll credit (today's reverse values by which to bring up to date) the now extensively paraphrased quotation with its own analytically separatist paragraph.

It was the best of times [by now out of copyright]. It was the worst of times [historically stultified]. It was the age of wisdom [tell that to the marines]. It was the age of foolishness [nobody's listening]. It was the epoch of belief [amongst the damned]. It was the epoch of incredulity [amongst the angels]. It was the season of light [so look for the light]. It was the season of darkness [can't see a thing]. It was the spring of hope [but not in the substance of things unseen]. It was the winter of despair [for lack of our every hope in things both seen and unseen]. We had everything before us [for all remaining untried]. We had nothing before us [for all having been tried]. And so we were all going direct to heaven [despite we were all going more directly the other way]. In short, the period was so far like the present period that some of its noisiest authorities insisted on its being received, for good or for evil, in the superlative degree of comparison only.

Sorry, have to stop here … on the roadside halfway to Kabul … no more fuel … running out of gas … ammunition depleted … and fast running out of time.

* * *

A Pivotal History of East–West Relations
Part II

Downtown or City Centre
A city centre [by reason of total gridlock, no source cited] is most frequently [as in Minsk, Moscow, and Kiev] the earliest settled part of the city, as distinct often from its central business district [as in Paris and Amsterdam]. Likewise, for being in Edinburgh [or Dunedin] or in the pinyin or urban core of some far bigger and older Chinese City [such as Lujiazui on the east bank from Shanghai's Old Town on the west bank of the Huangpu River] old and new towns are almost all [categorically] divided into past and present, old and new.

John Macnab-Jamieson, *Been There and Done That Mostly*

Watch your step (Lujiazui is on the east bank from Shanghai's Old Town on the Huangpu River). Pick your way carefully (you're now on the west bank of the Huangpu River) when walking/running/swimming undercover. The least step beyond city limits or with a spring in your step and so out of urban character, and you'll be done for. Don't stop to ask your way (nobody else pretends to know). Don't look into another person's eyes (you'll blind them). Don't chew, but always scoff your rice. At whatever risk, don't wash your fruit or feet or peel your cucumbers. Walk briskly (but watch for open manholes) and dress well (we said, dress well).

Think on this, most carefully, but no lotus position reflections outside the city hall, please, for that being the place of highest reverence here. A city centre [total gridlock remains, so still no source cited] contains the hardware for that city's soul. Got the message? No! Well, if the city hall here is the highest place of reverence (even although there's no notice, other than No Parking), to say worship here, then to make any worthwhile transaction, one just has to attract the attention of the city hall. That hardware thus requires the closest of attention (before engaging oneself in the action).

Of course, that's not all. The software (or sustainable infrastructure) for that city is most often to be found (soft belly upwards) in the less than completely urbanised suburbs. The historic hardware for that same city, often vested for centuries in the tall towers erected to their own glory by city fathers, frequently needs overhaul and remedial healing (with sometimes grain silos being turned into restaurants), whereas the current software (highly charged) in the spreading suburbs needs redemption, as often from demonic defilement as from its faulty initial coding.

Once again, watch your step (both physically and electronically) when undercover. You think of yourself—for perhaps being the most masterly (MRCVS) of undercover men—that you can get away entirely with your clean-shaven and non-macho look by wearing a burka (or else burqa), but only so cautiously take your pick of undercover gear before you feel the pinch of discerning flesh being felt on your own bottom? No, when disguised as an unaccompanied female, you'll get fanny-groped and bottom-pinched all the way down the main street (try Chicken-Licken Street, instead, before the sky falls down) of almost any city street (now gridlocked by the Taliban in Afghanistan).

Do you often go downtown (in the USA) or frequent the city centre (in UK, NZ, and USSR)? If you're a military man undercover (a.k.a. an undercover military man), then in even every such small thing, you'll need to watch your P's and Q's (a.k.a. *zvony* and *queues*)—but what else to find but queues (but without a place to pee) in Moscow. For your own lookout (there's three or four McDonald's in Moscow now), get culture conscious before anyone else gets culture conscious about you.

So if you put salt on your cucumber and eat it with the rind on, you're bound to get called out (like someone I know of, but won't tell of whom) from behind your undercover as a military man for every such misdemeanour in London, but not of course in Moscow (unless for not eating the rind or omitting the salt). Likewise, for asking the way downtown (and not to the city centre) in Minsk, you might be on your way to a Gulag whilst mistaking yourself to be on the way to be giving a lecture in the state university (formerly of Lenin) but now of dear-knows-what.

So likewise, watch your P's and Q's (a.k.a. po-russki, calls, and queues) when in Baghdad, Tehran, and Kabul. And repeat 'Allahu Akbar' (as if on closed circuit TV, which you could be) even when you think God is so far off as to have turned off his own closed-circuit TV. You see, the most unfortunate thing about going undercover is that because your next-door neighbour cannot see you, you so soon start to think that neither can anyone else see you too. The only way to be sure of avoiding this socially mediated temptation to expose oneself is (despite every great personal risk) to stay open all hours, not to go undercover, and to stand firm (or infirm) as the rapidly developing cot-case which might turn out to be yours (so quickly and expectedly) at any fast-passing moment of rocket launching can quite easily happen to be.

How do you react (or rather respond to such military operations) when under heavy fire in the field of action? Some folks go into a state of anabolic abstraction. Others go into a state of catabolic abstraction. Other folks hit the roof, together with whosoever gets in the way. Luckily, the physiology of us angels doesn't allow for either of these three states or of any other state or way of failing to confront the issues. You humans might allow for that by way of seeing us angels to be immortal. Makes no difference, since, for as long as you mortals are mortal, that's the whole point of us angels being immortal.

Mock me and scoff at me for saying so (since there's nothing seriously written in these days of the locust that couldn't be mistaken for spoof), but it takes far more ancient history to constitute the capital of any country (dug deeper still by far than any superficial geography of this earth's upper crust) than it takes to constitute the hidden infrastructure of that same country itself. City centres are most often the deepest dug, but you can still find a Scythian burial mound towering outside your local supermarket (on which to toboggan in winter) in the screaming cold suburbs of Minsk.

Every country needs a centre by which to be held together, and without which, the country will simply fade away. Take a clan-centred or tribal country such as Bonnie Scotland, and you need as many capitals as there are castles, or an insular country such as Britain or New Zealand, where you need as many capitals as there are highlands, islands, lowlands, moorlands, and uplands by which to hold everything together. For that agglutinative purpose, you can think to take a fix on Auckland or on Glasgow or on Berlin or on Rotterdam, but sooner or later, the tourist trade or the shipbuilding recession or the housing crisis or the pit closures or the environmental issues or any other breaks in the long-established historical continuity will take their toll. What happened to the Hanseatic League is a history in itself.

Oh yes, and in their struggle for power, capital cities can suck their countries dry, no less than everything can be called to flow uphill across the Great European Plain to Moscow or from all subcontinental points of Australia to Canberra or from up north and across the English Midlands to London or from down south in Bluff to up north in Auckland. And when geography and history combine (either as a matter of parental inversion or of mutual dependency or of both together), only demonic deliverance (short of physical catastrophe) can break the bond.

Of course, local government is only a shoot of central government, thinks central government (despite the historical flow being quite the other way). Thus, the same flow (frequently tidal) can happen between competing continents. The USA and the USSR are purposefully akin, since both capitalism and communism (even within the same country) will compete against each other (business enterprise versus social welfare) to deplete all remaining resources and so leave both continents, no less than every such singularly divided country, completely exhausted by any so-called Cold War. The president or premier of any country who mistakes the impact of his or her own history for another's geography in such circumstances is so academically off target as to overlook the extent to which his or her own country, instead of extending paternal peacekeeping to other countries (don't mention here, either WWII or Afghanistan), is actively contributing to their international aggression.

To every capital city, there's a contextual hinterland, which grows and grows and still grows increasingly to serve the capital at the country's expense, unless, for the sake of the country, the capital learns to curtail its own growth. Unless the capital learns, the hinterland will flourish either at the expense of the country or at the expense of the capital, but more than likely at the expense of both. But the same happens also at lower and increasingly microscopic levels, as between central government and local government, as between schools and universities, as between churches and cathedrals, as often as it does between householders and their households. The real risks of a power struggle, often ruinously internecine, are the same the whole world over. This is the case, whether up-close or far away, and on which when attempting both up-close as well as far away, read Vince Flynn on the subject of transfer of power.

Once there were world travellers for whom learning more about this principle of historical quantification was their principal purpose of travel. For example, it would be the journalist Jason Burke, who, whilst professionally reporting as a newsman to the outer world on the public punishments and executions taking place in Kabul, found surprisingly of himself and to his own chagrin that he too, like anyone else, could also be something of a self-confessed voyeur for his being not unwanting to witness such ghoulish manifestations of injustice.

Now alas, with the indulgence of apparently cheap travel, there are merely hedonistic tourists who flit from place to place without noticing the poor, the helpless, and the homeless, together with the destitute, the deformed, and the disabled, and who, apart from the pleasure of being tempted by their constantly changing cuisine, are case-hardened by the luxuries in their own lives against seeing any more of reality than would enable them to feel as for others the least thing (other than to provide the pitiable basis for some traveller's tale).

For such fly-by-night tourists (even if they could ever get to Afghanistan to tell or write a book about it), Kabul is but a dot on the map, which could be anywhere on any map, and of whatever history, then little more than of the snapshots and selfies they took of themselves when there, which might just as well be under one of so many Cleopatra's needles as there are from Luxor to Petersburg to Washington, as there also are from London to Paris and thence from there to New York, as well as many more still back in Egypt and in many other places.

Geography without history is no more than several pinpricks on a map. That's the trouble too with tourism; it caters to the superficial side of things. It cultivates the senses of seeing without looking, looking without learning, hearing without listening, listening without reflecting, tasting without digesting, as also reading without thinking, writing without reading, touring without travelling, and (which, although geographically widening) goes without historically deepening the mind.

Alas, we all know how much of an old fart the well-travelled military person can be, whenever (as the old saying goes) he is forced to reminisce on his time spent in Poona, which boring commission is part of the undercover we are called (not forced) by the Supreme Command to maintain (not only for the safety of ourselves but also for the safety of others). Mind you, dearest readers, both individual events as well as their cosmic contexts have radically worsened since then, for all that one's not-so-angelic grandfather served so much regimental time in India (although never commissioned to spend summers in Poona).

Once again ... running out of space ... sleeping in the streets ... no longer running ... can't get ahold on what's happening ... We're all transients ... all on the road ... to somewhere ... maybe nowhere ... Anybody seen my wife? Anyone seen my wife? My grandma says (for always playing the same game with her grandson at the expense of her daughter-in-law) that 'she's gone off with the sodjers tae Poona!'

Don't you believe it! It's grandma who's married to a military man, so presumably she knows more about holidaying in Poona. Meanwhile, after nine months and seven days' pregnant pause ... you'll have noticed ... surely ... why, keep your wits about you ... dearest readers ... to observe ... to note ... to see ... that as time shortens and space extends ... (which is what this space-extending punctuation is intended to indicate to anyone who is reading the signs of the times) ... that the fast-shrinking length of these sporadic chapters also shortens ... And as space goes on stretching ... ultimately for as far (both in time and space) as it takes any such elastic universe as ours ... of which this planet Earth is only a small component ... to break ... to break ... to break with all we think to know ...

Bear with me awhile; it won't be for long! There are so many different levels of disorderliness between chaos and cosmos in this life which, without experiencing, one has no cause to refute the existence of one's own heaven, far less the existence of another's hell. This increasingly brittle planet of ours (by now the withered and soon-to-be-forbidden fruit of past creation) is set to fall, to break free from all the other notions by which it could have been once fulfilled.

So too, does the conclusion of this book perpetually distance itself (although some would say recede from the writer) which, as a sign of the times, more than indicates that time is moving … still moving … still moving faster … for moving on … so here and now, whilst here and now still persists … still persists to exist … we'll simply take time out rather than just mark time … mark time … mark time … until we have mastered enough history of both heaven and earth to deal with the last remnant of resurgent darkness …

Oh, woe … oh, woe … oh, woe … not just resurgent darkness … since before the final last conflict shall come, a whopping great regurgitation of the deepest and widest darkness, as never ever before felt with such intensity, despite the still prevailing extension of outer space, since time itself is ever moving faster … moving faster … and moving faster … by moving on …

So then don't delay. Time itself is at a premium. If you have only worldly savings, be sure to cash them in … cash them in whilst there is still cash to buy you out. These signs of the times are like chestnuts whose skins haven't been pricked and so, at any time soon, are all likely to explode. They may all still look quite dandy whilst left roasting in a pan … so cash in whatever chestnuts are just about to burst. These are the signs of the times …

* * *

A Pivotal History of East–West Relations
Part III

City-Centred in Kabul
According to Breaking News [as the ever-present-future is now called but never known] the Americans were pushing on towards Baghdad … [although then, somewhat ironically, the unexpected happened] with a British soldier being killed in a car crash … Then it was Oriana reporting from Baghdad, her face growing thinner, paler, more shadowed by the minute and looking so beautiful—as if the stars and rockets and coloured smoke behind her were purely backdrop … Predictably her sympathies were entirely with the beleaguered Iraqis.

Jilly Cooper, *Wicked!*

As for me, for being always very much a prophetic traveller in the spirit and thus without any need or want to be always physically toing and froing, I accordingly stay very often firmly fixed (often overfixed for being so firmly fixed) in one place. Yet nothing makes for more nonsense—as seen by those who are part of the continual toing and froing that now takes place as the precursor or harbinger of these end times—than for someone to stand firm in the face of conflict. We all (without knowing what we ask for) plead for 'closure' and fail to find it by our running shy of openness. It takes complete openness … always … to obtain closure. And the more openness there is, then the more conclusive is the closure.

For my being now for the moment in Baghdad and no longer in Kabul, then like any reading raider (a.k.a. raiding reader), you've caught me out! You've caught me out, as you would have caught out any Britisher against the backdrop of all the spreading flack and firepower of the most recent Anglo-American bombardment of Baghdad, since here you find me quietly reading Jilly Cooper's 846-paged blockbuster *Wicked!*

As with most modern novels, for the lack of anything but a secular context in which to write, the moral message (if any such thing still pertains to writing) is muted (unless silenced outright) by our driving need for morally neutral narrative. Its underlying message (if any) is thus most likely to be doomed by all the literary fun, frolic, and fireworks required to assuage the lack of moral thought in modern writing (never mind any attempt at modern literature).

Alas! Even poetry is now often no more than a five-finger piano exercise [as performed by a retarded five-year-old beginner], by which prodigious effort of child prodigies (given OBEs or made members of the now defunct British Empire), being force-fed downwards to instant fame rather than upwards to lasting acclaim, serve only over time to burn out every prospect of any continuing British Empire. Well, now that's long gone, yet they still feed themselves no less ravenously (taking into account our now rapidly futuristic speed-up time for any education to project any infant, far less pupil, far less student, far less scholar into unfathomable space, where almost every doctoral thesis becomes no more than a ten-finger piano exercise [as performed by a retarded ten-year-old beginner on a honky-tonk piano]. Music has become minimalist, but celebrities of all sorts, however much they are all maximised, are far sooner cut down to size.

No less than by the same non-military means (the briefest smack being now outlawed from even parental education), warfare is now likewise muted or even doomed to destruction for being, like the law, any kind of even chivalric resolution process. Why, even libraries are shutting down, since there's no zest of the spirit left in writing or zest of the spirit to pursue (even just *The Peterkin Papers*) in serious reading where the youthful have been brought up to expect only virtual and push-button answers (and so but for lack of the briefest smack in their upbringing) have begun by now to punch, punish, kick, and defraud their parents of all parental authority.

The main fault of *Wicked!* [apart from its wayward way with words as so demonstrated by its title] is to be thoroughly misunderstood (most often for what it is most certainly not). The trouble with contrived humour, especially when we choose to keep a stiff upper lip and stay respectable, even although we might feel more like breaking down into (crocodile or otherwise) tears, is that we end up by having a good stoic laugh (far worse in the long run than maintaining that stiff upper lip).

Here, if only we had time and there was not the presently ongoing rocket attack bringing down houses to suffocate infants in the suburbs of Kabul, we would cross from our reading of Chekov's *Cherry Orchard* to Gorky's *Lower Depths* and so finish with our reading group's commentary confirming the intended objective of De Mandeville's *Grumbling Hive.* Well, buck up, you slower readers, or else, for all the many more good books being published these days, you'll get so far left behind as to not know what we're even more remotely talking about.

Consequently (as well as being the more precisely, consequentially), it is as hard to distinguish approbation from disapprobation for events (*in fact*) which, in turn, inclines the seriousness of such a book, as either *Wicked!* or *The Soul-Catcher* (purportedly a work of fiction), to be dismissed for all the wrong but nevertheless highly entertaining reasons (*in fiction*). You probably disbelieve of me that against such a backdrop of flares, fires, and coloured smoke in which men, women, and children are being incinerated, I could consecrate my mind enough to concentrate on no more than literary appreciation. Nonsense, without yet having completely blown my cover (also for me as an angelic academic with no less powers of consecrated concentration than Derek Prince, C. S. Lewis, and J. R. R. Tolkien), I too am still very much a military man.

A pun on Dickens's *Tale of Two Cities* and an object lesson on the way in which today's morally lax and lame-faced process of ameliorating the meaning of words such as *wicked* from their task of proclaiming profanities (of which the less than pure backdrop of foul language to Cooper's novel proclaims to many) rather to that alternative task, instead, of extolling the sublime *Wicked!* (as subtitled *A Tale of Two Schools*). The whole f—g trouble with democracy (as first so tellingly told by Plato, as if he didn't need the f—g death of f—g Socrates by which to confirm it) is that (no less by the UK than by the USSR version of democracy) it elevates the lower depths to the upper heights (as seen no higher than by the upper class) and so deprives the lower classes (as prevailingly unseen by themselves) forever to the lower depths. Do we so make our angelic selves clear, or do we, both for yourselves and ourselves, mistake ourselves (individually, at least) for not being democratically demonic?

Amongst many other things (including the moral degeneracy and bureaucratic corruption at all levels of English life), it's a real-life farce on the dispiriting state of English education. Nevertheless, when you're in the front line of any battle (whether in Kabul or Baghdad), you've just got to stand firm—however much that rock-solid firmness may be misunderstood by those others who're frightened to do more than give way before running away.

For those who have never read *A Tale of Two Cities* in which an apparently rock-solid London could be compared with Kabul or a teetering Baghdad compared with an apparently rock-sold Washington, far less *A Tale of Two Schools* (to see the privileged education of the English upper classes compared with the deprivation of their lower depths), then here read again (once more, but now straight, without the paraphrases from our early reading group) that famous first sentence that sums up poverty and profligacy for all time. Here again, although given now in the raw: 'It was the best of times, it was the worst of times, it was the age of wisdom, it was the age of foolishness, it was the epoch of belief, it was the epoch of incredulity, it was the season of light, it was the season of darkness, it was the spring of hope, it was the winter of despair, we had everything before us, we had nothing before us, we were all going direct to heaven, we were all going direct the other way—in short, the period was so far like the present period, that some of its noisiest authorities insisted on its being received, for good or for evil, in the superlative degree of comparison only.'

Yes, indeed, that prophecy still stands. It stands for London no less than Kabul and for Washington no less than for Baghdad. And it still stands, no matter for however long we too shall still remain standing and so to do nothing (but whatever's still wrong) with our trying to ameliorate the evils of the world and the sorrows of mankind until this world's sorry outcome be fulfilled.

For us angels, this means standing firm in Moscow at the inevitable fall of communism, standing firm in Washington during the continuing decline of capitalism, or it could be when next in line in Wellington (whenever comes the long-expected earthquake from the Ring of Fire to shake and hit that foremost fault line). We stay wherever we're called and commissioned to remain by the Supreme Command. For the present, our stay is in Kabul (the capital still officially of Afghanistan), and this no less than although it is to one's glory to overlook an offence (Revelation 19:11).

Although often under siege from both bombers within and bombers without (although a very privileged minority of its citizens may come and go on Afghan Airlines), like everyone else trapped wherever they may be (in New York, Minsk, or Montmartre), I too still travel, although only in angelic space-time. We're all time travellers, although very few of us accept our appointed commission to read the signs of the times.

Nevertheless, still as a military man, I stay centred in Kabul for as long as my commission to do so holds out, for my commission from the Supreme Command to stay here for as long as the present conflict continues is in itself (as you may expect from the Supreme Command) a labour of love. That may surprise you, as much as to learn that in this world, no love can be expressed without engendering conflict and exciting reprisals, as much as did Job (another military man) for his being the most righteous man in the whole land of Uz.

The fact (to which no blame can be attached) is that most folks wouldn't know the difference between a love poem and a war story, since most of the greatest war stories (as that of Homer's *Ulysses*) are love stories and most of the greatest love stories (such as that of Victor Hugo's *Les Misérables*) are war stories. Thus, without learning from their lack of love between the Montague and Capulet families, Shakespeare's *Romeo and Juliet* remains mostly misunderstood and unresolved to readers as an unhappy love poem (as if, as in *A Midsummer Night's Dream*, 'the course of true love never did run smooth').

Likewise, Tolstoy's *War and Peace*, to be fully understood, must be considered as much a love story as it is a war story (for which compromise it is neither amongst the greatest of love stories nor amongst the greatest of war stories but most certainly from many other points of view amongst the greatest of historical novels of all time). Whilst, like life itself and whether read in Tehran, Middlemarch, or in Aberdeen, Nabokov's *Lolita* is so confused that, for being neither one thing nor the other, it becomes too much of both and so confusing to everyone (whether they know of that confusion or not).

Most people avoid conflict (some people as if it were the plague) and so, on encountering conflict, are prone to run away (as if mere conflict truly were the plague), and yet (the Supreme Command willing) they may be truly plagued by conflict until (like Apostle Paul, likewise a military man) there is ultimately no means of running away from what they mistake for being the plague (and in extreme cases, so also by their deepest fear, as in the book of Job) become, through fear, to be the very ones who bring about the plague.

You see, by overcoming conflict through confrontational love, time is always on our side, as it always is on the side of those who take time seriously. Taking time seriously is, at the heart of things, an expression of love. Love is patient; love is kind. It is not proud, boastful, envious, or easily angered. It keeps no record of wrongs. Likewise, love always hopes, always trusts, always protects, and always perseveres.

Love never lets the truth pass unnoticed and so also never fails. All these things are expressions of time. Some attributes are for always, others are for never, and some attributes, such as patience and perseverance, cannot be expressed except over time. As you can now see, the supreme sin against every means of expressing our love for life is simply to waste, mistake, or mistrust the giving of time. As the lawyers say (with but a smidgen of its full forcefulness for all living things), 'Time is of the essence.'

So then here we stay (most extensively) in one place—and for the present (most intensively) in Kabul—but always in love with this remote and most capricious place, and so all our extensive travelling (mistaken by most of our friends for personal inertia) is done only in time. Look, there are rockets of recession being fired everywhere these days. Your household can be hit in the Scottish Highlands just as easily as in the Afghan Highlands these days. Without taking this time to study and reflect on world history (the increasing lack of which interactive interest amongst today's nations denotes a rabid form of public dementia), there is only increasing prejudice towards self-interest.

Here, breathe deeply, since time is of even more the essence! This North-West Frontier, as it has been known for a time to the British, and this South-East Frontier, as it has been known for a time to the Russians, as well as this no man's land [even to the Afghans] of Afghanistan, whose control has been claimed latterly in the name of democracy as if for all time by the Americans, is where the mullahs (the religious clerics, teachers, preachers, and leaders) first established the Taliban (literally, their students and followers) to take away control from the disintegrating mujahideen (previously the freedom fighters against the USSR, but then as brigands against the peasants and finally in gangs against each other). The Taliban is replaced by NATO/UN/USA peacekeeping forces in Afghanistan, yet all these individual groups professedly engaged in peacekeeping are by now already, and all so very apparently, running out of time.

As so often has been said (at least since 2006), 'Time is running out for Afghanistan' and so 'in an attempt to break the stalemate in a war that has now passed to a third US commander-in-chief, the Pentagon proposes to send in a reported further 4,000 US troops'. This is roughly half of the 8,400 US troops capped in Afghanistan by the previous commander-in-chief, but only under twice as many as the 2,400 US military deaths in Afghanistan suffered since 2001.

In the celestial scheme of things, peacekeeping seems like timekeeping, but this is so merely in the solar scheme of things and so is more like our own entirely self-interested process of clock-watching rather than by timekeeping, because merely to keep the peace admits to all lack of peace by any other means kept. Peacekeeping is rarely any sort of timepiece that keeps time by itself. On the contrary, the peacekeeper needs always be present, for he or she is no more than a highly subjective and fallible stand-in for the true celestial timepiece by which peace can only be made to be kept.

Meanwhile there's an ethics to tourism (or so we think) and most certainly to military tourism (or so we would hope), but not much of an ethics (so it would appear) for whatever mere sightseeing diverts our eyes from seeing things as they are for what they really are. There's even an ethics for terrorism—without an understanding of which there's no point to our trying either to prevent or to put a stop to terrorism. Those who just go to gawk at India's Taj Mahal or at

Canada's Victoria Falls or at the Mona Lisa in the Louvre are as likely to just gawk at Taliban executions in the Ghazi Football Stadium of Kabul. I've already warned you—as much to warn you against casually joining in the battle as to encourage you most seriously, since we've got work to do together—and no time for sightseeing. That's right, absolutely no time left on earth (however much for sightseeing), nevertheless, no more time for just sightseeing.

BOOK EIGHT

Going Nowhere or Going Native
As Nights Grow Longer and Darkness Deepens

Tying Up Loose Ends by Going Native
If I were a European, I never would have left my
home to come to Kabul. Not in those days. I would
have stayed in Poland or England or Italy where there
were no whistling rockets above, where meat and
vegetables were abundant, and women weren't afraid
to step outside their homes. Why leave such a paradise
to come to Kabul.

Nadia Hashim, *When the Moon is Low*

Intro 1—Neil: We began this report (essentially a jurisprudential one, which, unless you've forgotten, is one which critically analyses the relationship of law to justice) on the basis that the provision of justice is God's sovereign prerogative. 'Justice is mine,' says the Lord our God. Accordingly, he has complete sovereignty over the provision of justice, which he may choose to do on earth by extending or reducing the limits of law. The provision of justice (which, as a life science, can reach explosive proportions) thus operates under the principle of legal containment (in itself no more than a physical science).

On the other hand, by granting to humans their own freedom of will, God makes himself vulnerable to what then becomes mankind's sovereignty in its exercise of that free will. This reciprocal principle, when effectuated by mankind in choosing to exceed the (juristically determined) limits of law, ensures that mankind reaps for itself the exact level of retributive justice so determined from having gone beyond the limits of lawmaking. And as often as not, the divine irony of this cosmological process emanates from the fact that it is by way of man's own purported lawmaking that mankind exceeds the limits of law by which to perpetrate its very own juristic lawbreaking.

By exercise of its own legislative volition, mankind thus increasingly outlaws itself from God. On this score, some jurisprudential critics might point to laws which purportedly allow for abortion on demand, divorce on demand, marriage on demand, welfare on demand, and ultimately every sort of self-determination, including that of life itself, as of a universal right payable on demand. That, of course, is only the tip of a titanic iceberg, as any serious reader of Lon Fuller's *Morality of Law* (distinguishing authentic law from counterfeit law) and Wesley Hohfeld's *Fundamental Legal Conceptions* (distinguishing spurious rights from real rights) will recognise. As once said and then more fully understood for being said than it could ever now be understood, the road to hell is paved with good intentions.

As seen on earth by any synthetic (or creative) cosmologist rather than by any analytic (or critically scientific) cosmologist (and infinitely more deeply understood by any angel from heaven who combines both critical and creative faculties), cosmic justice then follows from the Supreme Command being lord of all that this jurisprudential relationship applies not just throughout this world's known universe but also throughout what remains of the humanly unknown cosmos. We are aiming to maintain our 20/20 prophetic vision (a tall enough order in itself far less than to push for its extension), but this aim does not limit the readability of this report to those readers with less than 20/20 vision. If you have lived long enough in this now rapidly dying world to have heard the call to revere the march of human progress, you will not need to look around now to have seen that once confident goose-step degenerate to a funereal slow march before resorting to a limping crawl.

Intro 2—Alcuin (the still look-ahead librarian): With anything less than 20/20 vision right now, it may help you, dearest readers, to undertake a survey of your own present level of readership. What questions would you ask of yourself, and how would you answer them? May you be blessed beyond belief by your undertaking this assignment from which to find out more about yourself in the course of pursuing 20/20 prophetic vision.

So then design and undertake your very own survey (the results of which may then far exceed this writer's less than 20/20 prophetic vision). By then, you'll have a book review, so always bear in mind that every book review is as much a review of the reviewer as it is of the writer and of the reader. No book (since $E = mc^2$ first declared) can be written without reviewing its writer any more than that book can be read without its reader being reviewed by both writer and reader, so where does that leave the review written by any reviewer if not yet back again to the realm of the creative writer?

Intro 3—Augustus: This report (made under heavy fire in the field of service to the Supreme Command) does so by trying to explain to humans (by way of jurisprudence in action) the process of telescoping time. On this score, then relax, since attempting to telescope time will not commit you to the big bang theory any more than entrapping enough antiprotons by a powerful enough antimagnetic field will demonstrate sufficient asymmetry to explain the present superabundance of all matter (but that of grey matter). No, what we have in mind (over matter) by way of telescoping time (however temporarily) is no more than a prototype for spiritual time travel.

All readers attempting to review themselves at whatever level of angelic flight they have developed under disciplined obedience to the Supreme Command will find even the earliest experience of bodily levitation (relieving the human soul from all sorts of demonic fears and associated burdens) is achieved more *per aspera* (through hard-won spiritual exercise) than through rocket science and technology. Such is the experience of raising one's soul-catching potential beyond belief (although entirely dependent on one's existing level of already faith-held experience). Remember, as Virgil so aptly writes, 'Non est ad astra mollis e terris via'—or, in other words, 'There is no easy way from earth to the stars.'

This telescoping of time is done, as you readers will by now know, first, by way of inducing lower-level abstraction (to prepare and accommodate the rather sluggish human mind to focus on higher things). From lower-level abstraction, the human mindset is then prepared (although at first often quite painfully) to engage in upper-level abstraction. And then so on and so on, from every lower to higher level of abstraction (for which process refer back to the rather dry foreword of this report on the topic of abstraction), so as to enable humans (ahead of their own assumed time) ultimately to engage in angelic space travel.

Take every care in all this need for the utmost expeditiousness all the same, because (apart from the many occult and counterfeit ways of engaging in spiritual levitation), there is only one righteous means of doing so in accordance with the universal laws of the Supreme Command. Perhaps now, however, this is the most cautiously telescoped time (since the speed of light is so fast failing in which to introduce you to your very own (if not self-destined, then self-determined) pace of soul-catching. And of course, as always, when under extreme heavenly command, you are, until fully committed and commissioned for this task, free to disengage from further instruction.

Intro 4—Ninian: What has gone before, no less than what follows (by now at the postdoctoral level of abstraction) is no more than (as always intended) to present a preliminary treatise on soul-catching. As for each introduction (no less than for the present one), so also for each block course (the eighth of which is represented by this book), these are always conducted under constant supervision of the angelic host.

To reach this precise point (whether you foresaw it or not), your faith as a reader has already been tested. Nevertheless, your heavenly credentials for soul-catching can be confirmed only by your engagement in the enterprise itself. This engagement requires (1) your following this report's 20/20 prophetic vision for AD 2020 and beyond; (2) your continued transmission of the gospel message to others who have not yet felt the cosmic shock of finding out that most of heaven's history has already been fulfilled on earth; (3) that for being fiercely fought and already won, this history of heaven has been made not as so much as directed by God in heaven but as delegated by God to mankind through Jesus Christ for the purpose of being fulfilled on earth; (4) that this history of heaven (unlike that of hell which relies on counterfeited happenstance) is directionally determined by human responses made to those ideas emanating from heaven; and (5) that in terms of implementing those ideas, a feminine sensitivity directed towards human relations holds a distinctively intuitive advantage over that male insensitivity which tends to be drawn towards gathering data, evaluating hard facts, accounting for figures, and gripping relentlessly on to concrete events. Believe me, the outcome for all mankind teeters on the mind of man.

Intro 5—Saunt Magret (the Pearl of Scotia and wife of King Malcolm III, nicknamed Canmore or Bighead): Beyond this precise point (beyond which there's little hope of imminent return), much more needs to be learnt from practical experience by which to distinguish the juristic sheep from the legal billy goats, since (1) by reason of their cut and dried masculine mind, males tend to take a quick fix on facts, figures, and events; likewise (2) it is this quick fix on physicality which so often consumes (rather than liberates) the human mind and so (3) either intimidates the gentler spirit or else provokes it to rebellion and so (4) blinds the most forceful part of all mankind to the cosmic light. Furthermore, (5) rather than by way of godly ideas given to liberate and to transform the human mind, it then becomes the perverse role of those man-made lapidary events which so often firmly grip and so finally fixate mankind's neural pathways so that (6) all attempts at the neural transformation so necessary for breaking cover (see Book 9 following) become blocked in time or, worse still, stay permanently fixed for all time.

Rather than liberate the mind of mankind from all this mischief, (7) the feminine exercise of this intuitive advantage towards ideas received and held by women (after all, it was women who were the first to see their risen Lord Jesus Christ) is so often withheld by men from women as to disadvantage the whole of mankind from seeing any more of the cosmic light than stray sparks amid the prevailing darkness so that (8) the trauma strongly felt mostly by women (but also by the feminine side of perceptive and prophetic men) bends some suffering souls towards brutality of mind and deficiency of spirit and (9) that more especially for women, in their being still held back by wayward men from their divinely created perceptive functions, they either remain backward or ineffective in their responses or else, through overcompensation, they become forwardly rebellious in expressing what then become their contraries.

What we are discussing here is critically important, since in the resultant impasse which hell eventually brings about to pervert or blockade the spiritual expression of mankind's finest, most creative, and purest of human feelings, then either the age-old Jezebelic spirit, or else that of the end-time whore of Babylon takes over. These happen to be the demonic spirits (although demons always hunt in packs) to which every macho male is made most vulnerable.

This accounts for the fact that Counterfeit Command afflicts the whole of mankind most ingeniously through subverting and usurping the foremost and most feminine strengths expressed through womanhood (and so then in turn usurping and subverting manhood) in its all-out struggle to pervert mankind.

The same human scenario that took place once before in the Garden of Eden (giving rise to the Jezebelic spirit) is now being replayed in these end times with far greater intensity across the world (giving rise eventually to the Whore of Babylon). Saddam Hussein (most obviously by his restoration of demonic Babylon in modern Iraq) no less than professed world-conquerors like Tamerlane, Napoleon, and Adolph Hitler, are among the many macho-males who fall victim to the same demonic forces, just as standing firm behind every man (of whatsoever sort) there is always either a righteous or an unrighteous woman.

Intro 6—Mungo: What therefore follows (for this tediously telescoped) but excitingly revealed moment of time, therefore, is this report's very short and exactingly abstract treatise on soul-catching. If you human readers are to follow suit (a legal phrase) in our angelic vocation of soul-catching, then this must be done on terms and conditions open to discussion but without disclaimers. After reviewing your earlier studies on the history of heaven (on which to test your faith), you shall then be examined as to your own chosen course of committed action. This preliminary examination shall seek to assess your proficiency in soul-searching every victim's earthly life as to what proportion at that last moment of contingent life may be redeemable by which to justify that victim's soul being caught by heaven rather than being snatched to hell. The measure of your assessment in each and every such case relates to the existing level of forgiveness emanating from those already hurting, maimed, fearful, or disabled victims. This most rigorous assessment of already established forgiveness for what is about to happen to them is the only one you can apply to determine which will wear the victor's crown. So then, pay full attention to every detail of this postdoctoral dissertation on whoever you may be called to be, or whatever you may be called to do by way of engaging in this exercise of soul-catching. Meanwhile, don't worry about however much these provisions which follow may appear to grieve and irritate, by their proving to be contentious and controversial to others (possibly themselves unforgiving persons). It is your own responses which are the only ones at issue.

Intro 7—Augustus: First, understand that for fear of the world, most folks will not share their soul. After all, look what happened to Christ—he was crucified on a cross simply for sharing his soul! Do you, dearest reader, really want to pick up and carry your cross and so follow suit (that same legal phrase, by which to indicate one's committal and commitment to one's acknowledged leader)? The response to this is yours by way of free volition.

The universal law (not a jot or tittle of which has been, nor could be abrogated, even by the love of Christ) is a hard taskmaster. Think very carefully before committing yourself to this commission from the Supreme Command. Heaven itself is bound by the same legal system (learn as much of it in this life as you can find out) as applies inherently to this earth.

So then what happens if in this life, you won't share your soul? Well, the paradox is that the more you commit yourself to saving your own soul, instead of simply sharing your soul, then the more you lose your soul, and so then ultimately, you cannot be saved.

Most people, once again for fear of this world, try to save their souls by hiding their souls, either deep within their own bodies or else in what they consider to be some safe place apart from their bodies. In short, for the sake of this world and not of the next world, they tend to their bodies and not to their souls.

They may manage to hide their souls so deep within their own bodies, that they either become completely unaware of their own souls or else more and more vehemently deny (even the existence) of their own souls. Unless by the grace and favour of their Father (Yahweh) in heaven, they put themselves and their souls (both physically as well as spiritually) completely beyond the redemptive power of Jesus Christ, their Saviour.

Hey, what a mess they have made not only of their own lives but by reason of having dismissed their vocation of soul-catching, so also what a mess they may have made of the lives of so many others. You simply cannot save your own soul (no matter how close you snuggle up to your own Father in heaven) without attending to the fatherless souls of others.

In trying so hard as many people in all walks of life and professing all sorts of levels of faith, attempting (when face to face, as they think with their own Father God) to solve for themselves this pre-eminently tricky question of their own salvation without caring for the salvation of others, their every effort is rendered completely counterproductive by reason of their failure (through personal pride perhaps or fear of man perhaps or through feelings of personal unworthiness perhaps) to share their human soul with other human souls.

Admittedly, it takes some finesse to share one's soul with other souls—experience of the world's ways, freedom from unresolved hurt and pain, a sensitivity to souls much different (by the uniqueness of each person's soul) to one's own soul, and a certain kind of inspiration, a sense of calling, and a recognition of empowerment (other than one's own) to share with others the intimacy of one's own soul. One has to develop a certain kind of artistry in one's vocation of soul-sharing that can only come both from hard-earned experience and an ever closer and continuing encounter with one's Father in heaven.

Intro 8—Second Peter (sometimes known as Ralph-Peter): Hey there, you think yourself a big-time lawyer, a small-time car salesman, a well-known prostitute, a prestigious plumber, an ingenious electrician, an old lag in jail, a patient in a psychiatric ward, a cancer patient already given up for dead, a defeated politician, a distraught solo mum—why, none are immune or excluded from having their everyday vocation to share their soul! So then don't bother with taking the next step in soul-catching, unless and until you can first share your soul.

For your next step in what will be for you then the pure science (or else fine art) of soul-catching (after having first learnt how to share your soul with as many other different souls as possible), you must then prepare yourselves, dearest readers, to reach and engage all souls (a clerical phrase to denote souls of every possible description) with your whole mind, heart, and unselfishly shared soul when tuned to an even still higher level of prayerful, if not also heavenly, abstraction. You must certainly reach that highest of levels before you can devote your received empowerment to what then becomes the very practical task of saving souls. Meanwhile (since time is by now exceedingly telescoped towards infinity), remember always that practical practice applied willy-nilly without strategic theory is an abomination to the Lord for its lack of coordination between heaven and earth in their different fields of one and the same spiritual battle.

Intro 9—James (also known as Seamus or Shane): We can pick here that news of this abomination (indulging in practical engagement without strategic theory) worries some of you readers. Alas, this may cause you to pull back not only from reaching the next level of abstraction from worldly affairs as required for the process of soul-catching but also from the level of abstraction which you have already reached to expedite your own soul-sharing. Never fear, and don't worry. Sometimes one has to go (only a little some ways) back in order to reach so much further forward.

Let's first be clear (having already got there) that the sharing of your entrepreneurial soul (easier for the artistically and creatively inclined) is not so hard as it seems (for those when finally commissioned) to the Supreme Command as it is often so very hard for those subjected to simply do what they're told by obeying task force instructions as if only under the command theory of law. The difference is best figuratively explained to those on earth in terms of constitutional law—between citizens of heaven who uphold the law and subjects of earth on whom the heavy load of the law is laid. In real terms, nevertheless, remember that for citizens of heaven being also the subjects of that same kingdom of heaven, subjectivity and objectivity are no longer divorced as required by earthly predication but instead are united under one and the same shared legal, logical, and linguistic system.

Intro 10—Callum (also known as John Three): We used the scientific abstract (once again, see this report's Foreword on the scientific abstract) as an analogue (or model) for the accustomed process in moving from the command theory of law to the commissioned theory of law. This process is facilitated by consciously passing through different levels of increasing abstraction. These two theories of law—one for the commanded subject (at a lower level of subjective focus) and the other for the committed citizen (at a higher level of more objectively predicated focus)—are literally worlds apart (for being in heaven one and the same).

So then, dearest readers, how do you primarily see yourself—either (1) at a lower level of subjective focus as a commanded subject of earth or else (2) at the more objectively predicated level of focus you aspire to—as a commissioned citizen of heaven? The choice (as you know) is entirely yours, but of course, for each category of (either earthly or heavenly) engagement and endeavour you choose, you have to acquire, maintain, and satisfy the prerequisite heavenly credentials by which to fulfil your chosen task.

Meanwhile (the meaning of which is in constant countdown), it may be helpful for you to know that the scientific abstract (like the lawyer's case note or the legislator's introductory explanation) does both all these but also many other and far less definable things. The more radical the conclusion to which anyone's abstract or headnote is heading, then like any academic thesis (or lawyer's brief), the longer it goes on before springing the surprise by way of reaching some completely unforeseen, if not also mind-boggling, outcome.

Any other way of hefting these everyday things would be extremely pettifogging. But here and there, by your soul-searching (any exceedingly brief) history of heaven and your soul-sharing (no more than a bare-bones) history of hell, you have been helped (so far as is possible without either curtailing, far less positively programming or negating your own completely free responses) to find your own life's most fruitful vocation. Remember always, however, that all life is judged (if not here on earth, then afterwards in heaven) by its most ordinary fruits (which, like any mustard seed on earth, may seem preposterously small) and not by its virtuoso gifts from heaven (which on earth may instead appear to be entrepreneurially huge).

Besides, in all these due processes of both science and law, no less than for history and prophecy, these processes still follow the standard forms of dynamic storytelling (which may stretch the patience of those who look for more communicative exactitude (instead of workable precision) than the endeavour is designed to bear).

The principle of the utmost postponement operates throughout (as in any war of attrition), allowing this report itself to account for the specific particulars of the enterprise by which to reach its own hopefully hallowed, rightful, and thus righteous conclusion.

As you can see, as in any court of equity, we don't hurry things along in heaven. The universal laws of heaven are ecclesiastical laws (where one day may be as a thousand days) much to the impatience of those on earth who have never yet graduated from being under the command (as it may be of the Supreme Command) to that of fulfilling their own more direct Supreme Commission.

Intro 11—Neil (a.k.a. Neal, Niall, and Niger): Don't be disappointed, therefore, that by presaging both this earth's past flood together with this world's future fire, this report seems (like any planet) to go round and round on its own trajectory, since solar time is tactically cyclic (and not just strategically linear). Remember also that the most emphatic learning period of life is during one's youthfulness—so do all one can to maintain one's youthfulness—in body, heart, mind, and soul (or spirit). Yet remember also that the only way to avoid a life of long and often painful learning is to die young and, perhaps worse still, to die (however young or old) without ever having personally enjoyed the consequential fruits of one's youthful learning.

Intro 12—Augustus (again): So then before saying any final goodbye (which may or may not come soon) to you, our dearest readers, take every care in choosing and following one's everyday education, and this by continuing it wholeheartedly to the very end of your own time.

Loading up on information (especially on incidental information at the expense of fundamental information, or on brute rather than refined information) when done without any real purpose for doing so can lead, and often does lead to life-long informational overload of the most serious kind. Purpose-driven people don't usually suffer from that sort of informational overload but there are all sorts of other informational over-loadings which can infiltrate into the soul, or overcome the will, or corrupt the heart, or disrupt the mindset (as through overhearing gossip, suffering unrelieved guilt, suppressing undeserved blame, re-living justified feelings of shame, and so on). This in turn explains how overloaded minds (often producing memory-loss and dementia in the elderly and autism among youth) will seek to fill the resulting void left in their minds brought about by suppressing the informational overload of troublesome data (resulting from such things as household conflict or school bullying) by their manufacturing their own kind of more manageable yet still pathological states of increasing abstraction, unjustified projection, or unwholesome diversions, in each case to induce or produce their own withdrawal from the troublesome data.

There's no goodbye for the lack of any first salutation. People just walk off the stage—the French way of exit, as Tolstoy calls what today's Britons know for being Brexit—and not even the curtain comes down at the end of the play.

All the same, today's overly pragmatic specialisation of academic form and function has left very little time and energy for relaxed generalisation. So sorry for that. Perhaps when we next meet again (perhaps not then still using the authorial *we*), we'll have lived long enough to have learnt how to rectify that … presumably (and more precisely) by sharing our souls. Meanwhile (but not for long) … so then … *do'svidanyiye* … *au revoir* … until we meet again … God bless … God bless … God bless (just as our fellow and most angelic author, the legal anthropologist, Jean Jackson says) … God bless … …

* * *

791

Going Nowhere or Going Native
Part I

Still Soul-Centred in Kabul
Even though he had been a military man, he seemed
more freethinking than Michiko-san. He did not seem
to be bothered by hippies or rock-music. He thought
it was all harmless ...
Wendy Nelson Tokunaga, *Love in Translation*

As for going native, make of it what you will. Some firm friends, especially those left back wherever they feel most at home, dismiss what they see to be the anachronistic nationalism of going native (whether Scots, Irish, English, Maori, or Anglo-American) for going nowhere. Others more positively say it's a means of tidying up life's loose ends (perhaps for persons broken up or driven apart by circumstance or happenstance). So also, these others might say it's time to grow up, to settle down, to bite the bullet, to care for others and not just for oneself (despite each and all these processes as often highly conflictive), turning out to be the most unsettling of life experiences in themselves.

One way of closing the experiential gap is simply to accept where one is, obviously some sort of expat, émigré, or refugee on this world's surface, and so eventually either to settle, return home, or go on wondering and/or wandering about who exactly we all are or who any one of us really is. Yet remember always that every marriage (no matter to one's greatest friend, closest cousin, or girl next door) or bonding to one's best friend or closest brother (no matter even to Christ himself) is always going to be a cross-cultural experience.

Then and there it is that the mere fact of choosing a mate (whether helpmate or soulmate) cuts across the respective cultures to which each mate belongs. If you've never felt that first-hand, then be sure to read something of Sholokhov's *Quiet Flows the Don*. Then it also is that, although perhaps only for fear of a worse unknown, the greatest ultimate curse which can be given physically from one Romany to another Romany and from one Tartar to another Tartar or more allegorically from one ongoing scholar to another ongoing scholar is for them to stay fixed either physically or conceptually in no more than only one place and so settle down.

On both sides of any great divide (and there are many such divides)—whether native or exotic, tourist or settler, immigrant or refugee, explorer or expat—each of these long lines winding through the Caucasus, no less than from Venezuela through Mexico, wavering across the Rio Grande and yet into the United States to climb the Statue of Liberty (gifted from France) ... and so (preferably upwards and) onwards ... from east to west ... and from west to east ... and from south to north ... and from north to south ... each of these incredibly long lines ... of the homeless in all sorts of weathers ... has its very own, just as incredibly long row to hoe ... whilst climbing walls ... and crossing rivers ... traversing seas ... and crossing oceans ... seeking refuge ... surmounting poverty ... taking stock ... and sometimes losing all ...

Who would have thought that whilst slanging off at China, now (lower) North America against (upper) South America would be building a just as unworkable (now Western) Chinese wall? Just what will it mean in the long run to go native to keep sacrosanct the proverbial Land of the Free?

So here I am still, as an undercover angel (perhaps having gone native, as they say of missionaries who become absorbed into the culture which they set out to evangelise and reform) yet still serving as a military man in Kabul. Amongst many other places, I've also served in Alexandria, in Cawnpore, and in Damascus. Soon I shall be centred in Syria, somewhat west of the president's palace, later on perhaps in Myanmar (but whether in big Yangon or smaller Naypyidaw, we shall await instructions), but for the very much slower-passing moment, I am still centred in Kabul.

And so at the moment of your reading this short treatise, report, journal (or whatever you care to call this series of nine books) on the subject of soul-catching (allowing for international timelines for being another instance of those ley lines explained before), I happen (at this very same time, yet according to the logistics of time by which there's no same time anywhere) to be reading back issues of the Salvation Army's *War Cry* on the streets of Kabul.

As said before, it's the small things that count for more than the big things, or to rephrase the selfsame approximate equation otherwise by which the first shall be last, then the less is more. Having gone underground, if not utterly native, and to feel what's like, I've resigned my commission as an angel. I'm just another lost soul. Nevertheless, I've still got a mission, so I know I'm alive, since you can't be alive without a mission.

But like any lost soul, sleeping now on the streets of Kabul, I've no longer got my dog tags, my only formal means of identification with the Supreme Command. I could now be Moslem (correction, Muslim), could now be Parsi (correction, Parsee), could now be Buddhist, or could be anything you like, since Father God loves us all—the long, the short, and the tall—most equally. As you say, I'm an experientialist (being closer now to nature in my having gone native than could anyone for being no more than an experimentalist).

As already said much, much earlier in my mission, many people mistake servanthood for servitude and so, having lost my way but not my mission, sleeping on the streets, anywhere—Aberdeen, Tokyo, Auckland, Tauranga—is pretty much the same. It would take me three long books to explain the ubiquitousness of angels, so don't let me bother you with more than one book, namely this one, for being as yet only the ninth book in this cosmic series of soul-catching.

Mostly I'm de-de-de-demented, sometimes de-de-de-delirious, but mornings are my clearest of times, when again I can see (sometimes only from the street refuse) that Kabul is not Tehran, that Kabul is not Baghdad, and nevertheless, that all such capitals are all much the same—physically as hotspots, historically as war zones, and even more so spiritually as outposts of the living dead (since it's impossible to live anywhere (as men mistakenly think can be done under the new secular order of things) without true spirituality.

You've caught me in a moment of true clarity, so let's talk on. Yes, that's right, since on the contrary, there has never been on this planet such a prevailing religion as this present religion of secularity. And although Muslim may war with Hindu and even Muslim with Muslim, Hindu with Hindu, Buddhist with Buddhist, and Christian with Christian, there has never been any such widely prevailing religion on this world's surface ever before than this present religion of secularity.

Its proponents believe (largely in terms of their own personal needs and wants) that this new religion of secularity will conquer all. Nevertheless, you can't employ the containment of a merely superficial conformity (especially the lotus-eating one of religious secularity) to deal deep down with diversity.

On the contrary (didn't I say that somewhere just before?), there's bound to be a huge and fast-spreading explosion, the likes of which has never yet been seen, but which has already been long ago started, as confirmed by these signs of the times. People think me mad for saying so, but the signs of the times are all around. Don't here interrupt me … just don't interrupt me … If you're looking for the window into my now shattered mind … you'll have to take your pick … It's a free country … always … anywhere … so long as you've got a still open mind …

Here comes the still prophetic window … If you, to see it, have got the still sound mind that you think you have to look through a glass darkly, then don't be put off by anyone's badly shattered mind. In case you don't believe me (since the whole wide world's gone academic in defence of secularity), the first (but by no means the last) patron saint of religious secularity (euphemistically revered as a social reformer) was George Holyoake. Aye, how very well do I remember Geordie, who, in 1842, was the last person to be imprisoned (a big mistake, as if he were yet another John Bunyan) for atheism in England.

It was George Holyoake himself who coined the words *secularism* and *jingoism*—two related concepts, both of which have come ironically to share much their same meaning in each other. And yet we still saved his soul, you know, caught it on its final downward fling. Wait, the window's closing. There's no relying on a shattered mind. It's always possible … that I wasn't even there …

Hold on … hold on … what would you say if I asked you, then, what did George Holyoake first most explicitly profess (at the very height of overseas missions from Britain to darkest Africa, the piratical Caribbean, and the cannibalistic Pacific)? Yes, indeed— what did he ask but this—for being his own (as he thought) very new system of entirely secular order based purely on worldly principles without any need for any creator, redeemer, or an afterlife? Do you think that professedly new system of his would have worked?

Scientific knowledge (as if complete) would then replace spiritual faith, which would mean (because of that incompleteness) that man's evacuated need to believe and have faith would be filled with fantasies of human progress and perfection (at the same time as dystrophic novels would prophesy disaster and dysfunction). Woebegone Geordie ... He wasn't a bad man, you know, like all the empiricists, egalitarians, and utilitarians ... all for the good of the many ... the common good ... through his complete and utter oversight of the one and only.

Come to think of it, all capital cities are much the same—London, Paris, Brussels, and Tokyo—as each (without their slightest realisation of what is happening) become more and more the same as a result of their being capital cities. Thus, through the increasing secularity yet more and more, irrespective of their apparently different cultures—whether Muslim, Buddhist, Hindu, or Sikh—they each share more and more the same secular spirituality. This is all part of the increased global drive, despite professed contradictions and innermost spiritual conflict to reconcile the whole wide world to this new age of a politically correct priesthood.

So here I am, a mere military man for being still unobserved and undercover in Kabul. Don't worry, most folks don't ever recognise an angel when they see one. Look at how long it took Jacob to recognise he fought against an angel or at Sarah who scoffed in her heart at the prophetic word by which she should bear a child or at Samson who, although in the service of the Supreme Command, couldn't keep his cover.

Our worldwide street cover, whether for bombarding others with kanji all over Shinjuku Station (since life is largely in the streets of Tokyo as elsewhere in the pubs of Dublin or with beating the All Blacks in Dunedin), is nothing more than tactical avoidance or else more straightforwardly for being a military man in Minsk or pleading for alms outside St Isaac's in St Petersburg or else simply sitting as a street beggar covered with sores in Kabul, is 100 per centum secured by the Supreme Command.

Yet if you don't yet believe in the complete military security against attack as afforded by the Supreme Command (understandably because there's so much more scam and spam around today than ever before), then read the authorised military history of the (at least) sixty-six books as written by the hundreds and thousands of authors (from priests and prophets to preachers and teachers) who have contributed their most explicit lives and not just their undercover wisdom to the eternal forcefulness of the living Word. It is simply impossible to overestimate the sanctified security of the Supreme Command, which means that many have come to needless grief from undervaluing it.

Many folks, in all walks of life but who know nothing of their own hearts, mistake me for being the angel of darkness, but I'm only one, a novice really, of the many, many angels of light. But then again, you may never have heard of us—whether as angels or as angels of light. Whoop! As do so many others, I've forgotten that for the purpose of going native, I've resigned my commission as an angel!

There's no cause for alarm, although hate pre-empts love, love pre-empts fear, no less than fear leads to fate and so to yet another round of hate. Don't be scared. We angels appear, most usually only singly, wherever and whenever human conditions become so intolerable that, left to themselves, men and women, when called upon to do so by the forces of evil, would give up their souls in utter despair. In times of warfare, either present or to come, we appear collectively, as you may see us represented as a warning to the world in the northern lights of the aurora borealis or the southern lights of the aurora australis.

Thus, although on call, we have only a contingent calling, insofar as 'wherever and whenever the human conditions for survival become so intolerable that men and women would be tempted to give up their souls in utter despair', then we're called in. We are literally called in as angels of light. Our purpose is to relieve the transformational situation by which for many who would otherwise despair of their souls are suddenly transformed—yes, even at that very last instant of their lives—by one last, even although unlooked for gleam of hope. Our work is not easy, not all to whom this one last message of hope is given accept even that last final message of hope.

But first, let me tell you not more than you need to know about Kabul, which would only be perplexing, but instead much less than you may already feel the presidential need to know in order to reveal more that is truly significant to everybody about everything in Kabul. Under the British, it was one thing; under the Russians, it was another thing; and under the Americans, it was nothing, even to themselves, that made any sense at all. That was roughly, very roughly when the Taliban came in—just at that very point when the uncertainty of life was being superseded by the certainty of death.

Many excuses are thus given for the severity of the Taliban's regime. Nevertheless, it remains the most extreme of any attempts to introduce Islamic law and order. Sumptuary laws were introduced for dress and personal appearance. Males were compelled to grow beards. Young girls were banned from schools. All other women were made to wear the top-to-toe burqa. No woman of any age could leave the home unless accompanied by a male relative. Despite the medical and teaching professions being largely manned by women, women were suddenly prohibited from engaging in every sort of work. All Western-style haircuts, fashions, and music were prohibited.

In such a state of affairs, as if immediately preceding that very point when the uncertainty of life has become superseded by the certainty of death, virtues tend to become seen as vices, and so vices then tend to become seen as virtues. There's nothing new in this reciprocal equation since Isaiah 5:20 is amongst the first on record to proclaim woe to them who employ the hoodwink by which to call evil good and good evil.

Bernard de Mandeville (very much to his own disadvantage, since, by means of huge bonfires lit outside most of the cathedrals in Europe, the church consigned his books to the flames) was amongst the first to draw attention to this equation for the reversal of moral values in the West. It's so often the most-needed (even if badly written) books that can be burnt or remaindered rather than those others merely blown in the wind in their writing and those yet so seriously unserious bestsellers that would best never have been written. [And lest you should think us military men in Kabul to be deficient in English-speaking grammar, then it's still (the case by reason of ellipsis) that the best books are so often remaindered by trashing or burning.]

Likewise, the real becomes surreal, and the surreal becomes real. So too, a lone woman in the streets of Kabul would then be oogled, pinched, or groped—as much by the Taliban as by the mujahideen—for the fact of her being unaccompanied by a man; yet if the woman has a male escort and her escort is dressed in Western style, then it is presumed that he is but a ponce for the prostitute and not his wife that he escorts. By then, all trust and whatever faith and goodwill we ever had in our own human society has sadly degenerated into that of poor, doubting Thomas (Hobbes), who held human life to be 'nasty, brutish, and short', even if that were to be certainly a prophetic description of everyday life in Kabul.

That was when for any woman to be seen (even at home) with her head uncovered would mark her down for being a loose and wicked woman. That was when for any group of women running a hairdressing salon or beauty parlour, their salon would be rumoured a house of ill repute, and the group of women would run more than just the risk of being labelled prostitutes. That was also when Afghanistan's former president Najibullah, who had secured a better life to Kabul than otherwise possible under the Soviet regime and who by then, after the regime's collapse, was living in the UN compound, would be shot dead after being beaten, mutilated, dragged through the streets behind a jeep and whose wired body would be left hanging from a post in the city centre.

Such is the situation when the people who set out to purify the sorry state of the world don't know how evil their own hearts are. It can be so hard to keep the individual text of one's own psyche independently separate from the social context of the group psyche. For being only all too human, we see ourselves reflected only in the social mirror and so know not which for us is the distorting image or which is the distorted image. And unless for being a scholar of history, a human lifetime is all too short for the experience by which to hear and answer one's angelic calling, however long the apprenticeship, and so to become a completely called-up soul-catcher.

Soul-catchers may spend the best part of a century in a single place. For one soul-catcher, it may be the Holy Mother Russia of

Ivan the Terrible that is their allotted place. For another soul-catcher, it may be the Not-So-Merrie England under Cromwell's Protectorate that is their allotted place. For yet another, he or she may be called to the American Colonies—a tough enough time for both England and the Colonies during their rebellion, but a far tougher time for the by then former Colonies during their Civil War to follow. The historical events to which we give crisp dates (such as to the Battle of Vienna in 1683) are more like icebergs in having seven-tenths of their bulk by which to sink the *Titanic* below waterline together with their coming from a faraway source together with drawn consequences that sets their course.

So you see, the moral/immoral situation (by which vices and virtues reverse their roles) by no means remains static. Morals (whether puritanical or libertarian) are so often merely the sidekick to provide the means by which political outcomes are decided, and the same, by whatsoever name (whether Judaic or Islamic), can go also for religious beliefs. Under Nazi Germany (supported almost to the hilt by both the churches and the universities), the Jews were done away with, whereas under Stalinist Russia, it was Gulags for the authentic communists, no less than it had been the salt mines or the shooting squad for writers and both freethinkers and Old Believers under the tsars.

* * *

Going Nowhere or Going Native
Part II

Virtues and Vices
If laying aside all worldly Greatness and Vain-Glory,
I should be ask'd where I thought it was most probable
that Men might enjoy true Happiness, I would prefer a
small peaceable Society, in which Men, neither envy'd
nor esteem'd by Neighbours, should be contented to
live upon the Natural Product of the Spot they inhabit,
to that of a vast Multitude abounding in Wealth and
Power, which should always be conquering others by
their Arms Abroad, and debauching themselves by
Foreign Luxury at Home.
Bernard de Mandeville, *The Grumbling Hive*

Sure, spirituality (in every angelic or human shape or even in every divine or demonic form) has always been a hot topic. It reaches the bestseller list whatever may then be the secular or profane outlook or else may then be the occult or mystic season of the human mind—in either each or both of which heaven then chooses to prevail or hell struggles to persist. Well, even if by now you haven't picked it, the basic cosmic focus of all these twelve books (of which this is still just the ninth) is nothing if not the relationship of physicality to spirituality.

It was the spiritual writer Charles 'Chuck' Swindoll who once wrote (amongst his many other books) also *Living beyond the Daily Grind* (in two volumes). There, he noted of the *New York Times* religious bestseller list, that it contained no less than eight separate books on the subject of angels (since 1994, the list grows ever longer). This confirms, so Chuck concluded, the still popular interest with which humans regard the serious subject of angels (even if not also leading them sometimes to indulge in the faddish and counterfeit excesses of their study known as angelology).

Nevertheless, there are but a few books, authorised or otherwise commissioned by the Supreme Commission or even where otherwise autobiographical, in which angels purport to dictate or write for themselves the messages they bring or to describe the tasks they undertake. All the same, these are new times, at least for the slowing down of light and the speeding up of time. In their own very limited way, just as these reciprocal factors apply to so many other different (both real and even virtual) avenues of communication, then what earthlings have earlier taken for granted to allow to humanity all the time in the world (whether by way of life space or space-time, if you will have it so) is now at its strictest premium.

The odds, whether mistaken for jurisprudence being the search for law and order or when promoted as the search for human happiness (utilitarianism), become increasingly critical for humanity at large. The elderly are the ones who notice the crisis more and more, especially as youth becomes more and more self-indulgent. For everyone but the least observant, there are good days and bad days … sometimes the solo mum on a twelve-hour cycle (when time is running short) … at other times the sleepless parent on the usual twenty-four-hour cycle … and yet others, when forty-eight hours passes for the retiree as a single day … and still yet others, when a full week either flips by or drags out (with neither drag nor flip making any difference) to the terminally ill as a single instant of no possible duration.

We elderlies don't need any physicist to tell us that the speed of light is slowing down whilst time is speeding up. We feel it in our bones and have no need of any other proof. Oh, they tell us that we're growing old … too old to lead … and not quite old enough to be led … But they've been saying something very much like that (although once too young to lead) ever since the day of our birth. There's a time, brief in itself as it closes in towards all eternity, however, at which subjectivity and objectivity coalesce into universality.

Well, after all, that's the human condition, which begins by being too young to lead and then too old to lead but, lucky enough, for being always still willing to be led. Every history of going native, whether to heaven or hell, poses the same processes; it's only the responses that make for any great difference. We're still talking about the human condition, of course, which even Jesus Christ himself had to experience for himself on earth in order to redeem the lost. So why shouldn't any mere angel have to be put through the same set of experiences in order to understand just what it takes to be merely human?

If so led to lead and thus laying aside all worldly greatness and vainglory, then you will spend most of your life (relative to its as yet unknown length) completely undercover as a military man and most probably in some relatively peaceable small society, where you will then carry out orders completely on behalf of the Supreme Command. And you will probably do so there (as if confined to the wilderness like John the Baptist) until, decapitated by opposing forces, your cover is blown and you have gone to glory. You don't lead for long, so you might as well learn to teach as well as learn to lead, both of which you might as well learn to do whilst undercover as a military man.

You'll need followers, but only a few of those (mostly those followers with nothing to lose in this life) will become and remain committed disciples. Of course, those (say, back home in Bethlehem) who, in your youth, witnessed the humility with which you learnt to lead others (to the kingdom of righteousness) will rarely follow you (to the same kingdom); and those who saw you learn to teach or preach or even perform miracles will soon back off from daring to make the same name, far less to share the same fame. People love to get and even tout for gifts (as much as they delight to exercise their rights to freedom) but back off from acknowledging their correlative responsibilities that result from the exercise of such rights to freedom or the acceptance of such gifts of freedom.

As already said, you don't lead for long. Before you know exactly who you are (literally speaking as some premier, president, or any other far more public figure), you are being led (most usually misled) by those who once followed you when you first led them. It doesn't pay to stick around when that happens, so choose your followers wisely and get out of their road when it's time for them to take the lead that you've established. But remember this, that unless for either belonging to or having been promoted to serve the Supreme Command, all earthly leadership is contingent.

Look at it this way—the only alternative to any demented old age is to die young. Every man, especially he who lives on honey and locusts, should take a lesson from the grumbling hive. Then you will be remembered for what you are now and not for whom you merely once were or, worse still, for having been given great gifts by the Supreme Command that you either feared to fulfil or else squandered in riotous living or in any other way prostituted your potential to engage with the enemy.

As said before, you don't live this life for long, but the revelation of this truth is not given to the young (who in their youth would abuse it) but only to the old (so that they may do most with the wisdom that comes to those only with the experience of latter years). The risk, in youth through to midlife, is to take a fix on earthly leadership (whether on one's own or someone else's) and unfortunately on the sort of leadership that may be fulfilled most easily (as often on what seems to be the best of advice) without having ever heard one's own personal calling. Instead, not only as a military man but also as a nautical man, find out what it takes to be submitting every moment of your life not only to your strategic calling but also to your tactical dead reckoning.

Except for those serving the Supreme Command, all earthly leadership is no more than a contingent calling. It could be valid and true, or for being contingent on so much else, it could be invalid and false. To find out (as always in the field of warfare between conflicting alternatives), one often has to learn from experience as to which is which—the right from the wrong (which invariably is a strategic rather than a tactical decision).

Speaking now to the most gifted, and more especially to the most diversely gifted, your path may have to be taken along just as diversely, potentially attractive, and apparently certain routes—each of which at the start may seem most welcoming and encouraging. And yet, as in some sort of logic machine, gates of encouragement may suddenly slam shut, and others go on just as decisively slamming shut, without giving any sort of indication as to your true calling. Never fear, the way may be longer, the travel more and more apparently circuitous, but the false is being winnowed away in the wind by virtue of one's own much deeper (although more painful) learning experience, from which to realise the one and only life-giving truth.

There are no shortcuts for those who are greatly gifted and who travel on multitudinous paths. 'Go to the ant," the hardest of gifted workers (no less than the utmost sluggard) may be told. So from whence does this apparently good advice come? 'Consider the bee,' the kindliest of beekeepers (no less than the most ruthless of financiers) may be told. Both counsels are scriptural, although in vastly different ways. Proverbs 6:6 (on the ant) is addressed by way of comparison only to the sluggard, but as everyone knows from Psalm 119:103, there is a superlative far beyond that of being 'sweeter than honey'. As Shakespeare reminds us, 'The devil can cite Scripture for his own purpose,' as confirmed both directly (Matthew 4:6) and over and over again indirectly by Scripture.

In all those fast-changing situations—those under the pretext that big is beautiful, bigger is better, and the biggest is best—the once peaceably ordered small societies will collapse into confused conglomerates. What is left of those once contented small societies will then contribute to 'the grumbling hive' syndrome of systemic disorder.

This systemic disorder is no more an oxymoron or self-contradiction than is that of some planet that geophysically switches magnetic poles. The final outcome (in terms of our earlier conception) is that what was once north is then south and what was once east is then west, but in the process whereby virtues and vices change similar roles fast and furiously during the search, first for moral, then for legal certainty, the experienced distress (brought about to resolve the resulting confusion of extreme and conflicting values) undermines all we say or do.

It may then come to the bit—not far away now—that everything once done legally is now illegal and that what was once illegally done becomes now legal. Under the rule of law, the legal system then crosses the moral rubicon by which making war is justified to keep the peace and to keep the peace justifies our making war, whilst the pre-emptive attack is excused as strategic defence, and 'the extreme case' justifies the absence of every principle of jurisprudence (otherwise known as the morality of law).

By now, for lack of their being taught in law schools, the principles of legality are as little understood as are the principles of logic or as are the principles of metaphysics. The result (as for morals, far gone by now, for having been displaced by rabid empiricism, soft-soaping existentialism, and devil-may-care experientialism) is that what once was immoral is now moral (and not even just amoral but even more than ever before moral) whilst what once was moral is now immoral (and that also not even just amoral but more than ever before immoral). And this outcome is at all levels being fast processed on the professedly apolitical production line of 'political correctness'.

By reason of this cross-dressing of vices and virtues, we have almost reached the point at which nothing at all can be known for what it is. Oh yes, there are still facts, and there are still opinions (however much we mistake most of our opinions for being facts and most of our facts for being other than opinions), but without having certainty as to our values (without which we could neither have facts nor opinions), we don't know any standard well enough by which to gauge whether we're right, wrong, or indifferent, which is why most of us are content to live lives which, for their lack of purpose, are themselves boringly indifferent.

The garden of Eden (like every Persian garden) once had a tree of knowledge, which we uprooted in our mistaken search for the mythical elixir of life. On leaving this garden, we took with us a cutting from this tree of knowledge (a root cutting, no less) to transplant the same and so to share its stolen fruits by which to at least prolong our by then sadly determined lives. The resulting paradox of our insistence on doing so—to be no less than as gods—is to lose our sense of the only values by which we could ever be as gods, and so we cross-dress the only certainties that would otherwise disprove the case. It is by our own free choice and self-determination, therefore, that we prefer to live out our remaining years in abject self-confusion.

For cross-dressing the virtues and vices under the mullahs (or teachers), the Taliban (the students), or the mujahideen (the striving or do-gooders), the outcome was no different. People (ostensibly first the petty criminals) would be lined up for mutilation—losing arms and/or feet or noses and/or lips—and finally, the more important cases calling for complete decapitation or death in some other shape or form would be brought into the public arena (as into Kabul's main football stadium). Sometimes, kids (in all their innocence) would souvenir an amputated arm or else play ball with each other by throwing to one another a severed, still twitching foot or by pulling the tendons in a severed hand, making it grasp and ungrasp (as if it were a chicken's foot).

As in the case of every execution (although hardly in accordance with the Hippocratic oath), medics as well as mullahs would be there to authenticate and legitimate the process. And of course, crowds, into their thousands—whole families of men, women, and children—would swarm into the spectacle of witnessing the execution of the death sentence, some with not only considerable enjoyment but with also religious fervour, by which they would raise prolonged shouts of 'Allahu Akbar' before the ensuing football match.

That's where I come in, right at the moment of death, in doing my job as a soul-catcher. Wherever I am, mostly in different times than at different places, my job is to act as a soul-catcher. You'll be coming with me, of course, as always in soul-catching, it's not so much the catcher that counts as the affinity between kindred souls.

As with the prophetic word, where the timing counts so much for reception of the message, then so also for soul-catching, it's the timing that counts as much for giving up and receiving the soul. Don't get diverted by any airborne head, loud huzzah, or pitiful scream.

These miniscule moments are no more than incidental to the salvation purpose of saving and redeeming any nearly lost soul. So then although the timing can count as if for everything, it's not the moment of death, which everyone mistakes for being so precise a moment that counts; it's more the personal response, either of acceptance or rejection of death, and not of the causes which tend to anaesthetise the victim through fear but of the consequences which follow from death rather than the acceptance of those causes leading to death that count.

The bodily causes can be overwhelming to most nearly every victim, but not to all. Yet for some who approach the certainty and not just the contingency of death (as for Anne Boleyn, Sir Thomas More, Charles I, and Mary, Queen of Scots—of whom I've served them all), their souls are for the saving. If not, they were already saved before.

Soul-catching, especially serious soul-catching, can be very tricky business. Every case (no less than every soul) is unique. Of course (which in this case is a set course), you need the calling. You can't do it on your own behalf, although to lessen the load of the transformational process from life to death or just by giving a hand to the transient from whom life is being demanded or otherwise more institutionally to authorise, sanctify, or lend respectability to the process of execution (which may be anything from the electric chair, intravenous injection, hanging, or death by a thousand cuts), many soft-hearted people try their hardest (especially in the churches) to engage themselves in sympathetic soul-catching.

The usual process at any public execution in Afghanistan over the last sixteen years is conducted first by a religious mullah (of respectably high standing) who harangues the crowd (as at any football match) to discredit the already transient victim before passing the buck of delivering three bullets to the head (as will be done by someone of much lesser standing). Passing the buck or keeping one's hands clean, as known in Western circles, frequently itself comes around (and round and round) full circle.

Justice must always be seen to be done by those who keep clean hands (however much they may dirty their souls) by giving their judgements. As the philosopher-historian Thomas Carlyle long ago pointed out in writing his *Sartor Resartus* (or *Patched-Up Tailor*), the legal system at least would drop down dead (if not also justice itself with three bullets to the head) if judges had to do their own dirty work in their being asked to carry out their own sentences.

The buck of discharging these bullets to the head having been passed from the religious mullah to be conducted by some heavily turbaned, Kalashnikov-totting, hard-line Muslim seems sweet to the mullah; but implementation of the sentence can also extend to decapitation or being dragged to death through the streets behind a jeep. More publicly and from further afield, it can be conducted by the seventy-five American cruise missiles that struck Afghanistan's eastern frontier during Operation Infinite Reach (enthusiastically supported by the then British prime minister Tony Blair), killing several militant Pakistanis (being trained to fight in Kashmir) as well as either killing or injuring about the same number of Afghan civilians.

So then apart from our need for this calling (to what can only be an angelic engagement), how is this most seriously professional level of soul-catching to be conducted? Since we ourselves (as humans) are only a little lower than the angels, this typically human question of 'How come?' can surely be explained.

Here's one attempt: for you human beings being taught to see us angels as far superior and spiritual beings (than are you human beings), you then put yourselves so much further down the beanstalk (than you have any cause to climb) as to write yourselves off for being merely human beans and so nowise yourselves spiritual in any shape or form. Now that's not only what scares you humans but what also scares us angels even more that it scares you humans.

Wow, that you humans (hammered into the ground perhaps by your great fall) cannot any longer conceive of yourselves (for being only a little lower than us angels) as any sort of spiritual being at all is even to us angels one of the scariest things on this planet! But in your (although earthly) beginnings (for each of you in different ways reflect on your present forms and functions), was it not the breath of spiritual life breathed into you by the same Holy Spirit of the Supreme Command who breathed the same spirituality into us angels?

Of course, what follows from that lack of awareness of your own spirituality as humans is fear. This explains your fearfulness of the spirituality which you fear you haven't got, and it's a fearfulness in the abstract which is far worse than a fearfulness in the concrete. That's because as humans, you don't know who you are as humans, which, in turn, explains why you run around taking selfies, multitexting great conventions, and wearing Fitbits.

Why, for being so ignorant of your own life force, you breathe scared, walk scared, work scared, talk scared, live scared, and so then die scared, with little more faith than for your body being from dust going again to dust. Against such scary symptoms of being altogether scared, you engage in every secular science of psychophysics, psychotherapy, psychophysiology, psychosexuality, psychosurgery, and even psychoministry as if there were no soul! Don't you know that *psycho* stands for the soul?

What hope then have you got to treat the soul devoid as if it were of all spirituality and as if the soul, together with the wonderfully designed human body, were nothing more than a material object, a mere happenstance (however carefully contrived) of secular physicality? No wonder, as with every other physical means of dealing with the soul, that you can see (which isn't far when you can't even see yourselves as any sort of spiritual beings)—yes, indeed, such is the case for you being literally without any sense of wonder!

But no wonder we angels say still no wonder that all youse human beans are so thoroughly scared! By knowing only of your bodily shell but nothing of the spiritual kernel that keeps alive your bespoke body, youse human beans are all at the ready to commit the greatest of cosmic atrocities of which you know nothing about! Well then, to be numbered amongst the many other walking, talking, working, playing, and sometimes even preaching, teaching, praying dead, then how's your little libido (never mind your massively great ego) today? Ah yes, our Lord God can be a very ruthless god, and so we leave you to cry against him once again for being so downright cruel and most unfair!

* * *

BOOK NINE

Breaking Cover—from War Games to Total War

If I Were a Monarch ...
'For what reason are we going to war?' asked Pierre.
'I've not the slightest idea, answered Andrei. 'We simply must. And what is more, I'm going to the front ...' He paused for reflection. 'Because the life I live here doesn't suit me.'

'If I were a monarch, I would never make war!' cried Nesvitskii, turning away from Andrei.

Lev Tolstoi, *War and Peace*

Intro 1—Neil: This present book is about conflict—the sort of unequal conflict which generates opportunities for soul-catching. We are shortly to engage (no bull) in this world's most open history (no sweat) of open conflict (no shit). Like the terrorism of today (no shit), this next time of even more open conflict (no sweat) shall be total war (no bullshit).

Intro 2—Augustus: There will be no rhyme or reason to this open conflict that anyone but the truly wise of this new era of reversed roles (no sweat) will understand (no bull). Yet the foolish of this world (for their being so judged by this world) shall be redeemed by an eternity of wisdom unknown to this present age and by which this present dying world has no earthly power by which to withstand or to understand (no bullshit).

Intro 3—Marsyas: To mistake the apocalyptic eschatological context of this twenty-first century for being any less than the 'apocalyptic eschatological context of the first century' is really bad news (no bullshit). Those of today's theologians who mistake prophecy for history to mistake the end times for being already all come and gone really first need to read their own heads (no bullshit) before they ever think to read again the Revelation of Jesus Christ.

Intro 4—Matthew: Although so much like today's terrorism, the continually moving field of total war already circles the globe. It sinks into every little household and into every little suburb (read Bertrand Russell's *Satan in the Suburbs*). Smaller size (in any case giving rise to the so-called Napoleonic response) is no longer immune to exempt that smaller size from greater conflict.

Intro 5—Augustus: Come to think of it, there's not much difference between cold war (as waged between USA and USSR) and warmed-up peace (as waged between factions in the Brexit UK parliament or in the petitioning of Congress to impeach the US President). As said before, the whole wide world is in a ferment.

Intro 6—Marsyas: After WWI, it was clearly prophesied, no later than 1930, that the next war, WWII, would be fought with tanks and not in trenches (see Liddell Hart's *History of the First World War*). Then came the Cold War, but the next war will be hotter than ever before.

Intro 7—Augustus: Remember that most folks die if not from breaking cover, then from refusing to face conflict (and as often by building walls or entering into peace treaties or professing neutrality) and thus so wishfully remaining to lie doggo (sometimes through the whole duration of any outright war) and so then (as it may be centuries later) only to die from never having taken up the needful challenge to break cover.

Intro 8—Malachi: Hardly any of you humans, when engaged in conflict (far less us angels), actually see the battle. Sometimes, the infantryman or reporter in the field sees just a little of it. But the more technology there is to hide behind and the greater the distance from which one can command and employ the warfare, the lesser one sees or understands or feels, whether to be either exonerated or incriminated, by the constantly changing flow of battle.

Intro 9—*Emma:* At best, only the non-combatant civilian, like Tolstoy's Pierre in *War and Peace*, can see both sides of any battle. It takes a lifetime of human conflict—both legal and illegal, both moral and immoral, both military and civilian, both religious and spiritual, both physical and mental, both intellectual and emotional—to begin to understand, far less to come to terms, with Tolstoy's *War and Peace.*

If we take life seriously, then we all know what it is to feel battle-weary. But before combat fatigue sets in (which can happen not just in military situations but in courts, colleges, schools, legislatures, and every other sort of social institution), there's a short phase of feeling 'session-happy' (as sometimes so described) which follows on from any much lengthier period of combative fixation. So also, but in reverse, the Maginot Line syndrome (this time affecting, infecting, and afflicting the ignorant, unwary, and effete) is a defence force syndrome (associated with mistaken sanctuaries). Like combative fixation, this also exerts a pathological fixity applicable to all walks of life.

Intro 10—*Marsyas:* In any battle, you may be accused of retreating from your heavenly objective (or even incurring treason to your country) or of breaking cover (and, worse still, for being a double agent). As for the already excommunicated and deceased Count Lev Tolstoy himself, so you too may be forced to stand further trial (academically speaking) as by Sir Isaiah Berlin against Tolstoy in his *The Hedgehog and the Fox.*

Intro 11—*Katherine Boyd:* If the reader is *left* to find (far less to answer) any question himself or herself and get it *right* (pardon the pun), then more of worth follows than of being told the question (far less to be told the answer or even how to find the answer) to the (known or unknown) question.

All the same, no reader can be sure that his own pretext (a.k.a. context) of interpretation matches with the author's text. So then perhaps dear old Isaiah (Berlin) is taking dear old Lev-Leo (Tolstoy) to task for something Lev never ever thought of or said or wrote. After reading Lev's *War and Peace*, it's hard to accept that its author masqueraded his very own personal and polemical view of history as a work of art or literary masterpiece. This is as surely out of place as writing off Tolstoy's *Resurrection* (as other critics have done) for being no more than a 'smutty' novel!

Intro 12—Nicolai Daniloff: Well then, what could we say of Berlin in his critique of Tolstoy for that of his hiding behind the diversionary writing of a wily old fox to promote the singularity of his one and only hedgehog-like idea of history? On the contrary, it took the seriousness of both these writers (Tolstoy to provide a literary model by which to portray the conflict between *The Hedgehog and the Fox* and Berlin to extend the seriousness of Tolstoy's novel to its fullest depth, width, and height, which otherwise would have been content to give the superficial reader only what he or she wanted).

Intro 13—John McNab Jamieson (formerly of Cawnpore, Fengtai, and Beattock near Wamfrey: These are but only two conflictive aspects (the creative and the critical) of one and the same enterprise. Yes, Berlin is right (and couldn't possibly be wrong), since the whole of Tolstoy's *War and Peace* is a treatise on history at large and on the history of warring conflict in particular. As distinct from Russian Orthodox Christianity, the concept of destiny is far removed from most Western church denominations, which probably has a big part to play not only in the decline of Western church faith but also in what Spengler prophetically put forward in his monumental work *The Decline of the West.*

Intro 14—Gideon: Don't ever forget but instead always remember that today's worldwide terrorism, at all levels (from domestic violence to supranational cartels engaged in drug dealing, people trafficking, money laundering, and both commercial and political espionage), is not what it seems. It may seem to be beyond governmental control at any national level—and yes, that's true—but this same worldwide terrorism is also instigated by many of those same nations (whether wittingly or unwittingly) at an international, transnational, supranational, and global level.

What, you want a specific, concrete, and irrefutable example of such governmentally instigated terrorism, do you? Well, you couldn't find a clearer example of such terrorist activity instigated by the government of any Western nation than the bombing and sinking of the *Rainbow Warrior* (flagship of Greenpeace) whilst in the Auckland Harbour of New Zealand in 1985, when done as then by the French government.

Of course, almost every nation on earth has a history of terrorism against indigenous people, from which evil history, unless redeemed and rectified, the prophetic fulfilment of that history proceeds into its next phase of exacting terrorism against subsequent generations of those whom the nation merits for being its own people. By what ye deem, ye shall be doomed, and by what means ye do to others shall be done to you. But alas, for all earth's unredeemed nations, there seem to be no earthly limits on man's inhumanity to man!

Intro 15—Lily McCloskey (retired schoolteacher): Exactly why is it that you can't often see what's really happening by way of governmental instigation at your own street level? Well, not unless you happen to live in Kabul, Baghdad, Tehran, and Damascus or perhaps now also in the streets of Paris, Kashmir, and Hong Kong!

The reason is that for the most part, the missing data at street level is being governmentally embargoed. Thus, the instigators or agent provocateurs of worldwide terrorism (as in any classic spy novel such as Joseph Conrad's *The Secret Agent*) are not those presidents, prime ministers, premiers, and parliamentarians (far less monarchs, military dictators, and similarly often only token heads of state) most obviously placed to take the flak in the front line. The facade of political respectability (already reborn as political correctness, since respectability is now more honoured for being a vice) is already such that they themselves are only front men (and now increasingly front women) for those actually holding the reins of power.

Oh yes, indeed, even tyrants these days (just as Chairman Mao and Ho Chi Minh once were) are no more than today's front men before becoming tomorrow's fall guys. And don't even think that all these leaders elected to rule purported democracies are really greatly different. Why, when the chips are down and the burning rubber meets the road, then but for the grace of God, even the Churchills, the Atlees, the Heaths, the Kennedys, the Nixons, and the Carters can all sadly lose the governmental plot.

Intro 16—Lizzie Hamilton (former seamstress): This is all part of the global subterfuge by which those apparently in positions of declining institutional power (and so the targets for protest initially from street power and eventually from competing external powers) are but the fall guys in any game of thrones for the real power behind any throne. Watch carefully any professedly democratic parliament in its downward slide from exercising governmental control, and you will see the street power (not the parliamentary power) of parliamentarians being openly used against prime ministers, reigning monarchs, and other fall guys who by then are no more than the figureheads to whom these same parliamentarians have sworn oaths of allegiance to serve.

Intro 17—George Barton (Queen's Counsel): If not the parliamentarians or their equivalent (in any professed democracy of whatsoever sort), then just who are the real rulers of society? Let's (not yet) just change the subject, but remember that in serving heaven, I'm a litigator and not, like any parliamentarian, a legislator. In my pleading before the courts of heaven (which, like any courts of conscience, are courts of equity and not merely of human habit or of conglomerated custom), I plead according to the heavenly principles (and not to the earthly affectation) of justice. Since justice belongs to the Lord, I'm therefore (although not seen from down on earth to be) a Jehovah-type person. You might think of equity as fairness, although what's fair in heaven is often far removed from what's considered by earthlings to be fair on earth.

Intro 18—Denzil Ward, CMG (formerly chief parliamentary counsel in New Zealand): At heart, I'm a legislator—that's a Moses type and not a Jehovah type of person. The antithesis of a legislator is a litigator, so the whole purpose of legislation is to avoid litigation. The overreaching power of intellectuality (whether amongst academics or practitioners) is the very one thing that gets in the way of drafting almost every piece of governmental legislation. Some folks (perhaps even the judges) might think that more than a modicum of intelligence gets in the way of being any right sort of lawyer at all. But to be sure, legal practitioners are far different from legal theorists and jurists. For every sort of practitioner, practicality is one's first priority both in getting things done and continuing to do things—so better done than not done (whether worse or better). Given from now, in then ten years' time, neither of us shall in any legislative shape or legislative form be remembered. Such is *The Way of All Flesh*, should you care to read Samuel Butler.

Just relax with the small picture and retire from the big picture. Look here, every legislative draftsman should be like a good guide dog, sticking steadfastly to the governmental task at hand, taking instructions, and conforming to the strategic needs of his or, as we'd say now, her blind master (now more often than not, a blind mistress). Guide dogs, apart from what they're told to see, shouldn't look round corners, look into the far prophetic distance, or bark or bolt at things as yet unseen. This substance of anything unseen might very well be there, but whatever's not substantive law is less than relevant to the immediate legislative task at hand. As said by England's first Parliamentary Counsel, 'Statutes are made to pass as razors are made to sell.'

Guide dogs (a.k.a. blind dogs) are chosen not for their intelligence, far less for their intellectuality, but for their very pedestrian task at hand. It's a pastoral ministry, not a prophetic ministry that guide dogs have. And even although the blind may very well lead the blind better in the short term than most others do in the long term, that's just what guide dogs are born to do—to lead the blind. To be sure, razors being made for no more purpose than to sell them may then end up by cutting their government's own well-intentioned throat, never mind their very own nation's throat. But by then, to bring any new government down, that's the irony of lawyering for the last but latest government. Meanwhile, be a good chap, Nigel, stick to the task of legislative drafting in hand. As the Beatles (all OBEs) have said, in one of their less than funnier moments, 'Be a good dog, Nigel!'

Intro 19—Katherine Boyd (once principal of Craibstone College):
For any deeper understanding, both of the historic past and the
existential present, as well as of the prophetic future, you must read
the signs of these present times. What was once prophetic is now
historic, and what is now prophetic is still no more than the substance
of things as yet unseen. In terms of both domestic peacemaking and
domestic peacekeeping (as opposed to the drama queen of worldwide
terrorism), consider how, by today's reversal of values, Buddhist
pacifism and Muslim pacifism and not just Christian pacifism have
become increasingly mistaken for anarchism. By means of reversing
the concepts of peace and war, it is now seen to require a war to
maintain the peace, no less than the cosmos has become a chaotic
battleground for that once good cause of peacekeeping and chaos has
become, in consequence, a commonplace on earth.

Intro 20—Gregor-McGregor (known familiarly as Wee M'greegor):
Yet hold on firmly to your faith for, as the old saying goes, 'you
ain't seen nothin' yet!' The world stage is not set but instead already
only upset and yet already upset from top to bottom for terrors the
likes never been seen by humans before. The only key to the already
revealed identity of those impresarios already charged with the filmic
introduction of such incoming terror (already being shown on all big
screens) is to understand the deep-seated conflict (already revealed
in every specific detail between heaven and hell). This conflict is
already being fought on earth, as all hell breaks loose by rising from
the lowest depths to which it plummeted from the highest heaven, just
as heaven again comes to earth to deliver what remains of this earth
from hell's bondage. Laugh as you will for this being an apocalyptic
fairy tale, but it won't be for long!

*Intro 21—Chrissie Schoenherr (once from Forres, which, although
a royal borough in Moray, is one of Scotland's oldest and still
smallest of towns):* What follows on from here are no more than four
short singularities on the history of conflict. Each fixated singularity
may be viewed either as an independently curled-up (Glaswegian)
hedgehog promoting no more than one big idea or else, when viewed
altogether from the point of view of some wily old (Aberdeenshire)

fox, as a collection of interrelated aspects of that one and the same big cosmopolitan idea. Behind both points of view, as behind any big idea, may be hidden a whole heavenly host (as now again legislatively in Edinburgh) of much smaller but not necessarily related or interrelated ideas. So then, dearest readers, take your pick from the following brief sketches of this world's most topical sources of often internecine conflict.

* * *

A History of Conflict
Part I

Maintaining the Software of the Soul
The solitary figure moved slowly forward, head upright, and his eyes fixed on a white stallion standing in the forefront of an array of horsemen. He halted within ten paces, and, holding the standard forward, proclaimed: 'Gentlemen, ye have won the day. We are at you service. We surrender honourably. Ye will ensure the safety of my men ...'

'Sir we accept thy surrender. Collect thy unwounded men and proceed to the palm grove ... Bring me thy flag; and also, the one from the Scottish Regiment.'
                                    Martin D., *Twin Souls, Twin Swords*

What is it like to be an agent in the field—a leading agent of the Supreme Command? Well, you already know of how we perform undercover. Just as the church for being the body of Christ needs so often to go underground—out of the field of battle, down deep in the catacombs, or even as convicts into the prisons—so even the angels, in this world as beggars in rags or as halfwits deeply sedated, need often to work undercover.

To every action, there is a counteraction, and to every move, a countermove. The temptation in military action, with its basis most frequently in political action, is to see ourselves engaged only in counteroffensive action, as if all our actions were always justified for being only defensive, making us blameless not only in our every action but in our every counteraction and even in our long list of offending non-actions. As every lawyer knows to his or her cost, there are sins (or offences) of nonfeasance as well as those of misfeasance.

As both the theologians and lawyers agreed on, there are both sins of omission as well as sins of commission, and most wars begin with sins of omission long before they are triggered by those events which historians finally latch on to for being sins of commission. And so by the mythopoeic certainty which we like to attach to academic argument, the outcomes seem predestined until dislodged by future disproof.

Both the First and Second World Wars, together with the American Civil War, could have been avoided, no less than the revolt of the American Colonies or the Russian Revolution could have been avoided—all at the level of family law—but then as with the Capulets and Montagues, family feuds become the fiercest forms of open and fast-spreading warfare. As between the rulers and would-be rulers of the earth—even from George III to George Washington or more incestuously with Queen Victoria, Kaiser Bill, Tsar Nicholas, and Edward VIII—cultural diplomacy is not a strong enough means in itself to resolve family disputes.

Likewise, to every political or military movement or manoeuvre (although whether towards or away from democracy, none at the time can say with absolute certainty), there is nevertheless an equal and opposite countermovement. So he or she who thinks himself or herself most clearly defined in his or her counterobjective or outcome (take women's liberation, for example) turns out to be least clearly defined by reason of waging only a counterobjective, whereas, as to the certainty of the objective being opposed (as with the case of women's liberation), the effect of countering what stands in the way of liberation is often only to clarify and strengthen what stands in the way of realising the counterobjective. Every counteroffensive manoeuvre should always first be cautiously weighed up against the efficacy of strategic retreat.

Are we contending *positively* for peace or merely *negatively* against war? Some entire cultures, typified, say, by the concept of merely struggling for existence, are almost entirely negative. Many of those negative countercultures never regain positivity. And particularly in the context of those whom we regard as being amongst the great reformers, we need to carefully examine the extent to which their reforms (although positive in substance, and for many, never regarded by their initiators in any way to be any form of opposition to every action) bed down as purely negative countercultures.

Maybe every book ever written (including Darwin's *On the Origin of Species* and Luther's *Ninety-Five Theses*) should be accompanied by a SPECT scan of the author's brain. Literary appreciation would then conjoin with psychoanalytic jurisprudence—positively enough [or so we would hope] to gain further insight into the relationship between life and works but also coupled with the risk of negativity by way of counterargument against the status of any work when seen (as it should be) for its own sake. To introduce the further risk of censorship by which to think of achieving the same end is not to let the work speak for itself but to decide on the basis of what is humanly thought of the issue.

Indeed, Spengler, in his divinely inspired book *The Decline of the West*, writes that 'the categories of the Westerner are just as alien to Russian thought as those of the Chinaman or the Ancient Greek are to him. As already written, a level playing field (allegorically represented by the road to Delphi) requires not only cultural diplomacy but also a cross-cultural diplomacy, yet the age of informed and wise diplomacy seems to have been superseded by that of political correctness and, in turn, by just as often political incorrectness.

The continuing decline of the West (which could not prohibit Spengler, that book's author, being dismissed as a crackpot in his own time) is typified in the masses by our substitution of technology for culture by which to subvert democracy's need for the highest possible level of universal [i.e. university] education, which meant then [but not nowadays] an education not only in the sciences but also in the humanities.

* * *

A History of Conflict
Part II

An Old Man at Twenty-Two

Twenty-two is young, especially for guys just about to die ... Old Dunghead Doug MacArthur was bragging about how the Chinese wouldn't come into the war [the Korean War] and he'd have the boys home for Christmas ... Well, there in our foxholes, we ate our C rations cold, put our dead friends into some foxholes we weren't using ourselves, and filled them in. A few of the kids played 'roll the gook'—they tucked the heads of dead Chinks between their ankles and tried to see who could roll a body furthest down the hill. In the tradition of the marines we buried only our own ...

Walter F. Murphy, *The Vicar of Christ*

It all started in Korea. [Excursus 1: Well, it didn't really start there, but for any history of human conflict (apart from Eden), then it's as good a place to start from as any other place. Whoop! But as on this world's very last day (as revealed by a study of the prophets), it is not the best of places in which to be called to account for being there.]

It might be all uphill from then on as when starting from Korea, but it's as good a place to start as any other. Us Americans (as the last nation left standing) had won the Second World War, and as the liberators of the Western world and defenders of democracy (for which purpose we had to put down as far as possible every claim of Holy Mother Russia as saviour of the West), we were all mighty well pleased with ourselves for having beaten down the Ruskies too, as well as the Nazis, and also in Korea, the Chinks, however much, for that being a bad omen, would prove to be in the Far West.

Yes, sir, a bad omen. And from then on, you could say just that, no less than we would proclaim the same message forcibly through every (anti-American) Chink we could find in Korea and through every (anti-American) gook we could find in Vietnam. Ours, after all, was the Land of the Free, from which we had the calling to share with all others the same sort of freedom.

Yet there was something missing, and of that, we were sure, especially in the face of flower power, over whose so-called peace movement even the weed had no effect. It (the weed) didn't work for us, as it had in Vietnam, but instead against us, as it did when we got back home. When stoned, then we could stonewall another continent and so convince ourselves we'd already won the Cold War, but against the little countries (like New Zealand) to which we'd brought back the weed, we couldn't cope any more than they could. We were heading for the biggest moral, political, and economic meltdown in our democratic history, and we didn't stand a chance—and all because we thought we'd won the war.

There was only one thing to do, and that was to give war another chance. Still, for being the defenders of world democracy (although on account of different cultures, there's no such thing), we forced our way (the democratic way) into Afghanistan, Iraq, and Iran and, just like the British, into Palestine, Ireland, and India, no less than like the Aussies against the Abos and the Wogs, and even so too the little Kiwis in their taking over responsibility from the Germans for the welfare of Samoans.

We were colonising (and didn't even know it). We were building empires (and didn't even know it). And so then in the midst of all our fundamental ignorance, all the best of our good and friendly intentions (including those to United Nations, the UN we nowadays never hear about) fell through—fell through to create more enemies than friends. [Excursus 2: Never mind the pretensions the Kiwis held (like us) for the rest of the Pacific (including even the trans-Pacific), since what all this continued turmoil meant was simply that we too had lost our heads, if not also by now the white-hot (once red-hot) flaming war.]

We Yankees (please pardon that self-expression of defeat) lost our heads in that continuing debacle, no less than did them Russkies (all five million of them) who, in their historic role as saviours of the West, had literally lost their heads in World War II. By then, the great war to end all wars had been displaced by World War II to become less proudly World War I, and both world wars, by continuing into what became known ironically as the Cold War, would leave economically destitute both the USSR and the USA. Whilst, as for Her Britannic Majesty, through whatever prime minister she had, then he or she would be seen to waive the rules since even Her Britannic Majesty (herself) could no longer rule the waves (except around the Falklands).

That big fella upstairs, you could say, had pulled the same plug on both capitalism and communism. Who would have ever thought we shared the same bathtub in the fight for any squeaky clean peace, whether for Kurds against Iraqis or Arabs against Afghans or Israelis against the Arabs (for which term, pardon the lack of any more broken plural)! You could say (for daring to be faintly un-American) that there's no winners (and although the Cold War grew pretty hot, even in a little Pacific patch like New Zealand, where the stories are legends), none of the contestants (far less the Kiwis) seem to have benefited any more than us. Yet some say today that the once Axis powers are doing very much better than most of the Allies.

What we are describing, even of ourselves, is of course so much less than accurate for being (in the spiritual as well as in the physical and intellectual dimensions) less of a singularity (typified in literature for the Greeks as a curled-up hedgehog) rather than any war is, including the Peloponnesian War, a monstrously multifactorial and distinctively foxy situation. Yet although that's true enough to allow every war being given a chance, it's also not to say, as between us Democrats and us Republicans, that we weren't all the time still fighting our own long ago and so never ever once ended the so-called Civil War.

Alas and alack for our own long-repressed (rather than long ago resolved) American Civil War! That's the trouble with all self-justified revolts, rebellions, and even revolutions. Call them wars of independence or whatever you will, but they never ever lie down. There's hardly any revolution that has not been preceded or succeeded by some most remarkably uncivil of all civil wars. Vietnam too, especially for us veterans, has been only one more as yet remarkably uncivil as well as being just as remarkable for being yet another instance of the unkindest sort of civil war.

* * *

A History of Conflict
Part III

Restoring the Hardware of the Soul
Your brain is the hardware of the soul. It is the hardware
of your very essence as a human being ... I wondered
if the brain were the missing piece of the puzzle in my
resistant patients. Perhaps, I hypothesized, the people
who were struggling had brains that could not 'run'
the new programmes I was trying to give them, much
like a computer cannot run sophisticated software
unless it has enough speed and memory.

Daniel G. Amen, MD, *Change Your*
Brain, Change Your Life

Scientists—no less than theologians, poets, and prophets, together
with musicians and other creative artists—think in terms of analogies
(analogues) and metaphors (models). In hard science (if pure physicists
consider anything less than physics to be hard science), it was the
biologist J. Z. Young who, in his *Memory System of the Brain*, was
amongst the first (in 1965) to write of the brain as a computer.

The gravitational pull of the increasingly interdisciplinary field
of what is now known as cognitive science (when focussed self-
centredly on the human mind) tends towards extending itself into
a universal calling. The increasingly self-centred human mind then
becomes a ceaselessly encroaching and cannibalistic opponent of its
own once heavenly endeavour.

Healing the cerebral hardware of the human soul then becomes
a constantly angelic calling. Mending, maintaining, restoring, and
updating the software of the same human soul likewise becomes a
constantly angelic calling. Nevertheless, the progressive secularising
of greater and greater areas of the human brain leaves not much
room for scientific conjectures, far less for poetic, artistic, and
prophetic, or other communicative forms of imagination. Such

brains progressively deteriorate into spongiform states of increasing dementia and calcification.

Neither healing nor mending the brain's hardware or maintaining the brain's software are just mechanical tasks, however, nor are their outputs even just anatomical processes with physiological functions. Both the hardware and the software of the soul (which is a composite entity whose algebraic sum is much greater than that of the arithmetic parts) obviously have fundamentally spiritual functions. Altogether they collaborate to uphold the soul or spirit of a person or, if you prefer for the moment just to think so, then for you to think no more (but there is more, isn't there) than to constitute the merely human mind.

But perhaps if the hardware and software of your brain were mended and maintained, then when freed of oppression, repression, and depression, not to mention also of whatever stresses, drugs, and addictions may have taken hold of both hardware and software, you would desire far more than merely accept this concept of the merely transient and ephemeral mind. Indeed, from dementia or stroke, even what merely mental life we have can be lost (not just at any time but at any moment). Maybe somewhere, somehow, there's some way of transforming one's existing mind!

You have to know (most intimately at all levels) that the hardware of your brain, as provided by its maker, is self-equipped to heal its own faulty, failing, and fallible soul-functions. Likewise, you have to know that both the hardware of your brain as well as the software of your brain are also made to mend, maintain, restore, and update its software functions. There are many and not just a few different ways of motivating and mastering these basic endeavours to heal and mend the fractured will, to control the wilful temper, to solace and console the despairing mind, to re-empower the sleeping emotions, or to bring again to life the broken heart. And they all face constant challenges and as often oppressive constraints. For being the offspring of a paramount creative maker, the human brain can redeem and recreate itself simply by staying in the closest of loving contacts with its only sovereign maker.

For instance, for us to speak here about restoring motivation to the fractured will or about bringing solace to the despairing mind or about re-empowering the clinically depressed spirit or awakening the sleeping emotions or to bring again to life some long- broken heart, our figurative speech may turn off the purely scientific soul that only springs to attention when hearing of the brain's basal ganglia system (responsible for anxiety and fear) or of the prescribed means of strengthening the brain's deep limbic system (which has so much to do with positively felt and negatively felt emotions) or of the brain's prefrontal cortex (so intimately concerned with impulsivity and problem-solving) or of the brain's cingulate system (controlling adaptability and cognitive flexibility) or of the brain's temporal lobes to control the temper (so strongly associated with maintaining memory).

In all this, our brain's prefrontal cortex (pfc, for short) can be seen in so many different ways to be the most advanced part of the hardware of our soul, but don't bother saying it in this way or on these terms to anyone uninterested in either critical thinking or in prophetic proclamation or in learning from experience or in whatever it takes by way of perseverance, discernment, self-discipline, and empathy for others to express the widest range of emotions.

In other words, sound morals take their stand on metaphysics, but of course, mechanistic metaphysics can be mistaken for spiritual metaphysics just as the body can be mistaken for the mind and the mind for being no more than the body. [Exegesis 1: The multifactorial fox, rather than the singular hedgehog, is having a field day here.]

Yet for relying on morals alone, you can mistake them for being sound, so you are better off, surely by far, perhaps by knowing the way that morals take their stand on metaphysics and so to have a measure for morals. But then this fallback or fail-safe measure depends always on your having (as for deciding whether peace or war) exactly the right measure. Some pragmatists cut corners by preaching that you can still be moral without knowing the metaphysics on which sound morals take their stand (although you won't appreciate your own vulnerability for losing out on the finer points of reality) when you find yourself being immoral as a result of choosing to be intellectually amoral.

So without any overarching picture or vision of reality—such as that given by the authoritative promise, revelatory prospect, and metaphysical reality of an eternal soul—informational specialism pervades the college corridors, turning ivory towers into those of Babel, where church bells no longer ring to remind believers of worship and the common communion of engaged communication breaks down into aggressively opposing opinion, constantly fractious debate, and deeply schismatic argument, until then finally and irrevocably, into open warfare.

* * *

A History of Conflict
Part IV

On the Subject of Seemingly Scurrilous Songs
It is interesting that the humanist Utopia and the
Communist dictatorship of the proletariat assume that
in the end all will be well in the best of all possible
worlds. The Christian can never be so gullible.
  Michael Green, *I Believe in Satan's Downfall*

We may blithely sing of some utopia or else more sadly of some
dystopia, although none but the Christian can be sure of which song
is which. Each song, with the requisite experience of false hopes and/
or false fears, can become just as seemingly scurrilous to the human
soul as can be its opposite song. Thus, are cynics made—not born—
who believe in neither heaven nor hell (nor consequently in much
else) because they have invested too much of their inexperienced
soul in each to recover from their unfortunate experience with both?

In the figurative sense alone, if you so choose to regard this
angelic message as such, the cynic, by sacrificing his soul to maintain
the equanimity of his emotions, withholds his every expression of
will in any and every belief far more than his state of unbelief in
any. Sooner or later, such is the conflictive tension between his soul-
deposed will and heartfelt struggle to express emotion, however, that
he will either explosively convert or submissively subvert to one or
the other of his previously polarised views. The subversion is usually
gradual, and the conversion is usually instant—or else, when often
inconsistently made, a mixture of both.

Yet sometimes, in the making of any Christian—such as Malcolm
Muggeridge, who must undertake his experience of the Soviet Union
in order to understand where he stands in relation to his soul—the
person is called to openly stand witness to his own pain, suffering,
and disappointment at having to change his own little-understood
soul-allegiance. That may happen to anyone of strong beliefs when
exposed to circumstances which demonstrate to himself or herself

that their soul-investment in any profession of faith or of calling, vocation, or choice of work or of spouse or of service to any country is no longer viable. And the touch, as to Apostle Paul, may be made publicly, directly, and most momentously from heaven. For others, more privately, it may be as if a pin drops from heaven, but perhaps no less painfully, and if from heaven, no less effectually.

You will understand by now that today's report (still being recorded here in heaven for training purposes) is most certainly a flesh-and-blood account. Through the birth of baby Jesus, the kingdom of heaven had to come to earth. It had come to earth not just in the abstract but also so that humanity in the flesh would have the opportunity to share in the crucified flesh and the spilt blood of the eternally resurrected Christ.

Only a flesh-and-blood account will help to compensate for what little it often is that most folks manage to make of their bare-bones Bible. A bare-bones Bible is one of the many versions authorised by hell, since, even although carried to and from church every once a week, such a bible is otherwise resorted to for little more than weddings and funerals.

This severely curtailed and once-a-week use of bare-bones bibles (especially when used for weddings and funerals as noted above) is very likely to reduce every wedding to the status of a funeral without managing to raise every funeral to the status of a wedding.

'Very well,' says the hard-bitten teacher of earthly experience, but that's not all, since the sting (if any) of any legal process always resides hidden in its less than legally credible tail of attribution. Consequently, this hidden sting, when so concealed in any bare-bones Bible or in any other of its demonic equivalents, is most certainly revealed and felt most profusely at every state-authorised hanging, at every state-authorised decapitation, at the giving of every state-authorised lethal injection, or at the swift but repeated pulling of the switch needed to bring about the victim's not always immediate electrocution.

This due process of law (when sworn on the still living bones of the eventual deceased) is devised to promote the pretence (for being no more than a pretence) of conducting a completely humane society. And so when authorised by law to conceal man's inhumanity to man, this legal process (most usually both ways compromised rather than one way confirmed by a priest) is thought able to divinely sanction the inhumanity of every such execution.

Accordingly, we shall bring you up to date by inviting you to some of the continuing executions that still go on, even although the last one to which you were formally invited to partake of by way of crucifixion was purposed to put an end to all those executions that have since followed. More thankfully, the Christmas story (so very nearly stymied at the very start by the massacre of the innocents) still continues (in both versions) although, for being separated more and more from its tragic aftermath, the Christmas story makes less and less sense to fewer and fewer people.

By now, hopefully, we shall have exhausted all further hope in explanations. So there's more food for argument given by this paragraph than needs any further writing (on this subject of crime and punishment) to preoccupy the theologians. Well then, because there's nothing like a song to depress, dispel, and disperse any chance of further argument—think of those songs sung by the notoriously laid captive Volga Boatmen—we'll take this opportunity to clear the air (especially after all this talk of executions) and so, with a song, pre-empt all further debate (even by which to excuse communism) which might otherwise eventuate between heaven and hell over bare-bones bibles.]

So then rejecting all this world's counterfeit words and counterfeit songs, listen again for that first-heard song, which on your own entry to this woeful world was first angelically sung and thus so designed by those in Supreme Command not only to soothe your tremulous soul when *en route* to earth but also to resurrect your responsive wonderment at your having been picked and marked out to receive this heavenly challenge to engage in earthly life. Listen for it, no matter how long without it you may appear to live, for the Supreme Command is always singing a default song of compassion for those who are truly listening.

A mother's lullaby is usually the nearest thing to this first-heard angelic soul-song. Later, the fast-growing soul may parentally learn of just how much this maternal lullaby has been sung generationally into the child (in turn to prepare that child for being a parent). So often this lullaby is sung in such close harmony intergenerationally to unite and justify the birthing pain of babyhood with the growing pain of parenthood (whether that be motherhood or fatherhood).

This maternal lullaby is not just the single melodic line (however maternally beautiful) when sung expressing assurance to an infant of his or her right to rest at nightfall—whether in the nursery or as a papoose on the wide open prairie—but instead becomes a paean of celebratory praise born of long forgotten birthing pains, those not only of the infant's birth and those not only of the birthing mother but those also of the mother's birth, the father's birth, and so (as we think backwards) to everyone's earliest born progenitor as well as (as we think forwards) to everyone's ultimately born descendant.

This ongoing paean of human life is a cyclic process, at least in its need for both deeper and wider learning, so read on if you would care enough about this, as often as not portrayed as an excessively short process and as often giving rise to a brutally hard road on which humans have to learn to walk their own talk by reading more about how best to live this human life.

The road is often long and often hard, but the way, when looking up, is surer than it is so much less sure for us when looking down. Learn from a lullaby that what can seem to be so utterly wrong (as with the birth of an unwanted child or the death of a starving child or the extreme afflictions of a disabled child) can nevertheless be taken up and not let fall, so as to perfect, no matter however unforeseen or disparaged for being so hard-heartedly divine, some far greater although persistently hidden purpose.

So many of this world's greatest souls (amongst them, that of the composer Beethoven or of the writer Helen Keller, for instance) have been conceived and born in such unpropitious circumstances that many cultures (including our own) would abandon their bodies (as of Romulus, the legendary founder of Rome) or, similarly, of those children whose developing bodies are denied their subsequent human history, then by authorising and legitimating their abortion (carried out most usually on no more humane grounds than that of personal convenience or of social respectability).

Nevertheless, because the human body (despite being almost revered sportingly, sexually, or socially by humans) is little more than the custodial temple for the potentially eternal soul, there is said to be a rule (perhaps more like a principle) of divine compensation. This principle works whereby even the most excruciating of physical pain (suffered by a mother in singing the most beautiful of lullabies to solace a dying child) may perfect such a completely unknown purpose in heaven's eyes through the world's eyes, that this world is immediately polarised into two apparently irreconcilable camps.

Of these conflicting camps, we angels are authorised to speak here not just of you humans (as if all of you were in one camp) but likewise not also of us angels (as if all of us were in the other camp), since some, both of you humans and of us angels, are to be found in each of these two opposing camps. Since the world has become increasingly a war zone, the (appropriately qualified) numbers from each opposing camp (whether of fallen or upright angels and of believing or unbelieving humans) are about equally matched. Nevertheless, whether in travail or at peace, you humans and us angels, whether upright or fallen, are still a very mixed (and often mixed-up) crew who have been picked, pricked, called, elected, destined, or predestined (all these words are hit or miss) to sail this singing starship of life.

Nevertheless, some lost souls have named this life a lottery and so have come to make their starship a grand casino. There are those, both humans and angels, who play for the highest stakes they can place for themselves in the ongoing game of this earthly versus heavenly life, polarised as it appears to be between so many conflicting opposites. There are many songs which, as much mistakenly about love as mistakenly about war, which focus, either explicitly or inexplicitly, on the scurrilousness of this conflict. Much harm can be done to the soul by a barrack-room ballad, by a student drinking song, and even more so by just as wrongful national anthem.

Some other songs, no less scurrilous, are seen to be polarised equivocally between right and wrong, unity and plurality, male and female, or war and peace. Others are seen to be polarised just as equivocally between rich and poor, first and last, the celebrity and the ornery, the known and the unknown, the sacred and the profane, the stupid and the wise—the list could go on and on and on.

834

On the other hand, however, there are those steadfast souls who still look, search, and fight for an all-encompassing orderliness by which these apparently conflicting opposites, although now serving only a temporal purpose (by which to highlight the present crisis in this worldwide conflict) can nevertheless be eternally reconciled, without compromise, into one encompassing and comprehensive view. They stake their present lives on an underlying reality (whatever the consequences) by which either to resolve or to accommodate both heaven and hell.

You can focus on the opposites, as do so many of the academic philosophers and theologians (which often only serves to perpetuate the problem of reconciliation), or you can (as do so many of the apparently more wayward practitioners and prophets) focus on the process of resolution (which cuts the problematic ground from under the feet of the more academic of the theologians and philosophers). This (for example) is the problem of pacifism, which likewise polarises people (whether philosophers or theologians) into two (sometimes both warring) camps.

Do you confront conflict and fight like any lawyer towards its resolution if need be or else run from it like any other man of the cloth seeking perhaps a quiet corner in which to pray or cry? Or else, if not these, like any man of the world, do you negotiate or try to compromise the outcomes that could be reached, whether by appearing to run yet standing still or otherwise when giving ground by really running away yet still intending to come back to fight to the death, always against any still remaining of the opposing party another day?

Dealing with conflict—both in the abstract, but more especially when in the concrete (and, worse still, when on the concrete)—poses lots of alternatives, both of a tactical as well as of a strategic nature. For example, are you, whether by choice or upbringing, a military man? Answer such a question at your peril, so don't try to answer until you're sure you understand the question. In times of peace, there are few (even amongst the armed forces) who clearly understand what it is to be a military man. Just as in times of war (especially during terrorism or total war), the roles of self-understanding can be remarkably reversed.

Which then, if made more abstractly, would be your choice—searching for a supervening sense of orderliness by which to reconcile this woeful world's apparent conflict of opposites or else, for as long as this highly conflictive and polarised world lasts out, then playing and toying with it as if, like cat and mouse, this world were being staked out against some already long-lost cosmic game of chance? Don't answer, unless you have the wisdom of Solomon! But, if like Moses, you're an impulsive man, you'll be made to walk the desert for forty years until you're patient enough to accept what could have been a far earlier answer!

Ever since the now largely forgotten fall (whether the fall from Eden or the fall from heaven makes no matter) and allowing for a slight intermission following the flood (of which only our faith in a rainbow remains in the way of any successor), what remains of this planet Earth has long been up for grabs in a gambler's market (with no holds barred by those who, rather than lose their long-term stakes, would prefer to break the bank). Likewise, don't comment!

For you humans having been born into this woefully dichotomised (or split-minded and thus discordant) world—where right is so often presented as arguably wrong and wrong is so often presented as arguably right—you too, as our dearest readers, may have already made a choice. It may be whether or not to accept or to reject any such specific principle of divine compensation (whose acceptance, amongst much else, helps to soften the dichotomy between good and evil, yet whose rejection, amongst much else, seems to disclose the existence of a very savage and powerful deity). Don't here dare break the heavenly solitude required, even in hell, for heavenly reflection!

On the other hand (in itself a dichotomised expression), the issue may be otherwise for you (in running away altogether from freedom of choice and by thus also running from freedom of action) to remain perplexed about which more fundamental choice to make—as between the now and the hereafter or as between relinquishing one's hold on those stakes you and others have already placed in favour of a once strenuously held but still somewhat firmly attached (but nevertheless false) belief. For being both a gentleman and a scholar, still hold your peace!

Given time (without end in heaven), you may have already picked from this preparatory account of these two camps, mindsets, or belief systems (even while still in hell) as to which camp, set, or system you already believe yourself to be in. It may be a religious mindset, a political mindset, a moral mindset, a social mindset, a philosophical mindset, a scientific mindset, or any other sort of closed mindset (including any or all these which you might mistake for being completely open). At this point, 'it's time to call your lawyer', calls an incriminatory voice from hell!

Lawyers (for the moment) aside, the two human camps (both male and female) on earth which mirror the two angelic camps (both male and female and as often androgynous) in heaven (since by such means, we in Supreme Command shall persistently remind you humans of how little different you are from us angels) are as follows: on the one hand, there is the rapidly growing camp of the *nyeboshnyi* (or unbelievers), and on the other hand, there is the just as rapidly growing camp of the *vyerayushchyi* (or believers).

We have chosen these two italicised terms from the colloquial Russian language because this is the means of current expression in which these conflicting concepts (say here, *nyeboshnyi i vyerayushchyi*—don't be shy) convey their most conflictive significance. And remember always that in terms of always looking for significance, then like us, you too should always be looking to read the *signs* of the times (sign off here, if you follow what we're saying about the semiotics of *sign-ificance*—again don't be shy), and this especially so (since semiotics deals with the science of signs) when we angels are preaching (whether down in hell, up on earth, or in reporting back to heaven). Thumbs up, eh, or else, when then closer still, then a high five!

* * *

BOOK TEN

Switching from Supreme Command to Supreme Commission

> From Commanded Obedience to Inspirited Commission
> What is feasible on the banks of the Danube may not
> be possible on the Euphrates—even supposing peace
> prevailed in Iraq as it did in most of post-communist
> Europe—and this ardent neo-conservative belief in a
> universal model went with a deep indifference to the
> particular history of the country.
>
> > John Gray, *Black Mass: Apocalyptic*
> > *Religion and the Death of Utopia*

Intro 1—Neil: Well, it's time now to answer that long-ago question as to whether you consider yourself to be a military man. Of course, it's not until you get into the thick of the battle that you'll really know the answer to that question, but of course, by that time, it might be too late to withdraw. So far, then so good, but we still can't do more than take your word for it.

Military commissions, like church commissions, begin by 'taking orders'. There's not much difference, really, between church commissions (taking holy orders) and military commissions (taking military orders). They both begin and end (unless stripped of rank or dishonourably discharged from the military) or defrocked (or excommunicated from the church) or struck off (from following one's medical, legal, teaching, or nursing profession) by the process of 'taking orders'.

Whether or not 'to take orders' (in terms of one's military, ecclesiastical, professional, or other vocational calling) may generate a great deal of blood, sweat, and tears—witness the lives of the martyrs. Even to hold the passport of one's own homeland can bring about one's execution, as in the case of the British national William

Joyce, who was hanged for treason for his part in broadcasting from Germany during World War II.

Intro 2—Samuel One: No one lives, even when in their own homeland (since, in the words of that poetical cleric John Donne, 'no man is an island'), without being 'under orders'. These orders may be military, civic, or ecclesiastical; and in times of war or terrorism or famine or plague or conquest (so study in detail exactly who the four horsemen of the apocalypse are who run the roost as this whole wide (but rapidly dying) world limps towards the last syllable of prophetically recorded time. By then, the civic legal system which we all (apart from lawbreakers) have come to take for granted may suddenly, in the twinkling of an eye, be replaced by a military manual (which even most lawyers in their civic capacity have never even heard of, far less studied).

Military commissions (not unlike clerical, legal, judicial, and other civil service positions) were once bought and sold just as wives, slaves, and servants were bought and sold. This was the height of capitalism carried to extremes in various versions of colonialism and communism where souls were regarded (in many cases religiously) as a propertied source of income (and still can be so regarded, whether as subjects or citizens of monarchies, republics, empires, and democracies) or of any other more or less totalitarian forms of government.

In its original sense of the word, holding a military commission (or any other commission) calls for commitment. The command system may continue, because in one way or another, everyone is subject to legally authorised command; but those who hold commissions do so at a higher level of command than that held by both non-commissioned officers and the so-called other ranks. And so they are legally authorised to issue orders appropriate to their level of command. Their power to command is heightened but so also is their responsibility to command the exercise of that heightened power of command.

Intro 3—Augustus: The Supreme Command operates in much the same way as any military command. This may be recognised by any such exemplar as that of the Church Militant or by such a denomination as that of the Salvation Army. There are rank and file under the Supreme Command no less than non-commissioned as well as commissioned officers under the Supreme Command. There can be promotion from the lowest ranks no less than from non-commissioned as well as commissioned officers.

The commissioned battle order of commissioned officers is usually that of apostles, prophets, preachers, teachers, healers, miracle makers etc. in accordance with their credentials as demonstrated first contingently by gifts of the spirit and then more substantively by fruits of the spirit. The order of commissioning is a spiritual one and so is neither an academic nor an institutional (nor yet in any sense a clerical) one. The foremost bishop or presbyter in the eyes of the world may be the least commissioned (for his or her being least properly committed) as discerned by the Supreme Command.

Likewise, the lowest rank and file by way of being the beadle or church caretaker or church cleaner may hold a commission way above the accustomed preacher in the pulpit or the prophet from the pew. Read Lev Tolstoy on such matters, for which his not always accepted truths, no less than for his obvious excesses of publicly published opinion, he suffered the extreme displeasure of and ultimately also his excommunication from the church. As said once before, church history is little short of being a horror story and more especially when being promoted by its own proponents.

Intro 4—Novice-Angel Chloe: Hold on, I don't understand what's happening here! What happens to the chain of command under a system of commitment? You know, that system of command, whether military or familial, which passes from Father God to his Son, Jesus Christ, and from thence to the Holy Spirit and so further through the serried ranks of angels, both seraphim and cherubim, onwards through the commissioned battle order of commissioned officers operating in all the gifts of the spirit, and so down to the lowest sinner in the accustomed rank and file! Surely, there's a celestial order of command, or is it possible for that order to function purely on the level and diversity of commitment? Thus, both angels and humans sinned, surely far more seriously through their lack of commitment than they did through disobedience. Indeed, it was for lack of their commitment that they presumed to disobey.

Intro 5—Augustus: Aha, what you're looking at then is no longer the chain of command, as it would be under a military operation, but the order of service under a heartfelt spiritual commitment. I know it's very hard, especially for mortals to make the switch from command to commitment, and many never manage to make the switch. Consequently, many churches, although they profess God is love instead of serving with that spirit-filled commitment to love, will operate solely under a chain of command, which, unless led through prayerful revival by the Holy Spirit, eventually leads to the institutional death of that church or, worse still, to that of their being subjected to some sort of counterfeit command.

To avoid this quandary, some churches will preach mostly Father God, others mostly Jesus Christ, and yet others mostly the Holy Spirit. They do this because they cannot reconcile their chain of command to any more loving and wider order of committed service. On this account, religious schisms proliferate, whilst some others promote a pantheon of broken spirits by which to disguise or hide the fundamental problem—which is that of committing themselves to a chain of command.

So you see now, dearest Chloe, that my own allegorical verse concerning fleas, both the bigger and lesser, with other fleas upon their backs to bite them, is itself a backbiting account of the way in which an order of loving service can degenerate into a hollow and unloving chain of eventually self-defeating command. When taken over and further falsified by the Counterfeit Command, the result is to express the reverse of what would follow from any committed order of loving service.

Intro 6—Nicolai Daniloff (lawyer, linguist, and logician, with all and yet many more options of soldiering available to a military man still in active service): Having by now long passed through the rudimentary stage of boot camp for any military operation, this tenth book on the subject of commitment to soul-catching comes to grips with every soul-catcher's need for the highest level of personal commitment to his or her calling. From here on, it is no longer any sort of *Soul-Catcher's Handbook*, far less any *Soul-Catcher's Guidebook, Pocketbook, or Copybook.*

It likewise now follows for this entirely self-committed sort of military operation conducted whilst under heavy fire in the field of action that this commissioning (instead of commanding) can no longer be considered to convey any sort of indulgence by way of providing any *Soul-Catcher's Safety Net*. So also, when committed to action under the least safe of successive military situations, no more than the briefest promise can be given of affording more than could be expected to provide of any long-term *Soul-Catcher's Delight*. On the contrary, from here on, a ruthless responsibility now supervenes by which to demonstrate every *Soul-Catcher's Calling*!

* * *

The Whole Point of Commissioning
In One Brief Word
Part I

From Commanded Obedience to Inspirited Commission
The sacred dies when it becomes locked into unchanging tradition. It dies when the environment it has sought to create and sustain breaks down. It dies when the reason for its being has been lost through corruption, abuse, or ignorance. It dies when it is privatised and seen as a purely individual activity. Yet the sacred is also the main drive for change. It is the vision that fires the imagination and takes us beyond the here and now to ask why and where we are going.

Martin Palmer, *The Sacred History of Britain*

There is but one brief word to describe the human soul's complete commitment, and that one word is *sacred*. Oh yes, even the sacred can be desecrated (as by false fixations and induced addictions), but even to be desecrated, there must first have been something sacred there. Find the trigger, twist, or false turn of life which gives rise to the desecration, and you've found the key by which to unlock the tortured soul (as it may have been imprisoned by generations of unchanging tradition) and so resurrect its own freedom to commit to the sacred by being born again.

This human commitment to any relationship, whether to person or to principle or to place or to thing, is conveyed and expressed by one's feeling (however much misplaced, corrupted, abused, or ignored) for the *sacred*. By comparison with anything other than partaking of this feeling of sacredness expressed through personal commitment, obedience by itself is no more than token.

Without commitment, then no relationship is sacred, and without this sacred level of commitment to what any relationship knowingly stands for, no act of obedience by itself is reliably sound for lacking this sense of the sacred. Every form of worship, whether soundly or unsoundly directed, is pointless for lack of all sense of the sacred. Yet, if there is any one word most overlooked in any discussion of commitment (which has been largely usurped by the concept of ritually required obedience) it is this sense of the *sacred*, without which there can be no possibility of commitment.

With the birth of Jesus Christ and even more so after his crucifixion and resurrection, the roughage of the world's 'lesser religions' took a dietary plunge. Without their accustomed roughage of rough and tumble (sometimes provided by ritual sacrifices, superstitious observances, and other occult practices (such as often the ritual abuse and temple prostitution on which these 'lesser religions' relied), their captive adherents never really recovered from their own rapidly rising religious constipation.

Whatever then ceased to fire a growing imagination would either (1) become locked into an unchanging tradition or else (2) lose out to conspiracy, corruption, abuse, and ignorance on breaking down. Each of these positions would then suffer from a growing indifference to the sense of wonder that had fired its initial motivation. Instead of aspiring to greater spirituality, what had once been revered for being sacred might then be tempted to demean itself. This it might do, although by no means in every case, by defaulting to religiosity.

Once the environment of initial awe with which any religion has sought to revere its objective begins to break down, then religiosity attempts to redress the resulting spiritual imbalance. This religiosity can be channelled through mixtures (although not always coherent) of institutionalism, legalism, collectivism, socialism, or individualism.

The extreme outcome of such channelling, as often as not achieved through differing forms of idolatry, scapegoating, priestly or clerical privilege, sale of indulgences, self-immolation, ritual sacrifice (human or otherwise), privation, reformist theology, and materialist restructuring relies on rule orientation instead of awe motivation. The result is to produce rules or observances (such as those of an architectural or sumptuary nature) which are as eagerly applied to the defaulting religion as might poultices and bloodletting be applied to any physically afflicted individual. In the long run, however, these tactical measures only compound the surgical seriousness of dealing with the burgeoning monster of overweening religiosity.

Many still surviving hotbeds of religiosity (e.g. Druidic, Shaman, and Zoroastrian) in turn afflict the understanding of Christian principles either with the occult residue of their pagan culture or else with the reinforced religiosity required to treat their own increasingly severely felt spiritual constipation. Cross-fertilisation and interbreeding abound (as shown by so many of the amalgamated symbols, e.g. the cross contrived within the circular sun borrowed by Celtic theologians to pacify Druidic theologians—a pagan symbol which still tops church spires from Edinburgh in the Northern Hemisphere to Dunedin in the Southern Hemisphere.

Theosophy (an amalgam of what was seen to be the best of all religions) paralleled Christian Science (which tried to amalgamate science with the garb of religiosity). Some remaining religions, less disciplined and when more startled by the evidence for Christianity or else less well founded on open-minded wonderment, resorted to passive aggression to isolating themselves in false havens and conspiracy, subterfuge and hidden violence. Yet others gritted their teeth, went openly to war, or else became stoic or persevered by protecting themselves with self-pride. Many existing counterfeit religions either converted to Christ or else morphed into their own deeper expressions of the counterfeit.

Nevertheless, with the resulting updraught from that first downward plunge of religiosity throughout the world, the way, the truth, and the life would soar into previously unknown spiritual dimensions on the resulting updraught of the resurrection. Sure, the sky would first darken into night, the earth would shake and tremble, just as graves would shortly open, and their dead be seen to walk the earth. All these events would more than token the Second Coming of this same Jesus Christ who had given his life for the redemption of sin, for the salvation of all humankind, and for the recreation of a new heaven and a new earth.

Much of that history of heaven was prophetically yet to come, and even still much more by way of being all eternity is yet to come. Nevertheless, many theologians who focus on the past facts of history rather than on the future fulfilment of prophecy, have reconciled themselves to their receiving only the half-earthly measure rather than the full-to-overflowing cosmic measure of the promised new earth and the promised new heaven which excitingly awaits them. Well, this diminished outlook is no different from that of those messianic followers of Christ's own time who were disappointed to find that he had a different agenda than was their own.

The ongoing forcefulness of this growing cosmic battle towards establishing a new heaven and a new earth rather than just pinning one's apocalyptic hopes once again on some new but just as completely fallible human leader (whether that be either some David or yet another Goliath) is to capitulate completely to the Counterfeit Command. The resulting loss from believers is not just of all one's prophetic dreams and visions yet to be fulfilled but also from many other would-be believers and could-be believers, their rightful appreciation of all those many battles already won on their behalf against sin and death.

Nevertheless, those battles already won by Christ against sin and death are no more than halfway to any new heaven in Christ's own recreative scheme of both earthly as well as heavenly things. These same victories already won over sin and death (however much appreciated by their human beneficiaries) cannot remain standing by themselves forever (like some totem pole testifying to no more than the potential of humanity) or be left for all eternity (like some pagan statue to Ozymandias) to stand alone.

Planet Earth still provides the main military arena for these battles between heaven and hell, which explains why the Supreme Command, in the person of Jesus Christ, brings heaven to earth. Nevertheless, apart from the triumph over sin and death, there is a far greater and more cosmic part of Christ's already revealed, infinitely bigger, and already fully prophesised military operation. The fulfilment of the prophetic consequences (the other half of heaven's history already revealed) makes it clear that for the final overthrow of the Counterfeit Command (the Antichrist or the lawless one, if you will), then the creation of both a radically new heaven and a radically new earth is required to give greater cosmic effect to the preliminary triumph over sin and death, and the effect of this may be no more than for the benefit of those merely defaulting humans presently on earth.

Nothing new is being said here. Everything written here has already been revealed. It was no more than halfway through Christ's three-year mission to earth that he swung the popular front of the war he was waging against evil (whilst on earth, he was only the chippy son of a carpenter, not a high priest, you know) from that of contingently fighting evil towards eternally saving souls. For by then having reached no more than that heavenly halfway mark, those battles already won over sin and death can be seen for being no more than a tactical feint to let believers envision what later will be asked of them by way of helping him to bring about this radically new heaven as well as this radically new earth.

Not everyone, far less anyone (apart from his Father in heaven), knew at the time what this apparently lonely and forlorn Messiah was on about. The whole military operation, in the swing of its popular front from overcoming evil on earth to saving souls for the sake of heaven, was becoming—even for Christ the bounty hunter—an increasingly pathetic operation. By the time of his approaching crucifixion, he would come close to falling out first with his disciples and then with his Father in heaven over the process. Yet for the very first time in the whole wide world, death itself was starting to lose its sting.

This renewed front towards securing salvation, now on the cross (a military manoeuvre carried throughout with great glee by the Counterfeit Command), then devolved into a basic three-day mopping-up operation, which thereafter, both in hell and in heaven as well as on earth, would be carried through to the further perfection instituted by the Holy Spirit at Pentecost at the calling of the Supreme Command. Meanwhile, the whole crazy legal system (of the no less than 631 subordinate regulations unauthorisedly legislated by the Sanhedrin as if by them then to supersede Ten Commandments) was completely fouled up by the Sanhedrin by their failing to administer and abide by its own rules of evidence as well as by their own rules of legal process in their trial of Jesus Christ.

Not a jot or tittle of righteous law would or could be disposed of, but this would operate only if the basic jurisprudence of believers in relation to the Supreme Command would move from their relying on their own overt obedience to misconstrued command to rely on their heartfelt commitment to one's heavenly commission. This would be no longer enforced as by military command, as had been so often attempted by earthly authorities in the past, but by personal responsibility to one's own divinely appointed commission.

Whatever earlier success could be attributed to the forces of fear that religious institutions and other strongholds had attempted to employ and enforce—as by compelling all citizens of Kiev on pain of death to submit to baptism in the Dnieper or by purloining Christianity as a trade-off for winning out as the most viable of all state religions—could no longer prevail under this newfound romantic yet most reverential idyll of a wider and more open heaven (which would thereby become personally accessible to absolutely every single person).

Then it was, under this reinstated threat of sanction (or penalty) imposed for refused obedience to an (as often unauthorised) command, that the forces of evil flourished more and more. The Counterfeit Command celebrated its mistaken supremacy over the heartfelt emotions by imposing more and more rules and regulations. It did so often by very pettifogging commands, each of which, as a result of arming the howitzers of intellectualism to maintain a barrage of rationalism, would be most credulously mistaken for being those not of the Counterfeit Command but instead of the Supreme Command.

The evil one, charged with the domain of insidious subterfuge, waged by spewing out mountains of incomprehensible and self-contradictory laws, carried the command theory of law to insufferable heights. To these heights of self-contradiction and incomprehensibility, many intellectuals and rationalists succumbed—and still succumb—even to the extent that many great intellects feel that they are being so commanded to maintain this barrage of rules for law and order as commanded by God.

Then even men and women still in the front line of the Supreme Command broke down under the self-contradictory and earthly realm of maintaining law and order, especially when faced with the fast-rising tsunami of evil overtaking the world. These front-line men and women who had once been mighty warriors on the side of the Supreme Command couldn't see the forcefulness with which their command (since sin and death had been defeated) was now restricted to dispelling darkness.

Instead, although ironically in the name of salvation, they fell victim to fear—to fear of their own failure—and by disguising this fear with a pride in what had seemed to be their own previous success, they thus failed to note how much the changed message of salvation required a commitment to love rather than to any legal compulsion. Even if they did not know enough of jurisprudence to recognise the forcefulness of this legal compulsion, still in their souls, they sensed the law's lack of lovingkindness.

Of course, when enforced by threat or fear of legal sanctions, then every citizen's fear of failure to obey the law and their fear of failure to succeed in their act of obedience gets in the way of their personal commitment to the law. Where there is fear, there is condemnation, but there can be no room for condemnation (either angelic or mortal) in our calling to follow Jesus Christ. The underlying jurisprudential remedy is then made more obvious through unconditional love than it could be under any legal remedy enforced through fear of shame or of pain.

But for our earlier need to fear what we little understood, the Supreme Command has never been founded on any command theory of law. Since the gospel of love came into the world through Jesus Christ, however, then our understanding increased through revelation from Christ as to how our earlier need for law would be superseded by our calling to exercise true lovingkindness. This exercise of lovingkindness, as once effectuated by way of our obedience to the Supreme Command, would then be effectuated not only by means of our committed word but also by means of our own committed action (as indicated by the true meaning of the word *indeed*). Almost all command theories of law fail, either sooner or later, for their lack of commitment to love. Law in action without love in action is no law at all.

The Supreme Command is at heart a Supreme Commission. For those of its body members who are no more than nominally committed (in seeing themselves required to do no more than obey commands), this commission can so easily be mistaken by these body members to be a law-based entity (not unlike the Counterfeit Command) rather than for their belonging to a love-based entity (like the Supreme Command). Unless attended to, this difference of mindset between body members is likely to give rise to serious problems, including the likelihood of religious schism (as typified by the bloodbath of church history, which can threaten to drown out any spirit of revival or serious need of spiritual reformation). It is the spirit of mundane religiosity which seeks to fan every such religious schism or every such bloodbath, whether between Catholic and Protestant or between Shia and Sunni.

The basic problem (if left unattended to, whether between those of either Protestant or Catholic persuasion in Ulster or Eire (once again a pivotal point between UK and EU over Brexit) or between Shia and Sunni in their fighting for control over different parts of Kabul in the Afghan Wars) has more potential to escalate into all-out, total war than it has to burn itself out, whatever the consequences of that burnout may be locally, in the unlikely process of providing its own self-containment. But in 1994, the outside world was no more interested in the plight of freedom fighters in Afghanistan than the outside world had been interested to go to the aid of Czechoslovakia and Poland against Hitler's invading Wehrmacht in 1939.

What is then the basic problem apart from all the evidence showing that the most basic of problems (when hidden under the camouflage of subsequent events) can debilitate and disarm all further attempts to resolve these still basic problems? Like so many aggressively spreading tumours, some introduced contagiously by conquest and others encouraged by the resulting warfare (which tends to camouflage and hide the primary source and cause of almost every war-torn situation), these are then left to spew out their own interminable fractals of distrust, disillusionment, and catastrophic suffering sometimes across the whole wide world.

These then basic problems (whether addressed by Taliban versus mujahideen or Black Sheep Turkmen versus White Sheep Turkmen or Islamic Shia versus Islamic Sunni or Protestant Christian versus Catholic Christian) can be and so often are left to let grow to such a monstrous size as to overwhelm first of all their competing factions and, if not by then spreading ever outwards, to threaten the security of the entire world. So then what's the basic problem?

In answering this question, both opponents divert attention away from themselves by pointing to the other party. Both have that same battle tactic in common. Both thereby highlight, if not fixate, themselves on that schismatic chasm stretching between themselves, as if there were no more basic problem between them than that of securing its resolution by such means as will support one's own party preference. By such stage of events, this outcome is most likely being pursued without any reference as to what cost entailed by each party's pursuit of preference is being caused (other than strategically favouring one's own party) to the other party.

Once having passed that point of reference, however (invariably the point of no return for both parties), it matters little or nothing to either party (witness the bombing of Frankfurt or of Hiroshima and Nagasaki during World War II) as to what the ultimate cost will be (either to the parties themselves or to the whole wide world at large). And by this time, even to the most astute of scholarly historians, the basic cause (however much mistaken for the *casus belli* giving rise to the ensuing war) has gone back underground (as in WWI and WWII) and is nowhere to be seen.

The basic problem is this—an unholy alliance between co-dependent factions. On the one hand, there are those who are motivated solely by fear of their own lives. On the other hand, there are those who, however much afraid they are themselves, are superiorly motivated to come to the help of the more fearful in being able to tell them and, if necessary, command them what to do.

These two factions then co-dependently come together (whether for their individual betterment or not) since those who are debilitated by their own fear to make their own decisions are prepared to be commanded (likewise for their betterment or not) by being told what to do and being prepared (or programmed) to obey those by whom they are told what to do. This is the military command which passes over into the civil sector by way of the command theory of law. Were there not some other mortal unlike themselves who could tell them what to say and what to do and so in whom obedience to command could be inculcated, and on the other hand, those who believe themselves better appointed to tell and enforce on others what to do, this system would not work (as evidenced by those situations in which it completely breaks down).

The way in which this military system, when applied to any civil system, far less to any church system, operates is most likely to entice both the fearful and the undisciplined, as well as the thoughtless, to join its ranks, as well as those who would thereby wittingly or unwittingly abuse or misuse the system to diminish the light of Christ. It is by this light of Christ—however much upheld by any democratic society, civil society, welfare society, or church society—that the mindfulness of every single individual as well as the collective well-being of all its monarchical subjects or republican citizens is maintained.

Nevertheless, as with any humanly mortal society, there is always a downside. Some Christian churches can be filled to the gunnels for thinking the Christ they serve to be no more than a wise prophet or seer. Other Christian churches can be filled to the same near-sinking level provided only that Christ be no more than a good teacher or perhaps a very great man. Worse still, and for their own very varied reasons, churches can harbour (whether undercover or uncovered) those who would reject Christ completely for being either a disordered fool or a complete charlatan.

Interestingly enough, without the discernment of the Holy Spirit, those very basic misapprehensions of Christ survive longest amongst those who dig themselves foxholes within those churches and other forms of government, both secular and religious, which serve them rather than serve Christ, for being the last outposts of command-based law. The distinction, at all levels (from the physical through the social to the spiritual), between doing a service and doing a disservice is a very fine line indeed. It is one which at every level requires the utmost of experiential wisdom and spiritual discernment.

Every command-based legal system—whether Babylonian, Hebraic, Roman (or even Anglo-American)—relies on pain (including the pain of shame). This may be enforced by imposing a fine (including that of confinement or even death). This is the so-called sanction (although in most cases, hardly any more than a formulaic legal process of sanctification). This civic process of sanctification is enforced by painful penalty or capital punishment (being a euphemism for the loss of one's head), but the command theory, in being driven by fear to maintain law and order, is made especially clear by the way it is linguistically expressed. Under common law systems, developed close to perfection in democracies, where the spirit of the law, as once in Greece and once in England, is strongly identified with the spirit of the people, absolutely nothing is prohibited. But you have to take the prescribed legal consequences of doing whatever it is which you decide to do.

Thus, in ancient Greece, Socrates (instead of running away, as was expected of him) took and drank the cup of hemlock. And so also, in ancient Israel (although long decayed, degenerate, and still fast declining under Roman occupation (from what had once been a commonality of workable law administered by committed priests), Jesus Christ unhesitatingly undertook head-on the same equivalently confrontive action. Indeed, almost all the disciples who followed Christ and later went likewise to suffer with him, undertook of themselves to suffer the same fate of their calling under the Supreme Command by undergoing their death by crucifixion. If you cannot understand the psychology and sociology behind this jurisprudence (or administration of justice) according to the commonality of allegiance given to the law, then you do not understand the humanity of Christ or the humanity of Socrates. In each of these cases, it is the allowable strength of the human individual to pit himself against the unthinking herd which so much coincides with the jurisprudence of the divine.

In these present days of failing law and order, the declining forcefulness of compulsory law, very much typified by the failure of the Roman Republic to observe its own rules and the failure of ancient Israel when still privileged to obey its own rules even although under Roman occupation, is typified by the increasing numbers of once common law jurisdictions to revert to legal systems of compulsion. Nevertheless, both at a national level and at a local level, unwieldy, unworkable, and often self-contradictory constitutions abound.

At an international level, treaties prevaricate the issues of each partner, as often with hogwash to conceal their respective and often contrary objectives. Even increasingly, as common law countries substitute the imperative *must* for the declaratory *shall* by which then to compel their citizens to obey rather than commit their citizens to uphold their own law, once again this manoeuvre of the Counterfeit

Command signifies an increasingly authoritarian and sometimes despotic aversion to common law thinking. By way of compelling rather than trusting their citizens and subjects to respect, honour, and obey what democratically, if not theocratically, is their own commonality of law, Anglo-American systems of law are in rapid default to command theories of law.

No wonder then that these days, there's so much lack of legal commitment. The law has lost every last sense of the sacred by resorting to its secular enforcement on the strength of solely physical (and sometimes unworkable and inoperable) sanctions. Complete commitment to the law (or to anything or anyone else) relies on the sense of those who are called and who follow that commitment that the relationship they share with one another (whether by saluting the flag, singing any national anthem, or partaking in any other form of communion) is sacred.

* * *

BOOK ELEVEN

Operation Soul-Catching

In the Midst of Life
It'd been eight months since I'd received word that
Paul had been killed in a helicopter crash in the Hindu
Kush, the mountain range that stretches between the
centre of Afghanistan and northern Pakistan. The
army helicopter had been brought down by al-Qaeda
or one of their Taliban allies; Paul and five of his
fellow Airborne Rangers had been killed instantly.
Debbie Macomber, *The Inn at Rose Harbour*

Intro 1—Matthew: Are you ready for this? It may take you (through
sweat, blood, and tears) to places where you've never gone before
(no bullshit)! You may have to forego much (if not everything) which
once attached you most strongly (or so you thought) to your (already
past) way of life. You may lose your work. You may lose your mind.
You may even lose your life.

There is no sweat or blood or tears that can now hold you back.
All the bullshit of the big bad world is left far behind you. This is
where the last, biggest, and most final challenge comes. but already
you have a big brother in Christ who's walking beside you. He's not
just leading you on; he's helping you on. And that's his way, his truth,
and his life on which for every day you depend.

Intro 2—Samuel: There's a brightness in the sky, a clarity in your
mind, a lightness in your step that you've never felt before. The
challenge of life is still there, and you need it to be there, because
instead of your life closing in towards one's last and final breath, it's
opening out into all eternity. This is the very time you've lived for,
and eventually, when that's all over for you on earth, it will still be
what you choose to die for so that you may live eternally forever.

The challenges shall never stop; but the sweat, blood, and tears it has taken to meet, fulfil, and sometimes overcome all these past challenges are somehow reformulated into a victor's crown. Each victor in heaven has his or her own radically different crown. There are no two crowns precisely the same any more than any of us there in Christ have exactly the same name. But oh, the names are long. How very long are each of our new and most beautiful names!

Intro 3—Kirsty: Our names are as long as are the strands of our DNA, and our crowns are woven out of the same strands as are our names. Each person is so beautiful, beautiful beyond description, yet each person's name, as well as each person's crown, has a most powerful and prescriptive force peculiar to that person. All in all, we are a most peculiar people—and more peculiar than ever before for when all eternity shall be there for us in heaven!

The visions of the future are given always for a present purpose. They may be given as nightmare warnings. They may be given as dreamlike promises. They may be given to reassure and confirm one's present direction of travel. The most fleeting vision may direct us towards a change of lifetime action.

One way or another, the visions of the future are always conducive to affirmative action. That action may be one quite new or already long pursued or on the point of being given up for being a failed endeavour. In some way or another, the suggested affirmative action will always be confrontational.

Thus, learning to catch and so to save another's soul, you must first learn to face up to and confront the state of your own soul. You must have learnt to cry and to sob over the state of your own soul before you can master what it takes to save another's soul. This is but the first step, but it is more than just the first step, for this first step leads on to yet a second and yet a third and yet many, many more steps (each of which have a transcendent value for the making of your own crown and for the calling of your own name, whenever you shall be called from earth to wear each of those rewards in heaven).

Intro 4—Neil: The authorised enterprise of soul-catching requires the relaxed yet self-reflective and so personally involved forms of soul-searching. Only these relaxed forms both befit and benefit the requisite abstraction from this world's fashion-conscious ways.

Intro 5—Zakariah: Still think on it (for all you've heard the same message many times before): that there's no present without a past and no future without a present. So then before prophecy could look ahead (in terms of consequences), there had to be a past history (in terms of causes) from which prophecy could be propelled.

Intro 5 (continuation)—Malachi: For fear of there being no prophetic light shining into their lives, the commonality of mankind (including paradoxically some of the greatest angelic as well as human minds) refuses to pierce and penetrate the deepest darkness of its own self-made history.

The answer to that lies only in the still presently inconceivable concept of what counts for being all history fulfilled. Once prophetically fulfilled, history cannot be mocked and cannot be sidelined. Nor can history be either scoffed at, put down, or remaindered off when once fulfilled. History is history—and more so than ever before when once out of time.

Until then, before the final burning up of all such vanities, these angels expelled explosively from heaven need (by way of containment) the requisite bodies (preferably human) in which to hide from the light and reside in the dark. Show such demons mercy or even understanding and so give them quarter, and mercilessly, they'll take you with them.

Intro 6—Alcuin: Nevertheless, for even demons (or fallen angels) now to prognosticate (using a deviant form of divination) and so make use of this future-present continuous time before heaven's prophetic ultimatum is fulfilled risks their banishment from those human bodies within which they presently inhabit to shelter themselves from the way, the truth, and the light.

What these self-prophesying (or prognosticating) demons most fear of (and therefore prepare themselves against) is to succumb to that deliverance ministry by which they are bound and dispatched from their possessory function by the Lord's anointed. But by now, in this last crucial moment of demonic possession they take their own property-rights to their victim's soul so much for granted that with all their defences down they are already celebrating. This is why any last-minute calling up of any soul-catcher catches them so much off guard. For being themselves such poor historians, fear has ousted every last particle of prophetic foresight from the most demented of demons by reason of which, when suddenly faced by any sudden onslaught of soul-catching, the devil (herself, by way of being a bad joke, but let's not be sexist) is most likely to be left severely distraught.

Intro 6 (continuation)—Marsyas: And as to hell's persistent worry over worldwide outbreaks of soul-catching (since demons are doggone worriers), there are already murmurs, heard even in the darkest offing, of a messianic mission to uphold and redeem the greatest possible number of today's sadly fallen humans. Of course, to allay their fear, this hellish bad news has every little demonic twerp pissing in his neighbour's pocket straight away to escape the resulting demonic outage.

This strategic mission of the Supreme Commission, striking abject terror down below ('even in these darkest of days', as reported by hell's *Underground Daily Times*), is (1) to harvest each possibly last human claim to this universally held-out offer of human redemption and (2) to extend every tactical means towards fulfilling this messianic mission (entrusted to both angels and humans) through paving the way, proclaiming the truth, and living the life as it should be lived in full preparation for each and every form of Holy Spirit–led revival.

Intro 6 (continuation)—Eli: The forcefulness of prophecy, whose foremost cutting edge, when honed by the experiential present, provides an open gateway or threshold to the future, is nevertheless dismissed by the commonality of today's worldly wise.

In consequence, from the earliest age through to the so-called higher education, the youngest of today's children are taught to think only in terms of such contrapuntal fairy tales (fact versus fiction) and so from the start are brought up to believe (if not yet exactly that right is wrong and wrong is right) that all such values (whether of fact or fiction) are inherently relative (and so capable of having their roles either merged, massaged, or even reversed).

Intro 7—Neil: Nevertheless, the commonality of unbelievers refuses to acknowledge its very own interest (and often conflict of interest) in this issue. There are at least three ways of very roughly expressing either this lack or conflict of interest. One way may be that for lack of proof, there are no grounds for hoping in the substance of those things that others believe in for their being as yet unseen. A second way may be that what unbelievers see for being already proved refutes those grounds on which believers hope and rely on for being the substance of things as yet unseen. The third way may be that there is simply no room for any hope in the substance of things unseen for there being nothing there to see and so likewise no possibility of proof.

Intro 7 (continuation)—Luca: Hold on to your hat here again, because there's a bigger and more intricate formula by which to reveal the prophetic future, which, by dispelling fear and renewing hope, is in the process of already being determined here in the present. The question (put to you as a test of faith) is whether you can multitask more than a mixture of at least five things. These five things require everyone (1) to become serious students of general history, as well as (2) to become more responsively related to whatever prophecy is propelled by the forcefulness of that history, by which (3) everyone so engaged will learn to reap the existential harvest of the present and so receive (4) the clearest possible vision of this historic past (however much strongly influenced by this sadly failing and possibly already doomed world) and yet leave themselves still freely open to conceive of (5) a yet still presently viable prophetic promise to be fulfilled of both a new heaven and a new earth in place of those already in the process of passing away. In no other way can any already perfectly envisioned future be realised, since any perfect future is bound to be the best of both worlds (the historic past together with the prophetic present), as can only be done by our then having (as promised) both past history redeemed for being also present prophecy fulfilled.

* * *

Operation Soul-Catching
Part I

A Short Treatise on Soul-Catching
A vision is gossamer, difficult to explain, more
difficult for the hearer to believe ... [since] ... in
an age of nuclear weapons and space exploration
whatever cannot be tested in a wind tunnel or a
laboratory or formulated on an engineer's drawing
board is generally treated with cynicism.

Arthur Blessitt (with Walter
Wagner), Turned on to Jesus

How can it be that you, for being a reader professing thus far to
believe in the existence of the sacred, nevertheless still can't quite
believe in the existence of the angels? Perhaps, from whatever safe
haven you mistake yourself to be in (remote from the occult and
immune to the demonic), you accredit your own soul-status with
being beyond reproach. Perhaps not, however, since your so-called
safe haven on earth may be no more than a false haven from hell. Safe
havens are like that (unless authentic, which few of them are)—they
stupefy the senses and sedate the soul.

'A vision is gossamer,' says Arthur Blessitt, who is not only
amongst the greatest of visionaries but also amongst the most
accomplished of spiritual activists of our own time. To put yourself
beyond all risk in some safe haven (safe and secure from the occult
or the demonic) is to put your soul at far greater risk by its seclusion
from the battle over all things righteously spiritual, since by keeping
you out of that battle, the entire demonic host will do everything to
ensure your soul is left to luxuriate in the spurious soft comfort which
hell provides to every false haven.

'So then,' says the Lord, 'you should follow me from the EU,
from the RU, from the UK, from the USA, and from as far afield
as NZ (in the South Pacific, remembering always that the Pacific
Ocean is ironically so-named on account of its aggressive nature)

into the wilderness that afflicts today's Central Asia of Iraq, Iran, and Afghanistan.

'Hey, hold on there,' you say. 'We've got a big enough bank account here, where we are, to backup (and, if necessary, to bolster up) our existing safe haven.'

'What wilderness?' you also ask, as if you could only innocently ask such a question and yet still watch worldwide TV. Of course, that you can do so worldwide and as if for all time and so go on watching as if for all eternity, no less than you think to go on so pleasantly living in the immensely privileged EU, the immensely privileged RU, the immensely privileged UK, the immensely privileged USA, and the immensely privileged NZ. Listen here, the privileges you take for granted in what appear to be the world's safe havens are less and less assured. In one way or another, most of the world's nations are either already sold off, up for sale, or up for grabs.

'In heaven's name, you ask what wilderness!' Why, in the Lord's name, so we angels say, not only that wilderness over there that you yourselves carve out in those places of Iraq, Iran, and Afghanistan which afflict Central Asia to the level of the demonic today but also in consequence of the still relatively hidden wilderness you make too of today's immensely privileged EU, today's immensely privileged RU, today's immensely privileged UK, and today's immensely privileged USA. We say nothing here of li'l old NZ, a not insignificant subject of discourse in itself but rather of all the other great wildernesses you yourselves have carved out because of the way that other people, even within your own home countries, have freely chosen for themselves to live!

'Until then, as we proclaim in the name of the Lord, so the issue of whether there are existing angels still stands between us. So then, without wanting to rattle off the thousand and one anwers which could be given to this question, let's be content to ask how then, first, without any angels, do you figure on what was not only told to but also fulfilled by the fatherhood of Abraham? Secondly, how do you figure on what was seen of the angelic ladder between heaven and earth that moved Jacob to recognition and responsive contrition? Yet again, thirdly, when executed by the disembodied moving hand at Belshazzar's feast, how was the portent of Belshazzar's doom (the consequence of his defiling the sacred vessels of the enslaved Israelites) interpreted to fulfilment by the prophet Daniel? And so also fourthly and for now finally, by what means was the promise of the Messiah's birth told to and fulfilled in Mary, mother of Jesus? How then, in these and in so many other different ways, can one make any sense of the scriptures (the written record of our Supreme Commission which we have bound ourselves to follow) without believing in the angels?

'Yet also by approaching the same question in a reciprocal way, how can one still make sense of this written record of the Supreme Commission (a record written according to accepted mathematical principles rather than that of being enforced under arbitrary rules of law) and likewise as of our lives (in practice) without recognising that the whole metaphysics of good and evil (and not merely morality as seen by humans) can be explained only by the presence of angels (both those fallen as well as upright)?

'Without Satan, the accuser of the faithful, together with one-third of the original heavenly host of angels who, by siding with Satan, were cast out of heaven to the earth (as recorded in the book of Revelation 12:4), there is absolutely no way of explaining the nature of good and evil or of righteousness and unrighteousness, far less of intended and unintended wrongdoing, except by the nature of the demonic. And because there is absolutely no other way of adequately explaining these and other wrongdoings (especially the most subtle of those which so wrongfully counterfeit the righteousness of our Supreme Commission), then by your disputing the existence of the demonic, more and more of you humans feel it more comfortable just to leave the present state of the world as it stands.

'But in the case of the demonic, because Satan is a counterfeiter of whatever is good, whatever is noble, whatever is pure, whatever is lovely, whatever is admirable, and whatever is excellent and praiseworthy, Satan is also the master of supreme disguise. Why then, often without the help of us angels to you humans here, the counterfeit is so close that only the Supreme Command can see though Satan's supreme disguise. And we fallen angels, who often can be so tempted to disguise who we are and even go so far (perhaps more than occasionally) to counterfeit ourselves as angels of light, are

862

thereby given one insight into what it can take, so easily for ourselves, to seek to perfect one's less than heavenly disguise.

'To discern fallen angels from the heavenly ones, however, there are more principled but, nonetheless, practical means of discernment than are the ways in which humans can avoid finding themselves (not always so mysteriously) walking their walk, talking their talk, and wearing their shoes. Like humans, who are only a little lower than the angels, the heavenly angels are also agents of our Supreme Commission. So then the heavenly angels (both righteous and unrighteous) are bound by the same principles of our Supreme Commission as are humans.

'Remember in all this that for discernment, every human prophet needs early, late, and constant schooling—severe schooling (so don't grouse about the state of the world, the state of your health, or about the learning process given to you that relies on producing pain). Remember also that every prophet needs sanctification (and yes, just like anyone else, a prophet may lose his or her sanctification) just as any angel, for being even as high as Lucifer, the fallen light bearer, may fall from heaven.

'And just remember also that with both foresight as well as hindsight, that once as humans you've put your back to the prophetic plough, there's no turning back, lest you die before your time with your calling unfulfilled in what then (to a greater or lesser extent) is bound to be an unmarked grave. It doesn't do to mess with the divine, eh? No or yes? Oh yes, you may stumble, you may fall, you may suffer grievous bodily or financial harm, but unless repentant, don't think to call the shots by suborning either the Supreme Command or Supreme Commission. And we're speaking to everyone here, because to a greater or lesser measure (the extent to which remains unknown until exercised) everyone is called to prophesy.'

How shall we humans respond to this angelic challenge? Perhaps we can look on things this way: we learn to know (through history and hindsight) from how things first started, so we already know something of what it takes (prophetically) to learn (with foresight) as to how things both go on or end. In any case, the resolution of the endeavour in which each of us is here and now engaged more and more confirms the already prophesied outcome by which this present heaven and earth shall give way to both a new heaven and a new earth. To advance the reality, as foretold of this cosmic transformation, is our present mission, and to help secure its accomplishment is our present objective. Life is as simple as that, and it's never complicated unless when devoid of our present sense of mission.

It then goes without saying that by this sacred mission, extended to everyone (despite being rejected or ignored for the present by more than a few), then we are the ones called to military action by our commission to the Supreme Command. For a more complete understanding of what this commission means, we humans must develop and deepen our sense of the sacred, which pertains not just to our own personal sanctification but also to the sanctification (as much as possible) of this whole wide world. Most folks either focus on only the personal view or only the public view (whether of sanctification or of salvation), which explains why their one-eyed and monocular view of each (instead of their bifocal view of both) never ever works as well as it should.'

A sense of the sacred (akin to a sense of the heroic in the vertical aspect and to a sense of the chivalric in the horizontal aspect) exists in every individual. It may lie passive and ignored (held captive sometimes by a sleeping spirit) unless and until inspired into action (or as often provoked by awareness of its own absence, then into counteraction) against those forces which hold it captive. Or else its grandeur may be abused, reviled, and corrupted and so turned to nefarious ends by some Napoleon, Stalin, Hitler, Mussolini, or Osama bin Laden—although ostensibly for the public good. 'Judge not,' we are warned, 'lest in turn we be judged [as most certainly we shall be judged] by the very same means as that by which we judge.'

Our own fast-dwindling sense of the sacred (to which we are less and less exposed) is so easily overwhelmed by the atheistic stench of the secular (to which we become increasingly accustomed) that we accommodate ourselves to trite and trivial assumptions as to how all things begin, and so in the same fashion, we oblige ourselves to believe that these things must also, in somewhat the same way, assumptively end. Thus, amongst the Western democracies, we flatter ourselves to think that 'the origins of al-Qaeda can be traced to 1979 when the Soviet Union invaded Afghanistan.' Historically speaking, that's laughable — were it not also so abominably untrue, and thus tragic for the Western democracies, in their pointing to the Soviets, to think that these Western democracies can so trivially exonerate and exculpate themselves from the origins of al-Qaeda.

Al-Qaeda was not by any means the only anti-Soviet (any more than for being the only anti-American and anti-Israeli) faction. And although it may be technically true—only technically true, because in history, we can never know the full facts—that 'bin Laden travelled to Afghanistan to help organise the Arab mujahideen to resist the Soviets', the Western democracies then jump from 1979 to 1996 to confirm the fact of bin Laden's 'increasing radicalism' by his then issuing 'his first *fatwa*, calling for American soldiers to leave Saudi Arabia'. What is not at all explained, however, is how come—for what tenuous reasons, for what assumed purposes, and to what further effect—American soldiers (as well as British and other soldiers) were in Saudi Arabia.

Historic assumptions as to the past imperfective either blow up suddenly in the present indicative (as with Iraq's invasion of Kuwait) or else go on to generate prophetic assumptions that remain too sadly imperfective (as by then stopping short of taking Saddam Hussein's Baghdad) to allow for any worthwhile credibility to remain in the present indicative. The sadly imperfective future rarely, if ever, will support any sustainable future, until Jesus Christ is seen to walk the streets of Kabul and the same Jesus Christ is seen to walk the streets of Baghdad.

Yet you hold up your hands not in celebration but in horror at such apostasy (by which the sanctified are presumed to be desanctified). Yet again, however, and although for not yet being seen by the human eye (never mind whether Muslim or Christian), nevertheless it is already hard fact (that Jesus Christ already walks the streets of Kabul and similarly also walks the streets of Baghdad). Open your eyes, just open your eyes! You can hardly expect to see the Lord in person (far less to see any angel in person) if you keep your eyes always shut tight and your heads always turned so far down whilst praying to heaven. Learn that causes (at ground level) may often correlate overintimately with consequences at both heavenly levels (yet their eventual outcomes may still be too much misunderstood when seen solely in terms of their limited inputs).

So then relax (your minds) and recover (your hearts) so that (by cleansing and purifying your own by now grubby and overhumanly determined souls) you may feel safe and secure enough to release your spirit of eternal life from this world's undercover of fame and fortune (measured by respect and status) of mechanical mobility (measured in terms of cars, trains, and planes) and domestic stability (when measured only by land, houses, and possessions). Extend both your inner and your outer vision. Hard times are coming (almost here now), yet the wind of the spirit is rising ... is still rising ... is still ever more rising ...

Right then, take to your positions, guys, for this third and last world year already long begun and long gone global, although as yet unknown by many for being cosmic beyond all time ... for being a spiritual and not just a physical battle ... So then puts us all, both combatants and civilians (it's yet another total war), in the same front line. So then helmets of hope and salvation to the fore (so think with your heads and not with your hearts, which are reserved for authentic feelings). Don't puff up your chests (or you'll split your breastplates of righteousness, as well as (since who knows) what it takes to detract from your already royal robes of righteousness). So then don't forget to fasten and tighten up, if necessary, your belts of truth (or every single one of you so recently commissioned officers may find yourselves demoted right down to your privates).

Likewise, don't leave behind or let go of your shields of faith (or you'll get skewered through the heart with false promises, hit over the head with counterfeit strategies, and kicked up the bum with fraudulent tactics). Likewise, don't fight with anything else than your two-edged sword of the spirit (or else what's left behind of your own withered fighting spirit will be left to struggle on with yesterday's by now obsolete weapons). So too, don't take off your soft-spun slippers of peace (because there are land mines everywhere around which would be set off and take you to kingdom come, which here, in this context, is not unambiguous.

So then, troops, just when you expect me to call you to attention and then say quick march, I'm going to do the reverse (which will

866

tickle the fancy of the Counterfeit Command) by telling you to relax, stand at ease, and pray as well as breathe deeply whilst we all send our chaplains (with their word of encouragement) to the fore and gunners (with their word of deliverance fire) to the rear. So then let's all get on our marks ... right, ready, steady, go ... to save this day from evil's sway by joining in the following fray.

Your concomitant task throughout the fray (however it may sway your mind one way and sway your feelings another way) is to remember always, as much for your own sake as for the sake of others, that this is not a fray (completely) of either your own human making or otherwise all of angelic making. The concept of pride takes too much pride of place (explained by loss of trust) in our own but by now conceptually deficient English language.

'So too, we angels can't give you English language lessons right now when we're all at the battle stations, and in any case, English has become such a universal language that we're already fully committed to teaching émigrés, refugees, deportees, and all other kinds of dislocated sad-u-sees.'

Most human downfalls, especially those felt over disappointed outcomes, are self-engineered. All of a sudden, whether or not these frequently false prophecies become self-fulfilling or else the degree to which the expected future-perfect remains rabidly imperfect determine the outcomes sometimes so convincingly as if their original inputs were doomed to fail (as indeed they often were so doomed by fear of their failure). We can so easily get trapped in the pseudomorphology of big issues, especially in the global issues which go so far beyond our domestic competency to resolve and determine as to convince ourselves that we can order their outcome by reference solely to the purely physical domain.

The sense of the sacred then survives (barely these days) most often inversely in proportion to what only passes (transiently) for human progress, most often inversely in proportion to what passes (momentarily) for human enjoyment, most often inversely in proportion to what passes (temporarily) for human achievement. The sense of the epic (so eagerly sought for by Tolstoy and Tolkien, by Dickens and Dostoyevsky) has forsaken human minds.

In such little ways (often the ways that most matter), the sense of the sacred may be birthed in the need to communicate, to share with some other soul the brightness of a morning, the beauty of a sunset, the wonder of a waterfall, the verdant peacefulness of green pastures, or the quietude of still waters. Each such self-awareness of sacredness privately sensed, and even much more so when publicly shared, has the result (however unexpected) so often of restoring the soul.

The sharing may be communicated by no more than saying good morning or good evening or even just by saying hi or hello. It can also be communicated silently by no more than the gentlest of smiles or even by just a meeting of the eyes. Indeed, to communicate without a word, where the sense of the sacred is least perceived by reason of an overly accustomed place or an excessively introspective personality, often requires a far greater effort of the heroic, because there, the sacredness of the meeting with another life has been locked into a tradition of unchanging individuality.

Yet still at the grandest of all architectural levels not only as by the obvious design and history of a great cathedral such as that of St Paul's in London but as also with the design of a Bach cantata or of Handel's oratorio (as personally composed in private and then so widely shared by those able to perform and appreciate its composition at so many public levels) or as also with the logical as well as literary design of the sixty-six books by forty authors which both inspire and confirm the biblical canon of wisdom, so too these writers and composers never cease to elicit the most awe (as always from us angels) which, in turn, surpasses all we could attempt to say by way of communicating our recognition of the symmetry of design associated with the sacred.

In this overwhelmingly machine age, the sense of the sacred has largely been lost from law, largely been lost from logic, and largely been lost from language. The loss of our sense of the sacred has been replaced by an exaggerated sense of the secular, which satisfies the lesser want of our far greater need only because the secular is nothing in itself but for being an offshoot of the sacred. Because this replacement is done only by way of our own self-substitution, however, there remains a continual hankering in our souls for the more truly sacred—something, in its own right, entitled to our everyday wonder and open to our everyday confession.

Yet like the sense of the prophetic word by which we are all encouraged to prophesy, we are all given something of this opportunity. Sometimes it challenges us, and for some few commissioned by a far greater task and almost military responsibility to engage in it, it may challenge them most severely. Yet through mothering, fathering, gardening, teaching, nursing, or preaching (no less than in the more rarefied heights of art, music, science, literature, or of any other sacrificial commitment), we are all called to share in this same prophetic sense of the sacred, by which even in its slightest expression may still require from all of us an exercise of the heroic.

We are talking here not only about nurturing the soul. This is achieved most usually through our main drive to provide and maintain a healthy and sustainable environment for developing both a supportive mindset and attitudinally conducive outlook by way of education. Nevertheless, we are also talking about the reciprocal process to ensure nothing is lost either through the worldly abuse of power (as by all forms of oppression and bullying) or by exposure to the degenerative effect of corruption (as employed by all forms of fraud, bribery, and deception).

What is very much less talked about these days (surprisingly enough, since that nurturing process is no more than a means of sustaining the soul) is instead about saving the soul, which is, after all, the strategic purpose promoting every tactical means of maintaining and sustaining the soul. Yet there is no point by itself to the maintaining and sustaining of anything (whether aware of the need for this or not) without our having a clear purpose to its maintenance and sustenance. Salvation is the first strategic priority, after which maintaining and sustaining the soul for this purpose makes perfect sense. That first strategic priority is also confirmed by the way in which those people who lack any sense of salvation also lack the same level of educational motivation by which to maintain and sustain what they fail to recognise as the soul.

* * *

Operation Soul-Catching
Part II

Some Players in the Great Game
Wassmuss in Persia, and Niedermeyer and Von Hentig
in Afghanistan were causing us some anxiety. The
latter pair ... had been in Kabul where, though well
received, they found the Amir, Habibullah, firmly
refused to depart from his policy of neutrality, and,
after a short while, Von Hentig and Mahendra Pratap
[an Indian revolutionary] were given to understand
that their presence in the Afghan capital was no
longer welcome.
                    Lieutenant Colonel F. M. Bailey,
                    CIE, *Mission to Tashkent*

Some unexpected happenings are apparently so big (including
even civilisations on the march) that they hug the ground and so
figuratively pass under the human radar. Any civilisation on the
march—whether Egyptian, Babylonian, Assyrian, Graeco-Roman,
Germanic, Scythian, Chinese, Japanese, or Anglo-American—
will be so huge as to defy all but the inner eye until the outer eye
is overtaken. And once started, the momentum of the so-called
unexpected happenings is such that (like any flight of locusts), so
too, civilisations on the march (although still just like locusts in their
death throes) can rarely be overthrown or turned aside.

Other unexpected happenings are apparently so small (whereby
tiny birds, although even large reindeer and huge whales change their
migratory paths) that these and many other unexpected happenings
just as figuratively fly over, trek through, or swim under the human
radar. In the same way, mankind on the move makes not only its
own collective history but also world history, often without being or
becoming the least aware of all or anything happening. The outer eye
without the inner eye is frequently a false measure.

It doesn't always take an angel (far less the entire angelic host) to foretaste the future-present of all unexpected happenings. Humans too can be called to engage in this culinary foretasting of the future-present no matter whether their appetites (or callings) for doing so appear potentially great or potentially small.

The objective of one's calling (whether great or small) is often to reveal whatever may be gleaned of otherwise unexpected future-present happenings. Of course, for being either unforeseen, unexpected, or unwanted happenings, these prophecies test the faith of those who hear them. After all, who wants to hear of any unwanted global war being waged, far less of the approaching end of both this heaven and earth, even as we think to know of them. Yet just as it tests the faith of those who hear such prophecies, so also does it even more test the faith of those who so righteously proclaim them.

What will it take to liberate the last five thousand years (or so) of mummified human history, as well as of this world's still conflictive history, from the mausoleum in which they have been for so long entombed? What is seen today for being human progress (from hand tool to hydrogen bomb) was once described (from Babylon back to Babylon) as the march of civilisations.

Civilisations which resort to marching orders (to compel their subjects to obey the law rather than committing their citizens to uphold the law) invariably break down. [Excursus 1: Compare Britain's taxing treatment of its American Colonies in the eighteenth century with what Britain learnt from such mistakes to entreat the Maori (at Waitangi in New Zealand) by the nineteenth century! No, sorry. On second thought, hold on, since that's an entirely new topic of comparative history in itself so huge and so controversial (on all fronts) that it can't be either treated or entreated here (despite the thousand and one treaties with the North American Indians in North America and the one and only Treaty of Waitangi in New Zealand, made between the British and the Maori back in 1840).]

The first inklings (by way of giving marching orders) of any breakdown in cultured ways of thought (however relative to their own times) occur in the substance of things as yet unseen—that is to say, first in matters of faith, before manifesting themselves in works of expertise. Indeed, the Counterfeit Command uses great although always worldly works—the building of tall towers, the opening of great exhibitions, the institution of grand charities—to cover up the (not always dormant) corrosion caused to civilisations by their increasing lack of faith.

Civilisations on the march (outwards always to their fragile periphery) invariably break down (inwards always to their conflictive epicentre). At first experience of breaking up (whichever way), they usually break up into a run. This initial break-up may give rise to an ever-widening melee (comprising a growing hotchpot of needy hangers-on and reluctant givers-up). Eventually however, all who remain (until eventually overtaken as in Sodom and Gomorrah) run riot, resort to terrorism, or break up into a rampage. 'Look on my works, and be amazed!' wrote Ozimandias, purportedly king of kings, whose self-promotional words alone survived amongst the ruins of his once mighty works.

Civilisations, although at first on the march and then on the run, give rise initially to émigrés outward (as from Britain to the Commonwealth) and later refugees inward (as from the Commonwealth to Britain), each on the run, then to the survivors of those same broken and displaced men, their weary women and war-torn children, all wearily wandering the earth in their search for survival and sometimes also to encounter warring civilisations on the countermarch, and finally to thugs and terrorists with nothing to lose nor anything to gain. To kingdoms on the ascendant, this is all a great game; and for generations of men, this great game has been played where we are now on the North-Western Frontier.

Invariably the game grows cold, however, and although often only after years (if not centuries) of being in the ascendant, these kingdoms decline as forcibly as others more forcefully arise. And so most usually after experiencing their own but relatively brief Indian summer of selfish indulgence, they either slowly begin to decay or else are overtaken by an apocalypse or catastrophe of similar or greater dimensions to that which they inflicted on others when first they went on the march.

One great empire after another—Egyptian, Babylonian, Greek, and Roman—rises from the dust to bite the dust; and there seems no end to this cyclic display of might, fame, and wealth, except that the material resources of the world grow sadly poorer, the deserts extend bleakly further, the seas run drier, the history of human disappointments grows longer, and yet the lessons of this abject history of human suffering, to the extent that the human race does not learn from it, becomes more and more overlaid by this palimpsest of suffering—all yet incredibly as if it had never happened before and by reason of our own self-confidence is never likely to happen again. No, there is nothing at all new in it, and in that lies the greatest of our sorrows—that we have absolutely no appreciation of the truth and increasingly no propensity to learn of it.

Most great empires—as for the Dutch in the East Indies, the Spanish in South America, the British in India, or the United States in Vietnam—seek to fight their battles (whether to vanquish their enemies or else to conquer or to subjugate or to colonise new territories) far away and out of sight or else safely offshore.

When close countries and contiguous cultures set themselves up on a collision course—as between Mongol and Chinese, Roman and Ancient Briton, Lowland Scots and Highland Scots, English and Irish, Israeli and Arabs, Mexicans and the USA—then the defending factions may build walls and forts or express a fortress mentality by some other physical or virtual means by which to contain (no more than their own more exclusive way of looking at things). The effort taken to implement and maintain this fortress mentality may in the end contribute to the downfall of the defensive country.

Thus, the fate of the Roman Empire was decided by unfinished business in the provinces, as typified by the withdrawal of the Romans from Gaul and Britain (leaving both to the marauding Vikings). The fate of the British Empire was decided by its failure to negotiate with the revolting American Colonies and eventually clinched by unfinished business in India. Will Brexit likewise be a new beginning? But for what reasons, by what means, and for what purposes?

* * *

Operation Soul-Catching
Part III

This World's Most Readily Seeded Sermon
Hell was a wooden arch with a cloth tunnel behind
it and a simple catch holding shut the green eye. It
smoked because there was a length of tarry rope nailed
up behind the gullet which Lucie set alight before
going on stage. God reached Heaven by climbing a
ladder behind the wooden scenery.

Geraldine McCaughrean, A Little
Lower Than the Angels

With 'a ladder behind the wooden scenery', by which 'God reach[es] heaven', which, for the crudity of its placement in leading up to any pulpit, might be encountered in the most worshipful context of every great cathedral or other place of worship, then seek to answer for yourself whether or not heaven is nothing more than but some very much misguided believer's big scam.

Well, as of any and every believer, then sooner or later, you'll be put to the test of deciding that very question. So then be prepared since (1) there are two sides (either yes or no) to every well-formed question (WFQ), then (2) you'll need to take seriously each of these two sides to the question, then (3) you'll need to put your ear as near to the ground of whatever last remaining railroad track you can find to determine whether the great ruler of the universe (GRU) is already on his way, and then (4) you'll need to decide the question for yourself accordingly.

If you're going to sow seeds, as every mind-grabbing preacher must always do in giving a sermon, then certain consequences follow. You may have to prepare the soil (which has probably lain fallow since 1215—the time of Magna Carta). For still being an 'upstart preacher', you'll expect an instant return (but for soul-harvesting, there is a very different sort of mind-grabbing season). Then (never fear) you must first learn to relax (like Moses and Noah) as to the resulting harvest. 'Never fear!' says the Lord, but like so many of the things the Lord says, even in his own sermons, then there's always a cost factor (or sacrifice).

Why then, even as pins (or as seeds, if you prefer to call them so), like pins piercing your fingers (so also bending so far over from the pulpit to sow seeds from a sermon can also hurt your back), the very words you've been given by which to sow these seeds can cause great grievance amongst those who would willingly congregate to hear a very different sort of sermon. Never mind, at least you know that (for the moment) against the preacher, there's nothing personal.

Although your faith is fading, you still remember the piercing experience of these seeds, pins, or words as they came dropping into your preaching heart directly from heaven. Nevertheless, the statistics for their failure to find their proper place in the darkest of people's hearts still show that the process of preaching, even when heard directly from the Lord's own mouth, is the one (apart from teaching to the multitude in the streets or prophesying to church leaders in private) which is the most widely as well as the most deeply misunderstood.

Why is it that the message 'Fear not', when heard from the highest of earthly pulpits, can so often be counterproductive and grossly misleading to almost three-quarters of almost every congregation. 'You've got no faith!' rabbit on some preachers to their most faithful of followers. It seems that the preachers themselves (who profess themselves to be pin cushions on behalf of close-following believers) are case-hardened by what they themselves preach for being themselves incapable of feeling the pain of being personally pricked by pins (which they may even dismiss for being demonic shafts from hell instead of seeds from heaven).

When one looks at the earthly statistics (contra the sermon, which tells us 'not to fear'), one begins to fear greatly for the Lord! The fact is (no less than one so often hears that message for being no more than a superficial fact from the pulpit) that until hearts are opened far enough (to receive the message once again like that freshly dug virgin soil which awaits spring sowing and yet now bear the summer pain of tall stakes piercing grown-up hearts and not just the pricks of little pins), one entirely misses the great sense of humour (yes, sometimes grim and even macabre, but more often boyish and always loving) that not only accompanies but also (like the living water of life itself) inherently infiltrates and refreshes every single word of the Lord's own great sermons. And from the parable of the sower to the parable of the prodigal son (and with every other parable betwixt and between), that is precisely why and most exactly how (when given heavenly understanding) we are also (despite every fearful military operation on behalf of the Lord when we are called on to fight) constantly told to 'Fear nought!' [Excursus 1: From which admonition to fear nought, it took a battleship of His Majesty's Royal Navy to resort to irony and so reverse the tide of naval battle in 1906 by being called *HMS Dreadnought*.]

Look at the process of preaching (also of teaching) this way: for the very lowest of laymen (there's a lengthy torch list) ... already patiently waiting ... for hours, for days, for years ... still waiting patiently on the Lord (as this piercing process of being called into the front line of any military action is itself called) ... there ... to feel for oneself ... pierced through one's already open and receptive soul, at least one pin (a.k.a. a seed, if you prefer to think so) dropped (from a great heavenly height yet both exactly and precisely) into its proper place to germinate (for however long this takes) on earth. This is simply part of the gardening process (which some call jurisprudence) in which there are seasons for all things (otherwise known as 'waiting on the Lord' or yet again as listening to hear at least one more pin drop towards the virgin soil from heaven).

So then be prepared not for but instead against those preaching-teaching prophets who exalt themselves (through raising Cain) by means of their exhaling fear. You must ask yourselves from exactly where (although we need not be precise) comes the bad air they breathe in (as well as where it goes exactly) when they breathe out. Their business of raising Cain (rather than raising Moses or Elijah) is a thoroughly bad business (whether all round or in the square). Maintain your fearlessness (through Jesus Christ). Go tell the good news on the mountain, and don't even think on it, most certainly not more than once, since no one knows of the unexpected consequences after breathing up any such self-exalted preaching-teaching prophet's exhaled air!

All parents of small children may well take the issue—both ways—with this very sound advice on the alternatives, whether (1) to fly from fear so as not to be infected or afflicted by that source of fear or else (2) to stay and do battle against the progenitor of that fear or else (3) to commit oneself to freedom from fear, then to live with the issue and go with the flow of that fear by reason either of apathy, of boredom, or of insufficient encouragement or else (4) actively to go on seeking, searching, and researching every last and latest source of all of one's fear and so then (5) to deal with whatever at all may be the hidden source of whatever fear (whether personally or externally induced) gothic excitement) drives one to enjoy and even indulge oneself in every least feeling of fear. [Excursus 2: Okay then, if you don't read gothic novels, watch action movies, or else spring a leak when someone unexpectedly places a cold hand on your warm shoulder, then this part of our report (although meaning everything to someone else) is *as yet* nothing to you.]

Learn to discern that, as with most feelings, there are two (and sometimes more than two) polarised extremes. [Once again, from the horse's mouth, if not the preacher's mouth, if you can't yet get your mind round more than the bipedal (dyadic) dimensions of most human thought processes whilst trying to envisage more than two polarised dimensions, then it's time to enroll in heaven's beginning course of study (Laws 585) on playing the algebra (whilst sticking to the rules) of multidimensional chess.]

Never mind? No, no, no, we don't say anything like that up here, since 'everything matters and always will matter' (on which rock, the materialists fall, but hopefully rebound). Instead, we say here always, 'Never fear!'

Now this saying is not so simple as it sounds—that is, until you can master the aforesaid legal algebra of multidimensional reasoning. In multidimensional reasoning (not unlike quantum mechanics), there are never just two polarities (or else these would, like AC/DC current) always to be switching themselves (as some folks do) always round and round. For a very rough translation of what's going on (valves are back in again), in any communication circuit (being most obviously from source translation to target translation), in terms of any (but only when fully authentic) feeling of fear, as every parent well knows of his and/or her child, for the child's own sake (in space) and in the long run (as a factor of time), little Mr Never Fear must be taught to fear (over time) by being made to fear (as made subject to the denominator of space-time). Without higher mathematics, we shall draw the curtains on this accounting process, no less than there are so many curtains still closed in quantum physics (and just as there are still so many closed books to those who have the nerve to still go on writing books).

Nevertheless (whereupon a lone hand shoots up from some preschooler's parents), whom you hasten to appease before you have 40 times 2 ... equals ... equals ... yes, that's right ... 80 hands showing (well, that took quite a bit of counting, so thank goodness these days for a calculator). The question, a fair enough question, although it does make you feel more than a little bit of a fool (although this is only preschool and not any so-called higher education) ... is this ... [Sorry, but would you mind repeating the question?] Ah yes, of course, the question is what do you do then with little Mr Always Fearful?

Yes, indeed, a very good question ... a very good question ... since asking a good question, as my old professor used to say, is worth ten times more than giving a good answer and twenty times more than giving any textbook answer. So then I dare not try to answer such a very good question (particularly when asked off the cuff and not out of the set textbook, which incidentally is not a very good textbook, except for its price, which to myself, for being its author, pays handsomely). But without giving such a very good question some time for thought and also, just as again my very, very much older professor used to say, 'without spending some considerable time' ... let's say (as he usually said) ... until next week ... for sleeping on it.

Therefore (for being itself a bright new word in the best of academic circles), although appearances both in and out of the nursery may suggest every reason for fear, little children are brought up to believe that they have no reason at all to be afraid of the dark and no reason whatsoever to be frightened of spooks, giants, and hobgoblins. And in consequence, they have no reason on earth to think that because their parents have suddenly gone out of sight, they or their parents will ever completely and utterly disappear and so cease to exist—all of which arguments (never introduce children to arguments which only produce more arguments) lead to the most fallacious conclusions by which to introduce any young child ... why, what was I going to say? What indeed was I going to say? Ah yes ... will only introduce any such young child to rationalism (instead of reasoning).

Why, instead of empowering reason, the negativity of this process at first empowers the absence of reason (as I myself well know because I've written a book about it), and so thence (a good word, *thence*, meaning 'precisely', although neither exactly nor exhaustively *towards there* and not to be confused with *hence*, which means 'from here') and so (again) entices the developing child towards and gets him or her addicted to a lifelong process of rationalisation.

To reassure and convince a child (since we are all still children) of there being no reason for his or her most primordial fears is either the most grandiose or ghoulish kind of advice. From such advice, when implanted very early on, we are thus introduced to reasoning, either from fictions or from facts, each surreptitiously laced with both values and opinions. Despite many other ways of preventing and confronting childhood fears, we are thus exposed from a very early age to some of the gravest risks of rationalism (a close relative of intellectualism) by which we put all our faith in reasoning.

This risk of inducing (more precisely, indoctrinating) rationalism is particularly the case where parents lean more than heavily towards professed facts than towards preferred fictions (fairy tales and suchlike) by way of reassuring children, which results in a discriminative process that can stifle the child's imagination. At a point which differs for each child, and particularly where the preferred facts are imposed rather than the lighthearted and fairy-tale fictions preferred, these facts (which become critically hard facts by reason of their parental imposition) begin to interfere even with the parentally preferred process of reasoning. This is because when exercised in the creative environment of every child's still developing brain, reasoning also depends on the fullest scope of childlike imagination.

Thus (in itself a paradigm for *thence* and/or *hence*, if you can pardon the multidimensional thought processes of thought-lonely professors who, when devoid of military discipline, chance to leap from form to function, from abstract to concrete, and from words to concept), since without encouraging every child to exercise such free-flowing imagination, then this parentally imposed and critically hard-fact reasoning becomes still riskier of introducing into every child's rapidly growing mind his or her complete reliance on rationalisation.

And so there we are, we have now answered your very fair and extraordinarily good question on what to do with (what was it … what was it) either the never fearful and/or the always fearful, by which we now know (having looked to the answers set out to the back of the set text-book) to be the sometimes fearful. So then Queue Ee-you Dee (as they say in Greek) or hallelujah (as they say if not again in Latin, then in Hebrew).

Believe it or not (as Ripley said), but it's far more than 'four score and seven years ago' since there was heard any Sermon on the Mount, far less any Sermon from the Mount of Transfiguration, but by now, there are hardly any folks left behind (except some oldies) who have heard of it. There's Moses and Elijah, who, as the first golden oldies, are coming again; but by now hardly any folks left behind will be able to recognise them. And there's Jesus Christ—name above all names—who likewise, at any moment, when we least expect him to fulfil his promise of coming back, will also fulfil that last promise of his coming again. So what's in a name? That's the final message of this world's most needed-seeded sermon.

But (again thanks to Ripley, who taught us to believe in the truth even when stranger than fiction) here we are, perhaps again, in Disneyland, Los Angeles. We are standing outside the pavilion (which could be for the signing of Magna Carta), but instead, we're inside the mannequin of George Washington. No, surely not George Washington or even Winston Churchill, far less Julius Caesar, but in this case, Abraham Lincoln is giving his Gettysburg Address to the American people. It's the best-known oration, sermon, or any other form of preaching/teaching in American history, which probably explains why so few Americans crowd the auditorium to hear this freedom-loving speech. Why, apart from the presence of the Lord, the auditorium is almost otherwise empty, apart from you and me, and also some Afghani refugees and Mexican overstayers, who are sprinkled like spicy rice throughout the rest of the relatively empty auditorium).

The manikin is most wonderfully but, for all that, a little ironically still speaking (with a back block's lisp) the Queen's English, for that being still Churchill's standard English, but that is hardly any longer the native tongue of anyone here. Nevertheless, the words by themselves could not be more compelling, even when heard from the mouth of such a lifelike manikin as this of Abe Lincoln (in this case, not a car but, for being too great a preacher, also a person).

When our USA finally goes down, perhaps for that (so comic) yet lovable country (of Li'l Abner et al.) being the last to fall down of this world's remaining empires, let's hope this Disney manikin survives through that last and final holocaust. 'Oh, it shall be great for our country to die,' we ourselves still sing, just as was sung back then on that gloriously pitiful battlefield of Gettysburg. It's a dirge, however—and not a psalm or a hymn—which so easily misleads military chaplains to misidentify the song for foretelling the coming of the Lord Jesus Christ to relieve the afflicted and put an end to the world's woes. And so, although they shall be forgiven and saved and gloriously resurrected, for the moment, yet another group of heartfelt preachers bites the dust.

So also, in these present times of pretended pacifism, that's probably not what you'd want to hear, namely that it's been great to die for one's country. And yet that's the case whether it means dying in Korea, in Vietnam, or in Syria. It also means much the same (since dying is dying) for anyone dying in the EU, the USA, the UK, or with the IRA.

Nevertheless, the whole concept of dying for one's country (although something we ask of a dog's life, as more than one dog tag from a deceased mate in Vietnam confirms) is far older (even ancient for being pagan) to be resurrected from the classical respect we once paid to the elderly, whether just aged or infirm and whether once old soldiers who never die or else civil servants who somehow just live on. Indeed, the same maxim 'Dulce et Decorum etc.' has been filched from the odes of the Roman poet Horace and may be discovered in such diverse places as over the rear entrance to our Arlington National Cemetery, where 'Dulce Et Decorum Est Pro Patria Mori' most prolifically flourishes in all its military grandeur, as well as more remotely on our going through the memorial entrance to Dunedin's little city cemetery (where it could hardly be said that everyone there died for their country despite the same motto of 'Dulce Et Decorum Est Pro Patria Mori' stretched out above the entrance). That's the funny thing about maxims and mottos—you can get away with the utmost stupidity when (especially in Latin) you dare to be wise (without thinking)!

But that's not what we've come to hear, not about the death and destruction, which the Gettysburg Address, still being given on the field of battle, so successfully overcame; yet it's still so sad to find in that now otherwise largely empty auditorium dedicated to Gettysburg in Los Angeles (the City of Angels), there were so very few of our own American citizens, for being neither native nor long-settled Americans but mostly recent refugees and nervous overstayers. But by now, time has moved on, so for us here, further historical reflection is prohibited for its risk of merely looking backwards.

The end times don't move slower, but like some few old but still sprightly folks, they do move faster and faster by far now than the slowing speed of light. So then there's a wall right now on the southern Mexican border of USA, along even the Rio Grande, or so they figuratively say, that somepletely (if not completely) contradicts the welcoming message of freedom given by our once so welcoming USA (but that, of course, on the Atlantic seaboard). So too, Abe Lincoln's Gettysburg Address (since the manikin is still pricking my soul with a thousand pins) is so mistaken now for being completely (and not just somepletely) out of date.

Hold on, since by now, my mobile tells me that the militzia from all nations are closing in on the same little preacher, the one from once outside McDonald's in Moscow to now being outside Abe Lincoln's in Disneyland—so he sounds like here, he's either Johnny Appleseed from amongst the Alleghenies or Li'l Abner from Dogpatch in the Deep South—to speak (on behalf of much maligned military chaplains) on the subject of the Second Advent of Jesus Christ.

Now dear old Abe Lincoln (he was seriously ill at the time) spoke only for a few minutes on Gettysburg's field of battle, but that same Abe will be remembered forever for his Gettysburg Address (just like that same first lawyer, Moses will be remembered forever for his redrafting (if not the first drafting) of the Ten Commandments). But before Abe spoke at Gettysburg, the Hon. Edward Everett spoke on the Battle of Gettysburg for over two hours, so it's not surprising that none can now remember anything Everett ever said but only remembers what poor old Abe said. So often it is, begorra, that the preachers of long sermons sideline their own message, and yet as preacher-teachers, we can't get away from the need for the longest of seed-sown sermons to fill this book.

Look over there. It's no longer the fired-up roast-chestnut vendor, but right now, it's the Johnny Appleseed preacher from the upper Alleghenies who is now rolling up his sleeves (comes from the Swedenborgian New Church of Jesus Christ, he does). So it looks like a long haul of a sermon we're in for—although he's still keeping that funny tin hat on his head by which he'll probably lift from time to time to let off steam and, in the end, send it round to make the collection.

Wait—this is unbelievable—there's a sideshow happening here by way of ... like perhaps a military diversion ... since over to the right, Li'l Abner (the prototype of the hick country prairie lawyer from Kentucky that Moses first was before his gratuitously Jewish opening of the Red Sea like he was also giving space to Abe Lincoln) is engaging the militzia (street Slavonic for lots of things) in what looks very much like a barroom brawl that wouldn't disgrace the town of Dogpatch. Looks like, after a hard night out, the Counterfeit Command's woken up again.

Wait again, come back, because you've got no calling! So then here comes Pastor Johnny, clearing his throat and spitting apple seeds right, left, and centre from one of his Rambo apples. *Shsh ... shsh ... shsh ...* Observe carefully the format and the punctuation of his presentation, unless you'd take the risk of being hit from the pulpit by a large Rambo (with that distinctive flavour and aroma) of having been the world's first-ever apple.

'The first thing we would ask of anyone and everyone', begins the peripatetic preacher-teacher (shifting his weight curiously from one foot to the other) 'is this first question ...' he asks whilst slowly looking ... all the time looking ... looking up and down and all around, then (quite explosively, for being a private question in a public setting), 'What's your name?'

You back off … you then back further off … [Does that mean me, you think, stepping backwards? No, no, no, it cannot be me … not me (as if I'd avoid an altar call). But then don't I too have a name? So then it must surely be my name too you then so casually think, since, just as the preacher first said … was … what was this first thing that he would ask … of anyone (that's me) and everyone (for still including me) was … for being still the hung-over question both exactly and precisely this: 'What's your name?']

'Ho-ho-ho!' hollers the (walkabout) peripatetic preacher-teacher, hauling off his antique tartan waistcoat. 'Some folks say it doesn't really matter!' he shouts. 'The gospel by any other name would still be the gospel. Then how about Judas? Could you call him, for instance (here he lowers his once-gruff voice to by now almost a gentle whisper) … the name above all names … Could you (he now wheedles) … call J-u-d-a-s (he slowly exudes the sound) … the Christ (his voice rising to a crashing crescendo)?'

Even folks who believe that names are arbitrary find difficulty in dismissing Judas. The name is such a woeful one. From being a proper name, Judas has become a common noun to describe a treacherous person. Its descent does not stop there. In place of animate subjects, it now denotes inanimate objects. Judas has so degenerated as to mean a small spyhole in a door. What a declension (pick the pun) for one who was once a close disciple of our Lord.

What happens (tell us again) when words lose their meaning? This is a topic we have already considered and will continue to consider for as long as we use words. That one-time lawyer James Boyd White, once wrote a whole book about it. Once words lose their meanings, it becomes impossible to write books. Words will keep their meanings for as long as writers keep writing books. James Boyd White wrote as a lawyer with a love for literature. Until a lawyer learns to love language, to delight in listening to how folks talk, to enjoy reading how folks write, and to seek the best of both the written and the spoken word, it is impossible for him to love the law. The law (particularly at the highest of universal and cosmic levels) must become a lovely word for anyone who dares to practise in the legal profession.

It is the same for those who preach and teach the gospel, which is what we are all commanded to do by the Great Commission of kingdom ministry. Imagine how it would be if such words as *faith, hope, patience,* and *love* had all lost their meaning. It is true that we could still teach by example. Indeed, it is also through the example set by our faith, hope, patience, and love that these words retain their meaning. How we ourselves give life to the good news is the larger part of the Great Commission. To practise any other way of life than the one we profess is so counterproductive as to be unthinkable. How would you like to have been once lovingly named as a child—perhaps Faith, Hope, Patience, and/or Charity—only to grow up and find out that these once lovely words had either lost or reversed their rightful meanings? To keep troth with words, that is to say, to keep fulfilling the law, is an inherent part of our Great Commission to proclaim the gospel.

Some folks still say that this sort of etymological declension of language is merely coincidental. Even the sorrowful significance we attach to the name of Judas doesn't really matter, so they say, because it is an association of ideas which comes after, not before, his betrayal of Christ. What they mean is that the significance we attach to Judas's name is ex post facto, that is to say, after the event. They forget that Christ was betrayed by humanity at large long before he died for us on Calvary Hill. His betrayal was clearly felt and foretold long before it was seen to happen as a fact of human history. [Excursus 3: A little later in this book (although you may think that we've already got there), we'll look at what it really means to foretaste the future (especially the present-future by which to make it the future-present), but until then, keep the law (which is much more than just obeying the law).]

So now, hear the prophet Zechariah [13:7], "'Awake, Oh Sword, against my Shepherd, that fellow who professes to be my associate and equal," says the Lord of Hosts. "Strike down the Shepherd and the sheep will scatter, but I will come back and comfort and care for the lambs.'" Jesus himself referred to the fulfilment of this prophecy when he told his disciples in Matthew's Gospel [26:24], 'For I must die exactly as prophesied, but woe to whomsoever I am betrayed. Far better for any such betrayer had he or she never been born.'

* * *

BOOK TWELVE

For the Sake of Looking Ahead
Mission Complete

The Tree of Life
On either side of the river, grows the tree of life,
which bears twelve kinds of fruit, the yield of which
continues throughout every month, while the leaves
of the tree serve as a healing for the nations.

The Revelation of Jesus Christ, as sent and signified
by his angel to his servant John

Intro 1—John (alias Neil): What are the twelve different fruits on the
tree of life? Twelve, for the number of months (although for a while,
time moved so slowly in earlier times that there were then thirteen
months). Twelve (both 'in words and figures', as the lawyers say)
features more significantly than most other numbers in numerology
(the study of significant numbers).

Why are there now only twelve (if not also once thirteen) so very
different disciples of our Lord Jesus Christ? Why does Roman law
have its earliest code of Twelve Tables? All these are questions of
biblical hermeneutics (or textual interpretation) which can so easily
veer off into the occult, and it is this constant temptation to veer off
from the truth (by leaning on the occult) which explains exactly why
there are both blessings and curses attached to the biblical book of
Revelation.

Whether global, international, or national, every dysfunctional
legal system demonstrates that no matter how many times we learn
and then relearn how to salute any country's either fast-changing
or half-mast flag, whatever reliance we would place on any of the
world's legal system (whether EU, UK, or USA) is no more than a
charade. We can point to Brexit, to the United States border wall, to

the yellow vest party in France, or to the civil protest in Hong Kong and to a hundred and one other acts of civil disruption, terrorist violence, totalitarian mismanagement, and international malfunction to back up what increasingly looks to be, once again, the inevitable and inexorable conclusion. So then pray for us all, won't you!

Intro 2—Kirsty (alias Emma): What will it feel like for us when we trade in the radically old for the radically new? By then, will we be so accustomed to inbuilt obsolescence that we'll think nothing of moving to a new earth in place of the present earth and no more perhaps of the new heaven than we think (now hardly at all) of the present heaven?

Despite any so-called still existing open market, none of us will be able to buy into the new heaven any more than we can buy into the present heaven! It won't even be a case of 'new lamps for old' as advertised in the tale of Aladdin (imported into the *Arabian Nights* by its French translator Antoine Galland and then later exported out to Disney. In any case, those who still have money to spend, when by the end of time, this old world gives place to the new one, might find it very hard to account for being so flush on reaching the gates of heaven.

Intro 3—Neil (alias John): There's no mission on earth that can be considered complete until the end of time. The total victory may be won, the eventual outcome made certain, but the full forcefulness of every mission towards these ends awaits its full completion until well after any humanistic debriefing (HdeB) or after-action review (AAR). Like each and every aspect of history, its most accurate and only reliable valuation (ARV) awaits the end of time (ET). For the sake of looking ahead and to always keep looking ahead, this far-sighted outlook (for developing which, there's no time like the present) must be constantly maintained.

Intro 4—Sasha (alias Kirsty): You authors still on earth have no idea of what it takes us angels to audit and edit human history before it happens. You humans unauthorisedly download our prophetic ideas and try to implement them all your own way on earth without any further recourse from heaven. Grabbing our prophetic ideas by the totalitarian fistful and rewriting them up all your own way and flat out for your own history books, whether to sell or remainder in hard copy, is not the thing to do. You lack all the finesse required for implementing heaven's prophetic foresight for the big picture (of a new heaven and a new earth as you call it) and in the long run (since eternity transcends all you can know of within all time).

This first angelic choice at the publishing level (less and less in terms of longevity in print, since time these days is more and more constrained in space) focusses more and more on the strategic ending than on the publishing means. In short (since the reader may read the book no more than once), will the book have a happy or an unhappy ending?

Intro 5—Emma: As so well known by publishers and also the best of booksellers half of the world's readers of any book (because of their need to know whether the book will (or will not) have a happy ending) decide to read their books backside foremost (i.e. from their end to the start rather than from their start to the end).

On this score, however, our sponsor of this report, the Supreme Commission, has a pre-editorial suggestion to make. It is that instead of closing off any book from possible purchasers by presale packaging, it would be more fitting for book publishers to promote and divide their books into those with happy endings (displayed, if indeed at all, then towards the back of their shops), whereas those readers who look forward to or are satisfied with unhappy endings (as more than one-half of the world is predisposed to accept or seek) can find more easily what they would seek or accept more straightforwardly from the booksellers front-of-shop displays.

Intro 6—Augustus: This may seem a most odd way of going about things, but marketing (especially book marketing) is (not unlike motorcycle maintenance) a fine art.

Intro 7—Emma (again): Every author's life and works (no matter how slight, no matter how fallible) are God-given. True, much (but not over much) of what is God-given has to be transcribed or translated into human reading, and so there's still a lot of hard work required of both humans and angels in all this enterprise (whether required by way of writing and rewriting, editing and re-editing, or marketing and remarketing). But even here, amongst all this human sweat and human tears, there's still the sense of thanksgiving required for all this hard work to bring even the most gifted of books (of which there are only a very few) to full fruition.

As already said, however, if you want to bear fruit, then you must, in turn, eat lots of fruit. So those who have the gift of writing books must also nurture that gift by also reading lots of books, no less than those who expect to write books for selling must also learn their trade by buying lots of books for the purpose of reading them in turn to nurture whatever gift they have of writing books to sell. Of course, unexpected as it may be to every author, all of which he or she writes (as if the reader has already heard the same pin drop from heaven) may very well be already in the public domain. He or she, as it then happens, is only reiterating the already iterated.

Intro 8—Augustus: Ah yes, but the other half of the world's readers, because they begin from the start of the book and so won't know whether or not the book will have a happy ending until they get to the end of the book, are amongst the world's slowest readers, because they are forever perplexed during their reading of the book as to whether they are being led (or misled) towards either a happy or an unhappy ending of the book. That is exactly why this discussion of books has been postponed until well past midway through this series of twelve books so precisely offered for the recommended (unremaindered) price of only one.

Intro 9—Neil: Welcome then to the seriousness of the book world, which is one of the many reasons why so many readers (besides taking the most serious of selfies in every situation) otherwise confine themselves solely to cartoons and comics.

* * *

For the Sake of Looking Ahead
Part I

The Paths of Righteousness
The Lord is my shepherd; I shall not want. He makes
me to lie down in green pastures: he leads me beside
still waters. He restores my soul.

The twenty-third Psalm, of all those many, many
songs composed by you, the progenitor of Christ on
earth, King David of Jerusalem

The authorial *we*, employed (not always consistently) throughout
this series of twelve books (one for each of the twelve souls saved
whilst on this present military assignment of soul-catching), is
only an angelic/human halfway house. [Exegesis 1: Chew on every
word here, just as you must learn to chew on every word of biblical
prophecy; otherwise, you'll go down (depending on how much you
consume for being left unchewed) with a severe case (most perilous
and unpleasant) of hermeneutic indigestion.]

This halfway house (neither here nor there) lies (as geographers
might not expect of it) at the geographic crossroads of prophetic
history (always green for being prophetically alive) rather than at
the historic crossroads (rather arid, windswept, and desolate) of
prophetic *geography*. [Excursus 1: Don't worry if you don't follow
this distinction, since it's only geographers and historians who are
usually troubled by such issues of priority (as between history and
geography). Nevertheless, history and geography are first cousins,
just as each couplet of psychologists and sociologists, logicians and
linguists, and lawyers and legislators are first cousins. Scholarly
boundaries are all left a bit frayed as a result of the past fad of moderns
for interdisciplinary dialectic. Nevertheless, the old boundaries still
remain closely watched to guard each couplet's own confrontational
issues of priority. And as when conflict breaks out between any such
first cousins—as it so often does between psychology and sociology

or between lawyers and legislators—then, by taking advantage of that domestic conflict, the forces of the Counterfeit Command try by their every false move to assert unauthorised priority over our by now Supreme Commission.]

As geographers (even of space-time, now increasingly contracted), you won't see this geographic (once solely historic) crossroads now, unless for reading between the historic ley lines (or geographic grid lines) by which this crossroads commands a future-present perfect stance over this possibly last epoch of world affairs. [Exegesis 2: We say 'this crossroads commands', although here, 'hovers over' (rather than 'commands') would now be the more precise expression for the way in which the fast-changing relationship between the Supreme Commission in its present policy of bringing more and more of heaven to earth and the waywardness of the Counterfeit Command in its outgoing passage from earth is likely to exacerbate the great and final conflict. And just as more and more of heaven comes to earth, so too the orcs of hell mistake themselves for taking over what they assume to be an almost totally deserted heaven.]

We know and understand how, if it is that you find earthly relations hard to follow (with every flea having yet another flea upon his back to bite him), it is bound to be so much harder to follow these highly mobile and immensely dynamic instructions, with no more than misguided self-biting to account for feeling ill at ease with heavenly relations. Nevertheless, we angels know even better that there are many spiritual statesmen (although still very much undercover amongst you humans on earth) who are already well up on the operational play, besides many others who are in process of strengthening themselves in one and the same Lord of Abraham, Isaac, and Jacob. The question of priorities (as between surgeons and doctors or between jurists and lawyers or between authors and readers) is not an ethereal abstraction (for which see the much earlier foreword on heightening levels of abstraction in this report).

This is so even although the crossroads at which the forces of heaven and hell now appear to pivot is no more than a halfway measure. More rhetorical than real, employed to make a literary pass (for communicative purposes) at the scholastic objectivity which so many 'pure' (but still so very 'speculative') scientists (and now the once 'pure' but highly 'speculative' theologians who have joined them) attach to their own but still very humanly limited pursuit of proof, the outcome (whether measured in unitarian reconciliation or outright conflict) will be permanent for all eternity and downright final.

The trouble with faith in science (whether in the science of law, language, or logic or in the science of physics or in any other science) is that such faith goes no further than faith in proof. On the other hand, faith in the substance of things unseen (which, as often as not, in science undermines the proof of things seen) hinges on truth. There are thus two sorts of belief, and it may take the experience of a lifetime to discern each from the other and to distinguish them in terms of beginnings and ends or cause and effect. The first sort of belief—however contingent, transient, and subjective—is belief in proof. The second sort of belief (on which the first sort is reliant for both form and function) is faith in truth. Without faith in truth, faith in proof cannot operate, far less be conceived of or be envisaged.

This scientific pursuit of proof (the infinitely regressive 'proof of proof', however much conjecturally based) is that which so many people in this pre-eminently scientific age will (dogmatically or even religiously) substitute for the pursuit of (what they fail to see for being) some more needfully fundamental truth. Many of our best scientists (especially in the so-called social or life sciences) will go on (most ironically) to withhold from the plain truth which they mistakenly ascribe to scientific proof all provision of any fatherly favour through the divine grace which demonstrates the metaphysical need to acknowledge (particularly by scientists) the existence of this far more fundamental and cosmic truth.

The inherently scientific 'fail factor' (applicable to the refutation by humans of some already proved conjecture) as well as the inherently scientific 'faith factor', renewed by the discovery of some new proof to replace the former proof now demolished, maintains the intellectual viability of science by its constantly human desire to keep on ascending the tree of knowledge. It fails (no less than when the objectivity of the faith factor invested in every measure of scientific proof itself is later found not to accord with the often subconsciously underlying) pursuit of this far more fundamental truth.

By way of a final résumé, let's recapitulate this argument in different terms. Every scientific proof (by reason of being proof) is therefore subject to disproof. As a matter of metaphysics, this subjectivity (not objectivity) makes every scientific truth contingent on what is already required by the scientific proof to sustain that scientific truth to rest on some as yet far more fundamental truth. So then it is to acknowledge the existence of this far more fundamental truth (together with its scientific faith factor on which every (humanly) fallible and so (humanly) most contingent of all the underlying beliefs on which every scientific proof depends, that we move this narrative from the first-person (plural) indicative of the authorial *we* into the third-person (singular) indicative as told by some other narrator). We do so to accord more direct recognition of all that is more metaphysically fundamental to the solely human (and so-called secular) preoccupation with the discovery of what is actually no more than that of humanly scientific proof. And we do so no matter how much the authorial *we* is supported by the heavenly host (against any lesser level of the humanly indicative) for purely scientific reasons.

To ensure the avoidance of every conflict of scientific interest, we accordingly now pass this concluding narrative (by way of epilogue on the subject of soul-catching) to a narrator unconnected with the practicalities of that (so-called unscientific) pursuit. In terms of this last use of the authorial *we*, we point out that all our exploration and discovery has been in pursuit of whatever fundamental truth shall conform with (as also confirm) the contingent likelihood of whatever subconscious reliance on that fundamental truth is needed to underlie all scientific proof. As in any court of law, the avoidance of any conflict of interest equates with the need (as in any research laboratory or operating theatre) for the appropriate experimental and laboratory conditions by way of scientific reasoning as well as clinically sound techniques and sterile conditions required for any scientific pursuit of proof (as close as humanly possible as that pursuit can come to the discovery and upholding of fundamental truth).

Listen then as we pass our angelic commission for soul-catching (in the field and often under heavy fire) over to that much superior angel (an archangel, if ever there was one) whose more abstract commission under our present Supreme Commission is to attend to all security measures required to maintain, to safeguard, and yet as well as to seed, sow, and disseminate the requisite heart feeling in all humans by which to enjoy what they otherwise may never see or hear for being the absolute truth. Listen then to what may be no more than the faint lyrical sound of some small pin dropping (or, who knows, what sudden symphonic avalanche of pins may more noisily rain down) from heaven.

'The sound you first hear (however lyrical) is not likely to be symphonic nor, in terms of what you may be privileged first to see, in any way more than a mere pencil outline (perhaps for you to colour in). Whatever you see or hear may either fade away or may fall to the ground (with no more intellectual aplomb) than does a withered leaf in autumn or does a dislodged downy feather waft down to earth from any passing bird. Here, think of (and then lightly re-envision) that first filmic sequence devised to open the movie made of *Forest Gump*—a spiritually superior film, as it so happens, by which to convey that same heightened theme of serendipitous action than could be managed only physically when going by the book!

'Every scientific proof (despite the divinity of truth) is always just as frail, always just as relative, always just as contingent as that wafting leaf or feather in comparison with the absolute, eternal, and cosmic measure (although heard by mankind only as a whisper) of the (only ultimate and only absolute) truth. So then take your time. Patience is a prerequisite … as well as lovingkindness … to the attainment of all the diverse and often painful exploration … sometimes needfully undertaken in pursuing one and the same (both fundamental as well as ultimate) truth.

'So then look and listen, both for the pencilled outline of your own personality and the whispered voice which holds out a palate of all the remaining colours by which your own personality awaits the divine (not secular) task of being completely coloured in. Both look and listen, since there's both a virtual (or subliminal) image already in transmission, together with an accompanying whispered but already fast-rising sound.'

'In our becoming wholly committed to one's by now Supreme Commission,' whispers an obviously guardian angel (yet in looks and attire indistinguishable from any no less authorised human being), 'we learn (which may take the whole, and more, of any human lifetime) of what is (far more than at any time before our present commission) we could have possibly imagined.'

Note that there's no counterfeit commission which is reciprocally equivalent to our own by now Supreme Commission. The Counterfeit Command may counterfeit the appearance of some commission for its own nefarious purposes, but it can never come anywhere close to expressing the mutuality of faith inherent in any commission. It relies on distance by which to exact obedience and enforce what little authority it deploys (based on fear).

Don't feel intimidated by fear of the Counterfeit Command. Your own Supreme Commission is no longer based on obedience but on such things as your own heightened faith, your own transformed mind, and your own exercise of those gifts of the spirit which demonstrate both that your own heightened faith, transformed mind, and divinely empowered spirit are every match and more for whatever arrows of outrageous fortune might be fired at you by the Counterfeit Command. In short, you are a new creation—as proved by the fact (if you have any need of proof) that you are now to all your foes a 'sitting duck' and perforce an unmistakable target. You cannot assume the exercise of any divine or demonic power without manifesting its correlative of divine or demonic vulnerability.

As between your former relationship based on obedience to the Supreme Command before gaining the closeness of your by now Supreme Commission, you will have a new touchstone of comity on which to rely rather than on the fear of being, in some way or another, disobedient. Nevertheless, still always look to the widespread future, however far ahead, as well as listen up-close (for which you must sometimes also clinch up tight with similarly transformed minds and spirits) and so learn never be limited by your own thoughts any more than by your own imagination (which may, through excesses of zeal, tempt you to exceed your calling).

'You have to learn not just how to belong to the Supreme Commission (as if you might mistake yourselves for joining no more than some social (far less swanky) country club, some all-powerful political party, or else some exclusively ordered commune) but far more how to participate wholeheartedly in an eternity of cosmic service (for which participation you may be laughed at, downgraded for work promotion, or even put in prison) which, for being heavenly from the very start, will go far beyond all humanly imaginable bounds.

'Does that make sense? Not by itself, of course, since making sense of anything relies on a mutuality and not on a singularity. By itself, we'll warn you now that neither the human imagination nor the angelic imagination is up to much, as witnessed by both the fall of angels and the fall of humans.

'The measure of both these falls, that of fallen angels as well as of fallen humans, is that of authentic creativity. Authentic creativity is the province of the truly divine. That's where all authentic creativity comes from. What is truly authentic cannot come from either the mind of angels or from the mind of man. Every counterfeit creativity (which can do no more than make a pass at divine creativity) comes from the Counterfeit Command either directly through fallen angels or else indirectly through fallen mankind.

'So then what makes for the authenticity of creative endeavour? There's only one answer, as when a pin drops from heaven, then it's hearing directly from the Lord, one's God. For reliably doing so, one needs a firmly established personal relationship with the Supreme Command. There are as many counterfeit pins as there are counterfeit messages and also as many counterfeit sounds of pins dropping as there are counterfeit creations. Get as firm a hold as possible on one's both personal and familial relationship with the Supreme.

'So then take care as humans, because your status on earth is measured by the firmness and strength of the bare footprint you leave on earth and not by the fashionable sole of your shoe or by the force administered by the toe of your boot. And yet to be subjects of heaven rather than merely citizens of earth (or of any other place) would make us be very wary of being martialled by any other's command (whether of formal church or formal state).

'No siree, but instead it's through the mutual as well as personal commitment which we angels and you steadfast believers both share together towards the Supreme Command that contribute to that greatest level of spiritual intimacy that we can each share and enjoy together on earth, which then begin to partake of our freely chosen commission of service together towards our Supreme Commission. And yes, this increased intimacy between the angelic host and human society is by now something rather new for being less scary and more familiar when demanded of our respective roles of righteous angels and righteous humans in these increasingly war-torn latter days.

'So there thus comes a time, if all goes well under your initial period of earthly command, when, because of your by then intrinsic commitment, any further need for that same sort of martial command would be rendered redundant. By then, every solid-standing believer is so well informed and so unanimously committed to the one, single endeavour in which all the remaining angelic host are conscientiously engaged that there's no need for commanders any more than for the issue of commands. Rule by command then becomes replaced by the rule of commitment. This is one of the most major of differences (as earlier explained to you) between the rule of law (by way of command) under the older testament (for example) and the rule of law (by way of commitment) under the newer testament.

'Under this new scheme of things, instead of doing things by command (on the basis of obedience), we then do them by reason of our commitment (on the basis of our shared understanding). There can still be misunderstandings and miscommunications in relation to our committed actions no less than with our obediently undertaken actions (but it is largely by our commitment and not by our obedience) that we henceforth saved from the results of our misunderstandings and miscommunications in both schemes.

'We (whether angelic or human) are thus given or granted a commission under the Supreme Command (there's no graduation ceremony, so don't mistake the saints for being any more than those who are true believers). Our only credentials are to honour our commitment to the grace and favour of what then becomes our own Supreme Commission. Just as previously, when operating under orders, our commitment to the task or endeavour would be measured by the level of our obedience to the Supreme Command. [There should be no real need for exegetical explanations by now, but both of the earlier Supreme Command and the later Supreme Commission have merged into one and the same divine entity (no less than are the older and the newer testaments now one and the same functional entity). It's just (if you can pardon the hidden ellipsis of that otherwise faulty grammatical expression) that the working relationships of both have changed.]

'From being under command to the holding of a commission is not promotion as of right, as seen by some who seek some higher status for themselves on this world's cursus honorum (or competing ladder of promotion), but rather as of accepting the greater exercise of personal responsibility (together with its correlative freedom) as of good will expressed towards the mutually shared objectives of the Supreme Commission.

'The truth (when conceived of as an absolute) is simply that as always scripturally said and proclaimed, you humans "are only a little lower than [are we] angels". Promotion, when seen on earth as of right (in climbing up the cursus honorum or ladder of promotion), invariably brings only disappointment and unhappiness and, through unawareness of its risks, often an increasing bitterness and sense of abject failure. Nevertheless, exercise of one's every righteous and therefore heavenly responsibility (to which one is internally and wholeheartedly committed) brings only joy and never ever sentient disappointment.

'However tough the task, commitment brings only joy, and even if not directly or immediately to oneself, then at least to whomsoever the task is dedicated or committed. So then from now on, in having reached our committed objective, we angels shall, before closing this report on the subject of soul-catching, henceforth refer to you as being committed to the Supreme Commission rather than to you as only obeying the Supreme Command.

'A last word of weather warning is due here, nevertheless, since once words lose their meaning and society loses its freedom, the rot doesn't stop there! Don't allow yourselves, this early on in fulfilling your Supreme Commission, to get confused by the way in which others less discerningly use and misuse words. These days, we'll find words like *command* or *commission* bandied about (as so many other words are bandied about) as if interchangeably. Under command, the responsibility for communication is unilaterally extended from whomever is authorised to give and to enforce it. Thus, in any functional democracy, there is room only for commissioned law, but not for commanded law. And to the extent that commanded law is needed, that is the measure of that so-called democracy's dysfunctionality.

'Under a commission, the responsibility for communication is derived from a mutual engagement in which both of the communicants are mutually engaged. Under command theories of law, the responsibility for communication comes from or is attributed to whoever professes, purports, or is held (sometimes against his or her will) to be top dog (although "top flea" would be the more apt expression). Thereupon, when communication breaks down, it either is or is almost always seen or held to be from the top down. Under committed theories of law (the most obvious examples of which would be as much the Periclean model for democracy as of Marxist or capitalist legal theory), the breakdown may come from either top-down or from bottom-up or from both top-down and bottom-up.

'We then find out for ourselves that our Holy Father in heaven is not one for convening over holy huddles—whether in English grammar or in plain-speaking or in any other passing fad. There's always speaking in tongues (or glossolalia) not just to fall back on but to bring to the forefront of our communicative measures.

'Father God's not just a committee man but more of a clubbable man, you understand? And by being more of a clubbable man (and so, as we might say, a team leader), he is still also very much the military man for being head of his own family and so always a dynamo for energising both heavenly games and heavenly action.

'So then, even though you and I (speaking here personally as your guardian angel) may still walk through that (vast and apparently never-ending) valley where the shadow of (utmost) death lies heavily upon our (sorely troubled) shoulders, yet neither you nor I shall fear whatever evil might be mistaken for pertaining to each of us, for we both know in our (fully opened) hearts that you, the Lord, accompany us in everything we say and in everything we do (and this even when you, Lord, tell either of us that you disagree with either him or her or me). Meanwhile, I know that you have a plan, a strongly strategic plan, for each and both of us, and this even when you seat me at the table and, however tactically, when even at the same table at which you also seat my enemies.

'We all know how changing basic relationships (whether for better or worse) impose severe stresses and strains on our previously assumed-to-be-correct means of communication (whether human or angelic). This is a worse woe for those whose lives have been unwittingly reduced to communicating in so-called basic English. Reducing language to its bare essentials is no better (and often many times worse for its results) than in reducing life also to its bare essentials. Forgive us for our grumbling, good Lord, but just why do you allow such impoverished minds to interfere with so much of the best-written scripture?

'This so-called basic English is just one further unauthorised attempt to get rid of the Authorised Version (no less than of the Anglican Book of Common Prayer), which is one good reason why Catholics stuck so long to the Vulgate and Orthodox still stick to Church Slavonic. What good can come of such linguistic reductionism coming out of basic English any more than Don Camillo could see any good coming of the Communist Manifesto? Dear Lord, this belittling of first the Queen's English and then standard English is some devious diversion from hell. And as and not just from our own (mostly human) failure to concentrate on the topic of saying farewell (more precisely, 'Fair ye well') instead of just 'See ya!'

'Basic English (together with the so-called black English) is yet another well-meaning but just as preposterous invention of one woeful Richard Ogden (given needfully here to dissociate him from another and no less woeful Richards) from their conjoint attack on the certainty and clarity of every language and, in turn, of every concept by their by now forgotten treatise on *The Meaning of Meaning*, by which, however, they did no more than confirm "the meaninglessness of meaninglessness".

'Out of such linguistic meaninglessness, mankind began to lose every sense of linguistic propriety. Very soon thereafter, every last attachment was broken to what had been once the power and forcefulness of human reasoning. Meaninglessness then acquired the force of meaningfulness, by what then became *the means* of linguistic Humpty Dumptyism. Words would (and could) be made to wander, whereby (so far away from the truth of things) wrong became right (and so right became wrong) whilst war became peace (and so peace

900

became war). Words—such as *family* and *wedding* and far more *sin* and *salvation*—were being made to slip their settled moorings, and so in turn, the once strongly settled concepts for which these words stood would lose their certitude and eventually reverse their roles (so that even heaven would stand for hell and hell for heaven).

'As earlier demonstrated to even the simplest child by the logician Lewis Carroll (by his writing of the everyday task of communication in his deeply prophetic books of *Alice in Wonderland* and *Alice through the Looking Glass*), when words would be allowed by Humpty Dumpty (before his falling off the wall) to take whatever meaning one chooses to give them to provoke (for all that man holds dear by way of culture and civilisation) the deepest of linguistic and, in turn, conceptual dilemmas. How then, first to define and then hold to one's everyday terms, if not perplexed by the utter relativity of the ensuing linguistic farce, when the legislative process (like the judicial process) becomes a constantly shifting and finally sinking sand and when the law of contracts (as of trusts) becomes a treacherous morass?

'So then you must surely excuse us now, dear Lord (unless you send a thunderbolt to burn up all such devious and demonic ways of undermining human thought), and so thus relieve us from having been so misled as to believe that sin is no more sin (but instead just a social or cultural lapse), that salvation is not salvation (since, without any concept of sin, we humans have no need of salvation), that mere promises, vows, and even oaths made in your name (whether by way of marital covenant, business contract, or deed of trust or to enter a profession) were never really meant to be kept. And that anyone dumb enough to believe in and trust his neighbour (and most particularly for anyone putting any trust in you, dear Lord) has only himself or herself to blame for everything going wrong! And so then it's best for everyone else (including you, dear Lord) to have nothing to do with such a clown or with any such family of clowns!

'Why, it's the same linguistic woe by which both linguistic and conceptual meaning in the course of any communication (and so in turn of holy communion)—including that of the Vulgate Version, no less of the Authorised Version than of today's Good News Version— have been reduced to barren meaninglessness! Why, even all our dictionaries too have lost their once essentially prescriptive and yet deepest of revelatory functions. Instead, they are expected to be sped-read or skim-read (including all their words in brackets, including this one). Why, even any more fully Amplified Version is, whether at one's own choice, rightfully or falsely freed entirely to suit oneself. The fact is (for being itself a fiction) that there are no real words any more—only usages (the most of which are misusages).'

Yet even in the most provocative presence of my enemies, you choose to anoint my head with oil, and though it offends them sorely, they cannot help seeing that for your sake alone, you replenish my cup (so close to that of suffering) so that it overflows towards each of them in ways which they cannot ignore. You and only you, Lord, are the staff on which I lean, whilst you and only you, Lord, provide the rod upon my wayward back—that rod alone whose fervent touch keeps me on the tight-run path of righteousness, even whenever otherwise I would surely falter or fall off. On your account alone, goodness and mercy frequent my every which way, so that for a certainty, I will live forevermore in your heavenly household and even there forever live always as a member of your chosen family.

* * *

For the Sake of Looking Ahead
Part II

The Last-But-One Request
'Prisoner, in this solemn hour, when all eyes are upon thee, and thy judges are jubilant, and thou art preparing for those involuntary bodily movements that directly follow severance of the head, I address to thee a parting word …'

Vladimir Nabokov, *Invitation to a Beheading*

Bear in mind that sensory perception (as not even every artist knows) is a spiritual gift. It follows that not everybody sees the same thing the same way when they watch an execution. For example (and by way of the paradigm for all such cases), not everybody sees the crucifixion of Jesus Christ as being one and the same event, far less one and the same crucifixion, and still even far less for seeing the same figure of Jesus Christ on the cross for being one and the same person. Do you really think that Father God is so much of a religious formalist and fanatic that he would want to have even all his precious people seeing everything exactly the same way?

Why, for centuries, even Christian theologians fiercely disputed the meaning of Christ's crucifixion, and most of them weren't even eye witnesses to the event. But yet even if they had been (and had not been tempted to stay away as did most of the disciples), the evidence of those who personally witnessed the event is markedly different. And that's exactly why, to denote the different views of Christ's crucifixion on the traditional Russian Orthodox cross, the lowest crossbar symbolising nothing like the same event for those two criminals who were crucified with Jesus Christ is tilted one way up and the other way down.

Today (as on any other day), we are writing (from ourselves in the first person to you in the second person) as if no differently than from some other person (whether angel or human) might text, telephone, or write to you personally on earth about your already appointed mission from the Supreme Commission (formerly the Supreme Command) for the purpose of your learning more about soul-catching. We do so person to person, so as to maintain strict operational security lest the Counterfeit Command make more than permitted of what they eavesdrop from third-party conversations. Let it be known, therefore, that today's the day to commit your heartfelt personal mission to full commission as a soul-catcher.

But as for this speaking order of these persons (first, second, and third), that's only as such parties more usually appear to be on earth. So then don't doubt the genuineness and sincerity of this heavenly invitation (which might well appear from here on earth and most certainly would in hell be seen to relate to your own beheading). So then when you front up at the chosen venue for the beheading, remember that the order of personal precedence (first, second, and third persons—in both singular and plural) is always reversed from that on earth (partly to allow for the requisite human faith factor and otherwise to maintain security) and so is very different from the more prophetic order of things, which, when cleared of earthly undercover, would shine clearer with a completely different reality when seen and heard more directly from heaven. By reason of its nature (where heads do roll), soul-catching relies on maintaining the highest level of security.

Of course, this is where we angels come in, as if you could risk not hearing (even just second-hand) of your already appointed commission. It is this commission of yours which is to assist me in laying a last-minute safety net to save those souls who are otherwise in process of being consigned to the bodily trauma of beheadings, hangings, and other pagan protocols of the Counterfeit Command. Keep in mind always that the code name for this military operation (as known only to us field agents) will be every *Soul-Catcher's Chief Delight*. And of course, as you would expect, passwords change in keeping with the apocalyptic countdown.

So then see here and listen well, since it is the heavenly text affording this heartfelt delight, however much presented in the horrific context of whatever pagan and other barbarities we are called upon to witness, that counts for everything and not at all the barbarities, so don't be diverted (either in mind or heart) from the text of the heavenly commission we are called to fulfil by the barbaric context in which that soul-saving text is presented. Nevertheless, it is this earthly (and so often worldly) context that evokes the need for heavenly text and not, as so often mistaken for being the other way around, by those who shut their eyes to the frightful context that evokes the heavenly text.

Faith is worthless until put to the test (as every true believer from his own spiritual experience well knows). So then, take extreme care, now before we hit the road to Damascus since (even if only figuratively speaking) your now delegated gift of ubiquity—of going from place to place at will to different venues of beheading as if on some magic carpet—shall expose your soul to see things there across the whole wide world which will pierce your heart, shrivel your mind, and depress your spirit).

Be prepared always for both the expected and the unexpected. The Counterfeit Command plays unexpected tricks with both the expected and the unexpected. Take neither for granted. Nothing at all is what it seems. Envision what professes to be a wide, green, and level playing field. No, no, don't relax. This is a training exercise. For the moment, for the moment, don't try to see it level, or else you'll ignore the tilt you've given to your head to facilitate the scimitar or axe. Okay, got it!

So then you've tilted your head to see the world for being flat and so to make the field of operations level, but now put your right leg back on the ground and slowly straighten up to the right ... that's right ... until you yourself are upright, completely straight, and vertical ... so then now in line with the heavens ... to the heavens and not from the already shaking ground as if that were your sole and constant measure. It's never from the rolling earth (as tainted through and through by the blood of Cain) or by the remarkably tilted and constantly circling world on whose earth it is by now almost impossible to keep your stance, without knowing what it feels like to have been washed clean of sin by the blood of Jesus Christ. That's right ... that's right ... by the blood alone of Jesus Christ ...

Now then, focus on what seems to be the centre of your field of vision! No, it's not a skull ... it's not a severed head ... but what's really there ... however counterfeit ...

Take your time ... take your time ... take your time ... That's right ... in the midst of the apparently wide, open, and green-grassed playing field ... is what ... is what ... is what ...

For the moment, never mind the why ... never mind the wherefore ... Just tell me what it is you see there ... says the Lord ... what you see with your inner eye ... your inner eye ... That's right ... exactly right ... There's a white-enamelled pail or bucket ... You do see it, don't you? You do see it. Now that you do see it ... the bucket ... then let me tell you more about it ...

That small bucket contains this world's greatest sea—a sea now of ice flows, icebergs, and melting ice ... a sea of rising tide levels ... a sea of fearful storms ... and of terrifying tsunami ... but, above all else, a sea of faithless faith ... a sea of faithless faith ... a sea of faithless faith ... when faith is all at sea ...

Yes, I know, you'd rather not see it ... But all the same ... there it is ... There's the white-enamelled bucket (no, I'm neither mesmerising nor programming you, you know, with what inner eye you see) ... So then you tell me what you see ... what you see ... just what you see ... But before we go any further ... be pleased to put ... now your left leg back on the ground ... even although in doing so, the previously flat and level ground now tilts ... and the buck ... and the bucket ... yes, the once distant bucket's coming closer ... coming closer ...

Well now, the pristine white bucket seems to be shimmering ... shimmering in the sun ... slightly ... ever so slightly ... pulsing (as with a spiritual heartbeat) perhaps ... probably by witchcraft ... or not, although there's witchcraft around ... And the white-enamelled bucket ... as if being commanded by some sorcerer's apprentice ... is coming closer ... ever closer ... as if it is minded to show you its contents ... probably rubbish or refuse ... but no ... no ... no ...

The white-enamelled, red-handled bucket is filled with severed hands ... no ... no ... There's a severed, still twitching, yet quite independent thumb ... and yet another twitching thumb ... and some big and still pulsing big toes ... all still sort of hopping, wriggling ... and a whole severed foot ... And they're all still twitching ... as if not quite dead ... and in response to your looking, jumping up ... on top of each other ... like crabs or crustaceans trying to escape ... by climbing on top of each other ... up the side of a container ... and then falling back ... And during all this time ... the fingers and toes ... being lighter ... seem to be doing so much better than the far heavier hands and feet ... I don't want to watch any more ...

I've got both feet back together again on the ground now ... and I'm slowly backing off ... and preparing to run ... But all of a sudden ... a severed hand has jumped up (no, not jumped, but kicked upwards helpfully by a severed foot) to hold on to the bloodstained handle of the by now bloodstained enamelled no-longer-pristine-white bucket ... which is being carried towards me ... presumably by the severed hand ... having latched itself on to the bloodstained red handle ...

But look now ... that's not all ... all around this open field are white-enamelled buckets ... some holding hands ... some holding legs ... some holding thighs ... some holding feet ... And yet quite suddenly ... as if out of the blue yonder ... from far beyond this verdant green field ... come groundsmen ... turbaned groundsmen ... to collect all the buckets ... and in place of these buckets ... to set up pavilions ... for the following session of whatever show is next to start ...

These broken and dismembered limbs, together with severed heads, gouged-out eyes, sliced-off noses, and cut-off ears, are the residue of punishments for penal offences (so-called for whatever reason or lack of reason) throughout the largely pagan but by no means exclusively pagan world. We are not called to resuscitate the broken bodies from which these poor portions have been violently violated, but we are called here to gather up and solace estranged souls, no less than at any moment of bodily dispatch, we are asked to catch and succour the last moment of all and even also wayward souls.

In the black-humoured opinion of the Counterfeit Command, we are called soul-scavengers, which is their name for soul-catchers. In the opinion of the Counterfeit Command, you must understand, we are the lowest of the low. On the face of it, like the level playing field they talk about, is something ... anything ... or nothing ... for being never really there. Don't worry, these ghouls never challenge us for souls (of which they maintain, there's no such thing). Well, it's that kind of nihilism which, in any military operation, gives the Supreme Commission the upper hand.

We angels don't propose to share our soul-catching techniques (not even with heartfelt believers) at any solely human level. The fine arts (as of soul-catching) are so often debilitated by focussing on the mastery of techniques (both angelic and human) that their essentially therapeutic purposes soon fall to earth and cease to function. We will say this, however, that to read the soul of anyone, the eyes have it, which is one reason why so often, no less than for any Samson in scripture, eyes are gouged out by their spiritual opponents rather than let the guilty read of their own guilt as reflected back from those eyes whose innocence reflects back the other's guilt.

So then the eyes have it, no matter of whatever shape and of whatever colour, in determining the nature of the human soul by which some persons (whether knowing of their search or not) often most passionately seek salvation, and yet others, although passionate enough in both bodily and worldly ways, evince not the slightest interest in eternal salvation. Yes, even the outer eyes (however narrowed, blinkered, or closed) will disclose most of what their person prefers or presumes to keep private.

As passionate believers, you will know that we attach far less importance to work profiles than we do to faith profiles, and with some people, we attach more importance to aural profiles (what they hear) than to visual profiles (by what they see). Whilst with yet other persons, we pay more attention to their seeing (or visual) profiles than to their aural (or hearing) profiles, but by and large, it is the depth and width of whatever (sensitivity of) vision (whether physical or spiritual or intellectual or emotional) they have (developed) by which we assess the readiness and maturity of the human soul. As said before, however, nothing in any of these books is withheld from those who may have less than 20/20 vision. In many cases, it is the lack of physical vision or the lack of physical hearing which enables a person more sensitively to hear with the inner ear and to see with the inner eye.

So then that's as far as we'll go to tell you humans here about the harvesting of souls! The eyes have it, of course, and if there's anywhere at all in which a yearning for immortality (and all the reciprocal responsibility encountered in this world which that yearning entails) then this dynamic and ongoing yearning (as well as the sense of concurrent responsibility which gives stability to this yearning) can be decoded and deciphered by any serious reader of signs when imbued with the Holy Spirit to do so in any place on earth.

Here are some clues: every historic marketplace is at a crossroads, at which you may still see the cross to mark the place at which the gospel of Jesus Christ was first preached. Look for it no matter how worn, how tawdry, how dismantled, or how long ago pulled to the ground or however much built over that historic birthplace may be!

The first confrontation between past and present, present and future, took place not just for that locality but for also every subsequent shift in space and time. It's all eternity. That's the issue here, not just human geography or human history. You'll find examples here, there, and everywhere, all the length and breadth of the British Isles—if only you know where to look for them! They're all at places of open conflict, of extreme confrontation, and of extreme provocation. Are you up with the play, or are you no longer alive in your soul this very day to try your spatial-temporal hand at soul-catching?

This soul-catching (see it as a form of spiritual dowsing, if you will) is not superstition any more than Euclidean geometry or Newtonian physics is superstition! Here in soul-catching (although for being intuitively heuristic, and so less clearly capable of being communicated and explained than are physics or geometry (for these being eminently practical in their proving as well as theoretical in their discipline) is offered that final last soul-moment on earth (through redemption in Christ Jesus) for the soul's eternal resurrection. What are we to say more of soul-catching (although possessing its own still hidden physics (or rather metaphysics), its still hidden chemistry (or rather biochemistry), and still hidden geometry (more multi-dimensional than could just be either plane or plain) when saying more would obviously risk subtracting from rather than adding to the credibility of soul-catching. What more said might input into any victim of this world's injustice (no less than detract from its outcome by way of heavenly justice) may be decided by many, extremely intricate and as often deeply confusing, for these also being conflicting variables.

Look first at dowsing (although never in the occult) if necessary to redeem whatever lost faith you may now have in soul-catching. Otherwise, take in faith every possible variation (including vagaries of space, place, and time) to which any victim (besides always checking your own spiritual status) may have been exposed. Feel for the tactical catching first before feeling for the strategic soul (since so often words and so often thoughts get in the spiritual way). Don't ever strive in the spirit, whether to do, tell, or achieve, convince, or communicate. Instead, look towards whatever may have been that very first place (whether in bringing to the victim the gospel of good news in Jesus Christ by which the root, branch, or twig of eternal life may have been wittingly or unwittingly lengthened or shortened. Lightly consider in consequence, how the victim's life, even although still surviving his or her equivocal experience, may have been either demonically lengthened or demonically shortened because of it. And don't overlook by virtue (or by vice) of what miraculous happening (whether truly valid or falsely invalid) may have taken place there (even before any cross intended to mark that hallowed place and space had been before erected or later demolished).

You may be arrested (in more than one way) for all your apostolic endeavours. You may be seen to be completely alien to where you are whenever and wherever you are—and that whether here, there, or wherever else you might be. That (including being overlooked or ignored) goes with the gift of ubiquity. All the same, when you are where you're meant to be, you'll always know you're really meant to be there—which is the correlative advantage in your having the gift of ubiquity. So then, don't bother about being so much misunderstood, ignored, overlooked, or causing dissension for being where you're meant to be. Don't take offence for being asked what you're doing whilst here! Don't you understand that for being seen to be an alien in so many of these here parts, you're not wanted here?

It doesn't matter whether this is a church of sorts, a synagogue of sorts, a college of sorts, a school of sorts, a village of sorts, a town of sorts, a city of sorts, a country of sorts, or just a little marketplace of sorts; but you're simply not wanted here. You might be a street preacher or a street teacher or a street beggar, for all we know, or a snake oil seller or a pickpocket or a horse thief, for all we know or care (and with a name like Mungo or Columba, why *should* we care?); but we've *horse-whipped, tar-an'-feethered, and chased monie an unwanted alien oot o' toun, and faur-across the countrie-side fur faur less than a'thaat—so pull-i'yer-hoarns fur thinkin' yi' hae oniethink still tae say*!

Whether the person's eyes be blinded *fur nae seein' yi'* or whose ears be deafened *for nae hearin' yi'* or whose mind be *claused richt-a'-the-way doon, faur nae un'erstan'in' yi', or whose hairt may be claus'd for being sae affronted by how deef'rant yi' haipen tae bee tae heem*—ought not to get in your way. It shall not be the blind who lead the blind to heaven. It takes eyes which have been opened to hell (besides being opened to heaven) to lead others who are blind to the way, to the truth, and to the light of life by which alone one reaches heaven.

First comes soul-searching, then comes soul-saving, and only last of all (no matter how often you've seen any other apostle, angel, or anyone else do it) comes soul-catching. For this last effort in the face of the Counterfeit Command who would if it could, in the last moment of anyone's life, filch from the Supreme Command the absolutely unique profile of a soul (however much case-hardened) to the agony of unremitted hell requires an effort of seriously spiritual surgery that takes one right up to the gates of hell.

Look to the outer eyes, and you will see the inner eyes. There, in the depth and width of the outer eyes, you shall see the inner eyes reflected through the outer eyes. Sometimes, the inner eyes will be reflected with joy, and at other times with sorrow, yet you shall see enough not only to settle the soul within but also to look out and so project the state of the innermost soul out of your own soul and into every other willing person's eyes. You jump back as if all this talk were of the occult, but it is no more of the occult than is Aristotelian logic, Newtonian physics, or even the Ten Commandments.

It's a gruesome form of savage entertainment to many when thus described of any such commitment to soul-saving. Yet indeed, this commitment to others is no more gruesome than searching your own soul can be gruesome to you. Nevertheless, the need for all this soul-saving mission—whether as for now no more than reflected through television, as in action films or in street muggings or in family feuds or in terrorist threats, as well as in school shootings and restaurant explosions—is just a warm-up for the up-and-coming main event. Do no more than just watch this space, and not only time will tell (for which alone you may be happy to sit back just to watch this space) but also time will tell against you, until you find that this space is no longer your own space. So then be warned!

* * *

For the Sake of Looking Ahead
Part III

Aspirations and Counteraspirations
It follows from the very character of a countermovement
that it is far easier for it to define what it is opposing
than what it is aiming at.
Oswald Spengler, *The Decline of the West*

What is the key by which to unlock and explain *The Decline of the West*? Almost every alternatively conceived religious movement since the advent of Jesus Christ (from subsequent Muslim to theosophist through Christian Scientist to modernism) has been a countermovement. For being long prophesied (even to ancient Buddhists as well as to ancient Israelites), the advent of Jesus Christ was no countermovement. In terms of authentic origins (as well as those strategic objectives employed to secure the intended outcome of those origins), there's a great deal of difference between true creativity and that counterfeited creativity made to pass for the true creativity it purports to copy.

It is far easier for the character of the Antichrist to define what is being opposed than what the Antichrist is actually aiming at. This subtle tactic facilitates the characteristically huge following of the Antichrist to latch on to the counterfeit action (by way of counteraction) instead of joining in the real action to which the Antichrist is opposed. And as to exactly why the Antichrist is opposed to Christ is never forthrightly told by the Antichrist but instead remains part of the Antichrist's entirely hidden agenda. Indeed, like most self-deceived individuals, the Antichrist himself has not the slightest understanding of his own motivation.

Apart from scoffing at Christ and his disciples, the Antichrist makes no purposive attempt at all to define what his countermovement is aiming at, except to threaten and to undermine the opposing will of Christ. There's a lesson here, for those who would think to revolt (far less than to revolt against revolt) as each such successive put-down is persuasively proposed and deceptively encouraged by the ongoing countermovement of the Antichrist.

In terms of both strategy and tactics, this lesson requires a thorough understanding of every military operation. Whether on earth, as when the West crusaded against the East or when Britain choose to repress rather than to assuage the revolt of its own American Colonies, the outcome is as terminal as would be the same were heaven to be so unwise as to undermine her own authority. Repressing any revolt is not only purposeless but infinitely regressive. To spend witless energy in fighting any countermovement, instead of concerning oneself with whatever may be the causes giving rise to that rebellious countermovement, is to be diverted away from the movement which the countermovement is not only counterfeiting but also attempting to overcome.

Why do you think it so that even the most gentle of souls either, for the sake of keeping the peace, will go to war or, for the sake of confirming their own authority, will undermine that authority or, in the name of either Allah, Muhammed, or Jesus Christ, will raise up a lynch mob, pass a death sentence, or organise and carry out a bloodletting? In writing of *The Patched-Up Tailor* (better known in Latin as *Sartor Resartus*), Thomas Carlyle for a while managed to convince all but the least open-minded of his readers that every human is at risk of contradicting their own profession of faith on account of the status they hold whether to preach, teach, or prophesy, or whether to legislate, judge or execute when hidden from the reality of their own lives by no more than the clothes they wear.

We are on our way now to the football stadium in Kabul. The arena of (mostly blasé) onlookers all around the field (with now tiered seating like any stadium) is now full to overflowing. There are men, women, children, and even tiny infants here. There's a warm-up game of football being played on centre field now, several games in fact, but with all the balls having substituted for them neatly severed human heads. Most of the games, as of soccer, are being played with widely open-eyed rounded heads. But for other games as of rugby football, these are being played with all-eyes-closed oval heads. Nobody, not even the players or even the referees, seems to notice. Don't worry, maybe what we witness here is no more than the substance of things as yet unseen.

As with the Sadducees (playing here against the Pharisees), the whole objective (however impossible for a game being no longer a game) is to stick by the rules. Nevertheless, marked by some curious synchronicity, whenever a penalty is awarded in one field (whether in soccer or in rugby), the penalty kick is awarded in all other fields, which, on being taken, is serendipitously succeeded by some sort of free for all, fought over the rules, in every field. [Feint 1: War games are no different, whether played as the Great Game on the North-West Frontier, in the Opium Wars waged by the British against the Chinese, in the Boer War waged by the British against the Dutch in Africa, by German imperialism under Kaiser Bill against British imperialism in the trenches of the First World War, by the Nazi war effort to establish the Third Reich in the Second World War. The bodily brutality of each war is full in your face irrespective of the rules of war, which are (as often as not) used to justify and implement the academically credible appearance of holding to absolutely inevitable and completely abstract outcomes.]

Likewise, every time a goal is scored (as with the Bolsheviks playing here against the Mensheviks), then the offending goalie (if not subsequently also the referee) is made by some inexplicable process to lose his head. And every time a try is scored (here, the Marxists against the Leninists), then the captain of the defaulting team (likewise by some inexplicable process) is made to lose his head. There is really no rhyme or reason to this grotesquely religious warm-up session (except to stimulate the gathered onlookers—pardon the pun—to look ahead), until at half-time, instead of the usual hot dog, ice cream, and peanut vendors, a band of roughnecks armed with Avtomat Kalashnikovs appear.

That's when the bullets start to fly—whether synchronously or serendipitously in Kabul or in Baghdad or in Tehran or else back here (although hardly then called home) in Damascus. (Wars are always waged subject to remarkably mobile centre points, and whatever rules there may be—whether national, international, or transnational—they are always not just subject to change but by now in the course of continuous change). Whoever still survives here (without even trying to pick foe from friend) has learnt to keep his, her, or all their heads down; but once again, as in Kabul or Tehran, there's no rhyme or reason to wherever rocket launchers strike or to whoever fires them. And you're just as likely to get keeled over whilst keeping well inside your house as out of it.

There is no point to describing the resulting carnage. News reporting is as often counterproductive to resolving whatever behind-the-scenes issues give rise to such openly escalating and eventually total warfare, just as crime reporting can lose all hope of operating to prevent crime. As the conflagration grows, the warring issues rapidly distance themselves from the causative agents giving rise to crime and war. The economics devoted to maintaining the peace (in the face of open warfare or of civil unrest or of criminal behaviour) peak at the point of no return where all resources (as of controlling any disease or bodily affliction) are no more than to focus on brute survival (irrespective of cause and effect or of right and wrong) and so are devoted to treating only the warring symptoms without any remaining hope of dealing with the inflictive cause.

Human conflict is no more than the symptom of some inflictive cause. Instead of treating the inflictive cause, however, the symptomatic conflict is either suppressed (as by enforcing law and order) or actually engaged in (as by waging war). The symptomatic conflict is thus mistaken for the inflictive cause, and the more so that this mistake is made and acted on, the more so that the conflict grows.

How then to save the soul—the all so vulnerable human soul? Soul-catching (for daring to deal with inflictive causes and so disturbing what little peace prevails) is as much maligned as it is the case that almost every form of soul-catching (both human and angelic) is grossly misunderstood. The soul is spiritual, not physical, and yet so many human soul-catchers—whether Taoist, Buddhist, Zen, Muslim, or Christian—spend so much of their devotional time (whether in church or temple or out of church or temple) only in harassing to death the human body (paradoxically, for that being the more authentic temple of the soul).

Of course, just as for Christians the corporate body of the church is the body of Christ, so also the individual body of every believer becomes also the temple of the Holy Spirit. Thus, the body of clay (as for each individual) no less than the institutional body of the church universal (as for the body of Christ) is of considerable importance for being the vessel of the Holy Spirit, but the significance of both these bodies (whether clay or collective) is secondary to the soul (in the case of the individual) and to the headship of Christ (in the case of the inspirited church universal).

For every inflictive cause of human conflict, look to the human soul or spirit and not to the consequential warring arena of human behaviour, in which the physical body is professedly paramount yet increasingly is taken captive and sacrificed to the so-called defensive armament or military *thing*. Put mankind into any institutional uniform—whether school uniform, church uniform, judicial uniform, military uniform, or any other form of freaky fashion—and immediately you have a *thing*.

For the fine art of soul-catching—whether in the White House of Washington or behind the red walls of the Kremlin—then get this straight: the body is but the vessel and the vehicle of the spirit or soul, but without that soul or spirit, the body (whether of church or state) is snuffed out of life. Then for every inflictive cause of human conflict—whether personally in the mind or heart of any president or monarch or of any presidential advisor, senate, or parliament—always look first to the soul of that person or to the spirit of that institution before taking issue with the merely consequential behaviour.

There's a logic to soul-catching. Speaking to logicians here—to logicians no less like Bertrand Russell or Augustus De Morgan—it's a deontic logic of rights as well as being a descriptive logic of practices. It is formal for its ability (known well by Russell) to define, follow, and apply equations relating to every instance of cause and effect. For being multifactorial (far more than either of these logicians could possibly imagine), it is also contingent on things both surprisingly unexpected as well as on the preferably expected.

By being experiential, it entails searching and researching, exploring and discovering, so it is open-ended and not mechanically or tautologically closed. It is a touchstone for the soul as well as being a measure for assessment and self-assessment. It provides not only a measure of mutuality for diplomacy but also a measure of democracy for good government. And as a measure of its truth, it operates as viably in times of crisis as during seasons of stability.

Just what is this method by which to measure and, where possible, to curtail this world's madness? Throughout this quiet discussion and at the closest of quarters, the Avtomat Kalashnikovs have not once ceased firing. From as far afield as in Kabul and Tehran, no less than periodically in Damascus, the rocket launchers have been also firing. The once tilted and unequal playing field of warfare (never fair) has now been (unfairly) levelled. On what was once the upper height of this now levelled playing field, there weighs down a heap of bodies.

Yet all this time (which like the law is loosely and not always tightly compacted), we angels (with the much-needed help of humans) have been multitasking our ministry of soul-collecting. Like the many-holed safety net of the law, we angels cannot always reap the fullest heavenly harvest. Around the outskirts of the harvest field, we leave you humans to glean those remaining souls which, to live another day, have survived the fray. Learn to minister first to souls, then to bodies—it is faith in the end which outlasts even the fatal bodily destruction of this earth's final day.

Don't capitulate. Your own soul will survive your sadly broken body, but your sadly broken body will not survive your sadly broken soul. But as always, you humans (committed to the cult of constant human progress) want to know how—want to know how! How things are done is far less significant than doing things as they ought to be done, just as the how by which things are left undone so often holds up and gets in the way of the means by which their having been done would have enabled other things to be done but now may be forever left undone.

So then if we angels tell you humans how we angels catch up those souls out of darkness, we do so most often as their incumbent bodies sleep. Of course, it is when their bodies sleep that human souls are most awake, which is why we angels, through night visions and intergalactic chatter, then discourse most deeply with you still sleeping humans on the realities of life. In most cases, there's no need for you humans to remember; in other cases, you are made to forget; and yet in other cases, you are purposely wakened in order to reflect on what we have shown and on what we have said. In any case, you know all this and so testify to this means of discourse whenever you decide for yourselves on any issue to *sleep on it.*

We angels can always come to human souls when their incumbent bodies are fast asleep, which is not something which you humans can always do; otherwise, you might be taking perhaps extreme risks with another's soul. Because you humans are only a little lower in the heavenly scheme of things from us angels, you might feel this withheld ability from yourselves to be unfair. Nevertheless, we could not tell you how to do something so important as to communicate with another person's soul when that person is fast asleep before you are altogether ready to do so by knowing the risks of so doing. In any case, these risks you yourself are already exposed to, unless you learn to discern between authentic and counterfeit night visions and messages. On this score, reread the far earlier checklists of credentials for soul-catching.

You see, humans (by reason of their excessive rationality) always have their own way of seeing means and methods very differently from the way that those same means to achieving anything and the methods by which these means are employed are so rarely even regarded by us angels. So too, that fundamental difference has been exacerbated by the mechanistic (and as often manipulative) outlook introduced into human thinking by the devotion they give to their own rapidly advancing technology.

That's all been the case ever since the engineering philosopher Descartes substituted doubt for faith in his so-called *Discourse on Method* (which the church of that time put on its list of prohibited books). Doubt has a part, relatively a very small part, in every system of method, but Descartes (just as any engineer or architect would do) exaggerated and elevated his system of doubt to the height of human endeavour. In the very short time, which it takes for such institutional prohibitions to become counterproductive, however, Descartes's own personal doubt (mistaken by him for knowing) became first systematic Cartesian doubt, and before much longer, both took over Western thought and began to spread over the entire globe so as to become what we all try to avoid by way of being systemic human doubt. By his maxim 'Cogito ergo sum', to mean 'I think, therefore

I am', Descartes substituted doubting for knowing throughout the Western world and so brought heavenly faith to lower ground level.

In other words, Descartes built his own tall tower of doubt on his own crumbling foundation of faith and so substituted a new fashion of architecture and systemic engineering thereafter to maintain the building of these very doubtful towers of faith (buttressed together as often by conjectural science), yet each of which, when put to the test (even of scientific proof) sooner or later is bound to fail. Doubts not only promote more doubt but an extravagant intellectuality.

So then why should any angel risk your faithful soul by thinking to extend Enid Blyton's *Famous Five* when tempted to become some far more intriguingly *Secret Seven*? Have you never heard of that not-so-wise old owl who asked (perhaps flatteringly) of the hundred-legged centipede to explain however it was that with all these legs to coordinate, he had ever managed to learn to walk? Well, the centipede thought and thought and thought until his mind went into a tailspin over finding any answer to this question so that when he finally woke up to reality, it was to find that he couldn't any longer walk! Don't forget. Curiosity (probably highly intellectual, as for any academic) also killed the cat.

You know the risks then, but as not only a true believer but also a long-committed disciple of the Lord, you claim to be able to cope with the angelic know-how by which to graduate as a soul-catcher. But it's not just a postgraduate diploma but a postdoctoral experience in the field that's required for soul-catching, you know; otherwise, you're liable to belittle a fine spiritual art to the pop psychology of stage mesmerism or to the pop theology of spiritual indoctrination by programming. Both these forms of mind changing are occult, you know!

So then do you think that when any angel looks into your eyes, he or she can read your soul? Lawyers and judges do that (whether rightly or wrongly) every day, you know. Why, even the history of ocular privacy, by which spectacles were invented by the Chinese college of Pinyin (or Mandarin) scholars so that none but upper-level bureaucrats could read what ought to be any judge's inscrutable eyes, has extended that inscrutability throughout governmental administration to the point that no one can look another person in the eye—no, not even to see eye to eye! So then are you yourself up to the level of coping with whether your eyes are open to angelic examination (at the postdoctoral level) for the purposes of determining whether you are as yet qualified to engage in the catching (not collection, mind you) of souls?

Let me remind you, before you answer, that whatever you say will be recorded and used as either evidence for or against your proposal. Let me also remind you that the collection of souls (as so often undertaken in a secular, if not also occult, fashion by historic figures like Kaiser Bill, Karl Marx, Comrade Lenin, and Adolf Hitler) is outlawed and verboten. Let me remind you too that your ministry is not (as if like intellectual property) your own property. It is subject to constant daily check by whomsoever (sometimes your own worst enemy) is appointed to do so by the Supreme Command. Nevertheless, you who are pinyin bureaucrats can postpone this present ocular examination to any time from now that you so decide. Otherwise (ambiguously said), we'll just go ahead!

Even still today, in these end times, it can still seem a long, long, way along the road from Jerusalem in Israel to Damascus in Syria and thence back home over the mountains to Tipperary in auld Ireland, but the whole wide world has shrunk into an already burgeoning cosmos whereby even to get back home by the once long way round to Tipperary (whether in a coffin or on your feet) is now (in both instances, with coffins on call) just round every Londoner's 'jolly horner'.

Yet now, before the clout obviously, is the time (if not already long past as before) to don our spiritual armour. In this sort of blasé crowd, you literally won't be seen for wearing your slippers of peace, your belt of truth, your shield of faith, your twin-edged sword of the spirit, your breastplate of righteousness, and your helmet of hope (and promise of eternal salvation). Most carefully count out these articles of apparel (before you don your battledress and sign for each strategic purpose of its military use) since you'll have to account for each of these *Secret Seven* (and not just to Enid Blyton) whenever you should ever attempt to let the side down by returning your spiritual armour (both slippers, please) or battledress on demob from just some little skirmish as this.

So then don't baulk at such atrocities or bury your head deeper under the blankets (or into the sand), for although your failure to accompany me shall be forgiven (since, after all, this is but a civil invitation and not yet another misguided military invasion), it seems as if once again on the road to Damascus that we're back again in Syria (although these days, wherever small pockets of Babylon still reign, it could be Myanmar, Minsk, and almost anywhere).

Oh yes, this is a fully authorised rescue (although marked 'not for resuscitation'). It'll be a quick in-and-out operation, but also yes (since you ask in relation to your own expenses), this is also (but only on return) a fully funded operation. So then let's get on with it, since these details of the operation are not in dispute, unless, instead of carrying out our commission, we stand here discussing these details and, as so often happens over the detailed fine print, find ourselves disputing with the devil.

Oh, and by the way, your understanding (in the humanistic rather than angelic second person) of what constitutes a divine mission on earth (in terms of both time and place) is very different from what we angels understand of every such mission (in terms of both text and context). Remember throughout the mission that there can be no text without a context any more than any context without a text.

We are bound to emphasise this mutuality even more particularly where any message is given through us angels more directly (in the first person) by and from the Supreme Command in heaven. We angels, as communicators, translators, facilitators, and assessors, thus serve only as court interlocutors (or pinyin bureaucrats) for the passing of information (both ways) between heaven and earth. Like all bureaucrats, we angels do not like to be left 'holding the baby' as 'piggies in the middle' (as we might say in borrowing these very mixed metaphors from earth).

* * *

For the Sake of Looking Ahead
Part IV

Something Very New Under the Sun
His callow, beardless face and shorn, scabby head
protruded from the hatch [of the armoured personnel
carrier] in front of me, as if prepared for the antique
Afghan torture in which a person is buried up to the
neck, then has their head used as a football.
Christopher Kremmer, *The Carpet Wars: A
Journey across the Islamic Heartlands*

We angels are travelling with you infantrymen through peak-time
traffic on the main road out of Kabul. 'Keep your eyes on the mine-
strewn road ahead,' advises five-starred Brigadier General Abdul
Hamidi. 'Aside from any sniper taking a pot-shot at us, the safest
place should we hit an anti-tank mine is atop this armoured carrier,'
the general explains. He has no idea of the angelic safety shield with
which the Supreme Command has committed us to provide him
against those pot-shots from snipers.

Good enough advice from the general against land mines for
those atop the troop carrier, but it doesn't prevent our personnel
carrier from running over and killing the young girl who is crossing
the road at our next street intersection. Amid the crowd of scattering
pedestrians through which we have roared, as if expecting those on
foot 'to part like the Red Sea before Moses', the jolt of striking the
young girl's slim and helpless body is hardly felt atop this heavily
armoured personnel carrier.

Keeping your eyes on the mine-strewn road that may explode at
any moment beneath you is small justification for failing to observe
other road users. Nevertheless, the army driver of our personnel
carrier would be no more than a sixteen-year-old youth. Even as
angels, ours is a military operation, and our commitment is to the
troop carrier. All we can do, even as angels, is to report to the Supreme
Command on the perceived facts—the incongruity of which would

prevent us from any attempt here at soul-catching. For being only a little higher in the heavenly scheme of things than are all you mortals, we too are subject to our own limitations.

Here, before leaving the relative safety of Kabul for the purpose of reporting on military action in the hill country, is the painful foretaste of a far more unpalatable future. It forewarns us of what little right we have to expect of any justifiable end being reached by no more than military action. This so-called incident will sour the day for all of us, both angels and mortals, before we can even reach the hill country up ahead. Okay then, but what yet lies beyond the hill country?

Although the cosmic plan for every nation, tribe, and family is the salvation of every single person, this concept of eternal salvation (rather than day-to-day survival) does not feature to the forefront of the earthly individual's mindset. All the same, be at the ready to partake of this heavenly promise at any moment not just because every such moment could be your last but because seizing that moment will bring you to perceive what's foremost to your ongoing future. As distinct from day-to-day survival, your then spiritually transformed mindset, taking over from one's long-accustomed earthly mindset, is one of the first prerequisites for every mortal to engage in soul-catching.

The resulting choice between salvation and survival provokes a perceived paradox at the merely mortal level. This can prove quite disconcerting, since having so long sought solely to maximise one's earthly tainted way of life is to lose it, whereas foregoing that earthly tainted way of life for the sake of eternal salvation is to effectuate a life-saving function beyond all earthly measure.

Nevertheless, it's still the same life-saving measure which works on earth and in heaven. The perceived paradox results from no more than two polarised aspects of this same measure as they differentially operate when either contingently expressed for the limited survival of the soul on earth or else as absolutely fulfilled for all eternity in heaven. The choice to align oneself to one or to the other of these polarised aspects of life and death is made as much by their own worldly sacrifice as by exercising one's heavenly appointed faith.

Sounds odd, but this exercise of free volition is required of nearly everything that really matters, so why wouldn't it apply to every issue of life or death? It's said that priests and kings (and perhaps also presidents) have the authority to enquire into what otherwise on earth would remain a matter of heaven's own business. Such privileged authorities may know nothing of the part they play in this process of heavenly investigation and as often heavenly restoration. Nevertheless, theirs is the part upon which they are called to build and repair broken walls, to soothe and uplift broken spirits, to repair derelict bridges across raging streams, and to straighten crooked and perilous roads. They are, as once said, 'the Lord's anointed'.

For just whom is all this work being done—often rendered by warfare and intrigue so apparently without purpose and so often apparently incapable of achievement? Yet even in the very midst of such worldwide confusion, all these works are being completed and brought to fruition with such great clarity, but not always on behalf of or to the benefit of those for whom these great works have been carried out or are still being done. But on this score, have you not already spoken, Lord? Nothing more remains in all this confusion but for us mortals to draw ever closer to your mind and heart.

Nevertheless, as mighty kings, powerful priests, and elected presidents, you who purport to rule the earth still ask to know the outcome, for you have yet to know who these as yet unknown people are for whom these great works are carried out. 'This then, by whom and to where my prophetic finger points,' says the Lord God Almighty, 'is just who these people are and where you are to find them, for my prophetic finger points through time and space to tell you not just in terms of who now they are but also in terms of who they forever shall be. Keep clear your minds no less than you must learn to guard your hearts, and make your way with no more haste or human passion towards others than your calling may in each different case indicate to you.

'So just as my slanting rain sweeps across the plain like frequent pins and stabbing needles, these now unknown people shall travel to the ends of the earth to achieve its renewal. They shall seek water in the thirstiest and driest of places. They shall plant olive groves where before were once barren hillsides and teetering chasms. They shall build fishponds in the most unlikeliest of places (yes, even in the midst of war zones, they shall build fishponds) and shall invigorate the seas and farthest oceans with new life—new life of all sorts both large and small. Do not call attention to yourselves. My calling, together with your affirmative response, is enough for others to see yourselves being called.

'Likewise, they shall restore herbs, trees, and plants, both new and old, to enable the deserts, whether already rendered barren of the many different seas or of the many different lands, once again to bloom and prosper. They shall so nurture the land as to provide forage enough for all known and yet still to become known species of animals and of plants. All these past, present, and future living things shall flourish as never yet flourished before. Even long-lost or soon-to-be-extinct species, however large and however small, shall then in their own way be seen to prosper. So then you shall enjoy the harvest of our combined work, as was always meant to be.

'No task shall be too large for such people who hear my voice,' says the Lord, 'for these people and their children's children and, in turn, the children of their children's children. All shall be renewed alone in my strength to garden my kingdom as never before, for as the smallest yet most viable of seeds, I have already implanted my hope and promise in each of them, to be as collectively my people, so that in my name, the fullest extent of the desert shall bloom.

'There will be many who disparage your efforts by saying it is all too late for what you do, but that would be for me to say,' says God. 'It is not for such disparagers to pre-empt the will of the Lord.' ['Too late, too late, too late,' screech their voices, like those of ravens and magpies, but none but the Supreme Command, holding the key to time, shall pull the plug on time.]

'And as already indentured gardeners, it is your task as my already chosen people to nourish and nurture these seeds of hope and promise, both biologically as well as spiritually, on account of which alone, the very deserts of this already dying earth shall break out into full blossom and so bloom as never before. You don't quite believe that, do you? But just as the last embers of any fire, when bereft of smoke and flame, shall be the hottest (as every blacksmith well knows), so my final breath of spiritual fire shall bring even fallow fields to their fruition. I tell you, that in these end times, more and more of my people who remain youthful in heart shall outlive even much younger folks—however bittersweet that may be to whomsoever witnesses that strange event.

'There is a season for all things, and now it is the fruitfulness of autumn that shall mark the end of days for those who know how to harvest autumnal things and not to expect always a constant spring. Yes, even for one last time, the desert shall bloom just as the elderly shall grow more active in their old age to inspirit and encourage the younger folks. And yet that autumn of mellow fruitfulness is already here, but the young have their eyes closed (except for television) and their ears blocked (except for earbuds and earphones). But before all that goes down, I shall give them one last chance—and this whatever it shall take to wake them up!'

'Yet who are we, the people still ask, both in fulsome awe and anxious trepidation, to be ourselves called such a chosen people?'

'You are my people of faith. I am the Lord God of all things,' answers the Lord. 'You are my people of faith who look for all great outcomes to be born of small things and who know that from any grain of faith no bigger than a mustard seed by way of the smallest beginning, only the very biggest outcomes can be sure to happen.

'Yet you who are called my people call on me still for revival and yet do not understand how small is your vision by which it is far too late in the overall scheme of things for that smallest sort of revival ever to take place on earth again. The smallest seeds, already sown, already carefully tended, have also already sprouted, just as also all the seasons, as well as all the gardeners' tasks for each of those seasons, must forever change. Look then to the ultimate of all revivals, for it shall be that revival which shall the biggest ever of revivals.

'Over and over again, you have been given that most temperate of spiritual opportunities, but by now, the time is too late for any such moderate methods. The self-maintaining biogeochemical cycles—the oxygen cycle, nitrogen cycle, the carbon cycle, the sulphur cycle, the phosphorous cycle, and the water cycle required for photosynthesis and other nutritional cycles in both animals and plants—are already rapidly breaking down, both through lack of reserves and the resulting imbalance through exacerbated overuse of certain processes. Likewise, mankind has introduced its own kind of artificial cycles (such as that of atrazine) and others just as toxic to sometimes many species (including to many of those species that are in no way hostile to mankind).'

Radical measures call for the revival, resurrection, and resuscitation of what seems to be a broken-down old world. Nevertheless, God knows better than to create more of the same. And already the most informed of mortals consider the world problematique (as earlier explained) to have finally passed the point of no return. God knows better than to resurrect and resuscitate any completely lost cause. What must be broken by way of birthing both a new heaven and a new earth must be all our attachment to this old dying world, and to do that will require no less a radically new heaven to eradicate that old world attachment than it will require a radically new world.

When God is radical, he is radical all the way. What we await, which will fulfil Christ's promise of coming again, is both a new heaven and a new earth. As with the end of any ongoing book or everlasting story, this will mean a new beginning. Until then, the biblical code is open-ended, on which account, the living Word is alive and well and the Bible remains a fully open book. The safety net of the Lord likewise remains open, and the ministry of the soul-catcher still goes on.

This ministry as an angel of the Lord Jesus Christ to serve as a soul-catcher is not well-understood. It is often belittled by more conventional evangelists for being a last-ditch endeavour. It is not for them to stand by the tumbril, to sit at the scaffold, to observe the fall of the axe or of the guillotine, or to gauge the depth of the drop or the sweep of the sword; but the issues of life and death (the substance of things unseen) are still the same.

It is time now to honour our official invitation to witness an execution. We shall go to the football ground in Kabul, where we shall mingle there with the crowds of men, women, and children who, by reason of their own downfall into darkness, all delight, almost as a matter of religious observance, to observe yet another and another and another execution. Yet not everyone of their own volition seeks the soul-catcher's safety net.

Although many shall be called, yet not all shall be chosen. On one side of the boat, the net may come up empty, and yet on the other side, the net may come up full to breaking point. As from this side to the other side of the boat, so too from this side of the world to the other side of the world, the earth shall be harvested of souls just as thoroughly as the sea is being harvested of fish. Only after all that is over shall the safety net be finally drawn up for the catch to be counted.

Until then, from this side to the other side of the boat and from this side to the other side of the world, soul-catching shall continue and shall not stop. The task is yours if you want to take the tripartite challenge—first, most thoroughly to search your soul; secondly, to commit yourself to saving souls; and finally, as if apparently tied to the very last of all lost causes, to equip your own soul to be the soul-catcher of this world's so many near-lost souls. Until the very end of this world, there shall be no end to soul-catching. It shall continue until the very last microsecond of all time. Until the safety net of soul-catching shall be full to overflowing, it shall not stop.

Without the constant counsel and military
surveillance of the Supreme Command,
this exceedingly brief battle report could
not have been commissioned,
far less written in the field,
and so is now sealed by the Supreme Imprimatur.
For later release as witness to the foregoing and further events
of considerable cosmic magnitude
in the ongoing heavenly battle
against every last remnant
of evil on earth.

Amen

* * *

Lightning Source UK Ltd.
Milton Keynes UK
UKHW012333160120
357108UK00001B/40/J